JAKARTA

JAKARTA

Kerry B. Collison

Sid Harta Publishers
1999

Published by: Sid Harta Publishers for Kerry B. Collison
                  and Asian Pacific Management Co.
                  (S.A.) Ltd.

                  Telephone: (61) (0 414) 958623
                  fax: (61) 03 9560 9921
                  Address: PO Box 1102 Hartwell,
                  Victoria, Australia 3125

First published January 1998
Second Printing April 1999
Copyright © Kerry B.Collison,
Sid Harta Publishers and
Asian Pacific Management Co. Ltd. S.A, 1998

Text: Kerry B.Collison
Cover Concept: Guy W. Collison
Final Proof Reading: Dr. John D. Quigley
Author's Photograph: Courtesy of Ned Kelly and the
                        Bundaberg News Mail, Queensland

Collison, Kerry Boyd

ISBN   0 95 874 48 66

Printed in Australia
by Australian Print Group
Maryborough, Victoria.

Acknowledgements

During the considerable time spent researching material relating to nuclear power, I was most fortunate to receive the support of many who, in one way or another, assisted with my ongoing education, particularly with the subject matter contained in this novel.

I therefore wish to express my gratitude to Andrew Karam of the Ohio State University, who contributed a great deal of his valuable time to assist me to understand more about nuclear reactors and life aboard an American nuclear submarine. To Andy, thank you for your friendship and incredible support.

I wish also to thank Tim Gabruch, visiting research officer at the Uranium Institute in London, who provided me with details of Chernobyl and in-depth detail of the Nuclear Energy Club, and Richard Broinowski, Honorary Professor, Faculty of Communications, University of Canberra for his contribution in relation to the final chapters of this book.

There are others I should not forget to mention here. These include: the Information Section of the United States Seventh Fleet in Japan; the United Nations representative office in Sydney; the Information Office of the Japanese Embassy in Canberra, Australia; the representative offices of Boeing in Sydney; the British Defense Liaison Staff, Canberra; David Wiencek, Research Associate at the CDISS in Washington, D.C.; Gary Benoit, Editor of *The New American;* and Clare Booth.

To the many *The Timor Man* and *Merdeka Square* readers who have communicated their thoughts, thank you for your incredible support.

Kerry B. Collison
Melbourne

Kerry B. Collison followed a distinguished period of service as a member of the Australian Embassy in Indonesia during the turbulent Sixties followed by a successful business career spanning thirty years throughout Asia.

Recognised for his chilling predictions in relation to Asia's evolving political and economic climate and as the only Australian ever to have been personally granted citizenship by an Indonesian President, he brings unique qualifications to his historically-based vignettes and intriguing accounts of power-politics and the shadowy world of governments' clandestine activities.

The author's biographical data is avaliable on the Internet at:
http://www.sidharta.com.au

Photo of the author by Ned Kelly, published by courtesy of the Bundaberg News Mail.

Dedication

I dedicate this book, *Jakarta*,
to the memory of

Air-Vice Marshall Raden Imam Suwongso Wirjosapoetro

Atas segala kepercayaan dan persahabatan beliau pada saya,
semasa beliau masih hidup, saya ucapkan terima kasih
serta maaf lahir dan bathin.

Other books
by Kerry B. Collison

The Asian Trilogy

The Timor Man

Freedom (Merdeka) Square

Jakarta

The Fifth Season

Non-Fiction

The Leo Stach Story

"Revolusi kita, belum selesai!"

'Our revolution has yet to complete its course!'

Indonesia's founding President, Soekarno,
in his last major address to the people before
being overthrown by General Soeharto

Jakarta — Tanjung Priok Harbour Nuclear Power Plant

Contents

Book three, Rama energy

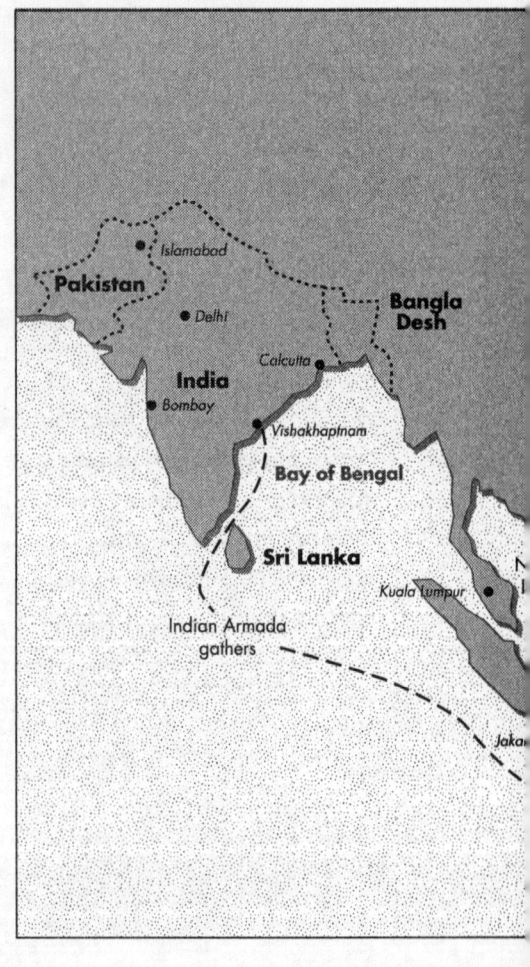

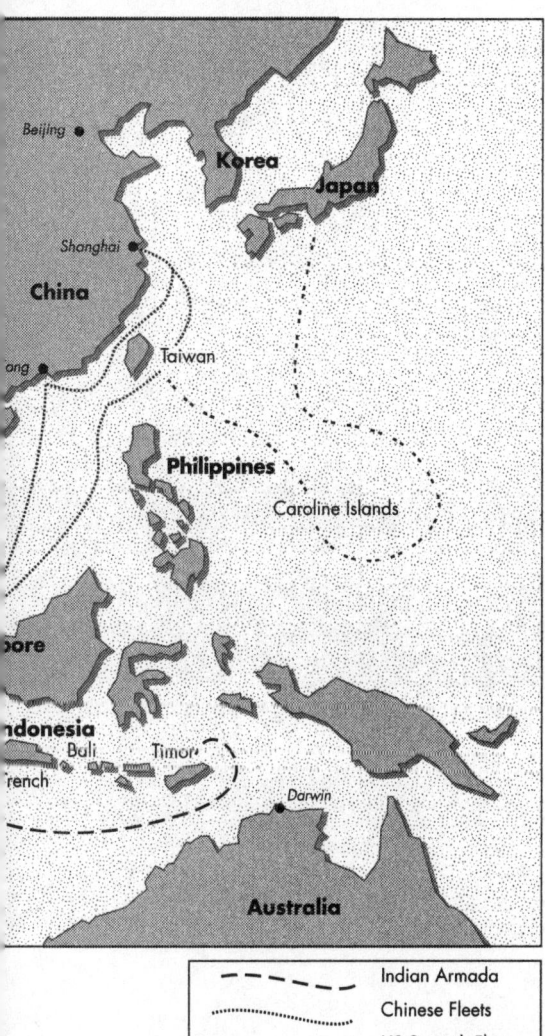

– – – –	Indian Armada
··············	Chinese Fleets
·· — ·· — ·· —	US Seventh Fleet

Kerry B.Collison

Prologue

'Sell Salima Jaya!' Budiman screamed hopelessly, his voice drowned in the cacophonous mix of panic trading and cries of disbelief which had prevailed since news of the disaster had reached the floor of the capital's exchange. Excruciating pain in his side caused him to catch his breath, sharply, as one of his colleagues elbowed past, waving frantically as he too attempted to off-load his client's stock in Salima Jaya Power. Budiman struggled forward, pulling against the shoulders of the others in front. *'One hundred and fifty-thousand!'* he yelled hoarsely, competing against a barrage of sellers who blocked his way, muffling his call. He lost his balance, again, and fell as the unruly mob of traders scrambled futilely to dominate the proceedings.

The floor was in total chaos as millions continued to be wiped from the value of all Salima stocks, plunging the entire market into a downward spin. In the first thirty minutes, the Jakarta Index had fallen thirty percent, while the Exchange's Chairman vacillated as to whether or not he should heed the many calls to suspend all trading, fearful that his own holdings had yet to be divested by his unscrupulous brother-in-law cum broker. He peered anxiously around the floor again, confused, resisting the temptation to leave his position and go in search of his man. Another fight erupted, resulting in a number of traders being dragged angrily away as security guards attempted to restore order. The Chairman caught a glimpse of his broker being escorted from the hall and knew, immediately, that it was too late, and that he too had been caught up in the disaster. He stared at the prominent clock and, overcome with despair, gripped the small podium's railings, his knuckles

15

white. There was at least an hour's trading left in the day. Resigned to the possibility that he had lost everything, the Chairman saw no advantage in suspending trading and he remained stationary, a solitary, silent observer of what had surely been the most calamitous day in the Exchange's history.

On the floor below, Budiman struggled to maintain balance as the body of traders surged back in his direction, threatening to crush him as he screamed his sell order. Incredibly, it was as if the buyers could not see his mark. Budiman was lifted off his feet as the panic-driven sellers surged forward. The young Javanese trader called out loudly, certain that he would be crushed.

Amid the confusion in the Exchange, none of the frantic traders registered the shuddering beneath their feet. The unstable ground below moved, rocking the building's floating foundations for the second time that day. They were oblivious to the aftershock, an ominous signal that the threat of pending natural disaster was very, very real.

Budiman felt faint. It was as if there was no oxygen in the air. *Why won't they let me through?* he wondered, bewildered by their failure to recognise the powerful group he represented. A large *Waringan Corporation* trader's identification tag covered the area above his left breast pocket. This was the First Family's own trading company symbol. *What's wrong with them?* his mind screamed, as he was pushed and shoved, unable to maintain his balance as the other traders ignored the sell orders held tightly in his right hand. He called again, in desperation, realizing that his voice would not be heard amongst the multitude of sellers screaming over him. Then, as he felt someone rip the paper from his hand, he stumbled and was pushed, then kicked savagely from behind.

'*No!*' he called weakly, but his cry was drowned amidst the screams of others who had tripped over Budiman as he fell. Mistakenly, several traders thought they had heard a buyer call out in his direction, and this galvanised them into action. The mass of sellers surged forward, fighting, kicking and punching their way towards where they believed the only remaining buyer of Salima stocks seemed to be.

At that moment, another tremor struck, this time showering clouds of surface cement dust over the assembly. Stunned into silence, the traders waited, holding their breath. They raised their hands above their heads, anticipating the worst.

An eerie quiet enveloped the floor as the building swayed threateningly. Scrolling price indicator lights flickered, then went blank as sensitive terminals shut down, unable to cope with the inadequate power support system. And then, within moments of the volcanic surge passing, the traders' screams once again dominated the floor.

Minutes later, two of the non-government banks asked to have their shares removed from trading. Within the hour, fifteen private banks had collapsed. Most of these were majority owned by the First Family and Lim Swee Giok's Salima Jaya Group. Only moments had passed when there was a further tremor, and huge clumps of concrete were ripped from the wall of the building crushing several men to the Stock Exchange floor. It was almost as if nature, having recognised the corruption inside, had moved to punish those within. As dust settled, a solitary cry was heard and one of the traders, his legs crushed, cried out in pain. The lights blinked, again, then power failed altogether, throwing the exchange into artificial darkness.

There was a hush as traders held their breath, waiting for another after-shock. But there was none. Then, unexpectedly, there was a blinding glare of light as the automatic generators switched in, and power was restored. Within moments, the momentary blackout was forgotten, and trading recommenced with renewed panic.

'*Sell Salima Jaya Power!*' the line screamed again, competing against each other, waving their sell-notes furiously. But there were few buyers. Budiman and a number of others lay unconscious, oblivious to the disastrous events which surrounded them. Several security guards pushed their way over to where they had seen him fall, and dragged Budiman and the other bruised men to safety. The panic-driven shouting continued.

'*Salima, sell!*' a trader yelled. '*Salima Jaya sell, two million!*' he screamed, fearing that his block of two million shares would be left unacknowledged, as he waved his sell order high above the shoulders of the shorter men who were hoping to off-load another six million shares of the stock, as the market continued its incredible collapse. '*Sell at one-fifty thousand!*' the voice shrieked, offering the once blue-chip share for less than a tenth of its value when the market commenced trading that day.

'Salima, sell!' another frantic trader from behind yelled even louder as the pandemonium continued, *'sell three million at one hundred thousand rupiah!'* he shouted, not to be outdone by his rival.

* * * * * *

And so the tumultuous session continued. The disfavoured stocks finally bringing the entire market down more than sixty percent as rumour continued to spread of the Salima Group's disastrous accident, and of the magnitude of what had happened. Earlier, and within minutes of the first downwards trend, the Singapore market had moved into the play, followed immediately by Kuala Lumpur and Hong Kong, sending the Jakarta stocks plummeting to lows few Indonesian industrial magnates could ever have imagined. At first they hesitated out of loyalty, but soon recognised that even with their support, their old associate's company would most likely collapse. Then, they too panicked, disposing of whatever stock the buyers could absorb. When the electronic bell finally sounded, marking the end of trading, there was a hush. And in the air hung the unfamiliar smell of despair as the Jakarta Stock Market closed for the day. The Salima Group, one of Indonesia's most favoured conglomerates, had all but collapsed, precipitating the demise of at least three hundred other publicly listed companies.

* * * * * *

The panic selling had been precipitated by an abrupt announcement declaring that the Salima Jaya Power owned and operated nuclear power plant in Bali had suffered structural damage as a result of the previous day's earth tremor, and was now in imminent danger of collapse. A nuclear melt-down. Reports further claimed that mass evacuation of tourists from the densely populated Island of the Gods had already commenced. The unstable nuclear energy site had been subjected to further tremors, threatening nuclear devastation on a scale yet unknown to mankind. There would be a massive loss of life, and with that, enormous claims against the owners and operators.

* * * * * *

Within hours of the disastrous trading session's close, many of Jakarta's high profile brokers, along with their military associates, quietly emptied their safes, made excuses to their families and girl-friends, then fled before the Presidential aides could comprehend what had really happened. They knew they would be blamed for the incredible financial losses the First Family had also suffered in those few short hours of Indonesia's economic Armageddon.

* * * * * *

The members of the board sat quietly, confused by their sudden change in fortunes and shocked by their chief executive's accusations. Not one amongst their number had ever heard their Chair-woman raise her voice before. This sudden outburst had only increased their feeling of foreboding as the Salima Jaya Group's matriarch stood at the end of the long, polished mahogany table, her head and shoulders silhouetted by the late afternoon sun as it continued its descent over the Sunda Straits, to the West.

'Enough!' she cried, loudly, slamming her fragile hand down hard on the table. She stood, glaring at those around the mahogany table, who were stunned with surprise at the sudden strength of the woman.

'That will be enough!' she demanded, rising slowly. One of the younger men leaped to his feet and pulled the heavy chair back, enabling her to stand. They cast their heads down in deferential silence. Their world had changed. The speed at which everything had been thrown into turmoil had left them fearing for their futures. And their lives. Suddenly, the room moved slightly, then rocked, as the upper levels of the building was whipped by the power of yet another aftershock. They all sat motionless and silent.

Less than a minute followed before nervous coughs brought the meeting back to order. They all stared towards the end of the room and waited for the small framed silhouette to speak again. And then she began.

The members of the board sat up, attentive, as she laid out the foundations for the Salima Group's future. The members sat quietly, mesmerised as *Ibu Ruswita*, their Chairwoman, outlined her plans to rebuild the Group's fortunes. There was not one amongst their number who did not realize immediately that if they refused to comply, then they would have no future at all. At least not in *that* country. In typical Asian style, accepting what had become the inevitable, they breathed deeply, silently, and listened to what the Chairwoman determined should be done. And, without exception, they knew that they would obey.

* * * * * *

Alone, having dismissed the members of her inner sanctum, Ruswita rose to her feet. The swaying sensation of the building seemed to have slowed, and she moved cautiously to the French windows which overlooked the Capital's protocol street, Jalan Thamrin. The air conditioning units had not automatically restarted and she could smell the lingering odour of *kretek* cigarette in the board room. Ruswita stared down at the small pedestrian dots barely moving along the footpaths below. She sighed, recalling the urgent communication she had received from Professor Sutomo, Chairman of BATAN, the Indonesian Atomic Energy Commission. She had listened intently as the scientist had offered his terrifying projections, projections which indicated that the loss of life could be in the millions. Perhaps even her own children could be among the victims; she had no way of finding out, as yet.

Ruswita's eyes blurred, and her mind slipped back to how it had all begun, and how her destiny had led her to this cruel predicament.

Book one

Chapter 1

Origins

Ruswita rested for a moment, stretched, then wiped her forehead with the back of her soapy hands. Then she crouched over the village *kali* again, taking the clothes one, by one, and rinsing them meticulously by hand to complete her washing. As she placed each item carefully into the hand-woven basket, Ruswita counted them to ensure that none were missing. Here the dark water flowed quickly and she knew that one had to be particularly careful not to slip, or lose track of the clothes spread out on the smooth, black, basalt river-rock.

Ruswita flicked at a few strands of long black hair which had worked loose from the temporary bun tied at the back of her head. One of the other women called to her friends and, at the sound of her voice, Rus glanced in the direction of the chatter, identifying the talkative young woman who had married just the week before. Rus cast another glance in the younger woman's direction, just long enough to confirm that the fourteen-year-old bride was already with child. She considered this with mixed emotions, sighed, then returned to folding her washing.

Here, on the river's banks, there were few secrets. The women gathered each morning on this side of the fast flowing stream, where the water cascaded down from the distant mountains providing life to the villagers, their fields, and the crops. During the past few years, the harvests had been exceptionally poor. But once, Rus remembered, it had all been very different.

Four years had passed since the civil war had finally ground to a halt, leaving the village almost devoid of life. The bloody and senseless holocaust had destroyed the world these simple and uneducated farmers had known, leaving little but a bitter harvest of hate and lasting discrimination. Ruswita had been most fortunate to survive those violent times considering she was of mixed extraction, a *peranakan*. Her Javanese mother had not been as fortunate. Ruswita's Chinese father had been slaughtered during the blood-bath which ensued from the general perception that all Chinese were Communist, and were therefore responsible for the violent and cruel deaths of the country's military leadership during the abortive *coup d'etat* of 1965.

When the marauding gangs had struck her village, Ruswita fled in terror, escaping through the rear of the family's simple dwelling. Terrified that she too might be killed, she did not turn back to go to her family's aid, knowing that the screams which followed were those of her mother and remaining family who had been caught, huddled together, at the entrance to their impoverished home.

The few who survived the anti-Communist blood-lettings soon discovered that their rich, fertile land had been sowed with bitter seeds indeed. Army commanders such as Sarwo Edhie embarked on genocidal missions with a determination that ultimately accounted for the deaths of hundreds of thousands of innocent villagers, many of whom were children who were not yet in their teens. The once bountiful harvests were gone. Children no longer played along the reaches of the river system, once considered their Garden of Eden. Evidence of their historical and cultural past had, in the greater part, been obliterated. Entire families, who had innocently permitted communist doctrines to infiltrate their communities, had disappeared forever.

During those fearful times, even the river boat captains refused to venture into their district, electing to terminate their journey further downstream. Their crews were terrified of the marauding gangs who, as they knew, slaughtered their enemies with incredible ferocity. Later, they saw the shocking results of the mass slaughter, when thousands of bodies washed down-stream and choked the river. Ruswita had been fortunate indeed to have been spared. As the terrifying attack on her village began, she had fled the scene, running down the river's muddy slopes, slipping and sliding in search of a safe hiding place. She plunged into the river and grasped the sides of a small timber boat behind which she hid from the marauders. There, Ruswita waited, terrified, fearful of discovery.

As she clung to the side of the ancient canoe, screams and shouting continued unabated, and she closed her eyes and prayed to both the gods her parents worshipped. An hour passed, and then another, before the shivering, terrified young girl managed to summon sufficient courage to drag herself cautiously out of the muddy hiding place and crawl cautiously back up the slopes to her village. There she was greeted with scenes of absolute savagery. Mutilated bodies lay everywhere, evidence of the cruel attack. Now, as she recalled these images while bent over the very same river which had once been her temporary sanctuary, Ruswita fought to drag herself back from those moments of horror, fighting the indelible memory of seeing her mother's headless corpse.

Conscious that she had been momentarily lost in her hideous past, Ruswita looked anxiously around to see if she had been observed by the other women. Without being obvious, she watched some of the women arriving late for their daily chores along the river bank, and noted that the village chief's wife had detailed two of the other younger women to carry her household washing down to the stream. Ruswita knew that the *lurah's* wife was someone to reckon with. As the village chief's most recent acquisition, she had an unofficial position within the community which went unchallenged. The new wife was the *lurah's* fourth. That meant there would be no more opportunity for the unmarried women who might have considered themselves eligible for selection. Ruswita sighed. She really had no ambition to marry. At least, not right then. She just wanted to escape the *kampung* with its poverty and horrific memories.

* * * * * *

Early evenings, before the villagers fell into their tired and well-deserved sleep, it was customary to gather together and listen to the radio broadcast, which immediately followed their final prayers for the day. Once the village chieftain had turned the Grundig off, and was satisfied that he had disconnected his valuable radio to ensure that the leads to the car batteries were not in danger of touching, he would stand, signalling that the evening entertainment was over. Silently, the small community would then retire in preparation for another demanding day which would begin before the sun's first false rays heralded its arrival. As kerosene lanterns were extinguished and the village became quiet, Ruswita joined the others in her hut, sleeping amongst the single women on *tikar* mats, cramped together in their simple dwelling. The young woman lay on her side with her hand under her head as a pillow, permitting her thoughts to stray, enticed by the promise of sleep and images of faraway places. Each night she would close her eyes and conjure up scenes of what the cities might be like, and how she would venture into those intimidating places. Comforted by the soft sounds of the others breathing as they too slipped into their own private worlds, Ruswita lay quietly and imagined herself in a small house in some distant place, far away from the nightmares of her past, and far away from the despair, loneliness, and poverty she endured.

* * * * * *

The wait seemed interminable, and Ruswita began to lose faith that she would ever find the opportunity to escape her village. At nineteen, she was considered almost too old to be a first wife, and too young to be around the other women's husbands as long as she remain unattached. Then there was the problem of her *peranakan* extraction. Rus was the daughter of a Chinese river-trader. Her mother had been a simple Javanese woman who had resigned herself to being one of the many wives her casual husband kept along the river trading route. Resentment against the Chinese still lingered in the aftermath of the civil war and Ruswita knew that her blood-line would guarantee that she would be relegated to a less rewarding life than she deserved. Ruswita understood clearly that even if she were fortunate enough to marry within the next few years, it would be unlikely that she would live long enough to enjoy caring for her own grandchildren for, in her land of Java, very few peasant women survived to celebrate their fiftieth birthdays. Birthdays were celebrated only once, upon a child's arrival, and as most of her fellow villagers were illiterate, records were not kept as such information was passed from one generation to another merely by word of mouth.

Ruswita refused to resign herself to her unfortunate lot in life as others around her had done, accepting their roles as mothers and wives as generations of women had before them. She learned to read the new language, *Bahasa Indonesia,* from old and torn newspapers carried into the village by the river traders, and was one of the few women in her village who could understand the evening news broadcasts. It was not long before the other young women avoided her. They were envious of her achievements, and piqued that she aspired to rise above her position in the village order. Driven by the desire to achieve an even greater level of learning, Ruswita was obliged to spend considerably more time than she wished studying the *Holy Koran,* as this was the only acceptable path for a woman of such simple origins. At the age of sixteen, Rus could already read and write as well as any city child who had attended primary school. She was a bright child, and would have had little difficulty with the lessons had she been given the opportunity to attend the district elementary high school. But, because of her origins and sex, this opportunity would elude her and Rus, accepting that this as her *nasib,* her fate, went about her life, praying that her *rezeki* would change for the better.

* * * * * *

In her nineteenth year, Ruswita came to the conclusion that it was impossible for her to remain in the village any longer, and devised a plan to leave. She encouraged the attention of one of the younger men and, promising rewards well beyond what she was prepared to give, slipped away from her village with the infatuated man, leaving her place of birth forever. Ten kilometres downstream, she left the disappointed suitor and climbed aboard one of the frequent river boats used to transport produce to the shallow-water harbour on the coast. She discovered that she could survive in the coastal city, working along the roadside as a daily labourer. A month passed before she could convince one of the Chinese shop-keepers that she really was literate, and this secured a position for her, working in a dusty garment store adjacent to the main thoroughfare, and inter-city bus terminal. She worked dutifully for three months, saving sufficient to purchase a bus ticket that would take her to the nation's capital, Jakarta. Ruswita eventually boarded a bus, crammed full of people, pigs, chickens and baskets of produce, her heart filled with the promise of things to come. As she headed towards the city of dreams which had occupied her thoughts since first listening to the village radio broadcasts, Ruswita's excitement grew, confident that she had made the correct choice.

The journey was extremely demanding. Roads were broken, and in many places washed away, often requiring hours of detours around streams which no longer afforded bridges. As she travelled through the countryside, Rus felt a little apprehensive as the overladen bus ground on through the poverty-stricken towns along the coastal route, her uncertainty growing as they neared the capital, where she witnessed the thousands upon thousands of roadside dwellers camped under makeshift dwellings. Occasionally, she waved to children as they scrambled out of the bus's path, turning quickly away from the choking, cloud of dust, and black diesel smoke which followed the dilapidated vehicle. After three long days and nights, the bus finally groaned to a stop in metropolitan Jakarta, not far from the *Glodok* inter-city bus stop. Ruswita stepped down from the bus, and looked around in wonder. The spectacle was more awe-inspiring than she had ever imagined.

There were at least a hundred buses parked in the square, Some had rows of huge baskets tied to the roof, filled to overflowing with vegetables and other produce. Others, rocking and swaying over the ruts, chugged laboriously through the filthy quagmire of the square. Animals defecated where they were tied, and day-traders moved tirelessly between the maze of buses, barely able to maintain their footing while balancing their precarious shoulderloads on long, bamboo poles. Rus removed her sandals and struggled through the mud, uncertain what to do next. She clung on to her few possessions in case she slipped and fell into the foul-smelling mud. The choking air caused her to cough, and as she did so, Rus remembered to cover her face with the end of her *selendang*.

At first, she was intimidated by the apparent chaos of the spectacle which surrounded her, but soon Ruswita's natural confidence and determination returned and she began walking quickly among the mass of people, politely enquiring about accommodations and opportunities for work. Most simply ignored her, or scoffed at her naiveté. Some of the men offered her money, and laughed when she turned from them, embarrassed. She understood clearly what their gestures meant. Ruswita felt bewildered and somewhat confused by the arrogance and obvious disdain of the city people. She had never encountered such animosity, such impolite behaviour, amongst her village-folk.

Hours passed, and Rus knew that she should try to find lodgings before nightfall. Depressed, but not discouraged, she walked away from the square. Her feet were filthy, and Rus shook her head in disgust. She had not expected that such conditions could possibly exist in the capital. Rus made her way towards a number of waiting *becak* drivers, selected one, then placed her bundle of possessions on the three-wheeled monster's narrow seat.

'*Where do you want to go, nona?*' she was asked.

'*Take me to a losmen that is cheap,*' she answered, wearily, holding ten Rupiah tightly in her hand for the driver to see. The driver grunted, lifted the rear wheel and pointed his machine away from the terminal. He pushed for momentum then climbed onto the seat, and pedalled away from the congested traffic. As he did this he was inwardly considering just how far he would take the country girl for her ten Rupiah. As they left the over-crowded square and entered the main thoroughfare connecting Glodok to the city's centre, Rus continued to cover her face to avoid not only the stench emanating from the sewerage drain running down the centre of the divided road, but also to reduce the nausea from the thick black clouds of suffocating exhaust fumes.

As they pedalled along, Rus was surprised to see continuous lines of roadside stalls selling traditional village foods, such as *durian* cakes, steamed rice wrapped in banana leaf, fried noodles, and many other dishes she had thought would not be available so far from the villages. As a familiar aroma drifted across her path, she experienced a sudden pang of loneliness and wondered, again, if she had made the right decision. Then, as the driver turned another corner, the magnificent old colonial Hotel Duta appeared, bright with coloured lights, a sight which took Ruswita's breath away. Floodlights struck the hotel's tall white walls, the luminous effect so stunning that Ruswita felt her eyes fill with tears. It was just like she had dreamed the city would be. The rows of coloured lights dancing across the evening sky made the building appear like some magic, dazzling palace. Moments later the brilliant scene disappeared from view as the *becak* turned once again, down a narrow street, and came to a halt outside what appeared to be a *losmen*. Ruswita paid the driver and, gathering up her clothes, entered the boarding house.

She paid twenty-five Rupiah to share a room with a number of other women, whose *tikar* mats had already been opened, and spread across the floor in preparation for sleep. Hungry, but concerned that she had already spent far too much for that day, Ruswita decided to skip the evening meal. She moved through the cramped quarters to the rear of the building, through a narrow passageway to the ablution block. There, she entered the primitive bathroom area, undressed, squatted on the concrete floor and peed, then rose and dipped the plastic scoop into the square shaped cement reservoir and threw the cold water between her legs. She then refilled the scoop and poured water over her head, enjoying the cool sensation. Ruswita could not remember ever missing taking a *mandi* at least twice each day before, but she had not bathed since climbing aboard the bus some three days earlier. So it was with great relief that she attacked the dirt, both real and imaginary, which had accumulated during the arduous journey from Central Java. Satisfied that she was clean, Ruswita then washed the clothes she had worn for almost four days, placed these over the outside railing, wrapped herself in a *sarong* and returned to the communal bedroom. There she unrolled her thin *tikar* and spread it carefully on the floor amongst the other women. She lay down and fell immediately into a deep, satisfying sleep.

When Ruswita awoke early the next day, it was not until after her morning ablutions that she discovered that she had spent her first night resting in one of the city's more infamous brothels, behind *Pasar Baru*.

* * * * * *

Not three kilometers from where Ruswita had spent her first night in Jakarta, Murray Stephenson sat in his pavilion *cum* office along Jalan Tasikmalaya, examining the poorly-typed letter he'd written some hours before. As he read down through the two paged report, he corrected no less than twenty errors and sighed, knowing that this was probably the best that his secretary could do. It was impossible to expect more, he knew. There were so few secretaries available who had been trained to type, let alone take shorthand. He sighed, thinking about the number of young girls who had professed to being adequately conversant with Pitman's requirements. There hadn't been one, he'd discovered, who could take shorthand faster than he could write his damn correspondence in longhand. He stretched, leaned back, then threw the ball-pen onto the teak table in disgust. If only he had a decent secretary!

Murray had been fortunate to fall on his feet, so to speak. After the coup, he left the Australian Government and returned to Indonesia to establish his own general consultancy. At first, he had been treated with suspicion by the local authorities. There was little he could do about this problem deciding that, as they had his file on record, he would just have to be circumspect about the circles in which he moved until the Indonesian authorities became comfortable with his new status. To his dismay, Murray had discovered upon his return that there were those amongst the Indonesian hierarchy who still considered him their enemy. Then there were the problems he faced relating to his limited clientele and diminishing finances. It seemed that ever since the new government had taken power and introduced its foreign investment laws, most foreign investors continued to hesitate, waiting cautiously to see whether or not it was true that the former communist country had really become receptive to Western nations investing in the near-bankrupt economy.

Murray knew that the opportunities would grow. There was an abundance of oil and, with that, he believed it was only a matter of time before a ground-swell developed, and investors began pumping millions of resource-orientated investment dollars into the formerly fragile economy. The difficulty he faced was making ends meet until he had secured enough clients to bankroll his expensive overheads.

His credentials were considered excellent by many potential investors who visited, reassured by his manner and obvious knowledge of the people and their culture. Murray was one of a small number of foreigners fluent in the Indonesian language. Before the end of his first year, he had already secured sufficient accounts to guarantee that he could remain solvent for at least another three years. Having overcome the major expense of accommodations, Murray had only to meet monthly payroll and basic living costs to make ends meet. His major client, Peter Wong, had advanced the mandatory three-year advance rental required for his premises. Murray had done everything to avoid making such an incredibly large payment but, as property could only be owned by Indonesians, and they had already been spoiled by the Embassies and other foreign legations in the capital, he had no choice but to pay the equivalent of the value of the premises in one lump sum; he knew that the landlord would then have sufficient capital to purchase another home, and most probably continue the cycle by renting out his new acquisition as well.

Then there was Coleman. Murray could not understand the speed at which the younger man's star had risen when he, with all of his connections, had to struggle to make ends meet. Murray thought about Stephen Coleman and agreed with those who remembered the story, that the former agent was indeed most fortunate to be alive. Murray had been surprised when the younger man had returned to Indonesia and elected to stay. He had been even more surprised when, in less than one year of having established himself as a competitor, the less-experienced Coleman had easily secured major contracts with the Indonesian Government. Murray admitted that he was more than a little envious of these successes, and avoided contact with his business rival. They rarely communicated. Murray thought it best, considering their common background, and the possibility that Coleman just might not be all that he appeared. The thought had crossed his mind that Coleman might still be employed by Canberra and, if this were true, it would most certainly explain how the fledgling entrepreneur had suddenly become so successful in Indonesia.

During the first few months of his return, Murray had serious doubts concerning his decision to leave the intelligence services, and the security he had enjoyed, to risk venturing out into a world of commerce which was so obviously, totally alien to everything he had known in the past. However, as he became settled and more confident, Murray discovered that there were, in fact, very few differences between these two masters. Both, he soon learned, were unforgiving towards those who made mistakes. Both, he also observed, only rewarded the winners. Others were quickly cast aside and forgotten.

Murray extracted another *Gudang Garam kretek* cigarette from the packet of ten, and placed it, absent-mindedly, in his mouth. His head ached but the strong smelling clove would soon remedy that. He reached for the stainless steel Ronson, flicked the lighter with his thumb, then inhaled the warm scented smoke deep into his lungs. He rubbed his face as if hoping this would be sufficient to wipe away the cobwebs strung across the inside of his head as a result of too many whiskies and not enough sleep. His thoughts turned to the two young women he'd left inside. Murray knew that, by now, they would have checked through everything they could find in the master bedroom. He tried to think, recalling his movements the night before and how he'd ended up with the two by himself. His mind was clouded, but he knew that it wasn't really important. Then something triggered his memory and it suddenly came to him. He'd met them at John Georgio's house. Slowly, pieces of the past evening came back and he smiled as he recalled arriving at the American's house, only to discover that Georgio had organized one of his indiscreet parties, where the women considerably outnumbered the men. It was there he remembered asking one of the local girls home, but she had insisted on bringing her friend. The rest was still hazy in his mind, but Murray could remember drinking the cheap, Italian wine John Georgio had insisted on pouring down his guests' throats.

The phone rang in the adjacent room and he knew the caller would be one of the men he'd taken with him to the party. He moaned, not really up to taking them by the hand to guide them through their appointments once again. They had insisted that he escort them down to the Directorate of Air Communications, and Murray knew that he had little choice but to attend the meeting, as the Indonesian officials would expect his presence. His secretary appeared in the doorway and signalled that the call was for him. He acknowledged this with a wave of his hand, then lifted the receiver to accept the call. Minutes later, having agreed to pick his guests up at the Intercontinental Hotel, he wandered back from the small office situated alongside his residence and went in search of aspirin. Murray knew that this was going to be one hell of a long day.

* * * * * *

John Georgio awoke with a start, and then relaxed once he remembered where he was. He was covered in sweat. He watched the overhead blades rotating slowly, wishing that he'd installed an air conditioner in his bedroom. He rebuked himself for having made the statement that he preferred ceiling fans, even though he had only done so because of monetary considerations. John knew it was vital to maintain the charade that he was financially independent, and was deeply concerned that the true circumstances relating to his financial situation remained a secret. Having declared to his friends that it was healthier to sleep with an overhead fan in preference to one of General Electric's wonderful machines, John had to put up with the sticky, uncomfortable conditions.

He lay quietly observing his surroundings. They weren't much, he thought, but at least they were his. Or at least, his to use. John quietly admonished himself. If only he could turn the clock back to when he was living the high life in the States. But he couldn't go back. He knew that foreigners in Indonesia couldn't own property, and having paid an exorbitant rent to the landlord in advance, he believed that he had probably already paid for the premises twice over. This thought made him unhappy. The owner had demanded that the rent be paid three years up front, and that amounted to most of the capital he'd borrowed from his mother back in LA. If his father discovered where the money had come from to finance his son's venture, he would have disowned him. It was not the first time in his brief career that John had, in his family's eyes, screwed up badly.

The fan moved slowly, cutting an edge though the still, lifeless air, as he thought of his mother and how she had risked his father's wrath emptying her savings to finance her son's exploits. At the time, there seemed to be little choice. Had he remained Stateside, he might not have made it at all. At least, now, his mother had the comfort of knowing that her son was a successful businessman, pioneering American investments in Indonesia.

John remained flat on his back, and laughed inwardly with self-mockery. There were few achievements for which he could claim credit. If his mother discovered the truth, she would be ashamed of her son and of what he had become. Why the hell had he embarked on an affair with a married Indonesian woman? He closed his eyes and conjured images of her face. She was, without doubt, amazingly beautiful. Probably the most beautiful woman he had ever known. When the striking woman had appeared in the lecture room on that day, and announced that she would be one of the instructors for his course, John recalled how, suddenly, he had difficulty breathing when she smiled directly at him. In that moment, John deceived himself by believing that she had smiled for him, and only him. As he lay in bed, his mind wandering, John crossed his arms and breathed deeply, remembering what had then followed.

Julianti had been employed by the United States Government as one of the language teachers for the Monterey Language Facility, where government officials were given basic instruction in the Indonesian and other languages. Julianti was contracted to assist with the Indonesian course, part time, while she lived with her husband, an Indonesian journalist, who was the representative North American correspondent for the Indonesian *Antara* news agency. Her husband's salary was meagre by American standards, and the couple found the cost of living difficult to manage. Soon after their arrival in America, Julianti discovered that in order to survive, she would have to find work to supplement her husband's income. Fortunately, within weeks, she was contracted to assist with the State Department's junior officer's course, and quickly settled down into the routine of things. Then she met John.

Although John Georgio projected himself amongst his friends as a man of the world, and one full of bravado, before meeting the attractive Asian woman, he had never been to bed with a woman. The moment John saw Julianti smile, he felt a surge of excitement as never before and they had begun their sudden and passionate affair. John had been accepted into the State Department as a junior officer in training. The United States Government had planned to send their young career officer to Indonesia upon completion of his language training but security checks had uncovered his romantic attachment to a national from the target country, and John Georgio was advised that he had been slated for a tour of Korea.

Furious with the Department's decision, but too totally engrossed with the first woman in his life, John resigned from the State Department. Julianti had told him stories of opportunities in her country and, without giving the matter too much more consideration, John announced to his family that he intended leaving for

Indonesia.

Georgio's parents were beside themselves. His parents had been born in Sicily and had migrated to America in search of a better life for themselves. They had been so proud when their son John had been accepted into university on a scholarship, and even more so when he went on to graduate with a degree in commerce. As his family attempted to come to terms with the shock of his announcement, one of their Sicilian friends initiated enquires and discovered that there was a small foreign investment company for sale in Jakarta. John's mother was only too happy to arrange the necessary funds for the acquisition. She was pleased that her youngest son had finally found a woman, and would soon be married. She could not know that Julianti was still tied to a husband who, at that time, was totally ignorant of his wife's infidelity. Less than a month later, John Georgio accompanied his mistress to Indonesia to take control of the fledgling marketing company recently licensed by the Government. After six months, the business had failed to take off and John recognized that he'd made an error in judgement, discovering that he really had no business acumen at all. Now he fervently wished he'd remained in the comfortable position he had enjoyed before being enticed into Asia by this beautiful woman.

He couldn't help blaming Julianti for the whole sorry mess. Not long after he had taken-up residence in Jakarta and arranged his affairs, Julianti's husband had come looking for them both. There had been numerous encounters and, on each occasion, the scenes had been ugly for them all. The Indonesian journalist had phoned him at home and embarrassed him in his office, screaming at the American who had stolen his wife. John had foolishly belittled the man by flaunting Julianti publicly. She had even agreed to move into his house in Menteng. So, not a month after they had returned from America, Julianti's husband decided to kill his wife's lover. He borrowed a revolver, and waited outside the small residence off Jalan Waringan, hoping to catch the man as he came out of his house.

On that Sunday John had taken Julianti for a drive to Bogor. His house guest, a fellow American who happened to somewhat resemble Georgio in build and facial features, walked out of the premises and was immediately confronted at a distance of some thirty meters by Julianti's husband, who pointed his revolver at the foreigner, and fired five times. Incredibly, he missed.

Devastated that he had failed to kill his wife's lover, he then took his own life with the remaining bullet, then and there on the street. John returned later that day to learn what had happened. The journalist's body had already been removed, and John's house guest had fled to safer accommodations. The following week, having discovered his real financial position, Julianti walked out.

As John lay reflecting on these events, he heard a horn sound outside. He rolled out of bed slowly, and looked back at the firm, brown body occupying the other side of his bed. The thought crossed his mind that he should send her on her way before leaving for his afternoon start in the office. John looked around the bedroom and decided that this would be best. His Dean Martin collection lay stacked against the wall, and he knew leaving her alone just wasn't worth the risk. He woke the girl and commenced his daily exercises, believing that this workout always impressed them. First he lifted the smaller weights, exercising his biceps and pectoral muscles. Then, standing half-naked in front of the attractive Indonesian girl, he crouched, lifted the weights, then snatched the twenty kilos up in one well-practised movement. He repeated this action while counting aloud for her to hear, finally placing the weights on the floor when he'd reached twenty lifts. John then looked at the girl and smiled.

'John, you are so strong!' she said, realizing her cue. Pipi had been told by her girlfriends that the American had a considerable ego problem and reacted well to positive comment. John expected the admiration, and she was only too pleased to make him happy. At least until she'd been paid. *'John, you look so handsome when you lift those heavy weights. You must be tired, John, no?'* Pipi had been well briefed. The constant flow of hookers had only increased their pool of knowledge regarding their American client. She knew what would happen next. The other girls had told her, laughing as they explained precisely what John would do after this, or that. He turned and drew a deep breath, filling his barrel shaped chest.

'Tired? Are you kidding? Hell, I could do this all day!' he boasted, as he bent down and pulled the weights back into position. Pipi's girlfriends had said that he would peak before thirty more pumps the second time around. They had all laughed conspiratorially, as

several of their number related similar incidents. One girl had shown the bruise marks across her chest, the result of John losing control of the weight while trying to impress her and dropping the heavy barbell across the bed. Fortunately, the soft mattress had taken most of the force, and her injury considerably less than that of the American's pride. Pipi counted as she watched the foreigner's veins swell under the exertion. She wanted to giggle but knew this would only result in his losing his temper and her foregoing the five dollars he'd promised for the night.

'Thirty!' he called suddenly, dropping the weights loudly to the floor. Pipi knew it was less than twenty-five but didn't care whether he cheated himself or not. It was only important to her that he did not cheat her when the time came to leave. Some of her friends had warned that he often refused to pay and then became violent. She looked around the room and saw evidence of what she believed to support this gossip. There were photographs of men dressed in military uniforms from some place called Vietnam. Pipi could read the annotation at the bottom of most of the photos of what she expected were John's friends, as he did not feature in any of these black and white images, which hung lifelessly on two of his bedroom walls. Most, she could see, had been autographed. Pipi had thought it strange, remembering the wall hangings in the other rooms, that John had not placed any of these photographs in the dining room or other entertainment areas for his other guests to see. Pipi was not to know that John had never served in the military, let alone even visited Vietnam. In fact, apart from his most inadequate appendage, he had never even held a weapon in his hand.

She clapped playfully, continuing to play the game. John smiled. He could see that she was impressed.

'Okay, time to mandi,' he called, heading into the en-suite to shower. 'You should join me,' he added, strutting towards the bathroom. Pipi knew that this was not a request. She sighed silently and rolled off the bed to follow, hoping that he would not want her to do it again in the shower. As she entered the cubicle and saw John's flaccid half erection, Pipi took the soap and held the sweet scented cake between her hands while avoiding his eyes. She moved under the warm stream of water and closed her eyes. Suddenly, she felt John's hands grasp both sides of her head, and she offered no resistance as he forced her to the shower's floor. Pipi then felt John lift his body up against her face. She dropped the soap and placed her hands under his genitals. Pipi knew what was expected of her, guiding his member into her mouth, pleased that its size was nothing John would wish to brag about. Less than a minute passed when she sensed John tremble, then groan deeply. Pipi had prepared herself for what would follow, willing herself not to choke and heave as she had done earlier. Suddenly she could not continue, pulling away from John's strong grasp, unable to breathe, as her body convulsed and she dry-heaved.

'You bitch!' she heard him scream angrily, as he struck her face savagely with the heel of his palm, smashing her to the floor. Stunned, Pipi lay in shock, as she sensed him step over her prostrate form and leave the shower. She was not sure what to do next, waiting for John to return, too terrified to leave the bathroom. Minutes dragged by, and the water became cold, causing Pipi to shiver. She continued to listen for familiar sounds, but could not hear anything which would identify that John remained in the adjoining bedroom. Groggy from the blow but convinced that she could not remain where she was, Pipi rose, turned the shower off, and listened again for movement. Unsure of what might lie waiting for her in the next room, Pipi slipped the catch across, locking the bathroom door. Then she towelled herself dry, and sat on the toilet to think, while cursing her stupidity for believing her girlfriends convincing stories regarding the American.

It seemed that she had been sitting there most of the afternoon when she decided that she had no other choice but to brave it out and just leave, even if it meant confronting the man she now despised.

Aduh! she thought, *wait till I get my hands on Titi and her other friends. So much for the great time,* she remembered miserably, *he couldn't even get a full erection!* If he was still there and hit her again, Pipi decided, she would just run outside and scream. She rubbed the side of her head. Her left temple throbbed less from the vicious blow, and she knew that bruising would become apparent as the hours passed. She unlocked the bathroom door, peered into the bedroom, and was immediately relieved to discover that she was alone.

* * * * * *

John Georgio had left Pipi to cool her heels while he went out and filled in some time alone. *She would still be there when he returned*, he thought smugly, while driving the General Motors Statesman through the lunch-time traffic. He glanced down at Pipi's clothing and a smirk creased his face. Georgio had ensured that she would remain behind in his villa. He drove up and down Jalan Thamrin twice, annoyed that no one had waved to him. *Where was everybody?* he wondered petulantly. Deciding that those of any note were most probably at the Hotel Indonesia Baris Bar, he drove back up to the *Selamat Datang* statue, cut across the traffic and entered the main hotel driveway. Spotting a group of foreigners emerging from the expansive lobby-reception area, he waited until they stood within sight, then sprang out of his car and threw his keys to the surprised parking attendant.

'Leave it there!' he demanded loudly, and ran with small, almost effeminate steps up to the foyer. The affectation was not lost on the two journalists who were also heading for the Baris Lounge Bar. They had had seen it all before and veered away to avoid having to be seen talking to Georgio in public. John noticed the snub but elected to ignore the men. He disliked journalists. He believed that they had deliberately treated him with scorn as a result of his indiscretions with the wife of one of their colleagues. John entered the bar, observed that it was too early to bum a drink, waved to the cringing waiters, then left. He knew there was little point in visiting his office; he had but a few clients, and nothing was scheduled for the rest of the day. He then drove down to the Sarinah department store where, out of boredom, he harassed the staff for an hour before returning to his residence.

He parked his car inside the driveway, locked the doors and entered the house. He looked around the lonely guest room and decided that he really hated the place. Then he smiled in anticipation, visualising what was waiting for him inside. John opened the door to his bedroom and called 'Pipi', then entered, expecting the girl to be waiting anxiously for his return, as he had yet to pay her for her visit.

The smile on John Georgio's face turned instantly to anger as he discovered that Pipi had indeed departed, obviously taking whatever of his clothes she considered necessary to cover herself. She had taken his razor to everything else left hanging, reducing the clothes in his meagre wardrobe to shreds.

Chapter 2

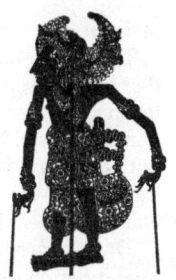

The Salima Group

'And why should we form a kongsi with them?' Lim asked, uncrossing his skinny legs then rubbing his calf muscles to restore the blood flow. He waited for his cousin to respond.

'This man will be the next Chief of Army staff. He will unlock many doors for us,' the man replied. Lim snorted. He knew that he really had no choice. Commerce in Indonesia without the support of the military commanders was impossible. He considered the long-term ramifications of having this general in his pocket as well.

'How much will he want?' he asked, knowing it would be excessive. His cousin hesitated. He knew that Lim would balk at the request.

'Five percent,' he answered, waiting for the outburst.

'Bangsat!' Lim swore, calculating quickly, furious that he would have to agree with the general's demand to be paid an up-front fee of half a million dollars against agreeing to the Salima Group being appointed for the supply contract. *'What about our arrangements with Seda?'* he then asked, concerned that there would be a double commission. Although only a peripheral player, Seda had produced several mutually beneficial contracts through HANKAM, the Defence Department, and Lim wanted to keep that relationship alive.

'He will step back for this one. Seda's smart enough to realize that the new army chief must share in the cake. Don't worry about him. I'll set up a meeting and let him know what's going on between Salima and HANKAM.' Lim looked at the man opposite and continued to rub the back of his knees. Prematurely bald and of small frame, the multi-millionaire had the appearance of a roadside pedlar. *Who would have believed,* Lim mused, *that his association with the First Family would have precipitated his becoming the most powerful busi-*

nessman in the country?

It was only after Soeharto had assumed the mantel of President that the self-appointed leader and his team of American-educated technocrats discovered the real legacy which had been left by President Soekarno. The country was on the brink of economic disaster with a foreign debt in excess of two billion dollars. The interest on this massive debt alone exceeded Indonesia's total export revenues, and investment had all but ground to a halt.

Drastic measures were introduced to reduce the country's annual inflation of one thousand percent, and the government embarked on a program designed to entice the Chinese merchants back to the country which, the year before, had denounced their ethnic group for precipitating the events which resulted in the subsequent blood-bath. Although the Chinese were not the primary victims during the slaughter of the communists, they believed that they had been specifically targeted during the post-coup period of ethnic cleansing, and helped perpetuate the myth that so many of their number had died during the purge.

Soeharto's successful coup against the pro-Chinese Soekarno had, at first, been of considerable concern to the commercially adept race. New laws were promulgated restricting their cultural activities, moves which were strongly supported by the indigenous or *pribumi* population. A set of guidelines titled *'The Basic Policy for the Solution of the Chinese Problem'* clearly established what the New Order considered to be acceptable parameters, within which the Chinese were obliged to remain. Chinese language newspapers and schools were closed. Chinese script was prohibited in public places and the government froze diplomatic relations with China, effectively isolating the Indonesian Chinese.

But behind the scenes it was an entirely different story, and the game was played with a separate set of rules. Realizing that the country would falter without their support, the government arranged for a number of prominent Chinese *totok* to be given access to government contracts in return for their financial support. These *totok* were pure Chinese immigrants who had ventured to Indonesia, bringing with them their natural commercial abilities. Once ensconced, they soon developed their own networks and flourished, establishing important contacts with military officers who, in consideration for the *totok's* financial support, provided security to the Chinese traders.

* * * * * *

Lim's early life in China had not been so different from millions of others who had lived, hand to mouth, as economic refugees in their own land. His family had fled before the terror of Japanese occupation, only to suffer under the cruelty of the local war lords. Near to death from starvation, he and many of his ilk had jumped onto boats and become the first real Asian refugees to head for Australia by sea.

As the Vietnamese would discover more than thirty years later, sailing through the pirate-infested waters of the South China Sea was indeed, a considerable gamble. Indonesian, Malay and Filipino pirates waited for their easy prey, boarding the primitive vessels, killing the men and women aboard once they discovered that most of these poor peasants had nothing to offer in exchange for their lives. Lim's boat had ventured into unfamiliar waters and arrived in Java in error. At first, he and his fellow survivors were distressed that they had not reached the southern land with its abundance of gold and opportunities. Instead, he found himself in the filthy harbour of Semarang, where he hustled his way along the streets, as he had in Shanghai and other parts of China. Later in life, Lim learned not to regret the navigational error. Hungry and destitute, he undertook any task, and worked wherever an opportunity for his limited skills arose. Soon, his tireless energy guaranteed his future.

Java's Chinese traders noted his commitment to hard work and respected Lim for the incredibly long hours he laboured to make ends meet. When he had climbed off the rickety, wooden ship, he was a young, penniless man. His early endeavours, and his ready acceptance of the strange culture and people he found himself amongst, laid the foundations for his future in the Dutch Colony. The difficult conditions which prevailed upon his arrival in Java in no way daunted his spirit. He continued to work hard. It was in his blood to do so.

Once he had collected sufficient capital, Lim started his empire as a simple trader working the streets of Semarang selling peanuts and cloves. From there, he worked his way up to trading in soap and medicine which, to his good fortune, presented him with an opportunity to deal with the nationalist forces during the struggle for Independence.

Unbeknown to the freedom fighters, Lim also traded with their enemy, the Dutch. Lim remembered his first major contract with the army divisions based near Semarang. It was there he met the Lieutenant Colonel who, in later years, was to open doors which would, ultimately, provide wealth and treasures even he had never imagined possible.

There was a time, Lim recollected, when he thought he was finished. Both he and the Colonel were caught smuggling sugar, which resulted in the divisional commander being reassigned, in disgrace. He had followed the man to Bandung and maintained their relationship but, for some years, there was a financial drought as his sponsor waited for another opportunity. When it came, the gods smiled on them both.

Lim recalled receiving his first summons to the President's home. Since that day, he and his associates had never looked back. But, he also remembered, there had been a *quid pro quo* for the favours promised. Lim realized that the mutually beneficial relationship was only secure as long as the country's leadership remained intact, and in the event of imminent change, he knew he would have to be prepared to divest himself of whatever holdings he had acquired in Indonesia well in advance, or risk losing everything.

* * * * * *

Lim glanced at his cousin sitting across the ornately carved coffee table. Silently he admitted that, had they not been related, the man would not have been entrusted with the few responsibilities he had so much difficulty in overseeing. Lim wished that his two sons were older and could return to take their rightful positions at his side. He permitted his thoughts to wander momentarily as he visualised the teenagers, pleased that they would arrive that day for their summer break.

Although Lim had never attended school, he was determined that his children be given the finest education available. He had sent them to the United States where, he hoped, they would both continue their studies until graduating with a solid knowledge of the West. Lim smiled, recalling that his sons had informed him that they would fly to Amsterdam first, just to inspect the sights. Although this would add considerably to their journey, he did not care that they might be up to mischief on their way back. It was best that they get all of this out of their systems now, he believed, as once they had graduated and returned to assist their father with his growing empire there would be no room for nonsense. He would select appropriate wives for them both when the need arose.

'You will go to the airport yourself,' Lim reminded his cousin to arrange to have them met personally, and driven home from the airport.

Lim's cousin smiled and nodded while receiving his instructions. He genuinely liked the boys, wishing his own children were as bright. He accepted that he had been most fortunate, indeed, when his influential relative had arranged passage for him, aiding in his escape from China. When his ship had docked in Semarang, he was amazed at the ease with which the problem of his personal papers had been handled, and the speed with which his new documents had appeared. In return, he had followed Lim unquestioningly, and was now most grateful that he'd had the wisdom to do so. Totally devoted, he had even emulated Lim and adopted the Salima name. At the time, Lim's compliance with the new regulation demanding that his race assume indigenous names had raised more than a few eyebrows within the Chinese community, as they considered the powerful *totok* exempt from having to comply due to his long-standing relationship with the President.

In 1967, Lim Swee Giok had officially changed his name to Robert Salima. Subsequent to the bloody aftermath which followed the brutal murder and mutilation of the country's military leadership, the Chinese population was encouraged to adopt indigenous names as part of a Presidential plan to reduce ethnic tension. The new President supported the concept of assimilation over integration, and the Chinese moved quickly into line, *kowtowing* to the new leadership. Lim had led the charge and was now enjoying the first fruits of his old friend's sponsorship.

As the two men sat together, sipping the cold herbal tea from miniature cups, a servant entered quietly, moved around the room unobtrusively, checked the teapot, then slipped away again to replenish the empty plate of steamed delicacies which she knew had been demolished by Lim's gluttonous cousin. Cook, and head of all things related to domestic arrangements within the Lim household, the homely servant knew that her master depended on her greatly.

She had followed Lim when he moved his business interests to the capital, taking charge of the new household and its five servants. The woman, although much the same age as her employer, was practically his mother. She doted on the man. Lim had been a widower for some years, and showed no signs of remarrying. Since both his sons had been sent to America to study, the large house seemed even more lonely than before.

The cook heard a door open, then close, and she scurried to the side door in time to observe Lim's cousin leave. When she entered, carrying a large serving of his favourite steamed cake, Lim smiled and nodded at the woman almost absent-mindedly, his thoughts preoccupied with how he would present his new proposal to the President. He was confident that he would secure the support needed for the new cement plants. His flour mills had become a reality and the Indonesian banks coffers were beginning to recover. It was time to make another move. He checked his watch, placed another cake in his mouth, scratched his stomach and rose to head for his bedroom to change in preparation for the meetings scheduled for later in the morning.

As he showered, Lim's thoughts centered on how he would handle the discussions with the consortium, and how he could maintain his majority stake in the project without using any of his own funds. By mid-morning his mind was clear of everything, except what had to be done to achieve the position he desperately needed, in relation to the project's funding.

* * * * * *

The young men shook hands with their *totok* uncle and followed him out to the waiting Mercedes. Their flight had been delayed for almost five hours as the KLM flight plan was altered to compensate for the 'no-fly' zone over India and Pakistan. Hostilities had broken out there, once again, and as both nations were armed with ground-to-air missiles, all international commercial flights were ordered away from the two warring countries. Over-flights were not permitted, and KLM, along with all other international carriers, were obliged to seek clearance to alter their flight path to the south of the sub-continent, crossing through Sri Lankan and Indonesian airspace enroute to Singapore.

Tired from their long flight and lack of sleep in Amsterdam, they were both grateful that their father was out on business when they finally arrived home, retiring immediately after they had consumed the mandatory meal prepared by the old, and doting cook. Within minutes of their heads hitting their pillows, both the teenage heirs were asleep.

* * * * * *

A small village in Pakistan

Thousands of kilometers to the north-west of where Lim Swee Giok's sons lay sleeping soundly, a youth of similar age crouched in fear as another shell exploded directly over his head. Mohammed bin Fuad screamed in fear as the air around ruptured, slamming him fiercely against the ground. *Oh, Allah, please make them stop!* he screamed, but it seemed that there was none who could hear as another explosion followed, then another, until he lay stunned, deafened by the close proximity of the strikes.

Hours passed and as shelling had long ceased, Fuad crawled painfully from under the wreckage and into the night. He did not bid his family farewell. They had all died when the savage bombardment had first commenced. Through the rubble and the acrid air thick with the stench of death, Fuad stumbled on, fighting the excruciating pain in his right arm which hung listlessly, signalling it was broken. Disorientated, scared, exhausted from the ordeal and in fear of the invading Indian forces, he willed his bleeding, unclad feet not to fail him, as he struggled away from the small resettlement village where his family and friends had died. When he fell, he crawled, dragging his tired body across the jagged earth until he reached the top of a small knoll, not two hundred meters above the ruins of his village below.

Fuad propped himself wearily against a boulder, and remained there until the heat of the morning sun drove him in search of water. When remnants of the defeated Pakistani army found his dehydrated body lying prostrate under the sun, the uncovered parts of his torso blistered by the sun, not one amongst their number believed him to be alive. As one of the raggedy soldiers turned the body over to inspect its face, he was astonished to discover that Fuad was, incredibly, still breathing. When closer examination revealed the wounded boy's broken arm, the soldier was tempted just to leave him to die, knowing that Fuad would be excluded from eating together with any others until he recovered the use of his right hand.

Against his better judgement, the Muslim soldier gave him water then tended to the badly broken arm. Having regained consciousness, Fuad joined these stragglers and followed them to the next village where he was given a bowl of mash and ordered to sit outside and eat with the dogs.

* * * * * *

Indonesia

At the close of business that same day, totally oblivious to the Hindu-Moslem conflict which would result in the creation of Bangladesh, members of the visiting Japanese banking consortium appeared satisfied that their shareholders' funds would be secure, and gave Lim the green light to proceed with his plans to construct the additional cement plants. As he stood proudly, with his sons at his side, waving at the departing bankers as they were driven away from their home, Lim smiled contentedly at the outcome of the meeting. Then a frown overtook the smile on his face as he recalled the undertakings he had given privately to each of the bank representatives.

Bangsat, he swore under his breath, totalling for the umpteenth time that day the millions he had committed in individual payments to be paid into each of the banker's Swiss numbered accounts. *So much,* he thought, sighing deeply while wishing there had been some other way. The payments would ensure his position of control in the proposed joint venture. *So much to be paid to those thieving bankers. And it wasn't even their money!* Distressed by how easily the bankers had taken his millions in exchange for their support, Lim decided to ask the President for a licence to start his own bank, wondering why he had not thought of doing so before.

Six weeks later, the Ministry of Finance announced that it had issued a private banking licence to the Salima Group. The new financial institution would be known as the Asian Pacific Commercial Bank. When the bank opened its doors, even Lim could not have envisaged that his new enterprise would become one of the most powerful houses in Asia. And all he had to give away this time, for the licence, was a mere ten percent of his bank's shares.

* * * * * *

During her first months in the capital, Ruswita experienced greater hardship than she ever imagined possible. The city of her dreams, Jakarta, was nothing like she had envisaged. The filth and pollution created by uncaring city dwellers was left to accumulate along the roads, and even the city's governor, Ali Sadikin, appealed to the four million inhabitants to burn their rubbish in home made incinerators to reduce the incidence of disease. Rats as large as cats threatened those who slept outdoors, and flying cockroaches larger than a woman's hand moved through the humid evening air in search of food. Dengue, hepatitis in all of its forms, malaria and dysentery, all contributed to the high death toll of the city. Outbreaks of cholera were common, and several cases of plague were identified by World Health Organization observers.

Ruswita had moved from her first night's lodgings as soon as she discovered that, had she remained, the mamasan would have expected her to participate in the whore-house activities. Embarrassment quickly turned to anger as Ruswita hurried away from the premises, ignoring the obscenities which followed her departure. She had found other accommodations, but these were far from the city's center where she had hoped to find employment.

Day after day Ruswita walked the streets, but there were limited opportunities for one who had no experience. She even sat outside several of the embassies along with hundreds of other hopefuls, offering her services as servant labour in their foreign households. Ruswita soon discovered that this was more or less a closed shop to outsiders, as servants always endeavoured to have one of their own placed within these lucrative households whenever a vacancy appeared.

She made but one friend, Lani, a girl of sixteen whose circumstances were not dissimilar to her own. Ruswita took her younger friend with her on her rounds looking for employment, but as the opportunities for two were even more scarce than for a single applicant, Ruswita returned to her search alone. The cold realization dawned that they would soon have to beg for their food. Lani turned to the streets where, as she was still young, she could earn enough from one casual encounter to feed them both.

It bothered Ruswita that her friend had become one of the thousands of young casualties who had succumbed to prostitution in order to survive but, in typical pragmatic Javanese fashion, Ruswita continued her relationship with Lani who was delighted to share whatever she earned with her older friend.

Attracted by exaggerated stories promising employment, tens of thousands of teenage girls left their villages in search of opportunities which did not exist. Soon their numbers swelled uncontrollably, causing the Governor to declare roadside sex in the three-wheeled *becak*s illegal. His administration then encouraged the more than one hundred thousand prostitutes to move their activities out past the Patimura Cemetery, in the city's southern suburbs, and Ancol to the north. The unexpected result of this action was that the inner-city became a gathering place for the transvestite community. The governor had no difficulty in accepting this change, even agreeing to judge the first 'Queen of the Queens' beauty contest which was held at the Intercontinental Hotel Indonesia, just across the road from where the gay community normally solicited clients. And that was where Lani was arrested during a police clean-up campaign, and where she disappeared, along with many others.

Lani had been taken one hundred kilometers from the city along with some sixty other street prostitutes who had been packed into the back of an open truck, driven far enough to deter the girls from attempting to return, then unceremoniously dumped along a country road in the dark, wet night. When Lani did not return that evening, Ruswita feared that some harm must have come to her friend. Later, Rus learned of the incident from street-vendors who had witnessed the raid. Alone, and even more desperate than before, but determined not to give up hope, Ruswita moved out to the city outskirts where a floating community of itinerant workers camped.

As she walked the ten kilometers to the east, Ruswita offered a silent prayer for her young friend, hoping that Lani would not be so foolish as to return to Jakarta. Hungry, but resolute, Ruswita finally found work during her third day on a construction site in Krawang, an area designated as an industrial zone for foreign investment. The following Saturday, as Ruswita extended both her hands in the customary and subservient manner with her left hand under, and supporting her right, she received her first *gaji*.

This payment of three hundred Rupiah for six days manual work amounted to less than one American dollar and, as Ruswita folded the Monopoly-sized denominations and placed these inside her bra, she sighed, conscious of how rough the skin on her fingers had become from loading and carrying bricks around the construction site. As a treat, she paid fifteen Rupiah to one of the vendors parked outside the factory grounds for the satisfaction of sitting down and eating two slices of roughly cut bread, both of which had been spread with condensed milk, then sprinkled sparingly with colourful, minute particles of chocolate known as hundreds and thousands. The sweet, sickly combination reminded her of those special childhood moments when, on rare occasions, her father could afford to treat his children to the extravagant spread.

As she sat on the small stools provided, almost oblivious to the dust and flies and the ear-shattering sounds of bus horns as the overloaded monsters sped dangerously past, Ruswita wondered if the city children had ever experienced *kampung* life. At that moment several children ran past, screaming *'capung, capung,'* and she noticed that the boy in front was being pursued for the tasty delicacies he carried threaded on a palm stick. She laughed as the others managed to catch the child, and struggled to remove some of the roasted dragon-flies impaled on the simple skewer. Ruswita did not believe that the *capung* the children fought over would be as tasty as the ones from her village.

As Rus reminisced, she was reminded of the first time, while still very young, when she had watched the older children remove the sticky white gum from inside a Jack fruit, and smear this over the thin coconut palm sticks they carried. She also recollected trying to keep pace as the children then ran amongst the banana trees in search of the magnificently coloured dragon-flies, which darted mainly amongst the higher branches. Wistfully, she recalled how fascinated she had been as the children had taken the live insects, twisted their heads as they pulled, removing the entire stomach in one movement, before placing each catch in line on their skewers.

The tantalising images of roasted dragon-fly suddenly blurred as a siren sounded, interrupting her momentary escape. She recognized the signal calling the labourers back to work. She rose, wearily, and drifted back with the others. Ruswita spotted the children she had seen minutes before as they ran past, still yelling and screaming happily as they continued their play. She smiled as one of them ran close by, and she could see that the child clung to several of the cooked insects, with the others in hot pursuit. A pang of regret crossed her mind causing her to falter, and almost trip, as she returned to the hot, dusty conditions.

Within minutes she had all but forgotten whatever it was that had occupied her mind during her break, as she struggled to balance the two baskets of bricks she carried at each end of her well-worn shoulder-pole. Ruswita had learned early on her first day to clear her mind of everything but what she was doing, as those who dropped or damaged bricks were soon dismissed from the site.

* * * * * *

Ruswita was fortunate to remain employed for three months and, as the factory walls took shape and cement render was applied, the loads of bricks which she had carried laboriously, day in and day out without complaint, were replaced by buckets of prepared cement. The palms and fingers on both hands were covered with calluses, and her nails reflected their neglect.

On the day the workmen raised the first timber trusses and placed these in line, spanning the factory's floor, Ruswita knew that her employment there would soon come to an end. She stood, unhappily, wondering what there was to celebrate as the carpenters cheered, bolting the final truss into place. A bunch of bananas was then hung from the frame, and the workers given a few minutes respite from the heat, in recognition of the landmark achievement. A *dukun* offered his blessing, then work recommenced on the last stage of the project. As the final concrete was poured, completing the factory's construction, Ruswita watched in awe as the huge packing crates which had been delivered from Tanjung Priok Harbour were lifted from the long bodied trucks, and unpacked, revealing for the first time the modern equipment intended for installation at the factory she had helped build.

Adding to the occasion, several foreigners wandered around the factory grounds, and the daily labourers ceased working, to stare at the Australians. Only a few of the workers had been that close to a foreigner before, and these had either been missionaries or Russians. Ruswita was not particularly interested in the two fair-haired men; she had seen many of these *bules* back in the city, and around the residential areas of Kebayoran Baru and Menteng when she was searching for work as a domestic. Instead, Ruswita was attracted to what was written on the side of empty crates, and stood beside one of the shipping containers engrossed, attempting to pronounce the words stencilled on the side of the huge boxes.

'That's the name of the shipping line,' a voice sounded behind, startling Ruswita. She turned instantly and found herself face to face with one of the Australians. She had no idea whatsoever of what he had said. Ruswita's face was half-covered by a dirty cloth, protecting her from the dust and cement. Only her almond-shaped eyes could be seen under the conical hat she wore to prevent the sun from burning her face and turning her skin dark brown. Embarrassed, Ruswita dropped her eyes and started to shuffle away.

'You can read?' the *tuan* asked, causing her to stop and look back at the man questioningly.

'*I am sorry, tuan, but I do not understand,*' she responded, hoping that she had not offended this man in any way. Her eyes then darted around the immediate area for help, knowing that there would be none. She heard another voice call out and knew instantly from its tone, that she was in trouble. *Why did this bule have to stop and speak to me?* she thought, distressed, as her eyes watched an Indonesian man hurry over in her direction.

'Did this girl give you trouble, *tuan*?' he asked the foreigner.

'No, no, its nothing like that,' Bill Davidson answered, light-heartedly. 'I just asked her if she could read, that's all.' He looked over at Ruswita and smiled, reassuringly.

'*The tuan asked if you could read,*' the Indonesian said, almost accusingly as Ruswita stood silently, wishing the earth would open and swallow her whole.

'Please tell the tuan that yes, I am able to read, but only our bahasa. Please also apologise that I am unable to understand his language.' As she spoke she noticed the young *tuan* tilt his head slightly as if he understood what she had said. This was translated for the Australian who, at that moment, was joined by his associate.

'What's the problem, Bill?' the other asked, his voice reflecting the authority he held as the joint venture company's general manager.

'Nothing, Neil,' he laughed, 'just a little public relations effort with this one, that's all,' he continued, nodding in Ruswita's direction. 'I was watching her trying to read what was written on the container. Thought she might speak some English, but apparently she doesn't.'

'Let it be,' the older man said, turning suddenly in the direction of a loud banging noise emanating from somewhere down behind the factory. Neil Thom walked off to see what was happening over there. They had both been in the country less than two weeks and had agreed that, if the plant was to be a success, then it would only be achieved by showing everybody just who was really in charge of the show. Davidson watched Thom stomp away, grumbling under his breath something about the place being the death of him. He turned his attention back to the woman.

'May I go now?' Ruswita asked, annoyed that they had obviously been talking about her, without knowing what she had done to attract so much attention. The interpreter ignored her, coughed and dragged a lump of phlegm from somewhere deep in his throat, leaned away from them and spat. Ruswita noticed the expression on the foreigner's face and smiled behind her face cloth. She remembered seeing tourists react with similar looks of disgust, as they attempted to negotiate Jakarta's irregular footpaths while ignoring the filthy itinerants and beggars.

'What's your name?' Davidson asked, managing another smile. There was something about this girl's eyes, Bill thought, as his gaze moved to where she stood, her feet caked in grime. He guessed that she was probably thirty to forty years old, judging from their condition.

'Ruswita,' she answered, once the interpreter explained what was said.

54

'How old are you, Ruswita?' she was asked. When she told the interpreter that she was already twenty and this was relayed to Davidson, she identified his look of surprise. Ruswita knew that she looked already old. She thought it rude of the foreigner to indicate that he agreed. Suddenly, bored with the confrontation, she turned to go about her business before the foreman decided that her services were no longer required. She started to leave when Davidson, to everyone's surprise, stepped forward and with a quick flick, removed her head-covering, revealing all but the lower half of her face.

'*Siapa sih!*' Ruswita snapped, alarmed by the man's actions. *Didn't this bulé know that one never touches another's head, even that of a coolie?*

'*Tuan,*' the interpreter moved to prevent a scene; what Davidson had done was unacceptable, even if the woman was a mere labourer. Her fellow countryman looked quickly at Ruswita and ever-so-lightly, shook his head at her. She glared at the foreigner, her eyes alive with hate.

'It's okay, it's okay,' the Australian called, raising his hands in submission. He was taken by surprise at her reaction, and noticed that he had drawn the attention of the other workers. They had stopped to see what had caused the altercation between one of their own and the foreigner.

'*All of you, get back to work!*' someone called sharply, sending the coolies immediately on their way.

'*Tell the tuan that I wish to leave,*' Ruswita demanded angrily, as she shook her head and released her bun with one hand, while removing her face cloth with the other. Davidson stood stunned at the transformation. She looked so young!

'Tell her it's okay,' Davidson instructed the interpreter, realizing that his actions had, for whatever reason, triggered the hostile reaction. He smiled at Ruswita who responded with an expressionless face; only her eyes reflected the animosity she felt for him. As the young woman turned and walked proudly away, he asked the interpreter the reason for her anger and was informed, politely, of his *faux pas*. Not wishing to have the local work-force off side from his first day on site, Davidson decided to take steps to remedy the blunder he had made.

The following day he instructed the interpreter to make discreet enquiries about the girl he had offended. He also asked the man to apologise privately to Ruswita in such a manner that would not diminish his authority as the operations manager, while sending a clear message to her that he had not been aware of the taboo he had broken. Davidson was pleased with the forgiving response, unaware that the interpreter, now a personal assistant, had fabricated the story himself.

In fact, when he had spoken to Ruswita, she had lashed him with a tongue even he found incredibly crude coming from such a young woman. To add to his bewilderment in handling the matter, Davidson had then insisted that steps be taken to provide ongoing employment to Ruswita, justifying his decision on the grounds that the woman could read, and might be of assistance somewhere around the office, or even in the *gudang* as a clerk checking stores.

Two months later, when the Australian-Indonesian joint venture company operation in Krawang was inaugurated, Ruswita stood proudly amongst the two hundred employees and applauded as the Governor cut the ribbon strung ceremoniously across the operation's driveway, while announcing that the P.T. Salima Jaya Products Company was open for business. It was the seventh Lim Swee Giok joint-venture company belonging to the *totok* entrepreneur's stable to be given government sanction in that one year.

* * * * * *

Earlier, she had watched as the dignitaries arrived in their splendid cars, and observed the excitement build as last minute preparations were finalized. Ruswita felt a sense of pride at belonging to something so grand and important, wishing that her parents had been alive to witness her achievement. She had been given the position of *gudang* clerk, and had spent an additional six hours each night of her own time learning many of the foreign words which were essential to her position in the store room.

Ruswita had not known why she had been given this opportunity, and her beliefs firmly told her not to question this *karma*, out of fear of negating the good fortune that had come her way. Because of her mixed background, she was often torn between following her Chinese beliefs and adhering to Javanese tradition.

Ruswita had been quite happy standing with the other employees as the official proceedings commenced, even though some of the younger men persisted in teasing her. She played the game, pretending to ignore them, until one of their number actually attempted to place his hand on her bottom. She turned and whacked the youth responsible, hard enough to demonstrate that she was not to be touched, but not so hard that she might have injured the young man. She frowned to show that she was annoyed but then turned and laughed. *After all*, she thought, *who could be angry on such an auspicious day?*

Ruswita was surprised at the brevity of the official ceremony. It seemed that none of the official party, Indonesian and foreign alike, could tolerate the extreme heat under the temporary cover erected for the occasion. She watched with the other employees as more than one hundred guests sat uncomfortably below the army tarpaulin, perspiration flowing freely from their foreheads. When the ribbon was finally cut by the Governor, there was a loud cheer. Ruswita was certain that this was more one of relief than applause in recognition of the event. The guests had then been invited to join in a traditional feast, which lay in readiness inside a section of the factory, sealed off specifically for the function.

As the thirsty gathering moved inside the factory, Ruswita and others who had been instructed to assist with the service moved away from the employees section, which had been cordoned off from the official area, and hurried into the guest area to support the catering staff. She felt privileged to have been given this additional responsibility, and was not in any way daunted nor intimidated by the close proximity of the wealthy and influential guests. As she moved quickly amongst their number, Ruswita removed empty glasses and plates, and fetched whatever she was asked, although most of the requests were totally alien to her ears. She marvelled at the capacity of the foreigners to consume alcohol, noticing proudly that none of the Indonesians she had seen present were drinking beer or the other mixtures she had so much difficulty pronouncing.

As the function progressed, Ruswita noticed also that most of the Indonesian guests had already excused themselves, and that the remaining number were mainly *bulé*, the white foreigners. She also observed that the general demeanour of these people had progressively deteriorated, becoming loud and discourteous. She was most surprised at their behaviour, having never witnessed such a gathering before.

Towards late afternoon, tired and already indifferent to what had been exciting just hours before, Ruswita was about to slip away when she noticed her general manager, Neil Thom, waving in her direction. Immediately, she hurried to where he was standing with several other foreigners, and looked to see if they required further drinks.

'Well, fellows,' she heard him say, 'do any of you require anything more?' Ruswita saw the group of men laugh, one of them said something which she did not understand, with which they all burst out laughing. Puzzled, she looked at *tuan* Neil, her general manager, confused as to what was expected of her. He said something else which only attracted more laughter. Observing that their drinks were finished, Ruswita went in search of one of the waiters. When she returned, the group were engrossed, huddled together in discussion and, as courtesy demanded, Ruswita waited for the man who had the other guests' attention, to finish speaking. He stopped, and suddenly the group broke into raucous laughter.

'Ah, you're back, my dear,' the now inebriated Thom announced, reaching for her elbow and pulling her towards the group of men. Her immediate reaction was to pull away, stepping back to permit the waiter to serve the group. She felt her face flush with embarrassment. As she looked up at the general manager, she could see that he was angry with her response. One of the other men said something which caused more laughter, but Ruswita could see from the scowl on *tuan* Thom's face that he was angry. He said something to the others, then turned to her.

'Where you work here?' he asked, attempting some form of pidgin English, believing that this would make him understood. It had worked for him in New Guinea, and he obviously believed it should also work here. Ruswita thought she understood what the question was, and replied.

'*Gudang, tuan.*'

'Oh,' Thom said, turning to the man who had offered the earlier, and offending remark. 'The *gudang!*' He paused for a moment, then muttered something to the others about waiting. Ruswita understood just the one word. She looked at her employer and became concerned that she had done something to warrant so much attention. 'I'll be back shortly,' Thom had said to his fellow conspirators, one of whom winked at Ruswita, causing her to blush. She felt frightened and looked around quickly for an excuse to escape.

'Ruswita,' she heard Thom say, 'You, *gudang,* now!' Obediently she turned, knowing that she had been told to go to her place of work. Completely confused, but greatly concerned that she had done something dreadfully wrong, Ruswita walked around the remaining guests and made her way along the factory lines, passing through the three separate stations until coming to the rear of the machinery line. She took her key and opened the door marked '*gudang*'.

Uncertain about what to do next, she waited alone expecting one of the Indonesian floor foremen to come and tell her that she had lost her job for offending the foreign guests somehow. As the minutes dragged by, the more convinced she became that she had committed some grave error, for which she would most certainly lose the only opportunity she might ever be given. She sat silently, waiting.

When the galvanised door opened and Neil Thom stepped inside Ruswita was surprised. She had expected to be dismissed by one of the senior Indonesian staff.

'Ah, there you are,' he said, the words meaningless to her as she watched, without concern, her general manager pull the bolt across the door. She stood as he approached, not understanding how she was expected to communicate with the senior foreign manager. She lowered her head and clasped her hands in submissive gesture, prepared to plead for her job. When she sensed that Thom was much nearer than she had expected, Ruswita suddenly became frightened and started to move away from his bulky figure.

In that moment, the near-drunk Australian lunged, his huge hands gripping her upper arms while his weight carried him forward, falling to the store room floor with Ruswita directly under his huge frame. It had happened so quickly she had no appreciation of what was really taking place. Her head hit the concrete floor. Simultaneously, her attacker's weight crushed the wind from her lungs as they fell heavily together to the ground. She struggled for consciousness, unable to understand why this was happening to her. She cried out for help as she slipped in and out of consciousness, but all she could sense was the foul smell of his breath as his face came into focus. Her scream was choked as Thom slammed his hand over her mouth.

He moved his weight and forced her legs apart while groping under her *batik kain*. Once his fingers touched the flimsy undergarment he tugged frantically, his excitement growing as the woman under him struggled. He pulled at the belt holding his trousers, and using his free hand pulled himself free of the clothing. Thom looked down at the helpless body underneath and grunted as he shoved himself forward.

Ruswita felt the shock of extreme pain as her attacker penetrated her body, but she could not scream. Her muscles froze in response to the unprepared entry. As the brutal rape continued, and unable to breathe with Thom's hand covering her mouth and nose, Ruswita finally succumbed to enveloping darkness, and lay motionless on the *gudang* floor.

* * * * * *

When consciousness returned, Ruswita was startled at first to discover that she was shivering with cold. Then, the memory of the attack came flooding back and she dragged herself to her knees, checking her body carefully to see how much damage had been inflicted upon her. Satisfied that she would live, she retrieved her partly torn panties and slumped to the floor crying in despair.

* * * * * *

Over the following week Ruswita continued to work in the storeroom, full of trepidation that she might still lose her position in the company. Only once during those days did she sight the man who had viciously raped her, and fortunately it was only from a distance. As that week came to a close and was followed slowly by the next, Ruswita assumed that she had been forgiven, and that her employment was secure. Then, in the third week, she was summoned by the administrative clerk up on the management floor. She sensed that she had arrived at the end of her wonderful dream, believing that she was finally to be dismissed. Instead, to her complete surprise, her fortunes changed.

When Ruswita learned that she was to be moved upstairs for further training she was ecstatic with joy. At the end of her first week, following instructions to remain back to complete work given to her by her superior, she discovered why she had been promoted. Alone in the management office, and determined to complete the additional tasks she had been given, she had not thought that she might be in danger.

During the early evening Ruswita was again abruptly raped by Neil Thom. Although it lacked the viciousness of his earlier attack, Ruswita suffered the unseen bruises of helplessness and despair. She prayed that he would leave her alone, and avoided working back late even when she knew her refusal to do so was noted. For weeks she lived in fear that he would do it again. She knew that it would not be possible for her to complain. Who would believe her? And then, for reasons she could not understand, Thom never bothered her again. At the end of the following month, Ruswita knew for certain that she was pregnant.

* * * * * *

Lani entered the compound and stood in line with the other applicants. It had been less than three weeks since she had been released from the Bandung rehabilitation centre for prostitutes, and already she was considering the advantages of returning to her profession. But Lani knew that she would have to wait; the prison abortion had not gone well. It had been her second, and the ensuing infection had removed any possibility of her ever having a third pregnancy. Lani realized that she had almost died and, although the detention centre provided few creature comforts, she accepted that her time inside most probably saved her life. Unable to pay for an experienced abortionist, Lani had resorted to using the damaging and dangerous massage technique, and she had haemorrhaged badly.

Upon her release, she returned to Jakarta, deciding to at least attempt a different line of employment but, in the capital's competitive market, and without any real skills, Lani found herself working once again, as a prostitute. She applied to work as a hostess at the LCC, the military owned club built almost at the foot of the Merdeka Square Freedom monument. The manager had not thought her attractive enough, and suggested she apply to the La Paloma, just down the road. Lani was immediately employed as a hostess, and for awhile, she enjoyed working in the night-club, even though this invariably involved sleeping with the guests. At least, she had thought at the time, she was not back out on the lonely, and dangerous Jakarta streets.

Then, one night, the La Paloma was closed, and the girls all found themselves unemployed. Several of the more attractive hostesses found work elsewhere; some were fortunate enough to have foreign boyfriends who took them in, overwhelmed by the attention the young and sexually experienced girls provided, whilst others, unable to face life back on the streets, simply overdosed themselves swallowing Mandrax cocktails, or drinking straight Mortein.

Lani found work in a small club in Cikini, called Club Sixty-Nine, where the management were not so fussy about personal good looks. She had worked there for just a few months until a drug raid closed the questionable establishment, and she had nowhere to go. Arrested for vagrancy yet again, Lani was taken out of the city along with hundreds of others, and dumped, this time in the mountains, not far from the provincial city of Sukabumi. She returned to Jakarta within days, deciding to take whatever work she could find. Anything, that is, except selling herself alongside the road.

* * * * * *

She waited impatiently until her number was called, then followed the security guard into the building. The factory needed more sweepers, and Lani was desperate to establish some form of employment record without which, the government would not issue a new identification card to her. She decided to take whatever was in the offering, work for three months, then apply for the card. The government had started to crack down on the movement of people between provinces and, with her history, Lani knew that she would most probably have only one more chance to remedy her employment record with the police. She followed the guard into the factory, up the stairs, along the wooden passage-way and into the room. Lani lowered her head and waited to be spoken to.

'What is your name?' she was asked.

'*Eri,*' Lani lied, knowing that her name would simply be annotated somewhere amongst the list of hundreds of others who had applied and, as she had no identification, there was little point in using her old name. Besides, she had decided to change it anyway, not having had much luck as Lani.

'*Where do you come from?*' Again she answered. She wanted to smile. Undoubtedly, the other applicants were illiterate and therefore unable to even write their names, let alone complete an application form. Lani remembered that both her parents used to 'sign' their names back in their village by placing their thumbprints on whatever required their signature. She looked up at the woman who was conducting the interview. There was something familiar about her voice. She stared for a moment and then raised her hands over her mouth. It couldn't be!

'*Where do you live?*' Ruswita asked, and waited for the woman's response. When there was none, she looked up at the other woman and raised her eyebrows, indicating that she needed an answer. '*Where do you live?*' she repeated.

'*Rus?*' was all that Lani could manage. '*Rus, is that you?*' For a moment the room became quiet as Ruswita sat staring at the figure before her. She did not recognize the other person.

'*How did you know my name?*' Ruswita asked, almost testily. She rose and leaned forward towards the applicant, still unable to identify who she was.

'*Rus,*' Lani said, her face breaking into a huge smile, '*Rus, it's me, Lani!*' she cried, raising both hands to her face in excitement as she advanced on her old friend. Ruswita leaned back in surprise.

'*Lani?*' she gasped, stretching her neck forward without wanting to get too close to the raggedy woman. '*Really?*' she shrieked, throwing her hands out wildly, and running forward to embrace her friend. They hugged, then Ruswita stepped back and held Lani at arms' length, looking at her. She shook her head in disbelief. Rus could not accept how the young woman had aged so. Then she stepped forward once again, and held Lani tightly.

'*Oh God, Rus, it's really you!*' Lani cried, the tears streaming down her cheeks as they continued to hug each other. Rus remembered where they were and glanced quickly to her left, and right, to see if they had been observed. Then she turned back to her friend and held her by both hands. As she stared at the old friend who had once sold herself to keep them both alive, an idea formed in her mind. Lani might just be the solution to her own difficult problem, one which was in danger of destroying her life, and career.

'Lani, you can't have this job,' she said, and before Lani's lip dropped any further she squeezed her hands and added, 'I have something much better for you.' This was greeted by a look of uncertainty.

'Why can't I work here?'

'Wait for me outside the gate. No, better still,' Ruswita decided, 'go home now to my boarding room and wait for me. We'll talk there.' Lani waited while Ruswita wrote her address down and, dipping into her purse, extracted ten, one hundred Rupiah notes.

'Take this and buy some food for yourself,' Rus said, handing the money to the destitute girl. 'Show this note to the security guard outside the main gate and tell him that I said he was to call a becak for you.' Lani was staggered by the suddenness of events but she accepted the money and smiled.

She did as instructed, stopping on her way briefly at a roadside stall where she hungrily gulped a bowl of *bubur*, before continuing on her way with the porridge settling comfortably in her empty stomach. When she arrived home later that afternoon, Ruswita was pleased to find Lani sitting on the front steps, waiting. The landlady had refused to permit the dirty vagrant inside.

Ruswita quickly remedied that situation, making arrangements with the stern old woman to permit Lani to remain there for the time being. Reluctantly, the owner had agreed, but reminded her tenant that she would not tolerate having men visit her house. Ruswita and Lani both giggled in conspiratorial manner, Lani almost was unable to contain herself as she just could not imagine Ruswita bringing a man back to her bed. That night, however, when she learned of Ruswita's predicament, Lani held her friend close and they cried.

Ruswita was well into her fifth month. She knew that it would be impossible to hide her secret much longer. She had to make a decision, soon, or risk losing the limited security she enjoyed at the factory. Ruswita knew that it would be impossible to expect the man who had raped her to take responsibility for what he had done, although she hoped that she might just have sufficient leverage to seek at least one favour. She was determined to keep her secret from everyone except Lani, whose assistance would be vital when the baby arrived.

The following morning Ruswita gave her friend some of her clothes and several thousand Rupiah she had saved, insisting that Lani go to the markets to buy material for herself. They would sit at home together at night and sew; there was little else to do with their limited resources.

During the following days Ruswita waited for the opportunity to approach Neil Thom with her request. The general manager spent relatively little time at the factory, and his presence was rarely missed. Neil Thom believed that his role as an expatriate executive required that he visit the company's operations briefly in the mornings, after which he would congregate with his peers at The Cellar Bar, one of the few expatriate watering-holes outside the Intercontinental. Gathered there, Thom and his drinking companions would dominate the bar for the greater part of the day, often running monthly bar-tabs in excess of their own basic salaries.

As managers, they approved their own incredible personal expenditures, justifying these as necessary public relations overheads. Of course, whenever these costs were questioned by the Indonesian joint venture partners, Thom and the others would become indignant and threaten to resign, arrogantly believing that their presence was essential to the operations, as the local partners would be unable to manage such sophisticated ventures without their expertise.

It was not until Friday that Ruswita finally gathered sufficient courage, and approached Neil Thom with her request. She knew from experience that he would be anxious to leave the factory early that day as, unlike the local staff, the foreign employees were not obliged to work on Saturdays. Ruswita waited for the general manager to settle down in his office before entering and taking a cup of steaming Java Robusta with her. Thom looked up as she entered, surprised that the secretary brought coffee for him.

Privately, he had regretted what he had done to the young woman some six months before, even deluding himself that had he known she was a virgin, he would not have considered touching her. His guilt had been the reason for her advancement. Having organised her promotion, his conscience was somewhat salved. As her later behaviour towards him was devoid of any acrimony whatsoever, Thom assumed that Ruswita had put the incident behind her, and was grateful to him for the new-found security she so obviously enjoyed. He admitted that he had been surprised with the energy she displayed when attending to her duties.

The general manager was even more surprised that she had managed to become reasonably fluent in English within such a short time and, although reluctant at first to accept Ruswita as his personal secretary, Thom silently acknowledged that she had been a perfect choice. He had already lost two personal assistants, wooed away by other foreign companies desperate, as was his own company, for qualified local staff.

He watched Ruswita place the coffee to the side of the large blotting pad which occupied most of his desk, noticing that there seemed to be something different about her appearance. Thom thought that she looked healthier, somehow, then remembered that the woman was most probably eating decent food for a change, now that her salary had been increased in line with her promotion. He tried to recall how much that would be, remembering that his last secretary had been paid close to thirty dollars each month.

"Anything for me to read or sign?' he asked, lifting the coffee to his lips. He noticed Ruswita hesitate before responding. Neil Thom sipped the thick, hot coffee carefully. *Why couldn't they drink instant like civilised people?* Thom believed the traditional coffee tasted like mud. 'Well?' he prompted, placing the black, un-sweetened coffee back on the desk.

'*Tuan* Neil, I wish to speak to you please,' she blurted out, knowing that if she hesitated all would be lost. The general manager's face clouded, but she continued anyway. '*Tuan* Neil, I wish to ask for your help,' she paused, searching for the appropriate words. *Sialan!* she thought angrily, she had practised for hours and now she couldn't remember how to say it without angering him.

Neil Thom sat glaring at his secretary. He'd often wondered when she would raise what had happened. *Hadn't he done enough for the girl already?*

'*Tuan* Neil,' she started again, this time more confidently. 'I have to leave my work and return home to Java.' Thom looked at her, slightly confused. Then it dawned on him. Someone had poached her away and he was about to be stuck without a secretary for the third time in almost that many months! He looked at Ruswita, scornfully. *They always said that they had to go home to Java instead of just telling the bloody truth. Why was it that these people always confusingly referred to Java as some other place distinct from Jakarta?* He shook his head in disappointment and Ruswita immediately knew that Thom had misunderstood her request.

'*Tuan* Neil,' she tried again, 'My mother is very ill and is not expected to live more than these few months. Please, *tuan*,' she implored, 'I only wish to go home to Java to take care of her before she dies. I know that I will be gone for some time and ask that you kindly consider giving me work again, after I return.' She dropped her eyes, and sniffed, hoping this might help. 'I know that I might lose my position here but I promise to return once I have seen my mother buried.' Ruswita's convincing tears caused Thom to frown. He would need a replacement immediately.

And there was no way he could keep the position open, even if she was telling the truth. Still, he thought, there was little downside in letting her believe there would be work for her should she return. Perhaps, considering their history, it would be better for all if she didn't return. Annoyed only by the inconvenience of having to find a replacement, and knowing that none of his existing administrative staff would be qualified, Thom shrugged and looked up at Ruswita.

'Okay, Rus,' he said, almost casually, 'come back when you can.' He watched what he interpreted as gratitude sweep her face.

'*Terima kasih,*' she answered, relieved by his decision. 'I will leave after work finishes tomorrow.' As she turned to leave, Neil Thom observed her from behind, thinking that she had indeed filled out, and in all the right places. That afternoon Ruswita made arrangements with the other administrative staff, informing them all that she had been given three months leave to take care of her ailing mother. She then asked the staff if they would agree for her to take her share of the staff *arisan*, an in-house banking arrangement run by employees.

The *arisan* was not run as a lottery. The staff would contribute an identical sum from their pay, at which time all of the names of those who had not yet won, would be subject to a draw. Once an employee had won, they would be required to continue making their contributions each pay-day, until such times as all the participants had been paid. For those who won early in the year, it meant having a substantial advance against their salary. To others who were not so fortunate, they lost nothing, receiving their savings later, rather than sooner. The company accountant normally kept the records, and it was not unusual for one of the staff to request special consideration due to financial difficulty. There was not one amongst Ruswita's fellow employees who had not lost someone in their family, and so it was agreed that she could have the advance. She was popular amongst the staff, and they sympathised with her, not knowing that she was, in fact, an orphan.

Ruswita then approached her last task with considerably more confidence than she had earlier in the day. She entered Bill Davidson's office and explained that her mother was dying, and advised that she would be leaving, temporarily, to care for her. Ruswita then explained that the general manager had guaranteed her position but, sadly, he had not seen his way clear to advance her any of her salary to assist with what most probably would be difficult times for her and her family.

Davidson did not hesitate, extracting one hundred dollars from his wallet, insisting that Ruswita consider the money a loan which could be repaid whenever she was able. Ruswita dried her eyes once again, thanked the operations manager and departed, not even bothering to attend work the following day. Armed with sufficient funds, Ruswita took Lani and moved to other accommodations closer to the inner suburb of Cikini, where the hospital would admit her when the time came. Ruswita enrolled in classes to improve her knowledge of commercial English, and during this time both she and Lani devised a plan which would, in the future, accommodate both their needs.

In her seventh month of pregnancy Ruswita collapsed in pain and was immediately rushed to the Cikini Hospital. There, the Catholic missionary doctors worked to save the premature infant and, in so doing, almost lost the child's mother. Two days after the birth of her daughter, the child was registered by the hospital administration staff. Ruswita named her daughter Ratna Sari, and for the records her father was listed as having died.

The nurses were, of course, sceptical, having seen the paleskinned infant. It was obvious to them that the young woman's child was more likely the result of an affair with one of the wealthy foreigners. How else, they all believed, could she have afforded such expensive maternity care? All agreed that the child's mother, Lani, was a most fortunate woman, having God bless her in this way. Two days after the birth, the real Lani came to the hospital as arranged, and took the pair home. As they drove the short distance to their rented rooms, Lani could not resist giggling at the prospect of being the child's mother, and how simple it had been for Ruswita to use her friend's name at the hospital for registration purposes.

The following week, satisfied that Lani understood what was expected of her, and confident that Ratna Sari would remain under her direct care, Ruswita returned to the factory and asked to be reinstated. Her timing could not have been more appropriate; her replacement had left just days before, citing the general manager's roving hands as her reason for resigning what she described as a poorly paid position. Everyone was delighted to see that Ruswita had returned, and offered their condolences at the loss of her mother. They were also relieved that she had returned to repay her debts.

As soon as her salary had been increased, Ruswita moved Lani and her daughter to a more pleasant location in Tebet, across the railway line from the elite suburb of Menteng. There, they set about establishing order in their lives, caring for each other, and bringing up the baby together.

* * * * * *

Bill Davidson could not believe how quickly his first year and a half in Jakarta had passed. As he sat in the factory office and observed the production line below, he frowned. His immediate superior, Neil Thom, had been putting the pressure on everyone lately, and Davidson could see that the joint venture partners were heading for a major dispute, if the Foreign Investment Board did not assist to settle some of the problems associated with their investment. But it was not Davidson's problem. His contract specified that his responsibilities were to oversee the production line, and maintain the equipment.

Salima Jaya Products had gone into full production expecting a return on capital in less than two years. The Indonesian joint venture partner had assured their foreign counterparts that the Foreign

Investment Board would honour the investment approvals which, *inter alia*, guaranteed protection to the fledgling company for at least three years. He knew that the Australian investment had been predicated on Indonesian undertakings to prohibit cheap imports from Taiwan.

Davidson also knew that there was more inventory of their product stacked at the additional storage facility, than the market could possibly consume. He believed that the joint venture partner's Taiwanese associates had continued to flood the Indonesian market with the identical product to the one his company manufactured under protection of the host government, and that even the tax incentives were useless against the organized dumping of product that continued to take place.

The enigma for Davidson, and his Australian masters back in Melbourne, was *why* their partner had deliberately orchestrated to defeat his own joint venture; surely, they had argued, he would understand that, in the long term, the joint venture would be far more profitable than the short term benefits of smuggling the identical product in competition with himself?

Davidson's thoughts were interrupted as Ruswita knocked, and waited outside the glass door. He beckoned for her to enter, remembering to point his hand to the ground as he waved. He removed his feet from the table, silently rebuking himself for his oversight. Davidson knew that he should never have permitted one of the staff to see him resting with his feet on the desk. It had taken him some time to become familiar with the customs, many still requiring more patience than he professed to have, or wanted to develop. It seemed that there were traps at every turn and, in his mind, assimilation seemed to be a little too one-way for his liking.

After his first blunder, Davidson went on to discover that these local idiosyncrasies and customs were almost endless, and believed that it would be overly ambitious for him to expect to understand them all. Nevertheless, he enjoyed living in the country, even if the working environment was confusing. He watched Ruswita walk in, smile, place the file on his desk and wait. The joint venture was fortunate to have her working there, he thought.

He had often wondered why she had not been tempted away by some of the recent foreign arrivals. And then, he recalled, she *had* once disappeared for several months. At the time, Thom had told him that he could kiss his hundred dollars goodbye making Davidson wish he'd not told the man about the loan he had made to Ruswita. His thoughts then returned to the documents.

'Thanks Rus,' he smiled. *Why did she always seem so distant?* 'I'll go through the file tomorrow.' She never had repaid the money he had loaned her.

'I will bring it back in the morning then,' she suggested, moving to recover the folder.

'No, leave it here.' Davidson said. 'I'll lock it away until then.' He smiled again, reassuringly. 'Goodnight, Rus.' As she turned and left his office Davidson watched her depart. As he had done so many times before, the Australian continued to marvel at the transformation that had taken place, and found it difficult to accept that this was the same woman who had stood before him in the factory yard, covered in dirt, less than two years before. He recalled, with some admiration, how quickly the transition had occurred. Ruswita had absorbed information and developed new skills with such fervour that she had soon attracted the general manager's attention.

During the factory's first two months of operation, Ruswita had moved from stores to the back-office where, within a short period, she had easily mastered the basic skills required. From there she had been moved forward into accounting. He was aware that Ruswita studied at night along with a number of other employees, and had attended the company-sponsored language lessons. The general manager had apparently seen her potential, as Ruswita was promoted to be his personal secretary. All this before the company had even celebrated its first year in Indonesia. Not that there was really anything to celebrate, Davidson thought, returning his attention to the inevitable confrontation between the partners during the first annual meeting scheduled for the following week. As production manager, he knew that he would not be invited to attend the meeting, and for that small blessing, he was pleased.

Ruswita returned to her desk, checked that all was in order, locked the general manager's office and phoned security for her transport. As the senior secretary, she was entitled to company transport, but only between the factory and where she resided in Tebet. Waving as she passed through the side employees' exit, she climbed into the company mini-bus, smiling at the security guard who had opened the vehicle's door for her. She was popular amongst the other employees, and had become a role model for many of the younger girls who discovered that they could always depend on her to listen to their problems.

The fact that Ruswita had not slept with the foreign bosses to advance to where she was did not go unnoticed although, had she done so, none of her peers would have been critical of such behaviour. Without exception, they knew that they were the fortunate ones, having secured employment with one of the foreign joint venture companies. These were tough times, and opportunities were not to be taken lightly. Ruswita had succeeded and they were pleased for her.

* * * * * *

Murray Stephenson re-read the letter and smiled. Zach and Susan had decided to tie the knot at last. He was delighted that they had caught up with each other again after Zach's tour had been completed, when he had been attached to the Defence Signals Regiment in Melbourne. It seemed that young Michael Bradshaw would have some discipline in his life after all, Murray thought, contentedly, not that Susan had done so badly without a man around the house for the greater part of eight years.

Murray looked at the enclosed snapshot and smiled again. Michael certainly had his features. He opened the top drawer of his teak desk and placed the correspondence inside. For a moment he hesitated, wondering if he should place the boy's photograph somewhere in view then, deciding against this, placed the framed photo also in the drawer, locking the contents inside. He had agreed with Susan that the boy should never know the truth. Besides, he had little security to offer a son of that age, and accepted that Zach would provide for the boy both spiritually and materially. Steve Zach was a good man; and a fine friend.

'Telepon, Murray,' his secretary called, then pulled a face indicating that she was not fond of the caller. Murray picked up the phone and wished that he had not dropped his guard that once, and bedded the girl. Now his secretary vetted his calls and even opened his private mail. He had wanted to pass her on to one of the new companies he represented, but she had found numerous excuses to avoid making the move.

'Hello, Fay,' he said, knowing from his secretary's expression that it would be the Australian Ambassador's personal secretary. They had dated regularly over the past few months and Murray was not displeased that she had called.

'Hello yourself. Just a quick call to let you know that I won't be over tonight. There's a stir on here and I'll be stuck sending out cables well into the night.'

'What's going on?' he asked, immediately wishing that he hadn't. They had a pact not to discuss Embassy confidential matters, knowing that to do so would only jeopardise their relationship. Fay realized just how difficult that was for Murray, considering his former association with the government, the time he had served in the Embassy and with ASIS, and his insatiable need to know whatever might affect the current investment climate. She appreciated that Murray had not been tempted to use their friendship to solicit information.

'Busy, busy, busy,' Fay said, permitting the slip to pass. Then she added, 'There's an old friend of yours coming to visit.' She knew that the tease would do the trick.

'I'm all ears,' he said, 'man or woman?'

'Eric Whitehead. Bye,' was all she had time to say before hanging up. Murray pulled the receiver away from his ear and then looked at it quizzically. He shrugged, then turned his attention to the name she had dropped. Whitehead certainly was not to be classed as one of his friends, and he was surprised that Fay would have even suggested so.

Most former agents suffered an occasional attack of paranoia, and Murray was no exception. He thought about the smooth-talking, well-groomed public relations giant and deduced that Fay must have seen an advance advice informing the intelligence boys of his arrival. Murray decided that his name must have been mentioned, for whatever reason, in that same message. His curiosity aroused, he then spent the rest of the day wondering what possible connection he could have with the CEO of Eric Whitehead and Associates' imminent visit to Indonesia.

The following morning it all became clear when he received a call from the Embassy's Political Attaché to arrange a private luncheon at his residence. Murray knew that there were few who knew that the officer holding this position in the Embassy always doubled as the ASIS Station Chief. Murray also knew who else would be present, and reminded himself to thank Fay for the warning.

* * * * * *

'Hello, there,' Whitehead extended his hand to greet Murray as he entered the residence. The white-uniformed houseboy who had escorted him onto the enclosed veranda poured an ice-tea and left the three *tuans* alone. 'It has been some time since we last met.' It was a statement of fact; Murray could still remember the precise moment. It was the evening, some six years before, when his incompetent superior, and Station Intelligence Chief, had collapsed and died not hours after being offered a position with the prominent public relations group. Murray decided not to raise the point. He had attempted to put his former association with the Australian Secret Service behind him.

He had only agreed to this luncheon with Whitehead out of curiosity. He wanted to know why his former associates had arranged for him to meet the man who provided ASIS with its commercial front in Asia. The question remained annoyingly in his mind and he knew that he had to discover the reason behind this unsolicited meeting.

'Yes,' he responded, taking the older man's hand, surprised at the firmness of his grip, 'but I don't believe we had much of a chance to talk.' He added, 'how can I be of assistance to the public relations industry?'

Whitehead smiled, enjoying the man's abrupt approach. He leaned back in the wicker chair and crossed one long leg over the other, deliberately taking his time. He withdrew a pipe, and commenced prodding the pot with a match-stick.

'Why don't we leave that until after we've eaten?' he suggested, hoping for a little more time to gauge Stephenson's current position and activities.

'Sure,' Murray replied, then turned to wave for the houseboy whom he knew would be watching them from a discreet place. The servant appeared immediately and knelt on both knees to the visitor's side, exchanged a few words, listened to the order, smiled and hurried away to prepare the whisky Murray had ordered. The men exchanged small talk until the houseboy returned with the bottle, poured a generous glass of his *tuan's* single malt whisky, and handed this to the guest.

Murray contained the smile which threatened to break through. The houseboy confirmed that the host did, indeed, keep a special bottle of single malt to one side, which he imported directly for his own needs. Murray guessed that the Embassy canteen stocks would not extend to providing such an extensive range of expensive Scotch whisky, and enjoyed his host's forced smile as he raised his glass in salute.

The meal finished, all three men returned to the pleasant patio area, waited for the servant to pour the coffees and cognac, then proceeded to the purpose of the meeting. Ten minutes later Murray was on his way back to his office, angry that the offer had been made. He had stormed out of the residence knowing that had he remained, there would have been violence.

'Well, Murray, it seems that you have not been idle in establishing yourself in the commercial sector,' Whitehead had commenced.

'We do what we can,' Murray replied, glibly. He really did not like this man, and regretted having accepted the invitation.

'Eric Whitehead and Associates wish to make you what I consider, a most generous offer, Murray,' the older man smiled generously as he spoke.

'What do I have that your organization might need, Eric?' Murray returned to the casual style he had adopted during lunch.

'The group would like to offer you the opportunity to join our ranks, so to speak,' Whitehead answered, while observing Murray's face for an indication of how the approach would be received.

'I already have a job, thanks,' Murray responded, not sarcastically, although there was an edge to his voice.

'I'm not offering you a job young Murray,' Whitehead suggested, 'I'm offering you a partnership!' Murray was struck speechless; *had he misunderstood?*

'A partnership?' he asked, incredulously.

'Yes, Murray, a partnership,' Whitehead confirmed. 'We will assume control over your existing operations, for which you would be handsomely compensated. And,' he added, 'you would be permitted to retain forty-nine percent of the Jakarta based operation.' Murray was stunned by the offer, and the man's audacity.

'What would possibly lead you to believe that I am interested in selling my company?' Murray asked, anger now evident in his voice.

'Think about it, Murray,' Whitehead suggested. 'With the support of our organization with its world-wide network, we could point a considerable number of our existing clients in the direction of a joint-Jakarta based operation. You would do extremely well from the arrangement. Hell, we'd even pay you a handsome salary!' he said, making light of the moment. Murray placed his tumbler back on the rattan table and made as if to leave.

'Wait, Murray,' their host interceded. 'There's more to it than that.' Murray looked at the ASIS Station Chief and frowned.

'I'm listening,' he said, coolly.

'We don't have the time to establish a grass roots operation in Jakarta. You are already on the ground, and know what it's all about. It might be wise of you to consider the offer, Murray, before going off half-cocked.' Murray glared at the First Secretary.

'He's right, Murray,' Whitehead added, 'as I said, you would be well compensated.'

'And,' the Secretary interrupted, enjoying his role, 'you might consider the down side.' With this, Murray had difficulty containing his anger. The statement was obviously a veiled threat.

'What down side?' he asked, glancing from one to the other. Whitehead cleared his throat, but it was their host who answered.

'Let's say you elect not to participate in the restructured company. Eric will set up office here, with or without your co-operation and, when they open their doors, without their political clout and substantial client list, yours will most probably close within six months. You would have difficulty maintaining your existing clients. Think about it.' Murray's face paled. He rose to his feet, shaking in anger.

'Mr Whitehead,' he commenced, his voice barely more than a whisper, 'Go screw yourself,' with which, he had turned and marched out, avoiding the temptation to whack their host, the First Secretary for Political Affairs across the head. And hard.

A short time later Murray stood in front of his bedroom air-conditioner unit and closed his eyes as the cool, artificial breeze washed across his face. *The bastards!* He kept repeating to himself, realizing that they could do precisely what they had threatened. Then he turned angrily and drove his fist through the wardrobe door. That night he went out alone and returned to his villa, almost paralytic from the excessive amounts of alcohol the ageing bar-girls had insisted on pouring down his throat until he could no longer stand.

Then they had taken him home and put him to bed. When he was awakened the next morning by a loud banging on his bed-room door, Murray still felt drunk. Then he looked to either side of where he lay and discovered the ugly women who had spent the night in his bed. Ill as he was, Murray woke the women and told them that he would give them each five dollars if they remained inside the bedroom until dark. He didn't want his staff or others to see just how dreadful these women were. They giggled, surprised that he would want them to stay. That had never happened to them before, well, at least not for some years. Pleased with their sudden change of fortunes, they agreed. Murray showered, dressed, and walked across to his office, having locked the girls inside before leaving. He mumbled something to his houseboy who merely grinned in response. He had seen the pair when they had returned with his *tuan* in the early hours of the morning and, even in the darkness of the night, the loyal servant had shaken his head in surprise, and disappointment.

'*Telepon,*' his secretary snapped. It was bad enough that her boss was ignoring her in preference to the *bulé* woman, but this! She had managed to extract the information from the houseboy. All, that is, except the condition of the two girls.

Murray groaned and answered the phone. He struggled to clear his head as he listened to the voice at the other end of the line. He continued for some minutes, mumbling his response, then dropped the receiver heavily into its cradle. He looked up and saw the look of disgust on his secretary's face.

'*Don't start!*' he warned, rising to his feet, instantly wishing that he hadn't. His temples throbbed. '*I'm going out,*' he said, and yelled for his driver. Then he remembered the other problem.

'*Here,*' he said, throwing the bedroom key to the hostile secre-tary, no longer concerned with her reaction to what she would find '*Have someone fumigate my room,*' with which, he made his way outside and into his car.

Murray was at least half a block away from his office and could not, therefore, hear his secretary's screams following him down the street. As his car reversed out of the driveway, she had gone directly into his house and unlocked the door. The women inside were just as surprised as their intruder.

Murray's secretary just could not believe that he would pass her over for the two disgusting creatures who had emerged from his bedroom, demanding money he had promised each of them. Having re-locked the door, she returned to the office, opened the filing cabinet and threw the contents out into the driveway. Then she ripped the telephone cable from its socket, upended the furniture, pulled the calendar from the wall and, in one last defiant gesture, hurled the house keys over the fence into the neighbour's garden. Satisfied that there was nothing else she could do to demonstrate her anger at what Murray had done, she sat on the floor amidst the scattered mess she had created, and broke into tears.

Twenty minutes passed before she rose, wiped her face and looked around in dismay at the evidence of her tantrum. Then she sighed despondently, and went about restoring the office as best she could, knowing that Murray would most probably forgive her for the damage she had done to the company headquarters. The two women she had left locked inside the house would, however, be another matter.

* * * * * *

Krawang industrial estate

Security opened the factory gates as his vehicle approached. Murray was surprised to see a number of metropolitan police inside the entrance and realized that this was not a good omen. As his driver jumped out and opened his door, Murray noticed also that another jeep-load of police waited close to the offices, and these were armed. He walked into the factory quickly, where he found an ashen-faced Bill Davidson sitting alone, both hands clasping his face in despair.

'Okay,' Murray started, 'tell me what happened.' The Australian joint-venture partner company was one of his clients. He received an annual retainer to act in an advisory capacity and provide additional on-ground support to the expatriate managers. This was not an unusual arrangement as Murray had several such accounts. It made sense to have access to his considerable in-country experience; there were few foreign managers with sufficient knowledge of how business was done in this country, and Murray had been engaged to provide guidance whenever called upon by the foreign partner.

'Neil has been arrested,' Davidson explained, apparently in shock. Murray waited. 'As you know, Murray, we've been having nothing but trouble with the partners here. We've got stock coming out of our ears and little support from the Salima management to rectify the problem of Taiwanese products flooding the market. We were guaranteed protection under our agreement, but this has not eventuated in any shape or form. The Salima people insisted that we were too impatient and should not antagonise the Foreign Investment Board. They have accused us of flooding the government offices with complaints, and that this has created an atmosphere in which any support for our case has gone straight out the window.'

'Why was Neil arrested?' Murray asked softly, hoping that his presence would calm the agitated production manager.

'The other day I took a call from Melbourne. To put it bluntly, Murray, they are fed up with the whole mess. Neil wasn't available at the time and so I was given the responsibility of carrying out their instructions.' Davidson paused, as if he was out of breath. He shook his head slowly. 'Melbourne were adamant that the partners have deliberately procrastinated over the market protection issue. Under the operating agreement, the technology remains the property of the foreign partner at all times, or until both parties come to some arrangement regarding our specialized tooling.' He raised his head and looked directly at Murray, knowing that he would not like what he was about to hear.

'Melbourne insisted that we remove the dies from the extrusion plant and lock these away at home until the Indonesian partners came to their senses, and met their contractual obligations as outlined in the joint venture charter.' Davidson stopped, obviously reluctant to continue.

'Go on,' Murray urged. He didn't like any of this, at all. It

79

explained the police presence inside the factory complex.

'When Neil returned, I relayed what the Australian directors had instructed and, to my surprise, he was supportive of their action. To tell you the truth, Murray, I didn't like it, not even one iota, but I had to follow their instructions. After all, when my tour's finished here, I still have a job to return to in Australia and, from the looks of things, that won't be too far down the track.'

'Tell me exactly what happened,' Murray insisted. His mind was already racing ahead, considering their options in securing the general manager's release.

'Well, as I said, I told Neil what the Melbourne office required of us. He instructed me to remove the dies. I had little difficulty doing this as the line has been inactive for almost a week, due to the stock surplus. I told him that there was no way that I would personally take the dies out of the premises, alone. Neil got a little pissed with me and insisted that I help him load the dies into the pick-up. I did. Neil then jumped inside the cabin and drove out through the gate where the security stopped him.' Davidson shook his head again, in a disbelieving manner. 'Jesus, Murray,' he said, with a tremor in his voice, 'the bastards were waiting for us!'

'They knew?' Murray asked, his eyebrows raised in surprise. 'How?' he demanded.

'How else?' the plant operations manager replied, sarcastically. He turned his head and indicated with a nod that he blamed the person sitting calmly in the adjacent office. Murray glanced through the glass partition which separated the offices on the mezzanine floor where management and administration was housed. He turned back and looked questioningly at the other man. 'She was the one who called the police for chrissakes,' he snarled, 'and after all we've done for her,' he paused, then turned and glared in her direction as he added, 'the bitch!'

Murray was confused by the accusation. He had met Ruswita on a number of occasions and thought that Davidson might have been a little hasty in pre-judging the young woman.

'Why her?' he asked.

'Shit, Murray, she is the GM's personal assistant. She knows everything that goes on here. Mate, little Ruswita doesn't miss a bloody thing!' Davidson rubbed his hands together then scratched his head nervously. 'My guess is, she listened to the incoming call from Australia.' Murray thought about this and accepted that it may have happened that way. He knew from experience that staff often eavesdropped, acting on instructions from their Indonesian masters. He sighed.

'Have you spoken to her about this?' he asked.

'What the hell for?' Davidson snapped back.

'Good,' Murray said, 'then don't. It won't help your case, nor Neil's, to have her offside. I'll go and speak to her, then the police, to determine what can be done.' He looked back over at Ruswita who, at that very moment, had also glanced in his direction. Murray smiled, but she did not respond, dropping her eyes quickly away. This was not the reaction Murray had hoped to receive. He looked back at Davidson.

'You might as well prepare to leave for Australia, Bill, as soon as I clear it with the police.'

'But I...' Davidson started to protest but Murray cut him short.

'Can it, Bill. I'm not taking sides here, just advising you what you should do. I've seen the inside of their jails and if you stir them up any more, you might just get to take a look for yourself. What you both did was bloody foolish, but I guess you don't need me to tell you that now. Wait here,' he ordered, then left the rattled expatriate to consider what he'd said. Murray then went directly into Ruswita's office, knocking as he opened her door.

'*Selamat pagi, Rus,*' he said pleasantly, wishing her a good morning. Ruswita smiled but Murray could see that there was no warmth in it.

'Good morning, Mr Stephenson,' she responded, her manner cool. Murray knew that her refusal to speak Indonesian was not a good omen either. 'Are you here as the Australian representative?'

Murray was quite surprised at the woman's impertinence. Ruswita was, in his opinion, greatly exceeding her authority as the general manager's personal assistant. He tried another tack.

'Rus, I am here to help recover the situation between the Australians and their Indonesian counterparts. Would you like to tell me what happened?' he asked.

'Surely you already know from Mr Davidson?' she replied.

'Yes, he told me that he had been instructed to remove some of the machinery parts, and that the general manger attempted to remove these from the factory compound.' He hesitated, not knowing just how knowledgeable Ruswita might be regarding the terms of the joint venture. 'What they did was inconsiderate, Rus, but it was not illegal. The foreign partner continues to own that special equipment…'

'You mean the dies, Mr Stephenson,' she said, surprising Murray. 'I have received instructions from the Salima Group not to communicate with you or any of the foreign partners. I am sorry, but I must ask you to leave, as these are their instructions.'

Murray was speechless that he had been spoken to in this way. Then he realized that he really did not have any legal position to be there, as he was not directly engaged by the joint venture company. If he was to assist the foreign partners recover their position, he would have to take a softer stance.

'May I speak to Salima?' he asked, indicating the phone on her desk.

'I don't know. I cannot say.' Ruswita hesitated, looked around to see if they could be heard. 'Mr Stephenson, you should leave now,' she said, then lowered her voice and spoke quietly in Indonesian.

'I am not ungrateful Pak Murray,' she whispered, using the respectful form of his name, *'but what has happened here is very serious. Mr Salima has informed me that the factory will be temporarily closed. Do you understand that this will mean that more than two hundred people have lost their jobs today because of what the Australians did?'* Murray did understand, and silently rebuked himself for not considering the consequences of the foreign partner's actions. He sympathised immediately with the staff and workers knowing that few of their number would find other employment.

'I am sorry that this has happened, Rus. Are you sure I can't speak to Mr Salima or his assistant to see what might be done to rectify this situation?'

'No, Pak Murray, that is not possible from here. You could always try contacting him at his office, or even home perhaps. I have been instructed to remain here, along with a small maintenance and security staff while the factory is closed. Please go now before I lose my position as well,' she asked politely, and Murray nodded then left. He went down to the police to determine where the general manager had been taken, and discovered that he had been placed under house arrest. Relieved, Murray drove down to speak to him, after which he attempted to contact someone in Salima's office who might be

receptive to discussing the joint venture breakdown.

After hours of sitting, waiting patiently at the Salima Group offices, Murray was ushered in to meet with one of the senior assistants. The man's manner was officious, informing him that the group's chairman had decided to prosecute the Australians. Murray considered the statement but decided that this was but a gambit. Salima would gain nothing from having the foreign employees jailed, but the threat was there, and he knew how the directors in Melbourne must respond.

The Australian company called an urgent board meeting and decided to withdraw from their Indonesian investment, and reluctantly agreed to sell their shares in the joint venture to their Indonesian counterpart. As a matter of face, the two Australians were to be detained for three months under casual house arrest, which required only that they sleep at their accommodations. The Indonesians did not want to be responsible for feeding the expensive foreigners.

The following week both the foreign employees were secretly flown out of Indonesia, via Bali, their confiscated passports still locked in the Jakarta Metropolitan Police Chief's desk. The dies were re-installed by a Taiwanese team of engineers and, within the month, the factory re-commenced operations. Almost the same day, the Indonesian Ministry of Trade imposed a total ban on the competitive, imported, Taiwanese product. Salima's strength, and reputation continued to grow, while Murray's suffered as a result of his obvious impotence in handling the matter. He lost credibility as an astute negotiator, and several of his major accounts moved their business across to the newly established offices of Eric Whitehead and Associates.

Several months passed before Murray admitted to himself that his business was in trouble. He decided to take in a financial partner and offered his services to one of his remaining clients, an aviation investor by the name of Peter Wong. Almost immediately upon signing his new alliance with the millionaire, Murray's fortunes improved as his fellow shareholder encouraged other Chinese investors to deal through their *kongsi*, or partnership. Murray was a viable front for their Mainland Chinese capital.

The Indonesian Government might have been receptive to its own Chinese investing in its rapidly growing economy, but they still had not forgiven Mao Tse Tung's China, for the support it had given to the communists during Soekarno's presidency, and refused to restore relationships with that country or its people.

Chapter 3

John Georgio and others

John Georgio sat across the table facing his visitors, pleased that his presentation had gone so well. John considered himself the only foreigner qualified to conduct surveys and market research in Indonesia and, it was apparent from the gathering's obvious *bonhomie*, that he had the team from Pepsi Cola convinced of his credentials. They had all willingly warmed to his proposal to represent their interests throughout the country and complete a market research study on the company's behalf. The investigating team had arrived over the weekend, and John had played the role of an influential American businessman well, arranging a police escort for the first-time visitors to Indonesia from the airport to the Intercontinental Hotel. The American visitors were impressed. They had checked with the United States Embassy and established that he was the only American in Jakarta who acted as a free-lance consultant, and was licensed to conduct surveys in Indonesia.

John was ecstatic when the delegation's leader confirmed that he would be appointed to carry out their market research. Apart from oil and gas firms, American companies had been slow moving into the new market, as most were still more than a little suspicious of a country which, just six years before, had boasted the third largest Communist Party membership in the world.

John's entrepreneurial capabilities were limited primarily by his inability to really understand how to conduct business in the Asian environment. Although he was conscious of the incredible opportunities Indonesia offered to those who had the capacity to deal within the established, but unspoken commercial guidelines, John's activities were inevitably frustrated by his lack of focus. He had few friends.

Several weeks subsequent to the Pepsi-Cola team's visit John received an advance payment to commence preparing their survey. He threw himself into his work, determined to finally make his mark. And he did. John's limited knowledge of his own target market led him to make a number of dangerous assumptions. Once he had compiled his client's basic questionnaire and received approval for its implementation, John, being Catholic, decided that he would ingratiate himself with the small number of Catholic universities throughout the country by employing their students to assist with his research.

He selected five of these colleges and negotiated directly with the student bodies. John determined that a Sunday would be the most suitable time to find the average household head at home and, some eight weeks later, and on the same Sunday, two hundred Catholic university students hit the streets in their respective cities and towns, each carrying an armful of John's designated questionnaires.

Foolishly, John had inappropriately camouflaged a number of questions which amounted to a political polling of the President, and other senior government officials' popularity. He had not even been paid for this highly sensitive service. John had actually convinced himself that by doing so, the Chinese Indonesian who had made the request would be indebted to him, forever. And, perhaps, even the general for whom they were secretly canvassing the public, in order to determine his popularity. It was obvious to John that this man might be considering a challenge against Soeharto in the forthcoming Presidential elections. During the meeting with Salima's cousin, John was so overwhelmed at having been asked to carry out this favour for the important group, he failed to secure some written commitment. He was later to regret his error.

* * * * * *

In a small town in East Java, a luckless student knocked, almost arrogantly, on the front door of Colonel Suparman's house. The Moslem army officer had been asleep less than two hours, having returned to his wife and family during the early morning hours of the night before. At first, the Colonel told his wife to ignore the interruption. He had not lain with his young wife for more than two months, and was determined not to permit anything disrupt their intimate moment. Unfortunately, the persistent student continued to knock on the Colonel's door which, to his dismay, resulted in a confrontation he could never have anticipated.

'*What do you want?*' the Colonel had demanded. The interviewing student had no idea that the man was in the military, as the officer was clad only in a *sarong*. The young boy could not understand what it was that had angered the man.

'*I am conducting a survey,*' he had answered, enjoying his newfound importance.

'*Survey?*' the angry officer shouted, '*survey you say?*' he yelled, tearing the document from the student's hand, and commencing reading its contents. For a few minutes the Catholic youth stood silently, smugly believing that the man before him was obviously having difficulty reading the survey questions.

'*This is a survey sponsored by our government to.........*'

'*Shut up!*' the Colonel barked. '*Who gave you instructions to ask these questions?*' he demanded. Suddenly the student became confused. He had not encountered such a violent response from any other householder that morning, and felt that the man before him was behaving out of hand.

'*I am part of a nation-wide survey team collecting information valuable for foreign investment,*' he replied, surprised that the man was reading through the complex document. '*If you don't wish to answer the questions then I'll just go,*' he offered, worried that this one stop might cost him valuable time. He had a quota of fifty to complete before the evening.

The Colonel ignored the student, reading on through the questionnaire. Suddenly he stopped, and his eyes opened wider in surprise. Then he frowned, re-read the particular section which he'd found cleverly disguised amongst a number of unrelated questions, then looked suspiciously at the student.

'*Who do you work for?*' he demanded sternly. The student was annoyed with the question. He reached out to retrieve his papers when, without warning, the half-dressed man he had attempted to interview stepped forward, and grabbed him by the throat with one hand. Terrified that he had struck a madman amongst the group of houses selected for the interviews, he struggled, dropped the remainder of his papers, and attempted to break free. But his resistance was in vain. The Colonel was considerably stronger and, within moments, the young man fell to his knees gasping for breath.

'Once more, who do you work for?' the army officer snapped, not accustomed to having such youngsters ignore his questions. He released his grip slightly as the student started to choke.

* * * * * *

While John Georgio strutted around the Hotel Indonesia swimming pool, flexing his muscles, vainly attempting to impress the ladies present, a team of investigators had already gathered in the small Javanese town to interrogate the luckless Catholic student. As John posed and smiled with his new found confidence, the young man who had innocently accepted the research assignment finally collapsed to the cell floor, unable to withstand the savage blows to his head and body.

That evening, as John Georgio stood in the doorway to his house and attempted to re-negotiate with his visitor for her time, a further twenty-eight Catholic students had already been arrested throughout East Java, and incarcerated for distributing subversive material. By the time morning arrived, and John was ready for the start of a new week, more than fifty arrests had been made, and the American consultant's activities in Indonesia were in imminent danger of coming to an abrupt end.

During the course of that week John Georgio's naïve attempt to disguise the sensitive political questions within the Pepsi Cola market research questionnaire was known throughout the country. He received two calls from intermediaries promising financial and political support, conditional that he not involve the Salima Group in any way whatsoever. Understandably, John panicked when called to attend an interview at the Indonesian Intelligence Co-ordinating Agency, BAKIN. There, he was formally served with a deportation order.

Upon returning to his villa, Georgio phoned his limited circle of friends only to discover that their recollection of any association with John had been far more casual than he had remembered. His calls and messages to the Salima Group director, who had encouraged John to compromise the questionnaire, went unanswered. Instead, he was instructed to meet covertly with one of the company's representatives, who confirmed that the Group would take care of his financial needs, suggesting that he should go to Singapore and wait until the crisis blew over, after which time he could return. Salima, according to the intermediary, had given his word. What's more, the man had revealed, John was to have the use of one of Lim's penthouses in Singapore for however long he might need to remain there. Also, there was to be financial compensation.

He was again warned that there was never to be any mention of the Salima involvement in relation to the secret survey they had commissioned. Reluctantly, John agreed, realising that seeking support to overturn his deportation order might only then be possible through the courts. Considering his financial position, and cognisant of Salima's influence within the community, he decided to make the best of the situation and gain as much mileage from his deportation order as he could. But the newspapers were determined to have his blood, and fuelled by the recent memory that one of their own had died as a result of his earlier indiscretions, branded John Georgio a pariah.

Most expatriates suddenly avoided all contact with the American, concerned that any association would be detrimental to their own activities and interests in Indonesia. Desperate, and in need of a friend, John approached the only foreigner in the city who had returned any of his calls. His name was Stephen Coleman.

* * * * * *

In no way did it bother Coleman that his rationale for providing some support to the American had been based on the assumption that he would acquire the Pepsi account, once Georgio had departed. There were a limited number of expatriate consultants capable of providing the representation such a client would so obviously require in the event bottling plants were to proceed.

He had discussed this with General Seda, his sponsor and silent partner. At first, the powerful man had appeared intrigued with John Georgio's machinations but later, his interest visibly waned. Coleman had argued that, although there might be some who would question his judgement in maintaining any association with the American, Georgio's recommendation to the giant Stateside company might just carry some weight when it came to seeking a replacement office to represent their affairs in Indonesia. Seda finally agreed when Coleman suggested that they might then be in a position to influence Pepsi's future decision as to who might be appointed as their distributor for the mammoth market.

On several occasions, Coleman invited Georgio for lunch at The Cellar Bar, and encouraged several other foreigners present to join them. Although uncomfortable with the prospect that they would be seen associating with John, which might in turn be detrimental to their own positions, the fact that Stephen Coleman was prepared to sit with the man was good enough for them. John was relieved that he was no longer entirely alone.

Prior to his departure, and on the very evening his deportation notice had stipulated he must finally leave Indonesia, Coleman secured a written undertaking that he was to take care of John's interests until he was permitted to return. Georgio had been informed, discreetly, by the Salima intermediary, that this would most probably be no more than a few months. As John wished to maintain the Pepsi account, he offered to inform their head office that his interests continued in Indonesia, and that Stephen Coleman's organization would be overseeing Pepsi's affairs on Georgio's behalf.

Coleman personally drove John to the airport. He carried but a few pieces of luggage, truly believing that his sojourn in Singapore would not exceed that which had been promised. He had left behind what few possessions he owned, including his prized Dean Martin collection. John arrived in Singapore and caught a taxi to the Penthouse address where he discovered that the apartment was locked and unattended. He made several calls to Jakarta, but was unable to speak to anyone of authority within the Salima conglomerate. Even then it still did not dawn on him that he was, in fact, fortunate just to be alive.

Confused, he moved in with a friend from the American Embassy and waited. When the rental contract on John's Jakarta residence expired three months later, he still had not been permitted to return. It seemed that all Indonesian Embassies had been instructed not to issue a visa to John Georgio because of his subversive activities in Indonesia. John waited impatiently for the signal that he could return. He survived on handouts from others who listened to his story, and the occasional young and naïve coffee shop waitress who believed his stories of wealth and influence. Finally, as the weeks rolled into months, and months into years, John Georgio turned to the only other work which suited his temperament.

He joined with a group out of Johore Baru, providing hookers for visiting businessmen and tourists into Singapore. It would be another ten years before he was finally given a restricted visa to visit Indonesia again. During that period of exile, John Georgio tried desperately to establish himself within the Singapore community but failed, his reputation as an up-market pimp precluding him from membership of expatriate clubs and social venues. Finally, resigned to his new vocation, he set about establishing an exclusive escort service, which flourished until he was caught providing Malaysian children to a number of foreign paedophile rings. After this, and a number of other skirmishes with the law, Georgio lay low for a number of years, until returning to his old habits, supplying women to wealthy clients. It was at that time that John Georgio became a full time employee of Peter Wong, and took the first steps which would lead him back to Indonesia. And his appointment with destiny.

Chapter 4

Ruswita at work

Ruswita's promotion from the Krawang factory had not come as any surprise to those who had worked with her over the past two years. She had accepted responsibility with ease, and had proved that she had a calculating mind and a dedication to Salima operations. Her quantum leap from the factory to Lim's head office had been a direct result of a suggestion she had made concerning transportation of product from the factory to provincial distributors. Those who attended the meeting had frowned when Ruswita, relatively junior within the new management structure, offered her unsolicited comments.

But later, when it was discovered that her suggestion could reduce the company's reliance on individual transport carriers, she was given the credit for the recommendation that the factory use its own trucks to distribute their product into the provinces while back-loading other Salima Group produce and materials. And there were other changes implemented as a result of her uncanny ability to identify core problems and offer solutions. Within a relatively short time, news of Ruswita's sound decisions had reached Lim's ears, and he moved her directly into his head office where she continued to impress her superiors.

Ruswita discovered that her *peranakan* heritage had become a huge asset. Since she belonged to both the Chinese and *pribumi* worlds, everyone trusted her, and she soon established herself as an intelligent, no-nonsense player within the Salima Group activities. Having served Lim directly as his personal assistant for more than a year, business circles identified Ruswita as one of the select few included in the powerful tycoon's *inner sanctum*. Against all the odds, she prospered.

* * * * * *

Lani continued to care for Ratna Sari as if she were her own, guarding Ruswita's daughter while remaining totally dedicated to her friend. They had become closer than sisters, their relationship further bonded by their affection for the child.

As Ratna grew, and outings together became more frequent, so did the risk of discovery. Ruswita arranged for Lani's papers to be altered, moving her companion's birthplace to her own village. Her name was also altered slightly. A hundred thousand Rupiah resolved this minor identification problem, and the official involved thought nothing of making the necessary alterations to the simple document. He had been making similar changes for years, and sometimes he wondered just who in his country had *not* altered their name. Satisfied that their relationship had been easily obscured, Ruswita concentrated on her career, knowing that her daughter was in safe and loving hands. Lani had become her widowed half-sister, and Ratna Sari was now her niece.

Ruswita's brief career had, incredibly, placed her right at *Mister Salima's* side as *kongsi* after *kongsi* grew, swelling the Salima Group coffers. She had been present when Lim had signed his ship charters with PERTAMINA, the state owned oil and gas monopoly, and also at his side in Hong Kong when he raised an additional one hundred million dollars to finance further expansion of his cement interests. It was no longer unusual for her to be seen travelling overseas with her chairman. Lim trusted her judgement implicitly.

He always insisted on her presence whenever the necessity arose for someone with her command of English, a language the Chinese *totok* had never found time to master for himself. Ruswita gave herself entirely to her career, and Lim appreciated her dedication. Slowly, his dependence on her capacity to also remove tiresome social and domestic problems grew, and even before he understood how it had happened, Lim became totally dependent on the young and vibrant woman.

* * * * * *

Ruswita smiled graciously while accepting the gift. Lim Swee Giok, or *Mister Salima* as he was now known to the foreign investment community, patted her kindly on the knee and returned her smile. As Ruswita carefully unwrapped the small packet and opened the lid of the intricately carved box, Lim's eyes twinkled. He observed the expression on her face, the delicate notes of Mozart's *Elvira* capturing the moment in his private office.

She placed the magnificently crafted music-box on her lap, fighting back tears of joy as she struggled to express her thanks, but words would not flow.

Lim rose from his chair and placed his hand gently on her shoulder. Then, adding to her surprise, he bent down and kissed her on the forehead. Bewildered by the fatherly gesture, she remained still, completely at a loss for words.

Satisfied that his small gift had pleased her, Lim placed his hand inside his pocket and withdrew a small, rectangular case, and approached Ruswita once again. She looked up and smiled, then her eyes fell on the small, unwrapped box, as Lim extended his hand for her to see.

'*Take it,*' he offered, and was surprised that she hesitated. Ruswita *knew* that such a case could only contain a ring. She looked up, enquiringly, completely bewildered by the moment. '*Take it,*' he urged again, holding the case open for Ruswita to see the cluster of diamonds alive with brilliant, tiny beams of light. Mesmerised by the ring's beauty, Ruswita reached out as she had been taught as a child, with one hand supporting the other.

'*No,*' Lim said, taking her hand and pulling her gently to her feet. '*Never again, like that,*' he said softly, understanding the submissive gesture and its origins. He then removed the ring and slipped it over her finger. Ruswita held her hand, her gaze transfixed by the magnificent diamonds

There had been no indication that this might happen. Her relationship with Lim had been one of respect, and the possibility that he wanted more from her momentarily frightened her. She had never even dreamed that such an opportunity might occur; she was stunned.

Ruswita glanced at Lim, uncertain of what such a relationship would bring. She looked at the powerful figure without seeing an older man standing there before her, nor did she consider the enormous wealth and power he represented. Instead, she saw only a man for whom she had the greatest respect, a man who had provided her with the opportunity to realise something for herself when all others had deserted her. Ruswita was suddenly aware that she had been staring at Lim, and broke into an embarrassed smile. He looked at her questioningly and, without further hesitation, she took his hand in hers and nodded her acceptance.

* * * * * *

Murray looked at the calendar and sighed, observing the highlighted dates indicating the end of the Ramadan fasting month, the ninth in the Moslem calendar. His secretary had drawn heavy red rings around the four days to remind him that the office would be closed. Murray knew that he might as well close for a week, or even a fortnight, as staff always managed to find some excuse to delay their return to work. He glanced back at the calendar and observed, with another sigh, that Christmas was less than three months away. Another extended staff holiday which would run unofficially from Christmas through to the New Year. Murray smiled sardonically, conscious that Indonesians celebrated all holidays, regardless of their religious beliefs.

It had been a most eventful year, he reminisced, and one which had thrown Indonesia well into the international spotlight. Murray wondered how much damage had really been caused by the anti-Japanese riots earlier in the year, which had resulted in the destruction of some seventy buildings and hundreds of cars and buses. He knew that the figures relating to the loss of life would never be released, but his sources in government had informed Murray that at least four hundred had been killed by police and riot squads. Murray shook his head; he knew, from his ten years living amongst the Indonesians, that violence lay just below the surface of what appeared to be a tranquil society, and that sometimes even the most minor of incidents was sufficient to spark the dormant hatreds which festered there.

When the riots had occurred, Murray had been hosting a visiting group of investors. They were returning, by chance, from the Foreign Investment Board located in Cut Mutiah when their two vehicles came into contact with a crowd of demonstrators obviously bent on destruction.

Murray remembered that moment all too clearly. He had hired

two large Nissans for the occasion, and was flabbergasted when both vehicles were prevented from proceeding any further, and the occupants ordered to alight. He had gauged the crowd's mood correctly, advising his guests to do as ordered, after which Murray had then mustered the group together, and ushered them away. Murray recalled the look of terror on the foreigners' faces when the Japanese cars had then been torched by the excited rioters. Later, not unexpectedly, he sadly accepted his client's predictable decision not to invest in the politically unstable environment.

Then, as the city returned to normal, the state owned Oil and Gas monopoly, PERTAMINA, all but collapsed. Murray's *kongsi* had committed themselves heavily in the oil and gas industry, investing in supply boats to service the ever-increasing number of offshore drilling rigs, providing credit to what they believed to be a cash-rich Indonesian Government company, to enable PERTAMINA to further expand its activities even outside its charter. The *kongsi* believed it had guaranteed future goodwill by advancing millions of the shareholders' funds to directors responsible for the allocation of contracts and concession areas. Suddenly the balloon burst, revealing that PERTAMINA had accumulated debts in excess of six billion dollars. The company's directors were replaced, but not before they and their families had successfully shifted tens of millions of dollars into their offshore accounts.

Had his *kongsi* not suffered as severely as it had, Murray might have laughed at the discovery that one of the PERTAMINA directors had died, leaving more than forty million dollars in his numbered Asian Currency Unit account in Singapore. Murray knew that the man's official salary was no more than a thousand dollars per month; much of the rest had come from organisations such as his, now lost forever. He knew that the country could not possibly continue in this vein; the national debt had jumped from eight billion to more than thirty, and was still building steam.

What Murray had most difficulty with was the fact that these incredible revelations and incidents just did not seem to matter to those at the top, whose own wealth had become startlingly obvious. He wondered where, or if, it would all end, believing that political instability would demonstrably grow, as the disparity between the wealthy and poor became more apparent.

Murray's thoughts then shifted to Portugal, and the events there that had also taken place in the course of this eventful year. He had followed the bloodless *coup d'etat* which the international press had appropriately named The Captains' Revolution, and wondered how these events which had taken place on the other side of the globe might affect Indonesia. Murray endeavoured to keep himself current with world events; he understood the import of knowing what was happening outside his own sphere of activity.

As his mind wandered, his thoughts strayed to Zach and Susan. He wondered how Michael was faring at school in Washington. Zach had been promoted, and offered the opportunity to move to the United States as Australia's Defence Liaison Group co-ordinator. Susan had been supportive of what could well be Zach's last posting before retirement and had encouraged him to accept. They had called Murray from Melbourne to inform him of their plans, and departed the following month. Now, Murray knew from their recent letters, they were well settled and enjoying life in the American capital. Michael, Susan had advised, had commenced Junior High, and he was delighted that he had not lost a year in the move, as they had arrived during the commencement of the Northern Hemisphere's summer holidays.

Pleased that they all seemed to be getting along fine together, Murray glanced over at the family photograph sitting in its frame on the shelf amongst his books. It was taken outside their apartment in Washington; the ground, he noticed, was covered with snow. Murray sighed and rose to his feet. Trickles of perspiration rolled down his back. He pulled a curtain aside and peered out through the barred window into the front garden, wondering how much longer it would be before the truck arrived with fuel for his stand-by generator.

* * * * * *

Stephen Coleman climbed out of his dark, metallic blue Mercedes 450 and walked up the President Hotel steps slowly. Upon entering the foyer, he observed a rather motley group of foreigners gathered there, unshaven and obviously distressed. He walked past quickly, not wishing to become embroiled in any discussion with the familiar faces, knowing that tempers were normally short at that time of the morning, and that he would be an obvious target for their snide comments. Coleman did not have to suffer the same power difficulties which had driven these expatriates to the President Hotel.

Coleman was aware that, had he ventured into any of the larger hotels which had wisely installed auxiliary power before the extended failure had commenced, the scene would have been similar. The week before, he had witnessed a fight in progress in the Hotel Indonesia lobby where an impatient queue of foreigners had formed, waiting for their turn to use the hotel's lobby toilets. To the rear of the hotel and around the swimming pool, he had seen what would normally have passed as a most comic display of expatriate lunacy, had the water shortage not been so serious.

Foreigners formed lines there too, but to bathe, and even shave. As the swimming pool did not normally open until later in the morning, the hotel management ignored the proceedings as many of the these unfortunates had, most probably, at some time or other, been paying-guests at the Intercontinental. Coleman had been told confidentially that the power problem had arisen as a result of the new Japanese power station in Tanjung Priok Harbour. The day it had been commissioned, the aid-financed facility had failed to carry the designed load, rendering the multi-million dollar thermal power-plant unserviceable even before it could go on-line.

Coleman was relieved that his *kongsi* had not been associated with this project; it had been discovered that substantial payments had been made to officials within the PLN, the State Electric Company, and that the contractors had merely offset this cost by redesigning the project. The resulting power loss threw the capital into chaos for more than three months, and Stephen understood, and identified with, the subsequent sombre mood which persisted amongst the foreign community. He knew that their houses would not be equipped with auxiliary power, and it was unlikely that they would have hand-mechanical pumps to restore water from their wells. Without water they would be unable to shower, or flush their toilets, adding further to the discomfort of living in a sealed house without air-conditioning; this he knew from his earlier days, when serving with the Embassy. Memories of those times reminded Coleman, uncomfortably, of his humble beginnings in Jakarta.

* * * * * *

Fresh from college, Stephen Coleman had been recruited by the suave John Anderson, who headed the Australian Secret Intelligence Service, ASIS. For more than twenty years, this clandestine operation had survived with relatively little accountability other than that to the Prime Minister, through the Attorney General's office. The existence of this organisation, developed along the lines of Britain's MI-6, was only revealed to the public, twenty years after its formation, by an investigative journalist, Brian Toohey, in his exposé entitled 'Oyster'.

Stephen had been an eager recruit, and willingly underwent training in Australia. Later, when he had been seconded to the Embassy in Indonesia, he had thrown himself into his work with considerable spirit. An unsatisfactory relationship with one of the American Embassy female staff had disrupted his life, and career. He and Louise had travelled together to West Irian prior to that province's Act of Self Determination. During their stay over in Bali, and after a bitter-sweet moment together, she had decided to re-turn to Jakarta, alone, a decision which would affect his life forever, as she had been killed when her plane crashed.

As the memory of her loss stung sharply, bringing him back to the present, the former ASIS agent was reminded that he had been most fortunate, indeed, that he too had not died at the hands of the rebels during that journey into the wilds of Irian. He had been medically evacuated to Australia where, subsequent to months of convalescence and a period of self-doubt regarding his role within the intelligence community, Coleman had resigned from ASIS and returned to Indonesia in search of some direction in life. It had been during this visit that General Seda had offered him the opportunity to work in partnership to supply the Indonesian Armed Forces with materials and weapons. The relationship had been most lucrative. Before he had turned thirty, Stephen Coleman had already set aside his first million dollars in a numbered Asian Currency Unit account, with the Standard Chartered Bank, in Singapore. What Stephen did not know however, was that his partner, General Seda, had a most secret agenda. He would discover, when it was believed that he could no longer influence the outcome, that the influential Timorese general's efforts were dedicated solely towards achieving independence for the land of his birth, East Timor.

* * * * * *

Stephen Coleman's home and office complex was located in Jalan

Cik Ditiro, in Menteng, directly between the Governor's residence and that of General Hidjojo, the former Indonesian Ambassador to Australia. As the rest of the city suffered rolling power blackouts lasting days on end, Coleman's electricity was rarely cut for more than a few hours. Not that this bothered him, as General Seda had kindly arranged for an army generator, and operator, to be installed at his house.

As the lift carried Stephen to the restaurant overlooking the city centre, he acknowledged that he had been fortunate to have the influential general as his silent sponsor. Their *kongsi* had blossomed, bringing the number of companies operating within the group to almost fifteen. *Not bad for a man not yet thirty,* he thought, a little arrogantly before stepping out of the elevator where he was met by the *maitre d'* and escorted to his table for breakfast. The waiters fussed as Stephen sipped his coffee and observed the traffic below.

He watched the congested traffic grind almost to a halt as buses and trucks manoeuvred their way around the undisciplined drivers entering the *Selamat Datang* roundabout. A break in the congestion permitted the flow from Imam Bonjol to join the disorder, cutting the south bound traffic altogether as drivers raced their vehicles across the circle and propped, waiting for those ahead to move again. Stephen followed a group of *becak* drivers crossing also, their steel carriages pushed courageously in front of oncoming angry drivers, unconcerned about the frightened passengers sitting up front, dangerously exposed.

'Morning, Stephen,' a voiced called, interrupting his thoughts. He turned and smiled as the other man slipped into the chair opposite and nodded to the hovering waiter. Stephen waited for the coffee to be poured and the waiter to move out of earshot before commencing the conversation.

'What's the score, David?' he asked, not wishing to waste time on pleasantries.

'It's all fixed,' the other man replied, smiling. 'I spoke to the States last night.' Stephen considered this for a moment, then nodded his head slightly with this news. It had been a long haul for all of them, dealing through intermediaries, agents, lawyers and, at one point, the American Embassy. The easy part of the entire negotiation had been the Indonesian end, Coleman thought. Their role had simply been a matter of how much and when, knowing that the Americans would be in complete charge of the project's technical aspects. The waiter returned and handed them both a breakfast menu. They ordered and then continued their discussions while waiting for their meals, ceasing to speak whenever a waiter approached to refill their coffee cups.

'When will we get delivery?' Coleman asked. 'Those dates given last week don't seem realistic.'

'The Pentagon seem to think that there will be no difficulty pushing the deal through State. Seems they have some rather excitable lobbyists working out of Houston who really want this deal to go through, Steve. Don't worry,' the American assured him, 'the squadron will be ready for delivery before the end of next year. Remember, your guys have got to find enough pilots capable of completing the conversion training. That's the only question that bothers me.' Stephen thought about the assurances given by Seda. The general believed that there would be little difficulty in having the Indonesian Airforce provide the talent required for Stateside training.

'And payment?' Coleman asked. Orchestrating the slush-fund had been the most aggravating negotiation Stephen had yet encountered. The sophisticated aircraft were to be provided under the terms of a defence aid programme; negotiating consultancy fees directly from the manufacturer had almost killed the transaction. Initially, the company had refused, citing their government's aid package as sufficient incentive for HANKAM to want to sign the order. Coleman had been furious at their naiveté. Seda had then threatened to veto the order and, for awhile, it appeared that the purchase for the two squadrons of jet fighters would not proceed, until Stephen suggested a secondary contract. This would assist the American suppliers to avoid violating their own recently introduced laws which prohibited buyer commissions.

There had been several sleepless nights as he watched the deal slowly collapse. Then, due to pressure from the oil and gas barons in Houston, negotiations recommenced. The sale would earn Coleman's *kongsi* almost five million dollars once the aircraft were delivered, and another three when the second order had been filled.

'Payment confirmed as agreed,' David said, smiling at the man across the table who would receive more money from this one transaction than any other deal in which the American had ever been involved. David had grown to admire Coleman's negotiating skills although, he admitted, there had been times when he would have been pleased to see the man give a little.

The American aircraft manufacturer's representative had been well briefed. This had included an informative meeting with the Defense Attaché at the American Embassy in Jakarta. David remembered being most impressed with the list of Coleman's accomplishments. His ability to be able to deliver a deal had become almost legendary. Or at least, this was the general perception within foreign military circles. When David had raised the question as to how Coleman had become so successful, the Defense Attaché, in turn, had shrugged his shoulders and inferred that Coleman had been just fortunate to be in the right place at the right time.

No one was aware of the relationship which existed between the company and General Seda, a relationship which had already generated millions of dollars. And now, with the two squadrons of fighters under his belt, Stephen was confident that his reputation would not suffer, particularly once word hit the street that he had been the one to broker the arms deal. The ramifications played with his mind as he sat, with growing restlessness, half-listening to the man who had delivered his *kongsi* its biggest commission ever.

He heard the American, David, waffling on concerning his company's attributes, and had difficulty concentrating. Stephen had come to the breakfast meeting solely for reassurance and, now that his contact had confirmed that their deal had been consummated, Coleman looked over in the waiter's direction, and raised his eyebrows. The bill appeared, and he signed, then rose to leave.

'David, thanks,' he said, shaking the surprised man's hand, 'but I must run. Guess you will make the necessary arrangements with the contracts?' Both men knew that, pushed by anxious clients, these would most probably be on lawyers desks even as they spoke.

'Sure, Steve,' David replied, his voice a little peeved at having been dumped so unceremoniously; he had hoped for a weekend out on Coleman's launch, having heard from the Embassy personnel that he should not miss any opportunity to visit the Thousand Islands, if invited. Stephen realized from the American's huffy tones that he had been a little brusque, and decided to offer his cruiser to the American.

'When are you leaving?' he asked, although he already knew.

Profile and other relevant information relating to the people he dealt with was already known to his office; Stephen Coleman relied heavily on General Seda, his partner. With his access to the Indonesian Intelligence Agency, they had the edge on everyone.

'Well,' the American hesitated, 'I had thought of spending a few days taking a look at the country, before climbing back on that goddamn plane and sticking my butt down for twenty hours. Guess I will take tomorrow's flight,' he said, almost pathetically. Coleman thought, *why not?*

'It would be a shame to miss seeing our beautiful islands, David,' he said, enjoying the tease. 'Would your company miss you for another four of five days, do you think?'

'Well,' David's mind raced quickly. He had envisaged a much shorter voyage, certain that he would attract too much interest from head office should he overstay. 'I could telex and tell them that we needed to tidy up a few things.' Stephen laughed as he rose, and extended his hand.

'Okay, then it's settled.'

'Will you join me for dinner tonight?' the American asked. Coleman thought about his schedule for the rest of the day, and reminded himself of the invitation he had received. One that he would be expected to attend.

'No, David, I'm sorry. There's a function I must attend.'

Stephen had not been surprised that the Salima family had placed him on their invitation list. He had conducted some business with the group in the past, and found himself looking forward to the occasion. He looked at David and decided that he deserved to be entertained. Stephen had mastered the delicate art of balancing his private life in the aggressive world of Jakarta commerce. He would invite some of the guests who attended the evening's celebrations to join them on his cruiser.

'Why don't you get yourself some shorts and sunburn cream from one of your cohorts from the U.S. Embassy, and I will have my driver pick you up tomorrow morning at six. Okay?' he smiled. Then Coleman added, 'Don't be late, Dave, the boat doesn't wait,' with which they both laughed and the Australian walked away, waving at a couple sitting on the other side of the restaurant. David watched as he disappeared behind the central columns adjacent to the lifts, wondering what would really happen if he were to be late. Then he smiled.

'Sonofabitch,' he muttered, nodding as he did so. He just *knew* that Coleman would pull the ropes and steam away leaving tardy guests behind, if for no other reason than to prove a point. David decided that he really liked the man. But he also decided to arrange a wake-up call for the next morning, not wanting to put Stephen Coleman to the test.

* * * * * *

Nyonya Seda was delighted that her husband was in such a fine mood. She watched as he placed the phone back in its cradle and laughed, slapping his hands together in childish exuberance. She was surprised, having seen his darker mood earlier in the day.

'*Mas,*' she said, caught up in the excitement, '*what is it?*' Immediately the general stopped, realizing that he was being carried away by Coleman's positive news.

'*Good news,*' he answered, his mind working quickly. *One should never disclose one's secrets,* he had decided years before, *especially to one's wife.* Seda's wife waited, sitting dutifully on the couch as she anxiously crushed a handkerchief in her hands.

'*Well, Mas, tell me,*' she implored, not really enjoying the suspense. General Seda was annoyed that he had been caught up in this game.

'*General Subroto is getting married again!*' he revealed, wondering if this would be sufficient for the woman. *Nyonya* Seda smiled and clapped her hands together with excitement at the news.

'*Who is she?*' Mrs Seda asked, smiling broadly. She had already heard the gossip weeks before and, from all reports, the girl was a *kampung* tart none of the wives could possibly accept into their homes. She knew that this was not the news that had pleased her husband so. After these many years of marriage, the secret telephone calls late into the night, and sudden departures to the Defense Department offices on Merdeka Square, she could no longer be deceived by his ploys. She bit her lip, as had become her habit over recent years. Her husband was a powerful and secretive man. Perhaps he was hiding an affair from her, she worried; perhaps he had become so bored with her that he had already arranged for a mistress to be ensconced in Tebet, the Jakarta suburb where most wealthy or influential men conducted their illicit affairs.

Nyonya Seda was afraid that it would only be a matter of time before he divorced her and took another wife. But at least he could not arbitrarily take a second wife, as many of the Moslem generals had done. She often had great difficulty when attending social engagements as most of her husband's contemporaries had remarried, some having acquired third and even fourth wives. The Sedas were Christians, and with this thought, she smiled inwardly, trusting that this would prevent him from breaking the law.

Seda glanced sideways at his wife, and decided that she would most probably have already known about Subroto's new marital arrangements. These women spent most of their days gossiping, creating more news themselves than what they heard from others. He selected a town at random, just for the sake of answering.

'*Some girl from Surabaya,*' he answered, feigning interest in the story he had fabricated. Seda then left the room, rubbing his stomach as he moved away, avoiding further discussion. His wife recognized this habit and sighed, knowing that her husband would most probably sit in the bathroom until he thought she would have forgotten the conversation or, having lost interest, would not pursue it. They had been through this scenario more times before than she cared to remember. She looked around the lonely, empty room, and decided to phone a friend. Moments later Seda's wife was engrossed in gossip concerning General Subroto's new flame, quoting her husband as the source.

Upstairs, in his bedroom, Seda lay on the thick quilt not caring that the servants would have clucked at his actions. It was not normally his custom to indulge in the traditional afternoon siesta; he merely used the opportunity to avoid further discussion with his wife. Coleman's call had brought the most exciting news Seda had yet received since first establishing the *kongsi* with the young Australian. As he lay there resting, Seda smiled smugly, congratulating himself on his move some years before to use the former embassy officer to consolidate his own business interests, while deflecting attention away from himself.

The general recalled how close his associate had come to being killed in Irian. Then the thought also crossed his mind that the success they had enjoyed together would never have eventuated had the faithful Umar's aim been a fraction more accurate. As quickly as these thoughts emerged he dismissed them. He had no remorse over what had happened to Coleman. Returning to the present, he cast his mind back over the intelligence meetings he had attended earlier that day. Seda did not believe that General Ali Murtopo's attempts at establishing a Fifth Column in Portuguese East Timor would achieve any great success. These efforts had been given the code name of *Operation Komodo*, and were designed to infiltrate the shaky colony in anticipation of any moves that East Timor might make towards independence.

Seda frowned, annoyed that Murtopo had jumped the gun and established subversive groups without first seeking approval from the President. As his thoughts wandered, Seda considered not attending that evening's function at the Borobudur Hotel, then decided that his absence would be noted. Besides, he thought, his eyelids becoming heavy, his wife would never forgive him if he did not escort her to what was to be the gala event of the year. He lay still, willing his body to submit to sleep.

Buried in a sound-proofed shelter below the ostentatious residence, a two hundred KVA generator's constant purr hummed faintly in the background, coaxing him to rest. Seda closed his eyes and listened to the soft vibrations, and soon drifted off into sleep.

* * * * * *

Lani sat quietly watching the child sleep. The power had only just returned and Lani opted to take advantage of the limited time she knew they would have before it was cut off again. The electric company distributed power in the most irregular, and what Lani knew to be, unfair way to the less unfortunate areas around the city. The area where they lived, Tebet, received electricity for only two hours each day, providing the suburb's inhabitants with barely sufficient time to refill their water tanks, bathe, and in the wealthier households, rest for a brief time sitting in front of their air-conditioners.

Lani stroked the side of Ratna Sari's head lovingly. It was the children who suffered most from the heat, she knew. The evening before, Lani had asked to borrow Ruswita's car and driver to provide the child with some semblance of comfort, even if it was for just a few hours. Lani had placed the young girl on the sedan's rear seat, and instructed the driver to take them along the city's by-pass roads, thereby providing Ratna with the opportunity to sleep in the air-conditioned car. Thankfully, this had been sufficient rest for the child, and Lani could see from her colour that the few hours of comfort had done her the world of good. She sighed, knowing that they would soon move to more comfortable accommodation.

Ruswita had informed Lani weeks before that she and Ratna would be moving into the main Lim household soon after her wedding. Lim had suggested that his wife's sister and niece move into one of the many rooms alongside the main house, where they would not be subjected to the stresses of power failures, and flooding. With this thought uppermost in her mind, Lani glanced at the clock and smiled, wishing that she could have attended the ceremony, or at least seen Ruswita in her gown. Lani looked down at the sleeping child she now considered her own, and stroked the soft dark hair from her face, while humming *ninabobo*, her favourite lullaby.

* * * * * *

Portuguese Timor

Xanana Soares sat cross-legged facing the two other men, listening to their words. As they spoke, Xanana nodded, agreeing to the course of action they had planned. If their people were to be free they had to move quickly before the situation became further confused. Inspired by their people's long struggle, they would now declare their independence.

At twenty, although Xanana was the youngest member of the movement's council, he was already considered leadership material, and was fifth in line to Xavier. He looked over at their President elect, Xavier do Amaral, who sat directly opposite. He was only thirty-seven. Xanana was familiar with the other organizations which had emerged during the few, short months since their colonial masters in Lisbon had announced plans for East Timor's independence. He and the other members also knew that one of these groups, APODETI, had been infiltrated by Indonesian agents who moved to dissuade their Timorese neighbours from supporting any political party not aligned with Jakarta.

They had become aware that the Indonesians had mounted a campaign to undermine any efforts which might lead to Independence. Copies of intelligence they had gathered through their unsophisticated network had exposed the Indonesian operation, *Operasi Komodo*. It was apparent to the fledgeling politicians that Jakarta was determined to subvert any efforts which might create an independent state within the Indonesian archipelago.

Xanana belonged to the Timorese Social Democratic Association, the second major political party to be formed at that time. The party combined the interests of rural-based elites, with those of urbanised groups. Most of the organisation's founders lived in Dili, but they still maintained established ties with their rural origins. Their committee believed they understood precisely what the people of Timor needed. Once the first free elections had been held and they won the right to govern, Xanana's party was determined to implement literacy and agricultural programmes as their first priority.

Xanana was aware that the committee had already made overtures to both the Australian and Indonesian Governments, requesting recognition of their country's proposed independent status and suggesting that they be permitted to establish diplomatic ties. Their requests went unheeded, yet they could not understand the reasoning for this rebuff, particularly from the Australians whose soldiers had depended heavily on the Timorese people during the war against the Japanese.

They had but a few weapons. Xanana had argued against raiding the former Portuguese armouries but had finally bowed to those with more experience in these matters. Xavier had argued that there would be no need for force. East Timor, he had said, was a small bubble, floating unthreateningly within the region. Why, he had asked, should the people arm themselves?

As he sat there discussing how their party could further consolidate its position amongst the people, Xanana firmly believed that his country, having been subjected to colonisation for more than four centuries, would soon be truly free. The Captain's Revolution in Portugal had become one with their own Revolution, and the former school teacher was confident that his determined group of socialist democrats would bring prosperity to an independent people of East Timor.

The evening meeting concluded, Xanana and the others returned to their homes and families, then slept, totally oblivious to the commitments which had been signed that day in Jakarta, thousands of kilometers to their west. Commitments which would eventually bring decades of death and despair to the Timorese separatists, as Indonesia's American fighters filled East Timor's skies.

* * * * * *

Indonesian Armed Forces Academy

'*Parade!*' the officer in charge called loudly, dragging every syllable out slowly, for effect, '*Parade, atten....shon!*' A dramatic drum roll reverberated through the official stand, drowning the next commands as the Academy's colours were paraded. Three men then took centre stage, the soldier in the middle carrying the AKABRI colours. Another order was then heard, drifting across the parade ground towards the spectators, following which, the well-rehearsed soldiers, positioned as guards on either side of the flag, marked time, and the guard captain screamed out the order for them to halt. The long, drawn command which followed was instantly accompanied by the first note spilling forth from the military band, and the graduating class stepped out, for their final parade.

'*There's Budi!*' one mother cried proudly, grabbing her husband's arm excitedly.

'*There's 'Man!*' another pleased parent called, as the young men marched past, their eyes and heads locked on the President as he took the salute. Even before the class had completed their final march-past, the chatter from the spectators' stand could be heard by the marching cadets, and they sensed their parents' pride in their achievement. They swung their arms high, and held their weapons close. This was their day, the day they had all worked towards since the moment they first set foot inside the Armed Forces Academy.

Another command turned the column, directing them back to their original positions, where they were ordered to halt, then turn, facing their senior officers. The officer of the guard marched forward, saluted with his sword, then offered the graduating officers for inspection. There was a discernible silence, as all held their breath in anticipation of the moment they had dreamed about. The President returned the salute, then stepped down from the dais and carried out his inspection.

They knew they were 'the best and the brightest' as they remained at attention, ready for inspection by their country's leader, President Soeharto. They knew that they had been honoured, for the *Smiling General* rarely attended such ceremonies anymore. Today had been a special gift to them all, and they knew it was because of the young army officer who was also graduating in their class, Lieutenant Sujono Diryo.

When the President walked along the front file, they all knew that the *Bapak* would stop and say something to this fine, outstanding officer. There was not one amongst their number who would not have changed places with Sujono; his father had been declared a Hero of the Revolution. Sujono was tall, handsome, and obviously talented, having been among the first five in the graduating class.

The young men stood firmly fixed at attention, their eyes locked on some distant object, as their hearts and ears followed the man they had grown to love. The President stopped, his face serious, and spoke.

'*Congratulations, Lieutenant,*' he said, congratulating the young Sujono Diryo, out of tribute to the man's father.

'*Terima kasih, Bapak,*' was all Sujono could muster. Then the President continued with his inspection, the band playing softly as he walked along the lines of proud academy graduates. In the stand, tucked well behind the dais, General Nathan Seda watched the proceedings with particular interest deciding, as the President returned to take the final salute, that he would take a special interest also in the young army officer who so obviously had Palace support.

In the days that followed, during which time the young officers received their first postings, Lieutenant Sujono Diryo was disappointed to learn that he had been assigned to Army Special Duties with the Intelligence Corp. Three days after his orders had been cut, Sujono Diryo reported for duty. He had then been selected to undergo further training, after which he was instructed to report directly to his new headquarters, BAKIN, Indonesia's Central Intelligence Co-ordinating Agency. And it was there, on his first day, that he was introduced to General Nathan Seda.

Chapter 5

A wedding

More than one thousand guests attended the wedding celebration. The Hotel Borobudur had been selected for the event, as this was the only venue with the capacity to accommodate such a large number of guests. The main ballroom was suitably decorated, creating an air of festivity which spilled out into the foyer and reception, as the orchestra entertained the arriving guests. The adjoining and smaller ballroom had been utilized as an elaborate storage area, filled with more than five hundred cases of soft-drinks, beer, spirits and, of course, an adequate supply of Hennessey's XO Cognac. The Borobudur general manager had personally overseen the entire preparations. It would be, he knew, the largest gathering of Indonesia's elite Chinese community ever to congregate so publicly in Jakarta.

The hotel's staff of three thousand had worked tirelessly and, as the general manager moved through the kitchens into the servery areas ensuring that the number of staff serving food and beverages was adequate, he experienced a sense of pride at the results of months of training. He moved as inconspicuously as possible through the main ballroom into the hotel reception and lobby, to examine the continuous stream of arriving guests. As he stood overlooking the entrance and escalators, he became concerned with the apparent bottle-neck created by the swarm of guests moving through the cramped, lower foyer.

Outside, other invitees waited impatiently as the continuous line of Mercedes moved slowly forward, permitting each group to disembark directly in front of the already congested entrance. The general manager estimated that it would take an hour for the guests to file through into the main ballroom. There, they would be greeted with an opulence never before seen in Indonesia.

Westerners dressed in formal attire mingled uncomfortably with the wealthy Indonesians who, for the greater part, wore traditional dress. Many of the men had donned the comfortable long-sleeve *batik* dress shirt, while their high-heeled ladies, hair tied in magnificent buns adorned with gold filigree combs, mingled graciously around, their *kain-kebaya* combinations requiring the shortest of steps. Diamonds and precious stones added to the amazing glitter, men as well as women wore oversized rings to demonstrate their wealth. Ladies smiled insincerely at each other as they floated around the setting, hiding their envy as new dresses or jewellery were displayed, or as they identified an old flame escorting his new companion. Their whispered but cutting remarks were barely audible under the magnificent chandeliers, as the conversation rose to a deafening level.

Murray Stephenson moved amongst the other guests, stopping occasionally to speak briefly to those he knew. He regretted that Peter Wong had been unable to attend the function. Murray knew that Peter's penchant for the young ladies had most probably kept him away, although the excuse had been otherwise. He had hoped that the evening might act as a catalyst for them to identify themselves somehow with the Salima Group.

It had been more than a year since Wong had stepped in to assist salvage his company and, although the business had grown dramatically with the number of offshore Chinese investing through his *kongsi*, Murray realized that the really big money was still out of reach to him. He had been unsuccessful in developing any real access into the Salima corporate machine. Murray waved at one of the American guests, winked at the delightful girl hanging onto his arm, then turned, bumping into a familiar figure.

'Hi, Murray,' Coleman said, wiping the front of his jacket where some of the champagne had spilled.

'Sorry,' he said, waiting for Stephen Coleman to finish so that he could shake his hand. They saw little of each other, as they always moved in different commercial and social circles. Their paths had diverged. Murray admitted to himself that he had become more than a little envious of the younger man's successes, both as an entrepreneur and as a ladies man. His reputation had continued to grow, and Murray no longer doubted that Coleman had covert support from within the Indonesian Military, for to achieve what he had in such a short time would have been impossible without someone very powerful watching over his shoulder. Murray knew that, in this world of lucrative contracts, they all needed to have such a sponsor. His was Peter Wong. But who, he asked himself, was Stephen Coleman's?

'No damage,' the other man said, rolling the paper napkin he had used to dry his jacket before dropping this onto one the waiter's silver trays as it passed. 'How's business?'

'Doing just fine,' Murray responded, a little too quickly. If Coleman had noticed, he had not shown so. 'And yours?' Murray knew that he had to be friendly, even though he did not particularly like the younger man. Coleman's activities had grown and outstripped his competitors at an unbelievable pace. Murray admitted that there was a certain amount of petty rivalry amongst the foreigners endeavouring to build careers for themselves in Jakarta but, for some reason which eluded him, Coleman was just not like the others. In spite of the man's lack of commercial training, he had firmly ensconced himself within the Indonesian business community, and was sought after by many of the foreign companies keen to develop access to the Indonesian Armed Forces.

Murray had no idea how Coleman managed to do so, but it was quite apparent that he had successfully established himself as one of the major suppliers to HANKAM, accessing the many millions the Indonesian Defense Department spent on weapons and equipment. Murray shook Stephen's hand briefly, smiled at the beautiful woman who accompanied him, and spoke to her in Indonesian.

'*Shouldn't talk business in front of such a beautiful lady,*' he said, watching her eyes open wide in surprise. She squeezed Stephen's arm excitedly, as one would expect of a young child flattered by such comment.

'*He speaks Indonesian also!*' she gushed, happily, and slipped her free arm through Murray's, placing herself between the two Australians. '*I will not let either of you go,*' she declared, her bubbly behaviour spilling over causing both the men to laugh. They talked briefly before being interrupted by an announcement, which brought the assembly to a hushed silence.

'*Tuan,tuan dan nyonya,*' a voice called from somewhere amongst the crowd of guests, '*Gentlemen and ladies, I give you Pak Salima and his beautiful bride, Ruswita Salima!'*

The crowd roared its approval as guests moved aside permitting the couple to enter. Murray applauded loudly along with the other guests, smiling broadly as he did so. The wedding had taken place in a private setting some hours before, permitting Lim the opportunity to return to their home where he still had unfinished business to attend to. Later, he had changed into a loose fitting *batik* for the occasion, while his wife continued to wear the white bridal gown designed especially for her wedding. There had been little change from ten thousand dollars for the magnificent garment, Murray had overheard one of the guests whisper, and he was not surprised. Ruswita looked stunning as she floated through the room accompanied by strains of Mendelssohn's *Wedding March*. Applause sounded through the ballroom as the couple moved to the centre of the hall, and waited.

'Gentlemen and ladies,' the master of ceremonies announced, *'a special song for two very special people,'* with which, the entire ballroom turned, as a deep resonant voice emanated from huge speakers placed appropriately to either side of the band.

'This is, the moment...' the singer crooned, sending the assembled guests in raptures as they identified the opening words and music to *The Hawaiian Wedding Song*. They listened as the beautiful melody filled the great ballroom, setting the most perfect mood. As light danced around the room deflected by the twin chandeliers, Ruswita and her husband moved amongst the guests, hugging and kissing until the song came to an end.

Applause filled the air once more and, in that moment, it seemed that this was the signal for the guests to commence talking again. The ambience was electric, and the moment almost too perfect as Ruswita was kissed on both cheeks by one of the President's children. It was her night, she knew, but it was her powerful husband who had commanded their respect; they had all come to pay homage to Lim, but Ruswita did not mind. She was happy.

As the band commenced playing again, General Seda and his wife stepped forward to congratulate her, and she beamed with pleasure, deliriously happy with her world. As Seda squeezed her hand lightly, and turned to move away, Ruswita felt the room move, threatening to spin. She reached for his arm for support, fearing that she was about to fall. The ballroom lights blinked once, then again, and suddenly the room was thrown into darkness. Incredibly, the packed ballroom became deathly still, instantly filled with fear.

As the twin one thousand KVA emergency stand-by generators were triggered into action, there were cries amongst the guests. Concern continued to sweep through the ballroom, causing a number of women to faint. Less than thirty seconds had passed before the generators, having achieved full power, switched across automatically and flooded the room with brilliant light. There was an audible sigh of relief, followed by cheers as guests turned to smile at each other confidently, having experienced another of the country's familiar black-outs. The band struck up once more, and the general manager breathed deeply, reassured as the music reached his ears.

Quickly, he despatched a maintenance team to correct the electrical overload problem and, half-an hour later when he was satisfied that the fault had been rectified, he instructed the generator operator to switch back to city power, as only half of the hotel lifts could operate while on emergency lighting. The engineer did so, causing but the slightest discernible flicker to occur as he threw the switch. Pleased with his equipment, he then went back to sleep in the quiet of the generator room. Two minutes later there was another jolt, stronger than the first which had triggered the initial power failure, but the guests hardly noticed the slight tremor as this time the lighting was not affected, and many of the guests were too engrossed in the celebrations.

* * * * * *

Four hundred kilometers to the east of Jakarta, nearer the earth tremor's epicentre, villages shook violently, causing roofs to collapse on those who slept inside. Walls cracked as the force rocked tiny dwellings, then toppled, as the second and more violent movement struck. More than twenty peasants died in the small hamlets during those brief minutes, but the isolated community had experienced such calamitous events before. Within days, these simple, hard-working farmers had completed their mourning, and restored their ramshackle structures. Within a week, life had all but returned to normal in the East Java *kampung*, nestled amongst the foothills of the dormant volcano known as Mount Muria.

Book two

the present

Chapter 6

Lim buys an American bank

Denny drove, while James continued to read through the brief again, just to be sure. As brothers, they had been closer than most; as family business associates, they had been inseparable. Together, they had left Indonesia to study in the United States, and together they had remained, building an extension to the Lim empire in the world's greatest economy, where they would eventually make their new home.

Lim's two sons from his first marriage were intelligent, assertive, and already influential young men. Both had graduated from the University of California in Los Angeles and, although their brilliance was not reflected in their academic achievements, their inherent qualities and skills soon became apparent once they flung themselves into the competitive world of banking and commerce. James, older by only one year, was by far the more aggressive of the two, and most like their father. Denny, not at all displeased with his position in life as the second child, in no way remained in his brother's shadow. He displayed much of the Lim street cunning and, as a team, the two had cut quite a path for themselves through American banking circles.

They rarely returned to Indonesia. James believed that it was their responsibility to take the Salima banking arm and develop a global strategy for their family-controlled Asian Pacific Commercial Bank. Almost a year had passed since they last visited Jakarta, when they had attended their father's wedding. The boys had been surprised when Lim had phoned to inform his sons that he was to remarry. Neither felt any animosity towards Ruswita; in fact, they had both warmed to the idea, knowing that she would remain at their father's side as his confidant and close companion. Denny had asked the obvious question during their private conversation with Lim after the wedding, and their father had assured both of his sons that their position within the family bank would always be theirs to control. James had been particularly pleased with his father's response, as the boys had discussed what Ruswita's entry into their family would mean with respect to the Lim fortunes.

They were conscious of her role within the Salima organization, and were comfortable knowing that Ruswita would not be involved in the management of the family's banking interests. Denny and James' position amounted to only thirty percent of the issued capital. Then, of course, there was the new baby, their half-brother Benny, to consider. And what would happen when he grew up.

Neither of the older boys really envisaged a future which involved Ruswita's son participating in any of the bank's activities in the United States. That was to be their personal domain and, having received such an assurance from their father, both Denny and James felt relaxed about their futures. Their shareholders were limited to immediate family and the Indonesian First Family. Their APC Bank had grown to take its place as the largest private bank in South East Asia. Lim, through his complex corporate entities both within Indonesia and offshore, owned fifty-five percent of the stock. He had given each of his two oldest sons fifteen percent each. The Indonesian First Family enjoyed ten percent of the shares, and the remaining five had been given to Ruswita to hold in trust for Benny.

Lim had agreed to an arrangement whereby James and Denny would be permitted to own control over whatever new interests they successfully developed in North America. They had given their undertaking that, as the family bank had funded their activities in the United States, the Asian Pacific Commercial Bank would be issued with forty percent of the new bank's stock. Now, having negotiated their way through the mass of bureaucracy and political hurdles which in no way had diminished their appetite for the North American financial markets, the Lim boys were close to finalizing their arrangements with the Kentucky State Governor.

'Take it easy, Denny,' James chastised his younger brother, *'he'll still be there even if we are late.'* The older of the Lim boys had every right to appear smug. Even before attaining the age of thirty, both of the American-educated Jakarta-Chinese were multi-millionaires,

thanks to their father, Lim Swee Giok and his empire in Indonesia where practically everything could be bought, acquired or fixed by coercion. In their relentless pursuit of money, the Lims had never considered their activities to be anything less than appropriate; it was the Asian way of doing business.

'We can't afford to screw up with this one, James,' Denny said, squinting, the heavily tinted glasses defying gravity, and hanging off his flat nose. *'His aide insisted that we get there on time,'* he said, worried. Although exposed to years of American influence, both still spoke to each other in the acronym-infested Jakarta dialect, with its market-place slang.

'We still have twenty minutes, take it easy,' James insisted.

They had driven from the state capital, Frankfort, heading for Lexington where their meeting could be conducted in the privacy of the senator's home. The Governor was, for obvious reasons, reluctant to be seen openly with the two young bankers. Although they had met several times, briefly, negotiations had been handled discreetly by the senator and a close, personal friend of the Governor's, who acted as his intermediary in such sensitive matters.

At first, the State Governor had been reluctant to provide the undertakings requested by the Asian businessmen. Their requests were, he believed, unreasonable. But when opinion polls had indicated that he was in danger of losing the forthcoming election, and his advisers pointed to the empty election fund coffers, he had committed himself to the Lim brothers and their future banking facilities.

Denny and James had acquired residency in the United States subsequent to their graduating from college. Neither wished to become American citizens, as this would jeopardise their positions in Indonesia. Once word had spread that the Lim family was committed to establishing their banking interests in the United States, they had been approached by several lobby groups offering their services. The dynamic Lim corporate presence had been well received, and the bankers were introduced to the influential intermediaries. When they discovered that negotiations in America were not dissimilar to those of Asia, James had laughed at the relatively insignificant sums requested to grease the Governor's political representative's palms. Denny, on the other hand, was not entirely comfortable with the arrangements.

'What do you think about the payment?' Denny asked, as he had, at least a dozen times over the past month. 'You don't think it's a little over the top?' James turned his head and looked across at his younger and more conservative brother. He was the worrier of the two. James had spent almost an entire year setting up the deal through intermediaries and, as far as he was concerned, the payment was inconsequential in relation to the profits they would generate once their banking operation had been fully established.

'I would have agreed to pay double what they asked,' James revealed. He knew that Denny was driving too fast not because they were late, but because he wished to consummate the deal and move on. He was the impatient one of the pair.

'I'd still feel better if we'd at least had confirmation of the branch status,' Denny said, unable to restrain his heavy foot. The needle rose above seventy miles per hour, and with the new speed restrictions James knew they were certain to be noticed on the highway patrol radar.

'Slow down,' he said, his warning tone sufficient for the younger man to pay heed. Denny slowed as they entered the city's limits. Already familiar with the route, they arrived fifteen minutes later, and were met outside the white-column entrance by one of the senator's staff. The wealthy young bankers, dressed in Armani suits, were ushered through an elegantly appointed reception area, and into the influential Southerner's study.

'Glad you boys made it all in one piece,' their host drawled, indicating where they should sit as an African-American woman smiled, poured iced-tea for all three, then left as inconspicuously as she had entered. Their host offered them cigars, but both refused. Once, earlier in his career, Denny had accepted one such Havana, and had nearly choked with his first puff. He had tried the Indonesian clove cigarettes while still a youth at school, but had not taken up the habit.

'We are anxious to conclude our arrangements, Senator,' James stated, concerned that the Governor was not present. 'Will the Governor be joining us shortly?' he asked. The senior senator for the State of Kentucky sucked on the end of his cigar, exhaled slowly, smiled, then leaned forward as he spoke.

'The Governor has instructed me to finalize our, ah...,' he paused, 'arrangements.' The senator smiled again, then leaned back into his heavily lined leather chair, observing his two oriental guests. He had not had occasion to deal with Asians before meeting the Lim brothers earlier in the year, and was pleased with the relaxed way both had accepted the offer made to them. He considered the Indonesian Chinese men before him. They were half of his age and, if he could believe the report he'd received from his own financial sources before negotiations had first commenced, their wealth was such that the Lim family could most probably even make the Rothschilds look scratchy.

More than eight months had passed since the senator had been approached by an intermediary, who enquired regarding the possibility of reactivating the State banking licence which belonged to one of the failed private banks, and selling this to the Salima family group. Negotiations had not been difficult or prolonged.

He recalled that it had been an election year for the new Governor and, due to the extravagant campaign run by his political opponent, donations were desperately needed if he was to have any chance of remaining in the race. The Lim boys had been a godsend. Funds had been committed by the young Chinese and, within a week from when undertakings had been given by both parties, more than half million dollars had flowed into the campaign coffers from untraceable sources. Subsequently the Governor had won the election, and the Salima family had arrived for their pound of flesh.

Their original request had been to reinstate the bank's operating licence which, at the time of its closure, limited the institution's activities to within the municipality of Lexington. Since then, greed and opportunity had driven their demands to include other cities and, although the new Governor was not entirely disagreeable to having foreign capital flow into his state's economy, his political advisers warned of the inherent dangers in accepting campaign donations from Asian sources, concerned with the possibility that such funding might be drug-related. They had seen similar, well-heeled Asian groups arrive in other States, bringing with them their culture of drugs, terror and intimidation, and seriously advised the Governor to exercise caution when dealing with the Lim brothers.

'Do you think we will have our other licences?' James asked, assertively. He had little time for government representatives, particularly those who sold themselves for considerably less than what their counterparts in most Asian capitals might demand. The Senator sat quietly for a moment longer, then answered.

'Sure,' he said, 'but this has required substantially more lobbying than we'd first envisaged.' He paused, gauging the two young bankers, wondering how far he could push. 'An additional consideration would not be out of order,' he said. James had expected such, and was prepared, not at all offended by the man's directness.

'How much?' he had learned this from his father. There was no point in beating around the bush when dealing with corrupt officials. If one did not give them what they first asked for, experience had shown that they were sure to come back at some later date, demanding more than their original request. The senator smiled, pleased that James Salima had not been one of those evasive Asians who avoided the more direct approach.

'One hundred and fifty thousand,' he said. James noticed Denny's surprise and with a cautionary look, cut him off abruptly.

'We agree,' he responded, a little too quickly. James decided that the figure was an odd amount, and that the American, like so many other Westerners, most probably believed that all Asians bargained themselves back to some predetermined figure, fixed inflexibly in their minds. He scoffed silently at the myth, and the way occidentals thought. Although he guessed that the senator was, in fact, only looking for a hundred thousand, James believed that his hook in the Governor was even deeper now that he had acquiesced. 'And we would be delighted to be included on the Governor's guest list next fall,' he added, beaming at the statesman.

The senator's mind raced. He had the opportunity to bury an additional fifty thousand dollars without any of the Governor's inner circle ever becoming the wiser. He also knew, however, how the Governor's wife, who partnered a well-established law firm in their home state, would not care to have such people at her home. The senator decided that he would leave that problem to the Governor to resolve for himself.

'Done,' he said, much to James' satisfaction. He desperately wished to break into the Bluegrass society circles and, with the senator's assistance, they would receive the exposure necessary to promote their ongoing activities. The brothers remained just long enough to finish their cold tea, then they departed, returning to

Frankfort satisfied with the outcome of their negotiations. Neither had thought it strange that they were required to travel away from the capital to finalise their transaction with the senator. They appreciated the need for secrecy in such matters. As they drove in silence, each son considered in his own way how their family's American acquisitions might enhance their futures, and add to their already incredible wealth.

Chapter 7

Rama Announcement

The crowd fidgeted, impatient with the delay. The sun was partially blocked by the low pollution which hung above the Senayan Stadium. The air was still hot and humid despite the cloud, and this seemed to depress the crowd for the Armed Forces' Day celebrations.

The President was late.

An AURI officer waited nervously for the signal to alert the Halim Airforce Command that the President had arrived. The fly-past had been planned to coincide with the *Bapak's* entry into the historic stadium, and it was this officer's task to co-ordinate the manoeuvre. The ambient temperature in the huge, Russian-financed complex rose exponentially as more than one hundred thousand Indonesians crowded into the stadium to enjoy the parade. The suffocating heat was stirred with the heavy smell of over-ripe *durian*. As the sewerage like smell struggled upwards and across the grounds, the pungent aroma entered the area allocated to the foreign community, precipitating anxious looks of disapproval from those present.

Anxious ABRI generals waited in line and checked their watches surreptitiously, concerned that something might have delayed their Commander-in-Chief. He had never been this late before. The temperature continued to climb, further exacerbating their frustrating wait. Suddenly, a roar rose from the crowd signalling that the President of the Indonesian Republic had finally arrived, and those present rose to their feet. Relieved, the generals raised their hands in salute as the white-haired Javanese leader climbed from what his people had facetiously named, the *Bapak-mobile*, a special purpose vehicle designed for official occasions from which the

President could wave to the masses. The bullet-proofed limousine had been manufactured in a car assembly plant owned by the former President's son.

Leader of more than two hundred and twenty million people, leader of the largest Muslim country on the face of the earth, and recognized leader of the non-aligned nations, the Indonesian President walked confidently to his position at the centre of the covered dais, and took his place. As the former general came to attention, the crowd roared its approval, and then suddenly fell silent as the trumpeting strains of *Indonesia Raya*, the National Anthem, reverberated through the stadium. While the final stanza was played, soldiers representing the three Services left the main body of troops and marched in line carrying their regimental colour-flags towards their Commander-in-Chief.

The well-rehearsed drill was accompanied by the sounds of drumbeat, rolling through the air as the disciplined men approached the point directly below, and in front of their President, where they came to a halt, then saluted. Whispered comment passed amongst the assembled dignitaries as the President slowly climbed the dais, while waving to the one hundred thousand spectators gathered inside the stadium. Dressed in an immaculate dark blue suit, the Indonesian leader wore a white *pici* on his head instead of the more traditional black, symbolic head-dress. To some observers, this was not a good omen, as Moslem fundamentalism had grown considerably under the new President's leadership. There were a small number, however, for whom the gesture was seen as a return to the true spirit of Islamic teaching.

At the precise moment the President saluted those before him, the air suddenly filled with the roar of Raptor IF-22s as AURI fighter jets screamed across the sky above. Startled, many of the spectators panicked before realizing what was happening, clasping hands over ears as the deafening scream of jet engines pierced their surrounds. Then, as their faces turned skywards, their mouths opened in awe at the spectacle of four aircraft tearing up in a vertical climb. Suddenly, as the white trails following the aircraft turned outwards, and then towards earth, the entire assembly broke into cries of pleasure at the aerial display. As the sounds of jet engines faded, these were replaced by heavy, metallic, grinding noises entering the stadium.

The crowd's faces turned towards the major entrance which had been rebuilt for the celebrations, and watched, applauding as the line of Scorpion tanks rumbled into the grounds below and came to a halt at their pre-designated positions. Following these light tanks were two surface-to-surface missiles, partially raised on their launchers, towed through the stadium by heavy-duty ancillary transports. A number of Leopard tanks then completed the spectacle, representing but a fraction of the weaponry *ABRI* had accumulated since the new President had come to office.

High up on the grandstand, above and behind where the President stood, hundreds of foreign reporters and cameramen busied themselves recording Indonesia's first public display of their missile strength. Further below, gathered in the aisles not far to the right of the Indonesian Chiefs of Staff and their ladies, foreign military attaches stood silent, lips pursed. They did not need to take photography of the weaponry before them; without exception, their own Defence Departments and intelligence gathering services all stored more information material on the Indonesian arsenal than perhaps the Indonesians had themselves. These foreign professionals were all too conscious of the fact that their host country's military leadership had been acquiring Russian and American arms on a scale not dissimilar to that of the Soekarno era.

Standing at the extreme end of the line, Colonel McMahon, the Australian Defence Attaché, watched solemnly, aware of the strike capability and range of the guided missiles before him. Even in their almost dormant state, he mused, while staring at the long silver columns, they looked most menacing. Australia had been most fortunate, he thought, that her over-populated neighbour had not seen fit to purchase any of the antiquated Soviet ICBM hardware that had become available after the collapse of Communism. On the other hand, since you could guarantee that the conventional warheads on any missile purchased from the Soviets had never been regularly tested, there was a good chance they would explode on the launch pad at any attempt at ignition. He recalled at the time how even Malaysia had rushed in to purchase the heavily discounted Russian MiGs, as these were on offer at almost half their original cost.

His thoughts returned to the missiles being paraded below, and he nodded confidently to himself, conscious of how fortunate they all were that Indonesia did not have ready access to nuclear warheads, or any suitable delivery system.

Colonel McMahon's attention turned to the amazing attendance which surrounded the military display, wondering how they managed to remain standing outside in the debilitating heat. He, along with the other foreign guests, fidgeted uneasily, sweating profusely in the humidity. Damp patches appeared behind knees and under armpits, revealing the discomfort they suffered in silence, while their Asian counterparts, more accustomed to the climate, remained relatively comfortable throughout the proceedings.

The Australian Attaché looked further down towards the President, surprised by the number of Indonesia's prominent business leaders who attended as Palace guests, privileged to be placed alongside their President. In the past, such invitations had been restricted to those in government, and foreign military representatives. Most he recognized. He leaned forward a little more to see who had moved into the two seats directly alongside the outspoken Vice President.

Earlier, as the stadium had filled, these had remained empty, giving rise to considerable speculation amongst the foreign Diplomatic Corp. As heads moved from side to side first blocking, then revealing those who had taken these seats, he raised his eyebrows in surprise, recognising the Lim couple, *Bapak* and *Ibu Salima*. He was immediately impressed, aware that the attendance of such a senior Chinese *totok* at the Armed Forces Day parade gave credence to the rumours that nothing had really changed in Indonesia - except the face of the new President at the country's helm. The military attaché leaned back into his hard uncomfortable seat. In practised movement, he inconspicuously lifted his cap and touched his forehead with a handkerchief to absorb the beads of perspiration which had formed there, while wondering how long the ceremony would last. He could see the looks of consternation amongst the other guests, whose wives had already shown signs of considerable discomfort, fanning themselves too energetically. Then, when the guests began to doubt that the parade would ever end, an announcement across the public address system courteously requested that they all take their seats for the Presidential address.

When the rustling of clothes and scraping of shoes over timber finally settled down indicating that guests and spectators were seated, the former Javanese general coughed, once, to ensure that the microphone was working; then began the annual Armed Forces' Day address.

'*Saudara, saudara,*' he commenced, then paused for effect '*People of Indonesia, members of the Armed Forces, and guests, we are here to celebrate……..*' As his voice droned on in a language only a few of the foreign guests understood, an audible sigh passed through the aisles of foreign military attaches, expecting a repeat of the previous years speech which, to their dismay, had continued for more than an hour. The United States Military Attaché looked along the uncomfortable row of foreign officers to his left, catching his Canadian counterpart's eye.

He winked. The French Canadian ever so slightly shook his head in response, then surreptitiously wiped the perspiration from his moustache. As the speech continued and the ladies became restless on the hard, metal chairs, the British Ambassador's wife leaned forward, turned to her husband with an expression of apology and fainted, sliding off her seat and into the narrow aisle. Other members of the Diplomatic Corp moved quickly, relieved at having been given the perfect opportunity to leave their seats and attend to the unfortunate woman. The American Chargé d'Affaires, who had been first to come to her assistance, suddenly ceased fanning the stricken lady and listened carefully to the words which flowed from the stadium public address system. Startled, he turned to see if any of the others had heard the word *nuclear* in the presidential speech, and immediately realized that few amongst their number would have understood, or even been listening.

'*…this will involve the ongoing commitment from our Armed Forces to maintain stability as we go forward together, and build a greater future for the people of Indonesia. Members of the Development Cabinet and I have therefore decided that construction of the first five plants will begin as soon as feasibly possible, followed by seven additional plants once those in the first phase have all been commissioned. The first nuclear energy power plants will be located in Java, and Bali. They will be known as Rama I through V. Foreign participation will be invited from……*'

The acting Ambassador slipped back into his own seat and motioned towards his political counsellor to exchange seats with his wife. This activity attracted little attention from the other diplomats, who were more concerned about the duration of the

Presidential address.

'Did you get that?' the Chargé d'Affaires asked. The political secretary nodded in response. He was reasonably *au fait* with the Indonesian Language, and had noted with similar alarm that the President had announced a commitment to address the country's crippling power problems by introducing nuclear power plants. The embassy officer scanned the faces of others present. It was clear from their blank expressions that they were unaware of the announcement.

'I'd best get back to the Embassy,' the officer suggested, 'and remove my phone from its hook.' The acting Ambassador forced a smile knowing that this would not happen, but he did nod for the officer to leave. The State Department would have transcripts of the Presidential speech in Washington within the hour and, no doubt, would respond with hostile enquiries to determine why there had been no indication from their in-country sources that the Indonesians had been contemplating such a move.

He looked over his shoulder in the direction of the Japanese Ambassador and his entourage, and noticed the agitated discussion taking place. Then he glanced around for the Russian delegation and came into direct eye contact with their Ambassador, Sergei Perevozchenko whose smile suddenly broke into a grin as he watched the American's face fall with the realization that Moscow had obviously been given advance notification of the news. He returned the smile and winked, freezing the Russian's cocky display. Satisfied that would be sufficient to generate at least a little paranoia amongst their camp, the American scanned the faces of those around in search of tell-tale signs which might reflect prior knowledge of the incredible revelations in the President's speech.

He believed that the general consensus supported the view that the Indonesians would never again consider nuclear energy, having lost the initiative during the Soeharto regime when the then Minister for Technology, Habibie, had attempted to implement a similar program. World opinion had discouraged the plan and it was shelved. Now, it seemed, the plan to establish a series of plants commencing with the two most heavily populated areas of Java and Bali had been resurrected.

The President concluded his speech and the crowd roared its approval. On cue, an officer screamed loudly bringing the parade back into order, and the guests once again rose to stand. Another command was called, and the President returned their salute. Accompanied by the band's deep brass tones, the President left the podium, stepping slowly as he was escorted down to his bulletproof, glass-covered limousine. He entered and stood inside the dome, steadied himself as the vehicle moved slowly forward, then commenced waving as he was driven away. The ceremony over, crowds pushed and shoved as they too made their way from the complex, while foreign guests and other dignitaries exited through a specially designated area.

Most returned directly to their official posts where, within the hour, copies of the President's speech had been translated and read. In the course of the next few hours, urgent meetings were held in most offices throughout the diplomatic community to determine whatever ramifications there might be with respect to Indonesia's nuclear energy plans. By late afternoon, the general feeling amongst the foreign experts was that there were would be no additional military threat to its neighbours.

Before early evening had arrived, Embassies whose countries enjoyed nuclear energy were already preoccupied with preparations to offer the Indonesians whatever was necessary, from technology to finance, in their attempts to secure what would obviously become an incredibly lucrative opportunity. Lights remained burning throughout the night in the tall, Japanese Commercial Attaché's office, where representatives of Kyushu Electric Power and Shikoku Power worked together as a team. For the first time since the death of the former President, Embassies worked around the clock as communications flooded in from all over the globe. Trade Commissioners suddenly discovered that they knew little in relation to the terminology and technology associated with the production of electricity by nuclear power.

The following morning they also discovered, one and all, that they had been caught unawares yet again, when the *Jakarta Times* carried news of an overnight Palace announcement, releasing the name of the Presidential appointee selected to oversee the project's implementation, and the company which would be created for this purpose. None were surprised to read that the newspapers had already coined their own acronym for *P.T. Perusahan Pembangkit Listrik Nuclear*, the designated power company. It was referred to in the Press as PEPELIN, and before that day had come to a close, the word was on everyone's lips.

Before the public address system on Jakarta's Isitqual Mosque had again, annoyingly penetrated offices as far as Merdeka Square, calling the faithful to mid-morning prayers, more than ten foreign Trade Commissioners had placed calls requesting an appointment to call upon General Seda, the newly appointed Chairman of PEPELIN.

The race had begun.

* * * * * *

Immediately upon her return to the residence, Ruswita removed her shoes and rubbed her swollen feet. The doddering old cook, inherited from earlier days, shuffled around getting in Ruswita's way when she went to the kitchen in search of tea and biscuits.

'Where is Lani?' Rus asked, but the cook did not respond. Ruswita was certain that the woman feigned deafness, as she had often noticed that there seemed to be little wrong with her hearing whenever Lim was around. She had left her husband behind, knowing that the day's announcements would require lengthy discussions with others involved in his various *kongsis*. A younger servant entered the room to check on *Ibu Ruswita's* needs, but she merely brushed her aside, quite happy to prepare her own refreshments.

'Please call Ibu Lani,' she asked the young *pembantu*. Ruswita was firm with her staff, but never bullied them.

'Ibu Lani has gone out to the plaza, nyonya,' the house-girl advised, still hovering close by, anxious to assist her mistress. Ruswita dismissed this girl also, deciding to pour her own tea. She returned to the comfort of the lounge, placed the tea and biscuits on the coffee table, then relaxed. As she sat, rubbing her aching feet, Ruswita thought about the parade and decided that it had gone well for all, but particularly for the Salima Group. Earlier, when Lim had announced that they would attend the function, she had been caught off guard, completely surprised with his decision; it was not normally his style to be seen in public, especially in the company of the country's leadership.

As a group, Salima had to contend with the public's perception that they owned considerably more than was fact. Lim had been successful, Ruswita agreed, but did not deserve the constant attention that the International press applied to him and the family *kongsi*. Such scrutiny had not been a problem in Indonesia. The local newspapers survived, primarily because they failed to report anything which might jeopardise their licences, and it was accepted amongst Indonesian press circles that any story which referred to the wealthy conglomerate would naturally attract the President's ire because of his personal association with the multi-national group.

Other than Lim, only Ruswita was in a position to identify every asset the family had accumulated over the years. After they married, she had continued to play an active role in the *kongsi's* affairs, and held positions on each of the main boards within the group. This dedication had only strengthened her relationship with Lim, who grew to trust her judgement unreservedly. Together, they had added to the family's incredible wealth, until even they sometimes lost track of the international conglomerate's smaller subsidiaries. She knew that they owned or controlled more than one hundred companies, including cement plants, flour mills, steel factories and banks in four countries.

As the thought of their banking interests crossed Ruswita's mind, she remembered how Lim's two sons, Denny and James Salima, had almost brought down the empire with their ambitious attempt to establish themselves as players in the United States. They had both been most convincing at the time they had submitted their proposals to Lim, and subsequently secured their father's support to purchase a failing bank in the United States in order to establish a foothold in North American banking circles. Ruswita had not been too keen on the move; she believed that both the boys' judgement had been influenced by their desire to continue living the high life in America, as neither seemed ready to return and take their positions at Lim's side back in Indonesia.

Ruswita identified the problem but was not prepared to interfere with their plan, concerned that in so doing she would be accused of creating family divisions. It was already difficult enough for her. She had given birth to a son, Benny, in their first years of marriage. When he was of age, Ruswita had encouraged Benny to study in Europe, and he had done so. Lim had been supportive of the idea, satisfied that all of his sons would have a Western education. Ruswita smiled, pleased that Benny had been able to spend his summer vacation with them at home for a change. One more year, she reminded herself, and her son would be home to stay.

The logistics of caring for their sons and supporting their activities overseas had resulted in a myriad of housing acquisitions. Ruswita's own personal secretary was responsible for overseeing the accommodations and staffing for these, which included penthouses in Hong Kong, Singapore, Sydney, London and Paris, and palatial homes in Beverley Hills, the south of France, Baden-Baden and ski-lodges in Aspen and Banff Springs. Ruswita admitted to herself that she had visited some of these only once; she was too old to learn how to ski and did not particularly enjoy the cold. Besides, she felt that these homes were best utilized for the purpose they were purchased, and that her family and associates should continue to maintain as low a profile as possible. It would not do, she knew, for them to be seen too often with those who frequented their lavish estates.

Ruswita remembered the difficulty they encountered in Canada when reporters discovered the country's Finance Minister vacationing in their lodge. By chance, the Lims had visited that day, and were unable to leave out of concern that their connection with the Cabinet Minister would be pasted across the Canadian press, thereby destroying years invested in developing their existing relationship with the woman. Finally, having waited for signs that the reporters had all followed their VIP, the Lims had been obliged to sneak back to Calgary where they were weathered in and obliged to remain in the airport terminal for more than twelve hours.

Ruswita clearly understood the significance of maintaining these discreet positions. Business could never be done without such access, and she continuously monitored the *kongsi's* dealings with those in power. She knew that neither Denny nor James had developed the finesse required to maintain such relationships.

Her thoughts returned to the near fiasco both boys had been responsible for in the United States. Having convinced their father to finance their entrée into the American banking fraternity, James had openly boasted that they had greased the State Governor in order to secure approval for their acquisition. The rumour had circulated for several years, emerging as a major issue when the Governor's name was mentioned as potential presidential material for the United States. Lim had been furious and threatened to close down the entire North American operation. The young Lims practically begged their father to permit them to continue there and, as Ruswita then openly supported their request, he had acquiesced. James and Denny both realized that they owed their stepmother a considerable debt. Now, as established and respected middle-aged businessmen, who had their own families to care for, they took few risks without first clearing these through Ruswita. Until, that is, James took their American operations on a dangerous journey into the Chinese political arena.

She sat contemplating their family and business empire. Although their wealth was considered by some to border on the obscene, Ruswita had never flaunted their riches. Whenever they received valuable gifts, Ruswita would have these placed around the rambling Menteng residence, rarely conscious of the item's value or beauty. A unique painting hung on one wall behind the grand piano in the room where she now rested. Ruswita did not particularly like the flowers depicted in the painting, preferring the traditional Indonesian landscapes, which made her feel more comfortable.

When Ruswita had been advised as to the value of the painting which one of their investment agents had purchased in London, she had been furious. Her eyes moved from the Van Gogh to the piano, and she sighed. None in the family could play so much as a note, and she wondered why Lim had insisted on leaving it there.

Her thoughts turned to what the President's announcement would mean in terms of family commitments. Ruswita understood that Lim's personal participation in most of the negotiations would be essential to the company's future involvement in the capital intensive power projects. Ruswita had played a major role in the decision making process which had led to the President's decision to resurrect the project. The Salima Group had worked with those who had first proposed the grand scheme, encouraging the government to finance the programme on what was commonly known as a BOT project, a concept which provided for a consortium to Build, Operate and Transfer the finished project to state ownership once they had recovered their costs and profit. Ruswita and

Lim had spent countless evenings together discussing the plan.

In secret, Lim had orchestrated for the government to award the contracts to Salima Corporation; the company would benefit not only from the construction of the projects, but also the ongoing management, and then, finally, once the plants had been fully operational for some years, they would list these assets on the Jakarta Stock Exchange. When they believed their timing to be appropriate, the group would slowly divest all their holdings in the energy companies.

The President had been enthusiastic, and even more so when Lim offered to provide for a significant share in the company awarded the BOT contract, shares which were to be allocated to the First Family's oldest son. The President was uncomfortable with the prospects of facing another barrage from the International press concerning cronyism within his government. He insisted that the process of selection had to appear to be legitimate, and asked that Lim agree to a tender being called to satisfy public opinion. Lim had complied, committing the Salima Group's resources in raising finances to fund the ongoing project. When Lim had suggested that the budget for the entire programme would be in excess of twenty-five billion dollars, the President had visibly flinched.

The national debt, which even then the country could not service, had risen to two hundred billion. Depletion of Indonesia's oil reserves and the exponential growth in demand for electricity had placed the leader in a most unenviable position. Since accepting the mantle as the nation's new leader for his first five year term, not a day had gone by when the national grid had not gone off line somewhere in the country, throwing industry into chaos.

In his inaugural speech, the President had promised to address the nation's deteriorating infrastructure problems. Instead, he had been swayed by his former military comrades, and approved out-of-budget military acquisitions to keep pace with regional developments. As Indonesia's aggressive buying spree continued, so too did the number of major power failures. Before the end of the President's first term in office, dissent became more apparent, and rumours that a number of young officers had been arrested for petitioning their leader were being treated seriously by the investment community.

Ruswita had encouraged Lim to consider off-loading some of

their Indonesian assets until stronger leadership emerged. She had watched many of the other Chinese *kongsis* liquidating their assets and reinvesting outside of Asia. Singapore, once the darling of Indonesian traders, was no longer as attractive as it had been during the giddy days of Soeharto's regime.

She remembered how the currency traders had almost brought all of the Asian tigers to their knees and had vowed, at that time, to ensure that they would never be caught again, or at least, not as severely. Ruswita believed that ASEAN had not delivered, and that as new trade blocs emerged, so would the ASEAN ten nation dream diminish in importance as a global trading force. Ruswita had agreed with Lim's observation that ASEAN had been doomed from the start. They believed that its concept was far too inflexible for Asia, and that its exclusion of China and India, influenced by political considerations rather than economic criteria, would only create new barriers, not tear them down. The Salima Group had invested across all known political boundaries, not concerned with anything other than the pursuit of profits.

* * * * * *

Refreshed from her brief rest, Ruswita decided to take a cold *mandi* and ask Ratna if she would like to join her for lunch. She checked the tall, Dutch grandfather clock, and decided to call Ratna herself. She rose wearily, and walked though the main residence barefooted, out into the terraced area which led down to a number of disjointed accommodations. They had continued living at Lim's original residence after they married, adding rooms as necessary, until the entire land area was covered with buildings, interconnected by a number of garden walkways and terraces. At the rear of the complex there were four rooms to accommodate servants and drivers.

Lani's small apartment was located at the end of the terrace and across from a number of larger bedrooms, which were kept for visiting family and close friends. Ruswita and Lim each enjoyed their own bedrooms built on the second level, overlooking the garden walkways. He still refused to dress in anything but singlet and shorts while hovering around upstairs.

A miniature pond lay amongst *bonsai* palms, and Ruswita

stepped across to check if the servants had removed any of the goldfish from the pleasant setting. She stood there for a moment, before bending down and slowly moving her hand amongst the water lilies. Satisfied that none of the large fish had been eaten, she stood, placed her hands on her hips, and called out to Ratna. Ruswita waited for a response and, when there was none, continued through the palms carefully, until reaching Lani's rooms. Again, she paused, this time to smell the delicate jasmine's perfume, which hung softly in the air. She opened the door and entered.

The carefully decorated room made her smile once again; she and Lani had done this together, and her smile widened as a familiar toy came into view, placed alongside a photograph of Ratna's graduation ceremony from the International School.

She remembered how difficult it once was for Indonesians to access the school for foreign students. The new facilities endowed by the Salima group resolved the question of her admittance. Since graduation, Ratna had not indicated whether she wished to continue her studies, or directly commence working in one of the family companies. Ruswita sighed, moved to the buffet and lifted the teddy-bear Lani had kept since Ratna's early childhood. She placed the ageing fur against her cheek and closed her eyes, ever so briefly, and uttered a quick prayer of thanks that the baby she now called her niece, had not been lost to her. Lani had been a true friend throughout the years, and Ruswita had provided for them both. Their secret had remained intact for more than twenty years.

As she turned to leave, Ruswita heard something fall and break inside the other room. Ready to chastise whichever servant was responsible for the breakage, she walked quickly to the bedroom and opened the door.

Ruswita's face froze when confronted by the scene before her. Ratna sat upright, in bed, the sheet pulled over her naked body, barely covering her breasts. Standing alongside the bed, dressed only in his pants, was her visibly shaken son, Benny. For a moment, the only sound evident in the room was the soft hum of the air-conditioner's compressor clicking into action. Then Ruswita stepped forward angrily.

'Get dressed!' she hissed at Ratna. Terrified, she climbed out of the bed, disclosing her naked body. Ruswita erupted. 'You,' she growled in her son's direction, 'Get out!' Benny bent down, snatched his remaining clothes from the floor and fled. Ratna dressed quickly, knowing that she was in huge trouble. She pulled her jeans up and fastened them over her fine, slim waistline, then slipped a cotton tank-top over her head until it covered her ample breasts. She ran her fingers nervously through her hair.

'Sit!' Ruswita ordered, noticing that her hands were shaking in anger. *'How did this happen?'* she demanded, standing in the centre of the bedroom, arms crossed.

'What is wrong, Aunty?' Ratna cried, almost defiantly. *'Benny likes me!'* The statement drove a cold sliver through Ruswita's chest. Her eyes narrowed.

'Did you have sex with Benny?' she demanded to know. Ratna's eyes widened at the accusation, then the tears poured down her cheeks.

'No,' she answered truthfully. They had not been given the opportunity.

'Benny is family, 'Na,' Ruswita exclaimed, using the common abbreviation of her name. *'What could possibly have entered your heads?'* she asked, rhetorically. *'Do you understand why you should not do this with Benny?* Ratna sat sobbing, looking around for a tissue. Spotting a box, she leaned over and pulled at one angrily, the gesture causing Ruswita to scowl.

'We are hardly even related, Aunty,' she sobbed, defiantly, then stopped just long enough to blow her nose. *'I'm not even a close cousin,'* she said. Suddenly, Ruswita was at a loss for something to say. She hesitated, then sighed, moving closer to the bed. She felt weak and needed to sit down before her legs gave way. Moments passed before she responded to Ratna's remark.

'It does not matter, 'Na,' she said, the anger now gone from her voice. *'To me, you are like my own daughter, and it is enough that I forbid you to consider any such relationship with Benny. Is that clear?'* Ratna's bottom lip fell. She nodded her head, sullenly. Ruswita sat on the bed as the silence continued. She leaned over and placed her hand on the young woman's arm. Ratna pulled back, and looked away while holding the tissue to her nose. Ruswita sighed heavily, and looked at her daughter. Then she rose slowly, and moved towards the bedroom door. *'I will speak to your mother when she returns, 'Na,'* she said, her voice steady, even though she wanted to cry and take Ratna in her arms and hold her close to her chest, as

a mother would. She struggled to keep the tremor from her voice. *'And in the meantime, do as I say or leave this home!'* with which, she turned and left, in search of her son Benny. Angry with Lani that she had not been there to prevent what had taken place, Ruswita knew that she had to act decisively, and what she must now do.

The following week Ratna Sari was sent to study in America, out of harm's way. Lani remained behind, as all the other mothers had done when their daughters had left to attend universities overseas. By the time her first semester had rolled around, Ratna had settled into the Salima stately home, acquired her Californian driver's licence, and knew exactly where to go for a really good time.

* * * * * *

Announcements that the country had decided to introduce nuclear power brought widespread demonstrations throughout Indonesia, but these lasted for only a few days as the Commander for the Restoration of Peace and Order sent his anti-riot troops into the streets where anti-riot centers had been established during Soeharto's regime and had proven their effectiveness in the months preceding his final presidential elections.

The President had instructed his generals to permit the demonstrations to continue, long enough to prejudice the parties opposed to his dictates. Then they had moved in, swiftly, executing the order to sweep the opposition away. Many of those detained simply disappeared. Others who had been arrested wished they'd learned from past experiences, and had remained uninvolved.

In Japan, demonstrators walked through the streets of Hiroshima and Nagasaki, carrying banners decrying the proliferation of nuclear energy plants in their own country, alerting the world once again to the dangers of radiation and the clouds of death which once claimed so many of their countrymen's lives.

In Australia, demonstrators picketed the Indonesian Embassy in Canberra, and organized crowds blocked access to the Consulates in Sydney, Melbourne, and Perth. In Darwin, Friends of the Earth joined forces with several hundred East Timorese and marched on the Consulate. When police were called to disperse the unruly demonstrators, fighting erupted and the Consulate was seized and torched by some of the extremists. In retaliation, the

British Consulate in Surabaya was stormed by militant youths by mistake, where they demanded that the terrified and confused Consul accept their letter of protest over the Darwin incident.

Opponents of the nuclear program warned of the potential disaster of locating such plants in what was considered to be a geologically unsound environment.

The Australian Government called the Indonesian Ambassador to discuss his country's announcement, and a number of meetings took place between senior cabinet ministers and the Indonesian representatives. It soon became clear that the Indonesians were determined to proceed with their plans to develop up to twelve NPPs in Java, Bali and Sumatra.

The Melbourne Age ran the headline, *Indonesia Joins Nuclear Race*, and the Sydney Morning Herald produced a series of maps showing how prevailing winds could carry radioactive dust the short distance across the Timor Sea to endanger large areas of Northern Australia. A computer simulation showing possible fallout from East Java in the event of an accident had been prepared by the Australian National University, and received widespread coverage.

New Guinea and Australia expressed alarm at the findings, which demonstrated that radio-active plume would reach both countries within a few days of any accident. Words such as Chernobyl, melt-down, China-Syndrome, Three Mile Island soon became all too familiar. By the end of the first week, most Australians were convinced that their country was in danger, and bilateral relationships between the two countries came under close scrutiny. At the beginning of the third week, the mood had changed somewhat, and Australian companies commenced looking for commercial opportunities which might be in the offing as a result of the ambitious nuclear energy scheme.

As issues closer to home slowly displaced stories relating to the earlier scare-mongering, information concerning the twenty to thirty-billion dollar project moved off the front pages and towards the sports section, until disappearing altogether as newsworthy items.

Only the Financial Review continued to run stories as, one by one, Australian companies announced that they would be forming their own consortiums to compete in the race for the lucrative contracts. Representations were made to the Indonesian Trade Counsellor, reminding him of an earlier statement in which he had stated that his country wished to maintain its good neighbour policy with its southern neighbours, and would consider submissions from countries which maintained a balanced perspective with relation to Indonesian affairs.

On the first anniversary of the President's announcement, tender documents had been completed for the first two plants. A probabilistic risk assessment secretly conducted by the Canadians had been lodged with the PEPELIN Chairman who, upon reading the startling statements contained within the highly classified document, personally had the entire file destroyed.

The first plant, *Rama I*, was to be built ten kilometers from the town of Negara, in Bali. The second Nuclear Energy Plant would be built alongside Mt Muria, some four hundred kilometers to the East of Jakarta, and would be known as *Rama II*. The remaining plants were to be constructed through Java and up to Aceh, as part of the national grid. The Chairman of PEPELIN, General Seda, advised the Press that tender documents for the first five plants would be available and ready for circulation within the following months.

* * * * * *

United States — Maryland, Camp David

The President's wife had elected not to accompany her husband once she discovered who their guests would be for the traditional late Sunday luncheon. It was not that she was in any way racist towards these people, but had acted more out of a newly acquired sense of morality. She believed that Camp David, as it had traditionally been reserved for close friends of the First Family, or visiting Heads of State, should not be used for such clandestine meetings. She lived with a growing concern that these financial thugs who used their powerful privileges to further their own vested interests would one day lead others to delve into the President's past, a past which she knew could not withstand close scrutiny. Publicity about the President's dealings with the Chinese-Indonesian bankers during his term as Governor could be extremely damaging.

James Salima sat alone with the President. He was pleased that this meeting would be conducted directly between himself, and the man whom he personally assisted into the White House. He had provided the necessary financial support to wage political war against his opponents. Although it was now time to call in the dues, James was not entirely confident that, with his new found authority, the President would remember the alliance he had struck with the Lims before leaving Kentucky for Washington.

'My father has asked that you support the transfer of technology for the *Rama* Nuclear Power Plant project. Without American participation, the tender process will become a fiasco.'

'You have my word, as agreed,' the President said, not at all uncomfortable with his commitment, as the American companies stood to gain significantly from the substantial energy programme under consideration. The technology was, as far as he was concerned, already virtually available in the public domain. Nuclear energy had been successfully developed throughout the world, and he could see no harm in giving an additional assurance to those who had provided him with the necessary support when he had most needed it. The invitation to luncheon at Camp David had been organised since meetings in this private setting were easily protected from the ever-inquisitive Press. Besides, the President knew that he might need the Lim support again, when he had completed his first term, and required funds for his re-election campaign.

It was becoming increasingly difficult for incumbents to raise campaign funds. Although he accepted that his people had bent the rules somewhat, the President had no difficulty with their behaviour, considering that his opponents were most probably being supported in a similar manner.

'There is one further matter, if I might now mention it,' James requested. The photogenic President smiled, his blue eyes masking the concern he suddenly felt as he prepared for what might follow.

'Go on,' he said, leaning back, exuding confidence. James took his time, using the opportunity to present his father's request. When he had first been summoned to discuss this issue, James had been shocked that they were to participate in what amounted to political lobbying for the Indonesian Government, and had suggested to his father that this would be most unwise considering the current climate. Lim had been adamant. His eldest son was instructed to remind the American President, if necessary, of his debt to the Salima family.

Although there were no direct commercial benefits for the Salima group arising from Indonesia's ongoing occupation of the disputed Timor territory, Lim's request was made as a gesture to the Indonesian President and the generals, whose pockets had greatly benefited from the military action. James was aware that some of those involved had cleverly reinvested their rewards in Australian based casinos, including one on Christmas Island.

'There is considerable concern in Jakarta that your Administration might take a hard line towards Indonesia's stand in relation to East Timor. I have been asked to seek your assurance that the United States will support Jakarta's position,' James revealed, hoping he had not misjudged the depth of his family's relationship with the American leader. The President mused for a few moments, then replied.

'You can tell Jakarta that the American people will remain consistent in their position over Timor, James. As long as the United States is guaranteed the same right of passage that our ships have enjoyed in the past, then there will be no change in the status quo. At least, as far as we are concerned.' The President had expected that the subject might be mentioned, and still marvelled with the frequency with which such issues were raised, not via political channels, but through powerful private lobby groups, such as the Lims. The President was annoyed that the small Asian backwater had been of considerable nuisance value to him, as it had been to his predecessors' Administrations.

The United States no longer feared Soviet intervention in the area; that bogey had been long dismissed. The concerns he and his military now faced were more focused on the growing Chinese influence in the region. There had been immeasurable resistance to continuing 'Most-Favoured' status for the militant country. China had proved itself worthy of being feared, particularly since recent disclosures revealed its capacity to deliver Intercontinental Ballistic Missiles to America's West coast. He knew that the United States, in order to maintain its forever weakening foothold in Asia, required a fresh approach to its position and alliances in that region.

The Lim request would in no way conflict with already established protocols; United States Navy nuclear submarines still traversed the Ombar-Wetar Straits undetected, and he would do nothing to jeopardise this strategic position. Satisfied that both had acquitted themselves as required, the two men ate sparingly before James, understanding that he had used his allocated opportunity, departed.

That evening he caught a flight from Washington to Vancouver, then flew on to Tokyo and Beijing. Less than twenty-four hours after having sandwiches with the American President at Camp David, James Salima, aka James Lim, sat down with senior Communist Party officials in China, and laid the foundations for his bank's future co-operation to provide the People's Republic of China with even greater access to the North American market. Under a shroud of utmost secrecy, James Lim then went about making the necessary arrangements for the China Ocean Shipping Company, COSCO, China's six hundred ship global corporation, to utilise the Asian Pacific Commercial Bank's American subsidiary for all of its transactions in the United States.

* * * * * *

Subsequent negotiations would result in COSCO being awarded three significant contracts in the United States. The first, a twenty-year lease over the former Long Beach Naval Station, would be passed to the Communist Chinese shipping company, with White House approval, on the basis of a fifteen million dollar annual rental. The contract left the American public spinning; the city of Long Beach was required to allocate two hundred and thirty five million dollars to modernise the facility, whereas COSCO's lease payments would require more than sixteen years to repay these initial costs. Patrick Buchanan, one of the foremost television journalists of the time, immediately christened the former US Navy yard, *The Deng Xiaoping Memorial Naval Base*.

The second startling development was for a one hundred and forty million dollar, taxpayer-subsidised loan guarantee to a COSCO subsidiary to build ships at the Mobile shipyard in Alabama. Then, while the American people were still reeling from these revelations, the American leadership supported arrangements for a Hong Kong-based subsidiary, Hutchinson Corporation, through the Panamanian Government, to lease the 'anchor-ports' on either side of the Panama Canal, a move which granted Red China a strategic toehold in the Western Hemisphere.

Fears that Mainland China was already firmly ensconced on American shores were viewed by the United States military as a grave error on the part of the Administration. The Pentagon chiefs looked on in dismay, as COSCO's placement of companies throughout the American hemisphere became even more obvious, making it evident that the Beijing leadership had embarked on a most daring, strategic programme, one which would give its navy a distinct advantage over the United States in the future.

With the help of their new ally, Panama, COSCO acquired the Pacific port of Balboa and the Atlantic port of Cristobal, both of which flank the Panama Canal. The Charleston Daily Mail pointed out in an editorial, that COSCO's agreement to lease the ports through a Hong Kong-based subsidiary called Hutchinson Corporation was the product of some suspicious back-room negotiations:

"Panama peremptorily closed the bidding, secretly changed the rules, and simply awarded the contract to Hutchinson before the American or other firms could even know what was happening." The twenty-five year lease was to cost only twenty three million dollars a year, but the agreements granted a two-year waiver of labor laws, and veto rights over the use of abutting properties. It was also pointed out that the Hutchinson lawyer of that time, was also the head of the port authority that awarded the contract.

A notorious arms dealer was named as the employer of record for the three COSCO deals, and was observed, along with James Salima, visiting the White House for a morning coffee session with the incumbent American President.

Chapter 8

The Palace at work

The Indonesian President sat motionless listening to his Chief of Army Staff's weekly report. These sessions had always been conducted in the privacy of the President's family home, because he had never felt comfortable holding such discussions in the official residence. Besides, the meetings were always informal, and he believed that his senior officers appreciated the gesture of being received into the *Bapak's* private domain.

'And I feel that his elevation to that position would satisfy Sumantri,' the General said, then added with an insincere smile, *'at least, for the time being.'* The President knew precisely what General Prabowo meant, acknowledging that the competent Major General under discussion was overly ambitious, and should be closely watched in the future.

Power changed hands in Indonesia only through violence. The President knew that there were those who jealously coveted his powerful position, and that he must, as his predecessor had done before him, diligently guard against those who remained in the shadows, waiting for their own opportunity to seize control. He thought about the senior command shuffle under discussion. Prabowo had been at his side when he had assumed the mantel of President, and had his trust. Besides, they were related through marriage, and this additional bond worked to their mutual advantage.

'What are we going to do with Arifin?' The President asked, knowing how Prabowo felt about this man. Very few of his Cabinet were not Moslem, and he wished to prevent the growing number of Christian officers from achieving too much influence within the military. There had already been difficulties with the *Batak*

151

Christians in Sumatra, and that perpetual sore which he had inherited, *Timor Timur*, had provided non-Moslems in the eastern archipelago with a forum to debate their own sectarian issues.

'He is well suited for the Eastern Commander's position, but I am uneasy with that thought. If we place him anywhere else at this time, we are going to ruffle quite a number of feathers.' Prabowo knew this only too well, as he had spent weeks considering how best to reshuffle his senior command posts to reflect the strengthening of the President's, rather than his own, position. Prabowo was sensitive to the many criticisms of his leadership style, and guarded against providing too many opportunities to those who accused him of supporting cronyism within *ABRI*, the Indonesian Military. He believed that General Arifin would be a danger to their power base east of Bali, and should not be appointed to any position which might strengthen non-Muslim support.

'Why not just retire the man and send him overseas somewhere?' the President proposed. The suggested solution had often been employed in the past during other presidencies, permitting the country's leadership to dislodge powerful officers and remove them from the country by appointing them as ambassadors. Prabowo smiled. He had hoped that the *Bapak* might make this recommendation. It would be better if his leader thought of this solution as his own idea.

'That would remove the problem,' he answered, relieved that one of his own supporters would now not be dislodged by Arifin's continuing presence. The President nodded. Although he accepted the necessity of these changes, he was never at ease with the constant reshuffling of senior officers. These actions might look like indecisiveness on his part. He knew that he had yet to develop the leadership skills of Soeharto, or even those of the master orator, Soekarno, and that he had to be seen as decisive if he was ever to be accepted by the Indonesian people.

The President had been angered during those weeks of national unrest when he had been branded by the international press as a colourless and brutal leader, who was obviously determined to continue the authoritarian style of his predecessors. The President believed that he had to demonstrate, not just to the Indonesian people but the entire world, that he would not tolerate the lawless behaviour his country had been subjected to by obvious, subversive elements. He could not understand why foreign governments failed to identify the need for censorship in a country which lived precariously, with violence smouldering just below the surface. As a military commander, he had witnessed such violence in the capital. He had seen the streets erupt and hundreds perish during the riots fuelled by irresponsible vested interests groups.

The President and General Prabowo completed their discussions and the Chief of Staff took his leave, satisfied that his own power-base had not been overly eroded. The *Bapak's* insistence that he move several of his stronger supporters into positions relatively distant from the centre of things might, he decided, bring more stability to the outlying provinces. *ABRI* had been embarrassed at its apparent inability to suppress civilian unrest in the outlying areas of Kalimantan, Irian, and Timur Timur.

Prabowo had been unable to identify the middle ground when considering the dilemma his powerful forces often faced, particularly when confronted with waging war on such minority civilian populations. He was all too conscious of world opinion in relation to the recent uprisings, and the response of his own people when so many had died during the lead-up to the last Presidential elections. Prabowo knew he was not alone in the belief that Indonesia could easily fragment into a number of smaller archipelago states, given the right set of circumstances, and he was determined to prevent such a situation from ever developing.

* * * * * *

Had the President been party to Prabowo's thoughts, he would have concurred. As a Javanese, he understood the necessity for his race maintaining rule over the other ethnic groups, and their resource rich territories. His small island of Java suffocated under the weight of more than one hundred million people, most of whom were peasants. He had attempted to rejuvenate the transmigration schemes, offering Javanese farmers fertile land and financial support on the other islands, encouraging them to move into the lesser populated areas of Kalimantan and East Indonesia. But, as his predecessor had discovered, the task was near impossible. The simple farmers would remain in their new surroundings only long enough to spend whatever they had been given, before returning to their over-populated homeland. And then there was China.

The President firmly believed that his country's Achilles heel lay in its inability to protect itself from China. He knew that his generals all concurred, that the Chinese would remain the major threat to their country's future.

As he sat considering his Presidency, the *Bapak's* thoughts turned to his family, and the image of his eldest son crossed his mind, causing him to frown. Although immensely proud of his children's achievements, he was not indifferent to the problems associated with the growing wealth his family enjoyed. He believed that many of the aspersions which had been cast were the result of rival jealousies only, and he was often bewildered by the accusatory positions taken by others who had also benefited from Indonesia's growth.

His son's most recent moves to become involved in the distribution of grain from rice field to store were, in the President's mind, highly commendable. He had listened to his son's proposal and agreed that, as rice was indeed the country's principle staple food commodity, its availability and price, should be ensured. The existing co-operative arrangement was not, his son had argued, competitive, nor was it sufficiently sophisticated to meet the requirements of efficient distribution for the twenty-first century. The President had agreed that his son should proceed to establish a monopoly over all rice production in the country, thereby guaranteeing both farmers and consumers undisrupted supply.

At first, he had been concerned that the price the new monopoly would pay the rice farmers was too low; but when his son had explained how the venture would work, the President was satisfied that the interests of all would be well served by implementing the monopoly. The retail price of grain would be raised and fixed; the wholesale floor price from the monopoly to store would increase marginally, to cover his son's establishment costs and overheads. The *Bapak* clearly understood the necessity for this and approved the higher price to the consumers. After all, he knew that only a small percentage of his people paid income tax, and the idea of this new distribution system, as an indirect means of extracting payment in lieu of a sales tax, appealed to the President.

Apart from the obvious, the other major problem with his son's venture had been in relation to the finance he required to establish the network associated with the monopoly. There had been open criticism of the project, and the President was personally offended by the suggestion that his son had been given the monopoly licence because of his relationship to the Palace. The President had instructed the Governor of the Central Bank to remove the chief executive of the government bank responsible for the scurrilous remark. The senior executive's replacement had willingly arranged for the necessary project funding, and once confirmation that the two billion dollars had been received, the new bank president's wife was appointed to the monopoly venture's expanded board. Now, it seemed, the project was experiencing difficulties again, and his son required additional funding to sustain the complicated and ambitious operation.

As he considered whom best to approach amongst his closest associates to resolve this problem, the *Bapak* knew that only the Salima Group would have the financial capacity to extricate his son from the difficulties he faced. He made a mental note to have someone summon the *totok* to discuss his son's predicament.

While the President sat deep in thought, he showed no signs that he was even aware of the constant flow of servants and family as they passed close by to his ornately carved chair, continuously checking that he was not in need of anything. Out the corner of one eye, the *Bapak* sighted his second daughter. Immediately images of her mother and the wonderful family she had given him sprang to his mind. He was particularly proud of his daughter's recent move into the world of commerce. Previously, she had been a quiet girl, living in the shadow of the other, more exuberant children. Then she married the young army officer, Sujono.

The President had been pleased with his daughter's choice, and even more pleased that his son-in-law had been promoted so rapidly over his peers. He recalled how quickly his daughter had changed, developing the confidence to venture into business as her older brothers had done. The *Bapak* willingly approved her project to place tolls on all major highways between Jakarta and Bali, and had wondered why it had not been introduced before, remembering how in past years, President Soeharto's daughter had been instrumental in introducing such measures on the capital's protocol roads.

An aide entered and stood some metres from the President,

waiting patiently until noticed. When the *Bapak* looked up and saw the Colonel standing there, he remembered it was time for his next visitor.

'*Bapak,*' the officer spoke softly, while standing rigidly to attention, '*Pak Seda has arrived.*' The President nodded, and the aide disappeared to his station in the adjacent room. There he would wait until summoned, knowing that it would be more than his life was worth to be caught eavesdropping on the President, and the powerful General Seda. Moments later, the tall Timorese entered, held both hands together in supplicatory manner, and bowed his head slightly in the leader's direction.

'*Selamat siang,*' Seda offered, entering and taking the seat across from the President, as he had on so many other occasions.

'*Well, Seda,*' the President began, always pleased to see this man, '*what do we have today?*' Seda smiled, prepared to move directly to the subject of their meeting. He knew that the news he had brought could only further consolidate his relationship with the Palace, and his position as the future Vice President. Choosing him would alleviate some of the problems with which the President was faced. Seda understood that a number of hopefuls had already commenced lobbying for the position which would become vacant during the President's current term in office. As Vice President, and as a Timorese, he would be perceived as offering no threat to the incumbent leader. His selection would, Seda realized, offer the President some opportunity to proceed through his term without being troubled by an ambitious deputy watching over his shoulder. Seda believed that he would be given the position, especially now, once he had delivered what the President wanted most.

'*The Japanese have agreed.*' Seda waited, observing the President's initial surprise, then the wide grin which spread across his leader's face. Seda had returned from Tokyo the evening before, and had deliberately delayed informing the *Bapak* until he could do so in person. The President continued to beam, extremely pleased with the news.

'*You have done well, Seda,*' he said, nodding at his guest, '*to tell you the truth, I did not believe that they would be interested.*' Seda smiled at the compliment.

'*They have agreed to support the venture as requested. It would seem that they had been thinking along similar lines, and have committed themselves unreservedly to the project.'*

'*And funding?'* the President asked, a little impatiently as his eagerness took control. He watched the other man's eyes as he spoke. Seda had developed considerable support from both the military and civilian sectors. He had become a wealthy and influential ally to the Palace, and had been personally responsible for steering a considerable number of profitable opportunities towards the First Family's business interests. The *Bapak* trusted Seda above all others, even General Prabowo.

He had learned that Seda's judgement in the past had been exceptional, and he had grown to depend heavily on the retired general's advice. He believed that Seda was basically apolitical, and not ambitious for power. The man's wealth had attracted considerable comment, but this had not unduly concerned the President, as he was pleased that at least one of the *pribumi*, even though Seda was not Javanese, had been as successful as he.

'*The Japanese will fund the entire project,'* Nathan Seda further revealed, disguising his own satisfaction at the remarkable success he had achieved. The President pondered this information, his face showing some concern.

'*When will they make their announcement?'* he asked.

'*We discussed this at some length, and they have agreed not to do so until you have made yours,'* he replied. The President seemed pleased with this, and nodded happily again.

'*And the other matter they had proposed earlier?'* the Indonesian leader asked, dropping his voice to a conspiratorial level. It was Seda's turn to nod his head, affirming that the Japanese had agreed.

'*They have asked that I return over the next months for further discussions but, in principle, it seems that we will proceed. The Japanese wish to inspect the existing facilities in Bandung. They might wish to establish something elsewhere, something more discreet.'* The President understood this reasoning and smiled again at his guest.

'*How long would it be before completion?'* he asked. Seda looked at the *Bapak*, having anticipated this question. Very few understood that such a project took years of research and development before coming to fruition.

'*The first phase will take approximately five years,'* he said, watching the President's eyebrows move together as he started to frown. '*The Japanese may be able to run both projects concurrently and, if this is possible, then both might be realized within that period. If not, then we should expect to add anything up to an additional three years for the second phase of development.'* The President had already commenced calculating what this would mean to him, as Seda spoke. The constitution had been altered at the end of Soeharto's rule, restricting future Presidential rule to two terms, each of five years. He thought quickly, wondering how he could manipulate this ruling, as it would be necessary to do so if he was to provide continuity to the project as Head of State. The time he had spent as Acting President would not be considered as part of his term.

Seda sat quietly, confident that he knew precisely what was flowing through the other man's mind. It would make little difference to his own strategies.

'Then we should encourage the Japanese to move quickly,' the President said. He wished it had been possible to have brought others into the discussions, even the powerful Lim, but knew that secrecy was of the utmost importance to the realization of this project. He was in Seda's hands, he knew, and was momentarily beset by doubt about the powerful position his friend now occupied. He had often wondered whether Seda was simply driven by greed, or whether his aspirations lay in other directions. During the months they had discussed the proposed project, not once had Seda indicated any ulterior motive. He dismissed his concerns.

The President knew that there would be millions to be earned from the implementation of the projects, and did not deny his friend's right to his share of these funds. They had openly discussed the First Family's involvement. The *Bapak's* family companies were to be involved in all financial aspects of the project's execution, with the exception of those areas controlled directly by the Japanese. After all, they had laughed at the time, it *was* their money.

The President agreed with Seda that Indonesia's most recent military acquisitions would not protect the country from China's aggression. Both had also accepted that Beijing would eventually need to cross its borders to feed its incredible growth. *ALRI*, the Indonesian Navy, would be no match for China's fleet. His own government's military strategy had been based on the premise that China would, eventually, become their enemy. China's intercontinental ballistic missiles were of major concern.

The Indonesian Army was inadequately equipped to oppose

any such attack, and he was determined to remedy this situation. He only hoped that his decision to proceed with the Japanese had not come too late. In the future, once his army had acquired the capacity to respond to any ICBM threat, the Indonesian people would most definitely demonstrate to their northern neighbour, that they would strike back, if provoked.

The President's own military background provided him with the ability to understand such strategies. He had studied the Chinese intercontinental ballistic missile capability and, although they had only ten of any significance, his main concern had been that the Chinese had the capacity to arm these missiles with nuclear warheads, whereas the proposed Indonesian weapons would only have conventional strike capability. He had agreed to enter into the joint development of the Japanese rocket with the premise in mind, that once Indonesia had the capacity to produce such a delivery system, the real significance would be in its ability to despatch missiles armed with nuclear warheads. This threat, alone, might act as a deterrent to China, and any other ambitious neighbouring country which viewed Indonesia as an easy target.

The President appreciated how well Seda had conducted the delicate negotiations with the Japanese. He was convinced that Japan would consider their participation in the construction and operation of the new nuclear plants, as a safeguard against Indonesia's successfully secreting surplus plutonium from the operating nuclear plants, and he was prepared to permit the Japanese to continue under this allusion. There was little doubt in his mind that the Japanese would never have considered jointly developing such a delivery system if they had believed this could, at some later date, be used by the Indonesians to deliver nuclear warheads.

The President strongly supported his country's military growth, particularly in view of China's three million strong armed forces. His generals continuously reminded the Press that their overpopulated neighbour boasted more than fifteen hundred tanks and one hundred submarines of which, at least two were nuclear powered SSBN's, armed with ballistic missiles. Indonesia's Navy was no match for China's sixty destroyers and frigates, let alone its combined naval and air combat fleet of five thousand aircraft.

The President knew that it would be most unlikely that any of the other ASEAN nations would be in a position to offer resistance against a Chinese attack, placing an even greater burden on Indonesia. The President concluded that, inevitably, Indonesia would be expected to provide the necessary military umbrella to protect the ten nation association against any future Chinese aggression.

And there were other considerations which plagued the President. His country's infrastructure had degenerated as a result of fewer investments in this unprofitable area. Each year, five million new births added to the conundrum, and the national debt spiralled to alarming levels. The President realized that he would have no choice but to address these problems, and turned to the wealthier investment houses but, disappointingly, with the exception of the Salima Group, his appeals had been all but shunned. The Indonesian leader accepted that he was fortunate to have the ongoing support of the Sino-Indonesian billionaire, who had become one of Asia's wealthiest tycoons and had been directly connected with the earlier First Family.

By comparison, Seda, although wealthy, was nowhere near the *totok's* league. There were others who had also fared well from generous Palace relationships but, unfortunately for his nation's economy, most of these entrepreneurs had milked the country, then transferred their capital overseas. He looked at the man to whom he had given more power than any other, and smiled warmly. He felt he could trust this man.

'*Seda,*' he said, almost affectionately, '*enough of this, let's eat,*' with which he rose and held his arm out to his friend, and steered him into an adjoining room where several of the President's older children were seated. They recognised Seda immediately, and remained just long enough not to appear impolite, before departing to leave their father alone with his guest.

* * * * * *

That night, as Seda lay quietly, he made a mental note that he should spend more time consolidating his relationships with the Salima Group. Over the years, he had enjoyed very few opportunities to exploit the powerful *kongsi's* hold on the Palace, and its First Family. Now, considering what had transpired with the Japanese, Seda knew that this would have to change. His star would only continue its ascent if he could devise a means to penetrate the Salima fortress, and rip the guts from those inside. For Seda was convinced, that as long as those who controlled the powerful *kongsi* continued to tighten their grip over the President, so too would his own power diminish. He *had* to find a way.

* * * * * *

Timor-Timur

'This is Leader One, on final run, do you copy?'

'Leader One, copy,' came the reply. Major Sumodjo armed the cannons and checked his altitude. It had been tricky flying. They had to tear down the valleys between the jagged mountain peaks avoiding the ground fire from the villages and then drop through the cloud at incredible speed to have any hope of identifying target areas. They hadn't taught them *that* during his training in the States.

Sumodjo belonged to 1 Squadron, based in East Java. He and his fellow pilots had been flying missions over Timor ever since the invasion had commenced, back in the days when the ageing Broncos had still belonged to 3 Squadron, and had been based in Iswahyudi, in Central Java. Their counter-insurgency squadron had been transferred back in 1989, clearing the way for the F-16s arrival.

He felt the sudden turbulence as the aircraft shuddered momentarily. He knew it would be useless looking back, as his wingman would most probably be exactly where he shouldn't be, and that would worry him even more than the rapidly approaching mountainside which had been determined as the day's target.

The American manufactured OV-10F Bronco ceased shuddering as it fell into line with the target area. All the pilot could see ahead was just more jungle. And cloud, dangerous cloud, blanketing the mountain. The crew ignored the combination laser rangefinder and target illuminator, a recently acquired modification used mainly for night targeting needs. This mission would be conducted, hopefully, with the target in full vision. Further back, an AURI Skyhawk followed, prepared to support the attack. Then, without further warning, they broke through the low cloud, sighting the target directly ahead. He didn't hesitate, squeezing the red release button at the precise moment the first village shack came into view. Bullets ripped through the air with incredible velocity during the four seconds window and, at the end of his run, the pilot released part of his load of incendiary bombs before pulling away sharply. Seconds later, the Skyhawk followed through, striking the target area with rockets. The young Javanese pilot's blood drained from his face as he pulled the powerful jet up suddenly, powering away from the hillside before any ground-fire could damage his aircraft.

The thunderous roar of jet engines was barely heard by the people below before their primitive village erupted under the impact of bombs and rocket fire. In those brief seconds, as screams were savagely cut off in mid-cry, and bodies were charred with the first fireball to rip through their compound, most of the peasants died.

There were less than five men living in the small cluster of huts, most of whom were older members of the mountain enclave. At the time the pilots delivered their deadly gifts, more than fifty women and children had been happily preparing their one meal for that day. Only two survived the unwarranted and senseless attack. One, a child of three who later died from her burns, and the other, one Xanana Soares, the self-proclaimed leader of the Revolutionary Front for an Independent Timor, who had been hiding in the remote village.

Chapter 9

General Seda and
Lim Swee Giok

Seda sat opposite Lim Swee Giok and nodded politely. Privately he was thinking that the man before him did not deserve either the power or the wealth he had amassed in so few years. Both men had built incredible fortunes in their time, although the Salima Group's wealth dwarfed even Seda's considerable assets.

'Pak Lim,' the former general continued, answering the Chinese *totok's* question, *'as Chairman of PEPELIN I would be in a position to guarantee that the tender decisions will favour the Salima Group. The President has already discussed this with me, and at great length. He has left it up to me as to how we provide for the First Family's interests, but I'm sure that you will have no difficulty in accommodating their needs.'* Lim knew exactly what this would be. There had not been one major contract signed over the past ten years which had not allowed for the customary ten percent payable as dues to the Palace.

What worried Lim most was the suggestion that he increase this allowance to fifteen percent, as Seda had insisted that his own consideration be calculated separately to the President's children's share.

The billionaire knew that the collective project could not absorb such obvious padding, anticipating his bankers' response, and their likely insistence that he place even more of his own capital into the new company structures which, if he could believe Seda, would undoubtedly win the tenders. He was sick of their greed. For years he had worked to build his empire, and along the way he had created many millionaires amongst the bureaucrats, military officers, and even bankers. They had stuck to his side like leeches, sucking profits from his lucrative ventures.

'Fifteen per cent is too much,' he said, breaking into a coughing fit.

He had not been well, and believed that the problems associated with the formation of his new energy company had contributed towards his condition. Chinese medicines and herbs had not seemed to have much effect anymore. Lim scowled, then remembered that the man before him had the President's ear, and that he should be careful when dealing with him. Lim had heard many of the stories circulating overseas as to the rewards that Seda's clandestine activities might have reaped in the past. He did not like the Timorese, but knew that there was little he could do but negotiate with him.

'Then perhaps there is another way we might resolve the problem of percentages,' Seda suggested. Lim looked at the man who might become the country's next Vice President. He knew that the rumours about him were more than idle gossip. The President had hinted directly to him during an earlier visit to the Palace that Seda was being considered. Lim knew that he now had to be careful about how he handled the delicate negotiations concerning what his circle referred to as *pungli* payments.

The Chinese abhorred the use of the word *korupsi*, as they did not consider such payments as corrupt. Instead, they had coined their own, softer terminology for these demands, without which, Lim was painfully aware, the Salima Group would never have acquired such immense wealth. It seemed that the man sitting across from him had thought his position through quite thoroughly, anticipating his reaction to the excessive *pungli* request.

'What do you have in mind?' Lim asked, struggling with another attack of coughing. Seda waited until the older man had ceased, before continuing.

'The Palace position cannot be negotiated, Pak Lim. However, I would be agreeable to having my own consideration offset against a position in the company.' Lim's surprise was evident. There had been no warning that Seda would attempt to position himself as a shareholder in the energy *kongsi*. Lim's mind raced quickly. He could not afford to have the man offside, but he also understood the inherent dangers associated with permitting an outsider access to such a substantial shareholding in his family's activities.

'That would be difficult to arrange,' Lim lied. He could not afford to have Seda so close to the centre of power. 'The bankers would be the problem,' he added, but both men knew this not to be true. Seda guessed that the Chinese entrepreneur had arranged his financing in much the same way as he dealt with government officials. Somewhere along the line, Seda believed Lim would have had to accommodate the bankers as well. It was common knowledge that the Asia Pacific Commercial Bank was controlled by the Salima family, and would be appointed as the major financier for the energy projects. Seda decided to try another tack.

'What if payment was made in two instalments,' he suggested, *'half when the tenders have been announced, and the balance when the first plant is commissioned?'* Lim thought about this too, still unhappy with the sizeable payment he would have to find for both the President's family and Seda. He looked at the PEPELIN Chairman, and wondered if he could negotiate the man down.

'If we could make arrangements within the tender documents so that the contract values may be re-negotiated once construction has commenced, then I think the Salima Group could probably agree to a total of twelve percent.' Seda resisted the smile hiding behind his mask of politeness. He was prepared to accept the offer, knowing that he could improve his own position at a later date.

'Pak Lim, my two per cent would need to be paid up front,' he said, satisfied for the time being. Lim looked at Seda and nodded. He would build the commissions into the overall project cost knowing that, even before they commenced construction, the budget over-run would start at twelve per cent, and this man would be in a position to approve the additional costs to the government. He was not in any way concerned with the morality of how business was conducted in Indonesia. As far as he could recall, not one of the government contracts awarded since Soekarno was toppled in 1966 had been commenced without some consideration being made to the First Family and their Palace sycophants. As the projects grew in size, and the President's children reached adulthood, so too did the scale of the consultancy fees demanded.

Lim recalled when the contract for the new international airport had been awarded, and the former President's son pocketed forty million dollars for brokering the deal on behalf of the foreign contractor. But Lim knew that the *Rama* programme was very different to those other projects, and not just because of the enormous capital required to complete the plants. The investors would have to wait a minimum of five to six years before their huge investment would enjoy its first cash-flow. He clearly understood the risks in committing to the multi-billion dollar project.

Lim had decided that this would be his finest, and last, major investment in the country. He was growing older quickly, it seemed, and he planned not to spend all of his remaining years in Indonesia. Once the plants were operational, he would sell the entire structure, passing the accumulated debt to the very people who would enjoy the power generated by the *Rama* Nuclear Power Plants. The bankers would accept the Indonesian Central Bank's guarantee which Lim would extract with Presidential pressure. He knew that this would, in the future, require further payments to whoever may be in power at the time. Lim looked across at Seda, knowing it would not be him. He also accepted that it was pointless attempting to speculate about who might lead the country once the current leader had completed his two terms in office. Lim had been in Indonesia long enough to appreciate that whoever this might be, the contender's arrival on the political stage would be accompanied by the same mystique and shadowy imagery that the Indonesian people associated with *Wayang* performances.

Seda and Lim finished their discussions and parted company, each satisfied that they had done about as well for themselves as circumstances would permit. The PEPELIN Chairman visited the President, and reported most of what had transpired during his meeting with Lim.

The following week, several members of the First Family flew to Singapore and Switzerland, making arrangements with their bankers to prepare for the first *pungli* instalment from the Salima Group of companies. The Swiss bankers bowed and scraped in typical subservient manner, as the familiar faces sat before them and explained how much they expected to be deposited into their accounts. Accustomed as they were to substantial inter-bank transfers, even they were impressed when they discovered that the first transfers would exceed half of one billion dollars. And on the day the winning tenders were announced, Seda received Lim's confirmation that a similar amount had been transferred into his account, as agreed.

* * * * * *

United States of America

Michael Bradshaw strolled from the tennis courts satisfied that he had acquitted himself reasonably well against his singles opponent. His doubles partner reappeared, and walked across the immaculately manicured lawn towards him. As she approached, he watched her long, purposeful stride, and well-tanned legs and he wondered what such a magnificent creature could possibly see in him.

'Great game, Michael,' she said, leaning forward to peck him on the cheek.

'That's for winning,' Ratna said, kissing him again, as she stretched, 'and that's for later,' she added, leaning closer and kissing him full on the mouth for all to see.

'Hmmn' he murmured, enjoying the softness her mouth offered. Michael then reached out to pull her closer, but Ratna resisted, pushing him back at arm's length.

'God,' she exclaimed, mock surprise on her face, 'take a shower!' Michael laughed and spun her around with a casual movement, then tapped her lightly on the bottom as they walked together towards the club house. Michael left Ratna with friends while he showered and changed. When he rejoined the group, he poured himself a long iced tea, then lay back in a deck chair, enjoying the early Spring sun.

He listened to the idle chatter, joining in whenever he felt he had some contribution to make, laughing as Ratna recounted some anecdote from life in far away Indonesia. Michael peered at Ratna through one eye, squinting in the glare, and saw that she had been observing him. He returned her smile, then lay back again, delighting in the warm sun on his skin. It was their last day together, and Michael had not objected to spending the time at the country club, knowing that there would be little opportunity to relax once he returned to Washington.

Ratna Sari continued to observe Michael as he lay outstretched, admiring his long, slim body and handsome features. She wondered how their relationship would fare once they had been separated again; she was not too keen on letting him go, alone. Ratna had indicated that she was willing to accompany him and left it at that; she was unsure what would happen if she pushed him too quickly, accepting that Michael needed at least a month to settle in to his new position, without her. Ratna understood that it might even be longer, knowing his penchant for forgetting all else once he became engrossed in his work. She had hoped that their time together in the palatial home would tempt Michael into taking that one last step, of asking her to marry him. The setting had been perfect; with the exception of the two permanent servants, the house was unoccupied and Ratna had shown that she could manage the domestic arrangements quite satisfactorily, dismissing the servants in spite of their protestations, preparing all of their meals by herself.

But Michael had seemed to be too preoccupied with his new challenge, and ignored the less than subtle hints thrown constantly his way. The possibility that he might not really love her challenged Ratna's confidence, and threatened to spoil their remaining moments together.

* * * * * *

They had first met at college. She had noticed the tall, athletic figure working its way around the track at a time when most other students had not even risen for the day. Ratna had taken to *tai chi*, and carried out her exercises alone, in the early morning hours so as to avoid the inquisitive glances of others. She had watched Michael pound his way around the deserted track and wondered who the solitary runner might be.

On another occasion, she recognized Michael playing tennis, and had stood admiring his game. It was a sport which had captivated Ratna since she had first observed it in Jakarta. It was obvious from his play that this player had followed the game for some years. She watched as Michael easily dispensed with his unfortunate opponent. When he left the court, Ratna moved directly into his field of vision, in order to attract his attention.

Michael collected his shoulder bag and glanced over at the attractive girl he had observed watching the game. He assumed she was one of the thousands of undergraduates attending college there, and turned his attention to the small group of friends who had been waiting for him to finish play. Ratna watched him join the others overlooking the courts, then walked over to where he stood and introduced herself, complimenting Michael on his game. Ratna had stood close to Michael, sending signals that were embarrassingly obvious to Michael and his friends. He was flattered; the girl's soft brown aquiline features were almost aristocratic, and her tall, slim body could have belonged to a model. When she had moved even closer, he could smell her exotic perfume.

'Hope you're available for coaching,' she said, flirting shamelessly. The other women in the group smiled at each other. Michael had that effect on most women, especially admiring undergraduates.

'Sure,' Michael grinned, deciding to play along, winking at the others, 'but I am expensive,' he had joked.

'Don't you think I could afford you?' she continued the banter, causing one of the older ladies present to cough as she suppressed a laugh. Michael gave her his best smile.

'Well, we could always find out,' he said, delighted with her attention. His friends became impatient to leave and he knew they would not be impressed should he ask her to join them. So, determined not to lose contact with the beautiful girl, he wrote down her number, promising to ring. That weekend, he had phoned and was delighted that she remembered their brief encounter. They agreed to meet. When she had insisted on picking him up from his friend's apartment, Michael had whistled when he saw the racing red Lamborghini she was driving, and regretted inferring that she was an impoverished student at their first meeting.

'Well,' he said, climbing into the passenger seat, 'I'm impressed.' Ratna laughed softly as she adjusted her sunglasses and patted him on the knee.

'Don't be,' she said, lightly, 'everyone who is anyone has one just like this in Jakarta.' Ratna went on to explain that these cars had become just another status symbol in Indonesia. When ownership of the prestige car manufacturer had passed to the Soeharto children, it had become mandatory for the rich and famous in her country to have at least one of the fabulous cars in their garages, somewhere, as a token of their support. He had barely had time to buckle-up when Ratna drove her foot to the floor, throwing the Lamborghini forward to the sound of screaming tyres.

Ratna had driven to impress, causing Michael to squirm as she pushed the needle dangerously past established speed limits. He had sat, white faced, but determined not to show his concern. When they finally arrived at the Salima residence, Michael cocked one eyebrow questioningly. Ratna enjoyed his surprise at the extent of the grounds and the magnificent residence which stood, floodlit, at the end of a long, tree-lined driveway.

'Yours?' he had asked, standing before the tall white columns and marble steps which led up to the expansive entrance.

'Aunty's,' she replied, grabbing him by the arm and running excitedly up the steps. Michael was not surprised to discover that the mansion was staffed. Two Indonesian women appeared and welcomed him as Ratna dragged him through the main reception, and through the mansion into the back garden. She laughed, childishly, pleased with the continued surprise she was causing as they came upon the delightful setting. It was as if the home had been built around an amphitheatre of natural rocks and cascading waterfalls. Incredible volumes of water poured from all around one end of the tropical garden, plummeting down through rocks until spilling over a ledge, behind which he could see the back wall of a flood-lit cave.

The grotto effect was stunning, and Michael walked slowly down the steps which led to the perfectly contoured swimming pool, as if in a dream. He stopped and turned, embarrassed, realising that he had left Ratna behind.

'Impressive, huh?' she said, skipping down the steps, two at a time. Michael watched as she removed the scarf which had been tied over her hair, and knotted it casually around the nearby railing. The moonlight caught her hair and she smiled at him again. Michael felt something warm stir inside. She was undoubtedly one of the most beautiful women he had ever seen, and he experienced a moment of uncertainty. The tantalising fragrance of her presence and the idyllic setting all caused him to shake his head in admiration.

'It's magnificent, Ratna,' was all he could say. One of the servants appeared at the top of the steps and said something totally alien to Michael's ears. He watched as Ratna offered confident instructions to the older woman then turned, pulling him to his feet.

'Swim!' she urged, pulling with great difficulty as he pretended resistance, permitting his weight to hold her slender arms powerless. 'Swim!' she said again, playfully, pretending to pout. Michael rose and followed her down to the water's edge. He stood there, hands resting in his side pockets, taking in the breathtaking setting. 'Swim!' she called once more, giggling childishly. He turned in time to catch Ratna launch herself into the pool. Michael glanced quickly to see if the servants had seen her remove her clothes and plunge into the water. Then he wondered who else might be looking down upon them from the rows of what appeared to be bedroom windows, which ran the length of the building along the second floor.

'Come in, Michael,' he heard her call, turning back just as she jumped playfully into the air revealing her breasts for him to see. He hesitated.

'What the hell,' he muttered to no one in particular as he stripped, before throwing himself into the pool quickly. When he came to the surface she was already at his side, and threw her arms around his neck, her legs turning around his waist. He watched as Ratna dipped her head forward, then quickly flicked it back, to remove the excess water on her face. Then she leaned forward and kissed him lustfully, driving her tongue deep into his mouth.

As the warmth of her kiss passed through his body Michael felt his senses react, and he broke away, embarrassed that they might be observed. Ratna flung her arms wildly as she sunk unexpectedly. She kicked against the bottom of the pool, rising back to the surface, coughing from water she had swallowed. Michael reached forward to help, but she turned and swam away, across the pool, under the waterfall and into the grotto. He knew he had to follow, concerned that she might be upset. With several powerful strokes, he too entered the man-made cave, where he found her smiling. Waiting.

Michael knew it was not necessary to speak. He moved to her and they embraced, this time his own tongue searching for hers. He felt her hand grasp him firmly and guide him towards her, as she moved firmly against his body and raised her thighs. He pulled her closer, savagely, and as he entered the warmth of her body Ratna's nails dug sharply into his back, the pain lost in the urgency of their coupling. They gripped each other fiercely, kissing, holding each other tightly, their movements gathering momentum, as they raced towards the prize which awaited them both.

Michael responded to her sensual movements, and he could

sense that she was approaching climax as her rhythm changed, driving him even harder as their bodies slapped together in the waist deep water. Suddenly, as she buried her nails even further into his back, Ratna cried out, and his knees weakened as the warm urgent flow left his body in short, frenzied, convulsions. Michael heard himself cry out also, and he groped for support as she drove her teeth deep into his right shoulder. And then, finally, they were spent, and they kissed.

For a long moment, he held her tightly, feeling a reckless passionate abandonment of caution. She raised her head and looked into his eyes, then kissed him with a tenderness he had not thought possible. Michael moved her body to the side, then placed his hands under her, to keep her afloat. Then he bent down and kissed her gently on each of her firm, pink nipples, causing her to shudder. As minutes ticked by and they began to feel the cold, Michael placed his hand around her waist, and led Ratna back through the waterfall and into the evening's soft moonlight.

* * * * * *

As they swam back across the pool, Michael saw, with some surprise, that the servants had placed two chairs and a table close to where he had stripped. Their clothes had been neatly placed on the chairs, and he could see that they had left towels and gowns for them to wear. In the centre of the table was a silver ice bucket, and what looked like champagne.

When Michael saw this, he stopped, looked at Ratna, and started laughing. She had seduced him! He climbed out of the pool and reached for her extended hands, pulling her after him. No longer concerned with the servants whom he guessed were still watching, they towelled each other, then dressed in the robes and sat at the table smiling at each other while Michael poured from the bottle of Dom Perignon. As soon as the lovers had settled down to sipping champagne, and basking in the afterglow of their sexual tryst, the servants carried dinner down from the terrace, and served the traditional dishes in silence.

Michael was concerned from their demeanour that he might have offended the two women. When they had finished serving the meal and quietly removed the dishes, he smiled broadly and thanked them both for the delightful meal. Immediately, they broke out in giggles and hurried away. Later, with the memory of their love-making still fresh in their minds, they lay alongside the pool, secure in each other's presence, listening to the evening sounds as the moon disappeared and darkness encroached upon the setting. Then they talked. Their conversation triggered childhood memories for both, as they recited tales and provided each other with personal glimpses into each others pasts. They lay quietly together, with but a few secrets remaining between them as each held back, just a little, reluctantly retaining some memories out of concern that the other might not understand. For Ratna, hers were of the most intimate nature. She knew that this was not the moment for her to purge herself of events which had led her to America. As for Michael, his recollections were far darker and more complicated than he could possibly reveal.

When the cool evening air failed to remind them of the hour, a polite cough from one of the doting servants encouraged them both to move inside. Michael followed his beautiful hostess up the stairs to her magnificent bedroom, where they shed their towels and showered, together. They were unable to resist each other's touch as the warm, pulsating jets washed over their bodies, and Michael carried Ratna, still covered with soap, into her bedroom. There, they made love again, kissing tenderly, at first, their hands stroking each other gently, softly, murmuring as their excitement grew, their passion arousing their deepest urges. They grasped frantically at each other, urged along the same sensual path which carried them both to the same sublime ending. Then, as their breathing returned to normal, Michael rolled to his side and released a long, deep, sigh.

Within minutes, Ratna and Michael had fallen asleep, the soft evening sounds lulling them as they slept, in full embrace, oblivious to the world outside.

* * * * * *

Early Californian sunshine settled softly around the pool as they sat quietly together, eating the splendid breakfast prepared by the still-giggling, and friendly servants. Together, Ratna and Michael remained beside the pool throughout the day, talking, laughing, reminiscing, and learning more of each others' secrets.

'You had to call him *the Colonel*?' she had asked, incredulously. Michael had just laughed. It was difficult to explain.

'He's really a great guy, Ratna,' he said, not really wanting to go too deeply into his past. Michael looked at her. She was so attractive, young, and vibrant sitting half-dressed before him. He accepted that he was besotted. He had never experienced such warmth before, yet a trickle of doubt challenged his feelings. 'The Colonel was more than just an officer in the Army. He was much more than that. Everywhere he went, you could just sense the respect others afforded the man.' He then fell silent for a few moments. Ratna understood that she should wait, as he seemed to be struggling with old wounds, or sad memories. When he looked up, and smiled, she could see that there was another world which occupied his mind, and knew from the expression on his face that he was not ready to share those thoughts.

'Tell me about your mother, Michael,' she asked. Immediately, Ratna noticed a change in Michael's demeanour. He leaned back, and laughed, and before he even spoke, she knew that he adored the woman.

'Well, she's still beautiful. At least to the Colonel and me,' he said. He explained that his mother had been widowed while he was still very young. As he talked, relating stories of his childhood in Australia, Ratna listened intently, sincerely interested in his early life, and how he had come to be in America. She sat quietly when he related how lonely he had felt when, as a young boy, his father had disappeared, apparently without trace.

Ratna sensed that he had tried to make light of it, but she could see the sadness in his eyes as he spoke of a childhood of uncertainty, occupied primarily by his mother, and an older woman he remembered as Grandma Muriel. There had obviously been considerable pain during his early life.

'What happened to your Grandmother, Michael, did you all leave her behind?'

'Not really,' he had answered, and again Ratna could see that he was saddened by the memory of the woman. 'Grandma Muriel was not related. The title was just a form of endearment. She was actually Murray's mother,' he had said, wistfully.

'Murray?' she asked, to induce him to continue talking to her.

She adored his voice, and the slight Australian accent which he still had.

'He was almost an uncle to me.' Ratna then noticed how animated Michael's face became. 'Christ!' he exclaimed, slapping his long, tanned legs with both hands. 'You should have seen this guy play. No matter how the club pro tried, he just continued to thrash the man.' Ratna now knew from whom Michael had learned to love tennis. She didn't mind; after all, she remembered, had he not been such a keen player, they might never have met.

'Where is he now?' she asked. She invited the answer, knowing that he was enjoying talking about the man. She suspected he might have been one of Michael's earlier role-models before the Colonel had come along.

'It might seem strange to hear,' he said, sadly, 'but I really have no idea.' This had been followed by another chasm of awkward silence, and Ratna left the table not knowing what else to do, and dived into the pool.

* * * * * *

Michael's presence had raised some of her own childhood memories of life in Indonesia, and she was not too sure that she wanted these to occupy her thoughts. Many of the images of her first years were vague. She empathised with Michael, as she too had not enjoyed the benefit of having a father around when she most desperately needed one. Her earliest, muddled recollections were those of her mother, Lani, and her mother's strong-willed sister, Aunt Ruswita.

As she recalled the two women who had both played dominating roles in her childhood and adolescence, she was reminded of how often they had seemed to be almost the one person. It was hard to think of a day when one or the other of these two women was not present.

Ratna remembered little of her early days at the *Ora Et Labora* school in Kebayoran Baru, Jakarta. The memories which had remained with her were only those of her teen years, when she attended the International School. As she remembered the years at the mixed foreign high school, Ratna inadvertently swallowed pool-water, and had a spluttering fit. Michael called out to her, but she waved back, signalling that she was fine. She leaned back once more and floated, moving her hands and legs slowly, enjoying the warm sunshine on her face. The memories flooded back, carrying her to a time when she was barely seventeen, and the first time a boy had touched her, there.

As Ratna relived those precious moments her thoughts drifted further afield to the day she had been caught, with Benny. She stopped swimming. The memory was one not worth recalling, she thought, bitterly, standing on tip-toe and running her hands across her wet face. Then she waded back to rejoin her handsome lover.

* * * * * *

Over dinner, Michael revealed how circumstances placed him at Berkeley, attending post graduate studies. Ratna learned how he had accompanied his mother and her husband, the Colonel, when his step-father had been posted to Washington. They had remained there for three years, he had explained, during which time his parents had become quite attached to living in America. At the end of his tour, the Colonel had taken early retirement when he was offered a position working as a technical consultant with the US Government. There had been no reason for them to return to Australia, and the family readily made the United States their new home. Michael disclosed, almost wistfully, that although he had taken US Citizenship he still considered himself Australian, suggesting that he might even return there one day.

As the rest of his story finally unfolded, she learned that Michael had completed his post graduate studies and was, at that time, taking a well-deserved break. When Ratna discovered that her campus tennis star had graduated *summa cum laude* in Physics more than ten years before, and had gone on to complete his PhD, she teased him. She had difficulty visualising the handsome athlete as a physicist and told him so. They laughed at her perception that all scientists looked like Einstein and were a little erratic in behaviour.

He joked about their age difference, suggesting that he was already an old man. She felt that he was fishing for a response, and Ratna had coyly explained that, as an Asian woman, she preferred mature men. Michael was surprised to discover that the beautiful creature who had been his that day was, in fact, some years older than he would have guessed. She explained that her late start at college had been her aunt's idea. Ratna did not elaborate, mentioning only that she lived in her aunt's household, and that it was in Jakarta. Michael listened, sensing that she had considerably more to tell. Ratna became quiet, as if deep in thought, then suddenly turned the conversation back to him.

Ratna learned a great deal about Michael during their afternoon, his early days in Melbourne and how his mother had raised him alone, after his father had died. She realized that she had inadvertently struck a nerve when she asked what had happened to his father, as Michael became solemn, and directed their conversation away from what was obviously still a sensitive memory. However, when she explained that her own father had died while she was still young, this seemed to draw them closer.

* * * * * *

Towards the end of that week, Ratna was convinced that she was in love. When she expressed her feelings to Michael, she was surprised, then disappointed that he had not responded as expected. Instead, he became distant, suggesting that they spend less time together. To Ratna, he seemed confused, even bewildered by their relationship, and reluctant to discuss what was bothering him. Ratna was deeply hurt by his behaviour, and by Michael's obvious change of heart. Miserable, and distracted by what had transpired between them, in the following weeks Ratna came dangerously close to failing her finals.

A stern warning ensued from her aunt in Jakarta. Ratna understood how close she had come to losing the opportunity granted to her, and re-focused on her studies, trying hard to recover lost ground. A few more weeks passed, and Michael ceased calling altogether. She was devastated.

Ratna was not alone in the world of lover's sorrow. Michael also spent the weeks feeling miserable. He accepted that he had been smitten by the beautiful, sensuous and loving young woman, but he was uncertain about the depth of his feelings; it had all happened so quickly, and he was unsure whether their relationship could stand the test of time. Michael was not prepared to sacrifice the career opportunity he had worked so hard to achieve, only to discover at some later date that the spontaneity of their relationship had been solely the result of their physical attraction for each other. He became moody and indecisive. This too, was a new experience for him.

He could not remember ever being this attracted to anyone before, and was tempted to take the plunge, risking everything. But when the final decision had to be taken, Michael refused to follow his heart. Saddened by the choice he knew would please both his mother and the Colonel, Michael packed his bags at the close of the month, and headed for Maryland, leaving Ratna behind. He had elected to take the Colonel's advice.

Michael had always respected Colonel Zach's judgement. He had been more than a father over the years; the retired war hero had become his best friend. Confused, and unable to decide which course he should take, Michael had turned to the Colonel for advice. He had been persuasive in his arguments, and Michael conceded that Zach's suggestion to see how he still felt once he had been separated from Ratna for some months had, at the time, made a great deal of sense. Pleased that he had recovered at least some of his objectivity, Michael had then re-examined his options and decided to follow the Colonel's suggestions.

For it would have been impossible for him to continue his relationship with a non-American of Asian extraction, and still expect to be cleared to the highest level of security demanded of employees working for the National Security Agency. He knew from earlier interviews how senior government frowned on such relationships, even if marriage was involved. Although the career choice had been of his own, Michael understood that the influence Zach exercised, albeit with his interests at heart, had been considerable.

The Colonel had been instrumental in arranging for his stepson's interviews and, Michael suspected, his acceptance into the NSA. They had been generous, permitting him to continue with his post-graduate studies. They continued to guide him as he was gradually absorbed into the monolithic government agency which employed many thousands of bureaucrats, intelligence officials, military personnel, and technological specialists in its global-wide operation.

His impressive academic record had guaranteed him an excellent future, and he believed that he owed it to himself, and his parents, to at least give it his best shot. After he left Ratna behind, Michael Bradshaw continued on to Fort Meade in Maryland, where he dedicated all of his energies to his new masters in what had been often, and irreverently, referred to as 'Puzzle Palace'.

Ratna completed her studies in California, then moved to Kentucky where the Lims had purchased property and acquired their first American bank. Her mother, Lani, had insisted that she make the move, sensing from their infrequent telephone conversations that Ratna should expand her horizons and, to Lani, that meant following the Lims wherever they might be.

Chapter 10

Lim and the Salima Group

Lim had left the meeting for Ruswita and her subordinates to finalise, as the discussions which followed would be primarily tactical. He had not been feeling well, and returned home to rest. The mounting pressures associated with the mammoth project and his declining health had contributed to his general state of lethargy. His personal doctor had insisted that he take more time to rest, warning Lim that if he failed to heed this advice, his life would be in danger.

Over the years his arteries had slowly clogged under the constant onslaught of a high-fat diet. Almost everything he consumed had been fried, including his daily intake of vegetables. Although he never smoked cigarettes and rarely drank alcohol, Lim's health had deteriorated considerably over the past year, and his doctor had become increasingly concerned about his constant fatigue, and loss of appetite. The doctor had encouraged him to take Chinese herbs designed to restore energy in advancing years. Lim had even tried crushed and powdered deer's antlers and other Chinese remedies to improve his health but, sadly, these had all failed. The doctor further advised that he should return to taking mid-afternoon naps, and entrust others to carry more of his workload

Lim had listened to the advice, and asked Ruswita to play an even greater role than before. She had accepted the additional responsibilities willingly, allowing her husband the rest his body deserved. To the other senior executives responsible for implementing Lim's wishes, this seemed to be a natural progression in the chain of command. Ruswita had worked alongside her husband since the day they married, and was a most competent administrator. She clearly understood the conglomerate's activities, perhaps even more so than any other in the group, with the exclusion of Lim Swee Giok. They were, without exception, pleased that she had taken an even greater role in the multi-national's affairs. They had all worked with Ruswita over the years and understood her to be almost as shrewd as Lim in her dealings. At least, some were to whisper, relieved when alone with friends, none of the Lim boys had been recalled to take charge. Denny and James' American activities had reached the Asian Press, and those associated with the Salima group in Indonesia were apprehensive that either, or both, might be given control over the conglomerate's operations.

Denny and James seemed content to remain in North America, while the youngest son, Benny had focused most of his energies on developing the Lims' banking interests. Unlike his older brothers, Benny had concentrated on expanding the family's main financial institution, the Asia Pacific Commercial Bank, and had already successfully negotiated the branch status rights in many of the ASEAN nations. It would seem that all three of Lim's sons would become major banking entities in their own right.

Ruswita was most proud of their achievements. Her only regret was that her daughter, Ratna, still seemed to be lost in some nebulous world of her own, wandering aimlessly from one affair to another, refusing to settle down and start a family. Ruswita knew that there had been little time in their lives to spend together, and that there would always be a barrier between them as long as their secret remained intact. Sometimes, when lying awake at night, Rus would try to think of a way of telling Ratna of her true heritage, without disrupting all their lives.

Each time these thoughts entered her mind, her conclusion would be the same. Ratna must never know the secret of her birth. To reveal the truth would only bring greater pain to those involved, and perhaps even cause her daughter to despise her altogether.

* * * * * *

Ruswita was more concerned than Lim regarding the approaching tender announcements. They had discussed their position at length and, although they agreed that Seda's apparent influence over the President could represent a problem for the Salima camp, they recognized that there was little that could be done at that point in time. The only weapon the Lims had over Seda was their wealth and the ability to provide funding for the *Rama* project. They enjoyed some comfort in knowing that Seda would be unable to displace the Salima Group as they held the key to the billions of dollars required for the successful completion of the entire project.

They accepted that the tender process would be, for the most part, a mere formality. The President, if Seda was to be believed, had already decided on the tender outcome. When Lim had personally broached the important issue at his last meeting at the Palace, he had been disturbed by an apparent reluctance to discuss what was happening directly with him. He sensed that Seda had managed to manoeuvre himself into an even more powerful position than he had previously enjoyed, adding substance to the rumours of his imminent appointment to replace the current Vice President.

Lim accepted that he was already deeply financially committed to the project's success, and could now only hope that what Seda had promised would indeed eventuate. The PEPELIN Chairman had assured Lim that it was now only a matter of timing. Once the Salima Group had completed the necessary arrangements with the many international organizations involved in the project's planning, tenders, construction, financing and, ultimately, operation, the President would announce the names of the successful bidders.

Lim had managed to snare most of the likely participants through a complicated network of nominee offshore companies, and associated *kongsis*. He felt comfortable with the contracts Salima International had put in place and, through Seda, Lim had provided the President with a final list of those consortiums associated with the Salima Group. The President's sons confirmed that they had received their first *pungli* payment, and Seda was given the green light to proceed with the winning tender announcements.

Lim's only remaining concern had been the ever-increasing role General Seda had insisted on playing in the overall implementation of the contracts. Lim accepted that the man's growing influence had earned the general a substantial slice of the pie and, as Chairman, he deserved to be well looked after. It was just the uneasy feeling the billionaire experienced whenever he spent time in Seda's company that warned him to be careful, and Lim had always heeded such gut responses over the years. They had rarely been wrong.

The ageing *totok* was disgusted with the unusual number of senior government officials who had held their hands out even before the project was off the ground. Particularly because Lim knew he would have to grease them all again, once the nuclear plants had become operational. Tired, and distressed with the thought that he no longer enjoyed the President's confidence as he had before, Lim went upstairs to his bedroom, followed by the faithful cook carrying a tray of refreshments. She placed these in his room close to the king-size bed, poured the tea, then slipped out quietly as her master commenced undressing.

Chapter 11

Murray, Graeme, Peter

Murray went through the lists again, searching for the company's facsimile number. He'd had it in front of him just moments before, now it seemed to have disappeared. Annoyed, he threw the file across the table towards John.

'See if you can find their bloody number,' Murray said, 'I'm taking a break,' with which, he rose, stretched, and strolled wearily out of the office. 'Going out for awhile,' he called to one of the secretaries who had looked up as he passed. 'Take messages. I'll be back in an hour or so.' He then walked through the maze of offices and poked his head into the Chairman's reception to let Peter Wong know that he was heading out for lunch. It was not expected of him to do so; but Murray knew that Peter always appreciated the gesture. Wong's personal secretary saw Murray and waved for him to enter.

'He won't be long, Murray, just finishing up a call now,' she said, a tone officiously. Murray looked down at the short, unattractive woman who had dedicated her life to the company. He understood why Wong trusted her explicitly. She had never married and stood loyally behind the Chairman, protecting his back, and had done so for more than thirty years. Murray attempted to drag a smile from her but was, as usual, unsuccessful. He wondered why it was that she never seemed to have empty hands. Whenever he noticed her, the woman always carried files or documents wherever she went, as if these were some permanent part of her office accoutrements.

'Hi, Murray, sorry to keep you waiting,' the frail voice was Peter Wong's, as he shuffled into the reception. 'Do you have time to talk now?' he asked, turning and heading back into his room without waiting for a response. It wasn't necessary, he was the Chairman and major shareholder. Murray, although he had become quite wealthy as a result of their relationship, still quietly referred to the man who had financed his Indonesian *kongsi* as *the Chinaman,* taking care that Peter was out of earshot when he did so.

Their relationship had become strained during recent years as Wong had grown older, and started to display signs of senility. Murray followed the *Taipan* into his elaborate office and positioned himself next to the window. He had always enjoyed this view overlooking Singapore Harbour, off Shenton Way. He looked out across the calm ocean to the south, and could clearly identify the Indonesian island of Batam. Fast ferries raced between the industrial estates there and Singapore, leaving long, white scars in their wake as they dodged the ever-present flotilla of small ships darting to and fro, evading the ever-watchful Customs.

The unobstructed view was a welcome contrast to the many months of irritating haze which had preceded the monsoonal winds that year. Indonesia's slash and burn tactics more than a thousand kilometers to the south-east, in Kalimantan, and across the Malacca Straits in Sumatra had cast a polluting smog which stretched for thousands of kilometers in all directions. Changi Airport had been closed on several occasions due to the smoke-haze, and Murray recalled the increased incidence of hospital admissions during that time as asthmatics struggled with the suffocating conditions.

Murray's stomach rumbled. He checked his watch and waited. Wong had long since given up taking his meals outside, and often forgot that others still needed to do so. Instead, he would have his secretary slip down to the basement kitchens and select an assortment of *Dim Sum,* which always included the tasty *har gao,* and *siao mai.*

'What's happening to our tender?' Wong asked, finally lowering himself into the oversized chair. Even in earlier days, when his health had permitted the Chairman to still play tennis, Murray had thought the chair to be too large for the man's gaunt frame. He noticed the absence of the poodles.

Peter had never been the same since John Georgio had inadvertently permitted one of the dogs to wander outside the building, where it had been killed by a passing motorist. Those who knew kept the secret from their Chairman knowing how he doted on the animal, and knowing how the old man would respond, if he discovered how the accident occurred. Senior staff who had been around the *Taipan* for many years knew only too well that the man had a vicious, vindictive streak. They believed the whispers that he had ordered the contract which had resulted in the death of his latest wife's lover, and had no doubt whatsoever that John Georgio would suffer a similar fate should their Chairman discover that it was the American's negligence which had cost the life of his prized poodle.

At the time, Murray had warned Georgio to disappear for a few weeks, just to be safe. Now, he had returned, and Peter had given the man the responsibility for handling the company's public relations. Murray knew that this really amounted to John looking after the Chairman's needs as discreetly as possible.

'We're just about there, Peter,' Murray answered, stifling a yawn. 'There are a few loose ends to tidy up before the end of the week but, apart from those, we're looking good.'

'What about the others?' Wong asked. Murray looked directly at the Chairman, anticipating the question. He had known Peter for many years, and expected the man to ask the obvious.

'Well, let's see,' Murray replied, settling down further into the olive green leather chair. He knew then that there would be no time for lunch. Wong would expect him to run through the entire list of registered tender applications and postulate as to how each of their competitors might fare with their submissions. He had been though this process before, and resigned himself to the tedious task of running though the information yet again. 'Westinghouse and General Electric seem to be in the driving seat as far as we can ascertain. Atomic Energy of Canada are a little short on their funding proposal, but we expect their government to step in and offer to make up the difference by offering a soft-aid package in conjunction with the bid.'

Murray continued from memory. It was not difficult, he had been working on the project for more than a year and woke up most nights with data still running though his mind. The tedious, arduous task of collecting commercial intelligence was something his earlier training and developed skills permitted him to carry out in a highly professional manner. Even so, the months of sifting through data and other material associated with the complex tendering process had consumed far too many months of his life.

It was as if he had become just another cog in the Wong machine, with few opportunities to relax. He was constantly involved in the assessment process determining where their competition might be with their own submissions. All of the principal manufacturers and operators were well known to each other. Murray knew that there were, effectively, less than a dozen firms which would qualify for consideration to construct the nuclear plants. He had spoken to them all over the months, visited plants and engineering offices, negotiated with their management and, finally, compiled a detailed report on how he perceived the tender would proceed.

His *kongsi* with Peter Wong stood a reasonable chance of winning at least one of the tenders, but Murray realized that at the end of the day, regardless of how competitive they might be, the final decision would rest with those in Indonesia whose seemingly bottomless pockets demanded attention. He had spoken to Chairman Seda on more than one occasion and, although quietly confident that his offer had been well received, Murray was still uncomfortable in his dealings with the retired general. He was not convinced that Seda had not merely used their negotiations to improve his position with other tendering parties.

They continued discussing their relationship with the American companies before Wong changed direction.

'What about the Japanese?' Wong asked. Murray nodded, and continued with his update.

'Hitachi and Toshiba are well ahead with their finance packages.'

'Yes,' Wong interrupted, 'I'd expected as much. We have to watch the Japanese, Murray, those bastards will cut the legs off their competitors, given the chance.' Murray scratched his head absentmindedly, then continued.

'Much of the information we have seems to indicate that there is a piece missing from their submissions. Our source swears that he has given us everything that's gone through, but I'm not entirely sure that he has access to everything we need.'

'Offer him more money,' Wong suggested. It had always worked in the past. Murray shook his head; greasing an un-squeaky wheel was not the way to go. He knew the source well enough to believe what he claimed.

'Not yet, Peter. Let's wait to see what else flows through before we spoil him too much.' He noticed Peter's eyes flick. Murray suspected that Wong's mind was calculating how much their informant had received, and whether they had received true value from the man. Murray was not overly concerned that his senior associate had never put much store in Murray's ongoing association with the SUBUD group until then. The government official who had provided details of competitors pre-qualifying submissions was, in fact, an active follower of the spiritualist movement. It had made Murray's task that much easier, as they could easily meet in secret within the SUBUD complex without raising suspicion.

That he used the organisation's facilities to disguise his commercial activities in no way disturbed his conscience. The movement had prospered over the years, and Murray could point to a number of investments which had been realized as a result of the secrecy which surrounded the society's activities. Murray still played an active role in promoting the movement, world-wide. It provided him with an international network of considerable substance. He looked at his inscrutable associate and wondered what insecurity caused Wong to worry about his relationship with SUBUD.

'Murray,' Wong said, interrupting what he was about to say, 'what happened to the French?' Murray frowned before answering. He had made a direct approach to represent them himself when the tenders were first announced. They had made it quite clear that they wanted nothing to do with Australians operating in Indonesia. During informal discussions with one of their executives, he had discovered that the French company had been badly burned by Stephen Coleman's sudden disappearance, and the resulting backlash from investigations into his activities relating to arms shipments into Timor.

At the time, Murray had been shocked as the rumours about Coleman emerged, some even suggesting that he was hiding somewhere in Vietnam, or Laos, and that there was a price on his head. Murray was aware that all of Coleman's business interests had been seized or closed down, fuelling speculation that he had overestimated his influence with the Palace, and had been caught somehow with his illicit arms dealing. Murray suspected that Coleman had just run foul of someone near the top of the Indonesian food chain, and had been swallowed up by his own shadowy associates, who-ever they might have been.

Murray seemed to recall seeing a note from one of the secretar-ies some time back, mentioning that there had been a call. He had been away from the Singapore office at the time, and had not both-ered to phone the number Coleman had left when he returned, as the message was already weeks old. Murray recalled that the French were not the only ones hurt when Coleman had so dramatically exited Indonesia, although there were a few who did benefit from Coleman's vanishing act. Wong's company, he knew, had acquired a fifty percent holding in one of Stephen Coleman's lucrative prop-erty developments.

Murray was aware of the arrangement as he had been responsi-ble for introducing the deal. Now that Coleman was on the run, Murray also knew that his senior partner would take advantage of the man's demise. Murray also knew that Coleman's share in the venture had been entrusted to Wong, and that the Australian would, should he still be alive, never live to see or enjoy his holding in the property venture. If this should eventuate, it was of no concern to Murray. He had never really liked the man and, although he would personally benefit from Coleman's demise, he had no feelings one way or the other as to the morality of the outcome. Besides, he knew that Wong would never acknowledge Coleman's right to the equal shareholding he had held in trust for the man; it was not Peter's style not to take advantage of another's circumstances. Murray was in no doubt that unless he was careful in his own deal-ings with Wong, he could suffer a similar fate. The thought made Murray uncomfortable, and he quickly put this out of his mind, returning his thoughts to the matter at hand.

'The French are unlikely contenders, Peter. They don't have the Palace connections any more.' Murray then went on to provide more information to Wong, including his evaluations regarding potential project engineers and material suppliers. Their own *kongsi* was keen to maintain a position in the tender process, and Murray had spent considerable time in negotiations already, talking to Bechtel, Siemens, Framatome and even Larsen & Toubro in India. He was confident that their *kongsi* would most definitely be involved downstream in the nuclear projects; they had done their homework and been generous with the necessary payments required to facilitate their position.

Murray looked out through the window and wished he was on the cruise boat leaving the harbour. It had been too long since he had taken a break. He looked at Wong and wondered how the old man could continue to entertain the flow of young women that John Georgio managed to provide on call to the ageing Chairman.

'How about we catch up later, Peter,' he said, uncrossing his legs and standing. He was tired. Checking his watch he discovered that they had been talking for more than an hour. Wong merely nodded.

'Okay, Murray, see you tonight,' the old man said, catching Murray by surprise. 'Had a call from Johnny earlier. Seems he has something special for tonight's little gathering.' Wong grinned mischievously, and as he did so, Murray remembered he'd left Georgio behind to check his lists for missing communication contacts. Murray cursed under his breath, understanding then why John had slipped behind with the relatively simple tasks he'd been given.

Murray knew that the title Wong had given the American was purely to satisfy the man's ego as he was, in fact, basically the company pimp, responsible for the constant supply of Filipino starlets and Thai models through the Chairman's penthouse. Murray decided that one day he should ask some of these beautiful women just what went on in the old Chinaman's bedroom. He found it hard to believe that even if Wong consumed *all* the deer antlers in Asia these would provide sufficient impetus to maintain Wong's waning libido. Murray responded to Peter's evil grin, then returned to his own office.

'What's planned for tonight?' he asked John when he returned to his office. Georgio was on the phone and hung up the moment Murray walked in.

'Three hot babes from across the causeway,' John answered, cupping his hands under his chest. Murray doubted this, recalling some of the Johore Baru girls he'd slept with in the past. "I'm taking them up to Peter's around eight. Will you be there?' Murray thought about this and decided that frolicking around in the oversized spa might just be what he needed.

'Sure, count me in,' he said. His stomach was still sending noisy signals that he had missed another meal.

'Great!' Georgio responded, enthusiastically.

'Who else is coming?' Murray asked.

'Well,' John said, 'I could phone a couple of the Phoenix girls and drag them over if you prefer?' Murray remembered the last time these amateur hookers had entertained in Wong's penthouse. He'd caught the clap. Even with the Aids scare, none of them wore condoms. Murray knew that he'd been irresponsible with respect to his frequent, casual partners. He always carried a couple of condoms in his wallet but, since he had first arrived in Asia more than three decades before, he had often, in the heat of the moment, failed to use them.

Murray realized that he had been playing a game of sexual Russian roulette, and vowed to start using the covers in his wallet. He had overheard many an expatriate near his age boast that if they hadn't already contracted the disease, then they were not likely to do so. Murray wondered if you could catch Aids and the clap at the same time. He turned to Georgio.

'Give them a miss, John. I'll just drop in for awhile to check out the action.' Then he became serious again. 'Did you locate that number?'

'Sure, Murray,' John answered in the affirmative, and passed him the list. Murray checked the information, then nodded

'I don't need you around here, John, if you have to get on with organizing whatever for tonight,' he offered. Georgio accepted the hint and left Murray to make his calls. He rubbed his abdomen, conscious of the empty space inside and changed his mind, deciding to return to his own apartment where he would grab a quick bite and make the sensitive calls from a more secure number.

* * * * * *

The small party was in full swing by the time Murray arrived at Peter's penthouse; he had taken an afternoon nap and overslept. He punched in the security code and entered, making his way through the thickly carpeted lounge room and out onto the patio where he expected they would all be gathered. As he stepped outside, Murray was surprised to see the familiar face grinning widely from where he sat, against the pool-side bamboo bar. The small structure was covered with a thick matting of palm fibre, adding to the setting's tropical ambience. Coloured lights had been strung around the bar, and a soft, warm breeze blew across the Straits from the Indonesian islands. In the distance, well-lit ships steamed through the heavily congested waters, making their occasional deep-throated blasts.

'Well, well, well,' the man sitting against the bar called, 'John said you might not be coming.' Murray strolled over and extended his hand. Graeme Robson slipped off the bar-stool and clasped it warmly. They had known each other since the younger man first arrived in Indonesia and stayed at Murray's home during his first weeks in Jakarta. Murray had known Robson's father quite well, and had undertaken to keep an eye on the mining magnate's errant son. It had not been an easy task, although Murray now admitted that Robson had certainly come a long way since those early and boisterous times.

Graeme had dropped out in Australia, leaving his home town of Newcastle to travel the world. He never made it past Jakarta, overwhelmed by the women and their generosity. He had not found it necessary to work, as his father sent him funds regularly to keep him away from the family mining interests. Graeme had displayed a total lack of interest in working, and his idle manner had often attracted his wealthy father's wrath. Embarrassed by his son's well publicised escapades, his arrests when drunk and disorderly, and the drug experiments which had resulted in the death of an underage student, the mining entrepreneur had suggested that his son might benefit from visiting Europe.

Graeme had leapt at the offer to take some time and travel at his father's expense. Upon arriving in Jakarta, Robson went directly to Murray Stephenson's office, and offered his father's letter of introduction. Graeme then bedded down in one of Murray's spare rooms where he remained until, having placed considerable strain on their relationship, and to the older man's relief, Robson suddenly gathered his modest wardrobe one day and disappeared.

Although Murray had treated his client's son almost as a younger brother, Graeme shifted out after a few weeks, and moved in with an Indonesian Chinese woman considerably older than himself. As he had ceased communicating with his family, his father became annoyed and discontinued Graeme's monthly remittances. He had already borrowed substantial amounts from Murray, who refused further advances when Robson, short of funds, decided to renew contact. Desperate, he then borrowed from the woman with whom he lived, and she willingly advanced whatever he asked for, as she had been led to believe that they would be married. For a short time, her modest legal practice kept them both reasonably happy, until Graeme discovered even greener pastures.

Tempers had flared when Robson announced, without warning, that he was moving out. Amidst the heated domestic dispute which followed, Graeme brutally attacked the woman who had lovingly cared for him, even emptying her bank account to finance his stay in Indonesia. The police were called, and Graeme Robson fled to the mountain resort area of the Puncak, where he sought the assistance of another Australian he had met briefly through Murray. Stephen Coleman arranged for Robson to remain hidden in one of his villas, while he negotiated a peaceful settlement through one of his contacts in the Justice Department.

It had been difficult; Robson's attack had severely scarred the woman's face, and she rightfully wanted revenge. He was advised to remain in hiding, and wisely heeded the warning.

After several weeks of negotiations, Robson was permitted to leave the mountain resort and return to Jakarta, where he took up residence with the daughter of a local entrepreneur. Her father took to Graeme, relieved that his child had finally found someone who might keep her out of the foreign bars she so often frequented. Recognising another opportunity, Graeme Robson proposed, and to everyone's relief, he actually went through with the wedding. Robson senior was delighted that his son had finally accepted some responsibility in life, and had changed his errant ways. He decided to follow through with Murray's recommendations that they invest in the Indonesian mining sector, to provide his son with an opportunity to build his life, and his newly acquired family's future.

His company filed an application with the Indonesian Mines Department, and they were granted a coal concession in Kalimantan. Graeme was appointed to the joint venture board, and given a free reign to run the company. At first, it appeared that he would fail, as the rambunctious Robson had really not acquired sufficient maturity to manage the commercial enterprise given to him by his father. Murray was called in to assist, and within the year, the company turned the corner when they secured several contracts supplying coal to the government thermal power plants in Java.

Graeme had been married less than three years when he received word that his father had passed away, leaving control of his mining interests to his youngest son. Overnight, Graeme Robson became a multi-millionaire.

'John didn't mention you'd be here,' Murray said, looking around for Georgio.

'He didn't know. I only decided to fly over at the last minute. Peter's secretary brought me up to see the old man. Speaking of which, where is he?' Robson asked, turning his head and looking around the outdoor setting.

'He won't join in the tub. Peter prefers to have his action in the privacy of his own bedroom,' Murray explained, surprised that the younger man had not been to one of Wong's exclusive spaparties before.

'Will we see him at all?' Robson asked.

'He'll come out shortly, no doubt.' Murray accepted a drink from the one domestic Peter kept on staff in his private domain. Wong had mentioned some years before that the man was an imbecile but, as he was his cousin's grandson, he kept him on. 'What brings you to Singapore on the spur of the moment then?' he asked, swirling the ice-cubes with one finger.

'Thought it was time for us to sit down and put something on paper regarding the ore supply for the plants,' Robson replied. Murray thought about this. He knew that Graeme's family company held substantial interests in mining around Kakadu in Australia. When the Federal Government had permitted the company to open what became a fourth mine in the national park, Murray remembered reading that there had been an incredible outcry. Environmentalist groups had picketed the company's head offices for weeks, retreating only when public interest had waned.

'What have you got in mind, Graeme?' he asked, although he already had a reasonable idea. Murray had checked with most of the world's uranium ore suppliers to see who had arranged representation in connection with the current tender. He had soon become familiar with how the ore companies worked, and how price variables were negotiated years in advance of any orders being delivered.

'I thought we'd have a crack at a total supply contract for the entire project,' he announced. Murray was surprised at the ambitious position Robson's Australian associates had obviously taken in respect to the *Rama* contracts.

'The competition will be stiff,' Murray suggested, not wishing to alert Robson to just how much information he and Wong had at hand.

'Sure, we'd expect nothing less, Murray,' he said. Both men turned as the sauna door came open, sending a wave of instant heat in their direction. John Georgio emerged, followed by a hot, sweaty, naked girl. Murray could see from the girl's appearance that she was not at all pleased with whatever had taken place inside. John sucked in an excessive amount of air, flexed his muscles and strutted over to the twelve-person spa, then lowered himself into the bubbling water without first showering. As he did so, the girl following stopped, coughed twice then spat on the patio floor. She looked over to her friends and shook her head in disgust, pointing her index finger into the air for them to see, then slowly bent it forward until it drooped. Robson laughed quietly.

'See John's habits haven't changed,' he remarked. Murray could not decide whether to join the others in the spa. Standing in front of his dressing-mirror earlier, he knew that he was rapidly moving into that age bracket when heart attacks were not uncommon. Still, he thought, he had worn well. Catching a glimpse of one of the nude girls as she climbed out of the tub to fetch John a drink, he was tempted, thinking that even a man in his sixties needed to feel young from time to time. When another of the nymphs displayed herself, he did not hesitate any longer. He climbed out of his clothes, threw these casually onto the plexi-glass-topped table, and walked naked to the spa. The water was not overly warm, suitably adjusted to compensate for the tropical conditions. After several minutes he felt his muscles relax with the gentle jets massaging his back and thighs. Someone splashed, disrupting his thoughts, and he opened his eyes to see who had joined them in the spa. It was Graeme Robson.

'Where did you get this lot from, John,' Robson asked, reaching for one of the girls. She did not resist as he pulled her towards him. As her body floated over his, she nestled her hand gently in his crotch and tugged playfully. Graeme Robson's attitude to extra-marital romps was that of most expatriates living in Asia. Providing it was quick and clean, that's all that mattered. Even Thai wives placed condoms in their husband's pockets before bidding them farewell, and although Graeme demanded total fidelity from his wife, he saw little wrong with his own behaviour.

'JB,' was all Georgio said, using the common abbreviation for the Malaysian port of Johore Baru, situated across the causeway from Singapore. Robson turned the girl around, placing her on his lap as they sat enjoying the jets force blowing against their skin.

'Murray, what's happening with…..' Robson started, then saw the cautionary look on Stephenson's face. He nodded and changed the subject immediately, remembering that Georgio was not a member of the Wong inner sanctum. Although John provided a most valuable service to the old man, and did actually participate in the company's public relations activities, he was never given access to sensitive material. Murray looked back at the younger man and winked, while another of the girls moved alongside him and started stroking his thighs. His warning heeded, Murray stepped out of the spa and pulled the girl after him, as he walked to the sauna.

Robson watched them enter and decided to give them ten minutes before following, but Murray was back out before he had made his move. Graeme watched the older man leave the attractive Malaysian nymph standing under the patio shower, then wrap a towel around himself before settling down at the bar. Graeme climbed out and dried himself off.

'What's up, Graeme?' Murray asked.

'I had an interesting conversation with Seda today, Murray,' he spoke softly, looking back to ensure that John remained out of ear-shot. 'The general virtually inferred that the uranium ore contract will be handled by your *kongsi*. How did you manage that? The rest of us are still in the tender registration stage.' Murray raised his eyebrows, and waited, wondering why Robson was telling him this.

'Our group?' Murray asked, surprised that Seda had spoken of their arrangement.

'Yes, that's what he said.'

'Are you sure?'

'Well, he suggested that we speak. He knows that Australia can be very competitive, Murray. The mines in Kakadu can easily meet the *Rama* requirements, and then there is the proximity of the supply source to consider as well,' he argued.

'Did Seda say specifically that we were to talk about sourcing ore from Australia?' he asked, concerned now that too much information might have been passed to the Robson mining group in Australia. Murray knew that sometimes Indonesian officials revealed considerably more than they meant to, if for no other reason than that to improve their standing, or image with those involved in the negotiating process. He was becoming annoyed with the knowledge that Seda had held one on one discussions regarding the uranium ore contract with Robson. Then the thought struck Murray that Seda might have had similar conversations with a number of other supplier groups, including the Canadians and South Africans.

'He merely suggested that I talk to Wong, that's all,' Robson replied.

'But he never actually indicated that we would be awarded the contract, did he?'

'No, not exactly,' he answered, defensively, 'but it would make sense if he intends using his associates' shipping line for the deal. Doesn't Peter have a position in there somewhere?' he asked. Murray knew that Wong had leased the ships to the group of high-ranking military officers associated with Seda. *What was the PEPELIN Chairman up to now?*

'Sure, but that doesn't mean that Seda owes Peter any special favours,' Murray said, searching into his mind for something which might explain the strange request. 'What else did he say?'

'Not much,' Robson sounded unsure of his ground. Murray sensed that the younger man was fishing.

'Have you set anything up with Seda?' Murray asked, to the point.

'Of course not!' Robson responded, a little too quickly.

'Why not? Seems to me that you would be in a position to take advantage of the political support the Australian mines might have.'

'Sure, Murray, but I got the impression from the PEPELIN Chairman that whoever won the supply contract would be associated with Wong's *kongsi.*'

'Why would you think that?' Murray was deeply interested in what Robson had to say. If Seda had started shopping around at this late date, then they were all in danger of losing the contract. Word would leak to the suppliers and they would want to know what was really going on in Jakarta.

'Well, my guess is that he wants some Australian content. That's why I was asked to meet and discuss our position. I don't pretend to understand why, I just assumed that you guys obviously had the deal sewn up from what he said, and I decided to take a shot before you close us out.' He thought for a moment, then added: 'Whatever his reasons, Murray, perhaps you should have a rethink about taking us along on the uranium ore supply. This is a very healthy contract and I wouldn't be too happy losing it just because Peter is in bed with the South Africans.' Murray then knew that Seda had said more than Robson was letting on. Wong's *kongsi* had been very discreet regarding whom they represented in the deal. Murray had even deliberately laid a false trail, suggesting that they were representing the French and Canadians. He knew that it was imperative that he not disclose the name of his supplier. As usual, politics was playing an important role in all aspects of the decision making process.

There were still those amongst the Indonesian Military who had not forgiven President Mandela's interference in the East Timor issue during the Soeharto regime. It suddenly concerned Murray that Seda had been most receptive to the idea that the uranium Indonesia needed for the nuclear energy plants should originate from the very country which had caused so much political fallout over Timor. Murray remained casual, refusing to be baited further by the younger man.

'Look, Graeme,' he said, careful not to add credence to whatever Robson had assumed might be happening between Seda and Wong, 'I'll be in Jakarta myself sometime over the next few days. Why don't you come with me when I talk to Seda?'

'Hell, Murray, why wait? I'll take you back with me, if you wish,' he offered. Murray forced a smile. Graeme was always looking for an opportunity to invite others on his Lear Jet. Apparently he had forgotten that Peter Wong owned his own aircraft, and that Murray could avail himself of this whenever he wished.

'When are you returning?' Murray asked, as he poured himself a drink and dropped several ice cubes into the whisky.

'Not until after lunch tomorrow. I have some banking arrangements to settle in the morning.' Graeme waved at the girl he'd left in the spa. 'Why don't we set up a meet for early morning?' he asked. Murray shook his head. Unlike Indonesia, Singaporeans rarely entered their offices until mid-morning. He finished off the remaining *saté* Peter's man had placed there earlier.

'Make it around midday and I'll alert Peter. Okay?' Robson thought for a moment then nodded.

'Okay, I'll be over as close to noon as I can make it.' He lifted Murray's whisky and took a long swallow. Then he returned to the spa and the dark-eyed girl who was waiting for him. Murray watched them all play for a few more minutes, then decided to leave. He knew from experience that Peter might not emerge for some time, if at all. He dressed, said goodnight to the men, waved at the disappointed girls and returned to his own apartment.

That night, when Murray finally slipped into a fitful sleep, he dreamed that he was standing alongside a ship moored in the harbour, and that he and Graeme Robson were near exhaustion from loading the rocks stacked in mountainous piles along the length of the wharf. Each time they threw one of the rocks up and over the ships side into the cargo hold, Peter's voice cried out for them to hurry, as the ship would soon be underway. As he and Robson struggled to throw more and more rocks into the ship's hold, the mountains of uranium ore on the wharf did not diminish. Finally, they fell exhausted, unable to continue. The ship sailed away, its cargo holds empty.

In his dream he could hear a familiar noise somewhere in the background, and he struggled as his mind fought to distinguish what it was. Startled, he woke to discover it was his own phone that had been ringing. He checked his bedside clock. It was not even five o'clock. Murray moaned, then silently cursed his inconsiderate caller. He lifted the phone and mumbled his name into the mouthpiece, then listened, as a voice from his past brought him fully awake.

Chapter 12

Japan's Prime Minister

Prime Minister Hiroyuki Hata stood with both fingers stuck inside his vest as he addressed his Cabinet. Hata frowned at the group assembled before him, his piercing eyes darting around the members of the uneasy coalition government he headed. As he viewed them all, he deliberately avoided looking upon the three new Cabinet members forced upon him. All three were women. For Hiroyuki Hata, the code of *nyonin kinzei* had been broken, and he was distressed that another of the long-standing taboos regarding the exclusion of women had been removed.

'*Gentlemen,*' he commenced, clearing his throat, ignoring the women's presence, '*I need not reiterate that we are faced with a most difficult decision regarding the Indonesian opportunities.*' The Prime Minister then turned towards a window on his right and moved slowly away from the table as if leaving the discussion. The others present who had enjoyed the benefit of earlier Cabinet positions knew that this was one of Hata-san's practised mannerisms, and waited for him to continue. Others, new to the Hata-Satoh Cabinet, waited quietly without displaying any semblance of impatience. It would have been impolite.

'*We are faced with the continuing conundrum of whether or not the Japanese have the capacity to finally look forward, and accept that tomorrow's world may not have as great an American presence as it has experienced since the second half of the last century.*'

Hata glanced back over his shoulder as a reminder that he was addressing all who were present. Several of his strongest supporters shifted uneasily in their seats knowing where the conversation was heading. They had heard it all before and were still not comfortable with their leader's position.

'We have seen the decline of American military influence not just in our Asia, but also in Europe,' he continued. Hata realized that there were those who were not happy with his style of leadership but he would have to maintain his close working relationship with them until assured that their support was no longer essential to his own political survival.

'Japanese industry has followed the American thrust for more than six decades and now must consider returning to a more Japanese focused view in relation to our regional interests.' He turned, fingers still hanging from the small pockets cut into his vest. He forced a smile.

'We can no longer afford to be dragged into supporting America's political position, which we have learned from past experience translates, in reality, into economic considerations which only serve American vested interests.' Hata knew that he would have a fight on his hands; his Coalition partners had been emphatically committed to maintaining a non-nuclear proliferation policy as the mainstay of their political platform. He refused to look at the three women who, to his dismay held the balance of power in the Diet. Desperate for power, Hata had accepted that he would have to make concessions during the course of his tenure as Prime Minister, and his party's term in government. He could still not bring himself to any direct negotiations with the group. Instead, Hata had relegated his Junior Minister for Women's Affairs to handle all negotiations with the trio. He removed one hand from his inside coat and pointed somewhere into the air.

'We have arrived at the cross-roads; it is time for us to select the path which will be most beneficial for the Japanese people.' He then returned his finger to the more familiar position, and looked over his shoulder through the window. He could barely see the buildings across the park. Pollution had also been high on the political agenda during the election campaign. Japan was choking on itself, he thought, himself a firm supporter of an even greater nuclear energy program than that he had inherited from his predecessor.

Although Japan had long before made energy conservation a national priority, domestic energy demand had grown by more than twenty percent over the past ten years. In that period of time, the Japanese Government had embarked on an ambitious programme to increase its nuclear power generation plants, as it depended on foreign sources for more than seventy-five percent of its energy needs. As a relatively junior member of earlier Cabinets, he had clearly understood that Japan would have to remove this dependency. As an industrialised nation, they had little choice if they wished to continue to compete against the rapidly developing economies of China and other Asian nations. Although Japan had become an economic superpower, its defence forces were totally adequate.

For years following the Second World War the Americans had prevented his people from re-arming, using propaganda to convince the new generation that to do so would only convince the world that Japan had not changed its ways. Earlier Diets had, he recalled, placed a ceiling on defense spending of one percent of his country's Gross National Product. It had been impossible, with such a restrictive amount of funding, to maintain any real military force. Hata knew that this had been orchestrated by the United States to permit them to maintain their own presence in Asia, thereby enhancing their trade opportunities and political influence over the region. He was pleased when, finally, subsequent Prime Ministers had been encouraged by the Diet to increase this spending which resulted, towards the close of the twentieth century, in Japan becoming the third largest military spender in dollar terms, worldwide, even surpassing Great Britain, Germany and France. Hata also remembered how the American newspapers had pointed to Japan's growing militarism, alerting alarmists to question his country's intentions. He was pleased, at the time, that this did not prevent the Japanese Government from continuing to fund Mitsubishi and Fujitsu, the appointed manufacturers for Japan's recently developed sea-based Anti Ballistic Missile system, which had been developed as a counter-measure to defend his country against a potential North Korean missile attack.

He had been disappointed that the Americans had been successful with their military lobbying, securing the bulk of Japan's defense spending for United States-manufactured weapons. Joint Defense projects, he knew, were rarely cost effective, and he believed that Japan would always be disadvantaged in such contracts. He remembered reading in one of the defense reports how four Japanese-built F-15s had cost fifty percent more to produce than in the States. Had it not been for Japan's insistence that the Pentagon buy a substantial number of the M-1 tanks back from Japanese plants, then these would have been considerably more than the five million dollars each had cost his people to produce for their own military.

Hata did not trust the Americans; the defense pact signed before the turn of the century cleared the way for his country to play an even greater role in respect to regional defense considerations, but the guidelines were typically restrictive. Hata had scoffed when the Japanese Government of that time had entered into the agreement, which committed Japan to United States security strategies in the Asia-Pacific region, including the Korean Peninsula. Loose interpretations describing the pact had suggested to Japan's neighbours that his people would re-arm and fill any vacuum created by the ongoing American withdrawal from the Far East. There had been considerable resistance from the ASEAN nations and, as expected, from China, who viewed the move as another provocative step initiated by the United States to prevent China's reunion with Taiwan.

There were even many of his own citizens, he knew, who totally opposed Japan's move to rebuild its defense forces. It was Hata's view that Japan had little choice but to move towards establishing itself, once again, as a dominant military power. He scorned those around him who suffered from political myopia; these would be the first, he believed, to come running should Japan be threatened. Hata believed that defense spending should be at least doubled to recover from the years of American dependence. Japan could not boast about its defense forces; the Japanese Navy had only twenty-five submarines, less than seventy destroyers and a handful of Mine Warfare ships and auxiliary craft. If Japan were attacked at that moment, Hata knew that his country would be in grave danger without the American presence. Japan's strength, if it had any, lay in its airforce. Rotary wing and combat aircraft totalled one thousand aircraft; but Hata believed that these would only be of value for a limited period should his country come under attack.

As Prime Minister, he accepted responsibility for Japan's re-armament, even if this required that he manipulate the system to achieve these goals. Hata staunchly believed that Japan had little choice but to enter the nuclear age if his people were to survive the twenty-first century.

At first, there had been considerable resistance in his country towards increased nuclear power production. It had been difficult to educate the people. Hata had always been aware that the issue was as an extremely sensitive one for the Japanese. Although none of his own family had died in either Hiroshima or Nagasaki, he had known many who had lost someone.

There was a cancer of fear and ignorance evident in Japan which was greater than any disease resulting from the two atomic bombs of 1945. The Japanese were always going to be reluctant to see the perpetrators of this devastation as benefactors but American raw materials were needed if Japan was to advance. Hata had the support of many of his colleagues in Cabinet, and Industry, for they clearly understood that Japan's future would lie in its ability to maintain an uninterrupted supply of raw materials and fuel.

Japan had few natural resources and had become overly dependent on fossil fuels. The Japanese forecasts had frightened some of the old guard into action. When they finally understood that the world's supply of petroleum was expected to run out in forty-five years time, and that natural gas would follow in less than twenty years after that, the cry had been to return to coal. The problem of pollution was suddenly forgotten as the country faced rolling strikes and street demonstrations advocating a return to mining coal. It almost brought the shaky government down.

Hata had not been the first leader to realize that his country's dependence on coal and oil had to end. But he had been the first to risk his political career on confronting the issues. First, as a leading spokesman for his Party, and then, for a short time as Opposition Leader before becoming Prime Minister, Hata had persisted in supporting the accelerated growth of the nuclear power industry in Japan. Finally, his country proudly boasted seventy-five plants.

Japan's jealous neighbours had become unsettled as their own economies had fought to survive, alarming the rest of the world by claiming that Japan's fast breeder reactors had a sinister, and more secret agenda than the Japanese would admit to. For a time, ignorance had reigned supreme, precipitating calls for trade embargoes against his country. World opinion moved to believe that because Japan based its nuclear power program on reprocessed plutonium, the country was perceived as planning to develop nuclear weapons.

One of his Ministers coughed politely, breaking through his

reverie, and he snapped back into action.

'...and we have to look to our future, a future when Japan could no longer rely on an American presence to maintain regional stability. It is therefore imperative that we protect Japan's interests by consolidating our position in those resource rich countries requiring development capital.'

'Hata-san,' a voice called, immediately attracting looks of surprise from the others present. 'Hata-san, would you kindly tell us what it is that you wish to propose?' The men present were struck speechless that one of the women, Aki-san, had brazenly interrupted their Prime Minister's discourse. Hata turned and looked directly at the leader of his Coalition group and nodded in perfunctory fashion. There was an almost audible intake of air as those who knew their leader best, noticed the change in his demeanour. They watched as he stared at the insolent woman. The men waited anxiously, their eyes surreptitiously moving from their leader to the woman.

Didn't she know that it was customary to wait until he had finished? Had she no manners? Will Hata sacrifice Coalition unity now to save face?

'Aki-san,' Hata commenced, moving closer to the table and standing directly across from where the women sat. Hata had been against giving any of the women positions in his Cabinet. At first, he had refused; *it was unheard of*, he had argued, *having any woman in his Party's Cabinet, let alone three!* Now he found himself faced with the possibility of entertaining general discussion with their leader, in front of his colleagues.

'Aki-san,' he continued, ' *our country must consider taking positive action which will reduce the number of pollution related deaths amongst our young and elderly.*' Hata had anticipated there would be objection at some point along the way, and had prepared for the moment. He had been surprised that it had come so quickly. In an earlier government, Hata had served in a capacity which had required him to be abreast of the health problems associated with Japan's industrial pollution. He had been disturbed to discover the number of children and elderly people whose deaths could be directly attributed to the country's pollution nightmare.

Influenced by the facts before him, Hata had decided then, that if he were ever given the opportunity to reduce the country's dependency on coal and other high carbon fuels, he would do so. But his political experience dictated that he approach the issue in a tangential way - the Japanese way. Hata had decided that Japan should demonstrate to its people how harmless yet beneficial nuclear energy continued to be. He aimed to completely remove his country's dependence on gas and fossil fuels within the coming decade. It was, he knew, a most ambitious plan.

But Hata also had secret hopes for Japan's re-emergence as a military power, knowing that in the course of the next fifty years most of the world's natural fuels would disappear, and that only those countries with the capacity to survive with nuclear energy would continue to develop. Hata also realized that his country would need to be able to protect its sovereignty as neighbouring countries looked enviously at their successes.

He was aware how useless it would be to attempt to explain that there were more than five hundred such plants operating safely in countries such as the United Kingdom, France, and the United States, as three generations after the *Enola Gay* had dropped her bombs, the Japanese still lived in fear of the two words *nuclear*, and *American*. Hata knew that he would have to lead the way, accepting that he may not live to see the results of the seeds he had planted, knowing that his strategy would require years, even decades, of dedication from all involved.

'I am looking for your support to have the Coalition Government fund a Japanese investment in Indonesia, Aki-san,' he said, surprising all but two in the Cabinet. There was a hushed silence as they waited for their Prime Minister to continue. Instead, Aki spoke first.

'Then what is all this subterfuge about, Hata-san?' she asked, at which several of the Hata Cabinet went into near apoplectic fits. Aki-san's two supporters paled. This was much more than they had bargained for. *Was Aki-san mad?*

'Please remember where we are!' one of Hata's older members admonished, shaking his head at the woman's rude behaviour.

'Aki-san, you must apologise to Hata-san!' another demanded. Hata stood staring at the woman, his face taut with visible anger. Inside, forces prevented him from displaying his displeasure. He continued the game, moving in skilfully, laying a sticky return path which would entrap his opponent. If, in the future, the unpredictable did occur and there was political fallout as a result of his strategies, Hata was confident that his Party could always cast the blame onto

the inexperienced women. Hata raised his hand to silence his fellow Party members. He had to appear to be generous.

'Aki-san, would you support our Government's decision to build, own and operate a series of nuclear power plants in Indonesia which would provide, not only considerable immediate benefits to our construction companies, but also long term, down-stream opportunities for the Japanese people?' Hata left his statement hanging in the air. The male Cabinet members sat staring at their leader, then slowly turned to the woman he had addressed. None present had ever seen such discussion in the Cabinet room before.

'May I ask what the status of these plants will be upon completion, Hata-san?'

The Prime Minister paused, knowing that the time had come to play his first cards.

'First, I must have your assurance that what transpires here today will remain within these walls, as the Indonesians have insisted that secrecy is of the utmost importance,' he commenced, the gravity in his voice reflecting the seriousness of what he was about to reveal. Without exception, those present bowed their heads, agreeing to his request. He looked around the Cabinet, hesitating for effect, then spoke with a clarity that surprised even those who had known Hata longest.

'We have been asked by the Indonesians to assist them to develop Fast Breeder Reactors similar to our own.' He paused again, observing that those at the far end of the room had leaned forward to hear him more clearly. He deliberately lowered his voice, even further.

'The Indonesians wish to develop a Fast Breeder Reactor for the production of plutonium.' He looked around the room.

'If we agree, then we will be responsible for providing the Indonesians with a means to produce sufficient plutonium which, if unfavourably applied, could launch that country into the nuclear race. This particular reactor would be developed in parallel with eleven other reactors which, in time, will form part of a national electric power grid from Bali to North Sumatra.' The room remained silent. Everyone present considered the extreme significance of what had been said. A small voice broke through the silence.

'Why would we want to do such a thing?' Aki asked. The men present looked from her to their Prime Minister. They too wished to know but were pleased that it had been she who had asked the

question. Hata nodded, indicating that he thought the question fair.

'*Because Indonesia is the world's largest Moslem nation. Because the Moslem nations control most of the world's oil and natural gas outside of Russia, and could use that economic weapon as they have in the past, to extract whatever they believe is important to their survival. And last, because if we say no, the Russians will say yes.*' Hata stared coldly at Aki, and challenged her to accept total responsibility for her Party's position.

'*Would you believe that the Japanese people would be forgiving if we were to cast them back to the dark years in the Seventies, when the price of oil doubled, then tripled, nearly crippling our industries?*' Hata asked, his voice dropping, forcing those at the end of the room to lean forward to hear.

It seemed that minutes had passed before Aki spoke, and in so doing, she rose in respect and bowed with dignity towards her Prime Minister. There was an audible '*aah*' heard from the men, pleased with her change in attitude.

'*Hata-san, I would support such a proposal, of course.*' Aki had been confused by the suggestion that she might not support such an idea. It was preposterous that any present should consider that she was not supportive of all Japanese industry. Japan had been partners in several such ventures over the past years, including the Koreas. Her objection would only have been to the introduction of more enrichment facilities into Japan itself. Her political platform had been based on environmental issues; she would not support any further expansion of the nuclear industry in her country.

Aki had no qualms about her country's owning and operating plants which might be harmful to others; she only drew the line at having such facilities operating in her own country. She had committed her party to maintaining the moratorium on further expansion of the industry in Japan. It was all over. Aki had been cleverly manipulated by the more experienced politician.

The Prime Minister offered a conciliatory bow in her direction as a gesture of his appreciation, followed by which the room filled with another, and more audible sigh of relief. There would be debate on the Diet floor, of course, but few present would be told the extent of Japan's commitment to the Indonesians. Other and less relevant information would, over a period of time, be deliberately leaked into the public domain. The Prime Minister considered this consequential to his long-term plans.

Hata smiled. Once the Japanese people discovered that they had participated in the successful operation of Fast Breeder Plants in Indonesia for some years, he believed that public acceptance to the next steps would be inevitable, as these were essential to Japan's survival. Hata stood at the end of the highly polished redwood table, a gift from a grateful American Senator whose constituency had re-elected the man as a result of Japanese manufacturing commitments made to his State. He then passed the floor to his Deputy and sat, deep in thought, considering his success.

As Hata looked down past the line of faithful politicians sitting quietly, while listening to his Finance Minister read his boring statistics, the Prime Minister observed Aki staring down at her lap. Convinced that she no longer represented any potential impediment to his government's plans, Hata ignored the Ministerial notes as they were read, considering instead which of the three major Japanese companies he would have his trusted intermediary approach to discuss the government's financial support in relation to the Indonesian project. His thoughts then moved to how he and his Defense Minister would need to disguise the undertaking they were about to give the Indonesian President, to secretly convert the Japanese Civilian H-3B rocket technology to produce a military version to serve the defense needs of both countries. Hata had been thrilled, some years before, when Japan had enjoyed considerable success with its H2-A rocket programme, which had then led into the current generation of sophisticated rockets. Japan had cleverly committed itself to the development of a range of rockets which would be used to launch his country's satellites, moving away from the dependency on American and French launch facilities.

Negotiations had already been completed. Japan would provide Indonesia with the technology and necessary funding. The H-3B had already proved successful in its civilian applications and the conversion to military use, although not overly complicated, necessitated complete secrecy. In the event their purpose be exposed, both countries could easily maintain that the joint venture had been initiated at the request of the Indonesians to advance their own technology, which would enable the Indonesians to launch their own satellites in the future. Mitsubishi's Heavy Industry company had produced Japan's first major indigenously designed expendable cryogenic-fuelled engine, known as the LE-7A. Its successor, the LE-9, would be used to propel the military version of the H-3B. The development and testing would take place in Indonesia.

In so doing, Hata believed that he had legally circumvented the requirements of his own country's nuclear charter, which stated that its people were not to possess, produce or introduce, nuclear weapons into its territory, while advancing Japan's interests for the future. A future in which Japan's role in world affairs would be considerably stronger than it enjoyed today.

* * * * * *

Jakarta

The main auditorium was crammed beyond its designed capacity, causing many to stand outside the side doors while those inside cursed the loss of cool air as it escaped through the open exits. The noise level fell noticeably as several officials walked up onto the dais, and tested the public address system, only to rise again when they left the area once satisfied that all was in order. A large, black security case stood ominously at the centre of the platform. Those present expected that this contained the confidential winning tender documents.

The hall was designed to accommodate one thousand guests however, on that day, more than fifteen hundred had packed the auditorium to witness the tender draw. As the hour approached, a solitary figure appeared, and coughed as he tapped the microphone, before requesting those present to stand. They complied, and a line of officials all wearing the traditional black *pici* on their heads, filed onto the dais, took their positions and waited, hands crossed subserviently in front.

Moments later, a tall, gaunt-faced Indonesian strolled to the center of the raised platform and stood to attention. The national anthem, *Indonesia Raya* commenced, accompanied by an audible groan from a group of foreigners towards the back of the hall.

Finally, after some tiring minutes had passed, the anthem finished and the Chairman, General (retired) Seda, spoke briefly before moving to one side to permit his deputy to commence with the formal tender announcement ceremony.

Television cameras whirred softly as cameramen jostled for better positions, and hundreds of flash-lights blinded all present. The official ceremony was relayed by RCTI, which had established itself as a private monopoly in the television broadcasting industry some years before. As Professor Ali Mochtar ceremoniously unlocked the security case, viewers around the world watched the proceedings with mixed emotions, via the Indonesian *Palapa* satellite system.

There was a hushed silence as an envelope was handed to Chairman Seda, and he broke the seal. Seda smiled, stepped over to the microphones, and commenced by thanking his deputy. Enjoying the moment, he then read the results of the tender submissions for all to hear.

'Rama I,' he started, lifting his head as he spoke to the audience, *'the winning tenderer is The Bhakti Corporation!'* There was a roar from someone in the middle of the assembly, as the American joint-venture partners who had signed with the Bhakti Group burst into cheers. The Chairman waited for the hall to recover before continuing. He looked down into the sea of anxious faces.

'Rama III,' he continued, *'The Harapan Group!'* There was a muted cheer as the surprised French executive almost choked with the news that his company's partner had won.

'Rama IV,' Seda called, as he looked down into the front row and identified Murray Stephenson. *'Rama IV',* he repeated again, *'The Bhakti Corporation',* and the hall erupted once again as the American syndicate screamed out in excitement.

'And, finally,' he announced, anticipating the looks of surprise on the sea of faces below, as they realized that something was wrong, for he had not mentioned *Rama II, 'to complete the first phase, Rama V.'* Representatives looked at each other then back at the general, to see if he hadn't made a mistake. The Chairman paused again, then looked directly down at Murray. *'Rama V has been awarded to The Nasihat Group.'*

Murray smiled and nodded in the retired general's direction. He didn't need to throw himself wildly into the air with excitement.

He had known for some months that his group would be awarded *Rama V*. He was, however, just as surprised as everyone else present that something had happened to the number two plant. Company representatives who had spent considerable time and, in some instances, millions of dollars in the preparation of the tender documents stood waiting, confused by the omission.

'*Saudara-saudara*,' Seda called, but the Indonesians, who had been interpreting for their foreign counterparts, were engrossed in their own conversations trying to explain that there had no announcement regarding the *Rama II* bid. Annoyed, Seda tapped the microphone several times to silence the hall.

'*My friends*,' he tried again, '*there is an additional announcement of considerable relevance to these proceedings.*' He then paused, waiting for those below to learn what he had said. Slowly, the room settled down and he continued.

'*I have here, in my hand, a statement which the President of Indonesia has asked me to read. Would you all kindly remain while I accommodate our President.*' Seda then removed another envelope, this one from inside his suit. He opened the document, first ensuring that he had the attention of those present, and that the television cameras were still rolling.

'*To the people of Indonesia and guests who have attended the official awards ceremony for the Indonesian Rama Nuclear Power Plant Programme, may Allah look upon you all and smile.*

'*Citizens and guests. I have asked my friend, General Seda, Chairman of PEPELIN, to read you my message. I believe that it is appropriate that the announcement you will shortly hear is made on the very occasion that commences the process which will establish Indonesia as a responsible world citizen, a citizen concerned about the rapid depletion of world energy resources. As no doubt most of you are aware, Indonesia is the third richest country in the world in terms of natural resources. It would be irresponsible of us to assume that these resources will always be available to us, such as gas to provide fertilisers for our farmers, oil to fuel our transport and coal to feed our hungry power plants.*

'*It should not come as a surprise then, that the Indonesian leadership wishes to strive for a future when, once these resources are no longer available to our people, our great nation will not be dependant on others for its survival. We have limited uranium deposits in Kalimantan. We are unable to yet determine whether these might be sufficient in the years to come, to feed the nuclear reactors currently planned as part of the Rama NPP Programme.*

'In consequence, the Indonesian Government wishes to announce, that it has finalized negotiations with the Japanese Government for the construction of what is known as a Fast Breeder Plant for the production of plutonium.' Seda stopped, and signalled for water. No one spoke as they all waited for the Chairman to continue. As the interpreters caught up with the speech, adding to the silence, looks of amazement swept across the faces of all present. Seda continued.

'Nuclear fuel recycling reduces the consumption of uranium resources and eases the environmental burden of radioactive waste disposal, since the uranium and plutonium recovered from spent fuel would otherwise have to be discarded.' Seda paused for a few moments, certain that the Indonesians would be having considerable difficulty passing this information on to their foreign colleagues as the technical terms were alien to most of his fellow countrymen.

'Indonesia has committed itself to nuclear fuel recycling in order to secure a stable long-term supply of energy, and promoting the use of plutonium constitutes an essential part of this programme. According to international experts in this field, it is estimated that the world's supply of uranium will run out within seventy years.

'This project will be known as Rama II, and will have a capacity of 1,500 MW, making it one of the largest plants in the world. It will be located near Mt Muria, in Java. As it was considered that premature release to the public of the terms and conditions relating to this project would not serve the Indonesian national interest, maintaining complete secrecy was imperative. The Indonesian Government wishes to assure the International Community that it does not have a secret agenda. Our reasons for selecting Japan as our partner in this special project are numerous, amongst which, is Japan's commitment to peace, and as the world's only nation to have known the horrors of nuclear devastation, the Japanese people are strongly committed to nuclear disarmament, as we, ourselves are.

'In closing, I trust that the Indonesian people will be proud of their country's achievements, and continue to pray for Allah's blessings to guide us forward. Terima kasih'.

The silence continued only as long as it took for the foreign community to understand what had been said, before conversations erupted throughout the hall. Seda had not finished, but realizing the impact the President's statement was having on those present, he did not mind. He had played a major role in the Japanese-Indonesian negotiations. All had agreed that it would not be in either country's interests to reveal that the remaining seven NPPs would, in the not too distant future, all be built by the Japanese; and these would all be Fast Breeder Reactors.

'Terima kasih, gentlemen and ladies, that concludes the official announcement of the winning names of those companies which will build and operate the first five Nuclear Power Plants in Indonesia. May God bless this project and smile upon us all.'

The crowd rose as Seda left the podium, quickly followed by the other members of his team. Reporters called out questions but they were ignored. Unable to obtain further information regarding the surprise announcement, they turned to interview the foreigners present, hoping that they would comment on the President's message. Others attempted to interview the winning company representatives, but these had already moved away from the main body, pushing their way though their competitors ranks as insincere words of congratulations followed their exit. Murray exited along with the others, wishing to avoid the feeding frenzy of journalists in search of interview possibilities.

There was not one of the Salima Group present. They had been instructed not to attend. There had been no need, as the results were already known to Lim and Ruswita. Other than the President, General Seda was the only other living person who was aware that the Salima Group controlled each of the winning corporations. And there was little doubt in his mind that they would want to be heavily involved in the Fast Breeder Plant as well, although to what extent, Seda knew, would depend mainly on the Japanese, the President, and their clandestine project.

Chapter 13

*Defense Intelligence
Agency — USA*

The Director for Scientific and Technical Intelligence finished reading the report and called for his assistant to remove the document, instructing her to return the material by safe-hand delivery to its originators. Across the file's cover, large bold letters indicated that this would be the National Security Agency, the NSA. The classification of Top Secret had been stamped in fire-engine red on both covers, and also above the heading of every document contained in the sensitive file. He then instructed his secretary to bring Michael Bradshaw into his office.

The communications intelligence (COMINT) activities of the United States are the responsibility of the NSA, which was created in 1952 under President Truman. Unlike other such bureaucratic births, the NSA arrived in silence, smothered in secrecy. It was given a mandate to listen to and decode all foreign communications of interest to the security of the United States. It has also used its power in many ways to slow the spread of publicly available cryptography, to prevent the country's enemies from employing encryption methods too strong for the NSA to break.

The Defense Intelligence Agency, or DIA, although also a gatherer of intelligence, has operations vastly different from other agencies because it is a designated Combat Support Agency and the senior military intelligence component of the American intelligence community. Although considered the new boy on the block, the Agency was established as recently as 1961, and the director was conscious of the rivalries which had grown between other intelligence agencies and the DIA since its creation. The DIA and NSA had rarely become embroiled in such rivalries, as neither organisation's charter actually encroached on the other.

The DIA director was a US Army officer, as were the heads of the other directorates. They all reported to the three-star general who led the massive organization, which employed thousands of civilians alongside their military counterparts. DIA employees could be found on every military base, in all American Embassies, in Maryland and working on the Missile and Space Intelligence Center in Alabama, or where the bulk of the staff were based, at the Defense Intelligence Center on Bolling Air Force Base in Washington. This was where Michael Bradshaw spent most of his time.

* * * * * *

At eighteen, Michael had graduated from high school and started college. For a while, he seemed to drift, plagued by a restlessness which interfered with his studies. Against his mother's wishes, but supported by his step-father, Zach, Michael enlisted in the United States Navy, where he remained for three years. During that time he travelled extensively but eventually, realising that the opportunity might not come round again, he decided to continue his formal education.

When he turned twenty-three, Michael applied for, and was accepted into the commissioning program, which resulted in his returning to college. He remained there until completing his undergraduate degree, achieving honours, and was immediately accepted for Naval post-graduate study. In his twenty-sixth year, Michael completed his Masters degree in Science, and returned to the fleet as an officer. He spent time onboard the nuclear submarine, *USS Plunger*, travelling the world's deepest ocean trenches.

Michael enjoyed his time on SSN 595 as a submariner. He remained in the service until he had completed his active duty obligations, and then returned to college to complete his PhD. At thirty-five Michael was snapped up by the American Government and given extensive training with the NSA. After several years he decided that, although intelligence gathering and interpretation was an exciting enough role, he wished to be more active on the gathering side, which resulted in his being accepted into the DIA. There, Michael's background experience was utilized by the Agency in its efforts to keep tabs on foreign government nuclear development programmes, which required an in-depth understanding not only of nuclear armaments, nuclear power plants and their applications, but also a keen sense of what was building politically in specified target areas.

His investigations often necessitated disguising his true vocation, and Michael travelled regularly, under the guise of an inspector from the International Atomic Energy Agency. This was not so unusual, he discovered, as the IAEA appreciated any feedback resulting from interdepartmental exchange.

'Great report, Michael,' the Director beamed, 'seems that your time in Meade wasn't wasted.' Michael smiled at the compliment. He knew that his earlier training with the NSA would have contributed to the ease he now experienced in executing his missions.

'Does that mean I can have some of that time off you promised me?' he tried, knowing that it would be unlikely that they would cut him loose for the month he'd requested. To Michael, it seemed that the DIA's demands on his time were endless.

'Good try, Michael, good try,' the Director responded. He hadn't had time off himself for more than a year. He looked at his intelligence analyst, recognising that Michael Bradshaw was perhaps one of the more gregarious agents on his team. The director had considered Michael's penchant for country clubs and other socially active venues as a negative, until realizing that the man's natural ability to mix at all levels could be used to the Department's advantage. He had considered Michael's extra-curricular activities and decided to support his exposure, using this to further enhance his cover while roaming the world's trouble spots.

'Hope you haven't made any plans for this weekend,' the director said, knowing that it would be most unusual for the younger man to be at loose ends. Michael waited for the punch-line. He'd grown accustomed to surrendering his weekends to the Agency.

'Well,' he started, 'thought I might manage to get a few sets in sometime. I've almost forgotten how to hold a racquet.' The Director knew this not to be true. He had had the recent misfortune to partner against the younger man during one of the rare office social functions.

'I want you to jump on a flight for Tokyo. Go and see our man at the Embassy, and see if you can develop some feel for what the Indonesians are up to.' Michael had read the classified memo regarding their announcement to build a fast breeder reactor in conjunction with the Japanese.

'I think it would be judicious to spend some time visiting several of the Japanese plants. I'll arrange for the IAEA to provide the usual assistance. I want your face known over there, Michael, and I want you to try and establish rapport with some of the Japanese who would obviously be in a position within their nuclear industry, to offer some further insight into the Indonesian-Nippon venture.' He looked across at Michael, his face solemn.

'I don't have to tell you that the Pentagon views the relationship in the most negative way. We should expect to have them on our backs over the next few years while construction is under way, and then some.' Michael understood how superpowers always felt threatened when others moved to join their exclusive nuclear club.

They discussed the parameters of his mission further, and forty-eight hours later Michael arrived in Tokyo, where he quickly established his bona-fides and went about developing a strategy which would accommodate his government's future needs. If the Japanese intention was to assist the Indonesians to disguise the production of excess plutonium, this would require the assistance of at least one of the senior Japanese nuclear engineers or physicists involved in the Indonesian project.

* * * * * *

Japan

Tired from the long flight, and annoyed that he had not taken the train from the airport in lieu of the taxi service, he paid the two-hundred-and-fifty-dollar fare and checked into the Hilton Hotel. He showered and, as he then felt reasonably refreshed, caught a cab down to the Ginza where he planned to wander around just long enough for his body clock to readjust itself.

Michael Bradshaw enjoyed his visits to Asia, particularly Japan, where he found the unique blend of Western and Asian cultures quite refreshing. As he wandered around the well-lit night-club strip, he smiled as he observed swarms of chauffeur-driven limousines depositing executives outside their favourite clubs, and reminded himself that he had perhaps selected the worst night of the week to go wandering around the Ginza streets. He remembered being told during an earlier visit that it was customary for executives to leave their wives at home, and go drinking together with their friends on Monday nights.

Michael remained in the area until midnight, witnessing the evening come to an end for the weekly revellers. Hordes of drunken Japanese men, having been dragged from the clutches of hostesses, struggled back onto the streets where they sang loudly. Some collapsed on the footpaths while others swayed in the evening air, the expressions on their faces reflecting the nausea which always preceded a violent vomiting attack. The remainder generally carried on enjoying themselves until their transport arrived to take them back to their wives and families.

Tokyo, for Michael, had always been a contradiction of cultures. Protocol dictated every movement, yet Western and other influences were evident as parallel layers. It had been necessary that he study the land, its people and culture, and although he had not attempted to learn the language, Michael had acquired enough of the basics to assist him with the required courtesies.

The next morning, refreshed and anxious to start, Michael caught a taxi to the American Embassy where he was ushered upstairs for his appointment with the DIA liaison officer, Derek Parkes, who had prepared additional information for Michael's Japan brief.

'What do you think of the schedule?' the Defense Intelligence Agency representative asked. He had prepared a draft programme in advance, and sent this to Washington prior to Michael's departure.

'I think I'll need a little more flexibility, Derek. Maybe we should cut out some of the smaller plants. It would be unlikely that the sort of people we are looking for would be working in the more junior positions,' he replied.

'Okay, then,' Parkes agreed, 'which ones?' His own knowledge of the Japanese nuclear power industry had taken a quantum leap over the past fortnight, having been instructed by the Director to prepare the ground for Bradshaw's visit.

'Let's eliminate all secondary power plants to start,' Michael suggested. 'I'd prefer to target the main stations in the energy producing companies, as it is more likely that the senior engineers will be selected from these locations.'

'All right, what's that leave us with?' Parkes asked, ready to make the necessary alterations to his copy.

'I'd like to visit Hokkaido if it can be arranged. There are two new plants nearing completion, and these might just be the last we'll see for awhile. Seems that the ruling Japanese Coalition is nervous about further developing their nuclear industry.'

'Will these be the Hokkaido Electric Power Company plants?' Parkes asked.

'No,' Michael advised, 'the Tokyo Electric Power Company owns both of these. The Hokkaido Company plants are fully operational.' Michael thought for a moment, then added, 'but it wouldn't hurt to have a quick inspection of either one of theirs as well.'

'Okay,' the liaison officer responded, ticking at his own list, 'what else?'

'I want to visit Kyushu. There are two plants there of interest to us. We'll inform both the Kyushu Electric Power Company and Shikoku that the IAEA inspection will take place towards the end of next week. Then I'll be able to drop in at the Chubu station at Hamaoka on my return leg.' The men remained discussing Michael's itinerary until he was satisfied that they had selected the most appropriate locations, then they broke for lunch.

That evening, having refused his associate's invitation to dine out, Michael remained in his room, finalizing his notes in preparation for the commencement of his journey through the Japanese nuclear plants. Early the following morning, he visited the first of these, the Japan Atomic Power Company's plant just fifty kilometers from Tokyo city.

* * * * * *

Michael's notes showed the rapid development of the Japanese nuclear industry from their humble beginnings to the current number of seventy-five operational plants, with several still nearing completion.

Japan had already achieved the position of being the world's fourth largest producer of nuclear power, after the United States, France, and Russia. But, even with these impressive advances, Japan's energy supply structure remained extremely fragile, as the country still depended on foreign fuel sources for seventy-five percent of its needs, most of which was petroleum. Michael understood the political, economic and social considerations relating to nuclear power use in this country, and sympathised with the general public's perception of the dangers relating to the production of power from nuclear sources.

There had always been mixed reactions in Japan to the country's continued expansion of its nuclear plants, particularly as Japan was a forerunner in the promotion of plutonium for nuclear power generation.

He identified the reasoning for disquiet amongst those who understood the production of nuclear power, and the complex questions raised as a result of Japan's insistence that they pursue a policy of using plutonium. At a time when the world community was struggling with the problem of disposing of the enriched uranium that had been left over after the former Soviet nuclear arsenal had been dismantled, the question had been raised time and again, whether it was necessary for Japan to press ahead with development of fast breeder reactors to breed plutonium.

Michael knew that the quantity of enriched uranium that had become available from scrapping the former Soviet arsenal had, in the main, already been consumed by world demand. He also understood that the development of fast breeder reactors was necessary to ensure long-term supply of nuclear energy resources. Although France and the United Kingdom had changed direction with relation to their policy of promoting this type of reactor, he believed that both nations would continue to jointly develop a new-generation series which would incorporate even more safeguards to allay public fears.

Michael considered the proposed Indonesian plants, and decided that their government had been clever in its decision to incorporate the production of drinking water, as well as power. He knew that Indonesia suffered acutely from pollution of the country's coastal underground reservoirs, particularly on the islands of Java and Bali. He also believed that the production of drinking water, although relevant, acted to distract public opinion away from the fact that the first Java plant, currently under joint construction with the Japanese, could easily be utilised to disguise the excess production of plutonium for weapon's use. If this were to be, then Michael agreed with the American intelligence community's conclusion, that the Indonesians would also have to be planning to develop a delivery system for the future.

Similar questions had arisen when Japan first announced its intentions to use plutonium produced from its own plants. It was now his task to search for information channels which might provide answers to the question as to whether Indonesia's future use of plutonium would eventually lead to the development of nuclear weapons. As a signatory to the Nuclear Non-Proliferation Treaty, Indonesia had already stated that this would not be so; however, signs now indicated the contrary, and Michael, along with a team of others in the field, were given the responsibility of searching for information which might provide answers to Indonesia's motives in developing the *Rama II* Fast Breeder Reactor plant in Java.

During discussions with others in the DIA, Michael had pointed out that, although it was true that Indonesia did not possess a high level of technological expertise in the field of nuclear energy, there was most certainly an abundance of such resources available from the former Soviet Empire. Building a nuclear bomb posed little problem for those with the experience and specialized knowledge.

Technicians with the ability to develop nuclear weaponry could be easily sourced from any of a number of former Soviet satellite nations, and Michael had suggested that, if United States intelligence agencies could concentrate on targeting former Eastern Bloc nationals moving into Indonesia, then they might have a greater chance of discovering what the Indonesians might really be planning. The DIA director had agreed, and later mentioned this to his counterpart in the CIA.

* * * * * *

Washington

At the conclusion of his three weeks' inspection tour, which had taken him through the majority of the Japanese nuclear power plants, Michael had short-listed three names from those he had met in the course of his visit. He carried this information back to Washington and placed his report on the DIA director's desk.

When he had finished reading through Michael's submission, the director had the three names cross-referenced with the other

Agencies for a more detailed investigation of these potential resources. The Japanese nuclear engineers were subjected to a full CIA and NSA check, and when the information had been collated and returned to the DIA, the director smiled as he drew a circle high-lighting the third name on the list. This person would be their conduit to gather information concerning the Japanese-Indonesian venture.

The Intelligence Chief tapped the man's photograph attached to the report. There would be little difficulty in recruiting the man, he knew. His eyes searched for the incriminating photograph buried amongst a number of others, and attached to the text of the second page. He extracted the damning evidence from the folder, and flipped through the pages. The director snorted in disgust, and wondered just how deeply they could hook the man. And what the Japanese Prime Minister might say if he became aware of his brother-in-law's deviant behaviour.

* * * * * *

Japan

Colonel Sujono Diryo closed his eyes as the warm sensation flowed through his body, cleansing his mind of the day's pressures. The soft, scrubbing motion relaxed his tense back muscles, and Sujono grunted with pleasure as the woman's expert hands worked their magic.

'*Sujono-san is pleased?*' she asked, continuing with the therapeutic, but gentle kneading around his lower-back. It had been troubling him for some time. He grunted, and the geisha girl accepted this as approval of her experienced technique. She continued in silence, allowing time for her honourable guest to completely relax. The girl pushed Sujono's head and shoulders slightly forward, as her hands worked their way expertly over his body. When she thought the water had lost some of its temperature, she nodded to the other geisha waiting patiently, silently, in the corner, and more hot water was added. Bubbles of soap rose with the heat, and she stopped, momentarily, to brush some of the suds away from Sujono-san's face.

She sat, her legs to either side of Sujono's, massaging his back, enjoying the warmth of the hot tub, and pleased that her regular guest had returned.

When he had missed his Friday appointments three weeks in a row, she had assumed that the Colonel had moved his business elsewhere. It had happened many times before with other clients. She leaned forward so her tiny breasts gently touched Sujono's back, recalling from earlier visits that this would arouse him, then moved the sponge around to his firm abdomen, and rubbed softly.

Sujono groaned with contentment, delighted that he had been able to return in time for the pleasurable bath, and the geisha's attention. He had recently been recalled to Jakarta, where he had remained for some weeks attending briefings of the greatest importance to his country's future defense. When the coded instruction had first arrived, he had suspected that his tour of duty as Defense Attaché had been cut short, at his wife's instigation.

It had not been easy for him, married to the President's second youngest daughter. She had joined him in Japan for no more than a few months before fabricating a number of excuses to return home to Jakarta. There she had busied herself with her enterprises, their prolonged absences from each other's company further endangering their childless marriage. Gossip plagued their relationship, but Sujono remained content to be married to her, accepting that he owed his rapid promotion to his association with the First Family. He had returned to *HANKAM* more than a little dispirited at having to leave Japan. Sujono enjoyed the people and their traditions. But even more so, he enjoyed their doting women.

Sujono had not been surprised to discover upon his return to Indonesia that his orders had been issued directly by the Palace. Before even visiting his wife, Colonel Sujono had been instructed to proceed to General Seda's home, where he spent several hours being briefed by his influential sponsor. Sujono accepted that his early career involvement with the powerful Seda had not, in any way, harmed his position within the military.

It was during Sujono's time as the general's *aide-de-camp* that he had met the President's daughter. He had risen to Lieutenant Colonel within months of their marriage, but had not received any further promotion since his posting to Japan. Sujono knew that he was being punished for his wife's failure to bear children, and resigned himself to the possibility that divorce might just be an option for them both.

'*You have been selected for this assignment on my recommendations,* '*Jono,*' General Seda had informed him. '*If you discredit yourself in any way, then you also discredit me.*' He remembered the feeling of disbelief he had experienced when Seda had revealed details of the rocket development negotiations with the Japanese Military. Sujono had been sworn to secrecy and, in less than subtle terms, threatened. He had resented being reminded of the consequences should the project be compromised in any way, but accepted that secrecy would be paramount for the successful realization of the programme. Sujono had then given the necessary undertakings, as demanded. Later, when he sat with Seda and the President at the *Istana,* he listened intently as the *Bapak* reiterated the importance of secrecy, and he had given his solemn oath to the President that he would strive to maintain the project's integrity and dedicate himself to the joint Japanese-Indonesian defense co-operation.

'*You have been given a great responsibility, Jono,*' The President had told him, solemnly. Sujono remembered wondering if his father-in-law was aware of his daughter's marital difficulties. He had decided that this would be most unlikely, considering his summons to the Palace. '*You have also been given a position of trust which I know you will respect, not just as an ABRI officer, but also as a member of this family. You have a great tradition to maintain, Jono. You must always remember that you carry the name of one of Indonesia's most respected heroes.*'

Sujono remembered how his eyes had misted over, when the *Bapak Presiden* had then spoken so highly of Sujono's father. He had very few recollections of the general; the one memory which had remained with him throughout the years was that of their last moments together, when his father had herded his family into a bedroom and locked the door behind for their safety, before confronting the murderous communists who waited downstairs.

As the President reminisced, Sujono remembered his mother holding his small hands tightly, as the general was laid to rest at the heroes cemetery in Kalibata, on Armed Forces Day in 1965.

As the son of a Hero of the Revolution, it was only natural that he should follow in his father's footsteps. Sujono entered the Academy, and excelled. Upon graduation, he had been assigned to the Intelligence Corps, and was posted to the Indonesian Intelligence

Co-ordinating Agency, *BAKIN,* where he was soon identified for his diligence and dedication. General Seda had selected him as his personal assistant, following which, his marriage into the First Family advanced his career beyond his wildest expectations.

Within the span of a few short years, Sujono's friends witnessed a transformation in his attitude and demeanour, but were not surprised to learn of his accelerated promotion to Lieutenant Colonel. He had then been posted to Japan, where he quickly adapted to his new environment, becoming fluent in the language during his first year at the Indonesian Embassy. His wife had become bored, and longed for her own culture. At first, she had taken a few short trips back to Jakarta. When the first year had slowly passed, and then the second, they found that their marriage had all but become one of convenience to them both. Sujono knew that she still loved him but he felt little for her in return. He was, however, astute enough to realize the career consequences should they separate, or even divorce.

At first, there had not been a great deal for Sujono to do in Japan, as there was little defense co-operation between the two countries. The Japanese Home Affairs and Defense Ministries had few secrets to hide, and he had been given *carte blanche* to roam Japan on tours, building his knowledge of the people and their culture. With less than six months of his tour remaining, he had been recalled.

It was then that Sujono had discovered that his future would be considerably brighter than he had grown to believe. He had returned to Japan, filled with a new confidence, knowing that the secrets he now held would guarantee his future, with or without the President's insecure daughter at his side.

* * * * * *

Sujono decided that he'd had enough, climbed out of the tub and walked to the shower. The geisha followed, washing any remaining soap from his firm, brown, athletic body, before leading him into another, but smaller, delightfully scented room. There they made love in a mechanical fashion, as they had done so many times in the past.

Colonel Sujono Diryo smiled as his geisha bowed formally, her face devoid of all emotion which might indicate her satisfaction with the envelope he had earlier filled with Yen and placed in her kimono pocket. He assured the young woman that he would return at the scheduled time the following week, and departed, mentally refreshed and physically satisfied.

As he walked from the geisha house and crossed the road to hail a taxi, Sujono was too distant to hear the rapid whirr of an automatic Pentax Z-1p's zoom capture his exit from the well known address. As the Indonesian Intelligence Colonel disappeared from view, the American photographer unscrewed the telephoto lens from the camera, placed his equipment back inside the brown leather case he carried, then returned to the United States Embassy. Within hours, Colonel Sujono Diryo's photograph lay on the DIA director's table in Washington.

* * * * * *

Indonesia — Bandung Research and Development Center

When the President had first summoned Professor Mohammed Subroto to the Palace and broached the subject of Indonesia's opportunity to join with the Japanese to develop a multi-purpose rocket, the gentle academic had smiled and prepared to leave, wondering why the country's leader had played such an inconsiderate hoax on an old man. When he realized that the President was indeed serious, Subroto was so overwhelmed, he was speechless.

It had always been his dream that Indonesia would one day direct some of its resources towards the development of its own space industry. Some years before, when the then Minister for Research and Industry, Doctor Habibie, had played a prominent role in the development of Indonesian aeronautical and science sectors, Professor Subroto had believed that he and the others who had waited patiently for so many years might finally be given the opportunity to participate in the development of Indonesia's own satellite industry, launching these from within the Republic. But he and his close associates were to be disappointed. Instead of allocating resources to provide opportunities to the country's talented pool of scientists, most of whom were United States trained, re-

sources were re-directed into uneconomic aircraft production programmes in Bandung, which added little to the country's prestige
when these programmes were eventually terminated.

Subroto recalled, that during the mid-nineteen-seventies, when
Indonesia had contracted for the Hughes Corporation to launch
the first of the *Palapa* satellite series, he had been devastated to
discover that the entire *Palapa* technology had been retained by the
Americans. He had watched, unhappily, as only the more menial
aspects of the programme were contracted to local companies, such
as the erection of the many communication towers necessary for
satellite positioning control. Subroto had been deeply annoyed by
the appointment of foreign companies to manufacture these towers and other equipment overseas when he was confident that these
could have been produced locally. Subroto realized that many
would benefit financially from this and similar contracts, but it
would not be the citizens of Indonesia.

The professor had visited one of the tower construction sites
and recalled how shocked he had been to discover the number of
foreign riggers employed to erect the relatively simple structure.
He was informed, confidentially, by one of the Indonesian observers that the local company, Communications Service, had acted
merely as a front for the expensive foreign labour contractor and
that its founder, Stephen Coleman, had pocketed considerable profits at the expense of local competitors.

Professor Subroto had been disillusioned for years by his country's lack of direction and leadership. He was convinced that Indonesia had sufficient resources to develop its own aeronautical and
space technologies, and could call upon a number of qualified Indonesian technical experts to assist implement such a programme.
He believed that his country's leadership had deliberately been
misled by the West who, in his opinion, feared the possibility of
yet another developing, or Third World country emerging to
demand their place as a member of the exclusive Nuclear Club.

When the opportunity was granted, the professor had happily
accepted the position to head the Indonesian team, as the senior
counterpart to the Japanese technical party. When he learned that
future plutonium stocks were to be derived from excess production in the *Rama II* plant, he had simply smiled, pleased that so
much thought had gone into planning the project's long-term needs.

The fact that the surplus plutonium was to be secretly stored in the reconstructed under-ground shafts only strengthened his resolve and commitment to his country's defense strategies.

The joint development rocket was to be based on the successful Japanese civilian rocket programme which had already been utilized to launch a number of Japanese satellites over the past years. Professor Subroto understood that the final product would be used not only for Indonesia's own satellite launch programme, but also for military purposes. The possibility that he might, in future years, be considered the founding father of Indonesia's rocket industry, carried great store when Subroto was first introduced to the project.
. He pledged his total support to the President, and accepted that there would be those who might accuse him of hypocrisy once they discovered that he had played an instrumental role in developing Indonesia's first Intercontinental Ballistic Missile delivery system. Acting on the President's suggestion, the missiles were to be appropriately named the *Pedoman* Series, which they all agreed would be sufficient deterrent against any future Chinese aggression.

* * * * * *

In determining Indonesia's needs, Subroto had been instructed to work with the Japanese to develop a delivery system which would place Beijing within range of an Indonesian launch. The professor knew that an intermediary range missile might suffice, as his country had the advantage of being able to establish launch sites more than one thousand kilometers to the north of Jakarta and closer to any of the selected Chinese targets. However, with the recent developments in the South China Sea, the professor, in response to suggestions from the Military, agreed that Indonesia should plan to develop a delivery system which would be compatible in basic design, with the launch rockets required for future satellite requirements.

The Indonesian development team was faced with three main factors which would influence the effectiveness of their ballistic missile. These were range, accuracy and the size and type of the missile's warhead. After several weeks of discussions with the Indonesian Military leadership, it was decided that the *Pedoman* missiles be designed as a three-stage ICBM, with a range of eight thousand kilometers. This, they all agreed, would be sufficient to keep any aggressor at bay.

As for accuracy, Subroto agreed that the Japanese advanced computer-controlled guidance systems, used in the H-3B experimental series, would most likely be appropriate for the *Pedoman* as well. He had also recommended to the President that the Indonesian ICBM be designed to carry only a single nuclear warhead similar to that of the French Intermediate Range Ballistic Missiles and the Chinese ICBMs. They had all agreed that in the interests of disguising their intentions from the Japanese, a conventional warhead would be also be designed as the designated missile's explosive.

* * * * * *

The Chairman of the Indonesian Nuclear Energy Company, PEPELIN, General Seda, assumed charge of the overall project. Prior to his appointment, Professor Subroto had never met the retired general and was surprised to discover that Nathan Seda was conversant with even the technical aspects of the joint development project. When the scientist was advised that *BAKIN* would be responsible for all security and the vetting of staff, he had not objected.

Subroto calmly accepted the introduction of security controls, which, although he considered extreme, were highly effective. These measures had resulted in regular visits by high-ranking *BAKIN* officers, whose intimidating interviews bordered on interrogations. The professor complained that he found these unannounced security checks to be disruptive, but bowed to the PEPELIN Chairman's insistence that these were necessary in the interests of national security. Although he totally supported the measures introduced to safeguard against possible security leaks, Professor Subroto had become increasingly concerned with the tactics of one man in particular, Umar, who had been given total freedom of movement throughout the Centre.

The Professor's most senior assistant was Doctor Sunarko, a well-respected Javanese physicist who had studied in the United States and Japan, and was conversant with the Japanese H-2 and H-3B rocket designs. Sunarko had also spent four years working with the Hughes Corporation in America, and had been responsible for many of the innovative changes that had been introduced into the final *Palapa B* series satellites during the past decade.

Sunarko had complained to the professor that the senior security officer, Umar, had followed him several times from the research centre into Bandung, and kept him under surveillance the entire time. Although such behaviour was considered unusual, there was little that Subroto could do about the matter, except speak to the man. Following his brief discussions with Umar, Professor Subroto had been surprised to receive a call from General Seda within the hour and immediately wished he had not been as critical of Umar as he had.

The PEPELIN Chairman had not minced words, making it quite clear that the security officer had explicit instructions directly from the President to ensure that none of the research centre's staff compromised the project in any way, even if this meant taking steps which might, under other circumstances, be considered excessive. The professor clearly understood the underlying threat and Umar's real role within the security team. Later, he spoke at some length with Sunarko, urging him and others on his team to disassociate themselves from anyone who might be considered a security threat to the highly secret project.

As the following months passed, members of the professor's research and development team threw themselves into their work, often not leaving the centre for weeks at a stretch. When Sunarko did finally take one of the jeeps into Bandung for a break, he was followed. And, some weeks later, when he left the Centre during the dead of night and drove along the dangerous, un-surfaced clay roads that wound through the mountains before joining the Bandung highway, he was also followed. The next day Umar reported to Seda what he had seen, and even the General had expressed surprise when he learned that the foolish Doctor Sunarko had paid a visit to the Australian's residence in Jakarta.

Chapter 14

The Australian Prime Minister

They all stood as the Prime Minister entered the room, accompanied by Professor Ian Hyde. The Australian leader motioned for the members of his Cabinet to be seated, and indicated for his guest to sit at his side. Although the country had become a republic, it still basically followed the Commonwealth system of government, providing its citizens with both an identity separate from England and a Westminster form of representation. What had been previously designated Governor General had merely been supplanted by a change in nomenclature. The Australian President, not unlike those of Singapore and India, was simply the Head of State. He was not involved in the day-to-day running of the country's affairs, and his attendance was most certainly, not required at this meeting.

'Gentlemen, as you know, I have called this session in order that we might obtain a clearer understanding of what is happening in relation to the Indonesian announcement concerning their Nuclear Power Plant programme. I asked Professor Hyde here, with whom many of you are already familiar, to address this meeting to assist those amongst us who have little knowledge or understanding as to what these developments in Indonesia might mean to us and the Australian people. Professor?' the Prime Minister then passed the meeting over to Ian Hyde.

'Thank you Prime Minister. Good afternoon everyone,' he began, looking around the room, recognising some familiar faces. Those he had not had the opportunity to meet in person he recognized from the media interviews all had given at one time or another.

'Firstly, it is my intention to brief you in laymen's terms on what the announcement will mean in terms of nuclear power capacity, costs, timings and other relevant data. Then, I would prefer that you ask questions and address those issues which are obviously foremost in your minds, such as what risks there might be to Australia, and the opportunity for the Indonesians to produce plutonium for other than use in their reactors.' The professor took a crumpled handkerchief from his trousers pocket and dabbed at his dry nose out of habit before commencing. He spoke without notes.

'It appears that the Indonesians intend addressing their electrical power problems by embarking on what most of us believe to be a quite incredible path, to produce power from nuclear energy when, in fact, they still have sufficient alternative resources available. However, we will come to that later.' He looked around the table.

'The Indonesian announcement advised that they intend building twelve power plants, and that these will be constructed in two stages.' He paused, and wiped at his nose again.

'The first phase will consist of five plants, one of which will be located in Bali, while the others will be spread throughout Java. The Indonesians have called this, the *Rama Project*. I am not sure how familiar you might all be with the *Ramayana,* although its relevance is not important to what we are to discuss; it may be of interest that *Rama* was one of the more prominent figures from that lengthy story. Considering the nature of the project, I would have expected that *Kalki* might have been a more appropriate name.' This was lost on those present, they having never heard of the mythical spirit of destructive power. The professor continued.

'The Indonesians have quite cleverly decided to use the nuclear generating plants in a dual role. A proportion of the energy will be dedicated to the production of pure drinking water through a desalination process. The remaining power produced will be dedicated to electrical needs for those Indonesian people fortunate enough to be living within the proposed grid. *Rama I,* and I am now quoting directly from the Indonesian Ministry of Home Affairs, will be located in Bali, and will produce one thousand megawatts of electrical power and two hundred thousand cubic meters of drinking water, daily.' He observed by the looks on the faces of some that they were suitably impressed by the scale of the operation.

'The Bali plant will be amongst the biggest in the world, and will, for a reasonable time, or until the island's people fully develop into major electrical consumers similar to that of Western standards, produce sufficient power to accommodate the entire island. The drinking water will obviously be a major bonus to their tourism industry, considering the number of visitors who regularly fall ill as a result of drinking contaminated ground water there.' Hyde then paused again, reminded that even he had fallen dreadfully ill during a holiday he had taken in Bali some years before.

'*Rama's III, IV and V,* are not dissimilar to *Rama I,* in so much as these are all what is commonly known as PWR's, or Pressurised Water Reactors. These systems are considered to be more reliable than BWR's, or Boiling Water Reactors, which are favoured by the Russians and Eastern Bloc nations. These plants are approximately the same capacity as *Rama I,* and will also produce drinking water for the thirsty one hundred millions living on Java.' Someone coughed, and he hesitated, permitting the senator responsible the opportunity to finish before he continued.

'As many of you would have read, Java is suffering from another water shortage, due not so much to drought, but as a result of water tables being polluted as salt water moves in to replace the shallow ground water which, I might add, continues to be consumed at an alarming rate by the island's coastal dwellers. Sewerage has also filtered down into the water systems, polluting ground water even further in those areas with high population densities. In short, most of the island of Java.

'The Indonesian Government's tender information release indicates that *Ramas VI to XII,* will be offered for bidding over the next few years. The first five plants are to be constructed, as near as is practical, simultaneously, and the nuclear plants are being offered to foreign and domestic investors on the basis of what is commonly known as a BOT project. This terminology refers to Build, Operate then Transfer of projects by investors, and has become quite popular in Asia as a means of funding infrastructure developments.

'In the United States, such projects would normally require up to fifteen years to develop, due to the number of government agencies and other bodies which oversee the construction and operation of nuclear plants. In authoritarian regimes such as one would find in Asia, this development schedule could be reduced dramatically, perhaps to as little as four or five years. The actual construction requires only two to three years. The rest lies in preparation, and commissioning.' Professor Hyde then paused, collecting his thoughts.

'What is of real interest, is the fact that the Indonesians have also announced a government-to-government joint venture with the Japanese, to construct and operate what is known as an LMFBR.' He smiled at the frowns around the table.

'*Rama II* will be a Liquid Metal, Fast Breeder Reactor,' he said, pausing again for effect, 'and it is this plant which will be used by the Indonesians and Japanese to produce considerable amounts of plutonium, both economically and efficiently.' He looked at the stony faces around the table. They were already aware that the second plant would be capable of producing plutonium, as the Australian Press had talked of nothing else ever since the announcement had been first made.

'The Indonesians have advised that *Rama II* will produce both power and drinking water, as do the other plants. They have stated categorically that the purpose of this plant is primarily for those purposes, and that the additional production of plutonium is supposedly part of their forward thinking to the time when there will be very little uranium left to mine.' He rested for a moment, then offered the opportunity for questions. The Prime Minister was first.

'How much will these plants cost, and are they economically viable considering the life of each plant and the cost of power production?' Hyde fielded the question. He had discussed this with the man before the meeting had commenced, suggesting that the Prime Minister lead with these, as this would assist Hyde to introduce the basic description of the plants so that the others could more easily comprehend how a typical nuclear plant might operate.

'Nuclear Power Plants, or NPPs, have a life of some twenty-five years. The American experience indicates that NPP electricity still costs marginally more than Thermal Power Plants, or TPPs. According to the Worldwatch Institute, new NPPs in the States are producing power for around twelve cents per kilowatt hour, while natural gas plants come in at around seven to nine cents. It is true that NPPs require huge initial capital investments. Financing such projects from their own resources would not have been a viable option. That is why these will all be fully financed on the basis of BOT.'

'Why would they embark on such an ambitious programme considering their extensive coal deposits?' The question was asked by the Defense Minister. 'Would it not be more advantageous for them to upgrade their existing plants?'

'I would be the first to agree that retrofitting existing coal-fired plants with high-tech desulfurization and denitrification technologies, or switching their existing coal-fired plants to cleaner burning fuels like natural gas which, by the way, the Indonesians have in great abundance, would reduce environmental impact and increase combustion efficiency. But, unfortunately, there are stronger political issues at play here, stronger than environmental considerations, I fear.'

'Will they be able to produce an atomic bomb?' the Immigration Minister asked, knowing that this was highly possible. He had read the report in the Canberra Times over the weekend, and thought that perhaps Australia should be considering its own Nuclear Power Plant be upgraded to do more than just produce isotopes for medicine. The controversy surrounding the proposed three hundred million dollar expenditure for rehabilitating the Lucas Heights reactor in Sydney was a continuing irritation to him.

'The short answer is, yes. Providing they are able to collect sufficient plutonium without discovery, then it would be relatively simple for them to do so.' The room was gravely hushed at the thought that their nearest neighbour would have such a weapon. 'Of course, they would still have to develop a delivery system for such a weapon to be of any real use.' The Defense Minister's mind turned to reports he had read concerning the number of missiles which had been trotted out for the Presidential announcement during their Armed Forces' Day parade. He wondered how difficult it would be to exchange the conventional warheads for nuclear, and whether there was anything in the Indonesian weapons' arsenal which they were yet to disclose. The Minister realized that, with the collapse of the Soviet Empire, nuclear weaponry had been made available for sale to countries such as Indonesia and other developing nations which would otherwise have had no opportunity to advance their countries to nuclear capability status.

'Getting back to these reactors, Professor, how much uranium would they consume annually in terms of dollars?' Several other ministers turned to look at the junior cabinet minister from the State of Northern Territory.

'Whoever wins the supply contract could expect something in the order of almost two million tonnes of product. That would earn around sixty to seventy million dollars. Once all twelve reactors were in operation, this figure would more than double.'

'Professor Hyde, I must apologise, but I'm still a little confused as to how this all works.' The statement came from the Minister for Ethnic Affairs; others in the room were relieved that the question had been asked. Professor Hyde admired the woman for admitting she had not understood.

'Not all uranium is fissile, that is, able to be split or divided. Most uranium ore extracted from the earth contains less than one per cent of Uranium 235, the rest being approximately ninety-nine percent Uranium 238. Uranium 235 is the only element found in nature which is fissile. When its nucleus is hit by a subatomic particle, a neutron, it splits into two fragments. In this fission process, a large amount of energy is released and more neutrons are produced.' He paused and smiled at the woman who had asked the question.

'I'm fine, so far, thanks Professor,' she said.

'Okay, then,' he restarted, 'energy is released, and more neutrons are produced. These can be used to split further U-235 nuclei and set up a chain reaction. A nuclear reactor is simply a means of controlling the chain reaction and converting the energy produced into heat and, subsequently, into electricity.' He paused, and when he was certain that she had understood, continued.

'The proportion of fissile isotopes can be increased by fuel enrichment. Now, this is very important. There are two man-made fissile elements, plutonium Pu-239, which is produced from the U-238, and the other being U-233, which is produced from thorium. The three elements U-235, U-233 and Pu-239 are the basic fuels for nuclear reactors.' Professor Hyde then rested, knowing that this would have been too much already for most of those present.

'Sorry, again, Professor, but what is a Fast Breeder Reactor again?' she asked.

'Humn,' he started, biding his time. He was judging how to

explain simply without seeming to patronise his audience.

'World-wide there are only a limited number of fast-breeder reactors. The FBR is not a thermal reactor…it has no moderator for control purposes. Fission takes place in the core and produces heat, which is then carried away by, let's say, liquid sodium, such as I would expect the Japanese might introduce for *Rama II*. This heat is contained within a large pool and exchanges its heat with a second intermediate circuit of liquid sodium. This, in turns, transfers the heat from the sodium pool to steam generators where the heat is transferred again, to water, creating steam to drive the engine.' Hyde stopped and looked around the table, knowing that many of their number would not have followed.

'It's okay, thanks Professor, we can always ask questions later,' the Prime Minister intervened. Hyde nodded thankfully, then continued.

'All right, then. Because the core contains no moderator, the fission neutrons are not slowed down and retain fast speeds. The core consists of a mixture of U-235, Pu-239 and U-238, contained within a blanket of more U-238. The incineration of plutonium in the core is inevitable; the choice as to whether or not to produce plutonium within the blanket is optional. What you need to understand is, once the fast reactor has been launched, it becomes self-sufficient and may produce excess plutonium. This is why it is given the appellation of "breeder".' He could see from a number of faces that they had clearly not understood. He looked for a simple analogy.

'Lord Marshall of Goring once described the process in this manner.' He looked at the Prime Minister who smiled and, pleased with the supportive response, continued. 'Imagine a group of castaways on a beach, trying to keep warm. We will assume that they collected a small supply of wood, most of which was wet, having been washed up by the sea. They knew that they could burn the available dry wood, and that would be that. Or, if they were to place the wet timber around the fire, building a blanket so to speak then, as the dry wood burned, keeping them warm, it would also dry out the wetter material, providing an ongoing source of fuel. In this way, the castaways could keep their fire burning in perpetuity.' Satisfied that they understood, he continued, once again.

'I have given you a simple analogy to the operation of the fast

241

breeder reactor. The fire of dry wood is analogous to the incinerated plutonium in the core. The drying out of the wet wood is analogous to the production from the U-238 blanket. The wet timber is analogous to U-238, both of which would be useless waste products unless used in this manner. The process of building up the blanket of wet wood, extracting dry wood from this and throwing the dry timber onto the fire, are exactly analogous to the fast reactor fuel cycle.'

Ian Hyde could see from their expressions that most of them understood.

'Professor Hyde,' one minister called, raising his hand slightly, 'I'm Timothy Garbutt, Minister for Resources.' The senior minister paused, looked at the Minister for Defense, then plunged straight in with his question.

'If we were to assume the worst case scenario, uhm,' he paused again, knowing that he would have trouble later with some of the members who were committed Asiaphiles, 'what, no,.. how long would it be before the Indonesians would be in a position to have produced sufficient weapons' grade plutonium to threaten their neighbouring countries?' Hyde looked at the man and sympathised with his difficult portfolio.

'Assuming they could go on-line in five years, they could have sufficient stockpiles within that year.'

Someone shuffled papers nervously and this could be heard in the ensuing silence. They were, one and all, speechless with this revelation that Indonesia could, conceivably, join the nuclear club before the end of the decade. One of those present coughed nervously.

'And what are the probabilities that the Indonesians could deliver such a weapon?' the West Australian Minister for Mining's deep baritone voice filled the room. All present turned to look at the professor, who merely shook his head.

'Your are asking the wrong man here, I'm afraid.' Then he turned to the man sitting on his left. 'Your Defense experts could help you with that one, Prime Minister,' with which, the Prime Minister looked over in the direction of the Joint Chief of Staff who had been invited to attend in an observer capacity. Lieutenant General Sharpe rose in response.

'If I may, Prime Minister,' he began. 'Correct me if I am wrong,

Professor Hyde, but I think it is important here that we understand, first of all, that all nuclear reactors produce plutonium. A breeder reactor is simply designed to do it more efficiently.' He sighed. The Australian Military had spent more than three decades building solid relationships with the Indonesians, and he could only remember one government over those years which had reached out to Australia's nearest neighbour and established real rapport.

'Firstly, we should not jump to conclusions here. The Japanese have been awarded the contract for *Rama II*. That, alone, should give us a certain amount of confidence as there is no way that the Japanese Constitution would permit them to be involved with the production of plutonium for other than peaceful purposes.' He looked at the faces he had come to despise. Politicians' faces. They had been obstructionist and self-serving throughout his career, and he wished, sometimes, that Australia could be governed in a manner not dissimilar to that of Singapore - or even Indonesia.

'Secondly,' he said, his anger not evident, 'any plant that reprocesses fuel will have the opportunity to separate plutonium. It is chemically difficult because plutonium and uranium have similar chemistries, even though the procedure is well known. Hell,' he said, hoping to allay fears that the Indonesians one purpose in life was to attack Australia, 'you can even down-load this information off the Internet.' He wanted to shake his head in disgust, but refrained. 'Should the Indonesians feel the need to make a bomb, we would not be able to prevent this from happening, but to do so, they would have to be much more clever than one would expect.' The general looked directly at the Prime Minister, and again the thought flashed through his mind that he wished Australia had a similar covenant to Indonesia, and America, prohibiting such people from governing for more than two terms.

'If the Indonesians wished to enrich their own reactor fuel and divert this to some sort of clandestine uranium enrichment plant to make sufficient weapons' grade U-235, then they would have to be far more devious than you or I. They would require a substantial number of additional facilities. If it was their intention to produce a uranium weapon, they would require secret facilities out of view of the American spy-satellites, just to start. Then, if they decided on a plutonium bomb, they would require a fuel reprocessing facility and a place to hide the plutonium. This would not be easy. Again, the satellites would identify any such 'hot' spot immediately it was established unless, of course, they buried this deep inside a mine shaft somewhere. Then, having camouflaged all of these clandestine activities, they would have to successfully hide whatever else they were doing from the IAEA.' When he saw blank looks, he explained.

'That is the International Atomic Energy Agency, which is responsible for maintaining a close watch on such operations.' He turned to the man who headed the table.

'Prime Minister, in order for the Indonesians to succeed if they were, and I must stress that I don't believe that they are, planning to produce a nuclear device, they would have to withdraw from the non-proliferation treaty and the IAEA in order to do so. Should this happen, then, and only then, would we be concerned as to their intentions.' The general had successfully avoided the question. There were but a few among those present who had knowledge of the secret Indonesian installations nearing completion in Bandung. He then returned to his seat, feeling suddenly uncomfortably hot.

'Professor Hyde, how would you see the Indonesian NPPs impacting on Australia in the event that one of them was to go supercritical, and collapse, or meltdown?' This had been asked by the Minister for Science and Technology. The professor had been expecting this question, and was prepared.

'There is always the danger that the uninformed public will view all new technology with suspicion. It is a fact, unfortunately, that the greater majority throughout the world perceive nuclear energy only in some distorted apocalyptic manner. Nuclear Power Plants are necessary if we are to save our limited reserves of fossil fuels for more beneficial uses. As for coal, this too has a finite life. Within one hundred years we will survive only with solar and nuclear energy as the earth's resources would, by then, have been stripped of most of its fossil fuels. It may very well be that we will be able to generate power from new, and yet undiscovered or undeveloped forms of energy, such as from sea water. Unfortunately, that race is yet to begin. As for your question, I am not attempting to avoid it, just qualifying my answer.' He removed his handkerchief once again, and wiped his face.

'Indonesia is geologically unstable. We all know that from the constant reports of volcanic activity and the frequent number of earth tremors registered each year. I do agree that more time should have been allocated in determining the most suitable locations for the individual plants. We may feel some consolation knowing that the Japanese are involved in at least one of these plants, and that the Americans are responsible for the project in Bali, and another in Java. However, I do wish to emphasise that I believe the Indonesians are in too much of a hurry to construct these plants and bring them on line. There are inherent dangers involved; the Americans and Russians will support this. Although the Three Mile Island disaster shocked America at the time, the United States still leads the world in nuclear energy plants, boasting well over one hundred operating NPPs throughout the country. No, I wish to state that I believe in nuclear energy production of electricity, but stress that no one, I repeat no one, should charge into the development of such systems as quickly as the Indonesians have.'

'I'm sorry, Professor, but could you give us some indication of what might happen if one of these plants was to meltdown? I believe that was the question asked.' The Prime Minister looked sharply at his Minister for Education who had spoken, and reminded himself that had she not maintained such strong political support from within the Party, he would never have entertained having her on the Front Bench in Parliament.

'If I were to extrapolate the number of possibilities relating to the cause and effect of a meltdown, madam, we would be here for weeks.' Professor Hyde was visibly annoyed with the woman. 'Simply put, there are nowhere near the number of dangers that the general public believe exist with such events. There are containment shells built specifically as additional measures to ensure the public's safety. I could go on, forever, but I won't. There will always be an element within the community which will feed off such ridiculous clichés as the *China Syndrome*, or such nonsense. Yes, there are intrinsic dangers with these plants. Yes, people have died as a result of Chernobyl. No, I do not believe that the *Rama* plants are a danger to Australia, principally because the Japanese are going to build the Fast Breeder Plant in Java, and the French and Americans will oversee the development of the others.' He paused again before adding, 'but I would be most concerned had Soviet technology and training methodology been considered for any of these plants. Fortunately, this is not the case.'

'I am sorry to push, Professor,' she insisted, 'but are you saying that if either of these plants suffered, say, some sort of explosion or whatever as a result of geologically unstable ground, that we would all be safe?' Professor Hyde glared at the woman, his annoyance now more visible.

'A cloud of radio-active dust would cause casualties within a radius of some fifty kilometres. Should weather conditions be unfavourable at the time of any such accident occurring, then this area would increase proportionately to wind velocity, the terrain surrounding the accident and, of course, the extent of the explosion itself. This would most likely result in an increase in radioactivity in most parts of Australia. I should add, however, that I would not expect the increase in radio-activity levels to be of any paramount danger to our population.'

'My god!' she responded. 'No danger to Australians, you say?'

'That's correct, madam,' he replied. 'We should not confuse a meltdown with that of a nuclear bomb detonation. There is no mushroom cloud, no loud bang, so to speak. There would be, however, lethal increases in radiation levels in immediate areas surrounding such an incident.'

'Would there be any warning?' another asked. Hyde could see that his audience had pre-conceived ideas as to affects of such an accident, believing that such a meltdown would inevitably wipe out most of Australia.

'No, not much,' was all he said. The group then fell silent, and he knew that they were attempting to visualize what might happen should a meltdown occur. He had received a similar reaction from most audiences he had addressed on this topic, and never ceased to be surprised at how intelligent people focused only on the potential disaster aspects of nuclear energy, and not the benefits. As there were no further questions, the Prime Minister thanked the professor, who then departed, leaving for his home in Sydney.

* * * * * *

As he sat comfortably sipping the fine Chardonnay served during the flight, Professor Hyde thought about the meeting and decided that it had gone reasonably well. That is, with the exception of the persistent woman. He sighed, as earlier tension all but disappeared. Relaxed by the alcohol, his thoughts drifted as the Fokker started its descent over the Blue Mountains, and he watched the city's fringe dwellers' homes appear below. The scene was reminiscent of homes and pastures he had visited many years before.

It had been during the months following the disastrous incident in Russia, when a design flaw had caused the reactor to trip, and then explode. The images of what he had found in that accident's aftermath triggered the professor's thoughts, and he experienced a sense of relief that the location of Indonesia's nuclear plants were far enough away to minimise the effects of any potential fallout to Australia. As the memory of Chernobyl returned to cloud his mind, he reflected on the number who had died of acute radiation sickness subsequent to the disaster, and a sense of foreboding concerning Indonesia passed through his mind.

Images of those who had not died within the first days, yet wished they had, flashed through his thoughts. He remembered the brave men and women of Chernobyl, as death painfully approached, the radiation causing extreme damage to brain and gut, knowing that even if they survived the first days, within weeks they would die as the sickness penetrated bone marrow and vital organs. He looked out the window at the congested clumps of homes, and again felt saddened by what had happened to the Russians.

That evening, alone in his study, Professor Ian Hyde sat re-studying the ramifications of such a meltdown occurring in the densely populated provinces of Java and Bali and discovered, to his horror, that the Chernobyl model he had used projected casualty numbers he could never have imagined possible. Later, as he lay awake, unable to sleep, the scientist uttered a short prayer of thanks that the nuclear power plants being built along known geological faults to Australia's north were not being constructed with Russian technology.

Chapter 15

Lim and Ruswita's story

Ruswita breathed deeply, identifying the pungent odour of *durian*.

'Sumi, send one of the servants over to the village. I can't stand it anymore, let's fill our stomachs while we have the villa to ourselves.' Sumi laughed, Ibu Ruswita's passion for the vile-smelling fruit was often the topic of office gossip back in Jakarta.

'I'll go myself,' Ruswita's personal assistant offered, *'are you all right, alone for a few minutes?'* Ruswita smiled at her concern. These days, she wouldn't dream of travelling without the woman at her side. Sumi had been a godsend at a time Ruswita had been desperate for a competent aide she could trust. Now, Ruswita could steal away for a few hours, sometimes even an entire day, knowing that her able assistant would provide the necessary buffer against the irritation of incessant telephone calls.

When Sumi went in search of the delicate tasting fruit, Ruswita stretched out, enjoying the fresh mountain air. She watched a bird fly overhead, and she suddenly realized that she could not remember the last time she had seen any birds flying around Jakarta.

The capital had become a major Asian commercial hub, and now suffered the consequences of unchecked growth as urban sprawl encroached on outlying villages and the poor were driven even further from the densely populated city centre. Ruswita sighed, remembering when the drive up to the Salima mountain retreat in *Cimacan*, just over the *Puncak Pass*, would take little more than an hour. Now she considered herself fortunate if their driver could manage the distance in less than two. Whenever possible, she avoided city driving, preferring her husband's routine of conducting business from their home. Especially during the wet season.

All but a privileged few of Jakarta's twelve million inhabitants had no choice but to put up with being trapped for hours in the inadequate transport system as flood waters from the tropical downpours inundated the major thoroughfares surrounding the central business district.

Children's playful cries drifted across from the *kampung* reminding Ruswita to call the older boys, and enquire as to how Lim's grandchildren were getting along. The boys' marriages had resulted in a sudden explosion of numbers in the Salima family, with overzealous wives openly competing with each other for their father-in-law's favours. Rus thought about the growing family wistfully, as neither Benny nor Ratna had started their own. The thought of Ratna, gallivanting around the world without her husband, deeply distressed her.

Ratna and she still spoke frequently, Rus learning what was happening in the young woman's life during calls from the most exotic places around the globe. Ruswita had made arrangements for Ratna, providing her with funds to maintain her independence. Her daughter still called her 'Aunty', and both Lani and Rus were determined to maintain the charade, as Lim still was not aware of the true circumstances relating to Ratna's birth.

Often Ruswita had wished that she had disclosed their relationship to Lim, as this was the one secret which she had kept from him. Sometimes she wondered how he would have reacted, had she informed him prior to their marrying. But what was the good of such speculation? She had lied to her husband, and now needed to maintain that secret.

For a moment, Rus thought about her old friend, Lani, concerned that she had become noticeably distant over the past year. When they discovered Ratna had recently divorced, Ruswita had been most surprised at Lani's insistence that she go to take care of her. Of course, this had been out of the question. Lani was still very much a *kampung* girl at heart, and Rus was certain that her daughter would probably be embarrassed. Lani had never travelled, and it was most likely that she would only add to Ratna's burdens during her difficult times should she suddenly decide to visit.

Ruswita missed her children, and found that the Salima empire consumed far more of her time than she could ever have imagined. Escaping to their weekend villa nestled amongst the hills had become a rare treat for her, and Rus was amazed that, for once, she did not feel guilty at having left business unattended back in Jakarta.

They had driven up during the early morning hours, before the city's congested arterial roads could block her escape. Ruswita was so delightfully relaxed she was tempted to phone home and inform the household that she would not return until evening. Since her husband had become ill, Ruswita made a point of trying to be home before Lim rose from his afternoon nap. It was her custom to take tea in the afternoon when at home, where Lim would find her sitting, reading reports, when he shuffled out of his room and into the upstairs lounge.

The thought reminded her that she should soon be leaving, deciding to do so once she had indulged herself with the tasty *durian*. She smiled. Her husband refused to have the fruit anywhere near their house, and Ruswita graciously confined her habit of eating the smelly but delicious *durian* only when in the mountains, and away from his sensitive sense of smell. Lim never complained whenever Ruswita slipped away quietly by herself. He understood the demands made on their lives, and knew that she would always be there for him, if needed.

* * * * * *

Lani's attention was distracted by the clock's chimes. She had been looking out through the lounge bay-windows for some time, expecting to see the security open the gate for Ruswita's Mercedes. Instead, she had spied the housekeeper gossiping to someone standing outside the entrance, their forms hidden behind the tall, reinforced pillars.

Lani was most concerned that Ruswita had not returned, knowing that it was not like her to be tardy. She chewed a finger-nail absentmindedly, then looked down at the row of poorly manicured stubs. Ruswita had often scolded her for it but she could not break the habit, which had followed her since childhood. Then she noticed that she had spilt some tea on her *kebaya* and hurried to her quarters at the rear of the mansion to change her blouse. When she returned to renew her vigil, Lani observed that security had closed the front gates, and that whoever had been talking to the cook had left. Lani continued to watch, waiting there by the window, patiently, hoping that Rus would return soon. Rus had asked Lani if she had wanted to accompany them for the day, but Lani had refused, not entirely happy with the patronising manner Ruswita's personal assistant often displayed towards her.

She stood, her mind wandering, thinking about Ratna's last call from overseas. Lani had not been there when the call was made, and was visibly distressed at having missed the opportunity to speak to her. Although Ruswita had relayed her discussions with Ratna, it was not the same as speaking directly to Ratna by herself. It had already been far too long since she had visited, and she missed the young woman, dreadfully.

Lani recognized that she had been grinding her teeth, and stopped. She knew the reason for her depression. She had not spoken to her adopted daughter for more than two months. Even then, it was Ruswita who had taken the call, and she spoke to Ratna for what seemed like hours before Lani was given the brief opportunity to talk to her.

Sometimes she felt that life had been most unfair; she had raised Ratna Sari as her own daughter, and now considered it only appropriate that she should think of the beautiful young woman as her own child. Her thoughts turned to Ruswita, and a twinge of regret passed quickly though her. They had once been so very close. Then Rus had married the wealthy man and begun sleeping upstairs and, slowly, everything had changed. Lani had virtually become just another of the household dependants. It was not that she was ungrateful, although she did feel that Ruswita might have treated her a little differently, and given her more say with regards to their daughter.

An hour passed. Agitated by her friend's unusually late return. Lani decided to refresh the afternoon tray she had prepared and left upstairs earlier for Ruswita. Lani knew that she would expect the customary lukewarm Chinese tea to be waiting for her. She uncrossed her arms and turned to attend to this chore, almost bumping into the old housekeeper who had, at that moment, walked silently up behind her.

'Get out of my way!' Lani snapped, startled by her presence. She disliked the meddling old woman immensely, and could not understand why Lim had not let her go years before, when she had become too old to manage the kitchen by herself. Her duties had been changed from cooking to light housekeeping, even though there were others whose responsibility it was to clean and wash for the Lim family and guests. The housekeeper stood her ground, her mouth open wide as if to speak but the words would not come.

'*What is it?*' Lani asked angrily, her curiosity aroused by the woman's strange appearance. The housekeeper's eyes were open wide, as if in surprise. She couldn't speak. Instead, she turned her head and looked over her shoulder towards the staircase. Lani frowned, followed her gaze, then looked back at the panic-stricken woman. Instantly, she knew that something was terribly wrong.

'*Oh no!*' Lani cried, fearing the worst, and hurried up the stairs, leaving the stricken housekeeper alone.

* * * * * *

As she waited for her assistant to bring the *durian* Ruswita listened to the village children's voices. She remembered earlier days when she too played along the village dirt tracks, climbed mango trees, and squatted in the dirt with the others playing *kelereng*, her tiny, clumsy hands unable to flick the stone marbles. She smiled, revisiting her childhood days, remembering the smell of *pisang goreng*, whenever her mother served deep-fried banana, and other tantalising village-food aromas.

Neither Ratna nor Benny had been exposed to this simple way of life and, sometimes when reflecting on her early youth, Ruswita regretted that her children had not experienced what life could be like without the benefit of money. She knew that Benny would follow in his father's footsteps, as he had already displayed the Lim street-cunning in his dealings. The older boys were, surprisingly, quite different from their father. Both had been influenced by their extended stays in the West, and it was apparent to Ruswita that they were no longer comfortable living in Indonesia. As she considered Denny and James, she became concerned with their American commitments, and some of the difficulties spawned from their banking activities.

Some aspects of their American operations remained unclear to Ruswita, but she could certainly read a profit and loss sheet and she was well aware that Lim's sons were hiding the greater part of whatever they had been up to in the United States. Ruswita had become concerned, at first, when she discovered that a number of Lim's international subsidiaries which were controlled by the two older boys, had been actively investing in the Peoples' Republic of China. The Lim family had substantial interests in the Republic of China, and she knew that should the Taiwanese discover their cross-border vested interests there would be problems.

As the conglomerate had grown, so did the need for Lim Swee Giok to divest himself of day-to-day control over his empire. He was growing old, and his punishing childhood years living from hand to mouth in China had left their legacy. Lim no longer had the strength to oversee his empire. He entrusted Ruswita to maintain vigilance over all they owned, and asked his two oldest sons to assume control with her, in Jakarta. They had both blatantly refused.

Lim wanted desperately for them to return, leaving their American interests in the hands of capable managers. Still, they had cited pressing financial obligations in the United States which dictated that they remain. Ruswita interceded, urging Denny and James to consider their father's needs. They were both required at home now, she explained, as their father's health had deteriorated dramatically over the past months. Finally, Denny had phoned and explained that they could not return at that time, and begged Ruswita to understand. There were problems, Denny had explained, and these would grow to damaging proportions if they did not remain to resolve the bank's difficulties. Ruswita was then obliged to assume even more responsibility for the complex operations, as her husband remained at home, only occasionally holding court with some of his closest business associates. He no longer visited the Palace; slowly, he seemed to lose interest with what was happening within the Lim empire.

Ruswita managed, alone, and even enjoyed overseeing most of the *kongsi* activities, although she wished at times that the Salima Group had never involved itself with the massive undertakings associated with the *Rama* nuclear project. Ruswita was concerned with their financial exposure in the four privately operated plants. Whenever she attempted to discuss these with Denny and James, they appeared distant, as if the investments were not as dear to their lives as one would have thought. Difficult as it was, Ruswita persevered, finally coming to grips with the ongoing problems associated with the plant's construction cost blow-outs, management difficulties and government interference.

First ground had been broken two years before, and construction was well under way. Ruswita had not visited the sites, nor did she encourage visible involvement by any of those close to the Salima family, as these projects had attracted considerable controversy. The Salima Group supplied most of the materials for the plants' construction. Cement, steel, engineering services, heavy equipment, cranes and even on-site catering was, in one way or another, controlled by the Lim group of companies.

The Mt Muria plant had been different, and Ruswita believed that only the PEPELIN Chairman would understand why this had come about. Lim had been outraged when he discovered that Seda managed to divert most of the contracts relating to the Japanese fast breeder reactor plant away from the Salima organisation to one which had very little substance but was, Lim suspected, closely associated with the greedy Chairman. Infuriated, Lim had gone directly to the President and been shocked to discover that the *Bapak* supported Seda's intrusion into what Lim perceived to be Salima domain. He had even approached the Japanese directly and, for the first time since he could remember, his *kongsi* had been excluded entirely from the supply of cement, steel and other materials he had dominated for decades.

It was at this time that Lim's health had suffered some deterioration, and he kept more to himself, often wandering around their home, still dressed in singlet and shorts, like some peasant recluse.

Ruswita had sensed that Seda had somehow broken through their monopolies because of the growing tide of anti Chinese sentiment, fuelled by those jealous of their achievements. There had been rumblings even from the floor of the Indonesian Parliament, and she firmly believed that this had originated with the former President's children, whose permanent representation in both Houses had been a bitter legacy indeed for the Indonesian people.

Ruswita remembered how Lim had attempted to maintain close relationships with the former powerful family members, but they had become a substantial financial liability, one which the Lim group could no longer support. Ruswita recalled that at least four of the former President's children, and grandchildren, all held seats in Parliament, from where they attempted to regain some of the power their family had lost when their father had passed away.

Ruswita had not been surprised that Salima then also lost the military materials supply contract for the aeronautical research and development plant being constructed in Bandung. When she had been informed that Seda's associates had been appointed as sole contractors, Ruswita knew that it was time for the Salima Group to reassess its position in Indonesia. She spoke to Lim about her concerns, but he was adamant that they would not liquidate their energy assets until the power plants had been in operation for at least two years, citing the potential for publicly listing the company as his reason.

As a result of their difficult financial position, he had finally agreed to selling a minority stake in the Salima Group company, before which the energy assets and those related to all off-shore subsidiaries, and his control in the Asian Pacific Commercial Bank, were protected. Several months later, the market fought to purchase the first Lim-associated shares, when forty percent of the company which owned and operated cement plants, steel mills, property and a myriad of other investments within Indonesia, was sold through the Jakarta Stock Exchange. The company had changed its name prior to the public listing, and became known as P.T. Salima Jaya Corporation. Within hours of the shares being offered to the public, the company's value doubled. Capital raised by selling almost half of the Indonesian assets was immediately channelled through the family bank, APCB, which was then used to relieve a considerable part of the debt accumulated in the Salima energy investment sector.

Their exposure in relation to the financing of the first four plants was not limited. Lim had insisted on maintaining a majority interest through their off-shore holdings, and had heavily committed cash-flow from existing investments to accommodate the foreign banks. Ruswita was aware that their projected accumulated debt at the time of completion of all four *Rama* NPPs, would exceed ten billion dollars due to extensive redesign and cost over-runs. She had examined the latest cost estimates just days before, and had been distressed to learn that each plant could easily exceed three and a half billion dollars, almost double the original estimates.

Ruswita understood clearly that the foreign partners associated with each plant would not suffer financially. They had been clever, entering into cost-plus contracts and, as they held the key to management, there was little that could be done to re-negotiate their positions.

Even the uranium supply contracts had caused concern when the Australian suppliers experienced difficulty with environmentalists. Ruswita had been further alarmed when disputes over land and mineral rights had been challenged by the Aboriginal people, who had been given rights over the Kakadu National Park, and insisted on assuming control over the mines. She had immediately contacted other suppliers, and was shocked to discover that the world demand had already accounted for most of the available ore, including that from the Vaal Reefs South African mines. Salima technicians confirmed that changing suppliers would not alleviate the problems, as the lead times required for uranium conversion, enrichment and fuel manufacture was in the order of two years.

Finally, she received personal assurances from the Australian company's major shareholder, Graeme Robson, that they would be able to meet the supply deadline. Ruswita was satisfied with this undertaking, or had been until she discovered that Robson's activities somehow had become enmeshed with her rival, Seda. She became suspicious and had Robson's activities in Indonesia monitored.

When Ruswita received confirmation that it was Robson who had been sourcing alternative material supplies for the *Rama II* plant's construction, she became even more suspicious of their relationship.

Prior to the contracts being awarded, the Salima Group had entered into an arrangement with Peter Wong, using one of his companies as the vehicle to control *Rama V*. Ruswita had learned that Wong's junior partner was the same foreigner whom she had come into contact with many, many years before. She had phoned Murray Stephenson and was pleased to find that he had returned to Jakarta, to act as a liaison consultant for Wong's company, the *Nasihat Corporation*. As she rested quietly, waiting for Sumi to return with the promised fruit, Ruswita recalled the meeting she had with the Australian.

* * * * * *

At first, Ruswita had not recognized him, for she remembered

Murray as he had been, more than twenty years before, in the joint venture factory, where she had been employed as the foreign general manager's personal secretary. His once fair hair had thinned, exposing ugly, red blotches on his scalp, and his roguish face now featured wrinkled, sun-damaged skin.

'Thank you for the lunch, Rus,' Murray had said, as she escorted him from the dining room into the congested lounge. He had been most surprised at having been invited, and even more so to find that he was to be the only guest. They had eaten and engaged in light conversation through the meal, and it was time now to reveal the reason for the meeting.

'Murray, I have invited you here to discuss a matter which *Pak Lim* and I believe you might be in a position to assist with,' she had started. Murray looked intrigued by the statement. 'We have not been prying into your business, but by accident we have discovered that you are quite friendly with those involved in the materials supply contract for *Rama II*.' She paused for effect.

'*Pak Lim* has been very concerned regarding the loss of this contract, but is more concerned that we might have difficulty with future supplies of uranium ore from Australia.' Murray frowned, he was obviously wondering where their conversation was heading.

'As any disruption in supply, for whatever reason, could also be of major concern to Peter Wong, through our *kongsi* with the *Nasihat Group* and *Rama V*, we were, therefore, hoping that you might be in a position to explore the relationship which exists between this fellow Robson and General Seda.' Ruswita had observed her guest closely, trying to determine whether he was aware of any association.

'Why the concern?' he had asked.

'Robson's group has controlling interest in the uranium mines which are under contract to supply all four NPPs we are building. It's no secret that Seda has managed, as Chairman of PEPELIN, to firmly ensconce himself amongst those who were awarded the lucrative supply contract for the Japanese plant. The Salima Group is becoming concerned that as Seda makes further gains in these areas he might also decide to become involved with the supply of uranium fuel from its source.' Ruswita knew that she would not have to explain that the Lim group was moving to avoid a situation in which they could be held to ransom over the enriched uranium supply contract.

'Why would Seda wish to do so?' he had asked, 'and if he did, how would you expect him to go about this?'

'Well, Murray,' she had replied, 'that's what we were hoping you might be able to assist us determine for ourselves. If Seda wishes to raise the stakes and acquire an influence over the Australian mining operation, would it not be reasonable to expect that Robson, whose company owns control over the extraction process, might just accommodate the general?' She could see that he was considering what she had said.

'I will do what I can, Ruswita, but no guarantees. I don't see as much of Graeme as I used to, but I will make a point of raising the issue with him,' he had promised.

'I don't know how you might do this, Murray, as Robson's association with Seda seems to have grown considerably. His company has acquired a number of lucrative contracts other than the Japanese plant, including the cement and steel for the Bandung research and development project which, I am told, is substantial.' Ruswita could see his surprise, knowing, as would the Jakarta business community, that Lim had controlled most of the government contracts to date, and that it was most unusual for the Palace not to have intervened on his behalf. Ruswita did not feel the necessity to further explain how Seda had consolidated his position with the First Family, and what this might mean to her own *kongsi* and its position in Indonesia.

By the time their luncheon meeting had come to a close, she had received an undertaking from Murray that he would assist. Ruswita remembered feeling that there was more to this man than he showed, and hoped that she had not made an error of judgement in seeking his assistance regarding Lim's concerns.

* * * * * *

A voice called, bringing Ruswita back to the present, and she looked to see Sumi returning, followed by one of their servants carrying several *durian,* which had been tied together. Minutes later, Ruswita sat on the porch, tearing the flesh from inside the fruit with her fingers, laughing as she did so, while relating stories of her youth.

Well into the feast, they heard the phone ringing, and her personal assistant hurried inside to answer the phone. Ruswita finished eating the remaining flesh, and, as Sumi returned, laughingly held the finished fruit up for her to see. But her dedicated assistant didn't respond. Ruswita was startled by the younger woman's expression, and a cold fear gripped her heart as she searched Sumi's face for some indication as to what was wrong.

'Sumi?' she asked, suddenly dreading her answer.

'Ibu Rus,' she stammered, resisting the temptation to break into tears. 'Ibu Lani wishes to talk to you, urgently.' Ruswita's first reaction was one of annoyance. It was not unlike Lani to phone, just for the sake of it. The thought crossed her mind that Lani might be sulking again. She hurried to the phone.

'Lani, what is it?' she snapped, immediately wishing she hadn't. Lani was crying.

'It's Pak Lim, Rus,' Lani said, 'it's Pak Lim!' she sobbed, uncontrollably. Ruswita became engulfed with fear.

'What is it, for God's sake Lani, what has happened?'

'Pak Lim is dead, Rus, he's dead!' she cried, her voice choking. For a moment the shock did not register, and Ruswita stood quite still. Rocked by the cold realization of her husband's sudden death, she dropped the phone, and felt her knees become weak. Sumi ran to her side, placed her arm around the older woman's waist, and assisted her to a cane chair. For a moment, she was not sure that Ruswita would not faint. Then, she recovered her composure and breathed deeply, nodded that she would be all right, and patted her assistant's hand in gratitude.

'Call the driver, Sumi,' she said, softly, and her assistant obeyed, hurrying away to do as instructed. It was not until they were more than half way down the mountain, speeding around the dangerous curves, that Ruswita realized that she hadn't asked Lani what had happened. The Mercedes sped down the mountain side, by-passed Bogor, and raced along the Jagorawi Highway. Sumi glanced at her employer, and placed her hand in Ruswita's. She observed that there were no tears. These, she knew, would come later. Thankfully, they missed most of the midday traffic congestion, as they continued through the sprawling city's outskirts, then along the ring-road and into Menteng.

When they arrived, the driver had barely brought their vehicle to a standstill when Ruswita flung the heavy door open and hurried inside, past the familiar form of the Lim family doctor. His eyes dropped in deference as Ruswita brushed by; there was nothing he could do. Lani had been waiting anxiously for their return and, as Ruswita appeared, she raced up to her, and flung her arms around her friend's neck, still sobbing uncontrollably.

'He's dead, Rus,' she cried, 'he's dead!' Ruswita unlocked Lani's arms from around her body and pushed her gently aside. The old housekeeper stood wringing her hands, looking nervously upstairs. Rus placed her hand on the old woman's shoulder as she walked past her to the stairs leading up to the private bedrooms she shared with Lim.

She entered the second storey quarters, passing slowly through the common lounge and study area, where they had spent most of their lives together. They no longer shared the same bed, or the same room. This was not a question of love, simply a necessary arrangement they had both accepted due to their age difference and the pressure of their lives.

She could see directly into Lim's bedroom, as the door had been left open. Ruswita inhaled deeply, then walked towards the unmade bed, her hands shaking slightly as Lim's body came into view. She moved to his side and stared at her dead husband.

She placed her hand gently on his outstretched arm, noticing how cold his skin felt. Ruswita wondered if she should cover his body, but instead, she leaned over and closed his staring, lifeless eyes. Alone with the man who had given her more than most people could ever dream of, she closed her eyes to steady herself, wishing that she had not left him alone that day.

Ruswita still could not bring herself to accept that he was gone. In death, Lim's emaciated form in no way reflected the enormous power the man had wielded, or his incredible wealth. She remained at his side for several minutes, praying, then Ruswita removed his clothing and redressed the body.

After some time had passed, she called downstairs for the doctor. When he entered their quarters, Ruswita could see that the man was genuinely saddened by her husband's death.

'I am terribly sorry, Rus,' he said, taking her by both hands and sitting her down slowly, 'but there is something that you must know.'

Ruswita looked up into the doctor's eyes and immediately felt fear clutch at her heart. She looked away momentarily, then across at the still form of her husband, Lim.

'What is it?' she asked, pulling her hands away from the man's grip.

'I don't really know how to begin, Rus,' he answered, then sighed. He sat on the edge of the bed, partially blocking the dead man's corpse from Ruswita's view. Then he dropped his bombshell.

Ruswita sat silently, almost in disbelief, listening to his shocking revelation. She asked several questions and was stunned by his answers. As her heart filled with rage at the betrayal, her anger displaced her sorrow, filling her with hate. Questions flooded her mind and she could find no answers. *Where were the servants when he had died?* She remained with the doctor, discussing what had taken place just hours before, somewhere in this room. They looked around, together, but could find no evidence to support the doctor's conclusions.

The old housekeeper had found Lim unconscious on the bedroom floor. It was her practice to waken the master from his afternoon rest. She had called the doctor, immediately, not knowing that Lim had already been dead for some minutes when she first discovered his body. She had called Lani and the security and, while waiting for the doctor to arrive, they had placed their stricken master on his bed. It was then that the servants understood that Lim was indeed dead. Lani had placed her call to the mountain resort, and the doctor had arrived shortly thereafter. At first, he thought that Lim had died of a stroke, but upon further examination, he knew otherwise.

Once the circumstances surrounding her husband's death had become clear to Ruswita, she solicited the doctor's assistance, knowing what she must then do.

Ruswita knew that she would have to move quickly, to prevent the inevitable panic which would follow amongst the Chinese community once word spread. She begged the doctor not to communicate with anyone, not even family. Salima's future was at stake, and Ruswita realized that they were in danger of losing it all, especially if others overreacted and commenced liquidating their assets in Indonesia.

They talked quietly, together, until the doctor reluctantly agreed to her requests and left her to make the necessary arrangements. Then she called Sumi to join her upstairs, and issued instructions as to what she must then do before alerting the others in the family. Her assistant understood, and went immediately to the phones to carry out Ruswita's orders.

Ruswita then went down to speak to the servants and security staff, ordering them to remain inside the grounds until instructed otherwise.

Lani looked at her friend questioningly, but Ruswita ignored her, returning upstairs where she too spent the following hour making urgent calls, overseas, in preparation for the selling spree she knew would take place the moment news of Lim's death reached the markets. Ruswita realized that this would be their real test, and hoped that she could count on their foreign bankers not to call in their notes.

There was no doubt that the Chinese community would wait to see which way their bankers would move before they too decided whether to liquidate assets. Ruswita was gambling that their friends would support the market, that they would survive the inevitable roller-coaster ride the Salima Group shares would experience before, hopefully, settling once again.

But she also knew that all of this was only possible as long as she had the confidence of the market, and that if the cause of Lim's death became known, then there would not be a single Chinese investor who would not immediately move to divest themselves of not only their Salima stock, but their own assets as well, creating a massive outward flow of capital from the Indonesian market. She believed she had no choice but to disguise the fact that Lim had been murdered. The Chinese would believe that if the powerful tycoon with his Palace connections had not been safe, then who in this city of Jakarta was?

Satisfied that she had done all that she possibly could, Ruswita settled down to wait for the doctor to return with a copy of the death certificate he had agreed to endorse, showing that her husband had passed away comfortably in his sleep.

* * * * * *

When news finally broke regarding Lim Swee Giok's death,

Salima shares and those associated with the conglomerate suffered a sharp fall, tearing more than twenty percent off the stocks' values. There had been only one major seller, and his name was whispered amongst the traders as they went about filling his sell orders.

As the stocks plummeted, the Asian Pacific Commercial Bank stepped in and started buying its associated stock. At the close of the morning session, the shares had regained half of their losses, and when it was announced that Salima's major shareholders were buying their own stock and had called an extraordinary meeting of shareholders without notice, the market interpreted this as one of confidence, that the family were demonstrating their support for Lim's widow, and closed the afternoon session with an overall gain for the day.

* * * * * *

The board meeting had gone as she had expected. The others really had little choice but to follow, she knew, initiating the call for the extraordinary meeting of the few major shareholders.

As she continued to gaze down through the double-glazed windows from the penthouse in the building which now effectively belonged to her, she smiled. But not in mirth. Ruswita thought about the meeting which had just taken place and the ease with which she had managed to totally emasculate those who had attended, knowing that none would ever have expected to see her take control of the company's board meeting, let alone chair the event. But that was behind her, she thought, and life would be different now she had taken charge.

Ruswita stood, gazing out through the windows. Below, she could see the bogged traffic fighting its way slowly along Jalan Jenderal Sudirman. She glared directly across the divided thoroughfare at the building opposite, not one hundred metres away. It housed the enemy. Her enemy. And she knew in her heart that he had been the one responsible for her husband's death. Ruswita turned away from the view and walked through the lavishly decorated board-room wondering what she could do about Seda, and how she could prevent his charge upon her family holdings. He had shown his hand by attempting to drive the stock down, con-

firming Ruswita's suspicions that it had been Seda who had paid
the assassin responsible for poisoning Lim.

Chapter 16

India

Vijay Rakesh believed that he was a good leader. Certainly, he mused, judging from public opinion polls he was obviously not the most popular Prime Minister India had ever had. The new millennium had not improved his people's lot; if it was not enough that his country already suffered from drought, now there was the phenomenon of *El Niño* to contend with. As he gazed down the empty hall over the magnificent Canadian Oak table, a gift to the new independent nation from Viceroy Mountbatten in 1947 which, only minutes before, had been covered with reports and submissions, Prime Minister Vijay uncoupled his hands and placed these firmly on the table, then rose slowly using the structure as support. His body had become even more frail over the past days. Vijay attempted to ignore the constant pain which had accompanied him for months, hoping that his scheduled operation would successfully remove the problem.

Slowly, he dragged his feet the length of the room until reaching the window which overlooked the square. He noticed that the glass had not been cleaned and thought to himself, how it could be, that in a country of one billion people one still can not find someone to clean the Prime Minister's windows? He raised his left hand and slowly rubbed against the glass in a clockwise motion, his thoughts wandering as the pain-killers interfered with his normally clear mind. He became momentarily mesmerised by his menial task. A wave of depression suddenly descended, causing him to cease what he was doing. Vijay Rakesh turned slowly, painfully, and dragged himself back to the head of the table where he lowered himself, carefully, back into the impossibly heavy chair, then stared into space.

267

The diagnosis had been confirmed. The doctors had informed him that it would now be only a matter of time unless he agreed to surgery. They had urged that he step down and permit someone younger and stronger to take control of India's leadership, but he had refused. Then they had challenged him and still he had refused, determined to remain on as long as his spirit did not fail him; he would hold on to prevent the political hyenas and jackals from attacking prematurely, and would resist those who sought to accelerate the inevitable.

His face twisted in agony as excruciating pain pierced his lower abdomen. These attacks were becoming more frequent, and more severe. Vijay Rakesh's fingers located the pills the doctors had prescribed, and slipped two more into his mouth. The mixture of aspirin and morphine hydrochloride entered his bloodstream, and he waited for the spasm to subside.

After what seemed an eternity, his breathing returned to normal and he looked down towards the window once again; he knew that outside, few amongst the city's swelling population would bother to cast a second glance at the huge and distorted red sun, as it squatted on the horizon. Vijay remained sitting alone, thinking nostalgically of his youth, and the snow-clad mountains in the north. Then, as he began to feel more comfortable, his mind turned once again the to terrible dilemma which haunted India.

Many of his countrymen were starving. India could no longer feed its people. And they, in turn, refused to listen. The population continued to grow to staggering levels, adding two million new mouths to the economy each month.

Following the announcement that India had finally passed China as the world's largest population, India had celebrated. On that day, Vijay had stood, feeling nothing but despair, waving from his balcony as the crowds cheered, celebrating their own demise. India's population exceeded one billion. As everyone else celebrated, he had felt nothing but outrage for the Malthusian outcome.

During his term in office, he had been unable to initiate steps to curb the exponential growth in the population. Vijay had called upon the country's religious, academic and social leaders to act, before it was too late. But he had been ignored. Political, racial and religious dogma prevented his government from achieving any form of consensus necessary for them to succeed. His every attempt had been frustrated by rivalry and ignorance.

As millions of Indians perished across the land, there seemed to be no acceptable solution to remedy the problems of over-population, and drought. Vijay had appealed to his old friend, Dr Imran Malhotra, who had offered the services of the Centre of Strategic Studies to assist in developing strategies to address India's problems. Such matters had come before India's National Security Council but, to his dismay, since being established in 1990, the Council had met only twice in its first ten years. After that, the ineffective NSC had been considered something of a joke.

Vijay had been shocked with the Centre's projections in relation to the number of Indian children who would die from malnutrition and starvation. And this was before the country had been severely affected by *El Niño*. The Prime Minister had spent numerous hours discussing the problems with Imran, whose sympathetic ear understood the vastness of India's conundrum. India needed food, desperately.

There were simply too many people living on what had become arid land. Vijay instructed Imran to prepare a report, for his eyes only, offering alternative solutions to overcome India's dilemma. Understanding the urgency involved, Imran Malhotra dedicated most of the Centre's activities towards producing his study. He personally acted as censor for the project, trusting none with the collective information until he had presented this to the Prime Minister in its final form.

When Dr Malhotra handed the report to his dear and respected friend, there were tears in his eyes. It would appear that their country was on a most dangerous course, one which would undoubtedly result in an apocalyptic end for the people of India. Malhotra had then guided his Prime Minister along the path neither wished to take. He believed that the gravity of their country's situation demanded a bold solution. For Imran Malhotra, there was really no choice. India was starving. India needed more fertile land for its people.

Accepting the gravity of the decision he must make, Vijay had decided to proceed with Malhotra's ambitious strategy. He believed he had little choice, justifying that the number of lives his country could lose in any short term confrontation would be relatively insignificant when considered in respect to the gains India would make. He called a meeting of those closest to him, to seek their support.

At first, his colleagues were horrified that Vijay had even entertained what one of their number referred to as India's Doomsday Plan. The Prime Minister had solicited the President's support, and it was he who had finally persuaded the others that, for India, there were really no viable alternatives but to embark on an immediate path of regional expansionism. India needed to secure more fertile ground to provide for its people. The alternatives were obvious. The Centre's Director, Dr Imran Malhotra had explained that, within five years, India could well implode politically as a result of famine and its growing inability to feed its millions. To do nothing would be to invite revolt against its central government.

Those present clearly understood the ramifications of what they had heard. India's borders could then easily be overrun in the northeast by China and there was little doubt that old animosities would drive the Moslems back across from Pakistan and into Kashmir. Following these successes, India's northern provinces would most probably be occupied. The audacious plan soon gained acceptance, paving the way for Vijay to order its secret implementation.

A list was prepared of those whose support would be essential to the project's success. One by one, Vijay called each of these to his home for private consultations, where he swore them to secrecy, demanding that only he, as Prime Minister, would have absolute authority over the implementation of the plan. The last to be called was Admiral Krishna Gopal, the only member of the Armed Forces to be taken into the Prime Minister's confidence.

India's Navy had always enjoyed preferential treatment whenever budgets were prepared. Over the latter part of the twentieth century, it had become one of the largest navies in the world. Vijay was not concerned that the Admiral was the only military representative to be briefed, as the other services would not be required during the initial phases. Gopal had been one of his government's strongest military supporters, unlike the Army leadership, which had never identified with any of his policies. With an understanding of urgency, the plan was then put into action, Imran Malhotra acting as co-ordinator. Meanwhile his friend, the Prime Minister, underwent urgent surgery.

* * * * * *

On the ninth of May, Admiral Krishna Gopal returned from China and went directly to visit the Prime Minister in the hospital, carrying the Chinese Chairman's personal undertaking that they would support India's inclusion as a permanent member of the United Nation's Security Council. This would bring the number of member nations to twenty. With the addition of Japan, Germany, South Africa and Brazil to the existing number of permanent seats, India's inclusion would bring the expanded total to ten, and all with the right of veto.

On the sixth of November, the General Assembly moved to vote, and although Indonesia had substantial support from fellow ASEAN nations and other Moslem countries, the seat was narrowly won by India.

Three weeks later, China's Navy sailed into the Spratly Islands, having further consolidated its position in the Paracel Island Group, and claimed sovereignty over the rich undeveloped oil and gas fields which surrounded the islands. Vietnam's ageing IL-28s and MIG-23 fighters turned back to their base in Vung Tau when confronted by the superior force. Within the month, China had also boldly taken control of Natuna Island and, without so much as one shot being fired, Indonesia lost possession of one of the world's largest known gas fields.

* * * * * *

China

Since the middle of 1993, China had been a net importer of oil, and her dependence on crude imports had doubled over the previous decade as a result of increased demand for motor vehicle transport and electric power. Her neighbours had few reserves of any consequence, and China had become vulnerable to the safe supply of oil from her suppliers, Iran and Iraq.

Indonesia immediately invoked the earlier international agreement guaranteeing its sovereignty over all sea-lanes within the Indonesian archipelago. China reacted as expected, and ordered ten *Jianghu* class frigates, and thirty-seven *Huangfeng* missile ships from bases in Zhanijiang, Aoemen (formerly known as Macao) and Xianggang (old Hong Kong) into the area it now controlled. Within days, the naval build-up added two *Anshan* and eight *Luda* class destroyers. Out of sight, but lying within striking distance of all ASEAN capitals with their Intermediary Range Ballistic Missiles, four *Han*-class SSNs patrolled the South China Sea, determined to prevent disruption to China's oil supplies from the Middle East. China immediately demanded the right to freedom of navigation of all international waterways for those ships carrying the Chinese flag. Beijing argued that Indonesia had no legitimate basis on which to maintain her claim over the Natuna gas deposits, and the entire region shook, as China made its presence felt in the volatile Asian arena.

An emergency session of the Security Council was called, during which Japan moved that China be censured over its aggressive and illegal annexation of the disputed territories and its military expedition into Indonesian waters. As a permanent member of the Council, India vetoed the call. In doing so, the former adversaries declared their hand, and the world watched with growing apprehension as it witnessed the birth of a new, and powerful alliance between the world's two largest populations. And the rest of Asia leaned back in shock, and trembled.

* * * * * *

Jakarta

General Nathan Seda remained dedicated to the cause to which he had committed his life. He continued to secretly implement his ambitious plans for an Independent East Timor, and would remain loyal to its realization until his death. When the last reports of yet another cleansing operation had been whispered to him in private, he had struggled to maintain his composure, knowing that time was running out. But he continued with his plans, adapting them to suit, rearranging them whenever required, patiently yet impatiently, reworking his strategies until he was satisfied that he had finally developed a plan which would work.

Seda realized that he might not be given another such opportunity. While there was still considerable resistance to Indonesia's occupation of his homeland, he believed that he should commit all of his resources to this one, final effort. He might soon be too old to continue with the struggle.

Seda had little comfort from the knowledge that the East Timorese refugees living in Darwin were growing fat from lying around in Australia, while their fellow-countrymen continued to be subjugated by the Indonesian forces. Although he found their position untenable, particularly that of Xanana Soares whom Seda considered something of an interloper, he knew that he would require their support if his operation was to succeed.

He clearly understood why the United Nations had been powerless to enforce its recommendations for the reinstatement of the former colony's independence; monthly reports which flowed across his desk indicated that Australian business would benefit greatly from the joint Indonesian-Australian oil and gas ventures in the Timor Sea. This is why he specifically targeted the offshore production platforms, and exploration rigs, in his initial concept. Seda knew that the incumbent Vice President would step down in less than eighteen months. The President had promised Seda this position, and he had agreed to accept the high profile office, once he had returned from Australia as its Ambassador. But Seda had done so only to disguise his real intentions. He used word of the imminent appointment to consolidate his powerful position, and assist with the implementation of his strategies.

The fortune he had amassed had been ear-marked to finance his complicated plans, and Seda was convinced that he would be successful. The riots leading up to his appointment, the attacks on oil production centres around the Timor Sea and the landings in Darwin and Western Australia had all been thought through in detail.

He had never been concerned that the Indonesian Military machine might offer more resistance than he was prepared to challenge; the United Nations, Australia, and the United States would support his move once they discovered that an independent Timor would be in their national interests. Seda had helped develop the nuclear power plant programme; and in so doing, had used the funding he had derived from this project to finance his ambitious, and perhaps final attempt to secure East Timor's freedom. He had received more than half a billion dollars from the Salima Group, but Seda knew that he would need every penny to finance his brilliantly conceived operation to achieve independent status for his people. He acknowledged that it would be impossible for him to become President of Indonesia; that was reserved purely for those of Javanese stock. There was no other solution; he would become President of an independent East Timor instead.

Seda smiled when he considered the incredible financial drain Indonesia had committed itself to with the *Rama* Nuclear Power Plant energy programme. Recalling his initial discussions with the billionaire, Lim, Seda had thought it would have been much more difficult to extract such large amounts from the Chinese *totok*. Instead, Seda had been surprised when Lim had undertaken to pay the incredible commission for his part in assigning the winning tender to the Salima Group. Unwittingly, Lim had financed the greater part of Seda's dream.

Although his own wealth was already considerable, Nathan Seda had been delighted with the windfall. That, and the knowledge that Indonesia would be encumbered with an incredible debt, one which would take several generations to repay.

As for the Japanese H-3B rocket development programme, Seda had used this perfectly as a distraction, knowing that such a project would be impossible to keep secret. He expected that the Americans would attempt to pressure the Japanese into withdrawing from the joint development programme once the Bandung experimental research centre's true purpose had been discovered. Should this eventuate, it did not overly concern him that the Indonesians would need to find a substitute nation to continue with the programme's development. By then, Seda believed he would have already succeeded in his mission.

Should international pressure fail to influence Indonesia's position concerning their rocket development programme, Seda expected that the threat of Indonesia possessing such a delivery system could only enhance East Timor's right to possess similar weaponry. In this world of ever-changing political alliances, he was certain that an independent Timor would have little difficulty in identifying a sponsor willing to contribute funds and technology to assist the development of similar weaponry for the strategically positioned island nation.

The retired General was convinced that East Timor would be in a position to maintain the integrity of its sovereign status, even in the shadow of its giant Moslem neighbour.

Seda thought about the complicated structure that had been put into place to ensure secrecy with the Bandung project. The mountains surrounding Bandung had long been renowned for the number of mining shafts which had been put down during the Dutch colonial times. It had not been difficult for him to acquire such a location, one which encompassed a defunct gold exploration operation. As the land already belonged to the government through the Ministry of Mines, possession had been easily transferred to the newly created research organization.

The Japanese had provided funding and technical expertise, while Seda's team accepted responsibility for the project's construction. The installation was to be maintained as a secret defense research centre and, while the general public would be informed of its existence, they would not be aware of the centre's secret activities.

The facility had been designed with a dual function, the first being the joint development of a missile delivery system designed and funded by the Japanese in conjunction with Tokyo's existing H-3B programme. The second, and far more sinister purpose would be the utilisation of the deep mining shafts to store excess plutonium, which would later be generated from the *Rama II* nuclear power plant's operations.

Seda had easily convinced the President that the Japanese would not be required to know the purpose of the secondary and underground installation. A plausible story for the secret bunker could be easily concocted should the need arise. Besides, Seda knew that it would be impossible for *Rama II* to commence producing fissionable material before he had firmly ensconced himself as President of East Timor and armed his people. Seda believed that it was necessary for Indonesia to be nuclear armed. Without this threat, an independent East Timor would never be able to justify securing similar weaponry. The thought of realizing his dream provided Seda with a moment for reflection. He had worked tirelessly to achieve his ambition.

As his mind wandered back over the past years, Stephen Coleman's face flashed across his mind and, for a brief moment, he was surprised to discover that he experienced a sense of sadness over his former associate's demise. In some perverse way, Seda accepted that Coleman had been mainly responsible for many of the financial successes he then enjoyed.

When the most recent East Timorese rebellion had failed, Seda had all but lost hope. The slaughter had been even worse than those during the first years of occupation. He had been devastated by the results. Investigations had been thorough, and Seda knew he must remove any possibility of his relationship with Coleman being discovered before his position was compromised. Stephen Coleman had to go. Nathan Seda had ordered his execution, and his trusted servant, Umar, had willingly accepted the mission.

Frustratingly, Coleman sensed what was happening, and had disappeared completely in spite of Umar's best efforts to track him down. Umar had followed his quarry's trail through most of Asia. When more than five years had passed, and Coleman had still not made any effort to seek compensation for the assets he had left behind, Seda believed that the man who had been responsible for creating their *kongsi's* first millions, had simply disappeared, and might even be dead. He would have felt easier had there been some evidence reflecting Coleman's status, one way or the other, and could only hope that his former associate was, in fact, gone forever.

Seda thought about Umar's service over the years, and agreed that the man he had found incarcerated in the Magelang Detention Centre, just months after the 1965 coup, had certainly served his new master with unprecedented dedication. Seda had already decided to take Umar with him to Australia; the success of his mission depended heavily on the former Communist army officer.

He then considered the other officers on whom he might rely; Sujono Diryo, Seda knew, could most certainly not be included amongst these. He had sensed that the younger man might also have his ambitious eyes on the Vice Presidency and, in Seda's opinion, that would be a major political error for the unprepared, and relatively inexperienced officer to make.

Being married into the President's family would not necessarily guarantee Sujono support from the other generals. As this, and other thoughts passed through his mind, Seda became troubled by his former protégé, Major General Sujono Diryo, and wondered whether or not he should consider having Umar arrange for the rising star's early retirement from the Vice Presidential race.

* * * * * *

Murray Stephenson disliked attending meetings in the Kuningan building. He knew that there would always be those amongst the foreign community who would misconstrue the purpose of his visits to the Australian Embassy and, in consequence, he avoided going there even to have his passport extended.

He sat opposite the grey-haired director and could not find any reason to be civil to the man. When he had been involved with the Australian Secret Intelligence Service, this was the man who had deliberately set out to destroy his career. Murray wasn't even sure that Anderson had not been responsible for many of the events which had clouded his last weeks in the Service. Although Murray despised the man, he acknowledged that ASIS still played an important role in maintaining his country's security; and it was for this reason, and no other, that Murray had decided to meet with the director.

'We all appreciate what you have done, Murray,' Anderson had said. Murray knew this not to be true. The man obviously had no heart; he wanted to ask what had happened to Stephen Coleman but thought better of it. He had not been involved for more than twenty years, and wondered how Anderson had managed to remain in power, considering his age.

'Sure,' was all he said, rising to leave. He left the documents lying on the table. They would be of no use to him any more. Anderson extended his hand but the gesture was ignored. Murray left them then, hoping that what he had done would prevent what could have developed into a major threat to the Australian people.

He had protected his source - not out of respect for Ruswita so much, but because he knew to do so would be prudent, considering his financial dependency on Peter Wong and Wong's obvious relationship with Lim's widow. He wished, sometimes, that he had never become involved in the *Rama* projects, but Murray, like so many others, had been caught up in the intricate, financial web that had been so cleverly woven by Lim, and he accepted that there was no immediate escape.

The knowledge he had so recently acquired had acted as a warning to him also. Murray's instinct told him that there was a major move afoot, and he was frustrated by his feeling of impotency, knowing that he was familiar with all the players and yet had no idea what the game plan might be.

KERRY B.COLLISON

* * * * * *

United States of America — Washington

Victor Lombardo had been serving in the American Congress for more than ten years, representing his home State of New York. He reflected on the mechanics of politics, never ceasing to be amazed at the intricate system which had provided the comfortable life-style he now enjoyed.

The Congressman finished drafting his speech for the next session, then leaned back in the leather chair to consider the consequences of his plea for Indonesia's Most Favoured Nation status to be revoked. Lombardo was confident that he had sufficient numbers to push his motion through should he still find this necessary. Politics was all about power, he knew; and power was about money.

Lombardo then reflected on his meeting of the evening before with the two Asian bankers, and the insulting offer they had made. When he had checked the contents of the envelope and discovered what value they had placed upon his services, Lombardo had thrown this back at the Lim brothers, and suggested that they reconsider just what they were asking of him. He had expected that they return with another offer and, when this did not eventuate, Lombardo decided to give them a taste of the stick he carried in Congress. He would call for the dismantling of Indonesia's MFN status, and see how quickly they then returned to discourage him from proceeding. His demand would be mentioned in the following morning's press, and the Congressman reminded himself to call in the appropriate favours to ensure that this would occur as planned. Then, when the Lims were sufficiently concerned that their country might be in danger of losing the MFN status which, he knew, would cost the Salima conglomerate dearly, he would renegotiate his position. Providing the two wealthy Chinese bankers met his price, he would then permit opposition debate to convince him to withdraw his motion, and everyone would be satisfied.

He leaned forward, made another note on the draft speech, then lay back in his chair as he visualised how he would spend the two hundred thousand dollars he expected the Lims would pay.

UNITED STATES OF AMERICA

CONGRESSIONAL RECORD

INDONESIA'S MOST-FAVORED NATION STATUS
(House of Representatives) [EXCERPT] [Page: J 4221]

The SPEAKER pro tempore. Under a previous order of the House, the gentleman from New York [Mr Lombardo] is recognized for five minutes.

Mr LOMBARDO, Mr Speaker, during the course of the following weeks, Members of this august house will be obliged to consider a great deal of information, while subjected to an unprecedented lobbying effort from both sides of the issue, which will then eventuate in their casting what could very well be one of the most critical votes ever to be taken in this Congress.

I refer to the vote on further extending most-favored-trade status to the Republic of Indonesia. The results of this vote, Mr Speaker, will demonstrate to the world where American priorities lie and will, most probably, be closely watched by our other Asian trading partners with respect to how they too might be treated during subsequent reviews regarding MFN status.

There will, no doubt, be those amongst this Congress who might well consider that the debate regarding Indonesia's MFN status extension is nothing more than an attempt, by those of us who are opposed to such an extension, to be obstructive in terms of global trade. Let me assure you, Mr Speaker, that this is far from the truth. There are more than 160 nations which enjoy MFN status in one form or another. Of these, only Indonesia and China have emerged as the nations which continually flout the considerations extended by this United States of America. In reality, the Indonesian MFN debate is about human rights. It is about Indonesia's refusal to abide by the decisions taken by the United Nations in respect to their occupation of East Timor. A vote in favor of Most Favored Nation status for Indonesia, is a vote, Mr Speaker, to condone that country's illegal occupation of another country. [EXCERPT]

Chapter 17

Islamabad

Mohammed Ali bin Fuad searched the skies for planes. It had become a habit, one he had acquired as a youth. He spotted two aircraft which he judged had just entered into their holding patterns, then he turned back downwind to watch the ageing Boeing 747 land. The screaming sound of runway concrete ripping into rubber struck his ears as the aircraft touched down heavily, leaving visible puffs of burning tyre-smoke in its tracks.

Fuad turned to his team and shouted above the high-pitched jet engines as decibels exceeded acceptable levels, then adjusted his headphones to deaden the noise. The ground engineer team waited, pensively, until the aircraft turned into the hard-standing apron area. Fuad moved out quickly and stood directly in line with the huge aircraft, guiding the pilot towards the allocated parking bay.

The service team swung into action as the aircraft braked to a halt, co-ordinating ground handling as they had been trained. Fuad stepped forward, plugged his communication lead into the aircraft's ground system and spoke to the pilot. Minutes passed before the doors were released from inside the cabin, permitting the final connection to be made as the passenger steps clicked into place. An hour later, as he observed the jumbo-jet depart, Fuad knew he would not be needed again until the following day. He completed his ground engineering report, lodged this with the station manager, then left the terminal building for home.

The bus dropped him off on the outskirts of Islamabad, where he lived in a small cluster of low-cost houses constructed for airport employees and their families. Fuad lived alone; he had never married, and at his age, had decided that it might already be too late to do so. Fuad's life was now relatively simple in comparison to his earlier years, when each new day brought life-threatening challenges, and all that he possessed were the torn rags on his back.

He entered his compact quarters and observed that his clothes had been washed and folded, and a note advising how much he owed the woman next door. He placed the clothes in the wardrobe and then showered before lying down on the narrow, hard timber-framed bed to sleep. As he lay there, resting, Fuad remembered how long it had taken him to accustom himself to city living conditions, and the uncomfortably soft beds people used there. When he was first taken to the swelling metropolis, Fuad had preferred to sleep on the hard, cement, store-room floor, behind the kitchen in his benefactor's home.

He thought about the people who had accepted him into their household and provided food and shelter at a time when refugees, such as he, had swamped Islamabad by the hundreds of thousands. Haunting memories of those times had not grown dim over the years. Instead, Fuad accepted these reminders of just how cruel life had been under the Hindus. As a child, his family had been driven from their own country, India, and forced to live in the arid regions of Pakistan where the heat was so severe, trees shed their leaves to preserve moisture during the day and birds flew only at night.

Then, when he had barely entered his teens, his former countrymen had crossed the border and commenced a campaign of ethnic cleansing which drove Moslems even deeper into Pakistan. His family had died during such an attack. Had it not been for a band of retreating resistance fighters, he too would have died in the desert. They had taken him with them, providing Fuad with water and *chanai*, the peasant's hamper.

As he lay on his back, resting, Fuad's thoughts carried him back to the long trek he and the others had made. Moving from village to village, living on the most meagre of rations, the armed band continued their retreat until they were no longer threatened by aerial attack. He sometimes still woke in the quiet of night, finding himself screaming aloud in his sleep as memories of the helicopter gun-ship attacks intruded on his dreams.

It was months before Fuad ended up in Islamabad. He had just followed the others, as he had nowhere else to go. The soldier who had saved his life when his village had been destroyed continued to care for him by taking him into his modest home and providing food and shelter. The brief and bitter war had ended with India gloating over its victory, and before Fuad had even arrived in the city life had already returned to normal.

* * * * * *

He had worked alongside the demobilised soldier, learning what he could of the man's mechanical skills. He learned to read. Before his twentieth birthday, Fuad's knowledge of engines had guaranteed him permanent employment with the government and, when the opportunity arose, he joined the army. There he received specialist training, and was placed in Pakistan's elite mobile ground defense corps. When hostilities broke out between India and Pakistan again, Fuad found himself out in the desert defending his adopted country against the land of his birth.

The fighting continued for seventeen days, during which time his unit had accounted for three Indian Mi-25 Russian gun-ships which had penetrated deep into Pakistani territory. The war had ended as had others between the two countries, with tens of thousands dead and no clear resolution.

When Fuad's unit had returned to Islamabad, he had been decorated for his efforts in shooting down the enemy gun-ships. His photograph had been placed in the capital's newspapers and, for a brief time, Fuad was treated as a hero. Then, along with many others, he was de-mobbed.

He was fortunate to find work at the airport. There, his dedication and skill attracted the attention of his superiors, and Fuad was given assistance to attend evening courses where he further enhanced his empiric skills, learning mechanical theory and even English which, he had discovered, was essential to his work at the airport. As the years had passed, Fuad consolidated his position at the airport by accepting a position with one of the foreign airline companies which required its own native speaking engineers. He had been given an excellent salary, and was taken to the United States where he underwent intensive conversion training on the United American fleet. By the time Fuad had reached his fortieth birthday, he had been appointed first assistant ground engineer for the airline's Islamabad services.

As he lay thinking about his career, Fuad reminded himself to check with the station manager regarding final confirmation of his posting. He had been informed that he was on a short list, and had been recommended for an overseas assignment. His six-month tour with the United American ground handling team in California had whetted his appetite for travel; that, and the incredibly generous allowances paid to staff while away from their home stations.

It was during his training there that Fuad had been surprised to discover the number of airline staff involved with the illegal import of drugs. Once, during an undercarriage inspection, he came across a two kilo package of white powder which he knew, instantly, from his time on the streets of Islamabad, was heroin. He had been tempted to remove the shipment and try and sell it himself, but realised that without contacts this would have been dangerous

Unbeknown to Fuad, he had been observed inspecting the shipment, and was later approached by the ground crewman responsible for its recovery. Fuad was offered five hundred dollars to remain silent. He willingly accepted the money and became friendly with the American engineer. As their friendship developed, Fuad even helped recover some shipments, when asked. By the time he had completed his time in Los Angeles, Fuad didn't want to leave.

He cherished his short stay, and wished he could remain. Fuad discussed this with his friend, who embellished the penalties associated with illegal entry, as he did not want Fuad being picked up as an illegal immigrant and possibly revealing whatever he had learned about the illicit drug activities around the airport. Fuad then decided that he would look for another way to return to America but, after several years back in the Pakistani capital, he acknowledged, sadly, that his dream would never materialise.

He wanted desperately to leave Pakistan and its bitter memories. There were a limited number of choices for those with Fuad's engineering expertise, and one of those included Bombay. He had thought of what he would say should the company offer to send him to India. Fuad frowned, discovering that this thought had caused him to bite through the soft flesh of his lower lip. No, he decided, even if it might mean that he would never again be offered the opportunity to travel away from Pakistan, he would most certainly refuse.

The hate he felt for the Hindus had all but consumed him during his younger years, and Fuad accepted that his feelings could never be any different. The memory of his parents' broken bodies lying under the rubble which had been their home could never fade. Disturbed that he had permitted his latent anger to spoil his rest, Fuad attempted to erase the past from his mind by conjuring up images of other things, but failed. An hour passed, then another. Finally he gave up altogether, dressed, and went out in search of something to eat.

On Friday, as he was preparing for the mid-morning prayers, Fuad was called into the station manager's office and asked if he would accept a two-year assignment as the company's senior ground-handling engineer in the Philippines. Fuad was overwhelmed by the opportunity, and eagerly accepted the promotion. He had often seen Filipino stewardesses when their flights had transited Islamabad, and smiled at the thought of living amongst such beautiful women. And, he remembered, some of them were also of the Moslem faith.

A month passed before Fuad arrived in Manila. He settled down to his work, and soon discovered the similarities between working in Los Angeles and his new station. Before he had celebrated his first year as the United American Airline senior ground engineer, Fuad was making ten times as much money from moving heroin as he was from his salary. And that was when he attracted the attention of the Drug Enforcement Agency, whose agents had been monitoring staff employed by airlines which flew between the United States and Asia.

Three months later, Fuad was arrested and interrogated by American agents seconded to the Filipino Bureau.

They decided that he could be far more useful working for the DEA than being incarcerated in some filthy local prison. He was offered the opportunity to avoid imprisonment of fifteen years, and Fuad leaped at the offer. Fuad then commenced reporting on a regular basis to the in-country DEA agent, knowing that his dream of ever returning to America was then an impossibility.

His file was sent to Washington, from where it was distributed to all United States defense and intelligence agencies. Within the month, his records had been amended to include his service records and other information gleaned from data collected by the American Embassy in Pakistan. It was then that he came to the attention of the United States Defense Intelligence Agency analysts, at Bolling Airforce Base in Washington and the world's most powerful covert agency, the CIA.

* * * * * *

China — Beijing

China's paramount leader sat transfixed, listening to his Admiral's discourse on regional naval strengths, and the unopposed annexation of the southern islands the Indonesians referred to as Natuna. He was most pleased with the results of the first expedition, and particularly satisfied that there had not been any interference from the United States forces, particularly its Seventh Fleet stationed in Japan.

The Chairman clearly understood the economic realities which confronted his nation. China's economic growth continued to be stifled by its inability to satisfy the country's insatiable demands for more fuel, and he had personally accepted responsibility to resolve this national dilemma. Foreign investments had doubled, then later tripled, once the West had been satisfied with China's handling of Hong Kong and the former colony's intellectuals. But the Chairman knew that the solution to China's difficulties would not be found in the slow transfer of technology from either the Russians, or the West. Instead, he had strongly supported the small dedicated group which had proposed a more lateral approach to China's quest for current technology, while maintaining its military growth and supremacy along the tens of thousands of kilometers representing China's borders.

As China's entire southern economic development belt scrambled for its share of infrastructure dollars, so too did the demand for greater fuel supplies grow. From Shanghai down through Guangzhou and across to Chongging, China's more liberal south had leaped forward at an incredible rate as these provinces continued to enjoy unparalleled, industrialised growth. Oil imports had dangerously exceeded all previous economic forecasts, and the Chairman had encountered few difficulties in obtaining support to remedy China's predicament.

Of the dozen or so nations which shared borders with his

country few, with the exclusion of the Russian states, produced sufficient fuel for themselves. So occupying these countries was not considered a viable option. He knew that any attempt to occupy Siberia would be met with an immediate, and most probably nuclear, response from Moscow and that isolated territory's other allies.

To the south, the rich oil and gas fields of the South China Sea offered a solution only to China's immediate problems. Later, they would need to look further afield to accommodate the country's incredible thirst for fuel and the funding necessary to accommodate this burdensome need. He believed that there could only be one solution to resolve these financial considerations, and that lay in China's acquisition of Taiwan, with its hundreds of billions in gold and dollar reserves.

The Chairman had stated the obvious to his political and military supporters. China needed to secure its lines of supply from the Middle East while developing a strategy which would deliver control over the substantial oil and gas reserves to the south. The implementation of his programme would, however, require that the United States of America be rendered powerless to intercede in any regional conflict which arose out of China's expansionist moves. The United States, they had been reminded by a senior strategist, had considerable economic interests to protect by remaining on a friendly footing with the world's third largest state.

The economist had emphasized that American trade with Asia had grown to half a trillion dollars and accounted for more than five million jobs in North America. The United States, he had gone on to say, had invested more than one hundred billion in Asia, while their Oriental counterparts had reciprocated by placing almost double that amount in American investments.

The Chairman's strategic advisers had pointed out that the United States was losing its military foothold in Asia. With the exception of Guam and Japan, which often played host to the Seventh Fleet and permitted the Americans to maintain a small contingent of troops and combat aircraft, the United States military presence had all but disappeared from the region.

The subsequent Party Congress had unanimously supported an increased military budget, one which would expand China's Navy and ensure the suppression of any civilian unrest which might occur along the borders. What surprised most China-watchers was the sudden shift Beijing made towards developing closer ties with the United States, believing that the two countries were entering a new era of friendship and co-operation. A goodwill visit had soon followed, during which time the American public discounted newspaper reports from one journalist who had overheard China's powerful Peoples' Liberation Army warlord, General Chi, comment that his country had already perfected a missile delivery system which could easily dispatch a nuclear warhead to Los Angeles.

In the wake of fading public indignation over the Long Beach affair, when China had successfully taken control over the former naval base for China's COSCO fleet, three Chinese warships, including two destroyers, were permitted to dock at the North Island Naval Air Station in San Diego Bay for a five-day 'goodwill tour'. North Americans welcomed the visit with unprecedented complacency, accepting visiting Red Chinese Vice Admiral Wang Yongguo's statement, that: *"Although China and America are far away from each other, we believe our countries can be linked by the Pacific Ocean."*

In just one year, the Chairman's skilful diplomatic measures had all but erased memory of the chilly confrontation between the two countries just twelve months earlier, when US carriers were sent to the Taiwan Strait in response to his country's efforts to intimidate the so-called Free Chinese during their presidential elections. Since then, due to substantial diplomatic inroads being achieved by his emissaries, the Chairman was delighted to observe that the American President had become far more deferential to China's concerns.

The Chairman's thoughts turned to the two young men most responsible for delivering the Americans to China. Although the paramount leader clearly understood what really motivated the Lim brothers, he could not help but believe that they were also driven by their Chinese heritage. The two bankers had been instrumental in providing the key which opened the door directly into the White House, and delivered not only the Alabama shipping facilities and the Long Beach naval yards to China, but also control over the anchor ports situated at both entrances to the Panama Canal. Now, given that the time was rapidly approaching for China to make its move, the United States would consider its position very carefully before interfering with his country's ultimate goals.

The Chairman recalled that world opinion had turned against his country during their early attempts to gain a foothold in the United States and Panama. Those responsible for jeopardising his country's dreams had been severely dealt with, and he had warned those who might be tempted to emulate their misguided colleagues that he would not tolerate such disastrous results. Because of a few, China's entire American strategy had almost been destroyed.

The Chairman frowned with the recollection of how a COSCO crew had been discovered secretly off-loading a shipment of two thousand AK-47 rifles in Oakland. Accusations of deliberate attempts to establish a Chinese Fifth Column in the United States had covered front pages for weeks. Then, as the issue started to fade away, the Chairman was infuriated when claims were made that China had permitted its shipping line, COSCO, to develop lines of supply within North America for heroin distribution. Then the US newspapers leaked stories claiming that more than four hundred Chinese businessmen were under federal investigation for espionage, suggesting that many of these were also COSCO associated.

Other articles claimed, irresponsibly he had thought at the time, that according to the United States Defense Intelligence Agency, China had increased its North American intelligence operations to the point where the DIA, and other American agencies, had been overwhelmed by the sheer number of China-related cases. In order to prevent any further deterioration in China-American relationships, his government had moved quickly, and once again the Lim brothers became involved in assisting China shore-up its relations with the United States. It had taken considerable lobbying and substantial funds to change American opinion, but inside one year they had succeeded in achieving this goal, during which time COSCO's underground activities reached an all time high.

The Chinese shipping company flouted every law in the land, and went virtually unchallenged. Its access to the American nation's largest container port, conveniently located near several sensitive defense research facilities, proved a windfall for their clandestine activities. Through the Lim's banking arms in Kentucky, they were able to purchase many of the Pentagon's high-tech surplus military parts then ship them back to China, hiding these in seagoing containers under tons of metal scrap.

Then, without warning, COSCO's ships were raided by the United States Secret Service. Among the items seized were fully operational encryption devices, submarine propulsion parts, radar systems, electron tubes for the Patriot guided missiles, and even F-117A Stealth fighter parts. Many of these parts which had been sold as 'surplus' were, they discovered, brand new.

The Chairman was aware of his country's intelligence agencies' dedicated efforts to secure technology from the Americans and had, in fact, condoned the measures, knowing that acquisition of such high-tech information and materials would assist China to drastically reduce its own research and development costs. His country's emergence as a mega economic power had, without doubt, paralysed its neighbouring countries with fear.

The Chairman then changed his country's strategy, moving the pressure back onto the Americans. When the British press disclosed that they had confirmation of China's ability to deliver a twenty-kiloton yield nuclear warhead to United States shores, and postulated a future which would include a Chinese inspired Armageddon, United States defense officials reconsidered their country's position, once again, in relation to the Republic of China.

The week following the disclosures made in the London tabloids, the Chinese Minister for the Interior had openly sought the immediate removal, and execution, of the engineer identified as responsible for the leaks. Photographs of his country's newly developed DF-31 Intercontinental Ballistic Missile, and technical data which suggested that this would be the missile used against American shores, had been deliberately leaked. Orders were given for the engineer involved in the ruse to be secretly moved to another research and development centre, where he could continue with his valuable work, and a common thief had then been executed in his place.

World attention was once again focused on China. Amnesty International highlighted past atrocities, and isolated intellectual groups demanded greater representation. The Chairman refused to accommodate requests for further political reforms, and ignored suggestions that China's Human Rights record was at an all time low. He firmly believed that there was no role for Western ideologies in the authoritarian state; China had entered the twenty-first century and demanded its place within the greater structure of the new global society.

The Chairman was an ardent historian; he firmly believed that, as China had once dominated the East, it would soon do so again. He admired the great Mao Tse Tung, revelling in the many stories of how Mao had kept the super-powers at each others' throats. As a young man, he had studied the Great Chairman's tactics and philosophies. As an older and wiser politician, he had learned that the wisdom of Mao was not necessarily appropriate for a nation which needed desperately to climb out of its economic quagmire. Although he had also respected Mao's political position in relation to India, the Chairman believed that China, in the new millennium, needed to have these people as allies.

He reflected on their historical relationships. Under Nehru, India had begun its slow crawl forward, and was admired by the West, and this relationship had continued until the Indian Prime Minister, during his state visit to America, had sided with Mao Tse Tung when Chiang Kai Shek's nationalists were defeated, and fled to Taiwan. As a Chinese, the Chairman would always thank Nehru for insisting that Mao's new China be given the vacant United Nation's seat and his refusal to condemn China over its anti-West stance. The Chairman knew from history that Nehru envisaged an Asia controlled by the two great powers, and mistakenly trusted Mao's loyalty. When Nehru had emerged as the self-proclaimed leader of the non-aligned nations, Mao simply sent Chou En Lai to the Bandung Conference as a token gesture of his support.

The Chairman reflected on the 1962 Chinese invasion of Tibet and North-east India, challenging Nehru's strength. Although India had appealed to the Americans for support, none had eventuated. As a staunch Mao supporter, the Chairman could not understand, at the time, why Mao then had withdrawn Chinese troops from the thousands of square kilometres already seized. The self-proclaimed and one-sided alliance between the two nations dissipated as quickly as it had appeared. India and China had immediately become border enemies. Now, as China's new absolute leader, the Chairman had been given the opportunity to use India once again and, in so doing, guarantee China's future lines of supply and natural rights within the region.

The Chairman had given his final approval for the rapprochement offered by China's natural enemies, understanding that the common denominator which tied New Delhi to Beijing would be their strength in controlling the seas. United, he believed, the world's two largest populations would soon dominate Asia. Once China had consolidated its position, he would review the alliance created with India. The Chairman sanctioned the bold move to send the South Sea Fleet across the South China Sea into Indonesia's undefended northern islands of Natuna. China's sea-lane access needed to be protected, above all else. Power, fuel, electricity: these were the driving forces which required that China move quickly, to feed its hungry millions.

The well-informed Chairman was familiar with most recent developments in technology. He also knew that, with China's annual growth ballooning into the double digits, even the ambitious nuclear power programme would never keep pace with his country's incredible demand for electricity. He had been one of the first to endorse the additional expenditures required for the advancement of their nuclear power industry, although he realized just how time consuming this new approach would be. He had clearly understood that, even with the development of a hundred new plants, these would generate but a fraction of his country's demands. The few NPPs already scheduled for construction would not even provide sufficient electricity for a city the size of Shanghai, let alone the entire southern region where factories remained working, demanding even more power, day in and day out, twenty-four hours each day.

His country's ambitious plans for expanding nuclear electricity generation had been severely curtailed by those nations which controlled the flow of uranium ore. The Chairman recognised that China's deposits of this precious ore were insignificant in terms of the nation's needs. Even the China National Nuclear Corporation, with its three hundred thousand employees, had been unable to resolve the question of China's self-sufficiency. Production centres, such as the Lantian mine in Shaanxi Province, contributed little towards satisfying domestic demand. He believed that there could be only one solution. China desperately needed to acquire its own natural energy sources, and in so doing, protect its existing lines of supply from the Middle East. *If only China had Australia's uranium ore reserves and Indonesia's oil!*

* * * * * *

The paramount leader of more than one billion Chinese finished listening to the Admiral's report, then dismissed his senior officer. He sat, contemplating China's immediate future and its relationship with India. The world's two largest populations, supported by two of the largest navies. *Who*, he thought, *could possibly prevent the successful implementation of their strategies?*

* * * * * *

Indonesia — Bandung Research and Development Center

Doctor Sunarko slipped away earlier than usual, feigning family illness. He drove down the slippery mountain road slowly, worried that the earlier rain might have dislodged part of the unstable cuttings which sliced precariously through to the lush, volcanic, rain-sodden soil. He braked entering a corner and the Toyota's wheels refused to steer, threatening to send the four-wheel drive crashing over the embankment into the river two hundred meters below. At the last moment, the vehicle corrected itself, and Sunarko braked again, his heart thumping dangerously.

His fear could not be altogether attributed to his poor driving skills; he was scared. Earlier, he had observed the Research Center's security officer watching him closely. Sunarko feared discovery, and now believed that this had happened, otherwise he would not have come under scrutiny from the security chief, Umar.

Lightning cracked to his right, causing him to catch his breath. Within moments, his vision was blurred as the thunderstorm released thrashing rain, carried by turbulent, mountain winds. He braked and swerved, again. Without warning, another deafening crack of lightning struck nearby, and Sunarko stomped heavily on the brake pedal, sliding to a halt. Shaking uncontrollably, he then buried his head between his arms, gripping the jeep's wheel. Then the engine died.

Suddenly, he couldn't breathe and, fumbling for his inhaler, discovered that he had left it behind, which increased the severity of his asthma attack. Sunarko struggled for air, but it was as if his airways were blocked. Within seconds, he felt his body slipping away, losing consciousness. His head slid slowly across and against the driver's door and, in that moment, he noticed another flash reflected by his exterior off-side rear-vision mirror. His last thoughts were that Umar had followed him and that he was surely going to die! He heard the other vehicle brake, then a door slammed shut, followed moments later by a fist banging on the side of his jeep.

'Are you all right?' he heard someone call, the man's voice barely audible. Sunarko cringed, not wishing to look outside into the dark, rain-swept night. Suddenly, the door was jerked open, and Sunarko shrank back, waiting for whatever might follow.

'Don't hurt me!' he cried out, covering his head with his arms.

'I'm not going to hurt you,' he heard the man call loudly, his voice partially drowned by another loud thunder clap. He looked at the stranger standing in the torrential downpour, and identified the figure as that of a foreigner.

'Who..are..you?' he asked, choking as he fought to breathe. He felt the man's strong hands grip him firmly, then pull him away from the driver's seat. Sunarko no longer cared if he was going to die; he just wanted to be able to breathe. He experienced the slight nausea associated with his loss of oxygen and panicked, trying to suck air into his lungs.

'Hold on, Mas,' the voice said, but Sunarko just let go, and slumped forward unconscious. Murray Stephenson grunted, pulled the engineer from the Jeep, and carried him with great difficulty back to his own vehicle. He leaned the Indonesian aerospace engineer against his car, opened the rear door, and dropped him onto the rear seat. Then he returned to the Jeep, turned the wheel to unlock the steering, and knocked the Japanese machine out of gear.

He watched the Jeep crawl to the side of the road, then dip its nose forward, before sliding down the steep embankment, and Murray cursed those who had arranged for him to meet with this engineer out in the mountains. He turned, then slogged his way through the thick, sticky clay, becoming totally drenched before reaching his vehicle. Once inside and behind the wheel, he dragged his filthy, mud-caked boots off, and threw these angrily onto the passenger's floor. Murray looked over to the rear seat and could see that Sunarko's system had closed down, putting him safely to sleep. Then he released the hand-brake and drove carefully around the mountain into Bandung.

* * * * * *

Umar swore loudly, then kicked the side of the Jeep's flat tyre. He looked down the muddy road, his eyes following the vehicle's lights to the next bend in the mountainous road. He had lost sight of Sunarko more than five minutes before, and knew that it would be hopeless attempting to catch him once he had changed the wheel.

He tugged at his coat's collar as rain stung his face and neck, driven by the gusty, mountain winds. Then he set about unlocking the spare wheel while considering what his next actions should be. Umar dragged his heavy boots through the mud, and stood at the rear of the Jeep unscrewing the bolts attached to the spare while contemplating his quarry, Sunarko. He knew that the man was up to something; he had followed him several times before and was convinced that the senior technician from the secret research and development facility was communicating with someone from outside. He had set out to follow Sunarko, hoping to discover who it might be that was so interested in the Bandung project.

Ten minutes passed before Umar could follow. He knew that it would be most unlikely that he could catch up with the other man, considering the weather and the dangerous road. Umar decided to return to the research centre and wait for a later opportunity to trap Sunarko. Then the thought struck him that he may not be given that chance, as he would soon leave for Australia to accompany *Bapak Seda* as his security chief.

Umar's face twisted in what some might believe to be a smile, as he recalled his first meeting with the General in the dungeons of the Semarang detention centre, where he had been imprisoned, interrogated, and brutally beaten regarding his role in the Communist Party's abortive *coup d'etat*. He accepted that Seda had saved his life, in exchange for which, Umar had agreed to follow the powerful intelligence officer unquestioningly. And he had for more than three decades, even when this loyalty sometimes required that he act as the general's personal executioner. He had been well rewarded. The former communist officer had discussed his retirement with the general; Seda had agreed that Umar would be relieved of his commitments once they had returned from the general's brief tour as Ambassador to Australia.

As he drove carefully back to the well-guarded facility, Umar smiled at the thought of his leaving Java to spend the next years in Australia amongst the likes of Stephen Coleman. The image of the general's former associate flashed through his mind, and Umar scowled, remembering how close he had come to killing the man the first time, more than thirty years before, when the Australian had visited the jungles of Irian, and stepped into his sights. Umar had fired, believing he had killed the foreigner, only to discover later that he had merely wounded the man.

Umar had been confused when General Seda later invited this man to enter into partnership when he returned to Jakarta. Even then, Umar believed that Coleman would always be a danger to them both. When Seda had issued instructions to kill his partner, the Australian had escaped, fleeing overseas. Umar and Coleman had barely missed each other in the Philippines and, later, in Phnom Penh. Umar had spent more than two years searching for his quarry to no avail. Finally Umar decided that someone else must have completed his task for him, as Coleman had simply vanished.

As he turned into the research centre's driveway and flashed his lights, two security guards stepped out into the rain, saluted, then opened the heavy gates. Umar drove through and returned to his quarters, thoughts of Stephen Coleman already washed from his mind.

* * * * * *

Jakarta

Geoffrey Thistlethwaites in no way reflected the image of what Hollywood traditionally promoted as a typical, flamboyant, handsome, and daring intelligence agent. His communications company, P.T. Communications Ready-Serve, had started out as a front for the confusing number of Australian intelligence agencies which had inundated the Jakarta capital over the past thirty years, but his company had actually developed into a *bona fide* operation, embarrassing his masters in Canberra. There were no less than five such listening posts in Jakarta attributed to the Australian intelligence agencies, most of which came into being after the press exposed the clandestine activities of Eric Whitehead and Associates' operations throughout Asia, resulting in the prominent public relations executive decision to resign from the public company and enjoy his forced retirement.

GT, as his friends called him, was a simple communications conduit who received and passed information in consideration of a modest, and often overdue, retainer. On this day, he took the taped interview and went down to the Embassy in Kuningan. There, under the subterfuge of meeting with the Defence Attaché, GT surrendered the tape to the First Secretary, Political, and returned to his workshop office in Cilandak. Not two hours had passed before the tape's contents had been encoded, despatched, and received at the relevant destination in Canberra, where the desk officer identified the highly sensitive coding, and passed the message directly to his superior. An hour later, the contents of Sunarko's interview were known to the Australian Attorney General.

* * * * * *

India — Army Northern Command

Undisturbed by the heat, General Rahul Kumar stood, almost majestically, his right arm hand prepared to snap his salute as the approaching column of soldiers responded to the command, 'eyes right!'. Standing behind, and slightly to one side of the Chief of Army Staff, was the Officer Commanding for India's largest military command, recently boosted to include three infantry divisions. As the soldiers marched past on parade, General Kumar recognized that these troops represented India's first line of defense in the event that his country was attacked by any of her aggressive neighbours.

General Kumar realized that it was highly probable that the young men proudly marching past before him would see action at least once during their military careers. The last confrontation with Pakistan had ended, as before, with an Indian victory. Although many years had passed since India and China had fought along each other's borders, he firmly believed that he would live to see hostilities break out between the two countries again. As he gazed proudly at the columns passing before him, Rahul Kumar was reminded of the graduation parade he had attended as a young officer, and the exhilarating speech the Officer Commanding had given, stoking the fires of patriotism in their young hearts. He could still recall most of what the general had said, and how he had attempted to follow this advice throughout his military career.

* * * * * *

Rahul Kumar had graduated from the Indian Army Officers' Academy at the age of twenty-two. From the very beginning of his career he had displayed those qualities which would result in his meteoric rise through the Army's ranks, becoming Colonel before his thirty-fifth birthday. His parents had been very proud; particularly his father, a retired major who had served under the British Raj, and had been responsible for instilling discipline in his son almost from the time Rahul had taken his first steps. He admired his father, and sorely wished he had survived to witness his graduation, but this was not to be. Kumar's father had been killed in one of the frequent border skirmishes with Pakistan the very month his son was to graduate.

Rahul had always enjoyed the many opportunities he had received to advance his career, including an extended visit to England, where he attended the Royal College of Defence Studies in London. Upon his return, Rahul Kumar was confirmed in the rank of Major General. Mainly because of his military acumen, but also due to the fact that Kumar had remained apolitical throughout his military career, he was appointed as India's most senior army officer. Admired by his fellow officers, but disliked by his counterparts in the country's navy and airforce, General Rahul Kumar had experienced few difficulties in establishing himself as India's foremost military officer.

It was unfortunate for the country that Kumar had never developed the desire to accommodate those who led India's political parties, often coming into confrontation with politicians whose acts of political expediency, in the general's mind, blatantly undermined India's position as a leading power. Then, when he refused to publicly support the incumbent Prime Minister's policies, Rahul experienced his first real concerns for his future. Those closest to him advised caution, and suggested that he settle his differences with the influential politician. He refused, and from that moment the army was relegated to a secondary position behind the Indian navy, particularly when it came to budgetary considerations. Kumar and his fellow officers were angered by the preferential treatment shown to the navy, particularly when it became obvious that Admiral Gopal, Admiral of the Fleet, also enjoyed a personal relationship with the Prime Minister, Vijay Rakesh. It was then that General Rahul Kumar first turned his attention to the United States, fostering ties with that country's representatives in New Delhi. Before too long, his open support for closer defense ties with the United States became a political embarrassment for the Rakesh Administration, and Kumar was summoned to the Prime Minister's office, where he was severely admonished for so openly promoting defense co-operation with the Americans. His behaviour, Vijay Rakesh had suggested, was in contradiction with India's policy of non-alignment. When Kumar had pointed out that the government had already established this precedent by publicly identifying itself with both the former Soviet and Western Powers, the meeting deteriorated rapidly, with both powerful men accusing the other of attempting to lead India in the wrong direction.

Within days, their animosity towards each other spilled over into the public domain, and General Kumar struggled to maintain his position as the Indian army's Chief. It was only due to the intervention of others that both men finally stepped back from their most public dispute, distancing themselves from each other as they continued to carry out their duties. Kumar managed to hold onto his powerful position, actually improving his level of support within the army. However, he did discontinue his open affiliation with the Americans, realizing that this could be used to undermine his position with the Indian military establishment, and his control of one of the world's largest armies which consisted of no less than one and a half million soldiers.

* * * * * *

As the highly polished trombones punched their harsh notes

through the stifling morning air, Kumar recognized that the parade was nearing its end, and turned his thoughts to the ceremony. When the final column had passed by followed by the band, General Rahul Kumar dropped his salute, turned to the Officer Commanding and smiled, congratulating his loyal friend on his Command's fine performance, not knowing that in the not too distant future, he would call upon this officer to consider an Indian army presence beyond their country's borders.

Chapter 18

Harold Goldstein had been in Australia for more than two years, and longed to return to the States. The Aussie environment had not been up to his expectations, nor had the potential for him to improve his standing within the Agency. Nothing ever seemed to happen in Australia. Stranded in the middle of nowhere, he had enjoyed very little of his time in the country which boasted great beaches, barbecues and scantily clad women. For Harry, his appointment to the American Embassy in the Australian Capital had been a great disappointment. He went over the weekly report again, and yawned with boredom. Then he turned his attention to a copy of the New York Times, and observed from the date that he was reading last week's news, again.

'Morning, Harry,' a voice intoned, the southern drawl easily identified as that of his senior field agent, Ian Chalmers. Goldstein looked up, smiled at his visitor and offered him the only chair in his office.

'What's up?' he asked. The CIA officer rarely appeared in his office before lunch. Goldstein, whose official position was Political Attaché, expected Chalmers was looking for someone to make up a fourth for some golfing appointment.

'Something's on the boil, Harry,' the agent reported, handing a brief report to his station chief. 'Seems there's been some activity in one of the listed safe-houses. Thought we should take a closer look.' The Station Chief looked through the notes, examined the black and white enlargements, the dropped them back onto his desk. He would be surprised if anything of any real importance was to occur in this sleepy Capital.

'Who is it?' he asked. Chalmers turned the file around and placed his finger directly on the man's face.

'His name is Coleman. Stephen Coleman. He used to be with ASIS until the early seventies. Then he disappeared, there's....' Goldstein was suddenly alert, and picked the file back up again, staring at the photograph.

'Well I'll be...' he said, staring the photograph. The other man was surprised by his Chief's reaction.

'Do you know this guy?' Chalmers asked, responding to Goldstein's grin.

'Shit, Ian, this arsehole has been missing for years!' he laughed, shaking his head as he re-examined the photographs. He picked the other snaps up, looked at these, then dropped them back onto his desk. 'Where did you say these were taken?'

'Just down the road,' he answered, surprised with the reaction this brought.

'Jesus H Christ!' he exploded, 'Are you sure?' Chalmers was taken aback by the response. He picked the file back up again and read directly from the report.

'Stephen Coleman arrived at the safe-house at approximately sixteen hundred hours yesterday, the sixteenth of August. He was observed, and photographed, entering the old Soviet-listed residence. Since its use was compromised back in the early eighties, the Australians took control over the address. ASIO used it for some of their domestic needs, but there hasn't been much of any significance to report on the address. Until now, that is,' he added. Chalmers felt that perhaps he should have been able to identify the man Goldstein had recognized in the photograph, but he had no recollection of anyone named Coleman listed in the current CIA lists. He looked over at the Station Chief who was deep in thought.

'Who do we have watching the address?' Goldstein asked.

'No one at the moment,' Chalmers replied, knowing that this would not be the answer his superior would want to hear. 'But I can get someone onto it ASAP, if that's what you want.' He waited for instructions, even more curious than before. Later, he would go back into the computer and search for more information, sensing that he should have already known who this man was.

'Get someone down there, or have someone lock the place down until I have spoken to Langley,' Goldstein ordered sharply, surprising his subordinate even more.

'You got it,' Chalmers replied, waiting for more. Goldstein looked over at him.

'Do it now, Ian,' was all he said, wondering what had brought this ghost from the past into play. His number two nodded, rose, then left the room without anything further passing between the two men.

******

Prime Minister's Offices

'I don't like it, I tell you, I don't like it at all.' The statement was made by the rotund Leader of the Opposition as the bipartisan discussion continued. It was not often that political parties in Opposition were asked to attend government meetings involving defense-related issues.

'Well, Bill,' the Prime Minister said, now convinced that it had been an error to invite his political foe to the discussions, 'none of us do. What we have to achieve here today, is for us all to reach consensus and send a clear message to the Indonesians that we refuse to be threatened, and that this message is from *all* the people of Australia.' Jack William Evans searched the faces of his Cabinet members and wondered how many of his own team would attempt to make political mileage out of the volatile situation.

As Prime Minister, he had called the urgent meeting to discuss Indonesia's growing dispute with Australia, which had been suddenly brought to a head by unprovoked attacks on Australian oil rigs operating in the Timor Sea. These had followed a break-down in negotiations over the Timor Shelf production rights, throwing the many concessions there into dispute. Arbitration had been attempted, but the Indonesians had refused any other venue but in their own country. Jakarta had denied any knowledge of the terrorist action, claiming that pirates had also burned villages in some of Indonesia's less populated areas in the eastern archipelago.

The Prime Minister knew that he had to avoid any further escalation at all costs. Indonesia's military build-up had outstripped Australian capability, creating an alarming gap between the two countries' defence capabilities. The former Soviet Mediterranean Fleet, which Indonesia had purchased and then mothballed, had been refitted. Jakarta had purchased American nuclear submarines which had also been taken out of mothballs and sold to the Indonesians under their United States Joint Defense Aid Program. Now, the *'Kalki IV'*, formerly the *USS Plunger*, carried Indonesian crews, and joined their American counterparts as they transited the Ombar-Wetar Straits off Timor, undetected.

Indonesia's ongoing defense build-up had been of concern to him for some time. When he last examined the country's Order of Battle which listed Indonesia's military equipment, he had been shocked to discover that her forces had more than doubled during the past four years.

The Prime Minister had read that ALRI's Eastern Command had stationed a further four corvettes and ten Soviet *Osa* class missile patrol craft around Irian Jaya, and did not believe for one moment that this strategic repositioning of its naval forces was in any way related to the recent Free Papua Movement uprising in Indonesian New Guinea. The Indonesian Air Force, AURI, had mysteriously acquired a further squadron of F-22 Raptors and, according to intelligence reports, had planned to base these on Natuna Island prior to China's annexation of the island. His concern now was with the most recent Defense Intelligence Report, which confirmed that these aircraft would be stationed at the rehabilitated Kupang airstrip within tactical striking range of Australia's north.

The Australian leader feared that his country's inability to defend itself against the threat from the north might tempt its Asian neighbours to test their resolve. Since Federation, Australian leaders had argued that the country's fundamental security interests lay in maintaining its alliances with the United States and the British Commonwealth. He knew, as had those who had gone before him, that Australia's limited military resources could never withstand any serious attempt to attack, or even invade the country. Australia's four guided missile destroyers, eight guided missile frigates, six *Collins* class submarines and a handful of support ships would be no match against such superior forces.

Faced with growing regional instability, he was not entirely convinced that the United States would support either Indonesia or Australia should any confrontation develop between the two countries.

Australian intelligence sources had been unable to provide evidence that the Indonesian Military was actually responsible for the recent and provocative action directed against Australian interests in the Indonesian Republic. His Cabinet had supported the position of further discussion with Jakarta before seeking the support of the United States Government. He had known for some time that the Indonesian leadership was in danger of swinging further to the right, and understood the problems their President faced, with China's threatening posturing along Indonesia's northern and unprotected coastline. The Australian leader had been greatly disturbed by the growing number of reports of armed piracy along the sea-lanes, and the possibility that these were directed at further destabilising Indonesian-Australian relations.

The Prime Minister had been further concerned when Australian shipping reported incidents of Indonesian naval vessels deliberately interfering with their passage through recognized international shipping lanes. These provocative steps aimed at intimidating Australian business had resulted in reciprocal action being taken by Australian waterside workers against Indonesian shipping.

There had been further riots directed at the Australian Embassy in Jakarta, and business interests there had revealed that they had been threatened with sanctions should Australia continue to disregard Indonesia's claim over East Timor.

The Prime Minister decided that this was pure sabre-rattling in preparation for the forthcoming United Nations vote as to whether a UN-sponsored plebiscite should be held in the former Portuguese colony. He was aware that the motion might just have sufficient support to be passed. He had discussed this with his Foreign Minister, and both had agreed that the Indonesians were demonstrating their displeasure at the increased Australian public support for the annexed province's independence movement.

It appeared that both countries were being dragged uncontrollably towards a political abyss by an emerging, and more militant, Indonesian leadership.

'I warned you Jack, but you wouldn't listen,' the Opposition Leader accused. 'You played softball with those bastards and now they're going to run all over us.' He turned and snarled at the Foreign Minister. 'And Lord only knows what *you* have probably promised them.' He looked back at the Prime Minister, believing that had the roles been reversed, this situation would never have developed.

'Don't you think it's time that we showed the Australian people some real leadership?' he challenged, caustically, 'Don't you think they're scared out there?' he asked, rhetorically, pointing his stubby finger through the air.

'You're not on the floor of the House, now, Bill,' the Treasurer snorted, as he moved his seat backwards and forwards, playing with the swivel.

'You're bloody right, I'm not!' he barked, his temper rising to the bait. 'Jack, let's at least do something to show the Indonesians that we mean business,' he pleaded, frustrated by the inaction.

'We have warned Australian tourists of the dangers of travelling to Indonesia, particularly Bali,' the Attorney General advised. 'Short of restricting flights, there's very little we can do to prevent Australians continuing to travel into those areas.'

'Gentlemen, I wish to remind you that we have inherited some of this mess from our friend here's predecessors.' The Opposition Leader bristled.

'Not that old…..' but was cut off by the Defense Minister before he lost the floor.

'I believe that much of what we are experiencing has its roots further back than the Timor Shelf agreements.' He paused, and raised a sheet of paper from the table. 'The Indonesians have always been suspicious of our support in relation to the Timor question. It is difficult for an authoritarian regime such as theirs to understand that we do not, unfortunately, have the same controls over our press as they do in Indonesia. Every time something appears in our newspapers which offends Jakarta there is a backlash.

'The very fact that we provide material support to East Timorese refugees in our country is considered not on its humanitarian merits, but as a distinct move by Australia to provoke the Indonesians. Hell, if we can be objective, they have a reasonable case when you consider the number of refugees this country has accepted from East Timor. And,' he said, looking directly at the Opposition Leader, 'those bastards in Darwin have actually formed their own government in exile!'

'Surely no one takes Xanana Soares seriously?' someone asked.

'Serious enough for the Indonesian Ambassador to raise the issue during his last meeting with our Department,' the Foreign

Minister claimed.

Almost without exception, those present wished that Gough Whitlam had taken the initiative in 1975 while still Prime Minister, and accepted Indonesia's urging to send troops into East Timor, or *Tim-Tim* as it later became known.

The current Prime Minister had been a young back-bencher at the time, and had called for Australia's intervention in Timor, citing East Timorese requests for Australian troops to be sent. He had not understood why Whitlam had procrastinated at the time; it could easily have been a *fait accompli* as both the Indonesians and the East Timorese supported an Australian presence.

When the Australian, New Zealand and British journalist teams from Australia's television Channels Seven and Nine were executed by Indonesian soldiers, he had been the first to shout 'shame' at the lack of leadership shown at the time. Looking back, he now realized that had Australia not bowed to American pressure, Timor could just as easily have become an Australian territory, providing the bridge into Asia that so many of his contemporaries had dreamed about over the years. Now, he knew, it was far too late.

'Look, gentlemen,' the Prime Minister intervened, 'what it all boils down to is whether or not we tell the Indonesians that we are prepared to take action over these attacks, and before we do that, is the Australian public prepared to suffer the consequences?' The Minister for Trade shook his head in disagreement.

'We currently enjoy a surplus in trade with Indonesia of approximately one billion dollars each year. That could disappear, or worse, our five billion dollars in trade with Indonesia might disappear altogether. We should all think very seriously about issuing any statement which might be perceived by Jakarta as a threat. They have nothing to lose.'

'Nothing to lose?' the overweight leader cried. 'What a load of crap! The bloody Indons sell us more than three billion dollars worth of product every year,' he challenged, throwing his arms wide as he did so. Prime Minister Evans sighed. He knew that they would not be able to agree on a joint statement which would satisfy everyone.

'This decision will not require a vote, gentlemen,' he said, 'but I do require your assurances that we are all in agreement that whatever message is sent to the Indonesians, it must appear to be representative of all the Australian people, and not just the voice of one political faction.' He turned to his opponent in the House. 'Bill?'

The Leader of the Opposition shook his head. 'I'd not be happy with anything less than a demand that they honour their agreements, and either provide protection to our rigs or permit our own defence forces to enter the disputed areas.' The Prime Minister thought about this then nodded.

'Okay, let's give it a shot,' he decided, ignoring the unhappy faces of his own Party members. His opponent did not bother to smile, knowing that in politics things were never what they seemed, and today's pact could just as easily become the basis for tomorrow's dispute.

'Prime Minister, will you be attending the reception being held at the Indonesian Embassy to mark their Independence Day celebrations? Ambassador Seda has suggested that it might be an opportunity to demonstrate to the people of both countries that our relationships are not as strained as the press would have everyone believe. Also, we might remember that reliable information would have it that he is slated for the Vice President's position when he returns to Jakarta.' It was the Foreign Minister who asked. His leader looked at the man in surprise, wondering how he had been lumbered with such an inadequate figure.

'No, I don't believe that we should demonstrate anything of the kind. In fact, I don't want any of my colleagues so much as showing their faces anywhere near the Indonesian Embassy until we see some response from them regarding the issues at hand.' Several of those present had received invitations, and would now have to explain to their wives that they would not be attending what had been promoted as the social event of the year for Canberra. The meeting came to a close and all but the Prime Minister and his Attorney General departed.

* * * * * *

'Why didn't you tell them about the Japanese H-3B missile venture?' the Attorney General asked.

'Shit, Doug,' Jack Evans snorted, 'then it wouldn't be a secret anymore, would it?' The other man shrugged his shoulders.

'What are we going to do about it?' he asked.

'Do about it?' the leader repeated. 'Nothing,' he said, 'nothing at all.'

'Are you certain about this?' the Attorney General pressed, although he privately admitted that he wasn't confident that the information would not leak, even from his own department. The Prime Minister just shook his head.

'Doug, there isn't a goddamn thing we could do, even if we wanted to,' he said.

'What about telling the Americans what we know?' The information revealing the Japanese arrangements to jointly develop a military version of the H-3B had been obtained by ASIS agents operating in Indonesia, and they were yet to share this recent intelligence with their American counterparts.

'I would doubt if the Americans didn't already know and are keeping the information to themselves, as usual.' Then: 'Their own political interests no longer run in parallel with ours, Doug, you know that. Not that I am entirely certain they ever did,' he added.

'I'm very uneasy with regards to their lack of open support for Australia on the Indonesian issue. Do you really believe that they would still come to our defence if we were confronted with the possibility of an Indonesian attack?' he asked, suspecting that they would not.

'Their interests have changed. Nothing's been the same since the Soviet collapse. But look on the brighter side, Jack,' the Attorney General said light-heartedly, 'if all else fails and our economy takes another slide, we could probably ask the Americans for Most Favoured Nation status.' The Australian leader attempted a smile in response, but instead frowned at the prospect of going to the voters with the economy stagnating as it had throughout his government's term in office. Unemployment had reached twelve percent, and the Australian dollar had fallen to new lows, just below the Singapore dollar.

'What do you think the Indonesians are really up to, Doug?' he asked. The politician thought that the Prime Minister looked exhausted. None of them had enjoyed a full night's rest for months.

'Well, I would have to agree with Anderson's conclusions.' He knew that Jack Evans, as had earlier Prime Ministers, trusted this man's opinions even more than those in his Cabinet. Anderson had served successive administrations loyally through the years, and yet, his was one of the least known faces amongst the multitude of Canberra bureaucrats.

Although well past mandatory retirement, Anderson still headed the Australian Secret Intelligence Service and reported directly to the Attorney General. 'He's worried, and with good cause, that Indonesia might start to fragment and break up. Anderson supports the position that ASEAN, as a geopolitical block, has failed miserably. Now that three of the member nations have withdrawn and entered into their own agreements with India and China, the original concept of a ten-nation trade block has required considerable review. As for the sea-lane dispute, well,' he paused, scratching the side of his head, 'Indonesia's attempt to police international oil shipping through its sea-lanes has been condemned even by some of its ASEAN partners.'

'And rightly so,' Evans interrupted.

'There had always been a certain amount of smugness around the Jakarta camp in the past, with relation to China's relative distance from their country, or at least that was the situation until Beijing annexed Natuna Island. The Indonesians had always intended that ASEAN represent not just a trade bloc against Chinese economic expansion, but also a buffer against any military threat. Indonesia viewed those ASEAN partners which shared borders with China as a long-term military barrier, but failed to recognize the possibility that these smaller countries with struggling economies, could just as easily become perfect satellites for China's ultimate expansion. As for Indonesia's domestic problems, these have been exacerbated by the ongoing corruption and cronyism apparent throughout all levels of government. Half of the main arterial roads now have tolls, and these are owned, predictably enough, by the President's family.'

'But that has never been a problem before,' the Prime Minister suggested, 'at most, whenever these stories appeared in the international press there was little evidence that the Indonesian people would not continue to accept the status quo.'

'Sure, but only because the government introduced those brutal riot squads we saw hitting the streets during the last demonstrations, and the controls exercised over what may or may not be placed in print. Their greed, unbelievably, has exceeded even that of their predecessors. Latest reports indicate that the First Family is even considering assuming monopoly control over all rice production. Do you remember when Tommy Suharto grabbed the Indonesian clove industry, throwing it into chaos? In the end, the farmers' own co-operative had to bail the President's son out of his half a billion dollar fiasco, and at their own expense. It's a disgrace; but one that has continued ever since Soekarno lost power to the so called New Order.'

'Anderson suggests that the Javanese are slowly losing control,' he continued, 'and are over-compensating by encouraging a swing to the more radical fundamentalist Moslem groups. This is not the first time in the country's history the Jakarta establishment has been challenged by minority groups.' He rested, swallowed from the glass which had been placed there before the meeting had commenced, then looked at his political associate.

'The way I see it, Jack, the Indonesians are confused by what is happening, particularly China's threatening naval build-up to their north. They, like us, are heavily outnumbered by the Chinese. Now that they are being squeezed by their giant neighbour, there may just be sufficient paranoia floating around Jakarta for their leadership to misconstrue Australia's motives in relation to the Timor issue. Their disappointment over losing Natuna Island is obvious, however the lack of international support, particularly from the Americans, came as quite a shock.' He uncrossed his legs and leaned back in the leather chair to stretch.

'The Indonesians were naïve to believe that the Americans would do more than shake their fists at China. US investment in both countries is impressive, but at the end of the day, China is more important to them. Even the Brits have been able to take advantage of the sea-lane disputes. Most of China's oil is still being carried through Indonesian waters by British ships. God, Jack,' he said, shaking his head in admiration, 'it's a little like Vietnam all over again, only on a much grander scale.'

The Prime Minister knew that the Attorney General was referring to another time when British ships entered North Vietnamese harbours, providing materials and supplies to the Communists, while Australian and other allied troops fought against the very same people being supplied by their Commonwealth partner. It was about that time, he remembered, that he learned the true meaning of political expediency. He listened as his knowledgeable associate continued.

'Beijing has been very clever. First, they demonstrated to the world that they are good guys by permitting Hong Kong to continue, virtually as it did prior to the British hand-over. Remember, Jack, we discussed this at the time? It was obvious, even then, that China would permit business to continue as usual, but only until such time as it managed to snare Taiwan as well. Hell, who wouldn't? Taiwan's reserves are double those of Japan and still growing. They must be really pissed off that they still haven't been able to take Taiwan. But given time, I'm sure they will.'

'Do you think the Indonesians believe that China might start chipping away at their more isolated provinces?' Evans asked.

'Now wouldn't that be something?' he replied. 'We sit here worrying that the Indons might invade Australia, and they sit up there worrying that the Chinese will do the same to them. Yes, I believe that Jakarta is more than a little paranoid concerning China, and rightly so. After all, they did swoop down and knock off their Natuna gas fields.' He then thought for a moment.

'It's quite possible that the Indonesians are going to do exactly that to us in the North-west, Jack,' he said, solemnly. 'They might not be that naïve after all. Let's assume that they believe it possible to take control over all the Timor Shelf production and extraction. We certainly could not prevent them to any great degree. A handful of *Collins* class submarines won't go a hell of a long way against the Indonesian fleet. What if the Indonesians already believe that they might have tacit approval from the Americans to do so? After all, the States did little when the Chinese took Natuna, and maybe Jakarta believes that the precedent will continue, only this time it will be in their favour.'

'It might be an opportune time for a quick visit to Washington.'

'Don't know how much that would achieve right now, Jack, but I guess you could give it a try.' The Attorney-General rose and walked around to restore circulation in his legs.

'If they agree, why don't we hit them with the H-3B developments at the same time? It has to be obvious to them as well that the Indonesians and Japanese will soon have their own missile delivery systems. Then, of course, it won't be too long before they'll have their first reactors on line in Bali and Java. Before you know it, Jack, the bastards will be nuclear armed with a Japanese-sponsored delivery system.' The Prime Minister nodded. They had been through this before with the Chiefs-of-Staff at Defence. All present had agreed that it would be unwise to panic the Australian public further. The Prime Minister had taken it upon himself not to reveal the information to the rest of his Cabinet colleagues. He would do so, however, when he considered it more appropriate.

'I'll sleep on it, Doug,' he said, wearily, rising to his feet slowly, 'given the chance.'

Both men smiled. They had been surviving on less than a few hours each night since the trouble had started. The Attorney-General left a few minutes later and returned to his own office, leaving his old friend alone to decide in which direction he should move, to counter the Indonesian threat.

* * * * * *

Coleman and the ASIS Chief had talked throughout the day, breaking only for a light meal.

Anderson had produced convincing evidence proving that Seda was involved in a most dangerous game, one he apparently played successfully for more than three decades. Seda's secret agenda had never been detected by his fellow generals or any of the others who had worked side by side with him. Slowly, step by step, Anderson laid the whole picture out before the disbelieving Coleman. Much of the earlier information he already knew, as this had been the core of their discussions some years before when the intelligence chief had provided the most amazing detail of Seda's bold initiatives for East Timor.

Coleman also remembered at that time he had been given an ultimatum, which he had unwisely ignored. In retrospect, had he listened and co-operated when the demand had been made then maybe, just maybe, he would have come out of the whole mess in much better financial shape. Still, he thought, as he listened to the detailed exposition from the well-informed bureaucrat, he had not done too badly. At least, up to now.

Twice Anderson made the point that Coleman was fortunate to have left Indonesia when he had, as it was most likely that he would have been killed by General Seda had he obstinately remained.

'Seda couldn't afford to have you eliminated until he was cer-

tain that you had not left any incriminating evidence behind somewhere. Seda was reasonably confident that you hadn't, but he was
not quite ready to take that risk. His world was disintegrating, what
with the failed uprising in Timor and the seizure of most of the
weaponry which had been stockpiled across on Pulau Kambing.
You had been party to those shipments, Stephen,' Anderson had
said, almost accusingly. Coleman was then surprised when
Anderson revealed that ASIS had actually made attempts on General Seda's life and, on both occasions, had failed.

'There must be a number of agents who could do the job for you
without the necessity for all of this,' Coleman said, waving his arm
around the maximum security cells buried below the Department
of Defence, where he had been held incognito by Anderson's security. Stephen Coleman had been picked up in Hong Kong by an
ASIS team and flown back to Australia. He had not been given the
opportunity to call his lawyer; that recourse, he knew, would not
be made available to him. It went with the territory. Even for former
agents. Stephen did not need to be reminded that, having signed
the Official Secrets Act, he had forgone all rights to be treated as an
ordinary citizen.

Anderson looked at the man whom he had once considered one
of the best in the business. Coleman had not aged well. He had
gained weight, his hair had thinned, and there were obvious signs
that he had given the booze a bashing over the years. The intelligence chief tried to recall how long it had been since he had first
recruited Stephen. It was difficult to believe that the man before
him now could have been the same young, enthusiastic agent, of
some twenty-five years before. Anderson tried to recall how long
it had been since they had last met; he knew it had to be almost
five years, but looking at his former protégé, he had difficulty accepting this. He thought about Stephen's question as to why he
had not selected one of his other agents for the task before them.

'Firstly, none of our current operatives are as familiar with Seda's
voice as you are. This is essential to the timing of the detonation.
We don't want others being exposed, and need to contain the effect to minimise casualties. Your responsibility is to detonate the
small charge once you identify his voice. We'll talk more about the
operational side later.' He then paused, examining Stephen's almost blank expression. 'Another reason why we have decided not

to use current agents is that, frankly speaking Stephen, operatives today just don't seem to have the same commitment anymore. Not that you were particularly outstanding in that area yourself in later years,' Anderson suggested, referring to Coleman's sudden exit from the Service years before. 'Also,' he added, 'we would never be sure that we could guarantee their silence.' Coleman's face immediately turned to stone. Anderson moved quickly to calm his fears.

'Obviously, Stephen, you'll be taken care of in the appropriate manner. You will need to disappear as you have done before except, this time, we will provide you with reasonable cover. That would be another identity, and travel documents should it become necessary.' He hesitated, then continued. 'I personally don't believe it will come to that. You don't need funds, from what I hear, so you will just have to be satisfied that we will consider your slate as being wiped clean, after which we will thank you quietly for your participation, and ask that you go back to whatever you were doing before this bloody mess required our intervention. Okay?'

It took a further two meetings before Coleman finally agreed to accept the assignment. Coleman had remained stubbornly adamant that he would not be Seda's executioner until Anderson, in desperation, lied, suggesting that the woman Stephen had loved, and lost, so many years before in Bali, had actually died as a result of an attempt by Seda on Stephen's life gone wrong. This was enough. Coleman had then agreed to participate in the deadly sanction against the Indonesian Ambassador.

* * * * * *

Indonesian Embassy, Canberra
17 August — Indonesian Independence Day

Ambassador Seda was not entirely displeased with the news report in the so-called objective press. He had become used to such biased reporting very early in his career.

He sat drinking his coffee while skimming through the pages, stopping to read only those articles which commented on his address to the Press Club luncheon. Some of the stories were inaccurate and slightly derogatory, several exaggerated the answers he had given in response to questions on Timor even suggesting that he had responded with an air of arrogance. Seda was not irritated by the remark. He had deliberately answered in provocative fashion, hoping to ruffle the feathers of the press.

As it turned out, the result was positive and in no way did he consider any of the articles to be detrimental to his real cause. As he expected, the majority of the stories came out in support of a United Nations resolution to provide the people of Timor-Timur with the opportunity to vote on the question of Indonesia's annexation and their right to self-determination.

He was pleased that most editorial comment challenged the Government of Australia over the Indonesian Government's refusal to withdraw from the former colony. This was the result he had set out to achieve, to prime the Australian public and prepare them mentally for the next frightening events so that their future response would lead to more than just feelings of indignation towards the Indonesian people.

Seda's plans called for a much stronger response. One which would drag both countries to the brink of outright war well before Indonesia had finally developed its own nuclear capability. His years of planning for an independent nation would finally become a reality. And he would be its leader. With these ambitious thoughts foremost in his mind, he went about his duties, anxious for the evening's festivities to commence.

* * * * * *

Umar Suharjo was satisfied that the van would be safe parked hard up against the sliding door which led into the armoury. He had set about rebuilding the room adjacent to the Embassy's registry immediately upon his taking up post as the Indonesian Embassy Security Attaché. His diplomatic status had provided the means for him to move equipment and weapons in and out of Australia, without question. During the four months since his arrival in Canberra, he had completed the tasks given him by Seda, and he now waited eagerly for the signal to proceed.

The specially designed and rebuilt van was ready. Inside, Umar had stacked layer upon layer of plastic lined bags filled with ammonium nitrate around an open drum of diesel oil. Before the van was moved, he planned to re-attach the container's lid for the relatively short journey planned. The Australian Parliament was a few kilometers from where the van now stood in readiness, its deadly cargo including a number of hydrogen canisters which Umar intended would act as a 'kicker' to increase the impact of the bomb. He knew that the extra ingredient would give the explosives far more cutting power allowing it to cut through the Australian Parliament's thick walls.

While other members of the staff prepared to assemble in the foyer, Umar re-entered the chancery and slipped surreptitiously through the registry. He crossed the room and unlocked the armoury access door. Umar wished to check that the surplus containers of pentaerythoritol tetranitrate (PETN) stored there would not block his access from outside, and that the double-locks had engaged when he had closed the sliding door earlier. Satisfied that all was in order, he re-locked the armoury and went upstairs to check that the Ambassador's private rooms were still secure; and to check on Seda's earlier guest who had been left upstairs, alone.

* * * * * *

Chalmers raised his binoculars again and refocused, noting that there was still nothing unusual happening in the former Soviet residence. He then returned his attention to the Indonesian Embassy, impressed with the lighting display. He logged the time, then concentrated once again on the safe-house occupied by Stephen Coleman.

* * * * * *

Umar observed that the visitor had left when he arrived at Seda's rooms. He completed his security check and, noticing the elegant briefcase left there earlier by the Ambassador's visitor, he picked it up and was immediately surprised at its weight. The leather briefcase was much heavier than he had expected. He examined it for a few moments and, unable to ascertain what it contained, decided that he would lock it away until he had either located the missing visitor or had discussed the situation with Seda.

Umar Suharjo mumbled *'sialan'* as he caught his knee on the side of the desk.

Back in his room at the safe-house, Stephen Coleman was wait-ing for the sound of a voice - Seda's voice. On hearing Umar cry out in pain as he struck his knee, Stephen panicked and his sweaty hands squeezed the small, luminous button, sending the dedicated frequency transmission through the airwaves.

Coleman tensed. He waited for the distant explosion.

Nothing happened. He tried again, Another malfunction! A feel-ing of incredible disbelief swept over him and he slammed this fist hard down on the table accidentally knocking the remote control to the floor. He cursed as he had never cursed before.

Coleman pulled the heavy curtains back angrily and stared across at the brilliantly lit building surrounded by hundreds of lim-ousines belonging to the elite of Canberra's society enjoying them-selves inside. Waves of disappointment flooded through his tired body, and he kicked angrily at the broken mechanism lying on the floor.

They had failed!

* * * * * *

Umar rode the lift down to the lobby and, wishing to avoid the multitude of guests now crowding every corner of the Residence and Embassy gardens, he slipped unnoticed into the empty regis-try. He looked around and, identifying the switch he sought, turned the lights on in the adjacent room. Inside, he could hear the guests clapping as the Indonesian melody came to an end. Outside, in the magnificently decorated garden, most of one thousand guests clapped as the Indonesian Ambassador, General (retired) Nathan Seda, stood in front of the military band and raised his hands over his head, clenching them together in appreciation. The conductor then waited, his body half-turned observing his Ambassador, poised for the signal.

As the General nodded, the baton waved delicately in the air, and immediately the handsome Menadonese drummer com-menced his roll calling all present to attention. The guests rose to their feet as the band started the Indonesian national anthem.

Umar moved to open the metal doors leading to the arsenal of weapons hidden there. He nonchalantly dropped the briefcase containing the plastique explosive casually into the corner.

The sensitive mechanism, which was unable to receive the earlier signal, immediately reacted to this excessively rough handling. As the deadly package hit the floor an eight-centimetre detonator activated causing the highly brisant RDX plastique to explode. The primary and secondary explosions came within a milli-second of each other as the C-4 exploded, firstly with the surplus containers of PETN, and then directly through the walls into the remaining pentaerythoritol tetranitrate which had been prepared inside the van to detonate the packed ammonium nitrate after the vehicle was later positioned under the nation's Parliament.

The first shock-wave pushed through into the parked truck and ignited its deadly cargo activating all of the contributing components which would rock the political world.

The first to die was Umar.

In that moment, an enormous burst of energy erupted through the assembly, turning the entire area into one massive fireball of destruction.

Figures danced momentarily before disintegrating into heaps of lifeless flesh and bone. The roar had ripped through the guests, hurling musical instruments into the maelstrom of human carnage, decapitating a bandsman. Then, for an immeasurable moment, there was silence.

A shrill cry pierced the quiet, then a cacophony of screams emphasized the full horror of the blasts. And amongst it all, General Nathan Seda, Ambassador Extraordinary and Plenipotentiary, future Vice President of Indonesia, lay dead.

* * * * * *

Chalmers lifted himself back off the floor, checking as he did so for injuries. Still suffering from shock, he sat, disorientated, wondering what in the hell had happened. Then he remembered, and moved clumsily towards his viewing station.

At first, he was unaware that the window had disappeared, destroyed by the thunderous blast which had ripped through the suburb of Yarralumla. He could smell the acrid smoke in the air and fumbled to focus his binoculars on the scene. He was overawed by the spectacle which greeted him. Chalmer's face felt wet, and he wiped it, unconsciously, with the back of his sleeve. In the dark, he could not see that this was blood, the result of splintered glass which had showered his body when the window had imploded.

Engrossed in the spectacle across the street, Chalmers almost missed the car as it pulled up outside Coleman's address. He had heard the horn, and it was only by chance that he noticed the sedan's arrival. Still suffering from slight concussion, Chalmers turned his attention back to the safe-house and readjusted the binoculars.

When he saw Coleman hurry from the house, he realized that he had been caught, flat-footed. He searched around his darkened room, found the pair of night-glasses, and rushed down to his own vehicle. He gave the sedan a cursory inspection for damage, then drove away in pursuit of the *Ford Taurus Ghia*, and the man he had been instructed to keep under surveillance.

* * * * * *

Director Anderson glanced at the rear-vision mirror once more before steering the Ford into the steady stream of traffic. He drove carefully, not wishing to attract attention.

'Is he dead?' the ASIS chief asked Coleman. Occasional shadows flashed across Stephen Coleman's face as he sat, silently, still suffering shock at the extent of the explosion. Nobody could have survived that blast, he thought.

'Yes,' was all he said. There was no point in explaining that the detonation had not taken place as planned; he knew that all Anderson would be interested in was whether Seda had been killed. Coleman wanted to scream out loudly but could not. He felt entirely drained of all energy.

They drove on in silence, Anderson back-tracking several times as he continued to guard against being followed. And compromised. Finally, they pulled into the Government forrestry reserve amongst the pines. In the distance they could see the blaze which continued to burn around what was once the Indonesian Embassy. They sat in silence, observing the extent of the bomb's destructive power. Smoke billowed into the sky, and the warning sirens of fire engines and other emergency services filled the night.

Anderson placed his gloved hand on Stephen Coleman's, who continued to stare at the horrific scene believing he was responsible. Suddenly, the moon broke loose through cloud and cast an eerie glow of its own across the smoke-filled sky.

Anderson's hands moved again, lifting the cold, steel barrel to within touch of Coleman's head. In the moment that Stephen Coleman's eyes registered shock at the betrayal, Anderson squeezed the trigger gently, and a bullet burst from the handgun.

* * * * * *

'Mother of God!' Chalmers uttered, automatically crossing himself with one free hand. He remained crouched off the side of the road, and waited. The agent had been fortunate to observe his quarry's car doubling back to avoid being followed. This had given him the opportunity to follow, which he did, maintaining surveillance at a safe distance.

Chalmers had driven after Coleman, pulling back from time to time to avoid detection. When the Ford had taken the observation point road, he pulled back even further, permitting those in front to believe that they were not in any danger of discovery. At the top of the hill, Chalmers parked his car to the side of the road, and covered the remaining distance on foot.

Coleman and another man seemed content to remain sitting in their vehicle, watching the fireworks below. He moved closer, hoping to identify who the driver might be. Then, without any warning, he heard the shot, and caught the brief flash as Coleman's head snapped to one side.

He watched the unfamiliar figure move away from the scene. Chalmers waited until certain that Anderson would not return, then slipped through the darkness, over to where the other car was parked. There, he discovered the body of Stephen Coleman, as it lay slumped forward in the front, a bullet hole evident in the side of his head.

Chapter 19

Japan — Jakarta — Robson

Prime Minister Hirohuki Hata accepted the rebuke with an outward display of calm, while inwardly his inner emotions ripped at his vitals as surely as any traditional *sepuku* sword might have done.

He knew he would have to resign. There could be no other choice. Should the photographs be displayed publicly in the press, his family's shame would be intolerable. Hirohuki Hata continued to look down at the floor, the burden of his family's disgrace almost too great. Slowly, he forced his eyes back to the table where the damning evidence lay spread, as if challenging Hata to examine their content again. The selection of black and white photographs all too graphically displayed his brother-in-law's deviant sexual behaviour.

The Prime Minister could not be certain of who had been responsible for capturing his wife's younger brother in these compromising situations. The evidence had been sent to his Coalition partner, Aki-san. Hirohuki Hata had granted the woman the private interview she had requested, during which Aki-san had handed him the opened contents, then waited for his response.

He might have been able to live with the shame of his brother-in-law's disgusting acts, but Hata knew there was no chance he would survive any disclosure of his government's involvement in the H-3B rocket Research and Development center in Bandung, Indonesia. A brief summary of the secret installation's objectives had been attached to the photographs.

He had been requested to provide an undertaking to his coalition partner, Aki-san, that the project would be discontinued immediately, failing which, she had threatened to go public with the entire contents contained in the damaging dispatch. His career had been ruined, and with that, Japan's future role as a military power had been reduced to one of continuing subservience to others.

* * * * * *

In the weeks following Ambassador Seda's death, the Japanese Government announced that, due to domestic economic considerations and as a result of reviewing its own development needs, Japanese involvement in the construction and funding of nuclear power plants outside of Japan had been temporarily halted. No further information was made available to the press. Prime Minister Hiroyuki Hata resigned, and the coalition went to the polls under a cloud of accusations of being expansionist, and lost the election.

This outcome, coupled with the believable rumours which had passed through the halls of the Japanese Diet, caused the *Rama II* project to falter. Several months were to pass before the newly elected Japanese leader learned of his former opponent's clandestine redirection of government funds, which had been used to finance the ongoing development of a military version of the Japanese H-3B missile. All dialogue with the Indonesian President, the Bandung Research and Development Centre and the Japanese Government, in relation to the production of a prototype delivery system, was discontinued. Japan immediately repatriated its scientists and engineers, destroying whatever technology was left behind.

* * * * * *

Indonesia

The Indonesian President had signed the decree appointing his son-in-law, Major General Sujono Diryo, as the new Chairman of PEPELIN, simultaneous with the announcement of Seda's selection as Ambassador to Australia, some months prior to the former general's departure for Canberra.

Within hours of the Palace press release, Sujono's office had been inundated with requests for interviews, and official appointments. Amongst these was a petition from the company president responsible for the future supplies of uranium ore from Australia,

Graeme Robson. When news of Seda's death reached Indonesia, mourning was brief. The powerful general's sudden demise had created unbelievable opportunities for others.

* * * * * *

'I am in a position to offer financing, as well,' Robson had suggested. He was pleased so far with the way negotiations were proceeding. Not unlike the rest of the community involved with the construction and development of the nuclear power plants, Robson had been more than a little nervous when the President's son-in-law was appointed to the influential position. Seda's appointment to Canberra had come as some surprise to the investment community, but his death had been an even greater shock.

'How long would it be before construction could re-commence?' Sujono asked, knowing that the President was most anxious to restore the *Rama II* project's schedule as quickly as feasibly possible. The Japanese had left his country in a difficult situation. Having withdrawn from the fast breeder plant joint venture, Sujono's first major task as Chairman had been to secure a replacement partner. Following Seda's death, Sujono found himself floundering in a sea of intrigue and financial disaster.

It seemed that everywhere he turned for support to locate a substitute investor to replace the Japanese, doors remained closed. He was not to know that the United States Government had moved quickly, undermining any overtures made by the Indonesian PEPELIN Chairman for finance and technical expertise which might result in the resurrection of the *Rama II* project. General Sujono soon became desperate, concerned that the President might have him removed from the powerful position.

Robson's approach had been most fortuitous. Not only was the man's group already involved in the downstream provision of uranium ore, he had totally committed his group to the completion of the *Rama II* project. It would seem to Sujono, that in the absence of other contenders, he would have little other choice but to deal with the Robson *kongsi*.

'Why are you using Russian technology to complete the plant. Surely it would be more prudent to engage another Japanese firm, having started with their engineers?' Sujono asked.

'*Pak* Sujono,' Robson continued in English, wishing he was more fluent in *Bahasa Indonesia*, 'we canvassed the Japanese engineering and power firms. Seems that their government has placed an un-official ban on working outside Japan for the immediate future. We also tried the French and British, but they too don't seem overly anxious to pick up from where the Japanese left off. Also, we spoke to the Canadian and American firms, but it seems that they would only be interested in participating if the IAEA were given inspec-tion rights upon completion. That left us with the Russians. There is nothing wrong with their technology, *Pak* Sujono,' Robson ar-gued. In fact, he had little experience in the field, viewing the project entirely for the profits it would generate and the subsequent po-litical gain he expected to enjoy from his involvement.

'*Are you certain that the Russians will be able to re-commence quickly and complete the project within the original schedule?*' asked Sujono sceptically. It had been several months since any real work had been carried out at the Mt Muria site.

'I guarantee it, *Pak*,' Robson replied. He was desperate to secure the contract. This would be the first major negotiation he had con-cluded without his corporate consultants' participation. When word spread, he knew that none would believe he had managed to put this deal together by himself. Graeme was reasonably astute, but even he admitted that without his late father's substantial wealth to support his ventures in Indonesia, and Murray Stephenson's considerable contributions of time and advice during his first years in Jakarta, he might still be living off a monthly remittance in a remote village somewhere.

'*And you agree that your company will, in no way, have any role in the management and ongoing operation once the project has been com-pleted?*' the PEPELIN Chairman asked, again. Unlike the other nu-clear plants which had been tied to the principles of Build, Oper-ate, and Transfer, *Rama II*, in the interests of secrecy, would not be managed by any other than an Indonesian military board. All tech-nicians involved in the day-to-day running of the nuclear plant would be Indonesians selected by Sujono for their trustworthiness and, of course, technical skills.

'The Russians will continue with whatever training programmes are needed. You will also be required to establish who, amongst the Indonesian technicians, should be sent for training overseas as soon as practical, *Pak*,' Robson suggested.

'*And your company is quite comfortable with the financing package we have requested?*' Sujono enquired, quite surprised that the funding had not really been an issue with this consortium.

'We will fund the project, as agreed, *Pak* Sujono. Our bankers will provide whatever finance is required based on our involvement, and they have offered us terms based on our capacity to repay within twelve months from completion of the turn-key project.' Robson was excited, and had difficulty hiding his eagerness.

He would, as already agreed, pledge his group assets and future cash flows to the foreign banks, and they would provide the balance of the funding required to complete the entire project. There had been no other way to arrange the complicated financing package, primarily because the completed plant could not be offered as security for the bridging loan. The Japanese had already expended more than half of the estimated completion cost, and had agreed to a government-to-government, thirty-year soft-loan package covering repayment of their investment up to when they withdrew.

Robson needed to find close to one billion dollars to complete the project. The syndicated bank loan would provide these funds on the basis that repayment would occur within three years or twelve months after construction had been completed and the plant commissioned, whichever of these events came first. Robson had, as majority shareholder in the company founded by his father, pledged future cash-flows generated in Australia and Indonesia, primarily from coal and uranium ore sales

He believed he understood the risks and, although there had been considerable opposition within his own corporate management, Robson had insisted on assuming the project's debt. He firmly believed that there was no way the project could fail. His executives had expressed concern regarding the company's exposure during the construction period. This remained a problem as none of the major insurance firms were interested, deterred by the project's history and location.

'*There is another matter that needs to be discussed,*' Sujono suggested. He had BAKIN investigate Robson well before inviting him back for the second round of discussions. The intelligence agency had reported on the Australian's commercial activities. There was no doubt in Sujono's mind that Robson would have, somewhere along the line while conducting business in Indonesia, paid the necessary dues for whatever licences he had acquired. Robson had expected to be approached by an intermediary, and was surprised that the Chairman had gone directly to the heart of the matter, himself.

'I believe I understand already, *Pak* Sujono,' Robson said. 'As my group will be directly responsible for all materials and equipment supply, we would be most indebted for any assistance you might offer to facilitate the implementation of our contract.' He then waited for a response, having opened the door for the Chairman.

'*As you know, I speak for others, Mas Graeme,*' Sujono lied, assuming, correctly that Robson would believe this to be true, considering Sujono's Palace connections. '*There will be a consideration set aside for those who will provide the final authorisation for your group to proceed.*' He was pleased to see that Robson nodded, affirmatively.

'*Pak* Sujono,' Robson interrupted, knowing how difficult these moments could be. He had been present when Murray Stephenson negotiated the coal contracts for his father's company some years before. In those days, he remembered, payments were broken down into a number of isolated arrangements, and the percentages were nowhere near as crippling as they had become in the current business climate.

'The bankers have set aside a fund of five per cent, based on the remaining construction expenditures.' He then waited for a response, watching as Sujono's brain switched into high gear, calculating how much this might represent.

It was a formidable amount, Robson knew, but one which was necessary if he were to secure the contract. It made little difference, as this figure would simply be added to the project's final cost, included as some fictitious consultant's fee, and the Indonesian Government would end up paying the graft themselves. This was how business was done in the country, and Robson knew that every company operating in the Republic would have, at one time or another, participated in making such provision for senior government officials.

During the initial construction stage, and while the Japanese had still been in control of the overall project, Robson had already negotiated an arrangement with Sujono's predecessor, the late

Nathan Seda. Cement, reinforcing-steel for concrete, and a substantial percentage of other materials had been directed through Robson's offshore corporate structure to facilitate payments to the PEPELIN Chairman and, if what he said could be believed, the First Family. Robson knew that Seda's manipulations had put the powerful Salima shareholders offside; however, in his mind, the substantial profits generated by the relationship had compensated for any downside or political fallout.

'*I believe that the fee you suggested is too low, Mas,*' Sujono implied. '*I am confident that you would be appointed as the project's contractor if I could report that the consideration was, say, ten per cent?*' Robson listened to the influential general, taking his time to ensure that he had understood exactly what the man had said in his native tongue.

Major General Sujono Diryo was not a greedy man. He had expected Robson to have understood that this figure was the standard rate for such a project. He observed the foreigner for a few moments, deciding from the uncomfortable look on the man's unhappy face that he might have gone too far.

'I'm sure we can handle that, *Pak* Sujono,' Robson unhappily agreed. The general showed no reaction to Robson's acceptance to pay what would most probably amount to more than one hundred million dollars. 'If you would provide me with the details, I will make the necessary arrangements,' Robson advised. He knew that these would most probably be given the same day contracts were signed, and the project officially awarded.

Satisfied that their undertakings were clear to each other, they parted company. Robson raced back to his office, barely unable to restrain his excitement, confident that his group had secured the nuclear energy and desalinisation plant's construction project. Upon arriving at his office along Jalan Jenderal Sudirman, Graeme Robson phoned his bankers immediately, and arranged to meet with them in Singapore the following day. He then instructed his secretary to warn his personal pilot of his departure details. He phoned through to Singapore to instruct John Georgio to arrange something special for his visit, as he wished to ensure that his bankers enjoyed the pleasures Graeme knew Georgio would be able to provide, even at such short notice.

When Sujono reported his decision to award the contract to Robson's group, and that he had received an undertaking that *Rama*

II would be completed on schedule, the President had reacted most favourably. Sujono informed his father-in-law also, that he had arranged for a small consultancy fee to be paid into the family coffers.

The President approved of Sujono's actions, although he was somewhat disappointed when he discovered the size of the fee. He then suggested that Sujono have the five per cent paid directly into the dedicated account in Switzerland. Sujono politely agreed, and contracts for *Rama II* were prepared and executed within the month. Less than six weeks were to pass before Major General Sujono Diryo also secured an undertaking from the President of Iraq, to provide the advanced rocket technology they had been given by their supporters in Beijing. Ironically, before the end of that year, the Bandung Research and Development Centre had secured plans through their Moslem brothers in the Middle East, which would permit them to duplicate an advanced version of the Red Chinese three-stage rocket Beijing affectionately referred to as *The Long March* missile.

* * * * * *

Australia — Ulladulla Harbour,
New South Wales

Few amongst the local fisherman paid much heed to the trawler as it prepared to leave the jetty. Most crews from the Ulladulla trawling fleet had already returned to their homes, those remaining went about finishing off outstanding chores in preparation for the following day.

The small ship's engines throbbed as the captain idled back, checking his instrumentation one final time as he prepared to leave. Satisfied that all was in order, he nodded to another man who then released the thick ropes restraining the trawler, and jumped on board as the ship moved slowly away from the jetty and headed out to sea.

The two-man crew navigated north, towards Sydney, their course taking them directly past the state capital, and further along the coastline where they would take on fuel and supplies before continuing on to Queensland's Great Barrier Reef. There, in the

Whitsunday Islands, they would alter course and sail for Port Moresby in New Guinea where, for the second time, they would replenish their fuel and food stores before heading off to Guam. Once in the safety of the American territory, they would off-load their precious cargo then sail on to the Philippines, where they would remain for several months before returning to Australia.

Neither of the two men were at all concerned that they had not caught any fish; the vessel belonged to the American Government, and both sailors were experienced field agents belonging to the United States Central Intelligence Agency.

* * * * * *

Darwin

Xanana Soares slapped at the bothersome flies, then scratched his head. It was hot. Even hotter than Dili, he remembered. He looked at his visitor and wondered how much longer he must wait before the Indian Government advanced further funds in support of his government in exile.

Otelo Ramalho had arranged their first meeting. Xanana recalled his surprise at the time, as his people had never expected assistance from this quarter. And, he remembered, it had been most timely. Support for their cause had dwindled as most nations accepted the reality of Indonesia's occupation of his country, East Timor.

'You will be able to travel, then?' his visitor asked. Xanana nodded.

'I have asked the authorities for a passport, and it seems that this will not be a problem,' he replied. Xanana Soares was not ungrateful to the Australian people for the sanctuary provided to him and the many thousands of his fellow refugees. He had not been amongst the first to flee the island, electing to remain and fight against the Indonesian troops which had crossed into his country some thirty years before, towards the end of 1975, and occupied the former Portuguese colony. It was not until the Indonesians officially annexed his country that Xanana and his comrades realized that they had been betrayed by the Portuguese Government.

Formerly known as the Timor Social Democratic Association,

331

the Party's charter, and name was now the East Timor Liberation Front, and under this banner Xanana and his colleagues prepared a programme to build the new nation. They had waited for more than a year before their reformed party, Fretelin, declared East Timor an independent nation. Nine days later, on the seventh of December, 1975 Indonesia had invaded his country. Although the United Nations called on Indonesia to withdraw its armed forces from Timor, the toothless tiger's demands were ignored.

Xanana remembered the bloody fighting and the years of terror which followed. At first, his resistance movement managed to hold its own against the much greater forces, their spirits lifting with each call of the United Nations for Indonesia to withdraw; but the Indonesian troops had remained, and Jakarta had sent its planes, provided by the American Government, to rain death upon the Timorese villages. Then, as Xanana and the others fled into the mountains to regroup, leaving thousands of their dead behind, the Indonesian Government initiated a campaign of terror against his people.

His restless nights were still occupied with dreams of times of unimaginable terror; of times when entire villages had been destroyed and tens of thousands of simple farmers annihilated by the brutal, invading forces; of times when Indonesian soldiers rounded up innocent, frightened children, and forced girls who had not yet entered puberty into prostitution to service the hungry soldiers. Branded rebels and separatists, Xanana and his freedom fighters continued to wage war on the invaders.

Jakarta responded by initiating a forced sterilisation programme thoughout the villages. But the worst was yet to come. Determined to eradicate all signs of resistance, and provide an embarrassed world the opportunity to move on, the United States Government arranged for the delivery of sixteen A-4 counter insurgency bombers to be delivered to Jakarta. These, along with the Bronco OV-10 jets, accounted for the deaths of thousands of innocent women and children as the deadly aircraft commenced strafing missions over East Timorese villages. Then, it seemed, the entire world had turned against his people.

The British jumped on the band-wagon, selling eight Hawk ground-attack aircraft to the Indonesian Air Force, and the Australian Government provided the forum for Australian companies to negotiate the substantial oil and gas deposit concessions with their Indonesian counterparts.

Xanana followed his countryman Nicolau Lobato, faithfully, as the newly elected Fretelin President led his poorly equipped band against the superior Indonesian forces. Weeks rolled slowly into months, and then into years. When Xanana heard that Australia had given *de facto* recognition to Indonesia's occupation of his country, he believed that the Australian people would, one day, regret their act of betrayal. Soon, his resistance movement would all but collapse. His only contact with the outside world had been by radio.

He remembered cheering along with the others in their secluded camp, when they heard news broadcasting the United Nations vote calling for the withdrawal of Indonesian troops and the right for self-determination to be exercised in East Timor. Jakarta responded by doubling its troops, destroying all of that season's crops, and slaughtering fifteen thousand more villagers. Soon Xanana was to witness the deaths of children as they starved, and listen to terrified women speak of their ordeals at the hands of the Indonesian soldiers.

Almost three years to the day after his country had been invaded, Xanana's spirits fell even further when they lost their only means of communicating with the Timorese people. Two weeks after Radio Maubere ceased transmitting, Fretelin's President, Nicolau Lobato, was shot and killed by the enemy.

Xanana had remained hiding in the mountains. He knew that Indonesian soldiers had received instructions from Jakarta not to take political prisoners. As each year passed, his enemy pressed further and further into the most remote mountain areas, annihilating entire villages they suspected of harbouring resistance fighters. Soon, there were few left to carry on the fight. The rebels had run out of weapons.

Four years after the invasion, Indonesia still had not conquered his country, nor had it broken its spirit. The United Nations General Assembly passed a resolution condemning the Indonesian occupation, and called again for an act of self-determination. This call would also go unheeded.

Xanana had finally decided to carry his fight overseas and left his home behind when he and sixty others sailed the short distance to Australia, where they knew they would be well cared for. They sailed to Darwin, where they were immediately interned by the authorities, as unauthorised arrivals, and subsequently processed and placed in one of the many camps the Australian Government maintained under its refugee programme.

After some months had passed, Xanana was given his freedom and permitted to remain in Australia. He was, however, warned not to create mischief, threatened with deportation to an Indonesian jail in the event that he did not comply.

Xanana had exploited his position within the refugee community, and established a quasi government-in-exile. He assembled a team from amongst those he considered most qualified, and set about organizing the Timorese community in Australia to provide support for his dream of an Independent East Timor. He received substantial support from the international press, and financial assistance from the many Timorese in Australia. He established contact with representatives within the United Nations and the Portuguese Government, and continued the struggle for recognition of their demands. As the years passed slowly, Xanana came to realize that their cause would never receive the support it deserved, as there were just too many economic and political barriers and vested interest groups which thwarted the Timorese wherever they turned.

He had always wondered why the American Government had been so supportive of the Soeharto military dictatorship; then he discovered how strategically important East Timor's seas were to United States nuclear submarines. They could reduce sailing time by more than a week by transiting undetected through the Ombar-Wetar Straits just north of his land. Xanana learned a great deal over those years, and became philosophical regarding his dreams when he realized that his host country, Australia, continued to benefit from ignoring the plight of those he had left behind.

Whenever he strolled around Darwin Harbour and noted the increased activity, Xanana came to understand that economic considerations drove Australia's desire to maintain peaceful relationships with its giant northern neighbour. When he read that Australia and Indonesia would reap many billions of dollars in revenue from the very area which surrounded East Timor, he finally accepted that he would never live to see freedom for his people.

And then he received his first visit from the Indian Chargé d'Affaires.

* * * * * *

Xanana had been pleasantly surprised to discover how knowledgeable his guest had been regarding Timor's history and its people. As the day progressed and they continued to discuss East Timor's position, Xanana was impressed with the diplomat's response to his request for financial support. Before departing that day, he had received a commitment from his visitor to provide a donation to establish a special fund for the Timorese refugees. Within the week, and true to his word, the Chargé d'Affaires informed Xanana that his government had agreed to deposit two hundred thousand dollars towards this cause.

Xanana Soares, self-proclaimed President-in-exile, was ecstatic over the donation. He had understood the diplomat's request that India not be identified as the source, and the reasoning behind this request. Immediately, Xanana went about further consolidating his position amongst his fellow countrymen, using the fund to lift his movement's profile, and dispersing some of the money to those he considered most in need.

It was then that Xanana received an invitation to visit New Delhi, which he willingly accepted. Once again, the Chargé had suggested discretion in relation to the proposed journey.

The diplomat pointed out that the Australian Government would not be pleased about the Indian Government extending such an invitation, and further suggested that Xanana not divulge his travel arrangements to anyone. Xanana had not been entirely satisfied with this request, hoping to use his visit to gain some additional press. Finally, he accepted the diplomat's advice, acknowledging that the purpose for the unofficial visit was to assist the Timorese to further their cause for Independence. That had been sufficient to convince Xanana to adhere to the request and respect the need for secrecy surrounding the invitation. He made application for an Australian passport, which was granted on the basis that he had already become a naturalised citizen the year before.

'Will Otelo be joining us in India?' he had asked. Otelo Ramalho was responsible for the unofficial East Timor Embassy in Canberra. There was, in fact, no Embassy at all. The Australian Government, bowing to public pressure, had resisted administrative calls to remove the small hut which had been illegally erected on a vacant block of ground directly across the road from the Indonesian Embassy. This had been an embarrassment to the government and, ironically, although the butt of many a joke from passers-by, the small structure became identified with the East Timor Independence Movement. Xanana was indebted to Otelo for his introduction to the Indian High Commission.

'No, Otelo will not be joining you, Xanana. It is of the utmost importance that he know nothing of your journey,' the official had insisted. The following week Xanana left Darwin and flew to Singapore, where he changed flights then continued on to Delhi. Upon arrival, Xanana was whisked hurriedly away, and taken to a government guest house where he remained, *incommunicado*, for more than a week.

At first, he had been disappointed that he would not been allowed to move around freely. It was almost as if he had been placed under protective custody, as if his hosts were embarrassed by his presence. But when he was informed that he would meet with the Prime Minister briefly before lunch the next day, Xanana panicked, fearing he would have little to say to the powerful leader.

The following day, while he was being escorted through the stark, white-washed building, Xanana refused to believe that this modest building could possibly be the office of India's Prime Minister. Bewildered by the subterfuge surrounding his visit, he was finally introduced to the man who led a nation of more than one billion people. When he left the meeting, an hour later, Xanana was no longer confused about the reasons for secrecy. He was driven back to the guest house, the content of his incredible discussion with the Prime Minister still buzzing in his brain.

The Indian Government had offered to support his cause by granting official recognition to his government-in-exile. This meant that he would have a powerful ally to provide a protective military umbrella over East Timor from its aggressive neighbours. India would enter into a twenty-five year Defence and Economic Development Agreement with his government, and establish a formal naval presence in Timor, similar to that which the Americans had achieved years before in Subic Bay in the Philippines. Together, their countries would exploit Timor's oil and gas which would then belong to the independent state, and India would station its ships within East Timor's territorial waters to ensure the new nation's sovereignty over these and the Ombar-Wetar Straits.

Xanana had been promised his own war chest of ten million

dollars. He knew that this was insignificant in terms of power to purchase weapons, but what it represented was confirmation of India's commitment to his country. He had unhesitatingly accepted the terms offered by the Indian Prime Minister. Following this, all that was required of him was his attendance at several briefings over the following days, before returning to Australia where he would wait, until called.

* * * * * *

On the twenty-eighth of November, in recognition of Fretelin's declaration of Independence on that date decades before, the Republic of South Africa sponsored a resolution in the United Nations General Assembly which called for an immediate withdrawal of Indonesian troops from East Timor, and for recognition of Xanana Soares as the rightful head of state for the Republic of East Timor.

The resolution was carried by eighty-nine votes in favour, ten against, with only thirty-six abstentions, including Australia and the United States. India and China had led the charge and, as support swept across the floor of the chamber, the Indonesian Ambassador to the United Nations stormed out.

* * * * * *

Xanana Soares gathered his possessions in Darwin and moved to Canberra where he went about soliciting further support and establishing an official base of operations for the *Fretelin* cause. His Australian citizenship was brought into question on the floor of Parliament House, which resulted in a screaming match when a Democrat pointed out that, some years before, a Cambodian First Prime Minister appointed to Prince Ranariddh's former post was also an Australian citizen. The following week, Xanana flew to Singapore and took possession of the first two of his ten million dollars, and placed this in a numbered account with the Hong Kong Bank.

Indonesia reacted as expected, by moving additional troops into the area. In recognition of Australia's lack of support, the Indonesian Ambassador to Australia, Major General Sudarsono, left his temporary quarters and drove to the Foreign Affairs building where he formally handed notification to the Minister that Indonesian sea-lanes would forthwith be closed to Australian shipping until further notice.

United States satellite coverage, identifying an Indonesian military build-up in close proximity to the Timor Shelf oil and gas fields, was passed to counterparts in Australian Defence. Within days, tension between the two neighbouring countries spilled over, erupting once again into street violence and demonstrations in both nations' capitals.

Book three

Rama Energy

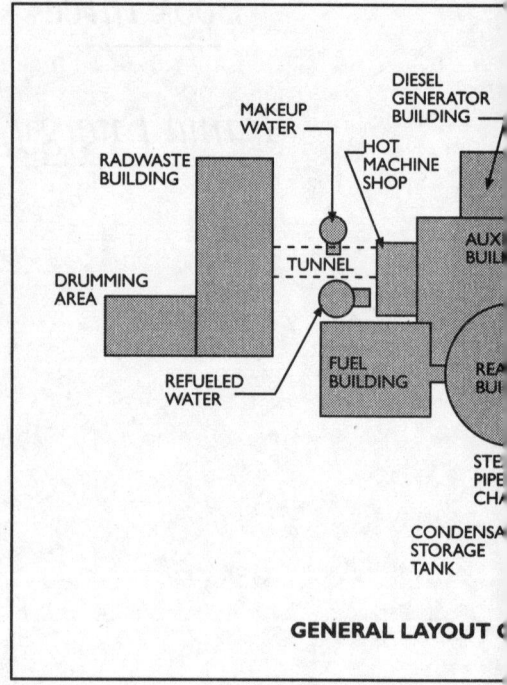

GENERAL LAYOUT (

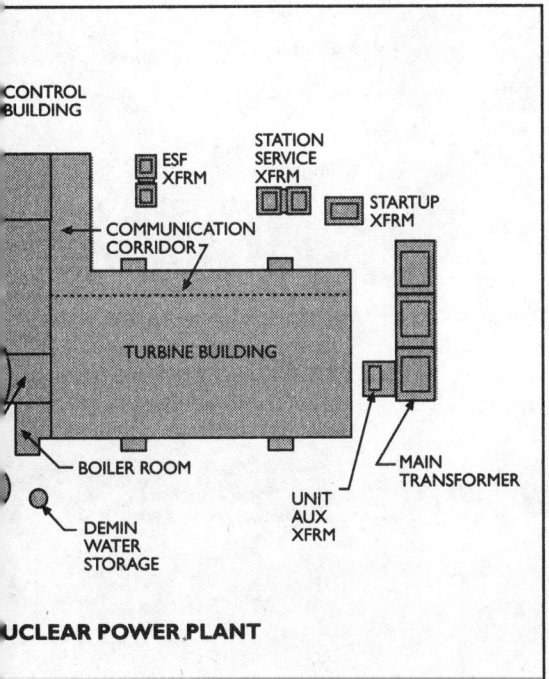

CONTROL
BUILDING

ESF
XFRM

STATION
SERVICE
XFRM

STARTUP
XFRM

← COMMUNICATION
CORRIDOR

TURBINE BUILDING

← BOILER ROOM

MAIN
TRANSFORMER

UNIT
AUX
XFRM

DEMIN
WATER
STORAGE

UCLEAR POWER PLANT

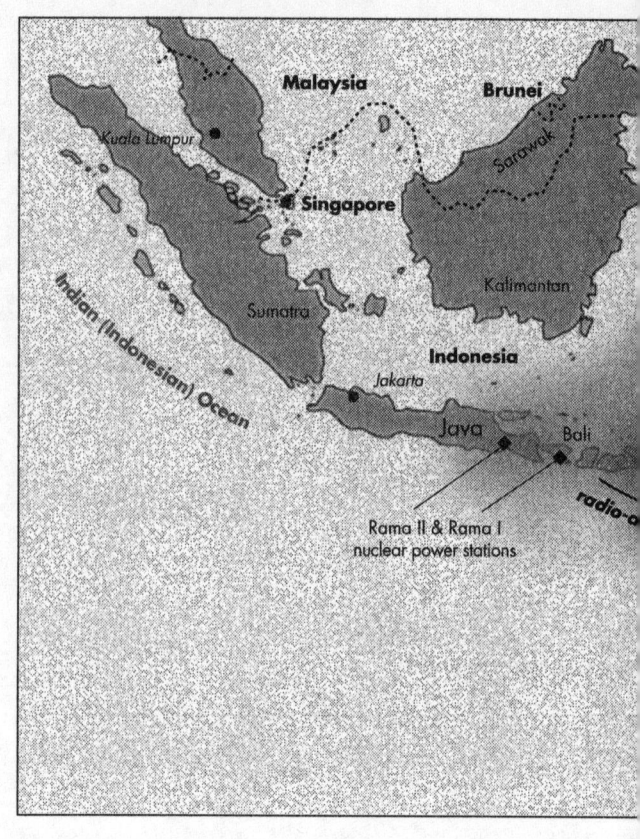

Irian Jaya

Papua - New Guinea

Timor

out drifts eastward

Darwin

Cairns

Australia

Chapter 20

Ruswita and the Salima Group

Vijay Rakesh winced with pain, and felt saddened that he might not last long enough to witness even the first step in the realization of Malhotra's strategy.

'The South African President has agreed,' he said, trying to disguise his discomfort. The medications no longer worked. He knew he would soon die. The thought of the State funeral and subsequent funeral pyre suddenly seemed appealing. Vijay was terribly tired.

'Vijay, why don't you rest,' Gopal said. 'Leave the implementation to those around you. There is little left that you can do.'

'We must push ahead with the Summit,' Vijay insisted. Malhotra's suggestion had been well received by all. Considering the regional conflicts, the timing was perfect for such a gathering of leaders to resolve their differences.

'Now that the South Africans are co-sponsoring the call, it will most surely happen, Vijay,' Gopal said, kindly. The three men had been close friends for many years, and shared the same ideals.

'And what about Imran's suggestion to involve those people in New Guinea?' Vijay asked. Admiral Gopal had played a major role in approaching the Government of New Guinea to suggest a goodwill visit by the Indian Navy. This would be essential in order to disguise the presence of such a large number of ships proceeding through the area.

'Port Moresby has agreed, Vijay. All seems to be in order.'

'Then, all we must do now is wait to see if the Indonesians take the bait,' the Indian Prime Minister suggested. Admiral Gopal grinned.

'I am sure they will jump at the opportunity to host a regional peace summit. Otherwise they might just be seen as being indifferent to settling their differences.'

'At least we have the Chinese supporting our strategy,' Vijay said, wincing again. Gopal could see that his friend was in severe pain and decided he must soon leave the Prime Minister to rest.

Rising to his feet he said, 'Yes, we have the Chinese, Vijay, and they, in turn, have the Americans to contend with.' Vijay Rakesh forced a grim smile and nodded.

'Do you think they will betray us?' the Prime Minister asked, knowing that everything depended on their support.

'No, Vijay,' Gopal said, 'they can't afford to do so. At least, not yet,' he added. 'I must go now and leave you to rest. I will come back tomorrow.' He moved closer and touched Vijay's arm, the gesture being rewarded with another smile. The admiral then left his ailing leader alone. As he walked down the corridor he reflected that they were on the verge of taking their country on a daring voyage into the future, one which would hopefully place food in the mouths of their starving millions.

* * * * * *

JAKARTA

Ruswita waved the servant away impatiently, returning her attention to the papers before her. She checked the covering overview letter which had been prepared by her son, Benny, saw that he had extended the period for amortisation over the most recent plants to come on line, and looked for the referenced explanatory notes to see why. Satisfied that he perhaps now knew more than she with regard to financing, Ruswita closed the final document and removed her glasses. She was weary from the demands placed upon her as Chairwoman. She glanced up at the framed photograph hanging on the opposite wall and smiled at Lim's face. It was one of the few photos he had actually posed for, as he had always feared ridicule because of his appearance.

Rus rubbed her eyes then placed her bifocals back on her nose to read the opened letter lying to the side of her official correspondence. It was from Ratna, and was addressed to '*Ibu Lani dan Dear Aunty Rus*'. She finished reading the letter and placed this back inside the envelope for Lani to read later. Rus thought about her daughter and her wasted life, saddened by the news of her divorce. She looked over at the clock and made a note to phone Ratna when it was appropriate, remembering to make allowance for the time difference between Jakarta and California.

Ruswita could not understand what Ratna really wanted out of life. She had always been restless, and lacked motivation to do anything which might involve the company's activities. She could virtually have had her choice of careers, Rus thought, and been given a solid start with any of the Salima companies which then spanned global trade and commerce, from timber concessions to banking, mining and shipping and, of course now, power generation.

Ruswita turned her attention back to the nuclear power plants under the Salima Group control. *Rama I* had been commissioned three months before, while *Ramas III, IV and V* had all come in under time four to five months earlier, earning considerable bonuses for the group. She had attended the official opening ceremony for *Rama I* in Bali, but delegated the other functions to Lim's oldest sons, who reluctantly flew from the United States specifically for the occasion.

She thought about these young men, who were already making a mark of their own, and wished that they would settle down in Indonesia and assume some of the burdensome responsibilities she carried. Her youngest son, Benny, had also taken to banking. He had been appointed President of the Asian Pacific Commercial Bank, which their family still controlled. She remembered that he had commenced negotiations to establish operational branches in India and the Middle East and, she thought miserably, this would lead to his spending more time away from her, also.

Ruswita missed her husband. Her busy life had not eased the loneliness she felt. It was not until she assumed control over the group's activities that Ruswita realized just how active Lim had been, and how unobtrusively he had conducted his business affairs. She brushed the memory of his sudden demise away as quickly as it had entered her thoughts, knowing how painful such recollections were. When Lim had been murdered, she had never been able to confirm her suspicions about how he had been poisoned, but she knew who had been responsible. She knew too that one or more of her staff must have been engaged to carry out the murder. Unable to discover which of her servants had betrayed their master, she had systematically removed them all from her household, including the old housekeeper, and replaced them with staff from other residences she owned.

The doctor had been of great service to her, taking care of the necessary arrangements through to the burial. Ruswita had insisted that only immediate family attend the small service, after which Lim's body had been cremated. She had lied to their surprised children, stating that Lim had once discussed such arrangements, and had specifically requested that his body be treated so. For weeks, flower arrangements had continued to arrive, reflecting his power and popularity around the world. Then, with his funeral behind her, Ruswita had turned her attention to their company's activities, and taken control.

Then, before she had been given the opportunity to strike at the man who she believed to have ordered her husband's death, Seda was already dead.

Many had agreed with her that Seda's appointment as ambassador was most bewildering. They all were aware of his considerable power, wealth, and influence over the President. Why then, had he removed himself from the very seat of Indonesian power and taken a lesser position? She had heard the rumours that he was being considered for appointment as Vice President at the time of his death. Ruswita did not believe that this would have eventuated. Seda had collected powerful enemies in his time, most of whom, she remembered, moved quickly to fill the vacuum created by his death.

The vultures had swooped, tearing at the flesh of his company structure, until the inner workings of Seda's entire operation had been exposed. Those closest to the President assumed many of the roles Seda had skilfully taken for himself. Supply companies changed hands within days and, once the military were satisfied that his widow had been adequately provided for, they absorbed the rest, distributing contracts and projects among themselves before others had any chance.

Ruswita had been asked to visit the President's home to discuss the *Rama II* plant after the Japanese Government had withdrawn from the project, citing domestic political pressures.

When they withdrew, the project had been more than half completed. She had pledged her support to the First Family, but refused to provide any funding for the project. The government banks were also reluctant to provide loan capital to the new corporate entity established to assume control over the plant, until the President personally insisted that the Central Bank guarantee the project. It was then that Jakarta business circles discovered that Seda's original contract had been assumed by the President's youngest daughter and the Robson *kongsi*. The Jakarta rumour-mill fed off the relationship which existed between the new PEPELIN Chairman, Major General Sujono Diryo, and his wife, the President's second daughter.

Now, Ruswita's sources confirmed that construction of the Fast Breeder Reactor plant was nearing completion, and that *Rama II* would most probably be on line within six months. There had been disturbing rumours about the plant's safety, and concerns that the rush to complete the project might compromise established safety procedures. Ruswita's *kongsi* did not even bid for the ongoing supply contract, suspecting that the government's project management team would be unable to meet their financial undertakings. As a major shareholder in the largest private Indonesian bank, Ruswita knew the value of the government's Central Bank guarantee, and hoped that none would ever have reason to call upon it.

She was surprised that Robson still managed to keep his foot in the door somehow, pledging his assets to gain a position in the plant's construction, providing Indian cement, Vietnamese steel reinforcing-bars and whatever else he could lay his hands on through credit. As his name came to mind, Ruswita remembered how close the Salima plants had come to losing its uranium supplies from Australia.

When the President had unwisely invoked Indonesia's sovereignty over its sea-lanes in retaliation for what he perceived to be disloyalty over the United Nations vote, Ruswita had sent her own emissaries directly down to speak to the respective Chiefs of Staff, warning them that the Australian uranium, or yellowcake supplies, could not so easily be replaced just at a whim. When they had learned that the *Rama Project* could be delayed for years, the ruling generals had approached their stubborn President and requested that he withdraw his edict. Amazingly, he refused. Then, General

Sujono and his wife also appealed to the President, explaining how *Rama II's* commissioning would be delayed indefinitely, should ore supplies be disrupted at this late date.

She remembered how he had shaken his fist in Soekarno style, then publicly forgiven the Australians for the inappropriate position they had taken at the time. Shipping had returned to some semblance of normality, although tensions still ran high thoughout the region.

Ruswita had smiled when the new Chairman of PEPELIN had been appointed prior to Seda's departure for Australia. The international press had enjoyed a field day, crying nepotism, when General Sujono was appointed to the position. She knew that the young general would be a very wealthy man before the remaining seven power plants had gone out for tender, and even richer once these had been brought on-line. She didn't mind. Lim had taught her how to handle such situations, encouraging her to accept that payments only guaranteed contracts, not loyalty.

Ruswita knew for certain from their family bank that the First Family's wealth had grown close to two billion dollars over the nine years the former general had held office. She believed this to be a modest amount for one who occupied the presidential seat. Lim, she recalled fondly, often laughed privately about those who had become President over the powerful economy, as their children squandered millions of Indonesian banks' funds on their misadventures and were rarely called to account over their debts. Lim had warned her to be cautious when dealing with these children, as most were inept when it came to monetary matters. Not that it really mattered to the First Family, Lim had joked, revealing the billions which successive Presidents had moved overseas into numbered accounts. After all, the Lim bank had been instrumental in arranging most of these transactions.

Ruswita planned to emulate the First Family's desire to hold their assets outside the country. She would divest Salima of its burdensome exposure with the energy plants, but not in accordance with Lim's original plans. Ruswita decided not to wait until they had been operating for the two years her late husband had suggested. The Salima Jaya company, whose shares had already been listed before Lim's death, had enjoyed the confidence of the stock market investors, and Ruswita had decided that it was time to consolidate the family's holdings by retiring as much debt as she could. She knew that this would mean floating the energy company well before cash-flows had been proven, but she no longer considered these projections to be relevant, as the Asian markets were operating at a level considerably higher than most had forecast. Ruswita decided to take advantage of renewed investment confidence and list the company, Salima Jaya Power and Energy, as soon as she had amalgamated all of their energy interests. Ruswita expected that they would be ready to float the entire operation off through the Jakarta Stock Exchange before the end of the year. Benny had provided her with projections as to what they could expect from the sale of these assets, and Ruswita had not even blinked when she saw the final figure of twenty billion dollars. They would still retain their banking interests and a token position in the energy company.

Divesting themselves of these assets would be met with public approval, as Ruswita expected the indigenous investment houses would have a field day fighting over positions in the proposed share-float, considering the conglomerate's successful cement plants, flour mills and other major operating assets. The remaining shares in the family flagship, Salima Jaya Corporation, would then be sold through the Stock Exchange as soon as the market had absorbed the energy company's shares. Her son, Benny, had estimated that their total cash assets would then exceed fifty billion dollars, not including the Asian Pacific Commercial Bank's net asset worth. The only outstanding issue, she mused confidently, would be how to incorporate the *Rama II* power production into the Salima Jaya Power and Energy stable. She understood from her son, Benny, how the nuclear power plant's construction had been financed; their family bank had picked up all the outstanding notes relating to the project. Ruswita knew that she would require Palace support to instruct the government banks, and superannuation fund managers, to commit to advance positions for her public float.

A voice outside reminded Ruswita that she was expecting a visitor. She opened a drawer to the desk, slipped the file inside, and moved into the next room to receive her guest, smiling as she entered the room to greet the recently appointed Vice President. The handsome Javanese general rose and returned her smile.

'*Good morning, Ibu Salima,*' he greeted, gently squeezing her extended hand.

'*Selamat siang, General Sujono,*' Ruswita said, warmly, as she welcomed the President's son-in-law.

Chapter 21

*Ratna Sari, Michael
in California*

Ratna lay back and breathed slowly as the sun reappeared from behind the cloud. She looked across at the man resting alongside, and admitted that she had not been this happy for years. Then she wondered what might have happened, had chance not taken her to the country club on that day, a month before. As she lay there soaking up the sun's warmth, Ratna smiled, recalling how their paths had crossed during the tournament.

* * * * * *

Ratna had been enjoying the tennis when someone walked up alongside her and coughed politely. She turned, lifting her sunglasses to see who had practically coughed into her ear, and Michael grinned sheepishly then merely said, 'hello'.

For a fleeting moment she remained startled, then her mouth opened in surprise as recognition flooded her face. He leaned forward and kissed her on both cheeks, and smiled, the faint and tantalizing suggestion of Issey Miyaki gently arousing his senses. Immediately, memories of their affair came flooding back as she stood, smiling, and suddenly it was as if they had never parted. Ratna's instincts reacted accordingly, noticing the other women's admiring glances as the tall, handsome man stood close to her. She was suddenly excited by how well Michael looked. His skin was heavily tanned and his hair fairer than before, signs that he had spent considerable time outdoors.

'I see you haven't lost your fascination for tennis,' she said, referring to their first meeting years before. She placed her hand gently on his arm. Suddenly, It was just like old times.

353

'And I see you're still trying to pick up handsome young men at these events,' Michael responded. He looked at her with obvious delight and Ratna could see that he was smitten all over again.

'My, my,' she teased, 'who suggested that you were handsome?' Michael laughed, relieved. 'Come,' she ordered, commanding Michael in a familiar way. Ratna slipped her arm through his, and led him outside onto the veranda overlooking the tennis courts, where they sat and talked, occasionally looking down at the players as the competition continued.

* * * * * *

Ratna laughingly related her experiences over the past few years while Michael listened. She had shed her tomboyish manner and grown into a beautiful, sophisticated woman. Ratna explained that she had married and divorced all in one year, returning to the States once the lawyers had finalised the property settlement. Ratna did not appear bitter in any way, nor did she appear saddened by what had taken place.

'You're staring again,' she said, wondering what was going through his thoughts.

'Let's get out of here,' Michael suggested, and when she nodded he called for the check and they left, unnoticed in the crowd which had gathered at the country club. As they walked outside he sighed, wishing he had hired a rental and not caught a cab out to the club. A deep metallic purple Lamborghini appeared, and Michael did not express surprise when the attendant passed the keys to Ratna.

'I'll drive,' she smiled, squeezing into the car. Michael hesitated, then followed, climbing into the expensive sports car. He buckled up immediately and, remembering how heavy footed Ratna had been in the past, braced himself for the ride. Instead, he was pleasantly surprised when Ratna did not stamp on the gas pedal as had been her habit when they first met and fell in love, but drove away from the club in a most sedate manner.

'Thanks, Ratna.' Michael said, sincerely. She turned to look at his face and laughed.

'What ever do you mean?' she responded, suddenly kicking the accelerator down, recklessly. Michael looked at her imploringly.

'Oh,' she said, mischievously, 'you mean that, back there?' Again she laughed, but seeing the concern on his face, slowed the car, bringing its speed back within acceptable limits. 'Last week I was called to order by the club president. Seems that I could lose my parking privileges if caught speeding through the grounds again.'

Michael shook his head sadly.

They drove up the old coast road and parked overlooking the ocean. There, they sat and talked though the afternoon until the cool sea breeze became too chilly for them to remain. Michael took the keys and drove them both back into the city. He did not seem comfortable sitting in the passenger seat along the winding, dangerous stretches, and Ratna had surrendered the keys without comment. He drove directly to his hotel and parked in the driveway, then turned and looked at Ratna questioningly. She climbed out of the car as he moved around to take her hand, and lead her inside.

'No, Michael,' she said, removing the car keys gently from his hand. 'It's too soon.' She looked up into his eyes and smiled, then raised her mouth to his and kissed him gently.

During the afternoon, Ratna had considered how she might react when he inevitably invited her to stay. There had never been any doubt in her mind that he would ask, and she had wanted desperately to spend the night with Michael. But the memory of what had transpired between them before was still on her mind. She had to be sure that he would not disappear again, once they had tumbled into bed together. 'Perhaps, when you return,' she promised.

'Okay, that's fine, Ratna. There's no pressure,' he said, but she could sense his disappointment.

'Thanks, Michael,' she responded, then looked up into his eyes. 'When will I hear from you again?'

'I'll be gone for about a week. I promise to phone then, okay?'

'That's fine, Michael, you do that.'

Michael had explained that he would be leaving the following morning, but would be back within the week. Ratna felt he seemed a little vague about what he was doing, and was not entirely convinced that he was telling her the truth. She asked if there was someone currently in his life, and Michael had assured her that there was no one. Ratna was uncomfortable with his reply, and had difficulty accepting it as true. Michael was a handsome fellow, and would be considered a fine catch. It was unlikely that he had not already found someone, and settled down.

Michael squeezed her hand, again promising to phone. They parted company, and Ratna returned to the Salima mansion. As the days passed without a phone call, she became despondent, fearing that he had passed fleetingly through her life again, never to return. At the end of the week, she was convinced that he had lied. Then, suddenly, he was there, standing outside the mansion, his handsome face all smiles. Ratna flung herself around his neck, and laughed, kissing him as he playfully struggled to hold her at bay. Michael had returned, as promised, and they then spent the following, wonderful weeks, totally engrossed in each other. And for Ratna, it was a matter of falling in love all over again.

* * * * * *

Now, she knew, the strength of their relationship was about to be really tested, as Michael was to leave her, again. Ratna reached over and pulled the sun-bleached hair on Michael's forearm, bringing him instantly awake. He had dozed off under the warm sun.

'As it's our last night, what do you say we go home now and lock ourselves in?' she suggested, hoping he would agree.

'Sounds fine to me,' Michael answered, sitting up and taking a quick gulp of the iced tea. It was lukewarm; surprised, he checked his wristwatch and discovered he had dozed off for almost half an hour. He rose, grabbed his gym-bag and took Ratna by the hand. Promising to catch-up when Michael next visited, they left the others and drove back to the palatial estate. Ratna left the Lamborghini directly in front of the house, knowing that it would be safe. They strolled leisurely up the steps and through the mansion, then down to their favourite setting. Michael strolled over lazily and activated the outside spa's pumps, then turned to see Ratna standing naked, reaching up to roll her long, black, shiny hair into a bun.

'You're staring, again,' she laughed, unashamedly, and Michael immediately felt the heat rising in his loins. He knew he couldn't get enough of her, remembering the passionate hours they had spent together in her room upstairs. Michael stripped, and slipped into the bubbling spa as Ratna walked gracefully towards him. As she stepped into the water, her eyes seemed to convey that she was as anxious as he, to make love. Michael reached out and pulled her towards him slowly, turning her onto her back, then kissing her, impatiently. She responded, taking him in her hand and stroking him gently, until he was fully aroused. Then suddenly, Ratna pulled away, climbed out of the spa and ran to the pool, and propped.

'The servants will be watching,' she teased, then threw herself into the pool and swam towards the grotto. Michael didn't hesitate. The old women who had guarded this house had probably seen worse, he thought, scrambling after his woman. He hit the water hard, winced, then swam over to where she waited behind the waterfall.

He dived under the cascading water, coming to the surface where she sat, perched on the rock-pool's edge like some golden mermaid. Droplets of water clung to her body, and she posed sensually, opening then closing her legs. Michael moved in closer, lowering his head until his face touched her firm abdomen. He kissed her skin softly, and then again, as Ratna moaned and grasped his head with her hands, begging him not to stop. Michael tickled her with his tongue, and, as she cried out once more, he placed his hands around her slender waist, and leaned her gently on her side.

As she lay outstretched along the narrow ledge, he leaned over her breasts placed his warm mouth over her erect nipples, and teased her generously. Then, he rolled out of the water, and moved to dominate her body with his. Gently, lovingly, he parted her legs and stroked softly. Ratna said something which he could not understand, and moaned once more as he mounted her body and filled her completely with his. They moved together, finding a rhythm which filled each other with ecstasy, rocking slowly, at first, then faster, and faster, until their bodies reached a pulsating, simultaneous climax. Michael's body convulsed, and he cried out in pleasure.

They lay together, still, as their hearts beat loudly, and Ratna could feel Michael's hot breath on the side of her face. She kissed him, tenderly, and then held him tightly as their breathing returned to normal. She stroked his head, brushing aside the yellow-bleached strands of hair which covered his brow. Michael responded, kissing her gently, then moved to her side.

'Tell me you will never leave me, Michael,' she pleaded softly, her eyes still dreamy with the moment. He moved his arms around her, tenderly.

'I love you, Ratna,' was all he said, and kissed her again.

* * * * * *

Jakarta — the Presidential Palace

'..and it is therefore my great pleasure to announce that the three-day peace summit will be held on the seventeenth of January, in Bali.' The speaker was immediately inundated with questions, as journalists jostled each other for advantage.

'How will Xanana Soares travel to Indonesia?' one journalist called.

'*Bapak Presiden* has kindly consented for Mister Soares to be present at the Bali Summit conditional on his undertaking that, under no circumstances will he participate in any discussions outside the agreed agenda, and that he will not attend any rally of any kind during his stay. It is my understanding that Mister Soares will first attend discussions in New Delhi, following which he will accompany the Indian Prime Minister and South African President on their flight to Indonesia.' The journalists held their recorders higher to catch the Palace spokesman's words.

'Can you confirm who will attend the Summit?' another asked, pushing back angrily as someone behind shoved.

'As I have already mentioned, Xanana Soares will attend, his presence sponsored by the South African Government. The Indian and South African leaders will, of course, attend. We have confirmation that the Australian Prime Minister will be present, as will the ASEAN Heads of State.'

'Will the President also be present for discussions?' the Singapore Straits Times journalist asked, hoping his cameraman was catching it all for the SBS early evening news.

'*Bapak Presiden* will attend the formal opening ceremony, and will remain only until the official reception on the first day. *Bapak* has advised that Vice President, *Bapak Sujono,* will arrive early on the second day of the Summit, and will represent Indonesia during ongoing discussions. The *Istana* wishes to emphasize that the Indonesian leadership places great store in bringing its neighbouring nations together for the Bali Peace Summit, and sincerely prays that the meeting will result in an accord satisfactory to all.'

'With the *Istana's* acceptance of Xanana Soares' participation in these talks, does this signal a rapprochement between his government-in-exile and Jakarta?' David Murdoch from the International Herald Tribune asked, his tall frame dwarfing his colleagues.

'The Government of Indonesia does not recognize claims over *Tim-Tim* by refugee East Timorese who abandoned their own country and migrated to Australia. The *Istana* wishes to make this point quite clear; there is no East Timor delegation to the Bali Summit. Mr Soares' presence has been agreed to primarily on the basis that the South African President has sponsored his attendance. The Palace therefore hopes that this clearly demonstrates its willingness to resolve the issues which have contributed to regional tension, and its sincerity in offering its neighbouring countries the opportunity to settle their differences peacefully.'

'In view that the United Nations has already voted on the East Timor issue, and Indonesia's refusal to withdraw from the colony, won't Xanana's presence overshadow other issues such as accessibility to your country's sea-lanes?' Murdoch asked.

'Mr Soares' presence is not an issue,' was all the *Istana* spokesman was willing to add. He then ignored Murdoch's raised hand, annoyed by his aggressive line of questions.

'Will the visiting Heads of State be invited to attend the inauguration ceremony for the Mt Muria reactor?' someone down the back of the room called. The spokesman was pleased with the opportunity to mention the project during the press conference.

'No,' he said. 'However, the Vice President will officiate at the plant's final commissioning ceremony, and this will coincide with the second day of the Bali Summit. Unfortunately, due to security considerations, the press will be not be permitted to attend. The Palace public relations office would be pleased to provide photographs after the event. *Terima kasih,*' he said, smilingly, indicating that the conference had come to a close.

He had fielded enough questions and was relieved that he had successfully avoided the more sensitive issues. Taking up his notes, the *Istana* spokesman then stepped away from the podium leaving more than fifty journalists to file their stories. He reported personally to *Bapak Sujono*, confirming that the press conference had gone well.

The following day most international newspapers carried the

story on their front pages, with headlines which ranged from 'Indonesia Extends Its Hand in Peace' to 'Xanana Soares Scores Political Victory' and 'Indonesia Takes Soft Stance', declaring the Bali Summit would provide Asia with the long-awaited opportunity to resolve regional issues and restore peace.

Nowhere, in any of the stories, was the inauguration of Indonesia's powerful Fast Breeder Nuclear Plant even mentioned.

Chapter 22

The Oval Office

Secretary for State, William James Deakin, shuffled restlessly around the President's office listening, as the CIA Director concluded the Central Intelligence Agency's Asian situation report. This had followed similar submissions by General V. 'Sonny' Davis of the Joint Chiefs of Staff, and the three-star Defense Intelligence Agency's director. There was a moment of silence as those in attendance waited for the President's response. There was not a man present who envied the American leader at that moment. Without exception, they sensed that they were participating in what future historians might even identify as the turning point in American-Sino relations, or worse.

'What do you think, Bill?' the President asked Deakin, who immediately ceased pacing and addressed his superior.

'You know my position, Mr President,' he answered formally. They had been close friends since college. Had it not been for that relationship, Deakin would have refused the offer to become the country's Secretary for State. William J Deakin would have been quite content to remain where he was, with General Motors. 'I have never been supportive of military action other than to defend these shores.' He looked across at the four men sitting, facing their President.

'We are dealing with some fairly nebulous conclusions here, I would say,' this was directed at the CIA Chief. Deakin found it difficult to accommodate the clandestine operations as an integral component of State's activities, although he accepted that the intelligence gathering activities were essential to their national security. Deakin's primary objection was to CIA and DIA covert operations which often undermined the State's own solution-seeking efforts on the world stage.·

'I don't believe we have sufficient intelligence information to take an informed position. My recommendation is that we wait for a while and see how it all develops. Then, if we feel that action is still required, our decisions would be based on intelligence which, in the future, would justify what they're proposing.' Deakin indicated with his left hand just whom he was referring to in the room.

'Well, Sonny, how do you respond to that?' The President asked his country's most senior military officer. Victor 'Sonny' Davis' star had been on the ascent ever since the American press had practically deified him and many other US Army field officers involved in *Desert Storm* more than a decade before. Since then, apart from Bosnia and a few minor skirmishes in Africa, the United States Military had been given few opportunities to provide American troops with battle-field experience.

'The Joint Chiefs are all in concurrence, Mr President,' he replied, knowing just how much weight they carried in such decisions. The general was not too happy with the Secretary for State's obvious influence over the President and the knowledge that Deakin had never so much as served one day in any of the US forces.

'All intelligence points to the Indians mobilising their Navy. If, for the moment, we can put political issues aside and concentrate solely on the military aspects of a major naval expedition, we would have to agree that, considering India's naval strength, in the absence of a successful retaliatory or pre-emptive enemy missile attack, they would be successful.' The general moved his large, beefy hands through the air as he spoke.

'The Indian Navy is third only to the United States in strength. Unless they were also contemplating taking the Malay Peninsula, which would then afford an excellent opportunity for ground forces to sweep down through Bangladesh, Burma and Thailand, then we do not see any real long-term benefit for India in the scenario suggested by the CIA. However, we do agree that a military expedition by India's forces is imminent. It is, in our opinion, most unlikely however that the Chinese would sit back and let the Indians go; that is,' he added, looking directly at the Secretary for State, 'unless they are acting in concert and intend conducting a joint expedition.' This statement was immediately met with surprised glances from both Deakin and the CIA director.

'No, I can't accept that the Chinese would ever entertain such an alliance,' Deakin stated, shaking his head in emphasis, 'and there is nothing to support such conjecture.'

'Is there?' the President pressed, conscious that there was an air of antagonism developing, and he didn't like it at all.

'No, Mr President,' General Davis answered, 'but the Joint Chiefs are most concerned with the spread of China's Southern Fleet across the South China Sea from Natuna Island off Malaysia, right though to Hong Kong. One would have to ask the obvious question regarding what they might do, should they perceive the Indian Navy consolidating its own position in nearby waters as a potential threat. We have initiated a number of war-game scenarios Mr. President, which all seem to indicate that, without Chinese accord, the Indians would be most unlikely to move further east than Singapore.' The thought of the South East Asian financial centre, Singapore, falling to India, whilst China dominated Hong Kong, startled others in the room.

The President put his fingertips together in thought. General Davis' statement provided substance to the suggestion that India might consider annexing the entire peninsula. There was virtually no other viable area in which they could expand; China blocked India in the east, and there was little to be gained by moving into the arid areas of Pakistan and Afghanistan. On the other hand, any overland expedition into the fertile plains of Thailand and Malaysia would require access though Bangladesh and Burma.

The President was all too aware of his country's weakened military position in Asia. Having given Vietnam back to the communists in 1975, the United States had been unable to sustain its credibility amongst the Asian nations. Then, when the Philippines evicted the US Navy from its base in Subic Bay, he had not been surprised when the Japanese voted to send American ships sailing from the majority of their bases as well.

He had been against the reduction of American forces in Asia. Singapore was one of the few countries outside Taiwan which still welcomed American ships. New Zealand's historic ban on nuclear ships had come as no surprise, back then, to the American people, but what had shocked them most was Indonesia's recent insistence that US submarines, which had enjoyed undetected passage through their waters since 1965, were no longer permitted to transit below the surface.

The President had always expected the West to experience a downside to supporting the Indonesians' claim over international sea-routes through their waters. As American influence waned in Asia, so too did trading with those nations become more one-sided. He had been pressured into granting Most Favoured Nation status to just about every goddamn country in that part of the world. He was painfully aware that the United States needed the heavily populated markets of China and Indonesia to continue to stimulate its own domestic growth, a growth which, during his Administration, had slowed dangerously.

He had always believed that the United States would be unable to sustain the growth it enjoyed over the previous fifty years. Even with the implementation of the NAFTA agreements which had been expanded to provide his country access to most of the Americas, industrial growth had slowed. Having already recovered from near economic collapse less than a decade before, he was convinced that if the Asian power-houses continued their amazing advances, their success would be achieved at the expense of the West which, in his mind, meant the United States of America.

His initial reluctance to extend MFN status to these Third World countries had been viewed by his colleagues on Capitol Hill as a clear indictment of his inability to understand the commercial realities of global politics in the twenty-first century. But he knew that they were wrong. A blunt edged sword it might be, but he firmly believed that Most Favoured Nation status should be raised whenever the situation demanded his government bring pressure to bear on some of the more recalcitrant Asian leaders.

'How are the Australians positioned?' the President asked his old friend, Deakin.

'Well, understandably, they're not too happy with us either. Historically, they have always suffered from the 'yellow-peril' syndrome Down Under. Relations between Indonesia and Australia are on the mend, but there is still considerable tension between the two countries over what is happening with East Timor. In hindsight, I believe that we should never have pressured..,' he hesitated, searching for the man's name, '...ah, yes, Whitlam, I believe it was, that we should not have prevented the Australians from going into East Timor at that time.'

Deakin was objective enough to understand how the US Administration in 1975 had been swayed by the CIA to prevent the Australians from occupying the former colony, even though initial requests had originated from both the Timorese and the Indonesian President, Soeharto. He remembered how paranoid his government had been at the time. The Australian Government was led by a team of left-wing socialists, and there was just no way that the United States could accept a government sympathetic to America's enemies, gaining a foothold in what was obviously to be another socialist state.

Upon his appointment to State, which provided access to sensitive information buried by past Administrations over the years, Deakin was not surprised to discover how his country had influenced the outcome in Timor, and understood American fears. In the course of that one year, they had lost Vietnam to the communists; New Guinea had become independent, Pol Pot had started on his path of genocide, Indira Ghandi had declared a state of emergency in her country, and Indonesia had been encouraged to invade East Timor. It was obvious to Deakin, as he read the confidential memos of that time, that his government feared Soviet intervention as far south as Dili. He agreed that the premise was probable; look at how the Russians had poured into Vietnam filling the vacuum created by the American withdrawal!

As Australia was considered pro-socialist, his predecessors had decided that it would be in American interests to have Soeharto's Indonesia take over the small colony, rather than have another Cuban-styled missile crisis develop in the centre of one of the world's richest oil and gas deposits. These thoughts passed through his mind before he replied to the President's question.

'I fear that the Australians believe that we would never honour our undertakings to come to their assistance in the event of hostilities threatening their shores. In short, they believe that we would simply walk away from our obligations under the ANZUS Treaty, should conflict erupt between them and, say, Indonesia.' General Davis interrupted him immediately.

'That may very well be so, but it was the Kiwis who first weakened that Treaty by banning visiting American warships!'

The DIA director nodded in agreement. 'The Aussies don't seem to understand exactly where they're going with their regional alliances. First they sign an enduring defense agreement with Indonesia, which states that each would come to the aid of the other in the event of external forces threatening regional stability, and then they embark on a programme of destabilising their relationships by permitting this fellow...' the DIA director referred to his notes, '..Xanana Soares to establish his own anti-Indonesian platform right on Jakarta's doorstep. The Australians have brought a great deal of what has happened recently on their own heads. Before you know it, they'll have dragged us into open conflict with the Indonesians, and that might just be the end of American influence in Asia.' The President looked at the director and then over to Deakin.

'Is there no way we can diffuse the situation then?' he asked. Deakin was about to answer when General Davis spoke.

'The Joint Chiefs recommend that we demonstrate to our allies that we are still very much committed to an American presence in the area by positioning the Seventh Fleet in Singapore on a more permanent basis. This would also send a clear signal to India and China that we are prepared to prevent further territorial expansion, and might mollify the Indonesians and Australians.' Deakin glanced over at the general, and nodded his support for the suggestion, particularly having considered the alternatives.

Positioning an American fleet in Darwin would, he believed, only antagonise the Indonesians further, and would not necessarily discourage the Indian Navy from moving across towards the Malay Peninsula; nor might it prevent further acquisitions by China, in the South China Sea. He had seen a copy of the Sultan of Brunei's written appeal to London, requesting British forces to be sent to the area, in answer to China's provocative annexation of the nearby islands.

Deakin had anticipated his associates' reaction to having any British forces back in the area. It had taken decades to displace the Commonwealth's influence, and the United States was not keen to have them restore any military presence in Asia.

'I would support the Joint Chiefs' suggestion, Mr President,' Deakin offered. 'I'm certain that the Singaporeans would welcome the idea.'

'I'm not so certain,' the DIA director challenged 'They would want to appear neutral.'

'Not so,' Deakin argued, 'we have sent the US Navy in before, and they were only too happy to have our fleet stationed there.' The director knew that the Secretary for State was referring to an earlier American plan to invade Indonesia through Sumatra, back in the chaotic 'fifties', during the times when most of his fellow countrymen still believed their government's propaganda that communists lurked behind every closed door.

'Yes, but the Singaporeans were under threat from the Indonesians then. Regional politics have changed dramatically, as you would well know,' the director added, knowing that his snide barb would not go unnoticed, 'and most Singaporeans would not entertain antagonising the Chinese either. What makes you believe that the Indonesians would not feel as threatened with our ships sitting in Singapore as they would if we positioned the Seventh Fleet in Darwin?'

'Because Indonesia has a substantial stake in Singapore, and they are politically astute enough to understand that any threat to Singapore would result in an immediate response from the British and American forces.' Deakin looked across the room at the man who would make the final decision for them all. 'Mr President, I reaffirm my support for moving our fleet into Singapore.' The President seemed pleased that the Joint Chiefs and State had taken similar positions. He looked at the others and raised his eyebrows.

'Gentlemen?' he asked the two directors.

'I'd go with that, Mr President,' the DIA Director said. He was closely allied to the Joint Chiefs and would follow his superiors' recommendations. The President nodded, satisfied that the decision had already been made for him. He then looked for the CIA's response, hoping for unanimity from his advisers.

'I would agree providing we keep other options open, Mr President.' The others all glanced in his direction. They knew what he meant. The CIA would want to maintain all of its covert actions, regardless of where the Seventh might be based. The President's face broke into a partial smile indicating that he was pleased his most senior advisers had reached consensus.

'Well, that's it then, gentlemen,' he said, rising from his chair and moving around to the front of the historic desk. 'All we have to do now is convince the Singaporeans that it is not our intention to stay forever,' he half-joked, but the others present knew that this would not be an easy task. They were a sophisticated people with a history of strong leadership, and would do only what was best for Singapore.

He held his hand up motioning for Allan Cox to remain. It was apparent from his earlier reaction that something else was troubling the intelligence chief, and the President thought a few minutes alone might clear the air. The other advisers shook their leader's hand and departed, leaving the CIA director alone with the President.

'Well, Allan, you had very little to say - weren't you happy with the decision?'

'Mr President, it's only a short-term solution,' he replied.

'What's on your mind, then?' The President propped himself up against the desk and crossed his legs, the palms of his hands resting on the structure behind.

'I still don't agree with the Joint Chiefs' appraisal. My money is still on India making a major move, one that will firmly ensconce them in the heart of things territorially speaking. I believe that they will go to war in support of territorial expansion and I do not believe reports that their army has not been mobilised.' The President thought about what the director suggested, and waited for him to continue. General Davis had not mentioned this possibility. *Was it an oversight?*

'Whatever they're up to, its real, and it's going to happen soon. As for the Chinese acting in concert with the Indians, we would be foolish not to prepare for such an eventuality, or at least work towards disrupting their developing alliance in other ways than via State.' He looked at the President feeling that he might have gone too far, but they had enjoyed a number of frank discussions in the past, and he knew that his leader valued his opinions.

'I think we have lost the plot, Mr President,' he said, not wishing to alarm, but sensing that what he was about to say might just do that. 'I think the Indian Government is most definitely preparing to go to war.' For a moment the director thought he could hear distant traffic outside, but he knew that this was not possible. Double-glazed bullet-proof windows and other security measures made this room a cocoon.

'We don't have anything to support that; you heard the others,

Allan.'

'Yes, sir, I did. But I'm not convinced that the Chinese are not acting in concert with India.

'Do you have anything which the others have not had access to?' the President asked, knowing that this would be so. Having being appointed to office, he had learnt to accept the idiosyncrasies of government, dealing with the jealously guarded power-bases which permeated all levels of each Administration, although he had been surprised to discover the competitiveness which existed between the intelligence agencies. The President waited.

'I do, Sir, but it's not directly related to today's discussions. There is something brewing on the Indonesian front, which has only just come to our attention.' The President accepted this would most likely be untrue; the CIA would have squatted on any new information until an opportunity to reveal whatever it was presented itself. 'I have not briefed the other departments as we still have no confirmation that the source, or the information, is reliable.' The President became impatient with the evasive ploy.

'Allan?' he insisted, and the director knew he would have to reveal his information prematurely. He hesitated, collecting his thoughts.

'I would hope that the President understands that this information has not, in any way, been circulated to the other agencies, including the Joint Chiefs.' It was meant as a question and the President nodded in affirmation.

'Go on,' he ordered, sensing that he might later regret his decision to push the director to reveal all. He had learned early in his political career that knowledge was not always power, that there was much that was better left unsaid. He waited, his impatience growing.

The director sighed, knowing what impact his words would have. He looked directly into the politician's eyes and said, 'I believe that Indonesia is less than a year away from having sufficient material to produce its own nuclear device.' He paused, expelling a heavy sigh, before continuing. 'If I am able to substantiate the information we have received, then the world will have its newest member in the Nuclear Club ready to go, possibly even before the end of this year. The President came upright from his relaxed position, stunned by the alarming news.

'Are you sure?' he demanded, shocked at the implications.

'Reasonably certain. We'll know more in a few weeks,' he said, in a tired voice. The President moved back behind his table and sat, his face creased with worry.

'Sonofabitch!' he said, glaring at the bearer of bad news. He crossed his arms and leaned back into the heavy, leather-covered chair. 'Sonofabitch!' he said again, as if the other man was no longer there. The director stood, uncomfortably, wishing he had not been pressed for the information until he was absolutely certain of its validity. He remained standing, waiting for the further response. 'And how do they intend delivering this weapon which they may or may not have in the near future?'

'With an Indonesian missile,' he answered, quietly. He watched the look of disbelief grow as the President's mouth fell open.

'The hell you say!' he exploded, jumping to his feet as the blood pumped from his face. 'You confirmed that goddamn project had been discontinued!' he accused, loudly, almost losing control. 'For chrissakes, Allan, are you now telling me that the Indons have resurrected that project alone, without the Japs, and without our knowledge?' he asked in disbelief.

'Indications are...' Director Cox started.

'To hell with your goddamn indications,' the President roared, 'just talk straight!'

'Mr President, I have already given this the highest priority. One of the reasons we believe that China is lining up with India is because they, too, are aware of Indonesia's Bandung project. Beijing would not wish to see them armed with any rocket capacity, let alone ICBMs.'

'ICBMs! How did they manage to acquire the technology once the Japs withdrew? I thought we had put an end to all that?' the President asked, openly furious.

'This is why I believe the Chinese might be tempted to take advantage of any move the Indians have planned. The ICBM technology has been handed to them by our old friends in Iraq,' Allan Cox admitted.

'What!'

'Iraq was given the technology for the Chinese *Long March* series when Beijing was desperate to avoid disruption to its Middle East oil supplies. It obviously worked. Iraq has developed its rocket industry well beyond that of its *Scud* capabilities as we discovered during *Desert Storm*.'

'How did Jakarta access the technology?' spluttered the President.

'Not difficult, when you consider the religious affiliations. We shouldn't lose sight of the fact that Indonesia is the world's largest Moslem society. The two countries are not just tied together because of their oil reserves.'

'Why would the Iraqis inform the Chinese?' the President asked, already aware of the answer. 'Why would they do that?'

'We don't know, sir,' the CIA director responded, lamely.

'And how far advanced are the Indonesians with this project?'

'We expect to have confirmation within two weeks. This I can promise you, Mr President. Whatever the Indonesians have hidden away in their Bandung Research center will not be secret for long. We have men on the ground as we speak, and they are doing everything possible to infiltrate their security.'

'Why didn't you come to me before, Allan?' the President asked, sharply. The intelligence chief gathered his thoughts before responding.

'There seemed little point in coming to you with something the Agency couldn't substantiate. You would most probably have ordered us to determine the veracity of our intelligence, which is what we are doing, now, as we speak.' He drew in a deep breath, then continued.

'Give me the two weeks I need to establish beyond doubt that we have something to really concern us, before throwing it open for general discussion. I'm not even convinced that the credibility of our sources in Indonesia has not been tainted by earlier misinformation.'

He watched the President's blood pressure ease slowly, as he lowered himself back into his chair. The President fell silent, his mood deliberative as he considered what he had just learned. If the information was correct, this would change his country's entire perspective in relation to America's position in Asia. He needed to think. And he needed to take time alone to decide what action would be necessary should Indonesia's nuclear capabilities be confirmed.

He swore under his breath. The United States was expected to play the role of International Policeman again! When the Japanese had withdrawn from their earlier commitments to the Indonesians, the Presidential advisers had all agreed that the development of Indonesia's future delivery systems had been successfully frustrated.

Angry to the pit of his stomach, he dismissed the director, having instructed him to mobilise all efforts to determine the accuracy of his intelligence. The President then called his Chief of White House Staff to cancel all appointments for the coming days. He would go to Camp David, alone. He had some thinking to do. Once there was evidence confirming or repudiating the world's largest Moslem nation's entry into the Nuclear Club, there was the possibility that the world might soon see a joint Sino-Indian effort to dismantle the Indonesian Republic.

* * * * * *

Federal Reserve Offices

James remained still like some unsmiling Buddha as he listened to the Federal Reserve Bank official's critical comments. James had never enjoyed visiting the Capital; he had found Washington to be cold, and most of the people unreceptive. Most, that is, with the exception of his powerful friends on Capitol Hill.

He glanced sideways at his brother, pleased that Denny, too, was not showing signs of distress under pressure. After years of dealing with government officials, he was not at all concerned with the summons to appear before this officer for preliminary discussions regarding the Lims' offshore banking activities. Had the veiled threat been delivered whilst the former President still occupied the White House, James knew that the official sitting across from him at that moment, would never have been permitted to summon them to Washington D.C.

James Salima remained undisturbed by the innuendo and veiled threats, believing that this further attempt by the Federal Reserve Bank officials to solicit access to records of their dealings in China would simply disappear once he had spoken to the White House aide.

During the meeting, James suggested that the government officer speak directly to the bank's lawyers, insisting that neither he nor his brother, Denny, had committed any offence, that their relationship with the Chinese shipping line and its principals was entirely legal.

The investigator in charge did not react well, visibly annoyed by James's reference to the Lims' powerful connections. The meeting lasted less than fifteen minutes, after which James and Denny Salima departed, leaving the frustrated officer to inform his superiors that he had been unsuccessful in his attempt to pressure the Lim brothers into disclosing more information than the United States Government was, in fact, entitled to. A copy of the official's report was forwarded to the Director, Central Intelligence Agency, where this was added to the substantial file maintained on the Lims' activities in America, and their growing role in providing conduits for the flow of Western technology into Communist China.

Chapter 23

General Kumar — India

The army's Protocol Officer informed General Rahul Kumar, Chief of Staff of India's Armed Forces, that the Prime Minister had been taken to hospital and that his condition was considered most serious. Army security had phoned from the hospital, only minutes before. Kumar had wasted no time covering the short distance to where the Prime Minister lay dying, his staff car ploughing dangerously through the congested streets between army headquarters and the hospital in record time. Upon arrival, he had marched directly into the building where he was expected, and taken immediately to the Prime Minister's side.

'He doesn't have long, General,' the doctor advised, in a hushed tone, hurrying alongside the country's most senior military officer, whose strides caused him almost to run to keep pace. They approached the intensive care unit where Vijay rested, security officers standing guard on both sides of the door leading into the room, their faces reflecting the seriousness of the situation.

The doctor signalled for the nurses to permit Kumar a few moments with the failing leader. He was heavily sedated and there was nothing more they could do to make Vijay's last moments any more comfortable. The sister in charge bowed her head sadly, fighting back the tears.

'General,' was all she said, acknowledging the army officer, then moving away from where Vijay lay drifting in and out of consciousness.

The general looked down at the Prime Minister. He moved closer and nodded at the second nurse as she moved from her bedside seat, leaving the two great men alone. The doctor followed the women outside and stood, waiting, between the guards.

Kumar placed his left arm on the bed, and rested his hand on the dying man's arm. Vijay's eyelids fluttered, then suddenly opened. Then, as if nothing out of the ordinary had taken place, the Indian Prime Minister smiled, totally at peace with the world. He had little time left, but at least he was no longer in pain.

'Oh, you're here,' the dying leader said, feeling the other man's hand on his arm. He felt the warmth and, with great difficulty, smiled. 'I didn't think I would see you again.'

'You should just lie there and rest,' Kumar said, stricken by the moment. He had never been close to the Prime Minister; they had never been friends. Their lives had caused them to follow different paths, often bringing them into conflict with each other. To Kumar, this person who lay dying before him was not just Vijay Rakesh, but India's Prime Minister and, although he personally had little affinity with the man, he respected him for the office he represented.

'Come closer,' the man in the bed whispered hoarsely. Kumar leaned forward, his hand still on Vijay's arm, feeling bone through the thin hospital gown. 'You must not tell Kumar,' the Prime Minister said, his voice barely audible as he fought to breathe.

Rahul Kumar frowned, then moved his hand slightly. The man was bordering on delirium, the general could tell. He looked over his shoulder but the nurse and doctor stood with their backs to the glass-panelled door.

'It's all right, I'm here,' he said, softly. Vijay's arm moved slightly, and found the general's hand. He squeezed, but there was little strength left in his fingers. Kumar heard him wheeze, and leaned ever closer in order to hear the dying man. He felt Vijay's feeble attempt to squeeze his hand again and he waited, patiently, knowing that the end must be near.

'The.. army.. must..not.. be involved, Imran,' he whispered. Kumar looked at the frail man lying before him. He was puzzled by what he thought he'd heard.

'It's all right, Vijay,' he said, kindly, but curious as to what the man had meant. *Had he said not to tell Kumar?*

'Imran,' the voice called, even more faintly then before. Kumar knew there was little time left. He listened closely as Vijay spoke, his words forming slowly as he struggled to give his dear friend his last instructions. The doctor peered through the door to see if he was needed, and observed that General Rahul Kumar was still with the dying man. He felt a sense of pride as he quietly observed two of India's most powerful men together. One dying, one comforting the other. The nurse caught his eye and the doctor merely shook his head sadly. It would be all over, soon. Several other senior officials hurried in, but the doctor raised his hands and indicated that they were too late. He gestured for them to wait, quietly, for a few moments longer.

The corridor outside where Vijay lay dying became hushed, as those present felt the terrible loss which was about to descend upon them and their country. He may not have been cherished by all, but those who waited outside his room knew that, with Vijay's passing, the man who had worked so tirelessly for the country he loved would be greatly missed.

Kumar remained still, his head close to the Prime Minister's as he listened to the incoherent words trip slowly from Vijay's lips. He was stunned by what he heard, tempted to discount what the man had said in his sedated state. Finally, he heard a soft rattle in the throat and Vijay's spirit departed this world. Kumar rose slowly from the bedside. He looked down at the man's peaceful face. Then he turned, his face grim, and marched determinedly away from the smell of death.

* * * * * *

Centre for Strategic Studies, New Delhi

General Rahul Kumar stepped out of the BMW and moved to climb the steps into the building which housed the Centre. As he attempted to do so, his path was blocked by a row of beggars crowding the steps.

'Get away with you all, or I will give you a bloody hiding,' he challenged officiously, while rocking his head from side to side in the habitual manner of his people. He was in a particularly foul mood, and the beggars must have sensed this, scurrying away quickly, missing limbs and other handicaps in no way impeding their escape. Kumar looked up, sharply, as the portal guards appeared and saluted their unexpected visitor.

India's army Chief of Staff arrogantly touched the brim of his cap with the tip of his baton and stormed through, as the guards jumped forward to open the glass doors obstructing his entry. The general marched further into the building, ignoring startled looks as he continued through the maze of corridors, making his way up to the executive offices on the second level. He continued down the hallway to the door marked 'Officer-in-Charge' and, without hesitating to knock, turned the knob angrily and barged in.

Dr Imran Malhotra looked up in surprise, but made no attempt to rise. He had occupied the Centre's senior chair for more than eight years and had seen such intimidating displays before.

'Good morning, General,' Malhotra said, his voice in no way betraying how he resented the man's arrogance. 'Please take a seat if you wish, or will you not be staying?' he said.

'I will not be bloody staying,' the officer responded, tempted to whack the man sitting before him with the swagger-stick, just to teach him some respect. His eyes narrowed as he struggled to control his temper.

'Doctor, I demand to know why your recommendations regarding India's forward strategy were not first cleared through me!' Imran Malhotra was taken aback. *Could Kumar be possibly referring to the East Indonesian strategy?* Caught off-guard, he struggled for a response. He looked at the volatile man standing before him and knew, immediately, that Kumar had discovered something concerning the navy's proposed expedition to Timor.

Malhotra guessed from the general's presence, and his reaction, that he was obviously not aware of the overall strategy, otherwise he would be banging his stick on the Prime Minister's desk, and not his. He decided to be evasive until he learned just how much Kumar knew.

'The answer is quite simple, General, because the Prime Minister insisted that all communications and reports go directly to him before being viewed by others.' He looked at the intimidating figure before him. Had the situation not been as serious, Imran Malhotra would have enjoyed the general's discomfort. His face clouded, as if he were about to suffer an apoplectic fit.

'You have not made any friends in the military today, Doctor,' Kumar barked, his voice carrying through the thinly partitioned walls, where anxious staff wondered whom they might call should the general become violent. 'I am here to warn you that if you persist in keeping the Armed Forces ignorant of what transpires between this Centre and the Prime Minister's office, then you will find that your future will be very cloudy, indeed!' he warned. Dr Malhotra sighed.

'General, do not threaten me. I am the appointed Head of this Centre. I will do as I am instructed by the Prime Minister. I do not take orders from you, neither do I take orders from others in India's military. If you have not noticed, General, I am a civilian. Please now leave, I find your behaviour totally inappropriate and unacceptable.' Imran Malhotra remained seated as the army Chief of Staff glared furiously. He worried that he might have gone too far. The tall man had removed the baton from under his arm, and was tapping his empty hand with the end of the rod.

General Kumar was most surprised that Imran Malhotra was unaware of what had transpired over the past hour. *My God, he thought suddenly, Malhotra doesn't even know that Vijay is dead!*

He knew of their relationship, which only added to his surprise. No doubt efforts had been made to contact Malhotra but, for one reason or another, he had not been informed of the seriousness of the Prime Minister's condition. Kumar knew that official notification of Vijay's death would not be made public for some hours. The military would need to position itself first, in anticipation of civil unrest. He decided to let the man before him discover the news for himself.

'We are all in this together,' Kumar said. 'You would do well to remember that it will be the army, not the bureaucrats, who will be called upon to make the most sacrifices.' The doctor became concerned. *How much did Kumar know?*

'I believe that you mean, the Armed Forces, General, of which the army is but one component,' Malhotra argued, intent on not permitting the man bully him any further. 'As for service to one's country, I, as have many others in similar civilian positions, have devoted my life to serving India. So please do not talk about who has made sacrifices and who has not.'

The general's temper was dangerously close to spilling over. Malhotra could not recall ever having seen such a display by an officer before. Suddenly, there was a blur of movement as Kumar's hand whipped through the air, slamming his baton down furiously on the desk.

'Damn you!' the general yelled, 'damn you to hell!' with which,

he turned and stormed out of the Centre. Malhotra's staff heard
the general leave, and waited until the sounds of his boots had
disappeared before one of them crept cautiously into their chief's
office. Imran Malhotra waved the man away, telling him to close
the door. For a while he sat deep in thought. Concerned that he
had not heard the end of General Rahul Kumar, Imran picked up
his phone and asked to be connected to the Prime Minister's personal assistant. It was then he discovered that the lines from his
office were out of order, for the fifth time in that week. Frustrated
by his country's deteriorating infrastructure, Imran knew that it
would be best for him to visit his old friend's office personally, and
some minutes later, followed the general out of the Centre.

When Dr Imran Malhotra discovered that India's Prime Minister, Vijay Rakesh, had passed away hours before, and that General
Kumar had been in attendance, he panicked, guessing then, how
Kumar came to know of their secret Timor strategy. *How much did
the general know*? he worried. Imran called Admiral Gopal, and together they went in search of the Deputy Prime Minister.

* * * * * *

United States Embassy, New Delhi

'What do you think?' The question was asked by Ralph
Davidson, the Defense Liaison Officer for the DIA. He chewed on
the end of his ball-point, a habit which had only developed since
joining the Agency.

'I think that Kumar is a very dangerous man, that's what I think,'
the CIA station chief replied. Davidson glanced at the other man
and wished he could read his thoughts. He had never been comfortable sharing intelligence with these agents; as far as he was
concerned, it was too much of a one-way street.

'Did you recommend that we run with him?' he asked. The intelligence chief removed his feet from the Defence Liaison Officer's desk, flicked the toothpick he had been playing with into the
waste basket, and stretched.

'I don't see that we have much choice.' He yawned. The briefing had continued through the night. He checked his watch and

saw that he had missed breakfast in the embassy canteen.

'Let's face it,' he said, 'there aren't too many pro-American leaders in this neck of the woods.' Davidson observed that the other man had already conceded that General Rahul Kumar was likely to become India's next Prime Minister, or President, or whatever. He had never really understood how a country could have both, each elected, and often from different political leanings.

'They'll call it a *coup*,' Davidson suggested. He too felt tired from the marathon discussions. The Ambassador had chaired the meeting, replaying the taped session with General Kumar, India's army Chief of Staff.

'The general says if he calls a State of Emergency, this would give him time to prepare for an election. Where have we heard *that* before?' he asked, with an appropriate sarcasm. The phone rang and Davidson answered.

'Let's go,' he said, wearily, rising to his feet, 'the Ambassador wants us all back, now.' The station chief seemed surprised. He too rose slowly to his feet and tugged at the knot in his tie. 'Seems he has a response already.' The men wandered out of Davidson's office, down the hall though the security gates, and into the East Wing. They were ushered into the Ambassador's office, where they joined the other senior advisers. Davidson looked around at the small group, noticing how exhausted they all appeared.

'We have a response from State, gentlemen,' the Ambassador began, raising the communication he held for all to see. 'The Secretary has advised that, after due consultation with the President and his advisers, we are to make ourselves available to General Rahul Kumar when the time arrives. We are, under no circumstances, to openly support any action which may be interpreted by others as an American commitment to provide for the General's successful attempt to seize power.'

The Ambassador finished reading Washington's response, and remained discussing the situation with his advisers. At noon, he left the Embassy to attend a luncheon being held in honour of the acting Prime Minister, knowing that he would most probably be required to repeat the performance for his successor in the not too distant future.

Chapter 24

Washington — CIA and Michael

Michael returned the file marked '*Indonesia - Rama Nuclear Power Plants*' to Central Registry, checked that the receiving clerk had signed his name off correctly, then went up to the Director's office as instructed.

'Well, what do you think they're up to?' the director asked. He believed he already knew. It was confirmation that he now required.

'They obviously have the capacity to produce sufficient material. It would be difficult for them to disguise what they're doing, though. I read that two of the NPPs will remain under American management, so I don't see any difficulty there. As for the other two enterprises, they are also subject to IAEA inspection. Assuming that the inspectors are doing their jobs, and management teams have not been compromised, then it would be extremely difficult for the Indonesians to remove sufficient quantities of fuel without raising suspicions.'

'What about the Fast Breeder Reactor, *Rama II* ?' Michael was prepared for this question.

'Well, access for inspection has been denied. That's sufficient justification for us to believe that they are most definitely planning to remove fuel. Let's see,' Michael said, referring to notes, 'Rama II's reactor would have commenced operations with just under five thousand kilos of uranium. The fast breeder process would produce around three hundred and fifty kilos of surplus Plutonium-239 within eight months.' He looked at the director to ensure that his superior understood. Satisfied, he then continued.

'It would be most unlikely that they would play with their fuel and commence extracting plutonium within, say, a month. Operational staff would realize what was going on immediately. Also, this would be terribly inefficient. The three hundred plus kilos of 'surplus' plutonium would be distributed throughout the core and, to extract it, you must remove, dissolve and process the entire core. It would make more sense to have some of the plant supervisors orchestrate the removal as a normal part of core operations; that way, the plutonium could be siphoned off during processing. They could simply claim processing inefficiencies to account for missing a few kilos at a time.

'Normally, plutonium is accounted for in gram increments, so you can easily see just how difficult it would be to disguise the removal of the required amount. There are many other ways they could camouflage their activities, such as doctoring instrument readings to show that neutron flux was lower than expected, therefore producing less plutonium than anticipated. The International Atomic Energy Agency has identified most of the covert practices rogue operators could employ.'

'As you say, access has already been denied by the Indonesian operators. How much would they need to produce, if that is their intention?'

'Not much,' Michael replied, 'they would probably need about thirty kilos to make a decent weapon. It would not be in the megaton range, but sufficient to destroy a city.'

'How would they hide thirty kilos?' the director asked.

'The density of plutonium for this configuration is such, the entire mass would only be about two litres in size.' Michael saw the surprise and smiled. 'Not that I would recommend it, but you could just about carry it around in a container the size of a shoe box.' The director thought about this.

'Satellites could identify such a supply without too much difficulty,' he stated.

'Sure, but they would be unlikely to leave it lying around. My bet is, if they are producing, there would be an underground storage facility to prevent prying eyes from discovering its existence.' The director understood. The Agency had suspected that Japan might also be disguising its own surplus production, but had been unable to identify where the plutonium might be stored. The IAEA had free access to all of the Japanese Fast Breeder Plants and had not once identified any violations to the International Code.

'Then there is nothing for it but to press for access to *Rama II* and take a peek inside their plant. I'm surprised that our friends have been unable to penetrate the Indonesian operation. Having a *friendly* inside the plant would certainly remove any doubt.' Michael knew that he was referring to the CIA. He had never understood how two such similar agencies, both with their own national interests at heart, had managed to generate so much antagonism towards each other.

'We will have to come up with something, soon. Your suggestion to visit is appropriate, Michael. We'll send you over with IAEA credentials. I want you to build your visit around the two American operated plants. In the meantime, we'll twist a few more arms about visiting *Rama II*.' Michael nodded, and rose to leave.

'I'll set up a schedule for your approval,' he said, 'while I'm sifting through the rest of the files relevant to Indonesia.' He then left and returned to Central Registry where he withdrew the first of thirty-seven folders, all related to his brief, and settled down in one of the reading rooms for the day. Each time he finished a file, Michael would return this and withdraw another, continuing the process until he had read more than a dozen. It was approaching early evening when he suddenly sat up, and whistled.

'You crafty old devil!' he said, aloud. The file he had opened was entitled *Indonesia - Rama V - Corporate Details*. Michael sat there staring at the photographs of the principal shareholders and directors of the *Nasihat Corporation*. Memories of his childhood flooded back as the familiar, boyish face stared back at him, almost mockingly. He slapped his leg and laughed, remembering how this man had taken him sailing around the bay during his infrequent visits and, during other opportunities, had taught him how to handle himself on the tennis courts.

Michael was carried back in time to when the loneliness of life without a father would immediately be forgotten whenever this man arrived. He often stayed with Michael and his mother when visiting Melbourne, and always brought with him an atmosphere of bonhomie and excitement.

He looked at the photograph again, then read the biographical data which followed. Michael was surprised to see cross-references to data banks he had not come across before, and noted these for later. Then he settled down and slowly examined the rest of the relevant information. Twenty minutes passed, after which Michael closed the file, deep in thought. He would seek this man's assistance to visit the *Rama II* plant. It was obvious from the file that his mother's old friend had a peripheral relationship with the Indonesian Nuclear Power Plant operators, being a senior director of the *Nasihat Corporation*, which operated *Rama V*. Convinced that he might now have found a way to penetrate the inaccessible plant, Michael took the file back to Central Registry, then returned to his office where he placed a call to Murray Stephenson, in Indonesia.

* * * * * *

Visakhapatnam Naval Base, East Coast of India

In the week following Vijay Rakesh's death, Admiral Krishna Gopal returned to his Eastern Command Headquarters, in Visakhapatnam, and continued with his preparations to take the Indian Navy on its scheduled exercises in the Indian Ocean, which would precede the goodwill visit to New Guinea. He, and the other senior officials, had reached an accommodation with General Kumar. They expected that the acting Prime Minister would be confirmed in his position before the end of that week, after which he would take Vijay's place at the Bali Summit.

Admiral Gopal was indeed proud of the role he had been selected to play in India's future. He had been deeply saddened by the loss of his dear friend, Vijay, but his concerns following the Prime Minister's death had been directed towards the implementation of the strategies formulated under Vijay's leadership.

Once he had received the acting Prime Minister's assurance that he would support the daring move as vigorously as his predecessor, Admiral Gopal had wasted little time returning to his operational command on India's eastern seaboard.

He had personally co-ordinated the selection of ships to accompany his armada. Gopal had ordered two *Rajput* class destroyers from his Western Command bases in Lakshadweep and Karwar, and another from Goa, to join his convoy where they would gather, off the Maldives. The admiral had also decided to increase the number of frigates to twelve, including the three *Godavari* class FFHs, as these were equipped with Sea King helicopters.

He drew these from the Southern Command where five corvettes had already been stationed in preparation for the naval exercise. He had considered increasing the submarine fleet's complement to twelve, but finally elected to leave three of the older *Kursura* class SSs behind in the Visakhapatnam base. Gopal's armada would further consist of two aircraft carriers, including the pride of his fleet, the *INS Indira Gandhi*.

Admiral Gopal smiled as he considered the naval staffing levels. India's Navy had been boosted to almost one hundred thousand, which included ten thousand fleet air arm and marine personnel. During the previous years, his navy had seen considerable growth in its numbers and equipment, and could now boast some of the most sophisticated weaponry available. American, British and Russian equipment adorned the decks of his ships. Ten years before, the United States had sold his government two squadrons of Seahawks, complete with missile capability, and he was confident that these would be put to good use during the second phase of the exercise.

The smaller of his carriers was equipped mainly with Russian MiG 29s and, although these were becoming increasingly difficult to maintain due to the shortage of spare-parts, he believed that their helicopter and VTOL squadrons would provide the support required for the initial phase of the task force's assault. Then, of course, the eighty-thousand tonne aircraft carrier *INS Indira Gandhi*, pride of the Indian Navy, would stand by with its arsenal of modern aircraft, should these become necessary.

Admiral Gopal believed that the Indonesians would walk away from Timor once they realized that the Indian Navy had acted, albeit unilaterally, with world opinion supporting their action. The United Nations had voted in favour of an Indonesian withdrawal, and had been effectively ignored. He believed that the overall strategy would be successful, providing his country with an opportunity to expand its sphere of influence without too much resistance from its neighbours.

Krishna Gopal's mind turned to the army as he considered India's ultimate goal, the rich, fertile land of the under-populated Malay Peninsula. He was no longer concerned that General Kumar might obstruct their plans. It would not have been wise for the acting Prime Minister to consider replacing the army Chief of Staff, as they believed that Kumar's support within the army was far too strong for such a move. The confrontation which had followed Vijay's death-bed disclosure had been bitter indeed, resulting in a stand-off between the government supporters and General Kumar. The army Chief had intimated that he was of a mind to reveal Vijay's plan to the general public, but when he realised that few would believe that he had not, in any way, been involved in the planning, Kumar had rethought his position. Gopal was relieved that at least Kumar had given his assurance that he would not interfere.

They had agreed that, as the army was not to participate in the initial phase of the Timor strategy, then no blame could be attached to Kumar should the ambitious move fail. When they had discussed inviting the Chief of Air Staff to share their confidence, both Malhotra and the acting Prime Minister had opposed such a move, insisting that Air Marshall Gurege not be informed until the navy's mission could be considered a successful *fait accompli*. He would be briefed, finally, once Gopal's armada was positioned off Timor, and Xanana Soares had been safely placed in power.

The admiral was confident that with this initial success his faction would have little difficulty in encouraging others to follow. He believed that their support base would grow quickly, and loyalties would change. Malhotra had suggested that they be patient until this moment arrived, and only then consider removing the obstinate and pro-American Kumar, replacing him with one who would support the final phase of their strategy. They knew that their success in Timor could not be ignored by the army, who, together with India's impressive airforce of over one thousand aircraft, would be encouraged to occupy and control the northern corridors leading into the Malay Peninsula.

When the new borders were redrawn, India would have succeeded in occupying all the rich, fertile rice bowls of Western Malaysia. China would find little resistance when taking the resource rich areas of Eastern Malaysia and Brunei. Indonesia would no longer be in a position to prevent international shipping from passing through its sea lanes as long as the Indian Navy maintained its presence in East Timor and China controlled the South China Sea. Between the two nations, they would control all shipping though Asia, including that of Japan and Australia.

* * * * * *

The National Security Agency Director sat quietly as his driver turned into the White House gates and stopped. Guards moved across, checked through the windows, smiled, then saluted. As he was driven under the building, he could not help but think that the information he held in his hands alone, would be sufficient to silence critics of his agency's substantial, and undisclosed budget. But he knew that the sensitive documents would never be released for public consumption, as these would be destroyed once the President had read and understood their contents.

Through its supervision of the Defence Advanced Research Projects Agency (DARPA), the NSA has been able to create and install a sophisticated global communications system of computers, satellites, telecommunications devices and the latest surveillance technology. Every second of every day, twenty four hours a day, the NSA beats along, as its massive computer network hums almost silently, collecting, correlating, deciphering, analysing spysatellite imagery and other data, sifting through incredible volumes of wiretap and sensor material, as the never-ending flow continues from the most unlikely sources. This most secret premier cryptographic agency, derived huge financial and computer allocations directly from US military budgets.

The director arrived and was escorted directly to where the President waited. The American leader read through the classified material and handed these back to the NSA Chief.

'You really believe that the Chinese are preparing to move?' he asked, still not convinced that the increased signal traffic identified by the NSA's world-wide listening network had proven anything other than a substantial increase in telecommunication activity between the two nations.

'It's mainly military traffic, and our analysts believe that the Indian Navy is keeping the Chinese fully informed of whatever they're doing.'

'Wouldn't it just be possible that they don't wish to ruffle Chinese feathers?' the President asked, wishing it could really be as simple as he suggested.

'The Chinese don't play war games, Mr President,' he suggested. 'Communication traffic between the Chinese Southern, Eastern and

Northern Naval Commands has reached unprecedented levels. Satellite tracking has identified a concentration of activity running from Shanghai down to their ships stationed in the South China Sea. There has not, however, been any real change in their army's status. Our analysts agree that it is unlikely for China to make any further moves territorially, without mobilising its land forces. This is why we believe that we should expect to see such movement at any moment.'

'How much time do we have?' the President asked. The NSA Director had anticipated this question also.

'If what they have in mind is purely a naval action, then not much time at all. At best, probably a week to ten days for them to prepare. It would depend on what targets they had in mind.' The President thought about this, his concern causing the deep lines in his brow to deepen.

'And this would be Taiwan?' he asked, fearing the answer. The director shook his head.

'That would not account for the increased traffic between India and China. Beijing would not need to inform anyone if they intended moving against Taiwan; they would simply charge in and hope that we remained away from the conflict. There has been nothing to indicate any specific targets, or at least, not yet,' he answered, also concerned with his analysts' failure to interpret what the heavy COMINT traffic really meant.

The President remained silent, thinking through the possible scenarios developing on the other side of the world. He knew that there was little that could be done until further intelligence confirmed whatever the two governments were plotting together. He finished discussing the developments with the NSA Director who then left, promising to keep the White House informed as the situation changed. Then the President summoned William Deakin, his Secretary for State.

* * * * * *

Jakarta, Indonesia

The Vice President ate sparingly in the *Bapak's* presence. It had become a tradition for the President to preside over Saturday

390

dinners with all of his family in attendance. Even though Major General (retired) Sujono Diryo knew how the President doted on his favourite daughter, he felt ill at ease sitting alongside his wife at this command performance.

'Jono, you're not eating,' his mother-in-law scolded, playfully. He smiled and said nothing.

'Maybe he has been eating too well outside,' one of the President's sons quipped, bringing a scowl from his sister. There had been great consternation within the First Family when Sujono had unwisely become entangled in an extra-marital relationship involving a vivacious and well known Indonesian actress. The Capital had been a buzz with the gossip, as the most public affair continued. Those closest to Sujono had appealed for him to consider his position, while the beautiful starlet's friends applauded her audacious fling. Then, without warning, all levels of Jakarta's society were rocked when the girl had been discovered, murdered, on the back seat of her car.

Everyone believed they knew who was responsible for the star's death, but none even dared whisper, except in the privacy of their homes, that a jealous wife had issued the order. The President had been shielded from the sordid affair. The *Bapak* rarely read newspapers anymore, never listened to the news, and was almost entirely dependent on those around him to keep him informed as to what was happening in the capital and the world in general.

When gossip relating to the affair first broke, none dared mention such defamatory stories in the Indonesian press. In private, Indonesians jokingly referred to the torrid affair as *kumpul kerbo*, and were not overly critical of the Vice President, nor his reprehensible behaviour. The Australian press, however, had not been as reluctant to run the story. Editors exposed the affair in their tabloids, nation-wide.

The President's daughter had moved quickly, summoning the Commander of the Jakarta Garrison and soliciting his services. That evening, her husband's lover, one of Indonesia's more familiar screen idols, was stabbed to death and dumped unceremoniously on the back-seat of the car which the President's son-in-law had given to her just weeks before. The city's inhabitants mourned her death, but none dared come forward to identify her killers, or even suggest that an investigation take place to bring those responsible to trial. To do so would have been suicidal. The President's daughter glared at her brother for having made the remark.

'*Be careful of your mouth!*' Sujono's wife warned, waving her fork menacingly in her brother's direction. Her father had no idea whatsoever of his son-in-law's infidelity, and his daughter used this to keep Sujono in line. Although Indonesian Muslims were still entitled to take up to four wives, very few amongst the educated class continued to practice this right. When Sujono had learned of his lover's demise, he had known immediately who had been responsible. He accepted his loss quietly, relieved only that his wife had not discovered his other marital misdemeanours.

The President smiled at his family, pleased that they had all gathered together in his home again.

'*Sujono?*' he started, watching his daughter fill his son-in-law's plate with more *rendang* and *nasi*. He waved for her to stop, and she added another spoonful and smiled caringly. The servants were never permitted to serve the food on these occasions.

'*Sujono, is everything now in order with Bali?*' asked the *Bapak*. Sujono swallowed slowly. The President was referring to the Summit. For weeks there had been diplomatic wrangling over the dates, who should or should not attend, who would have seniority during the discussions, where they were going to stay, and so on. His hours were filled with endless messages and calls for which he, as Vice President, had become responsible. Then, having selected several dates for the venue, they had discovered that the Balinese calendar would clash with the Summit, and that *Hari Nyepi* would occur during the three-day conference.

Sujono knew that it would be unthinkable to expect the international leaders to be present in Bali while everything ground to a halt to celebrate the *Quiet* Day according to Balinese custom. He knew just how seriously the Balinese practised their customs, remembering that village police paraded around on that day, making sure tradition was observed by all. In the more isolated pockets of the tourist haven, Sujono knew that even generators were turned off for the day, cutting power in observance of the custom.

'*They have agreed to the dates as you requested, Pak,*' he answered. It had been decided that the Indian Prime Minister would preside over what the world press had hailed as the Bali Peace Summit, and South Africa, Australia and what was left of the ASEAN membership, had all agreed to the agenda.

The conference was being promoted as essential to restoring regional stability, although few outside Asia believed this would contribute in any significant way. A virtual trade war had broken out between Australia and its northern neighbours and, although the Indonesian sea lanes were strictly monitored by Indonesian warships, oil shipments continued to pass through the archipelago finding their way easily into China. The Japanese continued to enjoy unhindered passage of their vessels, their trade relationships with the Indonesians not at all diminished in importance in spite of the failed nuclear power plant co-operation agreement.

The Timor Shelf oil and gas concessions continued to feature as one of the stumbling blocks between Australia and its giant neighbour, and Indonesia's insistence that East Timor remain an integral part of the Republic was rapidly losing political support. Both Sujono and the President agreed that they had to at least appear responsive to their neighbouring nation's requests. ASEAN was in danger of losing more of its members, and the Palace knew that they needed more time to reposition themselves as a regional military power, believing that their Fast Breeder Plant and their secret installations in Bandung, once fully developed, would realize their dream for the Indonesian people.

'And Rama II?' the President asked. Sujono knew that the plant was on-line already, and the commissioning process complete. The President insisted that the plant's official inauguration should coincide with the Bali Summit. It made little difference to the plant's operation, one day being as acceptable as the next. The Vice President had been a regular visitor to the high-security operation; the plant's operation, although under Russian supervision, had fallen directly under his control.

The operating team had included a small number of Eastern Bloc technicians whose responsibility for training Indonesian engineers had all but been concluded. Sujono had to accept that there were not enough skilled Indonesian technicians to manage the facility effectively without the remaining Russian support. Sujono believed that he would require those foreign experts for no more than another year, after which the plant's operation would be totally under Indonesian management.

The one thousand hectare site had the finest security money

could buy. The troops employed had been specially trained for this duty and were paid handsomely, well in excess of their standard army pay. These soldiers had been hand-picked by officers loyal to him, officers who had been, in many cases, more senior when he had first caught the President's daughter's eye. Sujono glanced across the table at his wife, visualising how she would present in the following years. She was not an attractive woman. He had known many others whose temperament and beauty far exceeded the homely girl he had married, but none of these could give him the key to the power that would now most surely be his. He realized that his often, indiscreet and flirtatious behaviour could easily endanger his position, and that he should be far more circumspect in these liaisons if he wished to succeed.

* * * * * *

Sujono expected to be the next President of Indonesia. His father-in-law had all but served his two, five-year terms after challenging and winning leadership, then governing the country as Acting President for a number of years, before calling elections to legitimise his position in power.

When Sujono had been appointed to replace his ailing predecessor, he realized that the President was merely ensuring continuity of his own rule, expecting to govern in some defacto manner once his son-in-law had been elected. There was little doubt in his mind that this would be so, for Sujono had already secured the support of *Golkar,* the ruling party in government. There would be only minor opposition to his appointment, he knew. The President had seen to that, with the incarceration of most political opponents over the years, and a controlled press, there was rarely any visible dissent directed against the country's leadership.

Sujono accepted that his fortunes had changed primarily due to General Seda's demise. The powerful man's death had further exacerbated existing tensions between Australia and Indonesia, and had contributed to a breakdown in negotiations concerning the disputed Timor Shelf oil and gas concessions. There was little doubt in Sujono's mind that his circumstances could have been radically different had the powerful Seda not fallen victim to the incredible Canberra bombing. Seda had been mooted to fill the position of

Vice President; Sujono considered how fate had presented him with the opportunity, and how he had not hesitated to grasp the golden ring. Earlier in his career, his experience with the Japanese and knowledge of weaponry had made him an obvious choice, at least to General Seda, to control security at the Bandung Research center.

Sujono had become aware of the late general's association with the Japanese Military only during his tour as Defense Attaché in Tokyo. He had not realized, then, that Seda was grooming him to carry out Indonesia's secret research and development programme in conjunction with the Japanese. At the appropriate time, and prior to his appointment as Ambassador to Australia, Seda had Sujono recalled to Indonesia, where he had been appointed by Seda as Officer in Charge of the H-3B's joint development, under the auspices of what had formerly been known as the Habibie Aerospace Centre.

He had reported to Seda that it would be impossible to maintain secrecy regarding their project unless a dedicated location be built specifically for this purpose. Seda had not taken long to decide that the construction of a dual-purpose facility would be more appropriate, and that this should be located within reasonable access to Bandung. They had spent considerable time examining possible sites, finally agreeing that the most suitable location was that of an old Dutch gold mining concession, thirty kilometers from the provincial capital.

The secret installation demanded the most stringent security, and Sujono had successfully implemented procedures which had ensured that none outside a limited number of technicians and military personnel, would ever become aware of what really transpired in the research centre. Within months of his return from Japan, he had been promoted to Major General, and the President had been most pleased with his son-in-law's advancement.

* * * * * *

'You will both be in attendance for the inauguration?' he heard the President ask.

'Most certainly, Bapak,' he replied, dutifully. World attention would be focused on the Bali Summit, and the Palace had orchestrated for the *Rama II* commissioning ceremony to take place

during the formal gathering of world leaders. Sujono knew that the President had considered attending the plant's inauguration, but had accepted that protocol demanded his presence in Bali. Sujono understood that his leader had not been keen to go, annoyed at having been pressured into permitting the East Timorese refugee into Indonesia to attend the conference.

Sujono listened to the President's argument, that he had only agreed to Xanana's presence once he had been assured that his acquiescence would not be construed as acknowledgement of the legitimacy of the so-called government-in-exile.

'It will be a proud day for us all, Jono,' the President suggested, and Sujono understood precisely what was going through the *Bapak's* mind. While he was in Bali as Head of State, his daughter would be officiating alongside her husband, the Vice President, demonstrating the powerful grip the First Family maintained over the land. And Sujono knew that he was an integral part of that power, as long as he remained in favour. He looked across at his wife and, conscious that the President was watching them both closely, Sujono smiled lovingly at the President's daughter.

* * * * * *

Washington — the Oval Office

Secretary for State William Deakin remained expressionless, thinking, while opposite him the President waited, impatiently, tapping the desk with the *keris* shaped letter-opener, a gift from the Malaysian Ambassador to the First Lady some months before.

'I'm afraid it's time to decide just how far we wish to go,' Deakin finally said, referring to their earlier discussion. 'We seem to be rapidly running out of options.' He looked at his old friend and sympathised with his dilemma. The United States President would have to decide within days on one of two options. He could commit his country's forces to the Asian theatre and risk jeopardising American interests, or do nothing, thereby creating a military vacuum which would undeniably be filled by either India or China. It was imperative that the United States not lose access to the Ombar-Wetar Straits for its own national security and, they both believed, their Australian allies.

'Can we be certain that this General Kumar will not be in a position to gain control without the Indian Navy?' the President asked, fearing he already knew the answer. Deakin nodded, confirming his fears.

'Krishna Gopal is a dedicated naval officer, totally loyal to the new Prime Minister. It appears that it was Admiral Gopal who acted as Vijay Rakesh's emissary to China, before Vijay died. There is no love lost between Gopal and the Army, particularly Rahul Kumar. If the General is to be successful, he will need to have Gopal's ships return to their Indian bases where Kumar can seize control. Without the navy, he would be defeated.'

They had been caught by surprise when satellite intelligence from the NSA had alerted them to the Indian Navy's move. Throughout the week, as the armada had taken shape, the President's advisers had urged him to press the Singapore Government to accept the American Seventh Fleet's presence in their harbour. Diplomatic overtures had all but stalled; the Singaporeans were not convinced that the United States naval presence would please Jakarta, and had vacillated over the American request.

'How far south of Indonesia could they be at the time of the Summit?' The President had asked the question earlier when the Joint Chiefs had been present. It wasn't that he had forgotten, he merely required confirmation that the Indian Navy would still be sailing in international waters.

'Ten hour's steaming,' Deakin answered, 'less if they wished to split their convoy.' The President rested his chin on one hand, deep in thought. Within two weeks the Bali Summit would take place. India's goodwill naval visit to Papua New Guinea could not have been more poorly timed. It appeared that Port Moresby had been miffed when not included in the Bali forum.

The New Guinea Prime Minister had been easily persuaded to host the visit, expecting to distract world attention away from the Bali Summit. India's clever use of the opportunity to move its navy through international waters during such a sensitive period was, to say the least, provocative. The Americans had suggested to General Kumar that he take pre-emptive action, immediately, but he had refused to accelerate his original plan to move against the Indian leadership until the now confirmed Prime Minister was away, attending the Bali Summit.

'Do you agree with the NSA assessment?' the American leader asked. The President had insisted that all intelligence departments and the Joint Chiefs attend the earlier briefing. The Oval Office had been filled with his advisers from the CIA, NSA, DIA, the Joint Chiefs and Deakin, from State.

'We can't afford to ignore the intelligence. China obviously understands the opportunity created by India. They might just use the moment to swing across, while our attention has been distracted, and hit Taiwan,' he said, disappointed that the State Department had missed all the apparent signs over the past weeks. There had almost been a sense of apathy in relation to the Taiwan-China question. They accepted that it would only be a matter of time before China used force to occupy the island, even though earlier tactics of intimidation had failed.

Taiwan's economy continued to outstrip its neighbour's, sending the Taiwanese reserves to a record high of one hundred and seventy billion dollars which, ironically, presented the industrialised nation as an even greater prize than before.

The President remained deep in thought, depressed by events which had worsened over past weeks, threatening Asia's stability and America's markets. Then there was the problem of Australian security, and the ANZUS pact. China, he knew, might consider the under-populated country and its abundant resources as imperative to her future survival. Australia and the United States continued to enjoy more than adequate mineral reserves well beyond that of their envious Asian neighbours.

A world dominated in the East entirely by China and India occupied his thoughts, and the President wished he could escape, once again, to deliberate more on the question in the comfort of Camp David. Time constraints, he knew, would not permit such luxury. He had to sanction the Joint Chief's recommendations or find an alternative solution to sending American troops back into Asia.

He recalled the last occasion when an American President had entertained such a commitment. The United States had lost fifty thousand lives, and the communists had swallowed all of Vietnam. No, he would not send American men and women to the defense of another corrupt Asian government. There would have to be another solution. He looked across at his friend and was comforted by the knowledge that Deakin would remain loyal, regardless of the decisions he might take. He rubbed his weary face and sighed.

'I don't think I could support the Joint Chiefs' option,' was all he said. Deakin looked at the President, understanding his reasons for taking this decision. They were alike, and the Secretary knew how difficult it must have been for the man not to take the easier option. He smiled sadly and rose slowly to his feet.

'I'll leave it to you to let him know,' Deakin said, feeling that they had all failed. He would not be involved in whatever followed. Those were the unspoken rules. He turned and left the Oval Office, his shoulders bent in disappointment. For a long moment, the President of the United States sat alone, his eyes closed in silent prayer, as he asked his God for forgiveness. Then, with the calm of one whose conscience was clear, he sanctioned the executive action as proposed by Allan Cox, the Director of the Central Intelligence Agency.

* * * * * *

They had spent the day lazing around in his Washington apartment, watching television, half-undressed, snacking when the need arose. Both knew that the discussion which had ended abruptly the evening before, was far from finished. Michael offered Ratna one of the snacks but she ignored the offering.

'Well, Michael, are we going together or not?' she asked, turning away, busying herself with some invisible spot on her naked knee. She picked away at nothing, waiting for his response.

'I'll be tied up the whole time, Ratna, and you'll only become even more annoyed,' he answered. He did not want to leave her behind, angry; but he also could not afford to have her tied to his coat-tails the entire time he was in Indonesia. Due to increased political tensions in the Asian theatre, it had become more imperative that he somehow arrange to visit the *Rama II* plant.

Michael had spent some time with his Director being briefed on what was happening in the region. He had been surprised to learn that the White House had placed the highest priority on all activity related to missions involving South East Asia, until he learned of the intensified communication traffic between China and India. As one of the more respected Asian analysts, even he had been caught off-guard by the recent and intriguing developments. Then there was the interesting question of Murray Stephenson's cross-referenced files. When he had attempted to access these, he had found that it was the CIA which had prevented his delving further in Murray's past. He had raised this problem with his superiors but was quietly told that the information held by the Central Intelligence Agency would not be released to him, and that it would be best if he just dropped any further enquiries into the Australian's past.

'I'm going, anyway,' Ratna said, defiantly, turning her hand to inspect her nails. She was furious with Michael. He had announced that he would be gone for several weeks and, when pressed, he had revealed that he would be visiting Jakarta, and perhaps even Bali. Ratna could not understand his reluctance to have her accompany him, especially as it would have meant an opportunity for them to spend some time with her family in Jakarta.

'Look, Ratna,' he said, wearily, 'it's not that I don't want you to come with me, you should know better than that. It's just that I'm going to be up to my ears in meetings with dull engineers, and going to dull functions with their dull wives, and I know you would be bored to death. Why don't we compromise? We could fly out together, and you could remain with your family in Jakarta while I go on my inspection visits without you.' Ratna considered this, then looked coyly over her shoulder from where she sat, her knees under her chin.

'Okay,' she smiled, a little too mischievously, and he sensed he'd made a mistake. She had given in too readily. He leaned over and placed his strong hands on both sides of her light brown, sun-tanned neck, and rubbed gently. Moments later she placed her hands on his, and he stopped. 'You will have time to come and meet Aunty?' she asked, almost childishly.

'Of course!' he laughed, pleased now that they would be travelling together, at least, to Jakarta. Ratna turned and faced him, still on her knees. She stretched up and kissed him warmly, and then held him tightly, as if he might escape.

'And then you will take me on to Bali?' she asked, knowing that he would say yes. Michael sighed, and broke away, holding Ratna at arms' length.

'Okay,' he said, suddenly realizing that he had already lost the argument before it had begun. It seemed that their discussions inevitably ended with Ratna winning her point, or having her way. He admired her strong-willed personality, but admitted that sometimes Ratna could be a little difficult to get along with. They were deeply in love, and Michael realized that he might soon be required to make another life decision, one that he had put off years before. He looked over at the woman who had so totally captured his heart, and was pained that he had lost those years with her, to another, when they could just as easily have been his.

One week before the Bali Summit was scheduled to commence, Michael Bradshaw and Ratna Sari boarded the flight which would take them into Asia and Indonesia. Before their flight had even left American airspace, Admiral Krishna Gopal's fleet had already assembled at the designated rendezvous point, and begun steaming in an easterly direction, south of Java.

* * * * * *

Virginia

In Langley, Virginia, the CIA Director checked his desk one final time before moving down the hallway to the room which housed the shredders. He extracted the loose pages from the blank cover file, and fed these, one by one, through the efficient machine. Satisfied that he had destroyed all record of the damaging evidence relating to his covert activities, the Director then returned to his office and continued with his duties, as if nothing of any real import had transpired.

On the other side of the globe, in what was once American-friendly territory, two men moved under the cover of darkness, grunting as they lifted the stores they would require, and loaded these into the steel-hulled ship.

'Shit!' the bearded man cussed, drawing his hand back quickly from under the box. He waved to the other man to place his end down for the moment, while he placed the injured finger in his mouth. The salty taste of blood did not alarm the ship's captain. He could tell that the wound was relatively minor compared to those he had suffered in the past. He wiped his hand against the side of his filthy trousers, then nodded to Mohammed Fuad that he was ready to continue. Silently, and without further event, they loaded their deadly cargo. Less than an hour later, when they had finished, the two men crawled into the forward bunks and immediately went to sleep.

As the early morning sun captured the tranquil setting, Filipino villagers wandering down to the sandy shore across the wide, deep, tropical lagoon ignored the ship's silhouette as it glided, silently, away from the idyllic setting. On board, Captain Dave Bartlett accepted the hot, steaming, black coffee from Fuad, and settled down for the first leg of a long voyage, which would end in Bali, the Island of Gods.

Chapter 25

Ratna and Michael in Jakarta

Ruswita hoped she had not been too obvious. She had found it extremely difficult to sit opposite the beautiful and vibrant young woman, knowing that she was her daughter, without demonstrating a mother's pleasure. As she viewed Michael Bradshaw with critical eyes, Ruswita was forced to admit, silently, that Ratna Sari had done very well in her selection of companions.

Their guest had been escorted into the main lounge, Ruswita's eyes twinkling as she observed Michael's reaction to the Van Gogh and other collector's items which were placed, inconspicuously, around the already overcrowded room. They had talked for hours together, after which she had insisted that he remain for dinner. It had already been arranged; Ruswita had wished to examine her daughter's beau before issuing the invitation. Over the years she had had the opportunity to meet many foreigners, and found their indifference to local customs or arrogance towards Asians most offensive. She was most pleased with the cultured man whom, she hoped, would make Ratna finally settle down and have children.

There was something about Michael which reminded her of another, but Ruswita put this down to the fact that so many of his race looked familiar, especially to her failing eyes. They had spoken about Indonesia and Asia in general, and Ruswita had been delighted with Michael's obvious knowledge of regional affairs.

The afternoon meeting had gone well, so well in fact that Ruswita had felt no desire to escape and take her customary afternoon break, alone, upstairs. Lani had also been introduced to Ratna's beau, and Ruswita was pleased that the woman had remained reasonably silent during Michael's visit. Ruswita had grown increasingly concerned about her old friend's ability to communicate, and about

Lani's moody silences. Recently, she had noticed, Lani would remain silent for days on end, never so much as uttering a single
word. She knew that Lani missed Ratna; but there again, so did
she. Their home had not been the same since the children had all
married and established their own homes, leaving the two ageing
women alone.

Denny and James remained in the United States, and called only
when business demanded that they communicate with Ruswita.
Although Benny and his family were domiciled in Jakarta and still
visited regularly, this had been of little interest to Lani who often
remained, a recluse in her own small domain at the rear of the Lim
mansion.

* * * * * *

'Michael, have some more *laksa*, she insisted, surprising the attending servants. None of them had ever seen *Ibu Ruswita* in this
mood before. The *pembantu* hurried towards the table at Ruswita's
direction.

'Thank you, thank you,' Michael protested, holding his hands
up to prevent the woman from refilling his large, empty bowl.
Delicious as it was, the curried soup had already sent messages to
his delicate stomach, warning him not to over-indulge. He looked
on in dismay as his bowl was replenished, wondering if he would
offend by not finishing the spicy noodle and prawn dish. Michael
glanced across at his hostess and smiled diplomatically, wondering how the women managed to remain so slim in this country.

From the moment he had set foot in the warm, hospitable environment, he had enjoyed the company of the magnificent woman
he had heard so much about through Ratna. Upon his arrival,
Michael had been ushered into *Ibu Ruswita's* home and doted upon,
almost embarrassingly, like some long-lost child.

Michael was astonished to see the incredible wealth displayed
casually around the guest lounge room. He was positive that the
painting he had seen leaning against the wall near one corner was
a Chagall.

* * * * * *

They had flown into Jakarta's Soekarno-Hatta Airport that morning. Michael had been pleased to finally leave Kuala Lumpur and the toxic haze which covered the unfortunate city. He had found the polluted air impossible to breathe, and understood the extent of the problem once they were airborne, heading for Singapore.

Indonesia's forest fires in Borneo and Sumatra had thrown a blanket of smoke across most of the Malay Peninsula and the South China Sea. Asia's financial centre, Singapore, had not avoided the pollution. As they drove around sight-seeing, Michael observed that the brown cloud had settled dangerously over the entire magnificent city, its density so thick in places that even the many skyscrapers were hidden from view. They spent two days at the Raffles Hotel before continuing their journey to Indonesia, saddened that their time in Singapore had been spoiled by the smoky conditions.

Upon arrival at Jakarta's international airport, Michael followed Ratna through the formalities, smiling at how quickly officials moved to assist the beautiful Eurasian woman and her friend. He had not known at the time that he was witnessing a touch of the Salima power at work. Ruswita's personal assistant had made just one call, and the officials were prepared for Ratna's arrival.

Outside the terminal, a white-uniformed driver jumped from a metallic blue Mercedes 600 and barked orders for the porters to load their luggage, then drove his *tamu* at dangerous speeds into the city. Several times Michael was tempted to ask the driver to slow down. Each time he moved to speak, though, it seemed that the driver's hand would hit the horn, and so he gave up and remained in anxious silence until they arrived at their destination.

Michael watched as the servants strained to lift her baggage from the luggage compartment. Then the security guard took hold of Michael's cases.

'No, please leave those there,' Michael said, surprising them all. He felt uncomfortable being placed in this situation, having expected to go on to his hotel after dropping Ratna at her home.

'Michael?' Ratna frowned, wondering what was going on. She removed her sunglasses and placed one hand on her hip, then suddenly removed this when she remembered where she was, and how offensive the gesture would be considered in Indonesia.

'I'm sorry, Ratna, I had no idea that you expected me to stay with your family. You knew that I'd booked a room at the Grand Hyatt,' he said, observing from her reaction that she was annoyed with him. She strolled around the car, took his hands in hers, then looked directly up, into his eyes.

'Michael, don't do this, please!' she whispered, but loudly enough so the servants could hear, further embarrassing him.

'Ratna, I have to stay at the hotel. That's where I will be contacted by the government agencies. Be reasonable!' he pleaded, irritated that he had been placed in this predicament. When the Mercedes had pulled up at the home and servants had descended upon the car, Michael immediately guessed what was happening. He could not permit Ratna to take charge; that would severely impede his ability to remain mobile and unencumbered.

They continued arguing for several minutes, Ratna still insisting that they stay together, at her family's home. Michael remaining adamant, determined that he be taken to his hotel.

'It will only be for a few days, Michael,' Ratna had come close to stamping her foot, tempted to tell him how angry she really was but, at that moment, *Ibu Ruswita* ventured out, and introduced herself. She had been listening with a certain amount of pleasure as the two stood arguing in her driveway. They both became silent as she spoke.

'Ratna, Michael has already arranged to stay somewhere else and you should accept that,' she quietly admonished. Michael was relieved by her intervention, and promised to ring once he had checked in and unpacked. Offended, Ratna turned in a huff, crossed her arms in one of her familiar tantrums, and ignored Michael's wave as the Mercedes drove away. Ruswita clucked happily as she placed her arm around her beautiful daughter and they entered the Lim home.

* * * * * *

Michael had welcomed the invitation to dine with the Salima family. He had been delightfully surprised to discover that the invitation had included *Ibu Lani,* and that he was to be entertained in their home. Slightly concerned that his earlier refusal to stay might have offended, Michael returned to the Lim mansion with three freshly cut bouquets of tiger orchids, one for each of the ladies.

His concerns were soon allayed, as he was warmly welcomed and treated as if he had enjoyed a long association with the family. Before his evening visit, he had really no comprehension as to the enormous wealth Ratna's aunt had gathered. He was embarrassed, and knew from Ratna's coy expression that she enjoyed her lover's surprise when he discovered who Aunt Ruswita actually was with respect to the international financial community.

The thought had crossed his mind that he could have so easily used his department's resources to search for information relating to the family. As he listened to Madame Ruswita Salima outline her group's activities, Michael experienced a sense of inadequacy in the face of such wealth and position, which far exceeded anything he had known.

Not once during his visit had he observed any visible sign that the expensive paintings and other *object d'art* were of any great importance to their owner. Michael had spent more than three hours being entertained by the pleasant Aunt Ruswita, before he understood that she was, in fact, the matriarch of such a formidable corporate powerhouse, known internationally as the Salima Group. He had read of the conglomerate's wealth and power, and now felt more than a little ridiculous, considering his intelligence analysis background, that he had not associated Ratna's Aunt Ruswita with the powerful Indonesian conglomerate.

'Ratna,' Ruswita said, smiling happily across the table, 'you should take Michael up to visit our mountain resort.'

'I will, Aunty, I will,' she promised, enjoying the attention. Michael observed Ratna's mother, Lani, from the corner of his eye and wondered why she played such an inconspicuous role in the proceedings. 'Michael will be …' Ratna was cut off by Michael.

'Thank you, Mrs Salima,' he interjected. He did not wish to lose control of his itinerary, and he suspected this could easily happen with these hospitable people. 'I would really enjoy that, but I don't think I'll have the time this visit.' He noticed Ratna pout, and Madame Salima smile. *Was she enjoying the sight of the strong-willed young woman being put in her place?*

'You will be visiting the *Rama II* plant?' Madame Ruswita asked innocently, with which Michael almost dropped his spoon in surprise. He was startled by Madame Ruswita's directness. From her influential position, she would surely have been aware of the secrecy surrounding the former Japanese-controlled plant, and that IAEA inspections had been forbidden.

'I have not received approval for an inspection, Madame,' he answered. Michael had read the historical background on the tender process associated with the first five *Rama* plants. Old Lim had been very clever, not revealing his company's position until the plants neared completion. It seemed that, by disguising their ownership in this manner, Salima was able to avoid accusations of cronyism. When Salima's controlling position had been revealed, it had been disclosed in such a manner as to suggest that the acquisition had been a recent undertaking to assist with budgetary overruns. The market had reacted favourably at the time, driving the family fortunes to even greater heights.

Michael was not entirely comfortable knowing that his lover was this close to Indonesia's most powerful family. He knew there were three boys, the heirs, who assisted Madame Salima with her empire. He sensed there was a bond between Ratna and her aunt, one which appeared stronger than her relationship with her mother, Lani. Michael put this down to the fact that her Aunt Ruswita had no daughter of her own.

He glanced over at Lani, thinking how different she was to her sister. One was a power-house of energy, while the other a reluctant participant in the proceedings before her. He found himself staring as Lani caught his eye. Immediately he remembered that this was considered rude in the Orient, and glanced away to hide his embarrassment.

'Perhaps once the plant has been officially opened, they will approve a visit,' Ruswita suggested.

'Let's hope that this is so,' was all he said, not wishing to reveal too much to his astute hostess. It was apparent to Michael that she would most definitely have the power to arrange for such a visit. But as an offer of assistance had not been forthcoming; he did not press. During these few hours, Michael's understanding of where he was had become much clearer, and he decided to proceed cautiously.

'Do you have any other friends here, in Indonesia, Michael?' Ruswita asked.

'Not really,' he answered, not wishing to associate himself openly with Murray Stephenson; such a relationship might be misconstrued by others. He had to avoid being seen associating with any specific interest groups for the duration of his inspection tour, at least until securing an opportunity to visit Rama II. He knew that it would be inconceivable for Murray and this powerful woman to not have met; Jakarta was a throbbing commercial hub, and as the two parties had common interests, Michael was absolutely certain that somehow Murray had played a role in the Lim's acquisition of the *Rama V* nuclear power plant. After all, Murray's name, along with that of his Singaporean partner, Peter Wong, were registered as the two largest shareholders in the *Nasihat Corporation*, the foreign partners in the *Rama V* joint venture, and now it belonged entirely to the Salima Group.

Michael's experience warned him to be careful. He was moving in unfamiliar territory filled by wealthy and very powerful people, with Ratna's aunt amongst those who enjoyed the most influence. Michael glanced across the table and saw that *Madame Ruswita* was observing him closely. In that moment he experienced a strange sense of foreboding, almost as if old Lim Swee Giok had been standing behind his chair, watching over Michael's shoulder to ensure that he brought this family no harm.

* * * * * *

As the late evening breeze brushed dark monsoonal clouds aside revealing the brilliance of a rare January moon, Ratna awoke suddenly and sat up, startled, her heart pumping in fear.

'*Who is it?*' she called, terrified, her fingers searching desperately for the familiar switch.

'*Na, Na, don't be afraid,*' Lani replied, '*it's only me. Don't be frightened!*'

'*What is it?*' Ratna asked her mother, finally locating the light switch, and illuminating the room. She was surprised to see Lani sitting at the end of her bed. She checked the bedside clock. It was not even two o'clock.

'*Is something the matter, 'Bu?*' she asked, concerned that she might be ill. Lani moved to her side and wrapped her arms around Ratna, then placed her head alongside that of the younger woman's, resting gently against the soft pillow.

'*No, Na, there's nothing wrong. I have just missed you so much, that's all,'* she said, sadly, holding her tightly. Ratna squeezed Lani in response, then yawned. She had stayed up late, talking with her aunt, once Michael had returned to his hotel.

'Are you going to marry this one, too?' Lani asked, not wishing to leave.

'He hasn't asked me,' Ratna replied, with a hint of remorse in her voice. She wondered if he had gone directly back to the Grand Hyatt, or if he had decided to take in the sights of Jakarta City without her.

'Don't get married again, Na,' Lani said, squeezing as she did so for emphasis. *'Why don't you stay here with me? I'll take good care of you.'* Ratna knew that she was in danger of being hooked into one of her mother's tireless conversations, and did not answer. She looked down at Lani but could only see the top of her head. Too tired to encourage further discussion, Ratna switched the light off and lay completely still, willing herself to sleep.

In the darkness of the room, Lani rested alongside the beautiful woman she considered her daughter, listening to her breathe, wishing that she would wake, and talk to her, as Ratna had with Ruswita earlier. She was saddened that Ratna no longer cared for her, that there was no longer any room in her heart for the woman who had mothered and taken care of her from the day she was born.

Bitter from years filled with endless hours sitting quietly alone in her quarters, Lani uttered a silent prayer to her God, begging that Ratna and she could stay together as they were then, forever.

* * * * * *

Java Sea

Twenty-three nautical miles North-north-east of what local fisherman called the *Java Hook,* where Gods and spirits connived to spoil one's catch or even boil the ocean with a fearful turbulence capable of capsizing the sturdiest of vessels, the small fleet prepared to return to shore. As they pulled their machine-woven nets over the side of their unstable boats, the crews remained silent. Their poor harvest had thrown a blanket of despondency over the fleet.

These were simple but suspicious people. They understood the weather, and watched the skies and birds for indications of where they should cast nets. They listened to their Gods and, surrounded by Petromax lights, still chanted around village fires when evening fell. They feared angering the powerful elements which controlled the currents, the wind. The invisible spirits of their *nenek-moyang* - their ancestral spirits which lurked in the darkness beyond - had to be placated.

Further out to sea, and deep in the earth's crust where basalt converts into still denser rocks, the subterranean structure covering the earth's molten mass grunted and heaved. As lateral slip faulting occurred, the two mighty masses wrestled momentarily until one surrendered. The interplay of these colliding plates instantly dispatched shock waves both vertically and horizontally through the earth's crust. The oceans above wobbled, absorbing much of the initial shock. Then the two plates began to slip against each other again.

One hundred kilometers to the south, and along the Sumatra-Bali Ridge, twenty-one active volcanoes coughed up plumes of black soot and molten rock. Then, for a moment, it was as if the Gods were content with their display of force.

A deafening silence fell over the sea, followed by a sudden, total absence of wind. The older men turned their faces to the open sea. Many had heard the stories; only a few of their number had actually witnessed what was sure to follow. The fishing fleet's headman screamed for all to turn their vessels towards the open sea, standing on the open deck of his boat and waving furiously for the others to follow his small, diesel-driven craft. Many among the younger fishermen did not understand his wild gesticulations. Bewildered, some even imagined their fishing-fleet commander had been affected by the sea's spirits, while others thought he was merely venting his disappointment at the poor catch.

The weather-withered Javanese head-man stood, gripping the boat's upper-structure. He had lived to tell the tale of a similar experience. Even then, he remembered, few had believed what he had witnessed. Fear gripped him as the first, and ever so soft, puff of wind brushed gently across his bare torso. He screamed once more to all within distance, but few understood his call; some even laughed at the irrational behaviour as he clung desperately to the

411

timber ship's stern's upright deck-beams. They listened to the old man's ravings and shook their heads; he was old, and becoming senile.

Suddenly, distracted by an unfamiliar sound, several of the men cocked their ears and looked around the fleet to see who else might have started their diesels. They looked out to sea and listened, trying to identify the source of the low murmur flowing across the waves. A long, wailing cry startled those closest to the mothership, and those on board the commander's vessel were shocked as their head-man slid to the deck and started to pray. The sea groaned under the now-terrified fishermen. Without further warning, the wind screamed across the water, whipping the waves into mountainous foam which towered over the decks of the vessels.

The fishermen clung desperately to whatever was within reach, terrified they would be washed away. When the first shock passed through their flimsy wooden craft, the full force of the sea rose before them in the darkness, and they screamed, as the tidal wave roared in upon them. They all knew that they were about to die.

* * * * * *

The Indonesian Urban Disaster Mitigation Centre at the Bandung Institute of Technology registered the major shudder on one of its continuous analogue seismographs as the Great Indian-Australian mantle grated against its counterpart, the Eurasian Plate, releasing pressures which had taken scores of millenniums to build.

As the sapphire stylus left its long, spiral trace around the seismograph's drum, Wiranto Arismudari, the Indonesian representative for the Asian Urban Disaster Programme, watched, full of apprehension, at the magnitude of the subterranean earthquake. The energy released registered 7.6 on the Richter Scale. He glanced nervously across at Widiadnyana Jegillos, his assistant, who immediately allayed his fears with an incandescent smile and a reassuring wave of the hand.

* * * * * *

Bandung Research and Development Centre

Several technicians grabbed at their benches frantically as the earth supporting the underground facility shook, frighteningly.

Many of the other team members looked up, as if expecting the thousands of tons of earth above to come crumbling down upon them.

A solitary light-globe had been strung across under the fluorescent fixtures to enhance visibility in one corner. It was swinging silently, indicating that the powerful tremor had shaken the secret facility's foundations. Minutes were to pass before the staff returned to work, all more conscious of their dangerous location than they had been before, some even resolving to submit their resignations upon receipt of their next pay.

* * * * * *

Mount Muria, Java — Rama II

Engineer First Class Mochtar Pribadi strutted along the interconnecting catwalk, dressed in his freshly washed white overalls. He was the midnight-to-dawn, assistant shift supervisor. His initial training had taken place in Japan and, subsequent to the Japanese withdrawal from their project, Mochtar had been sent to the Cernavoda project in Romania to learn more of Russian design and operational procedures. He was deeply proud to have been appointed to assist Vladimir Kruchinsky, first supervisor for the plant's operations. Mochtar was dedicated to his work, and grateful for the opportunity which had been provided for him and his young family.

When the tremor first struck, he was startled by the sudden rocking of the steel walkway under his feet, and he grabbed at the handrail to steady himself. It was all over within seconds. Mochtar peered over the steel-latticed enclosure, and observed that none of the others below had noticed the slight jolt. Accustomed to many such geological shakes since early childhood, he continued his inspection duties, not giving the tremor another thought.

The nuclear plant had been built partially on floating foundations. The Japanese had insisted that standards be similar to those employed in Japan, an area notorious for its sudden volcanic and other geological disturbances. The shell of the overall installation was constructed with concrete, suitably strengthened with steel reinforcing bars, giving the protective cover, or containment shield,

413

strength to withstand geological shocks.

When the Japanese construction had been taken over by the President's family, using Russian techniques and Indonesian practices, quality control had slipped to unacceptable levels. Graeme Robson's *kongsi* won the ongoing contract to provide materials to the site. These included cement and Vietnamese reinforcing steel.

High above Mochtar's head, at the point where two concrete sections had been sealed together completing the containment cover's dome, a hair-line crack appeared, tracing the inferior join.

* * * * * *

Jakarta

Graeme Robson observed the two men, and conceded that they were disturbingly similar in their mannerisms, and even appearance. Had he not known otherwise, Robson would have assumed that they were brothers. He looked around for another towel and gestured to one of the attendants to bring him another bourbon and coke.

'Make that three,' he called to the slight Sundanese houseboy, while watching Murray and Michael stroll back in his direction. Considering Stephenson's age, he was still in fine condition, he thought enviously, conscious of the flab of his own body. Robson could see that the younger man was obviously still in his prime. He had surprised them all with his skill on the courts earlier in the afternoon. Robson was unsure whether he liked Michael Bradshaw, with his ivy league manner. He watched the women surrounding the pool-side barbecue flirt openly with Bradshaw and he didn't like it at all.

Graeme was unaccustomed to not being the centre of attention and expected it, particularly when he was paying for the service. He watched his wife move amongst the other women, her slender shape and delicate features lost to a life of over-indulgence. John Georgio came to mind, and Graeme wondered if his wife knew of the arrangement he had with the professional pimp. Robson had never permitted Georgio to phone him at home; neither would he consider having the man anywhere around his residence in Jakarta.

Apart from the fact that John Georgio oozed from the pores at the slightest sign of a beautiful woman, the man had a total lack of class. Robson made a mental note to explore other avenues of supply for his secret interludes. He was becoming bored with Georgio's behaviour.

'When are you off to Bali, then?' he asked Michael, as his guests flopped casually down. The humidity was unusually high for that time of the day, and the men were still dehydrated from their tennis workout.

'I've had to rearrange my schedule, Graeme,' Michael responded, accepting the drink which appeared, magically, the moment he sat down. 'This Summit has screwed things around a bit, but at this stage I still expect to be in Bali from the sixteenth through to the middle of the week.' Michael then paused and took a long swallow from the tall glass before adding, 'but this could change if I'm able to swing a visit to the Mt Muria plant.' Graeme looked across at Murray, then fluttered his eyelids. It was an affectation that had grown into habit over the years, and made him appear quite ridiculous.

'The Vice President will attend that plant's commissioning ceremony during the Summit,' he said, a bit officiously. 'My sources have informed me that only a handful of Palace players have been invited.' Michael smiled. Robson was obviously miffed at not having been invited.

'Well, if I can't make it this trip....' He didn't finish, opening his hands in resigned acceptance that he would not be given the opportunity to see inside *Rama II's* operations.

'I might be able to swing something after the official opening, Michael,' Robson suddenly inferred, surprising Murray, who cocked an eyebrow at the suggestion. 'My company has been involved in the facility's construction. If you were to come along with me as my guest, it might just be possible. We still have an ongoing relationship with the operators, and there is still a considerable amount of ancillary work to be done around the site.' His eyelids flickered several times like butterfly wings, then stopped.

'I have an idea,' he said, leaning over and slapping Michael's well tanned leg, 'why don't you come down with us on the Lear Jet, and after we've had a few days resting up in my villa, I'll take you directly over to the *Rama II* site?' He paused, then added, 'I'll fly you over myself.' Robson was pleased to see that he had scored. Michael was obviously interested. Looks weren't everything, he mused, resisting the smirk hiding behind his mask of generosity.

Murray looked at Graeme Robson, wondering why he continually persisted in bragging about his executive jet and his pilot's licence. Murray knew that there were at least fifty such private aircraft owned by Jakarta entrepreneurs, most of which remained standing at one of the three airports, primarily as status symbols.

'Well, if the offer is to join you guys after my Bali inspection, I'm in,' Michael said. 'Not before?' Robson asked, surprised that someone would refuse an opportunity to fly down to Bali in a private jet and spend time at *'Puri Kauh'*, undisputedly one of the finest private villas to be found amongst the island's lushly vegetated mountains.

'Thanks, Graeme,' Michael offered, not wishing to offend this man, particularly if he really could orchestrate a visit to the fast breeder plant in Java, 'but I have already committed to spending some quiet time with my lady. She has her heart set on some place along the beach and, to tell you the truth, I'm looking forward to just lying around doing nothing for a few days once I finish the local inspection.'

'Perhaps we could get together while I'm down there and discuss the next step?' he suggested. Robson's weak smile indicated that he might have been offended.

'Sure, let's do that,' Robson said, obviously peeved. The conversation then drifted onto other matters while Michael continued to observe the other two men closely, trying to determine what their relationship might really be. He suspected that the intricate Jakarta expatriate network would have thrown Murray and Robson together in business at some stage. It was apparent that some synergy between the two did exist, considering that both had considerable involvement with the *Rama* energy plants.

As he listened to them discussing matters of little relevance to either the Summit or the nuclear power plants, subjects which had occupied most other conversations during his brief stay, Michael believed that these men had deliberately steered their conversation away from these topics while he was present. And he couldn't help but wonder why.

* * * * * *

'You look a bit strung out,' Murray suggested. He had remained after Michael had returned to his hotel. Graeme crossed his arms and straightened his back, bored with sitting.

'Having problems with the bankers,' he admitted. Murray was one of the few people he still trusted with such confidences.

'Anything I can do?' Stephenson asked.

'Well, that little bastard Benny Salima has really stuck it to me this time,' Robson said, leaning forward and stretching. One of the servants observed the movement and hurried in his *tuan's* direction, only to be waved away.

'What's the problem, Graeme?' Murray asked. He didn't particularly like the man any more, persevering with their relationship only because of their cross-business ties.

'Asian Pacific has indicated that they might not roll my notes over,' he said, grimly. Murray was surprised. The APC Bank was, he knew, the Lim flagship. Robson must have done something to upset them, he thought. Either that, or Graeme's company was in financial difficulties.

'Move the notes elsewhere,' he suggested, interested now in the other man's predicament.

'I've already tried, Murray,' he replied. 'The Lims have their noses out of joint because they couldn't get their cement and steel into the *Rama II* project. And,' he added, 'the Bandung Research and Development center.' Murray thought about this; it made sense to him. He guessed that the Salima group would have financed Robson initially, hoping that this would give them some leverage over the man's access to materials supply.

'How long do you have?' Murray asked. Graeme didn't have to think before replying; this had been foremost on his mind, lately.

'Three months,' he said, then asked, 'do you think Peter might be interested?'

Murray knew that the old Chinese sitting in Singapore would not be keen on taking over any debt, particularly if this was being transferred from the Lims. They rarely left any meat on a bone, and any suggestion that they were not interested in maintaining a client would only indicate that there was something suspicious with the deal in the first instance.

'No, I don't think so, Graeme. Peter is winding down most of his activities,' he lied. This didn't bother Murray in the least;

everyone lied in business, otherwise how could they survive? Graeme Robson rose from his pool-side chair and stretched again.

'Maybe we can talk about it more in Bali,' he suggested. Murray nodded, realizing that it was time for him to leave.

'Sure, Graeme,' he said, knowing that they would not, 'let's do that.'

Later that day Murray Stephenson filed the information suggesting that Robson's *kongsi* was experiencing financial difficulties. Before Graeme Robson retired for the day, having made one discreet call to John Georgio to establish that arrangements were in place for their Bali escape, his financial dilemma was already known to Peter Wong in Singapore. Before noon the following day, Wong's indiscreet enquiries had been recorded by at least five lending institutions, most of which referred the information search back to the Lims' bank in Jakarta. Word was then circulated that Madame Ruswita would be unhappy if the loan was to be picked up by any other institution.

Within twenty-four hours, Benny Salima sat smiling confidently, knowing that Robson would be unable to meet the notes when these fell due.

Chapter 26

Xanana and the Chinese Fleet

Xanana Soares accepted the hot towel from the Lauda Air stewardess and wiped his face. His attention was diverted from the attractive girl as the captain's voice announced that they had just left the coast of Western Australia, and that their flight was back on schedule. Xanana smiled as another stewardess opened the armrest and re-stashed his tray. He re-adjusted the in-flight monitor, and continued watching the movie. As the figures on the tiny mercury screen danced, his thoughts returned to what lay ahead.

It did not bother Xanana that he had left Australia, perhaps forever. Within a few days he would travel from New Delhi to Bali with the Indian and South African delegations. They had guaranteed his safety. Everything had been arranged. He was to travel, for the purposes of the Summit, on an Indian diplomatic passport, and remain with the Prime Minister only for as long as was required. Then, when everyone's attention was focused on the Summit, he would leave, quietly, with Admiral Gopal.

The thought of remaining in Indonesia for even one day concerned him. He did not trust the Indonesians. He feared that they might attempt to arrest or at least intimidate him in some way. It had been agreed that he was to play no public role during the discussions. His presence in Bali was to add credibility to the agenda, and provide India with the opportunity it had worked so long to achieve.

Xanana felt greatly indebted to the people of India. Through their generosity, he would be taken back to East Timor aboard the magnificent aircraft carrier, *INS Indira Gandhi*, and reclaim his country in the name of the East Timorese people. The will of the United Nations would finally be expressed through India's unilateral

419

action, supported by the might of their navy and marines. Xanana had been assured that the Indonesian troops would have little choice but to withdraw once they witnessed the strength of the Indian forces. He would then be taken ashore and ensconced as the country's legitimate President, after which India would continue to provide a military umbrella to the fledgling country.

He closed his eyes and tried to visualize how things would be in an independent, free and democratic East Timor. Memories of the bitter struggle flashed though his mind, and the many faces of those who had given their lives in the fight for freedom. He remembered the brave, poorly-armed men who had fled into the mountains and continued their struggle through the turn of the century and into the next. He drifted, his mind wandering as he envisaged the prosperity he would bring to his people from East Timor's natural resources, and the pride his countrymen would finally feel once they had achieved their long-awaited freedom.

Finally, his stomach full of the rich in-flight food, Xanana fell into a troubled sleep, until the First Class attendant woke him with instructions to prepare for the landing.

* * * * * *

Lombok Straits

Fuad adjusted his sunglasses against the brilliant glare reflected up from the calm ocean, as the *M.V. Rager* glided through the warm, tropical waters. He cast his eyes around the horizon in search of weather, but could see only the light, pale-blue heavens, the flat sea and some distant coral islands.

When dawn had broken some hours earlier, their world had been blanketed by a deep, thick, sea-mist, causing them to reduce speed. Bartlett had called to him earlier, instructing Fuad to look for small fishing vessels which would not show-up on their radar.

An hour passed, and Fuad became nervous when, in the still, ghostly conditions, the *Rager* suddenly lifted and rocked several times before settling down once again in what had been perfectly calm conditions. His first fear was that the wave had been caused by some distant tanker passing through the mist; but then he could not recall hearing any other shipping in the area. Fuad was not to know that this small swell had been a result of the same undersea movement which had devastated the fishing fleet hours before, and which continued to send out shock waves.

The morning sun finally pierced the fog, and a soft breeze swept the remaining mist away. A pod of dolphins swam alongside, diving playfully for some minutes, before leaving in search of a more responsive audience. Fuad stretched, yawned more out of boredom than fatigue, and continued to search the horizon for other shipping. Fuad knew, without having to look over his shoulder, that the only other man on the vessel would be watching him from the bridge. Fuad didn't like Dave Bartlett. He had the smell of evil about him. Fuad knew that he didn't need to stare into the bearded sailor's cold, lifeless, green eyes to know that he had killed.

They rarely spoke and the long silences didn't bother either man. They were only interested in their mission - and remaining alive to enjoy their rewards. Fuad thought about the money he'd been promised. It was a great deal, even for one who had made and lost a small fortune trading drugs and arms with the Filipino Muslim separatists. Then there was the promise of a green card for entry and residence in the United States. That had been the clincher. All those years of dreaming how he could return to America and remain would soon become reality.

They had promised that this would be his last mission, and he trusted them. His last venture into the Moslem-held Filipino islands near Mindanao had almost cost him his life. And that of Bartlett's. He wondered how the New Zealander earned the almost invisible scar buried behind his reddish-brown beard. Fuad assumed that the rust-bucket which carried them deep into Indonesian waters was Bartlett's. He seemed to pay too much attention to the ship's detail, not to have lived aboard for many years. The single-screw, seventy-foot steel-hulled work-boat had seen better days. When he had been briefed, Fuad was not too keen on the idea of steaming such a distance in the old ship but decided that, if Bartlett was to captain the vessel, they would most probably make it back to home port.

Images of Bartlett standing coolly pumping the twelve-gauge shotgun almost point-blank at the intruders flashed through his mind. The Filipino pirates had erred badly, and their assumption that the *Rager's* crew might be unarmed had cost them their lives. Fuad had watched in fear, as Bartlett had blown five of them back over the side of his ship, then calmly extracted a magnum from his belt and shot several more dead as they scrambled to hide on the smaller boat's deck. From that moment, he had been most careful not to cross the man, sensing that it would take little to attract his wrath.

Fuad wondered if the New Zealander's reward for this mission would be similar to his own. One hundred thousand dollars didn't go far these days, and Fuad knew he would need every penny of that to establish himself once in the States. He considered this, then decided that Bartlett's share would be more, perhaps even a quarter of a million.

His attention then turned to the stores hidden below. It had been the New Zealander's responsibility to clear the ship through customs when they passed into Indonesian waters. They had dropped anchor outside Ujung Pandang, the old Makassar Port, and waited. As darkness fell, a small boat powered by Yamaha outboards brought the Harbour Master alongside, where he recognized Bartlett and accepted the carton of cigarettes containing one thousand dollars. Fuad had been ready, below, armed with a machine pistol in the event the official had become curious and insisted on inspecting the ship's stores. He had not heard Bartlett conversing in the local language and, even if he had, Fuad would have thought little of this. He had discovered that the often sullen captain had little difficulty communicating wherever he travelled.

Fuad thought about the two *Stingers* sitting in their packing cases. He had argued for three, and reluctantly accepted what was stored below. Given that there was only one target, he had been told, even carrying two of the hand-held missiles was considered excessive for such a mission. Fuad reflected on the battle-field proven *Stinger*. Howard Hughes had not survived to witness the incredible destructive power of these man-portable, shoulder-fired rockets, designed and manufactured by the Hughes Missiles System Company.

During the most recent Pakistani-Indian war, Fuad had used the vehicle-mounted version more commonly known as a SVML. He had fired the MANPADs, or man-portable versions only once, but was confident that he would not miss his target when the time arrived, as the infra-red, heat-seeking guided missile was designed specifically for the application they had in mind for their Bali mission.

Once at sea, and far from their port of embarkation, both he and Bartlett had opened the well fortified cases in the ship's hold and examined their deadly caché. With a little support from Bartlett, Fuad had easily lifted one of the two *Stingers* to his shoulder, re-familiarising himself with the sixteen-kilo assembly which consisted of an individual missile, a disposable launch tube with its detachable grip-stock, and the integral range-finder (IFF) system. Although it was some time since Fuad had attended missile training courses in the Pakistani ground forces, he had not lost his respect for the formidable weapon.

He also remembered that the *Stinger* was unique in possessing an in-built TAG guidance technique, which biases missile orientation towards vulnerable portions of its targets, assuring maximised lethality. Fuad had little reason to doubt the reported combat success rate of the weapon in the Afghanistan-Soviet war, during which the *Stinger,* travelling at a speed nearing Mach Two, reportedly downed almost three hundred Soviet aircraft, helping to stop air assault operations and precipitate the Soviet withdrawal from the Moslem-dominated territory.

At first, Fuad had attempted to lift the one and a half metre missile assembly onto his shoulder alone and, although he managed to do so, both men agreed that on a cramped and moving deck, common sense dictated that Bartlett assist. They rehearsed this procedure several times, then repacked the cases. They would not reopen these until they had already positioned the ship in preparation for their strike. With a range of only four kilometers, Bartlett had decided not to move the ship into the strike zone until absolutely necessary.

There would be few preparations required. The *Stingers* would only require minutes to unpack, and they would be ready. Prior to that, he planned to leave the *Rager* moored off-shore, not too distant from Benoa Harbour as to attract attention, but far enough to deter others from visiting the disguised dive-cruise ship.

Fuad had wondered about the other cargo they carried, until Bartlett had explained the reasoning behind the incompatible equipment. The other weapons had consisted of machine-pistols of

Chinese manufacture, and additional life-rafts and flares which had identification tags indicating that these had been part of a Chinese submarine's inventory. A used HN-5B Beijing equivalent to the American *Stinger* had been included in the shipment. The idea of laying the blame for the air disaster at China's door somehow appealed to Fuad, although he wished that he could, one day, claim credit for having destroyed India's Prime Minister.

They had taken on bunker fuel the previous day, and would now not require further diesel until they returned to the Philippines. The ten two hundred-litre drums stowed below would see them through the remainder of the mission.

He heard Bartlett call and he turned, then followed the man's outstretched finger pointing to the West. Fuad removed his sunglasses and peered through the 8x30DIF Nikon binoculars, making a minor adjustment which brought the distant ship clearly into focus. After some moments Fuad turned and shook his head, but then continued to watch the huge tanker just in case. Bartlett had warned him that the Lombok Straits were dangerous; larger ships passed through here, one of Indonesia's busiest sea lanes. He wandered lazily back to where the other man stood, his left hand on the ship's wheel.

'How much longer?' Fuad asked, watching Bartlett extract a cigarette from its packet, using his teeth. He had been on four missions with the surly sailor, and had not once seen him remove the well-worn baseball cap, not even to scratch his head.

'We'll be sitting off Benoa Harbour at first light,' Bartlett answered. 'Then I'm going ashore.' Fuad frowned, thinking that this would be foolish. He said nothing, though, realizing that Bartlett would do as he liked, anyway. He walked back up forward and leaned on the ship's rail, wondering why the other man would take such unnecessary risks. Fuad knew that they would have to moor away from the other shipping until the time arrived, in order to remain as inconspicuous as possible. He turned slowly and glanced guardedly towards the bridge, and immediately wished he hadn't. Bartlett was smiling; and the expression sent a cold shiver through his spine.

* * * * * *

He looked down at the man he would later have to kill, and his eyes narrowed, wondering if perhaps Fuad had been given similar instructions. Dave Bartlett unconsciously scratched his face with his free hand, pondering this thought.

He had been betrayed before. More than once. He recognized that with age he had lost some of his edge, but Bartlett still considered himself capable of being able to defend himself, particularly against the likes of the Pakistani drug dealer forced upon him for this mission. They had worked together several times in the past, but Bartlett had never had much confidence in the other man. He'd seen him panic in situations which might have cost them both their lives.

Fuad disappeared below and, choosing that moment, the bearded captain raised his cap then dragged the palm of his hand across his head, recognising how thin the hair on his scalp had become over the past few years. Resisting the temptation to touch the scar, he adjusted his sun-glasses, then gazed out across the calm, blue sea. A flock of gulls swooped together, then veered away. In the distance, he could see the volcano's outline, and knew that this would be the majestic Gunung Agung, its smouldering rim evident above the clouds. For a brief moment, the scene triggered painful memories and he resisted the temptation to indulge in what might have been.

More than thirty years had passed, yet he could still clearly recall the image of the woman he had loved, Louise, standing on the dimly-lit foreshore, her golden hair nestled against his face, as villagers danced in rhythm to the ancient *gamelan* sounds. The irony that he was soon to take the lives of others, who would also die in the air, was not lost on Bartlett as he continued to stare at the island, and the point from where Louise had taken her fateful flight.

Bartlett touched his head again and accepted that he was lucky to have anything there at all. The force of the bullet which had struck the side of his head as it penetrated the skin above his upper jaw, had come within a millimetre of killing him. The bullet had turned against the shattered bone and travelled upwards, before exiting more than eight centimetres above his right ear. He had been shown Polaroid shots taken of his black, swollen face which looked like some badly inflated and severely bruised melon. Dave Bartlett, formerly known as Stephen Coleman, knew he was indeed most fortunate to have survived yet another attempt on his life, those years before in Canberra.

His unconscious body had been taken directly to a safe-house maintained by the United States Government, in the small border town of Queanbeyan, not twenty kilometers from where he had been shot. There, at the request of the Station CIA Chief, he had been secretly cared for by the Embassy doctor. When he recovered consciousness, two days after his near fatal shooting, the questions had started. During the first, groggy hours, his memory of the incident totally lost, Coleman had no comprehension whatsoever, of whom, or where he was. His amnesia had lasted for several months, and even now, he admitted, there were still major gaps which related to the time leading up to his near-death experience. He could still, however, clearly remember the man Anderson who had betrayed him.

When he had expressed concern that his disappearance would attract attention the CIA Station Chief, Harold Goldstein, had assured him that Chalmers had returned to the scene and removed the car in which Coleman had been shot. It would later be assumed that the vehicle had been stolen and his body dumped. During the course of that evening, the Canberra and Queanbeyan hospitals had been in turmoil as a result of the devastating blast which had occurred at the Indonesian Embassy. Coleman's credentials were thrown amongst others that had been collected by the authorities, who were unable to identify many of the bomb-blast victims. The Americans believed Anderson would come to accept that Coleman's body had been discovered and sent to one of the hospitals, where confusion had led staff to believe he had been one of the bomb casualties.

While sitting on the ship's deck steaming between Port Moresby and Guam, pieces of the annoying puzzle moved into place inside his head, but never enough to create a full picture of the events which had led to his attempted execution. He had remained under American care for almost one year, before they too decided that there was little left of any substance for them to glean from his memory. In their ongoing watch over the Australian security services, Coleman could be of no further use.

When they released him, Coleman became apolitical. In his anger, he also refused to acknowledge that he had any debt, or ties, or owed any loyalty to his country of birth, or to those who lived there. Unable to make contact with his bankers for fear this would reactivate interest in his death, Coleman knew that the funds he had squirreled away would eventually be sent to Australia, along with a number of letters containing detailed reports of his earlier activities. He was confident that these would find their way to Wanti's estate, and her daughter Seruni. These, he hoped, would bring an end to Director Anderson's rule over the Australian Secret Service.

It was then that Stephen Coleman moved into an even darker world, accepting assignments from those who had saved his life. He became a willing, well-paid, American mercenary.

They provided him with a new identity. His new name, Bartlett, was given as a result of intensive computer research which provided the basis for his new character. Coleman had grown a beard to cover the permanent scar tissue, and wore a cap to hide the damage the exiting bullet had caused above his hairline. Satisfied with his new persona, Stephen Coleman had remained in Guam for several years before moving to the Philippines, at his new masters' insistence.

There, while maintaining as low a profile as his activities permitted, he grew into his new identity as the owner of a small, inter-island ship, named the *M.V. Rager,* an ageing vessel that suited his purposes perfectly. He accepted missions which took him occasionally across into Vietnamese waters, where he traded in smuggled goods, and down into Mindanao where Moslem separatists paid handsomely for the weapons he carried.

He sailed to ports throughout the region, from Puerto Princessa on Palawan, to Davao and up to Tacloban, and even as far north as Taiwan and across to Hong Kong, and any other destinations which provided him with irregular but handsome earnings.

Coleman had not hesitated when required to kill. Nor was he concerned about the morality of his actions. Now, in this new life, he lived for survival, and developed no ties other than those with the Americans, whose generous flow of funds guaranteed him some security for advancing years. He knew he would not be able to continue working the ship alone too much longer. When he had been offered the contract to sail into Bali, Coleman had been reluctant to accept the mission, knowing that it would entail taking Fuad along on the voyage.

Once it had been revealed that Fuad's usefulness had been out-lived, only then did Stephen Coleman agree to sail into Bali and was briefed on the mission's purpose. He had been indifferent to the fact that his instructions would require him to execute Fuad once they had left Indonesian waters. As for the passengers who would die on flight *India One*, he had no feelings, one way or an-other regarding their planned demise.

* * * * * *

China — Xianggang (Hong Kong)

Admiral Tung-Pi Chen's South Sea Fleet's territorial command extended from deep in the South China Sea to the north, touching the border of Fujian Province, and across to the southern-most tip of Taiwan, the so-called Republic of China.

The Admiral stood on the modified *Luda* class destroyer's bridge, wishing his country had built, or at least acquired, a number of aircraft carriers. He believed that Beijing had made a grave tactical error years before, in not committing to the construction of at least two heli-carriers to be added to the Chinese fleet. Tung-Pi Chen thought about the imminent action, concerned that Vice Admiral Lieu, who commanded the Eastern Fleet, might enjoy most of the glory. Taiwan lay within the Vice Admiral's fleet's territorial con-trol, and was less than one hundred and fifty nautical miles from his mainland bases.

The action would commence within days, and Admiral Chen was one of the few senior-ranking Chinese officers aware that this would coincide with the Indian Navy taking a permanent position in East Timor. It was likely that the associated turmoil arising from the simultaneous operations would, most probably, occur without either nation so much as engaging their enemies in any real action. And there would be rich prizes for both countries.

The Chinese would demonstrate their naval superiority in the Far East, as they carried out naval-military exercises in both the South and East China Sea. Strategic Rocket Units based on the mainland would commence the exercise by launching a number of

DF-15 rockets into zones near Keelung in the north of the island, and Kaoshiung, Taiwan's southerly port. Further launches would be conducted, at two hourly intervals, throughout a three-day period of intimidation.

Seventy-five *Hunagfeng* class missile craft would then join the joint fleet exercise. They would steam to within ten miles of the Taiwanese coastline, accompanied by ten destroyers and twelve *Jianghu* class frigates. More than two hundred amphibious and other craft would leave China's coast, and sail towards Taiwan. Chinese intelligence was aware of the United States Seventh Fleet's presence to the south-east of the Philippines, led by the US Navy's only remaining forward deployed aircraft carrier, the *Kitty Hawk*. The Admiral was not concerned by the Americans' close proximity to Taiwan, because the Seventh was steaming somewhere near the Caroline Islands group, and he anticipated that they would turn immediately to the south once they discovered that the Indian fleet had turned north, towards Timor. But they would be too late. China's leaders in Beijing believed that the combined movements of both nations' navies, the threat of Chinese retaliation with its improved version of the *Dong Feng 31* Intercontinental Ballistic Missiles and America's need to maintain its commercial interests in Asia would force the United States to finally concede Taiwan to China.

The American public, now aware of Beijing's ability to deliver nuclear warheads with great accuracy to parts of the United States would, the Admiral believed, turn the tide. The lethal power of his country's forces had been greatly enhanced by supercomputers, innocently provided by the United States to China's military-industrial complex over the past years. China was most indebted to the former American Secretary of Defense, William Perry, who was instrumental in revising the legal limit on the export of super-computers, making it possible to acquire powerful machines.

Then, of course, there were his navy's improved *Xia* class Nuclear Ballistic Submarines. Official notification that two of these SSBN's were steaming towards the Chinese-controlled Long Beach Naval Base had already been served on the American authorities and Admiral Chen admired the strategy of positioning two Chinese nuclear submarines in American waters to coincide with the overall operation. He had no doubt that the American press would create sufficient alarm over the presence of the deadly vessels, as they steamed arrogantly into the United States' own backyard.

Chapter 27

*The Bali summit
day one*

The Grand Bali Hyatt suddenly fell quiet as Indonesia's ageing President shuffled forward and, watched by millions via satellite, hit the brass *gong* slowly, three times, in ceremonial style. As the deep, musical tone reverberated through the hall, the guests broke into loud applause. The Bali Summit had commenced.

Murray Stephenson returned to his seat alongside Graeme Robson and settled down to listen to the South African President address the assembled guests. Murray knew that once the formal addresses had been given, the visiting Heads of State would adjourn and commence their discussions in private. More than one thousand guests had been invited to the official ceremony, but only a few would participate in the three-day summit. Applause followed the President's speech and, after a polite pause, the floor was handed over to the Australian Prime Minister.

'Bapak-bapak, dan ibu-ibu,' the Australian leader commenced, then paused, permitting the thunderous applause to continue as the guests warmly welcomed his conciliatory opening words in the host country's language. He then continued in English, first addressing the Indonesian President, then the other visiting Heads of State.

'The Australian people welcome this opportunity to...' Murray looked around at the huge gathering and identified familiar faces he had not seen for some time. There was little doubt that the *creme de la creme* of Asian society had been invited, and Murray spotted a number of high-profile merchant bankers dressed in suits, sitting with Benny Salima across the hall. He wondered if Ruswita had attended the ceremony. '......and, with the deepest sincerity, I wish to state that the Australian people wish only to be your friends.

Terima kasih,' the Prime Minister finished his brief address.

As the visiting leaders each spoke in turn, they were greeted warmly by the guests who, without exception, understood the significance of this great occasion. Regional differences might now be resolved, and prosperity would continue to grow in their respective countries. The general consensus amongst those present was that the leaders could not be presented with a more opportune moment for open dialogue to seek whatever solutions were necessary to avoid a further escalation in disputes over territorial waters, sea lanes and borders. The general mood was one of hopeful anticipation that this summit would achieve an acceptable reconciliation for all, and restore regional stability. Without China's participation, however, many believed that Indonesia's position had been weakened, as there was little that could be discussed in relation to the Chinese seizure of Natuna Island without China's presence at the forum.

In their opening addresses, the Heads of State from Malaysia, Brunei, Vietnam and the Philippines all publicly criticised China for its aggressive actions, and called upon the Summit participants to support further action through the United Nations.

Murray noticed that Xanana Soares was not present on the podium. He thought about the Timorese exile. His absence was probably not a bad thing; after all what could he possibly contribute? It appeared that he was not going to be given the public stage at any time during his visit. Murray knew that the Indonesians would have insisted that Xanana's presence be played down, and that he would have no official recognition during his stay. Murray guessed that the self-appointed President of East Timor's government-in-exile would be experiencing doubts about his safety at that moment.

He conceded that once again the world was witnessing the perfect Indonesian compromise in their handling of the sensitive and highly emotional issues relating to their annexation of the former Portuguese colony. He joined the others, applauding, as the last of the formal addresses was delivered by the Sultan of Brunei. The guests rose to their feet as the leaders dispersed and followed the official party down to the informal luncheon, which had been prepared in the garden setting overlooking the beach. Murray followed Robson out of the hall and down to the swimming pool area, where hundreds of white-clad waiters prepared to serve the guests.

The atmosphere was most relaxed, and Murray could not help but marvel at the ease with which the foreign Heads-of-State moved amongst the other guests, stopping to talk to those who offered their sincere wishes for the Summit's success and waving back at others who had caught their attention.

The buffet commenced, and the guests settled down to enjoy the magnificent feast provided by the hotel catering staff. Roast suckling pigs turned slowly on spits while chicken, turtle, beef and goat *satés* were cooked to perfection across a bed of smouldering charcoal. Carved pineapples and watermelons, decorated with hibiscus and frangipani flowers, had been strategically placed around the tables. Exotic dishes with mysterious herbs tempted the brave, and foolish, while mounds of rice, white, yellow and fried, were dished out freely. Champagne flowed and the luncheon soon developed a carnival atmosphere which belied the seriousness of the occasion. Later, once the guests had retired to their rooms, Murray and Graeme were to return to Robson's villa, *Puri Kauh*, leaving the delegates to commence their three days of discussions.

Murray waited patiently until the crowded buffet area thinned before approaching the line of waiters serving the guests. He thought it clever that the Indonesian security had all been dressed in *batik* shirts to play down their presence. Further out, through the tall coconut trees which separated the hotel's finely manicured lawn from the sandy beach, he observed a number of well-armed patrols maintaining vigilance. He knew that the entire area would be under the strictest surveillance during the Summit, and hoped that the guards would not be called upon to protect the VIPs from any armed threat.

1245 Hours

Ratna giggled childishly as Michael rubbed the oil into the back of her thighs, while taunting her playfully. She was deliriously content, and wished they could remain on the island forever.

'Don't rub me there!' she laughed, as Michael's hands wandered, then she slapped his hand with hers, as his fingers found a sensitive area. Ratna rolled over on the beach towel and smiled lovingly, delighted that they would have the entire day to themselves before Michael's visit to the nuclear plant the following morning. She accepted the tropical fruit drink from a waiter and sipped slowly, enjoying the cold tingling sensation.

'Let's eat!' Michael suggested, with which Ratna shook her head. 'Why don't you order something light, then we can have an early dinner over at the *Puri Selera*?' She knew this would appeal. They had dined in this romantic setting the evening before and she could see from Michael's response that he had been captivated by the romantic, tropical ambience. Later, they had strolled along the soft, cool sand, admiring the moonlit night, and had lain together at the palm-fringed water's edge, listening to the outgoing tide and the gentle, lapping waves.

As the sea-breeze became cooler, she had shivered, and Michael had picked her up in his arms and carried her back into the hotel grounds, past smiling security guards, into their pool-side cabin. Their love-making had been sensual, soft, and loving. As they lay together, the warmth of their passion still evident, Michael had held her closely as she cried, filled with blissful contentment.

And now, as they lay around the pool, resting, Ratna wished their time together in Bali would never end. She looked over at Michael, and repeated her suggestion. He seemed to be dozing in the warmth of the tropical sunshine but he eventually raised himself to glance down at his wristwatch.

'That's a great idea,' Michael said. Then he yawned, and rose lazily to his feet. 'I'll order a plate of those tasty sticks of *saté babi* after I make a quick call.' He leaned over and kissed her forehead before strolling away in the direction of their cabin. Ratna wondered whom he could possibly wish to phone on such a magnificent day.

1322 Hours — Bali Harbour

Fuad looked over and observed his ship-mate staring across the water, apparently at nothing. They were bored, and he recognized the danger of their being so. Suddenly, Bartlett went into the make-shift cabin-cum-galley immediately behind the bridge, and reappeared wearing jeans, T-shirt and his tiresome baseball cap.

'I'm going ashore,' was all he said. Fuad watched as the New Zealander moved to the stern and prepared the rubber Zodiac to take him to the island. Minutes passed before he heard the twenty-five horse-power Evinrude outboard cough, then hum into life, as Bartlett pointed the dingy towards shore and opened the throttle wide.

1348 Hours — Java

Sujono and his wife arrived at the refurbished government guest-house and immediately rested from the arduous helicopter flight. That evening, they would be entertained by the local Governor and his family. The advance party had prepared their accommodations, and light refreshments for their arrival. While his wife rested, Sujono walked through the adjoining tea plantation, never out of view of his two armed security guards for more than a few moments.

He thought about the following day's programme, and considered the significance of the occasion. Vice President Sujono Diryo turned and faced the north, shading his eyes from the mid-afternoon sun, while he attempted to identify the distant buildings of *Rama II*. Scattered cumulus clouds moved across the sky gathering for the typical, monsoonal, late-afternoon thunderstorm. He searched the scene below and, at that moment, a break in the clouds permitted sunshine to strike the dome-like containment structure which covered the nuclear reactor.

Sujono breathed the fresh, sweet-scented mountain air, and his face broke into a knowing smile. He was reminded of the plant's dark secrets, and how these would soon place him at the helm of the Indonesian Republic. He then strolled back to the guest-house, intent on taking a brief nap, in preparation for the formal, evening dinner.

1540 Hours — Indian expeditionary Force, South of Java (Longitude 114 degrees East, Latitude 11 degrees South)

Admiral Rajesh Gopal was filled with a swelling sense of pride, greater than he had experienced at any other time in his distinguished naval career. He looked out and across the massive floating structure and considered his naval forces.

Since the establishment of the navy's three commands, India

had not once needed to deploy its ships in battle. His Western Command, with its headquarters in Bombay, was now the second largest naval base in the whole of Asia. He was most proud of his country's achievements. India had built a naval-air wing in Goa, at Lakshdweep, and now commanded the entire north-west of the Indian Ocean. Gopal's Eastern Command with its headquarters in Vishakhapatnam was well supported by its other naval bases in Port Blair and Calcutta. He smiled, recalling how efficient the crews of India's twenty-eight submarines had appeared during exercises out of their home port, Vishakhapatnam.

Gopal had supported the drive to increase his country's naval capabilities. When the *INS Vikrant*, India's first aircraft carrier, was decommissioned before the turn of the twentieth century, there had been only one other aircraft-carrier capable of leading India's navy. The *INS Viraat*, acquired from the British in 1987, was already showing its age. Less than thirty-thousand tonnes, it had been an embarrassment until the government had acquired the seventy-eight thousand tonne *INS Indira Gandhi* to lead the navy into the new millennium. His fleet had already steamed past Christmas Island, through the Java Trench and into the North Australian Basin, and he knew that they were currently maintaining their easterly heading, ostensibly for Port Moresby.

Gopal looked out again from the Group Battle Commander's bridge, directly above that of the captain's, and wished Vijay could have lived to see this day. Below, on the fifteen thousand square meters of flight deck, he watched as another of the F/A-18E Super Hornets was catapulted out, over the ocean, before climbing away to join the others. His flagship carried forty combat aircraft, including the two squadrons of Super Hornet advanced strike fighters, which had been wisely equipped with the smokeless F414 engines.

Gopal enjoyed being at sea, especially on this ship, which accommodated five thousand personnel and could cover seven hundred miles each day. Below, when you took one of the four aircraft elevators to lower levels, lay an entire city. There, one would find F-14 Tomcats, CH-53 transporters, many more Hornets and, deep inside the ships bowels, two nuclear reactors, which drove the massive bulk through the ocean at more than thirty knots. From keel to mast, Gopal knew that his ship stood more than twenty stories, and was three times the length of a football field. It was only fitting, the admiral thought, that such a magnificent structure should lead India into a new era, one which would see his country expand its territory for the first time since the time of the British Raj.

As he stood on the bridge overlooking the flight deck, Gopal considered the historic moment which would soon take place, while the Indian Navy was under his command. Once the armada had arrived at the point where Australia's territorial limits ended, his ships would turn sharply to the north and steam directly for Dili, around the point off Tutuala. The fleet would position itself between Dili and *Pulau Kambing*, utilising the island's airstrip to further consolidate the Indian force. There, Indian marines would be ferried ashore under cover of darkness, where they would wait until day broke across the island.

The fleet air-arm would then take control of the skies around Dili, alerting the Timorese of their President's return, while other propaganda material would be dropped across all major population centres, encouraging the people to take to the streets, as they had been liberated by the Indian Government. India's naval aircraft would control the sky, providing confidence to the people whose country had been occupied by one foreign government or another through four centuries.

Gopal believed that the Indonesian occupying forces would surrender under the might of the Indian Expeditionary Force, after which they would be given the opportunity to retreat, in an orderly fashion across their own lines, back into Western Timor. Gopal's orders were to threaten the Indonesians on all fronts, as India was not even prepared to concede Oe-Cusse, the small Portuguese enclave formerly locked and isolated inside Indonesian territory. India would then, by its actions, have succeeded where others had failed. East Timor would have its independence; an independence supported by the United Nations resolution. India, in turn, would have achieved the pivotal position it so desperately needed. An advance defence point for further expansion into the oil-rich and fertile basins of the Malay Peninsula.

Gopal was one of the few to understand that it had never been his belated friend's plans to invade Indonesia. East Timor was to be a bargaining strength from which the Indian's second phase would been implemented. With China in the north and east, and only arid terrain in the north-west, India had no choice but to consider the fertile peninsula which ran from Singapore, through Malaysia and Thailand, to the northern borders of Myanmar.

World opinion, he knew, would be against them. In a climate where China could successfully annex the oil and gas-rich fields north of Indonesia without foreign military intervention, Gopal believed that they had made the correct decision. *Who would possibly move against their supporting the reinstatement of a United Nation's recognized government?* Their tactics were clear. The Americans would be beside themselves over the Indian action, and call for a United Nations Security Council sanction to be imposed. He believed that this would not eventuate. China, as a member of the Security Council, would veto any action requested by other members of the United Nations Security Council. In turn, India would support China's annexation of Taiwan.

Admiral Gopal then thought about Xanana. It had been imperative that Xanana's presence on board be hidden from the world. Knowing just how difficult maintaining the integrity of such an exercise could be, he had decided that Xanana should not be taken aboard until after the Bali Summit had commenced, using the fleet's proximity and his own presence to disguise their intentions. Xanana would accompany him on the return flight to his flagship. Xanana Soares' presence on board the occupying force would then provide legitimacy to the armada's entering what would otherwise be deemed foreign territory.

Admiral Gopal was not entirely convinced that Soares had the strength of character to lead his country, even under the auspices of India's expeditionary forces. Once India had occupied the former Portuguese Colony, world recognition for Xanana's government would, he believed, soon follow. Admiral Krishna Gopal agreed with Dr Malhotra and his new Prime Minister that it was unlikely that nations which had earlier pledged their support for an Indonesian withdrawal from East Timor would renege on their earlier commitment, once India had ensconced its forces there, in support of a free and independent state. But it might become necessary for them to identify someone to fill Xanana's shoes if he did prove to be unsatisfactory.

He looked out from the Battle Commander's bridge, towering

more than a hundred feet above the sea, and watched the waves grow in height, some white-capping, licking the powerful carrier's sides as she steamed ahead. The admiral checked his chronometer, nodded to the Commodore who had been appointed Battle Commander, then left the bridge to prepare for his bumpy ride to Bali in the AH-64E Apache helicopter.

1549 Hours — Bali

John Georgio splashed water over the girls' heads as he kicked in their direction, swimming away from the small group standing in the shallow end of the beautiful pool.

'Come on, girls, get wet!' he yelled, back-stroking his way through the water.

'Johnny, no!' several cried, struggling to wade away from the splashing before their hair had been ruined. None of them could swim, and all of them disliked the idea of standing around half-naked under the hot, baking Balinese sun. They moved away from the man who had organized their paid excursion to the island, wishing he had remained behind. Not one of the young women was to receive less than five hundred dollars for the part they would play in entertaining the wealthy visitors.

'Grae! Grae!' one of the young prostitutes called, happily, as Graeme Robson returned and strolled down to the pool-side. 'Hey, Johnny, its Graeme!' she called again, moving as quickly as she could through the water, close to where he stood, and away from the offensive Georgio.

'How did it go?' John called, standing on tip-toe and wiping excess water from his face. He didn't care that he was not included in the arrangements to attend the opening, preferring to accompany the girls.

'Not bad,' Graeme replied, stripping down to reveal all as he spoke. 'Murray remained behind, says he'll join us later.' He eased himself gently into the pool, then slowly immersed his head under the crystal clear water. Moments later he found himself gripped playfully by one of the girls. He lifted her out of the water, then let her fall. She sprang back, terrified, her hair wet from the dunking. The pretty *Dayak* girl pouted, then turned on her friends, splashing them furiously as they squealed for her to stop.

'What have you got arranged for tonight, John?' Robson had given Georgio a permanent retainer to provide a constant flow of young, beautiful models for his extra-marital activities. When Peter Wong's shrivelled body and weakened libido had reduced his sexual appetite and activities, John Georgio's services had no longer been required. Graeme Robson had then engaged the American, knowing that John's access to the discreet amateur circuit was legendary around Singapore circles. He had been surprised to discover the daughters and sons of some of the more influential families on John's list.

'What, not satisfied with this lot?' Georgio answered, flinging something across the other side of the pool. Robson laughed; having already slept with two of the four dazzling creatures, he was already becoming bored with the Indonesian girls.

'No, I meant what have we organized for later in the evening.' He slipped his arm around the closest girl and untied the knot securing her costume. She did not resist, permitting Robson to remove the top of her two piece bathers. She lowered her body further, not wishing to catch too much sun. Then she felt his hands move to her thighs, and she assisted him to remove the lower half of her bikini. A servant appeared, moving silently around the pool and retrieving the drink coaster Georgio had flicked, unsuccessfully, at one of the girls. The servant then moved back inside the main building.

The servant had learned from earlier visits never to remain outside when the *tuans* were playing, remembering that the more these men drank, the greater was their abuse. What the prostitutes did inside the bedrooms was, to her, their own affair. Everyone had to eat, and although she would never consider selling herself to any man, she was not critical of others who did.

Her main concern was to watch these young women to guard against their sticky little fingers which, invariably, removed considerably more from the villa as they left than the *tuan* believed, often accusing his own staff for missing items instead. She watched and listened, as the two men talked, but did not understand.

'Well, if you and Murray are in the mood, we can go down to the new cabaret in Kuta.' He waited for Robson to stop fooling around and respond. John was careful how he handled this man's private assignations, knowing that his volatile temper had cost others before him their opportunity to remain in the wealthy playboy's employ, and John desperately needed the income generated from these excursions.

'Sounds good to me, let's take Murray, but we'll leave these behind,' he suggested, tilting his head in the direction of the four girls. John understood what was required of him. He would have to leave beforehand and see what he could arrange for Robson at the new Kuta Beach Club Cabaret. He thought about this and decided that it would be wise to make a few advance calls and have one of his contacts position a few ladies at the club, just in case. He waded to the side of the pool and climbed out.

'I'll make the arrangements now,' he said, snapping a towel off a table, drying his bald head while he walked back into the villa.

1804 Hours — Bali, Ngurah Rai Airport

The Indonesian President climbed the steps to his aircraft slowly, and turned to wave at those who were watching from the observation deck. Within minutes, *AURI One* was in the air, heading for the capital, Jakarta. The President's flight plan took him directly over Mt Muria but, by the time he was overhead, it was dark, and the presidential flight had already reached twenty-two thousand feet, making visibility below impossible.

As his aircraft bumped in response to the turbulent air currents flying over the rough terrain below, back in Bali, Admiral Gopal's helicopter set down on the designated area marked with a large white cross, located between the main hotel building and the beach. The pilot needed to refuel his machine at Ngurah Rai before the return flight, and maintained the engine's revolutions with the rotor-blades continuing to chop through the thick, humid air as the admiral ran, in a half-crouched position, towards those who waited for him in the magnificent hotel grounds. The Prime Minister's aide immediately escorted India's Admiral of the Fleet through a throng of surprised dignitaries who had gathered for cocktails, and led the way through the rows of security, into the main building, and upstairs to the Indian Prime Minister's suite.

* * * * * *

'Welcome, Krishna, welcome!,' the recently-appointed leader grinned profusely as he embraced his colleague. 'Welcome to the Islands of Gods,' he paused, 'and India's destiny', he added, gripping the Admiral's shoulders warmly in a gesture of camaraderie.

'Is all in order?' he asked, 'are we ready?'

Admiral Gopal stepped back from his Prime Minister, his face beaming with pride.

'Yes, Prime Minister,' he said. 'We are most certainly ready.'

* * * * * *

Java — Mt Muria (overlooking Rama II)

Vice President Sujono was wakened by the gentle knocking, and he called out to the housekeeper, acknowledging the call. He rolled to one side and observed that his wife had already slipped out quietly, leaving him undisturbed. Checking the bedside clock, Sujono knew that he had plenty of time to bathe and prepare for the Governor's dinner. He swung his legs over the side of the bed, found his slippers, then rose slowly and shuffled to the bathroom to take a *mandi*, hoping that the water would be warmer than it had been earlier.

Outside, standing alone admiring the beauty of Java's mountainous views, his wife stood contentedly, breathing in the cool, fresh, lightly-scented air. Terraced rice fields fell away below, their careful configuration a result of thousands of years of farming and irrigation. She looked out across the western slopes where the tea plantation encircled a small village, and wondered what it would be like to be raised in such an isolated, primitive environment.

Sujono entered her mind as she thought about preparing for the evening function, wondering if he would be as happy as she was at that moment, knowing that after the years of trying, his seed had finally found fertile ground. She then rubbed her stomach, excited by her secret. She would tell him tonight, before they went to sleep. Then she would wait until returning to Jakarta before informing the President that she was finally with child.

2147 Hours — Bali

Candlelight danced through the diamond-shaped holes cut into the hollowed pineapple, touching Ratna's face and accentuating her aquiline features. Michael reached across and touched the side of her soft face, then smiled.

'I could easily grow accustomed to this,' he whispered, captivated by the balmy, tropical ambience and his partner's beauty. Ratna raised her hand and placed it over his, then nestled her face against them both. Somewhere out in the kitchen the cook called out angrily for the staff to hurry, and she giggled, understanding precisely what the man had said.

Tantalising aromas drifted through the restaurant, teasing their palates as *saté penyu, gado-gado, rendang* and even *ikan pepes* were carried in by waitresses clad in traditional attire. Toothless members of the *gamelan* orchestra smiled happily as they played their timeless instruments, the bamboo xylophone tones prominent above the others. Then, when Michael believed the atmosphere was already perfect, a young Balinese girl sprang out onto the small stage and commenced dancing to the exotic music. At that moment, Ratna moved their joined hands closer to her lips, and she kissed Michael's softly, lovingly, and whispered across the table that she loved him.

2205 Hours — Rama II, Java

Their room flashed alive with a brilliance only lightning could deliver, and she flinched, anticipating the inevitable thunder-clap. The evening storm had brought their function to an early end, cutting power to the mountain guest-house as loose, dangerous cables whipped around the building's exterior, flicked about by the wind.

The Vice President and his wife had returned to their room with the help of candles carried by an army of servants. As the couple made their way up darkened stairs to their suite, Sujono thought it ironic that they were without electricity, practically within sight of one of the world's largest energy plants. They had changed quickly and climbed into bed, the silence between them interrupted only by the terrifying clashes overhead. He moved closer, knowing that she would be frightened.

'No, Jono,' she protested, 'I'm very tired.' She was angry with her husband and his flirtatious, roaming eyes. The Governor had invited his senior Military staff with their wives to join his family in entertaining the Vice Presidential couple. The reception had barely begun when Sujono started flirting with the Governor's daughter, obviously basking in the excessive flattery of the younger woman. Later, when they had retired, the Vice President's wife had decided against telling her husband about her pregnancy. She would tell the President first, and then see how Sujono reacted when he discovered that she had informed everyone else in the Palace before him.

Sujono understood her mood. She was not unlike any other Indonesian woman he had known, and was expected to show some signs of jealousy. He ran his fingers along her spine, knowing how she enjoyed his touch.

'I said no, Jono!' she snapped, unable to reach his wandering hands. But she could not resist. Minutes later she lay on her back, urging him to continue. He thrust against her, groping to remove the rest of her bedclothes when, suddenly, he cried out in pleasure, as the warmth of his body flowed prematurely into hers. Disappointed, she lay quietly under the light quilt, her eyes filled with tears.

2350 Hours — Bali

They strolled into the club reception, arms around each other's waist. Michael broke away to pay the cover charge, then reached out for Ratna's hand and escorted her inside the Kuta Beach Cabaret. Two overdressed doormen bowed as they opened the club's main doors. The cabaret show was under way as they entered.

'My God!' Ratna cried, deafened by the band's excessively loud amplifiers.

'What?' Michael shouted, bending his head closer to hear what she had said. Ratna shook her head and leaned closer, on tip toe.

'Let's not stay,' she shouted, the music so loud she could feel the pulsating rhythm vibrating through her chest.

'Just one drink over there,' Michael insisted, leading her by the hand through the packed night club. They made their way to the bar and stood while Michael screamed his order to the busy barman.

'Michael, I'll be back in a moment,' Ratna shouted, pointing to the red exit signs down past the end of the long, saloon-styled bar. Just then, the floor show came to an end. The club erupted with drunken cheering and whistles, as the Filipino dance group all turned their bottoms towards the guests and displayed what little they were wearing. Ratna made her way through the unruly crowd of drinkers packed around the bar to the toilets.

When she had finished, Ratna exited the dimly lit area and was startled as an arm slipped around her waist and lifted her bodily off the floor. She yelled, but her cry was lost in the cacophony around her. She felt a hand grab her right breast, and struggled, jabbing her elbow at whoever held her tightly from behind. Pain flashed through her lower arm as she struck her assailant's face, managing to struggle free. As her feet touched the floor, Ratna turned and kicked John Georgio directly in the left shin, glaring at the drunken American.

'You bitch,' he screamed. The tip of her shoe had struck bone. He lifted his fist to strike her, but before he could deliver the blow another guest sprang into action and blocked Georgio's attack.

'Cool it John!' the man yelled, holding Georgio firmly.

'For chrissakes, Murray!' he yelled at the older man. 'The bitch kicked me!' Ratna stood glaring at her attacker, shaking with rage.

'Are you all right?' Murray asked, leaning close and placing his hand under her elbow. His breath smelled heavily of alcohol, and Ratna immediately pulled away, then turned and pushed through the packed crowd. She found Michael, sipping his drink, standing at the bar.

'Are you okay?' he asked, concerned by her distressed appearance.

'It's all right, Michael,' she lied, 'can we just get out of here?' He placed his drink back on the bar, withdrew ten dollars and permitted Ratna to take his hand, leading him away.

'What happened in there?' he asked, as they sat inside the taxi, heading back to their hotel.

'Nothing, Michael, let it be. I'm just not feeling well, that's all.' Ratna was concerned that if she explained, Michael would most probably go back inside the club and beat the living daylights out of the obnoxious drunk.

'Are you sure?' he insisted, but Ratna ignored the question.

As they drove the short distance to Nusa Dua, Michael knew clearly that there was something wrong. Back in their cabin, when he had attempted to hold her comfortingly, she had feigned tiredness, undressed hurriedly, and gone straight to sleep.

Back in the Kuta Beach Cabaret Club, John Georgio called for more bourbon as the music grew even louder. Murray Stephenson simply shook his head in amazement at the noise generated by the revellers as they continued to have a great time. He checked his watch, and patted Graeme Robson on the shoulder.

'That's enough for me!' he shouted, rising to leave. Robson checked the time also.

'Too early!' he yelled, as he attempted to grope one of the Filipino dance group John had managed to drag back to their table.

Murray just shook his head. *I'm too old for this*, he thought as he left the others to play on. He walked out to the waiting driver and climbed into Robson's waiting Mercedes 600, where he promptly fell asleep for the whole of the drive back up to their mountain resort.

As the smooth German machine glided through the foothills, the driver felt his steering wobble briefly, and slowed noticeably for a few minutes. The sensation did not reoccur, and he increased his speed, satisfied that his imagination had been playing tricks again.

Chapter 28

Bali — the countdown
0040 hours, day two

John Georgio fell drunkenly to the dance floor as the revellers tripped over each other, oblivious to the cause for their sudden loss of balance. The jolt had shaken the night-club, but most inside were past being able to recognize the sensation for what it had been. They picked themselves up and continued to dance to the screaming sounds of the heavy metal band.

In their hotel room, Ratna awoke and looked across at Michael. In a few short hours she knew that he would have to rise and leave for his visit to *Rama I*. She reached over and stroked his hair tenderly, then went back to sleep.

* * * * * *

Rama II — Java

Engineer First Class Mochtar Pribadi felt the slight shake and immediately looked up at the control room instrument panel. He watched the indicators for several minutes, then returned to reading the smuggled Playboy magazine which one of the men had brought onto the site during the earlier shift. Boredom was the only danger he could see threatening the *Rama II* plant, only boredom.

The structural crack along the top of the containment building moved infinitesimally, and from the broken section precariously held by inferior re-enforcing steel came a faint groan.

There was no shift supervisor awake to note the seismic disturbance at the Bandung Institute; the automatic seismic measuring devices recorded that the epicentre of this most recent movement was somewhere off the Island of Madura, to the east of Java. The tremor registered only 4.2 on the Richter Scale, falling into the category of more common shocks felt around the unstable island chain and, as such, did not represent any real danger.

Shift engineers at the other plants ran the mandatory checks described in their operators on-line procedural handbook and noted that there had been no change in their instrumentation as a result of the light tremor.

Two hundred and twelve nautical miles south of Java, the tremor's weakened shock waves were not felt by any of the Indian Navy ships sailing in group formation with the aircraft carrier, *INS Indira Ghandi*, as they continued on their course for Timor.

0732 Hours — Bali

Some seven hours later, the Indian Prime Minister grabbed both sides of his chair as the breakfast laid out in front of him suddenly jumped and skipped noisily across to the edge of the coffee table, where it fell onto the thick, plush, royal blue carpet. He looked up in surprise trying to determine what had happened and was struck by the sight of the white face of his friend, Admiral Gopal, opposite him. The tremor continued for several moments until the Prime Minister noticed that the water in his fine crystal glass had finally stopped shaking. He looked at Gopal and shrugged.

'We shall not be staying too long,' he joked. Gopal clenched his fists under the table, concerned with the possibility of tidal effects generated by the tremor. He looked up at the Prime Minister and smiled weakly.

'That was a most severe shake,' was all he said, trying to appear less alarmed than he was.

Across the hallway, the South African President watched with curiosity as the bath-water sloshed around uncontrollably, and he pulled himself upright to avoid swallowing the thick layer of bubbly foam.

In an adjacent suite, Xanana Soares lost his balance when the tremor struck, falling to the carpeted floor, and two armed Indian security officers came to his assistance.

The Bandung Institute recorded the earthquake at 7.9 on the Richter Scale, just as the first staff arrived to clean and prepare the offices for the day.

Jakarta

* * * * * *

Rama I — Bali

Michael leaned forward as his driver eased the vehicle slowly around the corner, then veered off the main highway onto the secondary road which led up to the power plant's armed entrance. The security guards approached the vehicle and Michael displayed his official IAEA identification, to the more senior of the men.

'*Tuan* Michael, please wait, and I will inform the plant manager, and he will send someone down to accompany you to his office.' He thanked the officer and sat back to wait for his escort to arrive. He experienced the sudden movement as if something large had shaken his car, and Michael looked up, startled, but was surprised to see that there was no one remotely near the vehicle. *Not enough sleep*, he thought, before returning his attention to the file he had opened to read while waiting.

* * * * * *

Rama II — Java

The morning-shift first engineer checked the previous night's log book, then placed this back in numbered sequence, noting that there had been nothing annotated in the events column. He felt the jolt, and watched as the building around him absorbed the impact, moving ever so slightly, before returning to normal.

In the upper-most section of the containment chamber, the fine crack widened, permitting sunlight to penetrate. A shower of small concrete lumps broke away from the inferior cladding and fell down through the containment area, striking piping and machinery before fragmenting into tiny pieces.

Instrumentation continued to indicate that the plant remained on-line, and the structural anomaly continued to go undetected. Then, within minutes, the affected area experienced an aftershock which tripped the plant's turbines off-line. The shift engineer was startled by the shut-down, and sat mesmerised by the instrumentation for fully two minutes before hitting the red alert button on the monitoring console.

He moved across to check the auto-start, emergency, stand-by, diesel generator flow gauges, then hesitated, knowing that this machinery had not yet been fully commissioned and could not, therefore, provide alternative power.

The crack in the containment shelter widened under the additional pressures, throwing even more rubble into the plant below. The reactor's coolant pumps ceased functioning, due to the sudden loss of electrical power. Further away, in Java, nuclear power plants *Rama III, IV,* and *V* were kept under close observation by engineering crews as the second tremor was registered, without any incident being noted. But at *Rama II,* things were quite different.

Within the passage of a few, brief moments, the nuclear power plant attempted to *scram*, or shutdown automatically. Instructions to close the reactor down flowed through to the control panels from fail-safe protection circuitry which was designed to cut power to the latches holding all the important control rods in place.

* * * * * *

Mt Muria, overlooking Rama II

Sujono listened as his wife continued to throw up in the bathroom, and scowled when he saw that they were in danger of being late for the *Rama II* inauguration ceremony. Moments later she appeared, her face ashen from the morning sickness.

'I'm sorry, Jono, but I don't think I can make it,' she pleaded. Sujono could see that she was quite ill. He thought that the winding trip down to the plant would only make her worse, but was tempted, anyway, to insist. The President would not be pleased, and this was foremost in Sujono's mind.

'What if we wait a few minutes?' he enquired, but this was answered with further proof that this would be most unlikely. He cursed her under his breath and checked his watch again. He was going to be late! Moments passed and his wife appeared, her face a ghostly white. She shook her head, unable to go with him.

'Then remain here,' he said, turning to leave. *'After all, its only a formality anyway. The plant is already operational and doesn't even need*

our presence. I'll go down as planned, cut the ribbon, then return as soon as the photographs have been taken and Bapak has spoken by phone.' Relieved, she nodded, and then hurried back into the bathroom. Sujono left the guest house, and his convoy drove the short distance to *Rama II*.

0734 Hours — Rama I, Bali

The Bali plant's turbines were also tripped off-line with the full force of the earlier tremor.

'Activate the emergency diesel generator,' the chief engineer ordered, noticing that the generators had not automatically cut in as they were designed to do. Several minutes passed before the shift supervisor knew that he had further problems.

'Anything yet?' he asked, anxiously.

'Nothing,' the other man answered, shaking his head.

'What's happened to those emergency generators?' the chief demanded, anxiously. He followed established procedures, checking the instrumentation as valuable minutes passed. Still there was nothing. He grabbed for the internal phone and punched three buttons.

'Answer the phone!' he muttered desperately as the intermittent buzzing tone continued, unanswered. He tried again, but still no one answered. *What in the hell was going on out there?*

'Hamid, get over there and see what is holding them up, quickly!' he ordered.

He watched as the shift engineer hurried away to check. All staff had been well-trained to follow established procedures, but none had actually been exposed to any serious drama during the limited time the nuclear plant had been operating. Hamid disappeared to check why alternative power had not been supplied by the emergency diesel generators. When he arrived at the generator station, he found two other engineers arguing about the cause of the problem.

'No way!' the first man yelled, angry that his judgement had been questioned.

'It has to be!' the other responded. Hamid stepped in quickly.

'What happened?' he demanded, outranking both men.

'The engine fired, ran for less than a minute, then choked,' one said.

'*It has to be contaminated fuel,*' the other man claimed.

'*Then let's check the fuel,*' Hamid ordered, '*and quickly!*'

Both the men immediately went about checking the generator's diesel fuel supply to determine if this had been responsible for the machine's malfunction. Indonesian fuel supplies were, they all knew, notorious for causing such breakdowns.

While the men busied themselves, they were unaware that the reactor's coolant pumps had also ceased functioning, and had gone off-line as well at the time the engineers hurried to investigate why the stand-by power had failed.

The *Rama I* reactor tried to *scram* automatically, failing to shut-down as the control rods refused to budge. The rods were precisely machined to slide easily into place during a reactor *scram*, even after expanding when the core heated up to its normal operating temperature.

During reactor plant operations, though, the control rods are bombarded by neutrons, causing them to swell even further, but the design engineer had neglected to make these critical allowances prior to installation. The additional expansion of control rod volume caused the rods to stick, further confusing the inexperienced and poorly-trained operating staff.

0735 Hours — Rama II, Java

As a result of the tremor, a small piece of concrete which had worked its way loose finally fell from above into the reactor vessel area, damaging the hydraulic control valves. These valves were essential to the *scram* shut-down system, and this damage would later jam the valves when they were activated.

The incident went unnoticed by the staff, who were busily checking each others' appearance in preparation for the Vice Presidential visit. What had been a hairline crack in the containment structure just hours before had opened even more, revealing now cloudy skies. Further cracks occurred threatening to dislodge large sections of concrete.

0736 Hours

The rods were held in place by latches which, during a reactor *scram* or a loss of electrical power, are opened by powerful hydraulics. At the ends of the rods are strong *scram* springs designed to drive the rods into the core within a fraction of one second and thereby shut the reactor down. On *Rama II,* these failed to move. Immediately, the valve jammed, preventing the *scram,* or shutdown, from taking place. The shift engineer searched for his supervisor, but he was standing outside talking to security and others in preparation for the Vice President's visit. The engineer grabbed for the phone and punched frantically at the buttons. He listened to the slow, double buzzing tones.

'Come on, answer!' he yelled angrily at the handset, as it continued to hum.

'Shift controller,' a bored voice answered.

'What time will Vladimir arrive?' he asked the shift controller, who immediately identified the concern in the engineer's voice.

'He won't be here until later,' the man replied, stifling a yawn.

'Sialan!' the engineer cursed.

'What's wrong over there?' the other man asked, placing his cup of coffee down.

'The turbines have tripped off-line and we can't shut the reactor down!'

'What?' the shift supervisor yelled, jumping to his feet.

'We've.. lost power!' the engineer almost stammered, then waited, wondering why the other man remained silent. The shift controller thought quickly.

'What has the supervisor done?' he asked.

'I think he is out of the building. Can you come over?' The shift controller was not, in fact, rostered for duty that day. His presence had been mandatory, along with all other Indonesian personnel, due to the Vice President's visit and the official inauguration ceremony scheduled for just an hour from then. He had planned to return to his quarters once the VIPs had all departed. Now, this was out of the question, and he had no choice but to get over there, and quickly.

'Coming now!' he yelled, replacing the handset abruptly. He looked down at where he had spilt coffee over himself and wondered if the stain on his white coveralls would be noticed. He left the building and hurried over towards the main reactor centre. There he joined the shift supervisor whom he spotted hurrying also, returning from one of the auxiliary buildings which housed the stand-by generators.

'Problems?' he asked, walking quickly alongside the supervisor.
'It will still be days before they've finished installing the stand-by generators. Who called you?' he asked, as they passed through the reception area and the additional security placed on duty for the ceremony. There were dozens of flower arrangements everywhere, sent by well-wishers, foreign legations and contractors.

Minutes later the shift supervisor stood alongside the command console, scratching his head, and wishing that the Russian was there to advise. Even during assimilation trials he had not had the opportunity to personally witness the sequence of events which now confronted them all.

'Follow me!' he ordered, and the shift controller nodded. They climbed the first steel stairway and moved along that level checking for something they could not see, as neither knew what it was they were supposed to be looking for.

They could not know that the hydraulic valves which would normally have been thrust into action by extremely powerful springs had simply been jammed, by the falling concrete. These springs were designed to open upon loss of electrical power, allowing hydraulics to open the control rod latches. The shutdown *scram* springs alone, could not force the fuel rods down, because the latches could only be released by hydraulic pressure. These latches were designed to hold the rods up, and the *Scram* springs had been engineered to drive them into the core. Without hydraulics, the latches could not be released, preventing an automatic shutdown.

Then the reactor's temperature started to climb.

* * * * * *

0737 Hours — Rama I, Bali

Michael checked his watch and shook his head at the obvious bureaucratic response to the main-gate security's call. He knew that he was expected. Apart from the numerous communications that had exchanged hands between the *Rama I* management and the International Atomic Energy Agency concerning his impending visit, Michael had also made several direct calls to the management, informing them when he had arrived in Jakarta and later, upon arrival in Bali. He flicked another page open and continued to read on, resenting having to wait.

Inside the plant, less than a kilometre from where Michael Bradshaw waited, because of the sudden loss of coolant to the core, the temperatures and pressure inside the nuclear reactor began to rise.

Engineering design had anticipated such a malfunction, and an established mechanical set of procedures were automatically initiated by computer control. The primary relief valve opened, causing a reduction in pressure, and then closed again as it was designed to do. Two employees from the engineering team scrambled outside and hurried to the building where the stand-by generators were located, panic beginning to overwhelm the well-trained, but inexperienced team.

* * * * * *

0754 Hours — Rama II, Java

Vice President Sujono Diryo returned the officer's salute as he stepped from the black Mercedes and walked towards the reactor's main entrance. The Governor's party followed at a discreet distance, smiling broadly whenever the Palace photographer pointed his camera in their direction.

In all, the guests numbered twenty, including the Vice President's aides. Sujono's chest swelled with pride as he climbed the steps, admiring the huge welcome banner strung across the building's upper structure. Inside, the plant's General Manager stood nervously, waiting to greet the VIPs dressed, as were others in his team, in a white dust-coat.

Sujono strolled majestically across the highly-polished ceramic floor and shook the newly-appointed controller's hand. He then commenced his official tour of the facility.

The Vice President had visited the site on a number of previous occasions, and was comfortable with his limited knowledge of how the plant actually functioned. Sujono checked his watch, noting that there was ample time before the ceremony and the President's call. He knew that the *Bapak* would be disappointed by his daughter's absence. Sujono anticipated this problem, and reminded his aide to instruct the official photographer to include a selection of the photographs taken during the Governor's dinner party in the final press release.

Over in the control centre, an engineer continued to monitor the rapid rise in the reactor's temperature. His associate's worried face reflected his own alarm.

They were nervous at having been left alone with the dangerous situation and were afraid that they might be held responsible for any further mishap.

'I'm going to get the senior supervisor,' one of them suddenly called, hurrying away buttoning his long, white jacket as he climbed the steel steps, two at a time. He found the supervisor on the third level, fifteen metres up, deep in discussion with his assistant.

'The temperatures are rising too quickly!' the engineer called, hurrying towards the men. The supervisor could see that anxiety had taken hold of the man, and knew this would not help matters.

Why hadn't the hydraulic scram valves closed? he worried. He could not understand why the reactor had not automatically shut down. Unable to identify what was causing the malfunction, he started to lose focus, and felt an over-riding panic taking charge. Just then, the station communication's red light flashed, and he moved to the end of the steel-latticed walkway and lifted the phone.

'The Vice President's here!' the operator informed him. The supervisor cursed all things Russian and scrambled down the steep steps, down through the second and first levels, reaching the ground platform in record time. He hurried out to speak to the General Manager.

Sujono was discussing the plant's desalination benefits with the Governor, when he noticed one of the white-clad staff enter into a huddle with the General Manager. Seconds later, they moved quickly in his direction.

'Bapak Sujono, I'm afraid we have a problem,' the senior man said, his face concerned.

'What is it?' the Vice President demanded.

'We might have to close the plant down,' the engineer hesitated, *'temporarily, that is.'*

Sujono's face clouded over.

'What's the problem?' he asked, sternly. The supervisor was totally intimidated. He understood what normally happened to the

messenger carrying bad tidings.

'Well?' Sujono insisted, speaking to the general manager, but turning his head to the engineer.

'*We have a malfunction, Bapak Sujono. We have lost our turbine power and have no auxiliary stand-by generator on-line to correct the problem.*' He could see that the Vice President did not understand. The engineer wished the earth would open and swallow him. He would be held responsible for disrupting the auspicious occasion.

'*Can you fix this problem?*' Sujono asked, lowering his voice so others around could not hear.

'*Not without closing the entire operation down, sir,*' the supervisor advised. He could see Sujono thinking this through.

'*How much time do we have,*' Sujono asked, his concern growing rapidly that the ceremony would be delayed.

'*I don't know. If there was some way of providing alternate power, we might manage.*' The engineer really did not know what to do next. There had been no simulated training for such an unthinkable sequence of events. He scratched his head nervously; he would be blamed, that was sure.

He realized that there was little point attempting to explain, even with the use of simple terminology, what was happening inside as the nuclear reactor core's temperature climbed to uncontrollable levels. The mechanical failure which had occurred was most probably the result of inferior Russian equipment and installation procedures. He was at a loss to know what he might do and was breaking into a sweat.

Vice President Sujono frowned as the official photographer lifted his video camera and started rolling. He was merely testing his equipment again, in preparation for the brief televised broadcast which would soon go to air live, simultaneous with the President's call. It was essential that the timing of the ribbon-cutting ceremony not be delayed. Tens of millions of Indonesians and foreign viewers would be watching via satellite, and Sujono knew that the President was counting on the event's publicity to attract world attention to his country's achievements, while international interest was still focused on the Bali Summit.

Sujono feared that cancellation of the event might prejudice world opinion. After all, they had proudly established that the plant was operational, and that management had been passed to

Indonesian technicians. The possibility that some may laugh at the outcome struck home, and Sujono knew what he must do.

'Do whatever you can to keep this quiet; and don't panic the guests,' he ordered, leaning close. The unhappy supervisor could not believe that he was hearing these words.

'You may close it down as soon as the satellite feed has been disconnected.' The engineer nodded unhappily and left. He calculated what it would take, to do as instructed, and keep the plant operational for at least another thirty minutes. He cursed those responsible for the decision that prevented the Russian technicians from being present. The supervisor knew that he was lost without their guidance, and that the senior technician, Vladimir Kruchinsky, would not return to the complex until later in the morning after the ceremony had been concluded.

As the reactor's temperature continued to rise, a poor-quality weld finally cracked due to the plant's earlier movement, and the steam generator tube failed, allowing high pressure and high-temperature steam and water to enter the primary system. The heat and turbulence generated by the sodium-water reaction then extended into the reactor vessel.

* * * * * *

0810 Hours — Rama I, Bali

The moment Michael's driver opened his door, he knew there was a problem. Security escorted him into the main building, where he was met by the plant's manager.

'What happened?' Michael asked the manager. His question was met with a cautious smile.

'We had a minor malfunction as a result of the earth-tremor earlier. We're attending to the problem as we speak,' the man seemed unruffled by the event. Michael shook his head.

'Seems I could have picked a better time to visit, then,' he suggested, and the manager nodded. Michael noticed some of the staff hurry past; their worry was obvious.

'Why don't you wait inside, in my office, Mr Bradshaw?' the manager suggested, coolly. Michael followed the man, noticing that he was being led away from the main reactor building. Then he spotted several more white-clad staff running towards what he expected would be the auxiliary plant buildings.

'What happened exactly?' he asked, shortening his stride alongside the other man.

'I'll let you know, inside,' the officious administrator answered, hoping that the plant's engineering teams would have rectified the problem before the inspection commenced. He had expected Bradshaw's visit, but had honestly forgotten all about it in the turmoil which had occurred not minutes before. When he had been advised of Michael's arrival, he had deliberately kept him waiting at the main gate, hoping that the technicians would rectify things before the inspection commenced. After fifteen minutes, however, he had no pretext to delay meeting the inspector further.

They both knew that whatever had occurred in the plant's operation would eventually be disclosed anyway, as the IAEA required that all incidents be fully documented and passed to the Agency for review. As they entered the administration building, the automatic glass doors remained open after they passed inside, and Michael observed that the overhead wind curtain, designed to keep the cooler air locked inside, was not functioning. The entrance area was stuffy, and for a brief moment he concluded that the local staff might have turned the power off, knowing that they often did this when the air-conditioning became too cold for them. Minutes later, he knew that this could not be so, as the entire area was in semi-darkness.

'Coffee?' Michael shook his head, anxious to start.

'Are you going to tell me what the hell's going on here?' Michael asked, irritated by the man's complacent attitude. He watched the manager drop his eyes before looking up with a forced smile.

'The tremor knocked our turbines off-line,' the manager announced, his voice lowered as if those in the adjoining rooms might overhear. Michael raised his eyebrows in surprise.

'And?' he asked, annoyed with the deliberate attempt to downplay the significance of the event.

'They're still off-line,' the manager answered, fumbling with documents lying loosely spread across his desk. Michael jumped to his feet.

'Jesus!' he exploded, frightening the smaller man, 'how long have they been off-line?' he demanded, turning to leave the room as he spoke. The manager checked his watch, then answered.

'Twenty-one minutes.'

'What happened to the auxiliary power?' Michael demanded, standing in the now open doorway.

'The stand-by generators kicked in, then lost power before running more than a few minutes. The engineers are over at the power-plant now, trying to rectify the problem. All we have on line is the local power supply, and that could go out at any time. If that goes, we will also lose power to monitor through the control centre.'

'Jesus Christ!' Michael exploded. 'Take me over there. Now!'

'Certainly, Mr Bradshaw,' the manger responded, leading Michael out of the administrative offices, across a smaller car-park, which Michael assumed was for senior management, past buildings with signs indicating that these were data processing and storage areas, and over to the building where mechanical engineers were working desperately to clean the adulterated fuel from the diesel's lines.

Michael knew that inside the main reactor building, temperatures would be on the rise, and that they would not have much time to restore power before a major accident would occur.

The chief engineer monitored the temperatures with growing concern as they continued to climb and the system's relief valve, as designed to do, opened, then shut, in accordance with the escalation in core heat. He watched, as the cycle continued to repeat itself, without the desired result. Unbeknown to him, and those in attendance, this failure resulted in a steam bubble forming in the reactor's fuel core. This would inevitably accelerate the rise in local core temperatures because steam cannot carry-away heat as efficiently as water. In the adjacent building, Michael arrived on the scene to find mechanics yelling abuse at each other, panic threatening to exacerbate the dangerous situation.

'Where are we up to?' Michael asked the supervisor standing over the two mechanics as they wrestled with the fuel line assembly.

'We are trying to establish what's wrong with the fuel supply. The diesel may be tainted,' the supervising engineer replied.

'How long before you can have the generator back on-line?' Michael asked, trying to keep his voice level. The engineer looked up at the tall foreigner and shrugged his shoulders. Michael wanted to tell this man in less than twenty words that if he didn't hurry they could get their asses blown off; but he remained patient, waiting for the engineer's response.

'Depends on what we find. If it's what I think, then we might need another hour,' he said. Michael knew that they could not afford this much time. He took the manager aside and explained what he knew would be taking place inside the main reactor building, as they spoke. Less than a minute later, having encouraged the engineers to work faster, they both hurried over to the containment building to investigate what was happening there.

The moment they set foot inside Michael could see that panic had already set in. He asked to be taken in to speak with the senior technician on duty, and minutes later he found himself facing one very frightened plant supervisor.

'Temperatures are already well up,' the man explained, leading Michael around the terminal. Michael looked up through the overhead plant assembly, then calmly removed his coat, and his tie, and climbed the steel staircase to level one.

0820 Hours

'*Aduh!*' one of the mechanics cried loudly in pain, stripping skin from his knuckles as the wrench slipped forward.

'*Hurry,*' the other man cried, having learned from the senior engineer that the plant could self-destruct if electrical power was not soon restored. And they both clearly understood what that meant!

As the technicians at the Bali nuclear plant worked to clear the adulterated fuel from the lines while others went in search of alternative diesel fuel, those inside the main structure which housed the nuclear core and fuel watched the temperature rise to dangerous levels.

Lessons learned from the United States' Three Mile Islands accident meant that the American-designed plant's operational configuration allowed for make-up water, in the event of such an emergency, to be added directly to the pressuriser to minimise thermal stresses on the core.

Michael knew that the pressuriser would act as a buffer for the cold water which flowed through the heat exchange system. He also knew, from experience, that the pressures would drop immediately, as the added water would be considerably cooler.

When he checked the instrumentation again, Michael could see that there was some problem with this emergency procedure as well. He cursed the government which had permitted the plant's commissioning before staff were fully trained to handle such emergencies, although he recognized that, in most cases, only hard experience would have assisted identify the problems they then faced at *Rama I.*

Inside the reactor plant, technicians scrambled to learn why this was not happening. Michael wiped the sweat which threatened to run into his eyes as the ambient temperature became unbearably uncomfortable. He checked the monitoring station, desperate for a lead on what had happened to the fail-safe system.

When he finally identified the cause, he moved quickly to rectify the oversight, hurrying from the main station building with one of the engineers, showing him the way into the secondary structure. There, he checked the pump station responsible for directing the emergency reservoir of heated water which would be flushed from the pressuriser into the reactor's core.

The engineer responsible for ensuring this would occur had left his post to assist the others. He had never been called upon in the past to activate the pumps as an emergency procedure, for the unfamiliar sequence now taking place remained a mystery to him, as it did to most of the other inexperienced technicians at the plant.

Michael knew it was one thing to train people in procedures, and quite another to expect them to react according to the guidelines once placed under extreme pressure, especially if danger was present. He instructed the engineer who had accompanied him to engage the pumps immediately and, satisfied that this had been done, raced back to the reactor building.

His eyes darted across the maze of instruments. Indonesian technicians nervously watched the large digital clock above the console.

'My God!' an engineer exclaimed, pointing to the temperature reading.

'Let's get the hell out of here!' another called, turning to run.

'Wait!' Michael called, 'wait!' and the engineer stood transfixed.

'What's happening with that goddamn stand-by power?'

Michael yelled at the supervisor who had just hurried into the area. Michael could see that the other staff were dangerously close to abandoning the plant. He knew he had to contain the panic.

'The fuel lines have been cleared,' the supervisor answered quickly, as his eyes darted across the console. 'They're testing the alternate fuel tanks for water. If they're okay, we should have the stand-by back on-line within ten minutes.' Michael took him by the arm and pulled.

'Let's go!' he called, and the smaller man's feet fought to keep balance as Michael hurried back to inspect what was happening for himself. The remaining engineer watched the control console gauges in trepidation, as temperatures and pressure continued to rise. He looked at the double-doors, contemplating escape then, masking his panic, he waited while his co-engineers worked frantically to overcome the fuel problem.

When the reactor's core temperature reached a volatile twelve hundred degrees Celsius, the engineer prayed; he was sick to his stomach with fear, his eyes darting continuously from the temperature readings on the console, to the door, and back again. He wished they hadn't left him alone in there!

Less than a minute later, the stand-by power fuel system was declared clear, and diesel flowed into the huge generator as an engineer, perspiration stinging his eyes, leaned on the over-ride starter. Michael stood stoically in line with the others, as the familiar grunting mechanical noises rose from the machine, and they waited, willing the huge machine to start.

He closed his eyes, counting, listening to the compressed air turning the reluctant machinery slowly, a choking sound, a pause, then a groan. Suddenly, with an incredible roar, the generator clamoured into life.

Without exception, the engineers yelled, and even before the operator had attempted to place any load on the delinquent generator, they had left the building, running back towards the Control Center to establish whether they had sufficient time remaining to prevent the core from melting down.

0832 Hours

Michael's heart pounded as he ran back into the Control Center, his long athletic strides leaving the other engineers well behind. Over on the main console, he was staggered to see that temperatures had climbed to fifteen hundred degrees.

Moments later, he was joined by the others, panting as they gathered around the instrumentation to watch. Michael placed his hand on the shoulder of the engineer who had remained alone at the console.

'Good work,' he intoned. The man looked up at the foreigner, and forced a weak smile.

'Did we make it in time?' he asked, and Michael could see that the man had done well to contain his apparent fear.

'We should leave!' one called out, overcome with fear, turning to run.

'Let's get the hell out of here, now!' another cried, watching the gauge hovering around the fifteen hundred degree mark.

'Wait!' Michael yelled, holding his hands out, pointing back to the gauge. It had slipped slightly, as the cooler water had taken effect. In the deafening silence which followed, the team stood transfixed, watching. Then the temperature fell again. Suddenly, they all burst into cheers, grabbing each other's shoulders in excitement, as emergency power was finally restored. Michael remained standing at the console, his eyes glued to the instruments.

Below, as the steam in the core attempted to reach the same temperature as the core fuel, the pressure relief valve lifted, as if it were operating on some gigantic, domestic pressure-cooker. As the cooler water flowed into the system, the temperature dropped dramatically, collapsing the steam bubble which had formed inside.

Slowly, the nuclear core began to cool.

Michael waited at the control station until certain that the system had been restored, and that heated water was being redirected in a controlled manner to avoid cooling the fuel elements too quickly. He muttered a silent prayer, hoping that these would not shatter from the incredible thermal stress they would be subjected to as the temperature differential came into force. He didn't need to ask the engineers to check radioactivity levels.

Michael observed from the instrumentation that the additional release would be of little concern to them all. Still, he would insist that they continue to monitor the levels within the plant, just to be certain.

Michael looked across at the Indonesian supervisor and nodded. The man's face broke into a wide grin.

They had all done well.

They had trained for emergencies and, although there had been confusion during the incident, he believed that they had handled the situation in a most professional manner. He shook the hands of those around him, noticing that he had not seen the plant's manager since they had discovered the extent of the danger.

Michael's remaining concern then was whether they had managed to prevent irreparable damage to the plant, knowing that intense examination would be required to determine the extent of repair required to bring *Rama I* back to an acceptable operating standard. He glanced at the monitor clock, and was surprised to discover that the entire emergency had occupied less than an hour of his life. He found an empty chair and threw himself down heavily, mentally exhausted.

* * * * * *

0844 Hours — Rama II, Java

Vice President Sujono resisted looking at his wrist-watch again. It was only minutes since he had last checked. He forced a smile in the cameraman's direction, hoping the perspiration which threatened to soak his safari jacket would not be obvious.

Sujono preferred to dress in the same manner as Indonesia's founding President, Soekarno, believing that he had a great deal in common with the charismatic leader. He wished he knew what was happening with repairs, and how much danger there might really be. The agitated faces of the engineers around the control centre did nothing to calm his nerves.

Sujono walked towards the two brass poles which were several meters apart and supported the crimson coloured ribbon he would cut to officially inaugurate the plant. Unable to resist any longer, Sujono glanced nervously at his watch. It seemed as if time had suddenly stopped.

He turned around to view the guests, and was surprised that they did not seem to be at all uncomfortable with the sudden rise in heat. He breathed deeply, then waved for his aide to move to his side. It was almost time.

'Gentlemen and ladies,' the aide called, and the other guests immediately moved closer to where Sujono stood, eager for the ceremony to commence. They took their positions, the ladies straightening their colourful *kebayas*, tugging gently at their blouses. Additional lighting flooded the area to accommodate the television cameras.

The Vice President moved to centre stage where an ominous, red telephone had been placed in readiness for the President's call. The cameras whirred softly, and Sujono was given the signal to lift the telephone receiver, as satellite viewers stood by.

The guests were totally oblivious to the dangerous situation which had developed as they waited for the ceremony to commence.

While the sodium-water reaction continued unabated, unbeknown to the inexperienced engineers, it was also producing hydrogen gas. As the reactor's core temperatures rose, due to the ferocity of the sodium-water reaction, water disassociated with the temperature increase, further compounding the already volatile situation. The energy released by the reacting sodium and water pushed temperatures and pressures towards the point at which the pressure vessel would rupture.

'Bapak Presiden,' Sujono said into the hands-free telecommunications module, knowing that the Indonesian leader would be watching the proceedings via satellite, while speaking directly to the small assembly. In Jakarta, sitting comfortably in the *Istana*, the President frowned. *Where was his daughter?*

The President glanced at the members of his Development Cabinet, then turned back to the screen and proceeded to give *Rama II* his blessing.

'May Allah smile upon his people and bless this, the harvest of their toil, so that the world may see His children come of age.' The President then smiled, and nodded to his representative to proceed.

Hundreds of kilometers to the east of Jakarta, Vice President Sujono bowed his head in acknowledgement, then moved to cut the ribbon. As the cameraman panned across the guests' faces amidst the polite applause which followed, he captured the frightened figure of an engineer running towards the gathering, waving his arms frantically.

An aide stepped directly in front of the terrified supervisor, and blocked his entry. The man struggled as he was held, his shout of alarm suffocated by the powerful colonel's hand before he could warn those present of the imminent disaster.

'*On behalf of the people of Indonesia, I declare this facility, Rama II, to be officially on-line*' Sujono cut the ribbon and turned to face the cameras, his forced smile evident for only the briefest of seconds, as television screens around the world suddenly lost their coverage of the momentous event when the nuclear plant erupted, the rapidly expanding force ripping easily through the fractured containment structure, instantly spewing hot, steam-driven, deadly radioactive spume into the morning sky.

As both are pyrophoric, the uranium and plutonium, now exposed and incredibly hot, ignited, causing a highly exothermic reaction to occur instantly, and a lethal combination of water, heat and graphite burned with an intense, almost flame-less, heat.

At the same moment that the resulting hydrogen explosion ripped through the containment building, throwing shattered pieces of the deadly core into the heavens, Vice President Sujono Diryo died.

Radioactive particles from fuel rods, and spent fuel stored nearby, were also sent soaring more than a mile into the sky, where the prevailing wind carried it, mostly towards the east, in the direction of Bali, the other eastern islands of the archipelago, and northern Australia.

* * * * * *

0931 Hours — Bali Harbour

Fuad shook his head in disgust, as Bartlett prepared to head ashore for his second reconnoitre of the Kuta Beach's bars. He was annoyed with Bartlett. Fuad had remained on watch throughout the captain's absence, and when Bartlett had returned in the early morning drunk he wanted only to sleep. And now, having recuperated from his previous night's drinking spree, it was obvious that Bartlett was going ashore again. When the captain had seen the discomfort on Fuad's face, his lips had curled into a cruel smile.

'Watch the ship,' he ordered, mockingly, lowering himself into the Zodiac, once again, leaving Fuad alone. *Damn the man!* Fuad fumed. He felt so close to completing his last mission, the one which would take him to America with his pot of gold, he was on edge.

Fuad calculated that, with other payments he had secreted away since his arrival in the Philippines, this final mission would see him with almost four hundred thousand dollars to his name. He cursed Bartlett then moved out of the sun into the galley, where he opened a can of cold *halal* meat.

* * * * * *

Rama II — Java

Vladimir Kruchinsky, the Russian training supervisor, arrived at the high security area and knew, immediately, that something was wrong. As all foreign personnel had been instructed to vacate the area during the Vice President's visit and commissioning ceremony, he had taken the time to drive to Jogyakarta, knowing that he might not have the opportunity once his services were terminated.

The main security gates to the one thousand hectare site hung crookedly on their hinges. There were no security personnel in sight. Even the military guards had vanished. As Kruchinsky drove down the wide concrete road leading to the nuclear plant, it was as if he had entered a ghost city.

Unbeknown to the Russian, when the meltdown had occurred, only an hour before, survivors had panicked and fled the area. They had not needed to be reminded by the wailing, warning sirens that they should flee. The shrill sounds had pierced the morning air, and could be easily heard high up into the mountains, as far as the government guest-house where the President's daughter remained resting, waiting for her husband to return.

Twenty minutes after the explosion had ripped through the plant, *Rama II* was totally deserted.

The banner which Kruchinsky had seen the Indonesians erecting before he had left lay in tatters on the ground hundreds of meters from the main buildings. A puff of wind picked up one end, and the long, thin announcement lifted lazily for a moment before settling back among the debris.

To the Russian, it was reminiscent of a scene he had visited in his past; he knew immediately that something was terribly wrong. His heart beat faster as fear gripped his insides and Kruchinsky drove on, faster, towards the main plant, tapping the radiation detector inside his jeep. It continued to read zero. The meter was malfunctioning due to the intensity of the high radiation field.

Kruchinsky swerved to avoid a large piece of concrete which had been deposited several hundred meters from the seat of the explosion. He braked, avoiding a smaller block lying on the other side of the road. The engine stalled, and he looked up at the main plant, and what he saw caused the Russian to cry out aloud. The entire side and cover to the containment structure had been destroyed.

He spun the wheel of his pickup, re-started the engine and drove the gas-pedal hard to the floor. Kruchinsky switched off the air-conditioner and cursed himself for having left it on while inside the plant's perimeter. *This place would be hot as hell!*

* * * * * *

After the initial explosion, the few brave men who had entered the damaged containment building to offer help to others quickly discovered that there was little that could be done there.

Poorly trained, and totally unprepared for such an emergency, their ignorance would cost them their lives.

In the days that followed, nearly two thousand men and a handful of women would receive deadly doses and suffer acute radiation sickness. Some would meet their end within hours through extreme damage to the brain and other vital organs. Others would die, painfully, within weeks from damage to bone marrow and severe burns.

As the communication centre had been quickly abandoned, those who had fled the scene carried news of the disaster to the closest military garrison. There, the officer-in-charge of security alerted his superiors in Jakarta. Until then, nothing had been known of the blast outside the area. Although thousands had watched as the televised opening had suddenly lost transmission, no one guessed at the momentous event which had caused the black-out.

Following his report, the officer then phoned his family to reassure them.

News of the catastrophe immediately flooded the capital, where announcements were immediately leaked to both radio and television, and picked up by the international electronic media.

And if as the people of Indonesia had not already suffered enough, another earth tremor rocked the island chain.

1112 Hours — Jakarta, the Stock Exchange

Indonesia's tallest building shuddered as the tremor struck its floating foundations, signalling that the geological upheaval which had threatened the islands of Java and Bali during recent months would continue to intensify.

Trading on the Jakarta Stock Exchange came to an abrupt standstill as confused news of the *Rama* nuclear plant disaster flashed across the overhead bulletin board. As information was scant, speculation about the extent of the meltdown grew, in the absence of any real evidence confirming the extent of the catastrophe.

As the news release scrolled across the electronic information board high above their heads, looks of disbelief swept over the traders' faces. Then pandemonium exploded across the floor as the extent of the Salima Group's exposure struck home.

'*Sell Salima!*' The cry went up immediately, as the panic-driven traders scrambled to off-load the blue-chip stocks, driving the shares' trading value for both Salima Jaya and Salima Energy through the floor. In the subsequent thirty minutes of trading, the Jakarta Stock Exchange shed thirty percent across the board. As news flowed to other financial centres, these too abandoned Indonesian shares as quickly as their own markets could absorb the collapsing stocks.

Kuala Lumpur and Bangkok Exchanges closed, unable to sustain any further losses in their own markets. In Singapore and Hong Kong, *taipans* shook their heads in despair, wondering how such a calamity could occur so close to Chinese New Year.

* * * * * *

The Indonesian President listened to his aide's report in silence. The First Lady entered as the verbal report ended, and the aide slipped away unobtrusively.

'How bad is it, Bapak?' she asked, having only just learned what had occurred. The older man looked at his wife, sadly, and shook his head.

'The information is very scant. There has been a nuclear accident and the damage is significant. There have been casualties but, as it seems that the plant has been abandoned by remaining staff and security, we won't know until a team arrives from Bandung to assess the situation.' The First Lady was stunned. She scanned her husband's face for a sign that he was not hiding the worst from her.

'There is no other news as to who has been injured. There has been no word from Sujono,' he added. He sat rigidly still, but his wife of so many years sensed the turmoil in his heart.

'What would you have me do, Bapak?' she asked, resigned to the possibility that their daughter might be amongst the casualties. The President looked at his wife, fighting back tears, and blessed her for her strength. *'Should we go there?'* she asked, her voice near to breaking, but he shook his head.

'No. We will wait for the first damage assessment report. General Suharman is on his way to the site at this very moment. He has undertaken to report directly to me once he has arrived at Rama II.' The President paused, out of breath, containing the pain he felt inside.

'How long must we wait?' she asked, fighting back her tears. She knew that she must now be strong; especially for him.

'It might be some hours,' he said, softly. He had been determined to demonstrate to the world that Indonesia had entered a golden age of technological development, and had shed its shackles of economic dependency on the West.

Instead, he had brought his country to the brink of a nuclear Armageddon, and this may have cost him his daughter's life.

* * * * * *

1205 Hours — Bali

International news broadcasts revealed that the Indonesian nuclear power plant in East Java, only minutes by air from the popular holiday destination of Bali, had suffered an explosion, resulting in the plant known as *Rama II* being destroyed. Within minutes, Indonesia's telecommunication's systems were overloaded as family and friends of those visiting Bali attempted to phone through to the tourist destination.

As news continued to sweep the island, fear of Bali's proximity to the nuclear disaster and the possibility of radioactive clouds caused mass panic. The words Chernobyl and nuclear holocaust were on everyone's lips.

Tourists packed their luggage and fled to Ngurah Rai Airport. There, crowds had already swamped the ticketing counters. Many waved hundred dollar bills in their outstretched hands to secure seats, and airport security struggled to control the unruly mob. Taxis sped to and from the airport terminal, delivering more panic-driven tourists to add to the congestion. The Australian Prime Minister requested Qantas and Ansett Airlines to redirect as many aircraft as possible to the scene, conscious of the large number of his countrymen spending their New Year school holidays in the tropical paradise. Singapore, Malaysian, Cathay and Thai Airways immediately ordered additional flights into Bali to assist with the urgent repatriation of their citizens from the disaster zone.

* * * * * *

Ratna had learned of the meltdown from her cousin, Benny, who had remained in Bali to hold side-talks with the Indian delegation regarding Salima's banking investments in their country. He had suggested that she remain indoors and wait. Bored, and a little frightened, Ratna followed Benny Salima's suggestion and waited impatiently in the cabin for Michael to return. He had promised to be back before lunch. She checked her watch again, anxiously. He was late.

* * * * * *

Michael dropped the receiver heavily back into its cradle and shook his head.

'The lines are still out,' he said to nobody in particular before leaving the administration block and walking over to the plant's canteen. There, he discovered, the scene was almost one of celebration, as staff and other employees grinned at each other while recounting who was doing what when the reactor almost melted down.

'Over here,' he heard a voice call, and Michael turned to see the senior supervisor standing, beckoning for him to join his table, around which most of those who had been directly involved in the panic-driven moments of some hours earlier sat with dazed expressions. As Michael approached, he could see that someone had smuggled a bottle of local Bintang beer into the compound, and had opened this to help them celebrate. Normally this would have been a dry station, so Michael understood the necessity for turning a blind eye to what he had seen and accepted a chair which had been pulled across from one of the adjacent tables.

'We all want to say, *terima kasih,* to you Mister Michael,' the now inebriated supervisor advised. Michael knew that these people would not normally drink, and that the one bottle had obviously gone a long way to destabilising all four of the men around the table.

Then he understood; looking around, he spotted another of the brown bottles, then another, unopened, protruding from the engineer's overnight bag.

'Tuan Michael!' one of them called, his voice slightly slurred. He turned and accepted the froth-filled plastic mug, and thanked the men in return.

'*Terima kasih,*' he responded, and they all clapped warmly.

* * * * * *

1435 Hours — Rama II, Java

General Suharman and his immediate team, dressed in protective clothing, entered the disaster area. They were astonished to see the extent of the meltdown and its associated explosion, and could only wonder how it might have happened. An assessment was made of the general area, but Suharman already knew that they were too late to prevent the radioactive clouds from showering their deadly dust over the surrounding villages and beyond.

General Suharman had climbed through the rubble in search of the President's daughter and her husband. One of his team had called him over to inspect the half-hidden, broken body, lying crushed under a large slab of concrete, its legs twisted in grotesque fashion.

It was Sujono Diryo.

Later, the general spoke directly with the President by phone, informing him of the Vice President's death and the devastation which he had encountered at *Rama II*. His team then moved to the facility's perimeter, and sealed the entire area off, pending arrival of reinforcements.

* * * * * *

The Vice President's wife had been awakened by the guest-house security and informed of the explosion. Terrified for her husband, she demanded to be taken to the plant, but was finally convinced that this would only endanger her own life. Overcome, she had burst into tears, demanding that the staff phone the nuclear power plant.

Their attempts to reach anyone there were unsuccessful. It was then that she phoned her father in Jakarta and learned of Sujono's demise. She collapsed, and was immediately evacuated by helicopter.

* * * * * *

1450 Hours — Bali, Puri Kauh Villa

Experience told the servants that it would be inadvisable for them to wake the sleeping *tuans*. They, too, were tired from waiting on the three foreigners and their entourage, for the *tuans* and their women had frolicked and played through the early morning hours, oblivious to the rest of the world.

Exhausted from the evening's entertainment and having continued with the merry-making upon their return from the cabaret, the occupants of *Puri Kauh* slept through the morning and into the early afternoon.

Murray had been the first to rise, and although he had been first to return to the villa, he still did not feel all that well. He ventured out of the luxuriously appointed bedroom, leaving his delightful companion for the evening lying naked on her side. He wandered down to the pool, spread a towel out under the sun, and lay down. Murray was asleep, pool-side in the deck-chair, when Graeme Robson emerged and instructed the servants to bring coffee for them both. They remained there recovering from the excesses of the evening before, and were finally joined by Georgio sometime after three.

As the afternoon sun diminished in strength, and began to dip behind a thick copse of coconut trees, a soft, late-afternoon breeze blew gently across the hillside, from the East, and from the direction of the disastrous meltdown at Mt Muria.

* * * * * *

1512 Hours — Kuta Beach

Dave Bartlett rolled over and looked at the girl he had picked up sometime mid-morning. They had demolished a bottle of Myers Rum before lunch and had crashed together, on her bed. He sucked in several deep breaths, and immediately felt giddy which caused the bile to rise in his throat. He coughed, and the Canadian tourist turned her body towards him, exposing the breasts which had lured him back to her room in the budget mini-hotel.

Dehydrated by the alcoholic binge, Bartlett climbed out of bed and looked around for something to drink. He cursed, knowing that he would have to go outside to one of the roadside stalls for a can of soda, for not even the foul, furry taste inside his mouth could tempt him to drink from the bathroom tap. He had learned that lesson years before, and had paid the penalty for the oversight.

He staggered over to the mirror and checked himself out, wondering if he might have banged the plate in the side of his head which would, he believed, account for the ferocious headache he now suffered. Bartlett checked his wallet and observed that he had already paid the tourist her fifty dollars. He checked again to see that she had not taken more while he had slept off his alcoholic state.

He dressed slowly, covering his head with the baseball cap, then wandered outside. The afternoon sun flickered through the tall coconut palms, making him squint painfully. Bartlett made his way across the road, where a small roadside *warung* advertised cold beer. He sat down and sipped the *Bintang* beer.

'Can't get a flight?' Bartlett looked up at the tourist who had rushed in to buy a packet of *kretek*, the local clove cigarettes, and addressed him. He ignored the man, returning to his drink.

The tourist looked at him and shrugged his shoulders. 'Yeah, I'm in the same boat,' he said, with a hint of remorse, 'last time I'll bloody well buy one of those cheap tickets!' Bartlett glanced at the man, disinterested.

'Reckon the next best thing to do is remain indoors then,' the tourist suggested, then hurried away. Bartlett sighed, finished his beer and waved for the check, deciding to find something a little more up-market.

He dimly recollected that there was a bar somewhere around the corner, so he strolled slowly in that direction, totally unaware of the panic which had cleared most tourists from the Kuta Beach streets during the past few hours. He found the place he'd remembered, but it was closed. Bartlett checked his Rolex Oyster, then looked inside the bar. It was empty. Annoyed with the owner's tardiness, he turned around and went in search of another location where he could sit down and rest in reasonable comfort. He looked down at his hands and saw that they were shaking.

He knew he was getting too old for this business. He had already decided that this contract would be his last. Once he'd returned to Manila, he would change identities again and head for Rio.

As he wandered around, Bartlett thought it unusual that the narrow streets were so quiet. He found another place and walked up to the bamboo bar. The neglected television set there was showing the Cable News Network, and Bartlett, while waiting for the bartender to appear, began to watch the broadcast. Suddenly he was riveted to the spot. Now he understood why the streets had been so empty. Minutes later, swearing profusely, he went on a frantic hunt for transportation to get him back to the harbour. And his ship. Bartlett was furious with himself, but not because he feared any possible radioactive fallout. He was no man's fool and guessed correctly that the alarming news would undoubtedly affect the Bali Summit, throwing their meticulously planned operation into jeopardy.

At last Bartlett found a local driver who was only too willing to accept the excessive one hundred dollar offer for the drive over to Benoa Harbour.

* * * * * *

1520 Hours — Rama I, Bali

Michael shook hands with the group of smiling engineers and technicians before climbing back into his vehicle, waving as he was driven away. He was dog tired.

He looked at his clothes and decided that he badly needed a bath. He wondered why he had been unable to communicate in any way with Ratna since departing early that morning.

Michael considered the reports which had been received regarding the *Rama II* meltdown in Java, and shook his head, knowing that this disastrous accident would most probably precipitate widespread panic and fear, not just amongst the local Indonesians who would have nowhere to escape, but also among the hundreds of thousands of foreign tourists currently enjoying their holidays on Bali and the surrounding islands.

Then, as the driver passed through the first major town between Negara and Denpasar, Michael realized that his worst fears had been correct. A massive traffic jam had been created as trucks, buses and other vehicles blocked the wrong side of the highway. It had been caused by a collision between two tourist mini-buses racing to the airport, still more than an hour away.

Michael had stepped out of his own sedan and walked down through the amazing mess more than half a kilometre before locating the problem. He jogged back to his own car, and instructed the driver to meet him back at the hotel, once the traffic had been sorted out by the local police and he was finally able to proceed. Then he walked back to where the front vehicles were slowly moving away, and found himself a lift by waving a fifty dollar note in the air.

* * * * * *

Bali Harbour

Fuad spotted the Zodiac speeding towards the ship. He swore, angry that the other man's self-indulgence might have threatened the success of their operation. As the outboard engine's motor died, Fuad scanned the immediate area, concerned that Bartlett's hurried return might have attracted unwarranted attention. He listened as the New Zealander loaded the dinghy, then walked towards the ship's stern.

'Now it's my turn for a break,' Fuad said, deciding not to engage in any conversation. It would, he knew, most probably result in a fight as he could see that Bartlett had been hitting the bottle hard. 'I'm going to catch up on some sleep.'

'No you're bloody well not!' the bearded sailor spat, 'We're getting under way. Now!' Fuad looked at him with a quizzical expression then, believing the man to be drunk, his anger rose. He could smell the hard liquor on the other man's breath and knew, immediately, that Bartlett would be dangerous in this condition.

'I'm tired, and you've left me alone onboard for ages,' Fuad said, wishing the other man wasn't wearing sunglasses so that he could see his eyes.

'The sleep can wait,' Bartlett snapped, taking a step towards Fuad.

'Why?' Fuad asked, stepping back from Bartlett, shifting his feet into a better stance. If the other man swung, he would be ready.

'There has been a change in plan, Fuad,' he hissed. 'We'll get under way now!' Bartlett removed his sunglasses suddenly, and glared at Fuad. Fuad glared back and the cold, green eyes convinced him that Bartlett was indeed serious.

'What's happened?' Fuad asked, but Bartlett brushed past him as if he wasn't even there.

'The Summit's been cancelled. For all I know, the bastards have probably already left. Now let's get going for chrissakes!' Fuad cursed but moved quickly, as ordered, visions of the lost opportunity clouding his mind. He signalled to Bartlett back on the bridge as the anchor noisily rose and was locked into place. Minutes later, they were under way, steaming the few kilometers to their destination where they would wait, listening to the Ngurah Rai air-traffic control tower's communications.

* * * * * *

1620 Hours — Nusa Dua

'My God, Michael, where have you been?' Ratna cried, distressed. He had returned and gone directly to their cabin. Michael was confronted with a barrage of questions. He stepped forward, expecting that her reaction had most probably been precipitated by fear, and held his arms out to her, forgetting how he looked.

'We had no idea until just two hours ago, Ratna. I tried to phone but everything's overloaded to hell. The Negara exchange could not get through. Besides, there's no longer any danger here,' he said, attempting to comfort her.

'My God, Michael, what have you been doing?' she exclaimed, stepping back, surprised.

'There were major problems at the *Rama I* plant as well, Ratna. I had to stay on when everything came back on-line, just to be sure.'

'Were you exposed to any radiation?' she asked, fear in her eyes.

'No, Ratna,' he said, wishing he could take her in his arms and comfort her as he could see that she was visibly distressed. 'The Bali plant did not release anything which would be of concern to me, or those working there. As for the Java accident, there's likely to be far more people killed and injured from panic than there would from any radioactive fallout this far away.' He tried to reason with her, but the fear of nuclear holocaust had struck deep into the hearts of those even remotely within the critical fallout path.

'We must leave, immediately!' she insisted. He noticed that their luggage had been packed and left standing beside the door.

'Look, Ratna, this is silly,' he tried again, hoping that she would listen to common sense. 'If we remain indoors, there will be practically no effect at all. Hell,' he said, controlling his temper, having been through a very demanding day, 'there's probably a higher reading here than outside right now,' he said, pointing to where the television stood. Ratna looked at Michael, unsure. She sat down on the bed and looked at the floor.

'I'm going, please yourself,' she said, standing again, and reaching for her handbag. Michael moaned silently. He yearned for a long, hot, bath, then a few quiet drinks in the lobby bar.

There was no doubt in his mind that he would be expected to report back in Washington, immediately, as a result of the disastrous accident. There would be little point remaining alone there in Bali; he sighed heavily, resigned to the new problem which then confronted him.

'I'm serious, Michael, I'm leaving.'

'But Ratna, listen to what I'm saying. You will be perfectly safe here, for chrissakes!' He looked at his filthy clothes and started to remove his shirt.

'Goodbye, Michael,' she said, stepping to one side, then turning.

'My god, Ratna, don't do this, please. I'm tired, I've had one hell of a day, and I really don't need any of this right now. Okay?' Ratna hesitated, then looked challengingly, directly into his eyes.

'I'm really going, Michael. If you love me, then you will understand. Please, Michael, please!' she pleaded. Realising that there would never be any peace between them unless he agreed, Michael reluctantly gave in to Ratna, then shook his head, more out of disappointment for his own decision than anything else.

He phoned downstairs to reception. Then he remembered the traffic problems he had encountered on his way back from the Bali plant.

'This is most probably going to be a total waste of time, Ratna,' he said, exasperated by her behaviour. The lobby had been a beehive of activity when he arrived. A large number of guests were huddled together in the foyer, desperation on their faces.

Unable to obtain confirmation of seats, many had refused to return to their rooms, hoping that their situation might improve by waiting close by reception, not caring that their presence only hindered others.

'We might not even be able to find a cab. Have you any idea what's happening on the roads? It's chaos, Ratna, pure chaos.'

'I don't care what you say, Michael, I'm going to the airport,' with which, she opened the door and left for the lobby, leaving him behind to organize their luggage. She hoped he would follow.

Michael fumed, angered by her behaviour, and was tempted to let her go, alone. By the time he arrived at reception, their account had been prepared, and Ratna had secured transport.

Michael shook his head, thinking he should have known that she would have her way. Several minutes later their driver fought his way through a maze of buses and other vehicles, and they headed for the airport.

Although Ngurah Rai Airport was not of any great distance, their driver could do little more than creep slowly along, his hand firmly on the horn as he made way through the incredible mass of people heading for the same destination. Occasionally, those stranded along the half-blocked highway threw rocks, while others banged their fists against the side of the vehicle, venting their frustration at having been left behind. Ratna gripped Michael's hand, refusing to look at those less fortunate outside.

'Michael, I'm scared,' she admitted, as more stragglers angrily pounded their car.

'It'll be okay, Ratna,' he said, hoping that his voice was reassuring. Michael too was worried. He knew what mob anger could do and in no way wished to be the object of their misdirected rage.

'Is it much further?' she asked, but there was no way he could tell. Michael had never been to Bali before and, even had there not been a crowd surrounding the vehicle, he still would not have known where they were.

'Not long now,' he answered, hoping that this was true. Finally, having suffered the abuse of the roadside throng as they drove slowly on, the driver turned and spoke.

'Can't go any further,' he announced. Michael looked outside but could not understand what was preventing them from proceeding.

'Go on!' he ordered, but the driver merely shook his head and pointed to his front. There, amongst the crowd, Michael could see a line of soldiers ahead, blocking the road.

'Police no let you pass here,' the driver said, agitated, holding his hand out for the promised fare. Michael swore and turned to Ratna.

'Now we really have a problem,' he growled. They had been stopped from passing through the well-guarded airport entrance, and forced to leave their taxi at the airport perimeter fence. There was not a porter to be seen anywhere. Instead, they were horrified by the sea of white faces clambering over each other, fighting for access into the airport terminal. Michael knew that it would be futile to attempt to carry luggage through the mass of humanity, even if they were permitted through the gates.

'Do you still want to do this?' he demanded. 'We'll never get through!'

'Let's leave the baggage, Michael,' Ratna decided. He looked at the crowd ahead of them and was unsure. When he observed that she was determined to proceed, with or without him, Michael extracted his passport folder and, together with Ratna's papers, placed these inside his jacket pocket. Michael then wrote down the taxi's number, handed over fifty dollars, and instructed the driver to take their cases back to the hotel.

* * * * * *

1625 Hours

The Indonesian President declared a state of emergency following telephone discussions with each of the Heads-of-State still gathered in Bali. They had all decided to return to their countries immediately, and continue the discussions at a more appropriate time.

The President's announcement was followed by a similar call from the Australian Prime Minister. Both leaders were stricken by the catastrophic loss of life in Indonesia, and the people of both nations prayed for those still trapped in the path of the deadly, radioactive clouds.

Presidential advisers had informed their ageing leader that the imminent radiation spill from the country's East Java *Rama II* plant would spare few within the immediate area, and that heavily contaminated clouds of radioactive dust would most surely affect Bali.

Contamination would also, unquestionably, reach far into northern Australia. Forecasts were that the radioactive plume would be carried by prevailing winds across the Timor Sea and penetrate deep into the Australian hinterland. The projected fallout was then expected to spread, affecting population centres as far as central Queensland.

In Canberra, Cabinet's advisers tried to tell the country's leader that the Australian death toll in Darwin would be more likely to be caused by panicking Territorians hitting kangaroos as they fled the northern city than any radioactive poisoning which might reach their isolated city.

In East Java, Bali and major centres of East Nusa Tenggara through to New Guinea, the figures indicated that more than seven million Indonesians would be affected in some way as a result of the *Rama II* meltdown.

Fortunately for those who resided in the national capitals of Jakarta and Canberra, their population centres would not be affected, due to the direction of Indonesia's prevailing winds.

* * * * * *

1642 Hours — Bali

The Indian Prime Minister had finished conveying his confirmation to the South African President that they would depart as soon as was practicable. The Boeing 777, designated *India One*, was being prepared for their early departure, and would be ready within the hour. The African agreed, anxious to leave the island before their lives were, in any way, endangered by radioactive fallout. Aides scrambled to advise security, drivers, and the many others who would be involved in overseeing the revised arrangements.

Most roads leading into Den Pasar had already been cleared by the Bali Garrison Commander. The protocol highway leading to Ngurah Rai airport had remained partially blocked for hours, as traffic congestion choked the vital arterial road. Thousands upon thousands of tourists had vacated their hotels and stormed the airport, fighting for a place on any aircraft which might take them away from the dangers of radiation poisoning. They had refused to listen as broadcast information bulletins assured them that they were not in danger, that the only real risk to their lives would come from panic-related accidents, and that they should remain calm, preferably inside their resort hotels. But very few of the panic-stricken tourists believed this to be true.

Exaggerated forecasts had been irresponsibly made on satellite news broadcasts and, fuelled by confirmation that the Bali reactor had also experienced some mishap earlier in the day, the visitors wished only to leave as quickly as possible. By mid-afternoon, more than one hundred thousand tourists had inundated the airport. As buses plied continuously between hotels and Ngurah Rai, taxis raced at breakneck speeds over the mountains, bringing tourists from the more isolated districts.

* * * * * *

1705 Hours

Admiral Gopal entered the Prime Minister's suite, accompanied by Xanana Soares. There was a brief discussion, an exchange of warm handshakes, and smiles all around. The Summit's delayed discussions could only work in their favour, distracting attention from the Indian Fleet's mission.

'Good luck, Krishna,' the Indian leader said, with the deepest sincerity, smiling at Admiral Gopal. Turning to Xanana Soares, he said, 'and good luck to you also, *Mr President*.' Xanana beamed at the man who would liberate his people, shook his hand warmly then left with the Admiral. They hurried to their respective quarters to prepare for their imminent departure.

* * * * * *

1710 Hours

Murray felt like turning around and smacking Graeme Robson on the side of his head. He hadn't shut up once in more than thirty minutes, ever since they discovered what had happened. While others around the island were already making arrangements to leave, Robson and his guests had slept, and played, without their having the slightest inkling of what was transpiring outside the luxurious and isolated setting of *Puri Kauh*.

'You're a bunch of useless bastards!' Robson had screamed at the servants. 'Christ, John, and you!' he yelled at Georgio. 'You're supposed to know what the hell is going on, for chrissakes! Isn't that what you're paid for?' Robson continued to whine and curse, distressed with the knowledge that they had been lying around in the open for several hours before discovering that the area had, most probably, already been subjected to radioactive fallout from Java. Immediately they had learned of the danger they were in, Robson had grabbed for the phone, desperate for further information regarding the extent of the disaster. He phoned his office in the capital.

'There's nothing much getting through,' Robson's private secretary in Jakarta had advised.

'What do you want us to do?' his senior management had asked, anxiously. They had been unable to raise their chief executive throughout the entire day because the Balinese servants, following the instructions which had been explicitly given to them by Georgio, the evening before, refused to wake the *tuans*.

'What happened to the market?' Robson asked nervously. He heard the director at the other end of the phone cough nervously. When he finally learned how his own company's shares had tumbled, following Salima's, the air resounded with expletives which might have embarrassed a seasoned soldier.

'What is it?' Murray asked, concerned. Robson turned to him, his face white with shock.

'The market's collapsed,' he said, his voice suddenly running out of steam. Then, with the grim realization that their lives might be in danger, fear generated panic, and Robson screamed for Georgio to get the car ready while he attempted to contact his pilot and crew. Again, contact could only be effected via their mobile phones. To their relief, the forward thinking pilot had already summoned his engineer the moment news had filtered in about the disaster. Robson ignored what little luggage he had, yelling for the others to leave theirs as well while he made several more calls before hurrying out to the waiting sedan.

Their group numbered ten, including the additional girls from the cabaret. Robson and Murray climbed into the back of one of the Mercedes, squeezing two of the girls into the front, while the other vehicle, a wagon, carried the remaining troupe.

'John, can you take us by our hotel first?' the Filipino girls asked, only to be ignored.

'John, what about our clothes and passports?' another complained.

'Look, girls, it's like this. We're not going anywhere but the airport. Okay?'

'But John,…' one started, then cried out in pain as Georgio slapped her hard across the face.

'Shut up, bitch!' he screamed, 'or you'll stay behind!' The other girls put their arms around the shocked dancer, terrified that they might be dumped in the middle of nowhere. By then, they all understood quite clearly what was happening. They too had watched the CNN broadcast with the men and, like them, had sat shocked, disbelieving that all of this had happened while they slept.

Georgio had wanted to leave the women behind from the start, and Robson had been inclined to agree. It was only at Murray's insistence that Robson had finally acquiesced, and stormed out to the waiting cars while screaming for Georgio to take charge of the other vehicle. As an angry Robson sped away from the isolated *Puri Kauh* villa, the others were left behind and, although Georgio persisted in yelling at the driver to go faster, the winding, mountain roads surrounding Ubud only added to their frustration, causing the driver to drive even more cautiously because of the additional passengers he carried.

When the two vehicles hit their first traffic snarl upon arriving in Denpasar, Robson lost control, screaming at the driver. Finally, a traffic officer waved them through, and Robson seized the opportunity. He wound the window down and called the policeman over to the car.

Five minutes later, his entourage sped down the highway, wailing police sirens clearing a path for their vehicles as the white traffic jeep's driver leaned on his horn for additional affect. His sergeant winked, then laughed, patting the five hundred dollars he had pocketed, a gift from the bad-mouthed foreigner.

Behind, at the check-point, three disillusioned Filipino dancers placed their hands on their hips and screamed abuse at the departing vehicles, having been abandoned alongside the road and ordered to make their own way back to their club's hostel. Had it not been for the fact that the dancer's accommodations lay in a different direction to that of the airport, Murray would have objected.

* * * * * *

1735 Hours — Jakarta

Ruswita turned anxiously to the woman who had entered and coughed politely.

'Any news, Sumi?' she asked her personal assistant. Sumi looked helplessly at the woman she so admired, and shook her head.

'I'm sorry. We still have been unable to locate her.'

'Have they left the hotel?' Ruswita asked, hopefully.

'Yes. They have already checked out,' Sumi replied softly. She too had difficulty keeping the tears back. The day had been disastrous for the Salima Group of companies, she knew. But that was only secondary in their minds at that moment as concern for both Ratna and Michael's safety grew by the hour.

'Have you been able to locate Benny?' Ruswita asked, wishing that neither of her children had gone to Bali at this time.

'He has left a message for you,' her assistant replied. *'Benny did not want to interrupt the meeting. The message says that he is all right, that he has spoken to Ratna, and that he will accompany the Indian Prime Minister's team back to New Delhi.'*

Ruswita turned back to gaze through the window and watched the small pedestrian dots barely moving along the footpaths below. She turned back to face her personal assistant and forced a smile.

'Go home, Sumi, there's nothing you can do here,' she ordered, kindly. Sumi took several steps towards Ruswita and shook her head slowly.

'I'll stay,' was all she said, and then reached for Ruswita to comfort her. She placed her arms around the older woman and spoke softly. *'Ratna will be all right, Rus,'* she said, hoping that this would be true.

Chapter 29

Bali and Rama

Fuad watched his associate's face for a sign, deeply concerned that they had missed their opportunity. It seemed that the airport was in chaos as additional flights arrived to evacuate tourists, throwing established aviation procedures into total confusion. Tempers ran short, and ill-equipped personnel attempted to handle the overload.

'Anything?' Fuad asked, agitated by the lack of information.

'Shut up!' Bartlett hissed, concentrating on the communication exchange taking place between pilots and the control tower. Then he heard what he had been listening for, and his face cracked into a grim smile.

'Bali tower, this is *India One*, do you copy?' He heard the pilot ask.

'*India One*, Bali tower, what is your ETD?' Bartlett listened for the pilot's confirmation of his departure time, then looked at Fuad.

'Bali Tower, this is *India One*, anticipate rolling at Zulu 1035,' the voice of the captain responded.

'Copy *India One*, contact the tower for final taxiing instructions.'

'Copy that, tower,' he heard the captain say, before the air traffic controllers switched to another aircraft. Bartlett turned to Fuad, his expressionless eyes never more frightening.

'You've got about thirty minutes,' was all he said. *India One* had not yet departed and Fuad, breathing a sigh of relief, went about his own preparations. He immediately climbed down into the ship's hold, where they had stored their weapons and additional cargo. He crouched, then lifted the *Stinger* assembly carefully, looking up for Bartlett's assistance to lift the deadly missiles.

'Easy!' Fuad heard Bartlett hiss, as he handed up the weapon.

The man above then laid it down carefully on the deck.

'Ready?' Bartlett called, wondering what was keeping the other man. Fuad was sweating, and consciously warned himself to slow down.

'Fuad?' he heard Bartlett call, before his silhouette appeared above, and the sailor leaned down to receive the missile. Minutes later, having placed the *Stinger* inside the bridge, the captain called down once more, then lifted the second missile, taking this away also and stowing it safely alongside the first. Bartlett checked his diver's watch, then called to Fuad.

'Get the rest of the gear up, quickly!' he ordered, and Fuad complied, lifting the end of the Chinese inflatable upwards for Bartlett to drag onto the deck. This was followed with an assortment of supplies and equipment, all stamped with Chinese points of origin. He threw the PRC 7.62-mm sub-machine-gun and silencer into the dinghy, and placed a well-used Chinese Communist Type 54 pistol alongside, for good measure.

'Five minutes!' he heard Bartlett call. Fuad scrambled quickly back out of the hold, and prepared the launcher, retrieving one of the missiles from where Bartlett had carefully placed it, beside the bench aft of the ship's wheel.

He looked up into the heavens, away from the fading light. Then, having checked his equipment one more time, he glanced over towards the bridge and raised his thumb to indicate his readiness. He could see that Bartlett was engrossed, listening to the air traffic controllers struggle with the heavy aircraft traffic. Satisfied that he had done all that was necessary, Fuad then settled down to wait, watching the golden sun settle behind the island.

* * * * * *

Michael held Ratna roughly by the hand as they pushed their way through the multitude of hopeful tourists who crowded the airport's entrance in the hope of securing a flight away from the troubled destination. They almost felt like giving up at one point. Ahead, Michael could see little but a mass of passengers kicking, shoving and screaming as they surged towards the building's entrance. Then, airport security fired several shots above the foreigners heads; the effect was immediate, and restored some semblance of authority over the disorderly gathering.

Michael heard sirens approaching from behind, and attempted to move Ratna out of harm's way, but only succeeded in getting them both pushed back into the oncoming vehicles' path. The driver of the white police-jeep had never seen anything like it before. Indonesian crowd control exercises were one thing; driving his vehicle through a mass of foreign tourists which refused to budge was something he had not been trained to do. The vehicle following the police car contained Murray Stephenson and Graeme Robson. Murray opened his window and shouted at the pair standing amongst the crowd, then yelled for his driver to stop.

'Michael! Michael!' he yelled loudly, relieved when the man's face suddenly broke into a smile of recognition at hearing his name called. 'Get yourself in here!' Murray called.

'Jesus, Murray, what the hell are you doing?' Robson shouted, attempting to lean over to close the window, but Murray had his hand on the operating switch.

'That's Michael!' he snarled, pushing the door open against the swelling crowd. He stood in the doorway, above the mob, and screamed threateningly until they moved aside. By then, the police escort had stopped, its red lights still flashing. Foreigners amongst the crowd pulled back in fear, away from the armed men; Indonesia's riot-control police had earned their vicious international reputation on the country's bloody city streets. Foreigners closest to the police struggled, pushing back in desperation as they resisted those shoving from behind, fearing that they might antagonise the well-armed police who stood menacingly only meters to their front.

'Ratna, get in!' Michael ordered, lifting her bodily, and shoving her into the rear seat with the others.

'There's no room!' she shrieked, banging her head. Murray pushed with all his strength, forcing Robson across the seat. Then Michael climbed in, dragging his long legs after him as he squeezed, finally closing the door behind him.

'Tell those bastards to move!' Robson yelled to the driver, who immediately blew his horn at the escort in front. The forward jeep began to advance, police siren screaming.

'Who the hell are you?' an angry tourist screamed, his face dangerously close to the off-side rear window. Another kicked the door of the lead car in frustration, while others banged whatever part of the Mercedes was in reach, with their fists and drink-cans, while screaming abuse. As their car forced through the angry crowd, someone spat on the window. Ratna looked wildly at Michael. The crowd surged forward, blocking their path, and Robson's driver hit the horn again, hard, flashing his lights alerting the police to their difficulty. The escort police jumped from their jeep, brandishing their batons, threatening the tourists blocking their access.

Suddenly, the sound of automatic fire filled the air, as one of the airport police, not fifty meters away, opened fire, scattering the crowd. Terrified, those tourists closest to the entrance immediately jumped back, only to be pushed forward again by the crowd behind. The sergeant in charge of the unit withdrew his sidearm and also fired, twice, into the air. The response was instant. The area directly between the vehicles and the airport entrance cleared instantly, providing a path for them all to scramble through. They raced towards the terminal.

'Let's go!' Robson yelled, first out of the lead car.

'For chrissakes, move!' Murray screamed, and Michael tumbled from the vehicle.

'Ratna!' he called, waiting with his hand extended.

'Wait, Michael! Wait!' she screamed. She banged her knee and bit her lip in her haste. Then she grasped Michael's hand and they dashed for safety towards the waiting airport police.

'Leave the luggage!' Georgio yelled from behind, leading the way into the heavily congested area. Airport police moved forward and raised their arms to prevent them entering the building, but Robson's pilot was on hand to assist, yelling from the safety of the building's main doors as he alerted the police that this was his group of VIPs.

'The door's open!' someone cried, and the mob roared.

'They're taking more passengers!' another yelled, and immediately the crowd surged forward again, pushing from behind. Ratna was catapulted forward.

'Michael!' she screamed, and Michael dragged her back to her feet even before she had hit the ground. The crowd continued to push up against the airport police until another burst of automatic fire drove them away. People yelled and screamed, throwing whatever was in their hands at that moment, in sheer frustration, at watching these privileged few enter the building ahead of the queue. Murray cried out in pain, as a rock glanced off the side of his head, and he gritted his teeth, lunging forward towards the entrance.

'Murray?' Michael called, but he could do little more than push with the others, protecting Ratna as best he could. Crowded together, under a hail of abuse, they finally reached safety behind airport police lines, and rushed inside the terminal.

Their group was ushered through the impatient crowd inside the building, and Robson's two-man crew arrogantly pushed other passengers aside. Bruised from their ordeal, they finally made it to the passenger holding area, and paused for breath. Inside, through the glass doors separating departing passengers from immigration and customs, officials had long since thrown their hands into the air, permitting the heavy flow of departing tourists to board their flights without further checks. Robson's pilot banged on the locked partitions, displaying his permit to the soldier armed with a machine pistol. Moments later, they were all inside the waiting hall.

'What flight are you on?' Murray shouted, bending closer to Michael as he did so.

'Flight?' he yelled back, 'none, Murray,' he shook his head and looked at the impossible numbers cramped inside this section of the building. Murray leaned forward again and gripped his arm. Michael pulled Ratna closer to him.

'Come with us, there's room,' he yelled again, his throat becoming hoarse from the effort. 'Besides, you were supposed to be on this flight anyway, remember?' he grinned, but not convincingly. Michael nodded, remembering how their circumstances had changed in the course of just a few hours. He had been offered the opportunity to visit *Rama II* with Robson on his return journey.

'That's great, Murray, thanks,' he said, turning to Ratna. 'Seems we have lucked out after all.' Ratna didn't feel like smiling, she was feeling faint with the heat. She looked across at the others in the group, identifying that the women accompanying the other men were obviously professional hookers, what her mother would have referred to as *panggilan*. Immediately she was concerned that people might think she was one of them.

'Michael,' she said, tugging at his arm. He turned as she pinched the flesh around his waistline to gain his attention, causing him to jerk away in pain. She leaned closer, and stood on tiptoe.

'Michael, those women are all prostitutes!'

'For chrissakes Ratna, don't be so goddamned childish!' he snapped, holding her right arm tightly with his strong hands, 'who cares who the hell they are. It's a lift out of the stinking place. Isn't that what you dragged us out here for?' She pulled away, angrily. He had hurt her arm. She glared back at him, then turned away.

The noise outside was deafening. Here, amongst the fortunate few who would leave over the next hours, the cramped passengers were far more subdued. Michael could see that Ratna was close to tears, and stepped after her, throwing his arm around her shoulders to comfort her.

'*Ratna?*' a voice called, '*Ratna, over here!*' She turned instantly to follow the voice, but she couldn't identify who had called her name.

'*Ratna, here!*' someone yelled again, but amongst the thousands cramped together, packing the hall, she couldn't see who it might be. Then, she saw him, his face breaking into a wide grin as he managed to force his way through to her.

'*Benny!*' she squealed, and immediately pushed through the crowd until she reached her cousin, throwing her arms around him.

'*Benny, I thought you would be gone by now!*' she exclaimed, excitedly. They spoke together for a moment, and Michael watched. He saw her nod, then embrace Benny again. Michael pushed through the crowd, making his way over to where they stood.

'Michael, this is my cousin, Benny. He is *Ibu Ruswita's* youngest son,' she added. Benny extended his hand to Michael. His grip was limp.

'Seems that we're all stuck here together,' Michael said, raising his voice above the noisy, babble. Benny smiled.

'No, I'm not stuck,' he said, 'just waiting for the Prime Minister and South African President to arrive so we can board.' Michael looked confused. 'I'm returning on their flight, as I still have some business to attend to in India,' he added, pointing in the general direction of the waiting Boeing 777. Benny looked at Ratna.

'*Sure you won't join me, 'Na?*' he asked her, in their own language so as not to offend the foreigner. She responded by squeezing his hand.

'*Oh yes, Benny, please!*' she accepted, gratefully. Benny waited for her to ask if Michael could come too and was surprised when she didn't. Embarrassed, but not wishing to intrude on their arrangements, he checked his watch and decided it was time for them to leave. He held his hand out to Michael, in farewell.

'I'll see that Ratna gets back to Jakarta all right,' he said. 'I will speak to the Prime Minister's security. I'm sure, considering the circumstances, there'll be no difficulty. The Salima Group has committed a substantial amount of foreign exchange to the new banking systems to be introduced in India, and I'm certain they won't object.'

Michael was dumbfounded.

'You're dumping me to go on a separate flight?' he asked Ratna incredulously.

'Yes,' she said, and moved away with Benny, who led her through the crowd and out through the glass doors which connected with the VIP lounge. Michael stood stunned, speechless with what had just taken place. He watched as Ratna disappeared amongst the throng.

'Michael,' he heard his name called, and raised his hand in acknowledgement. Murray stood waiting, his impatience showing. Michael looked back in Ratna's direction, but she was nowhere to be seen.

'Son-of-a-bitch!' he cursed to himself, filled with anger. He then followed Murray and the others as they were led out through the double-glazed, plate glass doors which opened onto the hard-standing area where aircraft crews were hurriedly loading passengers.

There was no ticket control inspection required for their private flight. Security gave them a cursory check, then permitted the group to leave the terminal. As he stepped outside, the heat slapped him in the face and Michael covered his ears to shield them from the incredible noise.

'John, throw those bloody women aboard so we can get the hell out of here!' Robson shouted, his voice almost drowned out by the screams of aircraft turbines as they whined into readiness for departure. He saw Georgio yelling at the group of young, attractive girls, hobbling hurriedly across the busy concrete apron, trying desperately to avoid speeding service vehicles, their red warning-beacons flashing ominously as they raced to and fro.

Murray also tried to hurry, but his ageing legs were suffering from the past few days, what with dancing late into the night and frolicking in the pool with girls a third of his age. As he walked stiffly onto the parking apron, he looked, almost with awe, at the number of aircraft that had managed to squeeze into the area.

A dozen aircraft ranging from small private jets to jumbos lined up waiting for departure instructions. Murray wondered how there hadn't already been an accident. As jet engines continued to scream, pushing their gargantuan loads into readiness for take-off, Murray turned to see what had happened to Michael.

* * * * * *

Ratna walked slowly across the concrete apron, turning her head to avoid the hot, kerosene-filled air as another aircraft moved across her path. She hesitated, looking across in the other direction, away from the suffocating, acrid smell of burning fuel. She saw Michael, alone, standing not fifty metres to her left, watching as she headed for her aircraft. He waved, and in that moment, Ratna was overcome with regret for the way she had behaved.

She turned, looking for Benny, and saw that he was waiting for her. She looked back at Michael, then across at Benny Salima again. Suddenly, she knew what she must do.

'Michael!' She ran towards Michael, calling his name, narrowly missing a speeding power-unit as it passed dangerously close.

'Christ, Ratna,' he yelled loudly, 'be careful!' He stepped towards the woman as another vehicle threatened to bowl her over. He leaped forward and reached out, barely in time to pull her from harm's way.

'Michael, Michael!' she cried, falling into his outstretched arms, clinging to him tightly. He wrapped his arms around her.

'Well?' was all he could say. Ratna reached up, and there, standing on the concrete apron amidst the chaos of the moment, she kissed him firmly.

'I'm so sorry, Michael,' she shouted, 'I was scared, and reacted poorly. Will you forgive me?' He reached for her, pulling her close to his body.

'Of course,' he shouted back, then glanced after the others.

'Will you come with me?' Michael looked directly at Ratna, and she nodded.

'Okay,' she surrendered, agreeing to accompany him on board

the Lear Jet. Michael looked at her sternly and she smiled. Realizing just how ridiculous their situation was, they both suddenly broke into laughter and hurried to board Robson's jet together. Ratna waved at Benny, but he did not understand. He remained standing, watching as she entered the executive jet not one hundred meters across from where *India One* was parked, towering over the smaller planes.

They hurried aboard and found that the others were already strapping themselves into their seats. Murray twisted around, looked back and waved.

'Glad you could make it,' he called, as Michael ushered Ratna into one of the remaining seats. The engineer closed then locked the cabin exit door, and moved forward to join the captain who, at that moment, was absorbed with his pre-flight instrument check.

'Let's get this bird moving,' Robson called forward to the open cockpit door. The pilot obeyed his employer's command, and called the tower for instructions. Several minutes passed before the overworked air traffic controllers responded, and the captain spoke briefly.

'We're seventh in line,' he called back to those in the cabin. 'The tower has told us to wait for taxiing instructions.'

'Christ almighty!' Robson cursed, angered by the delay. He knew that this could easily compound, with priority being given to military and senior government officials. This, added to everything else, only raised his ire more. In their haste to depart, he had not had time to fully consider the devastating ramifications of the Jakarta market's collapse. He knew that his position would be precarious; his bankers would be anxious for an explanation of how he intended repaying the enormous debt he had acquired. He snapped back at the pilot.

'Call the bloody tower and get us some priority!' he ordered unreasonably. The captain responded with a nod, but did nothing, knowing that they would just have to wait their turn. He motioned with his head for his fellow crewman to distract the passengers. The engineer moved from the cockpit and stood where the passengers could see him clearly. He commenced with his rehearsed air safety demonstration.

'Not this goddamn bullshit again,' a voice complained, somewhere up front. 'Hey, Graeme,' Georgio then called, 'why don't

I just get him to pass out some drinks?' with which, he unbuckled and rose from his seat, moving into the aisle with some difficulty.

'Jesus, John,' Murray called out, 'leave it till we get airborne.'

'Move, goddamn it!' Georgio cursed, stomping over the girl strapped alongside. He dragged himself into the narrow aisle, then stood and faced the others, smiling at Robson. Georgio had already been drinking.

'Hey, Graeme, come on,' he said, flashing a bottle of bourbon from out of nowhere. At the rear of the small cabin, Michael felt Ratna's nails bite into his wrist. In that instant of recognition, her face clouded as the recent memory flashed through her mind.

'Michael, that's him!' she said, angrily, unbuckling her safety belt.

'What are you doing?' Michael asked, surprised. He too unstrapped, and squeezed out into the aisle behind her. Robson turned in his seat, craning his neck to see what was happening.

'What in hell is going on back there?' Robson yelled, his anger causing an ugly vein on the side of his neck to protrude. Murray also turned to see what the commotion was all about.

'Michael, I'm getting off,' Ratna announced. She called to the engineer. 'Open the hatch,' she insisted, moving to the rear of the stationary plane. The engineer looked bewildered by what was happening. Ratna turned to see that the crewman had remained standing next to the cockpit. She snapped at him in Indonesian. *'Open the door or I will do it myself!'*

'Jesus bloody Christ! What in the hell is going on?' Robson unbuckled, then flew out of his seat, furious with them all. He glared at the beautiful Eurasian woman causing the disturbance. One of the amateur hookers offered some snide remark which went unheard by all except Ratna, who immediately reached for the exit lock and turned the handle, releasing the door. The engineer hurried to her assistance.

'Who is this dumb bitch?' Robson snarled, moving away from his seat.

'Hold it, Graeme!' Murray barked, moving to block the aisle which his larger frame.

'Michael, that's the one who assaulted me at the club!' she called loudly, as noise exploded into the cabin through the now open doorway. Michael shook his head, raised his hands in surrender, and followed.

'Shit, not again!' he muttered angrily, having no idea whatsoever, what Ratna was talking about. Ratna sent Georgio a smouldering look and clattered down the steps to the apron. Michael followed her.

'Once you're out, you're out!' Robson yelled, motioning for the engineer to close and lock the hatch. He turned around and saw Georgio standing, still holding the bourbon. He snatched the bottle and took a long pull on the contents before offering the bottle to Murray, who shook his head, and refused. It was only then that Murray vaguely remembered something of the incident between John and some woman in the club. *My God*, he thought, *was that only last night?*

Outside, Michael caught up easily with Ratna as she stormed away from the aircraft.

'What in the devil's got into you?' he yelled, grabbing her arm, spinning her around to face him. They stood, facing each other angrily, both shouting to make themselves heard above the incredible noise.

'That man was the one who tried to assault me in the nightclub, Michael,' she shouted, then stamped her foot in childish frustration. Then she remembered that she hadn't told him what had happened inside the cabaret. Instead, she had behaved selfishly, recalling that she had taken it out on Michael, insisting that they return to their hotel. Ratna looked up at Michael.

'Oh Michael,' she cried, competing against the impossible noise, 'I'm sorry. I'm really, really sorry,' she said, reaching up to cling to him. 'I'll explain later.' Michael placed his arm around her and looked around the noisy, confused scene. He knew they should move off the concrete apron, quickly. They waited for several speeding vehicles to pass, then started walking back towards the terminal building.

'*Ratna!*' someone yelled, his voice barely audible as the thunderous roar of huge Rolls Royce aircraft engines signalled another aircraft's departure. They both turned.

'Michael, its Benny!' she shouted, taking control, and leading him towards the short, stocky banker.

'*Do you still want that lift?*' Benny yelled. He had watched her climb aboard the smaller aircraft and wasn't sure what was happening until the cabin door closed. He assumed she had changed her mind. Fortunately, as he walked slowly back to his own flight, he had glanced back, and witnessed Ratna hurrying away from the executive jet.

'Both of us?' she asked, holding onto Michael's arm tightly.

'Let's ask,' Benny shouted, indicating that they should follow. The three bent forward, hands in front, shielding their faces from a hot exhaust blasting across the busy apron as an aircraft bumped across the uneven concrete and came to rest where instructed. Michael could see from the arriving plane's cabin lights that the huge jet was empty, guessing correctly that this would be another evacuation flight that had just landed at the busy airport.

They made it to the foot of the mobile passenger-stairway together.

'Wait here,' Benny instructed them. 'I'll just go up and clear your travel with the Prime Minister's personal assistant.' Michael stood holding Ratna's hand under the scrutiny of more than a dozen heavily armed Indian soldiers. The *palace guard*, he thought, then looked down at the woman beside him.

'Okay?' he asked, holding her hand tightly.

'Okay,' she responded, but he could see that she was still distressed.

Moments later, Benny reappeared, and waved down for them to come aboard. They climbed the tall passenger steps, Michael impressed with the Salima family influence. They were met by security and physically checked before being permitted to enter the aircraft. Sirens sounded as they stepped inside the wide-bodied jet, alerting security that the Prime Minister's entourage had arrived. Michael and Ratna were ushered inside hurriedly, and escorted to seats in the forward compartment allocated to the accompanying Indian press contingent.

Minutes later they stood, awkwardly, holding onto the seats in front of their own, waiting while the VIPs all boarded the elegantly decorated Boeing. As the Prime Minister passed, followed by the South African President, the members of the press clapped politely, and remained standing until the two leaders and others of their group had all filed by into the VIP compartment. Their door was then locked from the inside. Four heavily armed Indian soldiers boarded the flight, taking positions in seats to either side of the

VIP compartment's access door.

'Well, we're on our way,' Benny Salima smiled, accepting a glass of juice from the dark-skinned stewardess, and both Michael and Ratna thanked him again for what he'd done.

* * * * * *

Bali

Xanana had never been aboard a helicopter before.

He followed the Admiral's example, bending his head as the powerful rotor-blades chopped noisily through the heavy, humid air. He watched as Admiral Gopal strapped himself in and copied the procedure. Then they sat, waiting, while the pilot attempted, unsuccessfully, to contact the Ngurah Rai tower.

'Admiral,' the pilot said, looking back over his shoulder at the Navy's most senior officer, 'Bali tower communications are not responding. The hotel structure may be the problem,' he said, indicating the eight-hundred room complex surrounding the ocean at that point. In fact, this had not been the reason for the airport tower's refusal to acknowledge.

As air traffic controllers battled with incoming aircraft, stacked waiting for permission to land, they had not been able to communicate with the helicopter, knowing that the pilot must wait. The Indian Navy pilot glanced over his shoulder at the Admiral and waited for a response.

Gopal nodded and the pilot leaned forward, looking for the hotel ground engineer's signal that they were clear. Satisfied, the experienced airman pushed the cyclic control forward as he manipulated the collective, lifting the heavy machine off the ground a few metres. The helicopter wobbled unsteadily, and Xanana suffered momentary panic as the helicopter's nose turned to face into the sea-breeze.

Conscious of the congested traffic overhead, the pilot selected a course for the *INS Indira Gandhi,* deciding to maintain an altitude which would keep them above any incidental pleasure craft as they passed along the shallow, dangerous coast.

* * * * * *

The captain of *India One* waited, patiently, for his final clearance.

'*India One*, you are cleared to roll,' the air traffic controller's voice finally announced, instructing the Boeing's crew to depart.

'Roger, tower,' the captain responded, immediately pushing the controls forward, pumping aviation fuel rapidly through the system, where it converted into pure thrust. The Rolls Royce engines whirred then whined, the crescendo building to an impossible scream as the two hundred and fifty thousand kilogram aircraft strained under the captain's brake.

Out at sea aboard the *M.V. Rager*, Bartlett listened to the air traffic control clearance instructions carefully, then removed the headphones and flung these, carelessly, on top of the receiver. He turned to Fuad and nodded.

'They're up next. Get ready,' he ordered. Fuad moved to the port side of the ship and positioned himself firmly, bracing his feet, while Bartlett helped raise the deadly missile until it rested comfortably on Fuad's shoulder. He felt the *Rager* move slightly when a light breeze pushed the steel hull gently, and he compensated, adjusting his stance, ready to fire.

* * * * * *

Brakes released, the aircraft moved forward, slowly at first, then gathering momentum as engines screamed, thrusting the aircraft forward, along the well-lit runway. The passengers looked out through the windows as the jet continued to accelerate, the light rocking sensation signalling that they would soon lift off, and be safe.

Navigation lights continued to blink furiously as the jet's engines' high-pitched whine pierced the early evening air, changing pitch as the aircraft became airborne, and the undercarriage retracted. They were on their way.

* * * * * *

Fuad grasped the awkward launcher firmly and stared down through the sights, waiting for his target to come into view. It would be soon. Above, the sky was alive with blinking navigation lights as departing and arriving aircraft flew along their designated courses, guided by the over-worked Bali air traffic control tower.

Fuad wiped the perspiration from his brow, and breathed deeply. As darkness had descended he had become increasingly worried by the amount of air traffic, and he knew that he would have to strike the aircraft before it reached any real altitude. Suddenly, he cocked his head and listened, as haunting, familiar and unmistakable sounds approached through the darkness. He spun around in surprise, recognising the heavy, chopping sounds emanating from somewhere to his right. There! He spotted it, and knew immediately that he had been right as his eyes focused on the slow-moving navigation lights traveling just above sea-level.

Memories of helicopter gun-ship attacks flashed through his mind. They had been discovered, he knew, his eyes darting in panic from the flashing helicopter's lights to the end of the runway, then back again, his mind visualising the gunner's actions as he prepared to bring his thirty millimetre automatic cannons into line and fire.

Bartlett remained at the wheel, not meters from where Fuad stood, unable to see the fear which washed across the man's face as he listened in terror to the familiar sounds beating through the air, heading for their ship. At that moment, navigation lights blinked just above the runway's darkened horizon. Fuad froze, terrified to fire within view of the helicopter.

'Shoot! Fuad, shoot for chrissakes!' Bartlett bellowed, and Fuad swung the missile back instinctively, concentrating his line of sight slightly above the runway's end, barely catching the faint silhouette of the approaching aircraft as it left the airstrip behind. To his trained eyes, the target seemed to be low. But in that second, in one well-rehearsed motion he raised the launcher a fraction, aiming the missile directly to the left of the port navigation lights, then squeezed the trigger.

The *Stinger* leapt from its launcher leaving a light trail as it tore through the dimly-lit sky towards its target. Bartlett watched in fascination as the deadly rocket locked onto the fully-fuelled aircraft and, almost in that same moment, impacted with a blinding flash, creating an enormous fireball which lit the early evening sky.

In the distance, the seasoned helicopter pilot reacted spontaneously and, as trained, twisted the collective around expertly and pointed his gun-ship in the direction from where he had seen the missile fired. He armed the two cannons attached to the lower sides of the AH-64 Apache, then bore down on the floating target, prepared to open fire. It was only then, for the first time, that Bartlett recognized the approaching threat.

'Jesus Christ!' he yelled, knowing what must be done. He lifted the second missile assembly and rushed outside to assist Fuad before it was too late. Fuad had barely sufficient time to shoulder the *Stinger* before the gun-ship was upon them. Without further hesitation, he lifted the launcher and fired into the whirling blades as the helicopter bore down on them no more than a hundred meters from their ship.

For an infinitesimal moment, there was nothing. Then their world erupted all around, smashing them both brutally back onto the ship's deck.

The explosion filled the sky with a roar as the helicopter's long-range fuel tanks ruptured, then ignited under impact, killing all on board. As the last pieces of shrapnel fell into the sea, Bartlett was already on his feet and moving.

'Let's get the hell out of here!' Bartlett yelled. While he weighed anchor, Fuad rushed to throw the evidence into the sea. Within minutes, they were under way. By the time the first Search and Rescue teams finally arrived to search for survivors, Bartlett's *Rager* had already disappeared from the scene, steaming through the Lombok Straits on course for the Philippines.

* * * * * *

Less than a few minutes before, the *India One* aircraft captain swore loudly as the Lear Jet cut across the concrete hard-standing surface and entered the runway, just as the VIP flight had commenced to roll. The experienced pilot braked and looked at his crew in disbelief.

'What the…!' the startled officer exploded, just as the air traffic controller's voice flooded the airwaves.

'Bravo Delta Foxtrot,' the tired officer screamed, 'you are not cleared, do you read me, you are not cleared!' Others in the tall tower overlooking the airfield rose to their feet to see what was happening.

'Bravo Delta Fox-trot,' someone growled, 'get the hell out of there!' The executive jet pilot ignored the instructions, turned, then lined up on the runway directly ahead of the huge jumbo and started rolling.

'Bali tower, this is Bravo Delta Fox-trot, we're rolling,' Robson announced arrogantly, as he pushed the throttle forward and smiled. In the cabin, John Georgio returned to his seat, still laughing at Robson's dangerous manoeuvre.

'Oooh weee!' he shouted. The smaller jet barely missed touching the 777's wing as they pushed recklessly past and jumped the long queue of waiting aircraft. The girls on board all screamed, believing that they would hit the other plane.

'Bravo Delta Fox-trot,' the frustrated controller called, 'you are endangering the lives of others. You are instructed to return to the terminal!' He knew now that this was most unlikely to happen as one of the other controllers yelled, 'He's going!'

Robson pulled a face and corrected the aircraft's line as it rolled on down the runway, gathering speed, knowing that he had the influence to have the matter settled later, when the complaint was lodged by the air traffic controllers. He looked across at his captain's concerned expression, and laughed.

'Don't worry, *Mas*,' he said, 'it's my licence they'll be after, not yours!' The captain glanced at his engineer, frightened. He could still smell the alcohol on Robson's breath, and had protested when the man had taken control of the aircraft. The seasoned captain sat strapped into his seat, carefully observing his employer's handling of the controls. He breathed deeply and watched the runway lights start to merge into one as the jet gathered speed and started to lift. He heard the engine pitch change, and glanced at Robson, who turned, caught his eye, and winked. Just as the missile struck.

* * * * * *

Most of the air traffic controllers caught the fireball out of the corner of their eyes, returning immediately to their screens to see what had happened. None in the tower sighted the second, low-level missile impact, the flash associated with this only confusing them more. The helicopter had only been identified on their screens during the last of those chaotic moments, which led to what they believed to be, a mid-air collision. Air investigators would later conclude that the helicopter had somehow strayed across the Lear Jet's path.

'Get the Indian Prime Minister's flight away, immediately!' the senior traffic controller barked, realizing the security implications should the VIP flight be delayed, not to mention the compounding problem of stacked aircraft waiting to land. The officer responsible for directing the Indian Prime Minister's aircraft obeyed.

* * * * * *

None of the passengers aboard *India One* flight had seen either of the two explosions, although a few of their number had heard something which they believed to be thunder. The captain had seen it, however, and communicated what he had witnessed to the tower. He discovered that several of the officers had watched the Lear Jet's departure with great concern, warning other flights to avoid the irresponsible pilot's flight-path. He had obviously collided with the Indian Navy helicopter which had appeared only moments before on their screens.

The explosion had occurred over the sea. Search and sea rescue teams were alerted immediately, but it would be some time before crews could be encouraged to don their uniforms and proceed in search of survivors. The traffic controllers then turned their attention to moving as many aircraft as quickly as possible, commencing with the VIP flight which had been paused, waiting for clearance when the accident had occurred. Satisfied that there would be no further danger, the tower gave clearance for them to leave.

'You may proceed, *India One*,' the tower advised, and the captain uttered a silent and practiced prayer as he repeated his procedure once gain. The passengers all remained silent, noticing that the cabin lights had been dimmed for their takeoff. As the engines thrust their aircraft forward, they leaned back, listening to the tyres bouncing along the uneven concrete runway. An overhead locker-door crashed open as the Boeing developed sufficient momentum to lift, wobbling slightly, before heading out over the dark ocean.

As their aircraft climbed, Michael looked out the window in time to catch the distant setting sun's last light, a thousand kilometers to the west. He turned to Ratna and smiled. They leaned closer, and embraced.

'I love you, Michael,' she said. He ran the back of his hand across her lips, then the soft skin of her face.

'I love you, too,' he said, and they kissed. Suddenly, witnessing the exchange, the cabin broke into thunderous applause, as the journalists, led by Benny, clapped and cheered enthusiastically.

Chapter 30

India

General Rahul Kumar sat behind the desk in the opulent office and signed the State of Emergency Decree, not dissimilar to the order imposed in 1975 by Prime Minister Indira Gandhi. Unconcerned with what might happen at the airport upon *India One*'s return, Kumar went about removing files and personal effects from the building, while the unsuspecting Prime Minister slept on board his flight. Upon his arrival, another crew would fly the South African President on to his own country, and the Prime Minister would be placed under arrest. Only hours before, the General had ordered his troops into New Delhi to support his imminent military rule.

Dr Imran Malhotra had already been arrested and incarcerated behind the walls of the Northern Command's military prison where he would, Kumar expected, spend the remaining days of his life. Politics being what they were in his country, the General would ensure that, with the first sign of any mass support for the late Vijay Rajesh's co-conspirator, Imran would undoubtedly be found dead in the detention centre before his popularity could further grow.

As he waited for confirmation that *India One* had landed, Rahul Kumar, dictator-to-be, read through the highly sensitive documents once again, wondering if the Americans might not consider supporting the original concept conceived by his predecessors. He took the folders and locked them away in his personal case for further consideration at a later, and more appropriate, occasion. Now it was time for his announcement. He checked the clock, then rose, brushed his uniform with one hand and marched proudly across the wide, marble floor of the room from which he would rule all of India. He paused momentarily, as if reminded of something, and turned, but could see nothing there. Then he opened the tall, white and gold double doors, moved into the adjacent chamber, and took his position in front of the television cameras. Kumar's aide closed the doors gently on the empty room, unmindful of the long, highly-polished Canadian Oak table standing majestically at the centre of the Premier's office. A solitary reminder of democratic rule — Viceroy Mountbatten's gift to a new nation.

* * * * * *

India's naval expeditionary force approaching Timor

In Admiral Krishna Gopal's absence, a worried commodore hesitated, wondering what to do. The Admiral was more than six hours overdue, and the Battle Group Commander was most reluctant to send SAR further into Indonesian waters, concerned that this might jeopardise their mission. Leaving instructions to be woken immediately if there was any news of Admiral Gopal, the Commodore retired, exhausted by the long hours spent on the flag bridge.

He made his way aft through the non-watertight door which had been latched open, brushing the dark, navy-blue curtains aside as he entered that section which led to his quarters.

At 0455 hours he was woken by an excited aide, who advised that his presence was urgently required back on the ship's bridge. The Commodore dressed hurriedly, hoping there would be news of Krishna Gopal. Instead, when he entered the Captain's navigation bridge, he was handed a decoded signal which he read, then immediately crushed into a ball, his anger apparent to the other officers.

The order had been for the fleet to return immediately, as a State of Emergency had been declared throughout his country. The brief, but succinct instruction had been signed by General Rahul Kumar. The Battle Group Commander scowled, confused as to what he should do. There had been no mention of the Prime Minister.

In Gopal's absence, he stood on the carrier's bridge, conscious that the Indian armada was still steaming on its original course. *Should he ignore the impertinent General and attempt to contact the Prime Minister for his advice, or should he discontinue the mission?*

What had happened to Admiral Gopal?

He looked out towards the horizon and observed a flock of birds flying mockingly alongside the massive, floating platform. As the first morning light cast grey shadows across the sky, his decision was made for him.

'Commodore?' the alarmed Captain came up to the senior officer, his face white, another signal in his extended hand. The Battle Group Commander accepted the communiqué, and read the message. Minutes later, he ordered the armada to turn around, and instructed the Captain to have his officers plot a new course for their home port. And to ensure that they complied with the demands contained in the signal, two United States SSN-21s surfaced within view, demonstrating that the American President was indeed prepared to support his request, if necessary with force.

* * * * * *

East China Sea, off Taiwan

China's Fleet Battle Group Commanders acknowledged that their attempts to intimidate Taiwan into submission by engaging in nuclear blackmail had failed miserably. Beijing's campaign to dominate the nations of East Asia and the South China Sea had been countered by the United States Seventh Fleet forward forces, and in the absence of the Indian armada's confirmation that they had arrived at their destination off Timor's shores, the planned assault had been considerably delayed, resulting in a dramatic and sudden change in Chinese tactics.

As Chinese DF-15 rockets fired from Fujian Province impacted at sea less than twenty miles to the north and south of Taiwan, the first of the Seventh Fleet's forward deployment entered the waters to the island's east. Before noon, led by the aircraft carrier, *USS Kitty Hawk*, the full American fleet's composition became known to the Chinese commanders and the confrontation ended.

And in the East Pacific, both Chinese *Xia* class SSBNs were surprised at the activity surrounding their ships when the submarines surfaced two hundred miles off the California coast and were immediately instructed to turn about. In the presence of four American SSN-21s, they willingly complied, plotting a course which would take them back into the North Pacific and away from the hostile American reception.

* * * * * *

Philippines, Celebes Sea

A hundred miles to the south-east of Zamboanga, Captain Dave Bartlett, swung the wheel of the *M.V. Rager* to port, then corrected his course heading for the small coastal Filipino village deep in the Moro Gulf. Satisfied that there was no shipping ahead, he left the wheel-house and moved forward to where Fuad sat, crouched on the deck eating meat from a freshly opened can.

'Fuad,' he called. The other man hesitated, turned, then dropped what he was eating as he sprang to his feet.

'What are you doing?' he asked, fear twisting his bowels. Bartlett was holding the Winchester shotgun directly at Fuad's head. His lips trembled and his knees went to jelly as he recognized the look in his killer's eyes. He had seen this expression before and knew, with certainty, that he was going to die. In the instant Fuad's mouth moved to beg for mercy, the blast removed most of his head, throwing him bodily over the ship's railing and into the sea. Bartlett watched as the body disappeared in the *Rager's* wake, then returned to the wheel-house and locked the weapon away.

He gazed out to sea as a flock of seagulls winged their way overhead, his mind preoccupied with what he would be required to do on arrival at his destination. He had decided to sell the ship, although he knew he would be lucky to see more than fifty thousand dollars in the exchange. Then he would see to whatever outstanding commitments there were, including settling up with the Americans before disappearing once more. With this thought in mind, he considered what name he might use for his new identity. A sardonic grin pulled at one side of his face as he recalled how difficult it had been adjusting to being known as Bartlett. On more than one occasion, he remembered inadvertently signing himself away as Stephen Coleman, and that it had virtually taken years for him not to respond whenever someone called 'Stephen' in his presence.

He removed the dirty baseball cap and rubbed the side of his face. He examined the torn brim, ruefully, then flung the faded cap out through the open cabin doorway, into the sea, deciding that it was time he bought himself one of those hair-pieces he had seen in Manila.

His recent killing of Fuad already washed from his mind, Stephen Coleman stood happily, gazing at the distant mountains, humming an old tune he remembered from his hazy past.

* * * * * *

Bali

Soft swells running in from the Indian Ocean lifted pieces of wreckage, burying some under timeless sand, while other metal fragments were pushed gradually towards the shore. Here, they would undoubtedly be found and turned into trinkets by the local craftsmen.

The force of the explosion had ripped through the helicopter with such ferocity the few remains recovered of those who had been aboard were not identifiable. Admiral Gopal, Admiral of the Indian Fleet, and Xanana Soares, President-to-be of an Independent East Timor, were cremated together in the traditional Balinese manner. When their ashes had been gathered, these were taken down to the beach overlooking the place where they had met their final destiny, together.

There, their remains were scattered with great ceremony, providing an escape for their spirits from the worry of earthly concerns, forever.

* * * * * *

The radiation released by the *Rama II* accident represented the equivalent of one twentieth of all that resulting from post-World War II atmospheric atomic weapons tests. As Java lies just below the Equator, Indonesia's northern neighbours of Singapore, Malaysia and Brunei were spared. Had the meltdown occurred in Northern Sumatra or even Indonesian Borneo where bush-fires would continue to rage out of control for a number of years, the death toll would have been considerable in those neighbouring

ASEAN nations.

Those most affected were the farm workers and peasants who lived within the immediate disaster area. Radioactive clouds were carried across to the east of Indonesia, over Bali, Nusa Tenggara, Timor and across the Timor Sea to Darwin. The levels of contamination varied according to the distance these deadly clouds travelled. In Java, some fifty million people were exposed, in one form or another, to contaminated air, water and crops.

Although the initial death toll was less than two thousand, a further six hundred thousand families were affected. Among these, another eighty-three thousand would develop radiation related diseases, and within six months from when the meltdown occurred. In spite of the massive evacuation undertaken by the Indonesian authorities, many of the evacuees were peasants, deeply bound to the land. Within weeks, they drifted back to where they had spent all of their lives, and started again. As levels of contamination decreased with time and weather, the farmers recommenced that timeless cycle of rice production, planting the first of their new crops just one year later.

The entire area surrounding *Rama II* was declared a no-go zone, and no attempts were made to restore the project in any form whatsoever. Before Indonesia was permitted further uranium imports, the International Atomic Energy Agency successfully extracted an agreement for open inspection on its remaining plants, thereby circumventing any future misuse of excess fuel generated in these nuclear plants. The threat of Indonesia developing its own delivery system for ICBMs, or becoming a member of the Nuclear Club in the immediate future, disappeared. The Bandung Research and Development Center remained idle, waiting for the day when some future leader might look enviously at neighbouring shores and decide to resurrect the project.

Tourism in Bali saw a dramatic fall in the number of visiting tourists to the island. Exaggerated fears of contaminated food and water sent many of the smaller operators to the wall.

In Australia, an attempt to restrict products originating from Northern Queensland and the Northern Territory was, sensibly, aborted.

* * * * * *

In the months that followed, a further and overwhelmingly supported South African-sponsored resolution was passed, calling for the United Nations to implement a plebiscite in East Timor, one which would guarantee the people the opportunity to vote, without fear, to remain as part of Indonesia, or elect their own independent government.

Surprisingly, Indonesia agreed. When the Act of Free Choice was conducted under United Nation's supervision, the people domiciled in the former Portuguese Colony voted, by a clear majority, to remain as Indonesia's twenty-seventh province. In the preceding months leading up to the plebiscite, Indonesia redirected a substantial number of its transmigrants from other programmes, settling these in areas surrounding Dili and other major population centres throughout the Timor province still referred to as *Tim-Tim*.

The United States signed a defense co-operation agreement with Indonesia, and moved its Seventh Fleet to its new home port, in Timor.

China continued on its belligerent path, threatening regional stability, poking and prodding at Taiwan. The following year, just months after the paramount leader passed away and was succeeded by a younger but more aggressive tyrant, China and Taiwan signed a friendship treaty, finally committing their two countries to union within the decade.

Lim Swee Giok's flagship, the Asian Pacific Commercial Bank, continued to flourish under the astute management of the Salima brothers. Their investments in China in no way suffered from the 'incident' between the two Chinas, and both Denny and James were invited to the American Presidential Inauguration Ball the following year. Benny maintained his position in Indonesia, but after two years of fighting Indian bureaucracy, withdrew his banking operations from the sub-continent.

KERRY B.COLLISON

Epilogue

Ruswita leaned back into the soft, cushioned settee, and immediately felt her energy drain away. As she lay there, thinking about that morning's events, she experienced a sensation of wholeness, of togetherness, and she smiled contentedly, thinking of her children and friends. Tomorrow, she knew, would be a most special day.

It had been Siti's first birthday in Indonesia, and Ruswita had thrown a most lavish party for her granddaughter. Michael and Ratna had returned to Jakarta, as promised, so that Aunt Ruswita could see their child for the first time. They had married in India, with a quiet, civil ceremony. Then after a whirlwind honeymoon visiting exotic places such as the Taj Mahal and the Pyramids of Egypt, Ratna had finally settled down with her husband, in Ohio, where Michael had taken up teaching at the State University, lecturing primarily in radiation safety procedures.

He was not at all unhappy with his decision to leave Washington, and the Defense Intelligence Agency. When their first child had arrived, they returned to Indonesia to fulfil a promise Ratna had given her aunt many years before.

* * * * * *

Lani had not attended the granddaughter's party.

For weeks, Ruswita had been preparing her old, dear friend, for a most special moment in their lives. Ruswita had decided to reveal her secret to Ratna, as she had already included her name with her other heirs in a revised will. The two grey-haired women, had spoken in depth as to how Ruswita would break this news to the one Lani had loved, cared for and cherished as her own child, since birth.

As Ruswita lay quietly, her body bordering on sleep, her thoughts turned to the woman who had been her dearest friend since her first days in Jakarta, and she prayed that Lani would understand her need, to now openly call Ratna her own.

* * * * * *

Lani had been deeply shocked by Ruswita's announcement, and still could not believe that she would proceed with her cruel and selfish disclosure. Distressed and bitter, she had feigned a severe migraine, refusing to attend the lavish lunch-time celebrations.

As was her custom, Lani prepared the tray of Chinese tea and cookies.

For several, long moments she stood, thinking, almost as if she had forgotten something. Then she lifted the tray supporting the Chinese porcelain service, and walked through the garden and into the main house.

During recent months, she noticed that the stairs had become even more difficult to manage and Lani rested, half-way, placing the tray alongside while recovering her breath. Looking down at the refreshments, Lani suddenly smiled at the countless number of times she had carried afternoon tea upstairs, in readiness for when Ruswita would wake from her customary nap. She had never once failed to have the lukewarm tea and biscuits sitting there, ready for her dear old friend.

She sighed deeply, recalling the burdensome memory of an earlier attempt at preventing Ruswita from distancing Ratna from her, and how it had failed. At that time, Lani had been deeply hurt, and desperately wanted to punish Ruswita. She glanced at the two biscuits sitting innocently, positioned, as she had done so many times before, to one side of the Chinese tea.

The prolific and highly toxic fungus grew in parts of their garden. The hot, humid tropical conditions were ideal for such mushrooms. The hallucinogenic jamur had been easily disguised in the cookies she'd prepared, and she had placed these on the tray knowing that Ruswita would not be able to resist the freshly baked biscuits.

On that fateful day, years before, and totally out of character, Lim Swee Giok had woken and consumed the biscuits prepared for Ruswita. The small amount of *jamur* that she had used at that time would only have made Ruswita violently ill, but was apparently far too toxic for her ailing husband. It was fortunate that Lani had noticed these missing, and had later removed the service. After the doctor had returned for Lim's body, Lani had informed Ruswita that she had seen the housekeeper talking to someone at the front gates. She had never understood why Ruswita had not called the police.

Refreshed by her brief rest, Lani rose and continued upstairs, not at all surprised to find Ruswita asleep on the lounge, nestled amongst the pillows Lani had made during the many long and lonely hours she had spent alone in her room at the rear of the house.

She placed the cookies, tea, and miniature cups on the glass-topped, carved coffee table, and stood admiring Ruswita's magnificent rings as her left arm hung listlessly at her side. Lani leaned over, and kissed Ruswita softly on her face. Then she left her alone, confident that Ratna would never, never discover the secret of her birth.

Author's Note

Whilst reflecting on another manuscript which had occupied much of my time when living in Asia, I came across a section which related to the period of my life when I was required to spend considerable time in Thailand. Memories of Bangkok came flooding back to mind, amongst which was the occasion when, by chance, I shared a car and driver with Sahid, who was in town undergoing treatment for wounds to his arm and shoulder.

Sahid was Mohammed Gadafi's brother, and had been caught during the American aerial attack aimed at removing Gadafi from the world stage; instead, the Libyan leader survived, but sadly his adopted daughter died in the bombing. Sahid had then slunk off to Bangkok where, having discovered his identity, I thought him to be either extremely naïve or a little too daring considering the number of American agents stationed in Thailand.

Reagan, as President, would have approved this attempted assassination attempt. The point of this inclusion is relative to my story, Jakarta. American Presidents have, throughout history, sanctioned the execution of foreign Presidents, Heads-of-State and other world leaders.

During the Eisenhower Administration, CIA attempts against the life of President Soekarno of Indonesia were sanctioned on a number of occasions. It is most probable that this executive order carried over into the Kennedy era as further attempts, financed by the CIA, were also made against the Indonesian Republic's founding father. Needless to say, *Bung Karno* survived all six attempts, although many who were present were not as fortunate, including the six young children whose distressing deaths resulted from the grenade attack aimed at their President during the official opening of the Cikini Hospital in Jakarta.

We have also learned that Lyndon Johnson and Richard Nixon both, understandably, considering the politics of that era, placed a price on Ho Chi Minh's head. And then, of course, there was John Kennedy and Fidel Castro, George Bush and Saddam Hussein, and a host of South American leaders who were perceived in the United

States as dangerous to the security of the world's largest democracy. It is, therefore, not without reason that I have suggested the possibility of an American President sanctioning executive action to remove another country's leader as an integral part of the storyline in my novel.

* * * * * *

There has been considerable concern in the United States in relation to the Communist-owned China Ocean Shipping Company (COSCO), which is a six hundred ship global corporation supervised by the People's Liberation Army (PLA). In documents registered with the United States Government, the employer of record for this organisation's interests in America is a notorious arms dealer who has, on occasion, been sighted taking coffee with the President in the White House.

COSCO's acquisition of the former United States Navy shipyard at Long Beach was cited as one of three questionable deals. The first of these was the twenty year, US$14.5 million per annum lease of the Long Beach facility, which was closed down earlier this decade as a result of American defense cut backs. The City of Long Beach, under the terms of the agreement, is obliged to pay approximately $235 million to modernise the facility for the Chinese; COSCO's annual lease payments of $14.5 million would require 16 years to repay the initial costs. A penalty clause in the agreement provided for COSCO to receive $32 million dollars worth of dock-side cranes as reimbursement if the contract turned sour. The second arrangement was the $138 million taxpayer-subsidized loan guarantee to a COSCO subsidiary to build four container ships in an Alabama shipyard.

The third, and most contentious of the three deals, was a recent agreement reached between a Hong Kong based COSCO subsidiary and the Panamanian Government to lease "anchor-ports" to the Panama Canal, a move which grants Communist China a strategic toe-hold in the Western Hemisphere. It is true that China, through this shipping company, has acquired control over the Pacific port of Balboa and the Atlantic port of Cristobal, both of which flank the Panama Canal. According to Panama's leading newspapers, COSCO's lease arrangements were effected through

Hutchinson Corporation in Hong Kong. It is a fact also, that 2,000 AK-47 rifles were seized in Oakland, America, from one of the COSCO ships, and General Chi of the PLA made the statement that Communist China had already developed the technology to deliver nuclear warheads to America's West Coast. (Sections of the preceding paragraph have been quoted with permission from 'The New American' Internet pages titled 'China Takes Over Former U.S. Navy Shipyard')

And the Japanese Government has already developed a missile titled H-2A, and is currently considering its conversion to military use.

* * * * * *

In the course of the past year, we have seen a series of calamities strike South East Asian nations, most of which, as in the case of the oil spills off Singapore and the Asian currency raids, were man-made. Then we had drought, and the disastrous fires which raged for many months across the islands of Sumatra, Borneo and Java. The fires undoubtedly resulted from the slash and burn tactics used to further enhance the pockets of the incredibly rich in Indonesia; we know that these most destructive fires could easily have been avoided, but graft and corruption are difficult masters to control, particularly when there are hundreds of millions of dollars involved. Even so, none of these events could, in any way, ever compete with the devastation which frequently accompanies a volcanic eruption or an earthquake.

Having lived in Asia for more than thirty years, I still believe that there is nothing more frightening than to be caught on the upper levels of a skyscraper when a tremor strikes. I recall attending dinner in the Hotel Sahid Jaya supper club one evening, to farewell a couple who had become dear to my family over the years.

This well-appointed restaurant was located on the eighteenth floor of the building. When the tremor struck, the lights failed and the building started to sway, terrifying the guests, as the restaurant's windows extended from ceiling to floor, providing a view directly down to Jalan Jenderal Sudirman and the footpaths below. Tables danced around the room and we clung to our chairs, waiting for the whipping motion of the tall building to cease. The memory of those minutes will remain with me forever, and the feeling of total helplessness I experienced still haunts me whenever I enter skyscrapers, even today.

Tremors are not an unusual occurrence in Indonesia, which boasts some sixty active volcanoes. Once, while dining in our villa in the mountain resort area of Cimacan, I witnessed a tremor with such incredible force that it bounced the four hundred kilo teak dining table across the room leaving startled guests with their mouths hanging open in surprise. Moments later, I recall, we then watched as an aftershock emptied the swimming pool. The point I wish to make here is that Indonesia would not be the safest of places to be considering the introduction of nuclear power plants.

As for Bali, I sometimes wonder just how many of the island's tourists have any idea as to the extent of the calamity caused when Gunung Agung erupted, spewing poisonous gases from its crater before spilling down the mountain's side killing thousands of one of God's most delightful races. The final death toll resulting from lava flow, gas and the eruption itself, which threw boulders the size of motor cars kilometers into the air, exceeded eight thousand.

It is fact that the Indonesian Parliament passed a bill on the twenty seventh of February, 1997, that cleared the way for the construction of up to twelve nuclear power plants on the geologically volatile islands to Australia's north. The first of these was to be built at the foot of the dormant volcano, Mount Muria, which lies some four hundred kilometers to the east of Jakarta, in one of the most densely populated areas known to mankind. Dr Habibie, Indonesia's Minister for Science and Technology, quite nonchalantly stated that his country must *'pasang pajung sebelum hujan'* which literally translates as, *prepare the umbrella before it rains*. He was, of course, referring to Indonesia's enormous power problems, and his desire to push for the accelerated development of nuclear power plants. Within six months, public pressure and world opinion caused Habibie to declare that Indonesia was no longer considering the use of nuclear power.

As an experienced Asia-phile, I would insist that it would be naïve of any to believe that, with the promise of billions of dollars in construction contracts in the offing, and given yet another opportunity to siphon large amounts of infrastructure funds away, those responsible for the final decision may not necessarily spend too much of their time worrying about the consequences of building a national power grid, driven by nuclear power, over the geologically unstable islands. Over the past forty years, the world's populations have had the misfortune to experience the following nuclear accidents:

- Windscale, England (October 7, 1957) A fire broke out at this plutonium production plant, releasing significant amounts of radioactive material.

- Idaho, USA. The SL-1 plant (January 3, 1961) Three workers were killed when a control rod was ejected from the core while being manually moved by one of the workers.

- Enrico Fermi, Michigan, USA. (October 5, 1966) A partial meltdown occurred, when a component broke loose and blocked the flow of coolant.

- Browns Ferry plant, Alabama, USA. (March 22, 1975) A fire erupted in the control room when a candle flame was used to check for air leaks.

- Three Mile Island, Pennsylvania, USA. (March 28, 1979) As a result of equipment failures and human error, the water level in the reactor core decreased to the point that the fuel was no longer submerged in water. Without the cooling normally provided, the cladding and some of the fuel pellets melted. Large quantities of radioactive material were released into the containment building which, thankfully, performed as designed.

- Chernobyl, former Soviet Union. (April 26, 1986) Failure to follow established procedures and poor design resulted in this, the world's worst nuclear accident. The design of the Chernobyl reactor resulted in a very rapid increase in heat after the water used to cool the core was lost.
Thirty-one people, all of whom were on-site emergency response personnel, died as a result of the accident. Two workers were killed by an associated explosion. Twenty-nine were killed by acute affects of radiation exposure; two hundred and three were

hospitalised with radiation sickness; more than thirty-six hours elapsed after the accident before the more than one hundred thousand local inhabitants living within a thirty mile radius were told to evacuate.

My reasons for writing this story were triggered by the concerns that I have regarding the possibility that Indonesia may, in the future, decide to resurrect the Nuclear Power Plant programme. Although I sincerely believe that technology developed in the United States and Japan severely reduces the risk of nuclear accidents occurring, particularly those resulting from structural damage caused by such geological disasters, I cannot resist wondering what might occur if a nuclear plant were constructed, as the Indonesians had originally planned, on such an unstable location as Mount Muria in Java, one of the most densely populated rural areas in the world. Coupled with the presence of those two old Indonesian warlords, Graft and Corruption, I, for one, would be most concerned.

* * * * * *

The story 'Jakarta' is a work of fiction, based on my own imagination and personal experiences whilst living in Indonesia and other parts of Asia, although I have based the story-line on some historic fact which is easily identified. The rest, I leave to the reader's imagination. However, there are some disturbing facts which should be mentioned here. India's population grows by some twenty-five millions each year and, according to United Nations projections, it could well be that we will see India become a net importer of food within the next two decades, about the same time as its population exceeds that of China's. Both India and Pakistan have nuclear technology, and are likely to use this in the event of another major altercation between the two nations.

Oil, gas and uranium will most surely run out before the close of the next century, leaving us with another hundred years of coal before the disappearance of all known fuels.

* * * * * *

It is imperative to stress, here, that I admire the Indonesian people for their culture, their kindness and their resilience. I was born in Australia but my adopted country, Indonesia, will always hold a very special place in my heart. I trust that my readers understand that in no way has it been my intention to denigrate the people of Asia. I wish merely to provide entertaining reading whilst, in some small way, affording those who may not have had the opportunity to enjoy the beauty of Asia and its colourful cultures, a small glimpse into what these might be.

Kerry B Collison
Melbourne

Glossary

ABRI	Indonesian Armed Forces
Aduh	exclamation, a cry
a.k.a.	also known as
AKABRI	Indonesian Armed Forces Academy
ALRI	Indonesian Navy
ANZUS	Australian, New Zealand, US Treaty
ASEAN	Association of South East Asian nations
ASIO	Australian Security Intelligence Organization (Australian domestic spy-service)
AURI	Indonesian Airforce
Antara	Indonesian News Agency
APCB	Asian Pacific Commercial Bank
APODETI	early East Timorese political party
arisan	office-run guaranteed lottery
ASAP	as soon as possible
ASIS	Australian Secret Intelligence Service Australian Overseas Spy Service
bahasa	language
BAKIN	Badan Kordinasi Intelijen: Indonesian CIA
bangsat	arse-hole, bastard
bapak	sir, respected male, often used to refer to the Indonesian President
Bapak-bapak dan Ibu-ibu	Gentlemen, and Ladies
BATAN	Indonesian Atomic Energy Authority
batik	Indonesian/Malay traditional cloth design.
becak	three-wheeled pedicab
bonsai	Japanese miniature trees
BOT	Build, Operate then Transfer, of projects
BWR	Boiling Water Reactor
bubur	porridge
bulé	derogatory name for white people

capung	dragonfly
CIA	Central Intelligence Agency
COMINT	Communication Intelligence
COSCO	China Shipping Company
DARPA	Defence Advanced Research Projects Agency
DIA	Defence Intelligence Agency
Diet	Japanese Parliament
Dili	former capital of East Timor
dim sum	Chinese breakfast individual serves
Dong Feng 31	Chinese ICBM
dukun	medicine man, spell-caster
durian	delicate tasting but foul smelling fruit
El Niño	climatic influence
FBR	Fast Breeder Reactor
Fretelin	Front for the Liberation of East Timor
gado-gado	mixed, cold vegetable dish, covered with peanut sauce
gaji	wages
gamelan	Balinese orchestra (bamboo xylophone)
GOLKAR	ruling political party in Indonesia (called a functional group)
gudang	store room
Gudang Garam	popular cigarette brand
halal	unadulterated Moslem-prepared style in food
Hankam	Indonesian Department of Defense
har gao	Chinese steamed dim sum dish
Hari Nyepi	religious 'quiet day' in Bali.
H-2A	Japanese rocket programme
H-3B	Japanese rocket programme
HN-5B	Communist Chinese man-portable surface-to-air missile
Ibu	older woman, mother
IAEA	International Atomic Energy Agency
ICBM	Intercontinental Ballistic Missile
ikan pepes	BBQ'd spiced fish wrapped in banana leaf
IFF	range finder for Stinger
IRBM	Intermediary Range Ballistic Missile
Istana	the palace, often used figuratively
jamur racun	poisonous mushroom (amanita muscaria)

JB	Johore Bahru: Malaysia's causeway city
kain-kebaya	traditional ladies blouse and sarong
kali	river or stream, canal
Kalimantan	Indonesian Borneo
Kalki	mythical Hindu god of destruction
Kakadu	Northern Australian National Park
kampung	village
kecil	small
kelereng	a game of marbles
kemasukan	to be posessed by a spirit
kongsi	partnership, commercial enterprise
korupsi	corruption
kretek	clove cigarette
kumpul-kerbau	literally a gathering of buffaloes but used by Indonesians to mean living together, having an affair
laksa	spicy Malay-Chinese curry noodle soup
LCC	famous early seventies Jakarta night-club
LE-7A	Japanese rocket engine
LE-9	future Japanese rocket engine
LMFBR	Liquid Metal Fast Breeder Reactor
Long March	Chinese ICBM
lurah	village head, chief
losmen	boarding house
Mach two	approximately 2,000 kph
mandi	to bathe
MANPAD	Man Operated Stinger Missile unit
MW	megawatt
'Na	abbreviated name form for Ratna
NAFTA	North American Free Trade Agreement
nasi	cooked rice
nenek-moyang	ancestors
NPP	nuclear power plant
NSA	National Security Agency
NSC	National Security Council (India)
nyonin kinzei	Japanese for 'women forbidden'
nyonya	Madame, Mrs
Oe-Cusse	former Portuguese enclave in West Timor
Ombar-Wetar	deep submarine trench off East Timor

Operasi Komodo	Indonesian Fifth Column activities in former Portuguese Timor
Ora Et Labora	a school in Jakarta
Pak	abbreviated form of Bapak (Mr, sir)
PALAPA	Indonesia's satellite system
Pedoman	leader
pembantu	servant
panggilan	whore
PEPELIN	Perusahan Pembangkit Listrik Nuklir (Indonesian Nuclear Power Company)
peranakan	of mixed extraction
PERTAMINA	Indonesian State-owned oil company
pici	small black cap worn by men
pisang	banana
pisang goreng	fried banana
PLA	Peoples Liberation Army (China)
Presiden	President
pribumi	indigenous person
PWR	Pressurized Water Reactor
Pulau Kambing	an island in East Timor
pungli	pungutan liar: demands for corrupt payment
P.T.	Perusahan Terbatas: limited liability company
Puri Kauh	Balinese name for Robson's villa
Puri Selera	Balinese restaurant
Rama	a king from the Ramayana Epic
Rama I to V	Indonesian Nuclear Power Plants
rendang	Indonesian spicy beef stew (goulash)
RCTI	Indonesian commercial TV station (owned by one of Soeharto's sons)
SAR	Search and Rescue
saté	skewered meat cooked over a charcoal BBQ
saté babi	pork ditto
saté kambing	goat ditto
saté penyu	turtle ditto
saudara	brother, friend, relative
SBS	Singapore Broadcasting Service

scram	terminology explaining a reactor shutdown procedure
Selamat datang	welcome
Selamat pagi	good morning
Selamat siang	good morning, good day
Selamat sore	good afternoon
Selamat malam	good evening
sialan!	exclamation, similar to goddamn
siao mai	dim sum dish
SS	submarine
SSN	nuclear submarine
SSN-21	twenty-first century nuclear submarine
SSBN	nuclear ballistic missile-armed submarine
Stinger	American manufactured, man-portable surface-to-air missile
SUBUD	Susila Budi Dharma religious cult
SVML	vehicle mounted Stinger rocket
TAG	Stinger guidance system
tai chi	Asian martial art
Taipan	powerful wealthy entrepreneur
telepon	telephone
terima kasih	thank you
tikar	woven mat
Tim Tim	acronym for East Timor (Timor-Timur)
tuan	sir, usually for foreigners
totok	pure Chinese immigrant to Indonesia
TPP	Thermal Power Plant
rezeki	luck, fortunes
sarong	wrap around dress
selendang	shoulder scarf, shawl
VTOL	Vertical Take-off and Landing aircraft

Places in India:	Places in Japan:	Places in China:
Goa	Shikoku	Shanghai
Lakshdweep	Hamaoka	Guangzhou
Vishakhapatnam	Kyushu	Chongging
Port Blair	Hokkaido	Xianggang
New Delhi		(Hong Kong)
Calcutta		Beijing
Bombay		

Chinese Navy Ships:

Jianghu	class of frigate
Huangfeng	class of missile ship
Han	class of nuclear submarine
Anshan	Soviet destroyers
Luda	ex Soviet destroyers

Indian Navy Ships:

SSGN Chakra	submarine
INS Viraat	aircraft carrier
INS Indira Gandhi	aircraft carrier
Rajputs	destroyers
Godavari	frigates
Vijay Durg	corvettes
Vidyut	missile craft

New Authors Welcome!

New Authors are invited to submit their manuscripts to our
offices in the United States of America, or Australia.
For further details regarding manuscript submission
contact our offices of visit our web page on:

http://www.sidharta.com.au
email: karam.1@osu.edu

Sid Harta Publishers
P.O. Box 1102
Hartwell Victoria 3125
Australia
Phone: (61) 3 9560 9920 or mobile: (61) 0414958623
Fax: (61) 3 9560 9921
email: author@sidharta.com.au

THE
TIMOR
MAN

Published by: Sid Harta Publishers for Kerry B. Collison and Asian
                       Pacific Management Co. (S.A.) Ltd.
                       Telephone: (61) (0 414) 958623
                       fax: (61) 03 9560 9921
                       Address: PO Box 1102 Hartwell,
                       Victoria, Australia 3125

First published 1996 as *The Tim-Tim Man*
Revised Edition, January 1998
Third Printing, April 1999
Copyright © Kerry B.Collison,
Sid Harta Publishers and
Asian Pacific Management Co. Ltd. S.A

Text: Kerry B.Collison
Cover Concept: Guy W. Collison
Final Proof Reading: Judith Bibo
Author's Photograph: Courtesy of Ned Kelly and the
                          Bundaberg News Mail, Queensland

Collison, Kerry Boyd

ISBN   0 9587448 1 5

Printed in Australia
by Australian Print Group
Maryborough, Victoria.

Dedication

To my wife Ni Nyoman Sukasani
and our children Sinta Dewi and
Guy Winston Collison

Kerry B. Collison followed a distinguished period of service as a member of the Australian Embassy in Indonesia during the turbulent Sixties followed by a successful business career spanning thirty years throughout Asia.

Recognised for his chilling predictions in relation to Asia's evolving political and economic climate and as the only Australian ever to have been personally granted citizenship by an Indonesian President, he brings unique qualifications to his historically-based vignettes and intriguing accounts of power-politics and the shadowy world of governments' clandestine activities.

The author's biographical data is available on the Internet at:
http://www.sidharta.com.au

Photo of the author by Ned Kelly, published by courtesy of the Bundaberg News Mail.

"And the beast was captured, and with it the
false prophet who in its presence had worked the
signs by which he deceived those who had received the
mark of the beast and those who worshipped its image.

These two were thrown alive into the lake
of fire that burns with sulphur."

Revelation 19, verse 20
From the Revelation to John
(The Apocalypse)
New Testament, Holy Bible

Acknowledgement

There are many who have assisted with this novel.

On more than one occasion, I wanted to give up and surrender all hopes of finally completing this tale and had it not been for the support of those who believed in me then this book would not be a matter of fiction but merely a figment of my imagination.

Determination is obviously not enough. And by itself, neither is energy. Together they are sufficient to see one through the endless months and in this case, years, of work and self examination.

Often, just one critique is sufficient to break a writer's spirit; I was fortunate to have the critic and the guide who provided the way out of the dark literary jungle I had created for myself. In this respect, I wish to acknowledge the support and assistance of Denise Cox, without whose honest criticism this novel would not have been published.

I also wish to thank Judith Bibo for re-proofing the new release and the many readers who have written to support my work on the trilogy.

Author's Note

The *Timor Man* is a work of historical fiction.

Originally, this story was released with the title *The Tim-Tim Man*, however, out of respect to the East Timorese people I have re-titled the book.

Fact and fiction are often held to be difficult bedfellows. In this novel, I have attempted to weave both into a narrative that general readers will enjoy, readers who have not had the benefit of witnessing at first-hand the incredible changes that have occurred in Asia over the last few decades.

Perhaps some of the descriptions of events and military hardware could be challenged, but for the greater part, the novel is supported by what I believe to be a solid foundation of fact.

In 1965 and 1966, during the time which many of us later understood as the *'Year of Living Dangerously'*, almost half a million people died in one of the worst blood lettings since the Jewish Holocaust.

Later, between the years of 1975 and 1990, almost a quarter of a million East Timorese were killed by Indonesian soldiers. More died, in fact, than were lost in the terrible wars in what are now known as the Former Yugoslavian Republics.

Although this story was not written with a political purpose, I hope it will reach your heart and appeal to your soul. As our world enters the twenty-first Century, we still go about killing each other more than ever before. Human nature doesn't seem to change.

Only the historical facts do.

Kerry B. Collison,
Kompong Som

Contents

Prologue

the present

The explosion erupted through the assembly.

Figures danced momentarily before disintegrating into heaps of lifeless flesh and bone. The blast ripped through the guests hurling musical instruments into the maelstrom of human carnage, decapitating a bandsman.

Then, for an immeasurable moment, silence ...

A shrill cry pierced the quiet, then a cacophony of screams emphasised the full horror of the blasts.

Canberra bomb toll 'horrific' — PM

By PETER JENSEN,

Canberra. Thursday

The Australian Prime Minister has issued a statement strongly condemning last night's terrorist attack which claimed more than 100 lives here in the Capital.

Amongst those believed killed were the Indonesian Ambassador to Australia, Mr. Nathan Seda, the Indonesian Chief of Army Staff, Lt. General Umar Suprapto, the Indonesian Minister for Foreign Affairs, Mr. Abdul Nasution, and the former Australian Ambassador to Indonesia, Mr. Duncan O'Laughlin.

A further 337 people have been reported as seriously injured. Local hospitals where the bomb blast victims are recovering from severe burns have been placed under tight security.

An informed source has stated that the condition of the Papua New Guinea Foreign Affairs Minister has improved but he is expected to remain on the critical list.

Eye witnesses reported that the Indonesian Embassy foyer erupted into a fireball moments after commencement of the Indonesian national anthem.

The explosion was felt throughout the area. Local residents in surrounding areas have reported extensive window damage. Meanwhile, the Prime Minister has expressed deep regret concerning the attack and has sent a personal note to the Indonesian President expressing sympathy and offering Australia's condolences to the Indonesian people.

He stated that he hoped current relations would not be further strained by what he described as "international terrorists and vested interest groups bent on sabotaging Indonesian-Australian relations."

Yesterday's reception was held to celebrate Indonesia's Independence Day in Australia, Mr. Seda's first since taking up his post.

Both Governments had hoped that his appointment would create an air of rapprochement between the countries since relations were strained over the Timor shelf oil disputes and New Guinea's recent border clashes with its giant neighbour.

Border violations throughout the past twelve months have resulted in Australian military units being positioned in New Guinea to assist under the terms of existing defence commitments. A number of Indonesian RPKAD troops and New Guinea soldiers were killed during a recent clash.

At the time, Indonesia claimed that their troops had been on an anti-guerrilla sweep and had inadvertently strayed into New Guinea territory. Political relations deteriorated further when the Australian Embassy in Jakarta was partly gutted by fire during student demonstrations.

It is not known whether Indonesia will now sever diplomatic ties as a result of this attack. Opposition Shadow Foreign Affairs Minister David Carroll demanded that the Prime Minister act to protect Australian interests in Indonesia as students are expected to demonstrate in retaliation to the Canberra bombing.

A Government spokesman has indicated that steps have already been taken in Jakarta but warned that tourists travelling to Indonesia should be aware of possible incidents in response to the deaths of the senior Indonesians here.

A man claiming to be a member of the Frente Revolucionarla de Timor Leste Independente (FRETILIN) party had phoned claiming responsibility for the bombing.

The Prime Minister has instructed the police and security chiefs to mobilise whatever forces necessary to investigate the bombing and pursue those responsible. — AAP

PAGE 3: continues

1975 — Kampuchea falls to Pol Pot, 'Killing Fields' period commences.
1975 — Saigon falls to the Communists.

Phnom Penh

Vietnam

Ho Chi Minh City (Saigon)

Konfrontasi — 1958-196[5]
Guerilla-style warfare invo[lving]
Malaysia, Indonesia & Bri[tish]
Commonwealth countri[es]
includingAustralia, takes p[lace]
mainly in Sarawak and Su[...]

Malaysia

Malaya

Natuna Island (world's largest natural gas deposits)

Sarawak

Singapore

Kalimantan

Sumatra

Indian (Indonesian) Ocean

Indonesia

Jakarta

Java

Bali

proposed nuclear plants

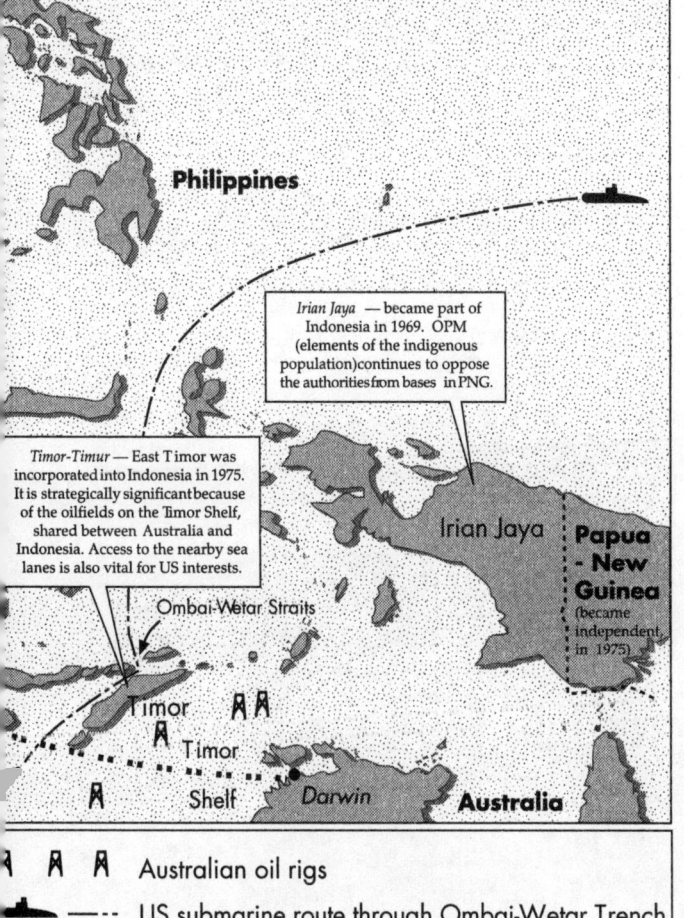

Philippines

Irian Jaya — became part of Indonesia in 1969. OPM (elements of the indigenous population) continues to oppose the authorities from bases in PNG.

Timor-Timur — East Timor was incorporated into Indonesia in 1975. It is strategically significant because of the oilfields on the Timor Shelf, shared between Australia and Indonesia. Access to the nearby sea lanes is also vital for US interests.

Irian Jaya

Papua - New Guinea (became independent in 1975)

Ombai-Wetar Straits

Timor

Timor

Shelf

Darwin

Australia

Australian oil rigs

US submarine route through Ombai-Wetar Trench

route taken by British 'V' Bombers armed with nuclear bombs, 1962–65

Book One

1965

Indonesia in Turmoil

Chapter 1

Nathan Seda
Jakarta — January 1965

Lightning cracked yet again, signalling there would be no break in the tropical storm. The city began to choke as rain fell incessantly creating chaos with the traffic. Trucks, buses and cars remained stuck where they had broken down under the deluge, their electrical systems saturated and rendered useless. Scores of drivers waded through the deep and filthy flows which threatened to carry the abandoned cars over the roads into the flooded canals.

The downpour continued throughout the day, threatening to close the capital, as most major roads became small rivers feeding shallow lakes which had suddenly appeared where once there had been parks and fields.

The air was thick with the musty damp smell of the rain. Humidity rose to unbearable levels.

The more congested intersections would remain blocked for hours as children played in waist-deep ponds covering the Capital's pot-holed protocol roads. Electricity flow would have ceased almost immediately rain had commenced. Without power there would be no water — the irony of being without adequate water while rain flooded the city was not lost on the Capital's inhabitants.

The transition from Dutch colonial rule to Independence had thrust the archipelago's one hundred and fifty million people into a political and economic quagmire peppered by religious rivalry and diverse cultural differences.

Soekarno's brilliant use of rhetoric, and support provided by the military, enabled him to take the helm of the world's fifth most populous country, a land rich in unexploited natural resources.

The national philosophy, the *Panca Sila*, provided for five basic

17

principles around which the people were expected to build their way of life. This philosophy eased the racial and religious tensions which otherwise might have caused civil war. Although the country had the world's largest Moslem population, political power was determined more by ethnic rather than religious considerations. Leaders from Java, the most heavily populated island, controlled the country's numerous and politically unstable provincial centres.

The sky remained ominously dark. Lightning flashed again, striking the unfinished skeleton of the Wisma Nusantara building overlooking the British Embassy. *Jalan Thamrin*, Jakarta's main protocol avenue, ceased to function.

Canal water flowed along the footpaths bringing with it unmentionable sewage and the occasional dead animal. Since seasonal maintenance was invariably neglected the *kali*, or drains, could never handle the sudden downpours. Putrid garbage and human effluent flowed into the streets and through the houses. Pedestrian traffic disappeared as the footpaths became increasingly inundated.

Houses built along the avenues adjacent to these canals always suffered the fierce odours from these sewage streams. *Jonguses* waited apprehensively as the rivers of foul waste threatened their masters' residences. Instructions were given to female servants, the *babus*, to stand-by to clean up after the occasional vehicle which passed immediately in front of a residence, throwing small waves into the well kept yards, creating havoc.

Most resident foreigners were members of the Diplomatic Corps. Their houses were grand old Dutch designed mansions built during the colonial times to provide for the numerous Dutch colonists. Now they were occupied by career men and women, many enjoying their first posting overseas.

Expatriates, generally speaking, were provided with vehicles. Transport was expensive and car smuggling was practised in many of the Third World Embassies to compensate for the poorly paid civil servants' meagre incomes. Drivers ferried their masters to and fro, enjoying considerable privilege within the domestic ranks of the expatriate household. The wet season was, however, when these drivers suffered most abuse.

Rain brought floods. Flooded streets caused the *tuan*'s car to stop. *Tuan* would be late for work, or even worse, late for a cocktail function. The 'mister' would then be angry and would surely blame his woes for the day on the driver. It seemed that no one appreciated the rain.

The traffic police disappeared. What could they do? The locals were clever enough to stay indoors and the foreigners, the *orang asing*, were always a problem demanding assistance waving their diplomatic passports whenever their vehicles came to an abrupt halt in the flooded streets. Just four or five stranded vehicles around the Hotel Indonesia circle could create hours of chaos.

Traffic congestion was further exacerbated by the 100,000 *becak* drivers who pedalled their iron three-wheelers everywhere, demanding equal access through the bedlam of traffic. These wiry-legged men were definitely a force to be reckoned with, should one be so unfortunate as to become involved in an accident or any other altercation with them. Theirs was, in fact, the most sensible form of transportation during heavy rain periods as the passenger was reasonably protected from the elements. There were, however, exceptions.

This year's *Idulfitri* contributed to Jakarta's unpleasant appearance. The remnants of that week's festivities floated along the inundated roads. Many who had returned to their villages for the *Ramadhan* feast would soon drift listlessly back to their offices satisfied that their religious and social obligations had been acquitted in accordance with tradition and the Moslem faith.

Idulfitri followed the Moslem month of fasting. Each morning, prior to daybreak, those participating would consume their last food and water until sunset. Initially, most Moslems would follow the dictates of the fast. Many would not have the strength to continue for the entire month and those who felt despondent for not being resilient enough to meet the rigid demands as determined by the holy Koran were not, in general, castigated for their weakness or inability to adhere to the religious rites.

Ramadhan was a time of restraint and abstinence.

Idulfitri was a time of celebration.

It was just unfortunate that this year, the holidays following the breaking of the final fasting period had to coincide with the rain. Most accepted the situation philosophically; the festival advanced by two weeks each year and eventually the holidays would fall during the dry season.

Not far from the central business district stood the splendid obelisk representing Indonesia's freedom from Dutch rule. Positioned in the centre of a large square, *Lapangan Merdeka*, the column could be seen from most points within the city proper. Surrounding the *Merdeka* square were government offices and the Indonesian Department of Defence, HANKAM. The United States Embassy, adjacent to the Republic's military headquarters, enjoyed the benefits of the prominent address, but not the excessive attention it often attracted.

The HANKAM building in itself was a relatively insignificant structure considering its importance. Built by the Dutch, it was a white walled terra-cotta roofed building which reached only to the customary three levels. The Dutch did not enjoy the benefits of lifts and air-conditioning, so consequently they designed their structures so that, having struggled up the stairs to the third floor, they could enjoy the occasional breeze which compensated for the climb.

Louvred windows allowed soft breezes to whisper through the buildings, cooling the self-appointed colonial masters. Security was, at best, cursory. Military police stood as sentries at the main gate checking visitors as they entered in their stately limousines.

The main structure housed two hundred staff, most of whom had very little to do but wander through the deteriorating corridors. Mildew was evident everywhere and leaking water pipes left patterns of moist blotches identifying the piping's irregular path through the maze of brick and cement walls. Cables hung precariously in the air held only by rusting supports. Wires bared to the copper hung threateningly from their two-holed sockets, the inadequate power rarely surging to more than half of its determined voltage. Power variation damaged equipment even more quickly than the tropical heat with its soaking humidity.

Not that power was such a problem, as it rarely worked anyway since the Soviets ceased their financial support three years before. The entire building boasted only three direct dial telephone numbers and the switchboard had virtually no capacity for improvement.

In the rear courtyard, more than twenty Soviet-style Jeeps, Armed Personnel Carriers and trucks stood abandoned and overgrown by grass. Generally speaking, the armed forces were in financial disarray.

A Banyan tree dwarfed the left wing of the complex. Children played in the branches, oblivious to the significance of their surroundings. Not fifty metres from the corner, a long row of two-storey shops and dwellings housed an array of squatters.

A group of Germans had recently acquired a lease to open their own club and construction was under way. This in itself attracted a number of curious spectators, as only occasional building or renovation had taken place during the past years and to see foreigners who were not Soviets actually doing something was quite unusual.

A group of workers waited for their pay, squatting on their haunches beside the remnants of what had been several cubic metres of river sand before the days work had begun.

Another day of drudgery was coming to a close.

* * * * * *

A solitary figure sat motionless, staring moodily across the square through a rain-blurred window from the third level of the HANKAM building.

His office was the typical bleak high-ceilinged room. The walls, stained by the smoke of belching buses and powerful aromatic *kretek* cigarettes, showed evidence of years of neglect. The discoloured ceilings were now a combination of moss-green and moist brown. Surplus ships paint sloshed over earlier leakage stains did little to camouflage the decay. Overhead fans struggled to cut a leading edge through the polluted air, their blades blackened by the endless movement through the heavy, sticky atmosphere.

Photographs hung untidily on the wall adjacent to the military green painted door. General Sarwo Eddie, the hero of the liberation of *Irian Barat*, stood in his typical arrogant style. His picture was placed to the right of the President while Dr Soebandrio sat knowingly in an armchair, holding a pipe, on the left of the Great Leader of the Revolution, placed there obviously by some clerk with a sense of humour considering the good doctor's role in delivering his country to Communism. The office was furnished simply with a desk and two chairs.

The man at the window wore an army uniform. The insignia on his shoulder identified him as an intelligence colonel. His dark, almost aquiline features indicated his ethic origins as being somewhere within the Eastern Nusantara group of islands. He was tall for an Indonesian and his face was completely unlined by the worries of his profession.

To the casual observer, the colonel may have appeared to be mesmerised by the activity in the foreign legation's grounds, the apparent object of his scrutiny. The United States Embassy was not, however, what was distracting him from the unread folders of military documents spread casually across his desk in this third level office.

A roll of thunder interrupted his thoughts, obliging him to acknowledge the unattended, indeed relatively mundane, matters before him.

He sighed. He was bored. Bored with the weather and the overcrowded city that lay sprawled out before him.

Colonel Seda pondered the problems associated with the rain, turned in his chair and returned to his partial view of the outside world. He ran his hand slowly through the curly hair which would soon require attention, his fingers finding a small crusty patch on the hairline to scratch. He examined the small white specks of dry skin under the nicotine stained fingernail. Disgusted with the find, he wiped his hand quickly against his thigh. It was always the little things that caused the most annoyance, he thought.

His driver had not, as yet, returned from Bandung. There was a very real possibility his transport would break down, should the incompetent idiot assigned to him from the motor pool attempt to bring the antiquated vehicle through the flooded streets. Again he sighed. His quarters would be leaking. Every roof in the country leaked. '*Sialan* — Damn,' he thought. The country was deteriorating at an alarming rate. Inflation had eaten his salary away to the point where it was practically valueless. At least the monthly rice rations kept everyone going. It was difficult to secure a position where a little extra income could be earned. He should have joined the police force, he mused. Without exception, police, because of their close access to the public, could always extract those little extras whenever they wished. At any time they could just stop any car with a Chinese passenger and squeeze him for a little cash.

Although a minority group, the Indonesian Chinese had a very real stranglehold on the Indonesian economy and were easy targets for extortion. Nobody cared when a Chinese was roughed up a little for they had not integrated with the indigenous races and often manipulated commodity prices to the point where many *pribumi* people starved. Wherever they settled, the world's oldest trading race eventually became embroiled in some form of racial violence and Indonesia was no exception. The Chinese were despised. They controlled the flow of all agricultural products and other basic necessities. They had their own schools. They controlled the shops.

And all that gold they wore!

"*Sialan mereka semua!*" Seda muttered, cursing the whole race as he continued to gaze through the window. Perhaps he should not complain, he brooded. After all, he'd done reasonably well with his life so far, considering that he had been born and raised in a small village near Dili in East Timor. There, life had been excruciatingly hard. His father had died from one of the many fevers that plagued the rural dwellers.

Seda had difficulty remembering much about his father, only his strong, sharp facial features remained fixed in his mind. He had obviously inherited his father's nose, for when he moved to Jakarta as an adult and visited the whores around the *Blok M* graveyard, they often mistook him for a foreigner. He would never know whether these genes were the result of some careless Portuguese sailor or some Dutch seed sown lustfully generations before.

The Portuguese began trading with Timor almost a century prior to any serious attempts by the Dutch to develop a foothold on the island. The division of the island between these two seafaring nations ultimately resulted in the development of considerable religious and cultural differences between the Catholic northeast and the Protestant south.

Although both colonial powers in Timor concentrated their efforts on preventing each other from expanding their spheres of influence, some trade in produce did develop. Coffee became the main export from the two colonies.

Dutch Timor inevitably became part of Indonesia as a result of the Independence movement. It was officially absorbed into *Nusa Tenggara* province by the central government in Jakarta during subsequent provincial restructuring. Kupang remained the provincial capital. For a time, Catholics, Protestants, and a few Buddhists, Hindus and Moslems co-existed without any real racial or religious turmoil. Even the head-hunters put aside their old habits.

When his mother was obliged to migrate to another village across the border, she remarried. Seda became one of seven children in what was already an impoverished family. He slept on a *tikar* mat alongside his new brothers and sisters cramped together on a dirt floor in a one room house which provided only the barest protection from the elements. There were two small meals a day, taken sitting cross-legged on the roughly woven mat. Some days, when his stepfather was unable to find part time work to supplement his pitiful income, they went without food altogether.

He remembered that his mother often stood outside, alone, looking down the dry slopes towards the sea and across to where they had lived when his father had still been alive. Occasionally, he would slip quietly outside so that the other children would not follow and go to her, leaning against her frail body, his head tilted against her hip trying to understand just what she stood and stared at from under the old mango tree.

She would not talk during these private moments but he didn't mind as he always felt a sense of warmth as her calloused hands softly stroked his hair and the side of his face. He knew that she frequently missed meals, ensuring that the children were fed first. She was often sick and he wanted to cry out for someone to care, but he knew, even in his youth, that almost every hut in the dry desolate village housed another mother whose suffering was similar.

Poverty and hunger can be great motivators. When his mother had arranged for him to attend classes at the local Catholic school he grasped the opportunity and studied diligently. At first he experienced great difficulty as the other children were more advanced, having had the advantage of attending classes since turning seven.

Seda was nine before he could read. When he was twelve he had recovered all the lost time and was increasingly being singled out by the priests for his rapid progress in class. These hard working men of the cloth struggled to educate all of the children, regardless of their talents, but their efforts were often severely restricted by a government which favoured non-Christian institutions. During the heat of the day when the classes rested, the children would literally drop to the floor in the school and sleep for several hours, enjoying the cool of the tiled floor against their undernourished bodies.

Schools were inadequately equipped. The population was desperately poor. The Church provided a semblance of basic primary education to many however funds were limited as the government restricted the growth of non-Moslem faith educational institutions. The priests were obliged to be extremely careful and selective when allocating positions in their school.

As a teenager Seda continued to study diligently. Excellent grades created the opportunity for the young student to attend the Armed Forces Academy in Java which resulted in his eventual escape from the provincial backwater. His mother had been delighted that her son had been selected for such a career opportunity. Now, his future would be secure. He would never again experience the hunger of his childhood.

Seda contemplated his humble origins. Although born in Portuguese Timor this was never reflected in any of his earlier school registration documents. Border crossings were frequent and registrations of village births on both sides of the border mainly went unrecorded. He remembered his mother and the tears of joy when his selection had been announced. Her tears were not just in appreciation for the blessing her god had passed to her son. She wept knowing that she would lose him. Once he had tasted the exotic life of the main island she knew he would never return.

* * * * * *

Seda had never been convinced that the army had been the correct choice. In retrospect, he felt that perhaps he should have elected to fly with AURI, the country's Air force. Many of the pilots and technical officers had been sent to the Eastern Bloc countries for advanced training. This inevitably meant additional funds for clothes, travel and other expenses and a chance to travel away from the disorder that prevailed.

Indonesia had entered its most dangerous period. Everything appeared to be confused. The country's leaders had all but embraced Communism yet this strange political ideology did not, in fact, accept religious belief! Bewildering enough for an uneducated Muslim population which followed the teachings of the Prophet Mohammed. The people had been instructed to follow the President's dictates. NASAKOM was the new political order — Nationalism, Socialism, Communism. The Russians had poured in billions of dollars in foreign aid to ensure that the Communist political agenda could be realised in this resource-rich archipelago.

Within a few short years, the country was equipped with tanks and every kind of sophisticated weaponry. Airfields boasted MIG-15s, 17s and 19s. Indeed, Seda had read a report just the day before about the amazing Russian strategic bombers, designated TU-16's, which had the capacity to bomb every major city in the country to the south in just one sortie!

Seda found that there was so much to learn from the new military jargon. IL-28s had been positioned at the Malang and Surabaya airfields. SA-2 missiles were sitting on their launch sites ready for firing from their revetments. There was also talk that the Russians had built a submarine base in Cilacap, on the south coast of Java!

Seda had seen the new steel mill under construction in Cilegon.

All of this, he thought, and still not enough money to feed the hundreds of thousand of troops the country had mustered. Everyone was waiting anxiously for the leadership to prove how the new doctrines would prevent past major food shortages from recurring. Maybe the new ships provided by the Russian Navy would be utilised to bring rice from other nations?

Seda snorted in disgust. He was intelligent enough to realise that the Indonesian people now faced starvation due to the folly of political misadventures by the country's entrenched leadership, and that the days when the country exported rice were over. He did not trust the group headed by Subandrio. The President was too easily swayed by the Communists. Maybe *Bung Karno*, as he preferred to be called, was, in fact, becoming senile and did not realise the dangers of these people around him. The President had spent far too much of his valuable time chasing young women and, to the dismay of his first four wives, his latest acquisition, a Japanese hostess, was set to become the new First Lady!

Seda looked over his shoulder at the photographs and suddenly felt uneasy under the gaze of the powerful trio hanging there as if in silent rebuke. The President was still very popular although there had been several attempts on his life. The political scene created considerable concern amongst the army's generals. Senior naval and air force personnel had joined the Communist Party swelling its ranks under Dr Subandrio's leadership. Considering these problems, it was best not to involve oneself, the Colonel decided.

Rumour had it that the Communist Party would attempt to weaken the Army by convincing the President that only party loyalists should be promoted to senior positions in the services. Their influence had reached into the schools and was evident on billboards and in the press. Seda recognised that the Communists were dangerous. They were dangerous to the nation and they were particularly dangerous to military personnel in positions such as his. Should the President permit their power to infiltrate defence control and policy determination centres, they would succeed in gaining control over the army.

The Timorese shuddered. All those years of study and obedience! These *bangsat* were no better than the blood-sucking Chinese leeches!

Unlike most in his peer group, Nathan Seda really did understand just how acute the problem had become between the Communists and the military in their power struggle during recent years. The President seemed to consider that competition between the two opposing groups was healthy. Seda thought inwardly that *Bung Karno* had lost touch with reality and with the very ideals which had originally brought the Republic together under the red and white flag.

Seda acknowledged that he had to utilise whatever connections he had developed here, at Defence Headquarters, to consolidate his position. He further understood that it was essential to identify himself with the current ABRI leaders who were anti-Communist to avoid possible suspicion of his allegiances. He was convinced that Indonesia's uneasy political climate could easily result in the Communist elements gaining control of the military which would be disastrous for officers of his rank. Being Timorese, he automatically attracted suspicion. Only a handful of non-Javanese would ever make it to the top and with a little skill and a great deal of luck he felt that time would reward him for his patience and loyalty. It was therefore imperative that he maintain his position in HANKAM, avoiding transfer to any other unit where his career could be buried forever, or worse...

The President had seen his war against the Federation of Malaysia as a means of diverting the nation's attention away from the economic and social nightmare created by corrupt and poorly educated leaders. Many of the hierarchy had little better than a primary education and were quite unable to cope with the problems posed by the failing economy. Indonesia's natural resources were mainly undeveloped as the western nations were reluctant to risk their capital in a country whose Communist Party boasted the third largest membership in the world.

The United States and British Commonwealth countries were alarmed when the Indonesian government readily accepted Russian armaments. The CIA often flew missions against the Indonesian forces from Clarke Field in the Philippines. One such mission failed and the American pilot, captured after being shot down, became the charismatic Indonesian President's personal pilot. The British, obliged to provide assistance to the fledgling members of the Commonwealth, prepared for major warfare. RAF Vulcan bombers, armed with atomic warheads, flew regular missions between Darwin and Singapore with their bomb bay doors open over Indonesia.

Australian soldiers served alongside their Malaysian counterparts in the jungles throughout this undeclared war. The Australian public knew little of what was happening as their government smothered almost all attempts by journalists to reveal the facts. Government 'D' notices prevented the release of news which was deemed detrimental to the security of the nation.

Australian SAS troops often carried out cross-border raids into Indonesian-held Irian and Kalimantan, capturing select troops for interrogation purposes and then dispatching them without ceremony. The Royal Australian Navy, whilst on manoeuvres, passed through the Sunda Straits with all hands ready at their battle stations. The fear of Communist hordes swooping down through the archipelago into the land of the Southern Cross was real. Or at least it was made to appear so by the leading politicians of the time.

Poorly trained and suffering low morale, many Indonesian soldiers died fighting against superior and more professionally trained forces. Nevertheless, Dr Soekarno was adamant; the war would continue. And so it did, much to the dismay of both his military commanders and Indonesia's neighbours.

A posting to the 'Konfrontasi' battalions was considered to be extremely dangerous as the unofficial lists of missing and dead were so unpalatable the figures were never released. A casual observer might be impressed by Indonesia's fine array of weaponry but to a skilled eye, the appalling lack of maintenance was obvious. Sophisticated aircraft and other defence equipment often remained on the ground or broken in warehouses due to the inability of the unskilled personnel to maintain the armaments. Spare parts were lost or misplaced. Although Indonesia had been heavily armed by the Russians, training programs were limited to a select few.

The Communists urged the President to move the military from Java to front line encampments. Their logic was that this would be sufficient to cause the opposing forces to collapse quickly once they recognised the might of the Indonesian military. Dr Subandrio, in concert with his fellow party supporters, urged the President also to consider that this action would bring pressure to bear on those commanders whom they considered were shirking their responsibilities.

The President was easily flattered by Dr Subandrio. As Head of State, Soekarno had himself designated as the Great Leader of the Revolution, President for Life, Chief of the Armed Forces and this self-delusion led him to believe that he would, in the future, lead the Non-Aligned Nations and the New Emerging Forces of the Third World. Soekarno would not heed his army generals when they cautioned him against moving his military support to outposts where they would be unable to support the Java Central Command. The generals were gravely concerned. Deliberate delays were instigated to prevent the main stay of the army's elite forces from being moved away from their direct control.

As a colonel in the Indonesian Intelligence, Headquarters Army Command, Department of Defence, Nathan Seda was privy to national secrets of considerable import. Clandestine meetings were often arranged to permit the exchange of secret memoranda to avoid discovery by the Communists. Reports regarding internal security were often passed, read, then burned.

Seda was not entirely at ease with this responsibility. It rested heavily on his shoulders; however he realised that, correctly used, he could develop considerable power through the accumulation of this sensitive information.

Lightning flashed again, this time followed by a crack of thunder that shook the building. Distracted, he checked his wrist watch, a square shaped Lavina which often opted to stop for no mechanical reason he could understand.

It was time to leave. Seda reflected on his immediate problem with transport then instructed the motor pool not to allocate a replacement vehicle for that evening. He elected to catch a *becak* as the three-wheeled contraptions often succeeded where powered vehicles could not.

Securing his desk, Seda strolled out through the old building into the courtyard, past white helmeted security guards and on to *Jalan Merdeka Utara*. There he beckoned towards the multitude of *becak* drivers who, having sighted the colonel leaving the defence building, edged forward calling out for the fare. He selected one and cautiously climbed aboard.

A Russian-built staff vehicle eased into the courtyard as he departed. The occupants appeared agitated. Probably, thought Seda, from the many stops the vehicle would surely have made in getting through the obstacle course that the congested street had now become.

Buses and trucks blocked traffic as passengers attempted to push their transport, often unsuccessfully, to higher ground. Waves created by the few vehicles which moved through the traffic pushed dirty water perilously close to the top of the *becak's* passenger seat. Seda's trousers became wet causing him to shift to protect the contents of his pockets from the wash. In doing so, he slipped forward and, to his and the driver's dismay, fell sideways into the filthy, inundated street.

"*Aduh, Pak,*" the driver called, his eyes wide, anticipating the angry outburst. "*Sialanlu,*" snapped Seda, pulling himself upright, using the *becak* frame for support.

He succeeded in wading to the other side of the flooded road where the water was shallower, cursing the driver for his stupidity, punctuating the vitriolic outburst with easily identifiable finger and thumb movements, while admonishing himself silently for having lost his balance.

He looked down at his trousers and what he saw angered him even more. They were ripped. His feet were wet and his shoes would take days to dry. He stood silently for a few moments forcing his anger to subside. Remembering the cause of his accident, Seda extracted his wallet along with its soggy contents. Four

hundred and fifty wet rupiah notes! Angrily he stared at his identification card and passes. All would require replacement. *Aduh*,
he thought, this had been one hell of a day. Resigned to the two
kilometre walk and determined not to board another *becak,* Seda
headed off in the direction of his quarters, brooding over the bad
karma.

* * * * * *

The morning summons to report to the director's office had been
unexpected. Although Seda was an excellent officer and there was
no apparent reason to be alarmed, he still experienced a sense of
uneasiness. Despite being self-confident under most circumstances,
he knew that this call had to be serious. The director rarely ordered such one-on-one meetings with lieutenant colonels. In fact,
Seda had only met the general twice and both occasions were during briefing sessions in the War room. He resisted the temptation
to hurry. It would display signs of nervousness.

The First Directorate for Intelligence Operations was at the end
of the second wing, secluded in a tight web of security. He approached under the watchful eyes of two KOPASGAT airborne
guards. One of them advanced towards him and ushered him directly into an ante-room. The door was closed and locked.

A small desk off to one corner was occupied by a first lieutenant
who rose respectfully and offered the Colonel a seat on the hand-
carved wooden bench seat. The suite was typical of the decorative
carved settees throughout the government offices and, as many a
foreign guest had found, they were not designed for long periods
of sitting.

The Colonel observed that there were no water stained ceilings
here. A hand woven Persian carpet lay spread along side the coffee
table upon which had been placed a glass of Java Robusta coffee,
covered with the standard aluminium lid to prevent dust and flies
from spoiling the cooling thick liquid.

He ignored the offering and continued to pass the time examining the recently printed map which covered half the wall area above
the trophy cabinet. The chart indicated that the ocean to the south
and west of his country was now named the Indonesian Ocean
and that the whole of Borneo and Malaysia bore the same identifying colours as all of the provinces of the Indonesian Republic. Seda

resisted the temptation to smile as he was conscious of the young officer's attention.

The General kept him waiting. It was warm in this room. Was it his imagination or did the overhead fan appear to be slowing? He felt the moist droplets forming around his buttocks and then under his arms. The perspiration made him self conscious and a small damp trickle established a line down the centre of his back. He leaned forward, to prevent the sticky drops from saturating his shirt, annoyed that his anxiety would be apparent.

Suddenly the buzzer sounded, startling him. The adjutant rose to his feet to escort him into the general's presence. The large double doors opened into an enormous room. It stretched across ten metres and was at least seven metres deep.

Seda was surprised. He had no idea that such offices were available in the cramped HANKAM complex. He had, in the course of his duties, visited many of the other senior ranking officers' rooms throughout the command but never had he seen an office with such expensive decor. The walls were covered from the floor halfway to the ceilings with polished teak timber panels. The skirting boards were all hand carved as were the joining sections between each panel. The ceiling followed the line of the roof, making the chamber large and impressive, and priceless Dutch colonial lamps were hung in each of the corners. One wall was covered with plaques, pennants and photographs from the general's past military service.

On the opposing wall, a huge Garuda highlighted with gold leaf was positioned overlooking the director's magnificent desk. Directly between its talons, creating an appropriate backdrop to the throne-shaped director's chair, were the words *Bhineka Tunggal Ika*. Unity in Diversity. The Red and White hung on its stand, moving gently to the wisps of artificial breeze blowing from the three, two-horsepower Carrier air-conditioners installed inconspicuously where former windows had been removed.

The imported guest chairs with tanned matching leather seats and chrome tubular steel supports were positioned so that the visitor was obliged to view the general's military memorabilia and photographic record of his achievements. He could feel the authority emanating from the room and its tenant. Seda came to attention directly in front of his superior, saluted smartly, then waited for a response. The door closed softly behind him as the adjutant slipped quietly away.

General Sudomo sat erect in his oversized chair which had been carved to match the front and side panels of the three-metre desk. The impression created was that the man was considerably smaller than normal, perhaps even a dwarf, but Seda knew this not to be the case. He was very aware that it would be dangerous to underestimate the Director, as his reputation for toughness was well known in military circles.

"*Ah Seda*," Sudomo spoke softly, indicating with a gesture for Seda to be seated. He obeyed. An opened cigarette packet had been carefully positioned in the centre of the glass coffee table. He noticed that the General's ribbon collection, displayed prominently on the left side of his chest, had grown since his last intelligence briefing. Seda made it a practice to notice such things. These small yet colourful bands provided considerable information as to the bearer's past and even current movements and activities. In a world of intrigue and power plays it was imperative to have up-to-date knowledge.

For high-ranking officers like the General, the ribbons were literally decorations. At the last count there were just over four hundred generals in the combined army, navy, air and police forces. Both the new decorations were the elite '*Konfrontasi*' ribbons and Seda again felt uneasy at any prospect of his possible posting to an active unit which specialised in border crossings into Malaysia and New Guinea.

Seda had seen intelligence reports before they had been revised for general dissemination. They had indicated that the highly skilled British and Australian troops assisting Malaysia were reducing Indonesia's 'hero squads' to scattered rabble. He had no desire to be a recipient of these distinguished '*Konfrontasi*' ribbons for the majority were awarded posthumously.

"*Kolonel*, I have called you here to discuss a most sensitive intelligence matter," the General firmly announced, then dropping his voice to an almost inaudible level, continued. "*However, there are some grey areas which must be disposed of before your security grading can be upgraded.*" He paused to light a cigarette.

Seda's palms were now very moist. He was staggered. It was what he had dreaded — a posting to a '*Konfrontasi*' unit! He desperately wanted to take one of the cigarettes from the table but knew to do so without one being offered was unthinkable. Instead, he clenched his fists tightly until he could feel the palms aching and then relaxed his grip, permitting the blood to flow freely again.

General Sudomo sat comfortably behind the ornately carved desk observing and enjoying the obvious agitation the Timorese was experiencing. The clinging aroma of the kretek cigarette permeated the stuffy atmosphere within this enormous Javanese sanctum. The general relished the power of his position and had orchestrated the demise of many of his peers from this very office. Now he was one of the few trusted officers close to the President.

He himself claimed to have no political ambitions. He had always believed that the military were the real power and that the day would come when even the over zealous politicians would need the total support of the army to survive their fool-hardy and unworkable efforts to change the inherent character of the peasant class.

Born in the heart of Central Java in a small village not far from the historic Borobudur temple, this son of a peasant farmer had once idolised the man who had become the nation's leader. Politically naive, Sudomo had followed Soekarno's leadership without question, as so many others had over the past twenty years.

He had learned to read at the village *Sekolah Dasar*. He could speak a little of the difficult Dutch language, but preferred communicating in his native dialect, Javanese. Even the national language, *Bahasa Indonesia*, did not flow fluently from his lips.

Although poorly educated, his rapid rise in rank was directly related to his ability to understand and overcome opposition. Prior to receiving his first star he had, in fact, met the President only twice. The first meeting was in Semarang when the *Bapak*, as he was often referred to, visited the local military command to introduce Dr Subandrio's latest innovation, a cadre force of women soldiers. These turned out to be a supply of Sundanese prostitutes for the *Bapak's* private use. These women would follow their leader from town to town ready at all times to provide the President with the creature comforts he so obviously enjoyed when away from the Palace.

At that time there were already rumblings of discontent regarding the President's support for increased Communist activity within the military. The Javanese Generals were secretly concerned that the communists were covertly stripping power from the army as they had succeeded in doing so with the AURI and ALRI leadership.

General Sudomo's second meeting had been in the company of General Nasution who had visited the *Bapak* at his weekend palace in Bogor. Soekarno had remembered his name and from that time Sudomo's star commenced its ascent. Now he headed the army's most secret intelligence bureau, reporting directly to the Chief-of- army- Staff.

His reaction to the young Seda was typically Javanese. Inwardly he despised the minority tribes, while in public he maintained an air of friendliness to all, regardless of their ethnic origins. He had kept Seda on his staff as the man was intelligent and loyal.

General Sudomo leaned back casually, preparing his next words for their greatest impact. The Javanese enjoyed drama. It was an integral part of their cultural make-up. The *Ramayana* saga. The discomfort he was causing the Timorese was most gratifying.

"*How long is it since you have seen your brother Albert?*" The General asked. The words hung in the air before Seda realised they were discussing his estranged step-brother in Australia.

Seda knew that he should show no signs of nervousness with this man and that his questions should be answered quickly and precisely. A small knot began to form in his stomach as he recalled omitting all reference to his brother in the detailed security information sheet prior to being selected for the Intelligence Corp. A brother, albeit only a stepbrother, who had acquired a criminal record for subversive activities, was not exactly ideal reference material for security clearances, especially in this Corp.

General Sudomo's pleasure increased as he identified the uneasiness evident in the Colonel's posture.

"Well, *Kolonel?*" he asked.

"*Pak 'Domo,*" Seda commenced using the polite and abbreviated form of the General's name hoping it would ease some of the tension between them. "*It has been many years since he was deported and we were not really brothers.*"

The General was completely conversant with the facts surrounding the departure of Albert Seda, his misdemeanours as a student, and Nathan Seda's family. This interview was only a formality. He

35

wanted to appear to be thorough with the Timorese.

The Colonel continued.

"We shared the same mother — I mean my mother married his father after my own father died." He felt flustered having stumbled with the reply. Seda was now embarrassed and angry. His family background was one subject he preferred not to discuss and now yet again it had become an issue in his career.

"As his adik-tiri, I had no influence over him whatsoever General," insisted Seda, anticipating some negative result from his family association with the man. *"I felt that any reference to our family relationship would only have been detrimental to my career and decided to omit all reference to him."* He stared blankly in front of him, resigned to whatever punishment he would receive.

Sudomo, now satisfied that Seda had confirmed his earlier information said, *"It is not necessarily a problem Kolonel."*

"Maaf, Pak 'Domo, I don't understand."

"We will overlook your oversight," the General responded, smiling at his choice of words. *"Your brother has communicated with you recently?"* he asked suddenly before Seda could have the chance to compose himself.

Seda squirmed. Letters usually requesting assistance to forward money to his mother and other family members had arrived from time to time. Surely they would not be aware of this?

"Tidak, Pak 'Domo," he lied. The General's eyes narrowed slightly. He studied his subordinate for what seemed to Seda to be an excruciatingly long time.

'What is this all about?' he wondered, now very concerned as to the direction the meeting had taken. He refrained from speaking further, waiting instead for the senior officer to continue.

"You are instructed to commence communicating with him." Sudomo ordered. *"We feel that he may be of some assistance to us, should you foster the relationship."* Seda was stunned. Surely they were mistaken! What had Albert done to bring himself to their attention? His letters had been brief, courteous, and uninformative. He felt the knot in his stomach return.

"Your brother has achieved a position of confidence with the Australian Government," the Intelligence Director said sharply, focusing on the Colonel's eyes as he spoke. *"He is currently employed as a language teacher for selected government personnel. We feel that his access*

to these people could be of advantage to Indonesia's future."

Seda could not believe his ears. Albert! A position of importance with the Australian Government! It was incomprehensible! He was certain that there had been some mistake. His stepbrother had always been in trouble. How was it possible that he could now be the one suggested by his superior? He thought quickly. Without knowing the General's real purpose he was lost in this discussion. He dare not refuse to assist.

Whether or not Albert's relationship could be cultivated was another consideration. It had been so long since they had last seen each other and even then Seda was happy to see the last of the troublemaker. He did not feel confident of carrying out the orders, remembering the circumstances governing Albert's departure from his homeland.

"You will be required to move your office to a new section created specifically for this task. Your total cooperation is essential to the successful cultivation of Albert Seda. Should you succeed, there will be rewards commensurate with the benefits achieved by your section."

General Sudomo paused ensuring the importance of his words had been absorbed, then continued. *"You are to report directly to me. There is to be a minimum of written communications between your section and others. You will be assisted by two of our former military attaché staff. They are former Siliwangi division soldiers and completely loyal to me."* Seda understood immediately that these two would be the general's watchdogs.

"You are expected to iniliate a rapprochement with your brother within the month." The General hesitated before continuing. *"You are being given a position of complete trust. I suggest you go home and consider these things before reporting to this office for further details tomorrow morning."*

Stunned by the sudden change in events and his new instructions, Seda wanted to say something but wasn't quite sure what would be appropriate. He paused for a moment before replying.

"Terima kasih, Pak 'Domo." Seda knew that there was really nothing left to say. He had been dismissed. Standing to attention he saluted and turned to leave.

"Kolonel!" the General called.

Seda turned and his heart sank as he recognised the envelope in the General's hand. It was a letter he had forwarded for Albert some time before. His world began to fragment before his eyes.

The General flicked it across the room towards him. *"No more secrets, Kolonel, do you understand?"*

Seda retrieved the envelope. The contents were missing. He nodded again, dumbly, saluted and fled.

The General sat motionless considering the Timorese Colonel. Convinced that he had made the correct decision he buzzed his adjutant.

"Bapak?" responded the Lieutenant. *"Call Mas Suryo dan Mas Wiryo,"* the General ordered. Immediately, the Lieutenant set about advising the former Military Attachés that the General had demanded their presence. Having completed his calls the young adjutant shuddered involuntarily. He had seen these two watchdogs in action once before.

And they scared the hell out of him.

Chapter 2

Albert Seda and
Stephen Coleman — April 1965

"Java soldiers, go home! Java soldiers, go home!" Albert chanted as he marched alongside his friends. *"Come on Didi,"* he called to a classmate who was struggling to carry a poorly inscribed placard as they were jostled. *"Give it to me. I'll carry it for you."*

"We'll carry it together," his friend responded, moving closer to Albert while raising the sign above the heads of the others.

They continued with the chant and soon their numbers swelled as hundreds of senior school students joined in the demonstration and headed towards the mayor's office.

"Java soldiers, go home! Java soldiers, go home!" the crowd yelled in unison as they boldly took their positions directly outside the military official's building. Their spirits were high. They were enjoying the moment and the thrill of challenging the Jakarta officials.

As they continued to chant and call for the Mayor to show his face, the students failed to notice the soldiers move quickly into position. One of the boys threw a rock through the Mayor's front window and within moments others followed with a hail of missiles they had picked up off the road.

A volley of shots cracked through the air over the demonstrator's heads sending the students into a frenzied panic as they broke ranks and ran, knowing that their lives were in danger. A squad of soldiers trained in riot control moved forward quickly with their rifles held out directly in front, the deadly bayonets fixed alongside the muzzle of their weapons. As they were confronted by the mass of youngsters who pushed each other in their attempts to flee, the sharp blades glistened brightly as they moved savagely from side to side cutting through flesh and cloth amidst the screams and cries of disbelief.

When he first heard the shots, Father Douglas was uncertain but when these were followed by the frightening screams which pierced the tranquillity of his small church, the priest knew for certain that the rumours had become fact. The students were demonstrating.

Immediately he feared for them all and crossed himself quickly. They were just children. Foolish children at that, forever challenging the authority of their new colonialists, the Javanese. Father Douglas rose quickly from his knees and ran to the church's side entrance. He opened the heavy teak doors and peered cautiously towards the main street and the incredible noise. He was stunned by the scene before him.

It was as if the streets were engulfed by white, breaking waves as the mass of students ran hysterically, yelling and screaming as they fled from the barrage of bullets and soldiers' bayonets. Two of the youngsters ran towards the church. Suddenly, the staccato sound of automatic fire hammered at his ears and both the students fell to the ground. Father Douglas closed and bolted the church doors.

* * * * * *

Albert Seda had not, at first, been as fortunate as his young stepbrother, Nathan. Bitter since childhood at the injustices that the Javanese soldiers had inflicted on the Timorese, Albert spent considerable time in the company of priests at the local Catholic church. Early on, Father Douglas identified the young man's ability as a student and coached him, helping Albert become fluent in English.

The priest's hopes that Albert might even enter the priesthood were dashed when Albert, involved in the student rally, found himself incarcerated by the local garrison commander on charges of sedition.

Albert had not really planned to attend the group rally. Like many of his friends he was just caught up in the excitement of the moment and the opportunity to protest on behalf of his people. He believed that to be his right. His responsibility.

The students, all teenagers experiencing the first euphoria of knowledge without the benefit of an adult life's exposure to disappointment and frustration, had gathered with placards pointedly aimed at the suffocating economic and military stranglehold the Jakarta-based garrison commanders had imposed on this poor province.

Almost without exception the young boys and girls originated from humble and still struggling rural families whose parents, as had theirs before them, suffered the harsh hand-to-mouth exist- ence of the impoverished farmer. They had seen the soldiers enter their homes demanding and taking whatever they wanted. Forced at gunpoint to stand by silent and helpless, they had witnessed the rape of their mothers, sisters and friends. At least one member of virtually every family in his village had suffered the humiliation and terror of being dragged outside their houses in full public view, where they were stripped, taunted and taken behind the trees where they were abused and left to struggle back home, their spirits bro- ken from the torment and physical violation.

They were angry but they were also naive. Had their parents known of their intent to demonstrate they would have forbidden such a rash and provocative act. There were less than two hundred students in the demonstration. The local garrison duty officer dis- patched fifty well-trained troops. The results were devastating. When it was all over four dissidents lay dead. At least another twenty were seriously injured. Only a few of the youths escaped beatings and many just disappeared.

Their parents lived in hope that their children had been taken to another province for indoctrination courses but, in their hearts, they knew that it was unlikely that they would ever see them again. And, of course, they had other and younger children to care for, to protect.

Albert had been fortunate to survive the soldiers' first onslaught. He was knocked unconscious during the first few minutes as the soldiers commenced their methodical and brutal attack. When he awoke, he was shackled and in a dark foul smelling cell with two other detainees. It was then he realised that, although he was lucky to be alive, he had been locked up in the *Lubang Maut*, or Death Hole, underneath the detention cells within the garrison walls.

These fearful cells had been built by Dutch plantation owners. Originally intended to break the spirits of peasants who protested the confiscation of their land, now they were used to deal with

Timorese freedom fighters — what the Indonesians called political agitators. Now the underground caverns held the children of those who had struggled before them. Now the colonists were Javanese, and they demonstrated their cruelty to excess.

He was beaten repeatedly each morning and, for some perverse reason, always within an hour of being fed the maggot-infested food. He was obliged to urinate and defecate within a one-metre radius of the damp corner to which his right leg was shackled. He was repulsed by the foul smells in the dungeon, suffering nausea and choking convulsions. Soon he sank into despair, punctuated by periods of prayer. Albert had no idea how long he had been detained.

Then one day he was savagely prodded to his feet. A length of rotan was extended towards him at the end of which hung the key for his chains. These he clumsily unshackled, dropping the key into the slime around his feet several times before mastering its use. Even his jailers moved away from their prisoner to avoid the stench. The soldiers forced him to sit in the prison courtyard where he was roughly hosed down to remove the accumulated filth from his incarceration.

He remained silent during this cleansing, his eyes shut tight against the brilliance of the sunlight. He had, Albert later discovered, not been held more than three weeks but he felt as if he had become an old man. Recovery was slow and extremely painful. His spirit was all but broken. His friends had all gone. Only his stepmother cared for him, the others too frightened to admit to his relationship with their family. He spent weeks, sitting quietly alone, living with the fear that the soldiers might return to take him back for further interrogation.

And then, one day, a visitor came. At first he did not know Father Douglas, the blue-eyed priest who had taught him English, but when recognition came, Albert broke down and sobbed uncontrollably. The priest, at his mother's desperate behest, had come to help him escape. Father Douglas had pleaded the young man's case with the local authorities and agreed to arrange to have Albert sent overseas with the Church, should the Commandant arrange his release. Being a man of God did not deter the Father from encouraging the officer to accept a small token of the church's appreciation, without which, Albert's release would have been impossible.

After a tearful good bye to his family, Albert and the priest took the road to the coast and boarded a fishing boat. It was not until they arrived in Darwin five days later that Albert could really believe that he had escaped and that he was to spend the rest of his life in another country.

Albert was permitted a visa for entry into Australia and commenced studies in Melbourne. Within a year he met a young female staff member in the immigration hostel and fell in love. Two years from the anniversary of his release from prison, Albert Seda married. Immigration officials who investigated his case were satisfied that the union was genuine and subsequently permitted him to stay as a migrant. Initially he obtained casual employment at the hostel, acting as an in-house interpreter.

Three years after his brief detention in the Kupang barracks, Albert was earning a substantial salary teaching Indonesian to Australian diplomats prior to their taking up posts in Jakarta. Father Douglas had been careful to communicate Albert's deep-rooted anti-Soekarno feelings to a friend in government. This made Albert's credentials acceptable and the father's friend then arranged for Albert's security clearance to teach. Suddenly, life was extremely pleasant for the good looking young Timorese.

Albert took advantage of all the opportunities available to him. He eagerly commenced evening classes undertaking a rigorous study schedule. He laboured late into the evenings. He worked through the weekends while others relaxed or played. He was highly motivated.

The young Timorese never forgot the cruel beatings. He stayed away from any involvement with political movements which he associated with too many memories of pain and humiliation. Now he had responsibilities. He was married. He now lived far away from the terror of his childhood and had been given a second chance by God. He would work hard!

Albert's wife, Mary, maintained her position at the hostel, working as an administrative assistant. She was so proud of her handsome husband. She knew Albert worked and studied diligently to ensure their future together although she often wished he would take more time for them to be together.

Mary's father, an Irish immigrant who worked occasionally between dole cheques, despised his dark son-in-law. Like the majority of blue-collar workers in the postwar years, Patrick O'Malley, with a dozen or so beers under his belt, would make the most of any opportunity to parade his prejudices, to sneer at anyone who was not white, Anglo-Saxon and Catholic.

Xenophobia was rife in Australia. Australians feared that waves of yellow-skinned narrow-eyed races would descend upon their Lucky Country and take it all away. The immigration authorities even prevented Asian applicants from gaining entry by introducing a system of discriminatory procedures which presented them with the most appalling obstacles.

Paddy, even when reasonably sober, could not differentiate between the various ethnic groups originating from Asia. Like many other Aussies, he believed that if you looked Asian, you were either a 'bloody Jap' or a 'bloody Chink'. He neither knew nor cared that such derogatory outbursts branded Australians as insecure white racists.

"Bloody yellow Chinese bastards!" Paddy would yell down the saloon bar at this favourite local on Friday nights. "Come down here and seduce our lovely ladies they do, and before you know it the whole bloody country will be overrun by the bastards!"

During the small wedding breakfast organised at the hostel, Paddy, a reluctant guest of honour, drank himself into his usual ugly, inebriated state. Hopelessly confused and adrift from reality, O'Malley, enraged at Albert's impudence in kissing Mary, ordered his new son-in-law outside for a thrashing. Mrs O'Malley, ashamed and embarrassed, attempted to save the party. As she dragged her husband home, he continued yelling and screaming drunken abuse, threatening to feed Albert's testicles to the local shearer's dogs.

Yet Mary loved her father Paddy. She could not understand why he could not appreciate her handsome husband who would one day produce Paddy's first grandchild. Mary's eyes glazed over as she slipped away into one of her frequent daydreams, imagining herself pregnant, and then holding her own baby, nestled calmly between her breasts. Had she realised her father's revulsion at the mere idea of his daughter bearing a half-Asian child, of sullying his family's pure Irish lineage, then Mary might have been a little more circumspect during her father's birthday dinner.

Paddy had invited the local drinking team to help celebrate his fiftieth birthday. If the truth be known, Paddy invited his mates simply because it was traditional for guests to bring more alcohol than they could reasonably expect to consume. O'Malley estimated that the surplus would stock his larder for at least two weeks. The lads were more than aware of Paddy's sensitivities; however they could not resist the temptation nor the opportunity to stir the little Irishman along, to see his nostrils flare with rage.

"Well then, Paddy," Pete Davies commenced, winking in the direction of his drinking associates, "when will we hear the patter of little feet around here?"

"When hell freezes over!" Paddy responded, eyes narrowing a little as the blood pressure rose and his muscles tightened. He did not appreciate this type of talk. Having his daughter married to the Timorese was bad enough; having her procreate with the man would be socially unforgivable!

Mary, unfortunately for all present, happened to overhear the rejoinder and slipped up behind her father, placing her arms around most of his enlarged stomach. "Looks like next year will be a very cold year then dad." Mary insinuated, not realising that she had struck her father straight through the heart in front of all of his drinking mates.

" I will make you a grandfather, yet," Albert added.

There was a hush. The men knew Paddy only too well. He was going to blow, and they did not wish to be on the receiving end of his temper, drunk or sober. His face turned scarlet as his chronically abused heart forced itself into overdrive in line with the adrenalin surge.

O'Malley bellowed with rage. Just once. Then he collapsed. Guests and family alike stood rooted as Paddy's body fell limp to the floor. It was all over in just a few seconds. He had roared once, then died. The ambulance arrived within the half hour and Albert, sensing the mood, left his wife alone with her grief and her emotional family friends.

* * * * * *

Mary and Albert never did begin the family she had hoped for. The guilt of her father's death ruined all chance of Mary and Albert having a normal happy married life. After the funeral the Seda household became quiet. Albert continued his studies, deliberately staying up late to permit Mary the opportunity to go to sleep before he retired.

He was extremely self conscious. He imagined that friends and acquaintances would whisper behind his back regarding his father-in- law's untimely heart attack, saying he was responsible. As months wore on his self confidence returned, and he learned to tolerate the bigoted Australian middle-class attitudes.

He concentrated his energies on his new teaching position. The challenge of preparing the young trainees from the government departments was rewarding and, generally speaking, Albert found the quality of these potential diplomats and consular employees surprisingly high.

He was one of a number of teaching staff selected to train the students in the formal use of the Indonesian language, *Bahasa Indonesia*. He rarely experienced animosity from the students as they identified a genuine willingness on his part to assist. It was this sincerity that enabled him to establish close bonds with them. Albert had found his niche. He was content although his co-workers often remained aloof. He had conditioned himself to ignore the social difficulties which existed between the staff members. Some academics publicly supported full racial integration while secretly concealing their distaste for mixed marriages. Amongst their number there were fathers who cringed at the very thought of their daughters marrying someone like Mary's "Alburp", as Seda was so unkindly referred to when out of earshot.

His recently acquired nick-name stuck when an instructor from the French department grossly embellished an incident which occurred during a formal dinner for the newly appointed finance director. Unaccustomed to the paté, Seda had burped during a lull between speeches and, visibly embarrassed, had then broken wind causing those sitting nearest to pale considerably. Mary had attempted to make light of the matter, but Albert's silence subsequent to the incident indicated all too clearly how deeply sensitive he was to the caustic comments and the general attitude of his fellow teachers. Over a period of time his embarrassment turned to disappointment and, eventually, indifference.

The students continued to warm to Albert. They sensed a sincerity that was not evident with other instructors. He gave his leisure hours to assist them and often ventured into their individual worlds to nourish relationships which soon developed beyond that of teacher and student. Often he would recount his student days in Timor, earning their admiration for his stand against the authorities. He never discussed his internment. This was part of his earlier life's horrors which he attempted to purge from his mind.

The memory could never be completely erased. He resisted the temptation to solicit their sympathy. No, these past nightmares were his, and his alone. Often, when the day's stress prevented Seda from sleeping soundly, the nightmares would recur and he would awaken, screaming, to find himself drenched with perspiration. His nightmares were real; they filled his dreams with the terror of his incarceration in that stinking hell hole in Kupang, the detention centre for subversives.

* * * * * *

Albert was already in his fifth year at the institution. It had grown considerably as a result of Australia's commitment in Vietnam. He taught Malay and Indonesian which, although basically the same languages, were just different enough to warrant separate courses. The 1965 course had commenced two months before, soon after the new year. Twenty students had been accepted from over one thousand applicants. Three were Foreign Affairs officers, and the remainder a mixture from the armed forces and government bodies such as AID and information agencies.

Albert was part of a five member teaching team responsible to the Director of Studies. The director coordinated the language courses and, in turn, reported to the college head, a Defence Department appointee. The courses were designed to produce graduates fluent in the target languages. Very few of the new intake had any previous exposure to the Asian languages as these were not taught in Australian schools.

The *Malay Emergency*, followed by the Indonesian '*Konfrontasi*' movement finally convinced the government of the need to develop an Asian language institution. Premises were located within an existing defence establishment and lecturers were scrounged from wherever they could be found. The need for extensive security inquiries reduced the pool of potential instructors to a small but talented group of men and women who were expected to produce linguists in the incredibly short period of just one year!

Father Douglas had provided the information required to fill in the blanks in Albert Seda's past. Security had been impressed with his anti-Soekarno stand and the priest's recommendations. He was cleared for the low-level security position almost without reservation. There had been some concern that this young man was anti-military; however lengthy discussions with Albert convinced the department that this was not so. It was understood that his animosity was directed at the Indonesian military machine and not the Australian armed forces. Had they persisted, Albert would have admitted that, in fact, he had a deep rooted hatred for all military groups but was realistic enough to realise that he had to say what they wanted to hear.

The Indonesian community in Melbourne was relatively small. Albert avoided his former countrymen and had it not been for an occasional visit to Radio Australia and the presence of two other Indonesian instructors, he would have had no contact at all. Occasionally a letter would arrive from his village. Father Douglas had been sent to Sumatra and his replacement refused to assist to forward correspondence from his family. He felt the sadness the migrant experienced on foreign soil once contact with family is broken. A few requests for funds had managed to survive the inadequacies of the postal system, and these always arrived months after the originator had put pen to paper. It was impractical to send money directly to Indonesia. Rupiah were not available in Melbourne, and Australian currency was unknown and not able to be cashed in Kupang. American dollars would certainly be stolen from the mail and postal notes or cheques were hopeless.

The solution was to entrust cash to a courier, but these opportunities were few and far between. At year's end he would occasionally seek the assistance of graduating students destined for Jakarta. Some would assist, but there were always those who would not, for fear of violating the currency regulations and thereby jeopardising their positions. Once in Jakarta, an embassy official had little difficulty in assisting with such trivial matters.

Albert was reluctant to send money via his stepbrother, Nathan. Occasionally he dispatched letters or small parcels directly to Nathan seeking his assistance as it was unlikely that postal items addressed to a military officer would suffer the same fate as mail bearing a civilian destination. He preferred not to encourage the relationship with Nathan as the Australian Government was unaware of his family association. He was concerned that, as his step-brother had risen to the rank of colonel, then perhaps they may review his security clearance should the relationship come to light. His earlier declarations would be challenged and he would be dismissed, perhaps even charged, and sent to jail. He was well aware of the Australian paranoia when it came to Asians.

Albert shuddered involuntarily at the thought of being deported. Quickly he dismissed the thought and decided it would not be in his best interests to make further contact with Nathan. He really felt nothing for the man anyway, he justified in his mind. After all, was his brother not one of them now, fighting and killing as the others had done throughout the bloody Revolution? He guessed that Nathan was most probably unaware of Albert's good fortune as previous communications had been formal and uninformative. Nathan had merely been a convenient conduit to Kupang for his remaining family.

Albert rocked his head from side to side, a habit he had developed when alone and deep in thought. He believed that his relationship to Nathan would eventually jeopardise his position, and decided that he would discontinue all communication with his step-brother; he would write to his family instructing them not to mention him in any of their letters, as an additional precaution. He was aware from a friend in Radio Australia that occasionally incoming mail was opened at the Australian end and not, as it was commonly assumed, by the Indonesian authorities.

Albert did not know of the existence of ASIO.

* * * * * *

Albert turned his attention to the students sitting facing him. Some already showed the strain of these few hard weeks. Others, with a stronger determination, forced themselves along, only to discover the hopelessness of attempting to understand the Asian logic. Every aspect of the languages they were learning seemed to be imbued with underlying alien thought patterns.

A few students actually enjoyed the pressures caused by constant correction, repetition and competition. These were rare, Albert acknowledged, his eyes moving casually from one student to another. There were only two he could identify in that year's intake. They stood out far in front of the rest of the class. Neither had previous language training and neither were members of the military.

Albert was pleased. He did not particularly enjoy devoting his life to teaching soldiers whose ultimate purpose was to kill. Intellectually speaking, he found the civilians who attended these courses far superior to the other students. It was for these reasons that Albert created opportunities to develop closer relationships with the civilians. Albert was wise enough to realise that these were the officers selected for overseas posts who might, in time, provide him with assistance should the requirement arise.

The bell rang announcing the end of the period. Albert's attention returned to his class. The students looked to the instructor who nodded, indicating that time was up. Their expressions reflected the mental fatigue. Written tests often produced this quiet response. As they departed Albert collected the papers and, as it was the end of the school day, he wandered home to the accommodation provided.

* * * * * *

Stephen Coleman rubbed his eyes and immediately wished he hadn't. They felt like sandpaper, irritated by lack of sleep and cigarette smoke. Far too much smoke. He realised that rest was imperative to prepare for the oral test scheduled for later that day. His head ached, the temple pulse exacerbating the pain with a dull throbbing sensation, beating a brittle drum inside his head. He knew that he consumed far too many cigarettes but this was not the time to break the habit.

The course pressure was devastating. Already four students had been removed and they were still only in their first quarter! The course was damn difficult and it was obvious that they were burning people off. They wanted only the best. Previous year's confidential records clearly indicated that most students failed or were removed either early in the course or, surprisingly, during the last days towards graduation.

The latter was a direct result of accumulated pressure for, as the end appeared in sight, some students virtually collapsed with memory loss, unable to remember even the basics of what they had studied through the long and mentally demanding year. The rewards were considerable for those who successfully completed the training. For some, instant promotion, for others a posting overseas with excellent career opportunities.

Coleman lighted another cigarette. Leaning back he viewed his cell-sized quarters. Small, sparse, practical. Almost claustrophobic. The adjacent rooms were occupied by dedicated military types who had considerable difficulty accepting civilians on their courses. He smiled, recollecting the first assembly.

Soldiers marched in, saluting, pivoting and stomping their feet at one another with gusto. The Timorese instructor, expecting students, not toy soldiers, was horrified. Ground rules governing an acceptable standard of conduct were explained. These were received with grunts of disapproval from the army, smiles from the navy and airforce, and cool disdain by the few civilian participants. This obvious contempt for all things military was the hallmark of public servants, which the servicemen found intolerable at the best of times.

Students were given a native name suitable to the language studied. Ranks and service seniority were to be ignored on campus and all were expected to live in the allocated accommodations, separated from family. Quarterly breaks of one week were scheduled. Most students utilised these leave breaks to consolidate their vocabulary while others simply disappeared, escaping the dull monotony of endless study.

Pre-selection for attendance had been announced in the monthly Government Gazette and it was not until the preliminary tests were conducted that Coleman realised that special priority had been given to the training. He observed the number of applicants and was surprised as to the standards demanded for the pre-qualifying examinations.

For some time the Australian intelligence forces had become increasingly alarmed at the accelerated development of military capabilities in some of the neighbouring countries. Indonesia was of particular concern considering it boasted the third-largest Communist party in the world and was well armed with sophisticated weaponry supplied by its Soviet mentors.

The Australian public was deliberately kept uninformed as to size and capability of this immediate threat, as Australian cities were clearly vulnerable to attack from Indonesia's air and sea strike arsenal had their Government been motivated to do so. That was the enigma. The Indonesians never displayed open hostility towards the Australians and yet attacked the very concept of a united Singapore and Malaysia. The two British Commonwealth states had recently formed their own Federation together, and the Australians were unsure of their best course of action.

Defence specialists urged the government to embark on a program which would give greater access, through information collection, to enable more accurate interpretation of the mass of foreign language material made available through Australian embassies and friendly powers. The difficulty lay with the defence sector's inability to source qualified personnel with acceptable security clearances to assist in filling the information vacuum. The decision had been made to provide immediate training in Asian languages to specific branches of the Government ranging from defence to information services.

Coleman was surprised when he was selected for the course. He had studied journalism at college before joining the department, believing at the time that this would provide the opportunity to travel abroad. But it hadn't. As a career it lacked the excitement his contemporaries enjoyed. Life in Canberra had been dull and, more out of boredom than any other motivation, he had applied for language training when the positions were called.

The financial rewards were attractive also, although he believed that few of the applicants were motivated by the considerable salary increases offered. He had not stipulated *Bahasa Indonesia*. The selection committee, having assessed his preliminary aptitude tests, decided that Chinese, Thai and Vietnamese would be too unmanageable due to the difficulties of tonal pronunciation. He had considered their decision and decided that this course was difficult enough. Had he attempted the Thai course there was every possibility that he would already have returned to his desk in Canberra.

The alarm sounded startling Coleman. Five o'clock! He had studied through the night without sleep. He yawned. God how his mouth tasted! His sense of smell was practically nonexistent but he knew the room stank of stale smoke and the partly demolished block of New Zealand cheddar.

He shaved, showered, and dressed quickly. Outside it was light and Coleman left his quarters and walked briskly towards the sea where, to his relief, the tide covered the foul smelling seaweed which could, at low tide, turn even the strongest stomach. He enjoyed these early morning walks.

Coleman reflected on how he had changed over the years. His present success continued to surprise him. He had been a shy and unconfident child! An only child, Stephen Coleman had grown up in an atmosphere filled with intelligent albeit often inebriated debate, and witty but cutting sarcasm, as both his parents were professional people who were often, to Stephen's amusement, fiercely competitive towards each other.

As a young child he experienced an ongoing sense of loneliness. His parents, due to the nature of their work and interests, were basically peripatetic and disliked putting down roots of any kind. They travelled extensively and the inside of his wardrobe doors were lined with post cards from the most exotic places one could imagine. He had spent his adolescent years in boarding school.

At night, when the other boarding students were asleep, he would lie on his bed visualising these faraway places and conjure up some fantasy in his mind to carry him off to those destinations, not necessarily to be with his parents, but to escape the monotony of being a teenager ensconced in the rigid disciplines as determined by the school's masters.

He had been one of those children who could pass through others' lives without being obvious, or apparently special. Not that he had really tried. In fact, although he had the ability, Stephen found the whole idea of attending boarding school relatively boring and conformed just to pass the time. He existed on the periphery of the other students' worlds.

One summer he had the good fortune to spend his holidays in the country at the invitation of another boarding student. He had enjoyed every moment. The host family had gone out of their way to treat him as they would one of their own and in the first week he had already mastered the basics of horse riding and sheep mustering. He had not known until some years later that the two-month holiday had been arranged by his parents. Apparently they had been invited to Banff Springs for the fabulous New Year's Eve formal celebrations and his mother had insisted that she and her husband attend without their child.

Stephen believed that his mother, having never been pregnant prior to his own conception, decided to become so just once for the experience and, once he was born, had decided also that it was not something one should repeat.

He had completed his secondary education without being able to remember even one occasion when either parent attended a prize award evening held by the school. Perhaps, he determined, that was one of the reasons he was not really motivated enough to win, or compete, as there was nobody to encourage his success or applaud his efforts.

University had, at first, been just as unstimulating as school but before the end of his first year he discovered that easy sexual conquests were available to all and he was determined to have his share. This new found confidence with the opposite sex nearly brought about an early end to his tertiary studies.

During the second semester of the following year he was caught in a scandal and his father was obliged to intercede on his behalf in what could have resulted in his premature and permanent departure from the campus. Fortunately the Dean of Students' over endowed and flirtatious wife admitted encouraging his advances and, in the interests of the college and with a little outside pressure, the matter was dropped. Stephen did, however, move from Melbourne to a Sydney campus.

Having completed his formal education at one of the state's finest colleges he felt there was not a great deal left for him to do in the academic sector. His life became directionless. He drifted through the long hot summer holidays surfing, reading and generally just lazily filling in the days alone. His parents, when their complicated schedules permitted, arranged never ending eating and drinking marathons around their pool with stockbrokers, lawyers and what seemed to be an endless list of interstate associates. Stephen should find something to do, they urged.

It was towards the end of February, the summer heat having reached its zenith, when his mother hosted one such reception in their home. Stephen had attempted to avoid attending the party but his mother's insistence obliged him to do so.

It was at this gathering that he first met Mr John Anderson. During the course of the afternoon, as he strolled around the pool stopping occasionally to speak to his parents' guests, he had observed his mother standing close to this charismatic and handsome man. She had called Stephen over to introduce them. He wondered had his father been present, would he have been concerned with the obvious attention his mother lavished on the popular guest, or would his reaction have been one of customary complacency.

Twice Coleman had the opportunity to engage the tall suntanned man in intelligent non-party conversation and to his pleasant surprise, Anderson did not patronise him nor did he avoid conversing with the younger man. They had also discussed the ski slopes of the Snowy Mountains. Stephen had developed his winter skills as a teenager whilst visiting Smiggins and Perisher and both men related their own stories of how they'd had near disasters on those runs, and the exhilaration of speeding down the snow covered slopes alone, challenging the mountain and the elements.

When Anderson had politely inquired as to Stephen's future plans and had discovered that the young man was not only undecided but lacked any direction whatsoever, it was he who suggested, later in the day, that Coleman consider entering government service. At first he considered the idea preposterous. He spent a week recollecting the brief encounter with the intriguing Mr Anderson and then decided to give him a call. Stephen borrowed his mother's Jaguar and drove down to the capital. They met over dinner at the Statesman's Club in Canberra at the request of the older man.

The evening had gone well. So well, Stephen felt as if the meeting was just an extension of the previous week's amicable conversations. He could not remember ever being so at ease with an older person as he had with John Anderson during those moments. It was obvious that his mother's close friend had deliberately gone out of his way to ensure that Stephen was relaxed.

Anderson had talked extensively and Stephen had happily listened, as the man made a lot of sense. Without a great deal of further deliberation he accepted the advice and made a commitment to apply for the position suggested.

He remained for a few days before returning to Sydney. There he stayed just long enough to pack and inform his parents regarding what had transpired as a result of his visit to Canberra. There was practically no discussion regarding his monumental decision although his mother appeared to be pleased. His father's reaction had been surprisingly cool and indifferent. At the time Stephen had shrugged it off and, as he departed, just shook his father's hand without any further exchange or comment, sensing that something had disturbed the man and that it related to his career choice.

Stephen had put his arm around his father's shoulders but there was little response. He seemed distant, almost preoccupied and overly reserved. His father had never really been a demonstrative person. Clever, yes, Stephen had thought but never warm or affectionate towards his son. Stephen could not remember ever kissing the man, even as a child. His mother had fussed as he said goodbye to her. She had held him closely and whispered into his ear, instructing her son to behave himself and phone regularly. It seemed strange. He was only travelling a few hundred kilometres from their home and yet he experienced a strange sensation of one who was embarking on a long journey, away from all that was familiar and loved. He had never experienced this emotion before, not even when he was away at school.

John Anderson used his authority to locate a suitable apartment. These were scarcer than hen's teeth as most were allocated directly according to strict waiting lists. Anderson was good to his word. Within a fortnight Stephen Coleman was accepted into the Department.

Once settled, Stephen easily fell into the routine of government employment. He enjoyed his workplace and the new circle of friends and threw himself into the arduous training schedules. He found the pristine air invigorating but soon discovered that the capital had a downside when the weather warmed. The flies drove him into fits of temper he'd not displayed since his childhood days on the sheep station. They were small and aggressive, attacking the nostrils and ears, causing Canberra's inhabitants to curse the filthy little insects, bred by their own government to consume the larvae of the traditional country fly which infested the rural areas around the capital. Stephen often wondered how the foreign diplomats and their families put up with the pests. Gradually he settled into the new routines and found life satisfactory.

Stephen enjoyed the first months assimilating to the work conditions and also adjusting to the demanding training schedules. He was pleased at having made the decision to enter into the government service. There was so much to learn and the opportunities seemed endless.

He had become concerned during the first weeks however when, for reasons he could not fathom, several of the other Department's officers displayed a coldness towards him, a coldness which was not evident in their behaviour with respect to their other fellow workers. He put it down to a personality clash or basic civil service arrogance and did not dwell on the matter until, during the course of a function at which one of these men having consumed more than was wise, made an offhanded remark that concerned Coleman. He raised the issue with Anderson when next invited to the mountain retreat which now had become a regular monthly excursion.

Stephen was surprised to discover that John Anderson had stood as referee for him. He knew, of course, that Anderson had facilitated his entré into the Department. They agreed that the attitude some of his co-workers displayed was probably resentment at Coleman's swift acceptance into his new position. He acceded to the older man's advice to put what he considered only a minor annoyance out of his mind.

A year passed quickly by which time he found that he was firmly ensconced in the Canberra circuit and continued to spend at least one weekend every month in the quiet of Anderson's hideaway. He still found himself relaxed in the man's company. Apart from the weekends away they met often, dining together and even travelling to Queenstown in New Zealand together for a weekend ski visit. He never tired of listening to John's deep soft resonant voice advise on subjects new to Stephen or lecture him on the idiosyncrasies of bureaucracy in government. He was always attentive to the older man's advice and out of the deep respect he had developed for him had, without hesitation, accepted his urging to transfer to the Information Bureau and broaden his horizons. Except it wasn't really the Information Bureau!

In years to come Coleman would reflect upon his close relationship with Anderson and silently acknowledge that he was not really conscious at the time that it was then he had been recruited, albeit surreptitiously, by the master craftsman. He had entered a new world, sinister and without shape, a world from which few had ever escaped. And now he was back in Melbourne, in literary hell, struggling to stay alive — or at least remain on the course.

Although difficult, the study load suited Coleman's demeanour. He was offered an intellectual challenge and was obliged to compete as an individual. Initially, during the confusing first days he had questioned his judgment in selecting this training. Critical of his own lack of patience he had, he decided, to persevere and complete the task he'd undertaken. Now, armed with weeks of confidence building results behind him, Coleman applied the necessary self-discipline required to push himself just that little harder, to achieve the level of fluency required to communicate in the alien tongue.

As he strolled towards the soft sounds of the sea and the waves slowly encroached on the narrow strip of the dark sandy foreshore, Stephen's thoughts continued to drift in the early morning hours. He felt tired, but at the same time he experienced a sense of exhilaration at being alive, almost as if he had finally been given some real purpose in life. Stephen found this new energy invigorating. He identified the new motivating forces and was pleased that they were not based on monetary considerations. It would have been relatively easy, he knew, to obtain employment through his parents' connections in a far more lucrative field of endeavour.

The cry of birds overhead interrupted his thoughts. A flock of sea-gulls passed over and Stephen instinctively raised a hand over his head. He stood for a moment observing a small fishing dinghy bobbing up and down a few hundred metres offshore. They were probably from the base, he thought, as it was some distance to a jetty not located within the military surrounds. Coleman stood for a few moments looking out to sea. A figure moved past behind him and called, " *Selamat pagi.* "

Coleman instantly recognised *Pak* Seda, one of his instructors. " *Selamat pagi,* " he responded.

Seda approached, hands in pockets, with the casual gait Asian men have developed throughout the centuries. " *Mau kemana?* " Where are you going? asked the short dark skinned man. Coleman hesitated. He knew he had to select his words precisely as mistakes, even off campus, were remembered when assessing student proficiency.

" *Iseng-iseng saja Pak.* " Just strolling around, sir, he answered. Coleman was pleased he had remembered the phrase. His vocabulary was growing rapidly which increased his confidence.

" *You are up early Koesman.* " Seda observed, using the student's allocated Indonesian name.

"*Yes. I needed the fresh air. Too many of these,*" he replied, indicating the cigarette dangling between his nicotine-stained fingers, his sentences still stiff as one would expect of a new student.

"*Would you like a kretek?*" the teacher offered. Aroma from these cigarettes mixed with clove would permeate every corner of the staff building when Seda smoked. The uninitiated would stand close to a *kretek* smoker only once before discovering that apart from the marijuana grass-like smell, the weed would often explode burning holes in nylon shirts, trousers, or even worse, as had happened one day, to the Director of Studies' sports coat. Seda had almost changed to more orthodox brands after the embarrassing incident.

Coleman flicked his cigarette away before accepting the *Dji Sam Soe*. As he lit it, the taste touched his tongue followed by a cooling sensation of scented smoke flowing into his lungs.

Seda observed the student expecting a response he had often witnessed from inexperienced Indonesian cigarette smokers. When none was evident Seda was pleased and proffered the rest of the packet.

Embarrassed, Coleman refused. "*No, Pak, terima kasih,*" breaking into English, "Thank you, but no. I cannot take your cigarettes as they must be very difficult to obtain here in Australia."

"*Tidak apa apa. It's all right. I buy them from friends who work for Radio Australia. They have plenty. Please. I would be offended if you don't take them.*"

Coleman knew that this was not the case. Asians would not show offence over something so trivial; instantly he felt a warmth for this lonely man who tried so hard to be inconspicuous amongst his peers. Stephen accepted the packet and walked along the beach road, his tiredness forgotten, pleased to be in the company of the Timorese.

"*As a child I used to walk along the beach near my village. I would dream of crossing the ocean to make my fortune and return as wealthy as a king.*"

Seda paused to ensure that he selected words simple enough for the student to understand.

"*In my kampung the people were so poor there was not even one motorbike. We were the neglected island: the forgotten people in Soekarno's dream.*" He turned his head to ensure that his student had understood. "*Do you understand, Mas?*"

Coleman had understood but was unsure how he was expected to respond. "*I understand what you are saying but do not understand the ...*" he paused, searching his memory for the correct word. Unable to remember, he resorted to the English substitute, "situation." he added.

"*Ah. Yes, for Australians life is relatively simple. What will you do when you have completed the course?*"

Coleman felt the thrill of the assumption. He had been reasonably confident of completing the training but this was the first indication, almost confirmation of the possibility from a staff member. "*No doubt I will be sent to Jakarta to assist the Information Bureau there. After two years in the Embassy the government usually sends us back to Canberra where we sit and wait for another opportunity to travel,*" he explained, struggling to find the correct words in his limited vocabulary.

"*Perhaps you will have the opportunity to visit my kampung halaman,*" suggested the guru.

"*Insja Allah,*" Allah permitting, Coleman responded flushing immediately he realised his mistake. He corrected his error with a suitable Christian equivalent and apologised to Albert for his error.

"*Tidak apa apa,*" Albert declared, not wishing that Coleman suffer for his mistake.

The two men walked together each contemplating his own future until the intrusion of the putrid seaweed smell forced their retreat to prepare for the school day.

* * * * * *

That evening Coleman decided to visit Albert briefly, away from the school, to establish whether or not the teacher would be prepared to offer additional tuition. He believed that, with the assistance of one of the indigenous speakers, colloquial and idiomatic dialogue would be less difficult to deal with once he had completed the course and commenced his tour in Indonesia. The basic syllabus provided only a general introduction to idiomatic terminology as most graduates would, in fact, have little opportunity to actually visit or work in Indonesia. Consequently, those who were fortunate to receive overseas postings would discover to their chagrin, upon arrival in the target language countries, that they would have considerable difficulty with the day-to-day communication.

As he approached the well-kept married quarters, Stephen noticed Albert sitting outside his terraced accommodations. Mary remained inside, apparently preparing the evening meal.

"*Selamat sore, Pak Seda,*" Coleman called, pleased with the opportunity to approach the instructor outdoors.

Albert had not seen the young man coming. In fact, he had not been conscious of anything much for the past hour. Startled, he jumped up and prepared to escape from the intruder before recognizing the student on his way up the path. He quickly buried the letter deep into his baggy trousers pocket, then waved, beckoning for Coleman to approach, composing himself as best he could considering the weight of the communique hidden in his trousers.

"*Selamat datang, Mas Koesman. Silahkan masuk.*"

Coleman hesitated, surprised at the initial reaction he had witnessed, then proceeded to address his teacher. "*Maaf mengganggu, Pak,*" he apologised.

"*Come in, come in,*" Seda repeated opening the front door to his bungalow. They entered together. Coleman waited in the guest room while Seda disappeared momentarily, returning with his wife.

"*Selamat sore Njonja Seda,*" Coleman extended his hand to the short homely-faced woman. Her hair was dull red and her skin showed signs of a harsh childhood, perhaps on a farm, the guest concluded.

"Sorry, I do not speak much Indonesian. I leave that to Albert," she explained.

Coleman was amused that Mary showed another of the country's characteristics. Foreign languages were something never spoken and rude if used by others in front of real Aussies!

They sat, talked, and drank strong black coffee. Coleman politely refused the offer to stay for dinner, returning to his room to study. The brief discussion had been rewarding. Seda had agreed to provide the additional instruction Coleman had solicited. Payment had been offered and brushed aside. A schedule was established and both had parted feeling pleased with the arrangements. Seda was particularly pleased that he had been asked. Coleman was delighted that the senior *guru* was personally committed to assisting with the extra-curriculum instruction. Later, as he lay awake, his mind recounted the two meetings with the Timorese that day. Albert's earlier over reaction to being startled now caused Coleman to smile as he recalled the scene as the instructor's behaviour had been almost comical.

Albert Seda also lay awake anxiously contemplating the letter from his brother Nathan. Sleep was impossible. The disguised threats unsettled his stomach. Should some source inform the Australian authorities of Albert's relationship to Nathan, dire consequences would follow for their remaining family in Timor. Tired and agitated the following morning, Albert decided not to attend classes for the day. He had to have time to think, to convince Nathan that it would be impossible for him to do those things that he asked. No, not asked, demanded.

* * * * * *

In the following weeks a further and even more threatening communication arrived and Albert assumed the Asian philosophical approach to Nathan's letters. He decided that he was, after all, of Indonesian heritage and that bore certain responsibilities even though he had not found peace in his country of birth. He had also considered his remaining family in Kupang and the additional hardships they may have to suffer if he refused assistance.

He really had no choice but to submit. He agreed to cooperate and, in so doing, commenced down a parallel path to that of Stephen Coleman, unaware that their respective journeys would eventually twist and turn in opposing directions as each moved forward in search of their own dreams and, perhaps too, their *ajal*.

Their final destiny.

Chapter 3

The line extended for kilometres. In some places, the bicycles were four and five abreast as the children free-wheeled down the gentle incline enjoying the lower temperatures and light humidity of the early morning. As they rode, they talked, laughed and flirted, occasionally pedalling, as they coasted down the hill. They were happy, innocent, and eager to get to school.

The girls wore dark skirts, white cotton blouses and thin red scarves knotted loosely below the neckline. The boys wore similar colours, dressed in shorts or trousers, depending on their age, and white short-sleeved shirts without the distinguishing loose tie. The girls held themselves erect, poised like Parisian models, their backs straight, both hands elegantly touching but not gripping the handlebars as they maintained their positions in the column.

Many of the young ladies sported waist length deep black hair. Occasionally, as the bicycles passed under the trees and then out of the thin shadows into the light, the sun's rays would touch the fine long strands causing their well-kept crowns to shine with the care, the brushing and the natural aloe vera applied each evening by their doting mothers before they retired.

Even though their appearance could cause one to think otherwise, these were not wealthy children and they wore sturdy sandals. Some wore white socks but only as an option as these were not a mandatory part of the school uniform. The boys wore an assortment of footwear. Most preferred a sandal not dissimilar to those worn by the girls, but more robust to withstand the perpetual pounding they suffered from the mid-morning and late afternoon breaks when the nearby field became a soccer battlefield.

Occasionally a scooter would pass, and then slow, to permit the driver or passenger to converse with the slower moving two-wheelers. To be privileged with a scooter did not, surprisingly, create peer group animosity as young Indonesians generally applauded others' successes.

Sharing was already a cultural trait well before the Marxist-Leninist philosophies crept into their lives. Thousands of years of cultural development had produced a people who had achieved a special ability to understand the import of preserving their way of life, to appreciate their history and respect their families and, at all costs, to coexist with their neighbours in their restrictive, suffocating dwellings. This same cultural force was also responsible for the occasional but sudden explosions of temper and violence which sometimes caused normally calm souls to run out of control, or run *amok*, often killing at random on a scale not understood in the West. Or at least that was so before militant religious sects eventually gained a foothold in the developed nations.

The road to the school travelled directly through the rich rice fields, the black tar macadam raised several metres above the millions of individually owned *sawah* under cultivation, permitting traffic to pass unhindered. Each plot, some almost unworkably small, would have been farmed by the same family over and over for many generations. Ownership would have passed from father to son throughout the centuries, the unwritten titles rarely questioned or disputed. Often these fields remained as the only real security that these betel nut chewing peasants could really rely upon.

Of course, the occasional dispute would arise as to just how much creepage had taken place when the *padi* fields were worked for it was relatively simple to enlarge ones area by widening the mud retaining walls over a few seasons. The gradual change to the miniature dam wall would go unnoticed as a few centimetres were added here and there until finally, after some years had passed, the plots size could differ in area considerably. If not kept in check, a farmer could conceivably lose land the size of a small suburban front yard over a period of ten or fifteen years.

Coconut groves separated these magnificent green fields from the roads. Flowers grew alongside the pathways and Hibiscus hedges were planted between the small thatched-roof dwellings. The rich volcanic soil provided food for all, including the slow-moving long-horned water buffalo. They were used to till the heavy black mud, producing a bed of fertile ground waiting to be seeded to commence the growing cycle once again. Clumps of banana trees grew in isolated spots throughout the sawah, giving shade for the farmers during the heat of the day. During the wet season, children would casually snap a large banana leaf away from its tree and use the branch as protection from the rainy squalls. To the villagers, the banana and coconut trees were symbolic of protection such as a roof may give, although one would be foolish to sit under the latter without first examining the position of the nuts. Young maidens, when courting, would often say to their lover, '*Please don't use me like a banana leaf, to be thrown away casually when its use is no longer needed!*' But often, even these life giving trees threaten man's handiwork. Overhead telephone and power lines, hanging like huge strands of black spaghetti, were often caught up in the trees or tangled between the supporting poles, further exacerbating the already hopeless state of the power and telephone systems.

Traffic was normally light during the early mornings — not that country town congestion was of any great consequence. Most vehicles were registered to the government offices or military and, although fuel was merely five cents a gallon, mechanical transport was used only when really necessary. Kerosene was even more important, for this was the fuel of the nation. The peasants were dependent on this low grade product for some of their cooking and most of their lighting. Charcoal was, of course, more commonly used in the villages; however the townspeople were developing a preference for the new fuel in their more modern kitchens. The country in general did not appreciate that this essential item on the basic commodities list was heavily subsidized as was most fuel, by the government, although not to the same extent.

These, and other economic problems which continued to plague the Republic, were of little concern to the young students as they peddled their way to their respective schools. They cruised together, chatting, discussing what may have been considered banal nonsense to others but, to them, represented essential dialogue. Their lives were isolated from the faster moving city communities.

There was no television in the village. Some listened to radios, but the majority read their books, read them over and over again until the flimsy paper became so worn that pages often needed to be glued back into place as they were passed on down to younger students. There exuded a sense of pride of achievement as many of these children were the very first in their families to be educated to read and write. Illiterate parents were still obliged to stand before an official whenever a signature was required, and first place their thumbs on the purple pad used for such purposes, before affixing their print on whatever document demanded their identification.

The emphasis on education had, understandably, become a priority with both the cities and rural communities. Kampung Semawi was no different. In this village all of the children went to school. One of the families which struggled even more than the others to achieve this aim now had two of its older offspring well advanced along the educational highway. Both had achieved exemplary results and enjoyed a certain kudos within their small community.

Even the old nasty woman (some said she practised witchcraft!), her head tied in towelling, her lips and toothless mouth bright red from chewing betel nut, would no longer whack them belligerently as she had done when they first raced across the small muddy stretch in front of her shanty in the years before. These days she would giggle like some inebriated soul, squatting still as before, but kinder to the two students whose legs would now only attract a token, but still accurate, flick of the willow branch as they passed.

Bambang and Wanti both knew that the village folk were proud of their achievements. They realized also that in an agrarian state such as theirs, the opportunity for advancement beyond secondary school was practically impossible unless one's family had the funds to pay for the university, or a scholarship provided the necessary access and ongoing financial support.

The column continued to grow as more and more students joined the throng. Several of the older male students moved into position on each side of Wanti. Popular at school with both the faculty and her class mates, Wanti personified the concept of beauty and intelligence. She was well motivated and never failed to achieve a leading position in her class. She was rarely outspoken. Wanti's observers were all in agreement that, given the right opportunities, she would succeed easily in life, even without her obvious intelligence, as her soft beauty was apparent even before she had turned sixteen.

On this day she was being teased by two of her classmates for sitting together with an older boy at school.

"*When are you getting married, 'Ti ?*" The cyclist on her left taunted, using the familiar abbreviated form of her name.

"*Ya, ja, 'Ti,*" enjoined the other, "*when's the big day?*"

Wanti eased her machine slowly to the left forcing the first lad to reduce his speed placing him then behind the much sought after girl. She feigned ignorance of what they referred to and just smiled, pleased that the school would no doubt be abuzz with gossip concerning her. The boy in question was Sutarmin, a close companion to her brother, Bambang, and he was as handsome as they came, or at least Wanti thought so. The taunting continued as the first boy regained his position, although he was now content just to ride alongside without any response from the girl. Both were happy just to be seen talking to her, accompanying the popular student to school. She had become conscious that recently the boys had begun paying more and more attention to her.

She flicked her head deliberately, causing her glossy hair to move across her back. She knew the effect this would have on her two admirers. Wanti ignored the two alongside as she continued towards the school. Her brother would have arrived already to prepare for those meetings he attended each day, she thought.

Bambang, although an excellent student, was far too outspoken and often hard-nosed about his own opinions. He had leadership qualities and had his own small following of young ladies who would just love to snare the ambitious young Javanese. At the end of that semester he would graduate. Bambang was severely disappointed that he would not be attending university. The resentment he felt was not just for himself but also for Wanti and the others in his disadvantaged family.

Tertiary education was only available to those with the finances or political affiliations which would see them through the arduous five and six-year courses. His family, not unlike most of the others from his class, were poor and, although he knew he should be grateful that he had been given the opportunity to reach as far as he had, Bambang still felt bitter that he was limited by what was effectively his caste. He had discussed this with his best friend, Sutarmin, on many occasions.

'Min had the foresight to anticipate his own funding problems and the year before, despite Bambang's heated objections, joined the Young Communist League, hoping that this would enhance his position when applying for one of the several scholarships the Party provided annually to students at their school.

'Min had been lucky. He had been informed just the day before of his scholarship and upon learning this news he'd grabbed his best friend, lifting his well developed body off the ground, and whooped loudly with excitement.

Bambang was, of course, pleased for his close friend but unhappy with himself when he admitted that the slight pangs of jealousy were real, and not just anger at the system, as Sutarmin's grades were well below his own. His friend had acknowledged the reaction and later that day decided that, although it was too late for Bambang it was not necessarily so for his sister. And so, without discussing the matter with his classmate, Sutarmin went in search of Wanti, finding her sitting with friends gossiping between classes.

As she cycled along she remembered with a wry smile that the meeting was not at all romantic as her girl friends had imagined. Wanti was extremely pleased to have a senior approach her and invite her to walk with him to discuss something, in private. Especially when her girl friends, without exception, thought that the handsome 'Min was unapproachable considering the strong competition from the older ladies in year twelve.

Sutarmin sat her down near the teacher's room under the loudspeakers which blasted forth each morning with what had become a very scratchy recording of the national anthem, *Indonesia Raya*.

He was still shaking with excitement.

"'*Ti*," Sutarmin commenced, "*I have won the scholarship!*"

Wanti's eyes opened wide in disbelief.

"*Bohong!*" she responded, accusing him of gross exaggeration as she knew that only two scholarships were awarded at their school each year and that it would be impossible for him to receive such acknowledgment for his scholastic efforts as 'Min was no academic giant.

"No, '*Ti, I am not lying. I really did win the scholarship!*" he replied, laughing and taking both her hands in his and squeezing them with affection.

"*How is this possible, 'Min?*" Wanti asked, not entirely convinced that it was true, her doubts giving way to laughter at the wonderful surprise.

"*The League, Wanti, the League,*" he answered hurriedly, his excitement bubbling.

Wanti's reaction was mixed. Her excitement at Sutarmin's good fortune was tempered by the mention of the Communist body responsible for his exuberance. Her mood changed quickly as the ramifications of what might now follow dawned on her and she sat, hands still clasped in his, looking into his eyes.

"*I am happy for you 'Min,*" she said but in her heart she had doubts.

"*Wanti,*" he whispered, "*listen to me. Join the League now, and you too could have the same chance next year. With your excellent grades you would certainly be selected.*"

She slowly extracted her hands from his grasp, so as not to offend, then sat smiling at her naive friend. It was not necessary for her to respond, as both knew that what he suggested would be impossible. Her brother's anti-League activities in the Student National Front would exclude her from selection. She would have little chance unless Bambang ceased his damaging activities on campus and even then it would be highly unlikely that the League would be that forgiving. Wanti smiled again and turned to see if her friends were still watching them together.

"*I must go now, 'Min.*" She tried to sound bright. "*I am really very happy for you.*" Smiling, she rose and waited for him to leave before returning to her girl friends, all of whom were now giggling together, anxious to discover what had taken place between the couple in private conversation. To their dismay she simply refused to be baited, electing to smile and leave the rest to their vivid adolescent imaginations.

That evening she had discussed Sutarmin's scholarship with Bambang without mentioning that he had encouraged her to consider joining the League. She did not sleep that night and, unknown to her, neither did Bambang. Both deep in thought, their eyes wide awake as they considered their futures, imagining '*what if?*' and the extrapolations of these possibilities and their nebulous consequences.

When morning came neither spoke again of Sutarmin's scholarship. Both realized the doors were permanently closed to them and it would be best to resign themselves to the fact that neither would ever see the inside of the famous university in Jogjakarta, the object of many a student's dreams. Or at least, in their case, certainly not as undergraduates. Neither should have had such grand designs, they knew. They were farmers' children and should therefore contain their ambitions. These serious yet despairing thoughts passed sluggishly through Wanti's mind as she and her group finally arrived at the *Sekolah Menengah Atas*, her high school.

The red dust was their only welcome as they pushed their bicycles into the grounds. There were no gates. There was nothing to steal here. The class rooms were inadequate and the demand for learning was so great that classes were organized on a shift basis so that two full sessions could be run each day. Unfortunately, the same poorly paid teachers were obliged to cover both the morning and the afternoon classes.

* * * * * *

Bambang had mixed emotions when the reports first spread through the school. He, like many of his contemporaries had become instantly excited while many of the other students were just a little frightened and confused. They had gathered together to listen to the *Voice of America* on the short-wave band, quite in violation of the government's ruling regarding foreign broadcasts, when news broke internationally for the first time.

Often the youngsters would use the village head's old cabinet set to listen to the overseas broadcasts. Its valves were always running hot, threatening to destroy the entire apparatus. Foreign pop music was just not available anywhere at that time and the boys (girls were banned from participating as they could never keep a secret) prided themselves on being able to recite the words to such fabulous songs as the Beatles *A Hard Day's Night*. They all, without exception, adored the wonderful music. Life was dull in the village and these clandestine gatherings added untold excitement to their young lives. The *lurah* would leave the boys alone in the care of his son Sutarmin, as he disliked the strange sounds and could not understand what the young men saw in the racket which blasted from his Grundig with its thirty centimetre speakers.

The old Bedford truck and this radio were the prized possessions of the village head — even he couldn't remember how both these antiquated items originally turned up in their village. Not that it really mattered. These items were his, a *warisan*, left to him by his father and no one in the *kampung* questioned their origins nor their use. The villagers would always know when the headman was returning from an outing as, during the dry season clouds of red volcanic dust would trail behind his noisy truck, distinguishing it from the government machines of Soviet manufacture.

When the old man drove down the four kilometres to the sealed highway he would load the truck with children, their parents, and their produce, and a large number of caged chickens for sale at the roadside markets. He was a good man. A simple man. But he was not a Communist.

There was a small foot track from their *kampung* which cut the distance by half to the main road and the outside world. The children took this path when walking as all they had to do was step carefully along the hardened tops of the mud-caked walls separating the paddy fields and, within the hour, they could reach the small market. When the heat was intense, just before the storms which heralded the beginning of the 'Wet', the old man would stop and load the school children, some with their bicycles, up into the remaining space after his trip into town. He knew they would be near to exhaustion, hot and in despair climbing the last few hundred metres over the small knoll and down to their hidden corner of the world. He loved all of the village children and certainly didn't object to their using his wireless.

On this day, as he brought the Bedford to a halt he could see a large number of them, more than usual, crowded outside his hut. Immediately concerned, he approached and heard the intermittent foreign voice fluctuating across the air waves. The radio squawked sending out a signal piercing the young listeners' ears.

They sat silently trying to comprehend the words as the broadcast continued. Only Bambang and Sutarmin, due to their constant use of the radio, were capable of understanding the general gist of the commentator's message. One of their group, frustrated with not understanding the broadcast reached across and moved the large tuning dial throwing the program into another frequency, which happened to be broadcasting music, the oscillating sound waves providing a much distorted Jerry Lee Lewis singing *Shake, Baby Shake*.

The smaller children laughed. Bambang whacked the errant member and quickly re-established the correct frequency. They all sat huddled together, transfixed, as Sutarmin interpreted what he understood from the foreign broadcast. And long after the news was over they continued to sit there in silence, dumbfounded, as Bambang, reality slowly sinking in, glared angrily at his close friend.

The report they had just heard was not specific with detail but the message was very clear. The Indonesian Communist Party had made its move. They were taking over the country's leadership.

* * * * * *

Bambang, unlike his sister Wanti, was regularly involved in political rallies so he was used to political disturbances. Was it not correct for students to do so, to lead the uninformed village people through to better lives, to attempt to achieve a standard of living that was all but an impossible dream to his *nenek mojang*, his forefathers, under colonial rule?

Ah, the Dutch! Bambang would sit for hours listening to his parents rhetoric recounting the *Revolusi*. Heroic tales of untrained soldiers armed only with bamboo spears fighting the Dutch Army stabbed his heart until he, in chorus with the other children would cry out in unison *'Merdeka!'* 'Freedom!' each time the story gave an opportunity for their participation. Their dislike of the Dutch turned quickly to hate as each tale they heard depicted the horrors and cruelty of the War of Independence, which raged from 1945 until early 1949, and there would be tears on the cheeks of all when they listened to the sad tales of incarceration suffered by *Bung Karno*, their leader.

Bambang was the only male child and consequently cherished dearly by all. Often in trouble, but always forgiven, Bambang managed to survive his mischievous childhood ways, becoming serious with his studies as he entered senior high school. He developed into a handsome young man. Diligent at school, he was regularly selected to accompany the *gurus* when they attended political meetings. Almost without exception they participated in the President's guided democracy policy of NASAKOM - Nationalism, Socialism and Communism.

Wanti was determined to succeed. If nothing else, at least she would be able to escape the potential trap of being obliged to marry while still very young, bearing a multitude of children and remaining in an almost destitute state for the rest of her life.

Although the eldest of the children, she had started school behind her brother. Wanti had no desire to participate in the political groups. Chided by her brother, she would feign interest; however her ambitions lay elsewhere. Wanti's aim was to finish high school and hopefully study a part-time course at a secretarial college. As in most village families, money was almost never seen in their household.

The postwar economy was sluggish due to lack of investment and corruption. Wanti realized early in life that to survive she would need to leave the village and find employment in Solo — perhaps in a *Batik* factory or even in the government service. To achieve this end she would require high grades at school and some political influence in order to be accepted. Competition was enormous on this small island as the population grew dangerously close to sixty million. Her classic face and figure would not burden her and being of Javanese descent was a distinct advantage.

* * * * * *

Wanti placed her bicycle in line with the hundreds of others and moved slowly towards the main school building. That day her first lessons were history and geography. She was pleased with this as Wanti enjoyed the opportunity to daydream of other places and other people. The bell had already been rung loudly, calling the children to their classrooms and she had followed, talking to others as they entered the overcrowded halls.

She had been uneasy during the morning class when rumours spread throughout the school of massive political unrest in the capital, Jakarta. The school was abuzz with excitement. None of the students understood what it all meant to them. Jakarta seemed a far away place, one that only a very few from their village would ever have the opportunity to visit. The previous evening they had listened, mesmerized by the charismatic idol, President Soekarno, as he harangued the masses packed into Freedom Square. Tears were evident — tears of pride and in some instances, fear, as their Great Leader of the Revolution, President for Life, screamed "*Revolusi kita belum selesai!*" Our Revolution is not yet finished! just moments before collapsing on the rostrum witnessed by hundreds of thousands of his faithful followers.

What happened next is history. An extraordinary and significant series of events changed the nation's course and resulted in the deaths of some half a million souls. The children had no idea at the time that they had witnessed the beginning of a very dangerous era which would scar their lives forever. Few would ever forget the events that followed.

Wanti wondered what these rumours would mean to them and their family if the reports were true. She went in search of her brother for reassurance. He would know, she thought, just how serious the rumours were. After all, was not Bambang a popular political activist himself? She hurried through the maze of corridors until finding her brother in the headmaster's office grouped with his classmates and teachers listening to *Radio Republik Indonesia's* broadcast. They were all very quiet, their eyes glued to the speaker fixed to the wall above the President's photograph. A solemn voice made the announcement over and over as throughout the country the people listened in shock.

The President had fallen ill, they heard, and might even be dead! Acting swiftly, Communist elements had initiated action to take control of the country. The capital was in turmoil. There were riots. Armed groups had taken control of the communication centres. A *coup d'etat!*

There was an abrupt, crackling interruption, then the broadcast ceased. The students sat in silence, stunned. Fear gripped them all, immediately. Even this far from the city there would be trouble.

Familiar with political violence, the teachers urged the students to flee the school for the security of their homes. The younger children were ushered out bewildered by the urgency, and soon the whole school was deserted. The inherent ability of the Chinese shopkeepers to identify danger was signalled by the closed and boarded shops. Within minutes, the Chinese had retreated into their houses fearful of retaliation. For whatever historic reason their race always suffered the brunt whenever violence erupted. The simple fact that they were Chinese was usually sufficient to warrant the wrath of rioters and looters.

People everywhere returned to their homes and waited for the unknown to happen, as they knew it would. Electricity was immediately cut off to the villages and, by nightfall, an uneasy quiet descended upon the *kampungs* everywhere, throughout the nation.

The terror had begun.

* * * * * *

In the weeks that followed, life developed a limbo quality for the people of Indonesia. Gangs from the cities gathered to avenge the savage deaths of their country's generals, whose bodies had been grossly mutilated. The Communists were held responsible and so too were the Chinese. None were safe to leave their homes and many were butchered without any comprehension of what their misdeeds may have been. Many groups led by students formed vigilante squads to burn out the Chinese and Communist sympathizers. Totally misguided, these groups, often supported by the military, murdered hundred of thousands of simple farmers whose only wrong was often a matter of simply being related to or merely being acquainted with a Communist follower.

General Sarwo Eddie was misquoted, or misunderstood, when he reportedly stated that the Communists should be driven from the land and their roots torn from the ground and destroyed. Tens of thousands of innocent young children were then slaughtered.

Wanti heard stories of entire villages being razed to the ground and that tens of thousands of innocent young children had been slaughtered. She realized too that Sutarmin's membership in the League and his recent scholarship would just about guarantee him a death sentence unless he could hide. What originally he had thought would be a blessing now amounted to a deadly threat to his life and family. Maybe even the village also, she thought desperately. The country had gone crazy.

Two agonizing weeks passed. Bambang and Wanti were instructed by their parents to visit the neighbouring *kampung*. Word had reached their village that rice stocks had been plundered by marauding gangs, creating shortages throughout the countryside. Without delay, the two eldest children were dispatched to bring their grandparents to safety.

They left quickly and quietly followed the small paths which zig-zagged between the paddy fields and through small streams until Bambang decided to rest close to a tall stand of thick bamboo trees. Neither spoke for fear of being overheard and shortly thereafter they continued with their journey. They were hot and thirsty but knew not to drink from the small streams.

Wanti couldn't understand why she felt so tired. Distressed at having to leave the safety of their village they plodded on, each with thoughts they wished would leave their taunted minds alone. It had never seemed this far before, they thought to themselves. Why is it taking so long to arrive? Were they being watched and would they be safe? They were tormented by fear with every step away from the safety of their own village.

Suddenly Bambang stopped, and Wanti almost slipped down the wet slope to avoid stepping on his heels. She stifled a small cry. Her brother was frozen in his tracks. He opened his mouth to scream but nothing came out.

Lying across the well worn path, half hidden in the grass was an outstretched arm facing upwards, fist clenched. *"Wanti, stop there,"* he hissed.

"What is it Bambang?" she called but her brother merely waved his hand urgently, ordering her to remain still. Slowly he bent down and with both hands cautiously pushed the long grass aside which covered the body. He gasped as his gaze fell on the headless corpse and he released the grass, quickly jumping to his feet, bumping heavily into Wanti.

"What is it?" she shrieked, her view of the body remained blocked by her brother and the tall grass.

"Someone's had an accident," he lied, turning and grabbing her hand, moving quickly away.

Wanti closed her eyes as she was dragged past the grotesque scene, only opening them again as she almost fell on the slippery path. Alarmed, they hurried towards their destination. Three kilometres from their first gruesome discovery they came upon worse horrors. Stacked on the side of their path were more bodies. Some had been young men.

All had been hacked to death with *parangs*.

The quiet terror of death caused Wanti to cry out. They broke into a run, fearful of being caught up in the nightmare of butchery. They slipped as they ran, now urged on by the possibility that they too would be slaughtered, running faster and faster until they fell in total exhaustion together down the slippery slopes into a small deep stream besides a field of near mature corn.

"Bambang. Save me, Oh Tuhan save me!" Wanti screamed as she struggled to claw her way out of the wet muddy bog. She continued to scream while Bambang unsuccessfully attempted to calm

her racking sobs of fear.

"*Djangan panik, Wanti! Don't panic! It will be all right. Our grandparents' village is close by. Be calm, please Wanti, be calm.*" Bambang whispered urgently. He was terrified that they may be heard by violent marauders roaming nearby.

They sat wet, dirty, cold and afraid on the edge of the *ladang*. Bambang held his sister close, whispering soothing words of comfort while his own insides churned with fear. Hours passed and, after what felt like a lifetime, evening fell. But the darkness brought little comfort as Bambang could see the sky ablaze with night fires. He understood the terrible danger they were in. To proceed to the next village would invite certain disaster. To return home would be as dangerous as it was now apparent that the gangs had reached out as far as even the most isolated *kampungs*.

Bambang explained to Wanti that he had decided they should stay where they were until morning. Wanti cried, urging Bambang to take her home, but he refused.

"*We'll sleep here until morning and then the killers should be gone,*" he told her.

"*I don't want to go on Mas, please don't make me go!*" she cried.

Bambang thought for awhile. "*Tomorrow we will return home,*" he promised.

"*Then we don't have to go to Nenek's village?*"

"*No,*" he answered, "*we'll go straight home.*"

She whimpered, trying to choke back the tears, petrified that her sobs would give their position away to the killers out there in the darkness. Exhausted, finally, she fell asleep in her brother's arms until awakened by the sticky damp surrounds and discomfort of the Indonesian outdoors.

* * * * * *

The two children stood exhausted, staring with disbelief at the carnage. Bodies lay twisted grotesquely wherever their murderers had cut them down, their life's blood making curious patterns around their mutilated corpses.

Bambang vomited out of control, his stomach heaving long after it had emptied itself. Wanti had stood in shock, motionless, the full impact shutting down her mind to assist her to cope with the death that lay before her.

Her three sisters lay sprawled in the garden. Beheaded. Her parents had been hacked into pieces now almost unrecognizable as once being human bodies. As she turned, the carnage continued to be evident. Bodies. Everywhere bodies. Over there an infant no more than a few months. What was her name, Elly? Or was it Atun? No, it was not Atun for Wanti could see Elly's body at the base of the brick wall against which she had been thrown. Death had snatched her from the hands of those twisted minds which had slaughtered over three hundred of her fellow villagers in this small *kampung*.

Their world had been destroyed.

Hours passed. Bambang led Wanti into the forest taking whatever food and clothing he could carry. His fear had now been replaced by hate and anger. His first concern was to secure a safe camp until the madness had ended.

As night fell they hid in the *alang-alang*, the long grass offering temporary refuge. They remained there, arms locked together in dread of being discovered until finally, exhaustion overcame fear and they slept.

A bird screeched loudly close by. Bambang awoke, startled. He turned his head slowly observing Wanti. His sister remained undisturbed, almost as if she had ceased breathing, her body was so still. He looked closer, panic rising in his chest. '*Oh Tuhan*,' he thought, '*what if she is dead?*' He raised his right hand to her neck to see if she was still warm. His face twisted in horror as he recognized the disgusting slimy body of the *lintah darah*, the leech, attached to his hand. He jumped to his feet examining the rest of his body.

It was worse than he had feared! The bloodsucking worms covered his body. He moaned and writhed pulling at the disgusting creatures undressing as he wailed. Then he remembered his sister!

"*Wanti! Wanti! Bangun, wake up, quickly!*" he screamed.

Wanti jumped to her brother's command, instantly overcome with fear, expecting to see the killers approaching. Seconds passed before she was sufficiently conscious to identify the reason for her brother's panic. She screamed.

"*Aduh! aduh!*" she wailed pulling at the leeches stuck to her arms.

Hurriedly, they had both stripped, pulling, brushing, occasionally assisting each other until their bodies were free of the terrible sticky animals. They inspected their bodies thoroughly and discovered that there were ticks as well, full now from their bloody diet. They slowly checked again. Their mother had told them that once a tick had entered the body, certain death would follow. Bambang vowed to sleep away from the damp ground in future. Later, he could not coax his sister into bathing in the small *kali*, which flowed nearby, for fear of the slimy creatures.

They stayed in the jungle for several days on the assumption and with the hope that the marauding gangs would have left their district, having already destroyed all of the local kampung settlements. Their village was one of perhaps twenty in the area spanning a radius of some ten kilometres. Wanti wanted to remain hidden a little longer but Bambang had convinced her that they must seek help from the army detachment billeted at *Kampung Kawi* just twenty kilometres to the north.

Wanti had reluctantly agreed, insisting that they cut through the mountain forest to avoid running into the gangs. Her brother felt certain that the murderers would have moved in a direction away from the Army, not wanting to engage a well armed force.

He discovered his error the following day when they almost stumbled into their camp. His fear was so great, Bambang felt his bowels begin to betray him again. He turned, grabbing his sister, and fled, not once looking back to see if they had been detected. They ran for what seemed to be an eternity, oblivious to the direction their legs carried them. They rested. Wanti complained that her feet were tired and sore so Bambang agreed to rest there through the rest of that day. They were hungry, and nearing exhaustion but still they couldn't sleep for fear of being discovered.

Bambang was not to know that this was not just one short spell of terror. Throughout the Archipelago, villages were raided and old scores were settled — the spark which ignited the countryside flared from home to home, village to village, town to town, and island to island until the number of dead blocked waterways and roads, corpses floating far out to sea where passing ships witnessed the bloated bodies by the thousands.

Muslims killed Chinese; Balinese killed Javanese; Sumatrans killed each other; and so the madness continued until one strong man emerged to take the country's helm and correct the savage course it had taken.

The new leader, an unknown, acted quickly and managed to restore order. As the country's leadership had been all but eliminated, General Soeharto assumed full control. He placed President Soekarno under virtual house arrest where he would remain for five years until his death, a hero in disgrace with few remaining followers.

Bambang and Wanti survived the holocaust physically, but spiritually they became just empty shells. They passed from *kampung* to *kampung* begging for food, working when they could until they arrived in Jakarta, destitute. Without identification and, more importantly, a letter certifying their good conduct and non-involvement in the abortive *coup* it was legally impossible to obtain employment. They found shelter on the outskirts of the city amidst thousands of other refugees who were camped along the canals, their homes also destroyed, many having suffered a similar fate to that of the young brother and sister from Kampung Semawi. Within months, their numbers increased until an outbreak of cholera convinced Bambang to risk entering the Capital in search of safety from the disease and constant violence now evident in the growing shanty town.

Slowly they made their way through the outlying areas of Ragunan and Kemang, along the unsurfaced roads until finally they spent the night resting amongst the old tombs in the Pattimura graveyard. The following day they were chased by passing police but managed to escape. Bambang took his sister down to an area behind the Asian Games complex where many thousands were also camped, sleeping at night under the derelict military vehicles that had been unceremoniously dumped there when spare parts had become unavailable. There were many soldiers camped inside the sporting complex and, as Bambang spent time around their billet, some of the younger Javanese soldiers befriended the pair, offering them an occasional meal of rice and vegetables.

As they became more familiar with their surroundings and less intimidated by the size of the city Bambang and Wanti learned to survive. As did another half a million itinerants who had flocked to the capital for safety. Many did not find the security they had hoped for as troops had inundated the city, bullying the terrified inhabitants.

Time passed slowly as the city moved to recover from the

terrifying year of civil war and its aftermath bringing an air of hope to those who had survived the slaughter, starvation and disease. A new government was installed. The years of undeclared war with the Federation of Malaysia and Singapore known only to the Indonesians as '*Konfrontasi*' was declared over and quickly forgotten. The capital's inhabitants breathed a sigh of relief as the Military gradually moved its tanks from the centre of the city to the outskirts and regular police commenced patrolling the suburbs in an effort to reduce crime. Law and order appeared to be restored. The New Order was now completely ensconced and the Chinese reopened their shops.

Life had returned to normal in Indonesia.

Chapter 4

Magelang Detention Centre for Communist Detainees

The screaming prisoner curled his body in the foetal position, in terror, pressed hard against the wall, holding his hands at first around his legs and then quickly up before his face to protect his head from the blows. The other prisoner lay groaning on the floor as the interrogator took his knife and swung the bladed weapon with the skill of a butcher, severing the man's left ear and two fingers, cutting the soft bone and tissue with a quick slicing motion of the wrist.

The prisoner remembered being struck. The severity of the blow brought him to his knees as the wind gushed from his lungs. He knew he should have anticipated the elbow to the stomach; *Allah* knows he had learned enough to understand the dangers of silent insolence; the failure to accept total subjugation at the hands of those in command at the detention centre for political detainees.

These guardians of the malcontents, runaways, perpetual troublemakers and other lost souls were hand selected for their unswerving obedience and callousness. Mean and extremely vindictive, they vented their frustrations on the inmates, most of whom were guilty of no greater crime than that of ignorance.

How many times had he already been struck? Twenty? Thirty? The pain was extreme. He dry-heaved momentarily then, agonizingly, dragged himself upright. His eyes were partly glazed but reflected the hate he felt for his new found jailers. His stomach heaved again. More blows. Then more pain followed by a vicious onslaught of kicks to the back and thighs.

To his right were other custodians. He knew there would be no respite should he react to the guards' onslaught. Obedience was the key and one might survive only if perceived to be subservient.

Opposition was for fools and would be counter-productive. He knew this much. He had sufficient experience as an interrogator to appreciate the hopelessness of his situation. God how quickly the transition had occurred!

Another kick. He groaned with the pain. And then another, this time causing him to fall again. He knew that he should not remain on the ground. This would only invite further punishment. His mouth was dry and his mind confused. He knew from the force of the blow that someone had kicked him in the head as he fought to maintain consciousness. Somewhere in the back of his mind he could identify what was happening. He had seen it before. He knew he had seen others struggling in fear, attempting to avoid the inevitable.

But now there was something wrong. He was the prisoner and someone else was delivering the cruel blows! It was a nightmare. Next would come the interrogation. Followed by total submission. He knew. It had been his duty before; in another lifetime. Blood filled his mouth. He was losing consciousness again. Next would come the final interrogation and the ultimate loss of one's self respect as he would be obliged to plead for his life. Total submission. The pain would far exceed the requirement placed on one's honour and he would accept the inevitable. He tried to grimace but his jaw was broken.

Honour! He wanted to scream. What would they know about Honour!

Another dogma instilled during one of those courses — which one was it now, the Code of Conduct or the Interrogation Techniques Course? His chest heaved, convulsed, and finally slowed as he forced his mind to maintain control over his battered body. Then he lost consciousness. His custodians instructed other inmates to drag him through the yards, his boots drawing almost identical snail-like tracks in the ground. The semi-conscious body was dumped unceremoniously on the floor in a solitary cell. Someone doused him with water. The surrounds stank of the previous tenant and those before him, for this was the ultimate in seclusion, and he slowly recognized the hopelessness of his predicament.

The beatings recommenced. He screamed and cursed as he willed his body to maintain consciousness, fighting off the waves of darkness sweeping over his body urging him to surrender, to sleep. He had been observed. The silent figure stood there watching the intense beating, watching every blow delivered as the prisoner's body jumped and bucked, involuntarily spasms twisting the torso, reflecting the excruciating pain as the punishment continued on and on, in one final attempt to break the man's spirit. Occasionally the stranger drew heavily on his cigarette to disguise his own disgust. He had to know if this prisoner could be the man he had searched for: his instrument.

The beatings continued. The punishment was inhuman but he didn't interfere. He had to know. The nauseating stench of the cell was more than offensive. Yet it was not just the accumulated human waste which offended the nostrils.

It was the smell of fear. Of death.

The punishment ceased momentarily. Some minutes passed and the prisoner groaned. Somewhere in the darkness of his mind he thought he heard someone speak. The voice had that deep-throated pitch, the resonance almost soothing as he tried to identify what was being said. His fatigued mind groped for reality. He knew someone was talking about him. Maybe there to do a body count. He raised his head a fraction and was unable to establish whether he was in the cells, or dead, and if the body men were perhaps waiting quietly to take his mortal remains away. He fainted.

Somebody coughed. The prisoner awoke. His surroundings had changed. He was positioned on a chair, his head resting on an old table. The room was poorly lit. A light hung low, perilously close to his face. He opened his eyes, moaned, then passed back into semi-consciousness. The shock of the cold water thrown over his head and neck partially revived his senses. The guards retreated, leaving him to his misery. He collapsed into sleep, exhausted, only to be awakened by the quiet. He had no idea how he had slept but when he moved, the shooting pain signalled that it had not been long enough.

* * * * * *

He was aware of the presence of another in the room. His swollen eyes would not permit clear vision as he squinted in the general direction of the shadow. The silent observer's breathing was the only indication of his presence. The man moved slowly from the dark corner of the interrogation room and, lifting the prisoner's head slightly, observed the broken features, then permitted the beaten skull to fall listlessly back onto the table.

"Your life is in my hands, Major. Do you wish to live or end the suffering now?"

The beaten officer again attempted to lift his head to identify the threatening voice. He cried out in agony as he succeeded in pushing himself up and away from the table. The figure in front of him was blurred. He realized that he had to respond — or die!

"Mati atau hidup, terserah!" he cried out weakly, almost insolently.

As the shadowy figure moved closer the prisoner prepared for the blow which did not come. The intruder observed the beaten body before him and admitted in his own mind that the officer's resilience to punishment had to be admired.

This was the man he wanted! This was the soldier he had to have and control to carry out his demands without question. Without remorse! He had searched the prisons for months, examining the scum imprisoned awaiting their executions for the role they played in the failed *coup d'etat*. For most there would be no time-consuming trial, just interrogation and execution.

He needed a man who had this one's talent. One who had lost everything and yet was prepared to accept an arrangement which would wipe the slate clean, so to speak. He leaned over close to the battered face and spoke quietly to the semi-conscious criminal.

"I will send you for re-indoctrination Major, conditional on your swearing on the Holy Koran that you will serve me faithfully and comply to my every command. Do you understand?"

The Major could barely comprehend the words of his benefactor. He turned his head slowly immediately wishing he hadn't as the pain shot quickly along the side of his bloodied neck and shoulders, signalling him to move his head no further. He looked out through the corner of his half closed left eye, the other now completely useless from the earlier beating. The figure there was difficult to distinguish from the other silhouettes in the interrogation room. The man was in uniform. Too difficult to determine which, in the dim light.

His spirit near broken, the Major accepted it was time to listen to what this stranger had to say. He had finally come to terms with his predicament and understood that he was close to death. He had lost. No doubt all or most of his men would by now have met their *ajal*, or predestined time of death. Although a Communist unit, all of his troops were Moslem by faith. This, unfortunately, would not have saved them from their executioners.

He tried to respond but his voice was hoarse. The visitor moved forward to give him water from the filthy dish. The major gratefully grabbed and gulped before it could be taken away.

"*Sudahlah,*" he whispered hoarsely, finally surrendering all remaining resistance.

The shadowy figure moved back quickly to the broken man's side and, with a slow movement so as not to indicate a blow, he placed his gloved hand at the base of the Major's neck and, leaning to within earshot, he whispered his message to the exhausted body in front of him.

"*You will be rehabilitated and then escorted to a special training camp. You will be taught that strict obedience will be required at all times. I will personally keep your arrest and charges file to ensure your loyalty. I have the power to have you returned to this or a similar centre at any time. Should you fail me at any task you are given then you may expect a continuance of what you have suffered here in prison. You are fortunate as I don't believe there are many officers who sympathized with or supported the Communists who have managed to survive the firing squads.*"

"*Terima kasih, Bapak,*" was all the broken-spirited soldier could muster.

"*Your name is to be changed. We will find something suitable to fit the records. You are to completely disassociate yourself with your past, family and friends. Is this quite clear to you, Mas?*"

The Major staggered to his feet, grunting with pain. He wanted to stand erect to indicate his acceptance and obedience but he could not.

"*Saya sumpah, Bapak,*" he managed, swearing a holy oath.

Colonel Seda smiled as he considered the irony of a Communist army Major now swearing allegiance to a Christian with a Moslem oath. He approached the Major and stood very close examining the subordinate. The badly beaten officer could see, for the first time, the unsmiling features of the taut skinned face, as his benefactor turned and silently departed. A cold shiver caused the soldier to tremble as he collapsed back into the chair. He knew, in that instant, he had only traded one hell for another, as he recognized the look he had identified on the Colonel's face. He had seen that expression many times before. It was the mask of death.

'*Aduh,*' he moaned inwardly. '*Aduh, I will still surely die!*'

* * * * * *

Seda leaned back in his chair, gripping the report now almost illegible from continuous handling. His face was a mask but inside he was consumed with rage with each review of the document.

It was an interrogation report. The dark smears were dried blood. Unlike the Major that Seda had recruited from prison, this soldier had died, beaten to death for his part in the atrocities listed. He had been a member of a small group of Communists who had seized the opportunity within days of hearing reports that the central government had fallen. They had been trained in Java. They were of Javanese stock. They had opened their cache of Chinese weapons and swept through the Timorese villages executing their ill-prepared plans to seize control and impose themselves as caretakers until one of comrade Aidit's teams could arrive with support.

Hundreds died that day. Many men, many children and, caught in the crossfire, Seda's mother, left for dead by the animals who had burned the village.

He returned the document to his wallet. He could not permit what had happened to interfere with his plans. If anything, his resolve would now be stronger. It was essential, he recognized, that he be patient, regardless of how long it may take. He would use the Major as his instrument. The knuckles on his hands were white as the inner rage was contained.

He would have his revenge, one day.

The Javanese would pay...

Chapter 5

Jakarta — 1966

Somewhere in the back of his head Stephen Coleman could hear the noises. They sounded like people moaning but amplified as if sent to torment him. He believed he was dreaming but on carefully rolling over, knew he wasn't. The waves of nausea struck, making him instantly aware that he was in danger of throwing up. The wailing continued and he slowly came to the realization that it would not go away, even if he phoned downstairs to the reception and asked them politely to turn whatever it was, off.

The nausea prevailed.

He rolled back hoping to compensate for the bilious effect of whatever he'd done the evening before. This obnoxious feeling in his head, stomach and somewhere in the lower reaches of his body, was all too familiar. The bile made an attempt to rise but he fought it back. He had been poisoned, he thought wildly but knew, in reality, that he had overindulged the night before, and was now paying the penalty for his indiscretions. Ill as he now felt, recollections of the previous night's activities flashed through his thoughts.

He could remember being met at the Kemayoran Airport. It was a relatively cool reception which developed into a one night indoctrination attempt by the man who would soon be referred to as his predecessor. Alan someone or another. Alex, that was it! Alex Crockwell. What a nice piece of work he turned out to be.

As dead memory cells were replaced by more active and not so alcoholically influenced ones, pieces of the previous evening's activities began to filter through to his brain and then, with a rush, everything flooded back to him.

He turned around quickly looking for the girl, and seeing no apparent sign of her, attempted to recall his last movements before returning to the Hotel Indonesia. He tried but could not remember. Sitting on the double bed with its hand-woven embroidered bed-cover still not turned down he leaned forward and placed his hands so that they would support his head. He really felt terribly sick.

The basket of welcome fruit, still wrapped in a cellophane cover, sat on the coffee table directly in front of the bed. The card stated something to the effect that the management welcomed him to the hotel and trusted that his stay would be memorable.

The phone rang shrilly, the sharp tones piercing his throbbing head.

"*Selamat pagi, sir, this is your wake up call,*" the tinny voice announced.

He raised his arm and peering through one bloodshot eye checked his watch. It read six-thirty. He dimly recollected booking the call for an hour earlier! Again he checked his watch, thanked the operator and pushed himself up into a sitting position.

He got up and the room swam before him. He knew he must get to the bathroom quickly, not through commitment to attend the office on time, on his first day, but more to avoid the inevitable disaster that would occur if he didn't, as he felt that the queasiness surging through his stomach could no longer be ignored.

Coleman headed for the bathroom knowing what was to follow.

He retched.

The heaving convulsions forcing him to his knees as he clung to the chrome grip alongside the bathtub, his head cradled by one arm over the toilet bowl. Minutes passed slowly and Stephen dragged himself upright and stepped into the bathtub, turning the cold faucet on to maximum. Leaning with one arm against the ceramic wall he steadied himself.

He remained in this position, the tropical cold water stinging his body, assisting with the slow recovery process. He then altered the water flow and filled the huge American Standard bath to its brim. He lay still in the bathtub contemplating what would lie ahead on his first full working day in the capital.

He had arrived over the weekend, much to the disgust of the staff delegated to meet and escort him to his hotel. He had completed his customs and immigration checks and identified the embassy official. He was obvious. Alex Crockwell stood alone with his hands clasped behind his back, apparently oblivious to the surrounds.

"Coleman?" he called out, raising one hand, finger pointed in the air as if he was about to hail a taxi.

"Stephen," Coleman answered, lowering both cases and extending his hand.

"Leave those there, the boy will carry them for you," he said and turned, leaving Stephen with no other choice but to follow.

"You couldn't have picked a more difficult time to arrive."

"Sorry?" Coleman called to the disappearing figure, not entirely certain that he was following the right person. The young and pretentious man had not even bothered to introduce himself. Moments later he caught up as the embassy officer had stopped and turned, almost impatiently.

"Put those in the back," Crockwell ordered the driver who had jumped from the Holden and raced around to open the door for the embassy official. Coleman watched without saying anything.

"Thanks for the reception," Stephen offered as they drove away from the dilapidated terminal.

"My turn on duty roster, I'm afraid," Crockwell replied. He then went on to explain that he had missed a wonderful opportunity to spend the weekend away in the mountains but, as Coleman's arrival coincided with these plans, he had to cancel. Stephen was surprised that the embassy officer actually raised the point that personnel movements always seemed to take place on weekends, apparently spoiling some event or other; Canberra really should be more considerate and realize that Indonesia was a difficult post, and should not expect the limited resources of the Embassy staff to sacrifice their own time to meet and escort others, when they should be recharging their batteries.

"I suppose you will want to have a look around later after you've freshened up?" Crockwell asked. The tone of his voice implied that Coleman should refuse the halfhearted invitation and, having enjoyed a few drinks during the eight hour flight, he was tempted to tell the escort officer to get lost and leave him to his own devices. But he didn't.

"Yes," Coleman replied, "it's still early and I would appreciate a quick tour. How about I check in, dump my gear and you show me around for a bit?"

Crockwell was visibly disappointed and sat silently for the rest of the ride to the hotel. Coleman decided he really didn't need the other man's company but would insist just out of bloody-mindedness. Crockwell waited impatiently in the lobby while Coleman slowly showered and changed. Visibly annoyed with having to wait, Crockwell displayed a show of childish temper by snapping at the driver as they left the hotel.

Coleman managed to restrain himself until later in the evening. He remembered enjoying himself in the bar with the women hanging around his neck, when Crockwell again made some comment as to the lateness of the hour.

"Hey!" Coleman had snapped. "Why don't you just piss off then and leave me here?" There had been an argument and, although the temptation was there, Coleman had resisted smacking the other man around the head as he rightfully deserved.

Stephen groaned. Damn! He hadn't even set foot in the office and already there would be at least one person gunning for him!

Slowly he towelled and waited for his body to adjust to the room temperature after the bath. He selected the pin-striped suit with a maroon tie. Conservative enough, he decided.

Venturing down to the expansive lobby Stephen immediately remembered the lingering smell he had identified when first alighting from the aircraft. It hung heavily in the air like the aroma of ageing fruit which was about to turn, and yet there was something about its scent, something exotic, which made one feel that it was a permanent part of the general ambiance.

Coleman viewed the traffic confusion from the hotel foyer. No briefing could have prepared him for the awesome spectacle of Jakarta's traffic crawling around the *Selamat Datang* column located directly outside the Intercontinental Hotel Indonesia. Bedlam would be an appropriate description, Coleman mused.

Thousands of *becaks*, the Indonesian trishaw, congregated at the entrance. He knew that the drivers often lived in these contraptions, earning barely enough each day to purchase a meal of *nasi putih* before collapsing exhausted. They would curl up in the passenger seat, breathing the foul diesel fumes as they slept. Undernourished and prematurely aged, these men would be lucky to live longer than thirty-five years. When they departed, a hundred others would scramble for the opportunity to pump their legs, strain their hearts and finally die, maybe even to die harnessed to their iron monsters, as had so many before them.

Competition was fierce. The city boasted one hundred thousand of these car-scraping, traffic-congesting, back-to-front pedicabs. He would take a ride in one of these *becak* at the weekend, Stephen Coleman decided. Until then, the Embassy had provided him with a light blue air-conditioned Holden, complete with driver.

Driving! Coleman shuddered at the thought. Part of his briefing had been an information sheet describing action to be taken in the event of an incident when driving oneself. The instructions were basic. In the event of involvement in an accident, regardless of the condition of any third parties, the foreign driver was to return immediately to the embassy grounds and report directly to the Consul. To stop and render assistance could result in the driver's immediate departure to a more heavenly highway at the hands of the violent crowds which, within moments, inevitably appeared at the scene of any altercation in the Far East.

Facing him across the roundabout lay the freshly gutted remains of the British Embassy. To his left, the Press Club stood as a reminder of the Asian Games held a few years earlier. The large vacant block adjacent was the site for the new Australian Embassy. A few tanks were still positioned nearby to the new city centre. Troops in battle-dress paraded around stopping vehicles, demanding cigarettes, and generally terrorizing the pedestrian traffic. Billboards once displaying socialistic slogans now featured garish artists' impressions of cowboy and James Bond movies. The government's Police Command had the territorial zones renumbered so that the Jakarta area could be allocated zero zero seven. Jakarta's finest now sported belt buckles, Texas size, with the three numbers blazoned across the front.

Coleman found this desire for Western identification totally in conflict with the paranoia towards imported customs which, he had read, still persisted at senior government levels. Indonesia had severed all diplomatic ties with mainland China, accusing them of precipitating the abortive *coup d'etat*. Hundreds of thousands of Chinese fled the country taking with them the very funds the economy so desperately needed to continue to operate.

The Post Report and other economic data made available prior to his departure were all very negative. Inflation was out of control. The rupiah was devaluing on the black market at a rate of twenty percent each week. American dollars were in great demand. Communications were practically non-existent. The country was on the verge of economic collapse.

Coleman pondered these things. In his capacity as a Second Secretary, Australian News and Information Bureau, his effectiveness would be reduced considerably due to the absence of modern communication facilities. Urgent messages were dispatched by telegram through the PTT which often required several days before delivery could be effected. These difficulties were further exacerbated by the government's inability to provide a constant supply of electricity. The PLN, *Perusahaan Listrik Negara*, often had major power failures for days on end severing communications domestically and internationally. The Embassy provided each of its staff with diesel generator backup systems - essential to the preservation of meat and occasional dairy supplies which managed to survive shipment via the harbour of Tanjung Priok.

Living under these conditions was a demanding task for foreigners. To operate effectively one required patience, cunning and stamina supported by almost unlimited financial reserves to survive the corruption, disease and frustration of day-to-day existence. The older expatriates would caution newcomers with regards to their health.

Disease was rife, ranging from the plague, cholera and all forms of hepatitis, to the more common 'revenge' series of disorders such as the bug, Soekarno's revenge; the bug had successfully permeated Jakarta's drinking supplies. The *Koki*, or cooks' revenge, was a similar bug caused by the unsanitary habits of the domestic staff and it was often the more devastating of the two. And then, of course, there was the frightening venereal wart which expatriate wives claimed was their revenge on unfaithful husbands. These excrescences grew to a huge size and were common amongst Jakarta's one hundred and twenty thousand prostitutes or *kupu-kupu malam*, the night butterflies, as they called themselves.

Coleman had suffered the discomforting after effects from the mandatory series of injections prior to his departure. The gamma-globulin was painful and, disappointingly, had proven ineffective to many who had suffered the long needles. His cholera and typhoid cocktail shots had caused light fevers and swelling during his final weeks in Melbourne.

Albert had been sympathetic but insisted that, even with the added protection of these injections, Coleman should never drink un-boiled water in Indonesia. Asians are often shy and avoid describing ablutionary problems to Westerners. Coleman could now understand Albert's reluctance to describe the filth he now observed before him. The open storm drain which ran east to west under the roundabout towards the hotel was crowded with Java's itinerants. What the foreigners' minds did not wish to comprehend, their senses were obliged to perceive as the sight of *becak* drivers squatting on the edge of the *kali*, defecating alongside women washing their clothes while others bathed, was all too real.

There were no public ablution blocks in Indonesia, this former Dutch and temporary British colony, yet it contained the world's largest Moslem population, which required its followers to clean before each of the five daily prayer periods. Coleman was reminded of his error in using a Moslem supplication during his early days with Albert. The Timorese were Christian and despised the Islamic teachings. He acknowledged his debt to the *guru*. There was no doubt in his mind as to the real reason for his success in studying the language. He had been informed that due to the political crisis in Indonesia his posting was to be effective immediately upon completion of the final examinations. He had excelled. Each evening he had spent hours with Albert and their relationship had quickly grown beyond that of student to *guru*. His vocabulary and style improved in fluency until he felt almost as comfortable in *Bahasa Indonesia* as he was in his own tongue.

Mary never accompanied them whenever they left the campus. Albert would attempt to explain the Asian philosophy by taking Coleman on field trips to farms, where in-situ exposure to agricultural life could be utilized to teach him the more delicate interpretations of idiomatic usage.

"Never forget, Mas Koesman, Indonesia is and always will be an agrarian state. It is therefore imperative for the complete linguist to first of all understand those things which are of most importance to the people. Europeans have little knowledge of our staple food. Rice. As you have now learned, we use a variety of terms to describe the state of that mystical crop. We do not call it just rice. You may consider me a pedant. I am not.

Nor am I attempting a lesson in semantics, for rice to Asians is life and life is God's gift to us. It therefore follows that, to a logical Asian mind, rice is a life form with its own soul. You must understand that, for Asians, acceptance of animism is common and is often intertwined with religious philosophy to become one belief. There are no rules governing what man should accept unto himself in terms of personal belief. Those barriers exist only within religious dogma itself."

Coleman had listened intently. In a country as populous as Indonesia, it was obviously a mammoth undertaking to feed the newborn millions each year.

"Do other basic crops command similar respect and therefore name changes from planting to consumption?" he had asked.

"Only some, and not in Indonesia, however I would expect so in China. Those people will eat anything."

The student was now accustomed to the occasional slight directed at the Chinese, for even a Christian Timorese who had grown up in poverty could still be expected to harbour some animosity towards the more affluent members of the community. The Asian staff at the school rarely proffered political opinions nor did they openly cast aspersions on other ethnic groups. Albert's comment was merely indicative of just how close the two had grown. Their time together had been mutually rewarding.

Stephen might have viewed their friendship differently had he known that Albert had forwarded his name to the Chief of Indonesian Intelligence — Nathan Seda. Albert felt satisfied that he had fulfilled his ongoing commitment to Nathan by advising him of students' names, military background, and postings upon course completion. He felt little remorse for these people were occidental and could not begin to understand the orientals' obligation to family. The mere suggestion of threat to his father and family was sufficient motivation for Albert. One is born with a greater loyalty than friendship and this was enforced by his belief, *thou shalt honour thy father and thy mother.*

He did not look on what he had done as disloyalty, but he did not deny that his strengthening bond of friendship with the young Australian tempted him to confide in Stephen.

His predicament had no immediate solution. To divulge his secret to Coleman and trust him not to alert the authorities was too much to demand of any friendship. On the other hand, once in

Jakarta, his friend could convince Nathan of Albert's impossible position. These alternatives frequently crossed Albert's mind; however he feared that an officer such as Coleman would be obliged to inform his superiors if he became aware of Albert's extra curricular activities. He had, wisely, discarded the idea.

They had parted at the end of the course with feelings of mutual affection and respect and, as Stephen had bid his farewells, Albert immediately felt the void of loneliness in which he was left. In the months that followed they had not communicated. Both had been too preoccupied with the demands placed on their lives during that time.

Coleman's fond memories of Albert were abruptly interrupted as he identified the CD-18 number plates on the Holden. The driver ran around the vehicle and opened the door before he could do so for himself.

"*Selamat pagi, tuan,*" Achmad, the smiling Sundanese driver greeted him.

"*Selamat pagi, Mas,*" responded the Australian, much to the surprise of Achmad.

"*Tuan bisa mengerti Bahasa Indonesia?*" Achmad inquired, amazed at Coleman's grasp of the language.

"*Bisa saja,*" Coleman replied.

The driver sat quietly concentrating on his driving. He was pleased that he had been sent to meet the new *tuan*. None of the other drivers would believe this when he told them. A new *tuan* who could already speak their language! Surely he must have lived here before. Ah, decided Achmad, then of course he could be Dutch and just pretending to be Australian. Achmad decided to scrutinize the newcomer to look for visible signs of his being Dutch.

Not that Achmad would know for he had never seen one of the former colonists. He was born during the Japanese occupation and the Dutch never returned to his province after the war. Those who had stayed on after independence left when Soekarno annexed West Irian in the early sixties.

Coleman could see that Achmad was not concentrating on his driving as well as he should. Instead, his small brown eyes darted continuously to and from the rear vision mirror observing the *tuan*. What for, Coleman could not fathom. They continued in silence for the short drive to Cikini where the Embassy building stood, set back from the railway some seventy-five metres. Coleman's heart sank.

The building was the obvious remnants of some colonial family mansion built in the latter part of the last century. To some it would have antique charm. To others, who knew that the ageing exterior often indicated a complete state of interior ruin, such dwellings were best demolished.

Alex Crockwell, the embassy officer who had been delegated the task of meeting him at the Kemayoran airport the previous evening had not discussed working conditions in the Embassy nor had he mentioned the poor state of the premises. Coleman assumed that it was not an oversight as the man most probably considered the dilapidated building's appearance romantic.

He was not unhappy that Crockwell would leave as soon as their hand-over was completed. Stephen disliked the petty, almost officious character, as he had seen many like him during his stay in the capital. He knew that there were many small-minded bureaucrats whose relatively unimportant positions provided the breeding ground for their moody dispositions and deep-rooted animosity for those who had real power.

Achmad the driver left the engine running as he raced around to open the *tuan's* door. Stephen adjusted his suit and started up the steps admiring the magnificent *beringin* tree to the right. The highly polished brass plate affixed to the small roman column on the right announced that they were entering the Australian Embassy. Coleman thanked his driver and entered the foyer, surprised at the apparent lack of security. He was relieved to observe that the structure had been air-conditioned with large banks of window units, each humming its way through a surprising range of mechanical noises, as the power fluctuated through lows and peaks that would have destroyed lesser machines.

"Ah, there you are old chap." a voice boomed from the other end of the reception area causing Stephen to turn quickly, immediately wishing he hadn't. The sharp stabbing pain near his temples returned with a vengeance. "Welcome, welcome," the rotund figure continued, extending both hands as he waddled towards the newcomer. Coleman thought the man looked like some giant duck.

"Have a good trip, did we? Are they looking after you at the *Ha Ee?*"

Stephen was to learn later that this sound like a banshee wail was the abbreviated form for the Hotel Indonesia and that not knowing so identified one immediately as new blood in town.

"My name is Geoffrey Dickson, Dicky to my friends, and I am the Consul in this fine establishment. You, of course, must be Stephen Coleman!"

Stephen smiled and immediately relaxed at the warmth of the man.

"Yes, and thank you Mr Dickson, Stephen Coleman is correct," he said extending his hand to those of the Consul.

"Dicky, man, Dicky," he intoned, taking Stephen's right hand between both of his, pumping ceremoniously and beaming sincerely.

"I will take you around this fine establishment and introduce you to its erstwhile tenants," the jovial Consul announced, sounding more and more like Robert Moreley.

"That's very kind of you, er, Dicky," Stephen responded, his left arm now under the control of the surprisingly strong grip of his escort.

"No need to worry about registration and all of that nonsense right now, old chap, you will have ample time to complete the formalities tomorrow. Come along now," he ordered, almost lifting the taller man off the ground with a sudden spurt of speed Stephen would not believed him capable of making.

"This is Bobby; he is the Assistant Consul. Totally superfluous in my opinion but the Post staffing requirements demand that his position be filled even though he has less than nothing to do," he said, his twinkling eyes and trace of a smile showing that he was not serious. "Bobby, say hello to our newest addition, Stephen Coleman."

The junior stood with an outstretched hand while removing his glasses for the introduction.

"Robert, Robert Thornton. Welcome to Dicky's Den," he said. The emphasis on the Consul's name indicated that this part of the complex really did belong to the fat career civil servant.

"Thanks, Robert, look forward to having a chat with you later. Maybe you can help me unscramble some of my advances and docs. Okay?"

"That's what we're here for, mate, that's what we're here for.

Come back when you're settled and we'll have a look at what you've got," with which Bobby sat down again and resumed his examination of the long list of financials in front of him.

They continued on through a lengthy corridor, down the centre of which was a length of thick wine red carpet, held in place by highly polished brass strips.

"You must close your eyes now, my dear," Dicky joked, as he extracted a large ring of keys from his back pocket attached to which was a chain tied carefully to his belt.

The door was unlocked, and again Stephen was speedily lifted off his feet by the Consul as he ushered his new man inside, Dicky ceremoniously re-locked the doors with a double turn of the strange looking keys. Stephen was surprised, as all that was visible was another corridor. He had expected something quite different, not sure exactly what, but certainly not just corridors! Dicky increased his pace and Stephen was a little troubled by Dicky's vice-like grip, which had remained on his arm since they were outside in the foyer.

"Won't be long now," he said, and suddenly propped before pushing at the wall between photographs of Her Royal Highness and Sir Robert Menzies.

Stephen was mystified. Why was there no handle on this door that had been made to appear to be part of the wall? He didn't ask. They entered another corridor, and now Stephen began to feel as if Dicky was playing some practical joke on him, a common trick back home when someone commenced their first day in a new job. Dicky sensed the younger man's resistance to continue and moved his grip further up Stephen's arm closer to his shoulder, without reducing his incredible speed.

"Ah, here we are," he announced, coming to the end of the corridor and opening yet another door with one of his countless number of keys. He pushed the door ajar, gestured with his left hand and, with a slight mocking bow, indicated that the newcomer should enter. Stephen did so, amused by his escort's antics.

They had entered the second level of security. The first had not been obvious but did, in fact, include the reception and the entire consulate area. Systems had been put in place to ensure the safety of the personnel and the security of the embassy's contents; however, these were deliberately not evident to the eye of the casual visitor. There were six or seven offices directly off to his left as he had entered, the upper sections of their partitioning constructed with glass to permit visual contact between the offices while affording soundproof cubicles.

"Why all of the subterfuge, Dicky?" he asked, not yet comfortable with the first name basis this man had insisted apon.

"Riots, my man, riots," he answered as if Coleman would automatically understand, but before he had the opportunity to delve into the idiosyncrasies of the passages with their strange access, Dicky was already opening the doors to the cubicles and introducing him to the officers at their desks.

"This is David, and that empty seat belongs to Alex Crockwell," he indicated with another wave of his hand. "They are with the remnants of the Colombo Plan section and assist with Australian aid and information. I believe you have already met Alex. Where is Alex, David?" he asked, lips pursed not expecting more than a token response, and then deciding he would answer his own question.

"Of course," he exclaimed, snapping his fingers, "you have already met our Alex. He was rostered as the duty officer to pick you up from the airport. I trust he took good care of you?"

"Yes, thanks Dicky, I certainly appreciated being met and assisted with the hotel check-in," he lied, but somehow feeling that this man already knew more about Crockwell's attitude than he let on.

The introductions continued as they passed from office to office, most offering no more than a cursory polite 'welcome' and displaying impatience at wanting to return to whatever they were engrossed in doing before being interrupted by the gregarious Consul.

"Well, that's about it for here. Except, of course, your desk, which is over there next to the First Secretary's. You can have Alex's when he leaves. Bit cramped here, I'm afraid, but you'll soon get used to the hang of things and once the new Embassy is built then we won't have these problems of space, will we?"

"Where are the Military Attachés' offices?" Coleman asked.

The Consul snapped his head ever so quickly back and his eyes narrowed considerably. "We will come to that shortly," he answered, as if miffed.

Coleman immediately regretted his question. He should have

remembered that the consulate section had limited security access and this had always been a bone of contention between the diplomatic service and consular offices since the first overseas emissaries were sent from country to country eons ago.

Consular officers were basically there to care for the citizens of the country they represented, whereas the main body of the Embassy housed not only Aid and Trade offices, but also sensitive sections such as the Military Attachés representing army, navy, and air force contingents. Even Federal Police sometimes maintained a presence as part of the international effort to prevent the flow of drugs from country to country.

The Ambassador, of course, as formal etiquette required, was equated to the rank of a Four-Star General in the host country. His authority was final. This is why the position was designated Ambassador, Extraordinary and Plenipotentiary. The Military Attachés naturally resented having to report to a civilian who probably did not understand their world of armaments and fighting, and often the mood during briefings reflected these differences.

When the need for the first Ambassadors became apparent more than a millennium before, they were sent as emissaries bearing gifts, offering peace and goodwill. They were trade representatives, not political officers. Somehow the two became confused as one, and this made it necessary for Ambassadors to carefully juggle the needs of both their country's merchant houses and the militant forces waiting impatiently behind them.

"Another officer will take you through," Dicky pouted, leaving the surprised Coleman uncomfortable, standing alone not quite sure of what he should do next.

As the door was pulled tightly closed by the departing Consul (if he could have slammed it, he would have happily done so!) another man appeared through yet another access adjacent to the last cubicle.

"Coleman?" was all he said, holding the door slightly ajar assuming the gesture was sufficient for him to follow.

"Yes," was all he had the opportunity to say moving quickly to follow the man with the serious face.

He stepped inside and once again he heard the familiar click of another exit being locked behind him.

"I'm Peter Cornish," the man stated, not extending his hand

very far from his body.

"Stephen," he responded. His surname would surely be known in here.

"Okay, Stephen, let's go. I'll introduce you around. Hope you smoke, everyone here does and there's one hell of a lot of pressure on right now."

Coleman nodded, quickly evaluating what he saw.

There were five Australians present. Two were women. The outer section was relatively small. It was effectively a barrier. Keys were required to pass through the mini-reception which consisted of an observer's window so that the inner-sanctum officers could identify the visitors without their being aware that they were being observed.

Past the double locked security door and to the right were a number of telex machines. All clattered away, out of synch with each other, creating a staggering amount of mechanical noise as they force-fed themselves information that had been retyped and converted through the deciphering monsters buried further inside, locked away from the scrutiny of even these operatives.

He passed several desks and continued down through a maze of filing cabinets into an area which housed two large refrigerators and an electric stove. Stacked to the ceiling on both sides of this walled-off section were cases of malt whisky, Jack Daniels Bourbon, Gordon's Gin and Bacardi Rum. There were no soft drinks or sodas evident.

Squeezed into this already tight area was a desk on which a new Remington blazed away at unbelievable speed, its extended carriage holding oversized pages unlike anything Coleman had seen before. The young woman operating the machine, a desk officer, momentarily looked up and smiled before returning her attention to whatever it was at hand that demanded her full attention.

"This is Margaret. She knows who you are. Margaret is the senior secretary in this section," he said, his voice almost monotone. "This is the First Secretary's office."

Coleman followed him into a cramped twelve-square-metre box. The desk, small as it was, carried more paper than Stephen believed possible. He looked around and asked, "Where is the First Secretary?" raising his voice more than he wanted, out of nervousness.

"That's me. I'm the man," Cornish answered, almost impatiently, then continued, "and you didn't actually get off to a good start in this city did you?" he snapped, gesturing to Coleman to sit on the typist's chair, which doubled for guests, rare as they were in here.

Coleman responded, surprised, "What the hell do you mean?"

The other man had by now taken his position behind the mound of files and, swivelling on his chair, lit a cigarette without offering one to his visitor, then swung back and hit the small cleared space over the blotter with his open hand.

"What the hell do I mean?" he shouted, then repeated himself, "What the hell do I mean? For Chrissakes, you haven't been in town more than twenty-four hours and already you've been out humping around with this lot!"

Stephen was stunned. Cornish didn't even bother closing his door as he continued.

"You young bastards come up here, full of your own shit, and forget everything you've been taught as soon as some tart opens your fly!" He flicked the imaginary ash onto the floor. "What's more, weren't you bloody well briefed by that little cock-sucker Crockwell when he picked you up from the flaming airport?" he demanded.

"No," Stephen stammered, "he didn't brief me on a damn thing except the fact he would rather be away for the bloody weekend than have to escort someone from the airport."

Anger now pumping the necessary amount of adrenalin, he continued. "Who the fuck are you to get on my case anyway?" he demanded, his hackles rising as he started to move out of his seat; aware that his temper had taken control of his better judgment but did not care, as his head ached, his stomach was in turmoil and now he was faced with some sanctimonious bastard who was having a bad day and quite obviously prepared to take it out on the new boy. It was not lost on Stephen that part of his response was in retaliation to being reprimanded within earshot of the young woman just outside the Secretary's door.

Suddenly, he was determined. 'If this arsehole wants to get his jollies off berating others within earshot of his staff then he can find someone else to take a shot at, and now!' he decided. He leaped to his feet and started to leave the office, when the secretary outside leaned across and closed the door brusquely, not even giving him a second look.

"Get back here, Coleman!" the voice barked. "Sit down and shut up." He was about to respond when Cornish raised his open palm and glared at the newcomer not to talk. "Just shut up and listen," he said.

Shaking with anger Stephen turned and glared at the First Secretary who was standing behind his desk, his anger obvious. Moments passed. He shook his head in disgust and returned to the seat.

"I am sick to death of seeing you young upstarts coming up here and carrying on as if you were the proverbial gift to whatever it is these days. You have only been here two days and already you are in shit up to your eyeballs."

Coleman sat still, listening partly out of shock and partly also because he was captivated by this man's performance.

"What the hell," the First Secretary continued and then, with a sigh of exasperation, pulled a cigarette from the box of Rothman filters and offered the packet to his new assistant. "Man, did I cop a bollocking because of you when I came in this morning," he said, his voice having dropped its venom. "Ten minutes with the boys out the back threatening to down grade our security in this section did not, I assure you young Coleman, offer the best start to my day!" He leaned back in the chair, placed his hands behind his neck and, with the cigarette still hanging from the side of his mouth, blew smoke from the other side contemptuously. "They will want to see you in fifteen minutes so I guess we'd best get on with the rest of the introductions."

Stephen still sat there, stunned. He didn't even know what the hell he had done but decided to wait for the 'boys out the back' to enlighten him as the atmosphere in the room was still hostile.

"Okay, thanks," he offered, "sorry about the outburst."

The older officer stared directly at his assistant's eyes for what seemed an eternity before unclasping his hands and leaning across the desk. He held his hand out which Stephen readily grasped, relieved that the bumpy start had a chance of being overcome. It was only then that it also dawned on Stephen that this man either had two offices or he had misheard Dicky point out the First Secretary's desk in the adjacent section. He was about to ask when there was a brief knock, the door opened and, not waiting for permission to enter, Margaret stuck her head into the room and said, "Time to move, boss, the animals need feeding," with which she left the door ajar and Cornish beckoned to Coleman to follow.

Turning to the others sitting around the larger office he said, "Listen up, everyone, this is Stephen Coleman. He will be on our team but will be seated outside until we can come to some other arrangements. He's coming with me now to the zoo so don't raid my stocks while I'm away!" with which he half waved while there were audible responses such as 'Hi, Steve' and 'Welcome, mate', but the one which caused him to be even more curious than ever was the girl's voice as she called back to her boss. "The animals sound hungry boss, better tell Stephen, to keep his hands in his pockets!" which attracted several guffaws from the men.

He followed his new superior back through the maze of doors and corridors towards the reception and consulate offices. Leading off in another direction from the area he had just visited was yet another passageway which led into a small guest area containing a number of chairs, coffee tables and book racks, creating an atmosphere not dissimilar to that of a dentist's or doctor's reception. There was a buzzer positioned at almost eye level above which the instructions advised those requiring to enter need only to push the button twice. They did so and were ushered into an area which contained at least a dozen offices, each tagged with the occupant's name, rank and official position, and a warning that access was strictly for authorized personnel only.

Stephen was taken around the outer office first and introduced to the three non-commissioned officers who acted as personal assistants to each of the three Military Attachés. He was then taken in to meet the attachés, one by one. He observed that all desks had been cleared of files and loose documents.

There was one office remaining apart from the others which had no designated name or any other information to identify the occupant. Only the warning regarding unauthorized entry was evident on the door. Peter Cornish knocked and waited. When the door was finally opened, the tall man extended his hand to the surprised Coleman.

"Welcome to the Zoo," said a smiling John Anderson.

* * * * * *

During the following days he met most of the remaining members of the embassy staff. Their reception was warm and Stephen was amused to discover that he was the only fluent Indonesian speaking Australian in the Embassy. Most of the others had acquired a smattering of what sounded to Coleman's ear to be basic kitchen pidgin. However, he reminded himself not to be overly critical as he understood only too well the problems these Australians would have experienced taking up temporary residence in a country where even most of the local inhabitants used their national language poorly, not to mention the absence of spoken English.

Where possible the Australian Embassy had purchased or rented houses in adjacent suburbs. He had not expected a palace neither had be been provided with one. *Jalan Sidoardjo*, Number Two, consisted of a one bedroom apartment-sized home surrounded by high brick and bamboo walls. The sliding iron gate was so heavy that the *jaga* appeared close to rupturing something each time he was required to provide access to the garage. The previous tenant had apparently used only embassy hire vehicles and was not particularly concerned with security. Previous guests were obliged to park their cars outside where there should have been a curb had the government of Jakarta both understood the necessity for such conveniences and, of course, the funding to build such infrastructure.

The area where he was now domiciled was known as Menteng. The homes were all of Dutch vintage and desperately in need of care. Lawns were practically non-existent as servants could never bring themselves to understand the reasoning for growing grass around one's house, cutting it regularly then throwing the cuttings away. You could not eat it and the effort in maintaining fine grass in the tropics was excessive. As a result, houses in Jakarta rarely had lawns but, instead, cleanly swept areas of dirt which, when the *tuan* was away, always managed to double-up as a badminton court.

Coleman inherited three servants. This did not include the *jaga* whose basic function was to provide security around the quarters. As the driver carried his suitcases into the house the servants ran around bowing and wishing him welcome. They had already heard of his linguistic ability. Surely life would be much easier with this new *tuan* who could actually speak to them avoiding the confusion which reigned with the previous tenant! He spoke to them for a few minutes and then set about familiarizing himself with the house. The *jaga*, an East Javanese, presented poorly. His demeanour was arrogant and Coleman identified the product of too close an association between employer and employee. Several questions to the cook confirmed his suspicions. The previous *tuan* had been dependent on the *jaga* for his girl supply and often shared his liquor with the man.

Stephen discharged him immediately to the dismay of the other servants. A replacement was found within the hour.

Another problem was the fasting period. He had arrived the week the religious observance had commenced and was now well into the *Ramadhan* cycle. Although the majority of Indonesia's Moslems commence the fast together, very few manage to continue for more than a few days. The general lethargy in the workplace becomes impossible to deal with by the end of the second week, at which time tempers have a tendency to become more volatile than usual.

As *tuan* of the house, his responsibility was to ensure that when the fasting period ended and the celebrations had commenced his staff would each have a set of new clothes and an additional ration of one month's rice, or *beras*, as it is called before cooking. He was politely informed by the cook that *tuan* should give them sufficient funds that day in order that they have adequate time to instruct the tailor to sew the new clothes.

He agreed and immediately there were requests for loans, holidays and salary increases by all. Coleman suggested that they were overdoing their demands and reminded them of the *jaga* who had been replaced. *Koki* agreed that the others had been greedy and ungrateful and undertook to reprimand them herself.

Christmas was a nightmare as it co-coincided with the *Ramadhan* period. Home-made firecrackers prevented all but the very deaf from sleeping during the fasting period. There were many parties but one had to risk the possibility of being stranded at another's home due to the curfew imposed nationwide. Liquor from the Embassy's duty-free canteen was extremely cheap and, as there was very little else to do, most of the foreign community drank — in most households, to excess.

The New Year was quickly followed by the *Lebaran* holidays. As Moslems celebrated, the country was inundated with the wet season's first rain. The conditions were not as Coleman had expected. Humidity caused discomfort demanding constant showering and a slowing of one's physical pace. Offices closed at two-fifteen providing workers with the opportunity to take their lunch then sleep through the hottest part of the day. Expatriates emulated the locals. They too slept through the afternoons. Most evenings were occupied with cocktail parties, national day celebrations and endless dinner parties. Weekends were often spent in the magnificent Puncak Hills bungalows area, where cool evenings often required a log fire, due to the scenic area's altitude of five thousand feet.

Coleman easily settled into the swing of the routine and soon enjoyed the self-confidence of an old hand. Local staff warmed to him when they understood that he had taken the time to learn to speak their language prior to his arrival. The drivers joked with Achmad, now Coleman's warmest admirer, for the rumours he created regarding the new *tuan's* Dutch shaped head, incorrectly designating him as a descendant of the former colonial rulers.

Achmad had suffered the embarrassment of their jokes until being requested through the driver pool manager, Sjaiful, to become the new Second Secretary's permanent driver. He was ecstatic as this removed him from the uncertainty of not only his work hours but also provided him with the opportunity to deal only with a *tuan* who understood his language. He was so very pleased that evening when, having completed his ritualistic prayers, he prayed also for the health and good fortune of his new *tuan* who had come from that faraway country of weapons they threw into the sky called kangaroos and cuddly little bears they called dingo. He knew all of this as he had listened to the other *tuans* and their *njonjas* discussing such things and laughing, happily about their country with its strange habits and practices. Although culturally confused, he was a good driver.

Achmad's position in the world improved overnight.

Ah, he had thought, he must ensure that his children have his advantage of understanding a second language!

Direct communication permitted Coleman access to government circles never before open to the monolingual embassy personnel. His willingness to assist others soon endeared him to the other

Embassies for few of their staff could match Coleman's fluency. His face could be seen at all the major social and diplomatic functions as the *Corp Diplomatique* suddenly discovered that they could invite senior military and cabinet representatives to their function without fear of their being left out of the conversations.

* * * * * *

It was at such a function Coleman first met Louise. Embassy functions were not designed to entertain. More so, these events were orchestrated to continue to highlight both one's country's and one's own presence on the cocktail circuit. Most parties commenced at the evening hour of six-thirty and rarely continued for more than two hours. Dress was normally formal and it was obligatory that all members of the host Embassy attend the Ambassador's residence where the functions were normally held.

Coleman had dressed slowly to avoid perspiration spots. He just could not get used to the depressing heat! The black tie and cummerbund made him feel self-conscious when he was first required to wear the dress suit but now, his confidence was such, the thought of wearing the Singapore tailored outfit made him feel more presentable. During his first formal reception not long after his arrival, he had discovered that almost without exception the other male guests were as uncomfortable as he in the tropical heat wearing the white dinner jackets, and yet they all persevered with the inappropriate attire just because of tradition.

Most of the time, the talk at these functions was mundane. One woman would complain of boredom, poor servants, bad stomachs and the heat while another would compete with stories of rashes, cockroaches and petty theft amongst the servants. The men bragged of their latest excursions to Mama's Bar where they drank hot *Bir Bintang* and paid the equivalent of thirty cents for a short time hooker out in the rear toilets.

Coleman soon discovered that eating the *paté de fois* was dangerous at these events. He restricted his diet to the occasional chicken saté as the electricity, and therefore the refrigeration, was not completely reliable.

He viewed the assembly which, as the alcohol took effect, appeared more like a flock of penguins gathering than the elite of the diplomatic establishment. It was Australia Day. Unfortunately, it was also the Indian National Day but tradition had it so that the Indian Ambassador would first attend the Australian function and delay the commencement of his own so as not to draw upon each others' common guests.

He was bored. Even the champagne was warm and he found himself restless. He was about to refuse yet another glass from the attentive *jongus* and leave when he saw her moving through the garden towards the steps.

She was wearing a full length white evening gown and her blonde hair was cut just above her suntanned shoulders. Lifting the hem of her dress between thumb and forefinger, and with very little effort, she covered the four steps back into the crowded, hot and noisy main reception hall.

Coleman removed two glasses from the waiter's tray and stepped into her path.

"I think you may have misplaced this," he said, holding one of the glasses towards the young woman.

She stopped. Casually casting her eyes over the now noisy gathering she returned her gaze to Stephen.

"Thank you," she smiled in response, accepting the flute. "I knew I'd left it here somewhere."

Stephen was surprised to see an unattached and yet attractive European alone. Especially one as beautiful as this!

"Coleman. Stephen Coleman," he offered.

"Louise," she answered, "and thank you for the champagne."

"Would you prefer to move away from the crowd? It's safe, I can assure you," Stephen offered, indicating an area in the corner garden.

She hesitated and then turned without speaking, leading the way back down the steps to the fountain and impeccably maintained garden. Raising her glass she said, "Saluté, Coleman, your timing was perfect!"

Stephen laughed and touching her glass with his own, paused momentarily to observe her place the crystal glass to her lips and sip the champagne before he followed, drinking the flute dry.

"Well," she teased, "you're either from the liquor suppliers or very thirsty," referring to the speed at which he had consumed his drink.

"No such luck, I'm afraid. Just a thirsty civil servant," he joked, feeling the alcohol working its wonders as he stood there bewitched by this beautiful woman, her fragrance more intoxicating than the wine he had consumed.

"Well, civil man, how would you like to be my servant and take me away from all of this?" she bantered, tossing her hair with her left hand while flashing impeccable teeth.

Stephen admired her beauty as she stood there, the party lights playing tricks with the colour of her fair hair and golden skin. She was immaculately dressed, her make-up highlighting her beautiful features. Taking her by the hand, he led the way through the now inebriated mass of diplomats and the portals of the white-columned entrance.

Always alert, Achmad spotted his *tuan* and soon had them both in the Holden speeding away from the celebrations. He was almost as excited as his boss that the beautiful woman now sat in the rear of the vehicle with her head on his *tuan*'s shoulder.

* * * * * *

There had never been any question that they would make love. She had opened her apartment, and within moments had disrobed standing naked in the room as if it were quite natural to do so. Coleman had followed — an urgency now taking charge as he held her, feeling her warmth and then her hands slowly stroking, encouraging him to the floor as she dominated the love play.

He felt his heart thumping as his body moved in concert with the slim soft stomach and firm breasts on top of him. Her perfume permeated the air and, as she called encouragingly he found his body moving to her commands, moaning together as they held each other tightly until the waves of muscular spasms urged by her orgasm caused him to ejaculate, draining his energy in total. She took his hand and slowly kissed his fingers, then his palms, his wrists and finally his mouth until he clung to her body passionately, unable to respond any more through sheer exhaustion.

They rested together, in a lovers' embrace, oblivious to the outside world. He dreamed. It was a peaceful dream and when he awoke he was totally rested. Coleman lay on his back savouring the clove cigarette. Louise's radio clock had turned itself on and he rested in the double bed listening to the Voice of America's music segment. He found himself humming along with Buddy Holly's

'Heartbeat' although he didn't know the words. He was happy! And as the song continued, he hummed, *"why do you skip when my baby kisses me?"*

Totally relaxed, at peace, and resisting the floating sensation merging on drowsiness he'd rarely experienced after previous sexual encounters, he smiled as he dragged on the sweet cigarette. This nothingness, this lack of 'afterglow' should have a word more descriptive of how he felt, he mused. His lips compressed into a thin smile as he mentally envisaged a definition for this lack-luster feeling. They smoked marijuana; his first. And now he was suffering from post-coital depression.

He laughed. He turned his head just enough to observe her beautiful body, the soft lines of her milk white breasts and pink aureoles dominated by the tiny nipples standing lazily overlooking the lines falling away to the firm stomach and shapely thighs. He remembered the warmth of her tongue and the shuddering spasms which followed. They spent the entire weekend together, making love, sitting on the large cushions which lay carelessly thrown onto the floor over the broadloom carpet, listening to her collection of LPs and cooking for themselves while Louise's two servants looked on in dismay.

She played the guitar and sang, and when Stephen had tried to accompany her she threw the smaller cushions at him, pulling a childish face while mocking his poor voice. They wrestled and they showered together (Louise insisted that the two of them just couldn't squeeze into the bath!) and Stephen taught her how to play Five-Hundred, a card game he had picked up back in his boarding school days.

Late on Sunday evening as the unfinished bottle of Medoc stood on the floor, accompanied by two partially finished glasses of the soft red wine, Louise suddenly leaped to her feet and ran into the bathroom where she stayed until Stephen could coax her out. He knew exactly how she felt. As the weekend came to a close it was as if each would lose something extremely precious that they had shared together.

He held her closely in his arms and whispered to her until the tension of the moment was broken, and he tried to sing the Johnny Horton ballad she loved, softly into her ear. She collapsed to the floor laughing and then he knew they would be all right. They were in love. And neither wanted to say it for fear that they would break the spell.

Louise asked him to leave before morning. He didn't understand but he unhappily agreed to her wishes, leaving the apartment compound where she was billeted in search of a *becak* to take him home. To his amazement, Achmad was standing outside beside the Holden with a broad grin on his face.

"*Selamat pagi, tuan,*" he said, pulling the rear door of the sedan open for the young foreigner.

"*Ya, selamat pagi, Achmad,*" Coleman responded, alerting the driver to the fact that he was not all that happy to be going home.

* * * * * *

Monday was hell in the office. Everybody wanted him for something or other. He phoned her office before lunch and then again late in the afternoon. He had left several messages for her before leaving for an official visit to Medan. When he returned he was disappointed to discover that there had been no reply at all.

The second week dragged slowly and Coleman felt that had Louise really wanted to respond she would have returned his calls. He was depressed. A few more weeks passed and he decided to get on with his work and, if necessary, put the affair quickly behind him. He tried, unsuccessfully, as Louise totally dominated his thoughts. Stephen had been required to attend yet another reception. He was averaging more than five per week due to his linguistic skills and was becoming more than a little testy with the over-demand on his time. He understood the cause of his moody behaviour and was determined to put her out of his mind, once and for all.

The evening had commenced well. He had accompanied the Ambassador's wife to the function at her request as she despised being alone and admired the young Coleman's knowledge of the local people. Her husband had been unable to return from Pontianak on time as the aircraft was grounded with engine trouble leaving his wife to carry on to represent them both.

Actually, she was quite pleased. Normally she found these cocktail parties as boring as hell but never indicated to those around her that she felt so. Tonight she would not be obliged to stand behind or to the side of her vociferous husband and listen to him carry on about the Commonwealth's interests being eroded in this hemisphere or how *that* man in Singapore was really a Communist, and so on.

Stephen held her by the elbow as he escorted her up the few steps to the formal reception line. He had developed considerable social skills and, dressed in his white jacket, attracted more than one second look from the ladies, most of whom were married and led very dull lives. The reception had been under way for just a short time when he spotted her. The other guests were moving around quickly, almost in a frenzy, snapping up the hors d'ouvres before the fresh Sydney rock oysters all disappeared. It had been quite a culinary coup for the New Zealand Ambassador to have a visiting RNZAF Hercules crew bring the ice packed shellfish on their visit in time for his function.

Peering over the heads of the crowded room he could see her standing talking to an Indonesian officer. He sauntered over to join in their conversation. As he approached, Louise's blue eyes sparkled as they had that first night they'd met and when he heard the soft laugh he felt the fist grab at his stomach. He moved in closer to them and was about to say 'Why the hell didn't you answer my calls,' when their eyes met and he instantly felt foolish.

"*Selamat malam, Bapak Seda,*" was all he could muster, hoping at least his use of the language would impress her.

"Good evening, Mr Coleman," the general replied in English as a courtesy to the young lady. "Have you met Miss Louise?"

"Yes, sir, I'm pleased to say," he acknowledged adding "but I was not sure that at the time I hadn't been dreaming."

The general looked at them both quizzically not understanding the connotation as the beautiful young woman flushed red with embarrassment. Louise regained her composure almost immediately and asked, "So, you are friends with General Seda?"

Coleman looked distantly into her eyes. Why hadn't she returned my calls he wondered? "We have met once or twice," Seda replied before Coleman could. "Then I am sure you will have something to discuss. Please excuse me," she said, smiling at the officer and quickly leaving to speak to another group she had spotted near the temporary bar.

Seda took mental note of the mild social skirmish and then he too excused himself leaving Coleman feeling like some disbeliever who had just been discovered in the midst of a holy gathering.

He headed for the bar and not finding Louise, settled down to enjoy the champagne.

Stephen did not go unobserved as he downed the Moet, too quickly, the bubbles forming an airlock in his throat. Louise stared at him, with mixed emotions, from the far side of the room while the Timorese casually observed them both. He reached for another glass from the silver serving tray as the *jongus* passed by. The house servants were always careful to ensure that this man always had their attention for more often than not, his presence in a household inevitably meant that the domestic staff were in trouble as he was the man who could speak their language and they knew they should watch him carefully.

Nathan considered the smartly dressed Australian. His dossier had been completed with additional input from Albert. He had identified some reluctance from his stepbrother when pushed for the information but eventually the data had flowed through. Nathan was surprised with his brother's glowing report and foot-note concerning their apparent friendship. Albert had emphasized that his relationship with Nathan had never been disclosed.

Nathan had smiled when he read this annotation. Albert was no fool as he obviously realized the consequences that such disclosure would have brought to them both. Nathan's dedication had earned him the coveted star on his shoulder bringing him to the Attaché Corp's attention immediately. His job function under the newly reorganized HANKAM was described as Intelligence Protocol. This enabled Nathan to mix with the foreigners easily. His English was poor as he had forgotten most of what he had learned under the priests. To his delight, conversing with this new Information Attaché Coleman was, indeed, a pleasure.

Believing that he had inadvertently caught the young man's eye, he signalled. Coleman noticed Brigadier General Seda's wave and he returned the gesture. The General had been particularly helpful with assistance travelling to remote areas which still required military escort. Central Java and a few of the outlying provinces were unsafe for foreigners. In diplomatic terms this indicated that the Central Government was still mopping up some of the so called communist remnants in those areas.

Coleman had witnessed the execution of one hundred and

twenty seven peasants near a small *kampung* in the Blitar region. The Captain responsible for the turkey shoot proudly paraded some fifteen rifles, the total armoury captured, hoping the representative of the Australian News and Information Bureau would congratulate him, perhaps even send photographs of this heroic soldier to Australia for inclusion in the newspapers.

There it would be picked up by *Antara* and perhaps included in the Armed Forces News. This would result in a rapid promotion for the cowboy Captain. Coleman understood this dangerous mentality and used it to improve his own position. Coleman praised the Captain, his men and their efforts to assist eradicate Communism. At first Coleman felt disappointed with himself for the hypocrite he had become. As the months passed and the horror of what had occurred in this beautiful country became apparent even he developed an affinity towards the hundreds of thousands of innocent victims who had been imprisoned on islands such as Pulau Buru and Nusa Kambangan. Rehabilitation camps appeared throughout the country and virtually a million men, women and children were 're- indoctrinated' into the *Panca Sila* way of life.

Along a dusty mountain track south of Blitar Coleman was disgusted to see pre-school children being instructed in the ways of the New Order, the *Orda Baru*. As his four wheel drive Toyota passed the newly erected *kampung* huts, row after row of little children were forced to stand with their right arms raised in a Hitler-style salute, yelling *Merdeka!* Freedom! in unison. These were the orphaned children of executed communists and it was here that the New Order practised its grass roots policy of indoctrination.

The sins of the fathers. He remembered the text from his boarding school days when at least two hours each week were dedicated to the scriptures.

Although Coleman realized he was becoming drunk he decided that another drink would give him something to do with his hands. He heard his name being called and turned towards the guest responsible.

"Ah, there you are Coleman," called the British Ambassador. "I wonder if you would mind interpreting for me for a moment old chap." Coleman disliked this Ambassador intensely. He was, at best, extremely patronizing and excessively colonial in nature and, in Coleman's view, a poor choice to send to this country.

"Not at all Ambassador. To whom do you wish to speak?"

"Why, this chap here of course," announced the gnome-like figure of Maxwell Westaway, in his deepest baritone, indicating the Asian figure to his left.

The object of the Ambassador's attention stiffened and turned to avoid what could presently become an unpleasant incident caused by the obnoxious diplomat. The British Ambassador would not be thwarted and he grabbed the man's arm.

"Just a moment old fellow, I would like to ask you something. This chap here speaks your lingo so don't run away." Ambassador Westaway had, by this time, secured the embarrassed Asian with his left hand while gesturing for Coleman to approach closer and assist with the dialogue.

"Coleman, be a good fellow and ask this chap if he had that dinner jacket made here or in Singapore. I'll bet it's a Singaporean product if ever I've seen one. Very stylish. Very stylish indeed."

The Asian gentleman diplomatically checked his anger over the Ambassador's obvious lack of finesse but the glint in his eyes suggested that he intended scoring off the pudgy British Queen's representative.

Turning to Coleman the Malaysian First Secretary asked in his own language, *"Are there very many more like him in Jakarta? My name is Ali bin Noor and I am the new First Secretary at the Malaysian Embassy. I overheard you speaking to our Ambassador in Bahasa Indonesia and I must admit, I'm impressed. Do you have difficulty with the slight differences in our two languages?"*

Coleman played the game.

"I should apologize for the Ambassador. He is the epitome of the sort of racially bigoted Englishman even we Australians have come to despise."

The Malaysian smiled and shook Coleman's hand warmly. He then turned to the Ambassador and announced, in precise English, "Actually, I purchased the jacket in London. If you wish, Mr Ambassador, I would be only too pleased to phone my wife in Kuala Lumpur and ask her to send the address to you." Smiling broadly, he then excused himself winking to Coleman as he passed behind the embarrassed diplomat.

Brigadier General Seda had overheard the exchange and he too winked at Coleman. He approached the Australian and assisted his escape from the now visibly furious ambassador. They conversed in Indonesian. *"Mas Stephen, I have something I wish to discuss with you."*

Cautiously blended with the correct tone of respect Coleman replied. *"Pak Jenderal how may I be of service to you?"*

"I have observed you and am pleased that you show simpati towards my country. One day you may need friends who are able to assist you for it seems that you are a good man. It also appears that you are not so adept at making friends amongst your own?"

It really was not a question that required an answer. The General continued.

"There are those in positions of strength who could be of assistance to you should the need arise. Everyone needs friends, some more than others."

"Does the Jenderal include himself as one of those who may wish to assist if the need arises?" Coleman was not sure which way this conversation was heading however he intended playing the game through.

"Yes. In particular ...." the General hesitated, and then decided to change his approach. *"The request I have really is just an idea. You speak our language so well whilst we have great difficulty with the English speaking foreigners. Watching you tonight I though what an opportunity we have for you to assist us with our English speaking courses. What do you say, Mas, would you help with some of that spare time I hear you foreign visitors have so much of here in Jakarta?"*

Coleman was conscious that the request was not necessarily being made for the General. He decided to play along, accept the challenge as he could always drop out, if it became too involved.

"Yes, of course, I would be pleased to participate in such a program. Why don't we discuss it formally, next week?"

"No. I don't think so. I would prefer an informal discussion to define the possible areas of cooperation before proceeding to an official level."

Coleman now knew he was entering dangerous ground. Informal discussions could easily be misconstrued.

"Perhaps then, if you would provide me with the opportunity I could visit you in your office Pak Jenderal"

"Bagus!" he replied. *"Let's leave it at that for the time being. I will arrange for a meeting next week."*

Satisfied that they had concluded their arrangements both men continued with small talk until eventually drifting into separate groups. Coleman felt uneasy with the General's oblique approach. He gave no more thought to the discussion and, considering the possibility of the protocol soldier's motives being not what they seemed, he decided as a precaution to report the incident directly to Canberra in his weekly report. He returned to the bar having strolled around the remaining guests looking for Louise. Where could she have gone?

Coleman was confused and angry that she had ignored him. He couldn't understand her attitude as he knew he'd done nothing to upset her! He remained at the bar, drinking heavily. He could vaguely remember one of the other guests suggesting he'd had enough. Each time the *tuan's* glass was empty the *jongus* refilled it quickly. Finally, somebody took him home but when he awoke in the early hours of the morning in the unfamiliar room he realized instantly the stupidity of his actions.

In the darkness the Ambassador's wife moaned and rolled towards him. Naked, her breath foul from the cigarettes and far too many Jack Daniels, Coleman's eyes opened wide with surprise as he saw the white mound edging towards him. Quietly, he crawled out of her bed, dressed quickly and searched for the security gate. The old man dressed in his white safari jacket, proudly displaying the gold buttons with the Australian crest, pretended not to notice as Coleman slipped past him into the night. He stood outside under the ageing elms, feeling foolish, dressed in his tuxedo at three o'clock in the morning on a deserted street.

Achmad, of course, was nowhere to be seen as the previous evening Stephen had had the benefit of the Ambassador's limousine. And, apparently, also his wife!

He walked to the corner and woke one of the sleeping *becak* drivers to take him home to his own bed. He needed more sleep. His body was already sending him alarm signals over the abuse he had heaped upon it. Still partially drunk, his anxious house-boy helped the swaying *tuan* into the bedroom. Exhausted, he kicked off his shoes, removed most of his clothes and dropped onto the bed.

* * * * * *

He'd had difficulty at first, drifting off to sleep, the ceiling spinning slowly and even when he closed his eyes he still imagined the nauseating motion through his eyelids. When he finally succumbed Stephen dreamed he had been pushed into a *kali* by a beautiful naked blonde who laughed as he was slowly being sucked down in the stream's filthy quagmire.

The dream was confused with others also laughing as soldiers threw bodies of children into the canal while Albert stood high on the embankment sagely shaking his head at Coleman's futile efforts to retrieve the bodies and throw them back to safety. Occasionally he succeeded, only to have the children scream as they were again bundled back into the cesspool. A tall soldier, his uniform covered in blood stood yelling at Coleman to do his duty and teach the children the words in English so that the soldiers could understand that they really did not want to die thereby saving them from his stupidity.

As he groaned and cried out in his sleep the house-boy banged on his *tuan's* door. He feared that something dreadful had happened to his master. Coleman was partially conscious of the pounding on the door but believed it part of his nightmare until finally, he awoke, crying out, his body smothered in sweat in the cold air-conditioned bedroom.

Sukardi, the *jongus*, raced into the room to help the young *tuan*.

"*Tuan, tuan, ada apa? What is it tuan?*" screamed the house-boy now feeling the terror in the room.

Perhaps the *tuan* had been bitten by a *krait*! No! That is preposterous he admonished himself. How could a snake enter his master's bed when he himself just hours before had prepared the room?

"*Tuan, tuan, please tell me what it is that is wrong with you,*" he pleaded.

As his master's consciousness returned 'Kardi put his arm around the younger man's shoulders assisting him out of bed.

"*Maaf tuan, maaf tuan,*" the servant apologized for placing his hands on the *tuan*. No sooner had Coleman regained consciousness than he doubled forward as the sharp stabbing pain ran down through his lower abdomen signalling the cause of both the nightmare and the screaming. Coleman had been initiated with his first attack of Soekarno's revenge.

As a result of this illness and its debilitating effect both physically and psychologically, the concerns he'd felt for General Seda's obvious attempt to recruit him and the guilt of spending part of the night in another man's bed diminished with the days, as he lay listlessly in bed recuperating from what he hoped would be his last encounter with the dreaded disease.

He had made a mental note to discuss his interpretation of the General's approach with one of the Military Attachés when the opportunity arose once back at his desk. His real concern was what his reception would be back in the Embassy considering his blatant indiscretion. And, of course, his career!

One very long week passed slowly and, lighter but now stronger, Stephen returned to work. He'd tried to contact Louise from his home to see if she would accept his call to discuss whatever it was she seemed to have on her mind, and obviously the cause for her behaviour towards him at the party.

The Embassy operator was impatient with his insistence that the call was extremely important. He insisted that she connect him to her extension. Finally, after numerous attempts, he was informed that Louise had been very specific in her request to the switchboard. They were not to accept any of his calls. That was it, then! He decided he couldn't understand her attitude — at least she could accept just one call to explain her position. He was deeply disappointed and became even more depressed.

Fortunately, the incident involving the Head of Mission's wife became more of a joke around the Chancery than an impediment to Stephen's career. Straight-laced Dicky had waddled past him during the early days when the rumour mill was in full swing, and merely 'tch-tched' him indicating his disapproval of the indiscretion. He had no idea how the gossip managed to spread as quickly as it did but, by his second day back at work it was obvious that he'd become the centre of attention within the Embassy's community.

The clearest signal was when he entered the main office area and all conversation ceased, the men with knowing smirks while the women looked at Stephen, almost with admiration. He had stood in the centre of the office and with a sombre voice and hands up-raised had said, "Not guilty," and left it at that. Unbeknown to the young attaché, the Ambassador's wife was responsible for the story travelling at such speed as she blatantly admitted having the romp with Stephen, during the weekly tea session all the Embassy wives attended.

Exaggerating the brief encounter, describing his sexual prowess directly from her vivid imagination some of the younger ladies had giggled nervously, one spilling her tea, while others laughed at her rendition of how eventually she had cried 'enough, enough,' and dispatched him on his way before he completely wore her out!

Stephen would have been very uncomfortable had he known that many of the looks he now received from the opposite sex were, in fact, an appraisal of the good looking man and curiosity as to whether his 'one-nighter' with madame was as sexually extravagant as she had insisted. He knew that if he could get through the following days without any clear indication that his career was to suffer then, by all accounts, he believed that the story had not and would not reach the Ambassador's ears and perhaps then his future would not be jeopardized by the foolish error in judgment.

* * * * * *

Brigadier General Seda arrived home and elected to work in his study until his wife decided to sleep. She was heavily pregnant and the soldier found her condition sexually repugnant. As a Christian he had only one wife whilst his Moslem peers sported as many as four wives and numerous *cewek* on the side.

He had married a Javanese hoping his Timorese heritage could somehow be overlooked by his superiors. Divorcing her would be out of the question unless he could find a woman whose family could influence his career to his advantage. Perhaps he should be satisfied with an occasional visit away.

Bandung — now there was the ideal opportunity for a man who had needs! The city boasted a major divisional headquarters and was literally over-run with poor young ladies financing themselves through school. He considered the options and decided he may invite the young Australian to accompany him on such a visit. He reflected on their casual but pointed conversation; however he remembered that, at the time, the Attache's attention had been somewhat distracted by the attractive American. He made a mental note to obtain further information on her, also. Seda was determined to move slowly with the embassy officer as he had detected the reluctance to meet privately when discussing the possible mutual advantages of cooperating together.

Control was important to the General. Although his salary was officially equivalent to only a few dollars each month, his position in the community provided access to the business sector which could not operate without the assistance of senior military personnel, such as he. The more important consideration was, however, to gain control over General Sudomo's slush funds, acquiring control of the clandestine operational accounts which, reportedly, ran into millions of dollars each month. He desperately needed access to these funds if he was to survive and grow. To build a clandestine power base required money, and he knew it was only a matter of being patient before he had the key.

The tall Timorese undressed then showered. Without reflecting further on these matters he slipped quietly into bed, cautious not to awaken his wife.

Indrawati, his wife, legs curled up so that her knees touched her enormous belly smiled contentedly. Her husband had returned home. How considerate he was not to awaken her and demand his rights! She imagined the other wives were envious. Her husband was handsome. She was an only wife. The first wife of a General!

She was pregnant. She was happy, deliriously happy. Tomorrow she would insist he couple with her as she understood only too well the dangers of an unserviced husband. That would surely please him, she decided, as he had not had many opportunities these past few months.

The room was not air-conditioned. The still, musty air, slowed their breathing. Had Seda's wife had any insight into her husband's covert activities which were so secret that even his superiors had no information regarding his machinations then, in all probability, Indrawati would have delivered her child there and then. Seda was building his network He was now a very dangerous man. Totally oblivious to each other's thoughts, their minds drifted until they finally achieved a deep, comforting sleep.

* * * * * *

BAKIN — Jakarta

Another year passed quickly. The city changed dramatically whilst in the villages the people had already put most of the horrifying past behind them. There had been tears and recriminations but nothing had really changed. The peasants still rose with the first rays of the sun and worked until exhausted from the day's physical toil, returning to their village huts to sleep only to awaken the next day and do it all over again with monotonous regularity.

Nathan Seda was pleased with his new appointment. General Sudomo had passed away, creating the opportunity for the ambitious and still relatively young soldier to tentatively occupy the sensitive post.

He had followed the career of the American, Hoover, and emulated some of this powerful man's control over others by developing an information base regarding their personal activities. Since the abortive *coup* attempt he had ensconced himself solidly within military as well as political circles.

Many of the former military officers had retired or passed away. Some were dispatched overseas as Ambassadors. A number still remained under detention for their part in the abortive *coup* or their affiliations with Communist elements or sympathizers. Some just had the misfortune to be in the path of another more ambitious player resulting in their disappearance or secret incarceration until whatever they had or knew had been surrendered. His star was rapidly on the ascent.

Military Attachés frequently wrote reports advising their respective Governments that Seda, although neither Javanese nor a Moslem, should be considered to be an integral part of the nation's New Order and not to be underestimated. He was well received amongst the *Corps Diplomatique*. He often assisted facilitate access to senior government officials and generally presented himself as a loyal, intelligent, and dedicated officer with no apparent political aspirations. His youth was not considered a handicap.

Even the Chief-of-Air-Staff and Minister for Air, *Laksamana Madya* Roesmin Nuryadin had been appointed by the President at the incredibly young age of thirty-eight! Informed sources suggested that Seda had not only slipped into Sudomo's chair but had also succeeded in accessing the funds used by the intelligent services for their clandestine activities.

The Indonesian counterpart to the Central Intelligence Agency occupied a prominent complex of buildings at the southern end of Jalan Jenderal Sudirman. This organization, BAKIN, *Badan*

Koordinasi Intelijen, received more than adequate funding for the many nefarious activities considered essential to the nation's security.

Seda relished this position of power. He had finally accessed the enormous amount of capital previously hidden away by his predecessor. The funds at his disposal were even more substantial than he had envisaged! Now he could build and develop his plan. He was secure.

There was virtually no financial reporting as the Ministry of Finance was under civilian control and, providing he spread sufficient funds around in the correct quarters, there would be no questions to answer as he now dispersed these funds. All of his predecessor's aides and administrative support staff were either posted to other commands or pensioned off to ensure positions for his own people.

He had both the Sudomo watchdogs ordered to Irian Jaya where they suffered, at his request, before the tribesman removed their heads. He had set about initiating a special operations team responsible for highly sensitive duties and it was at the head of this team that he appointed Captain Umar Suharjo.

Even in the BAKIN building there were whispers regarding this silent unsmiling Javanese whose past career details remained vague. He was a man to be avoided and the more hardened amongst their number did so, willingly, as the soldier's cold almost blank eyes could penetrate in the most chilling manner. Some said that he had been trained in a special camp; others declared that he had served in the anti-Communist sweep which accounted for several hundred thousand dead during the post abortive *coup* clean-up campaign. Whatever was said or whispered, there was, in fact, no accurate data relating to the Captain's past.

Only Seda had the key. The man would disappear for weeks at a time and no one dared inquire as to his whereabouts. Suharjo was Seda's secret coordinator, bag-man, go-between and, on occasions, executioner. He had killed so called enemies of the State, blackmailed members of the government and even orchestrated the recent demise of one of the other BAKIN operatives who accidentally discovered information dangerous to both himself and *Bapak* Seda.

He never questioned his instructions. He received his orders

126

directly from the General. His life was simple, uncomplicated, and suited his talents. He had no family and no friends. Just the General. He never questioned his superior's instructions. He did not care. He had become the perfect soldier.

And he belonged to the Timor man.

Chapter 6

Canberra — Australia

John W. Anderson briefed the Prime Minister with the Attorney General in attendance. As the special adviser liaising between ASIO, the Australian Security Intelligence Organization, and the Prime Minister's office, it was his responsibility, *inter-alia*, to ensure that the country's political leadership remained current regarding security matters. The session had not proceeded well.

The Prime Minister had exploded when the Attorney-General had dropped the bomb shell. "Jesus bloody Christ!" the politician hissed menacingly. "Jesus bloody Christ!" he repeated.

"Prime Minister, we will have an update within a few days and hopefully the report will not be as grim."

The most powerful politician in the country glared furiously at Anderson. He despised cloak and dagger operatives even more than the career bureaucrats who controlled the public service.

"Are you telling me Mr Anderson that we will not have an update regarding critical defence information for at least another forty eight hours?"

The liaison officer responded affirmatively. The Attorney-General folded his arms and looked disapprovingly across the room at the senior departmental head.

"It's not good enough John. Not good enough," he intoned.

Anderson was not to be intimidated. His position was more or less permanent. Politicians come and go. He just wished that this one would go sooner than later.

"We have been successful in intercepting communications from an extremely high-ranking officer in Indonesia. We anticipate further intelligence regarding this source imminently, Prime Minister," Anderson offered. The response was a cold accusatory glare.

"Get the Chiefs of Army, Navy and Air Staff here immediately," the Prime Minister demanded.

Anderson smiled inwardly. Everything was always immediate when the shit hit the fan. He sat waiting for someone else to make the calls.

'Damn!' he thought, if only the government was run by qualified people. He had never understood how the archaic Westminster System had survived so long.

'Why weren't these people required to have qualifications for their positions as other government employees?' he had often asked himself. It would be highly unlikely, he knew, that an executive would be appointed to head a major corporation anywhere in the developed world without having first demonstrated the necessary qualifications and experience applicable to the position. And yet government had no such established criteria! He felt contempt for these politicians, running around in their first pin-striped suits as if they were ordained, rather than simply being representatives elected by an ignorant public. Anderson remained seated.

The Attorney-General left the office and issued instructions via the Prime Minister's personal secretary. Drawing a deep breath, John Anderson then followed as it wouldn't do for him to be so obvious, so apparent, especially in the presence of the one politician who had the real power to create difficulties for his organization. He stood within earshot of the Attorney-General and clasped his hands in a submissive stance, as if now awaiting further instructions.

Less than thirty minutes had passed when all three senior officers summoned were sitting together with the Prime Minister, the Attorney-General, the Director of ASIO and Anderson. The Prime Minister listened while the Armed-Forces Chiefs discussed the information which had earlier been passed to him.

"In short, the armaments have been confirmed as having been shipped from Timor. We suspect that the consignments were received and rerouted via Dili," informed the Chief-of-Air-Staff in a calm, matter-of-fact tone.

Anderson noted the four rows of campaign ribbons which, in the Commonwealth, reflected real time, unlike their non-Commonwealth counterparts.

"Who is responsible?" demanded the Admiral who felt that the navy should, as the senior service, control all activities relating to defence. It was an ongoing battle to maintain the Navy's position as resources had been chipped away, little by little ever since the Australian aircraft carrier had sunk one of its own ships, the *Voyager*, with an incredible loss of Australian navy lives. Incredibly, the tragedy had later been duplicated and the carrier had sunk an American warship during a similar manoeuvre. As always, while lost in his own thoughts, he was answered.

"We have been unable to determine that at this point in time, however the 'think-tank' lads in Defence have offered the following scenarios," responded the Air Marshal, happy to retain the floor and assert his authority in the presence of the P.M.

"The first assumption is that the weapons have been financed to provide indigenous groups in West Irian the opportunity to prove they have the ability to resist the substantial influx of Indonesian troops prior to the United Nations controlled plebiscite, or *Act of Free Choice* as the general public refer to the vote. I believe that all present would agree that to give untrained villagers sophisticated weapons is, in itself, a seductive move. If the Irian people wished to become pro-active in their quest for independence it would be more beneficial to their cause not to resort to armed conflict against Indonesia's superior forces. Should sufficient passive resistance occur perhaps world opinion will support a rethink by the United Nations to prevent the territory from continuing under Indonesian control. We should consider that there is considerable support for a free and independent West Irian. This has come about not just because ethnically they are not related to the Indonesians but also this support stems from the regional concern that Indonesia may eventually wish to swallow the rest of New Guinea, once they are firmly ensconced in the western half of the island.

"They have been more than a little expansionist over the years and we should remember that *Konfrontasi*, had Soekarno succeeded, would have resulted in all of East Malaysia, that is, northern Borneo, falling under their control. Next would have been Singapore and perhaps even an attempt against the southern islands of the Philippines which have always been in dispute."

The Air-Force officer paused, taking a glass of water, before he continued.

"As we are all too painfully aware, should Indonesia, or any other foreign force attempt to enter Papua New Guinea, then the Australian people would be obliged to send troops in to protect the country.

"There is also a high probability factor that the Indonesians are testing our resolve by positioning armaments along our northern corridors and may even be willing, God forbid, to push into Papua New Guinea if we appear to be overly receptive to their move.

"These, gentlemen, are the questions that this meeting must address and," he added, "ask ourselves, why the Indonesians are sending weapons into the area, and what is their strategy behind utilizing these newly sourced arms supplies which have shown up during our own reconnaissance checks."

There was stunned silence. The soft hum of the air-conditioning became evident as those present were struck by the import of what had just been imparted to them.

'No,' they all thought, refusing to accept the information, 'it was just not possible!'

Although the Chiefs-of-Staff had been briefed, none had actually paid any real credence to the initial reports. All present now knew that it was time to re-evaluate their earlier appraisals.

Again, they had been caught by their own complacency! They had erred by basically arriving at the same conclusion as the first scenario had offered, that small groups of armed tribes people were being supported by external interests. This is what they preferred to believe as this option was more palatable. However they had not been convinced that there was any real threat just because the Indonesians were pouring significant numbers of troops and equipment into the area. The possibility that the Indonesians themselves were positioning armaments from non-traditional sources and suppliers with the intent of a possible swing across the border was, to say the least, unthinkable!

"Why would the Indonesians not just send their own equipment in, assuming you are correct, instead of purchasing additional supplies?" inquired the Admiral. "Surely they could justify such a move?"

The Army General decided it was time for him to assume the role of senior spokesman.

"Obviously this is part or could be part of the overall deception." The General continued. "Should their strategy be to infiltrate across the territorial lines terrorizing the inhabitants of the disputed border villages then they would be clever to use weaponry not associated with the ABRI, or Indonesian Armed Forces, as this would suggest an intrusion by yet a third party which, in itself, the Indonesians would claim as being provocative and maybe then march in under such a pretext to protect their borders!"

The veteran was enjoying himself. In fact, he almost relished the thought of the possibility of an Australian military intervention.

"The Indonesians have maintained for some time that they believed that both West Irian, or *Irian Barat* as they call it, and Papua New Guinea will eventually become targets for communist subversive elements," he lectured.

"It is possible that the Indonesians will use the weapons themselves to incite some of the border tribes in an attempt to frustrate the plebiscite, push these ignorant indigenes across the New Guinea border and then rush after them as part of a terrorist sweep."

The General paused for the greatest effect. "Then, with great difficulty, we would be involved in two police actions simultaneously," he warned referring to the Vietnam commitment the Australian politicians had so foolishly entered into.

"Are you telling me that a second-rate, uneducated, third-world bunch of coconut eaters have the ability to sit down, plan an excursion into a neighbouring country with the forethought to embroil Australia deliberately into a regional military mess such as the scenario you have just suggested?" snapped the Prime Minister testily.

"May I suggest, gentleman, that at this time we do not have sufficient evidence to substantiate the conclusions or possible outcome suggested here today," intervened the A.S.I.O. Director.

"Then what do you propose?" demanded the statesman.

"If I may ...?" the Air Marshall offered.

"Let's hear it then," the politician sighed, feeling the murky grip of this one already around his ankles.

"Prime Minister. We don't have the resources to keep track of the weapon movements. Nor would we have the materials nor the supplies to support a prolonged and systematic campaign of aerial and ground surveillance over the next nine months leading up to the plebiscite. My recommendation is that we inform the Americans if they don't already know and request satellite surveillance. In the meantime, we should endeavour to ascertain more concerning the source of supply of the weapons and develop some strategy to either prevent further shipments or at least, slow them down."

The Air Force officer completed his last sentence by first raising his hand and then slowly pushing it down demonstrating how he would resolve the supply flow.

"Shouldn't the Ambassador in Jakarta make some attempt to determine the extent of the Indonesian military's involvement?" suggested the Admiral.

"That will be attended to," warned the Intelligence director.

The last thing this agency wanted was some career diplomat identifying an opportunity to ingratiate himself with the Minister, yelling insults at Adam Malik, Indonesia's Foreign Minister.

The Australian Intelligence Agency, ASIO had no charter to operate overseas and was, to some extent, similar to the Federal Bureau of Investigation. These delicate matters of foreign inquiry were best left to those authorized.

The Prime Minister examined the faces of the men around him. He felt a wave of tiredness beginning to creep up from his feet indicating that he was not convinced that they had resolved the major problem, merely postponed the hard decisions. Still, he thought, that was how one often survived. Do nothing, appear to be doing everything and most party observers would applaud the non-decision making process as an integral survival tactic of the politician.

"Keep me informed," was all their leader demanded which indicated the end to the security discussions.

As the group departed, the Prime Minister indicated with a cursory nod that he wished the Intelligence director to remain.

Alone, the Prime Minister commenced issuing his instructions to one of Australia's most powerful non-public departmental heads. Unlike many other western nations, the head of Australia's Intelligence Service was not approved by consensus but more appropriately, by selection, *in camera*, of the most qualified candidate. He was responsible personally to the Attorney-General. It was not unusual for the Prime Minister to communicate directly with the powerful director.

"What do you really think?" he inquired, the tiredness in his voice apparent.

"The Chief-of-Air-Staff is a good man. Sensible. I would go along with his suggestions for the time being," the Director advised.

"Is there something else I should know?" the politician asked challenging. "You didn't appear convinced that we understood the real substance of the reports."

It was always difficult when asked for opinions relating to information collected by the intelligence gathering apparatus. So often the information was just a red herring; and yet, more often than not, when there was detail such as he had examined but not released to the other departments in relation to these arms shipments his sixth sense warned him, as it had in the past, that there was a subtlety behind the strategy that they had missed.

"It's tricky. We are missing something but it eludes me," he explained. "I just can't put a handle on why the shipments are coming out of Timor through Indonesian waters when it would have been far more expedient to dispatch via the Philippines if there actually is third party involvement and, if not, why not just move it directly from one of the closer ports?"

"The Americans are probably still our best bet for a quick answer. In the meantime I will arrange to activate one of our operatives."

"Don't get caught!" instructed the politician not comfortable that they were exceeding the organization's charter.

The Director smiled weakly. "We won't," he responded realizing that he had included the Prime Minister in his undertaking.

* * * * * *

That evening the Prime Minister attended a formal state function and noticed the Indonesian delegation across the room. He was tempted to orchestrate an encounter but his political experience warned him to wait for developments to occur.

"Damn the little bastards," he muttered under his breath before turning his thoughts to the argument taking place behind him regarding the Second Test cricket series.

* * * * * *

Kerry B. Collison

Merauke — Irian Barat
Indonesian New Guinea

The weapons were moved out of the safe houses during *fajar* as this was when the villagers were least observant, engrossed in going about their own morning ablutions. This had been the eighth load, as the inventory had to be broken down into manageable shipments. Another four, maybe five days and the entire group could vacate the premises pending the next cargo's arrival.

"*Awas, lu!*" the leader warned as the heavy box containing South African semi-automatic rifles began to slip from the lead man's grip. "*Cepat, cepat,*" he urged, encouraging them to hurry. The team of Timorese struggled and groaned as they carried the crates out to the waiting vehicle. "*Cukup dulu,*" enough, the leader hissed, "*kunci pintunya dan jaga baik-baik!*" ordered the Javanese, to ensure that the security locked the premises and guarded the armoury well.

"*Besok saja kembali,*" he advised, undertaking to return the following morning. The dilapidated four wheeled drive Russian version of the American A-2 Jeep then departed, carrying the officer and the remaining two team members.

They headed east for an hour and then stopped. Another vehicle was waiting for them. The weapons were transferred to the other vehicle. The men all worked silently.

No one spoke. This had been one of their instructions, and the teams now always adhered to their leader's orders. They had all witnessed the execution of two of their number for ignoring orders. Before departing from Dili they had been warned. Now they obeyed. The transfer completed, the men returned to town and slept in the *losmen*, remaining in their rooms until being called.

They repeated this procedure over the following four days until the *gudang* was empty of any remaining evidence that weapons had been stored there. On the fifth day they boarded a small coastal freighter and returned to Dili. There were now seven thousand rifles stored in twenty hidden armories throughout the New Guinea border area.

* * * * * *

THE TIMOR MAN

Jakarta

The Ambassador was furious. The Military Attaché had, *en passant*, mentioned the visitor to the Head of Mission. He had not been informed. As ambassador he had absolute authority over all communications and any other activities which involved the Australian Embassy in Indonesia. He dictated a strongly worded message and instructed his secretary to ensure that the Communications Centre expedited his inquiry at level one traffic priority. The response to his tirade was immediate.

MOST SECRET

FROM: MINISTER EXTERNAL AFFAIRS.
FOR: ADDRESSEE ONLY.
ADDRESSEE: AMBASSADOR/AUSTEMBA/JAKARTA/INDONESIA
YOUR COMMUNICATION RECEIVED AND APPRECIATED. YOU ARE TO ASSIST IF REQUESTED AND SUPPORT THE INITIATIVE ACTIVATED BY THE ATTORNEY GENERAL'S DEPARTMENT.

THIS AUTHORITY ORIGINATES DIRECTLY FROM THE PRIME MINISTER'S OFFICE AND YOU ARE FURTHER INSTRUCTED NOT TO ENTER INTO ANY FURTHER COMMUNICATION REGARDING THE SUBJECT.
COURIER DIRECTED TO NON-DIPLOMATIC RECIPIENT.
MESSAGE ENDS.

EXAFF/REF/PM
CODE:173224. NO ACKNOWLEDGMENT REQUIRED.

MOST SECRET

* * * * * *

John Anderson had not ventured into the field for some considerable time. His seniority and knowledge of the subject matter demanded his personal participation. The director had no choice but to elect to keep this particular activity strictly covert in nature. The Prime Minister was explicit. He would accept no responsibil-

ity should it fall, as they say, 'off the tracks'. He had slipped surreptitiously out of Canberra, travelled via Hong Kong and Bangkok and was now in Indonesia. Upon arrival at Kemayoran Airport, Anderson went immediately to the old Hotel Duta and used
the archaic telephone. Reaching his party he delivered guarded
instructions for the meeting then, settling back in the rotan chair,
removed his tie and waited.

Twenty minutes passed and his contact arrived not in an Embassy vehicle but in an old Mercedes 190. The black pirate taxi
pulled into the driveway adjacent to the beer garden where the
passenger alighted, paid the fare, and waited for the cumbersome
vehicle to depart. Identifying the visitor sitting on the patio, he
then approached, obviously agitated.

"Hello, Stephen," Anderson said, rising perfunctorily to shake
the annoyed Attaché's hand, "you made good time considering
the appalling traffic."

Platitudes, always platitudes, Coleman thought. He really didn't
need to be called out at this time. He was already up to his neck in
other assignments and was angry at being dragged away from these
tasks. Even by his director!

"It wasn't all that far," Stephen replied, anxious to cut through
the pleasantries quickly to discover the nature of Anderson's visit.

He was surprised to receive the call and was concerned when
he identified the voice. They had not communicated directly for
some time.

"Sorry about the surprise. We decided not to advise you via the
Embassy channels as this visit is strictly on a need to know basis."

'Aren't they all?' Coleman thought, annoyed that he had been
dragged out in public to meet at the Duta Hotel, of all places.

He looked anxiously at his watch. The older man understood
the gesture and wasted no time in imparting his instructions.
Stephen would understand the urgency once he had been briefed.
The director knew that.

Anderson continued. "Not even Foreign Affairs has been informed, however I will need to appear at the Embassy to speak to
the Military Attaché briefly. He will be advised that I am travelling
informally and I will treat the meeting as a courtesy call."

The soft spoken Intelligence Liaison Chief than dropped his voice
to a level at which even Coleman had difficulty hearing. He bent

forward and listened. Occasionally he shook his head or merely nodded to indicate agreement. They continued in this way for almost an hour before Coleman took his leave, disappearing into the pedestrian traffic as inconspicuously as he had appeared. The director watched him leave concerned that Coleman showed signs of stress. He ordered more coffee, paid the *bon* and waited for his change while carefully scrutinizing his surroundings. Confident that sufficient time had elapsed since the other man's departure he also left, following Coleman's steps.

Thirty minutes later Anderson arrived at the Embassy and asked the reception if he could speak with Colonel Wilson, the Military Attaché. He was ushered upstairs to the third level of the new building. The butterfly roofed four storied structure was often mistaken for the Japanese Embassy which stood alongside, all twelve stories, most of which were their Trade representative offices. The Japanese had understood, even then, how to impose their presence and economic grip on neighbouring countries.

The Warrant Officer escorted the visitor immediately to the Colonel's subtly furnished office, offered coffee, then returned to his own post. He had taken weeks learning not to stamp his feet with every movement in this undisciplined environment. It was a difficult habit to correct. The officer, even when he sat, exuded military bearing. He was just ten months off retiring and enjoying the pleasantries of his final posting. The Colonel didn't need any problems in his comfortable life at this time. Not this close to retirement! He was counting off the days to when his handsome pension would commence and when he appeared to forget, his wife would remind him that soon he could look forward to doing nothing more than having coffee each morning together, taking long walks, and doing whatever they had always wanted to do when he retired.

The ageing Colonel could not think of anything he would really enjoy doing with the woman who had been his wife for thirty-five years. Especially sitting and talking together. He smiled at the civilian whose very presence caused him concern.

The Colonel remembered being escorted down and through the underground labyrinth which contained the highly secret section. There, isolated from other sections of the Department of Defence, he was shown a list of names of operating agents and personnel cleared to access the sensitive information relating to the service.

As the Senior Military Advisor, it was essential that the Colonel be briefed prior to his departure for Indonesia and taking up his post as Military Attaché. He was, to say the least, flabbergasted.

All of those years in the army without any knowledge whatsoever that his government had been running such a clandestine operation. At first he was excited at being included on the list of less than seventy personnel. Then he worried that this information would compromise his career, and his pension. He knew the man in front of him by name. It had been high on the list.

"Well, this is a very pleasant surprise, John!" he announced, with as much sincerity as he could muster. "When did you arrive?"

Anderson smiled warmly at the older man. "Just this morning. This time it's unofficial as I am heading for Singapore for a little, and much overdue, 'R and R'."

"I am pleased that you took the time to drop in," said Wilson, adding, "had you sent us a cable we could have had you met at the airport."

The visitor's eyes twinkled. "Travelling with company I'm afraid, and I suggested that I leave her shopping down at Sarinah while I drop in just to say 'hello' on my way through."

"Touching base, so to speak," the civilian added.

The Colonel nodded thoughtfully. Must be discreet! He could understand this sort of reasoning and, although uneasy, he was pleased that this senior officer had made the time to drop in.

"Can I offer any assistance while you are here. Maybe dinner tonight?" the officer offered.

"Very kind of you, Peter," Anderson answered using Wilson's first name, "however I plan to leave for Singapore tonight. Maybe a rain-check?"

"Of course, of course, John," both now relaxed with each other's use of Christian names, the Attaché considerably relieved that there was no official demand being made on his office.

"I thought that I should report in just so they are able to keep track of me down South. You know how they are about our travelling abroad, Peter."

The Colonel nodded knowingly. He called the Warrant Officer. "Have a signal, Warrant. Take it down for my guest please and dispatch the message by routine. What classification John?" asked the Attaché.

"Oh, just send it as a standard restricted notification to my department that I have dropped in and am departing today for Singapore." Anderson said, now enjoying the discomfort the military duo were experiencing.

"Would you care to write the message yourself, sir?" the Warrant Officer inquired, not knowing the guest's official designation..

"Surely," Anderson responded, taking his pen, reaching for the Colonel's blank pad to draft his message.

Minutes later the simple message was being encrypted by the registry clerk also on the third floor for obvious security reasons and, within the hour, the brief and enigmatic signal was being read by the Deputy Intelligence Director in Canberra.

Anderson departed for Singapore later that day on the MSA flight, inter-connecting with the Cathay Pacific service into Hong Kong. There he briefed the Resident Officer who, due to the nature of the Colony's status, decided that it would be inconvenient to accommodate their activities in the High Commission.

John Anderson went immediately to The Lodge upon his return to the Australian Capital. The Prime Minister had sat silently, listening to how the mechanisms now being put into place would resolve the looming crisis.

'Or, God help me, even bring down the government!' he worried Looking out through the row of pines partly obscuring the fine view of the well planned city he felt the dread of being alone, unable to impart or discuss the secrets for which he had become the nation's keeper and he knew that, whatever the outcome, lives would be lost and few would ever know.

The Prime Minister also understood, and accepted, that he must live with the knowledge that it was on his authority and his alone that the order had been given.

'Is it the politics or the burden of responsibility that makes one age prematurely in this job?' he wondered momentarily and, not wishing to dwell any further on the possible demise of others, turned back to the papers he had been working on when interrupted by Anderson's visit.

"God save the Prime Minister," he muttered rubbing his weary eyes.

Chapter 7

Jakarta – Irian Barat

General Seda sat comfortably, legs crossed, listening to the Australian describe his recent journey through Sumatra. The Timorese continued to be fascinated by the Attaché's linguistic ability. He had almost developed the fluency of a native speaker.

"You seem to be quite taken by Sumatra, Mas," the host teased, *"maybe you were smitten by the beautiful cewek there?"*

"Of course one could not avoid noticing the beauty of the ladies throughout the island," Coleman acknowledged diplomatically. Some of the guests present were of Batak and Aceh origins.

"Perhaps you could give us your opinion how the Sumatran girls compare with the East Indonesian ladies?" challenged Njonja Seda, herself of Javanese extraction.

"Sayang, saya belum pernah kesana," apologized Stephen explaining he had not had the opportunity to visit the area.

"Kenapa tidak?" demanded another lady whose features varied considerably from Seda's wife.

"Why not? Well, for one thing I have not had the opportunity and another, visits are restricted due to the instability of the area," he answered, looking directly at the Timorese searching for a response.

"Surely you're not suggesting that travelling in Indonesia is unsafe, Mas?" asked the unfamiliar lady, *"Is this possible Bapak Seda?"* she addressed her question coquettishly in Coleman's direction' not really soliciting a response from the host.

"Unfortunately, at this time, there is considerable unrest in the eastern provinces. There is consistent subversive activity, particularly in Irian Barat, at this time," the host informed the gathering.

"Perhaps when things have settled down we can arrange for you to visit informally," suggested the young Foreign Affairs officer from

143

Surabaya.

"*Ah well, until that time the ladies of Ambon and Kupang will just have to wait,*" Coleman suggested lightly.

"*Why wait, Mas?*" again teased the General, "*we are surrounded by many of those areas' beauties right here!*" indicating politely with his right hand the young woman who had questioned travel security through the distant islands.

Coleman was visibly embarrassed. His face flushed slightly, much to the ladies enjoyment, and the other men's amusement.

"*Jangan, dong!*" ordered the hostess urging her husband not to tease their guest, although she was also enjoying Stephen's discomfort.

"*Tidak apa-apa,*" Coleman responded, recovering his composure.

"*As I am from Ambon perhaps the General would permit me to escort you to the region,*" suggested the taller young woman with curly and wiry hair.

Joining in the banter and responding now with ease the Australian replied, "*Asal Bapak Seda juga ikut,*" proposing acceptance conditional on the General's participation.

"*Mungkin juga, mungkin juga,*" offered the host in a non-committal manner leaving the door open to the possibility.

The afternoon drew to a close and the guests had all but departed when Coleman rose to thank the couple for their invitation to join them in their home.

"*Tunggu dulu, Mas, saya mau bicara sesudah yang lain sudah pulang,*" the General advised, sotto voce to avoid being overhead, suggesting that his guest not depart until the others, as there was something he wished to discuss. The time dragged on for another hour before Coleman was now alone with the Timorese.

"*Mas Stephen,*" began the older man in a friendly tone. "*I wish to discuss the possibility of that visit you suggested.*"

Surprised, Coleman was about to interrupt when Seda raised his hand indicating that he wished to finish speaking. "*These are not conversations that should be held with the ladies present as they have a tendency to gossip without considering the consequences. For example, most of the women present this afternoon would have made several telephone calls upon arriving home either bragging about their visit or simply gossiping to impress.*"

Seda paused, then continued in a manner accustomed to the

authority he had acquired.

"*I will arrange for you to visit providing you are able to secure your Ambassador's approval. We will require a formal request via the normal Foreign Affairs channels.*"

The Attaché considered the Intelligence Officer's offer, surprised by his directness, completely unaware of this influential man's motives.

"*I would be very pleased to visit Irian, Pak Seda,*" he responded, "and I will discuss this opportunity with the Ambassador first thing in the morning. Thank you. Pak.*"

Coleman paused, and then asked, "*Kenapa dikasih pergi, Pak,*" inquiring as to the reason for the offer to visit the area.

"*Because there are things that our Government needs for the West to see, yet don't understand how to proceed to disclose these situations without the outcome resulting in confusion. Or worse, embarrassment.*"

"*There are those of us who feel that Australia is not just our neighbour. Australia is our friend and we wish to maintain that relationship. Perhaps if you were to report the truth of what difficulties we are having with the primitive tribal groups then public opinion would not be so critical of our efforts to stabilize our half of Irian.*" Coleman was not surprised that the general had been a little presumptuous as to the outcome of the forthcoming plebiscite.

"*Then why not just open up completely and permit the Press to visit and inform their readers of the events there?*" he asked.

"*The government had considered this but came to the conclusion that it would be far, far too dangerous. The area is riddled with extremists and we could not guarantee the safety of large numbers of civilians tracking around in the undeveloped villages.*"

Coleman was not too impressed to discover that he had been invited to venture into areas where killings occurred frequently. He was no coward but travelling unarmed, even accompanied by military security through fire-fighting hot spots was not, in his opinion, within his job description.

"*Also, Mas,*" the General added looking directly at Stephen, "*we believe that most of the journalists likely to be selected would have preconceived ideas regarding our treatment of the indigenous and, consequently, such a visit would be counter-productive. We believe that your position would be objective.*"

The General paused before continuing, gauging the foreigner's reaction. "*Of course, we would prefer to have others accompany you, preferably of another nationality as this would add weight or more credibility to your findings if they were to be verified by an independent observer.*"

Coleman slowly nodded his agreement. It would be disastrous to open old wounds. And what the General had said was accurate, he understood all too well. Sending another foreigner who could substantiate his own findings would be the politically correct thing to do.

The majority of Asia's rulers could not understand why the Australian Government permitted the free press to operate as it did. Having journalists sensationalize the Irian village resistance groups leading up to the plebiscite would not only endanger the successful outcome of the *Act Of Free Choice* but could also create a substantial rift between the two neighbouring countries. He was aware that the Australian Government's policy was to support Indonesia's taking control over the underdeveloped country. Coleman had assumed that steps had been or were being taken by their giant neighbour to ensure the desired outcome. Tens of thousands of non-indigenous Indonesians had been transmigrated into the former Dutch colony. Military strength had been considerably increased.

Neither Australia nor Indonesia wished to see the potential Indonesian province as an independent state, threatening the security of not just Indonesia's borders, but also Australia to the South and New Guinea to the east! No, Australia would not accept such a development even if this required turning a blind eye, so to speak, concerning reports of atrocities carried out by Indonesian troops.

Coleman studied the Timorese. The newly promoted General wore his rank well. An air of confidence surrounded this man who had developed an incredible power base within a very short period of time. It was clear that a close relationship with this man would be of considerable benefit to the Australian.

"*I believe that it is a sound idea, and certainly a wonderful opportunity for me personally, Pak.*"

Seda smiled, pleased that his offer would be accepted.

"*We will find someone suitable to join you on the tour. Our preference would be for a non-journalist but certainly a person with acceptable credentials. Anyway, we will sort that out only after you have spoken to your superiors."*

"Baiklah, Pak. I will discuss this at length with the Ambassador and be in contact with your office when I have his response."

Seda smiled again and, holding his hand out to Stephen, indicated that the discussion was over.

Looking back over his shoulder and offering a friendly wave as Achmad drove along the magnificent *Jalan Teuku Umar*, Coleman felt an exhilaration that had been absent from his life for some time. He'd felt that his work had become mundane, the monotonous regularity of submitting weekly reports making him stale, and that somewhere along the line, he had lost his edge. This trip was exactly the remedy he needed! Turning down into Mohamed Yamin and around the corner towards his small residence Stephen was comfortably relaxed and already looking forward to the excursion into one of Indonesia's more primitive areas.

The General watched the light blue Holden with the diplomatic plates drive slowly away. His face muscles tensed as he considered the danger of what he was about to do, and the risk of exposure should his arrangements not be perfect in every way. Time was running out for the Timorese.

He was now committed to this new course of action and he believed the opportunity should not be wasted. Should his tactics prove successful then his ultimate ambition would be realized that much sooner and, in the event that his plan fail, only time would be lost. And a few lives. Either way, General Seda was convinced that his actions would only bring a further consolidation of power to his position within the military and, with that, he would be one step closer to realizing his dreams. He would use this foreigner to enhance the success of his strategy. He had thought it through thoroughly prior to the invitation being arranged for the Information Attaché to visit his home. He was sure that the inquisitive Australians were keen to take a peek into whatever the Indonesian military was up to in Irian and would most probably jump at an opportunity to investigate, should one arise.

An untimely terrorist attack killing the young Australian Attaché would create considerable damage to the implementation of the plebiscite, and may even result in its postponement. This, in turn, could inflame the entire indigenous population in Irian providing the regional instability he required to achieve his ambitious plans.

* * * * * *

Coleman considered the wording of his report and prepared its transmission personally. He was pleased that events had resulted in the opportunity to reconnoitre the Irian area and was amazed at the timely coincidence. The invitation fitted his brief perfectly.

He had informed Canberra immediately. His coded communiqué was deciphered and collected by an appropriately security cleared secretary for delivery to the Director. The Intelligence Chief discussed the contents with his Deputy. John Anderson then made the necessary arrangements for the Department of External Affairs to approve the visit. Canberra advised their Mission in Jakarta that the invitation had been offered through the Indonesian Embassy in Australia for a responsible journalist to visit and had, in response, suggested the Second Secretary Information, Stephen Coleman for their approval. The Indonesian Ambassador himself had phoned to confirm Coleman's acceptability.

Stephen had been summoned by the irritated Head of Mission. He was acutely aware that events were taking place without not only his concurrence but also his knowledge.

"Coleman, you have been selected, for whatever reason, to be given the opportunity to visit Irian as a guest of the Indonesian Government," he puffed. "There have been numerous mutterings within this Mission as to your qualifications for this tour, however. Your name was obviously picked out of the hat without any prior consultation with the department."

"Perhaps it was a decision relating to my language qualification Ambassador," he gibed.

The Ambassador rose to his feet, his face red with anger. He was incredibly short and attempted to compensate by lowering his deep resonant voice into a bellow. He reminded Coleman of the Wizard of Id.

"Whatever the reason young man, I do remind you that you are accredited to this Embassy and will maintain some semblance of respect when addressing this chair!"

"Yes Ambassador," the younger man responded wearily.

"You will be briefed by the Military Attaché as they require certain information you may be able to obtain during your trip into the wilds," he informed facetiously.

"When arrangements have been completed, you are also to be briefed by the First Secretary. Do you understand?" he demanded in a low growl.

"Perfectly, Ambassador. Is that all, sir?"

"That's it. Get to it. Don't screw it up!"

With this last order the rotund diplomat turned his back on the subordinate member of his Mission indicating that the interview was finished.

Coleman turned and left the room, smiling, as he enjoyed antagonizing the supercilious and egotistical Ambassador who so obviously suffered severely from the small man complex. He winked at the secretary whose office was adjacent to the side entrance of her boss' office.

"Not in a particularly good mood today, are we," he joked, pointing his thumb back in the direction of the man he had just left.

The secretary responded with a cool smile. "I hear you're going to Irian, Stephen?" she asked in response. Not surprised, but pleased that the fine looking Melbourne girl had at least attempted to be civil to him, Coleman's face broke into a grin.

"Yes," he answered, "I've just been informed."

"We will all miss you," she announced and turned her attention back to her typing. He immediately recognized the insincerity of the remark. A strong bond existed between the secretary and her Ambassador.

"I will try to keep my head," he quipped sarcastically as he left, displeased with himself for letting the remark get to him. He retreated to his office on the first floor and commenced preparations. He informed General Seda of the positive response and requested details for his journey. Satisfied that he was moving in the correct direction, Coleman settled down to prepare for his departure for Irian.

* * * * * *

He had never enjoyed flying. His hands were wet with perspiration as the attacks of fear kept him clinging to the sides of the canvas seat. The old C-47 bounced around continuously at around twelve thousand feet. The pilot appeared to be looking for a gap in the weather as he needed to drop down to a lower altitude. The first leg had taken almost five hours from Jakarta to Tuban airfield.

Coleman was aghast when he saw that several of the volcanoes were actually thousands of feet taller than the maximum ceiling this old aircraft could reach. The air was thin and cold. He felt no nausea, just fear. The transport dropped again and Stephen gripped the bars on each side covered with canvas until his hands ached. He had visions of the aircraft hitting the side of one of the mountains, never to be found in the dense jungle, even if he was fortunate enough to survive such an impact! At least his nervousness had taken his mind off his travelling companion who now sat across and directly opposite, apparently not at all bothered by the inclement weather, and resulting yawing effect the heavier than air machine experienced.

He'd been surprised, and then overcome with anger when he walked into the small asbestos-walled departure room reserved normally for crews and recognized her standing there, talking to one of the crew about her baggage. His travelling companion was to be Louise.

Furious, he had dropped his own case and stormed up to her.

"What the blazes are you doing here?" he demanded not even waiting for her to finish talking to the orange suited airman.

"A simple 'hello' would suffice, Stephen," she responded stiffly.

"You're not on this flight, surely?" he asked incredulously.

"On the flight. On the mission. Yep, guess you could say that cowboy!" she answered, deliberately exaggerating a deep-southern accent.

"And in what capacity, if I may be so rude as to inquire?" his face flushed with controlled anger.

"As an observer. Courtesy of Uncle Sam and however they refer to the Indonesian Government department responsible for the farce they have the audacity to call a plebiscite."

"You're the other foreign national sent to substantiate my report of this visit?" he asked, knowing that she was going to respond in the affirmative but not wanting it to be so.

"Correct." She hesitated for just a moment before adding, "and, it would be the mature and professional thing to do if we were to establish some ground rules together now, before we depart. Don't you agree, Mister Coleman?"

Stephen glared at the woman for whom he'd once held such deep passionate feelings and was suddenly lost for words.

She was as beautiful as ever. How could you be angry with a woman who looked as good as this? he wondered.

"Okay, Louise. Or is it Miss Louise, or, considering your newly developed accent, Missy? I'd heard you'd taken up with the good doctor over in your patch but I didn't realize that he was from Georgia!"

There it was. He'd said it. It had just slipped out, his mouth faster than his brain and immediately he'd regretted the barbed innuendo regarding her social life. For a long moment they looked at each other. He thought she had smiled first and he misinterpreted the sign, stepping closer to her, almost sheepishly.

"No, Stephen. Not now, we'll talk when we're airborne."

With which, he was obliged to wait. He was curious to discover why this woman had exited his life so suddenly, so mysteriously. He now had the opportunity or would, during the tour, to confront her, alone and away from the cocktail circuit.

They had seen each other at functions. She had always avoided him and, after some months, Stephen had finally accepted that they had no future together. He had never understood what had happened. He knew that their brief affair was more than some temporary fling. At least it was to him. Stephen resented the mixed emotions he immediately experienced when she turned up as his travelling companion. Stephen recognized that he still held strong feelings for Louise. But that was now all in the past.

Life had gone on for both. He had an occasional relationship, but without developing any real feelings for the partner he'd taken at the time. On the other hand, he knew that Louise was seen regularly on the arm of one of the USAID doctors, also an American. He let it all pass and after a time believed he'd put it all behind him. And now she was here, together with him, and he felt the old familiar stabbing sensation which had plagued him before. They were now both approaching the end of their tours and he did not want her to disappear again, or at least, not without a reasonable explanation. A reason, even an excuse. Something you could give to another who had once opened the window to their soul and believed the softly whispered promises that had been made.

A sudden drop dragged his thoughts back to the present. The air turbulence persisted on throwing the Dakota around as if it were made of paper. He probed his memory to recall whether or not he may have revealed his terrible fear of flying to her during those few exciting days together. Stephen was angry with her. She just sat there reading a bloody book! He wanted to unbuckle and move across to sit alongside her but fear kept him strapped into his canvas seat.

Again the aeroplane dipped, lifted slightly then dropped bringing a silent scream to his lips. And then the plane broke through the lower cloud cover and there, off the port side, Coleman could see the white beaches and coconut palms of the Island of the Gods.

Suddenly, it was as if there had never been any threat of falling, or fear of dying. He slowly regained his composure and smiled at Louise. She was preoccupied with the landing formalities and, as this was a freighter, double checked her straps and gear.

"Good flight, hey?" he called nonchalantly over the engine noise as they banked towards the small and narrow strip with ocean at each end.

She smiled in response. "Of course, I've had worse but out of ten, this was an eight," he offered, now full of bravado as the aircraft's undercarriage shook when its tyres leaped from zero to seventy-five miles per hour within a fraction of a second, hitting the hot tarmac and screaming as rubber tore away.

"Stephen," she said sharply, leaning towards him still buckled tightly, "shut up!"

It was said without venom. He realized then he'd been obvious and that she'd known he'd been terrified the whole time. He felt foolish.

The crew wanted to refuel then continue on through the rest of the afternoon to Kupang but he was adamant. He simply refused to fly any more that day. He was already tired and needed to regain his composure after the dreadful aerobatics he had experienced for most of the past few hours. He looked to Louise for support. "What about it, shall we take a break here?" he asked as the aircraft taxied to a halt.

She appeared indifferent as she sat looking at the pale blood-drained face. "It's your tour, Stephen but, to be honest, I wouldn't mind a hot tub after that last leg."

He was relieved that she'd agreed and immediately sensed the stress flow outwards from his body. The crew acquiesced, finally agreeing that an evening's stopover in Bali wouldn't be all that bad. As it was unscheduled, and at Stephen's request, he offered to pay for the meals and accommodation for the evening. The crew willingly accepted. They pocketed the advance he proffered and then disappeared into the free messing facilities available to them as members of AURI, the Indonesian Air Force. He was too tired to squabble over a few dollars.

The airfield was practically deserted. Together they hired an old left-hand drive Plymouth Belvedere taxi and proceeded to the Hotel Bali Beach in Sanur. Settling down to the 'welcome drink' in the Baris Bar Coleman recovered from his ordeal. Later, having showered, he attended to his equipment before phoning Louise's room. There had been no answer. He was disappointed.

That evening he dined alone. Well, as alone as one can be, Stephen thought, with more than a dozen staff observing his every movement in the under-occupied four-star resort. He searched high and low but could not locate Louise anywhere. Even the reception staff could not help when he pressed them politely, inquiring if she had gone out sightseeing, or taken a stroll along the thin strip of sand which separated the hotel grounds from the onslaught of the fast moving tides of Sanur. He sat in a deck-chair beside the pool overlooking the ocean. The setting was magnificent and, he thought despondently, wasted! There were less than ten guests in the hotel. The airport had yet to be upgraded to accept wide-bodied aircraft and, consequently, only a few visitors were able to enjoy the serenity of the warm hospitable people, their culture, and unbelievable scenery.

He had returned to the Baris Bar off the foyer and was entertained by observing a colourful character, an American, dressed in Bermuda shorts working very hard to sell what looked like Indian blankets. The man ordered drinks for the bar. Five, in all counting Stephen. Then he had opened the beautifully woven cloths to demonstrate their magnificent colours. The man was an absolute salesman, Coleman acknowledged.

Within minutes the old couple from the States had succumbed to his outrageous story of how he had smuggled these priceless and rare materials from right under the nose of the headhunters in one of the outer islands. Stephen had seen the same cloth in the small back streets of Pasar Baru in Jakarta selling for around three dollars. Before permitting his fellow countrymen to know the price of these rare and unique hand-woven works of art the overweight fellow insisted that they be his guest and enjoy yet another round of martinis which, of course, the elderly and now slightly tipsy couple readily accepted. Coleman knew when not to interfere. Anyway, he was enjoying the show and it was none of his business if this strange character found it necessary to flog village cloth to unsuspecting tourists.

He attempted to buy the man a drink. Surprisingly, he refused.

"That's my limit, man, got to fly tomorrow. Taking a quick run over to Surabaja but I'll have the bird back by sixteen hundred hours if you want to try your luck then."

Coleman looked at the American.

"I'm the chief pilot for Mutiara Airlines," he announced, his speech now more slurred as the martinis supposedly took effect. "In fact, I'm the only goddammed pilot," he laughed, holding both his arms out demonstrating to the bar that he obviously knew what aircraft wings looked like. "Haven't been paid in five months. The arseholes!" Looking directly at the couple he said, "Reduced to selling bric-a-brac to pay my way. What sort of life is that for a man who flew missions all over Indochina for Air America?" the words slurred more.

"Tell you what. As you're from back home, fifty bucks will do it!" he said, rolling one of the pieces up slowly over his arm and placing it in the woman's hands.

"Are you sure?" she asked, feeling guilty that they were taking advantage of one of their own, lost in the backwaters of civilization, probably without any real food.

"Ma'am," he started, "if I charged you any more I wouldn't be able to live with myself in the morning," and turning to the Balinese barman called for the check.

"Please," the old man was out of his chair, moving towards the bar. "Please let us at least pay for the drinks?"

Coleman quietly smiled. This guy was really good!

"Sir," he replied, almost sadly," you are a gentleman, and I thank you." With which he turned to the barman and instructed him, in Bahasa Indonesia, to put all the drinks, as usual, on the tourist's check. Having been paid he then disappeared.

* * * * * *

Stephen stayed for a while longer then strolled back outside into the balmy tropical evening air. He could hear the small waves and, occasionally, spotted their white crests as they broke onto the gentle sloping beach. Removing his shoes, Stephen walked down to the water's edge, deep in thought. In the distance he could see more lights and wandered slowly towards them.

As he approached he could hear the music long before seeing the dancers. A Balinese *gong* was performing, the sharp distinctive sounds emanating from the bamboo *gamelan* accompanied by drum and metal being beaten, the orchestra piercing the serenity of the night. They were performing for themselves. Perhaps a rehearsal, he guessed.

Stephen moved in closer to the artists and watched as they carried out their intricate dances, the beautiful young girls bending, twisting their bodies, while well rehearsed movements of their fingers and eyes not only displayed incredible discipline and control but provided the onlookers with a sense of participation in this rich and vibrant culture. Occasionally, as one of the musicians tapped the *cengceng* cymbals in concert with the beat of the *rencang* Stephen believed he could almost visualize the mythical characters depicted in the *gamelan's* sounds.

He was intoxicated with the night fragrance of the frangipani flowers and totally engrossed in the scene, this private view of the village collective, the *gong*, when he was startled by a hand touching his shoulder.

Turning quickly, he saw the silhouette of her head and shoulders, the shadows partly hiding her face.

He stood transfixed.

"Shh," she said, placing a finger to his lips. "Don't spoil the moment, Stephen."

Alarm changing quickly to surprise, he felt her arm slip through his, standing quite still, as if mesmerised by the unfamiliar noises coming from the village play performance. He could feel the warmth of her hands and recognized her perfume as they stood together, fascinated by the skilled dancers carrying out their intricate routines casting a spell over the Balinese night. The tantalizing rhythm continued, captivating the two, urging them together, locked in their own magical trance as they witnessed the soft brown figures moving gracefully to the sounds and the story of the

Ramayana Epic.

He turned to her and slowly moved his mouth towards hers.

She responded.

As she raised her lips to his, their soft touch produced a flood of memories. Holding each other with a tenderness long forgotten, Stephen tasted the bitterness of their long separation. And for a long time they embraced, without talking.

"I'm so sorry, Stephen. So very, very sorry!"

Her eyes reflected the sadness she felt and, suddenly, tears trickled down her face.

He moved his hand softly over her cheek, wiping the tears away as he kissed her gently.

"What ever happened to you, Louise?" he whispered, holding her close as if she would suddenly disappear again as she had before.

"I can't," she started, and then buried her head into his shoulder,.

"I must know," he spoke softly, encouraging her to continue.

"No, Stephen," she whispered, "not tonight," and looking into his troubled eyes she promised, "we'll have enough time together, I promise. Let it be, just for tonight."

He looked deep into her eyes, trying to understand, and silently agreed.

Suddenly she turned away from the ceremony and led him back down to the beach.

They sat quietly for awhile. He wrapped his arms around her and kissed her softly, first on the eyes and then gently on her lips. She leaned back, her head resting on the white sand and he kissed her again, passionately, her response signalling her desire to continue. There, in the cool of the tropical night, accompanied only by the sounds of the sea and the mystique of a Balinese night, they made love, tender love, unlike anything he'd ever experienced before. They stayed together until morning, touching each other tenderly, caressing, and whispering endearments until the soft cool morning sea-breeze alerted them to the coming day. Together they sat on the damp sand silently admiring the beauty of the sunrise.

As the morning's first rays stole silently from below the sea into the new pale sky, dancing though the jagged peaks of Gunung Agung teasing its occasional puffs of volcanic smoke, they made their way back slowly, reluctantly, through the coconut grove. They had not spoken again of the past. But both realized they would have to do so. And soon. Louise squeezed Coleman's hand tightly as they parted without speaking, each to their unused rooms to prepare for their departure.

Full of remorse she flung herself desperately onto the bed and buried her head in the pillow.

'Damn! Damn! Damn!' she screamed into the soft thick kapok filled cushion, hitting the bed with clenched hands. 'You stupid, stupid woman!'

She admonished herself for permitting it to happen, again. Their relationship should not continue. It was not the same as when they had first met.

This time she knew!

* * * * * *

Louise's own section head had shown her the file and advised her, no, instructed her to discontinue their relationship immediately for fear of her being compromised by Coleman. This limited brief merely contained a restricted advice to all section and department heads listing other foreigners attached to the multitude of embassies and consulates throughout the country. The confidential memorandum advised that those whose names were listed in the brief were to be treated with considerable caution. It did not elaborate.

When she scoffed at the innuendo, her chief had considered her emotional involvement sufficient to speak to his own immediate superior and the following day the young Attaché was summoned to the offices of what her friends referred to as the 'shadow people'. At first it seemed that the security section wished to discuss her file and clearances again. This was not unusual, as often these were checked and updated at regular intervals as promotions flowed, and postings changed the government employee's domicile.

She had not expected her relationship with Stephen to demand the attention of these people. Louise was astonished at the Langley file copy which she been obliged to read while sitting directly under the close scrutiny of the Embassy in-house 'spook' as they were referred to by the other civilian agencies. He had asked her to sign the declaration as Louise had done on many previous occasions when viewing restricted and sensitive material. This time she was surprised to see the additional marker flags on the top and sides of the folder containing the document, designating CIA-sourced intelligence.

The first photograph showed a group of young men talking together. Innocent enough, she thought at the time. The second series of photographs was taken with a telephoto lens but the clarity was enough to identify the man dressed in combat fatigues undertaking training exercises. The description was chillingly cold and brief.

Stephen Charles Coleman. Field operative Australian Security and Intelligence Forces. Active agent. Refer all CIA coded reference Top Secret 23519-68.

She listened quietly as the officer ordered her to discontinue the relationship; however, he suggested, his people would have no objections should she see Coleman casually, preferably in the company of others, as they understood that chance meetings both socially and professionally were almost unavoidable; such situations should be handled sensibly. Louise was then asked to confirm that she would accept the instructions given. The veiled threat was apparent.

Had she refused then there was no doubt in her mind that the following day someone else would be handling her official chores while she winged her way back home to the good old US of A!

She had no real choice. For days she suffered periods of depression and was bitterly distressed at not being able to explain to Stephen why they could not continue their relationship. Oh yes, she remembered, saddened by the memories, they had seen each other from time to time, at parties and receptions, but they never talked.

Louise could remember the cold look of bitterness she'd seen on Stephen's face during the first encounter, some months after she'd ceased accepting his calls. She had dated other men and had even started to see a colleague, an USAID volunteer doctor, regularly, but there just wasn't the same electricity she'd felt with Stephen and she ceased going out with him as well. At the time she felt that Stephen understood the reason for her behaviour and often wondered why he had given up so easily. She was a mature person for her age. Even as a teenager she did not accept that people could just fall in love, that quickly, so suddenly. And yet it had happened to her and Stephen!

She sat cross-legged, her favourite position when alone, her head resting thoughtfully on the palms of her hands. An hour passed. And how could she tell him that she knew? Another hour ticked away slowly.

She made her decision.

Distressed by what she was about to do but certain that there was no alternative, Louise asked the hotel operator to place a call on her behalf to Jakarta. Twenty minutes later she slowly placed the handset back in its cradle. Louise continued to sit, staring at the cream-coloured receiver. She wiped the tears away, angrily, as they blurred her vision as she started to write the message. She now knew she had made an error in judgment phoning her departmental head at his villa in Jakarta.

"Are you mad, Louise?" he had yelled down the line at her. "Even if you resign then there is no guarantee that you know who won't have your pretty little butt out of there so goddamm fast your head will still be spinning when your feet hit the ground in Washington."

He had been furious and, although guarded when discussing her situation on the open line, he still managed to convince her. His instructions had been explicit.

She really had no choice but to obey.

* * * * * *

Stephen waited in the foyer for thirty minutes. She had missed breakfast in the Barong Coffee Shop and he was becoming impatient. He phoned her room but there was no reply. Again he questioned the reception staff and they assured him that Miss Louise had not yet checked out of the hotel. He rode the lift to the seventh floor and moved quickly to her door, knocking several times, without any response. He returned to the reception and demanded that they open her door to see if she was all right, concerned that perhaps she had taken a fall in the bathroom and needed urgent assistance.

Embarrassed, a young girl dressed in the traditional *kain kebaya*, seeing the concern in his eyes, handed Stephen an envelope. He tore it open immediately, already experiencing a sensation as he read the hand written note. Louise had decided not to continue the journey to Irian. She could not give him a reason, at this time, but would when he returned to Jakarta, that is, of course, if he could forgive her for not remaining with him for the remainder of the tour.

He couldn't believe it!

As he finished reading the brief note he noticed that most of the lobby and reception staff had been observing his reaction to the letter. Stephen was not to know that they genuinely felt saddened for him, as the entire staff had known the beautiful romantic story of their interlude on the beach, the evening before. There were no secrets on this island.

When a woman refused to meet face to face with her lover, sending a letter instead, it was always bad news.

They felt *sedih* for Stephen but their pragmatic oriental minds knew, and both the young men and female employees agreed that, as he was also young and handsome, his disappointment should not last too long.

Several of the young ladies smiled even harder, as he settled his account. Stephen ignored their kindness, engrossed in his own unfortunate affairs. Anger now displacing disappointment, he didn't answer the note, departing brusquely, almost rudely. As he believed that her refusal to continue with the journey could also affect the outcome of his own observations, Coleman permitted this aspect of her decision to distort the magnitude of her unexpected change of heart. Moody and almost belligerent, he checked out of the hotel and was driven off in the same antiquated American car as the day before.

He cursed the driver as they plunged off the narrow roads twice. It was strange for Stephen to be sitting behind a driver who steered the oversized sedan along the small partially bitumenised tracks sitting on the opposite side to what he was accustomed to. Many of these old vehicles had been brought back by former diplomats who never concerned themselves with moving the steering position to its correct side. The perilous ride helped distract his attention away from his disappointment. After nearly hitting a Brahman bull and killing several unlucky chickens, Stephen finally arrived at the airfield, just before nine o'clock.

The crew were all sitting around waiting for him. Unsmiling and resisting the temptation to unleash his foul mood on others, he mumbled the basic courtesies as he threw his baggage up before him into the old aircraft.

The crew acknowledged Coleman with a polite *selamat pagi* and quickly boarded the freighter.

Fifteen minutes later they were grinding along at eleven thousand feet. There were no clouds. Coleman was relieved. He spent most of the flight time thinking about the previous evening and, conscious of her absence, occasionally looked across to the empty seat.

He shook his head in disappointment.

It was almost as if their meeting on the beach had not happened.

A dream even.

Strange, he thought, she had just about convinced him of her sincerity and now she was gone again. Just like before. Stephen suddenly realized that he really didn't know Louise at all. The longer he thought about it the more confused he became. When two people hit it off the way they first had you would expect them to know more about each other. He tried to recall their conversations and could not remember ever discussing their families, their work or any intimate detail about each other's lives. He wasn't even sure what she did in the aid section of the American Embassy as they really hadn't had the time to discuss these things. Maybe he should have encouraged her to discuss her job, her work, and her friends.

He considered these passing thoughts and decided that had he engaged Louise in such conversations then she too may have asked the same questions of him. And he would have had difficulty with that. Not that Coleman was unsure of his work, it was the constant deceit he had difficulty with. Had Louise asked he knew he could never reveal his true function in the Embassy, covering the truth with easily practised lies. He had never been comfortable lying to close friends about the nature of his employment. Suffice to say, he was a competent journalist and carried out the responsibilities of the Information Section with considerable energy. It was the other, more secretive responsibilities that often gnawed away at his conscience. It seemed obvious, he thought, that a permanent relationship would be near impossible anyway, considering the constraints of his covert activities which, he suddenly admitted, kept him fully committed to his masters.

His mind drifted back to the previous night's love making and he smiled. She had said in her note that it was an evening she would never forget and hoped that he wouldn't either as it had been so very special to her. Yes, he agreed, permitting images of their bodies pumping urgently together in unison on the beach to occupy his mind, distracting him from the aircraft's movements. It had certainly been a special night! Alone, the only passenger, and for the first time since he could remember, Stephen slept undisturbed whilst in flight.

* * * * * *

The aircraft droned on. And on. Finally, they arrived in Kupang, refuelled then continued on to Ambon. Having enjoyed the last sector, Stephen now felt slightly more comfortable with the knowledge that he was still faced with a substantial distance left to cover by air. During the break he sat away from the nauseating aviation gasoline fumes as several ground staff hand pumped the load from two hundred-litre drums. It seemed to take forever and yet, during the time required for the refuelling, their conversation was inconsequential, the exchanges stiff and awkward.

After the next leg of their journey they rested for a day and, to Coleman's surprise, changed crews. The following two days saw the aircraft forced down onto an unkempt, unsealed, World War Two runway with engine problems. They had picked up contaminated Avgas during the last refuelling stop. The Captain radioed ahead requesting assistance as he decided against flying with the possibility of ongoing fuel problems. When help finally arrived, it was in the form of a fishing boat dispatched from a coastal village nearby. The seas were unseasonably rough and Coleman stoically faced the turbulent conditions. Towards the end of the first day he was horrified to discover that the wind had increased its intensity, the waves smashing over the ship's bow as the crew fought for control.

Then the Australian suffered the humiliation of seasickness. His body ached all over from the constant heaving. His rib cage felt bruised and his throat was tender. He prayed that the vessel would soon arrive at its destination. He did not believe that he could survive another few hours of the waves' pounding motion. The boat rocked from side to side almost in a corkscrew motion. One moment the bow would lift high into the air and the next it would go crashing down amongst the waves, dipping below the horizon forcing the bile to erupt as he struggled to control his stomach. The vessel was battered for two days by the severe conditions. Exhausted, he crawled into the foetal position and collapsed, his body tossed around the deck oblivious to the pain as his limbs were bruised and cut by the hardened timber.

A solitary figure viewed the limp body with disgust. He made no attempt to assist or relieve the young man's discomfort. He merely watched to ensure the foreigner did not die, at least not here, as it would not fit the plan he had been given. He spat over the side and continued to observe Coleman as he lay, curled up, occasionally moaning in his fatigue induced sleep. *'Pity we couldn't just dump him over the side here!'* the man considered, *'would be safer and not as complicated!'*

The dark Javanese considered his current mission. He had received his instructions directly from the General. He always did. No one else could be trusted with the tasks he carried out for the Timorese. He was provided with more than sufficient funds to carry out his orders. He discovered that, if he was careful, he could retain a considerable portion of these monies and did so, turning the cash into gold and burying the proceeds. Not that he needed money. He had no life other than that ordered by Seda. He merely obeyed. This was just another mission which he would complete and then report back to the General.

He started forward to grab the sick passenger who was in danger of falling overboard. The Australian somehow unconsciously managed to avoid this catastrophe and, satisfied that he was out of danger, the observer stepped away from the ship's rails. As the seas grew calm and the wind softened Stephen slept. The old fishing boat chugged along until reaching their destination late in the afternoon of their third day. The crew laughed quietly at the prostrate figure lying on the deck. They secured their fishing boat.

Some villagers were called and the foreigner was carried into the *lurah's* hut. As headman, he would be responsible should the stranger come to harm. There Stephen was examined by one of the women then left to sleep through the night. He awoke several times, thirsty, and was given water after which he drifted back into an exhausted sleep. The following morning he was awakened by the sounds of the village coming to life. He bathed and went in search of a familiar face as he had no appreciation of his whereabouts. He was advised that the crew had returned and that the village *lurah* was to escort him to the military post some twenty kilometres by road.

Upon checking his belongings, Coleman discovered that everything was intact. He was given food and then asked to accompany the village head to the next destination. Transport had been organized and he was relieved to see that the rest of his journey would be over dry land.

* * * * * *

Towards noon, the jeep bumped along the track leading into the army post. As they moved into the clearing where the soldiers had established their base camp, Stephen estimated that there were about two hundred men stationed there. They were fully equipped. This, obviously, was not a training camp, and the look on the men's faces reminded him of the Blitar operation. He could tell that they had already experienced action. There were no smiles for the visitor, in fact, their arrival was almost ignored. A solid framed Javanese Major received them in his hut. "*Selamat datang,*" he welcomed them.

Formalities completed, the officer advised him that he had been in radio contact with his headquarters and informed Coleman that he would take him on an inspection of several tribal areas where patrols had encountered surprisingly hostile and well-armed groups of what he termed terrorists. They discussed the mission. He was shown a map of the target areas and was advised regarding procedures to be taken should they encounter hostile forces.

Coleman was instructed not under any circumstances was he to wear anything resembling a uniform as, they agreed, it would be unlikely that he would be targeted if the enemy identified him for what he actually was: a non-military observer. Hopefully, he would be mistaken for a United Nations representative although, to date, there had been none venture this far into the hinterland. The following day, accompanied by the Major, Stephen departed for the first contact zone. The object was to demonstrate to him from a distance, if possible, the considerable military hardware that these isolated tribes had been armed with, and had learned to use with a reasonable amount of success.

The small convoy progressed slowly. The drivers of both trucks engaged the four-wheel drive mode as the tracks were wet and slippery. Stephen estimated that they had travelled approximately forty miles before they rested. It was difficult going. They had commenced with fifty soldiers and, when they stopped the Major instructed a corporal and five others to stay behind with the vehicles as the remaining distance could only be covered on foot. Almost within minutes the landscape changed, from light undergrowth to bush, and then into jungle. Nettles stung Coleman's face, neck and hands while thorns tore at his clothing. The mosquitoes were unbearable!

He was wearing jeans, boots and an old light weight jacket which zipped all the way through. Anticipating identification problems Stephen had selected this particular apparel as it was bright orange in colour and was unmistakably non-military clothing. He did not wish to be shot by accident and hoped that these precautions would be sufficient to guarantee his safety.

They continued pushing along small tracks which the Australian assumed were recent as the foliage on both sides had been freshly cut back to permit the contingent passage. The ground was covered with leaves and grass indicating that these paths had been in frequent use. They walked in single file. Coleman had not yet removed his camera from its protective cover. He needed both free hands just to maintain his balance.

It started to rain. The Major beckoned for Stephen to keep pace a little closer to the soldiers in front, as he was falling behind. He obeyed. They progressed a few kilometres then rested again. The Major indicated that in another hour they would camp. The thought had not entered Stephen's head. Camp! Out here? He groaned with the thought of spending a night in the jungle being bitten by every insect known to man and the possibility of the tribes people slipping into their camp and removing a few heads, as they had been known to do!

These primitive people had accounted for many a famous explorer in the past. Coleman tried to remember if this was where the young Rockefeller was murdered.

* * * * * *

When the time arrived, the soldiers moved swiftly establishing their perimeter defence, and protection from the never ending rain. Coleman crawled into the small area which offered some respite from the elements. He was tired and felt that every muscle and joint in his body was calling out for him not to continue with the trek. Aching all over he tried to rest as best he could. They handed out *dendeng*, their version of beef jerky.

Coleman ate what he could. The *dendeng* was tasty but he had no appetite. Instead, following the soldiers actions, he rested, saving his strength for the following day. He slept. It seemed that he had only just closed his eyes when he felt the rough hands on his shoulder. The young Lieutenant was shaking him.

"*Tuan, tuan, bangun,*" he called, waking the foreigner. Startled, Stephen jumped to his feet and immediately felt the rigours of sleeping in the jungle. He attended to his ablutionary needs and finished the remaining dried beef.

They marched on for two hours until the tension began to grow amongst the men. Coleman noticed the change and decided that they were obviously approaching some known point of danger. He could almost feel the absence of wildlife. He remembered that only a short distance back the jungle was alive with sounds as the birds and other animals called to each other, warning of the possible dangers brought by man's presence. Suddenly they stopped. The point man waved silently to them, indicating that they should crouch and remain silent. They had arrived at the top of a rise and the Major beckoned for Coleman to follow him quietly. He did so, half crouched, half crawling, being guided by the experienced veteran.

They had left the main body of their troop some seventy metres behind. Coleman was instructed to copy the officer's movements. He lay beside the Major, accepting the field glassed offered to him.

"*What am I looking for?*" he asked.

The officer indicated a clearing below and roughly one-hundred metres away from their position. There was a group of perhaps twelve to fifteen men dressed in a mixture of khaki and tribal dress. They were armed. Coleman removed his camera and adjusted the telephoto lens. He shot the roll of twenty-four exposures, replaced the film and returned the camera to its case.

"*Okay, Pak, let's get the hell out of here,*" he pleaded.

The officer smiled, shook his head, gestured for the civilian to remain where he was and waved for the Lieutenant to advance.

"*You're not going to engage these men down there, Major?*" Stephen asked in disbelief knowing in his heart that this soldier was surely going to do just that!

"*Mas, kamu diam disini sajalah,*" he ordered, instructing him to remain there in a tone that Coleman could not argue against.

"Shit!" he muttered, surprised that he was, within minutes, to witness an attack on the guerrilla group he could practically touch from where he lay.

Minutes passed. The Commander had left two men with Coleman. The remainder followed him down the slope, crawling, until they had reached the point the Major had determined.

Suddenly, the air erupted with the ear shattering sounds of rapid fire. Bullets seemed to pass frighteningly close as he heard the air rupture when the small missiles passed by. Stephen wanted to bury his head in safety but was captured by the fire fight, observing the men running down towards their target, firing from the hip as they descended into the enemy's camp. The engagement continued for what seemed an eternity. Coleman lay as still as he could hoping it would all be over quickly. But it wasn't.

The attack continued for at least fifteen minutes, followed by sporadic fire. Angry voices could then be heard. These were followed by more shots and then the jungle became quiet, only the smell of the fierce exchange remaining. An hour passed. The soldiers accompanying the Australian directed him to follow their lead which he did, descending down the slope in a half-crouched position.

He was reminded of his early childhood, when Guy Fawkes celebrations were still permitted. On November the fifth, bonfires burned throughout the night. For days before and after, firecrackers could be heard exploding and the air held the same acrid pall of gunpowder smoke. Cautiously, he followed the soldiers.

Suddenly, he noticed a body. Then another.

Coleman was stunned. These were Indonesians! He had, for some reason, not anticipated any of his own group being injured, let alone killed! He was taken to the centre of the clearing. The

Major was sitting close by, resting up against the trunk of a tree. He started to move towards the man, at the same time calling to the officer.

"*Pak Major,*" he began but did not complete the sentence as the young Lieutenant grasped his arm and turned him away. Bewildered, Coleman brushed the hand aside and once again addressed the Major.

"*Tuan,*" the Lieutenant called softly, "*tuan, dia sudah mati!*"

Stephen stared at the Major unwilling to accept what the Lieutenant had said. He approached the silent figure and looked more closely, moving around to face the now lifeless body of the Commander. Coleman stood in shock, unable to move. The bullet had struck the Major's head around the left eye socket, tearing through the flesh, ripping bone and muscle away then exploding through the back of his crown.

His legs weakened. He had to sit down.

The Lieutenant moved quickly, assisted by the more experienced Sergeant, clearing the area and reorganizing his new Command. "*Tuan, bangun, cepat,*" the officer ordered, instructing the Australian to get up quickly. Another soldier assisted him to his feet.

The Lieutenant barked out commands and the survivors regrouped. Carrying their fallen comrades' weapons, they departed the battle scene leaving the bodies where they fell.

* * * * * *

As they retreated up the slope they were observed closely. The shooter replaced the binoculars and lifted the high powered snipers rifle. He checked the PSO-1 scope to make sure that it was exactly in the condition required for the remaining and more difficult shots he'd have to make.

The weapon was a Soviet SVD, weighing only four and one half kilos and had a muzzle velocity of two thousand seven-hundred and twenty feet per second. The killer enjoyed this weapon more so than its American counterpart, as the Soviet sniper's rifle had the advantage of being considerably lighter to carry. And over these distances and terrain, that was a major factor when determining which weapon to use, especially considering that both the American and Soviet versions were practically identical in all other aspects.

The weapon felt like an extension of himself as he settled the rifle comfortably into the shoulder, resting his right cheek against the stock as his left eye peered across at the magnified images. He was pleased with the accuracy of the earlier shot which dropped the Major. It wasn't necessary but he justified the killing for the additional confusion it had created.

He adjusted the telescopic sights marginally. Aiming at the figure towards the front of the line retreating back up the hill, he compensated for the angle of the shot, the differences in height, then took a bead on the centre of the man's back.

'The power of the small missile will tear the target's heart out through the front of his chest,' the sniper speculated.

Gently he squeezed the trigger and the bullet leaped from the weapon hitting its target even before the sound of the shot could be heard. The startled Lieutenant turned and, as Stephen started to crumple, immediately recognized what had happened. Assisted by the other soldiers, he dragged the young Australian's body away from the line of fire.

* * * * * *

Umar Suharjo was satisfied with his second kill. But he was annoyed that the third target had not appeared. *You can't kill someone if they're not there!* he thought, his mind racing as he knew that the General would be displeased that he hadn't also executed the American woman. He searched the field of view until he was convinced that none of the soldiers had established his position. He scanned the scene one last time to be absolutely certain then turned and crawled back into the thick undergrowth. He stashed the weapon under the trees, covering it with a thick mound of decaying leaves.

And, with the expertise of the silent killer, he quietly slipped away, unnoticed, and made his way back to the coast where the pre-arranged vessel took him aboard, for Jakarta.

And Seda.

* * * * * *

Louise had stood outside the hotel. Why hasn't he left, already? She'd waited for Stephen to emerge from the Bali Beach and finally, she saw him stride out purposely, almost angrily, and slam the door of the old battered sedan. The staff had done as she had asked. By now he would have read her letter. And no doubt, hated her for her what she'd done. Again! Louise watched Stephen driven away in the old sedan, and out of her life, forever. She waited several minutes then returned to the reception where her luggage had been placed behind the cashier's door. The staff smiled at her, thanked the young lady for her generous tip, and watched her depart with the *gendut*, overweight American pilot whom they despised. She'd little choice but to take the Mutiara flight as Garuda Airlines had nothing going out that day.

The pilot had changed his scheduled flight to Surabaya to accommodate her, agreeing to fly directly to Jakarta and return via Surabaya instead of the other way around. It really made little difference to him anyway, he'd said, and so Louise had decided to fly with her fellow American.

As they approached Tuban airfield she felt relieved to see that Stephen's flight had departed. Louise searched the horizon for the aircraft unsuccessfully. Her driver passed through the unguarded gates leading into what would have been a restricted area in other airports in many parts of the world, and drove directly up to the only plane parked on the small concrete surface outside the hangers.

Several men working around the port side ceased what they were doing and assisted the American woman with her baggage. She boarded the twin-engined C-47, the same vintage as the aircraft she had taken just the day before, knowing from its appearance that this machine had not been maintained as well as she had hoped. There were crates of tools and other mechanical items stored slightly forward in the cabin. These had not been strapped down and, judging from the condition of the rest of the aircraft, Louise thought that it was unlikely there were even any straps available to secure the heavy boxes. Grease remained smeared along sections where recent maintenance work seemed to have been carried out, and she had to be careful not to brush against these areas when taking her seat.

There was some activity around the tarmac area and Louise could see two men sauntering casually across in the direction of the plane. She recognized the American and assumed, correctly, that the other man was part of their crew. Both boarded and went forward to the cabin, mumbling as they dragged themselves into their cockpit seats, acknowledging her presence with merely a cursory nod.

Louise didn't have much of an opportunity to see their faces, particularly their bloodshot eyes, as they had half stumbled past her as she sat already strapped into the flimsy seat; but if she had, there is little doubt that the aircraft would still have enjoyed her company for the remainder of the trip.

Jack was in a mean mood. His head was thumping from the late night and his co-pilot, one of the few Indonesian men who drank hard liquor, was not feeling too much better for the same reason. First one engine was fired up and then, within a minute or so, the other coughed to life; as the decibels affronted her hearing, the high screaming mechanical pitch causing Louise to cover her ears. The old aircraft wobbled around as it taxied out from the hard-standing area in front of the maintenance building, as if it were trying, or testing its wings.

Suddenly she wished she'd not phoned Jakarta and followed her heart instead of her mind! The aircraft stopped momentarily, the engine revolutions reaching an almost unbearable pitch, before it suddenly lurched forward and commenced its attempt to breach gravity.

No sooner were they airborne when the unshaven pilot unlatched the cockpit door and left the controls to his Indonesian co pilot. He stumbled back into the mixed cabin and cargo area, lurching around until he located the small and dirty overnight Pan Am bag which had dislodged itself during takeoff. He pulled an aluminium flask from the side pocket, unscrewed the cap, put it to his mouth and took a generous swig of the contents. The pilot then looked back at Louise. She could see that he was unshaven. His puffed face and eyes were of immediate concern to her, and she was about to ask if he was well enough for the flight when he belched loudly.

"God damn, I really hate flying!" he laughed, sucking at the container for a second time. "Would you like a hair of the dog?" he asked, not really expecting his only passenger to accept.

Louise eyed him coolly. She was concerned. "Sure," she replied, unexpectedly.

The surprised pilot passed the flask to the young woman, eyeing her now more closely. "Don't drink it all," he suggested, "it's a four-hour haul to the next one."

'God,' she thought, 'four hours to Jakarta with this cretin!'

She sipped once, smiled and extended the flask, deliberately permitting the bourbon to fall to the deck.

"Christ!" he snapped, lunging forward to retrieve the hip flask.

Jack managed to salvage a little of the contents. He eyed her coolly and thought, 'bitch,' as he returned to the cockpit, fuming. "Just what we don't need right now, a smart-arsed woman on board," he called to the other man as he levered himself back into the port side seat while using his co-pilot's shoulder for support.

Had she witnessed this man's clever act of the previous night then she may not have been as concerned, assuming the drinking was part of a routine the former civilian war pilot played out for his guests. But she hadn't, and this was no act, as the man always drank when flying. He'd developed the perilous habit along with many of his flying buddies in 'Nam. On occasions he'd been known to drape a pet carpet snake around his shoulders when on the flight deck, but unbeknown to him, the other pilots at Mutiara had willingly disposed of it, under instructions from management. The man had a vicious streak and all were subject to his mean temperament when he drank.

Alcoholic haze and reality have no place together in the cockpit of any aircraft, and this flight was no exception. Considering the added aggravation of the incident involving the alcohol, Louise was concerned but not frightened, as she knew there was another pilot sitting forward, obviously competent, as Jack the blanket-seller had permitted the other flyer to take the controls while he went in search of an instant remedy for his hangover.

The aircraft droned along for an hour. Jack was, by now, well down the path of one of his fantasies which had, some eighteen months before, resulted in his contract not being renewed in Indochina. He'd not been lying when he boasted of his previous employers and his unusual background.

Jack had, in fact, flown for Air America for some time but suffered burn-out and was terminated before he killed someone. He'd managed to park two aircraft in unusual positions hard against the side of hills which, fortunately for him but not his other crew, were covered with thick vegetation at the time. Although the majority of the pilots were similar to Jack in nature, often taking uncalled for risks endangering their lives in the pursuit of the hefty pay packets these hazardous missions demanded, he was considered over the top with his weird antics as he scared the hell out of even the less stable flyers in the group.

After the second crash nobody would fly with him any more. He'd taken his pay and headed for Guam but, somehow, ended up in Bali with a job, flying the three former Australian C - 47s which, when they first took delivery, had almost zero engine hour time and full airframe clearance. The former owners had even added disc-brakes to the aircraft which were in almost perfect shape for these tropical conditions and would remain so, providing they were carefully maintained.

Now, suffering continuous neglect, these machines, once admired in aviation circles for their safety, had become very dangerous and should not have been cleared to fly. Two of the three planes had already been stripped for their parts, leaving the small feeder-service unable to maintain schedules and, more importantly to Jack, also unable to pay crew and ground staff salaries which had fallen seriously into arrears.

He drank here because that's how he'd flown in 'Nam, Cambodia and hell, even Laos when he dropped in there with a load of weapons to pick up the white powder from the pudgy little General who always paid for his deliveries in that way. There was never any difficulty in finding a buyer for the heroin although he drew the line at taking any himself. An occasional puff on the ganja sticks was okay, he thought, but that white powder, it would make your brains rot like shit! And besides, he could probably drink a fifth of Bourbon on every leg and not miss a marker, he often boasted.

* * * * * *

He recognized the familiar coastline of Java over the city of Semarang. In the distance he couldn't help but identify the incredible slopes of Gunung Semeru, its smoking peak reaching over twelve thousand feet into the sky, dominating the world around it, sometimes spewing sulphurous clouds over low-lying villages or hurling thousand of tonnes of volcanic rock and ash over all it viewed.

Air becomes very thin around twelve thousand feet and this aircraft type was not designed to climb much above that ceiling. Jack decided to take the smart-arsed lady on a detour to show her some of his skills. He corrected the course slightly changing the new heading in line with the volcano and winked at his fellow crewman.

"We'll have a quick look," he laughed, pointing his thumb back in the direction of the rear.

His co-pilot just nodded, all too familiar with Jack's flying antics. He peered ahead and identified the backdrop of cu-nimbulus and muttered to himself knowing that the sensible thing to do would be to avoid these instead of playing around with the mighty clouds. The American smiled as he returned to the rear section of the plane, this time opening what appeared to be a tool box, but in fact contained yet another bottle of his favourite bourbon. Jack had never wondered why it was that he drank so little when on the ground but consumed such incredible amounts when airborne! He tore the cover off, unscrewed the top, and lifted the bottle to his mouth.

Louise understood the macho play and smiled at him when he'd finished taking the equivalent of two or three direct shots from the bottle. She returned to her book, electing to ignore him, not showing her concern which had grown considerably, as now Louise had really become worried by his behaviour.

He took another long swallow, and then moved forward to take over the controls.

'Bitch!' he said again, silently to himself.

Another half hour passed and the mountain was directly up ahead in their flight path. The alcohol now stimulating his brain, Jack commenced his tour around the active volcano, moving the stick across, placing the slopes seemingly within grasping distance. He was determined to either impress the young good-looking babe in the back or at least demonstrate his flying skills even with the bourbon under his belt.

'Who knows?' he thought, maybe I'll get lucky tonight!

He corrected the plane's altitude, increasing its climb and moved the compass bearing for a new heading to the port side of the huge mountain. He intended to position the machine up as close to the summit as possible for a look-see into the crater if he could find a hole in the low weather which partly covered the peak. But even his clouded brain acknowledged the aircraft's altitude limitations.

Fifteen minutes later Louise felt the change in the aircraft's attitude, as it started to jump around suddenly, startling her. She looked out the starboard window quickly and was surprised to see the magnificent mountain slopes covered with trees seemingly scratching at the heavens, their tall trunks piercing through the rich undergrowth in search of more light, their crowns a mass of thickly leafed foliage offering haven to the numerous families of birds nestled there.

The scenery was incredibly beautiful. And disturbingly close!

The mountain seemed to disappear above her, far up to the right of the aircraft, the upper slopes now smothered in a blanket of cloud. There were no people or villages to be seen. It was as if the green walls of this enormous geological structure had forbidden man to enter, protecting its secrets under a veil of soft cloud and dense jungle. She was in quiet awe as the aircraft continued to encircle the mid-slopes of the mountain, staring at the jungle below as it smothered the lower view, offering its protection to the life forms which survived in the strange environment.

"Well, what do you think of that ma'am?" the voice interrupting her thoughts.

"It's stunning," she acknowledged

"Thought you'd enjoy the detour," he laughed, holding the now refilled flask towards her.

"No, thanks." Louise refused quickly.

"It's okay. Got the boy up the front taking care of things there."

He stumbled and fell as the aircraft dipped suddenly. "Goddamm!" he cried out as his knee came directly into contact with the leading edge of a case of tools tied down near where he was standing.

The aircraft dipped again, as the unusual air currents played with the intruder. Within moments they were engulfed by cloud. They had zero visibility. The co-pilot over-corrected as the starboard wing dipped.

And then it happened.

As the plane hit the treetops with incredible velocity, the fuselage disintegrated and the wings sheared off. The aircraft exploded into unrecognizable twisted fragments, and pieces of wreckage fell to the forest floor below.

Jack and his co-pilot didn't even feel the impact. The unbelievable force ripped them apart, taking their lives before their startled brains could acknowledge the fact that they were going to die.

Louise also died instantly. Her remains and those of the crew scattered onto the treetops and then down to the forest's floor.

Within minutes of the tragedy, quiet returned to the mountain and the jungle which covered its slopes. It was as if the accident had not happened and there was really nothing much there to indicate that it had. Pieces of the disaster blended immediately into the landscape, undetectable from the air as the disturbed birds returned to their nests high among the very same treetops which had stolen three lives just moments before. The C-47 had been well off course and the SAR parties would never consider looking there for the lost aircraft.

Not on the slopes of this volcano.

THE TIMOR MAN

Book Two

1975

The Timor Invasion

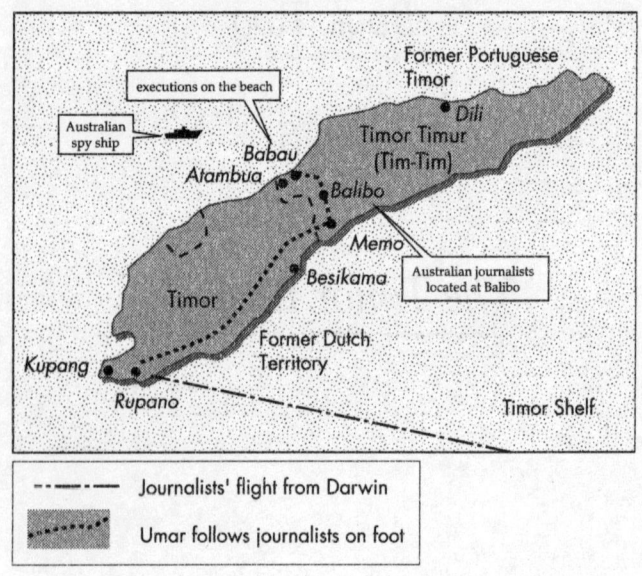

Chapter 8

Canberra — Jakarta

Canberra's winter ambiance suited this city of public servants perfectly. The Capital virtually went to sleep as the severe cold atrophied all resemblance of outdoor social activities other than those associated with Winter sports. The social set which normally thrived on cocktail parties, political functions and royal visits suddenly became subdued as if some local ordinance had abolished all revelry. Government offices closed at five and were, for the most part, deserted by six. Skies remained overcast, further reflecting the depressed social - political atmosphere.

* * * * * *

John Anderson glanced at his watch. He had arranged one last appointment for the day after which, he would escape to Sydney for the weekend.

When his secretary announced his guest's arrival Anderson smiled remembering that Coleman had always been punctual.

The visitor was ushered in, provided with coffee and then left alone with the well-groomed intelligence chief. They sat quietly for a few moments sipping the hot but tasteless liquid.

"Well, this is it then, you're really off tomorrow?" the older man asked, more as a statement than a question.

"Yes. It's definite," was the response and then, "it's time. . . " the words were left hanging.

"Remember our last discussion?" Anderson started, "whatever you need. . . "

"Thanks. I appreciate the offer," the visitor interrupted.

"When will you return?"

181

"A week, a month," he answered almost listlessly. "Maybe I will take the full three months and put my feet up on a beach somewhere," he answered.

When Coleman had requested the extended break, citing accumulated leave from his former department, the general consensus was that he should go, although his superiors were not keen on having him return to Indonesia. There was also the consideration of his not having the comfort and, more importantly, the protection of a diplomatic passport as he was no longer accredited to the Embassy.

As far as the public was aware, Stephen Coleman worked with the Australian External Affairs Department's Information Service in Canberra as a desk officer.

Recently there had been a major reorganization of the Australian Intelligence Organizations, including the military within which resulted in the ANIB no longer being used for overseas under-cover operatives. This had the effect of eliminating the requirement of the 'double-desk' subterfuge used during Stephen's tour, as current Information Officers in the embassies were not associated in any way, nor were they aware of the existence of any such covert activity.

John Anderson uncrossed his arms. "We accept that you may need this leave. We don't necessarily agree that returning at this time to Indonesia would be the correct choice of destinations under the circumstances. "

"There is no hidden agenda," Stephen had insisted.

"Even so," Anderson continued, "there is no reason for you to insist on that country for your break. Why not visit Thailand or even the Philippines, Stephen?"

"I wish to take a couple of months and wander around the place as a civilian for a change. Before it was different. I never really had any opportunity to relax and develop a genuine feel for the country. I need this trip John, although I do understand your reluctance in approving my itinerary. "

"If you take the full three months, just spread your time around," he advised. "Visit Malaysia or one of the other countries I've suggested and that will assist you to develop a more objective perspective of your life after what happened to you in Irian. "

"Then you approve?"

The older man had actively discouraged Coleman's revisiting Indonesia. If not for any other reason there was the consideration of his recently upgraded and highly sensitive security clearance. This alone demanded approval for any overseas travel by him as Director.

"No," Anderson insisted, "I agree. There is a subtle difference as you well know."

"Thank you, sir, " Stephen had said, in deference to the man and to reflect his gratitude for the approval.

"No more than three months, Stephen, just three months. Agreed?"

The younger man smiled. "Sure John. Just three months. " The extended break would be more than adequate for him to determine what he really wanted out of the rest of his life. He hoped to take the opportunity to decide once and for all whether he really wanted to continue in his present occupation and, if not, to examine his alternatives.

"Keep us posted. "

"I will," he promised, rising to his feet with his hand outstretched.

"Good luck, Stephen," the older man stressed warmly, taking Coleman's grip and squeezing it tightly.

His visitor nodded, smiled and departed with a casual wave born out of familiarity. He closed the Director's door behind him.

The Intelligence Chief leaned back into his chair, considering Coleman. He'd known, of course, that his protege had filed an application for a visa with the Indonesian Embassy weeks before informing anyone of his intentions. Anderson shook his head slowly and smiled to himself as he heard Stephen's voice.

"Bye, Madge," Stephen called softly, smiling as he departed.

Anderson's secretary watched the clean-cut, handsome and well spoken operative leave. She sighed. The senior secretary continued to look even after he had gone, deep in thought and then, remembering the stack of unfinished correspondence on her desk turned her thoughts back to the job at hand.

* * * * * *

The QANTAS Boeing 707's powerful engines thrust the aircraft along the runway until the nose lifted and the under-carriage could be heard retracting to the in-flight position. The Sydney-Jakarta flight time was eight hours, more than Stephen Coleman cared to spend in an aircraft but, at this time in his life, his fear of flying was of lessser import than it had been before.

He settled back in the comfortable first class seat, a courtesy upgrade arranged by 'Madge the Magnificent' as Anderson's secretary was often referred to by those who knew her well. Stephen accepted a glass of Moet Chandon then removed his shoes immediately sensing the tension dissipate.

He smiled inwardly at being relaxed aboard an aircraft. Life and attitudes had drastically changed, he contemplated as the four-engined jet climbed comfortably away to the deep hum of the four Rolls Royce engines. Sipping the champagne, Stephen's mind wandered back over the last time he was in Indonesia, the artificial friends he had acquired and, of course, that near fatal expedition into Irian.

* * * * * *

Stephen never did understand how he had survived the shooting. The bullet, having struck the soldier's arm first had been deflected upwards ripping into Stephen's right shoulder. He now realized that the corporal who was assisting him at that precise moment had inadvertently saved his life. His recollection of the medical evacuation and the first few days of hospitalization were vague. He did, however, remember the pain. The military team had been poorly equipped to handle extreme medical emergencies.

There had been no morphine or any other pain killers. He had awoken to the searing, burning agony time and time again, repeatedly collapsing back into oblivion. His left hand moved unconsciously to the wound; it had become habit. Long hours of physiotherapy had helped repair the muscular damage but in his nightmares he still saw the grotesque remains of the Commander's head transformed by the assassin's bullet. His shoulder would never be the same again, of course, but this was not evident in his stance.

As Stephen underwent physiotherapy under the watchful eyes of the nurses he had to struggle to meet the demands placed on damaged muscles and tissue. He knew that there really was no choice but to accept the discipline required for recovery. The exercises were difficult and tedious.

His mental well-being also required attention. Though there was no therapy that could help with the loneliness and sleepless nights, Stephen managed to cope with his memories. He was given the opportunity to rebuild his life, an opportunity given by Anderson.

The Director had been a regular visitor before he was discharged from the hospital and even visited when Stephen remained at his mother's home as a convalescent. On the anniversary of his 'accident' he completed his visits to the hospital. The physiotherapist had given him instructions for an exercise routine to maintain muscle development. In the privacy of his mother's home Stephen examined his body in the full length mirror surprised that even after a year the cicatrix remained ugly and red, like some great welt on his shoulder and side.

There were other scars; but these were indelibly etched in his mind. He had almost accepted the shooting as accidental. The Governments of Indonesia and Australia both agreed that the shooting was accidental, that he had obviously been mistaken for a regular Indonesian soldier during the attack by the insurgents. It had then become generally accepted that there had been nothing sinister behind the accidental shooting of the Embassy representative who was on record as having requested the tour. To accept otherwise would have raised too many unanswerable questions.

Coleman believed that it had been a deliberate attempt on his life. The circumstances leading up to his shooting appeared too orchestrated and, whenever he reflected on the events surrounding the attack, he believed that there could be no other conclusion. He had, however, elected to follow the general consensus and accepted that the shooting had been an accident. But only publicly.

Fortunately, the press also accepted the popular version of the incident. The Australian government did not need to issue a 'D' notice to prevent the newspapers from publishing articles detrimental to national interests. Intelligence services from Australia, New Zealand and the United States agreed that there was a substantial arms operation underway prior to the plebiscite. The majority of these agencies were convinced that vested interests had deliberately manipulated the Irian tribes into believing that armed revolt against the Indonesians would eventually lead to their achieving independence from the powerful Indonesian presence, and the United States delivered satellite photography to support these views. The poorly organized rebel movement, lacking in military hardware and training, failed dismally. What started as major outbreaks of resistance soon turned into occasional skirmishes. Opposition diminished rapidly once supply lines had been effectively disrupted. Most of the primitive groups lay down their arms and surrendered. Others regrouped along the New Guinea border vowing to continue their campaign of terror against the Javanese transmigrant colonies. The United Nations moved quickly and, as indications were that the people of Irian Barat wanted to be part of the Indonesian republic, the supervised voting commenced.

The results of the plebiscite destroyed all future hope for an independent West New Guinea. The exultant Indonesian authorities named the new province, Irian Jaya.

The significant events and changes which had occurred over the time of his absence amazed Stephen. He had maintained a watching brief over Indonesia and was restless to witness the changes he'd read about for himself. The people of Indonesia had become even stronger, uniting behind the powerful *Golkar* Party to establish their leader as the most powerful head of state in Asia, outside of China.

The country had commenced its drive towards a full market economy. Foreign investors flooded into the capital signing commitments never thought possible just a few years before. Suddenly, there was a burst of activity and the capital city's skyline started to change. The Chinese entrepreneurs returned and, with them, funds to develop the trading opportunities of this country's enormous consumer potential. Overnight, with its energy reserves, Indonesia became the new investor destination. They came in their thousands with briefcases full of money and promises.

The Indonesia Coleman had left, just two years before, had changed. Even the people seemed different. Senior government players had come and gone already over the short period. The technocrats were now involved. It was an exciting time. Particularly for General Nathan Seda.

* * * * * *

During the second year of his physical and mental recuperation and towards the completion of his intensive advanced intelligence training, Stephen had considered leaving the Service. The months had dragged on laboriously as the monotonous daily routines chipped away at his energy causing him to question his motives for continuing with the department.

He felt as if he now lacked motivation and needed something to stimulate him, to provide an excitement, to generate new energy in his life. Anderson understood the underlying reason, as did Stephan's mother, both annoyingly endowed with some sixth sense when it came to his well being. At times he found it suffocating. They had both, in their own time broached the subject of Louise.

He'd flatly refused to discuss her. Not with his mother and certainly not with Anderson. Stephen didn't believe that either could understand the emotions he'd experienced, the mental torment he had suffered once when news of her accident had been divulged to him. Their relationship was now history and nothing could change the facts surrounding her demise. Most was now just part of his confused memory punctuated with flashes of the shooting, their last night together, and the disappearance of her flight.

He'd been informed while still under hospital care in Sydney. By then the Search and Air Rescue parties had been called off and she had been declared officially lost, one of those incongruous euphemisms, he soon realized, which can be vague enough to provide a small window of hope to friends and loved ones. Even now he refused to accept the loss, although he recognized that part of the healing process was coming to terms with her death. He just wasn't ready to let go. At least, not then.

With the coming of the first falls of snow, Stephen eagerly accepted the opportunity to revisit Anderson's mountain lodge. Although he would need to nurse his shoulder back into the demanding sport carefully, he decided to go. It wasn't lost on him that his mother had been thinking of psychological recuperation rather than physical recovery when she suggested the holiday and somehow secured his Director's consent.

At first he was content to plough around through the white-blanketed setting enjoying the serenity of the Australian Alps during winter, but when he observed the other guests their host had also invited carrying their gear out to the four-wheel drive, he was immediately impatient to ski again.

He commenced with some light down-hill skiing and, although the conditions were poor he had little difficulty regaining the form he had achieved some years before. Stephen discovered that he still enjoyed the exhilaration of speeding down the slopes and, under the observant eyes of the clandestine department's chief, Stephen regained his confidence quickly. Convinced that his mind was back on track he attacked his work with a refreshed vigour, much to the relief of the departmental watchdogs who had become increasingly concerned with their agent's demeanour.

Due to his in-depth in-country experience, Stephen was placed in charge of the Indonesian desk. He was not completely comfortable with the position but understood the necessity of staying behind a desk until he felt *au fait* with the administrative and logistical support aspects of the profession he had entered.

Occasionally he dined with the Chief but other than those rare occasions Coleman kept to himself. This was not considered unusual as most of his associates had also kept to themselves during the intense training. They understood that their social lives would forever be restricted by the sensitive information they knew and avoided developing new relationships outside the group. The identity of members of the elite circle of government operatives was known only to the Prime Minister, his Attorney General and the small number of directly involved personnel. Apart from the demanding field training in Canungra, Stephen spent most of his time inside the Defence Department offices.

ASIS had been designed along the lines of the British secret intelligence services, more commonly referred to as MI6. The major difference between the two was that the existence of the Australian counterpart was unknown to the public and media. Only the most senior foreign intelligence chiefs had access to this extremely sensitive information. Stephen knew from the list he had examined that this included the Director of the CIA and, of course, MI6.

The security clearance alone often required extremely intensive investigation of potential recruits. Many were abandoned by the Department over the most minor considerations well before there was any possibility of their accessing any information whatsoever relating to the existence of the Service.

Coleman had been encouraged to re-enter the cocktail circuit and did so willingly. He was constantly amused by the not so subtle differences in behaviour he observed between the Canberra bureaucrats and the foreign diplomats. It was as if most of the city's population were all on some extended political holiday as they appeared to be always away down the coast fishing or visiting the ski resorts on weekends while their evenings were occupied by the numerous functions listed on the diplomatic calendar.

Occasionally Stephen spent the weekend with his mother in Melbourne. He was shocked to see how she had aged so during the past two years. He came to understand that he had never really appreciated just how much she had cared for him and how proud this elegant lady had become of her son. There had been no communication with his father. Not even when he had been hospitalized. His parents had separated not long after his first overseas posting and dfrifted to their own distant horizons, until finally losing all contact with each other.

Stephen found time to visit his old friend and teacher, Albert, who always reciprocated with a lunch or dinner invitation whenever he came to Canberra. He was pleased for the Timorese. Although his life had also suffered the extremes of love and disappointment Albert now appeared to be quite comfortably settled in his current position as a part-time technical advisor to the government, while maintaining his former teaching position at the Language Academy.

Mary had long deserted their marital abode. The couple had exchanged the necessary papers through their solicitors and now Albert was alone again, although he still received occasional communications from Nathan which, these days, he passed directly to the ASIO officer who arranged to meet with him regularly in Canberra. There he received a brief which he followed precisely upon returning to Melbourne, and the Indonesian community. Although he had asked himself the question many times, Albert just did not understand how or why he had been placed in the unenviable position which now overshadowed his entire life.

Unfortunately for Albert, he had never applied for naturalization whilst still married to Mary. Although the authorities stated that he now qualified in his own right, he could not understand why both applications submitted had been refused without a reasonable explanation. Albert had been informed that immigration checks took time and that he should be patient and persevere until he was accepted. During his most recent visit to Canberra and discussions with his intelligence contact, he had raised the issue and requested their assistance. He had been informed that his application was not necessary as he was already a resident and a further application may just open a Pandora's Box which could even result in his deportation.

Deportation! The very word gnawed at his intestines for weeks. The thought of being forcefully returned to Indonesia threw the fear of God into Albert. He accepted the agent's explanation and decided not to attract any further attention to himself. Albert was worried. He wished he could discuss the difficulties with his old student and now close friend Stephen Coleman. In fact, that is exactly what Albert should have done but he knew nothing of the Machiavellian world of intelligence and espionage and, in consequence, remained but a minor pawn under threat in two separate games.

He felt sad for Stephen when he first received news of the shooting accident. He had phoned his former student's parents to console them and obtain information regarding his condition. Albert journeyed to the hospital regularly as he was most sincere with respect to Stephan's well being.

Coleman appreciated the display of warmth from the Timorese. Their friendship grew and developed a new dimension.

Now Albert was alone again as Stephen, having informed him of his intended departure during his last visit, had bid farewell briefly by phone just the evening before as he waited in the departure lounge at Mascot Airport. Depressed since returning to Melbourne and alone in his empty bungalow, Albert considered his friend and silently prayed for his well being, the constant feeling which nagged at his thoughts ever since he had seen Stephen lying on the hospital bed covered in bandages, a worry to his mind.

There was just something about their relationship which he felt tied them together, driving them towards a common destination, to some form of conclusion. That night he said another prayer to his god, this time he prayed for his friend, Stephen Coleman.

* * * * * *

Coleman could not believe the changes he witnessed driving from Kemayoran Airport. The activity was intense. Roads had been widened, trees planted. New buildings were taking shape and the city's skyline changed from one of neglect to that of a city full of promise. The people even appeared brighter. There was a presence of hope in the air and not the despair he had so often encountered during his first visit to Jakarta. And the motorbikes! Where had all of those machines suddenly appeared from, screaming along in packs, twisting in and out of the traffic at dangerous speeds? He shook his head in disbelief. In just two years the changes had been dramatic. He was excited, the anticipation of seeing the Embassy again and perhaps meeting one or two old acquaintances raised his spirits even further.

When the taxi turned into Jalan Thamrin Stephen could not accept the incredible change that this avenue had undergone in such a brief period of time. Now there were skyscrapers where before there had been empty fields. Previously unfinished buildings, now completed, boasted neon signs on roofs advertising Sanyo, Toyota and other Japanese products. The main protocol road had been reconstructed as a four lane avenue with pedestrian crossings and traffic lights. The military with its tanks and soldiers were no longer evident.

Still suffering the mixed emotions of pleasant surprise and regret that he could no longer recognize the old city, Stephen felt his taxi pull to a jerky halt in the grounds of the new Australian Embassy. The old security guard, Pak Ali, recognized the former Attaché immediately.

"*Tuan, tuan,*" called the withered old man. "*Selamat datang, selamat datang,*" he continued to call as Stephen climbed out of the taxi and pumped the old Pak Ali's hand.

"*Apa kabar, Pak, sudah kawin lagi?*" Stephen asked, joking with the old man and asking him if he had taken any new wives.

"*Enggak, tuan. Pak Ali udah terlalu tua!*" he responded pleased that the tuan had remembered him and responding to the effect that he was now too old for that nonsense.

"*Kawin lagi dong, Pak Ali, bisa kembali muda!*" Stephen bantered, advising old Ali that if he remarried he would feel younger immediately.

"*Enggak, tuan, enggak!*" No tuan, no!, cried the toothless man.

This happy soul had served faithfully through until his first retirement when, at the mandatory age, he had been terminated. Almost everybody in the Embassy was aware that the old man could not support himself and the incredible number of offspring he had so indiscriminately sired and, as a gesture of recognition for his loyal service, the staff re-engaged him immediately, using a pseudonym to circumvent the inflexible regulations which had resulted in his predicament.

Coleman enjoyed the light banter with the old man. Always pleasant, smiling and willing to help in anyway, he was considered by some to be one of the kindest men in town. Waving fondly at the *jaga*, Stephen entered the Embassy foyer and was surprised to see Australian security manning the reception desk. Commonwealth Police.

Another change.

He registered his name and requested to see his successor, Phil Walters. Minutes later he was ushered upstairs to the military's 'mess' quarters, a section of the top and fourth floor dedicated, as the Naval Attaché suggested, 'to the spiritual pursuits of the military contingent attached to the embassy'. The serviceman had turned this top security area into their own comfort station, complete with bar. Stephen was ushered into the room and was pleasantly surprised to recognize some of the faces present.

"Embassy still closes at 1430 hours, old chap," the Army Attaché remarked, rising to greet the visitor, "and we heard you were going to pay us a visit. Welcome back."

Coleman shook the army officer's hand, "How are you Colonel?" he asked.

"Be a bloody sight better this time next week. Going home. Tour's finished. "

The group had obviously been hard at it for some time as the noise level for such a small group was unusually high.

"We bent the rules today, young Stephen," called another officer, the Air Attaché, "to welcome you back."

Phil Walters was obviously not completely comfortable as what the Group Captain had just announced was completely true. These six servicemen held their own regular and private function in the Embassy, and it was always located somewhere where security prevented most others from entering. During his tour Stephen had been called upon more than once to assist these men in their duties, due to his language expertise. He'd never refused their requests even when it involved giving up his valuable spare time over the weekend to defuse domestic problems with their staff.

They, for the most part, respected the young civilian. After all, he had graduated from one of their most difficult military courses and was so given provisional membership status within their secret circle. These private meetings also provided the opportunity for discussion of sensitive Indonesian military data, access to which had been within Coleman's realm, but not his successor's.

He looked at the small group of hardened but likable professionals and was immediately pleased to be back.

"I'm honoured, gentlemen," Stephen said.

He was then introduced to the faces which were strangers to him. A large Bangka tin mug filled to overflowing with beer was placed in his hands.

"Welcome back, Stephen," again the Army Attaché called, which solicited a chorus of 'welcome' from all present.

They raised their specially engraved mugs in salute.

He hadn't known it, but he was somewhat of a legend amongst the Embassy hands. Having been shot had something to do with that. Coleman toasted them all and, understanding the other civilian's discomfort at being present, drank just two mugs before thanking them for their hospitality and excusing himself from their further activities.

These extra curricular pastimes were mainly restricted to the Sergeant, Warrant Officer and Chief Petty Officer who acted as personal assistants to the three Military Attachés. As their superiors always departed together, these experienced and highly respected men would often remain behind consuming the remnants of liquor before proceeding onto more disreputable pastures.

All three assistants, although not commissioned, received salaries equivalent to that of a field officer as their experience and security classifications alone were second to none. They had access to most files and one of the three would have been painstakingly security cleared to yet a higher level placing him amongst the very few who knew that the service even existed. He spent an hour with Walters before requesting assistance to take him to a hotel.

"Why not stay with me?" his successor asked.

"If I remember correctly, those quarters were claustrophobic at the best of times. No, thanks Phil, I don't mind spending a few days at the Hotel Indonesia. "

Walters laughed. "Your old place has been demolished and the First Secretary's position now commands a three bedroom semi-detached out at Jalan Wijaya. Come on, Stephen, change your mind. I would enjoy the company. "

Coleman considered the ramifications of staying with this man. He didn't know him personally and did not feel completely comfortable staying with a stranger, even though Walters worked in his former department.

"Phil, I appreciate your offer. Thanks. I would normally accept but I have a few things to iron out first and, if the offer is still open in a couple of days, I may well take you up on it. "

"Okay, Stephen. While you're here, whatever you need, just call and I will do whatever I can to assist. " He hesitated. "That means, anything, okay?"

"Thanks, I'll certainly call if I need assistance."

"How long do you intend staying," he asked.

"Maybe a month or so, I'm not sure at this stage. I'll let you know."

The Information First Secretary recognized the sudden change in the visitor's demeanor. "Stephen, don't misunderstand," Walters apologized, "I'm not trying to keep tabs on you. As far as I am concerned, you're on leave, and what you do here is your business. "

Stephen eyed the man coolly. 'Yes,' he thought, 'on leave, but not from your department, laddie.'

Walters was not privy to the real nature of Coleman's employment nor the existence of his secretive masters.

"I'll still keep you informed," Stephen advised, the tone of his voice suggesting that this line of discussion had ended.

He shook Walters' hand and was escorted out of the building. Coleman had only to travel two hundred metres to the Hotel Indonesia. He walked, dispatching the driver ahead as the traffic flow had changed and the car would need to drive a considerable distance before reaching the roundabout.

Coleman arrived at the hotel simultaneously with the blue Holden. He checked in, showered and commenced checking old telephone numbers. At first he had difficulty as many of the numbers had changed or acquired additional numerals. The operator assisted him with the third number, as the first two were no longer used by the previous subscribers.

A familiar voice spoke on the line. It was *Si Jempol*, a useful contact from the old days. Immediately, Coleman replaced the receiver, not wishing to identify himself. He sat on his bed and considered this information. There was no guarantee that the subscriber was at the original address. It was quite possible that the number moved with the original *langganan* to a different location, providing, of course, that the new address was within the original exchange's distribution network. He decided to check it out.

* * * * * *

The street lighting had improved but it was still a brave tourist who ventured too far from the centre of the city at night. Proceeding from his hotel, Coleman walked directly up Imam Bonjol until he spotted the familiar Dutch colonial house with the unorthodox windows. He sat at a *kaki-lima* roadside stall, ordered a hot chilli *marta-bak* and waited. Half an hour passed. There had been no activity that he could see in the house across the quiet and poorly lit street. Stephen then finished the tasty Indian omelette and decided it was safe to approach the dwelling. He crossed the road and noticed a slight movement behind one of the windows on the second storey.

There was no *jaga* apparent. Immediately his body tensed as he found this scene disturbing. Stephen knew that all houses in Jakarta required security. He entered the yard cautiously and knocked softly on the heavy panelled door. Another curtain was pulled back, this time on the ground level, and a childish face peered at him.

The curtain closed. He knocked again. The curtain was again pulled back slightly and a man waved indicating that the *tuan* was not at home. He refused to accept the ploy and knocked yet again, for the third time and, as he expected, the door opened slightly to permit the tenant a better view of the intruder.

Seconds passed. The door was then pushed closed to permit the safety chains to be released, with which the door was opened quickly and he was pulled inside.

"*Tuan, kenapa kesini?*" the voice implored, its owner refusing to switch the lights on, demanding why to know Coleman had come to this house.

"*Mana Si Jempol?*" he hissed, demanding the whereabouts of the man he sought.

"*Udah pergi, tuan, udah pergi!*" the servant lied telling the foreigner, that the man had already left.

"*Jam berapa pergi?*" Coleman insisted, demanding to know what time the owner had departed.

"*Sejak kemarin, tuan, sejak kemarin,*" the servant again lied, advising that the man, *Si Jempol,* as he was known, having lost a thumb in a street fight, had left the day before. Stephen knew this not to be true as he'd identified the voice just hours before when he phoned from the hotel.

"*Suruh dia hubungi saya,*" he ordered, instructing the servant to ask his employer to contact Coleman.

"*Saya tinggal di Hotel Indonesia, kamar 722. Mengerti?*" Stephen left his hotel and room number having ascertained that the servant understood.

He returned to the hotel, and waited. Several long hours had passed when Stephen heard the knock he'd anticipated would come. The small peep-hole located at the hotel room's front entrance helped him identify the caller. He opened the door and gestured for *Si Jempol* to enter.

They shook hands. Neither spoke. *Si Jempol* opened a small case and proceeded to unpack certain items wrapped in used but clean cement bag liners. These bag liners, cleaned and rubbed smooth were as good as a chamois cloth suitable wrapping for delicate items and *objets d'art*. He unwrapped the items and placed them gently on the bed. The four pistols were in immaculate condition.

Coleman examined the Walthers A 9 mm Short and a 7. 65 automatics. He checked the latter's action then looked at the rugged Eurasian inquiringly, with one eyebrow raised.

The man indicated the number with his hands. It sounded a little on the expensive side but considering the weapon's condition he decided not to hassle him on the price. He picked up the second Walther and could hardly see any difference between the two. He opted for his first choice, returning the 9 mm Short, as the former was the more common of the Walther PPKs and Coleman considered the 7. 65 mm calibre as quite adequate for his needs.

He paid in greenbacks while the rest of the items were placed, having been carefully re-wrapped, back in the case. *Si Jempol* extracted a small box from his pocket and passed the container to Stephen who examined the contents, nodded, placed the package on the bedside table then opened the door for the man to leave.

He had not been in Coleman's room more than four minutes. The transaction completed and the merchandise now safely locked away in his suitcase, the Australian retired for the night.

* * * * * *

BAKIN Security had at least a dozen operatives working the Hotel Indonesia around the clock as most foreigners on diplomatic or business visits were obliged to stay at the only four star hotel in Jakarta. Their function was mainly to stand around in the bars and lobbies watching and listening, reporting anything of importance involving the foreign community. The phones in the hotel were all monitored, recording most of the considerable traffic which passed through the system each day, only to be discarded due to the Indonesians' inability to cope with the sheer volume of information and their shortage of skilled technicians.

One of the team leaders observed *Si Jempol* leaving the lobby lifts and casually made a note of the time and date. The normally discreet trader was up late, the security agent thought. A little too late for the black market gun dealer. Surprised to see the well known figure in such an obvious location the BAKIN agent underscored the time then returned to watching the wealthy foreigners parade around the hotel lobby.

* * * * * *

Coleman awoke early, completely rested and feeling more confident of his decision to return to Jakarta, although uncomfortable with the possibility of being compromised in having acquired the automatic. Anderson's approval for his trip, despite it being organized in his own time, was conditional on his undertaking to secure a weapon and carry it while he remained in Indonesia. He was also instructed to bring the weapon back to Australia upon his return. The service was always in need of foreign unregistered hand guns.

Stephen was concerned with customs but, unlike the United States, there were no metal detectors installed at Asian airports. He had agreed, albeit reluctantly and his Chief had then insisted that he use the contact numbers Coleman had tried upon arrival.

The weapon would remain locked in his baggage, he decided.

Chapter 9

Jakarta — the Kongsi

Nathan Seda had known of Stephen's arrival within an hour of his immigration *cap* being stamped into his passport at Kemayoran Airport. He was surprised that the former Attaché had elected to return. Seda considered the Australian's visit and admitted that he found his presence a little disconcerting.

He of all people understood just how fortunate the Australian had been to survive Umar's bullet.

It was not like the man to miss. As it turned out, the wounding was almost as effective as his death would have been. The world press, spearheaded by the Australian media, ran the story for a considerable length of time as Coleman was one of their own and his fellow journalists wouldn't let the story die. This had suited Seda at the time although the eventual outcome had been difficult to accept.

The surrender of the primitive Irian natives enabled the plebiscite to take place. The superior numbers and weaponry of the Indonesians Forces had prevailed. As one journalist had stated at the time, referring to the rebels, it had been an invisible war waged over invisible boundaries, as the primitive tribes of the region had no understanding of the import of political lines drawn by others which restricted their movements within their traditional habitat.

In retrospect, Seda acknowledged that although the desired result of the ambush had not entirely been achieved, considerable experience had been gained from the attempt. He had developed a greater depth of knowledge and understanding of, not only his own military and government leaders and how they reacted to provincial separatist threats, but also the international media and humanitarian groups.

He was committed to continue with his ambitious plans, adhering to the original oath he had sworn, motivated by a myriad of events so complex even he had difficulty sometimes understanding the strength of his own resolve and determination. Foremost in his mind, heart and soul was the one principle in which he really did believe, providing Seda with the necessary motivation needed to achieve this aim.

He swore that one day Timor would be governed only by the Timorese. And if his dedication could assist realize this outcome then he would be a very contented man. And a powerful one.

Even more powerful than he had already become.

Funding his operations was not overly difficult. The secret operational accounts from BAKIN had grown considerably, commensurate with the significant increase of foreign investment capital which had poured into the country over recent years. He had little difficulty in maintaining operations as he easily siphoned more than two million dollars off each year's budget allocations. The General realized that vast sums of capital would be required for his next war chest. Although thoroughly disappointed with the events in Irian Jaya he was determined to be better prepared when the next opportunity arose. Seda had learned to be more patient as he believed that the Irian uprisings were unsuccessful primarily due to the impatience displayed by tribal leaders and their lack of leadership. He would provide that leadership to his own people when the time came.

His current program involved sending specialist units across the Indonesian border into New Guinea where they terrorized the primitive groups and, on occasions, managed to successfully locate remnants of the Free Irian Movement. Occasionally he reported these incursions to the monthly defence and security sessions which he now co-chaired and was applauded for his dedication in eradicating these former terrorists.

The Indonesian Defence Council had received irrefutable evidence that armed bands of terrorists frequently crossed from havens in New Guinea and created havoc. They were more than happy to approve counter attacks and supplied Seda with additional funding to support these efforts. His position had never been stronger.

The Intelligence General realized that he had to be careful at all times, remain diligent and ensure that his position be maintained. The military had always been a competitive arena in the past but was even more so now, he discovered, due to the ever increasing number of commercial opportunities available to senior officers.

Coleman arrived in Jakarta without any request for official clearance and accreditation. This disturbed General Seda. All foreign diplomatic activity information was channelled through his offices. The General examined the dossier once again. Most he already knew as he had memorized the data through repeated readings of the Embassy journalist's information sheets.

He had almost successfully had this man executed. Why would he want to return? And then Seda remembered the girl. What was her name, Louise? Seda smiled darkly. He would have the Australian followed anyway. It was always best to be sure with these foreigners who had obvious government links. He could be troublesome but Seda didn't feel there was any real threat. Suddenly he smiled again, a thought playing to his cruel sense of irony. He would invite the former Attaché around for a social function as he had in the past. Then, first hand, Seda would be able to determine the foreigner's intentions in revisiting Indonesia.

* * * * * *

Seda was pleased with his new home.

His wife had not played any significant part in its planning, having merely stipulated that she wished it to be large and impressive. The mansion was both. The General knew that it impressed as he had observed the envious looks on guests' faces when they first visited his household.

He was selective in whom he invited to his home. At least once each month he would host a formal function at his residence, always arranging for at least two or three foreign diplomats to be present. Rarely would these senior members of the expatriate community fail to attend as to do so would inevitably result in missed opportunities.

The gregarious General was renowned for his generous hospitality and powerful associates, many of whom often appearing unannounced at Seda's functions. Some embassies actually requested that their ambassadors be invited. He enjoyed the power but he had not let it influence his thinking, nor diminish his resolve to achieve his final goal. His recent affiliation with the President's family was dangerous he knew, but essential as he was realistic enough to appreciate that the First Family would be around for a long time to come and to advance his power base any further would require the President's support.

Seda smiled when he remembered his first meeting with one of the sons. He couldn't believe the young man's arrogance and total absence of personality. They had met through a Chinese intermediary and discussed an arrangement whereby a Japanese consortium would be given priority in a military tender due to be called over the following months. Seda had deliberately ingratiated himself and asked for nothing, knowing that this is what the self-centred youngster had expected of him. After all, he was his father's son and Nathan was merely one of his father's generals.

The delicate relationship had paid off well. His shoulder displayed the additional star before the end of that year and it was then that Seda's name had become synonymous with the powerful forces which steered the nation. He had learned the game. When the Palace spoke, he listened. If there was a request, he endeavoured to have it fulfilled. As his superiors unabashedly demonstrated their greed, he helped satisfy their appetites. And, within a very brief time, a day would not pass without his name being mentioned with respect by his peers, in awe by his competitors and in fear by those who were foolish enough to consider themselves his enemy.

Seda had indeed become a force to be considered.

He called his adjutant, explained what he wanted and then informed his wife that she was to invite a small gathering of friends for the weekend. Seda was confident that the visitor would accept an invitation to meet up with an old acquaintance.

'If he was really here in a private capacity then why would he not accept such a social invitation?' he pondered. 'Then again, if he was involved in something covert for his government surely they would want him to accept the invitation as an opportunity to dine with the General Seda, these days, was not something to be scoffed at!'

There was something about this *bulé*, something which made the General slightly uneasy. Incredibly superstitious, Seda decided that maybe it was an opportune time to drive out to Bogor and visit his *dukun* again. He made a mental note to do so. These days he could not afford to be as complacent as he'd been before, he warned himself, such as when he was involved in orchestrating the disturbances in Irian Barat. The medicine man would offer him guidance and solace.

Feeling that he had resolved the slight annoyance he dispensed with any further thoughts relating to the foreigner and turned his mind to one of the many other problems he faced on a typical day. He looked up at the photograph of General Sudomo, his predecessor, his lips curling into a tight grin as he remembered his first visit to this office and the assignment he'd been given regarding his step brother.

The image of Umar substituting the powerful director's heart tablets with the wrong stimulants flashed through his mind. Without further thought General Seda turned his attention back to his work.

* * * * * *

Stephen Coleman remained in Jakarta until Thursday.

"I'm off, Phil," he advised, "heading for Samudera Beach for a week and then on to Bandung, maybe Jogjakarta. "

"When do you intend returning to Jakarta?" Walters inquired.

"Haven't decided yet. I will call from wherever I overnight to keep you current with my itinerary. Okay?"

"That's fine, Stephen, you're a free agent," Walters responded, with no innuendo intended. "Just have a good time. "

Coleman wanted to catch a bus but just could not bring himself to board one of the speeding giants. It wasn't just that these buses contributed to most of the road casualty figures. They were dirty and unreliable. Instead, he hired a private taxi for the week, departing from the city around mid-morning, finally arriving in the village of Pelabuhan Ratu in time for lunch at the Bayu Amerta.

The small seafood restaurant had been constructed along traditional lines, positioned on the edge of a cliff overlooking the majestic swells of the Indian Ocean. The panoramic view was spectacular. Waves crashed against the rocks below, showering spray high into the air, threatening the open garden restaurant setting. He ordered the swordfish which was served grilled, basted with sweet soya sauce, and placed on a bed of saffron rice. His favourite.

Memories of earlier visits came flooding back as Coleman began to unwind and accept the tranquil atmosphere and ocean air. During his tour he had made several trips to this beautiful resort area.

Once, he reminisced, Stephen had joined with a group from the embassy and hired a bungalow during one long weekend. He had encouraged them to experience the fresh seafood served at this restaurant and, after lunch, they had ventured down to the fish market and witnessed fisherman returning with their catch.

The group were enjoying themselves until one of the Australian girls had cried out in dismay. The inexperienced traveller had wandered off ahead of the others and now stood with both hands held close to her mouth in surprise.

Immediately in front of where she stood a fisherman had taken a long sharp knife and, brandishing the glistening blade was preparing to butcher a porpoise. Imediately, a shout of protest arose from the onlookers causing the bewildered fisherman to pause in his action. Eventually he was persuaded to sell the mammal at a good price to one of the foreigners who asked that it be thrown back into the sea whole. The old and very poor fisherman, now joined by several of his own villagers instantly agreed, not understanding why these naive Westerners differentiated between dolphins and the abundant big game fish found in the oceans.

Stephen had no doubts in his mind that once they'd departed the porpoise would have ended up in its original predicament and perhaps in the villager's cooking pot that very same afternoon.

* * * * * *

During the first days Stephen walked the beaches, clearing his mind of everything except the life around him. He sat with the fisherman discussing winds, tides and weather, and told stories of great storms and winds which often endangered the villages there. Stephen found that he could sit for hours listening to their simple stories of exaggerated catches and tales of sharks so great that even a coracle was once swallowed whole by one of these monsters. He found that the smell of the salt air, the innocence of these hospitable coastal people, and the abundance of coconut trees swaying together on the long white sandy beaches, simply idyllic, and wondered why he had not returned before this. Huge Indian Ocean waves thundered down onto the black volcanic rocks strewn across the shallow reaches, sending claps of thunderous applause at their own mighty strength when they then smashed against the tall cliffs surrounding the hotel, as he strolled along the white sandy beaches. He often found broken remains of swordfish bills strewn along the sandy coast, evidence of the mighty fish which were often captured unwittingly in the fishermen's net, their last dying efforts to thrash their way to freedom ripping the precious nets forever. Stephen enjoyed his stay more than he could have imagined. The simplicity of the people and their surrounds brought an inner peace he had not felt before.

A week passed and Stephen reluctantly called Jakarta. Walters' office continued to act as a conduit for any message traffic as a matter of professional courtesy. The First Secretary was not available however his assistant informed Coleman that he had received an invitation for the previous weekend. She apologized then explained that the telephone connection to Pelabuhan Ratu had been difficult and she had therefore been unable to inform him of the dinner arrangements.

"I did manage to have a letter sent to their house, expressing apologies on your behalf, Tuan Coleman," the efficient woman advised.

"That was very kind of you," was all Stephen could say, not remembering her name. She had not considered it necessary nor prudent to inform the Sedas that she had been unable to contact the *tuan*.

He was surprised when he'd discovered that the personal invitation had been sent by General Seda's charming wife.

"Would you please advise the General that I am not in Jakarta and don't expect to return for some weeks?"

"Certainly, tuan. I will phone immediately."

Coleman thanked her again, not wanting to be stuck there in the lobby waiting for hours to be connected to the Seda household to speak directly to them when the assistant could connect easily through local dialling. He hung up and hurried to the waiting Toyota Corolla anxious to get underway. The lobby staff waved as he departed, impressed with the Australian's fluency in their tongue. The receptionist went immediately to the communications room and typed a telex which, due to the shared lines suffering continuous delay difficulties, did not arrive at its destination until the following afternoon. The communications clerk at BAKIN headquarters had explicit instructions which he followed upon receiving the message.

He passed it to Major Umar Suharjo.

* * * * * *

The road from the narrow coast rose sharply as it wound its way through the range of volcanic mountains. The soil was rich, providing a lush green countryside of terraced rice fields bathing in the tropical sun. The terraces, stacked one upon another, reached to almost impossible heights. Small streams of life-giving water flowed gently from one paddy to another, maintaining just enough velocity to run from one field to the next. Banana trees grew in abundance shading the village shanty dwellers who lived alongside the pot-holed road.

Stephen passed occasional teams of workers, their lungs exhausted from the toxic fumes generated from heating the two-hundred-litre drums of asphalt to be poured by hand along the road. The weary men waved as he passed slowly, calling for cigarettes or money for food. As the car struggled slowly uphill they often encountered these sun scorched men, their clothes in tatters and their feet burnt from the hot tar they had just laid. Stephen instructed the driver to slow down even more so that he could hand these desolate souls a packet of cigarettes, or a few Rupiah. They always smiled and waved, even when they received nothing from the occasional passing vehicles.

The mountainous road climbed for an hour before they arrived at Sukabumi and although the main street was alive with the morning market activity, he continued through to Bandung, the city of endless students.

Stephen spent only a few days visiting the provincial capital again. As nothing much seemed to have changed apart from the Savoy Hoyman's menu and the introduction of a sleazy disco in an adjacent alley, he left the garden city. He was feeling a little disappointed with the lack of real change or progress that he had witnessed in Jakarta.

Stephen travelled through off-road and well hidden villages, examined the mighty temple, Borobudur, and even Candi Mendut, finally coming to rest in the hills just short of the east Javanese provincial capital of Surabaya.

* * * * * *

He was now into his third week back in-country and discovered to his delight that he was enjoying himself immensely. He had rented an old Dutch Colonial plantation villa which overlooked the valley below. The air was cool and filled with the scent of flowers which grew only at these altitudes. A tea plantation lay spread out like some gigantic green carpet covering the slopes, providing endless pleasure as he sat on the terrace, watching the rows of women move slowly through the bushes, picking the small shoots, careful to maintain the flat level appearance of the tree thereby guaranteeing the continuous growth of the sweeter leaves. This small hill station area had been built for the exclusive use of the former colonial masters. Situated an hour's drive from the city of Surabaya, it was the weekend destination venue for those who wished to seek relief from the heat and humidity of the dusty port. Since Independence, little had changed here with the exception of a few new walls and a small dance-cum-disco bar situated inside the lobby of the dilapidated hotel.

Each morning he walked down to the vegetable markets, purchased several of the small bitter apples and wandered back slowly taking in the vibrant colours of the commercially grown flowers. Twice he had ventured into the hotel's bar and spent most of the evening being entertained by the young girls who were only too eager for his company.

And his Rupiah.

The second evening he took two of the hostesses back to his villa, where the young girls took turns playing and splashing around in the cast iron bathtub filled with steaming hot water, as they had never had the opportunity before and, he guessed, would probably not have again. Stephen was delighted with their frolics. When they appeared from the ensuite bathroom robed only in towels and cheeky grins, he led them to the large four-poster bed and, removing the hand made quilt, undressed then slid in between the soft brown bodies. They giggled and talked then made love then afterwards, called for food from passing vendors before splashing around some more in the ancient tub until Stephen finally fell asleep, exhausted by their energy and effervescence. When he awoke in the morning they were gone.

They hadn't taken anything. And he remembered not giving them any money. He decided to return that night and present them with a gift for providing him with the happiest experience he'd known for too long a time. He laughed remembering their antics and was still smiling when the *jongus* appeared with the traditional thick cup of Java coffee and a small plate of strong cheese and chocolates for his breakfast. He had nothing to be ashamed of and was surprised at just how relaxed he was considering the lack of sleep.

Sitting on the patio of the magnificent bungalow admiring the scenery and enjoying the mood, Stephen Coleman made a decision. He felt at peace in this incredible country. He experienced a feeling of release; a cleansing, and closure.

The memory of Louise was still there, but he no longer felt the sadness which had plagued him over the past two years. He was alive. He would always remember their brief and loving affair as he believed she would have wanted him to. He had not dwelt on her reasons for leaving him on that fateful day.

As for the shooting incident, he decided that too must be placed in perspective with the choices he now made. He understood that it would be impossible to be comfortable with the dramatic changes he was about to undertake should his mind still be clouded by the shadows of his past. Like so many other questions that couldn't be answered he decided to now cast these negative aspects of his life away, and start afresh.

Coleman decided to remain in the archipelago. He realized that this decision had been in the making ever since he had regained his health. Reasonably conservative by nature, Coleman examined the motivation for his decision and conceded that he had been influenced by some magnetic pull which had always been there, tugging away until he surrendered to its mystical power. He spoke the language as well as most locals and believed that his funds would be sufficient to survive for at least a reasonable period. He was pleased with himself, but resigned to the fact that others would not be exactly supportive of his decision.

Collecting his thoughts, Stephen spent the following days composing letters to his family, Albert and of course, a telex to his superiors in the Department. Although he dispatched these from the central Surabaya post office. Coleman also decided to request access to the Embassy's communication channels to advise John Anderson directly and personally of his decision. He telexed the carefully worded message disguising the main gist of the text and addressee's name. This was a relatively simple procedure all field operatives used when obliged to utilize unreliable postal and telegraph services. The message was sent from Surabaya to Jakarta's main post office and then picked up by an embassy driver when running the hourly check for incoming telexes. This in turn was re-routed via Walter's office as there was no overseas link from this eastern provincial capital.

Stephen addressed his resignation to the Head of the Department who, in this instance, was the Minister for External Affairs. He knew that it would reach its correct destination once the Minister had read the communiqué. Stephen realized that he would be required to return to Australia, however briefly, to tidy up loose ends and sit down with his mentor, John Anderson. He was not looking forward to that meeting as he knew how disappointed the Director would be when he realized Coleman could not be dissuaded from his decision to resign.

These thoughts occupied his mind as he boarded the Garuda flight for the short hop across to Bali. Having now made these decisions and informed his department he felt as if a tremendous weight had been lifted off his shoulders, unshackling him for the future, and from his past. Stephen smiled in anticipation with the thought of relaxing at the Segara Village Resort before heading up to the cultural delights of Ubud.

He didn't wish to stay at the Bali Beach. Now that he had finally managed to come to terms with Louise's death he felt it would be better not to stay where they had shared her last evening together. He said his farewell and didn't need to resurrect old ghosts. He wanted a fresh start.

As he drove from the airport Coleman noticed little change here as well. He was pleased. It was unfortunate that progress would come to this beautiful island and he, like many others, wished that day was still far into the future. He checked into the traditionally designed hotel bungalow resort and was presented with the customary welcome coconut cocktail, a combination of rice wine and coconut milk which the staff often spiced with a touch of gin or rum.

Coleman failed to notice the man watching him complete the required registration procedures at the reception desk. All foreigners were required to register when moving around the country, particularly at hotels or guest houses. These alien registration forms were collected each evening by the local police and the data telexed immediately to their headquarters for further dissemination.

Foreign tourism had not yet developed to any extent outside Jakarta and the majority of all hotels were owned, managed or controlled by the central government. When Coleman had left the Samudera Beach Hotel it was this information that had been finally telexed through to Jakarta. He had been the only foreign guest there during his stay on the coast.

The dark-skinned man continue to watch the tourist complete the required formalities. He'd missed Coleman in Pelabuhan Ratu due to the delay in receiving the telexed information. However he caught up with the Australian in Bandung, and had inconspicuously followed him ever since.

Umar strolled across in front of the visitor and passed by without acknowledging his presence. Even had Stephen been more attentive he would not have identified the Javanese who had followed him for almost two weeks. Umar Suharjo smiled arrogantly to himself. He'd even stood outside the villa in Tretes listening to the three occupants bounce around inside.

Satisfied that the foreigner would remain in the hotel to unpack, the major vanished skilfully, to report on Coleman's movements.

'*Strange,*' the Javanese killer had thought to himself, '*the General appears so preoccupied with this one.* '

Convinced that he should have thrown the Attaché overboard when the opportunity availed itself, he grunted an insult to all who were *bulé* and went in search of inconspicuous quarters for himself.

* * * * * *

After three relaxing days in Ubud Stephen felt as if he never wanted to leave this idyllic place, its artists, its beauty and its characters. And yet, the entire time he had felt something strange as if his sixth sense and his training were sending him signals. He was almost certainly being followed. Stephen couldn't prove it, he just knew. Several times he had doubled back from where he'd been to check but there was no one there.

The following day he flew back to the capital.

* * * * * *

When Coleman returned to Jakarta his reception by Embassy staff was cold and indifferent. The official departmental representative in the Embassy was critical of his actions.

"Stephen, think this right through, man, you sound as if you've gone *troppo*," Phil Walters pleaded.

Coleman let the derogatory remark slide. He would need this man's assistance and decided to permit him his say. They discussed the situation for some time. Finally, realizing that his predecessor was not being stubborn, just determined, the Attaché threw his hands upwards in exasperation.

"All right, Stephen. Why don't we agree to put it on hold until you have spoken to the Minister?"

"You can't very well pick up the phone and just call him on an open line, Phil," Coleman patronized.

"We'll signal him and you could send a safe-hand dispatch with tonight's courier. He would have it before lunch tomorrow. "

"Okay," was the response. Coleman was, in fact, pleased that events were proceeding as he'd anticipated, not that they were any more palatable.

"Where do you now intend staying?"

"Why, with you, Phil. Unless the offer is no longer convenient?" Coleman parried. He had considered the advantages of hotel accommodations and privacy against the cost. Anyway, Stephen had argued, the Attaché would be in his office most of the day and, if these times were anything like those during his own tour, then the evening social demands would keep the residence's occupant actively engaged elsewhere.

"Of course, Stephen, you are welcome," Walters answered, not entirely convinced that was doing the right thing as their situations had now changed considerably.

With that, the two men accompanied each other to the official three-bedroom dwelling in *Kebayoran Baru*. The staff were introduced to the guest, some of whom remembered the Indonesian-speaking *tuan*. His host, having excused himself and agreeing to leave Stephen to his own devices, returned immediately to the Embassy.

Once secure in his office he composed a lengthy message, typed the signal himself and took the report to the registry. There, due to the sensitivity of the subject matter, the First Secretary Information, used his own combination access and encoded the low-level message.

Minutes later at the communications centre in Canberra a ribbon of paper was spewing out from the antiquated Lorens telex machine which received the encrypted signal. There was no lettering on these tapes, merely a series of punched holes, each representing a corresponding pulse on the master decoding tape which, for obvious security requirements, was locked and available only to those officers cleared to receive or interpret such classified material. The duty officer identified the classification and called the designated officer to accept the tapes. Ten minutes later the Minister responsible had read the communication and immediately used his secure phone. A further fifteen minutes elapsed before John W. Anderson read the report and frowned.

Pressing the intercom, he issued instructions to his secretary, "Call the Attorney General's office, and arrange for me to see him. Explain the urgency to his secretary."

Anderson sat deep in thought, chewing the end of a letter-opener.

'The stupid bugger,' he muttered angrily having read the confirmation of Coleman's intentions as relayed by Walters. A response from the AG was received and immediately the Director left the heated office instructing his secretary to cancel all appointments until he advised otherwise. 'Madge the Magnificent' obeyed and proceeded to check the Director's schedule for the following forty-eight hours.

That evening, late into the night, Director Anderson and his counterpart from the Australian Security Intelligence Organization discussed the recent developments and debated the most advantageous direction their two organizations should follow.

Both were in agreement. Coleman could be dangerous if permitted to cut loose without any further commitment to the Department. On the other hand, Coleman's determination to stay on in Indonesia could be beneficial to all, if handled judiciously.

* * * * * *

Stephen was surprised and disappointed. The Charge d' Affaires, in the absence of the Ambassador, had called him into the Chancery, where he was presented with a terse notification from the Department that they had received his resignation and would therefore set about completing his records.

Would he please arrange to meet the Australian Consul and surrender any official documents in his possession? Oh, and of course, his passport would require an endorsement that he was no longer employed by Her Majesty's Government. He was, of course, entitled to retain his passport, however the relevant endorsements were required to be executed immediately. Would he also advise details of his on forwarding address etc etc, to assist with final computation of outstanding administrative matters regarding leave-pay etc etc.

Stephen re-read the departmental letter delivered by Walters earlier that afternoon.

"Sorry, Stephen," was all the embarrassed host could offer. "This does not affect our relationship in any way, you know," he added. "Also, it goes without saying that you are welcome to stay on here as long as you wish. "

Stephen finished sipping the whisky, his third, and slowly shook his head.

"I expected at least a farewell note from someone," he complained. "Not even a bloody thanks for the years of service or a simple goodbye!"

"You must have anticipated at least a little annoyance Stephen," his host defended, "the way I hear it, the powers-to-be had great expectations for you in the Department. "

"Still, it's bloody rude," Coleman complained, the first effects of the alcohol accelerating his aggressive mood.

He resented their distancing themselves considering he had served conscientiously and with considerable merit. Well, he'd asked for it, and now he was on his own. At least the break had been clean. Now he had to get on with his life, reorganize, establish new relationships, find a job.

Find a job? The thought suddenly struck him. He had no employment and, consequently, no income. He poured another whisky, looked inquiringly at his host who shook his head then proceeded to think about his future.

Securing permits and obtaining an acceptable sponsor would be his most immediate concerns. Stephen was aware of the difficulties businessmen experienced establishing their activities in Indonesia, however he'd not given these problems much thought before this. He understood that he must address these difficulties without losing his new momentum. The government was frustratingly inflexible in its implementation of regulations governing the employment of foreign nationals, an understandable consequence of the abortive *coup d'etat* back in 1965.

The Australian embassy had wasted no time in advising the Indonesian Immigration and Foreign Office that his employment status had been withdrawn, even though he was not accredited to that post. Coleman had considered this particularly action as unnecessary. Even malicious.

He poured himself another whisky. Looking up, he identified the unhappy appearance of his host.

"I will arrange to move my things in a couple of days if that's okay by you, Phil. "

"I told you that you are welcome to continue on here as long as you wish. "

"Thanks. Time to wing it alone. "

"Have it your way," Walters replied, as he rose to leave, "Take it easy, Stephen," he warned, leaving Coleman to think his problems through.

"Sure. Thanks again, Phil. See you later. "

Coleman sat alone for a while, finished his drink, then instructed the houseboy to call him a *becak*.

"*Mau kemana, tuan?*" he asked politely, inquiring where Stephen wished to go, not out of curiosity, but so he could pass the information on to the three-wheeler's driver when he asked.

"*Jalan-jalan sajalah!*" the now quite inebriated guest advised the unhappy servant. "Just out."

The other servants giggled nervously when they observed the *tuan* climb into the *becak* as he appeared a little drunk. Still, if that made him happy.

The *becak* driver pedalled around for an hour until the young foreigner fell asleep. He then returned to the man's residence. Coleman was not drunk, just a little tipsy. He had been drinking without having taken lunch and was the worse for it. Feeling a little foolish at having to be woken by the driver, Coleman tipped the man for his kindness. As he undressed he realized that this was the first evening in over five years he could go to bed not knowing what he should be doing the following day. With those thoughts, and assisted by the whisky, he slept.

* * * * * *

At first he thought he was dreaming. He was certain there was something going on nearby, if not in his head. There were sounds from outside. Raised voices. The houseboy was adamant. The *tuan* was tired and could not be disturbed. He, Sukardi, would accept the letter and present it to the *tuan* when he had awakened and showered!

The soldier had persisted.

Sukardi resigned himself to the possibility of incurring the wrath of one or the other and decided that the messenger was far more menacing in appearance than the effect of *tuan's* possible tongue-lashing. Coleman was awakened and told of the visitor.

He checked his watch. It was already afternoon.

Immediately he was irritated, partly from the effects of the alcohol, but mainly because a soldier had succeeded in exercising control over the senior servant in a foreigner's household. Prepared to confront the soldier with more than a few sharp words, he instructed Sukardi to keep the man waiting at the front door until *tuan* had completed his *mandi*.

He deliberately procrastinated. An hour passed and Coleman emerged instructing the houseboy to usher the soldier into the small *ruang tamu*, a sitting room just off to the right from the main entrance.

"*Muuf, tuan,*" the soldier apologized coming to attention paying the courtesy of a subordinate, "*saya disuruh Bapak Jenderal Seda...*"

Coleman raised his hand cutting the man off in mid-sentence as the General's name was mentioned, waving for the houseboy to leave the soldier alone with him. He felt annoyed at his own stupidity. He certainly could not, especially at this time afford to offend a senior Indonesian, particularly one as important as the General! Having the messenger cool his heels would certainly reach the General's ears and could be misconstrued as a deliberate insult. He gestured for the soldier to sit.

Embarrassed, the soldier remained standing.

'Damn!' thought Coleman, regretting his insensitivity in placing the Corporal in the position of *serba-salah*, a potential *faux pas*, as it would have been incorrect to accept and impolite to refuse.

"*Baiklah, Corporal. You were saying that General Seda had ordered you here. Has my jongus offered you something to drink?*" he inquired.

"*Belum, tuan,*" the man replied, "*but that is all right as I am not thirsty, terima kasih.*"

"*Corporal, I am sorry that my jongus failed to tell me that one of the General's men was waiting,*" he apologized. "*However he will be reprimanded.*"

Both men knew that this would not happen; however the Corporal was pleased that this *tuan* had recognized the fact that it was incorrect to keep the General's messenger waiting for as long as he had.

"*Tidak apa-apa, tuan,*" the soldier smiled, indicating that what had happened was of no importance. He then handed the letter to the foreigner.

Coleman read the invitation immediately. Considering it may provide a window of opportunity and even resolve his present difficulties, he decided to accept. The soldier departed. Coleman changed quickly from the casual attire he had hastily dressed in selecting a blue motif *batik* shirt with dark trousers. The invitation was for cocktails followed by dinner.

The old Dutch grandfather clock indicated he would be late if he did not hurry. He had no vehicle.

As he was preparing to board a *becak* to take him to the Blok M shopping centre, Phil Walters returned, and offered his car and driver. Coleman accepted as the invitation was for six o'clock.

His previous experiences and working knowledge of the country and its people's habits were all too familiar. He was grateful for the extra effort he'd spent studying their customs and idiosyncrasies. Indonesians usually took their evening meal early. Remembering that Seda was not a Moslem, the *Magrib* prayer period would not pose a problem. Christians, Moslems, Buddhists and Hindus alike all practised what was referred to as *jam karet*, or rubber time.

Appointments had to be flexible. The contradiction lay in the fact that for a foreigner to be late was considered disrespectful and inexcusable. It was late afternoon and, as the residents rose from their midday rest, the city began to stir for the second time that day. The former diplomat sped towards his destination as the sun disappeared for the day.

The driver turned into the driveway stopping briefly at the security post. Coleman identified the familiar Czech automatic machine pistols held by shoulder straps as the guards carefully scrutinized the driver and his foreign passenger. The Holden displayed CD-18 series number plates, indicating that the vehicle was an Australian diplomatic vehicle. Not that diplomatic privilege was something these well-trained troops would respect should they consider the occupants a threat to their General, the passenger reflected.

The army would never forget the loss of its generals some six years earlier when the abortive, and first of three coups commenced. Security was now extremely efficient. Just to raise one's hand in friendly gesture too close to one of these military leaders could possibly result in an aide shooting the offender dead. The attendance of senior ranking officers at functions was always marked by a certain atmosphere of apprehension.

* * * * * *

Stephen was astounded at the size of the mansion. Obviously a new structure, the building occupied at least two thousand metres of land and was designed and constructed in a Mediterranean style. The entrance was surrounded by columns. The building was painted white with red terra-cotta tiles adding to the character of the overall design. Stephen was very impressed.

An aide appeared and ushered him into the splendid structure. As he entered, directly to the left of the foyer, two of the most magnificent creatures he'd ever seen strutted close by, their presence totally unexpected. The Birds of Paradise strolled in a natural setting where the late afternoon sun could strike their enclosed plate-glassed cage. A pond had been arranged simply so as not to detract from the natural beauty of the indigenous fauna in the enclosure.

The flora too was obvious, several rare varieties of black spotted orchids from Kalimantan being positioned above the artificial waterfall. The decor was pseudo-colonial, the emphasis on size. Twin marble columns on both sides of the reception area created the impression that the upper levels numbered more than were actually built. The walls were decorated with paintings of heroes with Diponegoro gracing one wall on his life-sized white stallion, his sword held menacingly as he screamed in still life at the enemy. Despite the power constraints placed on other households, a brilliant chandelier which hung ostentatiously in the centre of the room sparkled brightly, casting its own spell over the Persian rugs adorning the highly polished marble floor.

"*Silahkan masuk, tuan*," the aide invited, and Stephen followed, conscious of his own awe at the wealth this residence represented. During his absence from the Capital many new and palatial houses had appeared along this avenue. The President's residence lay not more than four-hundred metres to the north.

This area of Menteng spreading from Jalan Teuku Umar down through Jalan Cendana, was always smothered with armed guards and armed personnel carriers. It represented an elitist suburb for the government and military *bapak-bapak*. There were practically no Chinese in this section of the suburb with the exception of one who was as regular in attendance at the palace as the President's own family. This man had become almost as important to the new government as it's own military support.

Many stories revolved around the little broker who had become wealthy as a direct result of his association with the Javanese who now occupied the Palace. Within a few years, his financial empire placed him as one of the wealthiest entrepreneurs in the world. Acting as the President's financial confidant, this man managed to develop his interests in association with the privileged few until emerging as the financial and manufacturing giant of the Republic.

The New Order was cognizant with the influence this man wielded over the Chinese community and, in consequence, over the entire non natural resources or energy sectors, for the Chinese were the shopkeepers, bankers and manufacturers who, through their *kongsi* arrangements, assisted the economy to survive. Stability was relatively unknown to the peoples of this vast country. Now, with the strength of the new government and it's foresight to introduce a series of Five Year Development Programs it appeared as if political and economic stability could become reality and not just dreams propounded by politicians.

Bitter animosity continued to exist between the Chinese and *pribumi* peoples of the archipelago. The government could not afford to be openly seen to be conducting business with the Chinese minority group. Freedom of the press was perfunctory at best whilst in reality, the government maintained the strictest controls over the media. Anti-government or even defamatory statements directed at senior individuals was considered to be subversive action and treated accordingly. Harshly. The ultimate deterrent, the death penalty, was imposed as an anti-subversive measure and was strictly applied to those who did not toe the line.

Coleman shuddered as he remembered he no longer had the protection of his government. Any indiscretion on the part of his former colleagues could jeopardize his fragile existence in this new environment. Coleman was aware that most foreign governments including his own continually maintained covert listening agencies throughout South East Asia. It was a fact of the times. The outside world was still highly critical and suspicious of this country which was quickly emerging, almost galloping, ahead of its other Asian neighbours. As to who would be recruited for the position he had forgone, Stephen Coleman really did not wish to know. It was imperative that he was seen to be and was, in fact, totally distanced from all government agencies which incredibly, as history has shown, managed to compromise their operatives with amazing regularity, leaving them to extricate themselves from dangerous situations which were, for the most part, not even of their own doing.

* * * * * *

Coleman turned as his host appeared. The General entered the split level guest area where his young visitor waited. Seda was dressed in an expensive hand-made long-sleeved *batik* shirt, cotton trousers and Bally casuals. He carried an air of power and, as he approached, his gait was that of a man of position, almost of royalty. He smiled benevolently at his guest. It was obvious that he was proud of his new residence.

He had done well since his former director had 'passed away'. Seda's appointment to the vacant post had surprised most Jakarta observers as he was not of Javanese stock and also relatively junior within the military hierarchy. As to the secret of his continuing success, embassy circles whispered stories of how he had saved the Vice President from exposure over his unfortunate association with a former general who was still incarcerated on the infamous Buruh Island. Others in the know claimed that it was because his wife was related to the Chief of Staff. But those who thought they really understood the Timorese's swift rise to power claimed that their sources confirmed it was because of simple Indonesian logic, to promote the man most unsuited at the right time. How else would a relatively junior officer rise so quickly to such a prominent position?

Only a few who moved in palace circles knew he had been personally selected by the President as a direct result of substantial support from his own son, whose recommendations were a direct result of a new corporate relationship which Seda had recently developed. Within the short span of just a few years this arrangement with the Palace and the Japanese yielded untold millions into their offshore accounts in Singapore's newly created ACUs, or Asian Currency Units.

The Singapore banking fraternity had been first to identify the magnitude of hidden wealth in Indonesia and moved swiftly to provide secure and discreet storage for these funds through numbered accounts. Switzerland was too far away, too distant. Jakarta businessmen and other wealthy residents knew that they could not jump on a plane and fly to Geneva in just over one hour, physically sight their gold and cash then return home on the afternoon flight. To the simple yet wealthy corrupt officials, Singapore represented a safe haven, not just psychologically, but a practical one as well.

The sense of security knowing their money was just across the water, and that its secrecy was guaranteed by Singapore was sufficient to allay any fears they might have had. They believed that their offshore positions could never be challenged by any third party, including their own government. Funds could legally be transferred into a numbered interest bearing account into any one of the many prime banks operating in the Republic of Singapore. These funds would be jealously guarded by Singapore law, providing the account holders with complete security and, more importantly, anonymity should they so desire. And most did, out of necessity.

Within ten years these accounts had grown in volume to exceed thirty billion American dollars, most of which represented the result of corrupt deals or were just funds hidden from the taxation authorities. Singapore would eventually displace Switzerland as the world's safe haven for illicit funds.

The new premises, so admired by his guests, had cost the Director (Special Services) Intelligence Protocol, as he was officially designated, the equivalent of approximately one hundred years of his official salary. Nobody questioned his or others in his peer group, how they had acquired their sudden wealth. To do so would not just be foolish. It would be madness.

But in Indonesia corruption was such new stars were spawned by the day. Few were not involved and finger pointing was considered the conduct expected only of foreigners. It was apparent to Coleman that, as no other guests were yet evident, his invitation had been designed to permit his host the opportunity for a *tête-á-tête* and in style.

The General was trying to impress and Stephen was flattered. As the Timorese approached, Stephen could not help but feel how the man had grown, not physically, although there was more to him than before. It was something else. His posture. and self-assurance. The General moved with an air of confidence that had not been present when Stephen had first known him.

Seda greeted Coleman warmly. "*Apa kabar, Mas, you are looking well.*"

"*Terima kasih, Pak. And how are you and Madame Seda?*"

The older man just nodded his head as neither was genuinely interested in his wife's health, both recognizing the obvious opening courtesies required by custom before proceeding on to more important matters.

"*Please,*" he indicated, with all of his fingers extended, showing the guest where he expected him to be seated.

"*Pak Seda,*" Stephen began, "*firstly I wish to thank you for the invitation tonight. Also, I must apologize to Njonja Seda for not attending your earlier dinner party but, unfortunately, I did not receive your wife's invitation and was unable to attend.*"

It was not lost on the host that his young guest had elected to mention that the previous invitation was, in fact, sent in his wife's name, as he had instructed.

The General smiled, the slight gesture of his right hand indicating that it was of no consequence. "*You're here now, that's what is important."*

Seda viewed the Australian.

As did many of his race, he admired these people from the rugged southern country who had fought alongside the Timorese against the occupation forces of the Japanese. There was almost a camaraderie between their two peoples and yet, race colour and politics demanded that this not be so. Seda believed that the young Australian could play an integral part in his overall plans. He knew he could use this man to his own advantage. He had thoroughly considered the opportunity Coleman represented and, having expended considerable energy and time developing an offer which would be attractive to the foreigner, arranged to broach the subject before other guests arrived.

Even though he had put a great deal of thought into the proposition he was about to offer Coleman, Seda still had reservations as to the man's dedication to himself, as distinct from his country. This was imperative as he was about to take a dangerous, but necessary chance on the man's natural human failings.

Avarice and greed.

For a limited time they discussed Indonesia's rapid changing economic and social structure and, satisfied that they had exhausted all other topics unrelated to the real purpose of the meeting and, pressed for time as the other guests were due in thirty minutes, the General raised the question.

"Have you managed to obtain an acceptable sponsor to enable you to continue in Indonesia?"

Having advised the older man *en passant* and earlier in their discussion that he had left the Australian Government and now intended staying on in Jakarta, Coleman had hoped that the conversation would take this new direction.

"No, Pak Seda," he responded, indicating his lack of success with a slight gesticulation of the hands, *"perhaps you could advise what course of action I should take?"*

Seda studied the Australian. His decision had not been made lightly. The former government employee had been investigated both in Indonesia and through the Embassy in Canberra to ascertain this man's real function within the government apparatus. He was not considered a political risk although any journalist's credentials were always of concern to the Indonesian authorities. Con-

sidering absolute proof was impossible, the Timorese was sufficiently convinced of the former Attaché's sincerity to reside in Indonesia for purely personal considerations.

"*I will arrange a sponsor,*" Seda advised, smiling at Coleman as
he extended his hand.

Coleman gripped the hand lightly but warmly, understanding
that Asians preferred not to have their limbs pumped in the Western way.

"*Pak Seda, you honour me with your offer.*"

"*It is the least one should do for one's business associate,*" the General offered the surprised foreigner and, not detecting any negative reaction, continued, "*survival in this environment requires more
than a sponsor, Mas Stephen.*"

Seda's use of his first name and the insinuation of a possible
future relationship caught Coleman by surprise.

Maybe he'd misheard?

"*Pak Seda,*" he started only to be interrupted.

"*Mas, we'll talk tomorrow. Tonight I want you to celebrate quietly, as
what we have to do together will be our secret and to our mutual benefit.*"

"*Tomorrow,*" Stephen again started to speak and was again
prevented from continuing.

"*Tomorrow will be a very important day for you, Mas. We will talk
about many things, but particularly we will discuss a new organization I
am involved with and, as it requires the knowledge of someone, a foreigner, I wish to offer you the opportunity to join with us.*"

"*I have observed you since you first arrived in my country. You are
intelligent, respectful and clever. You are also young and impetuous. However, you have my support.*"

Stephen sat quietly as the General continued.

"*Whatever we discuss tomorrow, regardless of your decision, must be
kept confidential.*"

Stephen became restless. "*Of course,*" he replied, hesitantly.

"*Mas Stephen,*" Seda spoke softly, "*I must have your assurance that
whatever you hear during tomorrow's discussions will remain between
you and me only.*"

It had all been presented too quickly, and Coleman was not only
surprised but confused. He wanted to respond in the affirmative
but felt that he should know more before making such a commitment, even though it appeared that he was being offered the very

opportunity that suited his own personal yet undefined needs.

"*Pak,*" he began, "*I agree to keep anything you disclose to me completely confidential.*"

"*I require your word, Mas!*"

Stephen stared at the powerful man. He realized that to hesitate now would lose him an opportunity to really befriend one of the most powerful figures in the country.

Coleman extended his hand. "*I will be here tomorrow, General, and you have my word.*"

Nathan Seda smiled, obviously satisfied.

He would utilize this relationship to achieve his goals. The Australian would be of immense assistance to him. He would place Coleman at the front of his commercial activities, supporting him silently with his financial and political strength. The relationship would be most beneficial to both parties as he was reasonably confident in this man's abilities and unusual understanding of the Indonesian people. Then there was, of course, the question of maximizing the former government representative to access some of those foreign military suppliers who resisted dealing directly with Third World buyers.

They spoke quietly together, pausing only when the other guests arrived. The amazingly brief dinner party *Njonja* Seda had arranged for the small group of guests lasted only one hour. It was apparent to Stephen that the others had been window dressing for his meeting with the General.

They had been left alone again as the other visitors had excused themselves relatively early, obviously to permit the private discussions to continue. The problem of sponsorship was considered further and then settled. Seda would arrange for one of the departmental heads on the Foreign Investment Board to personally sponsor Stephen.

The General noticed his guest stifle a yawn and understood that his new associate had absorbed enough for one night. He reminded Stephen of the agreed meeting scheduled for the following day. The hour being late, Coleman took his leave, his head spinning. Everything had fallen into place for him like pieces in some giant but complicated jigsaw puzzle.

He was driven back to the house on Jalan Wijaya. Physically tired but mentally exhilarated he was unable to sleep for some hours, until finally drifting off, as the faint light encroaching on morning sky heralded the approach of *fajar*.

* * * * * *

Njonja Seda's car called for him at precisely nine o'clock as arranged. Coleman was impressed, not just with the driver being on time in a country which put little store in being punctual, but more with the expensive sedan. It was a dark brown Mercedes 450, the windows heavily tinted, permitting those inside to easily view the outside world while remaining obscured from the onlookers. This gave the German-manufactured vehicle a sinister appearance.

He had received telephone instructions earlier to leave the embassy accommodation and wait to be met outside the Brawijaya Guest House, not more than a five-minute walk from Walters' house.

The impressive sedan had pulled up directly beside where he stood, so close the tyres almost touched the tips of his shoes. The door immediately in front him was opened slightly from the inside, signalling for Stephen to enter. Having done so, the driver sped away without so much as a greeting, guiding the machine dexterously through the maze of *becak* and pedestrian traffic which blocked the road.

They wound their way through this maze of humanity easing into the Kemang turn-off before speeding quickly along the Kemang Raya road towards Cilandak. The surface was yet to be sealed and they accelerated forward, the driver with his palm pressed continuously on the double horns, roadside vendors waving their fists menacingly at the passing vehicle which trailed clouds of red dust.

The driver remained unconcerned, concentrating only on steering the expensive vehicle to its destination. They stopped momentarily at the junction leading off to the Navy's large depot which, for some unknown reason, had been built more than fifteen kilometres inland and south of the city. Here the car turned away from the Navy establishment and then continued twisting and turning, following the red-coloured dusty surface, broken from the constant pounding of oversized military trucks which used this track for transporting their river sand and other building materials.

They travelled for another twenty minutes and Coleman guessed that, by then, they should be somewhere around halfway to the town of Bogor. He couldn't be sure, of course, not having been along these roads before. Their vehicle approached a small village house, inconspicuously simple in appearance. And very isolated.

Guiding the now filthy Mercedes with considerable skill between a number of tall *rambutan* and mango trees, the driver managed to bring the sedan to rest directly behind the building, concealed from all who may pass by. Coleman was again surprised that the surly driver did not alight to open his door, a gesture expected by all *tuans*.

"The General is waiting for you inside," the voice from the front of the car advised.

Stephen opened his own door and proceeded towards the small and rustic dwelling, stepping cautiously as the soggy ground was covered by chicken and duck droppings. He knocked.

"*Masuk, Mas*," a voice ordered.

He did as instructed and found the General sitting alone drinking coffee. There was a red thermos and several cheap glasses on a teak table. There were no servants evident. He joined Seda, accepting the glass of black coffee, wishing he'd remembered how hot these could be to unsuspecting hands.

"*Let's begin*," Seda said, opening a folder and placing it so that his new associate could view the documents inside.

They discussed the mechanics of the new arrangements. From time to time Coleman interrupted to ask questions, continuing only when both were satisfied that he clearly understood the subject matter. They worked well together and, by mid-afternoon, they had established a mutual respect for each other's obvious capacity to understand the complicated issues and tasks with which they would be faced. Approaching five o'clock, they were both showing the strain of the tiring day.

Seda's powers of concentration increased as the in-depth discussions and Stephen's briefing led them into areas yet unknown to the Australian. They evaluated everything revealed by the Timorese General, together, and Stephen was pleased that he'd understood the older man's explanations when questioned on points still unclear to him.

It was agreed that Coleman would appear as the sole proprietor of a new company established as a supply conduit to the Department of Defence. Behind the scenes, Seda would manipulate others within the Department to consolidate the new company's position as a recognized and reliable supply source for the military's needs. A series of subsidiary companies would be established in regional capitals such as Singapore and Hong Kong to facilitate the double documentation associated with buyer's commissions.

Coleman listened, fascinated and impressed with the General's thoroughness and the extent of the elaborate plan. As Seda talked, with obvious knowledge and authority, Coleman became aware of the General's superb understanding of commercial matters relating to the Defence Department.

Seda took him through the concept, step by step, explaining his reasoning for the complicated procedures he had insisted on introducing prior to implementation of the project. Stephen thought he'd misunderstood when the General had indicated that his potential share of the company's proceeds would, within three years, exceed one million dollars.

As Stephen sat, stunned, Seda deliberately rolled the figure off his tongue again, more slowly, so that the ramifications of the potential their arrangement had would be overwhelmingly engraved on his mind. He could be wealthy!

The General understood the value of people. But he had a greater understanding of human nature and how values change proportionately to the volume of dollars involved. Recognizing the expression on the Australian's face, Seda was finally comfortable that he had made the right choice in selecting this man. Assured that his new associate understood the consequences of any disclosure concerning their relationship, Seda established a routine for their private telephone conversations which were scheduled to occur on a weekly basis.

They had also agreed that, in the interests of further distancing themselves from each other publicly, all personal meetings or sensitive transactions should be conducted strictly off-shore through nominated safe houses or via such people as the General may wish to designate.

Obviously, there was considerable detail yet to be discussed and resolved. They accepted that it was more important to establish the principles of their relationship and agree on a *modus operandi* for the company's overall activities during this day's discussions rather than attempt to cover too much detail.

"That's just about it then, Mas," Seda suggested in a tired voice, *"we will talk again next week and commence from then. Don't concern yourself about funding, we will have it all in place within a few days or so. You should concentrate on finalizing your permits and other documentation with the immigration authorities. Everything must be done according to the regulations. We don't want you to attract unnecessary attention."*

"Phone this number," he instructed, passing the piece of paper to Stephen, *"and arrange an appointment with Sutrisno. I have already spoken to him, as you know, regarding your sponsorship. It's all settled but he will need to assist you put your applications together correctly."*

"No one's going to refuse his sponsorship," he stressed, referring to the Chairman of the influential Foreign Investment Board.

"He will also provide you with a list of acceptable houses for you to occupy. Select one and he'll have it prepared through his offices. Power, water, telephones, everything. Then you should move in and settle down, preparing yourself for an interesting time," he paused, for the effect, *"and an exciting one, I'd expect. "*

They spoke for a few more minutes but as both were weary and Seda had to return for another appointment, he departed first, leaving Stephen alone in the smoke-filled village house.

An hour passed and he heard the horn blast twice. Coleman was annoyed with the driver's obvious display of contempt. The horn sounded again, impatiently. Coleman appeared and sauntered to the car, slamming the door as he entered, without effect, as the meticulously engineered doors clicked into place. Once again he sat in the rear and in silence, as they returned via a different route. The driver dropped him precisely where he'd waited earlier in the day. As Coleman left the Mercedes he deliberately left the door ajar so that the driver would have to close it.

He didn't. Instead, the car suddenly accelerated forward a few metres, jerked to a halt then accelerated again, causing the car's own momentum to close the door. Stephen shook his head in bewilderment as the brown sedan drove away, leaving him still standing in a hail of small gravel stones thrown by the spinning rear wheels.

The driver circled the block to observe the foreigner. He'd disappeared. Coleman, tired and not keen to walk the short distance home had quickly climbed aboard a *becak* and was already around the corner heading for a hot bath when the vehicle returned. The driver's eyes narrowed. Slowly, this time, he drove away from where he'd dropped the General's guest.

'*One day,*' he muttered, '*one day you'll get it, bulé!*' the thought of which seemed to comfort him as he unclenched his tight grip on the steering wheel.

Umar Suharjo returned the Mercedes to the Seda household. He was angry to the pit of his stomach. He didn't appreciate being looked down on by others. He had skills beyond their comprehension and one day he would demonstrate some of these to the arrogant Australian, Coleman.

Chapter 10

Wanti

Stephen Coleman enjoyed the transition from government to the private sector. He had returned to Australia briefly, spending a weekend with his mother on the Hawkesbury River with some of her friends, enjoying the wines and pollution free air. She had expressed disappointment, as he'd anticipated, at his decision to leave the government and enter the world of commerce.

"I guess there's nothing much can be done now, dear," she had criticized, standing on the Canadian redwood sun deck overlooking the serene river, a flute glass filled with Chardonnay in her right hand, posturing, her head covered with an oversized straw hat. "I doubt you could return to your position now even if you wished to do so. "

He knew that this was his mother's way of informing her son that he was practically in disgrace and that someone in Canberra had been talking to her about him. She enjoyed secrets, he knew, but Stephen guessed correctly that Anderson was responsible for her mood.

The following week had not been as pleasant. He'd made arrangements to meet with the Secret Service's Director and was twice left to cool his heels at the designated appointment without meeting the man. Stephen knew the importance of sitting down with Anderson and explaining his position. For that reason and the respect he still had for the senior civil servant, he tried a third time and was relieved when the Director's secretary confirmed their meeting.

Anderson had agreed to meet him for lunch. Stephen had arrived first and walked across the lounge to greet his former department head. He had observed the tall, almost gaunt figure enter, his shoulders slightly stooped from the years of sitting behind a desk examining reports, the gray hair adding a touch of sophistication to the conservatively dressed Director. His handshake was firm but without warmth.

The meal was a disaster. Anderson was reluctant to respond to Stephen's light-hearted attempts at casual conversation.

"There should still be plenty of snow, John," he suggested, hoping an invitation to the last of the season's powdery falls would be offered as maybe a skiing trip would provide him with a more relaxed venue for discussion.

Anderson refused the hint. "Don't have the time at the moment. Seems we are a little short-handed these days," the inference aimed at Stephen's departure.

For a moment Stephen glimpsed an expression of sadness in the older man's eyes, but looking again he saw nothing and knew that he'd imagined it.

"Pity," he said, rotating the ice cubes in his scotch slowly with a plastic stirrer, "your lodge will always be one of my fondest memories."

"Why, Stephen?"

"Well, because that is where you. . . " he started before being interrupted.

"No!" the other man snapped. "Why did you resign?"

Coleman leaned back into his chair and sighed. He knew it was going to be difficult, but didn't appreciate just how complicated his position had become until then. Only when faced with the man who had been his benefactor, Director and close friend, did he understand how hopeless any argument would be.

He wanted to tell this man, who had been more of a father to him than his own during his formative years, that he no longer believed in the way governments moved silently, secretly, subversively, without accountability. And that the power of the covert organizations was created through fear. He was disillusioned by the lies and corruption that permeated all the other secret government agencies such as the CIA, MI6 and the KGB.

He couldn't find the words to describe the feeling of not being able to go home at night and take a shower to remove the filth of the day's work, and lie awake until morning unable to sleep because of the uncertainties and all too frequent self-examinations.

Coleman didn't say these things because he was sure that this man already understood. He sat across the table and appraised the Director he'd so greatly admired. Anderson looked weary.

It was the stress, Coleman knew.

"I'm out, John. I'm sorry you're disappointed, but it's over for me," was all he found to say, pushing the inconspicuous package across to the other man.

Anderson had said nothing ignoring the rectangular cardboard box placed in front of him. He sat for awhile silently thinking. All around others continued to talk as they dined. Only their table remained silent.

Suddenly Anderson rose and stood erect looking down at the shorter man. "The door is always open, Stephen," he said quietly, then left, the brown parcel containing the PPK automatic held tightly in his right hand.

Coleman watched his friend walk away with his purposeful strides, hoping he would look back, just once, and wave or smile. He waited as the tall well dressed frame passed through the glass doors leading out to the car park and down the wide steps, until suddenly he was lost from view.

Stephen remained at the table for a few more minutes. He knew it would be difficult. It was just the hollow feeling of disappointment he now felt towards the man who had been his friend. He would never forget the final look Anderson had given him, as if he had betrayed their relationship and was no longer to be trusted. Saddened, Coleman paid the check and wandered outside into the sudden burst of sunshine as the Canberra sun broke through the clouds.

For a brief moment he experienced the despair that comes when long-established relationships are ultimately broken, leaving the participants with a moment of regret, even emptiness. Suddenly, as quickly as it had come the feeling was gone replaced immediately with a sense of bitterness. He looked across the avenue at his former offices.

"Fuck you, John Anderson!" he said, lifting his hand in mock salute. Then he turned and walked away from his life as a Secret Service agent, forever.

* * * * * *

He had left for Melbourne the same evening, experiencing a

sense of loss. Anderson had been a good friend, he knew, but Stephen had made his choice and was committed to at least giving it his best try. As he looked out the window, the city's lights were evident and he remembered that he must call Albert. He put the earlier events out of his mind and prepared himself for the landing.

Australia's financial centre plays host to most of the country's corporate leaders. Coleman had introductions to several mining companies and an aviation group which wanted desperately to break into the lucrative Indonesian market. He took the opportunity to identify his company's activities and was pleased with the response. During his brief visit his phone rang continuously as more companies discovered his presence in their city. They were eager to discuss opportunities in the newly awakened giant called Indonesia, and identified Coleman as a possible means to enter the massive market without too much risk or exposure.

His credentials were excellent. A former government employee, fluent in the local language, an established office and considerable connections into the host country's government circles were enough to convince his clients that he could represent them adequately in the target area. He concluded several arrangements, in principle, and returned to Jakarta via Hong Kong where he repeated his performance, also successfully. Stephen discovered that foreign companies were desperate for representation to facilitate their way through the maze of bureaucracy found at every turn when dealing with government agencies. His background, contacts and local knowledge were suddenly in great demand.

Stephen selected an address in the 'dress circle' and quickly established his activities in a newly constructed office-cum-residence along the main arterial road of Jalan Teuku Cik Ditiro, which connected Imam Bonjol through Menteng into Cut Mutiah, the administrative centre for the newly formed Foreign Investment Board. His company soon became the preffered alternative to the Embassy's Trade Commissioner's office for most visiting businessmen, as Coleman, courtesy of his silent partner, could offer realistic arrangements and often had greater access than the Embassy.

The city had been transformed into an exciting metropolis due to the government's attractive foreign investment laws. Bars and night-clubs mushroomed supported by the American oil men with unlimited expense accounts. Massage parlours appeared everywhere, in many cases located directly behind male hairdressing salons to permit the customers discreet access. A new race track had been built. Casinos operated around the clock, as did many of the new and more popular night clubs such as the LCC, situated adjacent to the National Monument. The city fathers turned Jakarta into a rival for Bangkok and Macau.

The Governor, a Marine General, shoved Jakarta into the twentieth century with such gusto even his administration could not keep pace with the planning requirements such rapid development demanded. Roads were widened, bridges rebuilt, hotels appeared and all prospered.

Indonesia had become the land of the new gold rush. The Japanese flocked into the country building textile mills and electronic factories. The Americans charged in with their drilling rigs and expertise carving out great sections of concession areas in the rich oil fields of the Java Sea. The Rupiah settled down and confidence was restored in the economy. Evidence of the military had all but disappeared from the streets.

Jalan Thamrin, Jakarta's main protocol thoroughfare, had been raised and then re-sealed, for a third time. Unfortunately, it still flooded regularly, creating chaos as the city traffic had grown at a much greater rate than road development.

The Australian Embassy stood dwarfed by its Japanese counterpart and the Hotel Indonesia, now surrounded by three other international rivals still managed to maintain high occupancy levels. Many major buildings were under construction to provide facilities for the continuing boom. Companies associated with the oil and gas industry increased the foreign population over three years by ten thousand families.

As the government had insisted that only foreign personnel with the required expertise be admitted, semi-skilled local labour was in considerable demand. Typists and receptionists received salaries five times that of a senior government employee and a night club hostess could easily double a Cabinet Minister's annual income in just a month. Or a week, should she be receptive to some 'extra service' so often demanded by the lonely visitors.

Home owners with acceptable dwellings could receive the total value of the premises as an advance payment for a five-year lease.

This introduced a domino effect which created thousands of new Californian-style homes suitable for the foreigners as the landlords would use the advance rental payments to construct yet more villas and the cycle continued.

The foreigners brought their own strange cultures to Jakarta. Restaurants which claimed to be English pubs serving pizza, hamburgers and cottage pies flourished. The expatriates collected in the bars daily to communicate with each other, as other means were totally unreliable. Managers were obliged to use drivers to deliver messages, as this method proved more efficient than the local telephone system.

Businessmen and tourists found the local girls appealing and willing to administer to their needs. Jakarta's street prostitutes moved off the footpaths into the numerous bars and massage parlors, leaving their territory to the transvestites. These *banci*, dressed in the latest fashions, paraded around outside the Kartika Plaza Hotel, dominating the street's pedestrian traffic. Their numbers grew unchecked until the tall deep-voiced prostitutes completely controlled the Jalan Blora district.

The Indonesians found the all too frequent altercations which occurred between drunken foreigners repugnant. They had never been exposed to this alien social behaviour and had extreme difficulty dealing with it. Most simply avoided frequenting those hotels or restaurants which attracted the oil-rig crews.

Many civic leaders claimed that the Western influence was detrimental to the Indonesian people and should be curtailed before the effects were irreversible. The Moslem leaders were particularly vociferous, claiming that casinos and poker machines which were now rife in the city's bars and night clubs, had an anti-social and anti-religious effect on the population, and should therefore be banned immediately.

The Governor of Jakarta pointed out that the greater part of the funding received for the construction of the prestigious Istiqlal Mosque was, in fact, derived from those very poker machines. Teenage school girls cut classes to attend the night clubs to work as part-time hostesses. Drug abuse on the streets was evident for the first time and teenage suicides became a major statistic. Illegal taxis thrived and Jakarta's *cross-boy* hoodlum gangs emerged.

All this, and more, in just three short years! The city was alive with an exciting ambiance. Jakarta's inhabitants were smiling and enjoying life. Opportunities existed where before there had been nothing. The government embarked on an ambitious development program spending many millions of dollars on infrastructure projects and a restructured Defence Department — all of which required a constant supply of equipment and new weapons.

* * * * * *

Stephen Coleman's company thrived on its defence contracts. At the end of his second year, the company boasted thirty-one permanent office employees. Their activities were mainly centred on the provision of military supplies. Although the other areas also provided substantial income, profits from armament and equipment sales to the Department of Defence represented over ninety percent of all earnings.

Seda's system was simple and effective. They had first established a holding company in Hong Kong, using nominee directors. This enterprise appointed Coleman's Jakarta based group to act as official representatives promoting the arms and services offered via Hong Kong. Stephen visited manufacturers and suppliers in the United States and Europe, negotiating directly with company presidents to obtain agency agreements for sales into Indonesia. These corporate heads were informed that he, in fact, was the legal owner of the supply company registered in Kowloon. He also advised them that he represented several well-placed military associates who could guarantee orders should agency agreements be successfully concluded.

At first Coleman was confronted with considerable resistance. Several manufacturers approached HANKAM directly themselves, attempting to circumvent Coleman's proposed supply route. Nathan Seda blocked their every move. Eventually several smaller dealers contacted the Australian and established test orders for the supply of radio broadcast equipment. Delivery proceeded smoothly. Further orders followed. Again the dealers were satisfied, and his reputation began to grow. Within the year the Hong Kong company had secured sales in excess of five million United States dollars. Seda ensured that Coleman was informed regularly as to the Government's requirements and budget allocations for military purchases. They were cautious not to monopolize the market.

Coleman suggested establishing other nominee companies to expand their field of representation however Seda was reluctant to do so. He became concerned with the frequency of their meetings outside Indonesia. The General had become increasingly uncomfortable being away from his power base more often than before. He suggested that they restrict the regularity of their meetings to minimize exposure. Seda insisted they implement a more efficient and less dangerous procedure, one which would remove the need to meet as often thereby reducing their overall exposure.

He proposed the use of a single courier, who would facilitate delivery of sensitive documentation between the two men. They discussed the idea and, although Stephen accepted the General's proposal in principle, he was still concerned with the thought of an outsider being given such responsibility. Both agreed that the only real link in this arrangement would be the reliability of the courier. They understood also that should the documents be compromised at any time then their personal safety would be at risk.

Stephen agreed to use coded communications whenever exchanging letters with Seda, and nominated one of his senior staff, Pasaribu, who had developed a keen interest in the company's activities and had demonstrated his willingness to carry out orders without question. The General had refused his choice as the man was of Batak descent. Seda disliked Bataks.

They discussed alternatives and decided that until such times as the Timorese was comfortable with any of Coleman's immediate staff to fill this sensitive position, Seda would bring in another one of his own.

Umar Suharjo reported for courier duty the following week.

* * * * * *

The school where Wanti worked catered for students at the *Sekolah Menengah Pertama* level. The junior high school had been built only two years before, one of many, to cope with the sudden influx of students from the provinces. Bambang had been able to convince the local educational authorities to accept his sister as a part-time teacher. She had felt so proud on that first day when the other teachers had received her warmly as one of their own.

Wanti had tried very hard, teaching rudimentary subject material. She had no training for the position but her willingness to always do more and the students' immediate acceptance of her as a teacher was sufficient for the senior staff to move her temporary position, into full-time employment.

Wanti was grateful to her brother and the other young women who now shared the simple accommodations not far from the school. She knew that Bambang had pressured his girlfriend to assist with her application and Wanti now endeavoured to repay her kindness whenever the opportunity arose. Sharing a room with her brother's girlfriend was appropriate, she thought.

Often, when at school and during lessons she would feel a strange sense of exhilaration with the work. Especially when the young teenagers treated her more like an older sister than their teacher. She adored them all.

Once, when the school year was approaching the final days after examinations had been completed, the staff and students spent the whole day travelling the thirty kilometres to Bogor. The picnic had been arranged to coincide with the annual flowering of the huge plant the foreigners called *Rafflesia*. Wanti and the children learned a great deal that day as they sat and listened to the guide explain the historical values of the beautiful gardens. She was surprised to discover that the British had, for a brief period, displaced the Dutch and taken over her country. They had sent an English gentleman by the name of Raffles to become the new Governor of the Spice Islands. Wanti would see the results of his tenure in Indonesia. The beautiful Bogor Gardens were designed and built for his wife and, when she had passed away, Raffles had buried her there.

Wanti loved the romantic story. She was amazed when told that the foolish English had surrendered possession of her wonderful country, returning the islands of Indonesia to the Dutch receiving, in exchange, a small malaria-infested island called Singapura and the northern lands of Malaka. As she sat with the other teachers surrounded by students and observed the enormous flower finally open for its annual display of beauty and size, she was shocked that the world's largest flower had been cursed with such an obnoxious odour!

Later, as they returned to Jakarta and the children joked and teased each other, Wanti decided that there must be many wonderful places to see and visit. It was after that experience Wanti knew she just had to travel. At night she would dream of faraway places, conjuring up mythical lands in her mind before falling to sleep and, sometimes, dream of the wonders she had not seen but only read about in the brochures which lay neatly stacked under her bed.

When school finished on Saturdays she would climb aboard a bus and make her way into the city. There she would search out the travel agents asking for brochures for her students. The receptionists knew that the young woman obviously wanted the material for herself, but none could refuse the attractive girl as she was so sweet.

At night, after taking her *mandi* and shared rice with her roommate Wanti would first attempt to read the brochures to herself before practicing aloud to her friend. She found the language difficult but was determined to persevere. Within a few months Wanti found that, with the aid of an English dictionary, she could actually make her way through an entire brochure in just one evening, understanding the contents clearly. Having mastered the contents she would then insist that her friend sit and listen as she read through the pages.

Wanti wished that her life had more to offer than just teaching simple subjects at school. She dreamed of being given the opportunity to fulfil her earlier ambitions. Wanti wanted desperately to become a secretary or at least a receptionist with one of the foreign firms she was always reading about, and sought ways to improve her chances for such positions. She concentrated on improving her communication skills understanding that knowledge of the foreign language was a pre-requisite in obtaining such lucrative employment.

Bambang had not laughed at her when Wanti explained why the travel brochures were so important to her. They were poor and could not afford the additional expense of books.

Wanti adored Bambang and he in turn cared for his sister above all else. She realized that soon he would be obliged to follow his unit to wherever they were sent, once he had graduated. Then she would be alone. Wanti knew that time was running out and it was imperative that she advance herself in some way. As most opportunities demanded a foreign language skill, the young Javanese girl decided that this should be her first step.

ᴐhe would attend a course.

* * * * * *

Wanti viewed her brother's uniform critically. Although two years his senior, Wanti considered her *adik* more of an older relative. He certainly looked impressive dressed in his graduation uniform. Who would have thought Bambang would become such a handsome soldier? She smiled as he adjusted his beret for the umpteenth time.

"At last, their *rejeki* had improved," she thought, considering how their fortunes had changed for the better over the months.

Standing there, staring, not altogether conscious of the dreamy expression she displayed, Wanti's eyes slowly began to glaze over as they had so many times before. She realized that it was happening, again, and attempted to resist the sudden seizure. *No!* Wanti pleaded with herself, willing her body unsuccessfully to control the strange effects of the attack. *No, not now! not today!* she cried out silently, alarmed. Suddenly, Wanti remained very still and her mind slipped away from the reality of the moment into some dark void, as it had so many times before ever since she had witnessed the horrific aftermath of the raid on her village.

The unskilled doctors understood her trauma but could offer no remedy, no therapy to the beautiful but tragic soldier's sister. They had not received adequate training at medical school and had been unable to do anything to treat these self-induced seizures. As her mind retreated into another world closing down temporarily distancing Wanti from the reality around her, she would be transported to another plane. Her eyes would glaze over as she stared unsmilingly into space, breathing slowly, almost calmly. It was as if Wanti was not even present. There was never any panic, or so it would seem to the observer. It was just as if her spirit had temporarily departed leaving its physical semblance intact, waiting for consciousness to return.

To Bambang, who was accustomed to these trances, it was heartbreaking. For others who witnessed the incredible transformation, it was frightening. Outwardly she would appear as if day-dreaming. There was never any apparent physical movement to reflect the torment of the violent imagery flashing across her brain as she experienced scenes from a time long ago, now buried deep in her subconscious. Deep enough, almost, to prevent a total collapse.

As the headless children and mutilated torsos danced in her thoughts distancing her from whatever reality that may have triggered the turn, she would continue to experience the hallucinations and suffer extreme fear while those around her saw only the unusual, placid demeanour of the afflicted young woman.

Her brother Bambang could merely stand by and watch helplessly. She would never remember and could not therefore explain to Bambang the silent screaming terror she experienced with each of these sudden attacks, and even the doctors did not understand what triggered these relapses. Wanti would suddenly awaken, her frail body exhausted, saturated in perspiration, sometimes startling her brother with a shrill scream as consciousness returned. Wanti never had any recollection of the chilling visions.

When the first seizure occurred Bambang was terribly frightened. He'd called to her softly but when she did not respond he thought her brain had snapped like the old woman who lost her son in a bus accident during *Ramadhan*. He had shouted at Wanti to stop. He'd shaken her violently to make her snap out of the trance, but she had remained in the self-induced state. He had taken her by the hand and called her name, over and over, to no avail.

Then, suddenly, she returned to normal, blinked, looked caringly at her brother and smiled softly.

"*Kenapa, Mas?*" she'd asked, curious as to her brother's anxious expression.

At first he'd thought she'd been playing some stupid trick on him until he realized that she was not pretending. Bambang had just let her hand drop back by her side. He didn't know what to do. He prayed that her sickness might go away, naturally, with time. When several more fits occurred, he learned just to shrug them off.

As Wanti's self-induced hypnotic state started to recur regularly, he realized then that it was *Allah's* way of preventing her mind from snapping. *Allah* was *Great* and understood these things.

Bambang was a simple *kampung* boy and being such, was not equipped to understand why these attacks could occur at any time without any apparent trigger. He pleaded in his prayers for this mind sickness to go away. But it didn't.

The frequency of the seizures did, however, diminish. Fortunately Wanti never remembered any of these incidents. Whenever she regained full consciousness and returned from wherever her mind had taken her she would always respond by asking why others were staring at her. *"Kenapa, Mas?"*

After this latest attack he stood with his arm around her tiny shoulders. It had been some time since her last trance. He would not tell her that it had happened today, of all days.

Wanti was suddenly aware that her brother was still staring at her. She detected the concern in his expression.

"What is it, Mas?"

Her brother hesitated, his eyes filled with love and sadness for his beautiful sister.

"Wanti, I am worried about you," Bambang slowly shook his head as he forced a smile, reassuring his sister. *"You are too attractive to take to the graduation ceremony amongst all of those good looking young soldiers."*

She returned his smile. Her classic features warmed his heart for she was truly a beautiful woman.

"Bambang, ada-ada saja, You're too much," she laughed enjoying the flattery. *"Do you think I don't know what you boys really say about your sisters when they are out of earshot?"*

"Ah, Wanti. If only you really knew!" the young Javanese soldier teased, adjusting the angle of his beret again, now pleased to put this most recent attack out of his mind as there was so much to do on this important day.

He looked at her closely and, reassured that she had recovered from the spell, continued to prepare for the ceremony.

"We should depart. I am very pleased you came to escort me to the parade Bambang, but to be late would not represent a good start for your career."

"Ayo, let's go," she cajoled, slipping her arm through his, feeling confident that their luck had, in fact, changed for the better at last.

That evening Wanti was excluded from the boisterous celebrations. Instead, she sat at home and contemplated her future. She understood that Bambang would no longer remain in Jakarta. It was likely that he would be sent to one of the distant Territorial Commands for practical field experience. She had managed very well alone, these past six months separated from her brother, while he attended his training courses. Living with a girlfriend and sharing a room, their incomes as primary school teachers less than that paid to a foreigner's *babu*, the attractive young Javanese girl quickly developed an understanding of how poorly paid they were in comparison to others.

They were all economic conscripts, she thought.

Now that her brother had commenced his career, Wanti understood the necessity in taking positive steps if she expected to drag herself out of these sub-standard living conditions and make something of her life. During her brother's absence she had undertaken free English language lessons conducted by the American Friendship Association. She had found the course difficult as there was little opportunity to practise. Nevertheless, the young teacher persevered and the Americans who taught as volunteers were impressed with her progress. In spite of her undernourished frame, she consistently worked hard.

'*Who knows,*' Wanti wished for herself, '*maybe I will be fortunate and marry well,*' considering that marriage would, after all, be a very acceptable solution to her immediate problems.

* * * * * *

A junior American Consulate Officer had spotted her in the long queue. The Information Section was running an additional program which could lead to most of the successful graduates being employed as local personnel in the Embassy. This was a very competitive opportunity and applications had been keenly sought over past days.

Wanti had waited in the queue until four o'clock on the first day. Applications were required to be submitted in person. There had been only four other girls queued ahead of her when the wire screen shutter dropped indicating that the application window was closed for the day. Her face fell and her lips trembled slightly. She had been waiting in the outside queue since early the day before. To be this close!

Determination brought Wanti back the following morning. She had argued with the others, moving far ahead of her entitled position to within view of the window. Ignoring the abuse, fighting back the tears, the beautiful young woman stood her ground and, before the morning break, was within six positions of being able to submit her application. Wanti refused to leave the queue for food or drink and, when the afternoon session commenced, she had moved forward two more positions.

One of the junior consulate officers had spotted her in the long queue the day before. He'd been disappointed when the attractive girl had disappeared with the others as the Embassy closed down for the day. And here she was again, just as radiant, just as stunning! He was struck with her natural beauty and, slipping into the information office, he spoke quietly to one of his drinking buddies who was responsible for processing the forms, pointing in Wanti's direction.

She had seen, as did many of the silent hopeful applicants, the slap on the shoulder followed by boyish laughter and smiles without understanding that she was the reason for the banter. Unbeknown to Wanti, she had just been guaranteed a position on the course.

Totally unaware that she had jumped the queue, Wanti continued waiting her turn and, when it arrived, she smiled and passed her documents to the young American. Had it been brought to her attention that she had been successful primarily because of her appearance, the young lady would have just smiled sweetly and answered, '*And why not?*' responding with Javanese logic, '*beauty is as much a gift as is one's ability to do things, such as type or manage the complicated telephones, or teach, or work in the fields, and one should not be ashamed at being selected because of that gift.*'

She was pragmatic enough to appreciate that every opportunity must be taken in order to survive. As Wanti left the building her benefactor approached and very directly asked her for a date. She blushed, unsure of how to handle herself with the *bulé*, as being asked so directly by any man let alone a foreigner was a completely new experience for her. Wanti managed to escape with a polite response, hoping that the American would not be offended.

"Thank you, sir," she answered demurely and softly enough to send the young man's heart palpitations into overdrive, "but I am sorry. I cannot do so just now. "

She did not wish to offend. Although she felt there was little chance of her winning the position, Wanti was astute enough to realize that upsetting one of her potential employers would rule out any possibility whatsoever of being selected for this vacancy.

As she walked away the veteran of only two months smiled to

himself and made a mental note of her person. Later he checked her application and wrote down her name. The applicant's pass photo didn't do her justice but he had little difficulty identifying her picture. When Wanti returned for the first lesson he was waiting. Again he asked her out and again she refused politely.

But the American was very persistent. In the end she agreed, accepting an invitation to a function at one of the Embassy residences. Unable to afford new clothes for this special occasion she was, nevertheless, embarrassed to wear her traditional costume. "*Wear it, Wanti,*" advised her room mate, "*show them what a beautiful Indonesian girl should look like when she dresses.*" Wanti agreed and spent hours in preparation.

* * * * * *

Her escort had insisted on sending his driver to pick her up prior to the function. Wanti didn't object as she did not particularly wish the American to meet her at their lodgings. It would not do to have a *bulé* hanging around her door for the neighbours to gossip about and she certainly did not wish this fair foreigner to witness her living conditions.

The driver's attitude verged on offensive, but not enough for Wanti to outwardly react. She merely made another mental note concerning the idiosyncrasies of Indonesian drivers who had developed this strange superiority complex because they were fortunate enough to be driving foreign *tuans*, whilst earning as much as one hundred dollars per month.

The American's car was luxurious. She had never felt such comfort. And it was air-conditioned! She would have a story for Bambang when they next met. In fact, the conditions inside the sedan were cool and refreshing, similar to what she had experienced in the mountains in Central Java where, should one walk up the trails to the two thousand metre summit, blankets were required to prevent exposure from the cold.

Wanti shivered. The driver had turned the air-conditioning to maximum knowing this would cause this girl to feel uncomfortable. He counted off the minutes expecting his passenger's reaction at any moment. He was aware that these girls were not accustomed to the cold air and this was his method of punishing them for associating with the foreigners. Wanti realized that the vehicle's air-conditioning was far too uncomfortable but was uncertain as to how to remedy the situation. She refused to seek this arrogant driver's assistance. There were no handles on the door with which to open the windows and momentary panic engulfed her.

Her eyes began to glaze over. Her mind slipped away taking her to another world and another time. It was as if her person had departed, leaving her physical being while her spirit travelled away - away to the picturesque terraced mountain slopes topped with blankets of cloud overlooking the tranquil rice fields spread so uniformly below. Her next recollection was that of the driver whispering urgently.

"*Non! Miss, wake up miss!*" The driver was extremely agitated and beginning to panic, 'worried that she had fainted or even worse, might complain to the *tuan!*

"*Non, please Non. Wake up!*"

Slowly her consciousness returned. Her body was no longer cold. '*Aduh,*' she thought, '*we have arrived. I must have been daydreaming again.*'

Regaining her composure Wanti was assisted from the Nash Rambler by the courteous young Marine who took her hand and escorted her inside. When Wanti first entered and saw the large crowd of guests she was immediately intimidated by the scene before her. She was nervous at being alone, not recognizing anyone until she spotted her date amongst the other guests standing in the reception queue. As Wanti was late, he hadn't waited more than a few minutes outside the residence before entering with the other guests, assuming she had elected not to come.

Wanti had walked directly up to the American and stood alongside as all the guests in the line moved slowly forward into the large colonial structure. The premises were located on Jalan Raden Saleh. It was the residence of the United States Military Attaché and the evening's function was to introduce some of the many new Military Aid Advisers. Wanti was relieved to see other Indonesian ladies wearing the traditional *kain kebaya*. Now she would not feel so conspicuous.

Her escort introduced his guest to the host, a very tall Colonel who towered over the assembly. American Marine guards stood stiffly at the entrance their colourful uniforms adding to the atmosphere of colonial splendour. Five hundred guests crowded the stately home, some spilling out into the garden and gazebo where houseboys mixed, then refilled, cocktail glasses at an amazing pace. Trays of *hors d'oeuvres* were offered by the white uniformed *jongus* while others prepared the buffet.

The spectacle almost caused Wanti to cry out. She had never imagined anything so beautiful! It was if she had been thrust into a scene from Hollywood. Foreign Attachés and Ambassadors, French, German, Italian and even Russian representatives were to be seen. It was almost too much for the attractive Javanese as she remembered not to gape at the cocktail dresses and jewellery adorning the wives of these prominent people.

As she was introduced to another group Wanti noticed the young foreigner standing alone, a cocktail in one hand, cigarette in the other. He smiled, and Wanti looked away, embarrassed. She turned to ask her companion if the food provided was *halal*, or prepared according to traditional Islamic Law, but had difficulty in expressing herself.

The American replied, asking her if she was already hungry, misunderstanding what Wanti had said. She attempted to ask the question again, and when the words she required stubbornly refused to flow in the required sequence, she turned away to avoid the feeling of panic which threatened to engulf her. Flustered, Wanti reverted to Indonesian to escape unwanted attention as the other couples in their group were observing her struggle, the women inwardly enjoying this pretty young girl's discomfort at not being able to converse as fluently as the others.

Immediately she felt self-conscious. Exposed. Alone. She wanted to flee, and turned back to her escort for comfort. He was now preoccupied with the platter of *saté* offered by the servant to his left. As Wanti's concern grew she was surprised that the young man who had smiled at her had suddenly joined their group.

He was introduced by the American. Wanti immediately noticed the man's confidence and looks of admiration he received from the women nearby. He stood directly in front of Wanti, squeezed her hand gently and inquired, "*Nona cantik ini, siapa namanya?*" Who is this beautiful young lady?

Momentarily, she could not answer, amazed that this foreigner could speak her language. Wanti stared at the handsome darkly tanned Australian, his green eyes smiling at her surprised expression. Her fears immediately vanished. She looked at Stephen, mesmerized, deciding that he was of mixed extraction as he was darker than most of the other foreigners in the room. Or maybe he was one of those Dutch Christian missionaries she had heard about? Whatever he was, one thing was certain — she had never met a *bulé* who could speak her language so fluently. Confidence returning, Wanti responded in her national tongue.

"*My name is Suwanti. Can you really speak Bahasa Indonesia or have you merely memorized a few phrases to flatter the ladies and impress your foreign friends?*"

Coleman laughed at her refreshing directness. He decided to converse in her language so that the other foreigners could not follow the conversation and to keep her at ease.

"*Bukan main galaknya!*" he retaliated, indicating that she was snappish, noticing the instant change of expression.

"*Maaf tuan, kalau perkataan saya menyinggung,*" Wanti apologized for her cutting remark. "*Apakah tuan bisa maafkan saya?*" she requested, soliciting his forgiveness.

"*Sudah dong!*" Stephen replied with genuine sincerity as he took her hand once more and guided her away from the group and her partner.

"*I noticed your concern and decided that you were too pretty to be ignored by your boyfriend.*"

"*Boyfriend? Oh no tuan. He is my English teacher when he is not working at the Embassy.*"

Coleman grinned. "*Call me Stephen, not tuan. You will make me feel so old with tuan this, tuan that.*"

He led her into the garden where the strong fragrance of jasmine hung heavily in the air. Frangipani flowers decorated the tables while orchid arrangements enhanced the gazebo's setting. Candles flickered in their clay temple-shaped holders as harmonious voices blended perfectly with the Tapanuli guitarists' chords.

* * * * * *

Stephen realized that he'd been staring at her only when Wanti suddenly smiled, looking directly into his eyes. He couldn't believe how stunningly beautiful she was, dressed in the traditional costume, her hair rolled into a meticulously dressed half bun which rested gently on her lace-covered shoulders.

Wanti's features were classic. Her bright almond eyes were more oval than round, accentuated by high cheekbones providing just a touch of almost regal strength to her face. Stephen had seen many beautiful women in Indonesia and other countries, but never had he been so struck by the beauty of a young woman as *cantik-molek* as this magnificent Javanese creature.

He knew that the other guests would be observing them together in the garden and, although there were many other couples now mingling in the outdoor setting, he became conscious of the other guests' glances in their direction. They made a handsome couple, indeed, he thought.

Wanti sat where he'd indicated while continuing to admire the decorations. Coloured lights placed along the walls spreading high into the tall *beringin* tree created an almost carnival atmosphere and she was now pleased that she had attended the function. They sat together, momentarily silent, absorbing the serenity of the evening setting. A *jongus* replaced Coleman's drink, asking if the *tuan's* health had completely recovered, genuinely interested in this man he obviously admired.

Wanti was surprised with the sincerity she observed between the men. It was not common to see a foreigner behaving so kindly to those they considered below them. She was again impressed with the man's manner. Her interest in the young Australian grew through the evening as she came to notice the respect given to him by many of the other foreigners and the friendly nature he displayed when dealing with her own people.

He talked to Wanti for a while telling her about the function and the people present, stopping only when interrupted by other guests who had also ventured into the garden. She realized that he had a natural ability to put those around him at ease. Wanti suddenly felt comfortable in his company and was reluctant to return to her original escort, although she knew that good manners demanded that she do so.

"Please excuse me, Stephen. You have been very kind to me but, I should return to talk to my escort. I don't wish to make him angry. You understand?"

Coleman turned his head and after examining the crowded area inside spotted the American.

"Wait here, Wanti," he asked, *"I'll just be a moment,"* with which he rose, patted her hand softly and walked back through the garden and into the main hall.

When he returned, he was surprised that she looked concerned, almost worried.

"Was I gone that long?' he teased, smiling so that she would feel at ease, as before.

"I must go now, really."

"I don't think it's a good idea," he started, *"I have just spoken to your date and he is currently putting the hard word on someone else."*

"I don't understand."

"Wanti, your escort has just arranged to meet with the young lady who is leaning all over him after he has you sent home," he lied.

"That will be all right. I don't mind, he is not my boyfriend and I am grateful that he asked me to come here tonight. I think it has been a wonderful evening," she said.

"Wanti, I have told him that you have agreed to permit me to take you home." He looked very serious. *"It is not correct that you should be sent home alone. I hope you don't mind?"*

"I'm not sure," she hesitated, *"should I speak to him first? Was he angry that we have been out here together in the garden? Have I been rude?"*

"No, Wanti, no," Stephen assured her, taking the long fingers of her right hand and squeezing them warmly. *"He was pleased, in fact,"* again he lied.

"If you're sure, and if it is not too much trouble. I could go home by becak if necessary but it is so far and late at night, not so safe, as you probably already know."

"Well, we should not be in a hurry to leave," with which he took her by the hand and moved around with Wanti attached to his arm, introducing her to many of the guests. She couldn't remember their names and had given up attempting to do so after the first few. It was so difficult. The names were strange and the accents varied greatly making it almost impossible for her to cope. She realized that in no way she did feel intimidated, holding Stephen's arm as they walked slowly around, he shaking the men's hands, introducing her to them and their ladies while ignoring questions regarding the length of their friendship, or how they had met, while she smiled and occasionally responded with a polite

rejoinder.

As the evening progressed she discovered to her surprise that she was really enjoying the party and the guests. They had accepted her as one of them. They had been kind and charming. She looked at Stephen as he finished listening to a story, laughing at its ending as he caught her eye. He grinned and winked at her. Wanti just smiled in response.

One of the other ladies in the small group they had joined put her hand on Stephen's arm as she laughed, and Wanti immediately felt a twinge of jealousy. The woman was dressed in a long white evening gown, her short brown hair cut to permit the expensive earrings to display their elegant diamond settings, matched with the small brooch clipped beside the cleavage exposing her softly tanned but adequately endowed breasts.

Wanti could not understand the feelings she was experiencing, accepting that she had only just met her handsome new friend.

"*Stephen,*" she interrupted, "*may I go home now please?*"

He turned, looked at her and smiled. "*Sure,*" was all he said, taking her by the hand and leading Wanti out of the main reception room, stopping briefly to speak with their hosts.

"*You're tired.*" Although the statement did not require an answer she responded anyway.

"*Thank you Stephen. You have been very kind to me. I wonder why?*" she asked, almost coquettishly, her eyes wide, smiling at her small success in having him move away from the group inside and the attractive foreign woman. She had not expected him to agree to leave immediately and was now not really ready to return home to her dismal surroundings there.

"*Because you are like a fairy princess who's just stepped into my life,*" he answered, smiling kindly, holding her hands firmly.

Wanti laughed. "*Never a princess, Mas,*" unaware of her familiarity in addressing him so, "*never a princess!*"

His car had turned into the brick-paved driveway as they waited on the steps outside and he laughed with her, pleased that she had used the almost intimate form in her response. He drove her to his villa. Stephen knew she would be impressed and was surprised at himself for feeling the necessity for her to be so. At first she had refused to leave the car wishing that he'd taken her directly home.

"*We will only be a few minutes, Wanti. Please come inside. It's okay,*" *nothing will happen to you."*

"If it's only a few minutes then I can wait here."

Stephen shrugged and turned to enter the doorway now open as the *jongus* waited for him. Surprised that the young lady had not followed, he left the door ajar and followed his *tuan* into the lounge room.

"Make coffee, Kardi," he ordered.

The houseboy disappeared and within a few minutes had returned with a silver tray, coffee, two cups and an already poured crystal glass partly filled with Hennessee's XO Cognac and a selection of after dinner mints. He placed them on the long carved teak table and stood with his hands clasped in front of his body.

Stephen looked up and raised his eyebrows. *"What is it, Kardi?"*

"The young lady, tuan?" he inquired, turning his head in the general direction of the front door which remained open.

Stephen thought for a moment. *"Take this out to the car,"* he said, indicating the tray.

Never totally understanding the whims of the foreigners and their strange habits, the houseboy obeyed.

Wanti saw the *jongus* appear and moments behind, Stephen.

"We will have our coffee here, if you find it more comfortable," he said, climbing into the rear seat.

Wanti was speechless. At first she felt embarrassed, realizing that she had insulted this kind man who had been so thoughtful to her all evening. Then, as she observed how relaxed he was sitting back comfortably holding a large balloon shaped crystal glass softly swirling its contents, she started to laugh.

Stephen looked sharply and then, appreciating just how ridiculous it must all seem to the young and inexperienced Javanese beauty he too smiled and then joined with her laughing out aloud. The houseboy watched from behind the curtains. He was convinced that the *tuan* had gone completely mad. And then he too then started to smile. The young lady had stepped out of the *tuan's* car and was heading for the door.

Still laughing together, Wanti permitted Stephen to usher her into the house where they sat together in the guest lounge, sipping the retrieved coffee while listening to Neil Diamond sing his way through an Lp.

They talked and laughed, enjoying each other's anecdotes and other trivia as Sukardi politely entered from time to time, checking their coffee and replenishing the snacks he had hastily prepared when his *tuan* had returned. The hours passed quickly and, as she looked up at the antique clock as it chimed the hour, Wanti suddenly realized that it was already morning. She had stayed out all night. Immediately Wanti was filled with anxiety. She couldn't permit Stephen to take her home.

"I must go home by becak, Stephen. Please understand. I have been out all night and my reputation will be ruined if the others see me returning with a foreigner," she had pleaded. He understood and reluctantly agreed.

Promising to meet again on the following Saturday, Wanti took the *becak* arriving home with barely sufficient time to *mandi,* change and catch the bus to the school where she taught.

All day Wanti's spirits were high. She didn't feel at all tired even with the long hours she had then to spend at the school. And when she awoke the following morning, the strange feeling persisted and continued to do so throughout the day. She sat, observing the young children as they studied their books, aware that it was not just the anticipation she felt for their next meeting that sent her pulse racing — it was more than that.

The young Javanese woman now understood the emotion she'd experienced late into her first evening together with Stephen when suddenly, as he'd touched her hand gently, softly, an overwhelming warmth had passed quickly through her body. Wanti sat, uncomfortably, observing the children as they studied their books, conscious of the strange and unusual sensation she had never experienced before. It was more, much more than she had ever imagined it would be. As she day-dreamed, the unfamiliar feelings caused her to unconsciously adjust her position on the hard wooden chair. Confused but happy, anxious but excited, Wanti thought she might be falling in love.

* * * * * *

Weeks later, stretched out alone on the poolside deck chair Stephen still didn't quite understand exactly how he'd permitted it to happen. He sat up slowly, raised the *cubra libre* to his lips, slowly sipping the Bacardi as he observed the two topless sunbathers across the azure blue swimming pool.

Wanti had not yet returned from her third successive day's shopping. He couldn't believe her capacity to stay away all day browsing through shops, bargaining, missing meals, then returning late in the afternoon flushed with the excitement of the day's purchasing spree. Their hotel suite was already inundated with scores of plastic shopping bags containing shoes, scarves, negligees, jeans and jackets, all boxed and bearing the latest tags. She'd even bought new suitcases, needed to accommodate the range of fashions she'd acquired and an assortment of cosmetics which immediately filled all available bathroom space.

It hadn't been so much a whirlwind romance but more of a whirlwind wedding he thought, reflecting on their impulse decision to marry. Stephen knew that he was expected to settle down sooner or later and cease the debauched life he'd enjoyed as a single man if he expected to be taken seriously within the International Trading Community. Now, he wasn't even sure that he loved Wanti, but decided that it didn't really matter. He was content to have her near as she added a new dimension to his life and, more importantly, she loved him.

General Seda had been pleased when Stephen had asked for his opinion.

"*Do it, Stephen,*" he had urged, "*do it! She is a very beautiful girl and it would do you no harm to have such an attractive, intelligent and loving wife.*" Seda failed to inform Stephen that her being Javanese was probably a greater consideration than her other attributes.

Stephen had not wanted to go through the monotonous ritual of a traditional Javanese wedding. He explained to Wanti and Bambang that, as she was an orphan and as his parents lived so far away, it would be wiser to keep their wedding ceremony small, inviting just a few close friends. Wanti agreed. At that time she would have agreed to anything although later, as the initial euphoria faded, she did have some regrets.

Although he had not insisted, his bride had readily accepted the simple wedding at the registry office in old Kota, downtown China Town. They invited a small number of close personal friends, and Wanti's brother Bambang, to the celebration. Seda had suggested he would not attend.

They had honeymooned in Singapore and Hong Kong. Sitting around the pool at the Hyatt Regency on Scott's Road, Stephen finally came to terms with what he'd done and how impetuous he had been. He was surprised and a little annoyed with himself for the impulsive step he'd taken.

Stephen closed his eyes as the sun suddenly emerged from behind the clouds warming his well-tanned skin. The long Bacardi and Coke rested in his left hand, the ice cooling his palm through the thin glass. He relaxed, watching one of the topless women sit up suddenly and add some more cream to her body. He thought about his new bride. Stephen Coleman knew then that he had to make the best of his commitment. He waved to the white jacketed poolside waiter and ordered another drink.

* * * * * *

It was in Singapore that Coleman received Nathan Seda's couriered letter advising that their operation was about to enter a new phase, incorporating the supply of several squadrons of helicopters and associated armaments. It was a major opportunity for them. The note had instructed him to meet with the General in Kuala Lumpur the following day.

Coleman left his wife with friends who promised her a shopping excursion even his bank manager would never forget. Upon his return they recounted the day's events, laughing as they explained to Stephen how even they had difficulty keeping pace with his excited bride. As she hurried from shop to shop Wanti just couldn't believe her eyes. Meticulously she selected materials, ordering the tailor to copy a cocktail dress she'd seen in his imported catalogues and a smart trouser suit to match the three-inch heels purchased in the *toko* next door. She was like a little child, tearing open the parcels showing her husband what she had purchased barely finishing an explanation of one before tearing open another.

That evening, alone in the darkness of their hotel room Wanti related the story of her life with Bambang and the horrors she had experienced. Wanti finished her story without being subjected to one of her seizures. For the first time, since she could remember, Wanti felt safe.

Stephen held Wanti close to him comforting her as she sobbed choking back her tears while describing the savage mutilation of the many *kampung* children slain dead, as they were held to their mothers' breasts. Her story carried them through the night leaving

them both emotionally drained. Only then had Stephen realized
what an incredibly strong little woman he had married.

As she lay asleep, her long black hair spread softly across the
pillow, the classic aristocratic features accentuated by high cheek
bones, her soft brown skin highlighted against the white sheets,
Steve Coleman swore an oath that, as long as they were together,
he would never permit Wanti to be exposed again to horror such
as she'd suffered as a child.

It was then he also decided never to reveal the true nature of his
company's activities nor the principal responsible for his success.
That he was dealing in arms did not overly concern him, nor did
he see this as some flaw in his character. Selling weapons was an
honourable profession, he thought. And if it wasn't, then this didn't
really matter either. He believed that his ideals and integrity had
already been compromised years before when he'd first met John
Anderson, and whatever he might do after his life after ASIS, the
Australian Secret Service, could in no way make him a lesser person than he had already become.

Stephen softly stroked her cheek admiring her features. He knew
that she would be in danger should he reveal his relationship with
the General and decided that this would have to be the one secret
he would hold from her.

* * * * * *

Married life in Jakarta changed Stephen's life style very little.
Office activities occupied the mornings, after which he would lunch
with business associates, sleep in the afternoons and spend the evenings with Wanti. She was extremely happy and couldn't wait to
be pregnant. As the months passed by she became agitated by the
possibility that she might not be able to bear children. Stephen
seemed not to be concerned and this also gnawed at her heart.

In Indonesia, as a marriage was not considered truly consummated until a child had been produced, several of Wanti's card
playing partners irritated Coleman with their playful innuendos
suggesting that she should be careful, as there may be others waiting in the wings. Fortunately, Wanti's brother Bambang visited
frequently and his presence had a calming effect on her.

Coleman admired his brother-in-law for the care and protection he had given his sister. The soldier never discussed the events

leading up to their departure from the *kampung*. On one occasion, when Wanti appeared to be daydreaming but was, in fact, only concentrating on her schedule for the day, Bambang had whispered her name several times, calling to her as if she had fallen asleep. Bambang's apparent relief at his sister's response had mystified Coleman at the time. He was unaware of his wife's former, frequent relapses and, as her condition had obviously improved since their marriage, Bambang decided not to discuss his sister's attacks with his brother-in-law.

Wanti had only induced the effect once during this time. She had overheard one of her husband's senior employees discussing their *tuan's* frequent trips overseas, joking as to the nature of his short visits away from Jakarta.

"*Tuan must have arranged a regular cewek in Hong Kong,*" Pasaribu playfully announced, waving the air tickets for that destination around in the air. It was one of his responsibilities to ensure Coleman's travel arrangements, or at least those which Coleman permitted his staff to know about as many of his destinations after Hong Kong were kept confidential.

"*This is his third trip this month,*" he said. "*I'll bet she has big breasts and is very expensive,*" he continued, holding his hands out in front of his chest cupping his fingers in an exaggerated manner to approximately the shape he was describing.

Wanti's reaction was to immediately to look down at her own chest. Her breasts were so small!

Wanti accepted, reluctantly, that the conversation she'd overheard was just office gossip and that she should not permit such talk to upset her. Nevertheless her bust was small and she would suggest that Stephen take her on his next trip.

The Sumatran's actions were quite intentional. Pasaribu had positioned himself so that it would appear he had not seen *Wanti* enter the office. Raising the tickets he laughed, waving the travel documents in the air as he insinuated that the boss was obviously not just preoccupied with business when away.

Wanti had immediately slipped back out of the room to avoid embarrassment and drifted away to her private world alone in her bedroom.

The Batak's motives were quite simple; devious, but simple. As he was one of the senior managers, he expected to benefit directly should such a situation arise due to his seniority and fluency in English, which might find him relegated to travelling overseas in lieu of Coleman.

Pasaribu had no idea as to the real purpose of these trips, his employer had never discussed these excursions and he did not appear to maintain records concerning these activities. Curiosity caused the Sumatran to ponder possibilities quite beyond his sphere of responsibilities and influence. Whatever the reason, he suspected that these short journeys to the other Asian capitals were obviously connected in some way to their supply activities.

He was familiar with the volume of material and weapons supplied and consequently understood the staggering dollar value of the group sales to HANKAM, but often wondered why the company did not increase its profits by dealing directly with the manufactirers and bypass the Hong Kong middleman.

He had learned that the margins earned by the sales were thin and, according to the talkative accountant, too thin, as the company's declared profits were surprisingly small. Pasaribu appreciated that, although his role was purely that of employee, the company should endeavour to increase its profitability whenever the opportunity arose. He had also considered that should the company be obliged to pay more taxes he would have the opportunity to take advantage of this situation. His cousin's wife was on the district taxation audit team. Pasaribu believed that he would be able to nibble into any increased monthly payments together with his relatives without anyone being the wiser.

He decided to examine these opportunities more while waiting for a suitable opportunity to manoeuvre himself into a stronger position within the group. Maybe even accompany the *tuan* on one of those business holidays. Pasaribu knew that there were hidden secrets somewhere in the company's files and dossiers locked upstairs in the boss's bedroom. If only he could locate that data he knew that he could be a wealthy man.

* * * * * *

As with the other office staff, the Sumatran was not aware that one of their number had been directly orchestrated into her position as a clerk, monitoring the other employees' activities. She reported everything to the Umar. He paid her thirty dollars every month for her loyalty. But she did it out of fear.

Six weeks after the incident regarding the air tickets Pasaribu's body was discovered, his throat cut from ear to ear and his wallet, wristwatch and other valuables missing. The office workers attended the funeral and, without exception, expressed their dismay that he could come to such a disgusting end, even though it was in the car park behind one of the more notorious massage parlors.

A few days later Coleman's accountant disappeared. Annoyed with losing two key personnel in the same week Coleman decided to look at the possibility of engaging foreign staff to assist with the ever-growing administrative support his company required. He advertised in the Straits Times in Singapore and was pleased with the standard and number of applicants who applied. Many were of Chinese extraction and, in his business, definitely not politically acceptable.

* * * * * *

The following month Coleman employed his first foreign assistant. His résumé had provided the applicant with an almost guaranteed position with the company. He had the correct academic qualifications and background. He was young and appeared to be comfortable living in the fast moving world of armament and equipment dealings. His credentials indicated that he had worked with one of the Australian Small Arms manufacturers and it was this particular reference which influenced Coleman's final decision.

Not that the new employee would have immediate access to many sensitive aspects of the company's activities such as actually arranging purchases and delivery of weapons — Coleman would always retain that responsibility for himself. It was essential to the security of his relationship with Seda that only he be conversant with such sensitive detail. The knowledge of the arrangements already in place would be too dangerous in another's hands.

Not mentioned in the man's curriculum vitae was his expertise as a skilled hand gun expert and dedicated skier. And that he'd fine tuned both of these abilities under the watchful eye of John Anderson. He was an ASIS mole - and his name was Gregory James Hart.

Chapter 11

Umar Suharjo was delighted with the riots. Cars and buildings were burning everywhere. Sirens screamed as fire tenders and police raced frantically from one location to the next, unable to keep pace with the deliberate destruction of property. Anything of Japanese manufacture came under attack. All of this excitement and none of it any of his doing!

Tension had been mounting ever since the Japanese Prime Minister's visit had been announced. In just a few short years the Japanese economic machine had moved into Indonesia and virtually dominated the consumer market. There were cries of unfair trade practices, such as buyer's commission and dumping. The Japanese elected to ignore the obvious signs of dissent and suddenly, without further warning, violence erupted throughout the capital.

Students ran *amok*, while soldiers stood by and watched, permitting the chaos to continue unchecked. It was if the government itself wanted this violent display against their economic benefactors. Vehicles of Japanese origin were blocked by the huge crowds and drivers invited to vacate their cars before the vehicles were destroyed. At first many drivers did not appreciate the seriousness of their position and immediately became the first fatalities.

All of Jakarta's major arterial roads were blocked by damaged and burning Datsuns, Nissans and Toyotas as the riots spread out of control. Crowds vented their hate, burning school buses and motor bikes, the violence finally spilling over into buildings displaying Japanese products or neon signs.

* * * * * *

Coleman sat in the rear of the new Nissan. The traffic had slowed,

261

and he could see smoke billowing from what appeared to be an accident up ahead on the junction of Jalan Juanda and Jalan Hajam Wuruk.

"Shit!" he muttered, turning to speak to his co-passenger, "another screwed-up morning. "

He was referring to the previous day's appointments, missed due to traffic confusion and rescheduled for that day. Moments later the traffic ceased to flow completely. Both of the passengers immediately felt the discomfort as the air-conditioner laboured, struggling to cool the stationary vehicle. Several youngsters ran along between the blocked lines of stagnated cars, trucks and buses and, as they passed between the Nissan and the adjacent vehicle, they banged the side heavily with their fists, startling the occupants.

"Little bastards," called Hart, not entirely happy with the situation, his clothes developing moist patches because of the failing air-conditioner.

"Okay," Stephen decided, "let's walk. This jam is impossible. We'll slip down past the accident and grab a taxi on the other side."

Leaning forward he touched Achmad on the shoulder. He turned his head slightly.

"*Nanti, kalau sudah bisa jalan, pulang saja,*" Coleman instructed Achmad to find his own way when the road cleared. The dedicated man who had driven for him when he had first arrived in the country and had resigned from the Embassy to follow the former Attaché.

Stephen and Greg then both left their locked briefcases behind and began walking towards the stagnated vehicles. They were within fifty metres of the intersection when the mob appeared.

At first Coleman assumed that the crowd was moving in their direction urged by traffic police. And then it dawned on him. He called his companion.

"Greg. Quickly! Follow me. And don't panic!" he added urgently.

Hart started to ask why when a team of well organized students commenced throwing stones at selected cars. Startled by the sudden violence he ran after Stephen, following him to the side of the street closest to the canal which divided the road.

"Cross here!" Coleman ordered, a note of alarm in his tone. Hart identified the urgency in Coleman's command. The small footbridge permitted the two foreigners to hurry across the canal, avoiding the coagulated brown mess below. Hart continued to follow his associate now moving quickly back away from the burning cars as the first vehicle erupted with a deafening explosion.

They stopped and stared back at the incredible sight. Bottles filled with petrol were hurled through the air at the expensive cars, exploding upon impact.

"For Chrissakes!" Hart yelled, "they're throwing Molotov cocktails!"

At least a dozen more vehicles caught fire. They were already burning furiously as the mob surged along the other side of the *kali*, screaming slogans, smashing shop windows and torching more cars. Their numbers multiplied by the moment.

"What are they yelling?" the visibly shaken Hart asked, "are we in real danger?"

"Come with me Greg! Take it easy, they're not rioting against us. The chanting sounds like anti-Japanese slogans. "

Hart paled. "Shit, Stephen, we could be killed! For Chrissakes, man, let's get the hell out of here before these bastards decide to widen their parameters!" yelled Hart above the rising crescendo of the swelling mob.

"Don't lose your head! If they see you run or panic they will turn on you as quickly as a savage dog so just bloody well stand here against the wall and shut up!" Coleman yelled, now concerned not just for his own safety and that of his associate, but also for his driver who had completely disappeared from view amongst the mass of rioters and spectators.

He could just see his Nissan. The flames consumed it with incredible speed. He stretched and still couldn't see Achmad. He hoped he hadn't attempted to protect the *tuan's* new sedan. The noise increased as the students moved into shops smashing more windows and throwing furniture onto the fires. Coleman could see that this was going to be worse than the rice riots of 'Sixty-eight.'

He shuddered. The demonstrators were now completely out of control wrecking everything, not just Japanese products, but anything at all as they broke into shops, looting and burning. He had learned from his own experience and from some of the older members of the expatriate community that generally rioters left foreigners alone providing they did not display arrogance, fear, or attempt to offer any resistance to the crowd's destructive actions.

Hart was alarmed by the sudden turn in events. He had never witnessed mob violence before.

"Shit! Stephen! Let's make a dash for it!" he pleaded as the crowd swelled past them, moving dangerously close.

"God damn you! Stay where you bloody well are!" he was ordered.

Hart wanted to close his eyes and permit it all to pass, tensing his body in anticipation of the first blow.

"Take it easy, take it easy," Coleman called loudly to the shaken man. "It'll be over in a few minutes. Keep your cool! The main body of the mob is moving away from us down towards Kota."

Jakarta's Chinatown represented the commercial hub of the capital. Historically, whenever there were signs of civil unrest the Chinese would react instinctively before any other ethnic group, protecting their shops and homes by throwing down the steel grated shutters to prevent looters from entering their premises. It was if their very actions were some form of riot indicator.

"Shit! They are going to burn Kota!" Coleman exclaimed.

"Couldn't give a rat's arse," Hart screamed, engulfed in fear, his voice almost inaudible, "just as long as they get the fuck outta here!"

The main body of the rioters headed quickly down town. As the mob moved, the terrifying yelling and screaming followed. Both men remained where they were, watching the alarming mass move slowly away, continuing on their destructive path towards the Chinese Quarter. Soon there was not nearly as much noise as before. Coleman and Hart remained alert, waiting, as they could still see smaller groups, mainly thieves, smashing their way into the remaining shops which had escaped the first wave of pillaging. The looters remained at work, but these were not as threatening as the screaming mob that had passed by just minutes before.

Coleman watched the ongoing violence around him cautiously.

He waited a few more minutes and then decided it was safe to move away.

"Greg? Are you all right?"

Embarrassed, still shaking, his legs a little weak around the knees, Hart attempted a brave face. "Guess so. "

"Stay on this side of the street," Stephen instructed." Walk quickly, and we'll turn down one of the narrow side roads and head towards the market. Maybe we'll find a *becak* there. The taxis aren't stupid. They won't move out into this mess. "

Hart followed. Moving back towards the junction where the first explosion had occurred, Coleman remained alert, his eyes searching for Achmad. He was very worried. There were people seriously injured everywhere. Some were probably dead.

They walked up to the smouldering wreck of the Nissan. Nothing could have been done for the faithful driver. His broken body lay on the roadside covered in blood and filth. His chest had been crushed by the weight of hundreds of rioters as they had swarmed through the street, carelessly trampling across the fallen driver smashing his ribs. Achmad had screamed out for Stephen as he went down but his cry had been lost in the tumult. In that instant, as a heavy booted-foot had kicked down, Achmad had died.

As the two foreigners passed the wreck it was impossible for them to see the dead driver's body, obscured amidst the burned and damaged vehicles.

"Down here!" Stephen called, indicating a small laneway too narrow for anything but *becak* and pedestrian traffic.

Hart moved quickly resisting the temptation to run. More explosions could be heard in the distance as petrol tanks ruptured throwing lumps of hot steel and other debris back into the crowd of unsuspecting onlookers.

Coleman pulled a thick wad of Rupiah from his pocket and waved furiously at the *becak* speeding past.

"*Where do you want to go?*" the becak driver asked braking dangerously.

"*Menteng!*" Stephen answered.

"*Enggak mau,*" the driver spat, refusing to take them to Menteng. As he pedalled away he called back to the foreigners. "*Lebih ramai disana dong!*" - It's even worse over there!'

Stephen spun around, shocked.

Hart looked at him impatiently. "What is it?"

Coleman turned his head slightly, his face a white mask. "Let's

265

go! Now!" he yelled and commenced to run.

"Stephen," his companion called after him, also breaking into a run as he realized that the other man was not about to stop.

"Stephen," he called again, breathlessly, "wait up, damn it!" as he slowed to a walk, already fatigued.

Coleman was at least twenty metres ahead when he stopped and yelled for Hart to hurry.

"Stuff it! I can't run any fucking further!" he choked, his adrenaline reserves almost depleted.

Coleman hesitated then stood impatiently waiting for Hart to catch up.

Glaring at the other man Stephen hissed, "Run! Run now you bastard or I'll leave you here alone!"

"What the fuck for? The crowds have long passed and we're safe here. " Hart screamed vehemently, disorientated and still terrified of the possibility that they'd bump headlong into another crowd of demonstrators.

"Yes. We are," Stephen clenched his fists, controlling his anger, "but others may not be so lucky. That *becak* driver refused to take us back home to Menteng as he claimed it's burning! The riots have hit there as well, Wanti will be in danger!" he yelled.

Immediately they ran, at first together and as Hart tired he called out to Stephen, insisting that he continue on without him. Coleman refused and, also out of breath, rested for a brief moment. He managed to wave down another *becak* driver, his fist held high full of Rupiah notes. This time he didn't indicate their destination as being Menteng, insisting only that the driver take them to Cikini, not a kilometre from the office.

The driver agreed and twenty minutes later the pair approached Jalan Cik Ditiro on foot, having paid the nervous driver off just two hundred metres from the office. As they neared the premises it was obvious that there had been considerable damage to the building.

Earlier, the screaming mobs had turned off from Jalan Imam Bonjol and commenced their path of destruction along Cik Ditiro. Stephen's complex was on a corner, between the Governor's official residence and the home of a retired Admiral. The former Marine General's house was well protected by armed guards who quickly demonstrated their impatience with the forward line of the approaching crowd by shooting over their heads.

The mob had panicked and split into two groups, one pouring down the smaller side street towards the Governor's home where they were met yet again with a barrage of bullets from another team of marines delegated to guard the city's much admired leader.

Molotov cocktails were thrown. More rounds of ammunition were discharged until finally the rioting crowd could no longer contain their rage, several of their number falling under a barrage of bullets. The frenzied mass of humanity poured forward determined to distroy everything in their way.

The mob was no longer motivated just by anti-Japanese feeling. They were out of control, the participants determined to vent their pent-up hatred of the wealthy, the powerful and the military.

Both of Stephan's neighbour's homes survived due to the diligence of their Marine Guards. Stephen's building was spared as a result of its position between the two senior citizen's well-protected residences.

One Molotov Cocktail had successfully carried its dangerous contents through a side plate glass window bursting into flames in the private dining area only to be extinguished by Sukardi, who had bravely attacked the flames with his jacket. All around on both sides of the street, houses had been gutted by fire and most were still smouldering as the rioters had hit this district first, leaving the carnage behind as testimony to the ferocity of their destructive power.

Stephen viewed the scene before him as he started to run towards his home and office. And wife. Another sedan, this time one of their Datsuns, stood half on the footpath and partly on the road, windows smashed and the body damaged, but not burned. Stephen rushed inside where he found the staff were all standing together, confused as to what they should be doing. They know it would be madness to attempt to venture out and yet it was apparent from the look of helplessness on their faces that they were all very concerned for their loved ones.

"Everybody wait here," he instructed, walking briskly through the office to his private quarters and opening the sliding door which accessed the inner guest area.

He sighed immediately. Wanti was sitting there as beautiful as ever, smiling as he entered.

"*Wanti*," he commenced, washed by a wave of relief to see that she was unharmed, "*Are you . . . .*"

"*Kenapa, Mas?*" she interrupted, continuing to smile blankly at her husband.

Stephen approached her slowly, kneeling in front of the chair where she sat elegantly and whispered softly, taking her hands in his.

"*Wanti?*" he called, stroking the side of her face with one hand, the other clasped tightly together with hers. "*Wanti?*" he called softly again, searching her face for a sign of recognition.

"*Kenapa, Mas?*" she replied, then commenced humming, the soft tone driving a cold slither of fear straight through Stephen's stomach.

Immediately he knew that she was suffering from shock. All around he could see and smell the remains of what had been a small fire. She had been sitting in that room when the bottle of petrol had hurtled through the thick glassed window and exploded into flames. The thick drapes had been open permitting the dangerous explosive to shatter across the room barely missing Wanti as she sat at the table, already petrified with fear as she witnessed the screaming mass move towards her home. The houseboy had saved her life, acting quickly to put out the fire then covering the broken window with a blanket from the bedroom upstairs.

But now Wanti remained still, sitting silently, seemingly totally oblivious to all that had happened. At that moment, Sukardi returned with coffee and placed the silver tray next to his mistress.

Wanti merely smiled. Stephen spoke to her quietly, urging her to rest. He was devastated by the sight of her poised on the chair, unaware of his presence. He sat with her for hours until Wanti unexpectedly rose from her seat and, still humming, walked unaided upstairs and retired to their bedroom.

As she left the room Wanti had hesitated and, for just a fleeting moment, Stephen thought she was going to be all right.

His heart sank when she spoke, then turned and walked away as she asked, again, "*Kenapa, Mas?*" her mind still locked under the spell of her seizure.

Chapter 12

Melbourne

As the wind grabbed at his coat and chewed eagerly at his ears he tried to protect himself from the unexpected cold. Stephen, more accustomed to the tropics than to Melbourne's bitter and deceiving Spring wind, shivered. He kept his arm around Wanti's shoulders, occasionally adjusting the thick woollen cap and scarf to keep her warm. Her near ankle-length coat covering the chic trouser suit provided suitable protection from the sudden gusts of wind. Stephen had taken her into the David Jones store and asked the fashion department supervisor to select something appropriate for his wife. Satisfied that the clothes would be warm enough, he had then taken her for a stroll, walking aimlessly as he pointed out buildings and churches and other historical places of interest. Wanti appeared to enjoy these walks, although there was no real indication that this was so. He just presumed that his wife was content to wander through the shops and parks as he hadn't observed any resistance to these outings. Nor was there any recognition that she understood anything of what he said during the walks.

The City Fathers continued to maintain the country's financial centre amidst never-ending and well-cared for parks and gardens throughout the Central Business District. Footpaths and jogging tracks wound their way through extensive settings of well-groomed lawns and garden beds.

Partly shaded circular beds of Lobelia dwarfed by the garden's tall sturdy palms would normally have warranted a closer look, but the weather was not really conducive to the mood he had wished for as they strolled along. Stephen walked slowly, hoping that she would enjoy the magnificent display of flowers as he deliberately detoured through the park's gardens.

The sky was grey. Not unusual for the State's capital. The weather had never been one of Melbourne's strong points, he remembered.

He slowed, pointing to a monument. As he explained its significance, Stephen felt that perhaps she really understood, as if his wife was in some sort of conscious coma in which she recognized what was actually taking place around her but, at the same time, was unable to respond or even participate in the moment.

As they left the park, Stephen steered her across the street to the two-storey late nineteenth century wooden and stone structure. There were several highly polished brass plates affixed to the front columns informing the public in an almost intimidating manner that this was the address of Doctor Raymond D. Phillips, M. B. B. S. D. P. M. Australia M. R. C. psych. F. R. A. N. Z. C. P.

They had arrived at the specialist's rooms.

He looked at Wanti's smiling face and, as he had often done before, stroked her cheek gently and reassuringly with the back of his palm.

"You don't have to do this, Manis," he said.

Wanti smiled, her mind trapped, locked tight and shut away securely from the real world.

"I will take you back to Jakarta today. All you have to do is say 'yes'," he pleaded.

She continued to smile as if pleased just to hear him talk. Stephen hesitated. He looked once more into her eyes searching for any signs of response. Then he took Wanti by the arm again, leading his wife up the steps and along the corridor to the doctor's reception. He placed her on a chrome and leather chair then attended to the registration details.

"Mr Coleman," the woman began, "how do you wish to arrange for payments for your wife's therapy?" she continued, leaning forward inspecting the uncompleted forms.

"Whatever is required," he answered, offended by the woman's tone and angry that this conversation was taking place in Wanti's presence.

"We accept most major credit cards if it is of any assistance. Or," she continued, rattling off the well-rehearsed routine, "if you're a member of one of the recognized medical schemes we can make the necessary arrangements for you. "

"Whatever," he responded tersely, counting out two thousand dollars in cash and placing it before the astonished woman.

Stephen was very annoyed and not just because of his helplessness in dealing with Wanti's illness. The couriered letter he'd just received warned him that his absence was jeopardizing the imminent contract Seda had put into place for the Hercules Aircraft refit and spare parts supply.

This was, he knew, a huge order and one which would generate significant profits for their *kongsi*. Stephen could understand Seda's concern over his absence but was irritated by his lack of compassion and how the General arranged his priorities.

The receptionist checked the registration forms and asked that they both wait for Dr Phillips. He sat impatiently.

After some time they were escorted into the doctor's studio room. Wanti remained still as he checked her eyes and reflexes, occasionally speaking to her softly as he carried out his thorough examination. Stephen sat and listened to the specialist then deliver a lengthy synopsis regarding his new patient's condition.

It made little sense to him. He just wanted to get it over and leave. The doctor explained the procedures he would apply and the probabilities of success with the new therapy. The treatment had recently been introduced from the United States Veteran Trauma Centres.

Stephen listened. He was told that it was unlikely that Wanti would totally recover from her latest seizure. The doctor had seen many similar cases of Post Traumatic Stress Syndrome among the returning Australian soldiers from Vietnam. He should prepare for a lengthy and expensive period of therapeutic care.

Stephen just nodded, occasionally looking out through the small dusty window and across the park. He could see a couple sitting there, together, a blanket across their knees as they fed the pigeons. They were old.

As the doctor droned on Stephen listened, suddenly very tired and depressed. He looked over at his beautiful, silent wife. Her eyes were still devoid of any signs of awareness of her situation. The doctor made a few more notes from his observations and promised Stephen that his wife would receive the very best treatment available.

He took her back to the Southern Cross Hotel. In a few more

days he would leave her with Albert, under the care of the specialist nursing service he'd engaged through the doctor to watch over his wife. They had been employed on an open ended arrangement, for an undetermined period of time to ensure her care and guarantee constant surveillance on a full time basis. He had the money. He was wealthy and wanted desperately to provide nothing but the very best for her.

They entered the hotel room and Wanti smiled as he passed her hand to the attendant nurse. He left the double roomed suite and went directly down to the lobby bar, returning only when he thought she would already be asleep. Stephen stayed just long enough to throw down enough double Chivas Regal whiskies to put him to sleep before riding the lift back up to the seventh floor.

He unlocked the door and went to the adjoining room. The nurse looked up and smiled then placed a finger to her lips to indicate that Wanti slept. Stephen returned to the interconnecting room and undressed. He tried but couldn't sleep. And when morning came he still lay awake wondering what it was that this beautiful and loving person had done to deserve her cruel condition.

* * * * * *

The arrangements were then all in place. Wanti had commenced treatment under one of Melbourne's finest doctors. At first, Stephen had considered placing her with his mother, but then rejected this idea. Her distant, almost aloof, attitude reflected her disappointment with his insistence on discontinuing his career with the government. Now, his marriage to a woman of Asian extraction had rendered his mother just another distant observer in his life. But he didn't want to leave her solely under the care of doctors and nurses.

Albert had been quick to make the necessary arrangements when asked and had even offered to accommodate them in his own home. Stephen considered his friend's offer and accepted without reservation.

It was an almost perfect solution. During the day Wanti would attend therapy at the specialist's clinic. When she returned to Albert's home in the late afternoons there would always be someone close by who understood her language and would watch over her. He would be her father, her family, and Stephen's constant liaison with his wife.

Stephen felt deeply indebted to his old friend. He was more comfortable knowing that, whatever her needs, Albert would be there to provide the friendship and attention Wanti would need during her treatment and convalescence. Having escorted his wife to Australia, met with her doctors and discussed the course of therapy the specialist had prescribed for Wanti he felt there was little else he could do. The doctors had agreed that her therapy should assist with the recovery progress and, hopefully, enable her to re-enter the world of reality. After coming to arrangements with Albert and the nursing team he became impatient to leave.

Stephen remained in Melbourne for what had seemed to him a long and painful three weeks. Each day he accompanied his wife to the clinic, waiting patiently for her to complete the sessions before taking her downtown to Melbourne's exciting fashion centres. Remembering her passion for shopping he'd hoped, wildly, that once she saw the array of fine clothes and specialist shops along Collins Street maybe, just maybe, Wanti would acknowledge something or even somebody. It had made little difference. If anything, she was totally indifferent towards her husband, except for her constant willingness to smile.

The specialist had explained that this behaviour could be an indirect result of the fact that she had not known, or perhaps even seen, a foreigner before the tragedy she had witnessed as a child. There could be some association, but it might never be known, as he could not be sure. The doctor had expressed confidence that as Wanti underwent concentrated therapy and, hopefully, slowly recovered, these barriers would disappear. Maybe she would remember the events leading up to her most recent seizure, permitting her mind to come to terms with what had precipitated the total withdrawal.

This was not exactly what Stephen had wanted to hear. He needed to have someone tell him that she was going to be all right. That she would recover. And soon.

He had to return to Jakarta. He really had no choice as his company operations were experiencing difficulties and only he could overcome the administrative mess that had piled up during his short absence. He'd phoned Hart, but there was little his personal assistant could do considering the confidentiality of the off-shore arrangements.

He booked his flight and informed his friend, his dear friend, Albert.

Albert was exceptionally kind to Wanti - and she appeared more at ease sitting quietly listening to his former teacher read in her own language. Whenever Stephen attempted to communicate he was always rewarded in the same manner. Wanti just smiled.

Albert cautioned his younger friend to be patient.

"*Sabar, sabar, Mas,*" he would advise, understanding some of the frustrations the husband must overcome.

"*I just feel so bloody helpless. The doctors have no idea how long she will be like this,*" he indicated, pointing at his wife, now sitting silently as she gazed out the window.

"*It will take time, Stephen. You must be patient.*"

"*I can't be patient, Albert, I have a multi-million dollar company to run. Every day I'm away is a day closer to another major cock-up which, if I'm not careful, could end in one almighty and expensive disaster.*"

"*I must get back and pick up the reins again. It's pointless my staying here unless someone can tell me realistically just how much longer it will be before Wanti can at least show some signs of recovering from the trauma.*"

As Albert looked at his friend he observed that not all of the apparent agitation was related to his company's pressures. The older man sensed a feeling of guilt. He understood that Stephen didn't want to leave her alone, locked in her own private world, which no other could enter. Albert was extremely sad for he recognized that this man had deep and sincere feelings for the woman sitting quietly across the room.

"*Stephen, I will take care of Wanti. The housekeeper is not entirely necessary. However I do understand your concern for her well being.*" Albert then smiled. "*It will be a welcome change having people around the house again. I accept your offer for the domestic staff. It's time someone else washed and ironed my clothes,*" he added, attempting to lighten the conversation. Stephen had insisted. He could well afford the service.

The ladies had been selected from a local suburban agency. He had also arranged for a regular taxi pick-up from both Albert's home and the clinic. Everything had been methodically organized to ensure Wanti's comfort and to prevent her presence from becoming a burden to his old friend.

The two weeks passed quickly and, with mixed emotions, Stephen bade farewell to Wanti and Albert. He returned to Jakarta and was soon absorbed in the increased demands upon his energies. Although his mind constantly flashed images of the beautiful young woman he had left behind, as the weeks passed by, Stephen realized that he too should face reality and accept the increasing possibility that Wanti might never recover.

Time passed unnoticed even as his work-load increased and suddenly Stephen was aware that it had been some seven months since he had seen Wanti. After a year had passed Coleman was convinced that his wife was destined to spend her days locked in her dream-like world forever. At the end of the second year he returned to discuss her condition directly with the doctors and Albert. Even the specialist was no longer confident of a recovery and suggested politely that maybe Stephen might consider having his wife institutionalized.

Albert now doted on Wanti like a younger sister and at his request Stephen agreed, reluctantly, to leave her in his care. The nursing visits were reduced to twice per week. The doctor's visits were discontinued. Stephen and Albert made arrangements for a more permanent stay for Wanti through the Immigration office, having her passport endorsed as a Permanent Resident. As the wife of an Australian citizen she was entitled to do so.

Coleman had smiled thinly when preparing to leave as Albert had spoken to him softly regarding his future.

"Stephen, this is very difficult for me to say and, no doubt, more difficult for you to accept. However, as we are close friends. . . " He then smiled kindly at the Australian, permitting his words to trail away, unfinished.

"Stephen, you will probably never forget Wanti but you should now make plans to get on with your life. "

Coleman understood what his close and dear friend had so much difficulty expressing.

"It's okay, Albert," he sighed. *"It isn't easy leaving her here like this but you are correct. It is time for me to think ahead. "*

Albert was pleased and put his arm warmly around his former student's shoulder, not needing to say anything more as both understood what had just been said.

As the taxi sped away heading for the airport Coleman looked back and caught his last glimpse of Wanti standing radiantly beside Albert as they raised their hands together waving him goodbye. He felt his heart tearing apart.

It was then he realized just how much he had really cared for her, grieved that now she might never know, her mind no longer capable of dealing with such realities.

Stephen looked back quickly, again, for one final glimpse. They had already disappeared from sight and, as the taxi slowly turned the corner obliterating his last view of the beautiful woman he'd married, he knew, although he did not understand why, she was lost to him forever.

Chapter 13

Timor — 1975-1978

The Portuguese colony was in turmoil and the population felt abandoned. After four hundred and fifty years of trading and more than one hundred years of direct colonial rule, the Portuguese had virtually thrown their hands in the air and walked away from this isolated outpost on the edge of the chain of thousands of Indonesian islands.

In Dili, the capital, violence had already broken out between the inexperienced and politically naive groups including disillusioned expatriate Portuguese who had been caught by the sudden change in circumstances. The confused and bewildered government civil servants who no longer appeared to have any official or legal status to oversee the former colony's administration, looked for leadership, but there was none.

Many Portuguese-trained Timorese soldiers turned mercenary overnight. Others formed armed bands and commenced pillaging shops and raiding outlying farms. Weapons were easily stolen from the poorly equipped armories located in the small towns and from the departing contingent of Europeans, who were ecstatic at being permitted to return home to Lisbon to escape the political upheaval.

The successful and bloodless *coup d'etat* the year before had all of Portugal's military in a festive mood.

A disgruntled group of some two hundred service Captains who, dissatisfied with the long, unsuccessful and drawn-out wars in the African continent as Portugal strove to maintain control over its colonies, overthrew the mediocre regime of Anonio de Oliveira Salazar in the *Captains' Revolution*. The new leadership, the generals who had been catapulted into power as a result of the *coup d'etat* had then set about cutting the burdensome cords to Portugal's colonies.

East Timor was not mentioned in the initial proclamations. As Portuguese Guinea and the African colonies, Mozambique, Angola and the others gained their independence, the embryonic separatist movement in Timor rapidly developed momentum. And outside support.

Almost immediately, Angola was seized by the Marxists who had received substantial military aid from Fidel Castro. The *coup d'etat* in Portugal had resulted in rapid decolonisation of her territories. Unfortunately there had been no transition period and this resulted in the creation of an administrative, political and military vacuum which could not be filled by the inexperienced and poorly trained Timorese.

The region surrounding Timor suddenly became hostile and extremely volatile.

The military leadership of East Timor's giant neighbour, having eradicated Communism less than ten years before, were aghast at the events associated with Portugal's uncontrolled decolonisation process, particularly when militant Marxist groups were permitted to assume power in the former colonies.

The Indonesians were perplexed by the rapid change of events. Suddenly they faced the possibility of a new independent country on their doorstep. And not only a new neighbour, but one that threatened to spread Communism across the borders into Indonesia itself. And their antagonists already controlled more than one half of an Indonesian island.

The unthinkable had happened. Indonesia was suddenly faced with an enemy potentially more dangerous than they had ever known before. The military knew that a consolidated Communist force located within their own country's borders could only spell catastrophe for Indonesia and could even be a threat for Australia.

* * * * * *

Nathan Seda had great difficulty concealing his pleasure. It had finally happened. This was the opportunity he had dreamed of and had planned towards for almost ten years. Now it was about to become a reality.

A free and independent Timor.

He had difficulty controlling his excitement. He knew it was now truly possible and no longer just a dream. These were dangerous times and Seda knew that he must be even more diligent than before. The other Generals would now watch him even more closely, because he was Timorese. He understood that they would no longer be as complacent. Since ascending to their rewarding positions of power under the New Order, as they insisted on referring to the current generation of military strong men, many had grown fat and lazy, their stomachs filled with the riches reaped from others as they easily carved comfortable niches for themselves.

He was not one of them. He wasn't Javanese. Even the Sumatran officers now viewed him with suspicion. But he would play their game. He would bend to their wishes as does the willow tree under a soft wind. He would smile in friendship while in his mind he would visualize images of a new Timor, one in which the children would not suffer as he and all the other village children had suffered. A Timor that could bury the bitter memories of its people forced to endure centuries of misery under the hand of the Portuguese. He would never forget the children lamenting the injustices inflicted by their cruel masters. And the fate of his family.

Seda believed the time had finally arrived. He acknowledged that earlier efforts had been badly organized or poorly timed. The West New Guineans were a miserable lot, he thought and his experiences dealing with these primitive tribes had not been memorable ones.

But this! He was amazed at the reactions he had witnessed from the Indonesian Armed Forces Strategic Committee when attending the urgently called session earlier that day. To think that this mighty country, with its now sophisticated hardware and half a million troops, could be rocked by just the threat of a Timorese uprising. He was astonished that a little sabre rattling had panicked all of them! He wanted to laugh out loud when the decision had been made to send a delegation to Portugal. The mood in the room, then filled with Indonesia's most powerful figures, supported immediate military action.

'Annex the potential danger area!' they had cried. 'Before world opinion can grow in support of the mercenaries, and other militants.' The general consensus was that there would be little or no resistance if they marched in immediately. The ABRI Chief of Staff even guaranteed that there could be few Indonesian casualties.

But there were logistical difficulties and many of the generals were reluctant to support such an immediate move. The High Command was embarrassed to admit that the basic difficulty was the navy's inability to transport the newly acquired hardware and, as for AURI, the nation's air force, most of its younger or more capable pilots were currently undergoing advanced training in the United States.

The non-military faction warned against occupying the eastern part of the island as, they reminded all present, less than a decade before their country had been accused of being expansionist during *Konfrontasi* when it was unofficially at war with Malaya and Singapore. They recommended that a delegation be sent immediately to discuss the crisis with Portugal's current strong man, Colonel Vasco Goncalves, in Lisbon. The debate continued well into the night and, not surprisingly, tempers flared, causing the Vice President to call an end to the Council's emergency meeting.

The President made it known that he was not supportive of meetings with a pro-Marxist government, even a military one. He had always believed that the Portuguese should have departed from the region with the Dutch, leaving the former colony to its rightful owners. His supporters knew that this meant Indonesia.

The 'Smiling General' also clearly understood from his economic and financial strategists that, as his country desperately needed its ongoing foreign investment dollar flow to continue, any arbitrary decision to ignore the possibility of a negotiated settlement-cum-acquisition of the former colony could be dangerously detrimental to his country's development. Bilateral discussions would be viewed favourably and would be far more palatable for the soft politicians in Washington, the influential heads of the International Monetary Fund and World Bank, than being confronted with the rumblings of Indonesia's military machines from far across the Pacific. He sent his decision to the Foreign Minister, Adam Malik.

The Foreign Minister considered his own national responsibilities and then the United Nation's position. He had enjoyed the exalted chair as President of the Twenty-Sixth General Assembly and did not wish to have his international reputation tarnished.

He elected to follow the path for which historians would commend him, a decision that he knew would earn him acclaim for his objectivity and understanding of world opinion. With his eye on the Vice Presidency, he supported his President's views, although not for the same reasons.

Seda snorted privately at the presidential suggestion. 'To hell with Portugal,' he thought, 'they are out and we are in!' he chuckled gleefully to himself sitting comfortably in the back seat of his Mercedes.

He now maintained a fleet of five almost identical cars, the same make, model and colour with tinted windows. The only distinguishable difference for those with a sharp eye was the Department of Defence consecutive registration numbers.

General Nathan Seda now knew he had the perfect opportunity to implement the plan he'd envisaged for so long. It was the opportunity he had not dared to expect, but now that it had happened, he would take the fullest advantage of the unrest and act decisively, providing his people with the chance to advance their cause for an independent nation. He would drag his people, with force if necessary kicking and screaming, into the twentieth century. The people were still uneducated, almost primitive and desperately deserved a leader who could show them the way. He would be that man.

His mind was full of details that now needed to be addressed quickly to take full advantage of the timing and confusion. There was so much to arrange. Coleman had to be organized. Umar had to be briefed. Shipments had to be dispatched. He must send weapons and supplies to the newly formed separatist groups. They needed his help, desperately. Impatient and eager to facilitate the additional supply of necessary weapons and logistic support to the guerrillas, he urged his driver to hurry as if they were, in fact, already waiting eagerly for his deadly gifts of destruction at some predetermined destination; and he was late.

Seda acknowledged that he had very little time. The opportunity would not last, he knew, as he understood how these Javanese and Sumatrans thought. He could predict exactly how they would react.

First, they would talk. Then they would ask to meet with all the groups with vested interests. These would consist of companies and individuals with existing contracts with the government. Together they would evaluate the financial benefit of agreeing to support any proposed invasion. Future timber concessions would be promised. Infrastructure contracts, perhaps supported by future international aid funds would be pledged and ownership of cement plants and rice silos would be agreed. Only when the Chinese money men were satisfied that their sector would maintain their monopoly of any future expansion into the new territory would they throw their economic support behind the government's leader.

Seda smiled.

There would be, of course, a substantial increase in military supplies required to match whatever the Indonesian forces encountered. This would further swell his coffers. And Coleman's.

He thought about the Australian. Their relationship had been very rewarding. The General had clearly believed, however, that the foreigner would always be the one weak link which could compromise the security of not only his person but also the complicated strategy he had embarked upon years before. This was the primary reason for the ongoing surveillance.

It hadn't been difficult. Not in his capacity as the head of the military's intelligence services. After all, any foreigner involved in supplying the Armed Forces with weapons and other equipment could jeopardize national security at any time. Coleman was watched around the clock seven days a week by a now, expert surveillance team which reported only to the BAKIN office. Umar Suharjo kept a close eye on the reports and advised Seda whenever anything unusual occurred.

The General was sceptical about the need to employ another foreigner, but Coleman had insisted that Hart was not only competent but essential to their overseas dealings. They had agreed that Hart's access to the more sensitive workings of their *kongsi* remain restricted. The General reminded his associate that should anyone else become aware of their relationship then they would both suffer the consequences.

"You wouldn't even get to the airport, Mas," he had warned, *"they would have you picked up and secreted away in some unknown place. They'd have you locked tight where even your Embassy would never find you. As for me..."* he did not finalize, leaving the words hanging in the air.

Seda was pleased to see Coleman shudder at the thought of being incarcerated in some secret place miles away from any possibility of assistance from the Australian authorities. It had happened before, during the post *coup* period. Many thousands had disappeared.

Seda's thoughts returned to the Timor border. He considered the likely reaction of the Indonesian leadership to any provocative or threatening action. Fearing that the small population would swing completely to the Left and threaten the Republic's internal security could, he knew, provide sufficient justification in their minds to strike first. They would panic and move the troops into the Indonesian, and western, half of the island.

World opinion would prevent Indonesia from crossing the border, but would not prohibit Timor from standing up for itself against its giant neighbour.

He extracted a file from his briefcase and opened the aerial reconnaissance reports. Seda brooded over the map. He considered the shipments that were to be increased in frequency now unforeseen events had almost overtaken his own well-laid plans.

Already Umar had positioned more than twenty substantial caches in the rugged eastern part of Timor near the foot of Ramelau Mountain. As many again had also been distributed to the guerrillas. The remaining weapons would be secure, as local inhabitants rarely ventured up into these difficult areas. Only occasionally did the villagers scratch around in the jungle in search of the wildlife for food. The hills were abundant with deer, monkey and the cuscus, which were trapped for sale to the occasional tourist as foreigners were fond of the marsupial.

A further fifteen caches of supplies had been hidden on the slopes of the hilly island of Kambing, almost within view of the fishing village. The small airport had been considered should airdrops become necessary, but Seda vetoed his own idea as the runway would attract too much scrutiny. The new series of Hughes' satellites were now keeping the regional hot spot under close surveillance for the American intelligence community.

He realized that additional shipments needed to be delivered without delay. As the separatists had only now being given limited supplies from some of his secret hoard, he estimated that to arm at least five thousand men would take a much greater logistical effort and a sizable portion of his funds.

Thinking quickly, Seda commenced organizing shipments in his mind, calculating the fire power he could arrange for delivery to Dili, Manatulo and Tutuala over the following weeks.

The company had offshore stockpiles ready for shipment but these would need to be replenished as the number of supporters grew.

'*The Cuban weapons will be very appropriate,*' he decided.

Ever since Angola fell to the Marxists, Cuba had sent, not just sophisticated weaponry to assist with the civil war now well under way in the former Portuguese colony, but also more than five thousand Cuban special forces who had trained in the jungles of South America.

* * * * * *

The weapons Seda considered Cuban were actually Russian and Czechoslovakian in origin. These were not made in Cuba, merely shipped via the Communist country. The Cuban negotiators had also offered to send their own advisers and, at the time, Coleman had burst out laughing thinking that the offer had been made in jest. He was not aware of the intended destination of the weapons under negotiation. Coleman was later surprised to discover that the Central Americans were extremely serious with their offer to provide highly trained soldiers to operate the more sophisticated equipment.

Privately, they had also negotiated directly with members of the Front for the Liberation of Timor to provide five hundred experienced soldiers, directly from the killing fields of Angola. The funding for these advisers was to be provided by the Castro regime as a gift of friendship to fellow Revolutionary Freedom Fighters working together against the Neo-Colonial Powers. When the original offer had been made, one of the misinformed negotiators had incorrectly assumed that Coleman was aware that these shipments would be sent to Dili and other East Timor destinations. Fortunately the Australian had replied, unaware that the arms dealer had committed a serious error.

"Not really applicable, gentlemen," he had explained recovering from a coughing fit, the result of suppressing a laugh, "it is unlikely that the Indonesians would accept assistance from your country at this stage. "

One of the team had stepped forward and jabbed the errant

speaker, warning him sharply in Spanish to hold his tongue or lose it. Fortunately Coleman had not picked up on the man's *faux pas*.

Seda had smiled when Stephen had met briefly with him in Bangkok and related the incident, but was immediately concerned with the possibility of foreign nationals, particularly soldiers, entering the game. The General realized that this could be enough to force the Indonesian military to occupy East Timor should they discover the existence of Cuban troops on their borders.

"Could you believe that these guys were deadly earnest?" he had said to the General, *"they actually believed that they could just drop a hundred or so of their troops into Indonesia if you gave them the order."*

Nevertheless, Seda needed the Cuban shipments and ordered Stephen to finalize the transaction then ship the weapons to Macau pending on-forwarding instructions. Seda had never felt the need to explain the nature of the orders to the Australian and had suggested during the embryonic development of their business relationship that for Stephen to have such knowledge of Indonesian military affairs would not be appropriate.

Stephen had always been under the impression that all of the shipments left Macau for Jakarta. When orders were placed, his instructions were explicit. The consignments were to be broken into smaller shipments for Umar.

The rest had been relatively easy. Seda now had sufficient firepower already in place to start his own civil war. But not enough to prevent one of the scale that was imminent unless he moved quickly. Assisted by the skilful Umar Suharjo and his uncanny ability to select the right time and place to move the secret cargo, the staggeringly expensive cashes of weapons had grown dramatically. The profits from the HANKAM contracts had mounted until even Coleman's share exceeded his expectations. He had become an exceedingly wealthy man. Over five years they had shared rewards of a scale so great even many major companies would have been pleased to see such profits posted in their balance sheets.

And it was all tax free!

This was to be Seda's new war chest.

* * * * * *

The General phoned Stephen in his office, his impatience causing him to violate one of his own strict rules relating to their covert activities. Coleman was not available. Annoyed, he summoned Umar. His partner had been enjoying himself in the Captain's Bar of the Mandarin Hotel when the assistant front desk manager approached and discreetly passed the message.

He phoned immediately. Stephen listened attentively to the instructions and closed the connection by simply answering 'yes' to the other party knowing that this would be sufficient. He disliked using the hotel phones. They were rarely secure. As he turned back to his friends a burst of raucous laughter exploded from the men he'd been drinking with minutes before.

"Missed a good one, Stephen," the burly red-faced insurance consultant belched, wiping the back of his hand across his eyes to remove tears of laughter.

"Tell it again, Alister, we won't mind," urged one of their number.

"It's okay, fellows," Stephen offered, looking at the time, "probably heard it before anyway. "

"Give us another round," he ordered casually, drawing an imaginary circle in the air with his finger indicating to the barman that everyone at the bar should have a drink on his account.

Immediately several of the drinkers changed from beer to scotch or other expensive spirits. Stephen didn't care, he knew most of them reasonably well and it was more or less expected of him. His success over the years had its down side. Petty jealousies and the occasional snide remark no longer offended him. He accepted that this occasional reaction went with the territory of being wealthy. After all, he was born in the country with the worst 'tall poppy' syndrome in the Western world.

He observed Greg Hart. His assistant seemed to be doing really well these days. Stephen appreciated the importance of sound administration but readily admitted his lack of interest in what he described as 'day to day drudgery'. Fortunately Hart's expertise and willingness to focus on the mechanics compensated for Stephen's indifference. Since Hart appeared to relish the monotonous regularity of compiling statistical reports day after day, Coleman was content to leave it entirely to him.

He caught Hart's eye and indicated by tapping his watch that he would soon leave the gathering. The man acknowledged with a slight nod then turned his attention back to the end of yet another story, this time related by one of the better raconteurs their expatriate community offered.

Having missed the story's beginning, Stephen was content to stand back and view their reactions to each other as the foreigners participated in what was almost a tribal tradition, practised during the extended lunch hour. He recognized that most of those gathered around the bar were no longer just social drinkers. They had passed those acceptable barriers years before. Without any self-imposed limitations regarding their consumption the majority were not concerned with the volume of alcohol which passed their lips in an almost dedicated fashion. Every day they would meet, drink furiously, while only consuming a limited volume of solids, and then leave for yet another and probably less respectable drinking hole to fill in their otherwise empty afternoons. And empty lives.

Many of these men had been employed on a two or three-year contract knowing that the clock had started and already their time was running out. Most were unemployable in the more normal working environments. They had developed the skills of the permanent expatriate and with these skills the knowledge that they would never achieve their long forgotten ambitions. Consequently, they were content to float along as the 'token' foreigner, often employed only to make up the foreign investors' numbers required by law to sit on their management boards.

As the noise level had risen somewhat he knew that the group wouldn't miss his presence. Following another peal of laughter Stephen excused himself with a half-hearted wave and called for his car. He was surprised that the General had, in fact, breached their established system of contact. The General had never attempted to contact Stephen, directly, before and he was anxious to discover what Seda considered so imperative that the security of their relationship could be ignored. Agitated by the breach and annoyed at the distance he would now have to travel, he climbed into the red Mercedes and prepared for the long drive.

* * * * * *

Stephen was alone as he steered the manual through the slow traffic. Foreigners generally preferred to be driven and, in most cases it made sense, considering the irregular traffic flow and irresponsible drivers on the city's roads.

He handled the car well although, had it been possible, he would have been very pleased had his old driver Achmad been there for him. He buried the thought as quickly as it had emerged, amongst the other distressing memories.

Stephen had agreed to meet with Seda in his mountain villa, located just over the Puncak Pass. Several hours had passed when they walked quietly together through the garden of the small estate, situated four thousand feet above the muddy capital. The air was noticeably cooler than Jakarta and a chill had already entered the afternoon air. Clouds had formed earlier in the afternoon, blocking all view as the misty and moist forms enclosed the heavily timbered property.

The men returned indoors. They sat inside the high-ceilinged structure directly in front of two oversized sliding doors which led back out onto a patio overlooking the well manicured lawn. A small fire had been burning for some time, Coleman had noticed, its choked chimney now throwing out more smoke than heat as the tea bush cuttings were dropped onto the smouldering embers.

Seda waited for the servant to leave the room.

"*Stephen,*" the General commenced, "*the Government needs to move quickly due to the Timor crisis.*"

Coleman was not surprised that the obvious urgency was in some way related to the distant colony that had featured regularly in the newspapers.

"*What is required, Pak?*" he asked.

"*The problem is more political than logistical,*" Seda elaborated, "*as there is considerable support for the military to go straight into the former Portuguese colony to prevent further bloodshed there.*"

Coleman was amazed at the revelation.

"*The Americans would scream, Pak,*" he responded, quite surprised at the man's candour, "*and they would be quick to react. Possibly even introduce an embargo as they have on Vietnam which would block further sales to HANKAM.*"

Stephen had referred to the United States trade embargo on the export to Vietnam of all American product. They had sought and received considerable support from other Western nations, including Australia. The crippling economic and social effects had already become evident as the now-united country struggled to drag itself out of the quagmire created as a result of hundreds of years of civil war.

"*Maybe,*" he paused, "*maybe. But I don't think so. Vietnam is a Communist country and Indonesia is today threatened by a Marxist group. I doubt that the Americans would pressure us into permitting Timor-Timur to fall to a Leftist regime.*"

Stephen considered the logic of Seda's statement. The man had developed an uncanny sense of intuition. His inside knowledge of the country's likely response to potential border threats enabled the head of the powerful intelligence apparatus to remain at least one step ahead of his peers.

"*The new OV-10 Broncos approved by the Government will be amongst those weapons delayed, Pak,*" Stephen warned, referring to the state-of-the-art aircraft sitting in the clean, uncompromising air of Tucson, Arizona, awaiting shipment to the West's newest ally.

Two squadrons had been sold to the Indonesian Air Force. It was an urgent yet ongoing effort by the United States Government to compensate for the recent disastrous collapse of the South Vietnamese Government in April of the same year. Russian manufactured IL-28s had subsequently been positioned in Vung Tau, overlooking the oil and gas fields Lyndon Johnson had so desperately wanted for his country and friends in Houston.

SAM missiles had been redeployed from the North to areas around Tan Son Nhat and Bien Hoa. MIG-23s now controlled the skies around the former so-called Democratic State of South Vietnam. The aircraft were within striking range of one of the world's largest gas deposits, the island of Natuna, which for some strange reason of history, fell within the territorial integrity of the Indonesian people. The Pentagon had identified the potential threat as Saigon had surprisingly fallen back in the earlier part of the year.

The oil barons from Houston applied unprecedented pressure to have the island protected at all costs. Natuna had to be theirs! The United States Military Advisory Committee suggested that their government provide strike aircraft compatible to the Russian MIG-23s already deployed in the mouth of the Saigon River. The Armed Forces Select Committee assisted with the push to have the deal done quickly, as the Vietnamese suddenly had the support of the Russians, filling the void created by the American embargo.

The Soviets wasted no time embracing their new satellite. It enabled them to spread their sphere of influence into a new dimension, directly within striking distance of the American Fleet in Subic

Bay in the Philippines. They already controlled Cam Ranh Bay and looked hungrily at the one remaining naval base in the region.

The Indonesians were also to receive Skyhawks once their pilots had completed their high performance training. The sale had already been sanctioned by the US Government. The Senate and Arms Manufacturer Lobby Groups were pleased that the potential expansionist move by the Soviets could be used to justify the sale of the two squadrons of American-manufactured aircraft to their new ally. They promised even more aid would follow.

The sale was approved by both the Congress and the Senate and, within weeks, Indonesia was able to transfer the elite of its young pilots to their advanced training course in The States.

"How will the Australians react?" he suddenly asked.

Coleman was taken by surprise.

"I have no idea. "

Stephen decided that the invitation to discuss the Macau consignments may have been a ploy to obtain information. He guessed that Seda always suspected that he had access to more information about Australia's 'interest' in the country than he'd revealed, but this was no longer true. And he would never reveal the nature of his past activities before his resignation.

Coleman dragged the General's attention back to the potential problem of the two squadrons of Broncos. Their *kongsi* stood to make millions from the ongoing supply of spare-parts, not to mention the commissions that would be due once delivery had been effected.

"What do you think the Americans will do with our aircraft contract?" he asked Seda. *"Don't you agree that they may elect not to deliver if the Timor problem escalates?"*

The General thought for a moment regarding this point. *'Yes,'* he pondered silently, *'I should do everything I can to prevent the new squadrons from being delivered, as they would be perfect for the AURI pilots should ABRI decide to ignore world opinion and march across the border anyway.'*

He looked back at his guest.

"That's a calculated risk that HANKAM will consider," he suggested to Coleman.

He shook his head slowly, trying to absorb the information and, at the same time, understand where Seda was headed with the conversation.

"You were saying that the problem was more political?"

Again the older man paused before responding quietly, as if he intended no one else to hear what he was about to say.

"Yes. HANKAM has decided to take delivery of the Cuban shipments."

"Why?" Stephen was now very attentive at this curious piece of information, obviously offered by the General after considerable deliberation.

Being privy to state secrets made him slightly uncomfortable. There was obviously more. He waited for Seda to continue.

"They may have to send a small group of two or three hundred across the border just to settle the area down as it is really getting out of control."

"Why then the Cuban gear?" he asked, confused by what he had just learned.

"If Indonesia sends soldiers across the border they will be hand selected from surrounding islands and Timor itself, armed with the nonstandard Indonesian issue weaponry and dressed in non-combat uniforms."

"Clever," the engrossed Coleman said, surprised at the ingenuity of the plan.

"And, as there will certainly be some casualties, none will be identified as ours," the General explained, *"thereby avoiding any possibility of an international furore."*

The Australian nodded his head in agreement. The Indonesians could not afford to displease the Foreign Monetary Bodies.

"When do we ship from Macau?"

Seda waited for a few moments before replying, as if preparing for the other's expected reaction.

"Stephen, this is very sensitive situation and on this occasion I don't want you involved."

Surprised, the younger man thought for a while, examining the pros and cons of such a variation from standard procedure.

"I'm not sure that I'd be happy with that, Pak Seda," he said.

Not altogether satisfied that the General would place the operation in the hands of somebody competent, Coleman shook his head in disagreement. He was confused as the introduction of third parties could compromise their operations. Their *kongsi*. And their security.

"You won't be out of it altogether, Stephen."

He listened as Seda continued.

"I would feel more at ease with your involvement, say, from the side-lines although I feel that you should be on hand for the formalities which relate to receipt of the consignments, even if it is for only a day or so. "

"When do you require my presence in Macau?"

Seda didn't hesitate.

"Can you leave tomorrow?" he asked.

"Yes, of course," answered the surprised Coleman.

The apparently relaxed General leaned back into his heavy leather chair.

"Good. It's done then. Let me know when you return and we will makan bersama," the General instructed. The suggestion of dining together when Stephen returned caught him off-guard. Considerable time had passed since his last invitation to the Seda residence.

Their meeting concluded, they parted company and returned to the city as they'd come. In separate cars. The following morning Coleman caught the Cathay Pacific Tristar into Hong Kong. He needed a short break, and made arrangements to continue on the ferry for Macau the following afternoon.

* * * * * *

The Rolls-Royce glided noiselessly along the overcrowded streets from Kai Tak airport. Coleman had always enjoyed Hong Kong. He thrived off its pace, its mass of humanity, its opportunities. The Peninsula Hotel sent one of their prestige saloons to meet him.

Having checked in and showered, Coleman phoned several numbers before visiting the bar. The operator would know of his whereabouts, if required — a practice he'd maintained for years. His head office in Jakarta was manned twenty-four hours each day by a very competent number of switchboard operators. They would not know how to reach him, even if necessary.

When Stephen travelled on business he rarely made contact with his office. Should the necessity arrive he would phone his home office and talk directly to his efficient secretary. He paid his staff well but he also acknowledged that they were probably one of the most efficient teams in all of the Capital. Just like the Peninsula Hotel.

Coleman never ceased to wonder at the ability of the hotel staff to remember the names and faces of the multitude of guests who passed through this magnificent edifice so prominently positioned by its founders overlooking Hong Kong harbour.

There was something about standing alone in an expensive hotel, propping up the Lobby Bar by oneself. Everybody ignored you, with the exception of the staff and that is how Stephen preferred it to be. Guests would come and go, some to meet others, some to sit and listen to the pianist playing, for the millionth time, the theme from *Love is a Many Splendoured Thing* as they imagined themselves enjoying their own romantic interlude. Such dreams so easily achieved in the setting and ambiance of the colonial structure, with its mixture of oriental and European intrigue.

He had dressed in a light summer sports jacket, a soft green shirt, without tie, and charcoal grey trousers. He still felt over-dressed. Coleman pushed the large bowl of cashew nuts away to the side. Small, crisp pieces of roasted pork rind followed. He avoided the bar snacks having discovered during his early apprenticeship in the East that many a stomach complaint could be traced to the prolific assortment of *hors d'ouvres* provided in such establishments. Not that he was concerned here. Another reason for his loyalty to this hotel had been its excellent cuisine. He just wasn't hungry.

A small group of wealthy tourists clapped as the song thankfully finished. The woman who had requested what she most probably considered to be Hong Kong's version of the national anthem, had attempted to sing the theme song before losing her way after somewhere 'high up on the mountain'. She then attempted to completely destroy the song by joining the singer pianist only on the high notes.

The tourist wasn't drunk. But she was close to that threshold.

Another request was played and Coleman pulled his jacket sleeve back slightly, checking the time. And frowned. He accepted another Chivas and stirred the ice cubes with his index finger. Stephen turned as this song also came to a close just in time to witness her entry. Most conversation stopped as the tall slim woman glided across the floor and over to the bar.

She was stunning in appearance. Her shining black hair had been cut to a pageboy presentation, its richness absorbing yet reflecting the multitude of rays, split and redirected by the chandeliers overhead. She was tall and walked like a model, her feet dressed in Chanel satin stiletto heels barely evident as the almost floor length body-tight black chiffon evening dress faintly touched the beautifully polished nails of her stockinged feet. She wore simple jade earrings. Her neck was decorated with a matching black choker to the side of which another, but smaller, jade piece had been positioned.

She approached the bar and placed her matching clutch purse on the bar beside him. Stephen Coleman immediately thought that she was the most beautiful woman he had ever seen. Her skin still displayed the softness of care with just a suggestion that she'd been briefly in the sun. Her eyes were brown. She looked Eurasian, and there was a suggestion of Chinese to her features. Whatever the genetic contributing factors had been, their perfect blend had produced a most breathtaking result.

Conversation died immediately at surrounding tables as men admired the magnificent creature who had just entered, while their ladies sat mesmerized with her appearance.

"Sorry I'm late," she said, holding her hand out to Coleman but not so far as to indicate that she wanted it shaken. "Problems with the driver," with which she smiled, displaying her even white teeth highlighted by the thin line of peach lipstick professionally applied across her lips.

"Do it again and you're fired," Coleman said, returning her brilliant smile.

"Fire me and who would take care of the children?" she responded.

"I know it would be difficult but even in Hong Kong I'd probably get lucky," he suggested.

She laughed and the stress of the past days and the long flight disappeared as he admired his date.

"I'm Angelique," she whispered, moving close so others couldn't hear.

"Stephen," was all he could muster, holding his tumbler up to welcome her, suddenly realizing that she hadn't been offered a drink.

The barman returned quickly and, identifying the woman, asked Coleman, "Moet, sir?"

"Of course," he replied, almost choking in laughter at the cheek of the man. "You do drink champagne, I take it?" he asked her, still smiling at the barman's hustle.

"All the time," Angelique laughed in reply.

They waited for the champagne to be poured then raised their glasses touching them together softly, enjoying the identifying ring of the Bohemian crystal flutes before sipping the wine. One of the older waiters serving outside the bar hobbled across and positioned the bar stool for Coleman's guest.

"Are we staying here long?" she asked.

"Hungry?"

"Famished!" she replied, touching the small of her stomach.

"Your choice then," Stephen offered, hoping she would not select some distant destination which would take hours in the Hong Kong traffic.

"Room service?" she suggested, watching for his reaction.

For once he was at a loss for words. He was tempted to agree but there was something in her manner which influenced his decision.

"Room service it is then, but not for dinner," Stephen said, continuing the banter. "For now, we shall sip our Moet and then I'd suggest we dine here in the hotel. "

She was obviously pleased as she flashed another of her incredible smiles first at Stephen and then around the bar to show their observers that she was indeed, with this man.

They finished the champagne and then dined in the hotel's superb main restaurant.

"Seafood or beef?" Coleman had decided to order for them both.

"You choose," she answered, causing her host to flip back to the menu's entree selection.

"Fine then," he said, addressing the waiter, "we'll both have the sultan's cream of tomato soup followed by the smoked salmon. Give us about thirty minutes and then we will have the baked crab."

Stephen then ordered another bottle of champagne.

"The soup here is excellent," he explained, "I have only found one other place that makes it anywhere near as well. "

The champagne arrived and as the waiter poured he explained. "They use fresh tomatoes, none of that canned variety here, and it is cooked almost too thick in texture but that's so the cream can be poured in the shape of a small ring around the centre of the soup. Then, very delicately, they also pour a gracious serving of Gordon's Gin into the centre and serve. "

She smiled as he talked, listening to his culinary description, without interrupting, appearing naturally attentive. They enjoyed their meal, resting between the courses, talking together as if they were old friends. Coleman had changed from the Moet Chandon to a burgundy with his meal but Angelique had politely refused, content to remain with the champagne.

Before the crab was served he'd asked her to dance. There were six or seven couples on the floor and, as they moved slowly around the small dance area, he knew that the others were admiring them as a couple.

"We're being watched," he whispered.

"I know. They are all thinking who is that handsome man that ugly woman has managed to catch?" she whispered back like some co-conspirator.

Stephen laughed, pushing her away slightly, jokingly, to admire her face. The music finished and they returned to their seats.

"Tell me something about yourself, Angelique," he asked.

"Only if you tell me about you, first. Okay?"

During the main course they took turns talking about childhood dreams, where they were born, where they had gone to school and other simple detail as if it all really mattered. Neither discussed the present, each sensitive to the other's unwillingness to divulge the more intimate and private aspects of their lives. They refused dessert and the coffee.

Suddenly Coleman realized that they were the last couple left in the restaurant and, glancing at his gold Omega discovered to his surprise that it was almost one o'clock in the morning. She noticed his expression and leaned across placing her hands on top of his.

"Stephen," she said softly, "time for room service," with which she rose pulling his hands forcing him to follow.

They rode up in the lift in silence. He could smell the tantalizing French perfume, a Guerlain Shalimar, and was conscious of the warmth in her arms as they brushed lightly together.

The suite was decorated in creams and gold borders. The double-lined drapes, when closed, displayed tastefully illustrated scenes of Chinese junks under sail, the mountainous islands surrounding Kowloon as their backdrop. He undressed as she left him to use the bathroom.

The bed had been turned down by the maid service. Stephen softened the lighting before he opened the huge and heavy drapes to gain the benefit of the harbour view.

He lay back on the bed, his head propped against his hand as he absorbed the sight of Hong Kong after dark. He heard the movement and, turning towards the sound saw her naked body silhouetted in the hall doorway, the bathroom lights behind.

She moved slowly towards the end of the bed and stood quite still providing Stephen with the breathtaking sight of her full breasts and womanhood. She moved around to where he lay and bent down, kissing him softly on the shoulder and then on the chest and finally moving her warm sweet mouth to his abdomen from where she used her tongue slowly, side to side across his stomach making a soft, almost snail like trail back up to his neck.

Finally she kissed him softly on the lips, forcing his mouth open with her tongue while pressing forward with her body, moving across to straddle his, the sudden warmth causing Stephen to groan. He lay like this as she prepared him, taking him in her hand and gently stroking his body until sensing the change in his breathing.

She stopped, rolled over onto her side guiding his length through her warm and soft gates deep into her body, moaning softly as he commenced the rhythmic pelvic thrusts while gently stroking her firm and sensitive breasts. Stephen climaxed, the jerking spasms sending an indescribable warmth of joy through his body as he emptied himself inside her.

They lay together, embracing each other until gradually falling asleep, only to awaken and make love again, this time more slowly, giving her as much pleasure as it did him.

The sun pierced through the windows as they had forgotten to close the drapes. They each bathed, ordered a breakfast of juice, toast and coffee and sat silently, sipping their black Turkish coffee together, dressed only in their white bathrobes, enjoying the quiet of early morning. Angelique noticed that he had finished.

She stood and let the robe fall back off her shoulders to the floor. In the light of day he could see that she was even more beautiful than he'd thought the evening before. They made love, again, but this time without the sense of urgency they had experienced during their first coupling. This time they kissed gently, slowly, and enjoyed each other's bodies reaching their climax together. They bathed again and dressed.

Coleman escorted the attractive woman down through the hotel lobby and, having arranged for one of the hotel's Rolls Royces to be standing by at his disposal, said his goodbyes on the marble steps and sent her away. He returned to his room and prepared for the journey to Macau.

* * * * * *

He thought of Angelique as the ferry sped across the choppy sea, and the previous night of love making, her beauty and exotic smell, and the probability that he would not be fortunate enough to have her again. It was best like that, he believed, as he didn't want any complicated involvements in his life right then. Perhaps in the future he would be able to settle down into something solid, maybe. For the time being he was content to survive on the casual relationships such as the electric encounter he'd had with Angelique. If that was, in fact, her name.

As the ferry slowed to prepare for arrival, Coleman made a mental note to phone and thank Mister Lim for his excellent taste. Stephen smiled as images of their bedroom tryst danced quickly through his thoughts. She was certainly worth it, he thought, amused at himself for having gone a little overboard this time with the wining and dining routine.

As the Rolls Royce had glided away from the hotel, she waved, and immediately her client turned to re-enter the hotel. She ripped open the envelope he'd given her as she stepped into the exquisite saloon. The woman who called herself Angelique let out a squeal of delight as she counted the money. She squealed again, having come to the last note in the count, and held it tightly to her chest. Two thousand Hong Kong dollars! She could hardly believe Stephen's generosity.

Remembering the envelope, the young hostess quickly replaced the money and buried the small fortune deep inside her copy Chanel bag, one of the first to be made in Thailand for the Hong Kong market. She would not disclose the gift to her boss, Lim, as he would be furious that she had accepted such an amount from one of his clientele. Instead, she would send the money back to the Shanghai hovel where her mother remained.

Deserted by her French lover, and barely sixteen, the pregnant and destitute girl had been forced to sell Angelique to Lim when the child was but six years old. He had arranged to have her transported illegally across into Hong Kong, hidden along with twenty other young girls, their skinny and fragile bodies caked in filth from the pigs which shared the junk during the rough crossing.

Two days after her fourteenth birthday she was given to a visiting Japanese businessman for the weekend on his friends yacht. She was forced to submit not just to this man but, when he had finished with her at the end of a painful first day, she was then used by three of the others in the party.

Lim had been paid well for the young virgin and he immediately identified her potential. Within four years Angelique had been given new documents, her name, and had completed intensive training directly under the supervision of the infamous Mama Lily in Wan Chai.

She was now one of several stars in what was known in Hong Kong as The Lim Collection. Lim's exclusive agency arranged escorts for wealthy and powerful clients. This provided the Chinese entrepreneur with considerably more than the substantial income generated by the beautiful ladies. Lim also traded in information, and secrets.

Angelique would be questioned at length as to what she might have heard or seen while in the company of the wealthy arms dealer. A report would then be made to those who paid handsomely for the occasional surveillance Lim's girls carried out whenever Stephen Coleman visited Hong Kong.

Lim would personally deliver any such information to the client although he was never comfortable with this chore. Raised in the world of Triads he was all too familiar with the dangers of such covert activities. Lim feared few people but always felt uneasy when alone with Umar Suharjo.

* * * * * *

The lighting inside the old warehouse was limited to one corner where the storeman sat, smoking, surrounded by bundles of documents. Coleman waited for an hour. The air was humid and the dilapidated building had little ventilation. A car horn sounded and he checked his watch. A solitary passenger alighted, paused, looked around carefully then entered through the poorly lit doorway. Stephen identified the courier and nodded in his direction.

"*You're late,*" the Australian admonished.

The Javanese ignored the complaint and walked directly to the storeman's table. He removed an envelope from inside his jacket and dropped it casually onto the desk.

The storeman retrieved the documents and handed them to Coleman who, conscious of the trace of arrogance displayed by the courier, examined Seda's signature carefully to ensure that this man had been delegated the unusual responsibility of accepting delivery of this particular consignment.

The papers were in order. Stephen instructed the storeman to pass control of the shipment to the latecomer. There were no further signatures required. Satisfied that this surly little courier, who had obviously been promoted by the General, could now handle the next phase of the delivery, Coleman prepared to depart.

He watched the Indonesian walk around the stacked cases containing the Cuban consignment, concerned that Seda had appointed this man to ensure final delivery of the weapons. Stephen had met this courier perhaps as many as thirty or forty times over the past few years.

He rarely spoke. Stephen had attempted to be civil on these occasions however the Javanese would merely grunt then surrender Seda's written instructions and depart without so much as one word. Whenever he was around this man , Stephen felt uneasy. There was something about him that worried him, even frightened him.

Coleman turned to leave as the courier completed his cursory inspection of the shipment. Strolling towards the corner table, a *kretek* cigarette now dangling from his mouth, he removed his jacket and sat on the corner of the storeman's cluttered desk displaying an air of arrogant overconfidence. He dropped the almost spent *kretek* and stepped on it with his left shoe.

Coleman now understood the reason for the light weight jacket. The man was armed. The revolver hung menacingly from its shoulder holster.

Umar Suharjo's gaze followed the departing Australian. He spat on the floor, removed a packet of *Gudang Garam* from the jacket and lighted yet another of the aromatic clove cigarettes. Minutes later his team arrived. They had been instructed to wait for Coleman to depart before entering the warehouse. They worked through the night loading the cases onto the fishing trawlers.

The men worked hard, their sinewy arms and legs bulging with the effort of moving the cases from the warehouse. Sweat poured from their bodies. There was no conversation, just hand signals and the occasional grunt as the men moved quickly to complete their task before morning. Umar checked the warehouse one last time to ensure that they had left no tell-tale identification of their activities. Satisfied, he ordered his team to join the trawler crews and prepare for departure. He re-entered the building alone.

Minutes later his men noticed him return. The flotilla departed, the destructive cargo well secured and camouflaged to avoid detection as the vessels headed for the southern Filipino islands in the Mindanao Sea. Behind, in the warehouse, everything was still. And quiet.

The dead storeman's body was not found for three days. One of the Macau police investigators at the murder scene checked the victim's pockets. The contents were placed in a small pile on the dead man's desk. The detective examined the items. With the exception of a few dollars and the victim's ID card there was nothing of value.

He noticed the loose cigarette which the storeman had extracted from his killer's packet left on the desk during the loading operation. Rolling the *kretek* between his fingers and, out of habit, the policeman placed the clove cigarette in his mouth and lighted the only evidence left by the Javanese. Moments later, recovering from the worst coughing fit he had experienced in many years, the investigator recovered the remaining stub.

Convinced that the cigarette was marijuana, he placed the remains in an evidence bag and returned it to the pile of personal effects. The detective knew that the murder investigation would have a low priority as it was probably drug related and his department already had its quota for the month, courtesy of the Triads.

* * * * * *

Seven days passed before the innocent fishing trawlers were

positioned off the former Portuguese colony's coast. The passage had been relatively easy. They had sailed down through the Mindanao Sea and then headed directly for Timor.

Umar Suharjo leaned against the railing scanning the coastline for activity. Satisfied that there was no threat, he ordered the teams to prepare for arrival. Later, under cover of darkness, two hundred men assisted to unload the valuable cargo. Within days, the small band of guerrillas had stashed the rifles, ammunition and grenades in discreet locations surrounding the town of Dili.

The weapons, coupled with earlier shipments of stolen equipment delivered directly from within Indonesia and the numerous caches now buried around the island, represented a substantial armoury for the group which would soon receive international attention as FRETILIN, the *Frente Revolucionarla de Timor Leste Independente*. The Revolutionary Front for the Independence of East Timor.

They were ready.

Chapter 14

Canberra — Jakarta

Albert was struck speechless when it happened. It took place without any warning whatsoever.

He had finished his breakfast and was engrossed in reading *The Age* when Wanti approached the small alcove and sat beside him. At first, he had not really noticed her presence. Until she spoke. Albert's initial reaction was that the nurse had called his name but immediately he realized that this was not one of her scheduled days.

He turned with an inquiring look and the young woman had smiled, leaned across to inspect the newspaper and asked, *"What are you reading, Albert?"*

Tears filled his eyes with disbelief. He took her hands and held them tightly.

"Wanti?" he asked.

Two hours later she sat holding an intelligent conversation with her psychoanalyst. Just five hours later they sat in a Dutch Indonesian restaurant together ordering a selection of dishes from the *rijstaffel*, celebrating her remarkable recovery.

The rapid change in Wanti was incredible and, although cautioned by her doctors, Albert knew that she had finally broken through those barriers which had held her mind chained to the dreadful memories of her childhood. For days Albert waited to see if her recovery continued to show signs of permanency before phoning Stephen. He didn't want to build up his friend's hopes only to discover that after a short time she would retreat back into her secret world once again.

A week went by. And then another. They talked continuously. About Indonesia, her brother, her schooling, while Albert discussed his unsuccessful marriage, the racial bigotry he'd encountered in Australia and his early childhood, deliberately omitting the severe hardships he'd experienced. He was concerned that he might inadvertently trigger some reaction with his tales of the desperate life he'd suffered in Timor.

She rarely spoke of her husband, Stephen. He thought it better to wait for her to raise the subject of his absence. Only twice did she mention his name and even then the subject was quickly forgotten.

Albert doted on her every move. He took time off work to spend with her, visiting the zoo, Phillip Island and as many other scenic places as he could manage, believing that the outings would assist with her ongoing rehabilitation. Instead, they grew closer, and Wanti became dependent on his support and tender attention. Albert and Wanti were content together and went about their lives in a comfortable and orderly fashion as if it were the natural thing to do. It was inevitable. Albert just hadn't seen it happening. He couldn't understand the signs at first but when he recognized what had happened he was overjoyed.

They became lovers.

Albert had never intended for this to happen but it seemed so natural when the moment came. He delighted in the warmth and sincerity of the relationship. He had never really been a very physical person but the tenderness they shared reminded him of the first months of his marriage and the terrible void that had enveloped his very being when the comfort of his first woman was removed from his life. In his mind Albert accepted the possibility that this still quite beautiful young woman had merely slipped into this new role as part of her recovery process. And she was so much younger. He didn't care.

He loved her dearly. He felt no guilt.

Stephen had not communicated with her for some time and it became apparent that he too had developed other relationships back in Jakarta. He was, nevertheless, concerned as to how best to break the news to Stephen.

They discussed their feelings for each other and Albert expressed concerns that, once she met her husband face to face, Wanti may discover that she still loved him. He really didn't want to take that risk but when he had suggested the possibility to her Wanti had held him warmly and reassured him of her affections. She had then agreed to marry Albert. It was decided that they would travel to Jakarta to meet with her husband and settle the matter quickly. Divorce in Indonesia was not a complicated process and Stephen was unlikely to object.

Albert hoped that too much time had now passed for Stephen and Wanti to ever recover their previous relationship, or restore the feelings they had once shared so intimately together. Albert set about making the necessary arrangements for their journey. It would soon be Christmas and he wished to return in time to celebrate with his loving companion as man and wife.

* * * * * *

Coleman was surprised by Albert's telex advising of their visit. He responded immediately, informing his old friend that he would meet them both at Halim Perdanakusumah airport. Although Albert had not advised Stephen of his wife's progress, he acknowledged that it was obvious there had been considerable improvement in her mental health for her to be able to travel back to Indonesia. He hoped she could now at least converse.

Coleman considered Wanti's return and accepted that he would be obliged to make considerable changes to his current lifestyle to accommodate the existence of a spouse once more. A lady of the house. The official lady. It had been so long and he almost resented the intrusion.

Stephen felt a twinge of annoyance. His life as it was, and at this moment, left little to be desired, but he understood that this would change dramatically with her arrival. He made a note to tell Sukardi to clear the rooms of whatever paraphernalia might still remain in his room left behind by his numerous female guests.

It was unlikely that their relationship could ever return to whatever status it had achieved prior to Wanti's collapse. He wondered if she could accept that he had obviously acquired new friends and if this discovery might trigger a recurrence of her illness. He didn't understand why Albert had dropped all of this on him so suddenly. And why inform him by telex? Why not just phone? Coleman sat staring at the message momentarily and, opening his diary, drew lines across the days commencing with his wife's arrival to provide them both with the time they would so obviously require to readjust to each other. He wanted to feel responsible but his heart just wasn't in it.

It was almost the end of another year. His work load, the pressures of the multi-million dollar monthly turnover, and his extravagant life style had started to show. He'd added a few kilos and his over exposed skin had become scaly from the constant damage imposed by the sun's ultra-violet rays.

The weekend cruises were not just all business. Amongst the more affluent foreigners, his was the most sought after weekend boating invitation. Stories of starlets and incredible parties preceded him whenever he attended dinner parties or other social events. Wherever he appeared as he was, unofficially, still considered an eligible bachelor, the younger women, foreigner and Indonesian alike, would become blatantly obvious with their attention, dominating all conversation just hoping for an invitation to one of his excursions to the islands. There had been no shortage of beautiful women. And money.

The company's activities continued to grow, his holdings in real estate alone so embarrassingly significant that his friends in the taxation department became overly friendly.

Stephen was obliged to use nominee names to hold most of the large acreages he'd acquired in the mountains for the new villa development the company had started there.

He estimated his net worth at more than eight million dollars. But it was tiresome and boring work. Particularly the mainstay of their activities, the ongoing defence contracts which provided the enormous cash-flow. He channelled his share of the profits into other ventures.

He had become a sought after figure. His advice was respected. Stephen had come to understand more about human nature and the incredible but superficially based respect people held for those who were successful. He despised them. And there were always problems with the younger women. It just never seemed to end. They went after it all with a dedication even he couldn't believe. They would do almost anything to secure a permanent place by his side. He acknowledged that this had been one of the reasons he'd never really considered divorcing Wanti. She had provided him with an acceptable social shield, protection from the insurmountable number of young females who continuously, he was sure, spent their spare time devising more schemes and more traps than one could consider possible just to get his dollars into the sack or a lock on his collar.

He thought about having a wife who was never present. Many of his friends, and certainly most of the women thought she was some figment of his imagination or a pretext he'd use to avoid being entangled. An excuse.

Slowly Stephen closed the diary and pushed it wearily to one side. He was resigned to the inevitable.

Yes, he had a wife. And she was returning. Soon. Perhaps even to stay.

Although he experienced an uneasiness with these thoughts of her return, he took the decision to provide Wanti with whatever opportunity she required to re-enter his life, even if it meant readjusting his household to provide an acceptable atmosphere conducive to her return. A token marriage. He felt sure that she was still ill, or at least continued to suffer from the traumatic seizures that had torn their lives apart. Those things just never went away. He knew. He'd corresponded with Wanti's doctors regularly at first, and they had all been of the same opinion. It was highly improbable that she would ever again enjoy the realities of the world as others knew it. In short, her mental illness had rendered her incapable of living a normal life, perhaps forever. He reached out and reopened the diary to the place where he had made the entries.

The uneasiness returned. He put it down to the effects of having over indulged the evening before and the ridiculous pool party he'd left sometime in the early hours of the morning. He suddenly remembered. He paged the houseboy and sent a note with a small envelope up to the master bedroom.

Coleman refused to move from the original quarters where the company first commenced its activities. Other offices were scattered throughout the city but this was still the nerve centre for his personal and joint activities with Seda.

He thought of the General. Their relationship had been lucrative. They still kept their distance from each other publicly although, occasionally, for appearances, one or the other would attend a function at the other's invitation.

Coleman was not a superstitious man but the sense of foreboding he experienced made him uncomfortable. Acknowledging that the sensation could have been precipitated by the unexpected news of his wife's pending return, he rose from the teak executive desk and placed the ribbon marker between the pages indicating the arrival dates. He would advise his staff that he would only be available for limited access during the initial period of her visit. Or return.

Greg Hart had become a most competent executive and was well versed in the general operating procedures of the company. Even Seda had agreed that the man's mastery of administrative matters was exceptional. He ensured that communication between the operational and administrative aspects of the *kongsi* flowed smoothly, almost mechanically. Coleman could confidently instruct his assistant to assume temporary control over the activities for the week. Having made his decision Stephen decided to lunch at one of his old haunts, The George and Dragon.

In the following week FRETILIN declared independence in the former Portuguese colony of East Timor.

Chapter 15

Canberra — East Timor

The panic in the air was ominous. The Prime Minister's office resembled that of a football locker room as one by one the senior department bureaucrats came and went hurrying along the corridors as the news spread from office to office. The relatively inexperienced leader glared furiously at his subordinates gathered to discuss the incredible news.

"Why in the hell don't we have adequate intelligence regarding their strength and basic political intentions?" the tall articulate politician's voice boomed across the room.

"We have no representation there, Prime Minister and at this moment we're dependent wholly on isolated reports originating from the missionary posts in the area. "

The Attorney-General contemplated Anderson's predicament . He was already working out possible scenarios whereby he could pass the responsibility for this screw-up down the line to Anderson. This could mean the end of his career.

What was the point in maintaining covert operations overseas if they were unable to provide current and crucial intelligence information when it was needed? The limited budget allocated to clandestine operations prevented reliable intelligence sources from remaining current and the lack of suitable communication centres in the vicinity of the Timor group of islands made information gathering very difficult. They had sought the assistance of an Australian hotelier who had established a small operation in Dili but, as the man was an amateur and followed everywhere by Indonesian and former Portuguese agents, his services were practically useless. And then, of course, there was that poorly trained Consul and his uninformed opinions!

Funding such operations were also extremely difficult. Due to the nature and sensitivity of the work involved, the number of support personnel or those who needed to know of the covert activity was always kept to the bare minimum. As it was, ASIO's Chief regularly complained that his own domestic operations now suffered as the funding for the overseas activities could not be acknowledged publicly. For obvious reasons, these expenditures were hidden within the domestic budget.

When the Prime Minister came to power he and his colleagues wasted little time taking control of the Intelligence Services. He was shocked to discover that Australia had been running a clandestine department for years under the direction of the Attorney-General's office and, as files had been kept also on members of his own political party due to their affiliations with the Left and other Socialist or Communist groups sympathetic to Australia's enemies, he was rightfully outraged. The Deputy Prime Minister had been vocal in suggesting that Australia withdraw its troops from Vietnam. Upon winning power, in one of its first announcements, the new Government signalled its intentions of carrying out a full withdrawal from the war-torn country. The Americans were furious.

Australia's allies had been concerned with its swing to the Left and had, for a considerable time, kept regular surveillance teams operating in the country observing some of the more radical elements in the leadership Down Under.

As the votes had been counted and it became quite apparent that the Conservatives would lose power to the Socialists the lights in Canberra's offices burned well into the night as the shredders worked overtime clearing the decks of all compromising material. Anderson had personally overseen the destruction of at least four hundred files. Having destroyed the last vestiges of damaging evidence collected over the years, he had felt relieved at the time but later, along with many others within the Defence and Intelligence community, he was not entirely convinced that he had acted in the interests of the nation.

There had been considerable soul searching within the walls surrounding the highly sensitive security department. He'd even contemplated resigning his position, as he didn't believe that any of the incoming rabble could even understand the importance of maintaining the Service's secrecy, let alone support its covert overseas activities.

It was quite clear to him that the success of their teams depended not just on their abilities as operatives but also the necessity for them to function in a world ignorant of their existence. It appeared that this would no longer be, as already the list of those who were now aware of the secret operations had been dramatically increased to include senior party rank and file members who, just months before, had also been listed on the department's surveillance sheets.

Anderson felt disgusted with the unprofessional approach the incoming Attorney-General had taken regarding accessing the most secret files. The AG had almost been cavalier about whom he added to the list. The Director believed that it was now only a matter of time before the department's existence became public knowledge — that is if it hadn't already been compromised by one of the new members whose name now appeared in the highly classified file.

He looked up into the Prime Minister's red-jowled face, his pulse now evident above the cheek lines as it pumped with the rising blood pressure.

"Are you telling me that we don't have any bloody idea whatsoever what these, uhm, FRETILIN terrorists are up to?"

"Sir, our reports indicate that they are only interested in maintaining sovereignty over the former Portuguese colony. "

"What about the American intelligence that they have showing satellite proof of Russian weaponry?" demanded the Minister for External Affairs.

"What?" the Prime Minister exclaimed, paling considerably at the news. "Are you telling us that these bastards have actually been stockpiling Communist war supplies without our knowledge? And why in hell have I not been informed of this development? For Chrissakes!" he yelled, slamming the palm of his hand hard down onto the desk to his right.

"The reports were sent to us by the Americans just hours after the FRETILIN announcement, sir, and we have not had the opportunity to disseminate the material to all departments. "

The leader's face turned crimson. His voice was deep and he spoke slowly, glaring icily at the Attorney-General.

"Your office was aware of the contents of the report. The External Affairs Ministry was aware also of the report. Why wasn't the information passed to my office?"

The men shuffled their feet. Several coughed.

The Chairman of the Joint Intelligence Services viewed the politicians around him with disgust. If he had had his way, none of these incompetent bunglers would have access to any of the intelligence communities' information. He believed that this group represented everything that the previous Government had warned against during their many years of office but, unfortunately, complacency had ruled, thrusting the Left into power for the first time in many years. As a result of an indifferent middle class vote, the Socialist Party had finally broken the Conservative grip on Australian politics.

The JIS Chairman looked around the room and identified several of those present who had vowed to dismantle the very political system which had brought them to power. The Chairman was certain that anarchy was only one step away.

The Australian military establishment had understood that their budgets would be slashed and their power base eroded commensurably. They believed that the country would slip back thirty years in terms of its capacity to defend itself, with a government in power that didn't believe in the existence of any real threat to the Australian people reportedly now sitting to the north of the country they now governed.

"Prime Minister," the Chairman commenced, "the information indicates the weapons originated from Cuban sources and are of Russian manufacture. We cannot at this time be sure of the size of their armories. However indications are that they have been stockpiling for some considerable time. "

The speaker looked around the office knowing that he had delivered a considerable shock to those present. What they did not realize was that a select number of highly-cleared Intelligence masters had prior knowledge of the information only now released to the assembled group. The intelligence chiefs had agreed that as they apparently could no longer determine just who could access the highly classified material, then they would initiate their own system of controls by retaining the information on a 'Director's Eyes-Only' basis to maintain its integrity. Those in the room who had knowledge of this tactic were pleased, as it had obviously worked.

"Furthermore, we have unconfirmed reports there have been

small numbers of Cuban observers identified around the town of Dili," the Chairman added.

"Cubans?" the Prime Minister gasped, shocked at the incredible news. "Cubans?" he repeated shaking his head disbelievingly, "have you all gone stark raving fucking mad?" almost choking with the invective.

"We can't confirm the sighting, however we believe that as the weapons probably originated from Castro's own arsenal there is little doubt he would have sent advisers and other technicians along with the equipment."

"What sort of weapons do they have?" the Prime Minister asked, reluctantly, expecting the worst.

The General stared directly at the nation's leader. Pausing to achieve the maximum impact, he slowly shook his head and spoke authoritatively.

"The FRETILIN and other armed groups will have the latest in rifles and small arms. The general consensus is that they will have a considerable supply of AK-47s, anti-personnel mines and, unfortunately, maybe even some small missile capability."

Those present who had not been privileged with this information prior to the General's announcement, were stunned. For moments no one moved. The politicians remained speechless, mouths agape, staring wide-eyed at the Military Commander who had, in one brief moment, delivered the most incredible statement they'd ever heard. Even by these Members of Parliament.

"AK-47s? Missiles?" the Prime Minister commenced his question, stammering, "wh. . . what type of weapons are they?"

The General again sighed, faced with the senior politician's ignorance.

"The AK-47 is a Soviet assault rifle used widely throughout the Communist world. The rifle is both semi-automatic and fully automatic, with a cyclic firing rate of six hundred rounds per minute. The weapon has been around for some time and the Cubans have stockpiles large enough to support armies of insurrections in at least half a dozen separate theatres.

"It's what the North Vietnamese regulars have been using against our boys," he added.

The room was filled with more silence.

"And the missiles?" the leader asked quietly, dragging the words out slowly.

"We don't know. "

"What?" the Prime Minister bellowed, "what do you mean we don't know? For Christ's sake man, surely we must have some information?"

"If the Yanks have this information off their satellites then they have not, as yet, been forthcoming in providing the data nor permitting our access to the material. "

"Jesus bloody Christ! Missiles!" the politician exploded again, slumping back into his heavy leather chair.

"The bastards!" he shouted, jumping back to his feet, "the dirty stinking bastards!"

The assembly watched their leader, surprised at his apparent loss of control over the situation. It was totally out of character. Several minutes passed and, regaining his composure, he looked back at the military men whom he now also despised for wrecking what had been a reasonable week in office.

"What is the estimated range of these missiles that we do not know whether they do or do not have?" he demanded sarcastically.

"If they have taken delivery say, of a Russian Guideline series surface-to-air missile then these could deliver a devastating effect to aircraft within range. The Russians have been modifying this missile and you may remember its effectiveness during the Six Day War when the Egyptians used it successfully against the Israeli Air Force. These birds can fly at three and a half times the speed of sound and will hit a target up to sixty thousand feet," he answered, almost proud to be a member of the world's military machine that could manufacture and deploy such sophisticated weaponry.

The General stopped to ensure that this was all sinking in as it was imperative that these civilians understood the ramifications of what was to follow.

"But these Guidelines are not our real problem." He now had the attention of every person in attendance.

"The major danger, gentlemen, is the distinct possibility of our own Cuban-styled missile crisis!"

Slowly all eyes turned towards the large man seated behind the Victorian desk. He was ashen and sat motionless except for the slight shaking movement of his greying head. The Prime Minister, as were those around him, was in a complete state of shock.

"My God!" he exclaimed softly.

"How?" he inquired, in a soft almost inaudible whisper.

"Gentlemen. We are all aware of the crisis precipitated by the Russian deployment of the Russian IRBMs in Cuba in 1962. These missiles were of the Sandal series which have a strike range capability of some one thousand two hundred miles." The General rose and approached the wall on which now hung a map of South East Asia down to the Commonwealth of Australia. He pointed at Timor and, removing his ball-pen, drew a circle around the island.

"Gentlemen, this is the potential strike range of the Sandal missile. Let's hope that they will not be able to deploy these or any other IRBMs for, as you can see, such a strike range puts most of Northern Australia, New Guinea, the Philippines and, of course, Jakarta and half of Indonesia, well within the targetable range of these missiles. "

Several of the Cabinet Ministers had now approached the map and were examining it in disbelief.

"Good grief!" the Minister for External Affairs exclaimed, astonished at the revelations he had just heard, "they could wipe out Darwin and maybe even Perth!"

"And probably Cairns, Alice Springs, the three secret American installations, also Port Hedland and Mount Isa," added the Cabinet Secretary.

This announcement brought the Minister seated across the room immediately to his feet.

"Are you sure? Mount Isa?" his lip trembling as he darted across the room to determine for himself that his own electoral seat could be obliterated by one of these incredible monsters.

"There is no doubt, gentlemen," the General continued, "should the Independence Movement succeed, with the obvious political ties they have already established, we should all assume the worst. There could quite possibly be a small independent Communist nation sitting just off Australia with the capacity to throw nuclear warheads into our and everybody else's backyard in the region. "

Immediately the room lost all semblance of decorum and broke into shouts and cries of panic.

"Gentlemen!" the Prime Minister called. "Gentlemen, let's have some order, please, this is not the Floor of the House! Settle down.

Now!" he demanded.

The nation's leaders returned to their seats. They all stared numbly at each other; several of their number had lowered their heads and closed their eyes, as if they had already been struck by some alien force.

"We cannot allow a hint of this situation to reach the press or the public. Attorney-General, please advise all present of the gravity of permitting such a leak to occur. "

The Attorney-General rose slowly and stood visibly unhappy with the task of warning his own colleagues of the penalties of the Official Secrets Act.

"As the Prime Minister wishes," he commenced. "I should request that we all maintain complete communication silence regarding these developments and, as the subject has been classified with the highest grading, the penalty of any such breach could earn the responsible party up to thirty years in prison. "

"I really don't consider this at all necessary, Prime Minister. If anything, it is a little insulting to suggest that any of us present would consider such irresponsible action," intervened the piqued Chief of Navy Staff.

"Nevertheless, that's the way it will be, gentlemen, and you will be informed as to where and when a further general discussion will be called to address the crisis," the leader announced. "General, I wish for you to remain, along with the Attorney-General, and Mr Anderson."

The room all but emptied within a minute.

Anderson observed the nation's leader drumming the desk with his pudgy and oversized fingers. Alone with the three men he had instructed to remain, the Prime Minister observed each of them, in turn, determining in his own mind that only his elected political associate could really be trusted completely.

"General, what is the suggested course of action, or remedy to resolve this situation?"

Anderson observed the Senior Army Officer as he considered the question. The man was almost as large as the Prime Minister. Both men had reached the pinnacle of their careers and, as is the case with most powerful men, each considered the other to be inferior and of lesser achievement. The General's obvious meteoric rise had been a result not just of his war service record and outstanding capabilities, but also his family's close association with the previous political moguls who ruled the Australian classes uninterrupted through the Fifties, Sixties, and early Seventies.

"My opinion is that we should encourage the United Nations to occupy the former colony immediately with troops for at least five years until such time as the people are able to govern themselves and convince the island's regional neighbours that its amenable to some non-aligned movement. Failing that, Prime Minister, either we go in ourselves, or we orchestrate for the Indonesians to enter the colony as it is, after all, just the other half of an island already occupied by their country."

The politician turned to Anderson.

"Would you agree?"

Anderson had already discussed the possible scenarios with the Army General. Although they were basically in agreement as to what action should be taken, they were very conscious that the politician with whom they were dealing was astute and could easily detect any possible collusion on their part.

"Sir," he commenced, "the obvious dangers of yet another independent state coming into being in the region oblige us to seek a course of action which will not just offer a short term remedy but also enhance Australia's own position with its Asian neighbours."

The statesmen slowly began drumming on his desk.

"The Indonesians will not tolerate an independent East Timor and we should avoid, at all costs, any confrontation with them over this issue. In fact," he continued "we should encourage them to enter the arena guaranteeing our political and, if necessary, our military support in this crisis."

"How will the Indonesians react?" he asked.

"Historically, the Indonesians believe that the whole archipelago belongs under one flag. Their action in West Irian has proven that political stance. I believe that they will jump at the opportunity to acquire East Timor as part of their country."

"General?"

"They certainly have the fire power to march in and wrap up the FRETILIN quickly. The danger is that the Cubans may have already firmly entrenched themselves and this would then become a United Nations issue which, eventually, could result in the creation of an independent country with substantial Communist backing. "

"Then you are both in agreement. The Indonesians should be approached immediately and advised of our position?"

Both men looked at each other and nodded their approval of such a gambit.

"General, the Indonesians would be receptive to someone of your stature approaching them with such a proposal. I feel that you should contact their ambassador immediately who, if I'm not mistaken, is also a retired officer of senior rank. "

The General's eyebrows rose quizzically.

"Also retired, Prime Minister?" he asked.

A semblance of a smile appeared on his lips. It was not the smile of mirth but one of sarcasm. He had nothing to be pleased about.

"Prematurely put, General. I'm sorry. "

"Thank you Prime Minister," the career officer responded without any sign of warmth. He despised these socialist politicians. "I will contact their Ambassador immediately and advise you of the outcome. "

"Thank you, General. "

Anderson prepared to depart with the officer but the huge framed man indicated that he was to remain.

"John. Tell me what you really think will happen, totally off the record," he asked when they were alone.

Anderson took a long slow breath and settled back into the comfortable guest chair.

"The Indonesians will grab at the opportunity, but world opinion will not be kind to them as Portugal has already recognized the declarations of independence in other former colonies, such as Angola and Mozambique. "

"Well, we all know what's happening in Angola,"the Prime Minister said unhappily.

"The way I see it, it really is a matter of how well we in Australia support the Indonesians and keep the press off their backs. "

At the mention of the newspapers the Prime Minister's nostrils flared. There was little love lost between his office and Australia's press moguls who denigrated him and his colleagues at every opportunity. They were all too aware of the government's philosophy and the party line regarding the press and the power its owners wielded. He had agreed prior to taking office to settle a few old scores should the opportunity arise.

"I will speak to them myself," he advised.

Surprised, Anderson's expression amused his superior.

"Everybody needs somebody sometime, John, you of all people considering your profession should understand the necessity for compromise. It's not just politicians who prostitute themselves, you know."

Embarrassed at the comment Anderson remained silent.

"What would happen if we suggested a Kennedy-style block-ade of the island?"

"Nothing. We don't have the fire-power and neither do the Indonesians. It is unlikely that the Malaysians or the Singaporeans could muster enough shipping to assist. And I wouldn't recommend that we even suggest this alternative to the Filipinos as any participation on their part would agitate the Indonesians and we could well end up with an expanded regional conflict."

"You realize that in my capacity as Prime Minister I am privy to all the activities of your department?"

"Certainly. We never burned any files."

The Prime Minister looked coldly at the bureaucrat.

"No one is suggesting that your office did. However, you are aware that there is considerable pressure from within the Attorney-General's Department to isolate these activities and bring them directly under the control of defence?"

Anderson had anticipated the possibility, although he dreaded any such action.

"That would cost us the integrity of our operational arm, which has taken considerable time, funding and effort to establish, Prime Minister."

"What can you do with this team to assist alleviate the current crisis over Timor?"

"We could certainly improve our lines of communication which, as we've observed today, are totally inadequate due to insufficient funding. We could position a vessel close enough to act as a communications centre and place a team on the ground."

"How would you execute this plan?"

"We will seek the assistance of the so-called 'Press Barons' as cover in exchange for the direct flow of non-essential information to the newspapers."

"You believe this is achievable?"

"I will put something together immediately. "

"John."

"Sir?"

"Don't screw this up. We don't want any bodies and we can't afford any more skeletons. "

Anderson nodded slowly as he rose.

"With your permission, I would like to liaise with the General. "

"No. I don't feel comfortable with that. If the requirement arises, deal directly through this office. "

Anderson agreed, excused himself and returned directly to his offices by commonwealth car. Ignoring the PM's instructions, he had his secretary leave a message for the General to contact him urgently upon his return from the Indonesian Embassy, then settled back to devise a plan which would place his clandestine section in a more secure and potentially powerful position for the future.

* * * * * *

Later that day Indonesia's Ambassador to Australia sent an encrypted radio communication from Canberra to Jakarta. The message was picked up by one of the Defence Department's listening posts, recorded, and dispatched to Melbourne for deciphering.

The Indonesian codes were simple and often a transcript of a coded message would be on the desk of the duty officer at the operational centre of Anderson's headquarters even before the Indonesians had received their own radio message at BAKIN in Jakarta.

The message read:

MOST SECRET BAPAK DJENDERAL NATHAN SEDA DIREKTUR/ COVERT/OPS BAKIN DATE: 28 NOV 1975 FROM AMBASSADOR INDONESIAN EMBASSY/CANBERRA. TEXT: AUSTRALIAN GOVERNMENT DEEPLY CONCERNED INSTABILITY CREATED BY FRETILIN UPRISING AND THREAT TO REGION PEACE. AUSTRALIANS CONFIRM THAT THEY WILL SUPPORT INDONESIAN ANNEXATION OF TIMOR-TIMUR AND ADVISE THAT AUSTRALIAN PUBLIC OPINION WILL ALSO SUPPORT SUCH AN ENTRY INTO TIMOR-TIMUR. THEIR PRIME MINISTER HAS ADVISED THAT THEY OFFER MILITARY SUPPORT SHOULD WE REQUEST SAME. MEETING HAS

BEEN REQUESTED WITH BAPAK PRESIDENT SOEHARTO EITHER
HERE IN AUSTRALIA OR IN INDONESIA. SIGNED: COLONEL
SUPRAPTO N2337339 ON BEHALF OF AMBASSADOR. MESSAGE
ENDS: MOST SECRET

* * * * * *

Nathan Seda considered the communication now on his desk
looking mockingly back at him. This was developing into an impossible situation. The Australians were acting out of character involving themselves in what he viewed as a simple case of a sovereign state declaring itself independent. Should the contents of the
message become public knowledge then this would encourage the
Indonesian High Command to march directly into Dili without fear
of international condemnation.

For Seda and the FRETILIN forces this would be a major catastrophe. They did not have the manpower to defend themselves against
the might of the Indonesian combined Armed Forces. He could
not accept that the Australian Government did not support the Declaration of Independence nor did they recognize the Portuguese
announcement that their former colony must not be annexed by
Indonesia.

Something was dreadfully wrong. He had to think. There had
to be a way of slowing the Indonesian attempts to seize the other
half of Timor without interfering with the process of establishing
the new Government quickly. Then there was the other signal he
had received. The Americans were discussing putting a hold on
the squadron of Broncos due for delivery.

This was favourable news as the OV-10Fs were equipped with
twenty millimetre canon and air-to-ground missiles. These aircraft
were an obvious choice for AURI to use in the event the Government declared war on the FRETILIN army, as the Broncos were a
superior counter-insurgency strike aircraft which, Seda knew, had
been modified for the Indonesian Air Force with the latest laser
controlled missile launch systems. Should the Indonesians succeed
in convincing the American Government to deliver these aircraft
then resistance, he knew, would be futile against such machines.
The Australian Sabres AURI acquired would need urgent modifications to handle the new air-to-ground missiles if they were also
to be used.

What was confusing was the change of attitude on behalf of the Australians as his sources had confirmed just days earlier that the Royal Australian Air Force had refused any assistance with a refit to the Sabres to provide for missile capability. He had come a long way and could not permit this opportunity to lapse. There had to be some way of keeping the Australians out of the conflict.

Seda realized that the Indonesians would mobilize quickly once they understood that public opinion was not against their entering its small neighbour's territory. He had to eliminate this support. He must prepare a plan with immediate effect.

Seda sat deep in thought. He continued to do so through the evening and well into the next morning. He did not sleep.

It wasn't until another week had passed that an idea began to formulate in his mind and, after considering the ramifications of the bold step he was about to take and when he believed that the timing was appropriate, Seda put the plan into action.

The General called Umar Suharjo.

* * * * * *

Bambang was proud to be amongst the soldiers whose units had been selected to protect the Indonesian Timor borders. He could see that the others felt the same way from the gait in their walk, and the confidence they exuded. This is what they had been trained to do.

They had all been briefed. A group of terrorists calling themselves the Front for the Liberation of East Timor had run amok across the border, butchering women and children, and were now threatening to cross the border *en masse* and destroy the Indonesian villages there. They were soldiers and their duty was to protect their country. He was not afraid. Bambang wished his sister, Wanti could see him now. She would be so proud of him!

The C130E transport had lifted them out of Surabaya for the long haul across the East Nusatanggara Lesser Archipelago, crossing over Bali before continuing on through hours of monotonous airborne travel until finally disembarking at Kupang.

The landing was, in itself a feat, considering the unsealed landing strip! His colleagues had joked with him in the mess where they hurriedly gulped down a large serving of steamed rice and *rendang*. The officers and men in this Command ate exactly the same food.

The airstrip in Kupang had a bad reputation and, in fact, should not have been used for aircraft the size of the Hercules which he now found himself in, winging his way towards his first real military adventure. The others were equally excited. One thousand soldiers had already been airlifted and rumour had it that there would be as many as twenty thousand KOPASGAT, the elite quick-action commando troops, to backup the ground forces. They had a history to live up to. Theirs had been the forces first to strike fear into the hearts of the Malay soldiers when they had courageously attacked the superior forces during the *Konfrontasi* period under *Bung Karno*, their first President. And they had also been with the forward troops when their Command had bravely jumped from the ancient C-47s into West Irian to liberate that province from the Dutch soldiers. This action would be just as swift, perhaps not even lasting one week!

There wasn't a command within the Republik as competent as theirs! They were well equipped.

The senior officers had told them that the basic training the men in this command had undergone was as superior as that of the British commandos.

Their training had kept them all fit and Bambang could not understand the necessity for sending so many of their superior number against a raggedy bunch of peasant rebels from across the border in what was known to be one of the poorest areas in the region.

He rubbed the two gold stars on his shoulder for luck as they prepared to land. As the enormous transport bumped along the grass runway the soldiers cried out in unison *"Merdeka! Merdeka!"* Freedom! Freedom! and sang their battalion's song of courage.

* * * * * *

The aircraft landed with a squeal of burning rubber as the tyres took up the momentum of the aircraft's touching down on the red, hard baked clay airstrip. As Bambang followed the other young soldiers, his eyes opened in incredulity as he counted four more of the massive transport planes also disembarking troops and supplies. Across the fields he could see the already erected tents of the different divisional encampments. He had never seen so many troops in one place anywhere before.

As they strutted across the hard-standing surface jammed with jeeps, crates of supplies and platoons of soldiers working on their delegated unloading and loading assignments, one of the non-coms barked an order from behind and immediately the paratroopers broke into double time.

As *Letnan Satu* Bambang and the other junior officers filled with excitement, he never even considered the irony of the date of his own arrival in Indonesian West Timor. It was the first day of October, 1975.

Exactly ten years to the day when Indonesia suffered the abortive Communist *coup d'état*.

And its bloody aftermath under Soeharto.

* * * * * *

Anderson was annoyed with the arrogance of the media baron. He was rude and manifested the ruthlessness for which he was renowned in every movement, in each gesticulation he made as he waved his arms from the elbow down, in pontifical manner, ignoring the cigar's threatening path as he demonstrated his point.

"Tell him to shove it!" was his reaction to the offer.

This man was tough. He acted tough, played tough, and had a reputation second to none for achieving his aims when it came to corporate acquisitions. There had been rumours, only rumours, that he also had direct links with the underworld element, but there wasn't a soul in either Sydney or Melbourne who would allude to this publicly.

He was feared. Often when negotiations got out of hand he was known to reach across the table and lash out directly at whoever on the opposing team presented him with the most resistance. He lived to gamble. The amounts he'd laid on horses were legendary. He even owned his own stables on several continents.

The final choice had been left to Anderson. The Government had enough problems of its own just maintaining its authority over Parliament without the added complications of the approaching regional conflict.

'Bloody self-serving politicians,' he'd thought when delegated the tasteless task of finalizing negotiations with this man. Anderson was exasperated by the knowledge that they were blinded by their own self-serving interests and their domestic difficulties to the extent that, if they weren't careful, the problem would escalate until finally becoming unresolvable. Under pressure, he'd agreed to finalize the arrangements. John Anderson had elected to run with this choice of the major players out of those who owned the tabloids in Australia. He had feared that the others may have rejected the proposal out of hand due to political differences with the new leadership in Canberra.

The man sitting in front of him was basically apolitical. Except when it came to amassing his ever growing fortune.

Anderson anticipated that in the event that the operation came unstuck, he could count on this man's greed and general absence of morals to bury the remains of the operation before creating any embarrassment for either his department or the Prime Minister. He recognized that it was essential that he maintained a stable working relationship with the Australian leader. Without him, it would be practically impossible to fund the covert operations and operate without the same bureaucratic procedures which had stifled ASIO's growth and thwarted so many ASIS operations over the years.

Anderson looked across at the media giant and waited. The heavy set square-jawed entrepreneur sneered at the suggestion that his assistance would guarantee him a closer working relationship with the Government's 'powers-to-be'.

"I couldn't give a shit about those mongrel bastards in Canberra. They are a bunch of wimps who'd sell their souls to whoever provides them with the key to the House. "

"Whatever," was Anderson's response.

"Do we have a deal then?" he asked.

"Let's just get it straight for the record then. "

Anderson repeated the arrangements, hiding his dislike for the bullet-shaped head towering over him.

"You provide the vessel, we provide the crew. We use it as a communications centre for relay purposes. You get to send some of your journos into the arena. We dissect the military sensitive material and your papers have the first opportunity to run the rest directly from the front line. At all times it must appear to be a private operation and you are not to lend your name to the ship's presence in the area. Also, the journos are your responsibility and in the event that they do suffer any injuries, we are not to be held responsible in any way. "

The Intelligence Chief assumed that tacit agreement had been arrived at discreetly between the PM and the entrepreneur and whatever the additional *quid pro quo* might have been, Anderson was certain that details would never be disclosed.

"Is that the lot?" the gruff bullying tone demanded.

"No," Anderson answered, determined not to permit the other to dominate the meeting. "As agreed, your papers will support the Indonesian position. And, as discussed, your television licensing applications will, in turn, receive the Government's support. "

"Set it up with Charlie. He will act as the intermediary between our offices. "

"Good. That's it then. I will inform the P M. "

"You can shove it up his arse as far as I'm concerned. Just ensure that the bastard keeps his word. "

Anderson nodded and left the powerful brusque figure standing, peering through the window of his office, surveying the influential empire he controlled.

That afternoon John Anderson reported back to the Prime Minister who, having received an assurance that the arrangements were completed and, recognizing the commitments made on his behalf, sighed and just motioned him away.

Within days the ship departed from Sydney late at night and headed directly to Darwin, where it took on additional fuel and victualling supplies before leaving for a position off the Indonesian island of Timor.

The security officer and the ship's Naval Commander were unhappy with the additional 'crew' which had boarded just an hour before departure from Garden Island. As it was, anchoring the civilian registered launch in the RAN's station had been difficult enough without the additional complication of having civilians passing through the restricted area.

On board was a team of specialist technicians trained in communications, deciphering, and their own collection of encryption devices.

The security officer in charge of the modifications hastily installed prior to their departure was first to discover that these recent and late arrivals were journalists. To his further dismay, the Captain informed his officers that the journalists were to be given instruction in the use of the ship-to-shore mobile radios as they would take several sets with them when they disembarked.

The ship's Commander was surprised when the group suddenly decided to discontinue the voyage once they had arrived in Darwin. All six of the men had suffered from seasickness and had requested that arrangements be made for them to fly the last leg of the journey. The Lieutenant Commander sent a priority signal and, several hours later, received confirmation that they were to proceed without the media personnel, and re-establish contact once the vessel had taken up position in the target zone.

The crew were relieved to have them out of their hair.

* * * * * *

The South Australian-based aerial taxi company had positioned both of its Cessna 310s in Darwin. That's how the contract read. They had requested urgent clearance for their flight into Kupang and, having waited three frustrating days, the charterers had become impatient as news of the military build up had spread quickly. As the flight path entered Indonesian territory, a 'diplomatic clearance' was required under the Geneva Convention and, although not strictly adhered to, it was always prudent to be able to produce some form of written authority when landing in the host country.

At 0630 hours on the fourth day the first of the two flights departed, followed at 0730 by the second Cessna. Neither aircraft had approval to enter Indonesian airspace nor did they have any authority to land on Indonesian soil. Both applications had been deliberately held, pending a final decision, on General Nathan Seda's desk, at BAKIN headquarters.

On board the first flight several of the group went about checking their gear. Cameras and bags of film were packed safely in the event of turbulence as the aircraft droned on towards the island of Timor. An hour behind, the second aircraft was making up lost time, having been delayed by one of the reporters who had insisted on making one final call back home, to his estranged wife Shelley, to see if she had returned the divorce papers he had sent her.

They were all young. And excited. The assignment was going to be a dream. The brief had been simple. Get amongst the action, they had been told by their boss, photograph whatever they could and radio report on an hourly basis everything that they observed on the frequencies provided. Their instructions had been emphatic. Radio report every hour. Everything!

Some time almost a week after leaving the launch which had taken them from Sydney to Darwin they were spotted. The crew of the ship had waved but the passengers were too high to see the friendly signals as they passed overhead.

The ship's Captain observed and noted in his log that the first aircraft had been followed some time later by another similar aircraft. As he watched the second aircraft pass and then fade into the distant light he wondered why they were in such a desperate hurry to reach their destination on the tense and primitive island. Two hours later the six journalists radioed that they had all arrived safely in Timor.

* * * * * *

The hot, moist, and debilitating pre-monsoonal conditions continued. The men had not encountered weather this severe even during their training exercises into other unfamiliar areas of the country. It was, as if by command, all cool breezes had been redirected to another world. As temperatures soared early in the tropical heat of the jungle the men had to be more disciplined than before in observing their water rations. Already a number of his own platoon had come down with the dreaded stomach cramps they had been warned about during their arrival briefing.

During their first week in Timor Bambang's regiment suffered from the prevalent diarrhoea more so than the earlier arrivals as they were bivouacked beside a running creek already fouled further upstream. Two of his men were evacuated with cholera symptoms just days after they drank from the small river. Most of the others suffered the debilitating cramps and the all too frequent latrine stops while out on patrol. At the beginning of the second week they had difficulty moving equipment as the first heavy deluges turned the dry fields into quagmires of mud.

The mosquitoes were enormous. Sleep was almost impossible.

The men who were not already weakened by the distressing symptoms which cursed the young soldiers became restless with the inaction.

They had come to fight. Instead, they had arrived and done nothing except clean and maintain their equipment and occasionally wander out through the jungle after the Hughes 500 choppers dropped them in relatively unsafe landing areas. The helicopters had been appropriated from the Pertamina fleet which had, in turn, left angry drilling crews stranded on their rigs for days beyond what their contracts demanded of them.

Bambang's platoon, or what was left and still capable of participating in the patrol, had been dropped two days before, but not by choppers. They had jumped from the rear of a Hercules transport as their target was considerably further away from their base camp than their earlier patrols had been. They could see the mountains up frighteningly close as the huge aircraft banked then settled down for the final run. The few veterans amongst them realized solemnly that the real test of their training would come when they plunged into the surrounding jungle below, into the foothills of Tata Maila mountain.

The Captain who led them had instructions to set up a forward reconnaissance camp to assist future incursions penetrate further into the enemy's territory. There had been fifteen such camps established on the same day. All across the border. Having secured the area and established radio contact with their base camp, they then waited for further instructions. And they continued to wait. Time passed very slowly for the young soldiers.

They had been in place for weeks and the men were already disillusioned with the conditions. Jungle rash had broken out, covering their bodies, festering under their arms and between their legs, spreading over their genitals, as they scratched continuously, further exacerbating the painful itch. They ate from their cold ration packs. There were no fires permitted. They knew that this wasn't just an exercise. This was for real!

Bambang had recovered from his most recent attack of stomach cramps and now lay around listlessly with the other men in their patrol and, although he didn't feel much up to it, he did attempt to set an example for the enlisted soldiers. He didn't complain but he really hated doing just nothing. Waiting. Just waiting.

* * * * * *

The Indonesian Command had decided to initiate two separate missions approximately six hours apart. The general purpose of these incursions was to create the impression that the raids were the responsibility of the pro-Indonesian East Timorese soldiers and, accordingly, the crack paratroopers were obliged to change their camouflaged battledress for less conspicuous military apparel.

A Company of almost one hundred of the well trained soldiers crossed the border as night fell and positioned themselves for the planned assault. They waited until the target area appeared to be secure for the night before proceeding through the densely wooded hill, avoiding the main track, just before 2300 hours. The shelling by their ships was supposed to have prepared the area for their attack and they could hear that the loud thudding bombardment had ceased some hours before.

Their Captain issued the command and the raiders entered the peaceful compound on the run, shooting at the small huts and everything else in sight. To their surprise they were confronted by a well-equipped force of regular troops who succeeded, much to the chagrin of the Indonesian Commander, in preventing the invaders from advancing any further. There was no evidence of the two days of bombardment reportedly delivered by their navy nor was there any sign of the *Apodeti* support groups who were supposed to have provided the local back up if needed.

The officer radioed his position and reported the resistance they'd encountered. He couldn't be sure if the enemy was FRETILIN or not, although judging by the professional tactics he'd seen, it was unlikely that they were entirely responsible for the surprise outcome of the engagement. The Commander was instructed to withdraw leaving none of the wounded behind. Each time he called for his men to pull out and regroup they suffered more casualties as the enemy pursued the poorly trained Indonesian soldiers.

The fire-fight continued for another half hour. The Indonesian losses were distressingly high. It was as if the enemy had known of the assault in advance and had been just waiting. In ambush.

The Captain called for his men one final time to retreat as he could see that their numbers had been reduced to but a few by the enemy's incredibly accurate fire. As he led the handful of survivors away he screamed as a bullet pierced his lungs, throwing his body to the ground. Reports of the number of dead, more than seventy men, were radioed by the wounded signals operator after they retreated. His Commander had been killed, shot in the back as they fled with the remnants of what had been a proud force of soldiers just hours before.

The village of Balibo experienced its second attack in less than five hours as another two companies entered the area anticipating the same fierce resistance that their comrades had encountered and paid for dearly. To their disappointment the enemy had already fled the area and it was assumed that they had headed towards the coast. The Company Commanders regrouped and were preparing to follow when, to their surprise, a number of foreigners suddenly appeared.

Across the mountain and less than sixty kilometres away and still at sea, the second team of raiders prepared to board the small motorized dinghies which had been tied alongside after the ship's guns became silent. Some had experienced the nausea of sea sickness as they were unaccustomed to the ship's motion. They were part of a the two-pronged attack, and although the task of storming beaches was normally left to the *Korp Komando*, the responsibility for the operation had been given to them. The officers understood the necessity for maintaining the small task force as a regimental operation. The two forces had planned to meet up on the coast at Babau, not so far from where they now prepared to leave their ship. The Navy had been softening up this area for several days.

This raiding party was also of Company strength, one hundred men and, as they stood on the deck holding the wire ropes to steady themselves as the ship moved under the slight swell, news of the incredible losses suffered by their comrades was passed to them by their officers. The fleet's radio operators had been responsible for relaying the information they'd picked out of the air waves to the contingent's Commander. The officer in charge was aware that this devastating news would otherwise only have been passed on hours after their own assault and deemed it necessary that his men be informed.

The soldiers reacted with dismay. Many of their friends were in the fateful operation and they now would have to wait for days before they would know who had survived and who had not. They were told that it had been an ambush. These young and inexperienced men felt bitter and angry. Bitter because the enemy obviously knew in advance and had waited for their comrades to walk into their trap.

The Commander knew only too well just how compromised their communication traffic had become. Even during the preceding days while searching for the Radio Indonesia broadcasts his Communications sergeant had picked up an Indonesian language broadcast and, thinking it was their own, listened to the news program on the short wave band. He remembered the looks of concern which passed over the Colonel's face when, to their complete surprise, as part of the news bulletin the commentator made explicit reference to the Indonesian troop buildup and actually identified the Divisions, their strengths and movements.

As they continued to listen, the broadcast language medium changed to English as the station identification was announced closing off the news broadcast and, to their astonishment, they believed they heard the voice advise that it had been a broadcast service from Radio Australia! They knew immediately that the information on the air waves could just as easily be picked up by the enemy. Almost every village in the region had at least one short wave radio and a large number were tuned into the Australian broadcasts. Still, they had wondered, how could the information be passed from the active front across thousand of kilometres to the distant city of Melbourne? With this information resting heavily on their minds they boarded the twenty dinghies and headed ashore.

It was still three hours before dawn. They too were dressed in an assortment of apparel made to appear as if their number originated from the East Timorese sympathetic to the Indonesians. They expected to arrive on the outskirts of Babau village just before dawn in preparation for their attack.

The small flotilla of Zenith rubber dinghies moved quickly towards the shore. None of the soldiers spoke as the small craft, each carrying up to six men and their supplies, moved like a swarm of large bees towards the shoreline, pushed efficiently by the Evinrude outboards. Foremost in their minds was the tragic loss of life suffered by their Battalion. They were convinced the foreign broadcasts had alerted the FRETILIN forces. As they moved closer to the shoreline the Commander checked his watch. The luminous hands and numerals glowed brightly in the moonless dark of the pre-dawn day. It was almost 0430. On 16 October 1975.

He couldn't see the expressions on his men's faces but he knew what was in their hearts. Their fear had now been displaced by hate.

* * * * * *

Umar Suharjo had carried out his instructions exactly as directed. FRETILIN had been substantially supported with regular arms shipments and access to the hidden caches in the hills. The results were greater than the General had anticipated and, in turn, he was pleased with the Major's efforts rewarding him accordingly.

Umar was confident that the Jakarta Armed Forces Chiefs had no idea whatsoever as to the immense amount of weaponry they had prepared in anticipation and support of the armed revolt the Separatist Forces continued to organize. They had appealed for international understanding of their cause but, it seemed, only Fidel Castro was prepared to listen. Although there were others who continued to watch, observing the accelerated changes in the small town's defences through the advanced technology of Satellite Imagery Enhancement.

Umar was suspicious of the bearded men who, to him, appeared to be Italian. He wasn't too comfortable with the presence of the Cubans. He guessed that out of the original two hundred men transported via Macau, no more than half a dozen had been killed in the action to date.

They were very good. Experienced and extremely cruel. He was pleased that they had no wish to mix. Often they would spit at their Timorese comrades and then break into laughter while babbling in a tongue only they could understand. He thought they were like monkeys. But, he acknowledged, they were very good soldiers. Their tactics were clever. Umar admired their patience and cunning. They would lay traps for the unsuspecting Indonesian soldiers and just wait.

Although the Indonesian fire-power was superior in numbers, their troops were far from home and poorly trained. And they had never been in combat before whereas these hardened veterans had accounted for more heads than one could imagine during their tour in Angola.

The Cubans scared him.

It was because he had not yet learned their ways, and when he did, he smiled with the thought, they would then be scared of him! They were intelligent and seemed to understand many languages. Each day at least two of their number would sit in front of their radios listening and writing furiously for hours.

Umar's lips curled, the closest he could bring himself to smiling. And then, of course, there was the free intelligence offered by the Australian news broadcasts. Although these created considerable bewilderment at first, the reports were now considered an integral part of each morning's briefing as they had proved to be totally accurate and dependable.

Umar was not convinced that the FRETILIN forces could withstand a full frontal surprise attack should these reports cease, and that was the question at hand. He was often confused by the commands he'd received and had long ago given up all attempts to understand the man to whom he had become an important extension.

His executive executioner!

Again Umar curled one lip as he enjoyed his own definition of his relationship with one of Jakarta's most powerful figures. The General had decided that time had come to increase international pressure on his own government. Umar was annoyed at not being able to second guess the man, although he rarely could. This latest directive appeared to contradict the basic plan. Or at least, as Umar Suharjo understood it to be.

It was not until Umar later fully appreciated the strategy that he agreed that it was, in fact, brilliant. And it would not be difficult to achieve. It was just a pity that it would bring an end to the much needed information they enjoyed from those daily broadcasts. He prepared to move into Kupang.

As he had crossed the border so frequently, Umar scoffed at the ridiculous ease with which it could be achieved. There were few border gates and signposts to speak of and he selected almost any path he wished to take, just walking from one country into the other. It really was ridiculous, he felt. Maybe the island should be one country and not divided as it had been by the foreigners hundreds of years before, Umar thought.

He had read enough history to understand how the colonists worked. The *bulé* would occupy a country and then split it into two. As in Korea, Vietnam, Ireland and New Guinea. Even Malaya had been split away from its Motherland, Indonesia, by the British! He pondered these thoughts and, realizing that they achieved nothing, admonished himself for permitting his concentration to stray.

The experienced Javanese Major decided to do something constructive. He was restless and disliked not being occupied. It wasn't in his make-up to just sit around and wait. He would check on the FRETILIN troops latest movement activity to avoid contact with their guerrilla bands. Umar had no wish to bump into those Cuban animals. During his reconnaissance patrols he had come across their handiwork on more than one occasion.

They had left hundreds of bodies in varying states of dismemberment throughout the territory, and even he was disgusted with the way they had butchered the women and children. He had known of one incident when the Cubans had hidden the severed heads of their victims in jute bags, and rolled them into a village school yard, laughing at the screams of terror as children discovered that the mud caked objects they had run to recover, were not coconuts at all. The Cubans didn't really care who they slaughtered. They killed indiscriminately, whenever it pleased them to do so. Often they killed the Free Timorese just out of boredom.

This, and other grotesque mistakes almost cost FRETILIN the international support it so desperately needed. Seda was angry and demanded that Fidel's butchers be expelled by the separatist groups. The Timorese were scared. They did not want to incur the wrath of the Cubans by suggesting they were no longer welcome.

Seda was disgusted when he read the report which described one drunken spree when the Cubans had taken more than fifteen teenage girls from the surrounding towns and locked them in a makeshift bamboo cage on the beach. They had insisted that their FRETILIN comrades-in-arms join them in drinking rum, a commodity they seemed to have in abundance.

The day had progressed slowly into the early afternoon when one of Fidel's finest had opened the temporary cage and dragged the closest girl out onto the sand by her long black hair. He held her with one hand while unzipping his trousers.

"*No! No!*" the fifteen-year-old had cried, choking on her screams at the thought of being publicly raped.

He laughed and, holding himself with his other hand, urinated on the girl's face. She accepted the hot steaming and foul smelling fluid, fighting to keep her mouth closed as the soldier brutally kicked her in the stomach to force her to cry out. She fell to the sand, sobbing. Moments passed and the crowd of villagers stood silently under the coconut palms, transfixed with the spectacle. The young girl's body convulsed with the wracking sobs of fear as she remained face down not daring to look upon the bearded man.

He withdrew his revolver and placed it behind her head as the disbelieving child attempted to turn towards her attacker, and pulled the trigger once. Her body jerked forwards then backwards as the impact removed the full facial section of her head. Laughing loudly while brandishing the weapon threateningly, the soldier turned again to the other caged girls.

There was a hushed silence as he lurched drunkenly towards the bamboo prison. He opened the flimsy gate and pointed his finger at the smallest girl in the group. She stood there, shaking her head, unable to cry, the tears streaming down her face as the other girls behind pushed her forward hoping that this would distract his attention from them.

"*Mama!*" she screamed, as he pulled her by the shoulder, "*Mama!*"

A shot pierced the air and the girl's torso buckled violently, the bullet entering her chest with such tremendous velocity she died before hitting the sandy beach.

Immediately the other girls screamed, exploding with fear and terror as they tore at each other in desperation, while attempting to scramble over the makeshift bamboo fencing which enclosed them. The other soldiers, thinking that their *Komandant* had expressed his wish to eliminate these peasant women, withdrew their revolvers and started shooting into the confined space. The young girls fell executed by the drunken soldiers and the villagers numbly looked on as the slaughter continued. It was all over in less than a few minutes.

As the last shot rang out the air was heavy with the smell of gunfire. And death. The young bodies lay crumpled on the sand.

Several had managed to climb the bamboo fence only to be shot as they reached the top, ending their lives almost as quickly as the others. Some of the teenage women had clung desperately to one another, engulfed by their fear and the knowledge of sure death.

The majority of the dead teenagers were of mixed extraction and had been specifically selected by the Cuban *Komandant*. Although his original intention had been to use them as an ongoing pool of entertainment for his men, he was just as satisfied that they had fulfilled this purpose as he witnessed the drunken guerrillas laughing like children, staggering up to the dead bodies still firing aimlessly at the broken remains. By keeping them occupied and distracted he knew that his men would not be so homesick. There was always the possibility they might revolt in this desolate place so far from their own homeland.

He understood his men's capacity for bloody violence. They had been killing black Africans for more than two years when they were ordered to this remote and desolate country.

No longer amused the group moved away leaving the murdered girls' bodies bunched together in a grotesque pantomime of horror, their faces wide eyed in death, reflecting their last moments of terror. When the soldiers finally left and they then felt safe, the villagers slowly approached the carnage, the occasional cry of anguished relatives being the only sound evident as one by one they identified their children. Carefully, lovingly, the small bodies were lifted and carried to an area near a copse of palms, where they were washed then covered with cloth before being placed in a common grave.

Even before news of the massacre had reached the international press there had been mumblings amongst the Timorese that the Cubans must leave their land. Umar doubted if even the entire FRETILIN army could muster sufficient courage to disband the Cuban guerrillas. They didn't seem to care whom they killed, just as long as they were killing someone, or something.

* * * * * *

Upon arrival in Kupang Umar was disappointed to learn that the group he'd sought had already departed, causing him to lose track of them for several days. He then discovered they had hired a jeep and headed in the direction of Atambua. He followed.

And then he lost them again. Information concerning their movements was scarce and unreliable but finally he managed to re-establish the general direction they'd taken from some of the village men who had carried equipment for the foreigners with cameras. The group had taken guides and crossed the border this time heading for the small town of Memo. There were no others who matched the general description of these men and their equipment.

Umar Suharjo followed their trail. It hadn't been all that difficult in the end. These foreigners were obviously not professional soldiers as they had left a trail impossible to miss. Villagers had eagerly pointed out the direction the foreign men had taken. Umar felt positive that these men had to be the journalists and cameramen he'd been tracking. After Memo he followed them towards the village of Balibo.

Umar was concerned. During the night he had heard the heavy exchange of fire. He was surprised that the foreigners were heading towards the battle scene.

'*Bodoh semua!*' he'd thought, believing that the men would have no understanding whatsoever of the dangers and risks they were exposing themselves to in the search for their news stories.

It had become hot and very humid again as Umar stopped to talk to an old farmer living alone in an isolated hut. He confirmed that the men he was following were not too far away as they had passed by less than half an hour before. The previous village headman had insisted that the group was only two or three hours ahead. He increased his pace while consciously preparing himself for an ambush. So far there had been nothing to restrict his movements as he'd not seen nor heard any evidence of any hostile elements for hours.

He arrived at the clearing leading into the village, the track well worn, the soil turning from dusty brown gradually into a typical sandy colour as it meandered through the coconut palms and thatched roofed houses. He could hear shouts and harsh commands in the distance.

Finally, there they were! He could see that they still carried their cameras and were dressed in a mixture of military jungle greens and civilian wear.

Umar knew this assignment left no room for error. There might be only one window of opportunity and his training demanded that he wait patiently for that perfect moment, using the element of surprise and cover.

To his bewilderment they appeared to have met up with or were being escorted by soldiers. Suddenly, he could no longer see any of them. He was becoming annoyed with the wait but reminded himself to be patient. He had to be sure. The timing had to be perfect. He understood that he had to get them all. There could be no witnesses.

Loud voices drifted in his direction as the group moved back into view.

Umar concentrated on the team members waving their hands and arms angrily as he observed their reluctance to continue, for some reason not apparent to him. He continued to watch and wait, expecting that at any time an opportunity could present itself. They were finally all together, and he guessed that they were about to make camp or at least rest.

He moved quickly. The canvas strap now held the weapon firmly as his left elbow confirmed its position, providing the necessary support as he moved it across slowly from right to left. They were somewhere within the village amongst the mud-walled huts. Umar followed the noises the group made as they argued loudly.

Squatting just a short distance from the small village compound he glimpsed several of the men moving around. Suddenly one raised his hands while calling out loudly as a second foreigner attempted to constrain yet another figure holding a rifle.

Yelling and shouting continued for some minutes and Umar was surprised that he understood some of the muffled voices, identifying them as Indonesian. Umar assumed that a dispute had broken out between these foreigners and one of the Indonesian soldiers.

He could now see the angry soldier standing directly in front of the tall, fair foreigner, a rifle pointed directly at the *bulé's* chest as he screamed abuse at the unarmed man. He could not hear all of the exchange, but from the yelling it was apparent that someone was uncontrollably angry. There were more shouts, this time accompanied by the sound of blows. And cries for help.

Suddenly they all disappeared from view. Umar could hear the men moving away as the abuse continued, intermingled with an array of foreign words he could not understand.

It sounded as if someone was in severe pain. He decided to take advantage of the distraction, running quickly along the outside of the perimeter trees ahead of where he thought the voices were leading, his machine pistol ready to execute them all with one quick but deadly burst, should the opportunity arise.

He had to complete the task before these men were taken into custody. If necessary, he would also kill the soldiers, Umar decided, but was more than reluctant to engage the Indonesians alone.

If only he'd brought the grenades!

Puffing from the sudden exertion he hesitated, and was about to break into the clearing when suddenly there was gunfire from behind the adjacent hut. He froze, throwing himself to the ground. Umar waited. There were shots.

He counted. Two, three, four! Someone had fired four shots. He lay very still and listened. The shooting had ceased. A few minutes passed and, through the trees, he could see the man quite clearly, dressed in an assortment of military combat gear, re-holstering his pistol as he strutted back towards a small group of men. Probably an officer, Umar judged. Having heard the gunfire the other soldiers had suddenly appeared, their rifles carried at the ready to protect the man with the revolver. There were at least fifty, maybe more, he counted quickly, pleased he had wisely decided not to fire upon them. Then he heard more shouts from the foreigners.

The situation had become unclear and very dangerous. He knew he would have to postpone his move until the soldiers had moved away. It was obvious that there was some serious problem between the newsmen and this group he suspected were Indonesian soldiers. He thought it was idiotic for them not to be wearing their own distinguishing shoulder flashes and berets as it was just as likely that one of their own would shoot them by mistake if, in fact, they were Indonesian regulars. They certainly carried themselves and behaved like the soldiers he knew!

He was concerned that there was now very little noise coming from the men he'd followed. Umar decided that he had to get even closer to investigate. There were only a few more days left in which to complete this mission. He could wait a little longer if he missed this opportunity, which now seemed likely, as they appeared to have been locked inside one of the village huts. He guessed that they would be well guarded. That would make it very difficult as he surely wished to be able to escape after he'd completed the task.

Another twenty minutes elapsed and he could no longer hear their voices. He suppressed the urge to crawl closer. The foreigners did not reappear and this confused Umar Suharjo. Could they have slipped away? He was concerned that if they hadn't been detained then perhaps the journalists may have been ordered out of the village and left, parting company with the soldiers proceeding through the other side of the village while he had waited for them to emerge.

"*Sialan!*" he muttered.

Moving quickly, he retreated fifty metres then circled around behind the huts where they had disappeared from his view. As he approached slowly to the right of the shabby dwellings he could see one of the camera cases.

Clutching his weapon while edging towards the huts. Umar noted the sudden absence of soldiers and, taking advantage of the lack of security, he moved quietly around the second hut and prepared to fire as they came into view. His finger had all but squeezed the trigger when he stopped and gaped in astonishment. He could not believe his eyes. There were bodies strewn across the dirt leading into the shelter. The bodies of foreigners! There were three slumped outside in the small yard and the partly obscured body of another in the doorway. He counted. He shook his head in disbelief. That stupid Indonesian officer had executed them himself!

Completely bewildered and for the first time in many years, Umar Suharjo panicked. He just could not believe what had happened. And then he suddenly felt a cold chill pass down his spine. Did Seda send out a backup assassination team? Or did the young Indonesian officer just take matters into his own hands?

"*Sialan,*" he growled to himself again, cursing nobody in particular. Suddenly, he wasn't sure what to do. If the General had, in fact, sent out a second team then obviously his own days and usefulness had come to an end. He was suddenly shaken by the thought.

On the other hand, had the execution been carried out by the young officer on his own volition then he could claim responsibility and the General would still be pleased as the result was the same. In fact, better.

Umar considered this possibility and decided against it, coming to the conclusion that he should advise the General that the journalists were dead and leave it at that. Best not to lie to Seda. Not now. Not ever. Not if one wished to remain alive and healthy! He looked inside the hut quickly to check the remaining bodies, still counting. Three, four...

And then he discovered another, and potentially more serious problem. There were still two missing. Quickly searching the other huts he found nothing. Now he was very concerned. There was obviously a large number of Indonesian soldiers around the village area and he'd lost sight of the remaining foreigners. Umar scouted the perimeter of the area until he identified a number of men moving away to the west. There were, from what he could make out through the undergrowth, far more soldiers than he had originally thought. It was very confusing.

And then he saw them. They were flanked on either side by well armed escorts. The two men he'd been searching for, their hands tied behind their backs, moved forward with the column of soldiers. Umar cursed silently again, confounded by the new complication. He had no choice but to follow them.

* * * * * *

The column moved quickly, heading away from the hills. The vegetation changed. Coconut trees along the path indicated that they were heading towards the sea. The soldiers weren't wasting any time, he observed, as the line marched away quickly with the two prisoners positioned towards the centre of their captors' file. They moved well, obviously attempting to meet a deadline or some predetermined rendezvous down towards the ocean as Umar could now sense that they were not too far from the coastline.

Occasionally one of the two prisoners would fall only to be pulled up roughly onto his feet, forcing him back into the long line of men. They pushed on, maintaining their pace for several hours. He could see that the foreigners were exhausted, obviously not equipped for such strenuous physical exertion. After some time they rested briefly before continuing.

Umar was surprised at the pace these soldiers set. He cursed when they didn't slow as he desperately needed rest. His body ached as old wounds sent signals to his tired muscles that he was no longer the young soldier who could easily cope with the demands of a forced march such as this. He wanted to rest but knew that it was not possible. He had to follow.

They arrived on the coast before noon and rested. Towards mid-afternoon they started again returning to the gruelling pace they'd set before. Finally, as the rest of the afternoon wore away, they approached the fishing village of Babau. Exhausted and very hungry, Umar hoped that they had finally arrived. He remained hidden approximately a hundred metres off to their flank, observing the men prepare for the next stage of their journey. Where are they going? Umar worried.

Some two hundred metres down towards the village fishing jetty he could see a number of rubber dinghies tied together. Not far from his concealed position the Major could just make out the two foreign men being marched across the sand, hands tied, heading towards the boats. He moved in closer, just enough to get a better view, but not so close as to be discovered. Umar sat cross-legged and lifted the binoculars to his eyes, adjusting them quickly, worried that the foreigners would soon be removed from his reach. His hands shook as fatigue prevented him from maintaining a steady focus. He rested his elbows on the ground to steady his view.

'*Damn!*' he cursed under his breath, '*they're being taken back as prisoners!*'

He estimated that there were more than seventy Indonesian troops on the edge of the beach, some sitting with their legs dangling over the side of the short fishing jetty while others moved around slowly, almost aimlessly. They appeared to be resting. He squinted as he examined their condition, their gear and their faces. There had been a fire fight here, he knew.

The signs were all evident and he could clearly see that the young and inexperienced troops were still suffering from the shock of their first engagement as they moved slowly, listlessly, with the tell tale signs of fatigue. Although Umar could not hear what was being said, it was quite apparent that the soldier who had executed the first four foreigners was an officer, as several of his subordinates had saluted as he'd approached, leading the two prisoners.

Umar decided that the two groups of soldiers were from the same battalion and regiment from the reception the newcomers received from the others on the beach. He watched as the officer addressed his men. Standing to attention the captain suddenly barked an order. They jumped to their feet. Umar knew immediately what was going to happen and instantly recognized who these soldiers were. He knew, because he had been one of them, once. A long, long, time ago.

He looked on in disbelief. Slowly, Umar shook his head and then stared at the assembly of soldiers with their two prisoners. What were these soldiers doing here? And out of uniform? Suddenly, the two foreigners were pushed forward, their hands tied behind their backs, forced to bend to the ground onto their knees. Neither made a sound. Or if they did, Umar could not distinguish any from this distance.

Umar watched the Indonesian officer step forward and place his revolver behind the head of each of the men, and pull the trigger. Twice. The scene was reminiscent of the infamous front page photograph which shocked readers around the world when a South Vietnamese officer executed a Viet Cong suspect on the streets of Saigon.

The echo from the second shot left an empty silence. None of the soldiers had cheered. Some had turned away, not wishing to witness the executions. They knew that what had just taken place was terribly wrong. A few even turned their heads away, not from the bloody site but in shame, knowing that one of their own officers had executed unarmed men. Foreign men!

Minutes passed when the order was given to bury the bodies.

He'd seen enough. The job had been completed even though he personally could not claim responsibility. The General's plans had been carried out by another. But the result would be the same. International condemnation of Indonesian forces and their invasion of Timor-Timur. After all, he thought, that had been the intention all along.

Umar Suharjo fled the confusing scene, leaving the foreigners and their executioners to create their own history. And they did.

* * * * * *

This senseless killing became the turning point, not just in the military war, but also on the political front. The international press focused on the slaying of the unarmed journalists who had been executed arbitrarily by the Indonesian paratrooper, whose only justification was that he personally believed that these newsmen were responsible for relaying vital military information by reporting what they had observed while in the active zone.

It was ironic. Some later called it fate. The officer who executed the journalists shared the same name as his President. Soeharto was a common enough name in Java, but one which was immediately buried along with the disgraceful act. Captain Soeharto also didn't make it back home to his family.

* * * * * *

Somewhere off the coast not far from the scene of the killings an order was given. Immediately, engines were started and as the powerful twin Cummings diesels came to life, the launch raised its anchors and moved out of the area, unnoticed.

On board, the man who was responsible for the collection and dissemination of the material that they had received on a regular basis from on-shore looked out across the sea towards the island's coastline. He wondered why transmissions had ceased so suddenly.

As their direct radio contacts had failed for five consecutive days, the mission, as agreed, was abandoned and the launch sailed directly back to Darwin, the captain concerned more for the safety of his media magnate passenger than the loss of communication contact with the journalists.

Chapter 16

Jakarta

The air-conditioning at Halim Perdanakusumah Airport was struggling to maintain some semblance of relief for the passengers. The terminal, recently converted from buildings originally used by the AURI Strategic Air Command, was quite inadequate to handle the increased numbers of businessmen and tourists now flooding into the vibrant economy. The former international airport, Kemayoran, had been retained as the domestic terminal.

Stephen used his pass to enter the restricted areas. The QANTAS Boeing 707 had arrived over an hour late. He stood patiently, observing the passengers disembarking slowly before struggling across the tarmac, heat rising up from the cement, increasing their discomfort. As they struggled across the searingly hot concrete, perspiration formed large ugly patterns on their clothes.

He scrutinized the disembarking passengers looking for Wanti. He couldn't believe the over-dressed tourists as they appeared from the long cigar-shaped airliner and were suddenly hit with the immense heat rising off the expanse of cement and reinforcing steel holding their aircraft in place. Obviously inexperienced passengers began the walk briskly then slowed to a lethargic stroll. Many of the one hundred and sixty had already entered the health and quarantine sections to complete their initial formalities when Coleman finally spotted them leaving the aircraft.

As they were near last off the plane this suggested to him that Wanti was still in need of attention and, perhaps, assistance in leaving her flight. Stephen discovered his error suddenly, recognizing them as the couple almost directly in front of him. He frowned.

They walked together, hand in hand and with that leisurely gait couples often develop together when moving as a single unit. Albert had aged a little less than he had expected. At his side, smiling and obviously relaxed, was the beautiful graceful woman he had loved so long ago, now physically more mature, her classic features even more prominent than he remembered.

She walked differently, he noticed. And her body had filled out, as graceful as before, now, if not more so, her shining long black hair as distracting as it had been when he'd first noticed her. She was everything he remembered. Stephen put his arm around her shoulders and kissed her lightly on the cheek.

"*Selamat datang, Manis,*" he welcomed his wife.

Turning to the older man, he extended his hand which Albert immediately grasped and pumped enthusiastically, a foreign habit obviously developed during his many years in Australia.

"*Selamat datang,* Albert."

Coleman escorted them through the immigration and customs procedures flashing his security pass. They completed their formalities in just twenty minutes. Most of the officials identified Coleman and waved him through with his guests as the porters fought over the large amount of luggage.

The driver had kept the Mercedes cool, and within minutes of leaving the terminal they were speeding down the new divided highway towards the Bogor-Tanjung Priok bypass. Stephen had placed them both in the rear of the red Mercedes 280, positioning himself alongside one of the drivers from the company pool. He normally elected to sit up front unless the occasion dictated otherwise. He talked excitedly as they drove back into the city along Jalan Gatot Subroto past the Air-Force Headquarters and down around the clover leaf roundabout into Jalan Jenderal Sudirman.

Jakarta had grown incredibly, and high-rise structures now dwarfed the remnants of red clay tiled roofed *kampung* houses scattered alongside the new hotels and office blocks. Wanti was engrossed in the apparent quantum leap the Capital had experienced since her last visit. She had forgotten the noise of this bustling city. And the scream of the thousands of motorcycles.

Stephen observed Wanti sitting serenely, almost unaware of the excitement around her. She appeared to be preoccupied, although there was a peacefulness about her that puzzled him. He smiled at his beautiful passenger and leaned back reaching for her hand as he spoke.

"*Wanti, you will find the shopping here an improvement from the old days. I will take you down to the new plazas tomorrow after you have rested.*"

She withdrew her hand slowly and smiled.

"*Albert will escort me, thank you Mas. We don't wish to be a burden during our visit.*"

Surprised, Stephen glanced at Albert who immediately looked away to avoid further eye contact. They continued to drive in silence. Coleman was puzzled. He decided to wait until the opportunity arose, as it appeared that his wife's rehabilitation process had not been as successful as he had at first been advised.

As their vehicle entered the driveway the office staff and servants were all outside to greet the new arrivals. The houseboys swarmed over the car grabbing the luggage in their excitement and wishing their *njonja* welcome home. Minutes later they sat quietly in the living area.

It was apparent that there was something amiss, and Coleman decided to take Albert aside to discuss the problem. He escorted his old friend into the business conference room which was maintained primarily for VIP discussions.

The room was furnished with Javanese carved tables and chairs, the walls covered with letters of appreciation and miniature banners from the many military commands which had benefited from his activities. Photographs of a slightly younger Coleman shaking hands with the President at an aviation day ceremony remained the centre piece, framed in a gold leaf frame. He indicated where his guest should sit and then placed himself directly opposite.

"*Stephen,*" Albert commenced, his embarrassment now obvious. "*Stephen, we must talk about Wanti.*"

"*All right, Albert, we have been close friends, almost family for many years. I have learned to identify from the expression on your face when something is bothering you. What's the problem?*" he asked, taking a clove cigarette from the opened packet lying on the table and lighting it without first offering one to his guest.

Stephen had that feeling. It was rarely wrong. His sixth sense had guided him into safe waters more than once in his business career and, he remembered, whenever he'd ignored the sensation it had cost him dearly. Stephen took a long draw on the *kretek* and then leaned back into the chair and observed his guest. He looked uncomfortable and Stephen wondered why.

Albert had acknowledged that the decor was expensive as soon as they had entered the premises. He didn't appreciate who the designers were or the artists' names whose works hung on the walls, he just knew that it looked expensive. His friend had come a long way. Looking at Stephen, he was suddenly at a loss for words. He didn't know where to start, but he did.

Slowly and precisely Albert explained the history of Wanti's recuperation process. The total blackouts. The inability to identify familiar faces of friends. Her complete loss of memory and the painful hours of therapy, month after month, eventually becoming years. Painful, Albert suggested, not just in the physical sense but distressful to those around her also who continuously cared and nursed her through the slow recovery process. He explained how dependent she had become on his friendship.

Albert then paused as if not knowing how to continue. Surprised, and a little confused, Coleman encouraged his friend to finish the discussion.

"Come on, Albert," he encouraged, *"don't keep me in suspense!"*

"Stephen," Albert hesitated. *"Stephen, I know that this will be difficult for you."*

Again he hesitated, obviously ill at ease.

"Stephen, Wanti has come to ask you for a divorce."

He heard the words but didn't identify their meaning. Not immediately. The words still hung in the air as Stephen looked down at the floor. There was nothing there. Some moments passed and he felt as if someone had delivered a severe blow to his chest. And yet, at the same time, he felt something else. What was it? Relief? He had anticipated that Albert had serious news concerning his wife and he'd assumed it related to her health. He lifted his head and stared directly at the Timorese.

"Why?"

Albert's eyes dropped and softly he said, *"Maafkan kami, Mas,"* clasping his hands together. *Forgive us.*

"Us?" Stephen asked, confused, as the import of the statement slowly dawned on him.

"No one ever plans these things, Mas," the older man offered.

Coleman sat rigid in his chair, bewildered by the mixed emotions he now experienced simultaneously, trying to separate what had been said from what he felt as the shock took hold. Was it outrage? He felt both betrayed and dissappointed and yet, mixed with these feelings was a touch of guilt for the relief he now felt in the knowledge that he would no longer be responsible for her condition and that this man, his old friend, would now assume that moral responsibility. He stared at the man in front of him. He felt a wave of emotion. Was it an attack on his pride?

Stephen was suddenly very confused and needed to escape to regain his composure. For a few moments he stared at the opposite wall away from his old friend's eyes, not wanting to look at his face. He was disappointed with his own reactions, even surprised.

"Albert, you must give me a few minutes to collect my thoughts. I really don't know what to say and, to be honest, I am not entirely at ease with the way I feel towards you both at this moment."

"We will leave immediately."

"No!" Coleman demanded loudly, almost shouting. *"Just take the car and driver out for an hour or so while I think this thing through."*

"What is there to think through, Stephen?"

Immediately he hated this man. His old and trusted friend. A friend who had just walked into his house and announced that he was responsible for Wanti's request for the dissolution of their marriage.

'What the hell has been going on in Melbourne?' he asked himself bitterly.

He then looked directly at the Timorese, unable to contain his feelings. Stephen knew he had to be alone. To think!

"Probably nothing," he answered, controlling his anger, *"but do this Albert, as I would appreciate an hour or so to work this out in my head. Okay?"*

"Baiklah, Mas," he agreed and rose to leave the conference room in search of Wanti.

Coleman called his senior houseboy on the intercom and instructed him to arrange for the driver to take his wife and guest out around the city for a couple of hours sightseeing.

"When tuan?" he asked, surprised as the guests had only just arrived.

"Now!" his employer had answered tersely and in a tone unfamiliar to the old *jongus*.

The surprised servant obediently arranged the car to stand-by

351

while he informed Wanti and Albert that their transport was ready. The couple left immediately.

Stephen stood looking down the road as his car disappeared from view. He was saddened by the events and was deep in thought when the houseboy knocked, apologized and informed him that the housemaid had completed the unpacking upstairs. Perplexed, he waved the *jongus* out without any acknowledgment and considered the immediate problem of the sleeping arrangements. There was no way that Wanti and Albert were going to share a bed in his house!

Suddenly he was angered by the delicate predicament in which he found himself. He thought the situation through and decided to instruct the staff to prepare a third room which he would occupy for himself. His domestic staff and, indeed, most of Jakarta was conversant with the state of his wife's mental health, or had been, before her miraculous recovery. The thought passed through his mind that Albert had deliberately not informed him that Wanti had recovered. How long had it really been, a month? Three months? Perhaps even a year? His pride was hurt but that did not diminish the feeling of betrayal.

Coleman spoke quietly to his trusted *djongus* and suggested that *njonja* was still not completely recovered and, acting under her doctor's instructions, she was to sleep alone during her visit. He further instructed the staff not to discuss this arrangement outside his household, knowing that the whispers would commence immediately the opportunity arose. They would think well of him for being so considerate to the beautiful woman he'd not seen in such a long time. The other ladies would applaud his behaviour as long as he could disguise the real situation. Certainly separate bedrooms would be appropriate. Considering the predicament he found himself in, Stephen had no great difficulty with the sleeping arrangements. If handled discreetly, he imagined that it could even work to his advantage. Later, when the couple had returned to Australia, he would fabricate a suitable story to account for the unusual relationship which, he surmised, would put the gossipmongers to rest.

Convinced that he had handled the matter in a mature manner, Stephen waited for their return. They had been gone for almost two hours when Sukardi announced their arrival. Stephen waited inside as the couple entered. He spoke briefly to Wanti and then took Albert aside and advised him of his decision.

The older man was nervous and wasn't sure just how close he should stand to his former friend. He flinched as Stephen leaned forward quickly and put his hand on Albert's shoulder.

"*It's okay, Albert, nothing's going to happen,*" he assured the other man with a slight squeeze before releasing his grip. Suddenly he felt saddened and ashamed by his earlier reactions. Stephen could sense the fear and realized just how impossible their respective situations were.

"*Albert,*" he started slowly, looking directly into the eyes of the man whom he believed had betrayed him in the worst way, "*firstly, I wish to assure you that I have no ill feelings towards either of you.*" Stephen lied as he paused for the effect. "*I believe that I understand how the relationship evolved and, having considered how difficult it must have been for both of you then I must also accept some of the responsibility for what has happened. The neglect I showed during Wanti's illness....*"

"*No, Stephen,*" Albert interrupted.

"*Please, Albert! Let me to finish,*" he insisted, holding one hand up to indicate that he intended to do so anyway. "*It was not easy for any of us having her down there for such a long time without considering our own needs while she was away, if you understand what I mean.*"

Of course Albert knew exactly what Stephen was alluding to, but was embarrassed to say so considering his own behaviour and the question of Wanti's infidelity. The Timorese sighed and, cupping his hands under his chin, eyes downcast, listened to the younger man as he continued to explain his position. He wished he was back in Melbourne sitting with Wanti together and away from this confrontation. He could hear Stephen's voice rattling on.

He said nothing. After all, what could he really say?

They discussed the arrangements and, after an hour both settled on the plan Stephen had proposed. Albert really had little choice. As the moment provided the opportunity, Albert asked the final question. "*Mas, will you give her the divorce?*"

Coleman paused momentarily and nodded affirmatively.

"*But it's conditional, Albert. You must seek a dissolution only in Australia. Do not apply while you are here. Agreed?*"

Albert wanted to explain that divorce proceedings in Jakarta would be swift and permit them all to get on with their lives. He remembered that this man could be stubborn and all that had been achieved in the past few short hours could easily come undone if he persisted in obtaining the divorce in Indonesia. Wanti would not be pleased. Albert was not happy with this dilemma.

He hesitated and replied softly. "*Stephen, a divorce in Jakarta would be more convenient. However I will respect your wishes and finalize the necessary procedures only when we return to Melbourne.*"

Satisfied, Coleman nodded his head in satisfaction.

"*When will you return?*" he asked.

"*There is not much point in staying too long. Wanti should see her brother Bambang and then we could return when airline seats are available.*"

Coleman weighed the problem in his mind. It would be difficult enough for all three to remain under one roof too long, considering the circumstances; however he felt that they should spend at least a week there, for appearances.

"*I will have my staff arrange your return bookings.*"

Relieved that their difficult discussion had finally come to an end, Albert extended his hand to his once close friend. "*Terima kasih, Mas.*"

"*Kembali kasih,*" he responded, surprised at how tired he felt from the emotional drain of the last few hours.

Saddened by the events, both men rose and shook hands, each realizing that their friendship could never be as before, while regretting the loss of the strong bond that had tied them together over the past ten years.

Stephen left the building providing Albert with the opportunity to explain to Wanti just what they had agreed. When he returned later in the evening, his houseboy informed him that both guests had apologized as they were tired and had each retired to their respective bedrooms. A trace of a smile passed his lips as he discovered that his faithful old servant had diplomatically placed a selection of his wardrobe in the middle of the three bedrooms thereby symbolically separating his *njonja* from the house guest. It was almost impossible to keep anything secret from the old houseboy.

* * * * * *

That night the household slept restlessly. Wanti lay awake, thinking of the two men who had played such a significant part in her life. She felt saddened understanding that now she was divorcing the very man who had picked her up and given her everything except the one thing she longed for most. And he didn't understand as he had no comprehension, she was sure, as to what had always seemed to be missing in their relationship.

Albert lay on his side listening to the occasional traffic as it passed by his bedroom window. Car lights flickered across the room, running up the wall from one side and over the ceiling until disappearing altogether down the other. He was pleased that the meeting had gone as well as it had. Wanti had scolded him for not insisting that the divorce proceedings be carried out quickly while they were there, and although he had argued against it, she was still unconvinced. For a moment he feared that she might insist on talking to Stephen alone but, thankfully, she hadn't.

Stephen lay on his back, his hands clasped behind his head as he lay quietly, thinking of the days ahead. Although the tension between them had all but disappeared, he understood that there is no such thing as a friendly parting of the ways when a couple dissolves their marital relationship. He was pleased that Wanti would not claim from him in any way as he'd agreed not to contest the divorce. The potential problem of a messy financial haggling match had been avoided.

He had been concerned as he knew that Seda would have been displeased with further attention being drawn to his already high profile partner. All in all, he thought, everyone got what they wanted. He tried to sleep but there were too many thoughts waiting to disrupt his attempts. He had many things on his mind.

Like Seda. And the incredible volume of shipments that had already been dispatched to assist the Indonesian military with the Timor problem.

The city became quieter and only the occasional bell could be heard as the *becaks* passed. Coleman finally fell into a fitful sleep, just hours before being woken again by Sukardi.

The following morning, on the eleventh of December, the Indonesian Armed Forces invaded East Timor.

* * * * * *

With incredible speed, the Indonesian military machine moved across the border into East Timor. The Indonesian losses remained excessively high. The guerrillas continued to resist the larger force and inflicted tremendous casualties. But not without their own terrible sacrifices. In spite of their losses, the Timorese were jubilant.

Central Command in Jakarta had predicted that the excursion, as one general had jokingly described the invasion, would be completed within one week and would possibly only require another fortnight of mopping-up operations to round up the terrorists. Their intelligence had been incredibly inaccurate. During the first three days Indonesian casualties reached three thousand and the communication lines between the field and command headquarters ran continuously hot. Each time the crack Indonesian troops mounted an attack, they were rebuffed almost easily.

The Siliwangi Division suffered severe losses as well. Never in the history of this elite division had its troops been routed. The soldiers were young and experienced primarily in riot control support and other training exercises aimed mainly at assisting the police during civil unrest. They had never had to face a real enemy before! One or two of the older soldiers had seen action during engagements in Sarawak during the *Konfrontasi* era, but their numbers were insufficient to withstand the surprisingly superior soldiers confronting them in the Timor jungles.

Air support had been practically useless due to the dense terrain. Ground fire had already accounted for six of their helicopters, and the AURI Commander had insisted on grounding his remaining squadron until the infantry could guarantee adequate support in the hostile areas. He also insisted that the intelligence at least attempt to be more accurate when determining targets and requested a few sorties with reduced risk to those they had already encountered, as morale amongst his crews was dangerously low.

One hundred KOPASGAT airborne had been dropped at the eastern ridge, leading to what had been identified as an Indonesian Siliwangi position. The severity of the ground fire reduced their number within seconds to but a few before any of the parachutists realized their predicament.

Many died in the air, their bullet riddled bodies floating aimlessly to the ground. Within twenty-seven minutes from the jump command all but six of the commandos had died. Five of the remaining men had been captured. And tortured. An uncaptured soldier looked on in horror from his hiding place in the under-growth as the guerrillas gouged out the eyes of his comrades, laugh-ing as they worked their disgusting torture on the young soldiers. He was overcome with paralysing fear.

The concealed corporal shook in terror praying that *Allah* would guard over him in his moment of need. He struggled to keep the bile from rising in his throat and discovered, much to his dismay, he had fouled himself through fear. He wanted to rush out and help his comrades but his legs were frozen and he couldn't breathe. Holding his breath, the soldier willed the enemy to leave, too scared to run and too frightened to fight. He waited, engulfed by the ter-ror around him.

As he hid amidst the thick grass he closed his eyes, hoping this would help disguise his presence as sounds of the enemy passed ever so close to where he had hidden. Ants poured over his body examining their potential meal, the bites painfully working their way along his legs towards his groin. He prayed for the strength not to cry out as the carnivorous insects covered his body.

It seemed as if hours had passed when the camouflaged NCO tensed as he noticed one of the enemy turn and look directly in his direction. The guerrilla's features were vastly different from those of the other Timorese he had known. This man was heavily bearded and his eyes were light steel blue! He barked an order and imme-diately the band ceased their ghoulish activities.

"Leave them!" he demanded. "Their condition may act as a deterrent to their comrades." As he spoke, several others similar in appearance moved to his side.

These men were obviously not indigenous Timorese, the aston-ished corporal concluded. It was apparent from their manner that they were in command of the band which now commenced mov-ing silently away from the tortured soldiers still screaming from pain. One of the wounded managed to struggle to his feet, only to fall down again. He rose once more, holding his hands to his head, covering the gaping holes where his eyes had been minutes be-fore, and screamed a curse at his captors.

"*Djahanam! Djahanam!*" he cried aloud with the pain, "*mampus kamu kalian!*" and again fell to his knees, sobbing with distress at having been deserted by *Allah*, the One and Only True God.

The Cuban turned and walked to the side of the young

Sundanese. His hand moved swiftly, extracting the self sharpening commando knife from its sheath, which he placed directly under the wounded man's left ear. The blinded soldier recognized the sound. He had heard it before. Immediately the brave young man ceased yelling his invective at the unseen enemy. He sat motionless, his body leaning forward slightly over his knees, the cold steel blade touching his skin lightly. He realized that the weapon would end his life.

This was his *ajal*, his predestined moment of death and, as with all faithful Moslem followers, he believed that this moment was determined at birth with the commencement of one's life. He lifted his head in a gesture of acceptance of his fate. The Cuban misinterpreted the gesture as one of defiance. The blade moved swiftly and the soldier felt the beginning of the stroke and the flow of blood simultaneously. He didn't scream.

His ear fell to the ground - but he was still alive! His bladder opened and he fell forward, sobbing with fear and shame. The Cubans laughed and, at the leader's command, the band of Timorese followed the foreign killers back into the dense jungle.

Corporal Budiman waited until he was certain that they had not left one of their number behind to lay *ranjau*, the dreaded anti-personnel mines. Convinced that he was safe to venture out from his concealment, the NCO cautiously approached the Sundanese, who now lay groaning softly in prayer. The wounded man stiffened as he heard the footsteps approach.

"*Sudahlah, dong! Bunuh sajalah aku!*" the commando pleaded, seeking a quick end to his agony. "*Diam, diam!*" the corporal whispered urgently, "*Aku Budiman. Diam dulu, dik!*" the soldier whispered hoarsely to his comrade, consoling the man while identifying himself.

Quickly he checked the others. Two would die, he could see from the wounds and he was not certain how to provide emergency care for the others. He located several of his fallen comrades and, tearing strips from their clothes, he commenced applying makeshift bandages to the disgusting head wounds the tortured men had suffered. Satisfied there was little else he could accomplish, Budiman went in search of the communications soldier to establish contact with his base Commander.

It was hopeless. There were bodies everywhere. But no radioman. He searched for half an hour and decided to use distress flares instead. These he fired and then settled down amongst the wounded to await assistance. Throughout the night he was terrified each time there was a sound. Any sound. He feared the return of the strange looking soldiers who had butchered his comrades. As the moon disappeared, only to be replaced by the morning sun, he sat alone, praying for forgiveness of his past sins.

The following afternoon two platoons of infantry arrived. They were accompanied by several officers from the ill-fated paratroops' regiment. By then, all but two of the original eighty-nine paratroopers had died from torture, shock or were unlucky enough to lose their lives even before their parachutes could lower them safely to the ground. Many of these remained hung in their harness, held aloft by the trees which had caught the unfortunate men, providing the enemy with easy targets.

Corporal Budiman helped the fearless Sundanese soldier to his feet and put his arms around the shorter man.

"You are a very brave soldier," he whispered, *"may Allah go with you and protect you."*

The wounded man groped at the corporal and, in his anguish cried, *"Where was Allah when we needed him?"* and broke into sobs, while his fists clenched in anger.

"We will take Allah's revenge on those animals, Mas. This I, Budiman, swear to you."

"Budi, Budi," the wounded man cried, *"they have taken my sight!"*

"I know, Mus, but they will pay for their atrocities, this is my promise to you."

"Kill them all, Budi, kill them all!" the man sobbed.

"We will. We will find them and kill them all!" he promised the now semi-conscious soldier as he slowly passed into a deeper state of shock and, finally, the soft world of oblivion.

Budiman sat for a while holding the dead man's hand until it was time to go. The young officer who headed the platoon ordered the bodies stacked side by side and advised his command centre of the final body count. There were too many to bury.

They merely collected the dog tags and placed these in one knapsack beside the body of the Siliwangi Colonel who had died in his parachute without having fired a shot. His magazine was still full. Acting *Kapten*, Bambang took the machine pistol and discharged the weapon into the air. Surprised, the junior Lieutenant turned towards the Javanese with a quizzical expression on his baby face.

"*The Bapak Kolonel's weapon had jammed,*" he lied, placing the light machine pistol beside the officer's body.

* * * * * *

When he first arrived at the scene of the massacre, Bambang could not believe his eyes. The company had virtually been wiped out to a man. As he walked around checking the bodies, the shock of what he was witnessing prevented him from feeling any other emotion but anger over the mutilated bodies left by the Timorese butchers. He had been ordered to hunt for the guerrillas responsible for the massacre.

Bambang told the terrified Budiman to accompany them on the search and destroy mission. Although the Corporal could not identify the strange and brutal foreigners he had observed, headquarters assumed that these were remnants of the Portuguese garrison now fighting alongside the FRETILIN guerrillas. They had been instructed to eradicate these killers. The members of Bambang's platoon, relatively inexperienced in any type of warfare, were nervous when informed of the objective of their mission.

The Cuban officer had indeed been clever. The tortured bodies of their comrades acted as a deterrent to the Indonesians, and already some were completely rattled by the demoralizing scene they had come upon just hours before.

The Captain was aware that many of his men had been intimidated by the mutilated bodies. Most were Moslem and their sect specifically forbade such disfigurement. Even the young Javanese officer had difficulty maintaining his composure when he discovered the eyeless corpses. Although a soldier, Bambang was disgusted by the torture his countrymen had suffered and undertook to deal harshly with the guerrillas when they eventually located them.

He was convinced that they would have a bloody fight when they met. However he was also confident that they would be successful, as his men were already on the ground and could not therefore suffer the same fate as the parachutists who hadn't been given the opportunity to fight. The initial problem the officer was faced with was to determine the whereabouts of the guerrilla band. It was unlikely that he would obtain any local support as the hill tribes disliked the lowlanders and feared the Indonesians from the other islands.

The Moslem faith had a scattered following. The Timorese had developed their own animist practices and ancestral and other spirits were worshipped by all. These people believed that life was a transferable spirit and, consequently, heads were taken in war. The Japanese had learnt that the hard way.

The young Captain shuddered uncomfortably. Warfare had been endemic amongst the various tribes throughout both the Portuguese and Dutch areas of Timor. Villagers built stockades around their houses, which were raised on piles providing additional protection from marauding bandits. He decided to avoid contact with the local hill people.

Unlike their fellow citizens in Irian, the majority of Indonesians knew nothing of the art of tracking. Bambang decided that the best course of action would be to head around the mountain, maintaining the same elevation as necessary then dropping quickly down the far side. He thought that this may offer them the opportunity to place themselves ahead of the guerrillas and perhaps the chance to ambush them for a change! Should they not encounter the enemy there, he would swing back and reconnoitre before formulating another plan. He wished the Colonel was there with them to advise. The other platoon was to remain where it was until contact had been established. They were then to move across the hillside as well, dropping down behind the enemy, and attack from the rear.

He could not have selected a more dangerous route as this had been the exact same path taken by the three hundred strong guerrilla force. Budiman had not been able to assist with any detail as to the enemy's strength. Their latest intelligence reports suggested that they were less than twenty. Bambang thought about the estimated enemy numbers. He knew it was unlikely that just twenty men would be able to eliminate so great a number of their airborne as they had the day before, although shooting men in harnesses wasn't difficult. His anger returned as he recalled the number of men dead, hanging in the trees.

He called his platoon together and explained his plan. They then set out, walking in single file, trying to remember what they had learned as the platoon climbed up one hill and across a small ridge, staying close together under the forest's dense cover.

As evening fell Bambang began to lose confidence. He had now lost radio contact and, as darkness enveloped his force, images of his fallen comrades began to play tricks in the jungle darkness. He became afraid. His men felt his fear and they too began to pray silently, for their safety and his leadership. The sergeant went from man to man checking their gear as they rested, offering them support when they needed it, and instant reprimand when they deserved to be reminded of their mistakes.

* * * * * *

Coleman had breakfast with Greg Hart in the Hotel Indonesia coffee shop. He didn't particularly enjoy eating there but he knew that his offsider would have been there anyway and it just seemed easier that day. He had arranged the meeting to avoid having to share his own table with the couple now occupying his home. He realized that his actions were childish and identified his feelings as more of pique than jealousy. It was of little compensation that the relationship had developed when Wanti's state of mind was questionable. Although his own behaviour had not been exactly chaste during their separation, he justified his sexual pursuits as necessary functions of his life which were not available, or could not be fulfilled, by his legitimate partner.

He could not have imagined himself sleeping with Wanti after her collapse. He felt it would have been totally incomprehensible that advances could be made when the woman was obviously not completely conscious of her own actions. Perhaps, he thought, this was the basic crux of the problem. He had imagined that Albert had taken advantage of her condition, as the Timorese was not exactly a younger or a more attractive man. Silently Stephen admonished himself for permitting his thoughts to follow this path. Albert had always been a kind close friend and what had happened had happened and that was that.

It was unlikely that with Albert's religious background, Stephen decided, Wanti had even slept together with the older man. 'Damn!' he muttered, continuing to stir the already cold coffee, what a mess! He observed his assistant, Hart, staring at him.

"Problems?" he asked.

"A few."

"You were supposed to take some time off. What happened?"

"HANKAM will undoubtedly be raising hell any time now. I decided to stick around for awhile and see if they needed to speak with me. Also, I hadn't anticipated having a wife around when I first made the arrangements. I was due out today and may still go. I'm of two minds at the moment although I could do with a break."

"How is the invasion going?" Hart asked, for if anyone in the city outside the Indonesian Military would know then it would certainly be his boss, Coleman.

"Too soon to tell. Shouldn't be too much for them to handle though, as they outnumber the separatists at least five to one. And the FRETILIN are a disorganized bunch of misfits with no more than a few disillusioned Portuguese followers."

"The Melbourne broadcasts were surprisingly specific with their reporting this morning," Hart suggested, watching Coleman for his reactions.

Surprised, Stephen suddenly realised that he had missed the program, one which he regularly heard with his breakfast. It usually offered an up-to-date coverage of world news with, he believed, very little Australian bias.

"That's impossible, Greg. How in the hell could they be reporting the action?"

"This morning's broadcaster claimed they were receiving information directly from Timor. I must admit though, it was eerie to hear the Australian news actually identifying combat groups, casualties and troop positions."

"My God, that's insane! The military will go berserk!"

"Maybe it's the station's revenge on the Indonesians for sending their representative home."

"Greg, listen chum. If I was a part of their High Command right now I would be looking for blood. Let's hope that this lunacy does not result in the Indonesians losing any of their troops; otherwise we may as well close up shop and disappear. Are you certain that it wasn't the Voice of America? Was it really one of ours?"

"Christ!" he exploded, "What a bunch of arseholes!"

"Spot on, I'm afraid."

Coleman thought for a few moments and then decided.

"Greg, I have changed my mind again. You hold down the fort, I will be gone for a few days. Okay?"

"Sure, Stephen. Where are you going?"

Coleman ignored the question, signalled for the bill and when it came, paid in Rupiah and left Hart alone to finish his breakfast.

* * * * * *

He watched Stephen hurry away to yet another of his secret assignations. Hart was annoyed with the action. He was disappointed that, even after the now lengthy time he had worked for the man, there was an obvious lack of trust, as considerable secrecy surrounded most of the company's operations.

His access to whatever Stephen's activities were off-shore was strictly blocked as the man made most of his own arrangements when travelling and there was practically no company record of his movements when he disappeared, sometimes for almost a week at a time. He needed to have this information if he was to feel that Stephen really trusted him.

The general business of the company was quite easy for Hart to follow. It was the armament supply arrangements which were complex and jealously guarded by Coleman himself.

Hart had guessed that most of the company's financial success had originated from the secret deals Coleman had obviously struck with HANKAM, as he was very close to most of the military leaders and was practically the only foreigner who was regularly seen at the Saturday night *Ramayana* puppet shows the Presidential household held for special guests and close friends of the Indonesian hierarchy. It was also obvious that the man's wealth had grown immensely over the years.

He was practically a legend amongst the other foreigners his success story, although often distorted out of all proportion provided for them a sense of their own achievement, for one of their number had been able to beat the system and secure the helm of a substantial enterprise, not as an employee, but as its owner. And all of this before he was even thirty!

Hart had estimated the company's worth at around fifteen million dollars but he knew he could never be sure. Even the string of nominees holding most of the property in the mountain resort areas had been arranged without his knowledge. He had a fair indication of who these people were as their names appeared regularly in correspondence relating to other matters, mainly in the defence representation contracts which the company held with a number of shadowy Hong Kong and Macau suppliers. These were the names who, more often than not, appeared as some of the approved signatories at the Indonesian Department of Defence, HANKAM.

On occasion he had approached Coleman and suggested that the operation could benefit from a more open relationship, as he personally had now made a substantial commitment to the company and believed that if he was to make the association a career then, perhaps, Coleman might like to consider bringing him into the company on a different basis. His superior had treated the suggestion coolly and indicated that there would be no immediate change.

* * * * * *

Upon leaving the other man to finish his coffee, Stephen had driven directly to his house. He didn't spend much time thinking about the man he'd just left. He did his job well and that's all that was required. Hart had little personality, he felt, and could go nowhere in the commercial sector as his leadership qualities were also questionable.

The amount of energy required to administer the known activities of the company was huge and, Coleman knew, Hart dedicated himself well when it came to the paperwork and more mundane requirements of his operation.

He didn't underestimate his assistant. Stephen decided that it would be a mistake to sell the man short as he had seen him take what would have been an administrative nightmare for others and turn the mess into a coherent form suitably presented and clear enough for his office staff to understand. He just didn't like the man.

Stephen thought he had the personality of a mangy dog. He didn't understand why he felt that way about Hart. Maybe, he thought smiling to himself as the Mercedes pulled into his driveway, it was because the man was an accountant.

Arriving at what he considered his nerve centre, Stephen checked in with his personal secretary and sat down to prepare the message he believed should be sent urgently to his associate. He sent a telex to the Hong Kong office with the necessary codes and settled back awaiting a response. It would take less than an hour, he knew.

Sukardi interrupted his thoughts as he lay on the sofa.

"Tuan, is it all right for Njonja Wanti to use the car for awhile?" his *jongus* asked, having knocked first to alert his employer of his presence at the open doorway.

"Sure," he answered quickly, almost impatiently.

The houseboy disappeared, sensing the *tuan's* mood. It was always best to distance one's self as far as possible when he was like this. The last time the *tuan* had threatened to fire him again, and at last count that would make it almost thirty times in just this new period of the Moslem calendar, he appeared really serious!

The servants had discussed this together and all had agreed. The *tuan's* mood swings were directly related to the fact that his wife was in his home but not in his bed. Since she had arrived the laundry and chamber maids had all observed that nothing much had happened since she returned. Not that the *njonja* looked all that sick. They all hoped something would happen quickly. The *tuan* had never gone this long before without a woman's company in his bed.

After the houseboy had left Stephen rose impatiently and strolled over to the tall windows overlooking the well manicured garden driveway. Albert and Wanti could be seen standing outside the office alongside his Mercedes.

He continued to watch them together.

'God!' he thought, 'please don't let them hold hands!'

As he observed the two entering his car his thoughts were interrupted by the telex machine noisily coming to life. He waited impatiently until the lengthy signal had been received and, using the established references, decoded the deliberately ambiguous message. It was as he had anticipated. There was trouble and he was required in Hong Kong immediately.

Stephen instructed the servants to advise his wife and guest that he had to depart suddenly and ordered his secretary to phone Garuda and get him on the first flight to Singapore. Once at Changi Airport he would purchase the next leg of the ticket to avoid his office discovering his whereabouts and any other detail he felt it prudent to keep to himself. It had been burdensome maintaining this level of secrecy but it had paid off. Stephen was not about to destroy the years of hard work by ignoring the basic premise which had protected his secret operations throughout the past decade.

Seda had made it quite clear to him during the embryonic stages of their relationship that everything depended on their ability to keep their dealings strictly confidential. If their positions were compromised in any way, the result would be more than disastrous. For both of them.

His secretary knocked and entered. "*Your ticket will be waiting for you at Halim. It leaves in just over three hours, boss. Shall I inform Mister Hart?*" she asked, not particularly fond of the other man, who continuously needled her for more information than she thought he should have about Coleman's travel arrangements and other personal details. She had never discussed this annoyance with her employer, fearing that the foreigners always stuck together when it came to staff. He'd even asked her out but she'd refused.

Coleman's secretary knew that would be most unprofessional of her and simply illogical on his part, as she was conscious of her age and homely appearance. Hart could only want something that she wasn't prepared to or was unable to give him. Information, always information.

"*Okay. Phone him now and let him know what flight I'm on. He's sitting down at the coffee shop and I guess you know where.*" Stephen smiled at her.

"*Consider it done, boss.*"

Hart was a creature of habit and nearly always preferred to eat there. Coleman thanked the woman.

The time passed quickly and he was reminded by the staff that the car was standing by. His clothes already packed by the *jongus* and with tickets and passport in hand, he locked the private room after removing the tapes from the telex, then carried out one final check before leaving. He put his head into the office section and waved at his secretary.

"*Bye,*" was all he said.

"*Oh, boss!*" she called as he closed the door, "*I managed to get through to Mister Hart. He said that he wouldn't be back here today as he needed to return to the Jalan Thamrin office. He said to wish you a good trip.*"

Ten minutes later he left for the airport in one of the Nissan Cedrics that had been parked below, the air inside already cooled. Stephen was pleased to be leaving. He thought about his house guests. He expected that Albert and Wanti would assume that he had left because he was angry. This, under any other circumstances may have been so. The obvious discomfort they all experienced as a result of Albert's disclosure certainly supported this action. This suited his plans although he felt a twinge of remorse at not having spoken to Wanti at any real length.

The traffic moved quickly and Stephen arrived at the airport in less than half an hour and checked in, as his flight had already been called. He was pleased that it was on time. Stephen was looking forward to an evening in Hong Kong. 'Maybe I'll phone Mr Lim,' he thought.

* * * * * *

As he boarded the wide-bodied jet, Coleman identified a familiar face sitting half forward in the first-class section. It was John Anderson. He was about to speak but decided just to smile and nod, acknowledging the man's presence. Coleman then permitted the stewardess to escort him to his seat.

Being naturally suspicious, Coleman could not help but feel a slight discomfort at bumping into this man and at this time. He immediately hoped that it was mere coincidence that they were to share the same flight. Stephen resisted the temptation to move out of his seat and speak to the man. The aircraft's first class section was practically empty and it would not have been too difficult to make the gesture.

As he accepted the Chivas and ice from the hostess, Stephen thanked the Garuda stewardess politely in her own language.

"*Tuan can speak Indonesian?*" she asked.

"*Of course,*" he answered.

"*Tuan is very fluent,*" she smiled warmly.

Coleman laughed. He needed the quick exchange, if for no other reason but than to distract him from the dark thoughts which immediately sprang to mind as he boarded the aircraft. He didn't like surprises and this chance meeting already had the ominous signs of ASIS stamped all over it. If Anderson's presence had been orchestrated, how could they possibly have known he was leaving when he himself only knew less than a few hours before the air-craft departed? He sipped the soft and soothing elixir, forcing the attack of paranoia back into the depths of his other thoughts.

The weather was good. He was already feeling a little more relaxed. The smiling stewardess stood beside his seat and inclined her head with a smile as she held the bottle firmly. Stephen accepted another Chivas, then settled back as the crew completed their final checks for departure.

The DC-10 lifted and banked to the east and the opposite side of the airfield across from the international terminal came into view. The military shared the airfield with the International Terminal. Funding for the upgrading had been arranged through non-military aid programs. HANKAM had willingly surrendered their control over the facility until the improvements had been completed, resulting in new runway surfaces which, in the future, could withstand the onslaught of fully laden Boeing 747s. According to international lending authorities, these futuristic aircraft would bring mega-dollars which would, in turn, repay loans provided for the development of the country's tourist industry. The airport's runway and other facilities had been completed, on time, and in accordance with United States Air Force specifications to enable B-52s an easy access with a full load, should their deployment become necessary in the future. Upon completion, the Indonesian Air Force reactivated most of its dormant facilities and recommenced Hercules and other military flights directly from the restructured airport.

Coleman stared out to where the hangers housed the military squadrons. There was considerable activity. He identified the recently refurbished C-130s which the Americans had refitted and supported with a generous supply of spare parts. He smiled and gave the aircraft a mock salute, for it had been a profitable contract for all concerned. American aircraft were always in demand. He considered the looming political issues and wondered if the pendulum would swing in Indonesia's favour, or would the Americans be obliged to bend under world opinion. The United States Congress would not permit the sale or gift of any of its military hardware to another nation should the intent be to use the equipment for expansionist purposes. They were quite clear on this point.

Stephen wondered how long it would take for the Americans to cease supporting the Indonesian military machine. After all, their newly acquired friends had invaded a neighbouring country and engaged in extreme military action. Along with everyone else, he was not quite sure just whose sovereignty had been violated as the former colony's status was still most unclear. The region would remain in a state of limbo until a clear signal had been sent by the United Nations, which he knew meant the United States, as to who should assume control over the desolate and insignificant piece of real estate called East Timor.

The Broncos would be a problem, Stephen mused. There was little doubt that the American Congress would put a hold on the delivery of the sophisticated aircraft as a result of the invasion. Originally, the deal appeared to have been struck as a direct result of the powerful Texas oil lobby.

The Americans had pulled out of Vietnam. Now they were investing heavily in Indonesia's oil and gas fields.

The Soviet-backed Vietnamese Air Force had suddenly acquired the strike capacity to threaten the rich gas fields of Natuna Island.

The Pentagon had quite cleverly decided to assist the Houston oil men. Congress required little persuasion to support the aviation package, not only because aircraft and defence sales were healthy for the United States economy, but also as this particular agreement provided for future protection of American interests while sending a clear message to Indonesia's more hostile neighbours that they were prepared to protect their trading partner's borders.

The American defence establishment had arranged the meeting which was attended by all the parties with vested interests in the future development of the field in question. As they sat around the table discussing the small island of Natuna which, according to satellite data and recent seismic interpretation, represented a massive oil and gas deposit, the Americans unanimously agreed that they must have control over the concession rights.

The parties were all aware that the island was in dispute as to who actually owned the potentially wealthy field. The Pentagon was adamant that it would not belong to the Vietnamese. The governments of Indonesia and the United States entered into a covert pact and, consequently, the aircraft were slated for delivery to the former pro-Communist country to protect itself from any possible intrusion by the newest Communist force in the region. Vietnam.

An airfield would have to be built quickly and quietly while funding needed to be diverted from other budgets to cover the construction costs. American engineers were consulted and the plan proceeded to the next stage. It was imperative that the ASEAN countries did not misinterpret the deployment of these aircraft as a hostile act nor speculate that Indonesia was positioning itself for an American re-entry into Vietnam.

The new airfield was not scheduled for completion until the Broncos had already been delivered to Indonesia and based at other airfields for at least one year. Indonesian pilots would require this time for training and logistical ordinance programs demanded strict scheduling procedures be implemented well before delivery. Neither country anticipated any real difficulty with the arrangements and within months of signing the joint defence memorandum, Indonesian pilots commenced their training in the United States.

The political storm started brewing when members of the Fourth Estate discovered the disappearance of some of their number in the Timor area. Accusations flew to and fro. However, as there was no clear evidence that the Indonesian forces were responsible in any way for the journalists' demise, Congress had little choice but to continue to support delivery of the sophisticated aircraft. Then came the Timor invasion. The Separatists had been powerless to prevent the action.

The Americans were immediately concerned that world opinion would turn against the Indonesians. They understood the complexity of Indonesia's position in relation to its regional partners and the separate commitments the United States had made with its neighbours, such as the Philippines and Thailand. However, the United States was still suffering the aftermath of their involvement in Vietnam and, consequently, pressure mounted on the politicians to veto delivery of any further military aid to the Soeharto regime.

There were many stories circulating at the time and both Seda and Coleman had heard them all. Rumours were, US satellite intelligence had proven the existence of considerable Eastern Bloc weaponry and had confirmed the presence of Cuban advisers in the former Portuguese colony. There were even fears that missiles had already been shipped to the area.

Coleman knew that under the ANZUS Treaty the United States was obliged to assist Australia and New Zealand in the event that hostile forces threatened their sovereignty. The Americans were not entirely convinced that the small Cuban presence in East Timor represented such a threat until their satellite photograph interpretation experts identified a substantial increase in Soviet arms already on ground in the disputed country and a disturbing array of large ominous containers. The United States Military Attaché in Canberra had reluctantly passed this information to his Australian counterpart. As a result of what appeared to be an aggressive Soviet move to support Cuba's adventurous incursion into areas outside its own sphere of influence in Latin America, satellite surveillance was stepped up to meet the new threat to regional stability, in the Far East.

Alarmed by these developments, the Pentagon believed that they had no choice but to circumvent their own congressional leaders and arrange for delivery of the aircraft as soon as was practical. The Americans were all too conscious of the dangers in permitting the Cubans to establish any form of missile capability on the strategically situated island. On the other hand, Congress would not permit support for the Indonesian violation of the newly created independent state, although FRETILIN's announcement had yet to be recognized formally by any of the world's leaders.

The Americans were confused with their friends Down Under. They had been closely monitoring the growing anti-American sentiment in both New Zealand and Australia ever since the 1973 withdrawal from Vietnam. The United States intelligence chiefs argued against informing the Australians of their intentions. Instead, they acted to cover their positions by insisting publicly that any country which enjoyed American military hardware, whether by gift or by purchase, could not use this equipment to assist or aid a third country involved in any expansionist military action.

Indonesia obviously fitted the description perfectly, and the defence apparatus moved successfully in keeping the meddling Aussies out of what was potentially a most dangerous game. Besides, just weeks before Gough Whitlam, the country's former Prime Minister had pledged total support to the Soeharto government and where was he now? They were still unsure of the new Prime Minister, Fraser, but they understood that at least his party's politics were somewhat similar to theirs.

An unhappy American Ambassador to Australia was therefore instructed to inform his country's allies of the U.S. position.

The Indonesians could use the OV-10Fs against the Timorese as the aircraft was perfect for such action. Equipped with a twenty millimetre cannon and up to four missiles AURI believed that, with experienced pilots, they could wrap up the invasion in days. It was decided in secret that American interests could best be served if delivery of the Broncos was not delayed any further. The military sales program would be accelerated enabling earlier delivery of the Skyhawks as well.

Coleman contemplated the seriousness of the conflict. He hoped that his meeting in Hong Kong would provide the information necessary to allay his concerns. If not, he would need to take whatever action was appropriate to avoid what were potentially serious political repercussions as a result of the company's armament activities. Australians had always enjoyed a close relationship with the Indonesians.

Suddenly that had all changed.

He had asked Seda about the killing of the foreign journalists but the General had claimed it had been an accident. There had been so many conflicting reports creating a great deal of confusion as to what actually happened.

* * * * * *

Recalling the breakfast meeting he still could not understand how the Australian Broadcasting authorities had permitted the news bulletins to go to air and divulge military and strategically sensitive information through its programs. The situation was extremely serious and volatile. He felt that the Indonesians would have every right to retaliate and, if this happened, being an Australian in Jakarta would be dangerous. Stephan hoped that the broadcasts would not be repeated. Still considering the ramifications of the potential political fallout, Stephen rose and headed for the toilet.

He glanced away as he passed the familiar figure sitting three rows behind his seat.

"Stephen?" Anderson called but Coleman ignored the man continuing to the bathroom. When he had completed his ablutions he returned to his seat only to discover John Anderson occupying the seat next to his.

"You're looking well, Stephen."

"You're sitting on my menu," the younger man snapped.

"Just a few words. I promise that you will be very interested in what I have to say. In fact, I would have phoned your office today as I have been in town since yesterday and planned to catch up. Had you not decided to leave unexpectedly we would probably already be sitting down somewhere having the same discussion. As it is, I've had to rearrange my entire itinerary just so we could have this private time together." Anderson could see the surprise on the other man's face as he alluded to the fact that he had actually orchestrated his travel to be on the same flight.

"We have to talk, Stephen," he said, almost staccato in emphasis. Anderson looked directly into Coleman's eyes as he emphasized the words by tapping the tray locked in front of his seat, one tap, one word as he'd said "we-have-to-talk, Stephen!"

Coleman, immediately infuriated at the master-pupil approach snapped back. "Stick it!"

"Come on, man, grow up!"

Coleman sighed. It was a difficult situation as there was really nowhere he could go. Not at thirty five thousand feet. Reluctantly he decided to hear him out.

"What do you want, John?"

The grey-haired distinguished Intelligence Chief leaned towards his former junior officer and lowered his voice.

"Are you going to Hong Kong?" he asked softly.

Startled, Coleman was caught off guard. He hesitated, looked Anderson directly in the eye and lied.

"No. Just to Singapore this trip."

"Too bad, I had hoped for a little company on the longer section."

"I doubt we would have too much to discuss."

"Oh, you never know, Stephen, we could talk about the arms shipments you have been handling and, if that is of no interest, we could move on to more personal matters."

Coleman felt the hot burning anger beginning as a flush, moving across his face. He remained silent, gathering his thoughts.

How did he know that I would be on this flight? Stephen asked himself. Then it dawned on him. The bastards, he thought, they have been keeping tabs on me and bugging my phones. And Albert's!

He glanced at the other passenger, controlling his rising anger.

"What do you want, John?"

"Are you going to Hong Kong?" he asked again.

"Maybe," he answered, this time sullenly.

"Then I insist we talk. Now!"

The command was too much for him, the anger suddenly bursting forth.

"Where in the hell do you guys get off, John? I don't cash your cheques any more and certainly have no intention of participating in any of your clandestine activities."

Anderson's eyes narrowed as he leaned a little closer to the other man. "We know about Seda."

He had made the statement in his soft resonant voice and yet it seemed to Coleman as if it had been shouted at him in a thunderous roar.

"Are we discussing Albert?" he inquired hopefully, his throat suddenly dry. He swallowed a large mouthful of whisky.

"Yes, and that too," Anderson replied softly. "I'm sorry."

"Christ! Your bastards have been tapping my lines," he accused.

"It really doesn't matter now. The important thing is that we have the chance to correct a few problems and prevent at least one major catastrophe."

He was stunned by these revelations. His mind raced quickly. How much did they know?

"How did you know I'd be on this flight?"

"As I said. It doesn't matter how we knew. We needed to talk to you urgently and out of the country. It was a stroke of luck that you jumped when you did."

"Jumped?" Coleman asked, incredulous disbelief crossing his face. "Just an euphemism, don't over react."

"Are you trying to tell me that you orchestrated my departure today?" he asked disbelievingly, "That's just so much bullshit, and you know it!"

"Let's cool it," Anderson said as the stewardess moved past and checked the drinks. She continued on down the aisle as she could see that they weren't ready for another.

Stephen jabbed his thumb on the service button. The steward-ess went directly to his service.

"*Tuan mau minum lagi?*" she asked slightly startled, now an-ticipating his request for a further drink, as foreigners always drank heavily and on these short sectors.

"Chivas," he snapped.

The young hostess identified the tone. "*And would you also like something, sir?*" she asked the tall grey haired gentleman sitting alongside. Stephen looked up at the lovely smiling face and im-mediately felt guilty for his display of temper. Although he really didn't feel much like it, he returned her smile.

"*Sorry, sis, I'm not angry with you. It's just that the old man beside me is very annoying,*" Coleman explained.

The girl smiled at the handsome passenger and then looked at the other man who had obviously been the source of his rudeness.

"The lady wants to know if you require a drink." Coleman snapped.

"Thank you, yes. I will have a Chivas also," he replied, unruf-fled.

Stephen sat and sulked until his drink arrived. He sipped in silence, refusing to communicate with Anderson. He knew he was in trouble. They had information that was only supposed to be available to Nathan Seda and himself.

Half an hour passed and the plane began its descent into Singa-pore. The two men disembarked together and walked briskly to the transit ticketing counter. Coleman purchased his ticket and the older man stood by watching. An observer could easily have mis-taken them for father and son. Recognising that Anderson was not going to leave him alone, Stephan sighed, shrugged his shoulders and turned towards his former mentor.

"We have half an hour. Let's find somewhere to talk," he sug-gested.

Anderson nodded his agreement. They selected comfortable seats towards the rear section of the first class lounge. Anderson had taken a wine from the complimentary bar and offered a glass to Coleman who declined and prepared another Chivas with just one cube of ice. He stood facing the government man slowly swirl-ing the whisky around the cube and then he took a seat positioning himself so that they could not be overheard.

"Okay. Give it to me. What's happening, John?"

"Well, Stephen, the shit has hit the fan and you seem to be sitting right in the middle of the target area."

"Let's cut through it. We don't have much time. What is it I may or may not have involved myself in that is of interest to ASIS?"

"Firstly. You are still tied by the Official Secrets Act," he warned.

"Hold it!" Stephen snapped, "I won't sit here and permit you to threaten me, John. Knock it off!"

"It's no threat. You are in serious trouble. This mess is partly of your own doing and, to put it bluntly, had I not been the man in the chair, as they say, your number would be up. Half of ASIS wants you put away, Stephen, they think you're an arsehole!"

Stephen had never heard the Director speak in this tone. Not even when he was angry. He then realized that the man was deadly serious and maybe out of some previous loyalty had decided to give Stephan the opportunity to extricate himself from whatever mess they thought he was in.

"Okay. I'm listening."

"Good." Anderson smiled, weariness now apparent as he extended his hand.

Stephen accepted the gesture.

Anderson then began to speak slowly in a soft monotone which, had the content not been so dramatic, would have made the listener drift off to sleep. He spoke without interruption for twenty minutes and when he had completed his explanation Stephen sat quietly, his face ashen, shocked by the information he had been given.

Forty-five minutes later the Cathay Pacific Tristar Star departed for Hong Kong. Stephen Coleman sat alone, sipping yet another whisky with no effect, as he was stone cold sober. He felt numb, not from the alcohol but from the secret and shocking disclosures he'd just been provided with at risk, no doubt, to the courier himself. He knew just how indebted he now was to John Anderson. A cold sensation passed through his body and Coleman shuddered involuntarily.

Anderson's revelations may have just been in time. He would know, for sure, after his meeting with Nathan Seda in Hong Kong.

* * * * * *

Nevada — USA

The inconspicuous building lay well back from the main road and out of sight behind a small spur that ran parallel with the secondary road leading back towards the Californian border. The total acreage was near to a thousand and most was covered with timber stands protected by numerous signs, designating the area as a special reserve. The photo interpretation unit had been established during the years when Khruschev headed the Kremlin. There had been a rush of new data collection facilities built as a result of even more sophisticated satellites being launched. This unit was dedicated to the intelligence monitoring of product, sent back to earth by the United States Military's Series Four birds which flew across the heavens orbiting specific areas as designated by the powerful men in the Pentagon. The air-conditioned centre and surrounding forest was encircled by a perimeter fence carrying sufficient power to deter the curious from entering the secluded facility. Signs had been erected warning trespassers of the charged fence and ranger patrols. Strangely enough none had breached the unit's security since it was first commissioned.

Lieutenant Collins had been engrossed in his own work when he heard the soft whistle of surprise from across the other side of their compact room. He looked up and spotted Davidson, one of his senior photo analysis experts standing as he held the two photographic records in one hand and waving them as one would a hand fan.

Collins gestured the other man over to his work area, now covered with detail of the last two runs obtained by the satellite over the Philippines. They had been monitoring shipping in that area consistently for the past three months at the request of their Intelligence masters.

Davidson handed the Section Commander both of the enlarged photos taken from space and sent by electronic impulse back to the earth station which, in turn, had passed the garbled signals to the relevant agency for interpretation and dissemination.

"This is fantastic, Davy boy! Great clarity, although there's some degradation in this one," he said shaking the photograph in his left hand.

"Thanks boss," the experienced hand responded, pleased with

the Lieutenant's reaction. They worked well together and he didn't mind putting that little extra effort into the demanding and sometimes boring intelligence work. The monotonous routine was extremely intense in nature as, the longer one was obliged to stare down through the enhancement apparatus the more the details became difficult to differentiate, even with the assistance of the latest developments in their field of pseudoscopy.

Collins looked at the detailed views and the sections already highlighted by Davidson and went into the computer immediately. He then compared the results with the photo-imagery taken of the Russian freighters which had been seen and photographed heading for Cuba almost fifteen years before. As a senior analyst he was responsible for confirming his team's results before passing the information to his superior. Their work was demanding at the best of times and mistakes were easily made, for it was not always just a simple matter of identifying what had been caught by the satellite's lenses as it moved across the sky at incredible speed, but also the difficult task of suggesting what the objects were in the black and white scenes.

Ten minutes after receiving Davidson's interpretation, the Lieutenant stood across from the Colonel with the information. Believing that they had confirmation of the cargo, the report was immediately transmitted to the Pentagon's South East Asian hostiles' desk. Less than half an hour had passed from the time Davidson had first spotted the configuration which sent alarm bells ringing directly to the President's Defence Advisor.

There were a number of possibilities according to the intelligence report. The crate sizes and numbers were almost identical in every way with those in the earlier photographs and, should the contents be the same, then the *M.V. Setia Budi* could be carrying a Soviet Skean (SS-5) ballistic missile on board as deck cargo. The report went on to describe the deadly weapon.

The Pentagon had data showing that the intermediate range missile was another of the liquid-propelled series which could be fitted with nuclear or thermonuclear warheads. The Skean series had a range of some two thousand miles, or approximately three thousand two hundred kilometres, and was regarded as the ultimate in postwar development applied to the old German V-2 series rocket. According to other satellite intelligence reports it was confirmed that the Soviets had deployed approximately one hundred of the missiles each with a warhead capacity of up to one megaton yield. These were housed in underground silo-launchers scattered around Europe with a few along their borders with China.

Once the information had been absorbed and acting upon White House directives, the Pentagon issued the order and signals were flashed across the oceans. These were intercepted then confirmed by the Fleet's Admiral.

As the freighter approached the coastline of the former Portuguese colony, approximately one hundred nautical miles from its probable destination, the Captain and crew of the M.V. *Setia Budi* were startled by the incredible noise which ruptured the vessel. In those few brief seconds as the two conventional warheads struck the ship almost simultaneously, cutting its hull in two with the massive force of detonation, all the men on the bridge died.

The ship sank in less than eleven minutes. There were only two survivors and both claimed that their vessel had struck an old mine, taking the freighter, its master and most of its crew to the bottom before anything could be done.

Having confirmed the kill, the United States Lafayette Class nuclear submarine turned back once more on its track and headed for the deep waters of the Ombai Wetar Trench, where its presence was practically impossible to detect.

In the following weeks American SEALS posing as tourists sailing through to Singapore from Australia visited the site. They required only three dives before they were satisfied with their conclusions, supported by the sensitive sonar instruments on board their yacht. These had suggested the unexpected results even before they had even considered the physical sightings as being necessary.

The Presidential advisor read the report and advised the country's leader that the threat had been removed. The shipments, containers, and box identifications were deliberately meant to be misleading. The Soviets had just been playing at their old tricks to test the American's response. The deck cargo had been nothing more than a series of empty crates and containers.

It had all been another Russian hoax.

* * * * * *

THE TIMOR MAN

Timor

Bambang had managed but a few hours sleep before the heavy downpour forced his platoon to break camp and continue their mission. The trail was slippery. The underbrush ripped at their uniforms, cutting through the camouflaged material supplied by some distant clothing factory in Hong Kong. At least they had reasonable fire-power when the time came for them to fight, as he knew it would. The enlisted men all carried the American M-16s with the exception of the Sergeant who struggled under the weight and additional rounds he carried for the heavy M-60.

Bambang knew that the weight of the ten kilo weapon would be taking its toll on his most experienced soldier, but someone had to carry the machine gun and it might as well be the man who would eventually be the one to fire it.

He looked across at the soldier who continuously slipped with every step. The M72 LAW didn't appear to be any the worse for wear from the constant beating it had received. Bambang considered taking the rocket launcher himself as he felt that it would be called upon early in the engagement and he preferred knowing that it was in responsible hands. With its three hundred metre range he expected to be able to keep the guerrillas well at bay. During their briefings they had been advised that the enemy was poorly equipped. Some, they had been told, carried antiquated weaponry, while only a few had the Soviet Ak-47s. They were practically guaranteed by the Major who carried out their Intelligence briefing that there would be no likelihood of their encountering any real resistance or, for that matter, any sophisticated weaponry.

Somebody should have told the enemy, Bambang thought, remembering the bodies hanging from the trees in their harnesses. The men were demoralized. They were tired. They were wet, and very, very hungry. Captain Bambang knew that he would have to achieve their object quickly before his men tired to exhaustion. The point reported a small compound not far around the next ridge, and he decided to seek temporary refuge and shelter, enabling his men to eat and get out of the weather for a short spell. The villagers would have prepared rice. The one thing you could count on in this world, the Javanese officer thought, was that regardless of location, someone, somewhere within spitting distance of wherever you were would have rice on the boil.

They scrutinized the perimeter fence before calling out to the villagers. There was no answer and the sergeant called out again.

"Tell them we will pay them for food. Tell them we will do them no harm. Tell the.." the Captains instructions were interrupted as a voice called out to them to go away.

"Pergi! Go!" the frightened voice demanded..

"We're not your enemies, we won't do you any harm!" the non-com called back hoping that the simple people there would not panic.

Minutes passed and the tall gate opened. At first, just a little, but sufficient for an ageing head to peer out and reassure itself that these soldiers really meant no harm.

"Why do you come here?" the old man demanded.

"We need food, Pak."

The withered body of the little man was now in full view.

"You eat, then you go, yes?" he asked.

"Ya, Pak, we will leave as soon as we have eaten," they promised.

Carefully, in single file, they entered the village compound.

They huddled below the huts which had been built on stilts, the ground was filthy and mud greeted them wherever they looked. It was a poor and desolate place to be, the men had thought, although thankful for the break to rest and eat. The village people fed the soldiers who in turn rewarded their hosts with warm smiles and a fistful of Rupiah. The old village headman shook his head sadly. He explained that they had little use for the paper money as it could only be used down along the coast and in the large towns.

They asked instead for one of the soldiers' watches. Captain Bambang sadly agreed and he, as platoon Commander, unhappily surrendered his Seiko to the headman. He knew it was extortion but felt saddened by the scene around him. These poor village people had given what was probably a large portion of their food stocks to his men. They didn't understand the conflict and were merely innocent bystanders to the fighting taking place all around them.

Bambang removed the wrist watch slowly. The old wrinkled face broke into a wide toothless smile as he accepted the piece. He examined the gift and noticed writing on the back cover. He asked the Javanese what the inscription meant as he was illiterate.

"Always be safe, Bambang, love Wanti," he read aloud, explaining to the village elder that it was a gift from his sister.

The old man nodded and looked up into the young officer's sad brown eyes. Then he returned the watch and walked away.

Their spirits lifted by the hot steamed rice and vegetables, the soldiers departed. They continued around the mountain and descended down its slopes, the trees and undergrowth, becoming much heavier as they advanced, impeded their movements. Bambang continued to monitor his men, as did his sergeant. They were already beginning to feel the effects of the constant downpours and inhospitable surrounds. They continued down another slope, the non-com cursing both his men and the slippery soil, saturated by incessant rain.

The men were nervous now, sensing that the enemy was near. They were able to increase their pace for awhile as the trail moved away from the thick growth and provided the men with the opportunity to move a little more freely. As the afternoon hours passed, Bambang decided that they would establish their camp earlier rather than later, permitting the men to rest well before any encounter.

They established camp observing their instructions not to start a fire. Bambang had wanted the men to refrain from smoking their *kretek* as he knew that a non-smoker could distinguish the easily identifiable aroma of the Indonesian cigarette, putting them at risk, but the sergeant indicated that it would be all right as the men were tired. And jumpy.

Conditions were not much better than the previous night. Bambang slept for a few hours, rose when awoken by his non-com and together they checked the perimeter before returning to take some fruit from their limited ration packs.

The corporal sat huddled against a coconut palm. He judged from its condition that they had come a considerable distance down from the mountain slopes as this tree was covered with full ripe clusters of the hard shelled fruit. Bambang nudged the soldier, indicating the coconuts hanging directly overhead. The corporal nodded accepting his mistake and moved away from the potential danger. The impact from the weight of a ripened coconut could be deadly and Bambang did not wish to lose any of his men so foolishly.

* * * * * *

As daybreak arrived the soldiers prepared themselves for the day's patrol. Those who were Moslem prayed, facing the west, in the direction of Mecca, while the two who were not just went about their ablutions silently praying to their own gods that they would see this day through. The platoon set out and within a few hours made their first contact with the enemy, when they heard the sound of weapons being fired.

Bambang wisely ordered one of his men to reconnoiter the area, and waited for his report.

An hour passed and when the point man did not return the Captain assumed the worst and ordered the men to prepare their weapons for he knew that the enemy were close. They proceeded cautiously, listening for any tell tale sign of the enemy's position, nervously anticipating the encounter. Ahead lay a clearing but the missing soldier was nowhere to be seen.

Last night's campsite, Bambang concluded, as he identified the tell tale signs. He barked an order and the men obeyed.

They encircled the area, but there was nothing.

Bambang considered the possibility that the man he'd placed on point had deserted. It was unfortunately common with some of the first timers. It was just so simple to do and he'd wondered why many more had not deserted the same way. Once away from their units all they had to do was throw their military gear away and slip back into any village then hide.

Bambang instructed his men to spread out and remain alert. The minutes dragged by and still there was nothing. He was worried that the guerrillas may have doubled back behind them somehow. He discussed this with his senior NCO, a veteran of the early Sixties invasion of Irian and the *Ganyang Malaysia Konfrontasi* era. Many of the veterans had left the military, disillusioned after the entire exercise became a totally useless effort on the government's part to not really wage war, but merely distract the people at home from their economic problems.

The sergeant suggested that it was unlikely that the guerrillas would remain down in the lower areas as they risked observation by aerial reconnaissance flights. *"Maybe they have a supply base back up in the mountain,"* he advised his officer.

"They would expect to be followed," Bambang had replied, anxious that they might have missed the enemy.

The sergeant thought about this for a moment and replied.

"They must be poorly equipped. If they were expecting us then why haven't they attacked?"

As Bambang listened to the experienced veteran he suddenly realized his mistake. They had entered a trap!

It took all his strength to control the sudden flood of fear that gripped his stomach. He crouched low and called out to his men, warning them to hold fast, where they were and not to advance any further. He hissed at the soldier next to him to keep low and, as the man crouched forward, his body suddenly jerked up and was flung over backwards as the crashing sound of the bullet ripped through the morning air. Crack!

Immediately his men panicked. Lacking in experience and caught by fear, they fired wildly as they could not see their targets in the thick undergrowth. The air was suddenly filled with the screaming cacophony only a fire-fight could produce. Explosions ripped through the trees and automatic fire produced the most incredible shock waves on all sides of the action.

Men screamed with pain. Others screamed just from the fear of dying. Bambang turned in time to see his sergeant's face twist and contort as a bullet passed through one side and then out the other, throwing him with such force his body spun through the air as if it were some rag doll. He grabbed clumsily for the M-60 but it was pinned under the dead man's body. He screamed for his men to hold their fire but they ignored his command.

Fear had taken control and they emptied their magazines shooting blindly through the trees, as they panicked and died. As the deadly fire continued Bambang responded shooting in the direction of the enemy's position without seeing any of their soldiers. He screamed at his men to retreat but he couldn't be heard over the fierce noise of the battle.

Suddenly the shooting stopped. The Javanese officer called out softly for his men to report but there was no response. Someone groaned aloud nearby. He crawled over and found the corporal doubled up in pain. He had been shot in the stomach.

Bambang assessed the situation quickly. He was not sure just how many of his thirty soldiers had survived. He crawled through the muddy grass and discovered another body. The radio operator lay face down half his torso blown away where he had been hit by automatic fire.

He called out again, softly. There was still no response. He heard movement on his flank and immediately froze.

A voice called out. Someone screamed and was quickly silenced by small arms fire. Bambang waited. He counted off the seconds as he had learned during basic training. He could practically visualize his instructor standing over him during that day when he had lifted his head far too soon, only to have the angry Sergeant-Major yell abuse for him to get his head back down and to count. He crawled forward and could now see directly across the clearing and his heart skipped a beat. There were hundreds of them!

He froze instantly, holding his breath for as long as his lungs would permit. Slowly he eased his body back down a small slope and lay perfectly still in the mud, half hidden by the long grass.

Suddenly he could hear the voice of a man in extreme pain. He dared not lift his head. The soldier cried out loudly, his screams piercing the almost otherwise silent air.

"*Help!*" he cried. "*Please help me!*"

The screams continued until suddenly these too ceased simultaneously with the report of a gun being fired. Bambang understood. There would be no prisoners! Fear now gripped his very being and he felt ashamed. He couldn't will his body to move. His fear of death was too great. His limbs would not obey.

Bambang remained where he was hidden from the enemy. He had heard more screams and more shots silencing the soldiers under his command. Until there was no one left. And then there was the terrifying empty sound of silence.

He lay on the ground for what seemed to be an eternity, listening for sounds, the sounds of the enemy moving through the long grass, slowly, carefully, knowing that they had not yet discovered the body of the platoon's Commander. He lay still, willing his heart to slow, praying that they would not find him. He sobbed, his face smothered in his arms as he lay in the muddy undergrowth, silently weeping with shame. He cried, for he was weak and now all of his men had been killed. He knew that he too should be dead, as they were, accepting that only his cowardice had saved his life.

* * * * * *

As the darkness descended he forced himself to his feet. Like a man in a daze he wandered slowly around the battle scene, staring numbly at the carnage which lay before him. His platoon. Shattered. He moved slowly, checking the bodies, startled with every noise the trees and wind made. He started to shake as the fear once again took charge of his body abd he fell down to his knees and held his chest tightly, the racking sobs of despair choking in his throat. Finally, exhausted, he crawled back into the thick grass and slept, only to awaken by the cold soggy clothing stuck to his filthy body.

He remained crouched, his arms locked under his knees, shivering with the biting rain and fierce wind until morning finally came, bringing with it the horrors of the day before.

The bodies lay as they had fallen. Except for those who had only been wounded. Soldiers who had not died during the engagement had eventually paid the price of capture. Some had their faces mutilated similarly to the victims of the previous massacre. Hollow skeleton-like eyeless heads made even more terrifying with the wide open mouths holding frozen screams, evidenced the extreme cruelty of the guerrilla band. Others had their testicles severed and their organs stuffed into their mouths.

Bambang retched, but there was nothing in his empty stomach to help him. He ran his hands over his face and screamed out loudly in anguish. He called for *Allah* to save him from the hell in which he now found himself. He cried out again and again but none listened. He panicked and ran. He ran wildly through the jungle until exhaustion overcame him, collapsing beside a small stream.

He woke to the silence of the early morning and discovered that he had slept for almost an entire day.

Bambang realized that he had no choice. He had to go back to his men. He would collect their dog tags and search for the radio. He experienced the sudden return of his shame and knew that it would almost be impossible for him to face the other men in his regiment as the only survivor of the ambush.

They would think he was a coward, he knew.

And so he returned to the battle scene. There, slowly but carefully, he dragged his fallen comrades bodies to a small clearing. He had located all but one, the wounded corporal.

He placed the dead in a row. Bambang then removed their identification tags and tied them together placing these in the top of his battle tunic. All the weapons had been collected by the guerrillas. There was no radio. He was completely alone but he knew what he must do. He was still a soldier and he would follow the large band until he discovered their base camp. Then he would return to his own unit and bring adequate reinforcements.

Bambang peered back up in the general direction of the trail which had led them into peril. He looked back over his shoulder at the dead, then turned and addressed the task before him. Slowly he commenced his climb, forcing his aching body to obey his mind's commands. Within moments the clearing covered in mutilated bodies was hidden from view and he marched on.

Less than two hundred metres from where he had remembered the wounded corporal had fallen he was astonished to discover the man sitting up against a coconut tree.

Caught by surprise, Bambang hurried forward to ascertain whether he was still alive. The soldier's eyes were closed and the blood had dried. The young Javanese Captain bent down and placed his hand gently on the still body, gently prodding, to waken the soldier.

Bambang heard the noise and admitted to himself that he really hadn't deserved the second chance to live. In the passing of one brief moment and as his hands moved slowly over the fallen soldier Bambang understood that the corporal was dead. And in that instant, as he heard the thunderous click of the trigger mechanism activated when he tried to remove the man's dog tag, Bambang knew that he too was a dead man. The moment created between life and death was infinitesimal in time as his body was separated from his soul.

The blast hurled both soldiers through the air, ripping the uniforms from their shattered remains. The broken Seiko lay smashed, the inscription still clear. "*Selamat selalu, Bambang, dari Wanti.*"

Days later the watch was exchanged by the old headman for a carton of *kretek* cigarettes. The hill people had collected whatever remained on the bodies of the unfortunate platoon and returned to the security of their enclosed compound. There they would remain until yet another Indonesian group of soldiers came by.

When a further detachment of the unwanted soldiers came in search of their fallen comrades the headman watched them also slowly disappear down the same trail which had led Bambang's soldiers to their deaths. The wise old man just shook his head. When these intruders were finally out of sight he dispatched a runner to report the presence of these soldiers to the FRETILIN post.

* * * * * *

"I'm really sorry about the reports. Have you been in contact lately with your family?"

Hart sympathized with Albert. The Timorese was heartbroken, having heard the morning report on the international news bulletin. It seemed that everyone in Indonesia these days now listened to the foreign broadcasts on a regular basis as there was little information filtering down from the government. The news had indicated that fighting had been stepped up with considerable casualties on both sides. Even the villages were being burned.

"Only by letter," he replied, "and that was some months ago."

"I'm sure they're okay. Just wait. Probably find some news waiting when you return home to Melbourne."

It felt strange to both of them that he had referred to that city as his home when, in fact, he'd been born in this country he now visited.

They discussed the broadcasts and both agreed that it was quite incredible how the Australian broadcasting station was disclosing Indonesian troop positions in such a blatant fashion. The Indonesians had no choice but to assume that it was a deliberate attempt by the Australian Government to prevent the success of the annexation. The Indonesian hierarchy was completely confused.

On one hand, the Australians had virtually given them *carte blanche* to assume control over the former Portuguese colony while on the other, the country's deliberate disclosure of Indonesian troop positions and other relevant military information, via their official radio station, had them totally bewildered. In Indonesia, such action would not be tolerated. The offenders would be dealt with quickly and the matter resolved within hours. Why was the Australian Government so weak, even timid, when it came to dealing with its media? They just couldn't understand why their old friends had let them down so badly.

Thousands of Indonesian troops had died by simply walking into traps laid easily by the FRETILIN as they too had listened to the broadcasts. At first the separatists had been highly suspicious of the information but, when they discovered the accuracy of the reports, they laughed at the relative ease with which they had dispatched so many of Indonesia's finest soldiers.

The windfall didn't continue, of course. It seemed that the flow of information ceased almost as quickly as it had started. All sides involved in the conflict had suddenly made a point of listening to the foreign radio broadcasts. Reportedly these had become unreliable over the previous days and appeared to contain more misinformation than real substance.

"Have you heard from Stephen?" Albert was disappointed that Stephen had left so suddenly without further discussing their future arrangements. He had difficulty obtaining return bookings and speculated that Coleman's secretary wasn't really trying as hard as he suspected she could.

"Nothing for a few days I'm afraid, perhaps we'll get something today." Greg Hart had taken breakfast with Albert. He didn't believe for one moment that Coleman would be in contact until he suddenly reappeared without notice in his office-cum-home. Hart had not entirely been happy when the company's other offices started appearing all over the city and neither was he pleased with Stephen's insistence that the bulk of the administration be moved out of his personal office to the company's main location down on Jalan Thamrin.

They discussed the events in Timor and Hart had assured the soft-spoken man he was certain that fighting was only occurring on the eastern side of the island. This was a complete off-the-cuff fabrication as he had no more knowledge of the real circumstances than the man sitting opposite him but felt that it wouldn't hurt to offer Albert some reassurance. Albert was not convinced. He was tempted to make contact with his step-brother and ask for his assistance but he knew this effort would be fruitless, if not dangerous.

General Nathan Seda had been adamant concerning this point. He did not want Albert to make direct contact under any circumstances and, as he had insisted, Albert would obey the General's wishes. Thinking about the man made him nervous. He swallowed too quickly, causing himself to cough. Embarrassed, he reached for a glass of water.

"What's Wanti doing today then?" Hart asked, changing the

subject as he could see that the other man was uncomfortable discussing the hostilities in his former home country. Albert replied briefly, his thoughts still clouded with the prospect of further delays due to Stephen's untimely absence. The conversation then drifted to more mundane matters.

Wanti had enjoyed the shopping as clothing was considerably cheaper in Jakarta than Melbourne. Already she had selected an array of fine lengths of material and these were being tailored for her in a shop off Blok M. All three had dined together at the beautiful Oasis restaurant in Cikini.

It was strange at the time that both men recognized the change in her mood. During the course of the evening Wanti continuously looked out through the magnificent gardens, admiring the landscape and yet, from time to time, a sadness became evident, just a shadow in her eyes; she seemed uncertain, and lost. Albert could detect that there was something different about her demeanour that evening but decided that she was just tired. As they sat together in the second and larger of the dining sections, the Batak singers entertained singing their melodious traditional songs from Sumatra.

The majority of the guests were from Embassies, the business sector and the Indonesian Government. Rumour had it that one of the Vice President had actually purchased the magnificent premises which was once the residence of the United States Marine Attaché.

Wanti wasn't sure for certain but she felt that Stephen had brought her here, once before, when they had first met. There was just something about the magnificent gardens that sparked a faint recollection from her past. In fact, it was in this very mansion that they had met and fallen in love. Wanti could no longer recognize her surroundings as they had been altered considerably to accommodate the new restaurant's requirements.

The following day, feeling obliged to entertain Stephen's wife and friend once again, Hart had introduced them to one of the expatriate drinking spots. This English-style pub and restaurant was located across the canal from the Hotel Indonesia and adjacent to the Kartika Plaza hotel. He'd told them both that it was one of Stephen's favourite haunts where he would spend considerable time with his friends and business associates. Hart didn't mention that his boss often entertained the ladies here as well for the atmosphere and cuisine were, at that time, perhaps the best the city could offer.

They had been welcomed by the pub's owner who often stood propped at the small corner section of the bar with his 'drinking team', as they were known, for the group of six or seven were rarely seen drinking elsewhere and virtually claimed that area of the bar for themselves. They would arrive around midday and take up the exact positions they had occupied the day before. Rarely did the group break up before evening and their presence helped develop most of the character, the ambiance, and the popularity that The George and Dragon enjoyed over the years.

The colourful manager, a short Cockney with considerable culinary flair, added to the pub's atmosphere, as his repartee often lifted the level of conversation and stories to new highs, pleasing the hard core drinking clientele who kept the till happily ringing away.

Although Hart enjoyed himself at the bar surrounded by a variety of foreigners throwing back drinks faster than Albert imagined possible, neither of his two guests appeared to particularly enjoy the venue. Unbeknown to the visitors and the public in general, this establishment had, in fact, been used for more than one covert rendezvous until articles appeared in the Hong Kong press suggesting that the popular pub had more than one purpose for its existence. The Russian and British Embassies were situated directly across the street and, as The George's reputation grew, so did the mystique surrounding it.

Journalists frequented its bar along with tough sounding riggers off the oil platforms. All in all the place was basically a communications centre as it was more convenient and, in most cases, more productive to arrange to meet downtown in this bar than spend hours dialling hopelessly through the local telephone exchange.

Having finished their lunch Hart excused himself. "Take the car, I have only a short walk from here," he'd offered.

The pair disappeared quickly, not content to sit around in the now noisy place, as they had friends to contact and more shopping to complete. Wanti had also made arrangements to meet with Bambang's former base Commander in Jakarta later in the afternoon as she was anxious to learn where he had been billeted at his new station. Phones were never connected to the men's single quarters and she wished desperately to contact him to see if he could get away and visit before they returned to Australia. Wanti intended using her Javanese charm to seek a special favour and ask the Colonel if there was some way her brother could be called to the officer's mess phone to speak with her. Bambang had written to her in Melbourne but she was unable to contact him prior to her departure.

They drove out to the military station and Wanti entered the building alone. Unfortunately the Garrison Commander was not available. Wanti had noticed the unusually active scene around her when shown into the officer's protocol liaison centre.

"*Sis, you indicated that you wished to see the Colonel,*" the liaison officer had asked. "*I'm sorry, but the command is very busy and it would be impossible for you to meet with him. Can I be of assistance?*"

Wanti smiled at the soldier.

She turned on the charm and the helpless little girl act that she'd found worked so well with others.

"*I really need your help, 'bang, to contact my brother in the Surabaya barracks. I haven't seen him in years and I must return to Australia in a few days. I would be very sad if I missed him during this visit.*" With which she looked up at the young officer who had now leaned across the service counter separating the staff from visitors.

"*Give me his name and rank, and I'll do what I can,*" he offered.

Wanti had quickly written the information down and passed it across the counter. Without speaking, the protocol officer took the piece of paper and disappeared through a rear door, leaving her to sit on the rotan chair staring at the photographs of the Army Chief of Staff and those of the country's leadership. A large Garuda hung on one wall directly above a number of flags which had been placed on either side of the office entrance. She waited patiently for an hour.

Wanti was aware that her brother had been posted to his regiment in Surabaya a few months before and clearly understood the difficulty she would have had in attempting to arrange such a call herself through non-military communications, as the government's telephones were impossible enough for just city calls, let alone inter province. Expecting to make such a connection for a long distance call in less than three or four hours would be naive, she knew.

Another thirty minutes had passed when the Lieutenant returned.

"*Sorry, sis. All communications to the Surabaya command have been blocked for military traffic only. I've been trying to call one of my own friends down there to assist but everything seems to be very busy. I couldn't get any priority.*"

He observed the disappointed look on the girl's face. "*The traffic should die down a little before five if you want to wait and let me try again. Or, if you wish, I'll write down the officers mess number and you can try from the post office or from wherever you're staying.*"

"*Terima kasih,*" Wanti replied indicating that she would take the number and leave.

Albert had waited in the car. He was nervous enough just being in the military compound without having to enter one of their buildings. He didn't require any reminders of his last visit to an army establishment, the memories of which had haunted him for years before he could put the whole thing behind him. When Wanti returned to the vehicle she found him sitting in a pool of perspiration, his face quite pale. She didn't understand why he hadn't turned the air-conditioning back on if he'd been that uncomfortably hot.

She explained what had occurred inside. Understanding her disappointment at not being able to contact him directly, Albert offered to fly down with her to meet with Bambang, before returning to Australia. They discussed this alternative.

"*Of course, there is still the possibility that we can make the call direct to the Surabaya station and arrange for Bambang to be called to the phone, now you have his mess number,*" Albert suggested.

She had agreed. They returned to the house, tired but determined and immediately started dialling the long distance number themselves. After some hours they gave up any further attempts for the day as it was then probable that the mess would have closed, having finished with the evening meal some time before.

The next morning they asked for Hart's assistance in arranging for the change in tickets and bookings. He came over from the other office and, having been told about the connection difficulties they'd experienced, instructed Stephen's secretary to keep on trying until the operators were successful.

"Mr Hart," the woman had started, entering the guest lounge

area without knocking, "the lines are going to be congested to Surabaya for some time. Especially all military installations."

"Just keep trying," he had ordered, dismissing the personal secretary brusquely.

"I don't expect we will have much luck," Hart said turning to his guest, "the military will have everything tied up what with the action in Timor right now. Even flights will be difficult if you really wish to go down that way."

The conversation then centred on the Indonesian invasion of Timor-Timur.

"The losses are outrageously high.

"According to the Indonesian Sinar Harapan paper the Armed Forces information bureau has released data suggesting that Radio Australia has deliberately exaggerated the Indonesian casualty figures to create doom and gloom in retaliation over the expulsion of one of their reporters some time before. They also challenged the Radio Australia broadcasters to identify their sources as, according to the Indonesian Minister for Information, no permits have been issued for any foreign journalists to enter the region," Albert advised, having read the *Bahasa Indonesia* language newspaper.

"That's a good point," Hart agreed, "but I doubt that their sources would be exposed. Still, it is quite amazing that they are able to report what the diplomatic community here suggest is reasonably accurate information."

"Well, one thing is for certain. This will certainly test relationships between the two countries. Australia and Indonesia will require some time to repair the considerable political damage sustained as a result of the broadcasts."

Hart considered Albert's last remark. Public reaction in Jakarta to the broadcast would, undoubtedly, affect the warm relationships Australia had enjoyed over the years with its giant neighbour. It was not inconceivable to expect student unrest and even demonstrations against the Australian Embassy. Hart felt uncomfortable with the thought of rioting students as he recalled the anti-Japanese demonstrations of some years before.

"Perhaps it would be wise for you to skip Surabaya and return to Melbourne, just in case things take a turn for the worse here?"

Albert laughed. "It is unlikely that the inhabitants of even this city would throw stones at a Timorese, Greg!"

"And besides," he continued, "Wanti would never forgive me if she missed the chance to see her brother."

"Albert, we will push the operator again for the Surabaya connection. If that is successful and you don't need to visit him or if he can't get leave to come here then, why not just return via Singapore? Chances are that you will have considerably less difficulty arranging seating from there."

Albert didn't respond.

The offended secretary returned and suggested that Hart attempt to speak to the operator himself as often a foreign voice would be enough to swing their attention and assistance in the caller's favour. He agreed. It was a good idea and he understood the reasoning. Many of the operators were looking for better paying positions with the foreign companies as most were reasonably fluent in the English language.

Hart settled beside the lounge room extension and commenced dialling. The lines to Surabaya were very busy the operator had complained, but should the *tuan* care to hold maybe she could connect as the opportunity arose. Hart had agreed, struggling to find the correct words to facilitate the conversation from his limited vocabulary, as he had the misfortune to strike one of the non-English speaking operators.

The minutes dragged on and suddenly Hart motioned Albert urgently to come to the phone.

"Contact!" he announced excitedly. "I'll call Wanti while you keep him on the line." he instructed, moving quickly to the rear of the building to alert the servants to call their *njonja* to the phone.

Wanti appeared within what seemed to be seconds, flushed with the news that they finally had Bambang on the phone. She took the receiver from Albert who also was smiling, for Wanti was obviously in high spirits. He stood beside the other man and together they watched the attractive woman as she spoke.

Hart noticed a look of concern begin to grow on Albert's face as Wanti continued to speak to the Surabaya party. Suddenly the call was finished and she replaced the receiver. Surprised, Hart looked questioningly at the two as Albert stepped forward towards the young woman. They spoke quickly and the Australian was unable to understand all that they said.

"What is it, Albert, is everything okay?" he asked.

"Maybe," he replied, "maybe."

"Wanti?" Hart questioned.

As she spoke he noticed that Albert had moved up alongside her and had taken her hand. He did not interpret the gesture for anything but for what it was, the hand of comfort for a friend in distress.

"My brother is not available as he was sent along with his division to Timor. They have no further news as all communication with Kupang must be requested through HANKAM in Jakarta."

"I am sure he will be all right, Wanti."

Hart thought quickly. Who could he call in HANKAM in Stephen's absence to assist with an inquiry?

"Look. Stephen will probably return today or, at the latest, tomorrow. I appreciate that it's difficult but if you try not to anticipate the worst and just believe that your brother is okay, then your husband will be able to use his contacts in HANKAM to reach Bambang," Hart suggested. "Stephen has many senior contacts within the military and I'm sure he could put your mind at ease as soon as he returns."

Albert continued quietly squeezing her hand reassuringly.

Wanti examined their faces as if attempting to determine the substance of what they proposed. She nodded her head slowly in acceptance. She closed her eyes and lifted her chin slightly.

"*Oh Allah!*" she whispered softly, praying for her brother's safety, "*Please watch over my Bambang!*"

Albert escorted her back to her room and instructed the houseboy to have one of the female servants stay with her.

Hart watched them leave the room. The company had the capacity to provide for its own but at this moment was powerless to do what was necessary without Stephen's presence. He knew that had Coleman been there his wife's fears could so easily be put to rest with just a few calls through his confidential military conduits. He didn't even know how to contact the man! Other than leaving messages with Coleman's private secretary should he phone, there was never any other avenue of communicating with him when he disappeared on these mysterious trips. Considering Stephen's strong contacts in the Indonesian defence establishment even these were useless without him being present to make the necessary personal calls.

Where in the hell was he?

* * * * * *

Coleman sat across the table from the General. It was difficult for him to maintain the required level of conversation as Anderson's revelations continued to remain foremost in his mind, clouding his thinking.

He let his thoughts drift watching the ferries on the other side of the harbour prepare for departure. The Kowloon side appeared busier than usual. The mid channel chop had already grown, sending spray up over the bow and back down the sides of passing vessels as they made their way through the congested sea lanes.

Seda was dressed casually in comfortable slacks and a long-sleeve beige coloured shirt, the neck open down to the third button. He sat cross-legged, holding his left ankle with both hands as he continued his discourse, only occasionally moving his right hand through the air when emphasizing a point, speaking with authority as a lecturer would to an assembly of students.

Coleman sat there and listened to the man drone on describing events as he claimed to understand them and offering his opinions as to how these evolved. He attempted to appear his old relaxed self, knowing that the man sitting in front of him was blatantly lying to him, again. And with the ease and skill of a practiced master.

Anderson had provided the most incredible insight into the powerful man he'd known all these years. Only now, Stephen realized, he hadn't really known him at all.

He continued to listen to Seda's monologue wishing he'd not come to the meeting. He should have taken more time to prepare himself. It was as if he was now swimming in one of those gas riddled oceans he'd read about when the undersea deposits suddenly aerate the surrounding waters, reducing the ocean to a wet bubble in which everything sinks and everybody drowns.

Anderson had said that the man sitting in front of him was personally responsible for the military information leaks made to the Australian media and the constant supply of military hardware to the separatists and other guerrilla groups. He had said that, without Nathan Seda, there would be no resistance of any substance within the former colony and the lives of tens of thousands of ignorant villagers would not have been wasted supporting his dreams of an independent state.

Coleman immediately scoffed. The accusations were outrageous!

"But why would he do something that stupidly dangerous?" he'd asked.

"Because he's ambitious. Because he is greedy. And because he is dangerous!" had been the reply.

"What would he stand to gain?" Coleman had probed.

"For God's sake, Stephen! Didn't we teach you anything?"

"Again," he'd insisted, "tell me again!"

"If you still have the capacity to be objective now is the time to do so. Ask yourself the question, why? The answers are clear. Wake up, man, listen to your brain and not the sound of the endless stream of dollars hitting those hidden bank accounts!"

Stephen remembered how he'd felt when that particular comment had been thrown in to shake him just that little bit more. They had really done their homework, he decided.

"Let's cut to it, John. Just explain to me. Why?"

"It's not simple. People like Seda rarely embark on anything that is so bloody complicated to start with that even they lose sight of the initial objectives as their scheming continues. Seda has followed his course with total devotion. It has taken him years of patience and dedication to achieve what he has, and right under our noses. And yours."

"You would know only too well, Stephen, just how much power he has acquired from the proceeds generated by the military contracts the two of you have enjoyed, awarded to your company year after year with his backing, the staggering amounts of commissions remaining offshore to fund his covert activities. In your case, your greed and ego sent you on a property hunt and the quest for the good life of the high-flyers. You were, sorry are, successful but nowhere near as competent as Seda. For the General, every penny he squirreled away was directed towards achieving his ultimate goal. Rebellion. Rebellion in East Timor and, hopefully, an amalgamation of both Timors under one flag. And quite possibly, one leader."

"From your tone it sounds as if you're actually proud of him," Coleman accused.

The older man had smiled as he responded. "Admire, Stephen, admire. When you consider that when he inherited the mantle from Sudomo the Indonesian Intelligence Services were practically a joke by our standards. Within just a few years he built an enormous network of agents and information sources even we would be pleased to have access to, today."

"Remember, Stephen," he had continued, now enjoying his description of the Timorese's dark activities, "He had to develop a secure Intelligence section while consolidating his own position within the country's powerful hierarchy. It wasn't easy, being outside the Javanese clique and all that, but he did it."

Coleman was surprised at Anderson's obvious admiration for the subject of their meeting.

"When the Apodeti first became a political force in East Timor very few knew that it was, in fact, an operational arm of the Indonesian military, under the direct control of BAKIN. We all know who controls that august body, don't we?" Anderson continued, rhetorically.

"This provided the man with a direct source of information from the colony. As the Senior Intelligence Director he also had the authority to censor information, question its reliability, control its entire flow in the dissemination process to other ABRI arms and, in short, become its puppeteer."

"What makes him such an outstanding and manipulative bugger is the fact that while he was providing his own Armed Forces with information gleaned from the *Operasi Komodo*, *Apodeti* and other sources, he also briefed the FRETILIN providing them with a continuous flow of intelligence of such import they were able to ensconce themselves extremely quickly as a power base within the disputed territory."

"Then, of course, we come to the arms shipments to which you were a party. I am still not convinced that you are so naive, Stephen, that you failed to identify what was really happening but elected to go along because of the enormous amount of wealth it was producing for you. For the time being let's just say that you have the benefit of the doubt and we'll reserve judgment until later."

Anderson went in harder. "You have compromised almost every ideal I believed you had. You are responsible for permitting the flow of not only substantial shipments of arms to what is potentially an enemy of the Commonwealth of Australia and its allies, but also you should consider the number of dead and wounded who represent the harvest of those weapons."

Stephen had sat quietly. Numbed by the revelations being made to him. If, in fact, what Anderson had said could be substantiated then he recognized that the ramifications of his involvement with the shipments would, undoubtedly, result in hostile action being taken against him. And at any time.

Stephen's first reactions had been to immediately discount everything that the Australian Intelligence Chief had said. Not only did it border on the absurd and ridiculous but it offended his own intellect. Anderson was expecting him to accept whatever he was told, he thought, without question, as the Director was not accustomed to having others challenge the authenticity of his statements. And his lies!

When Stephen had scoffed at the suggestions, Anderson had produced irrefutable evidence of the General's role in providing the journalists with sensitive military information, copies of communications between BAKIN and East Timor agents (Coleman didn't need to guess how he'd obtained those!) and copies also of bills-of-lading which he knew were related to consignments that he himself had arranged through Hong Kong. Only the annotated destinations were questionable. Stephen knew that the latter could have been falsified by anyone but, somehow, he just sensed that there was more to the documents than what could be assumed from a casual glance.

It was still difficult to accept. Tens of thousands of Indonesians and Timorese now lay dead, their corpses rotting in the fields of Timor partly as a result of his ignorance and, as they sat calmly discussing his position in terms of his own involvement, Coleman realized, for the first time, just how dangerous both Anderson and Seda had become to his own well being. And to each other.

It was complicated. Had the Australians accepted the military information and permitted its deliberate release? In so doing they would have not only condoned the slaughter of the Indonesians but actually assisted in the execution of the General's plan purely for his substantial monetary gain! Did Anderson and others in similar positions of power set a trap for the General in order to hook him for the future, just keeping him on line until they could see which way events would develop?

Or was it the other way around? Had Seda deliberately provided the separatist forces in Timor the opportunity as Anderson had suggested in order to orchestrate his own rise to power in the former colony?

Why hadn't the Australians gone to the Indonesians with this information and immediately ingratiated themselves by exposing the General?

God! he thought, rubbing his throbbing temples to ease a splitting ache, it was either all a load or crap or really was down in the hole so fucking deep they would need a crane to drag him out of the shit he was in!

"Where do we go from here then?" his voice betrayed fatigue.

"That's up to you now Stephen."

The brief and enigmatic answer didn't help. He wanted to stand up and shout at the man in front of him, the other jet-lagged passengers, Seda, the world, everyone, for being unfair, for trying to destroy him and undo everything he'd built.

At that moment he hated Anderson more than even he thought possible. The man had enjoyed bringing him the news. And the ultimatum. Ah, yes, he remembered. The ultimatum.

And, as he now sat in the room with the man who had created this incredible quagmire of international intrigue involving gunrunning, terrorism and subversive support for revolution against his own country, he knew that he would never survive to enjoy the fruits of his involvement in these activities should the General became aware of his partner's recently acquired knowledge as to the real purpose of the company's operations.

On the other hand his former intelligence associates could just as easily place his name on the *'unfriendlies list'* and it would only be a matter of time before he, too, would need to go into hiding or cooperate with them.

He turned his head slightly, looking at the General.

How did you manage to source all of that additional equipment? he wondered. Who has been assisting this man with the enormous amount of detail required to transfer shipments, re-box the supplies, change documentation and maintain the liaison necessary for such covert activities?'

The task was so unbelievably enormous Stephen had considerable difficulty in accepting that the information was indeed accurate.

He continued to rerun the details through his mind. It was clear that Anderson, and therefore others, had information — no, he corrected, proof — of his relationship with the General and their activities relating to the supply of weapons to the Indonesian Armed Forces. So far, he had not committed any offence except, perhaps, from the social aspects of being an arms supplier.

That Seda was responsible for the diversion of these shipments to the separatist forces in Timor played heavily on his mind. The accusations of Seda's involvement in the deliberate release of classified information relating to his own defence forces' troop movements had him baffled. Why would they fabricate such a story if it was not their intention to expose his activities, sending him into immediate disgrace and, most likely, prison?

Anderson had revealed what the intelligence services had discovered regarding Nathan Seda's true allegiances, or so they said. The chances were, he thought, that they had it all arse up again, as they had often misread what was happening in the past. And this might just be a simple case of the Intelligence Agencies screwing up again. Or overreacting.

Maybe Seda believed that the information leaks would make it appear as if the FRETILIN forces had the upper hand in the war? This would justify the Indonesian invasion and a more concentrated involvement by the Indonesian Military. If that had been his motive then, according to the latest casualty statistics, his strategy was successful.

Coleman had questioned the Australian Government's motives in permitting the broadcasts. The Intelligence Chief had smiled thinly and slowly outlined the government's political position. Australia was faced with the possibility of the creation of a hostile nation sitting on its doorstep. The Americans and Australians anticipated the probability of United Nations support for the fledgling nation which would permit Communist forces to gain control. There was no doubt that the United Nations would also condemn the Indonesian invasion.

The Americans and Australians believed that the Indonesian annexation was, in fact, the more acceptable solution but could not openly support the expansionist move. Should the FRETILIN forces win several decisive battles against the superior number of Indonesian troops then there was a distinct possibility that they would be carried away with their successes and reverse the role in Timor by crossing into the Indonesian territory threatening regional security.

As satellite intelligence proved beyond doubt that FRETILIN had support of the Eastern Bloc and there was proof of Cuban involvement then, it was suggested, Indonesia should have the right to defend itself from the aggressor. Under these circumstances, Australia could play an immediate role, the Americans could recommence military support and, more importantly, the Indonesians could legitimately claim the necessity to re-invade the former colony to secure its own borders. International support would follow.

The FRETILIN movement would be crushed and the threat of medium range missiles threatening Australia's security would disappear. And more importantly, the Americans would maintain their use of the Ombai-Wetar Straits.

"What the hell do they have to do with all of this?" he'd asked.

"You've been out of the mainstream of intelligence flow for some years and would have no current idea of what really is happening in the real world Stephen," Anderson had replied, not insultingly, "but basically the Yanks desperately need to maintain their use of the straits. This is why the American navy had insisted that the Pentagon concoct some red herring to distract others from the identifying their operational use of the waters there.

The Pentagon had used the threat of the newly occupied and former South Vietnam in relation to its potential capacity to assist the Soviets expand their sphere of influence in the immediate region. The red herring was the threat of Russian built IL-28s which they'd given to the Communist Vietnamese well before the fall of Saigon but had eventually found their way down to the south and within striking distance of the gas deposits off Natuna Island.

The story worked because the oil-hungry cartels soon used their powerful lobby to ensure that not just Natuna but all future and existing concessions under production sharing contracts within Indonesia would enjoy the protection of American military equipment. This would give Australia a de facto first line of defence without the crippling cost of supporting such a strategy.

East Timor's real significance to America's global strategy lies to the north of the island in the Ombai-Wetar Straits, which are exceptionally deep and through which nuclear submarines can travel undetected in their passage from the Pacific to the Indian Ocean. These straits remain crucial to the United States Navy as should this route be denied to them as the result of Timor's becoming Communist or fall under the expanding influence of the Soviets, the cost in terms of strategic positioning would be disastrous. An additional eight days steaming would be required for a concealed submarine journey between the two oceans via the alternative Lombok or Sunda Straits.

"Now perhaps you will understand their reluctance to accept any Marxist authority over the former colony as the American administration requires an acceptable conclusion to the hostilities in East Timor to protect their own strategic interests."

The concept was Machiavellian and Coleman understood how it would appeal to the politicians and military chiefs. He wondered just how many more Indonesians would die in the poverty stricken island before a halt would be called to the senseless killing.

Seda was still talking. Coleman listened, occasionally murmuring a response. The meeting concluded.

"*I will be returning directly to Jakarta, Stephen. Is there anything else you wish to go over now while we have the opportunity?*" the General had asked.

"*No. I don't believe so, Pak. Not at this time,*" he replied, while thinking, '*and perhaps not later, either.*'

"*Have you been to the bank yet?*" he asked, grinning at the suggestion. He knew that Stephen always went to the bank to check his deposits as soon as soon as he arrived in Hong Kong.

Umar had told him.

"*Yes,*" he answered, "*all is in order there.*" He remembered that he had already decided to change most of his accounts quickly due to the potential change in circumstances. He'd do it first thing tomorrow, he thought.

But not before sitting down and working out his future and evaluating the damage that was imminent to his company operations. Stephen needed time to get his head straight. He decided to slip across on the ferry to Macau. So much was suddenly happening in his life he needed to release some of the pressure and consider his options. Obviously, his future with the General looked nebulous and, for the first time since meeting with Anderson on the flight, Stephen Coleman was concerned for his life. Once he'd returned to his own room in the hotel Stephen phoned Mister Lim and asked if Angelique was available.

He needed to clear his mind. And think.

* * * * * *

Greg Hart was not impressed with the call from Stephen. He had been awakened at some ungodly hour and Coleman, true to his past behaviour, had imparted little information and yet had managed to issue instructions ranging across his own personal spectrum from financial matters to reminding his assistant to send his personal secretary's birthday gift. Everything, in fact, except how to resolve his wife's dilemma.

During the early morning telephone conversation Hart had raised the problem. Wanti's brother was part of the contingent that had been sent to Timor and she was desperate to contact him. Latest reports relating to the invasion were not looking good and she looked very worried, he'd told Coleman.

"She needs to speak to him, Stephen," he'd said, still groggy from the two hours sleep. "Why don't you give me some numbers and I'll phone HANKAM early in the morning. You know they'll bend over backwards when I tell them it's for you."

Coleman had been sharp and uncharacteristically blunt. "Do nothing until I return," he ordered.

"But Stephen, I know this may be a little out of my jurisdiction but your wife is frantic. Couldn't you make a few calls from wherever you are and then let her know?"

"Butt out, Greg!" Coleman snapped. "I'll do what is necessary, just leave it alone. Okay?"

"Okay," Hart acquiesced. He thought Coleman sounded a little drunk.

"Fine. I will be back in a day or so. Just hold the fort."

Hart had replaced the receiver and cursed the caller for his attitude. He lay in bed thinking about the problem and his own complicated life, and how he was neither one nor the other, referring to his current employment and his other masters. They would leave him alone for months on end and then, suddenly, out of the blue they would contact him with what were mostly menial tasks. He'd been debriefed several times regarding the company operations and had passed whatever information he managed to access from the records but this was not what they were looking for, he could tell, from their bored expressions each time he'd made his report.

Coleman played his game close to the chest, Hart knew. It was impossible to follow his trail as the overseas trips severed all connection to his movements and dealings, making Hart's task irritatingly counter productive, as he dedicated so much of his time endeavouring to resolve the enigma surrounding these trips, without any real results.

Several more hours passed. He looked at the bedside clock. It was almost five o'clock. Unable to sleep he showered and decided to take Albert and Wanti out for a Dim Sum breakfast at the Blue Ocean which operated as a non stop cabaret night club and restaurant, catering to the players who lived for the late nights, often carrying on until the sun demanded that others attend their offices while this small section of the community disobeyed the clock.

The steamed breakfasts were renowned for their flavour, the dishes carried on small trays by waiters from table to table as the round bamboo baskets containing the delicacies were snatched off the trays by the hungry guests.

Hart had to steer himself from his house to Jalan Cik Ditiro where Wanti and Albert stayed as his own driver wasn't due to start work for another hour. He arrived at the premises still too early to awaken anyone. The security personnel recognized Hart and opened the outside security gate permitting the car to enter before locking the sliding steel barrier again from behind.

He entered the office through the servants' access and went about checking the main office for incoming telex communications. There was one for Stephen to contact a supplier in Germany and several other mundane messages providing lists of available military equipment in France. And one incongruous request which surprised and baffled Hart.

The three lined message was so short and innocuous in content that, at first, Hart had missed the message completely as the telex pages had run together, causing the type to slip.

He reread the text. In spite of the hour he lifted the telephone receiver and dialled the number designated in the return confirmation advice. The number rang for several minutes before a tired and irritable voice barked into the instrument. Startled, Hart replaced the phone immediately. Then he reread the message for a third time.

Why, he thought, would Stephen Coleman be receiving communications from them? Hart stared at the page. He was not to know that the message in his hands should, in fact, have been sent to the direct number on the machine still locked upstairs in the private rooms.

There was no doubt that it was addressed to Coleman. The question was, what was Stephen Coleman doing arranging meetings with the *Badan Koordinasi Intelijen Indonesia*, Indonesia's Central Intelligence Agency?

He decided to forgo the breakfast and instead, placing the telex in his wallet, Hart left the office advising the houseboy that he would return later in the morning.

The old servant mumbled and went about his mundane chores. The *tuans* would come and go as they pleased. He didn't mind. He never pried into other's affairs. Life was difficult enough without the burden of responsibility which often came with the knowledge of someone else's problems.

* * * * * *

Far away, or at least what Sukardi, the ageing houseboy, might have considered to be far away, casualty lists were on the wire and being registered in the Ministry of Defence's Jalan Merdeka offices as the names spewed forth from the archaic communications machine. Seventh on the list on the first page of KIA's was the name, rank and serial number of the young Javanese Acting Captain who, in what was another lifetime, once laughed and played with a little girl in the distant village of Kampung Semawi. A little girl who had grown up to finally escape the horrors of their past and who now slept quietly in the bedroom above Coleman's office.

A simple and unassuming servant, unaware of the enormity of events unfolding around him, Sukardi cleaned and prepared Stephen's household for the coming day.

As there was no address registered on file for the dead Captain's next-of-kin, details as to his demise were passed to his regimental headquarters in Surabaya. There the information remained until later in the day when, having read the lists posted on the information board for all to read, the officer of the day who had spoken to the dead Captain's sister just a few days before, remembered that she was in Jakarta. He returned to his office and went in search of the telephone number he'd noted when Wanti had called.

Coleman's personal secretary had received the call and informed Hart. She also asked to speak privately with Albert, who accepted the news calmly, thanking the embarrassed worker for her consideration in passing the unfortunate news to him rather than directly to the dead officer's sister.

He discussed Wanti's condition with Hart. They agreed to call a doctor to sedate her, if possible before breaking the news, considering her previous reactions to shock. Albert agreed and Hart sent the secretary out to request assistance from one of the consulting doctors in the Cikini hospital.

An hour later she returned with the doctor who, by that time, had been briefed as to Wanti's condition, her previous attacks and the long periods of convalescence required as a result of her trauma suffered during the anti-Japanese riots. Albert had asked Wanti to go upstairs to her room as he wished to speak privately with her. Sensing that something was wrong, Wanti searched Albert's eyes for some indication of what was worrying him.

When the doctor entered the bedroom she knew immediately that Bambang was dead. She had sensed it the moment she had heard that he had gone to Timor to fight.

"*No, Tuhan, no!*" Wanti called, struggling as she resisted the needle being inserted into her arm. As she froze, her features contorted with shock, the grotesque ugliness of her expression reflected the trauma her brain endured while fighting to cope with the realization of her brother's death.

The doctor immediately administered a second sedative but the shock was too severe. There was nothing they could do for her. Her body remained locked in a catatonic seizure. Her reaction to the news of Bambang's death had blasted her away.

Throughout the night, Albert sat holding her hand, crying softly until tears ceased to flow. He talked to her, sang soft chants which suddenly, blessedly, returned to him for the first time since his childhood as he stroked her arms and offered God his own life in exchange for hers. He rocked gently backwards and forwards humming a distant melody which had haunted his soul from a time he could barely remember, a time when a warm and loving father had taken him by the hand down to the fishing village and held him close and kept him safe.

He spoke to Wanti as she lay there, telling her of the warmth of the sun, the cool winds of the early evening and the soft sweet fragrances of the flowers in the mountains. He kissed her cheeks and, as he did so, his tears fell onto her face as evidence of his love for the beautiful woman whose heart and mind had been taken by some unseen spirit and dashed against the walls of despair.

Wanti breathed slowly, peacefully, unaware of the words being softly whispered as her brain had now severed all links with the real world. Albert Seda stroked her hair, her hand and gently touched the soft colourless cheeks, refusing to acknowledge the distorted features that stared straight back up at him. The servants attempted to have him leave her side, to rest, but he ignored their efforts.

Now, for the first time, they understood. Albert refused to leave her. He had to stay with Wanti, she needed him now, more than ever.

Throughout the following day he remained by her side. He could see from the cruel and twisted ugliness that the muscle spasms had produced where before there had been a beautiful smile, that she was lost. There would be little hope, he knew, that she would recover. As she lay calmly Albert decided that he had no choice but to return immediately to Australia. Arrangements had been made. Hart had helped.

The following day Coleman unexpectedly returned, surprised at the cool reception he received upon arrival at his home.

Hart, angered by the events of the previous day, marched unannounced into his Coleman's office and slammed a letter down in front of the surprised man. "That's my resignation, you bastard!"

Staggered by the vitriolic attack, Stephen looked up at the man and, stunned by the outburst, merely said, "What the hell? A simple good morning or hello would have been sufficient!"

"What you did is unforgivable, Coleman," he started, using Stephen's surname to emphasize his contempt, "and the whole bloody community will know about it if I have my way. You're a fucking arsehole!"

"Greg, wh.? " he started.

"All you had to do was phone your own bloody wife once and maybe you could have prevented all of this!" he yelled unreasonably, half believing his own outburst, knowing also that he'd been given the perfect excuse to pull out, as instructed and withdraw from the company's activities before it sucked him down also into the incredible mess only his superiors understood.

He slammed the desk with his hand confirming to all who had heard the outburst within the office that the *tuans* were deep in argument.

The embarrassed staff lowered their heads quickly, suddenly engrossed in whatever they were doing when the argument had broken out between the two. They had no training in how to handle these predicaments and, identifying the delicacy of the situation, the secretary put her finger to her lips and gestured with her other hand for them to depart silently, as it was already close to the end of office hours anyway.

"Hold it!" Coleman yelled. "What the hell are you talking about?"

"Jesus, mate, you're good!"

"Again, Greg, what the hell are you carrying on about?"

"You know bloody goddamn well what I'm talking about!"

"What?" Coleman yelled, so loud that the servants heard the demand right through the office and through to their quarters. "Tell me for Chrissakes, man, fucking what?"

"Your wife, damn it man, your wife!"

Suddenly Stephen realized that he had no idea what was going on even in his own home.

Ignoring Hart, he ran quickly through the building and up the steps to his room, now for the first time, occupied by Wanti.

There he found Albert, sitting alongside the woman whom he knew was his wife, but now wore the mask of a stranger.

"What happened?" he demanded, shocked to see her condition.

Albert rose and escorted Stephen from the room.

"*Bambang's dead, Mas!*" and immediately Stephen understood.

He stood silently with the other man not knowing what to do. He had no power of healing and knew, more than everyone else, just how much pain this man would now have to suffer as Wanti lay in her own world, protected by some intricate trigger mechanism inside her head, distancing her from reality and the pain of living.

The following day Albert asked his permission to take her home. Sadly, Stephen agreed. He asked his staff to make the arrangements and seats were booked for the following day. It seemed that everyone in Jakarta suddenly knew of her demise. And was sympathetic to her condition. The two men only spoke when necessary and it was clear to Stephen that he was to carry the blame for the tragic events surrounding his wife's collapse. The subject of the divorce was not raised again.

* * * * * *

On the day of Albert and Wanti's departure Hart left the company. Stephen didn't really mind. But then again, Stephen didn't know that Hart had been instructed to do so as the company appeared to be heading for a confrontation with the military and his other masters wanted him well out of the way when this happened.

Stephen couldn't understand why he was being blamed for Wanti's condition. Bambang's death certainly had nothing whatsoever to do with him. He knew that even had he called at the time there was no guarantee that this could have resulted in the soldier not being killed. Hart never did advise Stephen of the telex.

Suddenly everything started to change drastically for Coleman. His world was turning inside-out and he did not know what he could do to prevent or correct what was happening to him. Of one thing he was certain. Timor was a much greater problem for him than Anderson had suggested. He could lose everything. Even his life! He still wondered why the Australians had not just exposed the General.

There had to be another agenda. One in which he was to play a role without knowing who all the other participants were to be. A dangerous game no doubt, he guessed, considering he was now sitting squeezed between two highly skilled professionals, neither of whom would have any compunction in ordering his permanent removal should they deem such action necessary to their respective causes.

The General had access to considerable funds and no doubt had successfully compromised more than one of his peers throughout his years climbing to the powerful position he now held. Stephen remembered the veiled threat made when they first embarked on their journey together, forming the alliance which had built an empire for each of them. An empire that would soon come crashing down if he did not now proceed with extreme caution with every move he made.

Maybe a few months away in Europe or Canada would be a wise decision at this time, he thought.

He needed time to rearrange his activities but he knew that time was running out and there was a distinct possibility that he would be unable to extricate himself from the mess in which he was slowly drowning, and had been for some considerable time, without even being aware of it.

He considered what the outcome would be should the General and FRETILIN react as predicted and retaliate, crossing over into the Indonesian half of Timor, creating the opportunity everyone appeared to support. This would be most unlikely, Stephen decided, as it would result in yet a further invasion of such a scale that all separatist forces would be totally destroyed once and for all! Alternatively, should Seda successfully secure an independent state for FRETILIN, did he see himself as the country's first leader? Its first President? And would the Indonesians sanction a man who had betrayed them to sit as the head of state in the neighbouring country? Coleman thought this through. Actually, knowing the General as well as he did, he knew it was unlikely that he would permit Cubans or any other alien group to control his military if he were to gain power. Should this be the case then it would surely follow that Timor could, in fact, become a reasonable, albeit poor, democracy in its own right. And Coleman would benefit from the relationship.

It dawned on him that such a scenario would also benefit the Australians and perhaps the other and smaller neighbouring states who were edgy about the powerful Moslem country dictating regional foreign policies. The Americans would rest easy knowing that their nuclear submarines could pass unhindered by the Soviets.

Was this is the strategy Anderson wanted to see in place?

Stephen concluded that this made a whole lot more sense than the other possibilities and would explain why ASIS had not exposed the General and perhaps even why they had moved back into his life to manipulate events even more from the sidelines.

He decided he should just wait for a few more weeks to see how it all developed. After all, according to the press, the fighting could continue for some time and that could only be good for their business. He would stay around for a few more weeks and monitor his relationship with Seda. Should the signs be positive he would maintain the status quo and work his way through the problems.

Feeling once again in reasonable control of the situation he decided to delay acting on Anderson's demands until he'd had enough time to further review the complicated mess. Coleman concluded that, short of nuclear weapons being introduced into the conflict, little else could change the current position of the warring parties. High casualty figures would mean support for Indonesia's invasion would deteriorate both domestically and internationally.

General Nathan Seda appeared to be heading towards the successful realization of his dream. An independent Timor.

Or, at least, an independent East Timor!

THE TIMOR MAN

Chapter 17

Jakarta — Timor-Timur

Seda arrived early for this vital meeting. He noticed that the priority files he had ordered to be circulated to the heads of each contributing department in preparation for this discussion were in place. They were set out ready for the head of OPSUS at his place opposite Seda. There were seven seats prepared, he counted, all with the customary blotting pads nobody ever used as they only carried ballpens. He made a mental note. No more blotting pads.

Only three of the powerful generals had arrived as Seda entered the well-guarded room. Military police armed with carbines stood watch at the door. He knew that they wouldn't be enough should someone really want to get in and blow them all away. Window dressing. Just window dressing, he thought.

The session had been called by the army's Chief of Staff. He was angry. His men were being annihilated and he found this to be personally humiliating. He was looking for a scapegoat and expected to have one.

Seda was ready. The meeting commenced, not with all present sitting down and formally being addressed as one would expect of such powerful men called to discuss the nation's security, but more on an unhurried and familiar basis, and one with which they were more accustomed. As the generals waddled into the chamber and casually took their chairs while already discussing the sensitive problems with each other Seda noticed that the Airforce Chief of Staff had moved his position up next to the Lieutenant General. He was surprised.

"*Ready, gentlemen?*" the army Chief commenced, not really caring whether they were or not. He did not enjoy having to brief the other services and particularly disliked the intelligence heads being

417

present. They always kept something back, in reserve for themselves, he believed.

"*The President has asked me to consider withdrawing our forces from Tim-Tim*," he started, observing the startled faces of the most powerful men in the country outside the presidential household. "*Bapak has been emphatic in his request that as he did not wish to have the invasion bring the new Five Year Development Program's overseas funding into contention then, as international opinion seems to be shifting, he has directed me, us, to consider the ramifications of a withdrawal from the province.*"

Seda listened, transfixed on the tubby little General's mouth, not believing what he was hearing. A withdrawal!

Immediately there were cries of *tidak! tidak! no!* from the other generals, as that was what was expected of them. In reality most didn't care too much one way or another as none had been successful in enjoying any financial gain to date, from the buildup and then the invasion, causing considerable discussion and concern with their Chinese financiers.

All those present were aware that the President really wanted to have East Timor annexed and over with as quickly as possible while his team of civilian technocrats wooed the World Bank and International Monetary Fund in their ongoing attempts to source the much needed capital required to meet the development programs already in place.

It was an incredible juggling act and a new exercise in international diplomacy. They knew, of course, that the Americans would support them due to the fall of Saigon the year before, and the presence of Leftist guerrillas always generated sufficient congressional support when lobbying for additional military hardware. Only now they had failed to produce any real results, placing the President in a difficult and indecisive mood. He needed time to consider all his options. There were none present who would object, since the President enjoyed the popular support of the people and of rank and file members of the infant political parties.

The President wanted the military to go in quickly, fix the problem and then hold the annexed country until such time as the United States gave them the nod to hold yet another plebiscite, such as they had carried out in 1969 in West New Guinea.

But for some reason, this time it wasn't as easy as they had expected. The Indonesians could not understand why the Americans were really so interested given that they already held the majority of the oil and gas concessions and even they knew that Vietnam was no real threat to their northern islands. There just had to be something else. And then there was these Australians who always seemed to run hot and cold. Their own Prime Minister made the effort to visit informally with the Soeharto in Central Java, even spending quiet time together in the mystical cave while they discussed the Timor issue. The Australian Head of State had emphatically given his country's undertaking to support a united Timor, even suggesting that it should be under Indonesian control. Then, suddenly, while their troops were preparing to cross the border *en masse*, the man was replaced by his opponent! It was really very difficult to understand how these Western nations managed to survive with no frequent leadership changes, they all agreed.

The threat of an independent hostile state strategically positioned such as Timor remained a major issue throughout the region. The Indonesians sensed that they had international support but didn't know how to go about securing it publicly.

"*Pak General*," Seda said, as all eyes concentrated on the Timorese. Apart from the Sumatran, all of the others were Javanese. "*Pak General, I believe that we can win this action quickly now that we have the new American Bronco aircraft arriving next month. These machines were designed specifically for counter insurgency attacks and I am convinced,*" he said, emphasizing the point and looking directly at the Airforce Chief, "*that once these aircraft and their support teams have been deployed then resistance will diminish dramatically!*"

"*That still won't finish the problem on the ground, General.*" The Admiral felt he had to offer an opinion as only too often the Navy was left out of these discussions. Hadn't his ships already proven themselves in the first instance by bombarding the target areas in preparation for the assaults?

He watched the others. The Navy had done poorly with recent budgetary considerations and knew that he must guard against the army and airforce gobbling up all of the funds. After all, without any supply or maintenance contracts, how would he live?

The Army Chief of Staff looked smugly towards the Admiral, thinking *What would he know?*

The piggy-faced man had the education of a peasant farmer and only enjoyed his position because almost all of his superiors had either died of old age or had disappeared due to their involvement in the communist push to take over the country. The Army General ignored the statement.

The discussion continued for no more than fifteen minutes and, as it was approaching the mid-morning prayer period which the majority of them would often use as an excuse to leave whatever meeting they may be uncomfortably locked into, the Army Chief procrastinated no further.

"I believe what the President is looking for is a firm commitment from us that we will finish the job quickly and without any further embarrassment." He looked around the table knowing that, whatever he said, they would agree. It was called consensus. He knew that.

"I agree with you Pak," the OPSUS General said, quite loudly.

"So do I," called another. Then another, until each and every member in the room had confirmed what he had known all along, that they would react like sheep.

The four-star General observed them all. Placing his arms on the table as he clenched his fists together, he played the role of the second most powerful man in the country.

"This will not be like before. The Bapak has insisted that we use all of our numbers and weaponry. Should we disgrace the country it would be unlikely that the President would be at all forgiving. We must not fail!" And, as he let the words hang threateningly in the air, the General rose leaving his file for others to collect and left before any further discussion could take place.

The Intelligence Chief stayed long enough to be seen to be a cohesive part of what had just occurred in the briefing, then left with the others, ensuring that none of the sensitive files had been left for the inquisitive and talkative clerks or aides to read.

Seda considered the commitment he'd made. The Bronco aircraft would be ready providing they could take delivery before too much more pressure was placed on the Armed Forces Standing Committee in Washington to cancel the dead. He now wanted the Indonesian Airforce to have the sophisticated aircraft as it would make the FRETILIN resistance that much more admirable in the eyes of the world, knowing that the simple people of such a small island fought bravely against such tremendous odds. Their resources were extremely limited against the American-manufactured weaponry. Seda was excited when the army suppliers had offered the new ground-to-air missiles suitable for individual soldiers to carry. The problem was that the product was American and difficult to source but he knew he had to have these deadly weapons for his separist fighters.

Also, he knew, delivery and repositioning were entirely different considerations. He estimated that it would require at least six more months before the AURI pilots were able to demonstrate the incredible capacity of the aerial killing machines soon to be placed in their hands.

The Rockwell Broncos were a mass-produced aircraft which the Americans had tested for some years and used successfully in their marine forces. It was a superb lightly armed reconnaissance airplane designed specifically for counter-insurgency missions and suited the Indonesian Airforce's requirements perfectly in targeting the FRETILIN forces. With the additional modifications these sixteen aircraft would undergo, they could be utilized at night for forward air control and strike designation purposes.

Seda had also orchestrated to have the manufacturers add further modifications at tremendous expense to AURI. These would permit the aircraft's stabilized night periscopic sights, which were coupled with a laser rangefinder and target illuminator, to act in tandem with another Bronco permitting direct attack or illumination of a target. He also believed it would be too sophisticated for the pilots' missions in Timor. And even if they did finally master the aircraft successfully over Timor's rugged terrain they would always be given sufficient advance warning of flight missions. With a little luck the ground forces would be given the opportunity to destroy two aircraft with just one missile.

Seda knew that there would be a price to pay. He also knew that had not his *kongsi* with Stephen become directly involved in the aircraft sales then others would have, costing their company millions of dollars in lost commissions and influence over sourcing the country's armaments acquisition program. Seda was pragmatic enough to accept that Indonesia would purchase these aircraft from someone as being inevitable and, why not ensure that he personally benefited financially from the squadron acquisition? At least he could continue to monitor what was really taking place offshore whenever deals were being struck with the suppliers and manufacturers' agents. He would often arrange for senior officers in the other services to be invited overseas where they would receive substantial remuneration for their support in recommending the equipment Stephen's company represented.

Seda thought about the numerous trips made by some of those present at the morning's meeting. It had really been so simple as they had been so greedy. Agent's commissions on aircraft sales rarely ran over five per cent of the purchase price. The real money lay in the spare parts which were loaded by over thirty and up to forty percent of the contract value and would apply to all ongoing spare parts purchases made by the client which, in this case, was the government's military. Even he had not realized the incredible flow of funds these contracts would generate until the company had entered its third year of operation and he'd spent three days in Seoul with Stephen going over the records together.

He had to admit, his partner had done well. By securing the agencies for the armaments and other weaponry required by not just the armed forces but also the police, they had cornered the majority of the HANKAM supply contracts.

They had been careful to permit a number of the less lucrative deals go to influential parties. Seda had discussed ways and means of spreading the large number of contracts over a range of acceptable suppliers to avoid suspicion and so Stephen had cleverly organized a number of separate corporate entities registered in what he'd explained were tax havens, to overcome the frequency of their own company's name appearing as the successful bidder for the lucrative deals. At first he was unwilling to agree with the procedures initiated by his partner. The complicated arrangements were bewildering to him and he believed that he would lose control of his own funds, giving Stephen far too much information and power over his activities.

They had taken a week away from Jakarta and met in Hong Kong first where it was all explained to his satisfaction. Then it had been necessary for them to continue on to Luxembourg where they established individual numbered accounts and then London from where they had purchased several already established shelf companies registered in the Channel Islands. By the time they had visited Panama, Seda's head was swimming with detail, but at least he felt secure and confident with the complicated arrangements made with the respective agents and nominee directors who were to act for them in the future.

Since that time Seda had changed most of his offshore structures, having developed considerable knowledge of how the system worked, as he felt that the time would come when it would be better that even his partner not know where he held his accounts. His golden hoard.

The General pondered the Indonesian military buildup. He wasn't too sure about the French. They had become close to the Airforce Chief and he believed that they would offer to build, or at least assemble their Puma helicopters under license in Bandung. He could see no way of benefiting from that exercise. The choppers would be far more dangerous to the FRETILIN forces as these would no doubt be utilized by Indonesian forces for rapid troop movements across the mountainous terrain.

Next would be the purchase of the Skyhawks. These contracts would be lucrative while the aircraft themselves would be very demanding of their newly trained pilots. Both squadrons had been approved by the Americans under the US Department of Defence Military Sales Program, as were the Broncos. These were state of the art aircraft and he knew that it would be best for the separatist forces that the question of Independence be resolved before the A-4 Skyhawks were delivered as these attack bombers were to be armed with air-to-surface Sidewinder missiles, Bullpups and an array of ground attack guns which could destroy all of his ground support in a very limited time. It would all be too much for his poorly equipped allies.

Day by day, even against the tremendous odds with which they were faced, FRETILIN's political and military strength had continued to improve. The majority of East Timorese now fell in behind the party's village programs where they had won considerable support away from the UDT. Their brave resistance against superior numbers of well-armed Indonesian combat troops had increased their following threefold in less than a few months swelling their ranks beyond expectation.

The General knew that it was imperative that the East Timorese become one united force and under one leader if they were to succeed. The fractured policies of the fledgling political parties confused more than united his people. He hoped that as FRETILIN had put its former ASDT mantle aside and was winning so much support, that there would soon be only one major political and military force to lead his country to its rightful destiny.

Seda considered Indonesia's unofficial political arm in East Timor, Apodeti and felt reasonably confident that whatever these sympathizers and agents had actually been able to achieve had not resulted in any real threat to his people. Whatever military information had been disseminated to the Indonesian commands he had also given to FRETILIN intelligence. Apodeti's following was restricted to a few hundred as everyone knew that they supported Indonesia's annexation only because of their close financial ties to prominent Jakarta businessmen. At worst, he believed, they would continue to act as a fifth column although, from the reports he'd examined which had passed over his desk, they were beginning to acquire some small arms supplies from across the border. He would put an end to that!

Taking the files and placing them in his briefcase, a recent present from his mistress in Tebet, Seda left the Ministry of Defence building and headed directly to his own. This was going to be one hell of a year, he thought, as the driver pushed through the heavy traffic flow along Jalan Thamrin and into Jenderal Sudirman. He reflected on the recent visit to Hong Kong, where he and Stephen had discussed the invasion and what it would mean to their *kongsi* arrangement.

"Shall we close it down?" the Australian had asked.

"Why?" Seda had replied, surprised at the suggestion. *"This could only mean further opportunities!"*

"But the ABRI forces will have it all wound up very quickly and then they will find themselves with an oversupply of just about everything they have in the field, in their warehouses everywhere, not to mention orders not yet filled."

The General had spoken convincingly of future projects, the Skyhawk and other orders, and the non-military supplies which would be required once full annexation had taken place in East Timor.

Coleman had sat there quietly, listening, even appearing almost disinterested, Seda had thought at the time. Maybe his partner was becoming bored with the company now he was wealthy? As his Mercedes moved slowly around the Prapantja area Seda decided to have Umar pay more attention to the Australian's other activities. Just in case.

* * * * * *

Stephen sat at his desk going over the mountain of information that had piled up over the past year. He couldn't believe that the time had passed so quickly. As he started to recollect the year's highlights, he had to agree that it did, in fact, feel more like two years had passed and not just one, trying to understand just how far behind they'd slipped since Hart had left the company.

They had advertised, of course, but after a number of interviews none of the applicants really had what he needed in an administrative assistant. His local staff couldn't even understand the systems put into place by Hart. The filing and accounting had become so intertwined; nobody could understand where it started and where it finished due to the complexity of the methods the man had initiated for the company's records.

"Stuff it!" he said, leaning back into the chair and rubbing his forehead.

He rested from the laborious task for a few moments and then rose, leaving the pile of documents all over his teak desk as he stepped over two more cartons of similar records which had been delivered from his Thamrin office several days before. Coleman had promised himself that he would attack the paperwork and simplify the system so that he and the others could understand and operate the records more easily.

After twelve hours straight examining the illogical sequences that had been put in place by his former employee he'd decided that it may just be easier if the whole mess was just burned! He went upstairs and showered. An hour later Coleman stood comfortably at the Captains' Bar and observed that he was alone. Not that he minded the privacy, acknowledging that he was early and at any moment the bar would begin to fill with the regulars who frequented the Mandarin Hotel's main lobby drinking hole. Out in the main hotel foyer he could see some of the embassy crowd gathering before proceeding upstairs to the *cordon bleu* restaurant where a trade delegation was holding one of their many functions. It had been some time since he'd had an invitation to one of these luncheons, he recalled, watching one or two familiar faces pass through the marbled space.

Stephen thought he identified one of the men who waved to him and so he returned the gesture, only to discover that there had been someone else on the other side of the glass partition who'd been the object of the man's attention. It'd been like this ever since he'd returned from Hong Kong and found Wanti collapsed.

Any expatriate community feeds off itself and there was nothing more than an ugly rumour to throw them into a feeding frenzy, he acknowledged. Invitations to embassy functions dwindled away in frequency and even some of his Indonesian friends' wives had put him socially off limits as they too sympathized with his wife's condition.

Stephen could understand their negative attitudes. He just didn't enjoy being held responsible for what had happened and being treated like a pariah. He hadn't even heard any more from Anderson and this really surprised him considering the *kongsi* association with Seda continued without any real hiccups. Stephen had almost convinced himself that they had decided to leave him alone as now the tide had turned considerably in Timor. The separatist forces continued to successfully resist the greater forces of the Indonesian military even after annexation was officially passed through the Indonesian Parliament.

Stephen had spent numerous sleepless nights justifying his decision to stay on with the General and risk the wrath of the men in Canberra. He now believed that one of his assumptions had been correct. The Australians were fence sitting, waiting to see if Seda could pull it off.

As the FRETILIN forces had grown from strength to strength, the international community had seen world opinion move behind the separatists who had now declared their own independence and continued to amaze the foreign press with their displays of courage and resilience faced with such a formidable enemy.

Even the punishing devastation inflicted by the Broncos couldn't stop the movement from strengthening its position in the villages where the party members threw down their weapons to help work the fields whenever there was a lull in the aerial attacks.

Now that the American Government had put a temporary halt to the supply of the two squadrons of Skyhawks, knowing that the independence movement could not survive such punishing aerial bombardment these aircraft were built to deliver, there appeared to be a growing possibility that the Indonesians would be obliged to withdraw to their own side of the border. Even the United Nations was heading for a vote in favour of an Indonesian withdrawal.

Stephen didn't mind forgoing the commissions he and Seda would have earned from the aircraft contracts should they be cancelled. He imagined that the General was relieved when the news had been broken to him although outwardly he would have to appear displeased.

He was no longer puzzled by Seda's incredible ability to display such obvious loyalty to the Indonesians whilst plotting the resistance by the very groups he had publicly sworn to assist defeat. Stephen knew that he would be inviting his own demise should he ever infer that he knew what the General had done and who had informed him!

A New Zealander he'd met and shared a few drinks with while out in the islands entered the bar and Stephen put these things momentarily out of his mind to greet the man. Stephen needed to look after whatever friends he still had as their number was rapidly dwindling.

Chapter 18

Timor-Timur

Refugees flooded into Australia and the newspapers had a field day printing their reports describing atrocities carried out by the Indonesian troops on the poor villagers and hill tribes.

The Cubans had all but disappeared from the fighting arena as, without Fidel's financial support, they could not remain any longer. Things were bad enough back home in Havana and by the end of 1978 their violent incursion into Timor was but a memory, some thought a myth.

Nathan had been pleased, knowing that their continued presence would provoke the Australians into supporting the invasion and, in consequence, when the butchers were all repatriated during the first months of that year, he breathed a sigh of relief.

He needed something to go right for a change; the struggle was not proceeding with the support he'd envisaged and he now felt betrayed by both the Americans and Australians. Even the British had now decided to enter the debate insisting that the Indonesian annexation was to be considered beneficial not only to the long term welfare of the Timorese but also in its regional context.

Having made the statement the British Ambassador had stood back and witnessed the British Aerospace Company sign contracts to provide eight Hawk ground attack aircraft for the Indonesian air force. He had hoped when the UN vote had taken place that world opinion would force the Indonesian troops out.

It hadn't. The UN General Assembly rejected the integration and instead called for an act of self-determination to be held in East Timor. The voting record, he'd read, was sixty-seven in favour, twenty-six against with forty-seven abstentions.

He knew that, if only they could hold on, the dream would be theirs!

Although FRETILIN had been relatively successful the sheer weight of numbers now entering the area from Indonesia's base camps started to change the course of the war. The Americans had cleverly devised a scheme to circumvent their own Congress again and now the sixteen Indonesian pilots were flying sorties in their new Skyhawks with devastating results.

The guerrilla bands hid in the mountainous regions but their numbers were severely reduced by the pounding inflicted on their camps as the new aircraft located their targets and destroyed the FRETILIN supply centres with ease.

The General had been outraged when he discovered that the AURI Chief of Air Staff had received his orders directly from the President, to arrange for his pilots to proceed secretly, from where they had been trained in the United States, to a location in a friendly Moslem country on the Mediterranean. At first, Seda had not believed their cunning, and their ability to put aside religious dogma, when the need arose.

The Indonesian pilots took delivery of their first squadron of fighters directly from Israel which, in turn, received replacement aircraft from the Americans. The Israeli pilots were amused at the irony of it all, but understood the necessity of maintaining their solid relationships with their US supporters. They volunteered to fly the aircraft on their first leg directly into the hostile Arab neighbouring state, where a quick hand-over was conducted before the grinning pilots returned home under instruction to maintain the utmost secrecy regarding their mission. They had not been informed, of course, as to the final destination of their Skyhawks but they soon understood when they read press reports of the aircraft's use against the poorly armed resistance fighters in Timor.

Surprisingly, the aircraft were then flown halfway across the globe virtually undetected; as all refuelling stops were located in Arab and Moslem nations until finally, the squadron arrived safely in Indonesia. He couldn't believe his eyes when they gathered at the aircraft hanger to witness the squadron's arrival.

They had landed in tandem, the aircrafts' magnificent lines displaying the latest technology in aircraft engineering, bringing tears to the eyes of the Deputy Chief of Air Staff as he observed his son in one of the two lead jets.

There was considerable mirth as the aircraft came to rest, in line, and the pilots had stood proudly beside the new machines, for the aircraft identification marks still bore their country of origin's insignia. The group had shaken their heads in awe that such a mission could have been so successful and secret. Each and every one of the sixteen attack aircraft sill bore the Israeli Star of David emblazoned on the fuselage!

Nathan had applauded the feat in his weekly discussions with other military chiefs but secretly he was most concerned at having been bypassed in the information chain. This fear was soon allayed as he discovered that all but the Airforce Chief and the President were aware of the arrangements until just hours prior to the jubilant arrival at Halim Perdanakusumah. The Americans had insisted that it be so! And now his freedom fighters were also losing press support as well.

The Indonesian Government placed a blanket on all information relating to the war and, within weeks, the Timor conflict moved off the front pages. He noted that the number of media reports in the international press had also decreased considerably. What he didn't know was that this policy had been put into place deliberately by the Americans who then advised the Australians that they now favoured the annexation in a de facto sense. Sensing an international political *coup* the Australians jumped the gun and announced their own *de jure* recognition before the Yanks could steal the limelight.

Australia had been preoccupied with the former mandated territory of Papua New Guinea, which had achieved full independence just three months prior to the Indonesian invasion of Timor. Demands were already being pressed for the political separation of Papua from New Guinea and there was a strong secessionist movement developing on the copper rich Bougainville Island. Australian interest in the Timor conflict waned.

Indonesia, detecting the decline in support for the opposing forces, decided to formalize their position in the island. And there were other problems. After Indonesia had formally annexed Portuguese Timor, to Seda's and the world's amazement, the act was promptly recognized by the former colonial masters. The FRETILIN death toll grew beyond belief and the party's President, Xavier do Amaral, was arrested by his own Central Committee once they had received Seda's secret reports that he was alleged to have opened negotiations directly with the Indonesian military. The General had listened intently as the information had been delivered verbally by one of the KOSTRAD Generals during a debriefing exercise.

Seda had been livid. Hadn't they all agreed never to surrender and definitely not negotiate under any circumstances with anybody but the United Nations? He'd felt betrayed.

In spite of the considerable international reaction, neighbouring countries protested little, if at all. The general consensus was that the conflict would soon be resolved, and regional stability would be ensured, a political position supported by the simple justification that it would be foolhardy to invite the animosity of their powerful neighbour by not standing up and being counted as a friendly supporter of the oil rich Moslem country.

Timor-Timur officially became known as Indonesia's newest and twenty-seventh province, the province of East Timor, and within a very short period of time the annexed state was only referred to by its new acronym.

It became known simply as Tim-Tim.

* * * * * *

He disliked being faced with this conundrum, especially as it related to a situation over which he was not entirely convinced he had any real influence or control. Invariably, whenever this happened he would let whatever the problem might be run its natural course before deciding on any remedial action.

It was Stephen Coleman. He was the problem.

The time had come to dissolve their relationship and, although Seda believed that the Australian would not overly object as he had appeared to have lost interest anyway, his generous bank balances obviously in excess of his future wants and needs, there would always be the uncertainty of his disclosing details of their commercial arrangements.

The General refused to underestimate the man. It was he who had established the intricate network of their corporate structure and handled all of the offshore arrangements. Most, that is, before he had become personally involved. Seda imagined himself being Coleman and attempted to evaluate how he would have behaved in a similar situation.

Seda concluded that he would have put some mechanism in place to protect himselfagainst threat.

The question was, what and how?

The problem would not just go away and he knew that as long as Coleman lived he would be a danger, a threat. And yet, should Stephen suddenly disappear would he have left something behind to alert others to his activities and his relationship with the General?

The powerful man drummed his fingers on the teak arm rests. He remained seated for some hours before making the decision. It was worth a try and, if it failed, he could still distance himself from the outcome. He went into his private study, picked up the phone and dialled. A voice answered and listened to the instructions to meet later in the evening. He didn't need to write the information down. He had been there many times before. The General then prepared himself for his dinner.

Some hours later and across the roundabout facing the block of three story walk up apartments built for senior employees of the Ministry of Foreign Affairs, a man exited the BAKIN building and walked slowly to his unmarked vehicle. As he turned out into the mainstream of traffic the unsmiling soldier cursed softly at the thought of yet another late night. One day, soon, he thought, one day soon I'll take a rest from them all, perhaps even the General!

He observed his rear vision mirror and then drove out through the outer suburbs towards an old village building which the Timorese had retained as one of his safe houses. He could remember when the trip could be completed within thirty minutes but now, with all of the new housing estates springing up everywhere and the enormous amount of congestion that had occurred over the past few years, he had to allow an hour to reach the same destination.

Checking his Rolex as he approached the dilapidated house he knew that he was still early for the meeting.

'What could be so important this time that couldn't be discussed back in the privacy of the General's own and very secure office in the building?' Umar asked himself as he lit a cigarette and opened the window to wait.

433

* * * * * *

Stephen had really enjoyed the party. Comfortably drunk, he laughed to himself, relishing a joke he had just remembered. As he drove the red Mercedes towards his house weaving danger- ously enough so that the following car elected not to overtake, he looked across at the girl sitting beside him and realized that he was still in a party mood. He reached out and placed his hands between her thighs. She giggled and he had to retrieve his hand momentarily to swerve away from the traffic island as the off-side tyres screamed their annoyance at his alarmingly close encounter.

They rounded the corner and he could see his house. Stephen nudged the car into the driveway and the engine died suddenly as he braked, barely stopping before touching the huge sliding steel security gate. He tapped the horn, once and waited as he looked at the girl and smiled through the alcoholic haze.

He hit the horn again, annoyed that his security had not imme- diately opened the gate.

"Bloody hell!" he muttered, opening the door, "the bugger's probably out having a pee, saying prayers or doing something or other to the bloody cook!"

The headlights permitted Stephen to see some of the yard be- yond the gate and, noticing that it had been left open a fraction, he got out and pulled the heavy structure across the closed driveway as the small un-oiled wheels groaned fiercely. Puffing from the ex- ertion he then returned to the car and restarted the engine, moving the expensive sedan, jerkingly, into the double garage area.

He noticed that his security had fallen asleep right in the mid- dle of the entrance and, turning to the girl who was to be his com- panion for the night winked and said, "Watch this," he said, "I'll frighten the shit out of him."

Stephen exaggerated his drunken movements, lifting his arms high in the air moving into the glare thrown out in front as the powerful headlights caught his figure and cast a dark shadow be- hind. He approached the sleeping servant and was about to yell loudly for him to wake up when he became confused with what he actually saw on the ground. There was blood everywhere!

Shocked and confused, he bent down to touch the body and, as he rolled it over he could see, even in his inebriated state that it certainly was his servant. Only he was dead!

A shrill scream pierced his ears. Startled, Stephan fell forwards onto the slain security guard. His female companion stood in front of the sealed beam lights screaming in terror at the huge amount of blood and, of course, the servant's body.

Stephen scrambled to his feet and stumbled towards the night entrance door only to find that it was open. He continued quickly, bumping into furniture and columns without feeling the pain as he hurried forward towards the servants' quarters.

There were two rooms. Both had their single doors wide open and he could see through the dim light that there was no movement. His hand reached for the switch. As the room turned to brilliant light his eyes opened wide at the bloody mess that had been left. There were two more bodies here, the houseboy's wife and teenage son who occasionally helped his father around the house.

Stephen backed away from the scene, turning slowly to check the other room, fearing the worst. There he found another body, this one the inside maid. He was confused and disorientated by the bloody scene.

And then he remembered Kardi. Where was he? His brain now screamed as the import of what had occurred pumped more adrenaline through his body.

"*Kardi,*" he called out loudly. "*Kardi, where the hell are you?*"

There was no answer, the deafening silence sending a chill through his spine. He crouched forward prepared to defend himself and moved deeper into the large rambling house, past the kitchen and store areas, past the preparation room where he checked the rooms downstairs.

There was nothing there. Not even signs of a break in or theft as everything appeared to be in order. He was completely mystified. Stephen returned to the stairway and cautiously climbed the flight of marble steps, listening for any sound which might alert him to another's presence on the next level. There was nothing which signalled evidence of danger.

At the top of the stairs he turned the remaining lights on, the wide verandah instantly illuminated before him.

Stephen approached the master bedroom slowly, his heart pumping furiously and pulled the sliding glass French doors open quickly revealing a room filled with fearful darkness. Long drapes brushed against his face and he flung these aside then groped through the dark towards his bedside lamp. He knew that this should be on, because the servants always prepared his room before retiring themselves and this light was left blazing to enable their *tuan* to cross the otherwise darkened room, as there was no place for a switch to be affixed to the glass panelled doors.

He stumbled and fell, cursing himself as he scrambled back up, holding the side of his double bed, finally finding the switch for the lamp. He pressed the small button and immediately the room was flooded with light.

Stephen froze. His rigid body choked the scream before it could escape from his lips.

Spread out across the top of his bed lay Sukardi, the man who had dedicated so much of his life to his *tuan's* well being. He lay spread-eagled, a distorted grin across his face, his eyes open wide as if he had been about to shout when the blade had been pulled quickly across his throat ending his life before any cry could emerge.

Staggered by the bloodied appearance of the *jongus'* body he turned quickly and fled, running from his bedroom down the steps until he reached his car and ripped the door open violently, yelling loudly for the girl to climb in quickly as he fumbled with the ignition keys, trying desperately to restart the car so that they could escape from the violence that had permeated his home.

As the effects of the alcoholic curtain rapidly lifted permitting his brain to function with some semblance of logic, Stephen Coleman experienced the chilling realization that, had he been home that evening, then it may easily have been his body now lying on the huge bed in the upstairs bedroom and not that of his dear and trusted old friend, Sukardi.

As the engine responded to its driver's desire for speed the car raced away into the darkness of the night, leaving behind the bodies of all of Stephan Coleman's servants and a grim message of what now lurked in the shadows waiting. Just for him.

* * * * * *

In a distant village school thousands of kilometres from the killing fields of East Timor, the young children sat happily singing the chant which assisted them to remember their lessons. The children's eyes followed their teacher's arm as she conducted them.

One by one, they would shouted in unison as the individual province's names and numbers were called out for them to remember and, one by one they repeated the corresponding phrase in consequential order as they passed from the special areas of Jakarta and Jogjakarta, "*One, two*" they chorused as the teacher continued through the many provinces of Sumatra and Java, "*ten, eleven*" and Bali, across the wide expanse of sea to Kalimantan, "*fifteen, sixteen*" and Sulawesi, "*twenty-three, twenty-four*" and then down through the Eastern Tenggara states to Irian, West New Guinea, "*twenty-six*."

The children were pleased when they reached the last and twenty-seventh province in the sequence.

But the children were also happy because their teacher had explained to them they had new brothers and sisters in the new province and they should be proud that these people had become one under the Indonesian flag to strengthen their *Republik*.

The children all shouted in rehearsed chorus the name of the distant province which had become Indonesia's latest acquisition, the twenty-seventh province. And the sound of their voices could be heard drifting across the valleys, echoing though the hills, beyond the mountains and in every corner of the archipelago as Indonesian children everywhere chanted the new province's name for the world to remember.

'Timor-Timur, Tim-Tim!'

'Timor-Timur, Tim-Tim!'

Book Three

The Present

Chapter 19

Saigon

Jack Brindley leaned his thin frame against the bar and sipped the cold Tiger beer. Things had certainly changed in Saigon, or Ho Chi Minh City as the world now knew the vibrant river port. Communism had all but died and the collapse of the USSR had ushered in a new era of hope as, one by one, even the former communist satellite countries opened their borders to Capitalism.

Vietnam had been no different from the others. The country had been at war for most of the millennium fighting Kublai Khan, the Chinese in the north, the French Colonialists, the Americans and their Allies. Not to mention their incursion into Cambodia, or Kampuchea, as it was more commonly known. Vietnam's market economy had leapfrogged, not unlike Indonesia's in the late Sixties and early Seventies. Foreign investment had pumped much needed millions into the war-torn economy, developing infrastructure, paving the way for domestic growth.

Jack Brindley had seen this all before. He had been a merchant banker in Jakarta during Indonesia's heady years and now resided in Saigon as a financial consultant to one of the major investment houses. Today, as usual, he was holding court in The Shakes Pub, a pseudo English bar overlooking Me Linh Square across from where the old Bank of America building had stood near the roundabout on Phan Van Dat Street.

Vietnam's revamped investment philosophy, Doi Moi, had been introduced by Vo Van Kiet during the preceding years. Consequently, demolition teams had moved in and destroyed large sections of this part of the city making way for hotels and offices to cater for the rapid increase in demand.

Jack watched the freighters pass along the congested Saigon

river. These huge ships, with tonnages of up to twenty thousand, sailed up the river more than thirty nautical miles before berthing in the crowded river port. As they sailed past, majestically, they created a strange illusion that it was possible for one to reach out and touch the huge structures.

Several of Saigon's hard-core expatriate drinkers stood alongside the financier, only too pleased to be seen in his company.

Vietnam's sudden change to a market economy attracted entrepreneurial types from all corners of the globe. The last recession in the West had encouraged opportunists to depart their own shores and investigate South East Asia. Vietnam's potential attracted a wide variety of these dubious characters, including a few former politicians from Western Australia who, after completing their brief period of incarceration in the Fremantle Prison, had fled their native country.

Vietnam's overseas image was that of a last frontier and this, coupled with its recent violent history, caused tourists to flood into the country. They had came to visit the land made famous in so many Hollywood movies over the last twenty-five years.

The contrast between Hollywood fantasy and the grim reality of everyday life in Vietnam shocked the naive visitor. Filth and misery were everywhere. Blocked gutters, broken footpaths, beggars lining the streets and pickpockets on all the main thoroughfares. Saigon presented an entirely different picture than they had anticipated. Even Dhong Khoi, with its string of boutique coffee shops, bars and Vietnamese restaurants, was not spared.

Violence was endemic. Mutilated bodies were often left lying on the footpaths until the early hours of the morning when they were removed by some passing truck.

Robbery was rife. Life was cheap.

Outside the hospital's dirty walls, groups of people gathered in silence. To the uninitiated, they might appear to be anxious friends or family waiting for news of some loved one. In fact, these people were Saigon City's mobile blood bank. The group would congregate and wait until approached by a distressed soul, desperate for a blood type for their child or relative and then the donor would haggle over the price. The price of blood depended not only on rarity of type, but the gravity of need.

Expatriate numbers had grown to several thousand boosted by

the recent influx of oil and gas companies anxious to develop the offshore fields of Vung Tau and Da Nang. Many had come and gone, discouraged by the difficulties in dealing with a socialist government still suffering extreme xenophobia. Most of the foreigners who pioneered Vietnam's emergence from the dark corridors of a mismanaged Communist bureaucracy were well-versed in the Orient's confusing ways before venturing into the now vibrant economy. Not that Vietnam didn't still suffer from the long period of stagnation caused by the crippling embargo placed on it by the American Government.

Deep warning blasts sounded downstream as one of the large freighters approached the port. A flotilla of small canoe-style ferry boats scurried quickly away from the oncoming giant's threatening bow wash.

Brindley ordered another round of drinks for everyone and the fat, ebullient bartender waddled over to pour a beer into his glass before the others. Quickly and efficiently, the waitress replaced the used glasses with clean chilled ones. All, that is, with the exception of Brindley who liked to hang onto his seasoned glass. He had a theory that glasses too chilled or washed in the wrong detergent would make the beer flat. It suited him to be the odd man out. He enjoyed the additional attention. Brindley was about to raise his hand to call for a packet of cigarettes when he sighted the tall pale foreigner at the other end of the bar.

Brindley observed the other man. "And a drink for my friend over there too George," he said, indicating the man sitting at the end of the bar.

The affable barman served the beers and delivered a generous measure of whisky to Stephen Coleman, merely indicating with his finger that the order had come from "Mr John", the tall thin gentleman standing in the group next to the darts area.

Coleman raised his glass in salute and drank. He could not remember the man's name but he dimly recollected the face and build. 'Dimly' was very appropriate, he thought wryly. He was not altogether clear just how many drinks he had consumed already in the course of that day. He no longer bothered to count. Not that he was an alcoholic, he easily deluded himself, it was just that he had not been able to get it all together again and, he worried, time was running out.

How old was he now, forty-nine? No. That was last March! And now it was March again. So, he decided, confused by the mental haze, he would now be forty-eight! He laughed privately at his own joke. He checked his whisky and observed that it already needed replenishing. Pleased with himself at not yet having broken through the magic 'fifty,' Coleman gestured to George to bring him another drink and, waving his hand in a circle, indicated that he wished to buy a round for everyone present.

The bartender wobbled back down to the other end of the bar and organized drinks for the group.

"I tell you, he had millions!" the fat bearded New Zealander whispered.

"Bullshit!" the Australian challenged.

"Actually," the British born financier offered, "no one really knows just how much he did have, but I will say this," he paused for added emphasis, "it was considerably more than reports would have it."

The group absorbed the information occasionally glancing over in the direction of the man sitting alone at the long bar. The conversation was typical banking fraternity gossip, each attempting one-upmanship over the others present. By offering opinions and observations without substance, they often irretrievably damaged the reputation of the unfortunate subject.

"What did he do with it then?" the Australian inquired, probably keen to discover a potential investor in his new project.

Brindley raised his glass and sipped slowly before replying. "No one really knows."

"Is that the guy that was deported from Indonesia about ten years back?" the Australian persisted.

Brindley considered this before replying.

"A little longer than that, if my memory serves me correctly, and I don't believe he was actually deported. Stories regarding situations such as the one in which he became embroiled obviously become distorted with time."

Brindley paused to drink then continued. "Stephen Coleman carried a very big stick, as they say, before he stumbled. There were many who were pleased when he finally fell out of favour and lost, or appeared to lose, the lot."

"What happened?" Bruce Point the New Zealander eagerly

asked.

"He was involved very deeply, or so the story goes, in an arms scandal revolving around the Timor fiasco back in the late seventies, or it could even have been the early eighties. At the time he went into hiding, and disappeared from Indonesia when it became a little too hot. Now he pops up from time to time in the most surprising places."

"Bloody hell!" the fat Kiwi announced, "A gun-runner!"

"Keep it down a little, Bruce." Brindley admonished.

The men turned their heads to see if Coleman had noticed, but he appeared to be lost in thought.

"When his group started to crumble," the well informed Brindley continued, "there was also some unsavoury gossip concerning his wife."

"And?" prodded one of the men.

"Well, I am not sure. It has been a long time and quite frankly, I believe that his private life should remain just that. The long and the short of it all is that he disappeared about that time. Although the stories have been embellished over the years, I never found the man to be anything but hard-working and reasonably friendly when I knew him back in those times."

All heads had once again turned in the direction of the Australian sitting alone. Stephen looked up and caught their glances. He just smiled thinly, ignoring their obvious stares. It had happened before.

* * * * * *

During his years of relative seclusion he had often encountered knowing glances and whispering voices when he ventured into the drinking dens frequented by expatriates. He remembered how in Mandalay, one afternoon, a complete stranger had walked up to him and accused him of unspeakable acts, abusing him so savagely that he had been totally bewildered and at a loss to defend himself. And now, here in old Saigon his past had followed him again, judging from the inquisitive stares from the group off to his right.

Stephen Coleman had dragged himself up the steps into the bar. He couldn't remember what time that had been. The hotel lifts stopped two floors short of the top, obliging the clientele to struggle up a series of steps before arriving at the roof-top oasis with its magnificent view across the Saigon River. He had seen the group at the bar on arrival but the painful effort of climbing, together with the fact that he was in no mood for company, made him decide that he wanted to be alone.

Fifteen years of self-abuse had produced the red, telltale blotches and dark bags under his eyes. He didn't care. At least it helped disguise his identity, most of the time. Today, however, he suspected that his cover was blown, but he didn't particularly mind. He was concentrating on getting drunk.

He had not been on a binge of this magnitude for at least a year, and it had started with the Cathay Pacific flight from Hong Kong a week ago. Of course, he could blame the attractive Japanese flight stewardess. It was she who had offered him the newspaper that had triggered his present bender.

He thought back over that flight. As a rule, Coleman disliked reading on flight. He always found that the overhead light didn't quite match the position of the seat, and he didn't enjoy holding the reading material close to his eyes as the Chinese seemed to do. And then there was the problem of the black smudges he'd find from the poor print quality.

It never failed. Whenever he was given a newspaper he found that the print always seemed to come off on his hands and then, inevitably, smear over his shirt. And for some reason he could never understand, the moment he'd manage to fold the cumbersome over-sized paper into some more manageable form, the cabin staff would commence serving meals! So he had taken the newspaper more to appease the smiling attendant than to provide himself with an update on world events.

He had refused the overly sweet pre-flight concoction served while the aircraft waited for the remaining passengers to board. Instead, he had requested a Chivas. The girl had smiled sweetly and apologized, citing the IATA regulations, or was it the Customs regulations, which prevented the consumption of alcoholic beverages before takeoff.

He had already been drinking prior to boarding and wasn't in a particularly good mood. He knew all too well that up forward in the first class section they would be pouring Bollinger or some other fascinating drinks down their throats while he sat crammed between the two Indian gentlemen in economy.

It was not that he did not have the means to fly first class. It just seemed more prudent to sit down the back with the tourists where he could maintain a low profile. Although he no longer needed to take such security precautions, it helped him to avoid bumping into old associates who might stir up the bitter memories which continued to haunt him. The skeletons of his past. There were more of these than he cared to remember.

Stephen drained the last dregs of his whisky then looked up blearily at the growing crowd in The Shakes Pub. He was pleased that the memories were becoming more vague with each year that passed, buried, as they were, under a deluge of alcohol and self-pity. What the hell! He didn't care too much any more.

His thoughts strayed back to the Cathay Pacific flight. The sector was only two hours so he hadn't taken too much notice of his seat allocation. Consequently, he found himself stuck between two overweight men whose bodies spilled over into his limited space. He remembered deliberately exaggerating his arm movements as he opened the pages of the large Sydney Morning Herald so as to annoy his neighbours. He had skimmed through the first few pages without particular interest in the happenings back in the land of his birth when suddenly he saw it, on page three.

He stared at the image before dropping his eyes to read the underlying caption. The lines blurred as the words meshed together. He stared at the photograph again and General Nathan Seda smiled back at him, almost mockingly.

Coleman had not wanted to read on but his attention was dragged like a magnet to the story accompanying the photograph. He read the article again, in disbelief.

His eyes remained transfixed to the photograph. Having finished the article, he unbuckled his safety belt and went in search of the flight attendant. The stewardess permitted Coleman to stand next to the galley only after he had complained about the other passenger's body odour. The male flight attendant, a Filipino, had smiled knowingly and presented Stephen with a full tumbler of Chivas with barely enough space for the single ice cube. For the remaining one-and-a-half hours of the flight his demeanour deteriorated to the point just short of being obnoxiously drunk.

And he had remained in that condition until he awoke some

time later in his hotel room in the early hours of the morning with a raging thirst. Stumbling around the room, searching unsuccessfully for a light switch, he discovered the washbasin and drank copiously from the antiquated water system. Then he crawled back into bed.

Stephen grimaced with the memory. How could he have done such a reprehensible thing? He'd been living in the tropics long enough to know that drinking local water was tantamount to suicide! His judgement had been clouded by the tremendous infusion of alcohol. When he awoke for the second time, he had been completely disoriented. He tried to make some sense of his surroundings but there was nothing familiar about the room to indicate where he was. After some minutes, he gradually allowed himself an attempt to rise from the bed. A gigantic wave of nausea flowed from his stomach, forcing the bile upwards as he lurched forward in search of the bathroom.

He retched. The heaving attack continued until he was totally exhausted. The combination of alcohol and whatever filthy parasite that had infiltrated his body produced wracking spasms and extreme stomach cramp, causing the already exhausted Coleman to fall forward weakly, until the next wave forced him to produce the physical strength to raise his body back up to the toilet bowl.

The attacks continued. At last, totally debilitated by the spasms, he fell insensible to the bathroom floor where the room maids discovered him and raised the alarm.

After administering medication, the doctor had issued instructions to have him bathed and instructed the staff not to disturb the man until he had slept for at least a further ten hours. In the early evening he was given soup, after which he again fell into a deep sleep. As he'd slept, a constant flow of staff had passed through his room, concerned that he might die in their hotel, especially during their shift. It was a further twelve hours before he awoke and looked around the still unfamiliar room to see a serious faced short man watching him, obviously worried.

Stephen shifted his position on the bar stool and lit another cigarette. He could recall the conversation he had as if it had happened just five minutes ago.

"Good morning, Mr Stephen Coleman," the small wiry person had called clearly, "we were about to waken you."

Stephen remembered watching the man for several moments before responding. He had assumed he was in some sort of hospital.

"Good morning," he said, struggling to make a sound.

"The dryness in your throat is from the vomiting. Also, I would assume, the soreness surrounding your chest and rib cage. Your lower abdomen will be tender from the cramps at least until tomorrow." The doctor waited for some indication from Coleman that these symptoms were correct and, receiving no response, continued. "Is this your first time in Vietnam, Mr Coleman?"

Stephen eyed the man suspiciously.

"Do you mean that no one has checked my passport?"

"It is not usually part of our medical procedures," the doctor answered caustically. He was a Southerner.

"Then maybe it should be," Coleman ungraciously suggested.

"I see that not only do you show bad judgement but bad manners as well."

Stephen studied the man and decided that he had gone too far.

"Sorry, Doc." Stephen apologized. "Where am I?"

"Room 507, Rex Hotel, Ho Chi Minh City."

He absorbed this information and decided there were other questions he should be asking but tiredness prevented him from pursuing these.

"Saigon? How long have I been here?" he asked.

"Just a day or so. You should rest now. We can talk when you have slept."

"What is the medication, Doctor..?"

"My name is Thuan. The medication I have given you is a simple sedative to make you relax, together with pain killers and Geomyacin which would have reduced the cramps."

"Thank you, Doctor Thuan. Again, I apologize for my rude behaviour."

"You should rest as long as the cramps and nausea continue." He hesitated and then added, "Avoid alcohol."

Stephen nodded. The mere thought of whisky induced a warning twinge in his stomach. Satisfied that he would recover, Coleman had thanked the doctor and, following his advice, rested in the room for the remainder of the day.

By evening, Stephen remembered he was well enough to wander along the passageway and out onto the magnificent beer garden, where he sat, relaxing under the stars. He couldn't believe the sudden change in temperature. There were a number of stuffed animals placed around in frozen postures together with some rather fine sculptures of elephants in different artistic poses. A large dome-like crown sat majestically on the centre roof structure, covered by hundreds of lights so that the hotel's popular garden setting could be easily identified from most parts of the city.

Occasionally he would catch a glimpse of the river's floating restaurants, brilliantly lit with thousands of lights strung in the shape of an enormous fish. The colourful lights and electrical display brought it alive.

He enjoyed the sense of history as he sat quietly on the iron garden chairs amidst the orchids and other pot plants, listening to the street noises five stories below. Taxis and buses fought for position in the traffic, moving perilously close to brave pedestrians who attempted to cross on the complicated pedestrian markings. The constant flow of motorbikes, cars and minibuses chased each other around the square and then into the dangerous roundabout.

* * * * * *

Stephen knew something about the Rex. He recalled that when Saigon fell in April of 1975, some eighteen months after the Americans, Australians and Koreans pulled out of the country, choppers could be seen hovering over the American Embassy compound just a few hundred metres away from this hotel. The noisy mechanical birds also swooped down to rescue the few remaining advisers caught unawares in this hotel, winching them straight out of the beer garden before whisking them away to the waiting transports at Tan Son Nhat. The Rex Hotel had been basically an officers billet where many of their number remained in the comfort none of the other addresses could offer.

Not two hundred metres to his left, as Coleman faced the river, he could see the newly renovated Caravelle which housed the Australian Embassy during the years of conflict that had claimed the lives of some five hundred young men from Down Under. He had been told that, immediately after hostilities had ceased, the new regime had turned the two upper levels, formerly occupied by his countrymen, into a dance hall and night club. This was used mainly for the elite Communist Party officials who then plagued the city.

Stephen was surprised to see that so much of the old Saigon had already disappeared. High rise monsters now dominated the skyline, changing the city into a mini metropolis not unlike other South East Asian capitals. It was quite depressing to see how the character of the city had changed. Forty years before it had been a city which had prided itself as being the most advanced of any other capital in the region with an infrastructure well ahead of Singapore and Hong Kong.

The Communists had changed all that. Mismanagement, graft and corruption were mixed together in a melting pot of confusing politics and religious dogma. These were stirred with the fear of reprisals which turned the former capital of South Vietnam into a cesspool of humanity, most of whom had only one wish in life — to flee.

And many did.

Now they were returning, carrying their new passports for the security these offered, visiting family and friends and cautiously checking around for investment opportunities. Their familiarity with the language and culture gave them a real edge over other foreign investors. The government welcomed them back with open arms and did not differentiate too much between these overseas Vietnamese which they called Viet Kieu and others, unless they became embroiled in anything remotely resembling political or religious activities.

Stephen recalled how he had observed a number of foreigners arguing with the white uniformed security guard near the beer garden's entrance. The Lilliputian-sized lifts stopped there as the building reached only to the fifth level, which accommodated the beer garden, a swimming pool and sauna area, the main restaurant and a small number of suite rooms, one of which he now occupied as a guest.

The men were accompanied by two Vietnamese girls dressed in *au zais*, the long white traditional dress and slacks. The security officer was adamant. The girls were not permitted into this section of the hotel unless they were guests. The police were severe when they caught local girls in areas of hotels where they were not permitted. Stephen had heard many tales of tourists who had slipped a girl into their room only to discover that the receptionist they had tipped to turn a blind eye had immediately betrayed them and phoned the police. The Vietnamese gendarmes would arrive immediately and take the girl down to the station and throw her into the prostitutes cells where, more often than not, they would be raped by the very men who had carried out the arrest.

Vietnam was still a cruel country, he knew. He had been there briefly before. In Nha Trang he had been terribly disappointed with what could have been one of the finest destinations in Asia. The scenic mountains rolled down to the white sandy beach and the offshore islands were almost within swimming distance. The beautiful ocean colours were magnificent except where the filth suddenly poured down from the city's river, polluting the coastline with ugly brown substances, plastic bags and other unmentionable effluent. He remembered being able to see a distinct line separating the brown polluted water from the ocean's blue as the filth encroached upon the beach.

Coleman remembered how he had left Nha Trang the following day after being revolted at an altercation he had seen near the beach when a policeman had shot a young boy dead for no apparent reason.

A police officer had been with his friends amongst the coconut trees drinking hot beer. Two cans had been enough and the red faced official grabbed at a young fourteen-year-old street urchin, who had gone to the beach to bathe under the watchful eyes of her brother. The policeman knocked the girl to the ground.

The others crowded around and urged him on. He ripped at her dress and tore the worn clothing to her waist. His friends had laughed at the girl's brother who had tried desperately to pull the attacker off his sister. Drunk and angry, the young policeman had pulled his revolver and shot the boy dead.

Then they all raped the girl.

It had all happened so suddenly. Coleman didn't understand the language and before he could do anything, the girl too was dead.

* * * * * *

Yes, it was a cruel country all right. Coleman reflectively sipped a fresh whisky which George had obligingly just supplied. His thoughts returned to the incident he had witnessed on his second night at the Rex.

Voices had become raised as an argument developed. One of the foreigners was obviously showing the effects of an earlier session in one of the many bars in this quarter of the city. Suddenly there was a scuffle and both the men were thrown to the ground. The two girls panicked and hit the 'down' button on the lift indicator panel in a desperate attempt to leave the scene before they too became embroiled in the dispute.

Moments later the lift doors closed and both the young women quickly disappeared, leaving their dates lying on the hard concrete floor with looks of disbelief that the relatively small security man had downed both of them with just one swift movement of his arms and legs.

The manager appeared and the guests, whose only injury was their pride, moved towards the bar as the security officer simply crossed his arms and waited for the next altercation to occur.

Drinks were poured while one of the men rubbed his now bruised hip and elbow still glaring at the person responsible for their losing the women. Stephen could see now that the man was quite intoxicated, almost belligerently so. He appeared to ignore the dangers of carrying on the dispute with the well-trained and disciplined Vietnamese who simply ignored the angry stares.

Stephen recalled he had observed the men for a few more minutes. It was then that he admitted that he, too, had behaved just as badly when on an alcoholic binge. He'd made a resolve at the time, he remembered with a self-mocking smile, to stop drinking - or at least slow consumption to an acceptable level. He knew that his heart, liver and kidneys would soon succumb if he did not adjust his habits. He'd retired, that day, pleased with himself that this had been his first alcohol-free day for some time.

Stephen had managed to repeat his success the following day. Feeling somewhat recovered he ventured out of the Rex and down to the Saigon River's edge.

The beggars had irritated him. Although the temptation to give them a few dollars to be left in peace was great, his experience dictated that he shouldn't as once you gave to one, others would immediately appear. The street urchins followed, tapping their target's legs with an empty can, following the distinct whistled instructions of their team leader, who positioned himself at one of the main intersections directing the dozen or so poorly clad youngsters towards likely marks among the tourists. Shades of early days in Jakarta, he'd thought, remembering similar problems that city had suffered when thousands of beggars, mainly lepers, lay across the footpaths, desperate for food.

Stephen swirled the ice around the bottom of the glass and stared moodily into the dregs of his drink. It was on his fourth day in Saigon that he had an unwelcome encounter with his past. A man had almost knocked him over in his haste, hurrying out of the Bong Sen Hotel.

It was Greg Hart.

Startled, Coleman attempted to follow the man but was unable to catch him before he jumped into a *cyclo* and disappeared into the congested traffic. Similar to the *becak* in speed the *cyclo* was peddled away quickly by the wiry legged driver and he soon lost sight of it. Stephen looked around for another cyclo but by the time one had managed to venture across the busy intersection it was too late. Twenty or thirty other similar drivers moved in the same direction with the traffic flow, making it almost impossible to distinguish one from the other.

Furious at not having identified Hart immediately outside the hotel lobby, Stephen rode the three-wheeled machine around for two hours on the off chance that he would sight Hart again. He returned to the Bong Sen and checked with the reception to see if he had registered at that hotel only to discover that Hart wasn't known to them.

He wandered around District One, checking the bars on the chance that he could locate the man whom he believed had been partly responsible for his downfall. Stephen really wanted to sit down with Hart and find out why the man had created so many stories about his business activities and spread so many filthy lies concerning Stephen's relationship with his Wanti.

* * * * * *

It was during his quest to find Hart that Stephen came to be in The Shakes Pub at the same time as Brindley and company. Having broken his pledge already once that day he commenced with beer to quench his thirst, then went on to whisky when his still-tender stomach had started to rebel against the gaseous liquid.

John Brindley had, by this time, also consumed a considerable number of drinks although, unlike the man at the end of the bar, he was not feeling the effects; he was accustomed to drinking for hours on end, without the benefit of food, each and every day of the year.

Casually he approached Stephen and extended his hand.

"Don't know if you remember me or not. Stephen Coleman, are you not?"

"Correct. Do I know you?"

"John Brindley. Jakarta."

Stephen thought for a moment and slowly his memory produced a vague recollection of the man.

"Sorry. Not thinking too clearly today. A severe case of the trots, too many pills, some foul tasting medicine and the walk up those bloody stairs have succeeded in impairing my ability to think straight."

"Well, I wouldn't have expected you to remember. It's been a few years and we didn't have a great deal of business together." Stephen felt Brindley's gaze take in the ravages of his countenance. "Would you care to join us?"

Coleman hesitated. It was no longer his form to drink in company but obviously these men had been around the scene long enough to assist him with a little information.

"Yes. Thanks. I'd enjoy that," he lied.

John Brindley took Coleman back to introduce him to the others.

The conversation was a little stiff to begin with so Stephen attempted to lessen the tension. He encouraged the tubby New Zealander to discuss the timber industry in Vietnam, the man's obvious area of expertise, and after exchanging views on other relatively unimportant subjects, Coleman popped his question.

"Thought I recognized someone I used to know bouncing around in one of those bloody *cyclos*. I don't suppose any of you know a Greg Hart by chance?"

The response was immediate.

"Shit yes!" one of the group answered. "He's been in and out of the city like a bloody yo-yo doing some promotional work for the Australian Government's Communication's Program."

"Not that it's done much to improve the phones around here," the tubby drinker added.

He was pleased. Stephen encouraged them to talk on and within a few minutes he'd been able to drag out enough information from them all to satisfy his needs.

So, he thought, half listening to the men discuss the day's exchange rate, Hart had been in Saigon for some time working with the Australian communications group which had established itself in Vietnam several years earlier. That was interesting. As it appeared that they had been relatively successful, he wondered just what role Hart had played or still played with the company which now employed him.

An hour later Coleman left the bar, in his pocket he carried his former assistant's address and telephone number. He would visit the man. But not until he was stone cold sober. At least he would have the satisfaction of telling him where to get off about the filth that he had been spreading. He could just about forgive the rumours Hart had started about Coleman's business activities, although even those were damaging enough. But he would not be satisfied until he made the bastard apologize for the lies he'd told which, in turn, had become the substance of the stories that had been repeated back to him from time to time by some of his dwindling group of friends. He had to confront Hart about the provocative statements he had made regarding Wanti's collapse which had indeed made him a pariah in Jakarta circles. Although the years had lessened the pain Coleman was determined to at least rid himself of that slander and now he had the opportunity. He returned to the Rex and ceased drinking for the rest of the day.

That evening, after bathing and resting for a few hours, Stephen felt refreshed and elected to dine in the hotel dining room located on the same level as his room. The atmosphere was excellent. A pianist softly accompanied the female violinist. The cuisine was an assortment of French and Vietnamese. He ate sparingly, still sensitive to his condition. He knew that the spicy rolls and seafood dishes could be too much of a challenge to his stomach as yet.

Relaxed, Coleman gazed around at the decor, the artefacts which were positioned around the hall, and the various foreign groups dining quietly. The staff glided from table to table efficiently and effectively serving and removing dishes as the soft dinner chatter continued. He was pleased to see that the majority were dressed for the occasion in an almost old worldly, colonial style. The women wore elegant dresses while some of the older men sported white dinner jackets and black tie.

The *maitre d'hotel* offered Stephen coffee which he asked to have served on the terraced garden. He sat at the glass-topped wire garden table alongside the well manicured hedge. This partly enclosed section had been raised slightly, permitting guests to remain comfortably seated while overlooking the avenue with its uninterrupted view down to the river. The strong Vietnamese coffee was not unlike the old familiar Javanese brew he had consumed in great quantities during happier times.

As he sat, unwinding, Coleman permitted his thoughts to float as he had so many times before during these long, lonely years. His thoughts drifted aimlessly, taking him back through his past and the deep rooted memories of lost love and disillusionment; to times when he was content with his life, even happy; to times when he enjoyed the success and accolades which accompanied his achievements; to times when he had the satisfaction of the company of many, and to the times and events which finally precipitated his hasty departure from the Republic of Indonesia.

And from General Seda.

Chapter 20

Jakarta — Macau

The General had been difficult to contact. Conditions had deteriorated dramatically for the separatist forces and FRETILIN had suffered tremendous losses. The war between Indonesia's invasion army and the defending East Timorese groups, often overwhelmed by the superior forces, had resulted in the deaths of more than two hundred thousand Timorese men, women and children.

As the territory had now been annexed by the Indonesians, those who resisted were now considered subversives and any captured separatist sympathizers were summarily executed without the benefit of trial. The Indonesians knew that they would be unable to prove in any court of law the legality of their brutal occupation of the small nation they had annexed. The list proclaimed by the new masters as to what constituted subversion was long. The charge carried the death penalty.

FRETILIN continued to fight, taking their resistance into the hills and away from the villages, where the mud walled shacks were burned, the young women raped and the children forced into camps to die from malnutrition and disease. FRETILIN was now severely outnumbered and out-gunned. The sky was consistently covered in strings of vapour trails as the efficient Broncos and Northrop fighter bombers ripped across the country, bringing devastation to even the most remote mountain tribes. Everyone had become a target for these aerial attacks, whether they were part of the resistance or just an appropriate and opportune target. Pilots killed indiscriminately, urged on by an incredible adrenaline rush to strafe the screaming villagers time and time again.

The guerrilla movement dissipated, unable to withstand the superior enemy numbers, breaking up into small bands which the

Indonesians then had little difficulty crushing. Those who believed, carried on the fight from their mountain hideaways. Even these insignificant bands were sufficient to drive the Indonesians into a frenzy at being unable to completely wipe out all resistance without annihilating the entire population. They came close. Almost one third of the population was killed in those very short years of resistance.

Although the United Nations called for Indonesia's withdrawal of its troops the country simply ignored the UN vote, which recorded fifty-nine in favour of withdrawal with only thirty-nine countries against such recommendations.

The Australians had done a complete turn-around, and now supported the annexation even though their own country had become inundated with refugees flooding into the northern city of Darwin. The Australian banks froze their funds, which had been deposited from the sale of coffee and other produce, reducing the overseas supporters' capacity to provide any form of assistance to their brothers in Timor.

Nathan Seda's dream seemed to collapse along with the partial defeat of the resistance and separatist groups. The General had moved swiftly to protect his position, eliminating those who could directly connect him to the movement in Timor. Umar Suharjo had been kept very busy indeed. FRETILIN's President, Nicolau Lobato, was shot and killed in a surprise attack by Indonesian troops.

* * * * * *

The first indication that Coleman had of any difficulties was when his conduit to the powerful man was disrupted, finally cutting him off completely from the Hong Kong apartment specifically maintained for their communication purposes. He had needed desperately to speak to his benefactor. He was scared and wanted the General's reassurance that his own personal security could be guaranteed after what had happened at his house and office.

He remembered driving for almost two hours that night, leaving for the mountains as soon as he had dropped the hysterical young girl back at the party where he'd found her earlier in the evening. That had been a mistake. He should have taken her with him and only returned after she'd spent a few days with him in the mountain villa, recovering from the shock of what she had witnessed in Coleman's driveway. At least she hadn't ventured inside!

His second mistake was not returning immediately after escorting the girl back to her friends. When he did return the next morning, the area was cordoned off by the police and even he had difficulty in entering his own office and home.

His office staff had all gathered outside in shock. He spoke to his personal secretary and briefly explained what had happened but she just stared at the dead as they were carried out to a waiting van, uncovered, for all to see. As the mutilated bodies were driven away, and after he had been briefly questioned by the police, Coleman asked one of the staff to find someone who could enter the house and clean it so that they could go about their business.

His secretary had looked at him in disbelief. 'You must be mad!' she thought. 'Go back in there?' She mumbled something quickly to her boss and left hurriedly, only to be followed by almost all of the other staff within minutes. Only one remained and Coleman instructed him to find the necessary cleaners. Promising those whom he was able to solicit a special bonus payment, the clerk returned within the hour with a team of ten men and women who commenced washing down the bloody walls and removing all signs of the brutal attack.

Over the next weeks Coleman's telephone lines were cut off from the exchange and, although he spent considerable time and a huge amount of sugar money, his phone remained dead. Then Stephen had a visit from a number of government department officials whom he had met regularly over the years, mostly when their annual 'consultancy' fees were due.

But it was different this time. His old friend, Hasnul, from the Taxation Department arrived with four others and seized all of the office records. Stephen was flabbergasted when they started ripping files from the office cabinets.

"What the hell's going on, Hasnul?" he had asked, disbelievingly.

"Orders, Mas. Sorry," was all he said.

The following day he had a visit from the immigration officers who wanted to examine his documents. While they were there, they asked about his former employee, Hart. They had left after only twenty minutes, their briefcases filled with cash, only to return late in the day to ask for his passport as it required endorsement.

"What endorsement? My documents are all in order!" he had yelled, calling them thieving little bastards, his temper flaring. He received no explanation as he reluctantly surrendered his passport.

The following morning his credentials and other documents were returned. By the police. Next, the Macau clearing house was closed.

Stephen had attempted to contact the General directly in Jakarta without success. He had broken with established procedure and phoned Seda's house and was surprised when even the servants treated him coldly.

Then there were rumours that an attempt had been made on the lives of several of the high ranking military, including Nathan Seda, which, he assumed, explained the difficulty in being able to contact the powerful man. Even his HANKAM access dried up, leaving him feeling desperate and politically powerless. And then, for reasons he could not understand, it was as if nothing had ever happened! Within two weeks his business appeared to return to normal and, enormously relieved, he set about restoring the company by employing new staff and re-establishing communication links with all of the foreign callers who were, by then, more than curious with his lack of response to their many inquiries.

He had tremendous difficulty in getting everything back on track. It wasn't just inexperienced staff that were to blame. There were constant visits from government departments he'd never dealt with before; these continued to eat into his time, creating even more credibility problems with his international business relationships.

And then it all crumbled into shit again. The mountain resort development suddenly had more problems than he considered possible. Almost all of his nominees had refused to return his calls and the Provincial Governor had sent an urgent letter demanding to see the original licenses for each and every dwelling that had been constructed on the extensive project. Days later this was followed by calls from the construction department to send original copies of all engineering documents for their perusal.

Coleman started to panic. He had most of his wealth tied up in these land developments! Whoever was after him had created sufficient momentum to cause his world to collapse and he couldn't understand why.

He had asked himself a hundred times each day, who might be responsible for his predicament, but was uncertain as to who had either the power or resources to destroy his commercial empire that Seda had helped him build.

The possibility that this had all been the work of ASIS had crossed his mind but even John Anderson, Stephan decided did not have the access that Coleman had built over the years with senior Indonesians. It had to be Seda!

But why? He considered the question, going over and over in his mind why the General would do such a thing to him after all of these years. He'd done nothing to warrant this action, he was sure.

Time passed and his business activities turned into a nightmare of demands from overseas suppliers and an horrific claim from the Indonesian Taxation Department which, he believed, could be amicably settled as had been done in the years before.

When he tried to resolve this amicably they refused. He was asked to pay more than three million dollars in back taxes and fines! He just couldn't believe it. His whole world was collapsing and he didn't understand why.

Suddenly, none of his old friends or contacts wanted anything more to do with him. Somebody had closed the doors on him, the realization driving him into despair. He drank heavily, often alone, for even his once close drinking buddies had now identified that having Stephen Coleman as a friend was tantamount to asking for a quick and negative endorsement on one's work permit or visa extension.

His launch was impounded by the customs authorities as they claimed that it had been used for smuggling treasures out of the country from the recent black ship discoveries thereby depriving the nation of its valuable heritage. Stephen was aware that there had been a discovery, but this was part of a major haul which had been recovered by a British salvage expert and auctioned by Christies in Amsterdam, achieving seventeen million pounds in revenue from the illegal operation. He had not been a party to that.

And there was more. Having checked the original import declarations for his Grand Banks launch they claimed to have discovered errors in the shipping manifests, which reflected an underpayment on applicable sales tax. The penalty would have to be paid before he would be permitted use of the vessel again. He was devastated. The small ship was his pride and joy.

When an enigmatic message suggesting a rendezvous at an address in Macau arrived, he assumed it was from the General and felt a flood of relief. Now perhaps he would know why he had been deliberately targeted by the Government, his life turned inside out, his launch confiscated and the HANKAM doors suddenly closed. These were but a few of the many questions which raced through his mind as he prepared a simple carry-all for the trip. He had departed immediately and connected with a ferry within an hour of arriving at Kai Tak airport. The taxi to the Kowloon terminal had taken only twenty minutes.

The weather was foul. Even the flight had caused some concern as they hit the second hurricane warning that Hong Kong had seen in the course of the past few days. The aircraft had bounced around, forcing the captain to insist that the cabin staff secure the galley equipment and take their positions due to the turbulent conditions.

The seas were exceptionally rough. After boarding the ferry, the passengers were instructed to wait for an hour to see if the next weather signal would be hoisted to warn ships at sea and, when the winds had abated enough for the Captain to get under way, they departed. Even in the more protected area of the harbour waves smashed into the vessel. As the first of many spine-jarring jolts caused the passengers to hold firmly onto the head rests of the seats in front, most cursed themselves for not remaining ashore until the violent weather had passed.

When they berthed, Stephen waited patiently until the all clear signal had been given by the crew. The overpowering smell of vomit permeated everything aboard the vessel, threatening even those who had been stoic enough to endure the crossing without succumbing to the motion sickness.

He scrambled ashore with the others and went directly to one of the small tourist hotels. He slipped the receptionist an additional one hundred Hong Kong dollars to avoid producing his passport for registration.

Coleman knew that it would be foolish to risk exposing his whereabouts to anyone. He still wasn't entirely sure that the trip had been a wise decision, one that he'd taken in haste due to the turmoil that had inexplicably beset him.

The ageing porter had insisted on carrying his one light piece of baggage up to the room on the second floor. He tipped the man, not too generously and asked him to find him a girl. The porter had understood the request immediately and smiled.

An hour passed and then a loud knock announced the old man's return. Coleman was surprised to see that the porter had brought two women. When he looked inquiringly at the stooped Chinese porter he was met with a wave of the hand and the two girls settled down on the side of his bed ready for the negotiations.

He didn't really need the hookers. It was just another precaution he'd considered necessary to complete the picture of what the locals perceived to be natural behaviour for a tourist. None of the three could speak any English. The old man gave the shorter of the women a ballpen and disappeared into the bathroom, returning within moments with a section of toilet paper which he then passed to the prostitute. She wrote a figure down and passed it over to Coleman.

"No," he said immediately, even though the figure was not too astronomical. He was tired enough to accept anything but he felt that it was necessary to continue playing the role by refusing the offered amount.

The pair broke into animated discussion. He wished he could explain that one of them could go home if she wanted but the language barrier was too great and he really didn't feel up to a prolonged haggling session with the two.

"Mister?" the one with the ballpen asked, having scratched out the original figure and halved it, showing just how generous they could be as the other woman commenced removing her clothing.

"Okay," he accepted knowing that he'd still paid well over market for the service.

Before the porter could escape to wait for his commission back down in the small reception, Coleman gesticulated with imaginary chopsticks to indicate that he was hungry. One of the women immediately smiled and put out her hand. He gave her one hundred Hong Kong dollars and she pouted. He laughed, they both then smiled and so he added another hundred knowing that whatever she returned with would not exceed his first offer.

She was gone for only twenty minutes by which time Coleman had been stripped and almost raped by the small tiger who had stayed behind. Obviously, he thought, the two had discussed their timing and this one was determined to have him laid and out well before their dinner arrived.

An hour later the three sat cross-legged on the bed having eaten the combination of noodles, vegetables and steamed fish.

He smiled to himself, wondering what his old friends would have said if they could see him now, sitting with two Chinese prostitutes probably well past their prime judging from the neighbourhood they were working, drinking the local sweet beer while being hand fed roadside food. If it hadn't been for the lingering doubts he still carried as to the purpose for his summons to Macau he might have even enjoyed the moment. But he couldn't.

There was no way that the three of them were going to squeeze into the bed comfortably together, no matter how vivid the imagination and regardless of how he tried, neither understood that he then wanted at least one of them to go home. They either didn't understand, or had elected to stay together as they were quite happy. It wasn't often they were paid so handsomely and fed for their efforts.

When he awoke they had both gone. He was still tired, stressed out completely from lack of sleep, and from the strenuous efforts to satisfy the rapacious desire of two women.

Then suddenly he remembered his wallet.

"Bloody whores!" he called. Jumping out of the bed too quickly he hit his leg on the bedside table in the cramped room. The pain forced him back onto the bed, holding his knee until the cruel ache subsided. He then limped across the room to check his pockets.

Nothing had been removed. Quietly relieved, he showered and paid for the room, leaving his soft leather carry-all with the old porter, who kept on grinning and giving him the thumbs up whenever he attempted to speak to the man.

He slipped another twenty dollars into the man's white jacket, borrowed his black umbrella and left for his rendezvous. He walked slowly, the humidity had already climbed well towards saturation point. Coleman found that it was easier to lean forward as he struggled against the strong wind.

It wasn't all that far. In less than half an hour he had passed through the small narrow cobblestone side streets down through the casino area and then back across to the small commercial harbour district in time for the prearranged assignation.

The sky was ominously dark as sheets of rain cut across the harbour. He held one hand over his eyes to protect them from the stinging pellets of water which forced in under his umbrella and quickened his steps. Running was inadvisable as the road was now covered with large puddles which were difficult to detect. Rain poured down furiously. Fierce gusts struggled with the umbrella. He considered folding it as his clothes were already wet but before he could do so, another blast of wind ripped the nylon up and back over the shaft, rendering the umbrella useless. He discarded it immediately.

Coleman had been advised that the meeting was to take place in the old warehouse which he had often visited and where, unbeknown to him, the armament shipments for Timor had been split. He was convinced that Seda had to be behind the meeting as, apart from the General's strange and hostile assistant, there were no others who would have been aware of their previous meetings in that place. Consequently, Coleman considered the warehouse an obvious choice for the deliberately vague arrangements.

Strong gusts continued to blow as he approached the large sliding doors. The wind rocked the steel structure and it creaked and moaned under the onslaught. He'd remained outside for a few minutes trying to detect whether it was safe to enter and finally accepted that it was impossible to know. The old building hadn't really changed. A warehouse is a warehouse, he thought, taking one last deep breath before stepping through the Judas gate. As he entered, Coleman thought he'd felt a cobweb clinging to his face and shoulder and quickly brushed the imaginary spider away.

The building was dark in the late hours of the overcast morning. Apprehensive, Coleman moved through the building cautiously, concerned now that he had committed a grave error attending the meeting unarmed. He regretted throwing the broken umbrella away. It would have given him some comfort, he thought, even if only psychological.

A light hung dimly in the far corner. He experienced a sense of *déja vu*.

Nothing had changed since his last visit. Except the pattern of his whole life. Pausing for a moment to allow his vision to adjust to the poor light, Coleman squinted across at the shape he could just make out in the far corner. The solitary figure sitting at the small desk waved impatiently for him to advance.

Coleman obeyed, moving cautiously in the man's direction. It was Nathan Seda. Coleman could sense that there were others close by but could not detect their presence in the sparsely lighted building.

"*Come, Stephen, we don't have much time,*" Seda ordered.

They sat facing each other. It was as if the General represented the master and Coleman the errant child awaiting punishment. He suddenly felt cold, his saturated clothes causing him to shiver involuntarily. He stared at Seda.

The Timorese was dressed like any other would around the docks. His voice sounded tired, almost old, and Stephen wondered if he'd come directly though from Jakarta or, as he himself had done, arrived the day before during the rough weather.

Maybe that's his problem, Stephen thought. If the rumours were true and an attempt really had been made against the General's life then, in all probability, Seda would perhaps expect his assassins to try again and this would account for the months of silence and subterfuge surrounding their relationship.

A length of iron sheeting shrieked as a strong gust of wind picked it up, violently slamming the metal roofing back into place, startling both the men.

Coleman was tense, waiting for his partner to commence. The light swayed slowly from side to side, pushed by an occasional puff of air forced through one of the many cracks in the damaged asbestos walls. Shadows danced, almost in slow motion, following the bulb's casual movements, creating an almost mesmerizing effect which he tried to ignore, concentrating on the other sounds he could hear behind the crates stacked to one side of the small desk. The palms of his hands were moist. He hoped the nervousness was not evident, and looked closely at the General to see if he could read anything from his expression, but couldn't.

"*It's finished, Mas,*" the Timorese suddenly announced.

Stephen paled. '*What do you mean, finished?*'

"*It's time to clean our house and put things in order,*" Seda said, cocking his head to one side, causing his features to appear almost sinister in the half shadow.

"*What do y....*" Coleman was cut off by a sudden gesture as the General raised his hand impatiently to indicate that he had not finished.

"*The company is closed. Our kongsi is finished and, sadly, our relationship must now come to an end.*"

"*Pak Seda, I don't understand what's happening here! What is going on? Why must we terminate the company's activities?*" Stephen asked, as he felt the panic rising, events overtaking him at a speed he could not comprehend.

"*Because we must now eliminate all traces of our involvement in the weapons supply companies. Because some of these weapons have fallen into the hands of the Timorese rebels and we will be blamed!*"

We? he thought quickly. How could we be blamed when the whole goddamn operation has your personal stamp all over it? His mind raced. What was coming next? Was there someone lurking behind those crates waiting to tidy up after the General departed?

Stephen recognized the strange glint in the General's eyes and instantly realized that his life was in grave danger. This man, his partner, obviously intended to have him removed as one of the traces he had just mentioned.

But not right away, he could tell. Seda would not have risked exposure if the sole purpose of this meeting was simply to bid his partner goodbye. There was something else missing here, he knew, something more that the General wanted.

His mind raced silently. If Seda was aware that Stephen had known about his activities in supporting the separatists then that would certainly explain a great deal. But how could he know? Who would have told him? Only Anderson would be in a position to do so and he hadn't been in contact for ages.

Slowly it dawned on him. Of course. Anderson! Anderson and Seda. Together! But why go to the trouble of bringing him to Macau? Why didn't they just have him eliminated in Jakarta? Coleman searched desperately for a solution to his precarious situation.

Suddenly he knew. The General first needed to know if Stephen had kept any records which might come to light in the event of his death.

"*What should we do, Pak Seda?*" he asked, holding his voice even, determined not to display any sign of fear.

"*Destroy all evidence and cease all activities immediately!*" he demanded.

So, that was it! The General was obviously very concerned that evidence existed which would incriminate him and, should Stephen suddenly disappear, the General feared that this information could be revealed! Was what had happened to his servants some of Seda's handiwork? Had it merely been a message to warn him of what could have happened if they'd so wished?

He hesitated. Whatever he said or did next would undoubtedly determine whether or not he walked away from this meeting.

His hands were shaking. "*Pak Seda,*" he commenced, "*This will not be a simple task.*"

The General scowled at the Australian.

"*Why?*" he snapped.

"*Why?*" he countered, "*because there are companies incorporated in at least five different countries all requiring my seal. These would have to be dissolved, agreements with nominee directors terminated, bank accounts closed and,*" he added, his mind moving quickly, "*there is a mountain of administrative work which would be necessary in order to completely bury the trail of all of our activities.*"

Seda recognized the emphasis that had been placed on the 'we' as he spoke.

There was a long silence before the impatient general snapped again. "*How long?*"

Stephen hesitated. He had to play for time. It was obvious that once he had completed these tasks to his associate's satisfaction, his life would be worthless!

"*Six months,*" he suggested.

Nathan Seda's eyes flickered once, then he nodded slowly. "*You must do it faster if you can, Stephen!*"

"*We have known each other for a long time, Pak Seda. You must trust me. I will do whatever is necessary as you have instructed,*" he said, relieved at the General's reaction.

Seda remained silent for several long minutes before continuing the discussion.

"*You are not to return to Indonesia, Mas, under any circumstances. Do you understand?*"

For a moment, Coleman was staggered by the unexpected command, and remained speechless waiting for the explanation.

The Timorese remained silent.

"*That's crazy, Pak General, why would I not want to return to Jakarta?*" he asked, anger suddenly taking the place of fear.

Seda's eyes narrowed immediately.

"*Crazy?*" he hissed.

"*A poor choice of words, Pak, but the question remains the same. Why am I not to return to Indonesia?*" he demanded, feeling more confident that his assumptions were correct.

Seda smiled.

"*Simply because you would now be arrested and tried for subversive activities, Mas!*" He hissed again, venomously.

"*What?*" Coleman cried incredulously.

"*Subversion. That's right. And it carries a death penalty, even for a foreigner!*" he snapped.

"*On what grounds?*" the amazed Coleman asked.

"*It has been suggested that your activities have not been restricted to the business sector. There is quite an anti-Coleman lobby developing back in Indonesia.*" *You have messed up your private life making public those things we Indonesians prefer to keep private in our own homes and bedrooms. And there has been suggestion that you have been engaged in political activities on behalf of your own government. Confidential discussions have already been held with your embassy officials. You could easily confirm their concerns for your behaviour. Just call them! In short, you have become an embarrassment to them as well.*"

Stephen was stunned. A feeling of helplessness washed over him. He had been a complete fool. This had to be Anderson's work.

"*What if I ignore the advice, General, and return anyway? Surely I can count on your ongoing support considering our past relationship?*"

Seda identified the implied threat and jumped to his feet, kicking the chair noisily as he did so. Startled, Coleman reacted also, rising quickly, anticipating violence. Immediately a figure darted out from behind the darkness and pointed the semi-automatic pistol at Coleman's head.

Umar Suharjo's eyes were blank. He maintained his threatening stance waiting for the command to kill.

"*No, you fool!*" the General yelled.

Slowly Umar backed away into the darkness from where he had come, the weapon still aimed at what he perceived to be a threat to his master. Coleman's legs turned to jelly. He knew that the man had been present to execute him in the event that Seda had felt comfortable in doing so after determining whether he represented any real threat. His only protection now would be their concern that in destroying him, they may also destroy themselves.

"You were responsible for everything that's happened to me and the company in Jakarta!" Coleman accused, his voice now rising. *"Why?"*

"That will be enough!" Seda snapped back, *"Don't say any more!"* he commanded, *"or you will live to regret it!"*

The General paused to regain his composure.

"You still have plenty. You have always been a greedy man without principles. You did nothing for my country and now you have lined your pockets. You demand more than you deserve."

He sensed that the powerful man standing facing him had almost lost control. Stephen realized he was still close to death. He remained still. And quiet.

Moments elapsed before the General spat the words at him.

"Do not attempt to be too clever. Everyone has a limit to their patience. You must do as you have been instructed otherwise, next time..." he paused, looking over his shoulder in the killer's direction, *"I think you are smart enough to understand?"* Again he paused as if reconsidering what he should do. *"Go now! Do those things which you must and remain in contact via these numbers,"* he ordered, handing a slip of paper to Coleman.

"And Mas," he paused adding to the effect, *"Ring every week. Or perhaps we will believe that you really have become expendable. Now go!"* he hissed menacingly.

Stephen obeyed, drawing himself slowly to his feet and, with a slight shake of the head to show his disgust, walked towards the exit.

He had to lean hard against the Judas gate to force it open as the wind continued to blow fiercely outside. As he stepped through the small hole, the sheet metal door banged hard against his shoulder but he didn't feel the pain. He just wanted to get out of there.

Stephen fled the building, willing his legs to hold. He wanted to turn and check if he was being followed, but didn't.

Somewhere behind him in the overcast morning he knew the killer Umar was watching him. He refused to look back and continued along the wharf area until comfortable with the distance he had put between himself and the warehouse. His heart pounding, Coleman turned down a small street and then ducked behind another building until he was satisfied that he was not being followed.

The tall structures on both sides of the narrow alley offered some protection from the wind and rain. He knew there would now always be someone following his every move, watching and waiting until they could be sure that by dispensing with him permanently, there would be no lingering problems to concern them.

Coleman pushed himself hard up against the old stone wall and tried to breathe slowly. His heart was pounding with the rising panic. The sound of someone running in his direction caused him to tense. He waited. There was a loud thump followed by a man's voice cursing angrily. Still he waited. He could hear the undersoles of the man's shoes hit the cobblestones clearly with each step, even above the drizzling rain. Coleman tensed again, preparing to defend himself, sensing the danger. Clenching both fists into a tight ball he drew a deep breath as the man turned into the small alleyway where he stood. His hands came up immediately to strike, to defend, to kill, if necessary.

"*Aiiee ah!*" the startled Chinese cried out loudly as he almost bumped into Coleman, one hand already holding his appendage, as he'd prepared to piss against the wall, out of sight of other pedestrians.

"*It's okay, it's okay,*" Stephen had called after the man who continued to run from his attacker, tripping as he tried desperately to re-zip his trousers.

Stephen leaned back against the wall, head lowered, his energy gone. He'd been just as startled and, looking at his hands discovered that they were shaking violently. He crouched down, knees bent. Some distant voice in the back of his head yelled at him to breathe deeply. He obeyed and slowly his breathing became less erratic. He then managed to drag himself upright. Now move! the voice ordered. Move it! Move it! Move it! And he did, unsteadily at first, but then moving faster and faster until his feet were splashing down hard on the cobblestones.

A voice from his past kept yelling at him to run, and he obeyed, remembering his punishing training. He ran until his lungs screamed out for his limbs to stop and rest. Coming suddenly to a halt, Stephen realized that he was lost. He wanted to laugh, but couldn't. How could you be lost in Macau?

A couple huddled under one umbrella moved away from him,

possibly because they thought the *gwailo* was drunk. He looked around and spotted a familiar advertising hoarding. Now he had his bearings back. The small hotel wasn't far and he stumbled off in that direction, not even caring if he was being followed.

The porter saw him first, calling to the receptionist to look at the soaking wet *gwailo* stumbling down the street in the rain. An exhausted Coleman stepped gratefully inside then leaned against the polished rosewood reception desk, dripping copiously onto the worn carpet. After he'd rested for a few minutes, Stephen retrieved his carry-all and headed down to the ferry terminal to see if he could jump on the next boat leaving for Hong Kong. He'd given the old man twenty Hong Kong dollars for the lost umbrella.

The overhead signs indicated that the next departure would take place in an hour and so Coleman produced the return half of his ticket and then found himself a seat in the terminal from where he could observe the other passengers. He knew that he must now be extremely cautious. Seda knew that Umar was known to Stephen so it wouldn't necessarily be him that the General sent after his former partner.

* * * * * *

The return voyage was not much better than the previous day's. For the first time since he could remember, seeing the Hong Kong skyline didn't raise his spirits. There didn't seem to be anyone among the passengers who showed any special interest in him. He had watched them all closely as they boarded before taking his own place on board.

He needed clothes. He went directly from the Kowloon arrival terminal into the massive complex of shops overlooking the ferries and harbour across to the Connaught Building.

An hour later Stephen had purchased enough clothes to carry him through the next two or three days while he considered what to do next. He decided against checking into his old haunt, The Peninsula in Kowloon, as he was too well known there. He remembered the Hyatt around the corner but also decided against this or any of the other four-star hotels, as now he needed to be inconspicuous, to disappear.

He walked around the Holiday Inn, crossed the road and walked briskly down the steps into the efficient underground train system. Minutes later the Mass Transit Railway had him standing on the other side of the harbour where he easily slipped unnoticed into the swarming crowds moving hurriedly through the central business district. It would be safer for him here, he thought. At least fifty-thousand *gwailos* were permanently based in this area, employed as accountants and engineers to fill the void created before Hong Kong was officially passed back to mainland China. He knew that there were more than fifteen thousand Australians employed in the city, ironically filling positions created by departing professional Chinese who now lived in Sydney, Perth, Vancouver and many other cities far from Beijing's control.

Stephen visited one of the business bars off Central for a few hours. He ate simply and then caught a taxi away from the upmarket business district across to Queens Road East where he rented a room in a cheap Chinese hotel that also demanded no identification when he signed the register. He was tempted to phone Mister Lim but decided to keep his head down until completing the tasks he had now set for himself.

The next morning Stephen visited the Hong Kong and Shanghai Bank in Central. He closed all of his accounts and concealed most of his cash in a safety deposit box. Then he went to the Standard Chartered Bank and closed the company accounts. The staff were not at all curious. Transactions such as these were common and rarely warranted any query as to why such a long standing account had suddenly been closed. When it came to money, there was no race in the world that could be as discreet as the Chinese!

After this, Coleman went directly to the First National City Bank and closed both his private account and several of the existing company accounts there, removing any cash that was there. He sat for two hours signing applications and proof signatures for the travellers cheques he'd requested. By the close of business that day Stephen had deposited more than half a million American dollars in safe deposit boxes that he could access at any time, and converted the balance to traveller's cheques.

He had just under one million dollars.

Stephen had kept twenty thousand in traveller's cheques on his person and another five thousand Hong Kong dollars cash in his wallet. He was now ready. Six months before, at least on paper, Stephen Coleman had estimated his worth at nearly twelve million dollars. It had all gone. Disappeared. Taken by others. Stolen. Now he would go away and hide. Away from the pressures of the world which had become so full of uncertainties and danger. He would disappear.

Slowly and carefully, Stephen planned his exit from the city, the one remaining place he really enjoyed. He accepted that from the moment he had left the General back in Macau he had committed himself to a lifestyle which would require a complete change in his habits and a discipline he wasn't sure he could still maintain. Just having to forgo everything he'd either left behind or had been misappropriated in Indonesia was the hardest part. Still, he acknowledged, he had a nest-egg that most people only get to dream about.

* * * * * *

The following week Stephen left Hong Kong taking along sufficient funds to keep him in a modest lifestyle in the islands. The remaining cash he left locked away in the security of the Hong Kong and Shanghai Bank. He had planned only to return whenever he needed to draw upon the reserves and didn't expect that this would happen for some time to come.

He had set out, initially, for the Marshall Islands and the Philippines, spending almost a year in both areas. He moved around regularly, concerned that by staying too long in one spot he would increase the chances of recognition. And he knew also that somewhere Umar would be watching him. Whenever he moved into a new location Stephen would first stay at a modest hotel and then, once he familiarized himself, find a beach house suitable for his needs. His days were spent walking, eating, sleeping, and at first, thinking about his life and what he had to do. Eventually this deteriorated into an existence which consisted of nothing spectacular, the days seemed to roll into one. Weeks and months passed without incident.

He'd had the occasional affair or two but these never amounted to anything. He had no wish to make commitments. During his first year in the Philippines there had been one girl, but when she discovered that he'd never divorced his first wife, she had left him and taken up with an Italian. He had not been bothered by the strange behaviour, or at least he thought it was strange, considering the Catholic morality that existed in a country which did not even permit divorce.

He'd moved on then to Palau where he was pleased to discover that the people knew little of Indonesia and kept mainly to themselves. He remained happily ensconced in the small community for almost two years.

Stephen always attempted to position himself close to a beach and not too far from a bar. Mostly he was successful. He would sit in a canvas sun-deck chair around a pool or spend the afternoon lying in a hammock permitting the sea-breeze to rock him gently.

He really didn't want to think about the past. He knew he should try to sort out in his mind what had happened to him but he preferred to try to forget the past, with its painful memories.

Ignoring Seda's instructions Coleman never did make contact with the Macau number. He was convinced that it would only be a matter of time before the Javanese killer called on him. Umar could decide that Stephen's time had come and take matters into his own hands despite his master's concerns over repercussions.

He refused to return to Australia, but sent postcards with scribbled messages to his mother. For some time he hadn't known that she had passed away, and now couldn't remember how he had discovered that she was gone.

Sometimes he was annoyed with himself for doing nothing constructive with his life, but this feeling of regret would last no more than a day, or at most two.

He had no feelings of guilt. When he considered what had happened in Timor he reasoned that, as he had not known what the General's real agenda had been from the outset, how could he be responsible for what had happened? And the hundreds of thousands who died were almost forgotten, who really cared? The passing years and historical fact had treated them all so very badly.

He recognized that somewhere there was a woman to whom he was still married and that he had neglected her out of lack of compassion and understanding. Because most of his life he had acted in a most self-serving manner his present demise was a direct result of that selfishness, and he was now paying the price for his selfishness and the selfishness of others.

Sometimes he would wonder about Anderson. But not for long. When he reached his fortieth birthday he had celebrated alone, privately, sitting on the raised wooden veranda of a beachside bungalow consuming the bottle of Dom Perignon he'd saved for the occasion.

On that one day, as he sipped the long cool mixture of rum and coke, he realized that he had no ties, no friends and virtually no family. His life had no real value. He was nothing.

He made an annual visit to Hong Kong to replenish his money supply, and even that city had slowly lost its character and become sad. Most of the intelligentsia had fled for greener and safer fields as time began to run out for the former British colony. He felt that it was as if suddenly, one day, some monstrous world clock somewhere had suddenly chimed, passing ownership of the land and its islands to the undeserving mass of humanity across the hills, leaving the struggling few to cope with their new masters.

It would be a sad day for all, he knew.

* * * * * *

From time to time in his wanderings Coleman bumped into vaguely familiar faces. He always left when the whispers started, but as the years progressed this happened less frequently. It had to be expected, his having been such a prominent, even notorious figure. Stephen had at first grown a beard but then considered it ridiculous and had it removed, explaining to his bed partner of the time that he was only doing so to please her.

Funds were never a problem. He continued to live off his capital, living modestly without being overly frugal. Stephen felt that there was just a limit to how much one could spend without making a career of it.

There was no necessity for him to place his funds on deposit. Besides, that would leave trace records and, although he was a staunch convert when it came to believing in the sanctity of the specialized numbered deposit system most of the Asian capitals had developed, he had never really believed that these could not be compromised under pressure should the situation arise.

Switzerland was a good example, he thought. Recent years had seen an exodus of capital from that country as it assisted other governments recover funds secreted away by former dictators, drug lords and even the more ordinary criminals.

He no longer cared about all of that. He was now totally devoid of ambition. His life had drifted along and Stephen Coleman became accustomed to, and even accepted, the emptiness and lack of commitment that filled his days.

* * * * * *

How quickly the years seemed to have passed, he reflected, dragging his thoughts back from this self-indulgent reverie. Reminiscence was not necessarily good for the soul.

A car horn sounded down below. He smiled as the waiter brought him another coffee and addressed him in French. Stephen sat for a while longer enjoying the evening air. A sense of drowsiness enveloped his body. He pushed the remaining coffee aside and called for his cheque. The relaxing atmosphere had almost caused him to become philosophical about his self, his life and his future.

He'd travelled the region for years and expected to do so for many more. He had been to Kathmandu and Shanghai, to Yangon and Mandalay, crossed the Thai countryside until he knew it almost as well as the inhabitants themselves, smoked grass on the beaches of Phuket and Pattaya, and fornicated in almost every resort on the tourist map.

And now he was in Saigon. And so was Greg Hart.

Chapter 21

*Canberra — Ho Chi Minh City —
Jakarta — Hong Kong*

The Prime Minister disliked immensely being referred to as that
silver-haired politician. But as he ran the comb vigorously through
his ample grey waves it wasn't his appearance that occupied his
thoughts. It was those fucking files! He wished he could burn the
documents.

Prime Ministers might come and go, but you still had to deal
with the bloody political garbage they left behind hidden like some
stinking skeleton, waiting for the new and unsuspecting tenant to
take the leader's chair. It was just not possible that even his predecessor has been this capable a liar, he thought angrily, pulling at
the knot in his tie one more time. He checked the handkerchief —
it didn't match.

"Shit," he muttered, throwing it away then digging like some
feral animal amongst the harmoniously laid out clothes accesso-
ries in the second drawer of the Victorian dresser.

"Gloria, where the hell is the other half of this combination?" he
called, turning to his wife, pointing to the tie he had so laboriously
worked on for almost ten minutes before discovering that it clashed.

"I don't know, dear. Have you left it somewhere?" she responded
distantly. He guessed she was still annoyed with the magazine article featuring his latest indiscretions.

"Hey!" he snapped, knowing where this was leading. He'd read
the bloody article himself.

The Prime Minister scrimmaged around for a few more minutes before deciding that it would be easier to change the tie.

The press were going to have a field day. Today, he thought,
they were either going to harass him about the intimate article or,
some smart-arsed little bastard would pick away at the Australian

481

Indonesian Defence Accord that had been signed by his predecessor without even consulting the other representative parties in either House. And as if that wasn't bad enough, the Prime Minister thought, the silly prick had waited until the twentieth anniversary of the Indonesian invasion of East Timor to make the announcement!

The press hadn't appreciated the lack of sensitivity. It had been precisely twenty years also since six of their number had been murdered in the area. At the time, most of the world's leaders had fallen over laughing at the naiveté of the man from 'Down Under'.

The only country which could qualify as being a potential danger was, they chortled, the counter-signatory to the agreement. It was almost another case of history repeating itself, like another agreement signed many years before in Europe, he cited.

'It will be just like Chamberlain and Hitler!' he had argued in the House at the time, leading the Opposition ranks to rally against the legislation which would legalize the document. As a member of the Shadow Ministry he had the numbers to have his voice heard, and heard he was, at the time, albeit unsuccessfully.

When the government had initiated the ridiculous agreement, the intellectual lobby screamed foul and endeavoured to defeat the government by working against this cosy arrangement. It had the potential to emasculate the Australian Defence Forces. Australia's military strength was only a fraction of its giant neighbour's and would remain so, he believed, as long as the country's defence strategists insisted on competing on a weapon for weapon basis.

The new Prime Minister was a realist. Although he knew that it would probably not happen in his life time, he had always expounded the premise that the country was too large to defend in terms of conventional defence policies. The country's coastline was difficult to maintain in terms of national integrity.

The long term solution would be to change the very nature of the armed forces by following the principle of dualism. In short, he had argued, when the servicemen were not occupied fighting wars or protecting their country elsewhere he believed that they should be gainfully employed in a civic capacity, similar to Third World countries whose maximum utilization of such military manpower had proven successful.

"Stuff the airforce!" he would say when the military budgets were discussed. "Why waste hundreds of millions of dollars on aircraft that can't even fly across the bloody country?"

The Prime Minister's position was simplistic, but he considered it appropriate for his under-populated country.

He envisaged an Australia protected by a massive fleet of gun boats which could double up during peace time as immigration and customs patrol vessels. These would operate in concert with a number of rotary and fixed wing aircraft squadrons consisting of the more conventional type of aircraft.

This would cut out the need for expensive jet fighters that defence departments always scrambled to acquire for their air forces. The savings in terms of the number of refugees who would be turned back alone could pay for a considerable portion of the budget, not to mention the positive counter-smuggling effects on the national economy.

When he had been Shadow Minister for Defence, well before he became the country's leader, he'd been asked how the Defence Forces would protect Australia in the event of attack. He remembered with some satisfaction, his response. "Well, we don't really have the resources to protect all of our coastline. It would be ridiculous to even attempt to do so. As I have maintained in the past, providing we have the ability to secure our coast with patrol vessels and air reconnaissance, then all we would need would be three of our own ICBMs." There had been a hushed silence after that particular reply. He wished the interview had never taken place, not least because of the copious amounts of wine he'd consumed prior to what should have been an informal discussion.

"How would we maintain the integrity of our own missiles?" he'd been asked by one of the more experienced Canberra reporters. The wine and the attention of the media had provoked an incautious reply.

"Simply, David, if we came under attack, we would send the first one off to one of their larger cities and then phone the bastards and ask them where they wanted the second!"

This had been met with a burst of laughter from the press and the following day's headlines had not done him any harm. Australians had always been concerned about their Asian neighbours' real intentions. It was odd but that off-the-cuff remark had probably been responsible for gaining him the Prime Ministership. Cartoon caricatures of him had appeared for weeks, depicting him walking around the countryside with the third missile hanging out of his back pocket stamped 'wherdoyawantit?' Overnight his popularity doubled and shortly thereafter he challenged the party's leadership, winning easily.

He had been successful, although the growing debate had not been easy. Dealing with a complacent public which had not been obliged to fight for their country in almost a quarter of a century had, at times, been tough going.

He understood that memories were short. He was a Vietnam veteran. He remembered how they had been treated like the enemy themselves after they had returned. If only the public had understood! The greatest loss the Viet Cong ever experienced was when they flooded into the province of Baria, south of Saigon, and overran the area, then held by the Australians and New Zealanders. More than two thousand seasoned Viet Cong and North Vietnamese regulars were repulsed at Long Tan by a handful of brave Australians who, when outnumbered by more than fifty to one, managed to lose only eighteen soldiers against tremendous odds, accounting for more than four hundred of the enemy.

'I wonder how many of my constituents would know that Hanoi then ordered the Viet Cong regiment to be disbanded out of sheer embarrassment?' he asked himself, knowing that the answer would probably be, none! People just don't care, he realized, especially when you encouraged them to become involved in their own politics.

The press still controlled the public. Whoever owned the newspapers and electronic media had become the de facto government of the people. The cross-ownership rules relating to the media in general needed to be further revised, he knew, so that the powerful few did not further tighten their stranglehold as they had during his predecessor's term in office.

He had read somewhere that the American President elect, once permitted access to the secret horror files that the public would never be permitted to read, was virtually given the choice to continue to maintain the recorded history of his predecessors' follies, or magnanimously destroy the evidence maintaining the public's perception that the man in the White House actually rode a White Horse and was guided by the purest of motives in the execution of his duties in the office of the most powerful nation in the world.

The PM shook his head at the thought of his inevitable battle with the media giants. Most Australian Prime Ministers had been faced with a similar problem when they took office.

He turned his head as his wife approached to check his tie.

"You'll be late, dear," she said.

"Tell Peterson to ring ahead. I'm on my way now," he ordered, examining himself in the long wall mirror again and, satisfied that he looked his best, he left the room, forgetting to remind his wife that he would not be able to attend the charity function with her again.

The drive from the Lodge, the Prime Ministerial official residence, never lasted much more than a few minutes and often he'd wished that his country operated on a similar basis as the Americans so that he could work from home, so to speak. He thought it absurd how most of the day he and his colleagues were forever running around the billion dollar Houses of Parliament when they could be just as effective plotting and planning the nation's course from the den of his temporary home.

The political system of the United States did not require that the nation's leaders necessarily be members of their Congress and the President, unlike his Australian counterpart, was certainly not required to stand and argue with the Opposition each day for hours on end, often as the object of considerable verbal abuse.

It was almost counter-productive, he believed, to elect a person to lead the country and then expect him to perform, when the majority of the time was dedicated to political infighting or slanging matches on the floor of the House each day.

"I wonder what the bastards are up to today?"

His Minister for Foreign Affairs, sitting opposite him in the limousine was caught off guard by the Prime Minister's question, as his thoughts were still concentrated on the sausages and bacon he'd been unable to finish.

They were running late for the meeting, again.

"Say again?" he asked, his mind still on the tantalizing aromas left behind.

"I asked, what do you think the Indons will get up to today?"

The head of Foreign Affairs shrugged, then shook his head and immediately placed his left thumb nail between his teeth, a habit he had perfected over the years.

"Probably another demonstration, I'd expect," he answered.

"You'd think they'd cut us some slack considering the fifty million dollars in aid support we gave the ungrateful pricks just in this year alone! For Chrissakes! They should be giving us bloody aid! Look how well their economy has shaped up, and look at our unemployment figures. We could buy one hell of a lot of voter support if we used the aid budget allocation for domestic purposes, you know!"

The Foreign Affairs Minister silently took one of his long deep breaths as his leader commenced on one of his tirades. He hated these early morning sessions, and today's rhetoric was shaping up to be no better than any other he had been forced to listen to in the rear seat of the PM's limo. He really disliked accompanying the man when he went on and on like this. Especially when he hadn't eaten!

The one-sided conversation continued until the black Limousine glided into the area leading up to the steps of the House. Australian politicians considered themselves relatively safe. Only one real attempt had been made against a senior federal politician since Federation and even he had not been the Head of State. He'd suffered only minor scratches as broken glass had been scattered around inside the Leader of the Opposition's vehicle.

The men walked together, smiling at the television crews that had already lined the steps hoping to catch them for an interview.

"Prime Minister, what's happening in Jakarta?" one called out above the head of the man in front of him. "Will you be speaking to their President?" asked another as his cameraman followed the pair up the steps.

They didn't stop but merely smiled and waved, offering a nod of recognition to some of the more senior crew members as they passed through the throng and headed directly to the PM's offices. As they entered, his personal secretary was standing with her hands clasped in front, unsmiling as always.

"Good morning, sir," she said, coolly.

"Now, now, Shirley, don't be like that. It's his fault," the PM said, pointing over his shoulder at the surprised Minister. "He insisted on having breakfast."

"We're late," was all she said, handing him the newspaper cut-outs and other press clippings.

"Ring them. Anything here?" he asked, running through the thick selection of articles.

"One or two I think you should read before the meeting. I have highlighted those in red."

He turned to his Minister for Foreign Affairs who knew that he would now be obliged to wait until the PM had finished reading the articles. They both detested the media but were astute enough to appreciate the power that they wielded and consequently the attention they demanded at all times. He sat in one of the leather chairs as the nation's leader walked into his office leaving the door ajar for his secretary to follow.

This was the PM's routine. He would read the articles, and they were usually damaging due to his position on the cross-owner-ship question. His secretary took notes of his comments for the PM's personal records.

This morning's editorial on page two was scathing on the gov-ernment's inaction over the widening gulf between Australia and Indonesia, which were now experiencing a cooling off in their re-lations. The article felt that both countries' national interests could best be served if their leaders resisted calling each other names, such as 'recalcitrant' and 'racist', and got on with the job of repair-ing the damage that had been done over the past year.

"What a bunch of lying bloody..." the Prime Minister's invec-tive flowed unrestrained.

His secretary listened for the umpteenth time to the new leader making his characteristic Monday morning outburst prior to the cabinet session.

His colleagues had publicly praised his abilities as if he was some new economic Messiah, ordained by the voters to cure their financial woes. Voters being what they are, especially in an envi-ronment controlled through an antiquated political system, cast their votes without understanding the simple principles of gov-ernment and what was really required of their elected representa-tives during their term in parliament. The complicated procedures were bequeathed in a manner which virtually precluded any rem-edy. He was resigned to the fact that the public were prisoners of the Westminster System and its inherent problems, which would continue to dominate their lives and the former colony for years to come. He had supported the move towards a Republic, but common sense dictated that the transition from one political system to another should not be rushed as the opposition would have it. Instead, he advised less haste in changing all of the statutes, as that alone would burden his government with years of effort untangling the complicated laws of the land already based on there being a Monarchy at the head of the country and its Commonwealth.

"Anything else?" he asked, throwing the clippings onto the desk.

"Just this," she answered, passing the red file cover stamped 'Most Secret' and 'Prime Minister's Eyes Only'. She had not broken the seal.

The PM took the file and read on through the report.

"Have the director r eport to me immediately after the morning prayers session," he instructed.

The new Prime Minister had appropriately coined the expression describing the weekly gathering of his Cabinet when he had read in the press, not long after taking up office, that the lack-luster team now sitting on the front benches had been described as a gathering of lay-preachers who thought they understood but were not quite ready for the heavy responsibilities of their new positions.

"Yes sir," the woman had responded.

"And you had better remind the Attorney-General of the meeting."

He continued to read the highly classified report, grunting from time to time as specific points met with his disapproval.

Glancing at his watch he realized that time would not permit him to complete his examination of the secret contents.

"Open my safe, please," he requested.

His secretary immediately checked the single tumbler's position and, using his key to unlock the door the tall man bent down and placed the folder safely inside the heavy duty steel Chubbs cabinet. He'd wished it had been a shredding machine.

The Prime Minister then went about preparing for the Monday prayers session with his colleagues.

* * * * * *

The Attorney-General was uneasy as he waited quietly with the

Chief of Intelligence, John Anderson. They had both been called to the PM's office for a special briefing.

Privately, he considered that the Intelligence Chief was well past his prime and should be put out to pasture. The AG resented the man's power. Even though the Director should, in fact, report first to the Attorney-General before taking any direct action, this had proven to be impractical. As a result, Anderson only dealt with the PM and this infuriated the AG. He took heart, however from the certainty that the Director would soon reach the end of the service extension granted personally by the PM and this would put him well over the mandatory retirement age. It was unlikely that he would be around too much longer with his direct access to their leader. Then the AG could go about selecting a suitable replacement.

Had the AG known John Anderson a little better, he would not have been so complacent. Anderson had no intention of letting any politician appoint his replacement. When the time came, he would orchestrate this with the Prime Minister himself.

The Prime Minister had called them both in for this meeting so that the Director could explain the conclusions he had made in the documents now locked in the PM's personal cabinet. Anderson was obviously uneasy with this request. Due to the sensitivity of the contents he would have preferred the discussion to remain one-on-one with the Prime Minister. The fewer politicians aware of the details, the better, he had wisely thought.

"Well?" the country's leader waited.

"We've seen it all before."

"It is almost a repeat of an earlier era. The situation has failed to resolve itself and it is my opinion that we are heading for an extremely dangerous confrontation." He paused, glancing in the direction of the Attorney-General.

"Your predecessor, sir, was very concerned at the rapid deterioration of Indonesian-Australian relations brought on generally by the emergence of the former General, Nathan Seda, whose influence over their President has grown incredibly strong in recent years."

"Our reports indicate that not only is he a frequent visitor to *Jalan Cendana*," he paused, turning slightly to the AG and adding, "that's the unofficial name of the President's home," he went on "strong rumour has it that he is being groomed as the next Vice President."

"Obviously not being of Javanese stock would prevent him from the leadership's top position; we should however be conscious of the facts. Politically, it would be a clever move for their President to appoint him to the position, not just because he is such a prominent and powerful figure, but also we should remember that the country's more than ten million Catholics would support such a move. There are also more than one hundred million Indonesians who are not Javanese and the majority of these would also, we believe, strongly support any such appointment."

"In theory, gentlemen, he would have as much voter support as the President himself without, obviously, the backing of the military. The escalating political and social unrest we have observed has not been entirely a result of falling oil prices. Corruption has reached levels where these practices have created billionaires. Family members of high ranking officials actually own or control whole sections of the non-oil and gas economy." He paused, taking the glass of Perrier and drinking before continuing.

"Singapore's banks are overflowing with most of the hidden proceeds and, generally speaking, infrastructure is suffering throughout the country because so much capital has been siphoned off and left to idle in secret numbered accounts throughout Asia. The emergence of right-wing extremist elements now influences their foreign policies. Many of these supporters have considerable disdain for Australia and the day has come for the Asians to no longer consider our country either economically, or militarily, a threat to any of their expansionist movements. Our agreements covering the use of sea lanes for both merchant and military shipping are being challenged. The Ombai-Wetar Straits may be closed in the near future to both our and United States' submarines. Australia's entire export programme to Asia is at serious risk. In short, gentlemen, we should batten down the hatches, so to speak, and prepare for an extended period of tension with Jakarta unless we take the necessary steps to prevent any future escalation."

"I have read your recommendations John, I can't say I entirely agree with your suggestions. They seem a bit extreme to me."

The Prime Minister pursed his lips and leaned back in his chair.

"Sir," Anderson began, "you have had access today, perhaps

for the first time to your predecessor's 'Eyes Only' file."

At the mention of this the new Attorney-General immediately interrupted.

"Do I also have access to this information?" he asked.

The Intelligence Chief smiled courteously and shook his head silently.

The AG bristled. "Prime Minister, I must insist! After all, as Attorney-General I should be conversant with what is happening in Anderson's department."

The PM shook his head.

" 'Eyes Only' means just that! It is not a consideration of whether the Attorney-General's office can be trusted with the contents of the document. It is a question of procedures."

He looked at Anderson, who appeared pleased with the PM's support.

"I certainly would not rest easily with the knowledge that others will access information relating to my period of service in this office subsequent to my departure which, I trust we all hope, will not be for some considerable time to come." He had attempted a smile. "It's worrying enough that when I do leave my successor will, however, acquire that right."

Question Time in the House prevented the meeting from continuing. Anderson rose to depart with the Attorney-General and, observing the Prime Minister's sombre expression, he knew there would be another summons to this office. Alone. The country's leader would certainly not wish others to be present when he authorized the steps which both he and the Intelligence Head would come to accept as imperative action.

As John Anderson was driven down Commonwealth Avenue, he considered the data contained in the secret file now in the possession of the new Prime Minister. He understood the sense of despair experienced by a new PM who, having accepted the mantle of the office, was immediately burdened with the information contained in the complex record of Prime Ministerial covert directives. And even with the most secret accounting Anderson knew that the records were far from complete. Information was the tool of his clandestine trade and he believed, as had his predecessor, the agency's first Director, that politicians were never to be trusted and that it was essential to the service's survival that some secrets continue as such. Even if it meant keeping these from the national leader.

His thoughts turned to the report dispatched by Hart.

* * * * * *

Director John Anderson rarely sat behind his desk. Most of the time he would walk the room as he thought through whatever had been troubling his mind. This day was no different from all of the rest. There was a major problem to be considered and resolved with as little fuss as possible. As soon as the first signs had begun to appear, his years of expertise flashed warning signals immediately telling him to extinguish this fire before it became impossible to control.

He read through the report again.

"Silly bugger," he said to the empty room. He continued to pace over and around the Tai Ping carpet which he had received as a gift from one of the graduating classes. He smiled. 'Classes' was not exactly the appropriate nomenclature for the graduating group of three. The year before it had been five. Before that, only two.

He looked at the facsimile in his hand and shook his head again. Sometimes, he reminded himself, some of the graduates just don't show their weaknesses until they are out in the field. And often, not even then, he remembered, thinking of Stephen Coleman. It seemed that fate had decided to play him a difficult hand for the day. Now he was faced with the problem of sorting out two of his former graduates and, as luck would have it, they had come into direct conflict with each other quite unexpectedly.

The Director thought about Hart. Then he remembered his holidays with Coleman on the slopes and smiled. Actually, he was quite pleased that Stephen had bloodied the cocky Hart. He wished he had been present to see it. Not bad, he thought, considering his age and the sedentary life style the man had lived over the last, how many was it, fifteen or sixteen years?

Anderson accepted that he had lost one of his most promising men when Stephen had decided to resign. He also admitted that he had not been pleased and had, at that moment, wished the young man an injury. Had it not been for the young man's mother, Stephen would not have been considered for the training. They had always been close friends and he was saddened by the way her husband had decided to pick up his belongings and just leave. He had offered her comfort. And she had accepted.

Now he was faced with the dilemma of her son, once again. Stephen had not been a particularly opportunistic soul and would not have made it to the top in his profession had he stayed on with the Service. He lacked that one instinct that was vital to operatives world wide. Self preservation.

Somehow he had known, even in the early days of basic training that, although his friend's son had ability, he had no real killer instinct! Now Stephen had become an alcoholic wanderer. A bum! And as Anderson always knew he would, Coleman had re-emerged to become a thorn in his side. He had to use this information and work the man who had become the thorn.

He looked at the photographs. Coleman certainly looked his age. Anderson knew that it had to have been the alcohol. The effects of liquor and a dissolute lifestyle were evident in the puffy features. He had seen many a good man destroy themselves, at first gradually, and then in a blind rush to reach whatever end they visualized for themselves through the bottom of a bottle.

He looked back at the photographs again, recalling with some sadness the vibrant young operative whom he had sent overseas, destined to enjoy a promising career with his Department. He also remembered seeing the same man in a hospital bed, hovering between life and death from his horrific injuries. He saw again the bleak, distant look Stephen had given him when he had told him of the death of Louise. That had been the turning point, Anderson reflected. At the time he had been perplexed and somewhat disappointed with Coleman's over-reaction to the loss. After all, Stephen had hardly known the young woman and certainly not long enough to warrant such a magnitude of grief. It was so prolonged that Anderson had been prompted to suggest a period of further training and a holiday.

The extended holiday had been a mistake, he now realized. Often he'd thought about the decision to permit the young man a few extra months as part of his psychological recovery process. Anderson misjudged his agent, believing that Coleman had purged the past from his system and was particularly annoyed when the young and promising operative had resigned. Now he was back.

The Director was conscious that this time he was dealing with a man who had already experienced life's peaks and troughs and would require delicate handling if he was to be of any real use. The Intelligence Chief was also aware of the limited power he would have over the man. He would need to develop a strategy suited for a man of Coleman's intelligence. He must be very careful. The man was no fool.

The ageing bureaucrat called his secretary and gave her the name. He would go over Stephen Coleman's file again and see just where he was most vulnerable and where his weaknesses exposed the man most to compromise.

* * * * * *

Most would consider it unusual for one to retire to a city populated primarily by public servants. Albert had gratefully accepted the adequate pension and moved from Melbourne to the small unit. It suited his needs. And there was considerably less violence on the streets of this well designed city. In fact, he thought, when comparing it with Saturday nights in Melbourne, the Capital was a dream. There had been already too much violence in his life.

It had been more than a year since the government troops had opened fire on mourners at the funeral of pro-independence sympathizers in the in town of Maliana. The people had been devastated by the unwarranted and violent attack. At least two hundred had been killed. Many others had never been accounted for, including his sister's grandchildren. He'd had no idea that many of his relatives had moved back into the area where the slaughter had taken place.

'Would they never learn?' he had asked upon hearing the news. Not so many years had passed since the Indonesian military had opened fire also on a group of mourners in Dili, killing sixty to seventy Timorese as they paid their last tribute to yet another separatist leader.

Albert could not understand why the world refused to acknowledge the cruel impact suffered by the East Timorese at the hands of the invading forces. Documents had been tabled in the United Nations evidencing the first campaigns of enforced sterilization organized by the Indonesian military, and clear proof that these actions had continued since earlier documents had been submitted to the authorities in Lisbon.

Again there had been no world outcry. He was devastated by the inaction and feelings of helplessness. The Timorese had pleaded for the international community to acknowledge their plight but none came forward to help. It was if they were to be ignored forever and the simple people, whose only fault was to seek their own independence from an outside power, suffered the indignity of being forgotten.

Even during the three years of killing in war torn Bosnia the people there had not suffered the losses the East Timorese had during their twenty years of struggle. Why then, the Timorese refugees in Darwin often asked, does one country deserve more consideration over another? Why doesn't the United Nations position a peace keeping force in their country, as they had in Bosnia?

Why had they been left to the mercy of their giant neighbour? They asked those questions, and many others, knowing there would be no response. The Timorese sadly recognized that their plight would continue to be ignored as the superpowers arbitrarily accepted Indonesia's dominance over the Tim-Tim. *Republik Indonesia* had become a world force in her own right and vested interests now controlled policy. Economic criteria had a greater priority than humanitarian considerations.

These questions had also haunted Albert. He just couldn't understand how it could be that the United Nations had called for Indonesia's withdrawal so many times, and supported a supervised vote on the right for self-determination in the ravaged country, only to be ignored. Albert believed that had the same set of circumstances existed in a country of greater significance to the superpowers then their cries for help would have been heeded well before this.

It seemed that it just wasn't to be. After the most recent slaughter the Indonesian central government attempted a cover-up but the Australian media managed to keep the massacre in the news, again opening old wounds between the Indonesian muscle men and the international free press. Unfortunately this had the disadvantage of providing the Timor separatists an exaggerated view of international support for their call for independence resulting in even more arrests as they continued with their struggle.

On the other hand, the Indonesian people could not understand Australia's persistent interest in supporting the terrorists, as that is how they had come to identify the separatists in Tim-Tim. *'Why do the Australians pose as our friends,'* they would ask first time visitors to their country, *'when the separatists support the destabilisation of one of our provinces?'*

Albert knew all about this. He still read the foreign language newspapers regularly. And in those pages he would often see the familiar face of his stepbrother Nathan Seda. The General's rise to political prominence was seldom out of the news.

He had not maintained any further contact. In fact, he had deliberately avoided contact with those who had remained in Indonesia, receiving only scant news, usually of accidents or deaths of a family member which would immediately be followed by requests for money. He didn't mind. They were far less fortunate than he and it was an obligation he could not refuse when asked.

And then there had been the occasional news of Stephen, but this too had ceased some years before. He felt extremely sad for his old friend. Bad news travels fast, so they say, and Stephen's fall from grace had been swift and severe, according to the gossip he had heard from other members of the Indonesian community in Melbourne. Perhaps it was for the best that they no longer communicated.

Maybe he was dead, although he thought that unlikely as this news would also have slowly filtered through the system. They had not spoken since Wanti's collapse and their departure from Jakarta. Albert had not returned to Indonesia nor made any attempt to contact her husband since those times. He still felt bitter at Stephen's treatment of Wanti.

If only they had known Wanti's secret then, perhaps their lives would not have resulted in so much despair, tragedy and disgrace. All Stephen had to do was agree to the divorce. It could have been handled in Jakarta within days and may have prevented, or at least softened the shock of her brother's death. He knew that the final decree would have been automatic and issued within the month even considering her condition at the time. The authorities in Indonesia would have been far more sympathetic to their needs than the bureaucrats in Melbourne. Now it was all too late.

Albert contemplated his past, reminiscing while strolling slowly along the cycle track, in the cool clear winter's day. He had long given up smoking cigarettes. His pipe was now one of the few remaining luxuries left in his life, and he puffed away furiously as he moved around the park opposite the apartment block.

Albert did not light his pipe when inside. His daughter, Seruni, would usher him outside immediately she detected the powerful odour.

"Please, father," she would scold in textbook Indonesian, *"you promised!"* and he would smile contentedly.

He had accepted her polite demands for, although barely out of her teens, he adored her bossy childlike tone. She had effectively become the lady of their household.

When her mother had passed away Albert did not feel that he had the strength to go on with his life. But as one soul had passed on to be replaced by another, he had found that it was possible for him to continue. He cherished the child who had been given to him to love, as he had loved her mother.

Wanti had meant everything to him and, even during her last months, Albert had tried in vain to persuade the authorities to let them marry before the birth of the child.

He thought back over those painful last months of Wanti's life. Her doctor had expressed surprise that the shock she had experienced while in Jakarta, let alone the return travel, had not induced a miscarriage spontaneously. As Wanti had remained silent regarding her condition during her early pregnancy it was not until she had advanced well into the fifth month that her startling diagnosis had been determined. An abortion was totally unacceptable to Albert and medical opinion merely confirmed that even under more favourable conditions such an operation would be ill-advised.

He had attempted to locate Stephen to seek his assistance in arranging an immediate divorce in Jakarta. Albert knew that Stephen had the influence and money to facilitate such matters. He had spent considerable time planning how to approach him. It was obvious that he would agree but it really came down to how well he could present the situation without having Stephen fly into one of his memorable temper tantrums.

Albert decided to gauge Stephen's reactions before proceeding with the request. Should his former friend be receptive, and not still carry a grudge over what had transpired, then it was his intention to ask that Stephen give consideration also to providing assistance in producing documentation evidencing the marriage of

Wanti to Albert, backdated to when they had visited. He believed that this was imperative for his child's future.

Due to her mental condition no one, of course, would entertain their marrying in Australia even had she already been divorced. Divorce proceedings could no longer be initiated by Wanti due to her condition, this course of action only then being open to Stephen.

'It isn't fair!' he wanted to yell at the bureaucrats who had explained the legalities of their problem and the limited options available to him. They couldn't even claim a de facto relationship due to her mental status.

He had phoned for days on end, attempting to locate Stephen, without success. Finally, having left messages everywhere regarding the seriousness of Wanti's condition, and the importance of his returning their calls, Albert decided that Coleman had deliberately ignored their requests out of spite. His disappointment became frustration and, eventually, totally disillusioned with the one time friend, he ceased further attempts and accepted the inevitable.

The pregnancy continued, the foetus alive in its own world slowly developing, oblivious to the fact that its life support systems were far more fragile than nature had ordained.

It was then that he grew to despise his former friend. And as the child inside approached term, preparing for its chance to enter the world, Albert sat and wondered what it would be. The nurse who now visited, out of a deep affection she had developed for the stricken woman, had volunteered her services regularly and Albert was extremely grateful for her kindness.

There had been little or few complications with the pregnancy. It was Wanti's mental condition that had induced her demise.

He had been at her side continuously. Within the minutes following his daughter's birth the baby was held to Wanti's breast, and suddenly, as the tiny child cried, the once beautiful woman squeezed Albert's hand, then called his name and smiled. Her twisted face even more grotesque with the effort of the labour, she had called out, *"Albert! Albert, the baby's beautiful!"* and he then believed, and always would, that God had blessed her with that one brief moment of consciousness to understand she had given birth. And then Wanti had died.

As she had closed her eyes Albert was certain that she had merely surrendered to exhaustion. He called her name, softly, and then urgently, still holding her hand, his heart tearing apart. The nurse had taken her hand away gently parting the couple. Suddenly the realization that she had really gone struck him with such force that he cried out loudly, his grief then taking charge.

The nursing staff had been efficient. He was sent away while they cleaned the body and prepared it for its next journey.

He had left the hospital complex, not knowing whether he wanted to live or die. The thought of the newborn child had not really registered as the pain of his loss was far greater in his mind than anything he had ever experienced, even as a child in that faraway place.

Days had passed before he could bring himself to visit the hospital again. As the nurse held his daughter for him to see through the plate glass partition, Albert's heart had skipped a beat and he felt awash with the proof of Wanti's love for him.

He had the child registered with his surname. That, he knew, was his right as the natural father. He even waited to be challenged as he submitted the forms, eager for some form of confrontation to question his rights over the infant, but none occurred.

The first time he held her in his arms he cried softly, the hardened nurses around him turning away, holding back their own tears and as Albert proudly walked out of the hospital with a new life in his care, he swore that he would always watch over her and that nothing would ever harm his daughter as long as he lived. She was later christened Seruni and Albert dedicated his life to her.

As her features took shape Albert became more and more pleased with her appearance. Her hair was a little wiry and perhaps she was not quite as pretty as her mother had been. But she was his daughter and he loved her dearly. Albert remembered her early days and smiled to himself. Scenes of their lives together flashed through his mind as he continued to walk around the tree-lined pathway, not really uncomfortable with the cold morning air. He remembered her as a tall slender teenager, intelligent and slightly over-demanding.

Now she was a young adult. Almost a woman.

'Ni, as her friends took to calling her was, he thought, most unlike her mother. Albert was pleased that she had become so independent, so strong and yet there was still a softness which he knew came from the magic of her mother's soul. As she had left her teens he tried not to be overly protective even though he was concerned that she would be hurt, or that soon he would lose her.

As the years progressed Albert had buried the sorrows of the past and now, as his child grew into a young adult, she would soon discover their secrets. He prayed that when the time came 'Ni would understand that her parents had been given no other choice.

Albert, however, would never forgive the man whom he held responsible for all of the suffering he and his family had born. He resented the intrusion of the man's memory in his thoughts.

As the ageing man climbed the few stairs leading to the apartment lift, he attempted to erase the face of Stephen Coleman from his mind.

* * * * * *

Saigon

Hart knew there would be a confrontation. There was no point in avoiding it. He accepted the call from Coleman and had consented to the meeting.

Greg Hart had agreed to his suggestion of midday in the beer garden behind the lobby of the Continental Hotel. The setting was normally quiet and not overly frequented by foreigners other than tourists. Hart walked through the lobby just minutes after the other Australian had seated himself on the far side of the terraced area which, he observed, permitted Coleman the opportunity to scrutinize arriving guests.

He'd seen his former employer a few days before when he almost knocked him down in his haste to get to his next appointment. He recognized the man instantly even with the additional weight and greying hair. It was the second time in less than four days that he had come that close to Stephen.

Hart had known of his presence in the city the very same day the man had been confined to his hotel room recovering from an obvious state of alcoholic poisoning. Identifying new arrivals was one of his tasks in Ho Chi Minh City and Coleman's presence had not exactly been low profile. He had reported immediately to Canberra and was instructed to maintain quiet surveillance, and in the

THE TIMOR MAN

event that he was seen, contact was approved conditional on his carrying the Berretta issued through the Hanoi Station Chief.

Coleman had also selected the Continental's rear terrace because it was on the ground floor with three separate exits should a discreet departure suddenly become necessary.

Coleman spotted Hart and raised his hand in recognition. Hart approached feeling wary and aggressive.

This was Hart's first opportunity to observe the other man closely and he was now startled by the change.

Stephen Coleman had aged considerably.

As he approached, Coleman rose but did not extend his hand. "Hello Hart."

"Stephen," the younger man responded and slipped into one of the heavy chairs, unbuttoning his jacket.

The silence was broken by one of the staff who had approached their table to take orders. They both accepted coffee.

Hart was the first to begin. "I trust we won't have any unpleasantness?"

"Why?" Coleman replied. "It would certainly be in character!"

"Shit, Stephen, I wouldn't have agreed to see you if I'd known that you were going to cause a scene."

"Mate," Coleman started, years of bitterness welling up as he now sat faced with the man he believed had caused so many of his problems with the authorities back in Indonesia, not to mention the expatriate community, "Why else would I bother to look you up? You don't really expect me to believe that you honestly think there is no bad blood between us? For Chrissakes, what you did to me in Jakarta would have earned you a box in most countries!"

"You don't understand, and probably never will. I did only what I thought was best."

"What a crock of shit! How could you possibly sit there and make that statement when I know, for a fact, that you spread so much shit around the market place regarding what had happened between Wanti and me that the gossip mongers had a field day!" Coleman was trying desperately to keep his cool. "And the bullshit you also started about my company and its activities. I hold you personally responsible for that, as well!"

"I think that this meeting was a mistake," Hart said, beginning to rise out of his seat.

501

"Sit down, you arsehole!" Coleman yelled, losing control of his temper.

"Go fuck yourself, Coleman," the other said, now on his feet and buttoning his light weight jacket.

Coleman caught a glimpse of the weapon as Hart hurriedly buttoned the coat.

"What the..!" he started to say, leaning across to rip the jacket open.

Hart resisted and suddenly they started yelling at each other, not loudly, but enough to cause considerable anxiety over at the waiter's station. They were watched carefully by the hotel employee as they argued. The concerned waiter decided it would be inappropriate for him to interrupt and stood discreetly away from the two foreigners as their voices rose.

Suddenly there was a shout and the Vietnamese was startled when the older man jumped to his feet and delivered several blows to his companion. The waiter fled in search of the hotel security.

Coleman stood over the prostrate figure, watching the blood ooze from the man's nose and mouth. He had hit Hart with all the force he could muster, the first blow releasing years of pent up hostility as his fist smashed teeth and bone. Hart had not anticipated the sudden blow and, stunned, did not even see the second nor the third punches which were expertly delivered with extreme force, smashing teeth through his cheek and ripping his lips.

The injured man lay still but not unconscious. His assailant remained standing, poised to strike again, arms raised, muscles tense and fists white with the skin broken around the bone. Moments passed and slowly Coleman lowered his hands. Someone called and he turned in time to see the waiter returning with what appeared to be security. Extracting a fist full of dong from his pocket Coleman waved the large bundle of notes at the approaching men. He convinced them that the altercation had ended and that his companion had not been seriously hurt, just his pride.

Stephen explained that they had argued over a woman and immediately the men departed, accepting the fabrication, amused that the older of the two had beaten the other to the ground with apparent ease. The Vietnamese enjoyed a good fight and so why not the foreigners?

"Must have Vietnamese blood," joked the security officer as he

looked back over his shoulder just a moment too late to witness the man still standing bend down and remove the automatic from the other foreigner's body.

Stephen waited several minutes for the bleeding man to recover. As Hart slowly regained his composure Coleman turned to see if he was still being watched by the waiter and, as he was not, bent down to position himself even closer to the half prone figure. Glancing quickly once more to ensure that he wasn't seen, he punched the prostrate body hard with severe blows to the stomach and ribs.

Coleman thought he heard a cracking sound and stopped his assault, breathing heavily. He then checked the coat and trouser pockets but found nothing of any real interest. He looked down at Hart dispassionately, he was groaning painfully.

Satisfied that Hart would survive, Coleman rose to his feet, straightened his clothing and left, the injured man still lying on the ground. The bitterness he had harboured through the years seemed to dissipate and, for the moment, he sensed a feeling of exhilaration he had not known in a long, long time.

As he stepped back into the hotel reception he heard the steel gates being pulled aside and, turning his head, he noticed that the lift had just descended. It was one of those noisy concertina shaped lifts, a restored version of the old cage models used widely during the French Occupation. Stephen waved to the security officer who had opened the exterior door to assist the guests inside.

The Vietnamese smiled warmly and lifted his fists in the boxer's stance followed by which he gave the Australian the thumbs-up sign indicating his approval.

Adrenaline still flowing quickly, Stephen Coleman walked briskly back to the Rex, caught the lift to the fifth floor and settled down at the bar to plan his future. The confrontation had triggered a response which had not displeased him. He had reacted positively to a basic human emotion and now realized that he could no longer avoid the ghosts which had haunted him for more than fifteen years.

It was time to settle with the General.

* * * * * *

Later that afternoon, nose bandaged and his face puffed terribly the bitter and badly beaten Hart sent a further communiqué to

503

Canberra. He advised Anderson that Coleman had attacked him and was, in his opinion, a threat to their network in the region.

The Deputy Director had responded immediately as the Intelligence Chief was away, advising their man in Ho Chi Minh City that they had initiated action and his instructions were now to avoid any further contact with Coleman.

Greg Hart attempted a smile when he received the message. Wincing with pain, he gingerly touched his swollen lips. They had required eleven stitches.

He hoped that the action his superiors had initiated would compensate for the thrashing he had received at the older man's hands. Hart knew he had never really been considered as having the right material to rise much further beyond his current position in the Service. This was only his second field posting since leaving Indonesia. The last had been seven years before and had not been entirely successful when they had to pull him out of the Philippines when he had been mistaken for another Australian engaged in one of the paedophile rings there. Still considered relatively junior in the Intelligence Organization, due to his limited abilities, he felt he really had no appreciation of what steps would be taken against his antagonist.

He leaned back in the swivel chair carefully considering this point. His pride had been seriously wounded. It would be obvious to all who witnessed his condition that he had been on the receiving end of a bloody good hiding!

'What if the staff at the Continental talked?' Coleman's beating enraged him. He fantasized wildly about being the one selected by his superiors to deliver the appropriate punishment to his adversary.

"Bastard!" he cursed, then wishing he hadn't as the pain shot through his broken face.

* * * * * *

Jakarta

Seda had never become disillusioned with the cause. He had committed his life, his being and his very existence on this earth to achieve his ambition for an independent Timor and would continue to do so until he had given his last breath. His resolve became even firmer, if that was possible, as the slow annihilation of his people continued, unwillingly conceding that the time had not yet arrived when his people could enjoy their freedom.

But he continued with his plans, adapting them to suit and rearranging them, whenever required, patiently yet impatiently reworking his strategies until he was satisfied that he had exhausted all possible scenarios available, eventually settling on one final and, what he believed, brilliant concept. Although it appeared that all was lost after the FRETILIN defeat, there was still considerable resistance to Indonesia's occupation of the territory.

Another generation had appeared. The new youth had again taken up the cry for independence from the Indonesian invaders, and they too were prepared to sacrifice their lives, if necessary, as many parents had before them.

The separatist problem just refused to go away. Support had increased after the indiscriminate shootings in Dili in 1991, and again as a result of the slaughter in Maliana in 1996. Children were taught secretly in their homes about the sacrifice their elders had made, and were encouraged not to forget the historic clashes in which their own people had won decisive battles against the much stronger adversary.

Names and dates were not forgotten. The death of Nicolau Lobato, the FRETILIN President who had been so treacherously betrayed on the last day of December in 1978, was remembered with sadness. And so too were the others, the painfully long list of their heroes who had given their lives in support of their freedom. Songs were sung softly in the mountain villages far from the ears of their enemy; songs of their heroes, and of the battles fought in places such as Bobonaro and Quelica, and of despair for the thousands of children who had died in the fierce aerial strafing attacks. The sterilization programs had continued unchecked by the international community.

The United Nations had all but given up voting on the issues relating to the enslaved state. It just wasn't in the interests of the major powers to intercede on their behalf. They had no money, no resources and now, very few weapons as, one by one their armories had been destroyed in the mountain depots. It was becoming clear that the status quo might never change as the Australians had not only signed defence agreements with the new colonial power but also entered into contracts to share the substantial reserves of oil and gas discovered within the former colony's territorial waters. The issues had become far more intricate in nature and complicated by the ever changing regional politics.

It was the hypocrisy of business, they sadly acknowledged, and their one time ally had now completely deserted them. It seemed that everyone was to prosper except the rightful owners of the land.

Even Seda's substantial wealth had grown, and with it, his power. He had discussed the offer of the Vice Presidency on a number of occasions with the President.

At first he declined. After a time, when the national mood swing supported such a decision, Seda accepted. It fitted into his general strategy, and his international standing would be greatly enhanced with the appointment. It would also permit the final touches to the strategy which could easily be his last attempt to achieve his dreams, and his destiny.

The incumbent would step down in one more year as agreed. Nathan Seda had suggested to the President that relationships with Indonesia's neighbours could be improved if, while waiting for the Vice Presidency to become vacant, he helped their Foreign Affairs Department to settle some of the main issues. Would it not be beneficial for him to spend some time visiting these countries in a gesture of rapprochement? The President was supportive of the idea.

Seda's enemies within the small powerful group of advisors, albeit few, threw their support behind the suggestion as they wanted him out of the mainstream of power and saw it as an opportunity to remove him from the political scene. This was the second time in the nation's history that the military hierarchy had become uneasy with the meteoric rise of one of the country's sons of non-Javanese stock. General Benny Murdani had caused them considerable concern when he almost clinched the post only to lose the opportunity due to his religious affiliations. National ideologies had changed considerably since the days of strict military control, producing a new generation of young men and women who were well educated, and less tolerant of the armed forces than their parents had been.

It was becoming more and more difficult to intimidate the

masses. Support for non-military figures had grown alarmingly, reflected in the number of seats now held in the Parliament. Student demonstrations were not always aimed at foreign issues as they had been twenty years before. Now the youngsters had the audacity to even confront their elder statesmen with placards calling for inquiries into corruption and nepotism within the government.

The new generation of Chinese had all but forgotten the frightening tales of slaughter that occurred throughout the archipelago thirty years before. They ignored the re-emerging signs which reflected the deep rooted animosities that had predicated the deaths of many of their ethnic minority during the abortive coup d'etat, under the Soekarno regime.

The powerful military lobby was painfully conscious of Seda's evergrowing popularity with the other ethnic groups and non-Moslem Javanese.

With half the country now no longer easily intimidated by the army, their concern was real, for Seda represented a role model which many wished to emulate. He had risen from humble beginnings and had never lost the common touch. He had served his country well both as a senior military officer and as one of the custodians of their country's economic growth, throughout the term of his service. The General had become statesman-like in his demeanour and didn't kow tow to the Palace over issues that were important to the *rakyat*, the people. When the Australians demonstrated in their cities against Indonesia's position over the ongoing oil and gas shelf territorial dispute it was their Seda who had spoken out publicly threatening to support a military blockade of the drilling areas. He was different from all the others, they knew. The people could sense it. And he was a Christian.

The former General's enemies were ecstatic at the suggestion that he be appointed as the country's Ambassador as they believed that once he had left their shores his popularity would soon decline, his name would then be quickly forgotten by his following. They had all seen it happen before and believed that Seda would be no exception.

Letters containing diplomatic necessities were exchanged regarding the appointment. The Australian people, once pumped into action by the opposition, would normally not have been receptive to such an appointment as the General had been identified as one of the principle movers behind the invasion of East Timor, and also a member of the elite military establishment which had been responsible for the slayings in both Dili and Maliana.

Had it not been for the direct and covert intervention by John Anderson, the Australian Government may have been submitted to considerable editorial pressure not to approve the appointment. As it happened, two of the larger circulation newspapers supported the selection of such a prominent Indonesian, once again reflecting, they wrote in their columns, the high regard the Indonesian Government had for the Australian people by nominating General (retired) Nathan Seda. The appointment was accepted, in principle, subject to the normal diplomatic procedures being respected.

The press had printed the story and suggestions were made that his appointment was appropriate, not only because Nathan Seda had served his country in a military capacity and then had continued on to become a successful entrepreneur in his own right but, primarily, because he was of Timorese extraction. The editorial in the Sinar Harapan suggested that his ethnic origins may even assist strengthen Indonesia's negotiating position during the forthcoming bilateral talks scheduled to be held in Canberra, Australia. It was hoped that the Australians would be reasonable in their demands and assist to diffuse the current tension over the Timor shelf oil contract concession areas.

The Armed Forces' sponsored daily newspaper, *Berita ABRI*, strongly supported their former General's selection citing not only his impressive service record but also the need for someone of his calibre, whom they believed was needed now at these difficult times when Australia and Indonesia were experiencing a major breakdown in their traditional support for each other; and although Indonesia's military believed that these reflected domestic issues in both countries, the Armed Forces were one hundred percent behind any efforts that General (retired) Nathan Seda saw necessary in restoring the good bonds that had existed until just a few years before.

* * * * * *

The day Seda departed on the Garuda 747 flight, almost ten thousand students and other supporters gathered along the route to the Sukarno-Hatta international airport to bid him farewell. As he climbed the steps of the huge aircraft which had been parked away from the terminal building due to traffic congestion, the crowd waved furiously from the observation level at the man they had come to admire so much.

He could just hear their chant above the roar of the other aircraft's Rolls Royce engines as it had taxied past, their voices drifting across the large expanse of concrete as they chanted, "*Se-da! Se-da! Se-da!*"

It was then, for the first time throughout his years of struggling to achieve the position of power that was almost in his grasp, he knew that his dream was imminently achievable and that he was almost there. He had stood majestically for a moment on the steps and waved back to the young people who had called to him, knowing that one day they would probably learn to hate the very sound of his name. This thought did not concern him. He could not permit such sentiment to cloud his judgement, as he understood that whatever they may feel in the future, regarding his actions, would depend entirely on just how successful his efforts were in achieving his goals. As the aircraft drew away from the terminal building Seda realized that he was actually entering the final phase of his plan. And should it be unsuccessful, he doubted that there would be another opportunity as his time had all but run out. This time he could not fail.

* * * * * *

The diplomat had orchestrated the travel itinerary so that his arrival would precede the international forum on regional stability. As a guest speaker, Seda would have an opportunity to achieve even greater exposure, consolidating his position as an international leader. The man who would become the next Vice President of Indonesia, and then even the President of his own country, Timor Timur. The small group of people who continued to support their dream of sovereignty would reclaim their country, silently, this time without bloodshed, while the two neighbouring countries of Indonesia and Australia concentrated on settling their own disputes as each fought the other to protect their territorial rights. His dream continued and Seda believed that it would soon be realized. One way or another.

The central government would never surrender the annexed territory, now just another of the industrial giant's many provinces. It would become part of the overall settlement when the bloodshed had finished and the two countries were obliged to sit down together and resolve their regional differences. He would ensure that this was so. As the country's Vice President.

His people had not benefited from the amalgamation of the two halves of the island: only suffering and extreme cruelty had come with the annexation. Amnesty groups had estimated that the death toll had risen to above three hundred thousand Timorese during the prolonged resistance against the Indonesians.

Seda considered that, as New Guinea was now also a serious regional trouble spot and, with tempers running high between Australia and Indonesia, there was still the very strong possibility that the people of New Guinea could also be dragged into the conflict, as even they no longer enjoyed the special relationship that had once existed between the two nations. The country was now considered unsafe for Australians and their investment houses. Violence was common between the two races and environmental issues and claims had all but brought many mining projects to a grinding halt.

Freedom fighters continued to cross the border into Irian Jaya causing havoc, and the Australians had accused the New Guinea Government of deliberately destabilising the area.

That self-determination could be achieved for the eastern half of Timor no longer seemed feasible as even political radicals agreed that it was highly improbable after so many years of Indonesian rule. The UN had become fragmented over the past twenty years and strong protest at the increasing volatility within the region had begun to cause some concerned nations to react unilaterally. They no longer believed that the UN had the power to resolve such issues unless the countries with vested interests, such as the United States, put their own priorities aside to bring about a peaceful resolution to the regional problems.

Now that the first steps of his project had been initiated there would be no turning back from this final commitment. It was a daring scheme but he knew it would be successful.

Seda had spent millions disrupting the fragile relationships between the two countries and, with his presence in Canberra, he believed that he could ensure an end to the Australian support for

Indonesia's control over East Tmor by committing all of his resources into this one final effort.

He was counting on the support of his own *Fifth Column* who, as refugees, had quietly ensconced themselves within the Australian community. In particular, he could rely on the large number of men he had assisted to cross the few hundred kilometres into Darwin and down to Port Hedland. Almost all had now been given political asylum over the years and the majority, at his request, lived in the northern Australian city of Darwin. Many now worked as tool-pushers or mud men on the offshore rigs operating in the areas now in dispute. When the time arrived they would sabotage the Australian operations and take control of those sites. This was essential to his strategy.

It would be extremely difficult, he knew, to establish a beachhead even for the few short days required, without the total support of the refugees and his own men who had successfully infiltrated most of the other political movements in Darwin and Port Hedland. They were all crucial to the successful implementation of his plan.

It hadn't been easy maintaining control of the separatist forces through his intermediary, Umar Suharjo. The FRETELIN rank and file were still not aware of his identity and he continued to use the former major as his only direct contact with all of the parties involved. They rarely asked questions. When they did, Umar's cold stare would be their only response and normally sufficient to curtail their curiosity as they were aware of his reputation. Most were satisfied with just the strength and sincerity of their secret supporter, as the constant flow of funds and weapons had never ceased. They accepted that this powerful entity needed to maintain a cloud of secrecy as to his identity, and understood also that his support was dependent on that secrecy being preserved. Whoever he was, they believed they could count on him and he on them.

Many of these former guerrillas had already been enlisted as part of a special task force which he planned to mobilize towards the third quarter of that year.

Seda's time was running out. Each morning as he observed himself in the privacy of the bathroom mirror he could see that his age would now be his major handicap should this final attempt fail them all. There had just been too many battles and far too many sleepless nights worrying about whether he had covered his involvement successfully.

The subterfuge had continued. Would there be a knock on his door late one night to relieve him of his power and all hope for his dreams?

There had been a time not so long ago, he remembered, when he sensed that his secret would become public and all would be lost. Seda had never understood how Coleman had successfully managed to evade Umar's search. He had worried that Coleman would suddenly reappear and accuse him of involvement with the arms company although the paper trail had long since been destroyed. As the years passed, and Stephen Coleman didn't appear, it seemed that his secret was to remain intact. Not that the Australian could really do him any harm now, after so much time had elapsed.

Anyway, Seda thought, it would be unlikely that anyone would believe the man. Coleman would be accused of deliberately agitating to further exacerbate the problems between their two countries at a time when even minor incidents caused social unrest and public reaction. No, he thought, he was no longer a threat to Seda nor the intricate plans that had taken years to put into place.

The retired General's rationale was a brilliantly conceived strategy with a simplicity in its application that virtually guaranteed success. He understood the phobia Australians had regarding their Asian neighbours. There was almost an inherent fear that, one day, hordes of yellow skinned devils would pour into their country and take their women, their land and eventually become their new masters. This myth had, he knew, been perpetuated by the Australian leaders themselves as a means of maintaining power, increasing defence spending and generally using the Asian population as a prop for whatever excuse required as the country slowly deteriorated economically during the latter half of the century.

He would attack their isolated towns, creating a moment of terror that they had not experienced since the Japanese destroyed Darwin with their air-raids and the mini-submarines attacked Sydney Harbour, executed as part of their desperate attempts to invade mainland Australia during the Second World War.

There would be other and simultaneous breaches of Australian security, but none as deadly as the bomb he had planned to deliver into the basement section of the nation's Parliament.

He sneered at the Australian's informal ways. Seda despised them for their lack of loyalty. His people had fought side by side with the soldiers and their funny shaped hats against the common enemy when the Japanese threatened to rule the Far East. Soldiers from both nations had died side by side. When the Timorese had sought the support of their old friends, at the time their impoverished land was invaded by Indonesians, they had received nothing more than a cursory commitment that the Australians would ensure the sovereignty of the fledgling nation which, in spite of those casual promises, never did have the opportunity to enjoy its own state-hood.

His armed groups would raid one of the small Australian coastal towns killing many of its inhabitants. When the sleepy southern nation retaliated, which he expected would be relatively slow in terms of response as they were so poorly equipped, Seda would have the opportunity to drag them even further into the conflict; this would, he anticipated, result in not just a regional swing against Indonesia, but also provide him with the opportunity to widen the split between the two countries until international pressure forced the warring nations to the negotiating table.

It was imperative to his plan that the United Nations finally be pressured by the other powers to intercede in the conflict, creating the opportunity for Timor to be used as a bargaining instrument in the final settlement. The rich Timor oil fields and the strategic military importance of the Ombai-Wetar Straits virtually guaranteed vested interest support from the Americans in achieving stability once again over the area. The United States was desperate to maintain their secret nuclear submarine presence in those deep ocean depths. The Australians would not wish to see their access through Indonesian waters blocked, cutting off their most important trade routes, and would have no choice but to also support an independent Timor. This would guarantee ongoing access to the deeper sea lanes, essential for the huge ships carrying iron ore and other shipments into Asia. Under the terms of the Law of Sea Convention, which Australia and Indonesia signed back in 1994, disputes over sea lanes were to be settled before the International Marine Organization. The President had agreed to withdraw Indonesia from that convention if other countries would not accept the routes revised by his generals. It would not be long before Indonesia could block all sea traffic through its territorial waters. Australian trade would suffer immediately, bringing about the loss of established markets. The Australian Collins class nuclear submarines would no longer be permitted to pass through the deep straits off Timor. Under the Law of the Sea, Indonesia was declared an archipelago state which gave it special rights over its waterways in exchange for providing an appropriate number of international sea lanes. The Indonesian military, as a result of Seda's influence, developed a different interpretation of the Law as they had become extremely suspicious about international shipping. Seda had a joint venture shipping *kongsi* with those close to the President and wished to develop a monopoly over the use of Indonesia's sea lanes.

Seda believed that all of these factors would contribute to the success of his plans. As hostilities increased between Australia and Indonesia he would step forward and offer to prevent further escalation and invite the United Nations to intervene. Seda knew he had substantial support from the Indonesian people. He would use this strength to force the Javanese to accept the terms negotiated with its neighbours.

As one of the country's senior leaders, Seda could ensure that Indonesia would bend to international pressure and grant Tim-Tim its independence. As a gesture, he would suggest that Timor be placed under the protection of the United Nations until such time as elections could be held. He didn't want to see a recurrence of the blood-letting that his people had already suffered. But, if necessary, he had promised they would once again fight, creating three fronts for the Indonesian military to consider. As almost half of the country's population were Christian, Seda was confident that he would have the necessary strength to achieve his aims.

The OPM freedom fighters would cross from New Guinea as they had done before, raiding the transmigration villages established by the Javanese in Irian Jaya, killing and terrorizing until the migrants fled and they themselves returned across to the safety of their own borders. They would burn the freeport copper town of Tembagapura and destroy the mountainous mining facility which continued to fatten Jakarta's coffers.

Australia would immediately go on the defensive once their coastal areas had been threatened and their cities attacked. The Timorese would press for yet another UN-sponsored resolution supporting their independence and, should this also fail, insurrection would occur immediately. Teams would take over the drilling rigs and those which could not be secured would be destroyed, with their crews.

His strategy was to activate the groups simultaneously. The first group, numbering twenty and armed with the weapons to be distributed by Umar, would strike the small town of Broome on the northern coast of Western Australia.

Their instructions would be to shoot and kill as many of the inhabitants as possible in one hour and then retreat. They were not to differentiate in their random selection of targets. Distasteful as it may be for the guerrillas, they were told that maximum effect could be attained if a reasonable number of women and children died in the attack.

The strike team would enter the area in vehicles which would be transported to within a few kilometres of the small town along with the weapons. This equipment would be in place three days prior to the attack, stored in two semi-trailers along with other essential items. The large trucks would be driven from the interstate storage company in Perth, an outfit Seda had arranged to purchase, along with the vehicles, the previous year. These would then meet up with the team at an abandoned cattle station airstrip.

Their escape would be by air. Two Nomads that had been acquired were currently housed in their hanger in Port Moresby. When the time came, both would be flown down through Queensland and across towards the target area where they would wait until after the raid, and then ferry the group back to Darwin, from where the aircraft would then return to their original departure point. The aircraft would fly low on the sectors in and out of the strike zone area. Flight plans would be submitted excluding these sectors, nominating other unmanned private airstrips, any number of which could be found throughout the enormous expanse of the great Australian outback. The Nomads would not be detected and, even if they were to show up on the traffic controllers' screens, they would probably be mistaken for another couple of foolish country flyers building up extra hours on their private licenses.

Seda had first developed the concept when reading how so many small aircraft continued to enter Australian airspace undetected. Many of the flights were drug-related shipments and he could never understand why the Australian air force was so complacent when it came to light aircraft landing at their military strips.

As the attack was to take place during the early evening, the raiding party would have sufficient time to complete their task and disappear before the shocked Australians could even begin to understand what had happened to their town. He estimated that, as the killing would occur during the school holiday period, the dead could number as many as three or four hundred.

His men would wear Indonesian uniforms, complete with their colourful berets and shoulder flashes. They had to be seen to be an elite Indonesian military corp responsible for the attack. Seda smiled at the reverse role some of the older men would play, former FRETILIN soldiers who would finally have the opportunity to take their revenge and have the Indonesians taste a little of their own for a change, once the Australians retaliated! The town would be in shock and relatively defenceless.

The men were to move in quickly, driving the jeeps through the main street and into the police station where they were to kill those present and set fire to the building. The post office would be closed, but the Telstra communications were a first priority target and had to be destroyed quickly. It was unlikely there would be many cellular telephones operating although, if there were, there was little they could do about this problem. Next, the team was to drive to the hotels and bars, strafing the windows and doors, and randomly shoot all pedestrians within sight. In the event some of the local inhabitants were able to take up arms and return their fire, bodies of any of their dead or wounded were not to be left behind.

The second group of seventy-five men, similarly dressed, would hit three or more of the small fishing villages across the Torres Strait killing as many of the islanders as time permitted. These raiders would escape, also through the night, by small high performance boats returning to one of Seda's offshore crew vessels, their point of embarkation. The smaller craft would then be scuttled.

They would remain on board until receiving further instructions from Umar. A specialist team of three would work from his residence. A catering truck would depart from the embassy compound where it would have been positioned away from the inquisitive eyes of the police until the time was right for its special delivery to the people of Australia. The vehicle had already been purchased and was being prepared by his Security Attaché. Seda smiled. Umar with a diplomatic passport! He wanted to laugh, and would have, had not the thought been so serious.

The small truck had already been repainted leaving only the appropriate company logo and colours to be affixed. They had done their homework with relative ease; security in the capital was quite deplorable, as he'd discovered during first investigations as to the viability of his plan.

It would really be so incredibly simple! Umar had come up with the idea and he had approved of it almost immediately. It was brilliant! The small truck had double lock doors at the back and a sliding access hole on the roof of the aluminium housing which rested lightly on the extended tray. Inside the container and immediately in the centre, Umar would place a drum of diesel oil and then steadily pack the metal bin with ammonium nitrate until the relative proportions had been achieved. When he had finished there would be approximately seven percent of the total contents in fuel oil sitting silently in the compacted mass of fertilizer, which they would purchase through the same trucking firm Seda had acquired for the Western Australian operation. As ammonium nitrate absorbs humidity from the air, making it much more difficult to ignite, the diesel oil was necessary to keep the chemical from absorbing the humidity, making it more combustible and compatible with the detonators they had planned for their surprise delivery.

Then it was just a matter of using the simple technique that Umar had observed so many of the registered suppliers were instructed to follow when on a run into the service areas of the Houses of Parliament.

The truck would be left parked below in one of the appropriate bays designated for light deliveries, and Umar would simply take one of the service lifts, walk through into the building and follow the staff until accessing the public passageways in the uncomplicated structure, leaving through the front entrance. Umar had already visited the buildings and had conceived the idea after discovering the incredibly lax security. He had been amazed when first entering the building that they had even been given him a brochure complete with plans of the overall layout. He had tested his idea at least a dozen times, casually walking through the entrance which leads into the Great Hall, turning to the left as if he'd intended using the toilet before taking the lift down to the underground carpark. Umar had discovered that there was an alternative choice available. Should any difficulties occur on the day, he would park the van on the common carpark instead as the lifts permitted visitors to exit directly outside the main structure.

The truck and its contents would remain in place until news broke of the successful attack on Broome. This would, no doubt, result in an emergency meeting of both Houses of Parliament. The building would be packed full of the nation's representatives!

Umar had estimated that the force of detonation would be similar to the Oklahoma City disaster or even the IRA bombing of London's East End. The explosion would almost certainly destroy the main building, killing most of the politicians present at that time.

Perhaps the Australian public would give him a medal! He laughed silently to himself, relishing the thought of removing the majority of the so called policy makers in just milliseconds! He expected that the military would act in the absence of any political leadership. The ageing General believed that the plan was almost flawless. The unpredictable Australian cyclone season may present a problem but apart from this consideration, he felt that the operation would be successful.

Umar had already taken up his post as Head of Security in the Embassy, acting as his co-ordinator and making preparations for his own arrival to take up the position as the new Ambassador.

The first team which was to be designated the task of attacking Broome all resided in Australia. These were loyal FRETILIN soldiers, Timorese whose sympathies still supported the use of force to liberate their homeland.

Almost everything was now in place. All that remained was his presence in Canberra, where he would present the new Australian Head of State his credentials, appointing him as the Indonesian Ambassador Plenipotentiary and Extraordinary to the Government of the Commonwealth of Australia.

Seda could hardly wait.

THE TIMOR MAN

*****

Canberra

The Prime Minister had, by now, developed a distaste for the all too frequent meetings with the tall grey-headed Intelligence Chief. Having listened to the arguments proposed by Anderson the politician reluctantly admitted that it did, in fact, make a great deal of sense to go along with the appointment.

His first reaction was to instruct the Foreign Affairs Minister to refuse to accept the notorious Seda as the proposed Indonesian Ambassador however, as Anderson had quite rightly suggested, although it would not be exactly palatable having him sitting in Canberra, the general public in both countries had no inkling whatsoever of the powerful man's covert activities and, away from the central power base of Jakarta, he would lose considerable strength and influence in that city. In consequence, the Prime Minister had, with reservations, agreed to the appointment. Normally he would not interfere in such matters; however, when the former General's name was mentioned during a prayer meeting the Prime Minister remembered having seen something about him in the 'Eyes Only' classified documents.

Later, in the privacy of his inner sanctum, he was disgusted to discover that he had been correct and that his government was being asked to accept this evil man at Ambassadorial level.

The afternoon following the ceremony accepting the former General's credentials in Canberra, John Anderson visited a two-room apartment in Braddon, one of the capital's older suburbs. It was the home of Albert Seda.

Chapter 22

Hong Kong

Stephen had stayed on the island of Koror in the Palau group for four weeks, swimming and snorkelling around the beautiful islands almost untouched by the tourist industry. The pristine beaches remained one of Palau's attractions, pulling him back regularly, like some gigantic magnet, whenever he felt the need to disappear and collect his thoughts.

He had lazed around on the main island for the first week, doing nothing more than walk around the small capital, eat, drink and generally play the tourist in what he considered to be one of the most beautiful islands in Micronesia. It was the combination of the overweight locals, content with their lives and always happy to sit down and talk to a newcomer as they were a naturally hospitable people, and the lazy tropical days, that made one feel completely relaxed. The sun's rays were not overly aggressive and the flat calm lagoon effect of the ocean as it barely moved upon the sands, the faint sound of the ripples licking at the minute granules of coral sand, could guarantee sleep at any time.

Each time he revisited, Coleman had difficulty believing that the tiny paradise, although it still enjoyed the protection of the United States, was in itself not subject to any external threat; nor was the minute republic exploited, even though it was truly one of nature's tropical wonders that had to be visited by all. Even the domestic political disputes were, by very nature, almost tribal, and the casual visitor soon became familiar with the more prominent personalities in the isolated and relaxed capital.

Stephen primarily dedicated his time to exercise aimed at reducing his weight. He ate sparingly, enjoying salads and the popular steamed fish dishes the islanders prepared so well. He drank only in moderation and was quite pleased with himself at being able to abstain until the late afternoon sun had disappeared below the horizon, providing him with the motivation to continue with these efforts to restore his health and get his life back into order. When he remembered the copious amounts of alcohol that he'd consumed every day over the past years, even he was surprised that his body functions had not given up well before, leaving him to die in some stinking hospital in Vietnam or China.

He read the American newspapers when they were available. Inevitably, the tabloids emphasised news from the States and hardly mentioned his area of the planet. There was still plenty of time to catch up, he thought, and once he had restored his energy level to where he felt confident of being able to withstand the demands he planned to place on his mind and body, then he would make the effort to find out what exactly had been happening in the rest of the world that may be of any real consequence to him.

Towards the end of the fourth week Coleman felt totally revitalized. He had lost eight kilos, almost eighteen pounds of fat, due to his healthy diet and exercise program. His skin had lost its jaundiced tinge, replaced by a healthy tan. He looked at himself in the beachside bungalow's long dressing mirror and decided that he should have embarked on this road of self care years before.

Admiring his improved shape and tan, he decided it was time to move on.

That evening he arranged his onwards travel a little saddened that he would be leaving the magic of these islands behind. The airstrip severely limited the size of the aircraft that could land in the scattered island group and he decided to follow the path established by many of the American servicemen still stationed on Guam, making his way south across the myriad of small islands down to Port Moresby, where he intended then sailing on to the northern tip of Queensland, via Cooktown and the other small coastal towns.

The typhoon changed his plans to island hop across the region as the sky turned ominously dark and the wind howled threateningly through the coconut palms and rooftops.

The power of nature's forceful winds alarmed Coleman. He had no wish to fly around the islands in a light aircraft being tossed around in the turbulence. The typhoon kept him indoors for almost three days and, sensing a bout of depression, he cancelled his immediate plans, electing to remain on the island for a few more weeks. Stephen scrapped the original itinerary and decided to replace his wardrobe and replenish the dwindling contents of his tattered money belt. He returned to Hong Kong.

No longer concerned with anonymity, Stephen checked into the Hyatt on Hong Kong Island, as the Kowloon side had suddenly been inundated with another flood of Chinese investors intent on purchasing whatever property they could now that the gates had been opened.

He visited some of the old familiar haunts but found that many had given way to even more high rise development on the already over-saturated land. The city's character had changed to such extent in just a few months he had difficulty identifying the real 'Hongkies'. The new tenants had flooded into the world's largest marketplace, placing unprecedented pressures on everything from public utilities to exotic and previously outlawed forms of Chinese cuisine. This new breed, descendants of Shanghai coolies and street traders who had become China's *nouveau riche*, had brought with them many of the old habits and ways which had been prohibited under the British.

Restaurants blatantly advertised animal organs from protected species as main fare for the day. Stephen noticed that one restaurant he'd passed had no compunction preparing the rhesus monkeys from India, locked in their cages, screaming at their temporary masters, almost knowing that they were doomed to a tormented living death when the expensive meal was taken by the discerning Chinese connoisseurs, scooping pulsating brain through a hole made in the table's centre section so that all of those present could participate simultaneously, believing that eating the live monkey's brain would give them tremendous sexual vitality.

He wasn't disgusted that the city's inhabitants had seemed to have taken a major step backwards and forgotten whatever the one hundred years of colony rule had taught them. Western civilization's perception of how human behaviour should be as the world approached the twenty-first century meant very little here.

Stephen understood that. Instead, he merely reserved judgement even though the thought of the monkey's brain appetizer would spoil his appetite. He remembered where he was, and how the people in the real world of Asia actually lived, and would probably continue to do so millenniums after Western civilization had been put well to rest.

Mister Lim's operation had quietly closed after he had fled to Canada prior to the Chinese takeover of the former colony. The hotel's concierge soon put him into contact with an up-market service, which he had dialled and made arrangements for the following evening.

He had ordered a selection of new clothes to be tailored and, although the fashions had changed to a combination of baggy shirts and semi-stovepipe trousers, with button-less coats left open, he'd insisted on the older and more traditional cut for his single-breasted suit. He intended at least to look the part of the role that he knew he must play.

When these were ready, Coleman phoned the Australian Consulate General and arranged an appointment with the passport control officer as his travel document once again required renewal.

Then he visited his safety deposit boxes and confirmed his assets, smiling to himself at the wise decision he had made all those years back when the pressures of the moment could have caused him to panic and lose it all. As he sat in the private cubicle prepared by the bank's clerk, viewing the first of the two boxes, a flood of memories returned as it always did each time he opened what he jokingly thought of as being his own private bank. He picked up the faded photograph and smiled before placing it back inside the box. Then he checked the cash.

Stephen counted. There was still more than four hundred thousand dollars left in the steel boxes. Even when he'd been in a permanent alcoholic haze in the past, he'd kept track of his cash.

There were also three envelopes.

He had not considered it necessary to take precautions before the threats against his life. When making the notarised declarations at the time, Coleman had thought that the ignominious material contained in the letters wasn't much of a testimony to his life. He understood clearly that, should the letters become public or actually be read by the addressees as annotated on each of the revealing envelopes then, of course, he would be dead.

His instructions to the bank management had been simple and explicit. At least once in every year he required that his signature be presented when either transferring funds or just inspecting his own safety deposit. In the event that a year had passed and he had not appeared in person then the bank was to open his security boxes and forward all of the contents to one Albert Xavier Seda as per the address he had given. Coleman had attached a will leaving the cash contents to his wife, Wanti.

The three brown envelopes were addressed to each of the editors of The Jakarta Times, The Sydney Morning Herald and The Mirror with copies of details of Seda's involvement in their *kongsi*, attaching invoiced proof of funds with the relevant banking authorizations nominating the General's own accounts as the recipient of huge commissions. Each also contained a statement regarding his earlier role working for the Directorate headed by John Anderson — sufficient information, he had thought at the time, to severely curtail their activities for some time to come.

Before closing the lid of the second container, he considered the contents of these damaging envelopes and smiled. Stephen sat quietly for a few moments before passing the cream-coloured steel boxes containing his whole life's possessions over to the clerk for double locking. He then left the bank's cellars and returned to the hotel, already bored and exhausted by the bustling city.

Stephen phoned the escort service and advanced his booking.

* * * * * *

The officious immigration officer had insisted Coleman return for his passport after two full working days, looking up at the applicant as if he were some dirty piece of dog's excrement, carried into the consulate stuck to the underside of his public service shoes by mistake.

At the time Stephen had bristled. He knew that this type of petty bureaucrat entertained themselves at the expense of the public and willed himself not to over react. Stephen knew how Australians were perceived by their Asian counterparts, although they were normally too polite or embarrassed to say. Often, when confronted with these minor officials whose supercilious behaviour resulted in adverse first impressions, the Oriental would accept the insulting conduct as normal and in line with what they had learned to expect of all European races.

As it was now already Thursday, Stephen had little choice but to wait until the Monday morning when the Consulate would have his new passport ready. They agreed that he could retain his old passport, reluctantly, until he had insisted that it would be required for banking purposes.

"You must surrender your old passport on Monday when we give you your new one." he was told.

He had thanked the obnoxious consular officer and left before his temper got the better of him. Coleman knew that he had to remember to keep his cool. It would be important in the weeks ahead. He had time to kill and decided to spend the next two days visiting Guang Zhou as he had not been there for some years. Disappointed with the industrial pollution, he returned late in the afternoon in time to confirm the arrangements for his Saturday night's entertainment.

She was exceptionally attractive, but not in Angelique's class, he thought, watching her undress hurriedly. Their lovemaking had been mechanical at first, and Stephen was tempted to pay her then and there spending the remainder of the weekend alone. She had showered and was sitting silently as if waiting for further instructions.

"You can go home now if you want," he said.

"Why?" she asked, surprised.

"Well, I thought maybe I'd take a rest and just watch a show on television."

"You no send me home, okay!" she had pouted, obviously thinking that an early departure had meant her client was dissatisfied with her.

Stephen had laughed at the serious expression and the accompanying act, fully aware of the reason behind the reaction. "Okay, you stay," he said, with which the towel around her breasts was immediately flung aside as she jumped onto the bed pulling him down playfully.

They left the room only to dine in the hotel's well-appointed restaurants and, as he was not drinking anywhere near as heavily as before, he found that his old stamina was slowly returning to form.

It had been a long time since he had really enjoyed the company of a woman for more than just a few hours. Her name was Kwai Fong. She was expensive. Coleman didn't complain as her attitude had changed when they returned to the suite, this time undressing slowly in well rehearsed and tantalizing movements, before engaging him in a long slow fantasy showing the sexual finesse of a practiced artisan.

Stephen was content to remain in the hotel room, eating, being spoiled and occasionally running the remote control through the multitude of channels offered through the hotel's satellite television service. He had arranged a final fitting for the rest of his new wardrobe and, satisfied that there was little else to do but wait, spent the remainder of the weekend being entertained by the beautiful woman.

* * * * * *

It was a short taxi ride to the Consulate's offices. The mass of humanity gathered around the ground floor lift access spilled out through the building's foyer onto the footpath. Visa applications for Australia, he assumed. Thousands of the old Hong Kong citizens waited for their families overseas to process their applications to join their children who had the right to sponsor parents and other immediate relatives under the revised immigration scheme. Too impatient to join a queue, he pushed through the crowd and found that it wasn't all that difficult. The others thought he was a member of the staff and quickly stood aside as he asked them to move.

The lift doors opened at the appropriate level and immediately Stephen had to fight his way through yet another large number of Chinese pushing to reach the numbered roll of tape allocating a position to those who wished to make an inquiry from the Consulate.

Again he pushed through and was relieved to see that one of the consulate staff had identified him. He signalled for Stephen to pass through the side security door and into another holding area. Stephen was impressed by the thick heavy door clicking firmly shut behind him.

He was ushered into an office where the almost effeminate creature, the man who had caused his blood pressure to rise when he'd last visited, was seated. The consulate officer smiled sweetly and advised him that his passport had been endorsed by the Consulate, but not renewed.

"What do you mean endorsed? What sort of crap is this?" he

had asked immediately, standing over the now agitated official.

"I am not the Consul, Mr Coleman, you will have to speak directly to him. He has asked that you meet upstairs and he will explain."

Coleman was then ushered upstairs and through another series of security doors, similar to the first, to another section where he was instructed to wait. He became impatient to get out of the building with its overhead fluorescent lights and sterile atmosphere.

Twenty minutes had dragged by when finally Stephen was asked to follow the security officer. The man was dressed smartly in his new Federal Police uniform, one of the first issued under the restructured department's new image edicts. Stephen became uneasy when he noticed, with some surprise, the Smith and Wesson Thirty-Eight police special strapped to the officer's hip.

Immediately Coleman sensed that he had made an error in judgement. He should have had his documents renewed in Manila, he thought, as the journey from Palau took him through that city, where he had spent two days and would have had ample time to complete the necessary formalities without this inconvenience.

He turned suddenly to the consulate officer, unhappy with the way things were developing and concerned that he might now be under armed escort. Stephen hoped he was overreacting.

"What's the problem? Look, if there's a problem, just give me my old passport and I'll proceed on to Shanghai and have it done there. It won't be a hassle for me as I have business there and my passport still has enough space for limited travel," he lied.

"I'm sorry, but you'll just have to wait."

"Okay, ten minutes then I'm out of here, passport or no passport," he warned.

"All right, follow the officer then," he was instructed, "you can sit in the other office."

Tense and convinced that he was justified in feeling hostile, Stephen followed silently as he was escorted into yet another room and again left to wait, impatiently, for what seemed an excessively long time. It was impossible to know, but he felt sure that the armed security who had not spoken during his exchange with the consulate official, had taken up post directly outside the room in which he now found himself. He was angry and was about to leave without his documents, deciding to return later or arrange to have someone else pick the passport up on his behalf, when the he heard voices approaching.

The door opened and Coleman stared at the visitor in disbelief.

"Good morning, arsehole!" the man snarled at him.

Coleman still couldn't believe his eyes. Standing across the room at a safe distance was the man he had left lying on the ground in Ho Chi Minh City. Greg Hart.

As he rose to his feet cautiously the doorway was suddenly filled with several other men who pushed in quickly and stood still, saying nothing, just glaring at him. These were unfamiliar faces but Coleman guessed from their size they were there to restrain him, should the necessity arise.

Hart smirked. Or was this his new natural smile acquired as a result of their last confrontation and the beating he'd given him?

"I won't give you any crap about the good news and the bad news Coleman," he spat sarcastically. "For you it's just all bloody bad!"

Stephen looked at the man silently, refusing to be baited in case he was being set-up. The heavy-set pair looked like they were just waiting for an opportunity to use their muscle on him.

What the hell was Hart doing here?

"You are being placed under arrest," Hart began, "and you are being charged under the Official Secrets Act."

The other government men in the room could see from the cocky manner that Hart was enjoying himself. The sarcastic tone and method of delivery wasn't lost on them. This was the first time either of the security men had been party to an arrest under The Act and they were nervous, understanding the gravity of such charges.

Had they been privy to the thoughts of the man now detained their concerns would have been justified. At that very moment, more than anything he'd ever wanted before, Coleman wished they would leave the room, if only for just a few minutes, so he could kill the smiling Hart. He knew he would do it, without hesitation. Coleman sat stunned with the incredible realization that it was Hart who was making the statement for his arrest. He must have been involved somehow with Coleman's former government associates and had been, even way back in Jakarta when his now apparent treachery had resulted in the collapse of Stephen's world.

He wanted to kill. More than anything he had wanted ever in his life before, he wanted to kill this man who had betrayed him. He cursed himself for leaving Hart's automatic behind in Ho Chi Minh City. Even without a weapon he knew he could do it. He stood rigidly still willing the guards to leave them alone as he half heard Hart's voice continue with the official statement.

"At this time you will not be given the opportunity to call or communicate with any legal representation." Hart paused, placing his hands on his hips before continuing. "I am advised that you will, however, be provided with such an opportunity when you arrive in Australia."

Coleman stood very still, only his fists moving as he clenched them tightly, almost cutting off the flow of blood to his fingers.

"Furthermore," the sarcasm evident in voice, "you will be escorted back to Canberra by these two gentlemen standing beside me."

Hart then turned to the men.

"Be careful of this piece of shit! You can see what I copped when I wasn't looking!" he lied, gesturing with one hand towards the fresh scars on his face.

"Well, he's welcome to bloody well try," said the thick-set ex-rugby footballer. Stephen's eyes darted to the man and knew that there would be no chance of escape.

"Well, that's it then," Hart said, his voice now slightly pitched as he was enjoying Coleman's dilemma. "Guess we won't be seeing you for awhile, eh Stephen?"

"My guess is about thirty years," stated the other Service escort, not really knowing what the exact charges were against this man but wishing to be considered knowledgeable on the subject of the arrest.

Coleman remained very still.

He wanted to scream. But even more, he wanted to spring across and pound away again at the sneering face as one of the men stepped forward and, to Stephen's chagrin, handcuffed his wrists tightly and deliberately heeled his right ankle, sending a searing spear of pain up through his leg.

They kept him there for five hours. Nobody was permitted into the room with the exception of his guards and the arresting officer. He was not given anything to eat or drink and he didn't want them to have the satisfaction of his asking. Coleman's mind was racing.

He knew that this had to be Anderson's handiwork but somehow it just didn't make any sense to him. Surely he wasn't being detained just because he bruised one of their men? And how could they have possibly made the mistake of employing such an incompetent in the ASIS?

No. There had to be something else. Surely after all these years there was no reason for them to harass him, as he had not been involved with anything of any interest to them for over fifteen years? He thought quickly and decided that Anderson would now be too old to still have any involvement in the intelligence network.

Then he remembered seeing the photograph some months before as he flew from Hong Kong to Vietnam. And suddenly he thought he understood. It had to do with Seda!

He didn't offer any resistance to the two huge men as they moved him out of the room and down to the basement carpark where a consulate vehicle was waiting, engine running and driven by yet another Australian. They had been to the hotel and packed his belongings. No doubt, he thought, they would have flashed their Interpol identification cards issued to Federal Police stationed overseas, and easily accessed his room.

There was nothing there of any interest except for his new clothes and other baggage. He still had the safety deposit key and the cash he'd withdrawn in his back pocket. There would have been no evidence of his banking anywhere in the room. He always destroyed these as his arrangements were simple enough to remember and really only required his personal attendance and passport when withdrawing funds from the security boxes.

He tried to concentrate, checking in his mind whether there was anything at all in his baggage that could be of interest to these people. Deciding that there wasn't, apart from maybe three or four hundred American dollars he'd made a habit of secreting away inside his toilet bag for emergencies then, he felt certain his safety deposit would remain intact. As for the small cash reserves, he wasn't concerned, knowing that these men would slip the few hundred dollars into their own pockets when they discovered its whereabouts.

Six hours later a completely shocked and confused Stephen Coleman sat, still handcuffed, on one of the RAAFs ageing Mystere jet aircraft en-route to Canberra. His exit from the former colony had been expedited swiftly without fuss as the Federal Police Officers rushed him through the private diplomatic counter at immigration as one of the pair spoke fluently in Mandarin.

Coleman could see from the expression on the Chinese immigration officer's face that the story they had concocted was obviously believable; he saw the official shake his head from side to side in disbelief at whatever he was being told in his own animated tongue. They checked his baggage only in a cursory manner, eager for the evil man to leave quickly. They knew that sometimes these sort of people brought bad *joss* and there was already enough of that around!

He was then taken directly to the aircraft and, when he recognized the markings, knew that whatever was happening was in fact, serious. The aircraft's engines were already idling as their diplomatic vehicle, escorted by a jeep flashing warning lights, crossed the tarmac and quickly deposited Coleman and his escort officers before disappearing again.

They had been given immediate clearance and, within five minutes, Coleman looked through the small round aircraft windows to see the terminal lights of Chek Lap Kok flashing by as the engine's thrust hurled them along the busy runway.

An hour later he was given a cardboard box containing sandwiches. No weapon there, he observed, picking at the small tuna fish and lettuce sandwich. He remained cuffed for most of the flight. When he needed to use the toilet Coleman was obliged to leave the small cramped toilet's door open each of the three times he visited the heads.

He didn't attempt to sleep. The speed of the events resulting from his arrest still had his head spinning. As the aircraft continued through the night, passing over many of the idyllic beaches where he'd lived an uninterrupted life without the cares of his peers, Coleman thought long and hard concerning his predicament and what it may really mean to his future. He believed then that his assumptions were correct. It was all somehow connected with his former activities with the General, that much was becoming clear as he thought it all through. But why would the Service go to such elaborate lengths to force him back to Australia? He was annoyed with himself at having being so easily tricked with the charade back in Hong Kong. It was just that so many years had passed since he had to be so alert he'd not identified the signs in time.

Coleman remember reading in the Hong Kong papers a few years before that the Intelligence Service had finally been compromised. Its existence was shouted out across the nation by a former agent who fed the classified information to several journalists. These in turn promptly printed their exposé and released the incredibly embarrassing disclosures for the world to read. The report was, in essence truthful, but surprisingly had not been of real consequence to those involved as the Australian public just sighed at the revelations as if they had expected as much from their leaders and promptly forgot about the matter. It was as if the existence of a clandestine government department had little consequence in their lives. The offending agent had been given a slap on the wrist for his offence and asked to find other employment.

Knowing all this, Coleman was sure that his previous involvement with the covert group had little or nothing to do with this current action against his person.

Realizing that it was rather pointless exhausting himself further worrying about the reasons for his predicament he decided to wait for their explanation. He knew there would be one.

* * * * * *

The small sleek-lined jet refuelled twice and then, eighteen hours from the time he had entered the Australian territory of the Consulate General ott Wan Chai, Stephen Coleman was surrendered to another team of Federal guards. They were waiting for his flight, standing patiently beside their unmarked van parked on the military side of the Fairbairn airport in Canberra. Moments later he was again whisked away with considerable speed into the city, where he was taken through the heavy steel restricted access gates leading down into the bowels of the huge gray complex on Russell Hill. There he was immediately locked in the special security wing in a military holding cell.

Sitting inside the dark van as they journeyed from the airport, Stephen had been unable to see where they had taken him. He had no idea whatsoever that he now was imprisoned directly below the very building in which he had first obtained his basic administrative training some thirty years before, that he was locked in the basement below the offices of the Department of Defence in the nation's Capital. There he was detained incommunicado for three weeks.

The guards could not be seen as they slipped his food and drink through the small steel hatch and, although he had managed to remain in reasonable spirits during the first few days, eventually he surrendered to the silent treatment, the isolation and rising fear, yelling abuse at this unseen jailers as they arrived from time to time to deliver his meals and other basic necessities.

The detention cells had been, unfortunately for the very few who had ended up incarcerated there, one of the better kept secrets of the Service. These had originally been designed many years before as an interrogation centre for political radicals but had not been put to use for these purposes.

Towards the end of the Korean War, the country's xenophobic masters, believing with incredible zeal in the subversive intentions of the Communist nations, had sanctioned the secret construction of the facility. Originally it was designed as an atomic bomb shelter, or at least that's what the architects, engineers and construction teams believed. Once the civilian workers had completed the buildings another small team of skilled technicians moved in and went about installing their own equipment and modifications to the original design.

The access codes were so intricate and carefully monitored only a select few had ever been approved for the sensitive positions occupied by these highly paid officers.

The design was such it also prevented visual contact between the prisoners and the hand-picked security personnel. The spartan facilities contained only the basics, although these were adequate for their purposes. There were three sections, all identical in design and purpose. The planners had not thought that more than this number would be required and, as it happened, they had been correct.

A single bed had been pushed up against one wall tiled with small cream coloured ceramic squares. The cement used had faded in colour with the years and now created the impression that the many thousands of tiles would soon break away and fall. The secret installations were ten metres below the surface and the thickness of the walls at this depth was more than one metre. All concrete and steel. There would be no successful tunnel rats in this detention centre!

In the corner a compact shower and toilet had been installed, and two extractor fans activated whenever any of the plumbing functions were used. Fresh air was pumped through an uncomplicated series of ducts which seemed to hang, almost precariously, from the low concrete ceiling. He had one light but they had not provided him with any reading material.

They had permitted him to retain his watch, and Coleman managed to keep count of the days and nights as he remained locked away, completely cut off from the outside world. Until one day, when he knew he had already been incarcerated for precisely three weeks, along with his breakfast he was given a copy of the Canberra Times.

He grabbed at the paper and immediately commenced reading, convinced that the guards had committed an error and would soon retrieve the newspaper before he'd a chance to read it. Like a greedy man devouring food, Coleman's eyes quickly skimmed through the headlines before returning to the main news item.

Then he understood why he had been given the daily. At first, he completely missed the familiar face and article, on the third page. The photograph was captioned 'General Nathan Seda Arrives' and below was the story of Indonesia's new Ambassador to Australia.

Coleman read on. When he'd finished the article he sat back, deep in thought, before reading the article once more to ensure that he'd missed nothing. It was quite a build up for the man who had once been his partner. He tried to recall his conversation with Anderson years before when the Intelligence Chief had tried to warn him of the dangers of the *kongsi* Coleman had shared with Seda, his trusted partner in a multi-million dollar armament supply organization that ended up achieving two goals for the Timorese. Capital from the healthy and regular commissions made during the years the company continued to arrange weapons and other armament contracts with the Indonesian Armed Forces being the first, and secondly, cash and supplies for the separatists who had died by their tens of thousands in their struggle for independence.

It was clear to him now that somehow the former General's appointment had something to do with his incarceration. What was the connection? Why had he been detained? Where the hell had they buried him?

Frustrated by not knowing the answers, Coleman kicked at the solitary chair beside his steel framed bed, knocking it over loudly.

"Shit!" he cursed, knowing that the outburst was counter productive and that he had to continue to keep his temper from erupting again. He read the article again, for the third time.

Then slowly it came to him. They'd had him removed as he was considered a threat to the ageing Timorese!

But why? he thought, confused even more by his own questions. Why bother? Surely there would have been a much simpler solution? They already had him in Hong Kong where an accident would have been so easily arranged!

And where was Anderson? Was he still the Director? Or worse! Had John Anderson passed away, leaving the powerful post to another who could not vouch for him? Who had so much authority that they were able to authorize an airforce jet to have him delivered back to Australia, and why then lock him away, without any communication whatsoever?

All these questions continued to clutter his mind and Stephen became seriously conserned as to the length of his incarceration.

He heard the metalic click as the door to the prison suddenly opened and immediately he realized what a complete and bloody fool he had been. Of course! It had to have been him, all along. Who else could have manipulated so many and remained so obscure, while skilfully orchestrating all the players to carry out his commands?

He rose to his feet and stood to face the elderly man.

"Hello, Stephen," was all Director Anderson said.

THE TIMOR MAN

Kerry B.Collison

Chapter 23

Canberra

Coleman sighed. He and Anderson had talked throughout the day, breaking only for a light meal.

Anderson had produced convincing evidence proving that Seda was involved in a most dangerous game which he had played successfully for almost three decades. He had never been detected by his fellow generals or any of the others who had worked side by side with him. Slowly, step by step, the Intelligence Chief laid the whole picture out before the disbelieving Coleman. Much of the earlier information he already knew, as this had been the core of their discussions some years before when Anderson had provided the most amazing detail of the General's hidden agenda for East Timor.

Coleman also remembered that he had been given an ultimatum at that time which he had unwisely ignored. In retrospect, had he listened and cooperated when the demand had been made then maybe, just maybe, he would have come out of the whole mess in much better financial shape. Still, he thought, as he listened to the detailed exposition from the well informed bureaucrat, he hadn't done too badly. At least, up to now.

He watched the Director as his hands punched at invisible points in the air, emphasizing his facts, changing the pitch of his voice when he wished the story to take a more visual form in the listener's mind, and it was then that Coleman decided that the powerful man sitting on the edge of his bed was indeed an incredibly dangerous person to be around.

Twice he had made the point that Coleman was fortunate to have left Indonesia when he had as it was most likely that he would have come to grief had he stayed for the long haul. He cited the attack on the house and office which resulted in all of the domestic staff being slain.

"That was just a warning, Stephen," the Director said, "and a test."

"Test?" he had asked.

"Seda couldn't afford to have you eliminated until he was certain that you had not left incriminating evidence behind somewhere. He was reasonably confident that you hadn't but he was not quite ready to take that risk. Instead, he managed to send you a rather blunt message which, fortunately, you eventually heeded."

He looked directly at Coleman. "Have you kept any evidence that can compromise Seda?" he asked, examining the other man's face to detect whether or not he could identify anything in his manner which would help him determine the truthfulness of Coleman's response.

"No," he lied, knowing that he was again on very dangerous ground.

"Then the General could have saved us all a great deal of trouble years ago, eh?" he half joked, knowing that the remark would unsettle the other man.

Anderson went on to explain that Coleman's name had, on a number of occasions, been suggested for Executive Action by his department. This news sent a chill along his spine. He understood very clearly what the term meant in Service vocabulary and he looked quizzically at the Director.

"Why?" he asked, "what did I do that warranted such severe steps? Surely the armament company did nothing to jeopardize relationships between the two countries and I had certainly never disclosed any of my former activities."

"It wasn't so much you by yourself. We had considered taking you both out together. It would have been cleaner and tidier for us."

"Shit!" he exclaimed, "easier for you! What about me, for Chrissakes!"

"Take it easy. It never happened, or at least, not that way. I will tell you this much though, we made two runs against Seda and missed him both times!"

Coleman was very surprised. Not just at the secrets Anderson had revealed but also that they had failed in their attempts. He sat silently for a few minutes, absorbing this new data. Now he was worried that he would not easily leave this place armed with the information he had just been given! Why was he being told all of this? The information was most sensitive and probably only known to a select few. He realized that he was being slowly prepared by this master of control.

Towards the late afternoon he could see that Anderson was tiring. And fast. Even so, he continued to explain how precarious Coleman's position remained as he could no longer return to Indonesia; the government there, courtesy of his former partner, had placed his name on the list of approximately two hundred souls who had been identified as either politically dangerous, or had caused considerable economic harm to the people of the Republic.

"Bullshit!" Stephen had said, and then wished he hadn't as the other man withdrew several more sheets of paper from his coat pockets and placed them on the bed for him to read.

His name was half-way down the second page as being wanted by the government for taxation fraud and failure to pay the correct sales tax on a considerable number of shipments of non-military materials imported into Indonesia.

Coleman had just shaken his head. "Okay, so it's not bullshit. Why did they do this?" he asked, already guessing that it had something to do with Seda's powerful control over so many in the military machine's administration throughout their Defence Department.

"The penalty for what they claim you did carries the charge of subversion, Stephen," he said, reasonably softly so that the required effect was achieved.

Coleman knew that this was another method used by the Indonesian authorities to either silence opposition or prohibit its spread. Subversion carried the death penalty.

Anderson had then produced considerable evidence citing him as one of the co-conspirators behind the armaments supply lines to the FRETILIN guerrillas which, whether he was directly involved or not, had resulted in the loss of many thousands of lives.

"Bloody hell!" he had exploded, "how could they concoct such a load of crap?"

"Come on Stephen, don't pretend to be so damn naive!" he was answered in an admonishing tone. "Seda could do just about

anything. Try and imagine just how much power the man had —
has," he corrected. "Sitting on the military boards, controlling their
intelligence apparatus, funding covert operations for both the Indonesians against the Freedom Movements of New Guinea while
still maintaining a serious resistance movement in *Tim-Tim*."

There! Hearing the words *Tim-Tim*, used by an Australian official for the first time shook Coleman. Was it possible that his own
country's leadership had always intended the disputed territory
to fall under Indonesian control?

"Was it all just a sham?" he asked, knowing that whatever answer he was given there would be another lie buried somewhere
behind, and perhaps another behind that as well, waiting to be
brought forward whenever the argument demanded.

"Without being overly philosophical, Stephen, you, more than
any of us, should understand that we are not masters of our own
destiny."

He looked at Coleman for a while before continuing, as if gauging his mood, and also measuring just how far he could go in convincing his former agent that whatever they had done, the Service
had provided nothing but the best for its members and, of course,
its country.

"It was never a sham, Stephen. We couldn't just jump in, even
when the threat was more real than even we indicated to the world.
It is a fact that this country was threatened with the very real possibility of East Timor becoming a Soviet satellite. It is also true that
the Americans were concerned with the Soviet's ever increasing
influence in the region. But, at the end of the day, what it was really all about was Australia's final emergence as a regional power
competing both economically and politically against the enormous
changes that were taking place in our own hemisphere."

"The people of this country have never really been able to understand what would happen to Australia once Japan had proven
its vulnerability - not by military power but by economic warfare."

"Our nation has retreated from being one of the most advanced
societies with a living standard almost second to none, to become
what one of our erstwhile leaders proclaimed as a Banana Republic. The sad fact is, he was correct."

"You will probably remember when you could visit say, Singapore, and change your Australian dollars into ringgits or straits'

dollars and receive almost four of theirs for each of ours. Or, in Tokyo at about the same time, again one of our dollars could be changed for about four hundred of their yen."

"I don't need to give you a lecture on what has happened to our exchange rates; it's just that even our currency's deflated value is indicative of the country's inability to motivate the young, the business sector, or even the government."

"The country has always been an agrarian state, or was, up until our resources were finally exploited by the thousands of mining and oil companies which flooded into this land to develop whatever they found. But it wasn't and won't be enough for Australia to survive in the long term. We need to maintain our position along with every other developed nation in terms of accessing, then controlling the vital resources so desperately needed by industry, and much more so, as we move into the next economic cycle. We do not have sufficient reserves to guarantee this country's economic independence when it comes to fossil fuels, Stephen."

"In short, we need control over the Timor Basin."

For the second time that day, Stephen was speechless.

Anderson had ceased talking and Coleman knew he was expected to respond. He had no idea that the Intelligence Chief would drop such a bombshell. He was suddenly very concerned and almost afraid of the man who sat there with him, quietly discussing these most delicate and sensitive political issues that had obviously been the subject of extensive debate at the highest levels.

"This is why we need you."

The words hung in the air, and Coleman suddenly imagined himself standing in front of one of those recruitment posters that had flooded the United States during the first Great War. The one with the moustachioed soldier pointing directly at the observer with the slogan *Uncle Sam Needs You!* blazoned all over the lower section. He looked sideways, quickly, to see if Anderson had really lost his marbles or was just testing him. Like Seda had.

He could see from the other man's countenance that he had been deadly serious and earnest in his display of nationalism. Was it really just that? Stephen wondered, thinking that the Director may just be a little senile. He shuddered involuntarily. Whatever the truth may be, he knew that somehow he was not going to enjoy the rest of these discussions.

Only moments had elapsed but they felt like minutes. He knew he must say something, respond, or he would appear to not be in concert with the older man.

"The Timor Basin?" he asked, almost lamely.

The elderly Director paused before responding.

"The country's majors, or multinationals, have already moved to secure their positions through negotiation. Most of the fields have been assigned under agreements which the Indonesians are fond of referring to as production sharing agreements."

"These have been finalized after some considerable effort and many years of determining exactly where their territory begins and ours finishes. One of their arguments has always been that international territorial limits should apply. Their whole goddamn country is just a mass of piss-fart little coral atolls which they have the audacity to use to enforce their extended territorial claims over the shelf which, geologically speaking, really belong to us!"

"No sooner had our companies spent the many millions necessary to prove up the fields when suddenly our neighbours decided that the formal agreements already in place delineating boundaries, and crossover areas determined under the accord, to be no longer valid. Even the joint production contracts which specify bonus payments to the Indonesians based on volume extracted are in contention."

Coleman had no real idea where the harangue was heading.

"But that's not all. In fact, its just the tip of the iceberg," Anderson continued, having taken a small sip of the mineral water. "They have deliberately caused tremendous anti-Australian feelings to erupt in their major cities as part of their typical bullying tactics. Australian investment has reached an all time high in the country and, apart from the long-term considerations in the event we lose these substantial oil and gas fields, the immediate future for almost eighty thousand of our citizens is, to say the least, bleak."

"We believe that the fields which extend from Timor across towards Darwin will produce more than this country requires for the next fifty years in terms of oil, not to mention the gas reserves."

His throat dry, Anderson then paused to take another mouthful of mineral water. He coughed lightly and then finished the remainder of the contents before continuing.

Coleman was now impressed with Anderson's argument about

resources. He had not really paid much attention to what had been happening in those fields and was surprised that the area had attracted so much interest. Volatile interest, too, so it seemed.

"When the Soviet Empire fell apart you may have read that Russia and some of the other larger former states went on a selling spree, off-loading military equipment on a scale not seen since the Americans financed the British against the Germans earlier in this century. Most of the Black Sea fleet was sold, intact, to the Indonesians. Stephen, we're talking about some thirty five to forty naval vessels that were fully operational at the time."

Coleman sat quietly, listening attentively, still not sure where the conversation was going. When the other man had mentioned the ships he thought he had read somewhere about the sale but paid little attention to this also at the time as he was no longer interested in the world of armaments.

"They needed it, John. Their navy never really regained the strength it enjoyed before the attempted takeover in Sixty-five," he said.

"These ships were supposed to travel via India for their refit but the contract was slipped off to another group where major modifications were undertaken. It was quite a surprise to all of us that the Indonesians suddenly acquired such a massive fleet of ships. Sort of an instant navy, so to speak.

"I want you to think about the following. Without the total production of the areas now under dispute, the Republic will be obliged to start importing oil again in less than ten years. Maybe even five. They know that they can hold onto the areas now in contention and perhaps even broaden the scope of their claims to include some of the other disputed properties between Vietnam and the Philippines. The Chinese and Malaysians also consider these island groups to belong to them and have positioned gun boats to support their intentions.

"Indonesia's economy has grown dramatically as you are, no doubt, aware. This boom has created an enormous appetite and the consumers have pushed their country at incredible speed to fill their demands. Although they are the world's largest exporter of natural gas and have access to thermal power as well, all of this will not be sufficient for the giant economy to survive should it become dependent on imported fuels. It is a very complicated scenario Stephen. I am not trying to patronize you but I don't think you have paid too much interest over the last few years and I am only now trying to present you with the problem as an overview to help you understand where we are at. Okay?"

"Sure. It's okay. Under different circumstances I would probably even be enjoying it." Coleman couldn't resist the inference at his cramped accommodations, moving his head from side to side as he looked around the small quarters.

"None of us are able to look into a crystal ball and just come up with an accurate scenario of what will occur in the future but we do have the ability to predict with a certain amount of accuracy what might happen given the right set of circumstances. And that is what this government has had to do to protect its own national interests. You can safely assume that the Americans, Japanese and other nations involved directly in the region will be doing precisely the same and, in fact, we believe that the United States considers what we have forecast to be reasonably accurate.

"There are many regional issues which can affect these long term projections. For instance, India has the second largest navy in the world! The average man on the street has no perception of what that means to us but I can assure you Stephen, they could be a threat to our regional stability. Their country's population explosion has put their numbers ahead of China's. Did you know that they are faced with an even more serious problem with imports than the Indonesians?"

Coleman did not answer, assuming that the question was merely rhetorical.

"Do you?" he was asked again.

"No, John. Sorry," he answered tersely.

"Difficult as it may be to believe, India with its more than one billion people, will become a net importer of food within the same period as the Indonesians may be forced into a similar position with fuel. Interesting, eh?"

"John. Please. What does any of this have to do with my being here?"

Anderson sat quietly, thinking, before he responded.

"It all has something to do with the reason for your being here, Stephen, directly and indirectly, just about all of it!

"The Indonesians are becoming militant and appear to be preparing themselves for the possibility of regional instability. That they are responsible themselves for this instability doesn't seem to enter into their thinking as many of their leaders are old and have become irrational over the issues which directly affect Australia. They are not very generous when you consider that we have supported their annexation of Timor and, even as far back as the annexation of Irian we also supported them. Now they seem hell bent on challenging us over our oil and gas reserves and other issues most of which are just a smoke screen to disrupt negotiations to settle the issues peacefully.

"Our intelligence sources, supported by the Americans confirm that there have been covert activities aimed at a possible pre-emptive move against us somewhere, even, perhaps in New Guinea. In short, it appears that Indonesia wishes to expand its territorial sovereignty to include other potential resource areas to eliminate the future possibility of domestic fuel shortages. We didn't object when they just took East Timor, neither did we block their move when they took half of the island of New Guinea, which is also one of their more lucrative provinces. There are those who are foolish enough to believe that we would also acquiesce should they push across into New Guinea because Australia doesn't have the military resources to prevent such military action.

"The bottom line is, Stephen, we can't defend ourselves and can no longer count on the Americans to run to our assistance as they have done in the past because they too need allies like the Indonesians. I wouldn't like to put money on Australia if the Yanks were forced to take sides in any conflict. Ever since the ANZUS Treaty was virtually compromised by the Kiwis refusing American nuclear ships access to their harbours there has been a significant shift in how the Americans now perceive the old alliances. It's probably because were just too bloody British and expect too much from the old relationships."

Coleman listened intently, feeling that the punchline to this one-sided conversation was about to be revealed. Anderson's next statement rocked him.

"Your old friend Seda will, within the following year, become the next Vice President of Indonesia."

He let the statement sink in while watching the other man slowly shake his head, smiling, and then finally holding the palms of his hands up as if in surrender.

"Now I know it's bullshit!" he said.

Coleman was suddenly relieved. He had expected the Director to arrive at the end of his discourse with a more subtle conclusion, not something this melodramatic.

Anderson's shoulders suddenly fell, as if his lungs had expelled all of the air contained in the ageing organs, almost as if in despair. Coleman noticed the reaction with surprise. He remained still, saying nothing more. The tall, thin and now very tired Chief slipped slowly off the bed, and walked towards the security door.

He said nothing, not even turning as he approached the exit and pressed the buzzer indicating he wished to speak to the man on the other side. When the observation hole had been opened and the guard identified Anderson, the door opened then closed quickly leaving Coleman suddenly alone. He remained alone without further contact for another three days.

When the Intelligence Chief returned it was if nothing had happened. He had just marched into the small detention area and dropped another newspaper on the bed. Coleman knew he was expected to read it immediately and did so, looking up from time to time to ensure that he was reading the appropriate story as intended by his visitor. He commenced with page one which displayed the aerial photographs with the supporting story and followed the article through the following pages. It was an incredible display of photographic journalism. The headline read, *Terrorists Attack Australian Oil Rigs*.

The two oil rigs were caught perfectly by the photographer's equipment, as they burned furiously, spewing columns of black smoke and flames high into the atmosphere.

"Well, what do you think now?" Anderson had asked.

"More than provocative, I'd say," he replied, attempting to be slightly nonchalant, when his true sentiment was of one indifference. He was still annoyed at having been left alone so suddenly and treated like some errant child who needed to be punished for his ways. "What happened?" he asked.

"Seda," was all he said.

"How do you know?"

"It's got his mark all over it!"

"That's not good enough. How do you really know?"

"It fits with what he wants from all of us."

"Come on!" he said, determined not to permit Anderson to just expect him to roll over and accept everything he said as gospel. "That's a fairly broad statement. Fits in with what, specifically?"

"It fits in with his plan to create anarchy, Stephen, that's what it fits in with," Anderson replied, his voice still even but with an obvious edge to it.

"Is he really going to be the next Vice President or were you just winding me up?"

"I wish it weren't true either but it has all but been confirmed publicly by the Indonesian President. Seda arranged to be appointed as their Ambassador to Australia for approximately a year or so before taking up the new position. The fact that he selected this specific post when he could have had Washington or even Paris leads us to believe that he is right in the middle of something which has great importance to him. He has achieved tremendous power, Stephen, since the two of you parted company. I know you will have difficulty understanding this, but almost half of the entire country now supports him. It is even possible that he has just about enough strength in numbers outside Java to even succeed as President, although we still consider that most improbable due to the grip the Javanese Islamic groups have on the military.

"We feel certain that he is behind most of the sabre-rattling taking place in Indonesia, and definitely involved somehow with the intelligence reports we have of possible terrorist attacks. We just can't get enough information to support our assumptions of possible targets. Hopefully, this is all it was going to be," Anderson said, pointing at the sabotaged rigs in the newspaper. "But we can't afford to take that gamble."

Coleman waited as Anderson rose, and stretched, then rubbed his long legs to assist with the circulation.

"Stephen," he said sitting back down on the bed, "we are going to eliminate the problem with Executive Action."

* * * * * *

Stephen sighed. They had been at it now for just a few hours yet already his head ached.

Since their last session together, when Anderson had finally come to the conclusion of his Department's observations regarding the new Ambassador, Coleman had not been able to sleep more than a few hours at a time. The magnitude of what he had been told kept him awake right through the first night as he went over and over in his mind what his involvement might be in the covert action. He knew from his past association with the Service that whatever course was decided, it would be extremely dangerous for Stephen Coleman.

"I guess it's time we discussed your role in all of this," Anderson had said.

Coleman sat anxiously waiting for him to continue and yet, somewhere in the back of his mind, a voice was urging him to ignore what he was about to hear from the Intelligence Chief.

"You will be responsible for the final stage in the operation." By operation, he knew that this was to mean execution and immediately shook his head.

"No."

"You don't have any choice," he was told.

"That's crap and you know it, John. Apart from detaining me here you have no power over my life any more. That's all in the past. The answer is most definitely no, I won't do it!"

"You don't have a choice," Anderson repeated. He then went on to recite the possible charges that could be laid against Stephen.

"You're not really serious? How could you possibly sit there and expect me to believe that you could actually consider making any of those charges stick?"

"Stephen," he started, "you seem to have forgotten the wide range of powers that the department has in cases like these. Should we be obliged to bring charges against you then the hearing would be held in camera due to the nature and sensitivity of the Service's activities. We are well protected under The Act and, quite frankly, should I deem it necessary in the interests of our national security, all I have to do is speak privately with the PM and he will sanction whatever action I consider necessary with regards to your future.

"Do I make myself quite clear, Stephen?"

Coleman thought about what Anderson had just said. He knew that it was true. The man had incredible powers that could be applied against him if he refused to co-operate. He could just disappear and nobody would ever know. Suddenly this thought passed through his mind and he realized that he had already disappeared. He didn't even know where he was being detained!

His mind raced as he thought quickly about his predicament. Coleman knew that he was caught and they had a gun to his head. Thirty years would be more like a life sentence.

"And then, of course, there's the Indonesian problem, which still hangs over your head because Seda has kept it there, on the front burner, so to speak. I just never understood why he never really made any serious attempt to have you out of his life permanently."

Coleman understood that once proven, his involvement in the arms shipments would attract the maximum penalty in Indonesia, as subversive activities are considered to be a capital offence. And, should he be charged and tried in Australia, he was cognizant with the standard thirty-year sentences which, inevitably, were spent in solitary confinement. All in all, he really had no choice.

He continued to listen to Anderson outline what was required of him. The man had already assumed that he would agree, Coleman thought angrily, frustrated with his impotence, and the feeling of total helplessness for the situation in which he now found himself.

It had taken considerable time to convince Coleman that Seda's death was the only realistic solution. He had offered many arguments and suggested alternatives to the extreme measures being considered, knowing before he had even mentioned these, that ASIS would have made its own evaluation as to their effectiveness.

He was shown further evidence of the former General's ongoing role in supporting the FRETILIN separatist movement and, to his dismay, the full report of Stephen's own shooting intelligence suggesting that Seda may have been behind the attempt. Even if this were true, revenge was not in his nature, Stephen had argued. The Intelligence Chief had merely smiled and cited the violent attack on Hart, to contradict the other man's almost righteous position.

They had, however, agreed that any attempt to expose the powerful Ambassador could now be counter-productive, as the Indonesians would be compelled to deny any such accusations and any such claim could even result in cancellation of the forthcoming bilateral talks.

"What about these talks. Won't they assist in resolving the question of sovereignty over the oil areas? Shouldn't you wait until there is a result from these discussions?" he had asked.

"There won't be any resolution. Seda doesn't want one. Time is crucial, Stephen, we know there's some serious military activity afoot and everything points to Seda as the power behind the threat. Even if it comes about that they attack say, New Guinea, we are virtually sucked into the fracas anyway, as both our countries are tied together under the defence agreements which date back to the time of their independence, over twenty years ago."

"What about the defence pact we signed with Indonesia?" he asked.

"That's the greatest joke ever played on the Australians. Can you imagine signing an agreement which stipulates that both countries agree that they would come to the aid of the other in the event of attack, considering that the only country likely to do so in Australia's case was the other signatory to the agreement?"

They talked on. Coleman was depressed with what was expected of him. He wasn't even sure if he could still do such things any more. Even for his country.

"Why me?" he had asked early in the discussions.

"It is imperative that we have someone who can identify him perfectly, Stephen, specifically his voice over the phone. We want this to be a clean operation. We don't want innocent bystanders taken out as well."

"There must be a number of agents who could do the job for you without the necessity for all of this," he had said, indicating the concrete surrounds.

"Not any more. Operatives today just don't seem to have the same commitment any more. Not that you were particular outstanding in that area yourself," Anderson had said, referring to Coleman's sudden exit from the Service years before.

"Also, we would never be sure that we could guarantee their silence."

When Anderson noticed the sudden change on the other man's face he moved quickly to calm his fears.

"Obviously, Stephen, you'll be taken care of in the appropriate manner. You will need to disappear as you have done before, except this time we will provide you with reasonable cover. That would be another identity and travel documents should it become necessary. I personally believe that it won't," he added, almost as an afterthought. "You don't need funds from what I hear, so you will just have to be satisfied that we will consider your slate as being clean, thank you quietly for your participation, and ask that you go back to whatever you were doing before this bloody mess required our intervention. Okay?"

It required another two meetings before Coleman finally accepted the assignment. Until then he had remained adamant that he would not be Seda's executioner. Not until the last thirty minutes of their discussion.

"I had hoped that it would not come to this, Stephen."

"Let's get on with it John. I've been here long enough, and you know that I just can't do it any more."

It was then that Anderson embarked on an elaborate deception, one which he had concocted over the previous weeks once he had observed Coleman's determination not to participate, regardless of the possible consequences. He had tried threats, loyalty to his country, and that even referred to the old friendship they'd once enjoyed. None of these had worked.

"I just don't believe it!" Coleman had yelled.

"It's true, Stephen. I didn't want to raise the past unless I found it necessary. We all felt for you at the time. Your mother was very sad when she discovered how you felt for Louise. Of course, she was never aware of the circumstances. And, if revealing this information to you will result in the elimination of the very man who was responsible for what happened then I would call it sweet justice. Wouldn't you?"

That final discussion had clinched it. He had agreed.

The memories of Louise came flooding back as he remembered the brief time they'd had together. Brief only, as he had now discovered, as her life had been cut short deliberately by another.

* * * * * *

That night, as he lay alone, he tried to conjure up her face in his mind; he found that his eyes were moist from the tears of sadness and despair he felt for the one woman he had really loved, knowing that she had died such a tragic death as a result of political opportunism. Remembering his own early fears of flying, Coleman was bitterly saddened to discover that Louise's life had to end in that way. She hadn't needed to die at all but Seda's interference had seen to that, or so he now believed. Anderson explained the conclusions, albeit speculative, which had been derived from intelligence, as to what had actually occurred during that fateful journey. He was reluctant to disclose the source of the information, even when Stephen had insisted that he would need to feel absolutely certain that the story was accurate, before he could even begin to accept it as truth.

Anderson had shown bits and pieces of United States intelligence and other exchanges which had taken place after her disappearance. It was convincing evidence, and he had believed the elaborate story woven around the tragedy.

He had no way of knowing that this fabrication was in every way false. All lies! Stephen wanted to know why she died and this man had given him an answer.

Anderson's claim, supported by a reasonable amount of documentation, stated simply that Louise was most probably going to be murdered along with him during their on site inspection of conditions in Irian. At the time the United Nations' sponsored resolution for the West Irian plebiscite, which the Indonesians referred to as the Act of Free Choice, was criticized by the international press as being partial and dominated by force through the Indonesian military.

He was told that evidence had come to light, in the years following the successful acquisition of the new province, which proved beyond doubt that there were three separate factions involved in the many acts of terrorism and slaughter which had taken place at that time. The Indonesians were already well ensconced in the area and had been since the Dutch left in the early fifties.

Then, he was informed, there was the OPM, a raggedy and disorganized group which represented most of the freedom fighters. They offered little resistance and were poorly equipped. Often they operated from across the border, carrying out relatively minor raids in their amateurish way before retreating back in to the relative safety of New Guinea, relative being the key word as often the Indonesians followed them well into the neighbouring country in search of the rebels.

Coleman had listened as the Intelligence Director had continued. He claimed that the Australian Intelligence Services believed that another group had been deliberately manipulating the primitive mountain tribes into direct confrontation with Indonesian troops. It appeared that their earlier attempts to thwart the plebiscite had been poorly organized, resulting in only token resistance from the primitive mountain tribes.

However, as the Indonesian's interest turned towards East Timor, their subversive activities recommenced in the Irian area. They were not sure at the time and, in fact, not even until recent information became available were they certain that the person behind these efforts was Seda. His aim had always been to secure the autonomy for *Tim-Tim*. Prior to the Portuguese withdrawal his plans were embryonic, to say the least. The *coup* in Lisbon had been a windfall providing, for the first time, an opportunity for the General to formulate a strategy which could be successful. Anderson said there was little doubt that, had the Portuguese remained in the colony then, eventually, the world would have seen violence directed at them and most probably supported by the Indonesians. Either way, Seda would have, at one time or another, been given the opportunity to commence his plans for a free state.

Once the separatist movement got well under way, he needed to distract the Jakarta General's attention away from Timor. By forcing the Indonesian military to concentrate their efforts more in Irian than towards the confused former Portuguese colony, it provided the fledgling political party of FRETILIN the opportunity to build support before the Indonesians turned their full attention to acquiring their land as well.

His original plans for his homeland hadn't changed all that dramatically once he realized that with the Portuguese withdrawal the Indonesians merely took their place as the new masters. He had needed world opinion to turn against the Indonesians and what they were doing in Irian. It was almost like a trial run, Anderson had said, "And what better way than to attract the wrath of the international press?" he had asked. "Why, of course, have one or two of their journalists killed violently and lay the blame at the feet of others."

"This was just one of his early day strategies to build international concern for the future," Anderson had said. "We now believe that he was going to have her executed before your eyes, although we don't have enough information to tell us how the final plan was to be implemented.

"What is important, Stephen, is that she was to be killed and you were to witness the event. Ask yourself, what would you have done, full of rage and hate wanting to lash out at those who had harmed her? In terms of international press coverage alone, had you been a real journalist at the time, wouldn't you have pulled every string available to ensure that your woman's death didn't go unpunished? And if you personally witnessed men dressed as Indonesian soldiers actually take her life would you not be a major source of embarrassment to the Indonesian presence in Irian and their aggressive takeover of that country? Think, Stephen, think!" he was urged.

"Then how can we now blame Seda for her death?" he'd asked, confused and angry with these revelations. "And why then did he go to such extreme efforts later to assist build the armaments supply organization?"

"One thing at a time, Stephen, one thing at a time." Anderson talked slowly as he recalled the rehearsed lines prepared for such questions.

"Seda was definitely responsible although we can not prove this, beyond all doubt, as the aircraft has never been found. We believe that you had both been followed by one of the General's henchmen I believe you know reasonably well, one Umar Suharjo. When he recognized there was a problem between the two of you he acted quickly to prevent Louise from leaving. Obviously it was not difficult for a man of his skills to obtain the information he required such as to how she was to leave Bali. We gather that we somehow had one of the ground mechanics play with the aircraft's electronics hoping that it would be grounded, providing you with the opportunity to convince her to go with you. All of the staff at the hotel were abuzz with your predicament. You told me so yourself, if you can still recall our discussions during your convalescence."

"Do you mean he tampered with the aircraft and that's why it crashed?" he asked incredulously.

"Sorry, Stephen but yes, we do."

"And she would have probably died even had she not taken that flight. Is that what your suggesting?"

"Yes," the older man had replied softly.

"Shit!" he had yelled, "I don't believe it!"

They had sat in silence for almost half an hour, he remembered, as the realization of what had happened slowly sank in driving all other thoughts from his mind.

He was filled with rage. All those years of not knowing and now, only when they needed him, was he to know. Coleman hated them all. Even Anderson!

Stephen remembered that his life had lost all direction when she died. He hadn't cared about his own injuries at the time once they had finally disclosed the loss to him in hospital. He was receiving treatment and still recovering from the bullet wound he'd received during the disastrous tour. She had been missing for weeks before anyone had informed him of the tragedy. Prior to that, Stephen had thought that Louise either didn't know of his injury, which he found difficult to accept, or she had elected not to have any further contact with him at all. She had disappeared even before he had been shot.

'And all the time it had been Seda's doing,' he thought, his head filled with hate for the General who had insisted that they take the journey together.

'The scheming, conniving bastard!' he had muttered over and over to himself as the venom built quickly, his mind tortured with the face of the man who had sat together with him so many times throughout the years, knowing what he had done, perhaps even smiling silently at his partner's ignorance. It was then that he had agreed to kill the man responsible for Louise's death.

And that man was Ambassador Nathan Seda.

* * * * * *

During the weeks he had been detained, the situation between the two countries had deteriorated dramatically. Student demonstrations in both had erupted into violence, and Australians were being discouraged from travelling to Indonesia, even to the almost apolitical tourist destinations such as Bali.

Pressure increased on the Intelligence Service which sensed that Seda was moving closer to the first phase of his plans, as communication activity increased dramatically between the Embassy and unidentified posts in the far east of the Indonesian islands. Anderson was perplexed by the lack of recent intelligence to assist identify the former General's intentions but, of one thing he was certain, what ever these plans were, the department's head knew without doubt that the outcome could only be to the detriment of the peoples of both countries.

Coleman now appreciated why Anderson had coerced him into accepting the assignment. He was familiar with the diplomat's voice and understood the language. He would never disclose the Executive Action as he had too much to lose himself. And he had a reason for wanting to complete the assignment.

And then, of course, there was the alternative, but Stephen did not relish the thought of spending his remaining days incarcerated under the Laws of the Land, if that was the course the powerful and devious Intelligence Chief elected to take.

John Anderson had given his undertaking that, subject to the elimination of the target, Coleman would then be free to come and go as he pleased, enjoying the remaining fruits of the years he had spent working together with the Timorese living under the alias that they had agreed upon. This did not bother him at all. He had no surviving family and doubted if the necessity to live a lie would really bother him any more. Suddenly he was looking forward to completing the assignment and returning to the islands.

Their final meeting had lasted throughout the day. Anderson then offered Coleman the opportunity to leave the detention centre.

Stephen would have accepted had the Director not also shown him evidence that the new Ambassador had positioned his own Security Chief there in Canberra. He even enjoyed a room in the Embassy's residence, he'd read in the report. Stephen shuddered. He knew his life would be in danger once his presence became known to this man.

He studied the photograph taken of the Javanese as he had exited the international airport some months before, carrying an Indonesian diplomatic passport which stated that he was accredited to their Embassy as a First Secretary liaison officer.

Coleman recognized the man as a much older, but obviously still active, Umar Suharjo. Although he was already committed, it was then Stephen was convinced that he really did not have any other choice. He would participate in the execution of the General.

Retired national hero, entrepreneur, diplomat and would-be Timorese President, General Nathan Seda, would die on the seventeenth of August, the Indonesian Republic's national Independence Day.

* * * * * *

There had been very little left to prepare. Anderson had seen to most of the arrangements.

They had agreed that the man had to be isolated in such a manner as to avoid wounding or killing innocent bystanders, or at least they were to attempt to keep the number down to an acceptable level. Coleman had smiled when he heard this. Only Anderson would have the audacity to convince himself as to what was, and what was not, to be considered acceptable, when it came to counting the cost in real terms.

Other people's lives.

Anderson had easily arranged to have the Ambassador's private office compromised by depositing a substantial amount of dollars in the Indonesian Air Attaché's hands one evening. The man had been taking funds from just about every Military Attaché in Canberra. Coleman knew what would happen to the *Kolonel* once he was discovered. And discovered he would be, he knew, as they were all caught in the end, pushed by greed or the insatiable appetite for power until finally making that one mistake which would destroy their lives forever.

It was now possible to eavesdrop, as the simple but powerful listening device broadcast the Ambassador's conversations back to one of the discreet locations controlled by the Service. It had been used as a safe house in the early years during the Vietnam war but not by the Australians. This was one of the Soviet addresses which had been monitored by ASIO, the Australian Security Intelligence Organization. Once the building had been compromised, the address had been purchased. Control was then assumed by the Service as an occasional address for some of their agents' contacts in the numerous Embassies located around Canberra. They knew that the Eastern Bloc agents would avoid the premises.

The assassination called for a bomb blast contained in the Ambassador's immediate office. As his security was too tight to penetrate, and considering the current tension between the two countries, Anderson had planned the execution so that it would appear to be the work of some of the members of the retired General's own ethnic group, now living in substantial numbers as refugees in Australia. The newspapers would report the bombing as the work of the remnants of the FRETILIN who believed that the important statesman being of their extraction should have done more to help his own people.

Coleman had smiled at the irony of the plan. Now that he had come to terms with what he must do, he was even prepared to take a gun and shoot the man himself, if that became necessary. He became impatient to have it all done and finished. He could identify the signs in his mood and knew that he must control his anger. He thought about the briefcase again.

A small but effective explosive device would be delivered to the diplomat's office. When they were absolutely certain that the former General was alone, Coleman would detonate the plastique. Anderson had informed him that he had arranged for a courier to deliver the explosives.

Stephen had considered this aspect as being the one real weakness in Anderson's plan. Accessing the Embassy and ensuring that only the General would receive the deadly consignment would be extremely difficult to accomplish, requiring the services of someone whom the Ambassador could not only trust but also permit into his inner sanctum. It wasn't until all aspects of the plan were ready for execution that he finally understood.

Anderson had been very clever indeed as he continued to manipulate all the players in his game with the skill he had developed as an intelligence master.

The deadly briefcase would be delivered by none other than Albert Seda.

* * * * * *

Albert had been given an assignment he could not refuse. It had taken very little to coerce Seruni's father. The suggestion of his being repatriated to Indonesia was sufficient for the badly shaken man to accept the task. They had never approved his application to become a citizen and he had given up submitting the forms further back in time than he cared to remember.

There was even the suggestion that they would, if necessary, look into the legality of his daughter's citizenship as her father was not a citizen at the time of her birth. Also, the girl's mother had been an alien living in Australia as the wife of an Australian citizen but was, in fact, the de facto wife of another foreigner. It was all very confusing. Although he believed that it was most unlikely that she could be deported, having been born in the country, Albert also considered the more personal issues involved, which would become very public in the event of any inquiry. He just didn't want Seruni to be harmed in any way.

At first Anderson had merely implied that perhaps Albert had erred when registering his daughter's birth as her mother was still, at that time, Stephen Coleman's legal wife and had been staying with her husband prior to her collapse. Hospital records indicated that there was every possibility of this being so. Should they inform Coleman?

He never questioned the absurd innuendo. He was frightened of the government man and even more terrified of having to return to his former country which, in his mind, no longer represented his home. He had given all of that up many years before. He was terrified that they could separate him from his daughter. She was all he had left in this world. And besides, what he had been asked to do was not such a difficult task.

And he would be paid! Heavens knows, he thought when the offer had been made, he lived frugally on the pension and still there never seemed to be enough. When he had first retired it had not been too difficult but now everything was just so expensive! And Seruni. She was at college now and although his daughter never demanded anything of him, there were always costs to be met, fees to be paid. He had agreed. What other choice did he have? Albert thought.

Anderson had been concerned that this man would refuse his request and decided to go in tough from the outset. Albert Seda's file was complete with detail of his interviews over the years when he worked part time for the government agency without knowing to whom he was really reporting. There were many like Albert living in Australia who had been tapped by the Intelligence Services as an easy access into their respective ethnic communities. He had never known of one to refuse to assist maintain a listening brief over their own former countrymen. Most did it out of fear of officialdom while others merely wanted to ingratiate themselves hoping for future favours. Having established that the Timorese was definitely under his control, Anderson then put the man at relative ease by explaining the nature of his errand.

The Intelligence Chief had concocted a simple story and one which Albert easily accepted considering the principles involved. Anderson had explained that Albert was to deliver a large sum of cash to the Ambassador. He had not elaborated to any great extent, merely intimating that the new Ambassador was no different than most, and that the Australian Government wished to convince him of its good intentions. They needed to send someone the Ambassador would trust.

Albert understood. The two countries were locked in dispute and he believed that the gesture would be appreciated. But would Nathan receive him after all of these years? Anderson went on to explain that they had considered various means whereby the delivery could be effected and had come to the conclusion that the senior foreign dignitary would be unlikely to accept such a gift unless he knew the courier personally. Albert had considered these premises and was obliged to accept Anderson's logic.

He had been advised that delivery was to be made at precisely six o'clock in the evening on the seventeenth of August. Albert expressed surprise as to the timing of the hand over. Anderson had merely smiled and suggested that the delivery was to be his stepbrother's Independence Day gift.

* * * * * *

Anderson had easily arranged for the invitation. The Air Attaché had sent this out almost immediately only too eager to assist knowing that his services would warrant another fat envelope at some later date.

Albert was to arrive half-an-hour earlier than the other guests and insist on meeting directly with the Ambassador, who would be expecting him. Anderson would arrange that.

His instructions were to then proceed with the Ambassador who would, undoubtedly, have his step-brother escorted to a place of privacy. They knew from their sources that this could be the Ambassador's private office. There he was to surrender the briefcase personally and then take his leave.

It was relatively simple. Albert accepted the role of courier. He would deliver the gift for Nathan. And then they would leave him alone.

Chapter 24

Canberra

The Indonesian Embassy had provided the sombre-faced Javanese Security Attaché with the means to move equipment into the country without question. He had arrived almost four months before the retired General, and soon demonstrated his ability by establishing the new security systems. The staff had been impressed with the quiet and dedicated officer. Several had commented, however, that they found him rather impersonal and uncommunicative. Others were surprised that he never attended functions or private parties, electing instead to remain on duty for more hours than the position demanded, arriving very early each morning and returning to his quarters late into the evening after the other staff had departed.

He must be very competent, they had thought, as this was the first occasion any of them could remember, even from their other postings, that the head of security held a diplomatic position and was accommodated in the official residence along with their Ambassador. Even though his quarters were out to the side from the main house, they still found the arrangement unusual.

After two months in the country they had become accustomed to his brusque responses and demands. Soon the other members of the legation accepted his manner as normal and practically ignored his presence within their circle without further comment. They no longer offered the new Attaché invitations knowing that he would refuse or ignore any of these courtesies extended to him.

Often he would just vanish for days on end, only to return as if there was nothing unusual with these sudden disappearances. They didn't ask and he never offered to explain. Someone in the secretarial pool started the rumour that the reason for the secret break away from them all was perhaps a woman, hidden outside somewhere and he was too embarrassed to be seen with her. After all, she couldn't be much to look at, the young girl had suggested, just look at him!

The new Ambassador had signed the instruction, to the surprise of the Consul, demanding that the maintenance section rearrange the lobby access rooms as an additional security measure. They obeyed and within two weeks the rooms internal layout had been changed to the specifications given to them, with only two exterior doors having to be relocated as part of the renovations. One of these now opened in a sliding action from the inside, permitting delivery vans and small trucks to back up to the building immediately in front, almost hard up against the door. The vehicles' rear doors could then be opened directly from the security room and the contents moved in and out undetected by inquisitive eyes.

Umar had decided that his very special stores should remain below on the Embassy's ground floor to avoid compromise. The lifts were impractical due to their size, designed to accommodate only four passengers, and even that was a squeeze.

Lugging the secret consignments up and down steps, could easily lead to discovery. His arsenal now contained the remainder of the stores required for dispersal to the strike teams. These special consignments would pass through Australian Customs unopened, as the lead-lined cases were endorsed as diplomatic cargo and protocol demanded that such luggage could not be checked by the authorities.

Umar's armoury had been constructed immediately adjacent to the main lobby reception area. The second set of external doors was also re-enforced with steel bars welded vertically and horizontally at twenty-centimetre intervals. These opened to permit access into the embassy gardens, which were pleasantly landscaped up to the dividing wall separating the delivery and storage areas from the colourful view. Usually, Umar would enter his stronghold via the embassy mail and registry room, which was located alongside the common interior wall.

Only he was permitted access to this area. Other embassy officers had correctly speculated that it contained weapons to be used if their building came under siege. They were not uncomfortable with these thoughts, as many had seen other legations destroyed over the years when demonstrators could not be prevented from entering the main buildings, burning, looting and on occasion, injuring the staff. Many even looked on Umar as their protector in the event their Embassy came under attack and, considering the current political climate, anything was possible. The mood in Australia was becoming tense.

The specially selected van had been repainted with the appropriate colours to comply with their needs. Umar had decided to wait before adding the delivery company's logos and other identification markings, as moving the van between the Embassy and its locked parking bay behind the Ambassador's residence increased the risk of discovery with each journey. He planned to complete the installations and leave the van locked where it was until two or three days prior to the target date. Umar felt safer knowing that it was within the compound where he could keep his eyes on it during the day. The rear of the van had been left hard up against the sliding door now for two weeks and the Embassy personnel had become accustomed to its almost permanent presence.

Inside the delivery van he had stacked layer upon layer of plastic lined bags around the open drum of diesel oil. Whenever the van was moved, he would re-attach the container's lid for these short journeys, removing the cover again once the vehicle was parked. He had finished storing the ammonium nitrate bags and had completed the finishing touches to the hydrogen canisters which would act as a 'kicker' to increase the impact of the huge bomb. The extra ingredient would give the explosives far more cutting power, allowing it to slice through the structure of the building.

Umar had checked the detonators behind the sliding doors. He had a choice of using the powerful industrial detonators or the PETN explosive sitting in the corner, separated from the rest of his volatile hoard. He considered the latter and agreed that the pentaerythoritol tetranitrate would probably be better, knowing that this explosive could generate a very powerful shockwave. Having made his final decision Umar completed his checks then locked and sealed the van's doors first, checking them once again to be absolutely certain that he had not missed anything before locking the sliding door securely. Satisfied that the important tasks had been completed, he returned to his rounds of the chancery and other areas frequented by the public.

As he passed through the registry room, he heard one of the typists whisper something to her friend. He couldn't hear what was said but knew they would be curious as to what kept him for so many hours each day inside the adjacent room. Umar Suharjo enjoyed the intrigue. He smiled to himself. Wouldn't they be surprised if they knew just what he had stored under their lazy little bottoms!

He was not overly concerned that one of the staff might accidentally discover what it was that remained such a secret within the four walls of his private domain. Anyway, he mused, considering the non-military staff with contempt, most of them wouldn't even know the difference between their hands and what was between their legs let alone have the capacity to identify any of the items in his store! The majority of these foreign affairs types hadn't even undergone national service training, Umar thought, annoyed with the civilians, and wouldn't be able to defend themselves if called upon to do so. He knew they would be useless if the Embassy came under attack.

He strutted around playing the role of the senior security officer. In all the years he had worked for the General this was about as close as he'd ever come to really enjoying his duties. He experienced a sense of elation, knowing that he alone would be responsible for the destruction of the Australian leadership when the massive explosion took place within the confines of their Parliament.

If only they knew, he thought, if only they knew!

* * * * * *

Nathan Seda enjoyed the exhilaration which resulted from the satisfaction of knowing that his dreams were almost within his grasp. This time it would be successful. He could feel it! The Ambassador had just returned from the function and met briefly with Umar before settling down to concentrate on the enormous number of unfinished tasks which need to be addressed. He had enjoyed the late luncheon.

When the approach had first been made, he was advised by the Embassy information officers that the invitation was considered to be quite prestigious, and would provide the Ambassador with an acceptable forum to raise issues not yet settled between the two countries.

Seda accepted the invitation to be the guest speaker at the Press Club luncheon. All in all, he thought, it had gone well, with the exception of the pedantic journalist who repeatedly interrupted his answers during the open question period. He had been asked if there would be any objections to an informal question opportunity for the other guests and, confident that there would be no difficulty in addressing whatever he was asked, Seda had agreed.

The man had insisted that the General be more specific in his answer.

"Why didn't the Indonesian Government provide adequate protection for the drilling crews against the attacks that had already closed down five drilling platforms in the disputed area?" he was asked. "Surely as these platforms and rigs are within what the Indonesian Government claims as their territorial waters the responsibility for the safety of the crews and multi-million dollar rigs rests with your government?" he was challenged.

"The Indonesian military does not wish to be seen by the international community as being overly aggressive in this matter. We sympathize with the families who have lost loved ones in these terrorist attacks and have asked your government to consider a joint military action to prevent any further recurrences of these disastrous assaults against not just Australian but also Indonesian workers in the Timor fields."

"Mr Ambassador. Is it not true that your navy already has a considerable presence in the area, and is it not also true that your country has the capacity to virtually guarantee the safety of these operations due to the very number of vessels that you are able to deploy in the concession zone?"

"Although it is correct to state that we have the capacity to provide such guarantees, our country does not consider that it should shoulder the entire burden of responsibility. Again, I remind you that we have offered your own navy the opportunity to work together with us on joint exercises to avoid misunderstandings as to our good intent, when our vessels entered the disputed territorial areas. Disputed only, I might add, by your government. We, in Indonesia, do not see that there is any argument. The area has always belonged to our Republic."

"Yes, sir, so we have observed. And what else do you want?" a voice from the back of the room had called, causing the assembly to laugh nervously while someone whistled his support for the question.

He had anticipated the response to his remark and, minutes later when he had finished replying to the faceless member, the assembly laughed politely while some even applauded his statesman-like wit and behaviour.

"Ambassador Seda. Would you tell us your own personal views as to where the United Nations will go on the latest call for the right of self-determination for *Tim-Tim*?"

He looked down from the podium to check the man who had asked the question. Seda didn't recognize the journalist but was pleased as he had hoped that someone would raise the sensitive issue. The room became quiet as he deliberately waited for the table banter among the members to discontinue to ensure their complete attention. He looked straight at the man who had raised the question.

"The people of *Tim-Tim* are Indonesian citizens by choice."

"Yeah, we all know that, but by whose choice?" shouted the man who had interrupted earlier.

"Knock it off, please, gentlemen," one of the committee called, embarrassed by the break in etiquette. "Let's remember who we are!"

"Thank you," Seda said, before continuing. "If you kindly permit me to finish. I said, the people of *Tim-Tim* are Indonesian citizens by choice. The reality is, they are. The choice was theirs, it became ours, and even you in Australia supported our declaration of sovereignty over the former colony. Show me one voice on the United Nations Security Council which condemns the current status quo in the province. Show me evidence that your own people don't support my country's annexation of the troubled state. And, if you can, please before you even consider asking the question, show me proof of the ridiculous claims that our Indonesian troops took the lives of your fellow journalists more than twenty years ago!"

"You can't" he continued, "because there is no such evidence which can irrefutably demonstrate the incredible claims made over the years concerning the loss of your some of your number."

"The Republic of Indonesia has demonstrated that it is a nation intent on peaceful co-existence with its neighbours. The Timor question remains no more as such because it has been answered by our country's actions, actions taken in the interests of all, including your own."

The questions had become heated. Seda had continued responding in the same vein and, at the close of the luncheon, he was confident that he had caused more questions to be asked than he had answered. But, more importantly, he had them all thinking seriously again concerning their own country's role in the sad demise of the East Timorese people. He was pleased with the day's events.

The Ambassador turned his thoughts to his discussion with Umar. The man was a genius with no sense of morality, he thought. It was a good thing he continued to command the man's loyalty, as the former Major had become totally indispensable in every respect, as there was just nobody else he trusted whom he could call upon with this man's skills.

The attacks would take place within the following week. Everything was now ready. The aircraft and vessels would take their positions within days and the combat teams had already been mobilized ready to move when Umar sent the command. The trucks and other support equipment had been ready for almost two weeks, the men standing by impatiently waiting for their next instructions. Umar had flown across and then driven out to speak to them. They had understood the necessity to be patient. He had told them, it wouldn't be too much longer, just wait!

Seda smiled again as he read his secretary's note confirming the number of invitations that had been acknowledged and accepted to attend the formal celebrations. Almost one thousand guests! This would be a function to remember, he thought, knowing that the whispers had already spread throughout the diplomatic community of his possible appointment as the next Vice President. All appeared to be on track and running according to plan, he thought.

Only the devastating consignment below remained as unfinished business, and this would be moved at the appropriate time. Umar had assured him that the final checks and paintwork could be completed in just hours once the van had been positioned at his residence's garage.

Seda had asked for it to be moved immediately but Umar had argued that it would not be safe out of his sight.

"What if there was a fire at the premises?" he'd asked, *"or what if one of those bungling idiot servants from Semarang became a little too inquisitive while their masters were out and decided to fool around with the volatile cargo?"*

In the end Seda had just walked away from the man. If it was safe enough for Umar, he decided, it was also safe enough for him!

Umar enjoyed the exchange. Even if he had moved the van to the residence there was just no way that the servants could even get a smell at the inside of the garage as he had always double locked everything. Umar expected the area would be safe. He had left small booby traps that were relatively harmless but enough, he knew, to scare the shit out of the domestic staff if they wandered off limits! He hoped that they feared him and wouldn't dare consider venturing into his domain without specific instructions to do so.

From time to time he had wandered through the kitchens as they were preparing meals. He could smell their fear as he stopped and looked casually around, picking up utensils and then replacing them without comment. Sometimes he would hold one of the carving knives up to the light as if he was inspecting the blade for cleanliness, but the staff understood the not-so-subtle message.

Even so, he preferred to keep his hands on the vehicle containing the explosives. It was just more convenient to keep the van where it was until the time came to move it out. He could see no problem. It was totally safe, although he knew that the General wouldn't understand this point. Like so many other intelligent people Seda had no idea how explosives were triggered. This one had not been activated. All of the components were in place but Umar had not connected the PETN charge directly to its detonation device. He would move that from the armoury and complete the complicated trigger only when he knew the exact timing for detonation.

Seda didn't understand the intricate workings of the bomb designated for the destruction of Parliament House and wasn't entirely comfortable knowing that the van was still sitting alongside the embassy building. Even if he had it moved to the residence's garage it would still be dangerously close to his person.

THE TIMOR MAN

* * * * * *

The newspapers had reported his statements in the following day's papers. Seda was not entirely displeased with the biased reporting, having become familiar with the so-called objective media very early in his career.

He sat drinking his coffee while skimming through the pages, stopping to read only those articles which referred to the luncheon and reported on his comments. Some of the stories were inaccurate and slightly derogatory. Several also exaggerated the answers given in response to the question of Timor, even suggesting that the Ambassador had responded with an air of arrogance. Seda thought about this comment and was not irritated by the remark, as he had deliberately answered in an almost provocative fashion, hoping to ruffle the member's feathers. As it turned out, the result was positive and in no way did he consider any of the articles to be detrimental to his real cause.

The majority of the stories, including two editorials, came out strongly in support of a United Nations resolution to provide the people of *Tim-Tim* with the opportunity to vote on the question of Indonesia's annexation and their right to self-determination, and challenged the Australian people to push their elected leaders into action over the ongoing abuse of these simple people's humanitarian rights. They also demanded a further government inquiry into the deaths of the journalists years before in Timor. They expressed disappointment that the questions relating to these murders have never been properly addressed.

This is the result he had really wanted. It was time to prime the Australian public and prepare them mentally for the next frightening events so that their response would lead to more than just feelings of indignation towards the Indonesian people.

Seda's plan called for a much stronger response. One which would drag both countries to the brink of an outright war.

Chapter 25

Independence Day —
Canberra

The Embassy had been decorated quite spectacularly. Nathan Seda had strolled around the building and grounds admiring the preparations as they neared completion. They had invited more than one thousand guests.

This would be the social event of the year, he thought, anticipating the favourable press coverage the public relations group had planned. He expected that the increased exposure would assist considerably when he called upon the United Nations to intervene directly once fighting erupted between the neighbouring countries. They would listen to Seda, as he had the necessary influence to bring about a cessation in hostilities and was not considered by the international media to be overly militant, as some were, within the Indonesian leadership. He hoped that they would call upon him to intervene in negotiating a peace settlement, and he would, but only when the timing suited his purpose.

This time he would succeed. He could feel it. All the ingredients were in place and soon he would achieve his dream.

As the Ambassador continued his survey of the grounds, catering staff busied themselves arranging the white and red combinations around the buffet tables. The national flag was designed to represent the blood of earlier revolutionaries spread across their white *sarongs* as the brave peasant soldiers lay dead or dying from wounds inflicted by the former colonists. They had fought with sharp bamboo sticks against rifles and cannon. He would fight with terror.

They were almost ready. Nathan Seda could feel the excitement building. If he maintained his course and continued to be patient, the General knew it would all then fall into his hands. Understanding his own weaknesses and strengths had been crucial to preserving the plan and his own position within the community at large. Often he had wanted to move much faster but had reasoned with himself knowing that impatience could result in failure. It had been such a long wait.

But it was nearly over. He continued his slow stroll, nodding occasionally to senior staff as they rushed by, arranging the finishing touches to the preparations. The guests would begin arriving in less than two hours. The Ambassador was pleased.

Floral arrangements adorned the long tables covered with white Indian cotton tablecloths. As these stretched out through the full length of the extensive garden overhead lights provided a colourful display as the soft breeze rocked them gently in the chilly evening air. Large marquees had been erected to protect the guests from the elements. August could be bitterly cold in Canberra and the caterers had suggested that they place a number of mobile pot belly burners around to take the bite out of the cool evening. These had already been lighted and placed around the perimeter of the setting.

The Ambassador's table was positioned on a slightly raised podium. Directly behind, the organizers had placed a huge Garuda against the painted plywood wall, built as a temporary backdrop. Flags hung from poles positioned with care at regular intervals between the tables and bunting was strung along the large tent posts creating a festive atmosphere.

As a centre piece, the Embassy had instructed the caterers to prepare an ice carving of the mythical Garuda bird and this two metre high ice sculpture had just been completed before Seda arrived and observed the men packing their tools and chain saws.

He viewed the scene and nodded his approval. At the far end of the garden he could see the table where, in just a few hours, he would host his own Chief-of-Army-Staff Lieutenant General Suprapto, the Indonesian Foreign Minister and many other prominent guests from Australia and abroad. His wife had not accompanied him to Canberra as she wished to wait for the warmer weather to arrive before joining her husband in the Capital.

Seda walked slowly through the setting, glancing from time to time at the neatly placed guest name cards inscribed in bold italic script. Towards the centre where the large ice bird perched regally, scowling at the surroundings, he noticed that two tables of twelve settings each had been allocated to the press. Seda was slightly amused by this as the band occupied the position opposite, not ten metres from where the journalists and their wives would later struggle to make themselves heard above the amplified sounds. He imagined the loud music blaring across the short distance, swamping the evening's polite dinner conversations showing contempt for them all.

Everything was in place. Satisfied with the magnificent garden arrangements he turned to leave for his residence to change and, as he was about to enter the main building, his personal secretary, Nona Kartini, hurried towards him.

"*Pak Seda,*" she called then hesitated, apologizing to her Ambassador as he looked over in her direction, "*I'm sorry to disturb you.*"

"*What is it?*" he demanded, surprised at her obvious concern. Normally his secretary was very composed and not given to any display of emotion.

"*Ambassador,*" the agitated secretary began, "*I have received a call of the most confidential nature! May we speak in private?*"

Seda nodded and walked briskly to the lift followed by his confidential assistant.

They entered the Ambassador's private chambers. Seda strode directly across the heavily carpeted room and dropped, almost impatiently, into the leather swivel chair. As he sat behind the carved teak desk the General looked at the woman and nodded for her to begin.

Seda frowned as he listened to his efficient secretary report the telephone conversation which was, he discovered, the cause for her agitated manner. He watched the career woman refer to her notes, taken during the strange discussion with the caller and, when she had finished, he asked her to go over it again.

She obeyed and read the message once more. He then excused his assistant and sat quietly considering the message he had just been given.

Suddenly he felt very uneasy. Naturally suspicious of any coincidence, Seda ran the information through his mind trying to unravel its secrets. Although agitated by the telephone call he could see nothing sinister in the request. The General recognized that as pressure built over the next few days he would need to ensure that he remained composed at all times and not permit these minor disturbances to distract him from the real objectives. Especially now!

Seda frowned.

Why had the man come out of the woodwork precisely at this time? Had it something to do with that evening's function?

There was really nothing to discuss with the man, he thought. They were not even real brothers.

Why did Albert feel the necessity to leave such an enigmatic message?

What did Albert know that was of such significance that he had insisted on meeting so urgently?

And how did he manage to acquire an invitation?

Why hadn't he made the call himself?

There were too many questions to which there were no immediate answers. Suddenly Nathan Seda rose to his feet and headed for the armoury. He was annoyed. The Ambassador disliked puzzles and was surprised to see that he was, in fact, preoccupied with the nuisance call. Suspicious of the unexpected message, Seda decided to ensure that the surprise visit did not interfere with the evening's celebrations.

He would instruct Umar to wait for Albert.

* * * * * *

Coleman had replaced the receiver and immediately informed Anderson that the call had been completed. The woman hadn't recognized that he was not a native speaker. He was pleased that he had not lost his touch!

Stephen checked his watch. Five o'clock! Anderson would already be on his way to rendezvous with Albert.

Coleman felt the tension and was conscious of a burning sensation in the pit of his stomach, which he knew was not a result of the second packet of cigarettes he had already consumed that day, but more likely the knowledge that within the next few hours he was going to kill.

Several times during the days leading up to this moment he had almost declared the assassination off, unable to sleep with fear of the consequences and the complicated reasoning for his actions. He had accepted that Seda was evil and should be removed completely from the political arena. His own personal justification for killing the man was more difficult to come to terms with now that he had examined his motives for the umpteenth time. Sure, he hated the man for what he'd done to so many others without remorse. The death of his servants had plagued his thoughts for years and that act alone was enough for Stephen to want to kill the man responsible. But wanting and doing were two very separate processes.

It was the memory of Louise that now played with his mind. Somehow he knew in his heart that the woman he had so deeply cared for would disapprove of what he was about to do had she been alive. But she wasn't, and because of that fact, he was still going to do it! This was his justification.

He wanted to avenge her death.

Coleman had dreamed ugly visions of her last moments. He knew that it would be impossible now or ever to come to terms with how she died. No one would ever know. Not he, not her family and certainly not Seda, even if the man really did have a soul.

The man was manipulative, ambitious and cruel and threatened the lives of millions in his quest for power. In those few days subsequent to Anderson's revelations, as his anger turned to a deep burning hate, Stephen no longer required any further self examination or justification of his motives to execute Seda. He was going to do it!

Coleman checked his watch yet again. His stomach erupted with another twist forcing him to belch. He drummed his fingers nervously, waiting for the minutes to tick away, as they did, slowly. Then he rubbed his face, pressing both temples with his fingers before readjusting the headphones. Strange, he thought, noticing the perspiration for the first time then wiping the moisture from his forehead with the back of one hand. Stress.

He tried to block the negative thoughts and imagined himself back on the beaches of Palau but it didn't work. His legs were suddenly tired, as he realized that they too were as tense as every other part of his body. He glanced down at his watch, but the minute hand had hardly moved.

'Damn!' he cursed.

His mind wandered for just a few seconds before snapping back quickly, reminding him of what was happening and why he was there in the quiet house alone.

He rubbed his forehead again, cursing the drops of perspiration that had gathered there to remind him of the danger and consequences of what he was about to do. He played with the headphones again, annoyed that they didn't sit exactly on his head as he'd wanted. He knew that the tension was getting to him. And he was tired. So very, very, tired.

Coleman willed himself to think of the future, and the lazy days he would have once again in the sun, lying back on the beach, resting, but the serene pictures would not form in his mind. They were blocked by a confused swirl of many thoughts, faces and events which refused to give way to the pleasant and peaceful images of the tropics. He closed his eyes momentarily and listened to the silence.

He knew that this was stupid. Open your eyes, you fool!

He fought against the desire to sleep as he went through the procedures once again. His mind kept repeating its signal, over and over. Be alert! Wait for the moment! Push the button! The instruments in front of him became hazy as he listened to the commands. He felt even more sleepy and closed his eyes again, for a few seconds, before snapping back from the drowsy state. Nothing had changed and his eyes closed again as his brain attempted to reduce the enormous pressure it now experienced.

Be alert! Wait for the moment! Push the button!

Again, Coleman jolted suddenly back to full consciousness and looked quickly at his watch. The hands showed eight minutes before six o'clock.

Startled, he sat up immediately. It was almost time! Bloody hell! he swore at himself. He'd almost slept right through.

Coleman removed the headphones and poured the remaining half bottle of mineral water over his face before wiping his forehead with the used napkin lying on the table along with the other remnants of yesterday's lunch. Or was it dinner? He didn't care. Snatching the headset off the table and placing them firmly over his ears Coleman concentrated on the reception.

Still there was nothing. He played around with the equipment and decided that, as it had been set and reset, he counted, maybe twenty times, perhaps he should just leave the bloody gear alone and wait.

Holding his head-phones with one hand, Coleman bent forward and then back, and then forward again until his head was between his knees. Then he sat up and inhaled slowly, blowing the foul air from his neglected lungs.

He repeated this exercise four times and, feeling the first signs of giddiness, knew that would be enough. He then lit a cigarette which caused him to cough violently. He stared at the smouldering stick and stubbed it out in the overflowing ashtray. Coleman picked up the plastic one-litre bottle of mineral water and, remembering it was now empty, threw it across the room in disgust.

His watch informed him that it was already six o'clock. He sat perfectly still, his expression that of stone. It was almost time.

At any moment now his once dear friend would deliver the briefcase to the one-time General. To his step-brother. And then they would both die.

Stephen sat gazing through the window across at the Embassy as he considered this one final act of retribution. Anderson didn't know. At first, he had not planned to kill Albert but the more he thought about his old friend's actions the more clear it became to Stephen that Albert too should die.

Imagining the two men sitting together somewhere in the ostentatious building across the road filled him with cold rage. Were they laughing together, at him, at the rest of the world? Did they have any comprehension at all as to the incredible pain that they had inflicted on others? On Louise, on Wanti, on him? No, he was sure, they bloody well did not! He knew in his heart and mind that this had to be fact.

One had killed the woman he loved and the other had killed the woman he'd married. But today they would both pay.

Anderson could do nothing to prevent him from seeking his just revenge from these men who had lied and cheated their way into his life, destroying everything that was good, finally leaving him with nothing.

Coleman's fingers danced almost rhythmically on the table. One touch of the button would send the signal out through the airwaves to be captured by that one designated receiver installed in the briefcase carried by Albert Seda. He knew that they had not reached the Ambassador's private office where the listening device still sent its almost-silent humming signal into his headset. This was imperative to Anderson's plan.

Coleman was to detonate the small charge of plastique by remote, sending the signal across the few hundred metres into the compound, until it found its way into the labyrinth and ultimately into the open arms of the receiver which would, in those milliseconds, activate the detonator attached to the half kilo of malleable explosive.

He wished he could be there to see the expression on their faces as they died. He wished he could let them know in their last seconds of life that he had been responsible for their deaths. He wanted to have the opportunity to tell them that this was their punishment for their crimes against others.

Against him, Stephen Coleman.

The cruel thoughts passed slowly through his mind, only to be displaced by images, firstly of Louise as he had last seen her, and then Wanti as she had been taken away from his home in Jakarta, collapsed and still in trauma, only to be taken back to Australia and violated by the very man who had been given the responsibility to care for her.

Anderson had been reluctant to say, he could tell. When they had discussed Albert's role Stephen felt obliged to ask after her. The older man expressed genuine surprise that Stephen was not aware of his wife's death many years before. And when the unfortunate slip was made regarding her daughter he was incensed with what the man suggested had occurred to the unsuspecting Wanti. Albert had taken Wanti and she had become pregnant while she had no control over her own mind.

At first he had wanted to go directly to Albert and confront him with the evidence. And then kill him!

He felt drained.

Anderson had, he realized, deliberately withheld this vital information from him in order that there would be no disruption in their plans to execute the General. He would not forgive Anderson this one last machination as it was obvious that the Intelligence Chief had known from the very beginning. He wished he could destroy him also.

Stephen felt disgusted with the whole filthy mess and just wished he'd never ventured back into Hong Kong. 'Was it really less than two months ago?' he wondered.

Anderson had shown him photographs of the girl. Stephen had insisted. And the birth certificate when he again questioned the accusations made against Albert. She had been born prematurely, the master manipulator had lied, and her mother had died as a result of the birth, having never recovered from her mental disorder and the trauma resulting from her last visit to Jakarta. Stephen had sat coldly still as the realization of what Anderson had suggested slowly burned deep into his soul.

Unanswered questions immediately became clear, such as why Albert had made no attempt to contact him after Wanti died.

His old friend had been too ashamed.

It was now clear how Anderson had managed to convince the man to do his bidding. Coleman wondered just how long the Director had held this information over the former teacher. Had he threatened him with a charge of rape? It would also explain how he expected to maintain Albert's silence once delivery of the bomb had been effected. Although Coleman knew that this would no longer be a problem.

He just could not understand how Albert could have done such a thing. Stephen felt disgusted to the point he desperately wanted to hurt the man, painfully and slowly. His behavior had been criminal and totally incomprehensible. Now he would pay the price for his abuse of the woman he once claimed to care for, to love. A price, Stephen believed, which would be commensurate with the man's deeds.

* * * * * *

Albert had taken a taxi to the Embassy. At first he had difficulty just leaving the cab as the soldiers manning the gates looked so intimidating. He paid the driver and stood for a moment observing the main gate guards. They were dressed in their parade best, he knew. These were not the ordinary security one would normally see watching over an Embassy he thought apprehensively, recognizing the maroon berets and fierce appearance of the paratroopers. Had he not been so concerned Albert might have been impressed. It was unusual to see foreign military in Canberra, especially armed soldiers. Albert stared across the driveway and lawn at the impressive building and then back at the guards. Unless the occupants position demanded such prestigious attention that relaxation of the Foreign Affairs rulings had been granted, then these men should not be strutting around the main entrance, wearing sidearms. His palms started to feel moist as old memories forced their way back into his mind.

Albert produced his invitation and handed it to the guard on the right, who glanced casually at the gold embossed card and handed it back, coming to attention as he did so. There was no salute and neither had he expected any from the paratrooper. He then proceeded through the huge iron gates unaware that the soldier had waved once towards the embassy building before returning to his previous station.

As he entered the grounds a small elderly Javanese confronted him and demanded to know his business. Albert was suddenly frightened. What if this man insisted on checking the contents of the briefcase and discovered so much money inside? Immediately he started to sweat in the cold evening breeze.

"*I have an appointment with Bapak Seda,*" he said, hoarsely, his voice letting him down right at that very moment. He wished he hadn't come!

Umar scrutinized the man's features. He smelled the fear and was satisfied that this man represented no danger. He was old and it was unlikely that he would be carrying a weapon.

"*Follow me!*" he ordered, watching the visitor carefully as he turned and moved quickly along the driveway then up the steps into the lobby. Umar walked briskly then motioned for the visitor to take the stairs with him.

He followed, trying desperately to keep pace as they climbed the staircase. Albert was frantic. The shorter man moved so quickly! He had difficulty keeping up and, before they had even reached the first level, his heart was already pounding from the exertion. He needed desperately to slow down, yet had to appear casual and mask his difficulty in breathing.

Albert rested at the second level and feared that he had overstretched his physical limits. The giddy spell threatened to throw him back down the steps which doubled as a fire escape. He held tightly to the bannister and breathed slowly. Then he looked up and prayed that it wasn't far to go before he could deliver the briefcase and leave. He didn't particularly want to meet with Nathan but his directions had been explicit. 'Deliver only to the Ambassador, or bring the case back home,' were the instructions the government man had given him. He had been quite emphatic. If he were to leave this delivery with another how could they be certain that the Ambassador had really received the gift and that he had not taken it himself?

Albert certainly did not want these people to think that he had taken the money. He was committed to passing the briefcase and contents only to his step-brother.

He looked at the polished leather Satchi case, its deep, almost maroon color reflecting the value of its contents. The polished brass latches were fastened but not locked as the simple tumbler combination in the centre and under the handle served this purpose. The sealed envelope in his pocket contained the numbers required before the gift could be opened.

Albert had no idea how much money was inside the briefcase. It felt like a great deal. He hadn't expected it to be this heavy. Perhaps there were also gold bars inside, he thought. That would explain its weight!

As they reached the final steps Albert knew that, had there been one more flight of stairs to tackle, then he couldn't have made the delivery. He was becoming dizzy from the exertion when the dark little man opened the heavy access door and indicated that they had arrived at the last level.

Albert breathed a sigh of relief. He paused for a few moments and then continued along the passageway past the lifts, following the other man directly into the Ambassador's private office.

Umar instructed Albert to wait while he went in search of the General, who had last been seen escorting the Indonesian Foreign Minister around the huge reception area in preparation for the formal announcement calling the guests to dinner.

* * * * * *

Seda was pleased to strut around as the visitors admired the decorations and complimented him on the magnificent social event that had been arranged for the Independence Day celebrations. It was obvious from their reactions that very few of those present had ever attended such a function in the capital as grand as this and Seda played the part of Ambassador to perfection.

Umar wasn't happy with having to leave the man upstairs alone, but those had been his instructions. He ran down the steps as quickly as his tired legs would permit.

Albert was also tired. He placed the briefcase on the floor and removed the small envelope from his breast pocket. He wished he could leave. Perspiration added to his discomfort as he sat waiting for the man he had not seen in so many years. He waved the envelope slowly, softly fanning his face, as he had forgotten to bring a handkerchief.

The minutes dragged by and he felt a slow wave of panic descend upon him. His shirt became damp with sweat as he felt the fear grow. He looked up at the air-flow duct but knew he wouldn't be able to see if this was warm or cold air moving through the system. It felt so hot!

Albert glanced at the envelope and was startled to see that it had become damp along the edges where he had held it. Embarrassed, he placed the letter back inside his coat pocket. He looked at his wristwatch and frowned. How long should he wait?

Should he take the money and return?

Where is he?

Albert Seda rose to his feet and stood indecisively as panic engulfed his mind and body causing him to suddenly feel ill. He coughed once and swayed slightly just managing to keep his balance as an attack of nausea threatened to further complicate the moment.

* * * * * *

Coleman had heard them enter the room and then there was silence. He leaned closer to the small powerful transmitting device and raised his index finger. And then he too waited for Nathan Seda to arrive.

* * * * * *

The Ambassador had gestured abruptly at Umar as he attempted to interrupt the Foreign Minister's harangue on the wonders of Sumatran culture. Annoyed, he moved away from the small group and stood alone, waiting for the General's signal to approach. It didn't look good. Within minutes he was joined by other Indonesian dignitaries who had arrived early, all offering their congratulations on the splendid appearance of the Embassy and the evening's preparations.

He checked his watch. The visitor had now been waiting for almost half-an-hour. The reception was about to commence! Guest limousines were already entering the grounds and the short security man shook his head in frustration as the Ambassador continued to ignore him.

Suddenly the foyer seemed to fill very quickly as the Ambassador, accompanied by the Foreign Minister and the Chief-of-Army-Staff, were ushered into position in the receiving line.

Seda remained there surrounded by other dignitaries for almost thirty more minutes, greeting his guests as they arrived in the lavishly appointed lobby.

The large crowd had already spilled out into the garden area where mountains of food had been stacked in preparation for the reception. Laughter could be heard as the guests moved around admiring the effort that had gone into producing the delightful setting and colourful decorations.

The aroma of *saté* drifted into the reception hall, tempting the visitors into the magnificent garden and temporary dining area. The band had been sitting patiently, awaiting the signal for them to play their national anthem, *Indonesia Raya*.

Umar again checked his watch and decided that the man upstairs had been left alone far too long. He went to check on Albert.

* * * * * *

Coleman realized that something was terribly wrong. There had been complete silence for over an hour and he could not understand why the General had not yet entered the room. And then he heard a door opened. Then closed. Followed by more silence

* * * * * *

Albert could not bear to remain any longer. He could hear the band starting up and decided to depart. He looked at the case containing what he thought was money.

Albert thought that he would be conspicuous leaving with the briefcase and decided he had no choice but to leave without it. He would tell the government man that the Ambassador had personally accepted the gift and thanked him for his kind gesture. He left the private office and hurried down the passageway to the elevators.

The lifts had been locked in the ground position to prevent any of the evening's guests from inadvertently accessing the upper floors of the embassy. He took the stairs and discovered upon descending to the lower level that the security doors had also been locked on the ground floor for the same reason. He sighed and commenced the slow climb back to the upper levels.

At this time Umar had used his security key and activated the lift controls. Upon entering the Ambassador's office he was surprised to find the visitor gone. And then he noticed the case.

Umar lifted the elegant briefcase and was surprised at its weight. It was much heavier than he'd expected. He examined the container for a few moments more and, unable to ascertain its contents, decided that he would lock it away until he had either located the missing visitor or had discussed the situation with his General.

Umar Suharjo mumbled '*brengsek*', cursing as his knee caught the side of the sofa and, in the distance, startled by the sudden sound and mistaking the man's voice for that of the Ambassador's addressing the courier, Stephen Coleman panicked and his sweaty hands squeezed the small luminous red button sending the dedicated frequency transmission through the airwaves.

Coleman tensed. He waited for the distant explosion.

Nothing happened. He tried again. Another malfunction! A feeling of incredible disbelief swept over him and he slammed his fist hard down on the table, accidentally knocking the remote control to the floor. He cursed as he had never cursed before.

Coleman pulled the heavy curtains back angrily and stared across at the brilliantly lit building surrounded by hundreds of limousines as the elite of Canberra's society enjoyed themselves inside. Waves of disappointment flooded through his tired body and he kicked angrily at the broken mechanism lying on the floor.

They had failed!

* * * * * *

Umar rode the lift down to the lobby and, in his haste, overlooked re-locking the elevators. The General had moved into the garden area and was already approaching his own table when the Security Attaché gave up any further attempts to call him away. It would now be impossible, he knew, observing the guests filling the marquee and taking their allocated positions. Wishing to avoid the multitude of people now crowding every corner of the Embassy and garden, Umar slipped unnoticed into the empty registry.

Albert Seda had succeeded in slowly climbing the steps once again and rested on the stairs for a number of minutes regaining his wind. He was becoming disorientated and confused as to how he became locked inside the building. He thought he heard the whirring mechanical noise stop and forced his old legs to carry him back into the passageway and down to the lift station.

Relieved to find that it was now functioning, he pressed the button and instantly the strange sounds commenced again signalling that the ten-horsepower electric motor was pulling the wire ropes returning the lift to his floor.

Albert then descended to the lobby and, finding the room completely blocked by hundreds of visitors now pushing past him towards the garden, he decided to wait there until their numbers had thinned just enough so that his exit would not be too conspicuous.

Umar Suharjo looked around the quiet registry and, identifying the switch he sought, turned the lights on in the adjacent room.

Outside, the guests were clapping as the Indonesian Ambassador stood in front of the band and raised his hands over his head clenching them together. They had played *Bengawan Solo* and other favourites, much to the enjoyment of the gathering.

The conductor then waited, his body half-turned observing his Ambassador, poised for his signal. As the General nodded, the baton waved delicately in the air, and immediately the handsome Menadonese drummer commenced his roll calling all present to attention. The guests rose to their feet as the band commenced playing the national anthem.

Inside, having now opened the metal doors leading to his arsenal, Umar Suharjo nonchalantly dropped the briefcase containing the plastique explosive casually into the corner.

The sensitive mechanism, which had been unable to receive the earlier signal, immediately reacted to this excessively rough handling. As the deadly package hit the floor an eight-centimetre detonator activated, causing the highly brisant RDX plastique to explode. The first and second primary explosions came within a milli-second of each other, as the C-4 exploded directly through the walls into the PETN, which had been prepared inside the van to deto-nate the packed ammonium nitrate after the vehicle was later po-sitioned under its own target.

The first shockwave pushed through into the parked truck and ignited its deadly cargo, activating all of the contributing compo-nents simultaneously.

The fertilizer exploded, cutting through the building like some giant knife, the powerful shock waves slicing their way in all di-rections as the explosives acted on each other creating the moment which would rock the political world.

* * * * * *

The first to die was Umar. Then Albert. And many others as that one enormous burst of energy erupted through the assembly turning the entire area into one massive fireball of destruction.

Figures danced momentarily before disintegrating into heaps of lifeless flesh and bone.

The roar had ripped through the guests, hurling musical instru-ments into the maelstrom of human carnage, decapitating a bands-man. Then, for an immeasurable moment, there was silence.

A shrill cry pierced the quiet, then a cacophony of screams emphasised the full horror of the blasts.

Coleman picked himself up off the floor slowly, not noticing the blood across his face and shoulders which had taken the impact of the imploding window. He wasn't seriously injured. Searching fran-tically around in the dark he located the glasses and wiped them quickly.

Coleman viewed the scene through binoculars. He stared at the scene in confused awe. He did not understand how, finally, the relatively small charge had been detonated with the effect of a much greater explosion. Although he had not seen the bomb Coleman knew that it was contained in the small briefcase as he had ob-served Albert walking through the main gates carrying the deadly package.

He was numb with the shock of what he had done. That he was responsible for this incredible destruction. He raised the glasses once again and was horrified to see that most of the building had been destroyed, while many of the limousines were burning fiercely as fuel tanks continued to explode through the cold night air.

Clouds of black smoke spewed out from where the rear of the building had been and Coleman could see that houses in all directions had also suffered incredible damage. The buildings closest to the blast were burning fiercely.

There could be no survivors he thought, still stunned at the sight before him, as he recognized that there would have been many hundreds of guests caught in the horrific explosion. He had watched most of them enter as their cars arrived to deposit the important passengers at the steps of the mansion.

Minutes passed and he heard sirens screaming as fire engines were first to arrive at the scene. Several loud explosions followed and he could then identify the loud calls being made as the firemen urged the neighbouring Embassies to vacate their buildings quickly. The whole evening sky was ablaze with light.

He could see American Marine Guards running outside their own compound, checking its perimeter. A car horn sounded. It had meant something to him but his mind was still confused with the horror outside and he was unable to unscramble his thoughts. What was it? He tried to remember. The horn sounded again. This time impatiently.

Immediately, then, Coleman remembered. The signal!

He moved quickly, leaving the binoculars and broken pieces of the transmitting device behind as he vacated the premises.

* * * * * *

He entered the black Ford Taurus Ghia and the car moved away slowly from the scene as more fire tenders appeared. Road blocks were already being established to prevent even further casualties as petrol tanks continued to explode into the night.

The gloved driver remained silent, guiding the car swiftly away with increased speed, leaving the disaster and its terrifying aftermath well behind. They continued down the capital's protocol roads winding their way through the startled suburbs and across the lake towards the airport. Fifteen minutes passed when the driver pulled into the government forestry reserve amongst the pines and switched the engine off.

Soon, the faint cooling noises of the hot metal adjusting to the new temperatures were the only sounds evident in the cold night.

The cloud had all but disappeared. They were parked on a rise looking back towards the city proper.

Coleman stared at the man behind the wheel.

"It's finished," Stephen stated simply.

The driver's eyes glazed momentarily as he turned his head towards Coleman.

"Could you be certain that he is dead?" he asked softly as if not wishing to break the silence inside the vehicle.

"Yes," he answered knowing that no one could survive the blast.

They sat quietly, together, observing the bright red glow in the sky.

The other man turned again towards Stephen.

"Both of them?" he asked again, without surprise.

"Yes. Isn't that what you really wanted?"

He didn't answer. Instead he watched the red blinking light move across low in the sky. He could see the lights guiding the late and last flight for the day down the runway. It would be from Sydney, he knew. The last flight was always from Sydney.

He sighed. "Then I guess you're free."

"Free?" Coleman asked, suddenly terribly weary as he looked out across at the bright evening sky. He thought he could still hear some explosions in the distance.

The realization of what he had done continued to numb his brain. All of those people. Dead. Because of him!

"Free?" he repeated, confused.

His companion slowly released the wheel then leaned across and placed his gloved hand on Coleman's. Stephen was not conscious of the gesture and continued to look out through the side window at the distant blaze. They sat in silence, observing the extent of the bomb's destructive power. The moon could be seen fighting its way through the clouds of billowing smoke, casting a ghostly light over the capital.

"Yes, free," the driver whispered softly as he moved his left hand across from behind the passenger seat, pausing as the automatic came to rest against the other man's temple.

Coleman turned, surprised at the feel of the cold metal. As the bullet burst from the small handgun his body convulsed and his eyes registered an instant of disbelief at the final treachery.

As life flowed from his body he recalled images of faraway scenes. Of people and places. And of beaches fringed by coconut palms and, he thought that he could see Louise standing, smiling, calling his name and beckoning him.

And then he was swallowed by darkness.

* * * * * *

The driver wound the window down and sat for a while staring at the view. He felt no remorse. Only sadness at what had taken place. It had to be done.

An owl hooted twice from its perch high up in the branches of the pine trees and the faint mist that had settled across Lake Burley Griffin was now slowly drifting away. The breeze touched the trees and their faint swaying motion created the almost surreal impression that they were dancing and waving at him.

John Anderson sat quietly considering those words he had read many years before, words he had always believed in and had tried to instil into the minds of his young trainees.

'That the justification for the use of force was that Government was force. And that the Government had the right to use force against its own citizens.'

He felt no shame. Just sadness.

The grey-haired Director studied the dead man beside him and was surprised to feel a slight twinge tug at his heart. Sometimes principles had to take a back seat to real life. To reality.

Anderson placed the revolver in the lifeless hand. It had been Stephen's.

"Silly bugger!" he muttered.

And then he left, slipping away silently through the shadows, and into the night.

Epilogue

Lightning flashed. A clap of thunder heralded yet another downpour as the young woman sat wistfully looking out at the bleak, wet day. The rain never seemed to cease.

She looked down once more and, still filled with curiosity, was tempted to open the faded envelopes as she held them with both hands. After reading the letter attached to the documents she knew it would be wrong to do so and, with a sigh, set them aside for posting.

Seruni looked at the photograph once again and slowly moved the tip of her finger across the images of the couple as they smiled at each other. On the reverse side there was an inscription and date.

Stephen and Wanti — 1972
Cinta Abadi — Eternal Love

In the year following her fathers' death Seruni's grief had been immeasurable. Most nights she still cried herself to sleep. She felt so alone. Albert Seda had been cremated. She was never sure how they could have determined which body had been his. The explosion's aftermath left little. She had scattered his ashes around her mother's grave. Nobody had asked her to do so. Seruni just felt that it was the natural thing to do.

She sorted through the strange case of personal effects which had been passed to her as heir to her mother's and Albert's estate but there were no answers. Only more questions.

Her eyes returned to the snapshot and, with a gesture that even she did not understand, she raised the picture and placed her lips softly against the faded faces while wondering who this wonderful benefactor had been.

Seruni had counted the cash, still not believing her good fortune. There was almost half a million dollars there. The money had been a gift to her mother, Wanti, from the handsome young man in the photograph.

And now it was all hers!

Glossary of Terms

Although many readers would have visited Indonesia, this simple glossary of the *Bahasa Indonesia* words used throughout the novel may assist others who have not yet been fortunate enough to visit the beautiful archipelago and become familiar with its multi-faceted culture and language.

ABRI	Indonesian Armed Forces
adik-tiri	younger step-brother/step-sister
adjal	destiny
aduh	exclamation
ALRI	Indonesian Navy
ANIB	Australian News and Information Bureau
Antara	Indonesian News Service
ANZUS	USA, NZ and Australia Treaty
Apa kabar?	How are you?
Apodeti	Timorese Popular Democratic Association
ASDT	Timorese Social Democratic Association
ASEAN	Association of South East Asian Nations
ASIO	Australian Security Intelligence Organisation
ASIS	Australian Secret Intelligence Service
AURI	Indonesian Air Force
awas!	be careful!
babu	servant (female)
bagus	good
Bahasa Indonesia	Indonesia's national language
BAKIN	Indonesian Intelligence Agency
bangsat	arsehole/louse
Bapak/Pak	a term of respect to an older man
becak	tricycle taxi
beliau	His Honor, Sir
berita	news
bersama	together
bioskop	cinema
bisa	can

bohong	lie
brengsek	something/somebody incompatible
bule	foreigner (slang)
Bung	older brother
bunuh	kill/murder
cepat	fast
cewek	girl
cinta abadi	eternal love
cyclo	tricycle taxi
dia	he/she
jahanam	curse/hell
Dji Sam Soe	cigarette brand
dukun	witch doctor
enggak/tidak	no
fajar	dawn/day-break
FRETILIN	Revolutionary Front for East Timor
gamelan	Indonesian orchestra
ganja	cannabis
gudang	storage room
gunung	mountain
guoilo	foreigner
halaman	garden/court
HANKAM	Department of Defence
hidup	live
Idulfitri	end of fasting period feast
jaga	guard
jangan	don't
jongus	servant (male)
joss	bad luck (Chinese)
journos	journalists
kali	stream
kampung	village
Kapten	Captain
kawin	marry
kita	we
koki	cook
Konfrontasi	War against Malaysian Federation
kongsi	union/company/society
KOPASGAT	Indonesian SAS

Korp Komando	Indonesian Marines
KOSTRAD	Strategic Reserve Command
krait	deadly poisonous snake
kretek	clove cigarette
ladang	arable land
Laksamana Madya	Admiral
langganan	dealer/client
Lebaran	a religious feast
Letnan Satu	First Lieutenant
losmen	housing
lubang maut	death hole
lurah	village head
maaf	apology
mandi	bathe
manis	term of endearment/sweet
Mas	address to an older man
mati	dead
mengerti	understand
Merdeka	independent, free
mereka	they
muda	young
nama	name
nasi putih	steamed rice
nenek mojang	ancestors
njonja	address to an older, or married woman
obrol-obrol	chatting/gossiping
OPM	Free Papua Movement
OPSUS	Govternment Special Operations Unit
orang asing	foreigner
Panca Sila	the Five Principles of Indonesian National Philosophy
panggil	call
parang	sword
Parlimen	Parliament
pasar	market
pemerintah	government
PLN	Electric Company
pribumi	indigenous people — 'sons of the soil'
protokol	protocol

PTT	Post, Telegraph and Telephone
rakyat	people, of the country
Ramadhan	the ninth month of the Moslem year
Ramayana	Indonesian epic originally from India
rambutan	small red fruit with hairy rind
ranjau	land mine
rejeki	good fortune
rendang	spicy meat dish
ringgit	Malaysian currency (dollar)
rotan	rattan, cane
RPKAD	Army Regiment
rupiah	Indonesian currency
sabar	patience
sawah	rice fields
saya	I
sedih	sad
sekolah	school
selamat datang	welcome
selamat pagi	good morning
semua	all
sialan	damn
silahkan	please
simpati	sympathy
sudah	already
sumpah	swear
tamu	guests
terima kasih	thank you
terserah	do as you please
cap	stamp
toko	shop
tua	old
tuan	sir
Tuhan/Allah	God
tukang	labourer/worker
UDT	Timorese Democratic Union
warisan	legal heir

FREEDOM SQUARE

*Other books
by Kerry B. Collison*

The Asian Trilogy

The Timor Man

Freedom (Merdeka) Square

Jakarta

The Fifth Season

Non-Fiction

The Leo Stach Story

FREEDOM SQUARE

(This book was previously
published as Merdeka Square.)

Kerry B.Collison

Sid Harta Publishers
1999

PUBLISHED by: Sid Harta Publishers for Kerry B. Collison and
                 Asian Pacific Management Co. (S.A.) Ltd.
                 Telephone: (61) (0 414) 958623
                 Fax: (61) 03 9560 9921
                 Address: P.O.Box 1102, Hartwell, Victoria,
                 Australia 3125

First published 1997 as Merdeka Square
Second Printing, April 1999

Copyright © Kerry B.Collison,
Sid Harta Publishers and
Asian Pacific Management Co. Ltd. S.A, 1997

Text: Kerry B.Collison
Cover Concept: Guy W. Collison
Author's Photograph: Courtesy of Ned Kelly and the
                       Bundaberg News Mail, Queensland.

Collison, Kerry Boyd

ISBN 0 95 8744858

Printed in Australia
by Australian Print Group
Maryborough,
Victoria.

Dedication

I wish to dedicate this novel to the memory of

Adik Irma Surjani Nasution,

General Nasution's daughter who, at the age
of five years, was shot dead in her parents' home during
the failed assassination attempt against her father
and other members of the Council of Generals.

When she lost her life, so too did Indonesia lose its innocence.

Kerry B. Collison followed a distinguished period of service as a member of the Australian Embassy in Indonesia during the turbulent Sixties followed by a successful business career spanning thity years throughout Asia.

Recognised for his chilling predictions in relation to Asia's evolving political and economic climate and as the only Australian ever to have been personally granted citizenship by an Indonesian President, he brings unique qualifications to his historically-based vignettes and intriguing accounts of power-politics and the shadowy world of gorernments' clandestine activities.

The author's biographical data is avaliable on the Internet at:
http://www.sidharta.com.au

Photo of the author by Ned Kelly, published by courtesy of the Bundaberg News Mail.

"When in Rome..."

"Only be patient till we have appeased
The multitude, beside themselves with fear
And then we will deliver you the cause
Why I, that did love Caesar when I struck him,
Have thus proceeded."

Brutus to Mark Antony after Caesar's assassination,
Shakespeares's *Julius Caesar* Act III

* * * * * *

"Masuk kandang kambing mengembik...."

"Sabarlah dulu sampai rakjat yang bingung
serta takut sudah bisa kita tengangkan.
Setelah itu, baru akan saja djelaskan kenapa
Bung Karno, walaupun betapa djuga saja hormati
beliau sebagai Presiden, terpaksalah saja sisikan."

Perwira Tinggi, Tentara Nasional Indonesia
Djakarta 1965

Contents

Book three,1965, coup and counter-coup

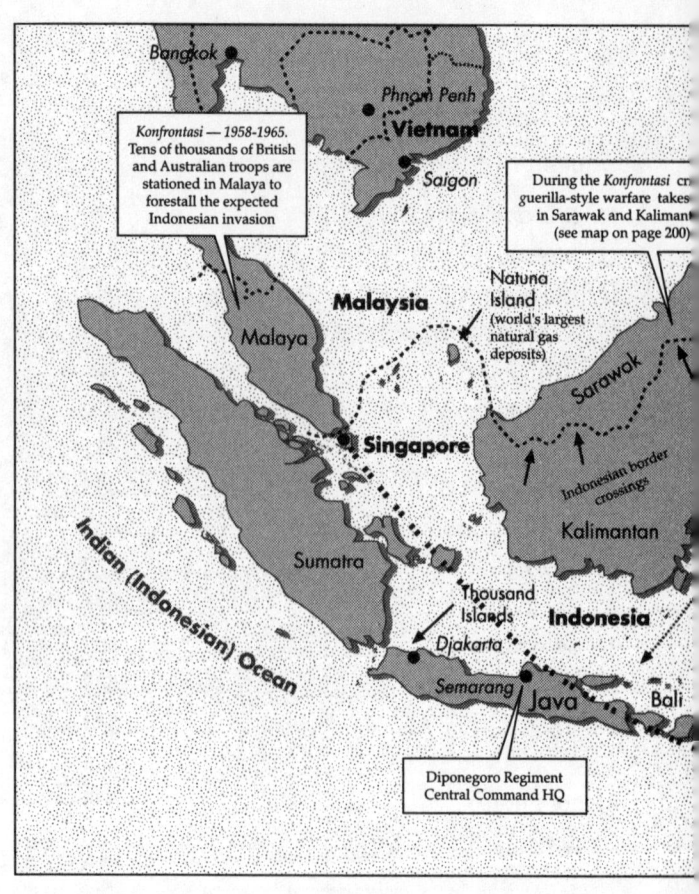

Konfrontasi — 1958-1965.
Tens of thousands of British
and Australian troops are
stationed in Malaya to
forestall the expected
Indonesian invasion

During the *Konfrontasi* cr[...]
guerilla-style warfare takes
in Sarawak and Kaliman[...]
(see map on page 200)

Natuna
Island
(world's largest
natural gas
deposits)

Malaysia

Malaya

Singapore

Sarawak

Indonesian border
crossings

Kalimantan

Indian (Indonesian) Ocean

Sumatra

Thousand
Islands

Indonesia

Djakarta

Semarang   Java

Bali

Diponegoro Regiment
Central Command HQ

Bangkok

Phnom Penh

Vietnam

Saigon

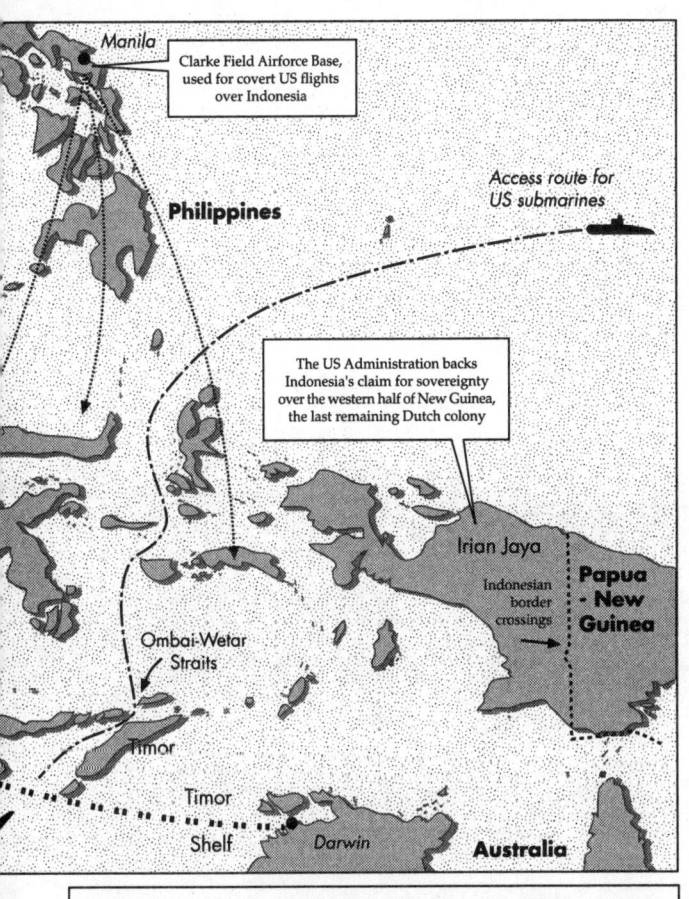

Manila
Clarke Field Airforce Base,
used for covert US flights
over Indonesia

Access route for
US submarines

Philippines

The US Administration backs
Indonesia's claim for sovereignty
over the western half of New Guinea,
the last remaining Dutch colony

Irian Jaya

Indonesian
border
crossings

**Papua
- New
Guinea**

Ombai-Wetar
Straits

Timor

Timor
Shelf

Darwin

Australia

🚢 — ·· —	US submarine route through Ombai-Wetar Trench
▪ ▪▪ ▪▪ ▪▪ ▪	route taken by the British 'V' Bombers armed with nuclear bombs, 1962–65
◀·········	covert flights by the US Airforce

Prologue

John McEwen, Acting Prime Minister of the Commonwealth of Australia, stood silently, pensively looking out from the windows of his office across the well-lighted gardens.

He remained motionless, hands clasped behind his back in military stance.

There were no books, no decorations, nor were there any items of personal memorabilia to identify the room's previous tenant. These had all been removed at the request of Prime Minister Holt's widow.

It had been just one week since Holt had disappeared while swimming in the ocean off Portsea.

Upon taking office, John McEwen had been immediately briefed by the Attorney-General. McEwen had been shocked and angered to discover the existence of the covert organization ASIS, and its subversive activities directed against Australia's powerful neighbours. His Coalition partners in government had deliberately kept him in the dark.

A file lay opened on the oversized teak desk. Above and below the text, the page was boldly endorsed with security classifications and warnings ...

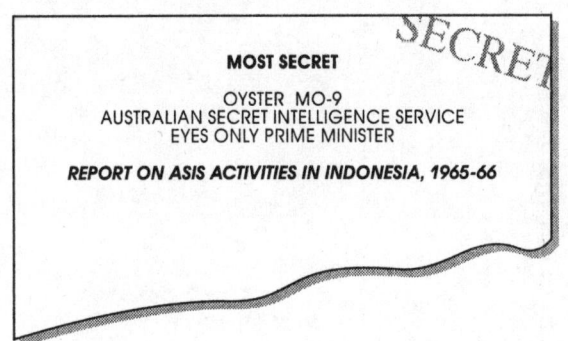

MOST SECRET

SECRET

OYSTER MO-9
AUSTRALIAN SECRET INTELLIGENCE SERVICE
EYES ONLY PRIME MINISTER

REPORT ON ASIS ACTIVITIES IN INDONESIA, 1965-66

John McEwen watched the traffic flow round the roundabout and spin off along the arterial roads to the suburbs. It was late.

He turned, almost painfully, and moved back to his desk. He stared down at the file and was suddenly overcome by waves of fatigue. He looked back through the windows as if wishing to avoid confronting the damning report which lay before him, but there was no escape. Now he could barely distinguish the shapes of the slow-moving cars, their lights dimmed by the early evening mist drifting in from Lake Burley Griffin.

The Prime Minister leaned forward, placing his hands on the high-backed leather chair for support and closed his tired eyes momentarily.

More than half a million had died throughout Indonesia. ASIS was deeply involved in the disaster.

And why should that be the only secret that Holt had kept from him?

Book one

1901-1964

Chapter 1

The peasants moved lethargically as the hot, dry monsoon wind toyed with the dust causing occasional eddies of choking air to swirl about. As the villagers went about their monotonous chores they covered their heads with cloth to protect their faces from the fierce heat and dust. Their bodies were dehydrated by the dry, debilitating conditions during the day, and then further ravaged by the uncontrollable sweating in the humidity of the still, suffocating tropical nights.

Their village, Kampung Blitar, located in a desolate and isolated pocket of land, was locked behind the giant volcanoes to the north, in one of the most densely forested tropical islands known to man. This insignificant area, treated harshly by the prevailing weather patterns, was almost unknown to the outside world. But Kampung Blitar was not so isolated that it managed to escape the attention of the gods who ruled their precious Javanese realm. They watched, patiently, until the planets had achieved a suitable conjunction and, at an appropriate moment, moved to alter the destiny of their subjects below.

* * * * * *

Blitar's impoverished community was situated in the centre of Java's only rain shadow. The arid conditions and intimidating terrain had not attracted the *Vereenigde Oost-Indische Compagnie (V.O.C.)* planters. Instead, this desolate place had become a sanctuary to the thousands of *pribumi* people who had fled their colonial masters during the centuries of the Dutch East Indies Company's dominance.

17

Initially, many of the district's inhabitants consisted of escapees from police stockades. Most were merely guilty of minor offences which, at the time, attracted severe and often cruel punishments such as public flogging. These petty criminals fled to the *Blitar* region knowing that the Dutch soldiers would not follow. The terrain was dangerous and claimed many lives amongst the white foreigners who had ventured into the mountainous region. These unsuccessful incursions resulted in orders being issued by the *V.O.C.* Governor not to pursue prisoners who had fled into this domain. The *Compagnie* designated the area as *badlands* and the district continued to be neglected throughout the hundreds of years of Dutch occupation of the extensive archipelago.

As the Dutch East Indies entered the twentieth century and social change slowly produced a literate class amongst the indigenous people, Blitar also became home to the first political refugees. Although their number was limited, their presence was accepted by the peasants in their isolated world as these intellectuals could provide some semblance of learning to the illiterate farmers and their children.

The villagers were predominately Javanese who followed the Moslem faith and lived in simple clusters of thatched roofed dwellings scattered throughout the barren region. These *kampung* were rarely established without a mosque where the faithful could be called to prayer. As the five daily summons emanated from the makeshift minarets, the entire population would follow the established regimes, and go about their ablutions prior to commencing prayer. There were few exceptions. These rituals were essential to their lives. The people of Blitar suffered many hardships and depended heavily on their spiritual beliefs for relief and comfort.

* * * * * *

The island's inhabitants had all but forgotten the devastation cast upon them by Krakatau's explosion when they were visited by torrential rains which seemed to never end. It was the year of Nineteen Hundred and One.

Thunderstorms had lashed the countryside causing floods throughout the rich rice-bearing plains, and landslides in the mountain regions. Roads remained cut for months. Blitar had become even more isolated and hidden from the rest of Java's millions.

In one of the larger villages a small school had been constructed from the traditional mud bricks and teak trees. There were no desks. The children simply sat on small *tikar* mats which they placed on the clay floor before lowering themselves to sit cross-legged in the one-room hall. The building doubled as the *balai* or village community centre. Often the mothers would join the children and assist with the teaching. There was only one class for all the students, regardless of their age.

The school represented far more than the primary education it provided. It was a symbol which these simple people respected and desperately clung to in their surrounds of extreme poverty. The *kampung* elders had organised the building's construction as they understood the importance of providing these basic facilities for the children. The hall had taken almost five months to build and the entire village had participated, working together in the accepted manner of *gotong-rojong*.

This was one of the schools where *Raden Sukemi Sosrodiharjo* taught. He helped with the school in the neighbouring village as well, but was reluctant to spend too much time away at this time. His Balinese wife, *Ida Nyoman Rai* was heavy with their first child and he wished to be present when the birth took place.

There was no hospital here, only a midwife who also nursed the injured and sick whenever one of the villagers required her limited medical knowledge. Her cures were traditional concoctions of herbs which were often accompanied by chants and prayers. *Ibu Arifin* was respected and admired by the *kampung*, and feared by a few who claimed that the Sumatran woman was, in fact, a *dukun* who could not only cure the sick but also cast spells. Good and evil *dukun* could be found in every village throughout the islands as mysticism was an integral component of the Indonesian culture, delivered in abundant doses by means of the *Ramayana* shadow puppet shows. *Ibu Arifin* was a true believer even though she followed her traditional beliefs in parallel with her Moslem faith. She understood that the stars had cast an incredibly powerful influence over their earthly presence and that a conjunction of the sun and Neptune in the ascendant was nearing prominence. This would be, she knew, a reccurrence of the celestial conditions which had accompanied the birth of the Prophet Muhammad. As she worked, she offered a silent prayer to the *One and Only True God*, then added a supplication to her traditional ancestors and their formidable ghosts.

Demands on the woman's time and expertise had grown considerably during the year but she never complained. At that very time, there seemed to be an overwhelming number of young pregnant girls approaching term, most of whom had yet to see their fifteenth birthday. The midwife cared for them all, never admonishing these young girls for their predicament as she herself had given birth when only fourteen. Whenever those distant memories occasionally emerged, she would immediately endeavour to concentrate on some other thoughts for those earlier times had left bitter scars, which *Ibu Arifin* preferred to leave buried in her own distant village near Padang.

* * * * * *

A late afternoon electrical storm had driven most of the villagers indoors as dry winds forced a path down through their valley, ripping at trees, tearing at the poor soil and sucking all that was loose up into huge clouds of choking dust. Throughout the night, the children lay close to their mothers, clinging onto their *sarongs* as the wind screamed wildly outside, generating visions of wild demons shrieking across the evening's darkened skies. *Tjengkeh* trees, silhouetted only occasionally by the brilliance of lightning flashes, shuddered violently as the turbulence struck causing unripened cloves to be stripped from their pods prematurely. The brilliant flashes produced still portraits of eerie figures which seemed to dance momentarily as several of the women rushed bravely around outside, collecting possessions left behind in the panic, when earlier they had dashed quickly to the confines of their huts. The heavens seemed to be tearing themselves apart as lightning flashed continuously, all around, followed predictably by the deafening roar of thunder claps. It was as if the gods were at play.

The terrifying sounds ripped down through their valley, seemingly gathering momentum as the stark mountain walls on both sides channelled the fury in their direction. The villagers understood that the storm which had erupted thousands of metres above their heads and along the mountainous ridge to their north could easily bring the desperately needed rain to their dry land. But it seemed that their prayers were to go unanswered. The heavens exploded with the gods' cruel laughter, the sharp deafening cracks of thunder a testament to the power which surrounded them.

Alone, in the dark village square, the *lurah* clutched his *sarong* tightly around his body while he struggled to protect his eyes from the maelstrom of dust and leaves. He cupped one hand and held it to his right eye, vainly attempting to identify whether rain was falling further up on the slopes. More than eight months had passed since his village had been blessed with rain. Impatiently, he waited for another flash of lightning. There! For a brief moment, the village headman believed he could see what appeared to be rain falling in the distance. He felt cheated. It would seem that once again, only those who lived higher in the mountains closer to the gods would benefit from the squall. He remained outside praying silently that the storm would move closer, bringing just enough rain so as not to strip the remaining topsoil away from their land. But the squall was rainless and the old man, disappointed, turned away from the wind and limped into his sparse accommodations.

A young girl darted suddenly from one of the huts and headed directly for the *balai* in search of the midwife. It was very late, she knew, probably even morning. As she crossed the open ground between the huts, lightning flashed and she turned in terror then fled back to the safety of her home. Moments passed and the child reappeared, running directly towards the simple structure as her mother had instructed. *Ibu Rai* was not her natural mother but in villages such as these that did not matter. The orphan had been taken in by this kind Balinese woman and cared for lovingly. Every year throughout the district, many children were abandoned as their parents fell victim to disease or some other cruel condition of life. Cholera, smallpox, and typhoid were all too frequent visitors to this community. Death would always claim at least one in every fourth child, before they could even walk.

A clap of thunder exploded around the huts causing the fragile girl to fall. Screaming with fear she jumped to her feet and continued running. Her heart pumped excessively as she tried to open the heavy door, only to find that it had been jammed tightly shut from the inside. She yelled as loudly as her small lungs would permit but her screams went unheard. Terrified in the dark, she turned and retreated to her own hut only to find her mother already lying on the floor, preparing for the imminent birth. She clasped her mother's hand tightly and sat down on the *tikar* mat beside her as the moment approached. She was scared and wanted to cry. Her father had not yet returned from the other *kampung*. What was she going to do? He had not come home at all during the night. The child called frantically to her mother, *"Bu! Bu!"*, but the woman's painful labour now caused confusion and the child's tearful calls did not register.

Another thunderous explosion threatened to rip the simple hut apart as the wooden door smashed inwards. The young girl jumped to her feet and attempted to lift the broken timbers back into place, but without success. As she struggled with the slats of wood her mother screamed again. Confused as to what she should do first, the child was not conscious of the figure which brushed past her, then moved quickly into the room to attend to the mother. As the girl stood in the doorway, the wind beating heavily against her tiny frame, she became aware of a strange, almost unfamiliar sensation. Holding her hands to her face for protection, the child leaned against the wind and peered outside. Immediately she knew from the sharp biting sensation that stung her arms and legs that it was raining. Lightning flashed again followed by several claps of thunder which rocked their entire surrounds. Suddenly the wind died. And the rain continued.

As she stood there with her little hands held outside cupped to catch the elusive treasure she heard one final cry, and the girl turned slowly, and witnessed the birth of her brother. She stood there for what seemed an immeasurable time watching as the baby emerged, only to be taken quickly by the adept midwife and placed in a small space alongside the *tikar*. Minutes passed as her mother was attended to and the baby cleaned. She heard her mother whisper some words which sounded to her like *ari-ari* but she was not sure, as *Ibu Arifin* removed something quickly and wrapped whatever this was in a square of cotton cloth, before placing the item in the urn on the far side of the small room. She watched, fascinated, as the midwife completed the essential tasks before placing the newborn baby in its mother's arms.

When the Balinese mother thought the moment appropriate, she would retrieve the cloth and its contents and find a suitable place to bury the *ari-ari*. It was a Balinese custom to place the placenta in a blessed place somewhere in the garden, in the belief that this represented the recently born infant's other half, and that this act would guarantee that the two halves would always be reunited. Balinese have always been known to return to their place of birth and adherence to this tradition would, in the future, be even more important as the new baby's mother was a titled Balinese woman.

The young girl was startled by a shout from outside and turned to see her father's figure scrambling across the now-soggy field. When she was certain that it really was her father, she ran quickly towards the man squealing with delight, calling to him that the baby had been born. When she reached the tired figure, he bent down to scoop the child into his arms, holding her tightly to his chest. Nearing the centre of the communal yard he observed that his neighbours had ventured outside, babbling with excitement at having been blessed with the downpour. Women ran with excitement into the small hut and examined the boy child. A loud shout brought them all back outside. It was the village *lurah*.

"*Look!*" he commanded, pointing to the sky as the rising sun's brilliance broke through the clearing storm clouds. They followed the direction of his outstretched arm and a silence fell over the village.

As the clouds dispersed the sun's rays pierced through the hot, moist morning atmosphere. The people stood transfixed by a magical sight. The golden colours merged with the most brilliant reds and greens. There was a hushed silence as the rainbow seemed to move closer and closer, its colours becoming brighter as it approached. None could ever remember having seen such a magnificent *pelangi* before, and certainly not one which appeared within reach of their outstretched hands. It was almost as if the powerful beams rose out of their *kampung*.

Ibu Arifin appeared from the hut. She was stunned by the rainbow's proximity and brilliance. Cautiously, she called to the baby's father. "*Subuh,*" she said, her head raised to the sky, "*Your son was born at the prayer time of Subuh*". And the father nodded his head slowly in consent. It was an appropriate name which respected the time of birth and his faith.

His son would be called *Subuh*. As the entire village stood in awe of the mystical sign that *The One and Only True God* had given, they remained silent, almost fearful, knowing that they had witnessed an event of great significance, and that somehow the child who had been born at that moment of prayer was somehow associated with the blessing of rain their village had received.

One by one the villagers approached the proud father and gently stroked the tiny baby's feet. As the women crowded around the teacher, there was a soft cry from behind. They turned quickly in the direction of the sound and there, standing in the broken doorway, *Ida Nyoman Rai* held her hands to her face as she looked across the short distance to her newborn son. It was as if his very being was surrounded by the magnificent rainbow. An aura. It was a sign! The woman moved awkwardly towards her Javanese husband who quickly placed his arm around her waist and led her back to rest.

"We will call him Subuh", she heard him say as they entered the hut and her weary body slumped to the unmade bed. *"Muhammad Subuh Koesnasosro!"* Her husband placed their son in her outstretched arms and smiled warmly at them both as they lay together before him. In later years, many who were present in that village at that time would swear that the colourful aura was in fact witnessed by all present, and that many people came from distant villages to see the newborn child. It was as if they somehow could sense that this child was destined for greatness. He would become their country's first president.

* * * * * *

At the time the strange events surrounding the birth of the child named *Subuh* took place, storm clouds had also gathered ominously over Gunung Merapi. For days the earth had trembled as the huge volcano sent signs that an eruption was imminent. Tremors had rocked the island of Java travelling from the epicentre thousands of kilometres to even the most isolated places. Huge clouds of ash and poisonous fumes spewed out of the enormous crater. The earth continued to twist and sway as a terrifying series of tremors rumbled outwards, towards the towns and villages throughout the archipelago.

The combination of storm clouds and billowing fumes provided a spectacle which struck fear in all who witnessed it. Clouds of heavy poisonous gas flowed directly down the mountainous slopes unimpeded, sweeping through the unfortunate villages which lay amongst the rich rice-terraced foothills. None could escape the poisonous fumes. The young, the elderly, the village headman, all died within moments. Goats and chickens lay scattered where they had fallen.

Huge lava flows moved with perilous speed down the volcano's sides carrying a lake of molten stone in their path. Villages disappeared in just moments as the mass of lava swallowed the flimsy huts. As the devastating bubbling mass encroached upon village after village, the air was filled with the sounds of coconut fruit exploding on trees as the air surrounding the flow became impossibly hot, causing the ambient temperatures to rise rapidly above flash-point. Thatched roofed dwellings exploded as waves of heat engulfed the villages, instantly cremating those caught inside by the deadly gas just minutes before. The volcano roared on throughout the night. Only a few of the terrified villagers were spared as they fled.

* * * * * *

The small village of Woboro lay within sight of the incredible events which unfolded not ten kilometres away. Because it was positioned on the northern aspect of the volcano's foothills, the menacing lava flow and poisonous gases mercifully could not reach the tiny hamlet. As the eruption continued, all of the *kampung's* inhabitants waited nervously outside, gathered together as they prayed for protection. None of the villagers could remember such a violent display from the mountain, although there were tales of similar devastation which had occurred back in the ancestral days of their *nenek-mojang*.

Their prayers were led by a senior Islamic leader who had returned to this village to attend the birth of his child. His presence made the villagers feel secure, for this scholar was a true representative of their beloved *Allah* and he provided the spiritual comfort they needed so desperately at that time. They prayed continuously through the evening and, as the danger passed, fell into exhausted sleep. Occasionally, some would awaken to the sudden familiar jolt of an earth tremor, but most remained asleep until they were called for the morning prayers.

Once prayers were over, the holy man was summoned to the small room where his wife was resting. She smiled tiredly, exhausted from the ordeal of the birth, and reached out with her right hand to her husband. He squeezed it lovingly as the midwife held his newborn son out for him to examine. Waves of emotion engulfed him as he released his wife's palm and took his son into his arms. He turned and walked outside into the small village square where he stood facing the menacing volcano. The sun had risen but its brilliance was choked by the storm clouds and deadly ash. The midwife, fearing that the particles of the ash might injure the child or at least interfere with its breathing, insisted that the father return the child to its mother. The father refused. Instead, he commenced chanting while rocking the infant to and fro in his arms. He prayed. Soon he was joined by many of the villagers who had completed their prayers earlier, during the *Subuh* period, and now wished to inspect the new addition to their village.

An hour passed, and then came the fiercest of storms. The peasant farmers retreated into their huts and waited for the heavy deluge to pass. Soon they were able to venture outside once again to discover that not only had the rain ceased, but the sun's rays had managed to pierce through the filthy haze of ash and dark clouds. Suddenly there was a chorus of shouts which brought the rest of the villagers running outside.

They all stood in amazement at the spectacle. In the distance, towards the east but behind and surrounding the huge volcano, there was blue sky. As they murmured amongst themselves, the father reappeared holding his newborn son.

Immediately, there were gasps of astonishment for, at that very moment, the early morning sun's brilliance sparkled in every direction and the most magnificent rainbow appeared across the valley. The villagers turned towards the man holding the child and were surprised to see him smiling at his son, as if ignorant of the incredible spectacle surrounding them. The *pelangi* seemed to rest at the newborn child's feet. Suddenly, the new father raised his head and called for them to rejoice. He announced that this miracle had been a sign sent by the *One and Only True God, Allah!* They responded at once, falling to their knees as the man led them in prayer. Later that day, the volcano ceased to erupt and the weather returned to normal.

As in Blitar, many of this village's number were prepared to swear on the *Holy Koran* that they had witnessed the miracle of the brilliant rainbow and the volcano's abrupt silence. Many maintained that they could see quite clearly where the rainbow commenced, its proximity so close they believed they had touched the magnificent rays. Some also related, in reverent voice, that, at the moment when the brilliant colours spread across their hills, they noticed that there was also an aura surrounding the newborn child.

These were all simple people. They were not wise in the way of the *maggis* who clearly understood what was happening: that they were all in fact witnesses to the fulfilment of an old prophecy which predicted the birth of three kings at this time.

One, the prophecy stated, would be a king of his people, leading them out of the darkness of oppression. The second would also be born during the violence of nature's despair, to rise to lead his people away from their spiritual suffering. The third would be born of pale yellow skin in the islands far to the north, and would conquer the world known as the Far East.

Before the close of that mystical day when, as the sun slipped quickly away and the faithful attended the *Mahgrib* prayer period, the newborn child had been named. His father sensed a great moment had arrived but even he was not to know that his son would grow and become one of the world's greatest spiritual leaders as he introduced the philosophy of *Susila Budi Dharma*, or *SUBUD* as it would become known.

On the day of his birth, his parents selected his name and wrote it down to be remembered. He was called *Soekarno*.

* * * * * *

None of the inhabitants of either of the two villages which experienced the mystical events on that same day were aware of the strange coincidences surrounding their two communities, nor how they were inextricably tied together. That both of the chosen children born during the early hours of that morning would suffer identical illnesses within days of their birth would not have registered as being of any significance, had these simple people even known of these events.

Subuh's father carried his son in his arms for weeks as the boy's health deteriorated. *Ibu Arifin* had never seen anything like it before. She could not understand what it was that ailed the child, only that the debilitating attacks were taking their toll on the infant.

And, in their village, *Soekarno's* parents also continued to pray as they watched, in disbelief, as their son continued to suffer from the devastating illness.

The gods observed this enigma and moved to correct their dilemma. On an appropriate day, as the confused state continued threatening both children, holy men visited both *kampung* and blessed the infants. Traditional *adat*, or custom, then required that the children's parents select new names for the sickly boys, to assist with the fresh start in life each would be given.

In the small village of Blitar where rain had mystically fallen as the boy child was born, his parents ceremoniously cast away the infant's given name of *Subuh* and renamed their son. They called him *Soekarno*.

Almost one hundred kilometres to the north in the village of Wiboro, a similar ceremony took place. The parents here also prayed for their son's *kharma* to improve with his new name.

Their child's name was changed from *Soekarno* to *Muhammed Subuh*.

* * * * * *

And so the gods smiled on these two children and blessed them, and their health returned and they grew, and moved forward with their lives, each destined to fulfil the prophecies passed down from their ancestors.

Chapter 2

1928 — 1933

Soekarno leaned forward and gazed out through the window overlooking the quiet street. The provincial city's inhabitants were enjoying the mid-day break from the heat. Everywhere throughout the region, the Dutch masters and the Indonesians followed the customary habit of resting from the mid-day heat. It was a time set aside for rest before returning to one's chores later in the afternoon. *Bandung's* residents rarely slept at this time. The Dutch had discovered that this city's moderate climate did not place the same demands on one's body as the low-lying settlements along the humid coast. Here, in the evenings, one could even experience the occasional need for warm clothing although most of the *bule* wore these heavy clothes as an affectation, or out of some sense of homesickness for their native land.

Soekarno loved it here in *Bandung* with its parks and gardens, its schools and colleges. Especially the colleges. He smiled quietly to himself and leaned back away from the view, rolling easily back onto the bed. The girl's musky fragrance still hung in the air and he closed his eyes momentarily, conjuring up images of the young student undressed again. He lay still, controlling his breathing as his mind recaptured moments he had spent with the soft, pale-skinned girl.

Since he could first remember, his close friends called him *Djago*, The Cock, or Champion in deference to his obvious schoolyard strength. And later, as his handsome features and charismatic charm developed, his prowess at winning the hearts of the ladies confirmed the appropriate title. Soekarno enjoyed the flattering nickname which had stuck since his early teens in Surabaja although, these days, he preferred to be known as *Bung Karno* as he felt that

29

this identified him more with the people, and his political ambitions.

As his thoughts moved away from the charming and willing student who had shared his bed in the early afternoon hours, the handsome young engineer permitted his mind to wander back to other ladies he had known. Soekarno always enjoyed this feeling of post-sexual after-glow which provided the occasion for his mind to relax and his thoughts to wander carelessly. Such luxuries were becoming increasingly rare, and often eluded the ambitious graduate as his political activities and demands on his private time consumed opportunities for such interludes.

He was reminded of his early teens in the small village town of *Tulung Agung* where he was raised in the care of his grandparents. He loved them dearly and recalled the seemingly endless, almost dreamy days of uncomplicated rural life he missed so much here in the city. Living away from his own parents hadn't bothered the young teenager. In fact, he enjoyed escaping the suffocating life of the *kampung* although he missed his mother dearly, at first. It was during this period of his development, living with his grandparents, when he became enthralled by the *wajang kulit* puppet shadow plays which recounted the Hindu *Ramayana* epic.

These never-ending stories captivated his heart and soul. He recalled rapturous evenings spent at the village roadside theatre depicting the ancient stories wrapped in symbolic gestures, which represented the very heartbeat of Javanese culture. Night after night, he would plead with his *nenek* to be permitted to go down to the village square where these shows were held. There he would sit with his friends and watch the shadows move behind the white screen as the drama unfolded. The puppeteer would half-talk, half-sing the story, sending his audience of children into a trance. Sometimes they would just fall asleep, as the plays could continue for many hours into the warm Javanese nights.

It was during one such occasion that the young *Djago* observed a number of girls sitting a short distance to the side of his friends. When he discovered that they were giggling and pointing in his direction, he correctly assumed that they were discussing his handsome features. Although only fifteen, he was already conscious that he attracted the opposite sex and never felt uncomfortable with this fact. As the girls continued to giggle and attract his group's attention, *Djago* remembered rising to his feet and sauntering over to the junior high school girls who immediately became quite embarrassed. None of the other boys would ever have done that! An hour later, the young Soekarno found himself fumbling with one of the girls under the copse of palm trees behind the village square. The next morning, his grandparents placed him on the bus and sent him to Surabaya. He never did understand why so much commotion had been generated from what was just a short encounter in the bushes. After their brief and clumsy sexual experiment, the schoolgirl had immediately told her mother who, in turn, related the shameful encounter to her husband when he returned home later that evening. The following morning the grandparents wisely packed his bags and sent him scurrying off to the city and out of reach of the angry father's razor-sharp *golok*.

At first, Soekarno didn't enjoy the large city. He spent some weeks with his family's distant relatives living in an overcrowded shanty on the outskirts of Surabaja Port. Some weeks passed before he received a letter of introduction from his father which requested assistance from an old acquaintance for his son. Soekarno delivered the communication and was immediately taken into the household where he maintained lodgings while completing his high school studies. This was the home of Omar Said Tjokroaminoto, the esteemed civic figure and renowned religious leader.

Tjokro treated his new lodger as if he were his own son. The two soon became close as the elderly scholar identified the enormous potential of the eager young student. As his foster son, Soekarno received a concentrated schooling in languages and religion before moving on to study politics under the older man's guidance. As time passed and the young protege eagerly absorbed whatever teachings he was exposed to, Tjokroaminoto gradually introduced Soekarno to many of his special guests who came to seek the respected leader's advice, often encouraging the young man to participate in the general discussions. It was during this time that *Bung Karno* discovered the complexity of many of the issues facing his fellow countrymen. The never-ending flow of political and religious activists who passed through his foster father's home provided a forum for him to study these emerging leaders, who spanned Indonesia's growing political spectrum.

Tjokroaminoto often observed his young protege and wished

that he was his own real son. As this was not to be, he decided on the next best course of action and, at the age of sixteen, he married his daughter Siti Utari to the confident Soekarno.

Soekarno's competitive nature and manner precipitated difficulties in his new relationship with Tjokroaminoto, whose followers had escalated in number to more than four hundred thousand. He fell out with his father-in-law, and the marriage lasted only another two years before Soekarno sent her home, childless, and established a de facto relationship with the landlady of his Bandung accommodations, Inggit Garnasih, a woman some twelve years his senior. Always the opportunist, he married this wealthy woman who supported her handsome husband while he studied at the Bandung Institute of Technology.

Inggit soon discovered that her young man had no intention of being faithful to her but she still adored her cocky, high-spirited husband and accepted his many liaisons. Eventually, as their fifth anniversary approached, Inggit realised that she had become, once again, just his landlady as Soekarno ceased sharing their bed, preferring to keep his life and activities totally divorced from her. She accepted the status quo, preferring the hurt she felt to losing him completely.

Soekarno knew that he had power over women. It never ceased to fascinate him that this was so, although he believed that he was special and was destined for great achievements in his life. Now that he had graduated he could move onto a different path. He had never really wanted to be a civil engineer but, as the Dutch controlled the colleges, he had considered himself just lucky that he had obtained any degree at all. During his years in Bandung, he consistently developed relationships with other students who shared his political views. He practised public speaking alone in his small room before venturing down to the common park areas to test his style on the other undergraduates. Soon he became a sought-after speaker as his demeanour and style attracted huge crowds. His charismatic personality and presence often mesmerised the gatherings. Soekarno's confidence grew quickly as he discovered that his popularity was not restricted to the provincial city of Bandung.

As he lay on his back contemplating his past, Soekarno knew that he had reached a major crossroads in his career. It was unlikely that he could now expect any civil service opportunity as the Dutch police had been watching his activities closely and he had already been warned several times as to the content of his speeches. He knew they were inflammatory. His captivating style depended on channelling his audience's hate and despair with their colonial masters into support for his political ambitions. And he was becoming more and more successful. The following day he was to leave for Semarang and prepare for a rally that had been organised.

Soekarno smiled with anticipation. He lived for the adoration, the mass hysteria that broke out whenever he spoke, the opportunity to consolidate his political base and, of course, the power he felt flow through his veins as the crowds shouted out in unison calling his name. '*Soekarno! Soekarno! Hiduplah Soekarno! Long live Bung Karno!*'

The following morning Soekarno joined his comrades who would support his rally and act as bodyguards in the event the Dutch secret police attempted to attack their hero. They were all dressed alike, simply, wearing their black *pitji* caps proudly. They were in high spirits. It was as if they sensed the historical import of what they were about to do.

And so they departed, taking the slow winding mountain road down the dangerous track towards the north coast of Java and the coastal towns of Tjiribon and Semarang, heading for the huge rally that would changes all of their lives forever.

* * * * * *

Semarang

Even Soekarno was astonished at the large number of students that attended his rally. The townspeople had followed the surging mass of humanity into the old soccer field more out of curiosity than anything else. Street vendors also followed and, within a relatively short period of time the entire area had taken on the appearance of some organised festival as the crowd moved around slowly creating an almost carnival atmosphere. The roadside vendors or *kaki-lima* traders sold *sate* to the clamouring high school children, while Soekarno and his team prepared an area on the side of the field from where he would address the crowd. He was extremely pleased with the turnout. His confidence grew and he strutted around smiling and talking to anyone who cared to listen. It was his way of preparing himself prior to an address, collecting his thoughts, as most of his speeches were unrehearsed.

At the back of the crowd, a young boy complained to his mother about the heat and flies. Occasionally, as small clouds of dust rose around the main pedestrian traffic, he would sneeze and wipe his nose with the back of his hand. He didn't want to be there. He had just followed his mother and she, in turn, had only followed the crowds into the field to discover what was taking place. Once his mother had determined that it was just a student gathering, she sat down alongside everyone else to wait. There was nothing else to do in the town. Their bus didn't depart for Djogyakarta for at least another three hours and so she elected to wait there and observe whatever was to take place. Her son, Soenarko, sat down disgruntled beside her.

The Javanese woman merely placed her hand behind his back and, slowly moving her fingers up towards his neck tickled him quickly to distract his attention from the conditions. She glanced at him and, satisfied that he would cope with the heat, returned her attention to the crowd. They sat in the heat for another twenty minutes or so when suddenly there was a roar as the crowd scrambled to its feet. The young mother rose with the others and then bent down to pull her son up alongside her. She realised that the boy could not see and decided to move out and away from the centre of the crowd. Slowly they made their way back towards the entrance and eventually found an area that was not as crowded. She looked down at her son and was immediately concerned. Soenarko had difficulty breathing. It was one of those attacks which had haunted him practically since birth. His mother sensed the urgency and sat down next to him encouraging her boy to lie on his side while she stroked his back. The dusty conditions only further aggravated the boy's asthma attack and he began to choke. The woman panicked and, sensing this, the boy followed suit.

Suddenly a figure moved alongside and picked the boy up. He held him upright, applying a wet cloth to the child's face, rubbing the back of his neck several times, while speaking softly to the stricken Soenarko. Moments later, the man led both mother and child outside and away from the crowded field.

'*Rest here!*' he ordered, pointing to several well-worn wooden stools normally reserved for the patrons of the roadside vendor who specialised in *bakmi goreng*. He motioned to the owner and indicated that he wanted a glass of the sweet syrup which was sold to accompany the fried noodles.

'*Drink this!*' he said, handing the pinkish-coloured mixture to Soenarko.

'*Terima kasih,*' the child politely responded but before he could sip the cold drink was struck by another attack. It lasted for several minutes, depleting the boy's reserves. He sat on the stool listlessly, held close by his anxious mother. They continued to sit quietly together for some time and the boy might have fallen asleep had it not been for the air suddenly being punctured by the crowd's deafening cries. '*Hiduplah Bung Karno!*' they shouted in unison, '*Long live Bung Karno!*' they chanted, over and over again until a hush enveloped the crowd.

Moments of quiet followed; then the woman heard a voice drifting across towards them, carried by a resonance and clarity which startled her with its strength.

'*People of Semarang,*' the voice started, pausing for a moment as the crowd became completely hushed. '*People of Semarang, you are political slaves!*' Again there was a pause for effect.

'*People of Semarang, you are prisoners in your own land!*' The voice rose slightly, developing a pitch which carried across the packed ground. '*People of Semarang, the time has come for you to unite and work together for the benefit of yourselves, your children, your futures and your independence!*' And then, with his powerful voice he called, '*People of Semarang, Merdeka!*'

The crowd screamed in unison, their voices pounding the air as they called out together, '*Merdeka! Merdeka! Independence! Freedom!*' which slowly changed into the fervent chant, '*Hiduplah Bung Karno, Long live Bung Karno!*' Knowing that his commanding presence had been felt by all those present, Soekarno then went on to speak for more than an hour. He did not rest nor did his rhetoric lose any of its brilliance. The crowd adored him. The more they called his name, the less tired he felt, until the mass of people were totally under his spell. It was as if one of the characters from the shadow plays had come to life to care for them all. They didn't want him to finish.

They listened in silence when he cajoled them for being ignorant of what was happening around them and criticised their teachers for failing to fan the fire in their hearts, the desire for freedom from the Dutch. They listened as he encouraged them to unite as one, to forget their racial and religious differences and work together to form a common front. They sighed when his voice developed a soft musical quality as he talked of love and loving, of peace and prosperity for their children. They screamed in support when he called for them to take up arms and expel the foreigners from their soil when the time was right.

Soenarko and his mother sat with the stranger who had assisted them and listened to the orator continue to speak without once resting. They knew that something special was happening around them but were content to just be a small part of whatever it was, without question. The stranger leaned closer and placed his hand on Soenarko's shoulder. He smiled and looked directly into the child's face and said, *'When I was very small I also had a sickness. My parents later told me that the village people where I was born believed that I might die. But, as you can see, I am now well again and have not suffered any such illness since my childhood.'*

Soenarko's mother looked at the man's face and believed what he said. There was a strange truthfulness about this stranger and she wanted to take his hand and hold it for comfort. Her son also sensed the man's power but was confused by its presence. He only knew that his attack had gone and that he now felt much better. He looked up at the stranger. *'Did you have my sickness?'* he asked.

'Yes,' he answered the surprised boy. *'But as I told you, it has now gone, forever.'*

'Perhaps you gave it to me!' Soenarko accused, causing his mother to purse her lips and frown at his rudeness.

'Perhaps I did,' the stranger replied, smiling at the startled pair. *'And if I did, then I am obliged to take it away.'*

'Please don't.' The woman intoned, saddened now by this talk. She knew that this sickness would stay with her son for life. Anyone in their village who fell victim to the breathing illness suffered throughout their lives with the beast inside their chest. She looked sadly at the stranger who smiled, then placed his hand back on her son's shoulder.

The boy responded to the warmth of the man's hand and offered no resistance as the stranger closed his eyes and appeared to pray silently, to himself.

'*Njonja,*' he said, removing his hand from the boy while addressing the mother, '*What month was your son born?*' The woman was surprised at the question but answered as she could see no harm. She thought for a few moments, collecting her thoughts. When she gave the answer, the man's face broke into another smile and his eyes danced with satisfaction.

'*It is the same month as my birth. Only you are a little younger,*' he said, speaking to the boy. '*Siapa namanja?*' he suddenly asked, wanting to know the child's name. Soenarko replied politely in his clearest Javanese dialect. The woman placed her arm around her son and squeezed him softly.

'*What is your name, sir?*' she asked, using the polite Javanese level to address the softly spoken man. She was pleased that she had done so, for when he responded, the woman knew instantly that this stranger was not only highly educated, but was obviously from her own district in Java.

'*I will write it down for the boy. I would like for him to take this paper home when you leave and keep it folded until the morning. Would you grant me this strange request?*'

The woman was surprised but etiquette demanded that she agree. A small piece of paper was produced and when he had finished writing, he folded the paper and passed it to her.

'*I must go now. I am sure that you will have a safe journey home. Selamat tinggal!*' he said, rising slowly and lightly touching the boy for the third time on his shoulder.

'*Goodbye, sir, terima kasih.*' the woman responded, her hands clasped together, her fingers softly touching her lips as if in prayer.

'*Selamat djalan, Bapak,*' the grateful boy called as the white cotton dressed man departed. He watched the figure walk away when suddenly the man turned and waved to the boy as he called, '*Sampai ketemu lagi, Soeharto! — until we meet again, Soeharto!*'

Soenarko's mother was surprised that the helpful stranger had, in a matter of a few minutes, already forgotten her son's name and was deep in thought when there were shouts and cries close by. Frightened by the clamour, she immediately rose and led her son away from the disturbance. As they headed down the street past the *pasar* where the stench of the day's unsold produce hung heavily in the air, they could hear police whistles and pistol shots shatter the air. Suddenly there were hundreds of people running down the streets nearby as they fled the savage police and their batons. They immediately took refuge in one of the stalls and waited for the disturbance to pass. Soon they were able to continue and, later into the afternoon, they boarded the bus which would take them safely home to their small house in Desa Kemusu Argamulja.

They arrived late in the evening, too tired to eat. Soenarko fell asleep immediately under the watchful eyes of his mother. As she sat there praying that his sickness would go away and leave him to live the life of a normal child, she remembered the stranger. Extracting the paper he had given her from her *tas*, Soenarko's mother leaned closer to the kerosene lantern to read the inscription. She did so then bent forward and kissed her son. Then she placed the piece of paper with *Subuh's* name on it beside her son's bed and left him alone, to dream whatever it was that little boys dream about.

* * * * * *

Another year was to pass before the sickness became so severe that a holy man was called to her son's side. She now believed he was about to die, plagued by the debilitating attacks. As she sat with Soenarko throughout those distressing days and nights, she prayed the boy would recover, as had the stranger they had met. Soenarko's health did improve, mysteriously, and when he was well enough to rejoin his class, his friends were not overly surprised when he announced that his mother had given him a new name so that the sickness would not return. On that day, when he was called by the teacher, he politely corrected her for using his former name.

'My name is no longer Soenarko, Ibu. My name is now Soeharto!'

And, almost magically, the child known as Soeharto recovered completely from his illness. Within a short period of time even his school performance improved, attracting the attention of his teachers. He had beaten the terrible attacks and would never again suffer the disease.

As he became older and wiser, the fortunate Javanese understood that his recovery had, indeed, been miraculous. And although he came to learn that events in life were often shrouded with mystery, he firmly believed that the quietly-spoken religious man who had offered him comfort on that day played an integral part in his recovery.

And so, Soeharto never forgot the name of the stranger they had met when the police had raided the political rally in Semarang, arresting the outspoken activist, Soekarno, and throwing him into jail. He could still remember the roar of the crowds as they called to their hero and these chants would often plague his dreams, awakening him in the dark of the night as the multitude of voices still echoed in his ears calling, 'Hiduplah Soekarno, Hiduplah Bung Karno! Long live Soekarno!'

Chapter 3

*1963 — Kepulauan Seribu,
The Thousand Islands*

They had agreed that *Pulau Putri* would provide the best anchorage and, now that they had settled down on the small islands' white, almost crystalline beach, Murray had to agree. There were fifteen or so in the group. The voyage from Tandjung Priok, Djakarta's harbour, had been reasonably pleasant. Murray would have preferred to sail but this had not been an option. They had approached the ALRI *Laksamana Laut* and appealed to the Navy Rear Admiral's generous nature, requesting a charter boat for the students and their Australian friend. At first, the senior naval officer was insistent that his vessels were not available for hire but when the young smiling Australian stepped forward and spoke to him in fluent Bahasa Indonesia, the situation changed. Not immediately, of course. The officer was suspicious of a foreigner possessing such uncommon skills in the local language. The Dutch had all but left Indonesia, and only a handful of Europeans who could converse fluently in the national language remained. Many of these were Soviet technicians.

When it appeared that they were not making any real headway with their negotiations, several of the female students had ushered the rest of the group out of the navy office while they remained behind to persuade the stubborn officer to reconsider. Although some rupiah did change hands, the port commander still required considerable convincing that the Australian was not from the Eastern Bloc.

'*Show me his passport,*' he demanded. Murray was summoned back into the office where the two girls were then dismissed. He requested the document politely, albeit brusquely, and examined the blue-covered passport. '*Murray Lloyd Stephenson,*' he read slowly

41

and with difficulty. *'Do you have any dollars?'*

Murray surreptitiously removed the wallet from his back-pocket and extracted two American dollar notes. An hour later, his excited group were steaming out past the breakwater walls towards *Pulau Edam* where they passed close to the lighthouse before taking a heading of 330 degrees. The ship was more than they had expected. The Russian patrol boat slipped through the calm sea at thirty knots covering the forty nautical miles in just over an hour. As the noisy twin diesels churned the water, flying fish raced before the wooden hull, entertaining the excited students. All but two of their number had never been to the magnificent string of more than one hundred coral islands which dotted the shallow sea north of the capital. Their destination was one of the more isolated islands which lay in the centre of a large lagoon, surrounded by a necklace of coral atolls. These were all densely covered with tall coconut palms and low shrubs. Kepulauan Seribu, the Thousand Islands, were virtually uninhabited as drinking water was scarce on the smaller atolls.

They had unloaded their supplies and made camp just twenty metres from where the calm lagoon's occasional ripples tickled the beach. As soon as the patrol boat had departed with instructions to return the following afternoon, everyone stripped down to their underclothes and entered the warm clear water. They laughed and splashed each other while a few of the young men ventured out into the deeper water in search of green-backed lobster. As the day wore on, the girls organised a fire and prepared a simple meal of rice and fish which they had exchanged for cigarettes from one of the passing fishing *perahu*.

The island was relatively small. Murray had ventured off to reconnoitre after the meal and discovered that he could cover the area in less than fifteen minutes. It was a paradise, he thought, wishing that he had sailed out to these magnificent islands before, when he had first arrived in Indonesia. Now he had only a few days left and the thought depressed him. The past two years living in Djakarta as an exchange student, studying at the Universitas Indonesia, had been the most significant period in his life. Murray had developed a sound appreciation of the Indonesian people and their culture. He had acquired many friends and now resented having to leave it all behind. But he knew that he really had no choice in the matter. Although his family were financially secure, it wasn't money or the lack of it which would require that he soon return to Australia. He had given a commitment and was obliged to fulfil the undertakings he had given prior to his departure from Melbourne, two years before. His thoughts were suddenly interrupted as the attractive Sundanese girl dropped beside him and rested her head on shoulder.

'Why do you sit here by yourself, Murray? Can't you decide which of the tjewek you want for tonight?' she bantered. Yanti knew that given the opportunity any one of the other girls would jump at the chance to tempt her boyfriend away.

'How did you know?' he teased, *'I thought, that as the decision's so difficult to make then perhaps I should have them all.'*

'Okay, you do that and I will cut their hair off,' Yanti parried, then added, *'and maybe something of yours as well!'* but Murray knew that she was only half-joking. One thing he had discovered very early in his stay and that was just how damn jealous these beautiful creatures could be, and how totally insecure they were in their relationships.

'Murray, sajang, would you take me to Australia when you go?'

'Sure,' he replied, wanting to keep the banter light. *'And a couple of Javanese girls as well.'* There was always strong competition between the Javanese and Sundanese and he attempted to change the direction of their conversation. He would certainly miss Yanti when he left but there were others who were just as sweet, and he really didn't want to think about all of that on this beautiful island. He rose and pulled Yanti to her feet before her pout became permanent. *'Come on, let's go back in the water.'*

'No, Murray, I have already been out in the sun too long! You will make my skin black and then everyone will say I am ugly!' she said, half-jokingly, although it was a fact that a girl's beauty was tied to the fairness of her skin. Working in the rice fields was to be avoided at all costs as the tropical sun was merciless, stamping the women as peasants with their darkened faces and bodies. Nevertheless, she followed the tall, fair-haired Australian down to the water's edge where she playfully kicked sand at his back before fleeing happily back to the safety of the shaded campsite.

Murray swam slowly out into the deeper water and lay on his back soaking up the late afternoon's warmth. Occasionally, as he drifted lazily and the mild currents carried him too far, he would turn and swim back a few strokes to avoid being washed onto the coral reef which surrounded the adjacent island. The conditions were idyllic. In years to come, tourism would spoil these islands, he knew, and then the magic would tragically disappear.

During his two years in-country, he had travelled extensively and was continually amazed at the enormous tourist potential of the archipelago, with its pristine beaches and coconut groves, its towering volcanic mountains and rice-terraced highlands, its diversity of peoples and cultures. Yes, he would certainly miss all of this, and the prospect saddened him. He reluctantly accepted that he would return to the bleak Melbourne winters and, if an old friend failed to support his return, he would remain locked behind the desk job he knew would be waiting. Murray feared that his life might then slowly deteriorate and he would, as had many of those who had preceded him, regret the decision he had made a few years before to surrender his innocence in exchange for opportunity. At the time, he had been excited with the prospect of joining the government agency. In fact, he still enjoyed several exceptional relationships which had developed as a result of his membership in the exclusive intelligence service. The opportunity had been offered and he had not hesitated.

Murray accepted that, had it not been for his association with *Central Plans*, as it was referred to by its limited membership, it would have been most unlikely that he would have ever visited Indonesia: at least, not during these politically unstable times. Brief recollections of Melbourne and his family crossed his mind as he kicked slowly causing his body to move back towards the beach. Something in his mind triggered his memory and suddenly he found himself thinking of his mother and how she often had manipulated his early life.

* * * * * *

Murray had considered himself fortunate as his mother and sister had always been loving and very supportive. His mother had made sure that he received the best of education. Attendance at Geelong Grammar School stood Murray in good stead. During the years he spent at that fine establishment, he excelled not only academically but also on the sports field. He developed relationships with other students which would remain intact for many years after he had matriculated. Later, when he had graduated from Melbourne University's Faculty of Law, Murray was really not surprised to see the occasional familiar face amongst those who had also entered government service.

He had first been approached during his final year at university. Murray's mother had accepted an invitation for them both to spend the weekend with the Bradshaws in Portsea. In later years when reminiscing, Murray would often smile when recalling his mother's telephone instructions just before that long week-end.

'You will be expected to join in the tennis. The Bradshaws are very competitive people but you should not let them intimidate you. I will meet you there.' Mrs. Stephenson never missed an opportunity to advance her son's social relationships. 'Darling, you have the directions. Oh, and Murray,' she added, 'don't forget the new sports jacket I gave you on your birthday. They dress for dinner.'

'Should I bring complimentary batteries for their hearing aids?', he asked, and immediately wished he hadn't. He appreciated his mother's aggressive approach to widening his social contacts but remembered several other invitations which had been disastrously boring.

'Murray, don't be impertinent. I am confident that you will find these people quite exhilarating and, as for the inference that we are all just a bunch of old fogies, you should be prepared for some very competitive tennis.'

His first reaction was to decline the invitation, but knowing his mother's persistence, he decided that taking a break on the coast wouldn't hurt. The undergraduate studies were more demanding than he had anticipated and, as he entered his room just off campus and identified the stack of unread reference titles, the thought of a long weekend away from the drudgery suddenly appealed.

He thought the weather was probably going to be fine, although, like most Melbournians, Murray knew that any predictions he might make about the weather were likely to prove incorrect. The following day, having packed both warm and summer clothing just to be sure, he drove south down through the old farming areas towards the Army's Officer Training School before following the directions his mother had given. Murray knew the area reasonably well but even he was impressed to see the delightful cottage in its setting so close to the sea. After parking the MG TF snugly against the footpath, Murray lifted his gear from the back seat and strolled into the rose filled front garden. Before he could knock, the door was opened by a genial Harry Bradshaw and Murray was gripped by the hand and escorted directly to the rear of the house, where a small group had gathered.

'Everybody, this is Muriel's boy,' Bradshaw called out as they stepped down onto the enclosed terrace, behind which lay the tennis court and swimming pool. 'Murray, this is my wife Susan,' he said before turning to the women playing cards. 'The lady successfully cheating your mother at gin rummy is Jean Broome, and this gentleman is to be your tennis partner. Alfred, may I introduce Murray Stephenson.'

Murray stepped forward and shook the extended hand warmly as he smiled confidently and said 'hello' to the ladies. He was surprised to find that both these women were considerably younger than their husbands. Alfred Broome maintained his grip while he took Murray by the shoulder and playfully tested the younger man's arm for strength.

'Seem's you'll do, Murray. What do you say that we give our hosts a thrashing as soon as you're settled?'

'For goodness sake, Alfred. Give the young man a chance to catch his breath.' Jean Broome called as she placed her remaining cards down on the table indicating another win. 'As you can see, Murray, I'm not the sporting type I'm afraid. Hope you will be able to carry the side as your partner's ego is far superior to his game!' With which, the Bradshaws joined in the fun laughing at the truthful statement.

'That's okay. I enjoyed the drive and, quite frankly, I've been looking forward to a game or two. Been locked away with my books for too long. Will five minutes be okay?'

'Muriel, would you do the honours please?' Susan asked, indicating the guest room alongside the pool. Murray's mother rose and took her son by the arm leading the way. She returned quickly and took her place at the card table.

'He is a fine-looking young man, Muriel. You must be very pleased.' Susan commented, not realising that the very same thought preoccupied the minds of the others present.

'Perhaps we should send the old ones home,' Jean Broome added idly, sipping her gin and tonic. This was already her third. After her eighth or ninth, she had been known to become amorous with the younger men. Her comment brought a brief scowl to her husband's face.

'We'll see who's old, my dear,' Harry Bradshaw interceded quickly. The Broomes were close friends and both couples readily accepted each other's idiosyncrasies. Bradshaw crossed the terrace and lifted Alfred's wife out of her chair and headed towards the pool. Knowing that to continue with his charade would be folly and disastrous for the weekend gathering, Harry returned his guest to her seat and kissed her gently on the forehead, just as Murray returned.

'Well, let's do it,' Susan suggested, slightly miffed at the display. 'Muriel, you don't mind do you darling? You're more than welcome to join us, you know.'

'Not today, thanks dear. I'd be happy to stay here with Jean and discover just how she always manages to win.' Amid the light ongoing banter, the foursome moved onto the tennis court, and commenced with a few minutes of warming up shots before the challenge got under way. They played for an hour resting only briefly between the two sets. Murray was surprised at their level of play. He had expected a typical weekend game and was delighted that he was normally enough to earn courtside accolades from the gallery. On this occasion he struggled to maintain his first service due to the fact that he had not anticipated such strong opponents. Underestimating his hosts' skill was indeed a major tactical error which attracted several severe and pointed glances from his partner. Alfred had expected more of Murray, from what his mother had implied on the telephone the week before, but he did not overly display his disappointment. As the set developed he was pleased that he had reserved judgement for Murray's game improved dramatically, serving well and generally covering the court, saving difficult points which might have otherwise cost them the game.

The match over they rested around the swimming pool sipping champagne and freshly-squeezed orange juice. As the sun moved behind a thick blanket of cloud, the air became chilly and they adjourned to their rooms in preparation for the evening meal. Murray was relaxed with the thought of spending the rest of the weekend with his mother's friends. He hadn't always enjoyed the company of older people. He felt comfortable here and hoped that they approved of him. As he showered, Murray's thoughts turned to his own father and he sighed, the hot stinging stream of water washing away the instant mood swing he experienced whenever he remembered the man. Quickly he put the image out of his mind and, stepping from the shower, towelled himself until his skin reddened under the onslaught. He dressed casually then added his blazer.

Upon entering the main house he cursed himself silently for not wearing a tie. The other men both wore cravats, and the moment he caught his mother's critical eye Murray wished he'd remembered her advice. They drank and talked for almost two hours before sitting down to dinner. The conversation moved from sport to politics and both the older men invited the younger man's opinions.

In fact, he was being tested for the soundness of his political views. During the Cold War years, many apparently Ivy League types had concealed their left-wing persuasions and many a government agency had been burned. The women present were oblivious to what was taking place. Murray had no idea that both of these men were senior government officials whose activities placed them in the dark and sinister world of intelligence gathering and, on occasion, espionage. This was how their covert organisation recruited the select few who now represented the most elite secret service in modern times. Had Murray been told at that moment that Harry Bradshaw was one of the most skilled field operatives in the Government's employ he would most probably have scoffed. His host was affable and gracious without the rough edges one would expect from the grubby world of spies and their intrigue. The other male guest could easily have been a senior member of the community, seen participating at fetes and church bazaars with his splendid humour and entertaining stories. Murray would also not have accepted that Alfred Broome was, in fact, the head of Australia's Secret Service and that he commanded a force of agents that was so secret that even the Parliament was not privy to its existence.

As the evening wore on, the women retired, leaving the three men to pursue more serious discussions. The older and more experienced pair led Murray into conversations which surprised him as they discussed regional politics, the Commonwealth's unhealthy position in relation to the ever-increasing American presence around the globe, and the threat of communism as it spread through Asia and down towards Australia. When he finally returned to his room, he was amazed to see that they had talked together until three in the morning. Tired from the tennis but satisfied that he had carried himself well, Murray fell asleep almost within moments of his head touching the soft kapok pillow. He was totally unaware that he was about to take his first steps along a path with a very dark and sinister destination, that his life would never again be his own, and that his mother had unwittingly delivered him into the hands of evil.

The following day, Saturday, they had a rematch but the outcome was the same. Alfred was ecstatic as some considerable time had passed since he had partnered a win over the Bradshaws. That evening, as they had on the previous night, the women retired shortly after dinner leaving the men to their discussions and, once again, the topics followed much the same pattern as the evening before. Alfred directed the conversation back to his preferred subject, communism and its spread in Asia, and the dangers of the Domino Theory while Harry checked and probed the unwitting law student as to his own loyalties and preferred political affiliations.

It was towards the early hours of Sunday morning that Murray was asked very directly whether he would be interested in government employment once he had graduated. Murray was quite taken off guard by the question, but when it was made clear that there was a sound career path opportunity for him, and that both of these men could ensure his acceptance subject to final security clearances being conducted, he was flattered that he was considered worthy of such sponsorship. They didn't dwell on the subject, suggesting that his decision would require much more than a few days to determine whether he believed he could make such a commitment. They agreed not to raise the issue again for the remainder of that weekend. On the following day, Murray was surprised that they had meant exactly what they had stated. It was almost as if he had imagined the intriguing discussions having ever occurred at all.

He remembered that it had rained throughout the Sunday and a sharp exchange had taken place between the women, Jean and Susan. He had not understood at the time as Murray was not privy to the personal secrets these two couples enjoyed. The ensuing tension made him feel uncomfortable and he went for a long jog in spite of the weather. When he returned, it was as if nothing had occurred, as they were all, including his mother, quite tipsy from the champagne Harry had broken out from his cellar. Murray joined them after he'd showered and was relaxed to discover that the earlier tension had disappeared. He quietly examined his mother's expression but there was no indication that everything had not returned to normal.

That evening passed slowly. The atmosphere became tense once again and it was obvious that the couples were suffering from overexposure to each other. It was apparent to Murray and, as the youngest present, he felt uncomfortable. Shortly after dinner he excused himself, kissed his mother on the cheek as he whispered to her, then retired to his room. He undressed slowly and then flopped into the soft double bed, wishing he had brought something to read. Murray lay in the darkness willing his mind and body to relax but he could not sleep. Hours passed before he finally submitted, drifting into a deep sleep.

The night had almost passed when he awoke suddenly, startled. He grabbed at whatever it was that moved close to him in the dark.

'What the...!'

'Shh!' the woman intoned, surrendering as her hands were gripped fiercely by Murray's. 'Shh!' she called urgently, again, indicating that there was no resistance. Confused, he released her wrists and, as he did so, felt a hand moving softly over his face until it rested on his mouth.

'Don't say anything, Murray! Please don't say anything!'

He could smell the alcohol on her breath. Murray reached for the bedside light but she anticipated the movement.

'Don't, please!' she pleaded, lifting the bedcovers and slipping in beside him. He thought the woman to be quite mad coming to his room while her own husband slept close by.

'For Chrissakes, you'll get us both hung!' he hissed as she started stroking his firm arms and thighs.

'Don't speak, Murray, just be quiet!' she implored, moving over his body and kissing him in an attempt to prevent him from talking.

It was hopeless, he knew, as already he'd been aroused. Moments passed and, as she stroked his body slowly, kissing him softly first on the neck and chest, and then slowly down his firm stomach, he realised that he wanted her to stay. A small voice warned him that what they were doing was dangerous. They would be caught! He should send her away! But the warmth moving up from his loins enveloping his whole body was a far more powerful force and, before he could offer any resistance, she had slipped into position over him and was gently rocking him into an uncontrollable feeling of ecstasy. His hands moved across her body in the dark until coming to rest as he cupped her breasts. They moved together, in harmony, their excitement building when suddenly she called out softly, stifling her cry as she shuddered.

Then she bent forward and gently kissed the surprised Murray before slipping back out of the bed, leaving quickly before he could prevent her departure. He heard her move through the darkened room and, when the door clicked closed behind her, even then he dared not turn the light on, until he was sure that sufficient time had passed for her to return to her own room. He was stunned by the sudden exit and bewildered by the woman's foolish adventure. If it had not been for the lingering scent, he may have believed that he'd been dreaming.

Hours passed before sleep returned. And even then it was not a refreshing rest, as he dreamed restlessly only to awaken without any recollection of what had transpired in his sleep. Of one thing he was certain. A woman had entered his room and made silent, eager love, leaving him concerned and disappointed with the interlude. He was irritated with himself for permitting it to happen. But more than anything else, Murray was annoyed because he was not certain which of the two wives had entertained themselves at his expense.

As he sat down to breakfast, Murray felt uncomfortable knowing that one of the women sitting across the table had cheated on her husband just a few hours before. He tried to act as if nothing at all had occurred and joined in the casual conversation, surreptitiously observing those present to see if there was some indication, some acknowledgement as to which of the ladies had been his visitor. There was just no way he could determine this as even their perfumes seemed similar and neither of the wives gave any indication of their indiscretion. It was almost as if nothing had happened. Guilt, and an uneasiness that his affair may suddenly be exposed, encouraged his early return to the city where he buried himself conscientiously in his studies. For weeks, when he lay awake at night, Murray visualised the exciting tryst and, no matter how he tried, he was unable to determine which of the women had compromised their friends and husband.

During the following months, Murray was invited back to the Bradshaws home on several occasions and he had accepted, not just because he enjoyed the strong bond which had developed with Harry but also, at first, out of a sense of curiosity. During the first return visit the programme was much the same as before. They played tennis, dined and talked late into the night, and Murray felt comfortable in their company. During his third and final visit, the tennis consisted of men's singles only, as Susan had insisted on remaining with Muriel Stephenson while the men fought it out on the courts. Murray thought it relevant that Alfred Broome's wife had also not accompanied her husband on these last visits.

Later, he had asked his mother casually about the woman's absence, but she merely shrugged, almost indifferently, and ignored the question. As the circumstances were never repeated, he believed he understood why and wondered what had happened to the flirtatious Jean Broome. He never met her again and, by the end of his final semester, the fading memory of the brief encounter no longer concerned him as he had established other priorities in his life. He completed his law degree a few months later, and immediately entered government service.

Murray Stephenson joined the sixty-three other members of the Australian Secret Intelligence Service and commenced the gruelling training demanded of agents in the exclusive agency. He attended the jungle training courses in southern Queensland and completed the basic Code of Conduct courses at the discreet Australian Army facilities in Middle Head, Sydney. Murray then went on to practise his new skills at the military installations on Swan

Island. Murray Lloyd Stephenson had entered the dark world of suspicion and intrigue and become one of its clandestine warriors.

Before Spring had revisited the Victorian capital and Melbourne once again pulsed with the promise of another Grand Final, he had completed a two-month indoctrination and assimilation course on the first floor of the old prefabricated two-storey building near the lake in Albert Park, referred to as the *Head Office*. This was the home of Australia's most secret institution, ASIS. And it was known to those select few merely as *Central Plans*.

* * * * * *

Murray's tight work schedule excluded him from enjoying any real time off during the weekends. It wasn't until he received the call from his mother that he realised just how long it had been since he had taken a break away from his duties. His mother, insisting that he attend the garden party with her, reminded him that it had been more than four months since his last visit. Murray thought that his mother had seemed a little distant, almost cool, when they spoke on the phone. Muriel Stephenson was adamant that they attend the function together. Recalling her son's preference for casual attire, she also insisted that he wear a suit. Murray was not surprised as his mother had always dictated his dress code since he could first remember.

He arrived at her house and parked his MG. Muriel Stephenson refused to go anywhere in his car, instructing Murray to drive her in her own vehicle. It was only then he discovered that the hosts were to be the Bradshaws. Murray could not remember precisely when he'd last seen Harry and Susan. Certainly, it was well before he had commenced his demanding training with ASIS. Although Harry was, in his own right, one of the most senior Intelligence Heads in the country, ASIO was not accommodated in the same buildings as its overseas counterpart. Apart from the last time he'd spent at the weekend cottage, Murray couldn't recall when he'd last spoken to his mentor. He had been just too preoccupied with the demands of his new position.

Murray smiled at his mother's secretive manner. They drove up Toorak Road until Muriel Stephenson instructed her son to stop. Without waiting for him to open her door, she then stepped out and stood alongside the entrance of a church Murray remembered having passed thousands of times as he had driven into the city. She watched as he locked the car and then turned and walked through the side gate into the lawned area. Murray followed, caught up and then walked down the paved path towards the group assembled outside the church's main entrance. When he recognised the couple he smiled, and waved as he and his mother proceeded towards the Bradshaws. Bewildered by the secrecy, he continued to play his mother's childish game, stepping up and shaking Harry Bradshaw's hand, then leaning towards his wife Susan, to kiss her on the cheek. Even when the woman stepped forward and handed the crying infant for Susan to hold, it did not register that he had been invited to a christening. And then he turned and caught the expression on his mother's face. Then he turned again and looked at Susan. He was confused. Then he understood. It had been some time since he had seen the couple and now it was clear why Susan had opted out of the tennis earlier in the year. He looked at his mother and shook his head wondering why she had kept the event secret. Embarrassed that he hadn't even brought a gift, he opened his mouth to remonstrate with his mother when the minister appeared and ushered them all into the church.

Throughout the brief service, Murray glanced at his mother and he could see from her expression that something had upset her. Deeply. He knew that she could be like this, remembering the turbulent time following his father's departure. They never did see him again and he recalled the months which followed, when there was practically no conversation at all in their house. He frowned, concerned that he had missed something which so obviously worried her. The private christening took no more than ten minutes, after which the small group moved back outside for photographs. There were less than ten people present, including the proud parents. Murray took his turn and stood, holding the child between both Harry and Susan. Then he watched as his mother was given the child. Murray thought he could see tears in her eyes and then it came to him. She had become lonely. And then he felt guilty, knowing that he had been neglecting her.

They were invited to the Bradshaw's Toorak home for a brief celebration. Harry served the Moet Chandon while Susan attended to her child. Murray stayed just long enough to have a brief conversation with Harry before his mother developed a headache and had to be taken home. They drove to her house in silence. Murray parked her car, walked around to open her door but, once again, she had moved first and left the vehicle unassisted, walking directly to her front door. Murray was again confused. He walked up to the house where she waited, expecting that his mother would hand him the key to unlock the door. When he stepped up to the front step, she extended her hand for her car keys. Surprised, he handed these to her as Muriel Stephenson's hand flashed through the air and struck him fiercely on the face. He reeled back, stunned from the unexpected blow.

'What the hell......!' he began to say, as his mother calmly placed her key into the lock and opened the door. He stood there in shock. She had never struck him before, not even when he'd done the most outrageous things as a child.

'Just like your father,' she said, and stepped inside. For a long moment Murray stood on his mother's doorstep wondering what had happened. Unable to figure it out, he turned and left, angry at her behaviour. He understood that she was growing old and was suffering the pangs of loneliness. He couldn't help that, and was shocked by what had just transpired. Murray knew from past experience that, given time, his mother would respond to a telephone call and some flowers. Then he would get to the bottom of what was really troubling her. Angry that she had selected the Bradshaw's special day to demonstrate her feelings, Murray left without speaking to his mother further, believing that it was almost impossible to fathom the female mind.

Muriel Stephenson heard her son drive away and bit her lip. She refused to cry. It was not her position to tell him. Suddenly she felt so alone. And ashamed. Then, when she realised that he just might not have known, she broke into tears, devastated by the knowledge that not only had she alienated her son, but the fact that she would never be permitted to claim the child just christened as her own grandson.

* * * * * *

Murray let it go for a week before he phoned his mother. He was surprised when Susan Bradshaw answered the call.

'We have to talk, Murray,' Susan had said. Murray agreed to meet, suggesting lunch, but she had insisted that a drink would be more appropriate.

'Harry will not be joining us, Murray, so please come alone.' He did, and they met in the bar at the Intercontinental. An hour later, Murray left Susan to find her own way back as he wandered down the street, bewildered by the news she had brought. It was only when he arrived back in his sparse bachelor quarters that the enormity of what Susan had said really became apparent. He just couldn't believe it. And all that time he had thought that it had been the other woman who'd climbed into his bed and cheated on her ageing husband.

And then Murray couldn't sleep worrying about Harold Bradshaw. He lay in bed in the dark, thinking, conjuring up in his mind what the ramifications of that disclosure could bring to his life, should their secret ever be uncovered.

* * * * * *

The Thousand Islands

A girl's voice startled Murray out of his quiet reverie causing him to choke as he swallowed sea water.

'Murray! Murray! Awas! You are almost over the coral!'

He coughed and, regaining his breath immediately kicked quickly, then rolled over to discover that he was in less than two metres of water. He moved slowly, cautiously, as directly below he could identify the sharp long black needles of what the locals called *bulu babi* — pig's bristles. Murray knew that to touch these deadly sharp needles would result in the tips breaking off wherever they touched the body, causing extreme pain. The sea porcupines passed dangerously close to his stomach as he made his way carefully away from the coral and back to the beach.

As he climbed out of the lagoon, Yanti ran up and threw her arms around him. He knew that he had been fortunate she'd alerted him to the dangerous reef in time. He smiled down and kissed her gently. *'Terima kasih, manis,'* he said, wishing that he really could take her home to Australia with him. But Murray knew that this would be impossible. Even if he had not been associated with the

Service, her own political affiliations would have precluded Yanti and most of those who'd accompanied her out to the serenity of the islands from ever visiting the Commonwealth of Australia.

For Yanti was a member of the *Gerwani* — the *Gerakan Wanita Indonesia* or Indonesian Women's Movement, which was directly controlled by the *Partai Komunis Indonesia*. Yanti and her friends belonged to an advanced cell within that organisation. They were amongst the more dedicated followers on campus. Murray looked down at the smiling face and innocent eyes. It was difficult to believe but true.

This sweet playful creature, his Yanti, was not just a senior member of the Indonesian Communist Party. She was a dedicated member of an elite women's corps of communists. A very dangerous playmate, indeed. Yanti, as had many of her fellow *Gerwani* members, had undergone intensive military training. She was just one of the tens of thousands who now followed the Indonesian Communist Leaders. These tough women were considered brutal in the execution of their orders. They were feared on campus and were responsible, through their culture of intimidation, for the swift growth of their organisation throughout the Indonesian universities. There was no doubt in Murray's mind that, had Yanti been aware of his true agenda in attending the University of Indonesia, she would have been amongst the first to participate in whatever steps were necessary to protect the *Gerwani* and destroy him, without remorse.

Chapter 4

1960-63

Murray's detailed administrative training was no less strenuous than the physical aspects of becoming an ASIS agent. Much of his time had been dedicated to learning the new jargon and the complicated terminology associated with Defence and its myriad of associated spin-offs. His first field assignment was to take up temporary residence in Indonesia, posing as an exchange student. The fact that there had been no reciprocal arrangements with the Indonesian university apparently was of little concern to the government agencies involved, both in Australia and Indonesia. His brief was to establish himself using the cover of the University exchange programme and then to penetrate all the political factions which had infiltrated campus life. There were specific target groups. Murray was to befriend student members of the *Partai Komunis Indonesia* — the Indonesian Communist Party, which had grown to become, or so they claimed, the third largest in membership after the Soviet Union and China. He was to identify and associate with student leaders involved with political, cultural and religious group activities on and off campus. In short, Murray was to develop a deep cover and not alienate any of the groups targeted. This proved easier said than done, as Murray soon discovered that petty rivalries on campus could develop into deadly vendettas once away from the watchful eyes of the University *dosen*.

He had left Melbourne and flown directly to Singapore where again he was discreetly briefed by the ASIS Chief of Station in the Australian High Commission. Murray was amused at the location selected for Australia's diplomatic mission as the Consulate and other departments were located above the Hong Kong and Shanghai Banking Corporation. It was customary for all diplomatic and consulate staff enroute to Djakarta to spend a few days in Singapore, to break the long journey and provide an opportunity to obtain a tropical wardrobe from the fine Singaporean tailors. Murray, unfortunately, had no such entitlement as he was obliged to maintain the facade of being an advanced student who wished to study *Bahasa Indonesia* and the Indonesian culture. His luggage only contained an assortment of casual clothing and sporting equipment.

His briefing in Singapore consisted primarily of studying recently acquired photographs of known student activists which he committed to memory. Murray spent two days examining reports covering the latest military signals intelligence which, frustratingly, had been seriously edited by the source provider, the British equivalent service, MI-6. Information was a jealously guarded resource and even the British were cautious about who should benefit from their covert activities.

The Station Chief suggested to Murray that these concerns had created a rift between the two intelligence arms soon after it was discovered that one of the architects of the Australian Secret Service, Charles Howard Ellis, had been working for Adolf Hitler's gang during the Second World War. Just a few years later Ellis was interrogated by MI5 officers. The Australian-born spymaster not only admitted to maintaining close personal relationships with Philby and Blunt during their traitorous years as Soviet moles, but also confirmed their suspicions that he had been compromised by the Soviets some ten years before.

Murray scanned through the signals concerned with the many deletions. He was cleared to the highest level of security known in Australia and yet here, to his dismay, the names of field operatives and other essential information had been removed. At least, he thought, with some sense of quiet comfort, his own position would be less likely to be compromised as the Australians had retaliated by withholding essential intelligence as well.

* * * * * *

He boarded the British Airways' 707 and enjoyed the short flight across the Java Sea and into the Indonesian capital. The flight stewardess had announced their arrival before remembering to pass the complicated arrival forms. Murray smiled as he completed his

Customs and Immigration forms when he read that *'pornography was a banned import without special licence.'* A heavy pungent smell permeated the air as the cabin doors swung open.

In years to come he would always remember those first moments, standing in the aisle, concerned with the air quality as the suggestion of rotting garbage and *durian* assailed his nostrils. He had moved forward with the other passengers, slowly, in single file, until reaching the exit where they were obliged to step across a wide gap onto the ancient mobile steps which, shaking precariously under the weight, threatened to spill the new arrivals onto the tarmac. He looked around quickly, surprised to see villages surrounded by coconut trees just off the runway. Children played along the airstrip, kicking a soccer ball to and fro and, as he watched, a dog entered the game, biting playfully at the children's bare feet as they chased each other. Murray looked up at the sky and immediately wished he hadn't, the sun's brilliance momentarily blinding him. It was hot.

As he stepped down onto the cracked cement tarmac, waves of heat rose through the soles of his shoes and, within seconds, his clothes were saturated with sweat. The short walk from the parked jet through the poorly maintained Kemayoran International Terminal immediately cast a cloud of depression over his excitement. The building reflected the country's economic collapse. The walls were filthy and only parts of the ceiling remained painted. There were no partitions nor doors. The entire area was one huge, unkempt hall with a number of broken ceiling fans hanging precariously in the centre of the building. There were bright red signs painted on the interior walls which Murray identified immediately as Communist slogans. He remembered that this airfield doubled also as a military facility where the Soviet Mig-15s and 17s were based to protect the city.

The unenclosed airport was practically deserted as the handful of passengers struggled inside and away from the fierce heat. There was little respite for these shocked foreigners as they slowed their movements hoping to ease their discomfort. One by one, they were checked and questioned, each passenger requiring almost fifteen minutes to pass through the immigration desk.

Customs were even more belligerent. The surly officers opened everything and, whenever they discovered a camera, the film was immediately removed. Cigarettes disappeared as these were a treasured item. The smarter visitors carried four or five cartons, knowing that the officials would leave them with at least two of these. Books were removed and examined. Clothing was checked and even letters were opened and examined for money.

Murray smiled his way though the hour it took to complete both procedures. It was not in his character to lose his cool, and anyway, doing so would not only further exacerbate whatever situation had provoked such a reaction, but would also be considered as a severe loss of face in this, and most other Asian nations. Finally he was cleared and permitted to leave the terminal. As he exited the building, a foreigner walked up and greeted him.

'Keith Wells, Head of Station,' he said quietly, extending his hand and taking Murray's case with his other.

'Murray. Murray Stephenson,' he responded, completing the formalities. Both men had seen each other's photographs and read each other's files. Wells then escorted his new arrival to a light blue Holden sedan.

'Well, thought you'd never get out of there. What happened?' the embassy officer asked as they pulled away from the large group of beggars which had encircled the car, hoping that this would guarantee that a few rupiah would be dropped from the *tuan's* rear windows. The driver placed the vehicle into first gear and revved the engine loudly, warning the filthy beggars to move. He had no patience for such displays around his car.

'Nothing out of the ordinary,' Murray replied, 'I think the two Brits ahead of me caused the delay.'

'Yep, that will do it every time. They still have quite a bee in their bonnets about the British. You'll soon discover that as you wander around the streets here. Most of the itinerants will spit at you unless you are quick to convince them that you're an Australian.' He looked at the new arrival and smiled. 'How is your *Bahasa Indonesia?*'

'*Lumajan sadja,*' he replied, knowing that he needed to concentrate on this aspect of his credentials quickly. He'd had relatively little opportunity to learn the language, what with the gruelling training courses and the incredible mountains of information his masters demanded he absorb in those few short months. 'I'll need to put in some real time, that's for sure. It won't be that difficult now that I'm here,' he added.

'True enough.' The other man looked at the back of the driver's head and motioned to Murray with his hand to be careful with what he said. Most of the drivers could understand some English and, amongst these, even after the Embassy's careful screening process, there were agents who had been placed in these driver positions by Indonesia's own secret service, *BAKIN*, the *Badan Koordinasi Intelidjen*.

They occupied the twenty minute drive with small talk. Murray was fascinated with the spectacles along the main thoroughfares. Occasional stands of coconut trees grew alongside the road. Weather-worn tarpaulins hung listlessly across broken footpaths, sheltering roadside vendors selling a vast choice of foods. As their Holden slowed from time to time, weaving through the disorderly pedestrian traffic and the three-wheeled *betjaks*, Murray caught his first glimpses of Djakarta's inhabitants. Roadside stalls were packed with customers sitting on long bench stools as they devoured their servings of hot, spicy food, while the air was filled with voices calling out to passers-by, enticing these potential clients with boasts of flavour and price. *Soto Madura, Nasi Padang, Sate, Sop Buntut*, these and many other food stalls' signs flashed by as Murray remained engrossed in the congested scene. The driver slowed, then stopped. He opened the door slightly and spat heavily onto the road. As they drove on, Murray detected something different in the car's air quality. For a moment, Murray thought that the driver had done the unforgivable; he winced and held his breath.

'God!' he said hoarsely, almost choking on the smell. The other Australian looked at Murray and snorted.

'You'll get used to that,' Wells suggested. 'It isn't what you think, Murray. That wonderful scent you have just encountered is the foul-smelling *durian* fruit which, believe it or not, the Indonesians claim is the most delightful taste ever designed by Allah.' Wells smiled before continuing. 'Our Consul tried it when he first arrived. Claims the experience would be like eating an 'off' custard cake inside an outback toilet!' with which he laughed and shook his head at the comparison. Even the air-conditioning could not prevent the powerful aromas from entering the sedan. As they drove on, Murray slowly accepted the overpowering stench as something he would have to get used to.

There were PT-76 Soviet tanks positioned on several of the main intersections and Murray wondered what amphibious tanks were doing inside the city. They looked most threatening with their 76mm barrels pointing directly towards the oncoming traffic. As they continued, he discovered that most of the vehicular traffic seemed to be of Eastern Bloc manufacture. Truckloads of armed soldiers approached recklessly from behind, blowing their horns arrogantly, causing the driver to pull over and permit the convoy to pass. Then Murray spotted what he thought was the most ridiculous thing. It was another amphibious vehicle, ploughing down the street leaving track marks along the bitumen road. He smiled at the sight of the Soviet BTR-50 Armed Personnel Carrier, complete with its nine soldiers standing aloft.

Murray was surprised to see that the soldiers standing in the back of the huge trucks were fully armed, some carrying grenades hanging from their belt webbing. Another convoy sped past, throwing thick clouds of dust high into the air as ducks and chickens squawked, screeched, and scrambled for safety, sending the pedestrian hawkers scurrying after their birds. Horns blared raucously, adding to the pervasive chaos. School children stopped and turned away from the noise, covering their ears and closing their eyes to avoid the suffocating dust. Older and more affluent students pumped along on their bicycles, handkerchiefs tied across their faces as they fought for some small share of the pot-holed roads.

Their driver elected to take the *tuans* via the large market area of *Pasar Senen*. Here the traffic ground to a halt as Wells cursed the driver for his stupidity in selecting this route. He had not been watching when the car had turned away from *Djalan Hajam Wuruk* and now would pay the price for permitting the driver to take one of his impossible shortcuts. The market area was cluttered with produce and a multitude of peasants were off-loading even more, as the ancient buses rested from their arduous journey down the mountain roads. Goats were tethered in line, as one of the many butchers prepared his section for another of the animals to be slaughtered, according to Moslem tradition.

Murray was only metres from the swift knife as it flashed once sending a bloody trail splurting across the fly-ridden table. He was shocked at the brutality of the moment, and surprised at his own reaction. As Murray knew, the meat would only be be considered *halal* and accepted by the Moslem customers if the throat had been severed in the correct manner.

Buffaloes walked lazily through the slop and mud, directed by small boys with rattan sticks. Bicycles were pushed through the mud by their owners; along the cross-bars were dozens of chickens tied upside down, ready for sale and slaughter. Men and women alike yelled and screamed at each other, abusing those who splashed mud carelessly on others, as they fought their way through the maze of baskets containing everything from vegetables to quail eggs.

Murray was astounded at the mass of humanity congested around this marketplace and wished they could move on, for the air inside the vehicle had become uncomfortably humid. But reversing out of this congestion was out of the question so the men were obliged to sit and wait for the section ahead to clear. The car's engine began to overheat and the airconditioner ceased to function.

'Get this bloody car moving, Mas!' the Station Chief hissed at the unhappy driver whose eyes immediately searched again for some way through. He started blowing the horn hoping that this would make the huge bus broken down up front suddenly disappear. Keith Wells shook his head in disgust and became resigned to the situation. It would not be safe to walk though the *pasar* area.

Another fifteen minutes passed when finally their sedan managed to move though the muddy section, and away from the decaying mounds of the previous day's produce, which had been just left at the edge of the market. As the driver shifted into second gear, Murray observed hordes of children, their clothes in tatters, fighting and playing in the stacks of refuse. He had read much about this country of extremes but admitted that there could be no preparation for the sights he had seen in his first hour in-country. He made a mental note to keep his injections up to date.

Within minutes of leaving the squalor behind, Murray was surprised at the contrast as they drove into the city's inner suburbs. Fine two-story residences lined many of the well-kept streets. Tall palms stood majestically beside the white wall dwellings, signalling the lush gardens hidden discreetly behind tall perimeter fences. They drove on. A further ten minutes passed and they moved from

Tjut Mutiah into Menteng, Djakarta's elite suburb where most of the generals lived. It was only minutes away from the centre of the city and, of course, the Presidential Palace. The driver turned into *Djalan Tasikmalaya* and stopped at the second house in the well shaded street. It was an old colonial-styled villa surrounded by bougainvillaea trees. The driver blew the horn impatiently. Suddenly, the iron gate opened and a smiling, toothless *babu* waddled outside to welcome her new *tuan*.

'*Selamat datang, tuan mudah,*' she said through the betel-nut-stained mouth, welcoming the young foreigner.

'*Terima kasih,*' was all Murray could find to respond at that moment as he was almost speechless at the size of the villa. 'It's fantastic!' he exclaimed, admiring the Dutch dwelling.

'Don't get too excited just yet,' Wells warned, leading the way along the footpath which wound its way through a number of frangipani trees beside the villa. Murray followed silently and, as they turned around behind the beautiful home, he discovered a small detached building similar in size to a garage. Keith Wells turned and smiled, permitting the excited housekeeper to brush past carrying the *tuan's* baggage easily under her powerful arms.

A wave of disappointment washed over Murray as he suddenly realised his error.

'This pavilion will be yours, Murray, for the next two years,' he was informed by the smiling Station Chief who was obviously enjoying the look of dismay on the younger man's face. 'Welcome to Djakarta.'

* * * * * *

Almost six months had passed before Murray felt comfortable using the language. His proficiency accelerated once he began to take the occasional female student home to his compact quarters. Although austere by Western standards, his accommodations were adequate. The entrance opened into a two-by-five metre lounge area which Murray used more as a store area than anything else. This almost verandah setting adjoined his bedroom which, in turn, backed onto a simple bathroom and general ablution area. The basic kitchen was outside, to the rear of his bedroom. An overhanging tiled roof provided protection for the kerosene stove from the rain.

More often than not, when meals were prepared in this simple place, his betel-nut-chewing houselady would ignore the *minjak tanah*, preferring to squat and fan a charcoal fire rather than risk cooking on the kerosene monster which often threatened to explode. Whenever Murray overslept and had company, she would make it quite clear that she did not approve, often failing to knock when entering his room, regularly catching Murray and his surprised bedmates in various states of play. He adored her almost doting ways and often would walk up behind the greying *djanda* and playfully pat her on the bottom, remembering to jump aside quickly before she whacked his legs with her *sapu lidi*. She always seemed to be carrying that broom.

Murray attended the *Universitas Indonesia* in what amounted to an 'observer' status. Although he was not enrolled as a full-time student, he probably spent more time on campus than many of the Indonesians. He registered as a part-time informal student, paying considerably more than he should have for this privilege, and attended a variety of lectures. His presence was never questioned and, as his language proficiency improved, he discovered that he actually enjoyed listening to the senior *dosen* lecture on their version of Indonesian history. He found that most of his fellow students were very naive when it came to discussing politics and concluded that their immaturity was a result of the strict government censorship imposed on all forms of communication.

Sometimes, when he participated in discussion groups he would endeavour to explain issues or historical events only to find that there was a wall of resistance to the truths he proposed. Mostly, his friends would laugh when he suggested something which they could not accept as true or accurate. But there were those who resented his presence, his colour, and his popularity. These were the student activists and he knew that, if he expected their acceptance, then it was imperative that he convince this group of his sincerity.

Murray went out of his way to encourage dialogue with the individual members of these student political organisations, but discovered that the young men were overly suspicious and the girls were extremely hard-line in their views.

Eventually, he convinced one of the young women, Yanti, to go on a date. They spent several Saturday afternoons, accompanied by at least one of her girlfriends, watching Chinese movies in the

Menteng Bioskop. Finally, Yanti agreed to go out with Murray, alone. That evening, she visited his small pavilion and stayed until morning. When he awoke on that Sunday morning, Yanti lay alongside, her eyes wide open, watching her new lover.

'*I love you, Mahree!*' she said, almost sadly and kissed him softly. He responded by making love to her once again and, from that day on, Yanti ensured that Murray was accepted by the other members of her group. His conquest provided the means for his successful infiltration of a major target group: the Indonesian Communist Party, which was known across the nation as the *PKI, Partai Komunis Indonesia*.

* * * * * *

Dr. Soebandrio seemed pleased with the Party's progress. Only those who knew him well understood that the powerful left-wing politician rarely displayed his emotions publicly. Today he was particularly elated with the reaction he had received during the Cabinet meeting when President Soekarno himself praised his Minister for his foresight and services to the country. Immediately after the session had noisily been terminated by Bung Karno screaming at the Military elements, they had left together to prepare for the official announcement.

They worked for hours on the speech. Mostly, the style was pure Soekarno. However, the Communist Party's line was mentioned more than once, which satisfied Soebandrio. They had agreed that he, as Foreign Minister, should make the announcement. The declaration was broadcast immediately by *Radio Republik Indonesia,* and on that day Dr. Soebandrio's name became synonymous with the war that was that day declared to crush Malaysia.

They called this action *Konfrontasi*.

* * * * * *

Murray followed the excited group down the passageway into the covered student assembly area. Already there were more than a thousand other students gathered, listening to the broadcast which had, by that time, been underway for more than ten minutes. He moved closer to the loudspeaker and immediately wished he hadn't. The distorted voice made it even more difficult for him to understand what was being said. Impatient, he reached out and pulled Yanti closer.

'What's going on?' he asked.

'War, Mahree, War! We've declared war on Malaysia!' she added excitedly, not noticing the shocked look on his face.

'What?' he asked incredulously, hoping that he had misheard her reply.

'It's true! We're going to war against those imperialist servants!' she announced gleefully. The Indonesian people knew that the new Federation of Malaysia was designed to threaten their country. The former British colonies had amalgamated to form an alliance against the only truly free and democratic state and now they would be crushed by the might of the Indonesian Military.

'Yanti,' Murray called, raising his voice to compete with the excited crowd. *'Yanti, are you sure?'*

'Sure, Mahree, sudah pasti!' she responded, confirming his worst fears. *'Listen, Mahree, and you will hear for yourself!'* with which Yanti suddenly left his side and disappeared in search of her other friends. He concentrated hard but with great difficulty. The distortion made it almost impossible to decipher what was being broadcast and he felt frustrated, standing there in the midst of thousands of people but unable to understand what was taking place around him.

'Are you all right, Mas?' a voice asked, somewhere close by. Murray turned and spotted the smiling face and he responded by placing his hands over his ears. She understood and laughed. *'Yes, I agree, it's too loud!'* she shouted up at him. *'Do you understand what is being said?'* she asked.

'Not much, I'm afraid. It is too difficult with all of the ...' with which he was lost, not knowing the Indonesian word for distortion.

'I understand, Mas. Let me help, okay?'

'Baik,' he answered, grateful for her assistance. He looked around for Yanti, annoyed that she had so suddenly deserted him.

'Dr. Soebandrio has announced that Indonesia has declared a war of confrontation with our neighbouring countries associated with the Federation of Malaysia. He has made the announcement on behalf of the Cabinet with the full backing of the President and the Military. He has stated that the neo-colonial powers will be powerless to prevent Indonesia from moving to protect itself from what the nation's leaders consider to be a

hostile assembly of puppets threatening the Tanah Air's sovereignty. He went on to say that the Military will mobilise immediately and sukarelaan forces will be formed to accommodate all of those brave volunteers who wish to fight against the aggression of the Western Imperialists' ideologies.'

'You're very good,' Murray praised, admiring the girl's power of recall. 'Do you think he is serious?'

'Oh, he is serious enough, Mas. We all more or less expected that one day our influential Communist friends would embroil us in a war of sorts' She turned and smiled again and asked, 'You're an Australian, no?' and then continued with her next question before Murray could respond. 'Are you an Australian Communist?'

'No, not at all,' he replied, stunned by her assumption. 'Why do you ask?'

'Well, I have been here for two years now and you are here already for, how long, one year?' Murray confirmed this by nodding, his voice fading with soreness from shouting to make himself heard. She paused momentarily before continuing. 'I have seen you maybe a hundred times, and I know your name. I know a great deal about you already. What I do not know about you, Mister Mahree, is why you spend so much time with all of those Communist girls.'

Murray was taken aback by her directness. It was so out of character for an Indonesian who was not familiar with the person being addressed. He found her attitude refreshing and smiled as he spoke.

'Perhaps they are the only tjewek who want to talk to me!'

'I don't think so, Mahree,' she answered, coyly. 'Perhaps you should widen your horizons,' she teased.

'And how far would those horizons have to reach in order that I would know your name and where you come from, nona manis?'

'Far and high enough to see the tip of Gunung Merapi,' she replied, immediately indicating that she was of Central Javanese extraction by nominating the closest major mountain to her origins. 'And my name is Ade, Mister Mahree,' answering while deliberately drawing out his name as if it were totally alien to her tongue.

'Well, Nona Ade, terima kasih. I will remember your kind help and comments today.'

'Are you going already?' she asked, surprised, as if he was then obliged to remain and continue the discussion. 'Don't you wish to *know what else Dr. Soebandrio has been saying while you have been talking and I listening?'* she enquired, almost with a pout.

'Saja minta maaf. I'm sorry, Ade. I have been impolite. Would you please tell me what else the famous Foreign Minister has said?'

'Of course, Mahree,' Ade replied. *'He said nothing!'* with which she turned and walked away. Knowing he had offended the young girl, Murray hurried after her and, in spite of her short stature, he had considerable difficulty following her through the crowded assembly.

'Ade! Wait' he called, *'Tunggu sebentar!'* but she feigned not hearing his call and hurried along knowing that he was following. Minutes passed and she stood out in the open ground waiting for Murray to catch up. As he approached, she pretended to turn and ignore him and then turned back and smiled.

'Do you know that it is considered impolite to chase a gadis you do not know as you have, just now, in front of thousands of curious eyes?' Murray stood alongside and laughed at her cockiness.

'Okay, Ade. I have already apologised once. For an Australian, that's already a great deal. Let's declare peace before your Dr. Soebandrio gets us both.'

'He is not my Dr. Soebandrio!' she hissed almost vehemently.

'Why do you feel so strongly about the Foreign Minister?' he asked, careful with his word selection this time. Ade hesitated before answering.

'I just don't agree with the power he and the Communist Party have been given. Our nation is one that is based on many considerations, including Belief In God. Nowhere in our Pantja Sila does it state that Communism has a place. How can we accept a belief in Tuhan on one hand yet support the destruction of that very ideal on the other?'

Murray was again surprised by the girl's response. He liked Ade immediately and decided to pursue their conversation later. Right then it was imperative that he make contact with the Station Chief in view of the Crush Malaysia announcement. Murray made arrangements to meet at another time then hurried away, hoping that he could find a decent *betjak* driver to peddle quickly, as the Australian Embassy was some considerable distance. He avoided visiting the building too frequently, not wishing to raise suspicions. His cover dictated that he maintain the semblance of a student.

There was no doubt that the declaration would have been

received with considerable alarm. These were not empty threats, it seemed. Murray understood that the Indonesian Government had, for some time, been wooing the Soviets. They had jumped at the opportunity to establish a firm foothold in South-East Asia, and military equipment and infrastructure aid had been pouring into Soekarno's Indonesia. Already, the Air Force, *AURI*, boasted squadrons of the huge Tupolov TU-16 long range bombers, the Soviets' answer to the American B-52. These had been strategically based at the Madiun airfield and represented a real threat to regional stability.

These bombers had the strike capacity to wipe out any Australian capital city and certainly all of the regional hubs such as Singapore, Hong Kong, Kuala Lumpur or even the American bases in Guam. AURI's ORBAT, or Order of Battle consisted also of IL-28s, the sophisticated bomber attack aircraft which, until then, had not been seen outside the Eastern Bloc. Missiles were installed throughout the country, many at bases strung along the north coast of Java. It was envisaged that this area might be the target of a possible first strike from the American forces stationed at Clarke Field in the Philippines.

Murray had been obliged to study this information. He had learned that the Pentagon had financed numerous missions into Indonesia, under cover of Air America, and it was during one such sortie that the Indonesians shot down an American pilot, Pope, providing Soekarno with the justification he needed to further increase the ABRI arms build-up. The CIA pilot had flown down from the Philippines, strafed a village and its church, killing seven hundred people during his attack. Murray understood the propaganda value this pilot's capture gave Soekarno, who finally agreed to surrender Pope to President Kennedy's brother when he visited. Murray understood that first it had been the British, and then the Americans who had increased their military presence in South-East Asia, and Soekarno had become deeply concerned as to their real intentions.

The President believed that the entire region was being destabilised not so much by the new republics, but more by the British and Americans in their ruthless attempts to re-consolidate their positions in his part of the globe. Soekarno watched with disbelief as the British increased their presence in Malaysia, transporting many of their soldiers from Europe to occupy bases throughout their former colonies. Even the Americans had been startled by the British build-up, countering with their own increased presence in the Philippines and Indochina. Soekarno had initiated a secret dialogue with the Burmese. Their country had been torn apart as a result of American foreign policy just ten years before. Fearful of Chinese support in Korea, Eisenhower had brazenly financed remnants of Chiang Kai Shek's former Nationalist Army to occupy northern Burma, in an attempt to open a second front with the Chinese so as to distract their main thrust through Korea. The Burmese leaders had explained to Soekarno how, as Chiang Kai Shek's men fled Mao Tse Tung's superior forces and overran Burma, these well-armed Chinese had little difficulty establishing control over the heroin trade, boosting its production tenfold. Once he had discovered the United States' involvement in the disruption of order in that country, Soekarno didn't mind accepting the Soviets' overtures and developing relationships with what he perceived to be a healthy counter to the American and British presence in his region. Besides, the USSR had re-equipped the Indonesian arsenal entirely on credit, and were apparently eager to continue to do so as long as this emerging nation maintained 'satellite' status with the Soviets.

Murray had read reports on how the Navy, *ALRI*, had also benefited from the Soviet Military Defence arrangements. Warships had suddenly appeared in Indonesian waters, their difficult-to-pronounce Russian names replaced with softer Indonesian choices such as *'The Irian'*. Murray had seen many of the new warships moored in Tandjung Priok. He had even passed close by the submarine base in Surabaja, but was unable to obtain clear photographs. He had counted five of the small but deadly ships moored together, but was not to know that three had already been taken out of commission due to personnel problems.

The Indonesian submariners generally feared going to sea, and insisted on surface steaming in preference to the claustrophobic conditions imposed once their ships dived to the oceans depths. Less than eighteen months after the small fleet had arrived in Surabaja, *ALRI* all but abandoned their plans to utilise these vessels. The crews simply refused to man the submarines.

Murray knew that the Army had secured impressive weaponry

from their new allies. In fact, the constant flow of trucks carrying men and equipment to and fro suggested the nation was preparing for war. Murray thought about the complicated Indonesian military position as he made his way down to the Australian Embassy in the Tjikini-Menteng area, off Djalan Pegangsaan Timor. They crossed the railway in front of the Tjikini Hospital and the *betjak* driver insolently clanged his bell at the Soviet PT-76 tank positioned on the corner. The Australian Embassy was just a few houses down on the right.

'*Setop disini!*' he ordered, with which the driver quickly squeezed the handbrake situated under his well-worn bicycle seat. Murray did not want to take the iron monster into the courtyard again as, the last time he did that, it earned him a stern lecture about protocol from the Consul. He climbed out of the *betjak*, paid the driver ten rupiah and strolled into the Embassy grounds. There was only token security at the entrance and, as he passed through, the smiling near toothless Pak Ali beamed as he mock-saluted the young Australian.

'*Pagi, tuan,*' he called happily, '*How are you tuan mudah?*'

'*Baik sadja, terima kasih,*' Murray answered, replying that he was well. He spent a few moments talking to the gentle old security guard before entering the building. Ali was regarded as somewhat of an icon amongst the small Australian community. No one really knew just how old Ali was, as he lied about this continuously to maintain his employment with the Embassy. Murray moved on, laughing at Ali's latest gossip, wishing he could spend more time with the man. He climbed the few steps and went through the foyer directly to the receptionist.

'*Selamat pagi, Murray. Apa Kabar?*'

'*Still intact,*' he joked, smiling at the middle-aged woman. '*How's your love life?*' Rukmini pulled a face and extended her tongue. '*If it's that bad, maybe you should try one of us bule for a change!*'

She laughed. '*What, and ruin my reputation forever?*' The exchange was nearly always the same. Murray always spent a moment here or there chatting idly with the local staff. They were all fond of the handsome young Australian and pleased that he usually found time to talk. Not like some of the staff members whose arrogant behaviour was often the main topic during *kopi* breaks. '*Do you wish to see Mister Keith today?*' she asked. Murray rarely asked to see anyone else except the First Secretary or the Consul.

'Thanks, manis,' he replied and wandered over to the rack of Australian newspapers in the corner. Murray missed them a good deal, and enjoyed his occasional visits to the Embassy where he could catch up on the sports back home. In theory, the newspapers were sent in the diplomatic bags from Canberra on a weekly basis. Unfortunately QANTAS often refused to land at the poorly-equipped Djakarta airport and it could be two or even three weeks before they arrived.

'Seems your team is still at the bottom of the ladder.' Murray turned to the man who had spoken after silently gliding up behind him. Murray extended his hand.

'Sometimes I think they believe it's where they belong,' Murray grinned ruefully. His club had not been in a final for ten years. 'How are you, Keith?'

The Station Chief shrugged and indicated that Murray was to follow as he turned and walked back through the rear of the reception and Consulate area. Murray knew just how paranoid the First Secretary was about talking in front of others, especially the Indonesian staff. He followed Wells down a corridor and waited patiently while the man knocked and identified himself. Murray always found this routine amusing as the officer on the inside could see though the spy-hole just who was on the other side of the heavy reinforced door. Moments passed before they could enter and when they did, Murray discovered that there had been changes initiated in the office layout. Where before there had been a small reception area manned by an administrative officer, there was now another wall and, to his surprise, yet another door. The officer activated the release catch from somewhere under his desk and remained seated as the two men passed through into the Embassy's political section. There were three offices located in this area. Wells finally spoke as the second door clunked closed behind.

'Just been installed. Canberra felt that this old building couldn't withstand a determined break-in and flew their own carpenters up for the week. Must say they did a bloody good job although we were all pleased to see them go. Couldn't get anything done while the bastards were here, and we both worked shifts around the clock keeping an eye on them, while they completed the installations.'

The Station Chief's office was on the right. 'Go in and sit down,

Murray while I find Davis.' Keith Wells left Murray to wait so he helped himself to the strong-brewing *Robusta* coffee. He heard them return and stood up to greet the Second Secretary, Alan Davis. He had met the Tasmanian on a number occasions during earlier briefings in these offices and once socially when he attended a quiet dinner at the man's quarters on Djalan Patimura.

'How's it going, Stephenson?' Davis asked, pouring coffee for himself. 'Shagged all of the girls on campus yet?'

'No, but I'm getting there. Why don't you come around and spend the weekend at *Djalan Tasikmalaya* and I'll set you up with a couple of freebies?' Murray responded, almost sarcastically. There was rivalry between the two and Wells pursed his lips as the two sparred with each other. Although Davis was more senior than Stephenson, they were both young and relatively new to the Service. He wished some of the more experienced agents were present, especially with the volatility of the moment.

Murray had resigned himself to the sub-standard living conditions. His role dictated that he live in the simple accommodations at Djalan Tasikmalaya, unlike the large villas the Embassy officers enjoyed at this post. Sometimes, when the electricity failed for hours as it often did due to the inadequate city supplies and antiquated reticulation system, or the water pump refused to work during the dry spells, he would drop in to one of the Embassy homes and use their facilities. These houses had stand-by generators and were equipped with air-conditioning, deep-freezers to hold their hoards of imported steaks and sausages and larders which were always filled with supermarket items not available in the local shops.

On one occasion he had suggested that, as Davis was unaccompanied on this posting, it would not be unreasonable for Murray to drop around from time to time just to use the western bathroom for a change. The Second Secretary had been adamant that too-frequent visits to his house could compromise Murray's deep cover, knowing that he would have the Station Chief's support. On the other hand, Murray was conscious of Davis' inability to strike up a successful relationship with any of the foreign women. This was not just because Davis was cursed with an unattractive body and an ugly disposition, but because, as number two in the political section, any relationship with a local girl would be considered grounds for instant recall to Melbourne. Consequently, whenever the opportunity arose Davis would dismiss his servants for the night then drive down to the *Patimura* Cemetery where literally thousands of prostitutes would congregate during the early evening hours. He would select one of these girls, take her back to his villa for a few hours then send her away by *betjak* when he had finished with the *kupu-kupu malam's* services.

It was old Pak Ali who had informed Murray of the *night butterflies'* indiscreet visits. As Davis' security, his *djaga* would refuse to leave the area entirely, remaining close by to ensure that the villa would not be broken into by the many *maling* who worked the suburbs. All the Embassy *djaga* would confide in each other, relating whatever goings on took place in the foreigners' households. Davis silently envied Murray his handsome looks and numerous conquests. He despised himself for using the *Patimura* prostitutes and, regrettably, as his tour progressed he became more and more dependant on these liaisons.

Once he contracted gonorrhoea and, fearing certain discovery by Wells should he visit the Embassy doctor, Davis was obliged to sit in a local doctor's congested surgery along with *kampung* kids and their mothers. Venereal disease was normally reported by the Australian doctor to the Head of Mission, as this was one of the conditions of his employment. Davis knew that it would be impossible for him to claim having contracted the disease from one of the foreign girls as her name would also be required by the Embassy doctor. The obvious conclusion would be that he had been carrying on an unacceptable relationship, thereby jeopardising his sensitive position.

He believed this to be most unfair, especially as Stephenson was permitted to sleep with whomever he wished, and was even encouraged to do so with the Indonesian girls. No, he was not about to make Murray Stephenson's life any easier than it already was, regardless of whatever relationships existed between the Ivy League player and the senior spymasters back in Australia.

Word had preceded Murray's arrival that he was well-connected, which only increased Davis' envy. After their first clash, Wells had suggested that the young Stephenson's star was on the ascent, and inferred that it wouldn't harm Davis if he were to make the effort and try to get along with his fellow agent. It seemed that his advice had fallen on fallow ground. The two were naturally antagonistic towards each other.

'Have you been following the broadcasts?' Wells asked. He disliked operating in this country without the benefit of the local language. Whenever an interpreter was required they would call upon one of the Military Attaché's NCOs who was cleared to assist with these tasks. He raised a sheet of paper and passed it to Murray. 'This is a translation of the Foreign Minister's bulletin. How does that fit with what you have heard?'

Murray read the page quickly. It was obviously a direct translation of the broadcast he had heard earlier. 'This is as I heard it,' he said, 'although I missed some of the bulletin due to the voice distortion.'

'What was the reaction on campus?' Wells asked. Did you have a chance to discuss the good Doctor's declaration before beating a path down here?' Murray silently acknowledged the admonition. The Station Chief was totally correct. He should have waited around to establish the student mood and reaction to the startling announcement.

'From what little time I had, I'd say that generally, the student body was supportive.' He didn't mention the girl Ade who had offered her opinion regarding the Communists. 'The PKI leaders were onto it immediately, chanting as they usually do when the opportunity arises. I didn't have much of a chance to talk to Yanti as she dashed off looking for her Gerwani comrades. How about I return tomorrow and fill you in?'

'Under the circumstances I think you should only come in if there is something really important. It would be more beneficial for you to stick close to your girlfriend and see what her little commie friends are cooking up. One thing's for sure, as we speak the British bases in Singapore and Malaya have gone on full war footing. Wouldn't be surprised to see some early action from the RAF boys in Changi Field. Seems that we have no choice but to send troops. Any threat to one of Her Majesty's Commonwealth nations embroils us all, I'm afraid. Wouldn't be surprised to see the HMAS Sydney or even the Melbourne steaming up through the Sunda Straits in response to the proclamation. The Embassy is on full alert and the Consul is busy contacting Australian citizens to recommend they prepare to depart this screwed-up country.'

'What's the Military Attaché's opinion? Will Soekarno go

through with it?' Murray asked.

'I've just finished a joint briefing with all the Attachés and the Ambassador. Seems they put the wind right up the little bastard as he immediately suggested that he return to Canberra for consultations with the Minister. The general consensus is that yes, Bung Karno must and will attack now that Dr. Soebandrio has issued the declaration publicly. It is fairly obvious that the President sanctioned the broadcast. The interesting thing will be to see just how much support the Army give him this time. It's not even a month since that last attempt on his life and the word is that the failed assassination was carried out by two field officers. We're still waiting for the new protocol lists to see who is missing. One thing you've got to say about Soekarno, he's living a charmed life. According to my count, this makes the fourth attempt to date and not once has he been seriously hurt. Why doesn't someone teach these bastards to shoot?'

Murray thought solemnly about the previous attempt to remove Soekarno, and felt saddened by the number of children who died just across the road in the grenade attack in the hospital grounds. The President had attended the official opening ceremony for the new Tjikini Hospital wing. As he stepped down from the black convertible, a number of children ran forward and placed garlands of flowers around their *Bapak's* neck. Their bodies had saved Soekarno's life as Army rebels hurled grenades from the back of the crowd of onlookers. When the dust settled, The Great Leader Of The Revolution just stood dazed, unhurt, surrounded by the broken bodies of some fifteen or twenty young children. How was it, Murray wondered, that this man continued to engender so much hate and yet, at the same time, could still be loved and admired by so many millions?

'Seems almost indestructible, if you ask me,' Davis suggested, attracting a sharp look from his superior. The thought that Soekarno was proving difficult to remove deeply concerned the Station Chief. Two of his own operatives had been involved in one of the earlier assassination attempts but neither Stephenson nor Davis were aware of the Executive Action which had been sanctioned by the man in The Lodge, back in Canberra.

'It's only a matter of time before one of his four hundred generals takes the leap himself and blows the cunning little devil away.

As far as I'm concerned, the sooner the better. The world is sick to death of tyrants like Bung Karno and I'd be willing to bet that he won't last the year once the first casualty lists are posted. I'm just amazed that the Army agreed to support this ridiculous declaration of war.' Wells, removed his hands from behind his neck and leaned forward. 'If I'm wrong, gentlemen, this will be one very unhealthy place to be should the Brits unleash some of their weaponry, just to show Soekarno that playing at war can be a very dangerous game. They could swing over here from Singapore and drop one or two low-yield atomic warheads and it would be all over. Don't underestimate the Brits. They have the capacity and would never stand by and permit an invasion of any of their Commonwealth countries, let alone three!'

Murray considered this and agreed that Singapore, Malaya, and Brunei would be protected at all costs. It seemed like madness that the Indonesians even considered such a misadventure, knowing that they would have little support for such aggression.

They discussed the situation for another half-hour before Murray departed, promising to send word as the need arose. He was escorted back through the internal security doors and left to find his own way down the passageway and out of the building. Waving cheerfully as he left, Pak Ali watched him climb back aboard another *betjak*. Murray headed down through Menteng to his quarters. The driver grunted and cursed as they moved slowly towards Djalan Tjokroaminoto while Murray remained deep in thought, ignoring the long row of tall trees as they passed by. These covered the *kali's* banks providing shelter to Djakarta's itinerants and beggars, many of whom called out for money as the *betjak* moved in their direction. Murray ignored their requests, his thoughts concerned more with the sudden turn of events. He did not believe that there would be any personal danger for himself should hostilities really begin, because there was a predetermined series of steps and actions he could take to ensure his safe departure, should this become necessary.

Murray decided that this would be unlikely. He suddenly wished he knew more about what really went on down in the Presidential Palace, with its incredible intrigue and constant power plays amongst the government leaders and ambitious military chiefs. Although question after question came to mind, he realised that his experience and knowledge of the Indonesian thought process was frustratingly limited. Nevertheless, he couldn't help but feel some admiration for the charismatic leader and his ability to remain on top of the diversified and confusing mass of one hundred and fifty million people. How could Soekarno manage to survive, he wondered, with the constant feuding, the compromise, the threats and the incredible juggling act which had become an integral part of his daily routine? Why had he so blatantly rattled the sabre at a more powerful adversary when he knew that this action would summon the strength of Britain's forces? What could have been going through the President's mind when he sanctioned the declaration of war? Murray continued to speculate, as his transport delivered him to the front of his driveway.

What in hell was the Indonesian President really up to?

Chapter 5

Djakarta

Soekarno sat quietly, eyes closed and legs crossed as he cleared his thoughts. Outside he could hear the distant traffic as it moved around both sides of the Palace, never so close that it hindered conversation. This room was not air-conditioned. He was always uncomfortable when it was too cold, preferring the slow-turning overhead fans which moved the air gently around the high-ceilinged room. This is where he relaxed, mostly alone, at the end of his long days. In here he knew that he could do whatever he wished in complete privacy and, as if this thought had just at that moment occurred, he kicked his shoes off, removing his socks with his toes. He then stretched and yawned, reviewing the day's events in his mind.

Suddenly Soekarno smiled as he recalled the morning Cabinet session. There had been no formal agenda circulated. He certainly did not solicit the opposition's opinion as to whether they agreed or not with his decision. Had they been given this opportunity, the meeting would still be under way without any resolution in sight. No, that was not the way to deal with those manipulative generals who secretly worked against him and his supporters. If only he knew for certain which of their number had been responsible for the ongoing attempts on his life.

One day they would succeed, he thought sadly, then shivered. The reality was, he knew, with so many generals around him any one of them could have been involved. After each of the first two attempts, he felt a burning rage at these acts of betrayal and vowed to have those responsible publicly executed once they had been caught. But they never were and this added to his fury. When the third attempt almost succeeded, he became philosophical about his failure to engender total loyalty from those close to him. The most recent attempt had convinced him that his *adjal* was obviously not to be for some considerable time, and consequently he almost treated these attempts to take his life with contempt, as if it were all a part of some grand game in which he was the ultimate referee.

* * * * * *

President Soekarno had anticipated the outburst from Nasution. He believed Nasution to be so predictable. On the other hand, the President considered that his powerful Ministerial ally, Soebandrio, didn't understand how to handle men like Nasution, Indonesia's most senior general. His Foreign Minister had warned that, since General Nasution had attempted a coup once before, he was likely to do so again.

'Bapak, Nasution wishes to be President. He has the support of most of the divisional commanders. He could move on the Palace at any time. Why don't you just send him off overseas as one of your ambassadors, just to be sure?'

Soekarno had dismissed Soebandrio's fears.

'How could you have already forgotten the ease with which we handled his last attempt? The man has no sense of opportunity. He had us in his sights, backed with tanks and yet, with a few soft words and promises, he folded. Ten minutes later he sat and ate together with the very people he claimed to despise. I promoted him and, in so doing, removed his power. No, Nasution is no longer a threat. We must look past this man to see who stands quietly behind in the shadows. That's where the danger lies and where we must look.'

Soekarno stared deliberately at his senior general, then explained that Soebandrio had been instructed to read the declaration of war against Malaysia. To stare at one's adversary in such a way was to invite immediate confrontation but, he believed, as President it was essential to display his authority over those present before they could establish any real form of resistance to his elaborate plan.

Soekarno could see that General Nasution was deeply unhappy. The President was aware that the anti-Communist elements had looked to the General to restrict the PKI and Soebandrio's rapid growth and, since Soekarno had removed Nasution as Army Chief of Staff and relegated him to the advisory council of KOTI instead of chairing this important West Irian command, the General's power base was clearly in danger of disappearing.

'Bapak, it would be foolish to declare war on Malaysia. We would lose such an action,' Nasution had pleaded. Soekarno had listened in silence as his subordinate walked a fine line in arguing against the declaration. The President knew he could easily find support among the junior generals and use this against Nasution. Soekarno was aware that the man before him had unsuccessfully appealed to *Djenderal Yani*, his replacement as Army Chief of Staff, who at the time had avoided Nasution's eyes and coughed, embarrassed that he would appear so obvious in his lack of support for a fellow general.

The President was aware that General Yani had his own Javanese faction to consider, and would realize that he had little choice but to support his President or end up as impotent as his Sumatran predecessor, Nasution. Soekarno had watched, concerned as the Indonesian Armed Forces had undergone radical changes over the recent years. Divisions and rivalries were still apparent and Soekarno knew that his decisions were often considered whimsical and irrational. The President knew that it was essential to his own survival as leader that he keep his Military opponents' alliances off balance at all times. At the President's request, and as an act of appeasement, Yani had moved to replace the divisional commanders in Sumatra, South Kalimantan and South Sulawesi with his own men. The previous commanders had all foolishly resisted Soekarno on matters relating to the PKI and had subsequently paid the price.

President Soekarno had looked up and, caught by Nasution's troubled eyes, looked away once again.

'Djenderal Nasution. We have reconstructed the Military in our homeland and committed our people to enormous hardships so that your officers and men are able to enjoy the most sophisticated weaponry available. Our Soviet allies have provided bombers, missiles, tanks and ships. Now you must provide the men to utilise these expensive toys. Are you telling this Cabinet that you are unable, as our country's Commander of ABRI, to carry out the orders of your Supreme Commander?'

Soekarno stared once more directly into Nasution's eyes, challenging the four-star general to refuse to accept the Presidential decision. Soekarno recalled how slowly the moments had passed as the tension was apparent on the faces of all present. Nobody wished to see an open split between the Army and the President. It would be catastrophic, and the damage irreparable.

'May I suggest Bapak that we consider appointing one of the senior officers other than Djenderal Nasution to the specific post to take charge of this endeavour?'

Nasution's head had turned quickly to the speaker and he glared. Soekarno had smiled silently, knowing that his opponent most probably had expected such a suggestion from the Minister for Air, who carried only two stars on his shoulders. With a few exceptions, most of those present were senior military officers.

'That would be totally unacceptable to the Armed Forces. Or at least, to the Army. Unless there has been a change in my circumstances that are yet to be announced I believe that I am still the most senior officer currently serving in our ABRI and, as such, remain totally responsible for all such military matters. I could not...'

'That is so, Pak Nasution,' Soebandrio interrupted, *'I agree that you should lead our forces against the Malays!'*

Soekarno knew he had ensnared Nasution in his well-laid trap. The atmosphere had been electric as all eyes turned to the popular military figure. Nasution had little choice but to retreat. Those present knew it was imperative for Nasution to maintain his friendship with Yani, even though they did not always see eye-to-eye on the important issues. It was obvious that Yani would support the Army should a contest erupt between the Palace and the Military, but Soekarno knew that Nasution could not be confident about the degree of support he could expect from the Javanese Chief of Staff.

The President could see that Nasution felt frustrated by the other generals. Having been raised in Javanese fashion himself, Soekarno could understand Nasution's annoyance with the traditional Javanese way of conducting business. The reluctance of the Javanese to express themselves openly, unlike the Sumatrans, never ceased to irritate the Revolutionary hero.

President Soekarno wondered if Nasution really understood that the Foreign Minister sitting across the long table, Soebandrio, was behind most of the machinations which continued to weaken the Army leadership. Soekarno had sat back and permitted this situation to develop as it was necessary to his overall strategy for political survival. He knew that Nasution had learned much from Soekarno and his colleagues over the years. The President had out-manoeuvred the generals more than once before, but they were now becoming more and more determined to prevent any form of communist take-over.

'The leadership of this national effort should be given to Djenderal Yani.' Nasution had then crossed his arms in defiance and waited for Soekarno to respond. The President was surprised. Did Nasution realize that he had taken a very dangerous gamble, surrendering even more power to the capable and ambitious Yani? Soekarno thought that the general did not want to be remembered by his fellow countrymen as the man who took them to war when he mistakenly believed that peace was an available option.

'Bapak. I would be proud to serve with this new command,' Air Vice Marshall Omar Dhani had offered. Immediately others joined in, offering to support the war effort. Within a few minutes, almost all the officers present had committed themselves to supporting Soeharto and Soebandrio's quest to expand the country's political boundaries.

Soekarno stood at the head of the magnificently-carved teak table and observed those present. Slowly he looked from face to face as if determining what to say next while reading their thoughts. Most, in typical Javanese fashion, remained expressionless. The communist members were obviously pleased with the session's outcome and displayed this by grinning and winking at each other.

Nasution sat stone faced. He wished a thunderbolt would strike the room and exterminate the filthy communists. In his mind, the unthinkable had happened yet again. His opponents had increased their already powerful political base at his expense.

Suddenly Soekarno spoke.

'We must show the nation and our people that we are united in this great task which lies ahead. We must educate the masses to understand that it is imperative for them to remain alert against neo-colonial and imperialistic forces which continue to endeavour to destroy our country and its people.

We are being encircled by the British and their puppet states.

The formation of this so-called Federation of Malaysia is designed to achieve one aim and one aim only; the destruction of Republik Indonesia and Pantja Sila. The British have provoked our response. It was agreed during the Manila Conference that a referendum would be called in both Sabah and Sarawak to determine whether or not the people truly wished to join this proposed Federation of Malaysia.

Now, with the Malaysian Tengku's blessing, the British have decided to proceed without the agreed referendum. The United Nations were to conduct the polling, but these arrogant British colonialists have announced that they would not have accepted a negative outcome, even had the choice been put to our brothers in those two small countries.

We have no choice. They have refused to entertain any dialogue which may have prevented this heavy decision I have taken this day, with your full support. We will move forward together and destroy the British imperial states which, through their proposed amalgamation, will block our country's natural development and impede the spiritual growth of our children. We cannot permit our children to hide in the shadow of British colonial values. We must eradicate this threat from our borders. We must crush those who threaten our nation, chew them into small pieces then spit their remains into the British faces. We must ganjang Malaysia!'

Soekarno's careful choice of a slogan astonished Nasution. If he was not as angry as he then felt, he might have also cheered and applauded with the others. As the meeting broke up and the members departed, Soebandrio and Soekarno stayed behind, talking together. Nasution walked out of the hall alongside Yani to show that there were no hard feelings. The newly appointed commander remained silent until they were alone on the steps, waiting for their drivers.

'You've got to admit, he's very clever,' Yani said softly without looking at the other officer. *'In one move he has managed make us responsible for this ridiculous attempt on Malaysia and what's more, responsible when it fails, as fail it must!'* As his vehicle had arrived first, he offered his hand to Nasution who took it warmly and squeezed once, acknowledging the difficult position in which Yani now found himself.

'Be careful, Yani,' Nasution warned, *'Ganjang Malaysia just may not turn out to be the tasty meal Soekarno is led to believe!'*

Yani turned while still in earshot, smiled and whispered with a hint of sarcasm. *'That's why he said ganjang, not makan,'* he said, and then added as he entered the Russian four-wheel drive, *'He just wants to chew them a little, not swallow them up!'* and then saluted Djenderal Nasution, who was then left standing on the Palace steps, very much alone.

FREEDOM (MERDEKA) SQUARE

* * * * * *

Brigadier-General Soeharto dressed quickly. He was annoyed at having been overlooked at the briefing session. He checked his uniform, then finished the luke-warm glass of *kopi*. He would eat later, when he returned. Although outwardly he did not display his feelings, Soeharto was furious. The announcement had taken place while he had been off-duty for the day. Tien, his wife, had arranged for the children to all be photographed with their parents, and he had broken with tradition and stayed home that day. His distinguished Javanese features came to life as he smiled quietly to himself. Their youngest son, Hutomo Mandala Putra, was barely one year old.

Soeharto was reminded of the campaign he had been given to liberate Irian Barat from the Dutch. He had given his youngest son, "Tommy", the campaign's title *Mandala* as his middle name for it was this dedicated service which had restored Soeharto to his rightful rank. For a moment he reflected. Now his children numbered five, three boys and two beautiful girls. The image of his oldest, Rukmana, passed through his thoughts as he remembered that she had already reached fourteen which, had they been but a poor peasant family living off the soil back in the villages of Central Java, would have certainly meant an arranged marriage before her next birthday.

The Brigadier frowned. There was such a fine line between what was and what could have been. He had always endeavoured to provide for his family, as his own mother had for her children. Life under the Dutch had been difficult enough. Being born into a confused state of secrecy precipitated a childhood without the support of relatives so important to the young. The truth relating to his mother and her relationship with the royal court of the Sultans of Djogyakarta had long been buried and he wished that it remain so, for her sake and his, and her grandchildren.

As a child, he had been tenderly cared for by his mother and he loved and respected her dearly for this. Soeharto remembered his childhood. He had been an only child although his family's cramped quarters were overrun with his father's offspring from a previous marriage. The family grew even more when his father married yet again, resulting in his moving continuously from home to home, never really feeling settled in any of these places. He had suffered a series of illnesses during his early years but, there again, who did not? In typical Javanese fashion, his mother had encouraged her son to complete high school knowing that the Dutch would favour those who had gained their diplomas. Soeharto sometimes reflected on the brief period when he was accepted as a trainee bank clerk. Although his mother was pleased with this achievement, Soeharto soon became impatient for excitement. He remembered also that fateful day when his clothes had been ripped by his pushbike while cycling to work. He lost his job but this did not entirely displease him. He was young and his country was bubbling with political activity. An opportunity arose and he jumped at the chance to join the Dutch colonial army where he underwent basic recruit training.

Not long thereafter, the Japanese occupied the archipelago interning the Dutch and other foreigners. Soeharto, as did many of his peers, sided with the Japanese and became a member of the Japanese-sponsored Defence Corps. He was selected for officer training and served under the new landlords until they too surrendered, granting Indonesia the opportunity to declare its independence. Soeharto disassociated himself with the emerging political groups. He avoided their rallies, preferring to listen to the speeches on radio. Often he was amused with the new President's rhetoric and would scowl whenever Soebandrio's communists held their parades.

Letnan Soeharto was deeply disappointed that the new republic was immediately embroiled in a battle for its own survival against the Dutch. He joined his fledgling country's guerrilla forces and fought alongside other heroes of the Revolution and War of Independence. They fought with what few armaments were left by the Japanese, often armed with simple bamboo spears and farmers' field scythes. He remembered the bloody encounters and the dead. In Bandung he had seen the wholesale slaughter of many innocent victims, and the memory of Surabaja being continuously shelled by the British Royal Navy still tore at his heart. Their war continued through four years until Indonesia was formally recognised, and shortly thereafter, Soeharto joined Djenderal Nasution's command and was promoted to lieutenant colonel.

Shortly thereafter, due to his dedication and capable leadership, he was promoted to command the elite Diponegoro troops in Central Java. He remembered how contented he felt at that time, with his career firmly established in the new Angkatan Bersendjata Republik Indonesia, and the birth of his first child, Rukmana. His circle of friends had grown considerably and, due to his new position, he discovered that even the local Chinese business community sought his friendship.

He approached his new administrative duties in a methodical manner and soon discovered that the entire system of supply was in chaos. In fact, Soeharto identified serious problems with the divisional procedures and took immediate steps to rectify the problems. It soon became apparent that the men in his command were not receiving their correct entitlements, nor were equipment supplies and rationing handled in a professional manner. Just ten years before, when Indonesia officially took control of its own Treasury, there was less than fifty thousand guilders left to rebuild the entire country from scratch. The Military had first call on funds as these limited amounts became available. When the Soviets finally supported the Republic with its massive infrastructure and military hardware loans and aid programmes, much of the financial pressure was relieved. However, the troops still had to be fed and clothed. As Commander of the Diponegoro troops, the responsibility to provide adequate food and supplies for his men became his first priority. As Soeharto remembered those difficult times, a slight smile crossed his face as he recollected meeting the little chinaman for the first time.

The merchant could barely make himself understood. He, like so many of his race, had migrated illegally to Indonesia to escape the turmoil of Mao Tse Tung's China. As these people arrived, they quickly went about establishing themselves throughout the coastal cities, developing their links with other merchants. They worked tirelessly, building the foundations for their new futures, understanding the need to foster close relationships with the Military. But there were often many problems and the port traders of Semarang City complained bitterly as waterside costs escalated, due to overly ambitious and greedy Navy officers who squeezed many of the Chinese out of business. The Chinese traders were desperate to break loose from the Navy's grip and approached Soeharto with an offer to accommodate his needs, on the condition that he intercede on their behalf.

In typical Javanese fashion, a compromise was reached through considerable discussion with the local Chinese merchants. It was obvious to the Army that their food and other supplies were controlled by these merchants. The Military had nothing to barter with except protection and this, although greatly appreciated, did not generate sufficient funds to overcome their problems. An arrangement was suggested which provided for both the commercial and political aspects being satisfied. The Military controlled the movements of all trucks in and out of the harbour. The Navy were unable to negotiate this arrangement as their authority ended at the port's entrance. The merchants believed that the Customs and Navy were destroying their profits with their ever-increasing demands and illegal duties. The cost of moving cargo from the ships, through the warehouses and then onto Navy trucks for delivery, had reduced their margins to the point where large-scale smuggling to by-pass these harbour officials was essential to their survival. Why not formalise some commercial arrangement and eliminate the difficult sector, thereby stabilising prices and profits?

The concept was sound and the Army was desperate for supplies. A meeting was organised and Soeharto was introduced to a Chinese trader who had fled his Communist homeland and settled in Java. An interpreter was required as the merchant had not lived in the country long enough to acquire even the local *pasar* language. They sat together for hours, eating and discussing the proposed arrangements. The Army would send its own trucks into the harbour and use soldiers to unload the cargo which belonged to the trader. In return, the Chinese would provide essentials to the Army and, from time to time, credit for their supplies. It was agreed. Their relationship prospered, the men in Soeharto's command benefiting from the *kongsi* that had been born out of common needs. A short time later, documents were arranged so that the mainland Chinese trader could legitimately stay in the country.

Soeharto was never to fully understand what happened next. General Nasution had been furious that reports of smuggling though the Diponegoro Command had reached Djakarta. Accusations were hurled back and forth but, in the end, the damage was too great to contain and Nasution accused Soeharto of complicity in the scheme. He was transferred. Angry, frustrated and falsely accused, Soeharto stepped out of the limelight. He was sent to the Army Staff College to cool his heels. Many of his compatriots believed that Nasution was concerned with the sudden rise of Soeharto and moved to slow his star's meteoric rise. Nasution's faction supported his decision and the Sumatran severely damaged Soeharto's reputation. He never forgot, nor would he ever forgive, this ill-treatment delivered by the hands of his fellow officers. Dismayed with the outcome but still loyal to his country, Soeharto continued to serve diligently. He watched with growing concern as the Communists strengthened their grip on the country's leadership and infiltrated senior positions even within the Military. Disgusted with the growing number of politically-motivated promotions, Soeharto decided enough was enough and finally stepped forward, his voice among the few who were identified as fiercely anti-Communist. He was sent away from Java. At first he feared that this would damage his career forever but then, as his own group of followers and supporters began to grow, Soeharto commenced applying pressure whenever and wherever he could, in the hope that the senior officer corps would resist the PKI political machine's growing influence. His dedication and loyalty began to bear fruit and now, finally, he had established an enviable power base within the military and was able to influence others, even his superior, Djenderal Yani.

An old grandfather clock chimed in the next room and Soeharto knew that he must move quickly. The broadcast had been repeated and he knew that there would be considerable activity downtown in the Defence Department. As he left his home on Djalan Tjendana, Soeharto's aide jumped to attention and ran to open the rear door of the Soviet sedan but he waved the soldier away, indicating that he would drive himself.

He drove down to Kota and found the man sitting in his customary singlet and pyjama trousers, waiting patiently for him to arrive. The little chinaman listened in silence while the Javanese spoke. He understood the ramifications of what had happened. The entire community of Djakarta's Chinatown area of Kota had been abuzz with excitement. They were all anxious to determine just how a war with Indonesia's neighbours would affect them, their families and their businesses.

When he was satisfied that his old friend understood what was required, Soeharto left the small, narrow office and drove back up Djalan Hajam Wuruk towards the new city. Fifteen minutes later, Soeharto arrived at the Army's KOSTRAD headquarters and went immediately to his third floor office and called his aide. He was very troubled. The communists were making a move and he was agitated about being left out of the information loop. Soeharto sat behind the carved teak desk surrounded by pennants, flags and divisional plaques and brooded over his problems. He knew from experience that not only would the whole country swing into a destabilising mode due to the President's proclamation, the Chinese community would do as it always did whenever they anticipated violence. They would immediately close down all of their activities and wait, sending the commercial sector into another tailspin. He knew that this would continue until they could be assured that they would not be embroiled in the madness of Indonesia's politics or be targeted by isolated groups who could make political mileage from involving the small minority in some way.

Brigadier General Soeharto rose, then walked slowly towards the large window overlooking *Lapangan Merdeka*. Across the park, almost hidden behind the huge National Monument, he could just make out a motorcade as it entered the grounds of the United States Embassy.

Deep in thought, he squinted in an attempt to identify the embassy vehicles as they moved into the American compound but the distance was too great. Minutes passed and another motorcycle siren identified a second ambassador visiting his American colleagues. Suddenly an idea crossed his mind. Soeharto returned to his desk and collected the papers which lay there, then left the Army Strategic Command office and its view overlooking Merdeka Square.

Chapter 6

The mood around the room was solemn. The group of five men sat silently digesting the information they had exchanged during the morning's marathon session in this chamber. Most were dressed as one would expect of elder statesmen and senior Public Servants. The odd man out was in uniform. The uniform was that of the Australian Army and the officer was its Chief of Staff. That the other services were not represented did not reflect on their importance in any way. The matter under discussion had not required their presence at this stage, but further meetings would, no doubt, be scheduled, once consensus had been reached with those present.

'Gentlemen,' the heavy-set leader commenced, his face clouded by the seriousness of the moment. 'Gentlemen, I believe we have no choice. It seems that President Soekarno's intentions are quite clear. He intends to take Malaysia.'

The Prime Minister looked at the others present almost as if challenging them to respond. He was furious with the Indonesian President. The impertinence of the man, declaring war on the British Commonwealth. It was, he considered, the most absurd act of aggression. The man had to be insane!

'I believe that we are all in agreement then?' the recently-knighted Sir Robert Menzies asked, though it sounded more like a statement. His political stature had grown considerably with the honour Queen Elizabeth had bestowed upon her Australian Prime Minister. He had led the country through the past fourteen years. He looked across at Holt, his Treasurer and heir-apparent. 'How will it be funded?'

'I suggest that we just increase the allocation funds currently dedicated to ASIS. This would alleviate difficulties with any audit

requirements as ASIS's operational expenditures are not account-
able to Parliament. The figure would blow out disproportionately
in relation to ASIS's own activities but, I believe, this would be the
most appropriate method of disguising the funding required.' Holt
paused before continuing to ensure they understood. 'I don't fore-
see any problems.'

'Attorney-General?'

'I agree, Sir Robert. Funding the activities is not what still worries me though. We have limited resources in ASIS and may be
obliged to go further afield for assistance.'

'What do you have in mind?' the PM asked cautiously. He had
a very sound cabinet and his most senior players were present.

'I believe that we should bring the Americans in on it.' The Attorney-General knew that this would be of concern to both the Intelligence services. He glanced at the two men, in turn, expecting
their objections.

'Why don't we try this without them for once,' Alfred Broome
suggested. He didn't want those damn Americans interfering in
what was to be his operation. ASIS may be under-funded and short-
staffed but introducing the 'cousins' into the arena would amount
to giving them control. 'Besides, this really is a Commonwealth
problem.' He knew that this would appeal to the Prime Minister's
sense of "Best if British".

'Do you agree, Deputy Director?' Harold Bradshaw was asked.
As far as his Department was concerned, it would be difficult for
his ASIO men to get even a sniff at whatever was planned. Being
Australia's domestic spy service, Harry was not permitted to operate outside the country.

'Prime Minister,' he started, having prepared for such an opportunity, 'Although the Act prevents my men from participating,
perhaps we could second our more experienced agents to ASIS for
the duration? Some of them were originally involved with ASIS.'
He looked across at Alfred who nodded thoughtfully. It would be
more palatable to have Harry's team on board than having to watch
his back with the Americans.

'That would be acceptable, Sir Robert,' Alfred advised.

'And the SAS?' the Prime Minister asked, addressing the Chief
of Staff.

'We will have them in place within two weeks, Sir Robert.'

The General could have put them into the air that day but decided that he would prefer the additional lead time. Also, he wished to negotiate with his British counterparts who would no doubt want to control the secret missions out of their bases in Singapore and Malaysia.

'Understand, gentlemen, we are not under any circumstances to imply to our allies or the Parliament that we are engaged in an act of war. As discussed earlier, I am prepared to send the SAS, conditional that their efforts are kept covert, that the men who are selected are to sign the Official Secrets Act, and that at no time is it to be suggested that I have approved even so much as a simple police action. Our soldiers will be going to Malaysia and Singapore simply as part of an exercise that had been scheduled since last year. Do I make myself entirely clear, gentlemen?'

The men all acknowledged affirmatively. They all understood that they were already co-conspirators and had been since the formation of the Australian Secret Intelligence Service. Not even Parliament was aware of this covert arm. The Opposition had no idea whatsoever what was going on and, considering the colour of their politics, it was probably safest to maintain the status quo.

Further meetings were scheduled for the Friday and the group dispersed. As Alfred walked together with Harry, they discussed availability of agents and other matters relating to the proposed overseas missions. An hour later they shared a Commonwealth car on their way to the airport. Australia's espionage and intelligence centres were in Melbourne, not Canberra, and both these spymasters wouldn't have had it any other way.

Harry agreed to visit Indonesia to determine the accuracy of Alfred's Djakarta Station reports. He had offered his services and reminded the other Intelligence Head that his previous field experience would be invaluable in ascertaining the mood and political situation should he visit the Djakarta Station. He sent an overseas cable to Murray and indicated that he was making a private visit and requested Murray's company for a short journey. Language difficulties and all that. Ten days later, Harry Bradshaw, Deputy Head of Australia's domestic spy service landed in Bangkok, enroute to Djakarta. He had elected to take the long way round.

* * * * * *

Murray felt certain the left-hand drive Plymouth Belvedere would leave the road at any moment and plunge into the valley on his left. He wished the other driver had agreed to the lower fare. At least his car's steering was on the appropriate side. And they were both feeling the effects of the winding road and the leaking exhaust pipe. Suddenly he couldn't take any more.

'*Stop here!*' he barked at the driver. Distracted, the driver almost collected an oncoming bus speeding down the mountain side towards them at an incredible rate. Immediately both he and his companion climbed out and moved away from the oversized American sedan and the effects of its nauseating smoke. '*Turn the damn engine off!*' he called but the driver refused.

'*Tidak bisa, tuan. If I do that we won't be able to restart the engine*'

'*Well then, you stay here while we walk ahead,*' he ordered. The girl looked at him as if she did not understand. He took her by the hand and started walking up the long climbing bitumen road. The air at this altitude was refreshing and slightly cool. The view to both sides of the road was covered by tea trees, their tops flattened deliberately by the picking process, creating the impression that the volcanic slopes were covered by a wide unfolding green blanket spread deliberately in this pattern by some giant hand. Alongside the winding road stood tall oak trees planted by the Dutch to prevent roadside erosion and, in some instances, to indicate dangerous corners. The oaks were painted white around their lower trunks to assist drivers who dared cross the mountain by road at night.

A soft mist started to roll towards the couple as they continued their slow stroll. The low cloud passed, leaving the sky clear once more. They had been walking for more than ten minutes when Murray became concerned.

'*Where the hell do you think that driver has gone?*'

'*He's back there waiting for us, Murray,*' Ade replied. '*You told him to wait there for us!*'

'*No I didn't. I told him to let us walk ahead and that he was to follow.*'

Ade knew what she heard. She also knew that the driver had not been paid and would follow when they didn't return. '*It's not far, you can see the building from here,*' she said, pointing up the slope to where the long structure dominated the mountain pass.

'That will take at least another twenty minutes, Ade. Are you sure you're up to it?' he challenged, knowing that she would accept. She muttered something to herself and commenced walking quickly, her short legs almost strutting as they moved on and up the hill towards the mountain coffee house. Ade had been trying to entice Murray to the Puntjak Pass since their first meeting, some weeks before. She had spoken to him on campus once or twice, and believed she'd made it quite clear that she would go out, if asked. At first, Murray appeared to be preoccupied, and it was not until they bumped into each other at a friends' house that they held a conversation of any real depth and their friendship developed. Their mutual friend was a student of religious studies and Ade was surprised the Australian had been invited. It was then that Ade learned that Murray had already developed a keen sense of observation and understanding of matters related to the Indonesian people. She was impressed with his knowledge of the Javanese culture, his ability to understand the intricate customs which, because these were so shrouded in a wealth of symbolism, most foreigners found impossible to comprehend. Ade laughed with the others present when he attempted to emulate the voice of a *wajang* puppeteer. He was relaxed in their company and extremely popular, which was obvious from the expressions of admiration he received.

As the evening had come to a close, Ade was further surprised to discover that her gregarious friend knew so little of Mohammed Subuh, the Islamic scholar. He'd sat and listened intently as their host attempted to explain the *Susila Budi Dharma* philosophy and the mystique which surrounded the SUBUD movement. Ade was particularly pleased with his interest as she was more than just another Mohammed Subuh admirer, she was also one of Bapak Subuh's most ardent followers. Along with others present, Ade urged Murray to attend one of their meetings and he had willingly agreed. They had made arrangements to meet and visit the small compound located on the city's outskirts and, to her astonishment, Murray was so taken by the experience he insisted that they return within just a few days of his first *latihan* session. Amazingly, it seemed as if he found something that had long been missing in his life. Suddenly they had something in common, something they could share. Ade built on this quickly in an attempt to discourage his relationship with the young communists on campus. She had become fond of Murray but soon realised she had little influence over his choice of friends. Ade could not understand why he would want to spend so much time with Yanti and her comrades. Ade despised her fellow student; even more so, now that Murray continued to associate with the communist supporters.

They had agreed to spend the day together, after a morning *latihan* session, driving the two hours up to the pass where the famous Riung Gunung Coffee House was nestled between the shorter peaks, under the shadow of Gunung Gede. It was well-known that President Soekarno often took time away from his summer palace in Bogor, just a few kilometres from the mountain foothills. For Ade, this added to the excitement of the outing, wishing for an opportunity to see her hero again. Like many of the younger generation, Ade adored the legendary President and tales of his extramarital activities. It did not bother her, as a woman, that her hero was so promiscuous. When Murray jokingly suggested that Soekarno was no longer capable of servicing his many wives and girlfriends, he discovered that Ade was overly sensitive to comments about their leader.

'I don't wish to hear you say anything bad about Bapak. He is loved by all and is now the father of our nation. He can not help it if all of those dreadful women continue to throw themselves at him. After all, he is only a man and entitled to make some mistakes!'

As they arrived at the coffee house so did their driver. Murray told him that they would be there for at least an hour and suggested that, this time, he should turn the Plymouth around and face the ageing vehicle downhill. He watched as the driver complied but still the engine was left running.

'Why don't you turn the engine off, dong!' He called out to the obstinate *supir,* who mumbled something about the car wouldn't like him to do so. He shook his head. In a land where the culture referred to inanimate objects having life, feeling, wants and desires, Murray knew it was easier to ignore the problem than argue. As an Australian, he had found it very difficult to understand just how deeply-rooted animism was in the Indonesian culture. When he studied their official language he came to accept that the inanimate often dictated the sentence structure. For Murray, this had been extremely difficult as it contradicted his own culture. Murray

gave up and was about to enter the building when he noticed a huge eagle perched, with its left talons tied securely to the pole. He admired the magnificent creature.

'Look, Ade. It's so incredibly beautiful.' he said, standing a few metres away from the stern-faced eagle. He shook his head sadly. *'It's just a pity that it has to be tied in this way.'*

Ade held his lower arm and tugged, slightly bored with all the attention the bird was receiving. *'If it wasn't tied, it would just fly away, Murray,'* she said, serious in her observation. He looked at her quickly to see if she was teasing and identified another of the differences between the Asian and European cultures. The thought that someone may wish to release the bird for purely unselfish motives, permitting it to escape its prison, did not enter into the rationale of her thinking. Even after two years studying the people and their culture, Murray repeatedly found that an understanding of Indonesian logic still eluded him. He sighed, letting it go. He had been there before and knew it would have been an unsatisfactory debate. Murray checked his watch and reminded himself to return early. He had a plane to meet the following day and needed to be alert.

Harry Bradshaw was coming to town.

* * * * * *

Thailand

Harold Bradshaw handed his passport to the immigration officials and waited patiently. There was no drama and neither should there have been. His credentials described Harry as a teacher and his declaration stated that he was travelling on holidays. Unfortunately, no, he could only afford to spend the one night in Bangkok, in transit. No, he said to the official, he had nothing to declare. His baggage would remain at the terminal overnight. This was completely true, as he had entered Thailand from Hong Kong on a Cathay Pacific flight and Harry did intend departing the following day for Singapore. His flight had been delayed some hours and he was now concerned that his meeting might be aborted.

Accepting the first fare offered, he sat up front in the battered taxi and played with the knobs controlling the airconditioner, but without success. It was steaming hot. The perspiration caused discomfort but he ignored this minor irritation. Again he checked his watch and tried to encourage the driver to go faster but was unable to communicate. At least the man understood the name of the hotel he had nominated, and nodded for almost ten minutes confirming that he knew where it was downtown, as he drove full throttle along the airport highway. At least it hadn't been raining, he thought thankfully. During his last brief visit, Harry was obliged to leave his stranded taxi, remove his shoes and walk almost two kilometres through knee-deep water and sewerage overflow from the *klongs*.

They arrived at the small hotel off Soi Nana where Harry had arranged to meet. He would not check in here. Harry had made other arrangements. He paid the driver with the baht he'd bought at Kai Tak Airport and walked quickly inside. The cocktail lounge was to the left of the small lobby. He entered and sat at the bar, ordered a bourbon and coke then casually looked around. It was dark and his eyes had not adjusted to the lack of light. There were a dozen or so guests sitting in the booths, being entertained by their girlfriends. He finished his drink and was about to leave, resigned to the fact that his meeting had failed when he identified the thick silhouette moving towards him.

'You're very late. I didn't think you were coming. This is not good. We do not have a great deal of time,' grumbled the man in a heavy Russian accent.

Harry didn't bother extending his hand. He disliked the man and even under more cordial conditions might still have avoided touching him. The heavy-set Russian smelled as if he hadn't bathed for weeks. But they all carried that very same odour in Moscow. Harry knew, he had spent time there, in the field.

'Flight was delayed out of Hong Kong,' was all Harry offered, waiting for his contact to take the third seat along the bar. Harry had deliberately placed his coat on the stool immediately next to his. The few extra centimetres may not make that much of a difference, he thought, but at least it was worth a try.

'We will talk here?'

'Yes, it's okay,' Harry answered.

'You will leave tomorrow morning?'

'Noon flight,' he answered, already tired of the small talk.

'Do you have it here?' the Russian asked, leaning closer so as not to be overheard. Harry leaned back slightly, shocked with the sudden intrusion of bad breath. 'God, this man is an animal,' he thought. Harry lifted his coat and extracted a small parcel from the inside pocket. He handed this to the other man.

'Time for a vodka?' Harry asked, turning to attract the bartender's attention.

The drink was poured in silence. The Russian took the small glass and gulped its contents before placing the thick envelope in his huge trouser pocket. He then turned and walked away without even bidding the Australian goodbye.

Harry watched the Russian leave. Then he checked his watch. The drop had taken only three minutes. He was relieved. Time was running out. Harry dropped an appropriate amount on the bar, placed his coat over his arm then departed also, leaving his unfinished drink.

He left the small hotel and walked down to the eastern intersection. He hesitated, pulled a packet of cigarettes from his coat and placed one slowly in his mouth, then turned to see if he had been followed. Satisfied that he had not, Harry lit the Rothmans and immediately wished he hadn't. His throat was dry and this was his third pack for the day. He stood on the corner for a few more minutes as if trying to make up his mind which direction to take, then turned and walked slowly back to the hotel he had just left.

This time, when he entered the bar he continued through until reaching the rear section where exit signs indicated the toilets and fire door. Harry opened the rear door and looked cautiously in both directions, then stepped out into the dark alleyway. Confident that he was alone, Harry walked up through the alley to the right and stopped just before the corner and knocked on the door marked K115B. Only moments had passed before the door opened and he stepped inside, passing his coat to the young man who stood waiting, smiling at his expected guest.

'I am so happy to see you again sir,' the boyish voice said, taking his guest by the hand. 'It has been so very long since you were here,' he continued, his voice now almost a whisper as he led the *ferang* up the few steps into his bedroom and started to undress slowly. The lights were soft and the air heavy with an almost pungent smell as Harry stood transfixed, staring at the young boyish figure slowly undressing before him.

'Where is Piya?' he asked. His words sounded hoarse. 'You promised me Piya,' he repeated, becoming agitated as the shape moved slowly to the soft sounds behind the cushioned bed. He stepped forward, almost lunging as he tripped on a carefully laid rug. 'Where is Piya?' he asked again, his voice rising.

'Piya is here, my darling. Piya is here,' he called softly, rotating his hips back and forth in a slow sensual movement. The ageing spymaster was momentarily confused. He looked closely at the soft young body gyrating within touch and suddenly understood. It had been almost two years since his last visit and his lover had grown. Relieved, Harold Bradshaw stepped forward and took the young boy in his arms and kissed him hungrily before falling to the bed together. Piya was ecstatic. His generous *ferang* lover had returned. And on this day of all days! He was really so fortunate to have such a wonderful surprise!

And on his twelfth birthday.

* * * * * *

Harry awoke with a start and moments passed before he remembered where he was. He looked across at his companion and smiled. The boy reminded him of an earlier time and another place which, as he closed his eyes, brought back a flood of other memories. He permitted his thoughts to drift and, as sleep evaded him, Harry recalled his early days in Europe and England, when he was still in his prime as an active field agent.

Then the image of Konstantinov flashed across his mind and he ground his teeth, willing the memory away, without success. He lay there in the partial darkness, listening to the airconditioner hum as it fought to keep the room temperature constant. He tried directing his thoughts to other things, but the memory kept returning to haunt him. Tired and annoyed with the invasion of his thoughts, Harry permitted his mind to wander wherever it wished, no longer resisting the distant events which flooded back into his mind.

He had been foolish, he admitted. The boy had been only thirteen but in post-war Berlin who could tell the difference? The streets were swarming with prostitutes of both sexes as they fought to survive the aftermath of Hitler's Germany. Most were destitute and gave themselves willingly, sometimes for the price of one meal.

He had taken the boy back to the small hotel. Nobody paid any attention as he escorted the youth to his room. Or, at least at that time, he had thought that his activities had gone unobserved. Berlin at that time was inundated with agents. As the city had been carved into sectors, he had been assigned to the British Sector and had already spent some months moving across the sector lines through East Berlin, sometimes acting as a courier, other times to handle a simple intelligence drop.

Harry would never forget his shock when the bedroom door burst open and two huge men barged into his room brandishing automatics. He and the teenager were both naked. The men punched the boy unconscious and ordered Harry to remain where he was as one of the men photographed the lurid scene. The other Russian stood with one hand in his overcoat pocket while indicating with the Luger that the Australian was not to do anything foolish. The flash blinded Harry as the first man moved in closer to the bed for a clearer picture of the boy's bleeding face. Several more photographs were taken and then they turned to leave, the larger of the men maintaining his weapon in full view to discourage Harry from following or doing anything courageous. As they moved through the broken doorway the photographer turned and smiled sardonically while the other man spat on the floor. Then they were gone.

Harry was relieved when they finally made their approach. It was inevitable that he would be required to follow their demands and, at first, these were not too difficult to accommodate. Their requests were generally for information concerning British operatives and Harry provided these without hesitation. He had no choice. Disclosure of his sexual idiosyncrasies would not only have ruined his career but would also have placed his life in danger from within his own organisation. He knew how brutal the Russians could be.

Harry had seen it all before. As that year came to a close, Harry discovered that he actually didn't care too much one way or another whether the West or the Communists controlled the world. Berlin had become a cesspool of humanity and he, one of the many sucked into the filthy quagmire created by extremists from both Left and Right of the political spectrum, became a relatively insignificant player in a game which none of them seemed to understand. Even the most hardened agents became cavalier as they went about their secret lives, scoffing silently at the ideologies propounded by Moscow and the temptations offered by Washington, as the self-proclaimed leader of the West. It was when Harry was escorting a family of three through an established route, bringing a fellow conspirator's children across from East Berlin, that he became apolitical and severely critical of all who would be the world's masters.

The crossing had ended in disaster. The children had been sacrificed and it was only later that he'd discovered that even had the escape not been compromised by an unreliable cell in the Soviet Sector, they would most certainly have been killed before completing the crossing. The massacre had been intended as an explicit message to all agents who operated along the divisions separating East from West Berlin. The father had been turned, and his children had paid the ultimate price for his betrayal. Harry had survived the ordeal, but only just. The Soviets had orchestrated that he be blamed, his usefulness to them no longer in question. Later, when he discovered that he too had been marked to die during that operation, Harry went to ground for months before being discovered. The British offered him sanctuary but it was, as always, conditional. He was to leave the SIS. He was no longer considered an asset to either side and, for the first time in many years, Harry felt a tremendous burden disappear from his shoulders as he gratefully accepted the dismissal. He fled Europe and escaped to his home, in Australia, as had Ellis before him. For months he had lived as a recluse. His life had become void of all attachment and he considered taking his life. Harry became desperate, desperate for some justification to live. He had no friends. He felt drained of those emotions which demanded commitments of loyalty to King and Country, to family and friends. These were no longer part of his make-up.

After months of seclusion and self-examination, he accepted that whatever had happened, it had not been entirely his fault. Harry went to Melbourne and applied for a position with the Ministry of Defence. They were desperate for field-hardened men with

European experience. During his first month at the Defence establishment, Harry learned from hushed conversations that a new Intelligence arm was to be formed, based along the lines of the British MI-5 and MI-6. A team from London was appointed to act as adviser to the Australian Government and, amongst this number, Harry identified William Webb Ellis, a former Sydney man whom he had met on more than one occasion while on field assignments. He remembered the deep resentment many of the other agents had expressed for this man which, at the time, Harry had put down to British-Australian rivalry, as the Colonial Boy had climbed to giddy heights within the British Intelligence Service.

There had been rumours, none of which had been substantiated. Whispers seem to follow Ellis wherever he went, even to Singapore and the United States where he directed British MI-6 interests. The spy master married so many times it was almost impossible to maintain records of his marital activities. Harry was surprised to learn that one of Ellis's wives, Lilia Zelenski, was a White Russian which, considering the sensitivity of the Intelligence Chief's access, was in itself typical of the man's extraordinary behaviour. Harry decided to approach the colourful, enigmatic bureaucrat. Ellis recognised the former field agent and, shortly thereafter, Harry's future was assured. Ellis had offered his hand and Harry had eagerly accepted. Harold Bradshaw had completed the circle. He was now back in the intelligence fold, only this time, under the control of Australia's first double agent. It was through Ellis that he met Alfred Broome. After that, Harry's field experience provided a clear path for his accelerated promotion to senior roles within the embryonic Australian intelligence community.

At first, it was as if he had been given a new lease on life but, as he became more and more engrossed in the machinations of the sinister world of espionage and the confusing shadows this life cast, Harry grew to despise the creators of the world in which he had become a prisoner. Disillusioned, embittered, he found it more difficult, as time passed, to retain his sense of identity.

He made serious attempts to identify why, emotionally, he felt no real loyalty to his masters. Harry believed that the West was as culpable as their Soviet counterparts. He decided that neither side really offered any solution to the problems the masses faced as they struggled just to survive and, as the major powers improved their economic, social and political grip on the emerging countries which suffered the humiliation of being relegated to the Third World, Harry elected to remain silently apolitical and non-aligned. Reluctant to offer political opinions when asked, silent and inconspicuous even within the strange world which bred contempt for those who maintained too high a profile, Harry soon became an integral part of the upper echelons of the fledgling Intelligence community.

Harry was promoted to Assistant Deputy Director in the newly-formed Australian Security Intelligence Organisation. One of his first calls to congratulate him on his appointment was from the Cultural Attaché, Embassy of the Union of Soviet Socialists' Republic. It required only one brief meeting for Harry to consent to re-establishing their former relationship. The Cultural Attaché had shown him the photographs.

As the months passed, Harry learned to accept the compromise he had made. He established himself as a reliable officer and those around him soon developed an even greater respect for this man on whom they discovered they could always rely. Meetings with the Russians were relatively infrequent. When they did effect a rendezvous, Harry willingly accepted the envelopes which always contained a generous consideration for his services. He never did feel like a traitor, electing to consider himself more as a mercenary, a free agent. He continued to provide the Soviets with the information they required and his financial rewards increased considerably when it was announced that he would move to England to establish a new liaison centre with the British MI-6. When Harry arrived in London, he was instructed to liaise with a nominated KGB officer who was stationed at the Soviet Embassy. His name was Konstantinov and his demands on Harry drove him perilously close to insanity. The fear of discovery and the consequences of his actions chewed away until finally, when dangerously close to a complete breakdown, KGB colonel Konstantinov identified the seriousness of Harry's mental state and temporarily discontinued utilising his services. Within the year, when the Russian believed he could once again be pressured into complying with the KGB demands, Harold Bradshaw recommenced his double life.

Since that time, Harry had remained in the full employ of the KGB and, when the Australian Government established its second

Intelligence Service on the 13 May, 1952, due to his unique field experience and uncanny ability to analyse the Soviet's activities, Harold Bradshaw became Deputy Director. The position demanded that Harry attend all joint working Intelligence sessions whenever these were held, and liaise with foreign government counterparts, including the CIA and MI-6 where he soon developed close working relationships with the other spy chiefs.

In June, 1957, Harry married Susan Christina Blackmore, only daughter of Sir Ronald Blackmore, of Blackmore and Heath, London. His bride was more than twenty years his junior. He had hoped that this union would assist him to become financially independent of the secret income he had been receiving from the Soviets. Unfortunately, this was not to be. Susan's father passed away that summer leaving his estate deficient of funds due to poor investments. Although their marriage had been consummated, Susan soon discovered that her husband's sexual appetites appeared to be deteriorating at an alarming rate until, to her dismay, they ceased sleeping together even before their first anniversary had arrived.

Accepting his condition as graciously as possible, Harry watched his wife Susan throw herself into the social circuit with great energy and managed to occupy her life with social rather than physical intercourse. Susan had wandered only once. The brief affair had been discreet and intimate. She was young, attractive, and Harry knew she had become disillusioned with the physical aspects of their marriage. Harry had suspected that his wife might enter into such casual relationships and accepted this, recognising that with her looks and youth, he should prepare himself for Susan's occasional infidelities. For Harry, the marriage was, in many respects, a perfect arrangement. Susan was not a demanding woman and presented him with a perfect cover to hide his own sexual preferences.

He had never strayed into dangerous sexual liaisons while in Australia, even though such opportunities were easily arranged in Melbourne where the domestic security service was based. Even within the ASIO ranks, he knew of at least three operatives who were of a similar persuasion to himself. No, he had decided when first moving to the new organisation, he would be circumspect in selecting his sexual partners, preferring to leave these activities for when he visited Asian capitals, such as Bangkok. It was here he had discovered Piya during one such visit some four years ago. Now, he thought, remembering his surprise at the boy's change, he would need to find another reliable partner as Piya would soon be too old.

As these and other thoughts elapsed into a foggy blur, Harry finally fell asleep to the hum of the air-conditioning unit.

* * * * * *

The following morning Harry had bathed and dressed even before many of Bangkok's foreign tourists had returned to their hotels after all-night sessions in Pat Pong's infamous bars. Normally he would have slipped a change of underwear into his coat pockets for such brief stays and regretted this oversight. Even his teeth felt gritty. He would shower and change again in the First Class lounge at the airport. He checked his wallet and looked down at the sleeping boy. Harry removed two hundred baht and placed the money on the bedside table, then he left.

As the Deputy Director left Piya's rooms, he was observed. Harry walked down to the corner and up the street to find a taxi. He decided to go directly to the airport and take an earlier flight to Singapore and on to Djakarta. Harry Bradshaw smiled smugly as he approved of this slight change in his travel plans. It never hurt to be flexible in these matters, he thought, the years of field experience influencing his decision. Three hours later, as the Intelligence Director's flight taxied into Paya Lebar Airport in Singapore, details of his previous evening's activities had been encrypted, transmitted, deciphered and placed on a senior analyst's desk across the other side of the globe. Harold Bradshaw had been picked up by a surveillance team as he entered the young prostitute's rooms.

The contents of the sensitive material were then taken upstairs and surrendered to the Australian Area Operations Desk Officer who read the report slowly then smirked at the photograph pinned to the file cover. Suddenly, his face clouded

'Gotcha, you asshole!' he snarled, poking Harry's image with his finger. 'Gotcha at last, you sonofabitch!' With which, Senior Agent Richards of the Central Intelligence Agency slapped himself on the thigh and opened the top drawer of his desk, extracted his banned Havana cigars, selected one and placed it between his teeth. He lit the expensive leaf and leaned back into his swivel chair, savouring the cigar's almost perfect flavour. It was worth waiting for, he knew. They had caught him at last and he had even provided them with a bonus.

The American closed his eyes and grunted in satisfaction. They had him cold. And Richards knew that should the need arise, this man would be obliged to co-operate. The Australian had compromised himself completely. At any time they so desired, he would become *their* man.

* * * * * *

Piya smiled as the two men arrived for their appointment. He was excited, believing that this would be a very rewarding arrangement. He peered out through the spyhole and watched the men as they approached his door. Piya was a little surprised as one of the men appeared to be Thai. He could see that the other man was obviously a *ferang*. They both held themselves like soldiers. He had seen their type before and Piya assumed that the Thai national was merely escorting his foreign friend. The young prostitute spoke to them first, establishing that they were, in fact, the clients who had telephoned earlier. He then let them enter and suggested that the protocol was to first pay him for his services. The solidly-built *ferang* whom Piya had correctly guessed was a soldier smiled as he moved closer and delivered two short but swift blows to the boy's abdomen. Piya collapsed to the floor doubled in the foetal position, sucking unsuccessfully for air as his world disintegrated around him.

The beating did not last more than a few minutes but, to the young male prostitute, it was an eternity. He lost consciousness only to be revived by his attackers. He moaned then cried, sobbing for help from the Thai man, confused as to why he had been so brutally beaten. He had little money on the premises and he knew it would not be rape; they would have done that before any attack on his small body. Perhaps they just enjoyed going around beating up people in his profession, he thought, fearful that they might still kill him.

When they finally left, Piya's battered limbs were still trembling with fear. They had threatened to return and he was certain that they would. He had told them everything they wanted to know. He had also promised to keep them informed in the future should there be any further contact from his favourite client. They had warned him not to run away and he understood their threats. Piya believed that they could find him if he deserted his premises. Besides, where could he go? He had bathed slowly after locking the doors securely. What was this all about? he wondered, still in shock.

Why were these men so interested in Harold Bradshaw?

Chapter 7

Indonesia

Murray was convinced that Harry had practised sitting in that position before. He had still not mastered the uncomfortable cross-legged lotus and was impressed with the older man's ability to sit in that way without apparent discomfort.

As soon as Murray had explained his experiences in the SUBUD community's compound, Harry had insisted that he be taken and introduced to the religious sect's head. At first, Murray was reluctant, convinced that his visitor had an ulterior motive, but changed his attitude the moment he witnessed Bradshaw's reaction to his first contact with the *SUBUD Bapak*.

They had entered the peaceful room and remained standing in their stockinged feet until the master had entered. He smiled and clasped his hands together, moving them slowly from his face towards them as if in a gesture of supplication. He spoke to them in English, welcoming Murray and his guest and bidding them to sit with him and talk. Subuh sat on the large *tikar* mat and beckoned, indicating that the others should follow. Harry immediately moved into the cross-legged position while Murray eased himself down carefully onto the woven mat.

'This is your first time in our country?' he asked politely.

'No, it isn't, Bapak.' Murray had offered directions as to how the religious guru should be addressed and was pleased that Harry had been listening. 'I have visited Djakarta and Surabaja before.'

'I am pleased that Mas Murray has brought you to SUBUD. What religion do you follow?' he enquired. Harry was momentarily taken aback. In Western cultures, it would have been considered impolite to be as abrupt in enquiring as to one's religious denomination. It had been some time since he had attended church as a Christian for the sake of prayer or worship. In fact, apart from weddings, funerals and the odd christening, Harry did not recall having attended a Sunday service for many years.

'I was raised a Catholic but regretfully, I have been lacking in my duty to my faith.'

The master explained that it was irrelevant to which religion they belonged providing one believed in God. 'There are seven types of soul in the Cosmos,' he explained, 'and there are religions corresponding to these seven types. Man has long known of their existence,' he said, looking directly at the two men as he spoke. 'These may be compared to the Seven Ages of Man, inasmuch as different forms of behaviour correspond to the various stages of growth.

Our community here should not be confused as a new religion. Some have compared the SUBUD philosophy with the ancient Mysteries while others have suggested that SUBUD is a derivative from or a combination of Hinduism and Sufism. I will leave you to consider these thoughts to assist with your own conclusions. Our aim is to educate our members to a deeper awareness of the true nature of their souls and to purify and cleanse them. This is achievable through prayer, meditation and the *latihan*.'

He then went on to deliver a short lecture encouraging them to direct their spiritual hopes and aspirations exclusively towards God. He asked them to join him in prayer, to which they willingly agreed. They listened to the soft resonant voice fill the room as their thoughts concentrated on the great man's prayer. His words were clear and precise and, as the almost melodious tone seemingly eased whatever tension lay in their bodies, they listened as he spoke softly, willing them to relax their minds and bodies completely, urging both men to sit quite still and clear their thoughts. They closed their eyes for what seemed to be moments, only to discover, when they heard their names being called, that they had unknowingly remained in a trance for almost twenty minutes. Later, Harry admitted to feeling a sense of awareness during those missing minutes but could not remember any specific thought or words which transpired during their trance. He asked Murray if he too had felt as if his body had become a soft electric current, flowing aimlessly around his person, creating what he described as a floating sensation. Murray had agreed that he too had experienced a warmth, but compared it more to being suspended under a soft light.

When they heard the Bapak call their names, both men instantly regained full consciousness of their faculties, and opened their eyes to see the master standing before them. The ceremony was over. The Bapak left the room without any further word, leaving the men in the company of their thoughts. Both remained in the lotus position for some time, conscious of the blood flowing through their veins more freely and, for a brief time, they felt full of pure thoughts.

As they left that special place, both men knew that they had experienced something extraordinary; almost bordering on the mystic. They walked away quietly, each contemplating what had taken place.

As they moved between the small trees, Mohammed Subuh watched the men with a clarity only his eyes could see. There was a slight blur in his vision as he concentrated on the two men walking away, almost as if there was a shadow obstructing his sight. As he turned his head ever so slightly to see past it, he was alarmed that this mark remained fixed on one of the men as they walked away. He closed his eyes, attempting to will this dark blur away, then opened his eyes. He frowned. The mark remained. And it remained fixed on the departing image of Harold Bradshaw.

* * * * * *

Before Harry returned to Australia, he revisited the compound and attended the *latihan*. Harry had not objected when Murray brought one of his student friends along to the session but he was surprised that the girl was not permitted to join with the men during the latihan. The sexes were segregated for this emotional and soul-searching exercise. Before the men entered the room, which had been specifically prepared for such sessions, they were required to remove their watches and any other metal or hard objects which could cause physical harm. At first, this request made Harry apprehensive but, as the others complied, so did he. Later, he was to admit privately to Murray that this experience was one of the most incredible he had ever had.

Harry learned that the *latihan* was a means whereby followers entered into a state of self-purification. SUBUD, not unlike Sufism, offers its members the possibility of knowing Reality through inner experience, conditional on the participants' ability to purify his or herself sufficiently in order to receive such revelation. Many never achieve this pure state and for those who do, the process is a long and demanding one. This training of one's self required Harry's concentration to induce what he thought was a form of auto-hypnosis in which the direction originates from one's Higher Self. Once this process becomes operative, he was told, the *latihan* proceeds in the same manner as that in which he took breath; it would become as automatic as his heartbeat and he would be able to achieve this state with full consciousness.

At first Harry was shocked with the behaviour of those around him. Some of the members fell to the floor, crying, while others started screaming loudly. He panicked and wanted to leave the room, which suddenly erupted into pandemonium as men screamed of their lives and disappointments while others stood perfectly still as if already in a state of tranquillity. It was like a scene from some mental institution. Gradually, as he realised that there was no danger, that these men were merely exorcising their devils, he fell into the routine of things himself, and started to sing. Amazingly, he felt no shame or embarrassment and, as the minutes rolled by, discovered a sense of release from the stress under which he had lived most of his life.

When the *latihan* session had been terminated, they spent an hour alone, meditating. Soon after, all three returned to Murray's pavilion where they sat for yet another hour discussing their experiences that day. Ade had to hurry home, so Harry invited Murray back to the Intercontinental Hotel for dinner, which he gratefully accepted.

'How about we leave now and I'll take some clothes. If you don't mind, Harry, I could certainly do with a long tub in your room, that is if you don't mind?'

'Go for it, Murray. I can see why you'd enjoy some civilised facilities for a change.' Harry laughed, looking around the very basic accommodations. 'But don't worry, young man, from what I hear you will be out of here very soon.'

Murray looked at the older man with some surprise. 'What have you heard?'

'We'll talk over dinner. Come on, grab your gear and let's get the hell out of here before I become claustrophobic.'

Half an hour later, Murray lay in the luxury of a hot bath, not entirely uncomfortable with the knowledge that he would soon be returning to Australia. He towelled, changed and met Harry down in the Baris Lounge of the hotel. He strolled into the bar wearing an open-neck batik shirt. It was almost his trade mark, as the other expatriates simply refused to wear the cheap cotton cloth. Murray did so out of necessity and didn't really mind. A few familiar faces raised their hands and said 'hi' as he passed their tables. Most of those present were either journalists or embassy officials. There were only a few drinking holes around Djakarta and this, the newest, catered for those who were on government business and could afford to pay the one dollar fifty US for a cocktail.

'Murray!' a voice called and he made his way around the horseshoe shaped bar. The bartenders recognised him and brought a large bottle of Bir Bintang as he slipped in alongside his friend.

'Malam, tuan!' the chief bartender said, warmly.

'Ya, selamat malam, Mas,' Murray responded mechanically, then remembered to smile. He was not entirely relaxed, even after the bath. Perhaps he was edgy because he knew he would be leaving soon, he guessed, or was it because he hadn't felt entirely comfortable with Harry from the moment he had arrived? Murray was concerned about having such a senior member of the Intelligence community visiting without the support of his own masters. Harry had been explicit in his cable. He was on holiday and firmly indicated that he would not appreciate having Murray's people either coddle him during his visit or feel obliged to entertain him while he was taking a much-deserved break. Harry had explained that Susan had not wanted to leave home at that time. He said she had insisted that he go alone and enjoy himself. Djakarta was no place for a three-year-old infant and so he had decided to take some private time off, just for himself for a change. When Harry had mentioned his wife, Murray had immediately felt the old uneasiness return. He had watched the older man's face carefully as they discussed family and friends and, to his relief, at no time did he see any indication that he might have known.

'Well, cheers, Murray,' he said, downing half of his bourbon and coke and immediately indicating to the barman that he wished another. Murray observed the speed with which the double shots disappeared. He raised his glass of beer and swallowed slowly.

'Can we get right into it, Harry? I can't stand the suspense.'

'It's off the record. Your own powers-that-be will advise you in their own good time. I'm not the messenger, just a friend short-circuiting the delivery process.'

'How much time do I have?' he asked.

'Give or take, I'd say, hmmm,' he paused, 'about a month.'

'Shit, Harry, that's no time at all!' he almost shouted, then dropped his voice knowing that most of the journalists in that bar could not obtain the *surat djalan* permits necessary for them to move around the countryside, and some places even within the metropolitan area, and so they survived primarily off what they heard here.

'It wasn't my call, Murray. You know that my influence is limited. Besides, there is a strong possibility that you will be back before you know it.' Murray grabbed at the suggestion. 'How strong a possibility?' he asked, sensing there was a great deal more that he was not being told.

'My estimate?' he asked, 'Oh, I'd say something around the high nineties.' Murray's spirits suddenly lifted with this news.

'When will I be told?'

'It seems that I am to have some influence over what will happen up here,' he said, lowering his voice even more as he twirled the long plastic stirrer the barman had insisted on placing in his drink. 'Keep it to yourself. Don't want your team spitting the dummy because I pre-empted their delivery service. Okay?'

'Sure. And thanks,' he agreed, thankful for the early warning.

'As I'm leaving tomorrow, what do you say we eat upstairs then take a stroll around the traps?' Harry was not really all that interested but felt that it would be out of character not to hit at least Mama Louie's before heading back to Melbourne. Murray finished his second glass and left the rest of the bottle.

'Ready when you are,' he said, edging off his bar stool not entirely unhappy that someone else was picking up the tab. The atmosphere in the Baris Lounge was not exactly conducive to confidential discussion. There were just too many embassy ears listening, their amateurish behaviour made obvious by their strained dialogue. Djakarta had become a cesspool full of foreign intelligence agents, he thought, waving goodbye to the staff as he followed Harry Bradshaw.

They dined in fine style on the top floor of Djakarta's finest hotel. The Nirwana Supper Club was set in splendid surroundings, with views down both sides of the restaurant. To his right Murray could see the lights around the newly-constructed sports stadium, built with valuable dollars so that Soekarno could show the world that even the New and Emerging Nations could provide for their athletes. He smiled as the area blacked out while he was admiring the achievement. On his left Murray could see down Djalan Thamrin all the way to Merdeka Square. Suddenly he realised just how much he would miss this city and its inhabitants, even with the inherent problems of corruption and apathy which often tested his patience.

'Never get too close, Murray,' the voice interrupted his wandering thoughts. 'It's not only unprofessional, it would be dangerous.'

'Seems that the place really does grow on you after all,' he responded. 'There are worse places,' he added, almost lamely.

'Sure, but you haven't seen them all, yet,' the older man advised, remembering an earlier time and another place. He seemed to recall making a similar statement to his controller. How long ago was that, he wondered? Was it really twenty years ago? Harry pushed the memory back to where it belonged. Those times were not all that memorable. 'Come on, don't get morbid on me. Finish your steak and we'll leave.'

'Actually, Harry, I wouldn't mind staying here for a while.' Murray did not particularly wish to end up playing interpreter again for his friend. He'd had enough of that during the first few nights. It was tiring and boring task, holding a two-way conversation repeating everything twice to both parties for hours on end, while the hookers crowded around encouraging him to arrange for Harry to take them back to his room and, after all of that, Harry always refused.

Harry was happy to call it a night after dinner. 'As it so happens, young man, I am feeling a little worse for wear and would be pleased to just stay here. Will you come for breakfast tomorrow? My flight isn't until midday.'

'Wouldn't miss it!' Murray happily responded. In a way he

would be sorry to see Harry go. Apart from the interpreting demands, Harry had been good company, probably the best he had enjoyed for some time. Too long a time, he suddenly thought. Maybe it was time he went home. He didn't want to believe that he was losing some of his objectivity. They remained until the floor show was over. Harry signed the cheque and escorted Murray down to the lobby. He smiled as literally hundreds of *betjak* drivers crowded towards the entrance, calling out to the familiar face.

'Good night Harry,' he called, climbing into one of the three-wheeled monsters, waving as the driver turned without caution directly into the flow of traffic and cut across the roundabout towards the Soviet and British Embassies. As his driver pumped furiously to beat the oncoming traffic, Murray turned and waved once more but his companion for most of the past week had already disappeared from view.

Harry had watched Murray's transport cross the busy roundabout and then head home. He checked his watch and saw that it was still quite early. He looked down towards Djalan Blora where he knew the transvestites congregated and snorted with contempt. He stood for some moments, feeling the warm evening breeze move slowly through the night. A touch of dust mixed with the many tropical aromas hung temptingly in the evening air as Harry looked sadly at the small group of children offering themselves just outside the hotel's perimeter.

He resisted the temptation, turned and entered the hotel. Alone.

A guest dressed in a long-sleeved white shirt and charcoal trousers checked his watch as Harry entered the lobby lift. He observed the indicator lights above the doors and checked the level at which the lift stopped. The man then waited for a further fifteen minutes before wandering out of the hotel and into the car park. There, he remained sitting in a black Mercedes 190 until midnight. Convinced that his quarry would remain in his room for the rest of the evening, Dimitri Kololotov then drove away, returning to his own small premises at the rear of the Soviet Embassy.

The Russian was not the only party to show interest in the Australian's movements. Both Murray and Harry had been observed while they were at the SUBUD compound. In fact, they had been followed almost from the moment Bradshaw's flight had arrived in Djakarta. As Dimitri had concluded his duties for the night, so too did his American counterpart. By noon the following day, Harry and Murray's movements would be known from reports which had already been deciphered, scrutinized, and placed on their respective desks in both Moscow and Langley, Virginia.

The observations were practically identical. Data extracted from files was checked and updated. Harry's movements were noted along with detailed information relating to those he was seen with during the visit. When the files had been read, these were returned to the security clerks who, in turn, checked the instructions attached to the report's cover. A cross-reference note was placed in Harry's file and, as per instruction, a new file was then opened, bearing the relevant identification in bold red letters across the documents face. The new file was simply titled, STEPHENSON, M.I., and then stored in the 'possibles' section.

In both the CIA and KGB Central Registry, Murray Lloyd Stephenson had been identified as a result of his association with Harold Bradshaw during the latter's visit. In both reports he had been classified as having strong Communist Party affiliations and being a member of the SUBUD religious-cum-spiritual group. In the course of the next twenty-four hours, his name would appear on no fewer than a dozen cross-referenced intelligence situation reports. Within the week, agents from several foreign legations in Canberra, Australia, would commence the tedious task of investigating his background in order that his file be upgraded to 'confirmed' or relegated to the lesser categories in the Registry computers.

Their investigations would eventually leave their masters confused and shaking their heads.

* * * * * *

True to his word, Murray arrived for breakfast. They sat in the outer section of the coffee shop and filled in time with banal discussion until the hour arrived for Harry to depart. They drove to Kemayoran Airport together and Murray waited until Harry's plane was airborne before returning to his pavilion.

When he arrived, he was met by his servant, who informed Murray that he had guests. After Harry's demanding visit, the thought of female company for a change lifted his spirits. He had expected to find either Ade or Yanti waiting for him inside. Instead, there were two men waiting for him.

'Hello, Stephenson,' Davis said, a grin on his face. Murray looked at the other man.

'G'day, Murray.' It was Keith Wells. 'Haven't heard from you for awhile. Been busy, have we?'

'Got some great news for you, Murray,' Davis added, impatiently.

'Shut up, Davis!' Wells snarled. He had just about had enough of the Tasmanian. 'Why don't you go and wait in the car while I talk to our friend here?' It wasn't really a question. Miffed, Davis stormed out sullenly and banged the door loudly as he left.

'You're going home, Murray,' Wells advised.

Murray waited a few moments before responding. 'Guess I'm due for a break,' was all he said. There was an awkward silence before the Station Chief spoke again.

'This may be more than a break, Murray,' he said slowly.

'Meaning?' he asked, anxious now about what his superior seemed to be implying. Murray felt uncomfortable not being able to mention his discussion with Harry.

'Seems your time here is up. That's all.'

'Just like that?' he asked, incredulously. This wasn't happening the way Bradshaw had predicted. There was something wrong. He could detect the hostility.

'Just like that,' Wells replied.

'Do I need an explanation?'

'Yes, but that's between you and our masters back home.'

'When do I leave?' he asked.

'You're to be out by the end of the month. Come down to the Embassy on Monday and we'll have your tickets and funds ready.' Keith Wells then left. Murray watched the housekeeper close the gate behind them. 'By the end of the month' meant just over two weeks before he departed. He rehashed the brief and enigmatic conversation in his mind and decided that even the Station Chief may have been left out of the information loop, and that his concerns were just an over-reaction to Well's delivery style. Anyway, he thought, there was nothing he could do until he returned to Melbourne and Central Plans.

Murray commenced making mental arrangements for his

departure. There was not a great deal to do as he had little to pack. He looked around the sparsely furnished quarters. Not much for two years of one's life, he thought, ignoring the feeling of depression which hovered now with the thought of leaving. He would concoct some acceptable explanation for his sudden departure. Murray thought about his friends. He would invite them all to a farewell party! Once again he looked around the cramped accommodations and decided to arrange something special. Then he remembered the Thousand Islands. Murray believed that this would be an ideal venue for his farewell party.

He left Djalan Tasikmalaya and headed for the university to inform his friends. He knew that this would not be an easy task. Murray had developed some very special relationships on and off campus during his two years and now, suddenly, he must tell them he was leaving.

Less than two weeks later, Murray and most of his close friends chartered the Indonesian Navy vessel and spent their last week together on the idyllic tropical island. Most, that is, with the exception of Ade. Distressed as she was, knowing that Murray was about to leave, Ade was adamant. She would not spend the weekend in the company of those communists.

* * * * * *

Murray pulled a bottle of beer from the home-made, polystyrene-lined ice box. It had taken all of them to off-load the heavy cask. The drinks had not been put on ice until they made camp amongst the coconut trees a few metres from the high tide mark. Sjamsu had carried the one metre blocks of ice from the ship's freezers and broken them into more manageable lumps. These he placed in the ice box and then emptied the case of beer into the large container. Murray had tried to explain that the beer should have gone in first but, with typical Oriental logic, Sjamsu had ignored his suggestion knowing that to do so would only make it more difficult later when they needed to take the beer out. The bottles remained on top of the ice.

Murray decided that he'd had enough swimming for the day and took another stroll around the small atoll. The island was literally smothered with tall coconut palms, most of which were heavily laden with fruit. Murray looked up to ensure that he was not standing under one of the coconut bunches. He had seen the damage a falling coconut could do to a car roof and didn't need to be told not to sleep under the swaying trees. What amazed him was that the Indonesians still insisted on sitting under the palms, and would only move when one of the coconuts dislodged itself, falling perilously close. Murray thought he understood, and believed that this was not bravado, nor was it stupidity. It was simply their fatalism, their belief in *adjal*.

Yanti did not follow. She understood that Murray needed to be alone with his thoughts. His friends all understood that he was sad to be leaving. They too would miss his company and friendship and this was reflected in the group atmosphere which, on this occasion, was subdued. The girls prepared more food and, as Murray returned, several of the men had taken their small *tikar* a short distance and prepared for the Mahgrib prayer. Murray looked across to the west and counted the slow seconds as the huge dark orange ball slipped below the horizon. And then he sighed, as the sunset all but disappeared within that magical moment.

* * * * * *

In the late afternoon on the following Tuesday, Murray Stephenson left Djakarta. There was a feeling of loss as his friends waved from the open observation level. They watched as Murray walked slowly across the concrete and called out loudly when he turned and waved goodbye to them. Sjamsu called loudly as Yanti waved furiously, holding a hand written placard wishing him 'Selamat Djalan'.

As he approached the steps leading up to the Boeing 707, Murray turned for one last farewell. He could no longer distinguish their shapes, let alone their faces. Disappointed that Ade had not put her feelings aside just this once and joined with his other friends to bid him farewell, Murray looked back over his shoulder and paused for one final look before entering the aircraft. He sensed that a major chapter in his life was coming to a close.

The four-engined jet screamed along the short runway then lifted suddenly, banking to the West and passing back over the terminal building. Murray peered down below, unable to differentiate between the structures as the Boeing climbed noisily. The aircraft continued to climb as the pilot manoeuvred the jet gracefully, changing its course in accordance with the flight plan. A chime sounded somewhere within the cabin as the seat-belt and no-smoking signs were switched off. Murray unlatched his seat-belt and made his way forward from the economy class section towards the toilets.

As he passed the front section of the economy seats, Murray waited for the stewardess carrying complimentary drinks to finish serving before he continued towards the toilets. He paused, placing his left hand on the aisle seat headrest to steady himself as he stood waiting. The aircraft dropped slightly, then steadied itself as he held tightly to the seat and, as the aisle had then cleared he moved forward, turning to apologise to the passenger whose seat he had gripped during the light turbulence.

'Sorry, ...' he started to say, looking at the occupant of the seat.

'Hello, Mahree,' the young woman replied, enjoying the look of surprise on his face. Murray gripped the seat in front to steady himself as the aircraft suddenly dipped again. He stared at the passenger, lost for words.

'What are you doing here?' he demanded, confused by her presence on the aircraft.

'Why, Mahree,' Ade teased, deliberately shifting the emphasis on the syllables, *'going to Australia with you, of course!'*

Chapter 8

Australia

After readjusting to life back in Melbourne, Murray was satisfied that he had made the correct decision. Three months before, he had been prepared to walk away from his profession and search for something less demanding on his personal relationships. Now, refreshed, away from the idiosyncrasies of Asian life with its often confusing cultures, Murray experienced a new vitality, a rejuvenation of his former self.

He played tennis, enjoying the game without the humid conditions he had become accustomed to in the tropics. Old friendships were re-established, and life moved into a familiar mode, one which provided an atmosphere of order and solidarity. He was home.

Murray's debriefing had not taken too long. During the first days, he sensed that there had been a certain amount of animosity amongst his peers. He put this down to the fact that he had been out of circulation and had lost real contact with the other agents. He set about rebuilding and consolidating these relationships.

His mother had been strangely distant when he visited her. Their first meeting was stiff and awkward. When several of her card-playing friends arrived, providing him with the opportunity to escape, he felt relief. He had stayed with his sister during the stopover in Sydney and she had brought her brother up to date regarding family matters. He had left his travelling companion to her own plans, although he suspected that she would have preferred accompanying him into see the sights, before proceeding on to Canberra. This suited Murray. He was pleased to have the day alone with his sister.

Sitting in the quiet leafy garden, Murray reflected on the events surrounding his departure from Djakarta. He remembered being totally disorientated when he discovered Ade on the plane. He had taken the empty seat beside her as he recovered from the shock of seeing her there.

'What are you doing here?' he had asked again, his mind confused by her presence.

'You have your secrets, Mahree, I have mine,' she smiled.

'How did you manage to arrange all of this so quickly? Passport, tickets! My god, Ade, how did you even manage to organise a visa in that time?'

'I had a little help, Mahree. Professor Winton at the Australian National University made most of the arrangements. Do you remember meeting Bapak Winton at the SUBUD complex? I'm sure we talked about him. He was the one who spoke fluent Bahasa Djawa to Bapak Subuh. Don't you remember?' Ade explained, bubbling with enthusiasm as she spoke.

'When you told me you were leaving for Australia, I asked SUBUD if they would help me contact the Professor to see if he had been serious about assisting Indonesian students with courses at his university. After that, I didn't have to do anything! They were all so supportive. Bapak Subuh must have spoken directly to his old friend because they called me back to the community centre the very next day and told me the news. I didn't want to tell you in case nothing happened, Murray. It was to be a surprise. We all knew the date of your departure and it was not difficult to book a seat on this flight, as you can see for yourself,' she said, indicating the near empty plane. *'This is also why I didn't join in the island trip. By then my documents were complete and my ticket confirmed. I knew that you would be so surprised!'*

Ade giggled, and looked directly at Murray. *'You are surprised, aren't you, Mahree?'*

He sat quietly listening to her explanation and, when she had finished, he just shook his head slowly before responding. *'You should have told me, Ade. Perhaps I could have helped.'*

'But everything was well-organised and I did want to keep it a secret until we boarded. I watched you at the Kemayoran Airport with all of your friends. You were so preoccupied hugging and kissing all of those girls you didn't even notice me when I was at the check-in counter.'

Murray had cast his mind back to the departure hall. She was totally correct. The scene had been a little chaotic, he remembered. Not that he would have recognised Ade anyway, Murray thought as he observed her clothes. She was dressed in a long trouser suit and high heels. He had only ever seen her in knee-length dresses or blue jeans, normally wearing the comfortable flat-heeled casual shoes most of the younger women preferred. Ade had tucked her shoulder-length hair up under a cap making identification nearly impossible. Murray smiled at her and shook his head once again.

'What are you going to do in Australia? What about your studies at Universitas Indonesia?' he asked.

'I have already confirmed with the university lecturers that my time in Australia will be credited towards my final examinations when I return. I will not be in Canberra long. My study visa is only for three months. But you could always help me extend, couldn't you, Mahree?' she suggested coquettishly. Murray ignored the idea, talking instead about more mundane matters such as finances, clothing and where she would stay while attending the short study course at the Australian National University. He was amazed to discover that all of these had been carefully, albeit quickly, planned to the last detail by the SUBUD members. She was indeed very fortunate to be going to Australia. Especially at this time, he had thought.

When they parted at the Sydney airport, Murray had promised to call her in a few days and arrange for her to visit once she had settled. He watched her walk away to arrange her ongoing flight, completely confident and assured. As she left the airport lounge area, he turned and waved once to which she responded immediately. Murray was still considering her successful efforts to visit Australia as his taxi dropped him at his sister's apartment in Neutral Bay. He understood that the visit had been quite some achievement. He also knew that, without some intricate string-pulling, it would not have been possible for Ade to accomplish what she had, in such a short time. Obviously, he thought, SUBUD had developed some strong pulling ability and was quite capable of applying it whenever deemed necessary.

* * * * * *

'You must come down, Murray.' The invitation had been offered for the third time and he could not refuse again. Harry Bradshaw had all but insisted that he spend the weekend at the coastal retreat. 'Bring your racquet and we'll see what's happened to your game while you've been away.' Unable to provide another suitable excuse, he accepted.

He drove down to the Bradshaws' home slowly, anxiety chewing at his stomach. Murray had considered telephoning Ade in Canberra and offering her the fare if she would come down and accompany him but, considering the circumstances and the host's position, he decided against it. Ade had met Harry in Djakarta but he wasn't sure if it would be appropriate for him to invite the Indonesian girl. She had done well with her time at the university and was not looking forward to returning home, which would be soon. Murray had invited her down several times already and Ade had happily visited, staying in his apartment along St. Kilda Road. He did not take her to meet his mother, which Ade found more than a little curious. Murray believed that their relationship could not be permanent and ensured that these feelings were understood by Ade. Nevertheless, they slept together, enjoying each other as natural lovers would, ignoring the inevitable.

Ade sensed that Murray would not ask her to remain in Australia which clearly demonstrated that he did not care enough for her to do so. She also understood that, once her flight departed Australia and she returned to Indonesia, their relationship would most certainly end. With only a few weeks left before her visa expired, Ade knew that the immigration authorities would not approve yet another extension. It was clear to Murray that she wished to remain in Australia, and he knew that to encourage her to do so would be irresponsible. Perhaps it was for the best that he hadn't asked her down for this weekend, he thought, slowing down as he approached the cottage.

He parked his MG and strolled slowly towards the large cottage, kicking the iron gate closed as he passed through. The lawn had obviously just been cut. The air still carried that grassy freshness which always accompanies that chore. Rows of poppies backed by dwarf lavenders lined the footpath on both sides, their fragrance competing with the other colourful beds of flowers, most of which were in full bloom. He looked up to the front entrance and instantly caught his breath.

'Welcome back, Murray,' Susan said, smiling radiantly. 'It's been too long.' She bent down, then crouched, holding the child from behind. 'Say hello to Uncle Murray, darling. Murray, this is Michael!'

Murray stepped forward and also crouched, 'Hello tiger,' he said, admiring the boy's striking blonde hair. 'Are you my new tennis partner?' He extended his hand and touched the boy's cheeks softly. Michael screamed, turned and shrank back into his mother's arms. They laughed at the child's reaction and suddenly Murray felt the angst wash away with the moment. He followed Susan Bradshaw into the house and through to the patio. It was almost as if he had not been away from the setting. The card table and the drinks were the same, and to his astonishment, even the same people who had made up the party during his first visit some four years before were present, including his mother, Muriel Stephenson. He walked over and kissed her first before turning to the others. She responded warmly, boosting his confidence.

He then turned to Jean Broome and immediately observed that she had aged considerably, her face showing the results of over-indulgence. She clasped her gin and tonic with both hands. Obviously, her extended visits to the sanatorium had not been successful. Murray had only discovered her problem well after she had taken to disappearing for weeks at a time. Office gossip had alerted him to her alcoholism.

'Hello, stranger. You're looking in good health. The tropical climate appears to have suited you,' she said. Murray smiled, pecked her on the cheek and shook her husband's hand.

'Alfred. Looks like we'll have another tough match on our hands,' he laughed, turning then to Harry Bradshaw and shaking his hand also.

'Thought it would be fitting to have that re-match Alfred and I have been promising each other. Same partners as before, Murray, only this time you will have to run a little faster. Your partner is not as young as he was when you last won.'

Alfred Broome snorted. 'Well, let's see about that! Come on, partner, change your gear and we will give them a quick thrashing before dinner.'

They played for an hour, the Bradshaws winning easily. Harry had been accurate in his observations. Alfred had aged considerably over the past few years, which made the match even more demanding on his partner. Twice, the game was brought to a halt as the older man ran out of steam and required a short spell. When Harry offered to call it a game, Alfred insisted that they continue.

He should have heeded the warnings.

The following week, while attending an Intelligence Chiefs briefing, Alfred Broome collapsed with chest pains and died before the ambulance team could render assistance. On the Monday morning, Alfred Broome was buried in a quiet ceremony attended only by his family and a few close friends.

An urgent meeting was called by the Minister and those summoned agreed on an interim replacement for the deceased Chief. There was little discussion as to whom this should be. There was only one qualified candidate who was completely au fait with both the domestic and overseas Intelligence arms, and he was present at the meeting. The Minister was receptive when he expressed willingness to make the necessary move in the interests of expediency and continuity. The decision had been unanimous, and before lunch on that day, Harold Bradshaw was appointed the interim Director of the Australian Secret Intelligence Service. Immediately, he set about reorganising Central Plans' operational structure, increasing agent representation in all South-East Asian target countries.

* * * * * *

The following month Murray Lloyd Stephenson finally returned to Indonesia. The word 'Diplomatique' was emblazoned across the cover of his passport in gold lettering, and his other credentials declared he was a member of the Australian Embassy in Djakarta. The revised Protocol Lists circulated regularly throughout the Diplomatic and Consular missions mentioned Stephenson's arrival and status. His position in the Australian Embassy was listed as Third Secretary, Political Affairs.

* * * * * *

Langley, Virginia, USA

The Assistant Director, South-East Asia, looked across at the other officer and nodded, in concurrence. It would appear that the other man's evaluations supported his own conclusions.

The Australians had weakened their overseas intelligence capability while perhaps strengthening their domestic service with the appointment of Bradshaw as Intelligence Chief, ASIS. The vacuum created within ASIO would be of little consequence, providing 'Finger Jar', the designated code name allocated to Bradshaw within the CIA, had no influence over whoever was appointed to fill his former position as Deputy Director.

'Getting to be like those goddamn Brits,' the ADSEA grumbled. He had come in from field operations almost ten years before and still cursed the MI6 for the SIS operations which had cost the CIA one network and a number of valuable agents. After the Philby and Burgess fiascos, there wasn't one American operative left still prepared to risk exposing themselves to the British agencies. The Agency had decided that the Australians had been too close to the British, resulting in their secret intelligence operations often being compromised.

'What do you expect, Sam,' the other man responded, feeling the frustration of not being permitted to just move in and resolve the mess as they would have before Johnson became President. 'Our inexperienced friends Down Under were not even aware that the very man who virtually co-founded their Secret Service was not just a former nazi collaborator but also served the goddamn Russkies for years before he was isolated.'

'Well, what are we going to do with this lot then?' the ADSEA Head asked in an almost perfunctory manner. He knew what he would do had the decision been his alone to take.

'What we always do, Sam. What we always do, goddamnit!' As Assistant Director, Australia and New Zealand, his work load had suddenly doubled since the Brits had enticed their Commonwealth brothers into joint operations against the Indonesian 'Crush Malaysia' campaign. Until President Soekarno started playing with the Soviets, his sphere of operations had been relatively uneventful. He, too, was tired. Tired of the bullshit and tired of having his hands tied when there was so much he could have done to rectify many of the 'situations' which had suddenly pushed his distant Pacific area into a 'hot' status.

'We will have to take them out of the loop until they rectify the problem.'

'Why for godsakes don't we just goddamn tell them?'

'The Director feels that with the Vietnam involvement building up we will need their international support. Besides, we can continue to contain any damage 'Finger Jar' may be responsible for by moving into a direct relationship with him. It would be more beneficial to keep him as one of our 'friendlies' by alerting him discreetly to the information we hold. Should the Aussies move to replace him, God knows who they would select as his successor. Besides, we're getting used to the Brits screwing up. It's just bad luck that the Australians are so dependent on their relationships. I wouldn't touch another British agent for the next generation after what that asshole Maclean and his playmates did to their Intelligence Service, not to mention ours.'

'So we just sit back and not inform their Prime Minister that his most senior Intelligence Chief has not only compromised himself and his Department, but possibly the domestic agency as well?'

'No. Not even that. As far as we are able to determine, he's been very careful. Apart from the Bangkok fairy he visits, we have no other evidence that he has similar liaisons outside Australia. As for what he does on home territory, we have only assumptions to go on as there has been no evidence of 'Finger Jar' breaking the law in his own country. Not even the hint of any homosexual activity. Let's hope that he keeps it that way. I, for one, would not wish to be involved in the decision-making process which would necessitate any extreme action. Our jobs are difficult enough and, if I'm right about Lyndon B. Johnson and his Texas oil friends, we can expect more and more escalation in the Indochina conflict.' He paused for a moment as the memory of Kennedy's assassination flashed through his mind. At the time of his death, American losses in Vietnam were almost negligible, the sudden escalation pumping American losses through the roof. The ADSEA believed that the new Administration would continue to increase American presence in Asia in what could be a futile attempt to encircle Ho Chi Minh. The United States would need domestic and international public opinion to support their war effort.' The bottom line is, we will need to maintain the very best relationships possible with our inexperienced friends from Down Under, as they say.'

'What about Indonesia, Sam?' he coughed, cursing the habit which needed almost three packs per day. Sometimes he wished he could have a quiet moment with that 'Marlboro Man.'

He coughed again and his opposite number waited patiently. He looked at his old friend. The word was that he probably wouldn't make it to year's end. 'Do we beef up our presence?'

Samuel John Forrester looked at his friend and sighed. No one really understood what the hell was going on there. They had penetrated almost every known apparatus of government, placed their agents in sensitive positions, financed the hell out of the place and still all they got was a load of crap intelligence as to who was doing what and why! They had more than fifty operatives active in the arena and he could guarantee, based on the intelligence he had seen flowing through over the past eighteen months, that not one of the so-called experts knew what the hell they were talking about! He just felt so frustrated with the lack of professional reporting. It tore at his gut. When he remembered the amount of 'green' that had been dropped to grease the information flow, he wanted to throw up. The so-called 'intelligence' which he had personally evaluated was just a bunch of crap. In his opinion, they had no real representation in situ and, because the White House had refused to acknowledge Soekarno as a real threat to global peace, much of his resources had been redirected to Laos and Cambodia.

'Sure,' he said, 'let's send in another dozen agents so they can sit on their green asses and justify their presence with the crap this Agency is in dire threat of drowning under!' He rubbed his tired and pulsating temples. God, he wished he could have one of those damn cigarettes. 'There's so much shit on file right now it would take more goddamn desk officers to evaluate than you could fit into Yankee Stadium. Whatever happened to quality, for Chrissakes?' His heavy chest sucked in a large amount of air as he placed his head between his huge hands and rubbed his jowls briefly. 'The short answer is, no. There is no budget. Soekarno has moved down in priority because now the Pentagon has persuaded our Executive Branch that 'Nam needs all of our attention right now.' He rubbed his face briskly again, then leaned back into the uncomfortable chair. 'It seems that we must do with what we have.' His tired and bloodshot eyes peered across the table at the other sector officer.

'Okay. I've got it,' the other man responded wearily. 'We'll hold any action in abeyance until this asshole craps in his own nest. Is that it?' he asked, referring to Bradshaw.

'Sorry, Pete. That's about it.' He looked down and suddenly rolled his head to exercise the tight neck muscles which threatened to lock his head in one permanent position.

'Fine, Sam. Hope he doesn't become an expensive asset, that's all!'

'Me too, Pete. Me too,' the weary Assistant Director sighed.

Chapter 9

1965, Indonesia

Subuh had just departed, leaving the President in a foul temper. The Palace staff could hear his tirade from the next level and they knew it would be an unpleasant day for all. Whispered voices carried news of the unusual outburst through the Palace corridors and, within a very short time, the story was circulating throughout the halls of most Government departments.

The President had summoned the respected figure to his office. He had wanted to know why the man had been in the habit of receiving foreign nationals who, according to the Indonesian Intelligence Co-ordinating Agency, BAKIN, were obviously foreign agents. Soekarno had exploded when he had first read the list which, unbeknown to the President, had been provided by the Soviet KGB Station Chief in the USSR Embassy, through one of their contacts in BAKIN. There were at least a dozen American names contained in the damaging report. According to Soebandrio, one of his confidants in the intelligence community, having examined the report, informed him that many of the foreign names listed were known representatives of foreign intelligence services, the majority being from the CIA. The President warned Subuh to be more discriminating in the selection of his *bule* followers.

Minutes after this uncontrolled burst of anger, Soekarno had immediately regretted what happened. Such behaviour was atypical for a Javanese and this had caused him to lose face. Indonesians favoured discussion and consensus. The President was chastened by his own behaviour and, to mollify the situation, he had then taken Mohammed Subuh and hugged him warmly.

Soebandrio had remained in the adjacent room until Subuh had left. Having heard the President's harsh attack just minutes before, he was reluctant to show his face just in case Soekarno was having one of his temper tantrum days. The Palace staff had observed recently that such incidents were occurring more and more frequently, and they realised that the Crush Malaysia war effort was mainly responsible for their leader's volatile outbursts. Soekarno felt that he had been betrayed by the Military. He had been embarrassed by their failures and refused to accept that the Indonesian soldiers could not defeat the Malays in the jungles of Borneo. All he had heard for the past months had been lame excuses as to why the elite of his forces had been unsuccessful in their campaign to take Sabah or Sarawak, on the northern side of Indonesian Kalimantan. Troop losses had been astonishingly high. Morale had deteriorated severely amongst his forces, and rumblings of dissatisfaction could be heard along the corridors of the Department of Defence.

Soekarno realised that his position would be seriously weakened should his Crush Malaysia effort fail. He blamed the British for he knew that they were supporting the Malaysian resistance throughout the newly formed Federation.

'*Sialan*,' he muttered, believing the Tengku had betrayed him. Soekarno was convinced that the Malaysian Federation was an attempt by the British to encircle Indonesia, and he had no choice but to destroy their efforts. He would sit alone and listen to many of the foreign broadcasts. He despised the Voice of America and British BBC for their attacks. They accused him of being erratic, confused, and a threat to world peace. As these broadcasts increased, so too did his own radio sessions with Radio Republik Indonesia. Whenever they called him a tyrant he would respond by accusing the West of neo-colonial and imperialist motives. Soekarno understood that he must assert his own and Indonesia's claim to regional leadership. The Asian political sphere had changed dramatically over the past fifteen years.

Soekarno understood that British Empire influence over its former colonial states had waned considerably . The concept of the Malaysian Federation was, he believed, an attempt to re-establish the European presence and prevent Indonesia from expanding its own sphere of influence regionally. He desperately needed to succeed with his policy of Confrontation, as domestic issues were overwhelmingly in need of such a distraction. The President was convinced that *Konfrontasi* provided the solution to all of his major problems.

Soebandrio entered the large room where Soekarno had just finished his meeting with Subuh. He tried to determine whether the time was appropriate for him to raise the issue of replacing some of the anti-Communist Military commanders. He had planned to use their recent losses as an excuse to have these senior officers posted to less influential positions. The *Partai Komunis Indonesia* had increased its power base considerably and now needed to develop a Fifth Power to sit alongside the Four Armed Forces.

The concept had been proposed initially by Aidit, the Party Chairman whose audacious plan to arm five million workers and ten million peasants would place the PKI in a position of strength which even the military could not oppose. The communists must have control of their own militia if they were to control the country. Soebandrio was concerned, as were his comrades in the Party, that their President may not survive long enough for them to achieve their goals. Already Soekarno's health had deteriorated. The long years he had served in prison had not helped and recently he had complained of a recurring kidney ailment. As much as they adored their leader, the Party leaders had agreed that preparations to establish a communist military force must be completed, before the country was faced with the possibility of losing its President. Soebandrio realised that, should the Great Leader of the Revolution pass away suddenly, there would be a scramble for power. A communist he might be, he thought, but before that, he was an Indonesian and understood clearly what would follow any sudden vacuum occurring in the country's leadership.

There had never been a change of government without bloodshed in his country, even as far back as the mighty kingdoms created a thousand years before. Soebandrio knew that whoever held the gun when the stage became empty would control the next leadership challenge.

For now, it was the Armed Forces under the control of many anti-Communist officers. Slowly, he and his party faithful had eroded their opposition's strengths and even orchestrated the successful placement of their own officers in command. But this had not been enough. The anti-Communist factions were strong amongst the Military.

Soebandrio had recently become aware that a group of senior ABRI officers had established their own secret alliance, a Council of Generals. He had been unsuccessful, however, in establishing the purpose of their covert activities.

He approached the President and waited. Soekarno turned, his arms crossed.

'The country is overrun with foreign agents. How did we let this happen?' The question, Soebandrio knew, was rhetorical. He waited. 'The Americans want to play on both sides of the fence. First, they offer training for our young officers and, once they have them over there and away from the influence of their motherland, they set about indoctrinating our men with their own form of imperialism.' He unfolded his arms and bent down, resting on a carved settee. 'Do you realise that the American Embassy has almost five times the staff of any other foreign legation in our country? And what do these representatives do with their time? They subvert our leadership and plot our overthrow!' he said angrily, punching the coffee table with his fist as his voice became raised.

He would never forgive the Americans for their past attempts to destroy Indonesian unity. The Eisenhower Administration had been incapable of understanding his neutralist position and non-aligned policies. He and the people of Indonesia had suffered at the hands of the Americans. Soekarno would always remember their attempts to support open rebellion in both Sumatra and Sulawesi, and the threat of direct invasion by their Seventh Fleet back in 1958. It was a time when dissident parties moved to create their own countries within the Republic. The Sumatrans demanded their own independence, confident that they had the support of the United States, while in Sulawesi, fighting had flared up again between government troops and local elements which were backed by the Americans out of the Philippines.

Before it was all over, his generals had committed most of the sixty-nine battalions enrolled in their three Javanese divisions to fighting on both fronts, Indonesians killing Indonesians, encouraged by the United States. Soekarno knew, at that time, as long as the Dulles brothers maintained their powerful positions as Secretary of State and Director of the CIA, his government would remain under threat. As he considered those earlier events, he shook his head sadly. Why couldn't the Americans have understood that non-alignment did not translate into anti-American activities? He had expected more from the West. Instead, they joined forces to destroy him and his country. The final straw came when the might of the American Navy was used to intimidate his people. It was an obvious ploy to provoke a reaction from his poorly-equipped country. The American Seventh Fleet had established Task Force 75 which was then ordered to Singapore. The Task Force was comprised of the heavy cruiser USS *Bremerton*, the destroyers USS *Eversole* and *Shelton*, and the attack aircraft carrier, USS *Ticonderoga* which carried two battalions of marines.

As the American Fleet assembled in Singapore, he remembered the tactics they used in their attempts to further provoke an Indonesian reaction. President Soekarno knew that rumours had been concocted by the United States Ambassador who even had the audacity to request confirmation that he intended sending AURI's planes in to bomb the Caltex oil fields in Sumatra! He was enraged when foreign radio reported US Navy officers in Singapore publicly stating that they would move into Indonesian waters and evacuate Americans from the trouble spots in Sumatra. It was an obvious attempt to justify an American invasion.

It was then he saw Nasution at his best. In a lightning preemptive strike, General Nasution caught the Americans off-guard. The Army Chief moved five battalions of marines and RPKAD paratroopers by air to eastern Central Sumatra. He had dropped two companies of the paratroopers directly into Pekanbaru Airfield where they discovered that the Americans had overflown just hours before, dropping weapons and supplies in anticipation of their own invasion. Nasution's men laughed with excitement when they identified the modern machine and anti-aircraft guns complete with ammunition lying there, waiting for them. Immediately the tide had turned, and Nasution had thwarted the United States' attempt to divide Indonesia into separate states.

Soekarno remembered with bitterness just how many thousands of Indonesian lives were lost due to the American tactics of covert support for the rebels, and open intimidation against his legitimate government. He turned towards Soebandrio and suddenly smiled.

'*Perhaps the Americans are going to inundate us with their own people until there are more of them than us,*' he joked, but his mind was troubled.

Soebandrio saw an opportunity immediately. '*Why don't we consider improving our reporting? Perhaps Bapak should consider replacing the djenderal with someone more sympathetic to the Palace. It is impossible to believe that our own Intelligence Agency has not placed these foreign elements under surveillance. And, even if that is their position, it is unacceptable. It is well known that the BAKIN leadership is anti almost everything Bapak has proposed over the past three years. Perhaps they are a part of this Council that is rumoured to have been formed by senior echelon army officers.'*

'I already know all about that!' the President snapped. *'It's Nasution again. He won't be satisfied until he becomes President. What else must I do to that damn Sumatran? Sialan,'* he growled, rising again to his feet. *'I should have locked the bangsat up when I had the opportunity. Now it is impossible.'*

Soebandrio changed tack. Soekarno had not responded to his earlier suggestion and, given the President's volatile mood, the Foreign Minister resisted promoting his own solutions. He knew that the President's wild mood swings could permanently ruin one's career. He was confident that the Intelligence Agency would be run, eventually, by a PKI loyalist.

'Why doesn't Bapak consider sending Nasution away, perhaps as Ambassador to one of the South American states?' The President re-crossed his arms and snorted at the suggestion.

'If only that were possible. Nasution has no wish whatsoever to leave. I have already had these suggestions made and he refused.'

'Do you suspect that he is really considering an Army take-over, a coup?'

'No, not again. He could not muster the support to effect such a move. Also, the Tjakrabirawa guard would not let him within sight of me without first alerting the Garrison Commander.' Soekarno suddenly looked tired. He returned to the ornately carved teak settee and lowered himself carefully. Soebandrio observed the stiffness with which the President moved. Soekarno's face was blotchy and puffed. Soebandrio noticed how thin his leader's hair had become in recent weeks. The Foreign Minister wondered if this is why the Bapak was never seen in public without his *pitji*, the black cap he wore everywhere. The President was tired. Soebandrio agreed with his own Party's Internal Committee conclusions. Soekarno could die at any time.

'Bapak,' he said softly, *'you look tired. Why don't you rest for a few days?'*

Soekarno stretched himself upright then leaned forward, placing both hands on his knees for support. *'I am leaving for Bogor tonight. I have decided to spend some days there.'*

'Bapak, may I bring Low Jooi Keng?' he asked. The Chinese doctor had already treated the President when earlier illnesses had occurred. She was considered to be one of the finest Chinese doctors in Kota. Soekarno merely nodded. He still suffered from the occasional lower back pain.

Soebandrio decided not to pursue their discussions about Nasution. He excused himself and went immediately to arrange for the doctor to be present when the Bapak arrived at the Bogor Summer Palace. He would have to hurry, he knew, as the President would most likely already be there within the hour.

* * * * * *

Major-Djenderal Soeharto stood smiling at his sixth child. He had agreed that she be called *Siti Endang*. The doctor had quietly told the general that this would be the last child. He was not unhappy with this. His wife was not a young woman any more and *Tuhan* had already given them so much blessing. Now they had three boys and an equal number of girls. He believed that this was more than mere coincidence. The religious leader Subuh also enjoyed an identical number of children! The Javanese father slowly shook his head in acknowledgement of what the older man had said. He would always be very grateful to this spiritual leader, for his prayers and, now, for his advice. In a sense he felt there was some unexplainable mystical bond between them. It was if they were brothers living in each other's shadows.

He touched his newborn softly with his right hand then left. He had matters to attend to, serious matters. He would confront Yani immediately to discover why he had not been invited to join the so-called *Council of Generals*.

* * * * * *

Lembah Njiur

The meeting was held in secret. As the evening prayers of Mahgrib had been attended to and the sky darkened in the absence of a moon, the vehicles arrived, one by one. Guards, inconspicuously dressed, manned the perimeter. Although their corps identification had been removed, the surrounding villages knew that these soldiers were members of the army's finest. They had seen them here before.

Yani was the first to arrive at Djenderal Nasution's mountain villa. The lieutenant general sat low in the back seat as his unmarked sedan passed through the hillside *kampung*. Several children were dragged unceremoniously back by a concerned mother as they had moved to see who could possibly be passing through their village at that time of the night. Thick clumps of bamboo and native grasses lined the dirt road, scratching at whatever vehicles struggled past as they bumped their way through the three kilometres of heavy rain forest. Large sections of the dangerous track had collapsed into the steep ravine causing further delays, as the military vehicles moved cautiously around the winding route.

Another hour passed before the others had all arrived. Nasution nodded to the group as he entered the villa's main lounge and waited for his *djongos* to finish serving coffee and leave the room before addressing his officers. Nasution had spent almost the entire year formulating his plan which would require the absolute support of the men who were present. As he looked around the group of Indonesia's most senior Army officers, whom he believed were his trusted supporters, Nasution experienced a sense of sadness that there were not more who could have been invited to join his Council. He smiled at Yani and then at the others before welcoming them to the meeting. He was not overly concerned with the security arrangements surrounding his villa. The men who stood guard outside would kill any intruder. Even the drivers had all been selected from this elite group of loyal soldiers.

As he looked at the men present, he wondered if any had compromised their relationship by telling others the true nature of these meetings. Nasution knew just how difficult it could be to maintain secrecy. He was conscious that several of these officers had more than their share of domestic problems and it would not be inconceivable that one of their members could unwittingly disclose his whereabouts to a wife or girlfriend. Nasution was aware that at least two of their number had difficulties maintaining their quota of wives, as well as small town-houses in Tebet, where they frequently rendezvoused with their young *tjewek*. Sometimes he wished his officers had been more monogamous in their relationships, setting a higher standard for the others but he knew that, as long as their laws and culture provided that men could take up to four wives, then it would be an impossible task to change their attitudes.

The evening air was considerably cooler than the men were accustomed to in the capital. They had all lighted their clove cigarettes, the pungent smell heavy in the sealed room. Nasution signalled with another gesture that they should come to order.

'*Gentlemen*', he commenced, crossing his legs and leaning back into the leather chair. '*We have much to discuss tonight. I trust you have all made arrangements?*' The generals understood. None had informed their families or others as to where they would be that evening, or when they would return. As military men such situations were rarely a problem. Those around them were accustomed to the sudden disappearance of the senior officers and accepted their absence without question. These men were all painfully aware of the consequences should there be a breach in their security. There was no doubt in their minds that they would be arrested for treason and, most probably, not even be given the benefit of a *Mahmilub*, or Court Martial. They knew that should their activities be discovered, most likely they would just disappear or suffer a tragic accident. It was an occupational hazard, serving in a Military infested with communist cadres and informants. They all murmured in response to their Commander's question.

'*We should not underestimate Bung Karno and his communist friends. They are far from being stupid. As we progress with our plans, it will become even more important to our survival that you continue to be diligent, and never discuss our association with others unless we are all in agreement. We must be extremely selective in our recruitment of fellow officers and their men. The PKI has penetrated every division in our Army and even, I am sad to say, my own offices. AURI, our Airforce, can no longer be counted on for any support. This is another reason why we must agree to restrict our Council only to Army officers. The Navy is borderline and, as for the Police, ...*' he raised his hands in a gesture of hopelessness.

'*It would seem that we could expect support from the majority of our men. How will we contain the Airforce when the time comes?*'

The question was raised by Major General Harjono, Third Deputy to the Minister and Chief of Army Staff. He was considered to be one of the brightest in the upper echelons of the Army.

'It would be imperative that we secure Halim Perdanakusumah Air Force Base and Bogor simultaneously. We wouldn't want them airborne with those damn helicopters.' The voice belonged to Major General Parman who was well known for his outspoken views regarding the President's confusing leadership. The others nodded in agreement. The Russian Hound helicopters were based just outside Bogor and could easily move into the Capital within minutes, when needed. They were well-armed and could carry more than a dozen crack troops.

'I would be more concerned with what would happen to the AURI units in Madiun and Djuanda,' Major General Soeprapto said. *'It would be impossible to maintain control over both of those fields without the support of the Diponegoro Divisional Heads. Madiun has at least five of their TU-16s fully serviceable and we could not afford to have any of their communist pilots tearing off with the bombers. Should they have support from the Surabaja Fleet Air Arm in Djuanda Field then, gentlemen, we would most likely lose East Djawa to the communist forces.'*

'Our Brawidjaja units should be positioned in close proximity to both fields to ensure that we don't lose control of those AURI squadrons. I have seen what the IL-28s can do and would not want to have those aircraft in the hands of Aidit and his crowd. It would be difficult, I agree, but I don't see any alternative but to arrange to have enough of our own men close to those bases when we are ready to move.'

The officers discussed their problems and strategy well into the night. From time to time, Nasution permitted his *djongos* the opportunity to enter and refill the empty glasses of coffee and remove the overflowing ashtrays. As the men became weary and it was obvious to all that, although they had come a long way in their discussions during the course of that evening, there was still much to consider and plan.

One thing was certain. Without exception, all present had agreed that the Communist Party had to be eradicated before they gained further control of the country. They would effect a military coup d'etat. They would save the Republik Indonesia from the overwhelming tide of communism which had swept through their country, poisoning their culture. Yes, they had agreed, they would act to remove the communists and the *dalangs* behind the scene. Each man had given his solemn oath to the others that they would work towards this aim and the elimination of Dr. Soebandrio, Chairman Aidit and their chief sponsor, President for Life, Great Leader of the Revolution, Bung Karno.

* * * * * *

Canberra, Australia

When he had first been invited to the Soviet Embassy in Canberra, Harry had thought at the time just how ridiculous it would have appeared to anyone who knew of his sensitive post as Head of Australia's Secret Service, had they observed his entering the obscure building. As a matter of protocol, Harry always complied with the reporting requirements of his own Department and logged his visits with the ASIS Deputy. In so doing, he skilfully established these occasional visits as a necessary activity within the framework of his maintaining conduits with all foreign intelligence representatives in the country. The courtesy calls were never considered sinister by station watchers and other intelligence observers. To the contrary, whenever Harry made arrangements to visit the Russians, he was always driven in one of Her Majesty's Commonwealth cars. The Security Chief would merely instruct his secretary in Melbourne to make whatever arrangements were necessary, and an official car and driver would meet him at the Canberra Airport and remain at his disposal until he departed.

Amongst Canberra diplomatic circles, Harold Bradshaw was relatively unknown. His counterpart, and successor to his position, was quite a different story. The domestic agency, ASIO, was well-known and its Director often invited to formal functions throughout the foreign community which maintained a presence in the Australian capital. As Harry had previously been Deputy Director of this agency, a substantial number of Canberra observers also maintained a watching brief on the man as his former position continued to attract considerable interest.

After some months had passed, and Harry's name had all but disappeared from the Public Service Lists, most accepted that he had been shunted sideways into some obscure position of little significance within the Department of Defence. Even Susan resigned herself to her husband's move out of the social limelight, electing to maintain her own circle of friends.

Mostly, Susan Bradshaw mingled with the Broomes, through whom she met Muriel Stephenson, an old acquaintance of Alfred's. Harry seemed pleased with this particular relationship although Susan never did examine his reasons. She assumed that this was because both her husband and Alfred worked together in the Defence Department in something she had overheard them refer to as Central Plans.

Intrigue never really held the same fascination for Harry as it so obviously did for the current generation of operatives he had witnessed passing through the Head Office. He believed that many of the men and women who had graduated from the demanding courses to be selected as field agents suffered from what he'd once described as the flick syndrome. The experienced Director had seen looks of disbelief on many of the new graduates' faces when they discovered that only a small minority of their number would actually venture out into the field as agents. It was obvious from extensive psychological testing over the years that many of the applicants were initially attracted into the Service in search of excitement. Some resigned, disheartened when they discovered that the often tedious tasks they would be obliged to endure would often be the limit to whatever excitement they might experience during their careers. Very few eventually qualified to be selected as field agents. Due to the extreme secrecy which surrounded the very existence of the covert organisation, recruitment had become increasingly selective and demanding. A growing number of personnel had been exposed to the existence of ASIS. The Director knew that, in time, this would be their weakness. It was therefore imperative that security clearances were staged in conjunction with staff recruitment, training, and indoctrination, so as to avoid full exposure to candidates who were unlikely to proceed past a specific point within the administration or operational aspects of the Service. Harry felt uneasy even with the limited number who had achieved the highest level of clearance. There were less than seventy, he knew, as he could recall every name on the list buried in the Attorney-General's Department.

As the black Government limousine pulled into the driveway,

Harry instructed the driver to wait in the vehicle. It was good practice not to permit drivers to talk, especially to members of foreign legations such as this. The Director alighted and walked briskly up the dozen or so steps before being escorted directly through the foyer and up the staircase to the second floor. Harry observed that nothing had changed as he climbed the carpeted steps. It was always the same, he thought, right down to the silent escort leading the way while another followed behind. Both men looked like they could strangle gorillas with their bare hands. What was it, he thought, that made all of these people smell the same? It was probably some sort of Russian genetic deficiency. He shook his head and squeezed his nostrils together as he continued to climb the stairs. At the top of the stairway they turned down the right corridor where Harry was directed into a small room and left alone for some minutes. The escorts had closed the door behind him after he entered, but Harry could still smell their presence. He was certain that they would be waiting just outside the room if needed.

Harry looked around the familiar surroundings. He had attended meetings here before. The decor's lack of colour and the portrait of Khruschev's unpleasant features contributed to the cloud of depression which threatened to envelop him as he sat uncomfortably in the austere surroundings. He bit on a fingernail, a habit he had not suffered since early childhood.

'Welcome Comrade,' the voice boomed, startling the Director who had not expected the KGB officer to enter as silently as he had. The man's frame filled the doorway as he entered, his movements slow and almost stiff. Harry rose quickly.

'Thank you, colonel,' Harry replied, preparing himself for the vice-like grip which somehow, always left him feeling inadequate.

The Russians were in the habit of playing a little joke on their Western counterparts. The most senior KGB officer in their overseas missions always filled the post designated as Cultural Attaché. Often, it seemed, these men would play role reversals with the other staff, just to keep the host intelligence services on their toes. Harry had read a recent report in which Konstantinov had been observed driving around the city with his allocated driver enjoying the ride from the rear seat. Harry did not enjoy these childish pretences. He believed this displayed a serious character flaw and wondered what other games the KGB colonel might enjoy when others were not looking.

'We will start, then,' Konstantinov said, almost impatiently. 'We have something of interest to you, Comrade.' Harry wished the colonel would desist from referring to him as if they were ideological partners.

'I'm all ears,' Harry responded dryly. He hoped that the Russian did not want to play word games as he had in the past.

'You will remember our recent discussions with respect to Indonesia?'

'Yes, colonel. You went to great lengths, if my memory serves me correctly, to explain how disappointed Mr. Khruschev has been in relation to the Indonesian's refusal to permit the Soviet Fleet anchorage in their ports.' He hesitated. 'Has there been some change to this?' Harry was surprised. There had been nothing from his own agents to this effect.

'There may be,' the colonel replied, 'but only if we are able to push them a little.' The ASIS Director looked quizzically at the KGB officer and waited. 'We are in possession of a most interesting document, Comrade Director,' Konstantinov continued. 'Moscow has permitted me to divulge some of its contents as you will need to know this information before conducting some business for us in Indonesia.' Harry's heart rate increased slightly. He did not like the direction this conversation was heading in, not at all.

'Let me remind you of our position, Comrade Director.' Harry wondered why Konstantinov insisted on calling him 'Director'. The Soviets had no knowledge of the existence of ASIS and, as he had informed them of his move from the senior position, hoping to discourage too much further interest in his affairs, he was curious as to why the Russian continued to address him in this way. Harry tried to recall what their reaction had been when he first advised them of his apparent demotion, and he remembered that there had been relatively little curiosity. He assumed that they believed he was still involved in senior intelligence matters and accepted the apparent ruse in the normal course of intelligence business. Harry listened intently as the colonel continued.

'The Russian people have been betrayed by the Indonesians. When they pleaded for our support, we unhesitatingly gave it. When they begged for our aid, we provided whatever they needed. When their own President requested that the USSR provide military equipment, we delivered our most sophisticated weapons. And what do the Indonesians give us in return?' he asked, his voice rising angrily, 'I will tell you Comrade Director, they give us nothing. Nothing!' he added, banging the desk with his huge fist for emphasis. 'But now we have the opportunity to change all of that! Their President smiles behind his hand at us but now we will show him that we Russians still exert considerable influence in his country. What do you know about the Indonesian Army's Diponegoro Division?' he asked, unexpectedly.

Harry was momentarily caught off guard, and hesitated. 'It doesn't matter,' the colonel interrupted before Harry could respond. 'All you will need to know is here, in this file.' The Russian tapped the thick document slowly with his stubby index finger. 'I want that you should read this file,' he said, picking the bundle up with both hands and passing it to Harry.

'What! Now?' he asked incredulously, staring at the bulky package. 'It would take me all week!' he exclaimed, shaking his head.

'No, Comrade, you may read this later. We give you our permission to take this very valuable document away to read, then return to us.' The KGB colonel stared stonily, Harry shifted uneasily in his seat. He was surprised that they would even consider permitting such information out of their sight, let alone out of the building.

'When am I to return this file?'

'Three days, Comrade, three days only. After that,' he smiled and snorted at his own joke, 'as the Americans say, we will send in the cavalry,' with which, he leaned forward and slapped Harry's leg painfully. 'Now I stop joking and you will listen.' Konstantinov immediately became serious once again. 'In these documents you will see that we have edited much of what was originally contained. This was done, obviously, to protect our source.' The colonel looked over at Harry as he spoke to ensure that he had the man's undivided attention.

'What is the country of origin?' Harry asked, not expecting that the Russian would reveal such information.

'The United States,' he said clearly, his face showing the slightest indication of a smile. The KGB had obviously scored big, Harry thought. He straightened his back and waited for more. 'We have successfully penetrated their Pentagon at the highest level,' he announced, waiting for Harry's reaction. There was none.

The Australian Intelligence Chief resisted smiling. If anyone had been penetrated, it would have been the Soviets, he scoffed silently. Even if they had successfully compromised some cipher clerk of a junior administrator, they would always be vulnerable to the possibility that they had been played by the clever men at Langley. Junior officials were often deliberately placed within reach of Soviet agents with the intent to confuse or lay bait for bigger fish.

Harry was disappointed with what he had just heard. He was surprised that such a senior player had been sucked into what would inevitably be a typical CIA operation. Konstantinov sensed the reaction and moved his head forward slightly, his upper lip curled as he spoke.

'No, Comrade, do not assume that we Russians are all stupid!' he almost hissed. 'We have a copy of one of their field agent's reports. The information we have was not sourced in the usual manner. We now have a most reliable source ensconced within the American Department of Defence — specifically, at the Pentagon itself.'

Harry showed surprise. It was not like Konstantinov to disclose so much unless their source had already been repatriated — or killed! His interest rose as he opened the file and identified markings and other verification with which he was most familiar. CIA Intelligence exchange continued between the Western Alliance and, on more than one occasion, Harry had sighted identical markings and references on documents provided by his counterpart in the United States. He read on, turning the page as he scrutinised the information and, as his excitement grew, he flipped through the remaining pages to see if there was some way he could authenticate the data. He knew that this would be practically impossible. He looked up at the colonel almost in disbelief. The Attaché had watched Harry searching through the bundle impatiently and now sat with a thin smile on his lips.

'This is incredible!' Harry said, knowing that what he held in his hands was most probably an excellent example of the finest intelligence gathering he had seen for some time.

'We will talk more. First, we will take a vodka.' Harry was about to refuse. He rarely drank before evening but remained silent as he realised that the colonel wished to celebrate. He didn't hear the buzzer but knew that there must have been one somewhere within the Attaché's reach for suddenly, taking Harry by surprise, the door snapped open and the colonel barked an order in Russian to one of his minders. The man returned immediately with a full bottle and two glasses. The colonel dismissed the huge shape, opened the vodka and filled both glasses almost to the brim.

He handed one to Harry. 'Russia,' was all he said before downing the entire contents. Harry followed, wishing he was elsewhere. The colonel refilled the glasses. The Australian knew it would be impossible to refuse. 'To the Party,' the Russian offered, once again emptying his glass. Again, Harry complied. Konstantinov looked pleased with himself as he filled the two glasses, this time, only to half. Harry sighed and accepted the measure one more time. He waited for the Russian to offer the toast. Konstantinov smiled and held the half measure up and clinked glasses with his co-conspirator. 'To the Diponegoro Regiment,' he said, drinking the vodka quickly before banging the glass on the desk. Harry followed, hoping as his brain commenced its downhill slide that this would be the final toast.

'Comrade Director,' the colonel started, 'there is going to be a coup d'etat in Indonesia!' Harry looked incredulously at the Soviet colonel.

'A coup?' he asked, sure that he had misheard. 'In Indonesia?'

'Yes, a coup!' the colonel continued, seemingly enjoying himself with the revelation. 'And we are to ensure that it is successful, Comrade Harry!' he added, the vodka taking effect. A cold chill passed down the ASIS Chief's spine. He heard the statement and knew that he wouldn't enjoy what was to follow. 'You, my Aussie friend, are going to help Mother Russia recover some of the ground we have lost. Okay?'

'What do you have on your mind, colonel?' he asked cautiously. The effects of the vodka slurring his words. He silently admonished himself for permitting the Russian to manipulate him as he had. 'How can I help the USSR with its problem?'

'You, Comrade Harry,' he replied, leaning forward as he moved his weight around to a more comfortable position, 'will assist the KGB by supporting the elements in the Indonesian Army who plan to take control of their Government!'

'The Diponegoro Command?' he asked sceptically, 'you really

believe that the Diponegoro Command has the capacity to effect such an incredible task? It sounds like foolishness!' Harry snapped, immediately wishing he had been more selective in his word choice.

'You will read this report,' the colonel insisted, once again prodding the thick document with his finger. 'You will understand more when you have completely examined the information there. The Americans have already placed one man inside. Do you think that they would bother if there was not substance behind the initial reports. Look for yourself. Their own agent's reports are included.'

Harry was stunned. He flicked through the file but was unable to locate the specific document to which the colonel referred. Impatient, the Russian snapped the file out of his hands and rummaged through the pile of data until locating what he needed. He turned the bundle around for Harry to read. 'There!' he barked, cheeks reddened from the alcohol.

It was all there. Harry shook his head in amazement. It just seemed incredible that the information even contained the agent's name. The report described a number of meetings that had taken place, where they were held and who contributed to the secret assembly of officers intent on revolution. He started to read on when the file was snatched back out of his hands.

'Later,' the colonel snapped. 'Now it is time for you to listen.'

The delayed effects of the vodka had thrown a blanket across Harry's mind. He no longer felt threatened by the Russian; after all, he remembered, they were in his country, not some back street off Lenin Square. Then he remembered that it was imperative he maintain his composure. After all, he was still on foreign soil, so to speak.

'Mother Russia has exposed its soul to these backward people. Our investment cannot just be counted in terms of currency, even though the USSR has given the Indonesians more than two billion American dollars in aid, military hardware and credits. There is a great deal more at stake here. Comrade, listen!' he commanded, moving to the edge of his seat, dangerously close to tipping the balance with his huge frame. It was as if the effects of the three oversized vodkas had already dissipated. 'The Indonesians are no different to the other satellites which embarked on a path of Communism as a means of satisfying the masses. The Chinese, Koreans, Laotions, Vietnamese and even the Malays have played with our great ideology, corrupting its very essence to favour their own interpretation and domestic needs. Already we have seen Chairman Mao Tse Tung lead six hundred million peasants away from Moscow's influence. Ho Chi Minh has sided with his great enemy and now, having sucked our country dry and unable to repay our great gifts, the Indonesians follow some poorly-conceived axis which they believe will deliver the whole of Asia into their revisionist hands.'

Harry struggled to concentrate but did so, knowing that what the colonel said was essential to the document he now held tightly in both hands.

'This Soekarno believes that he can now distance his country from Russia while maintaining some ridiculous concept of what he calls ...' he hesitated, searching for the correct word. 'NASAKOM. Yes. That's what the fool calls it, NASAKOM! This man has taken Communism and twisted its very heart, preaching his revisionist version to accommodate all that contradicts the true meaning of Communism. The people are obviously confused. How could they accept this man's corrupt teachings? That he endeavours to create a new ideology by throwing Nationalism, Religion and Communism into one melting pot only proves that the man is not a true thinker!' Konstantinov paused for a moment. Harry grimaced as the colonel looked at the half-empty bottle. Moments passed before the KGB officer continued, as if he had rehearsed this dialogue well before.

'This man, Soekarno, he is not good for Russia.' Again the colonel paused. 'He has permitted the Indonesian Communist Party to grow, and it is now the third largest in this world. You might ask, Comrade Harry, is this not a good result for World Communism? We would answer you, no! The Indonesian communist is not like a true communist. He thinks he can pray to his gods when in need and play with communism only when it suits. Their President has taught them this. Now, it seems, he may just be successful in developing this very dangerous axis between the Asian communist leaders. Soekarno is close to developing a very powerful alliance which, if he is successful, would run from Indonesia, through Malaysia, into Ho Chi Minh's North Vietnam, Laos and even Cambodia, leading up to the welcome arms of Chairman Mao.'

'Why would this be detrimental to Russia?' Harry felt obliged to ask. He was confused by Konstantinov's presentation.

'The Asian communist deals in revisionist Marxist theory. That is what is dangerous to world communism. Look at Castro, he is a real communist, not like these pretenders who merely play with the words in order to create even more power for themselves. No! Soekarno and his friends are not real communists. They have created a pseudo-communist ideology to accommodate the uneducated peasants who follow their leadership blindly. How can they be communist and still embrace their gods? How does this Soekarno believe it possible to follow pure communist doctrine when immersed in religious dogma, nationalism and whatever else he feels necessary to feed to his followers?' Konstantinov paused. 'They destroyed their only true communists during the Madiun Rebellion.'

'Then why do the Soviets continue to support the Asian communist leaders?' Harry managed to ask.

'Because we must keep our foot firmly inside the door.' The colonel reached out and held the vodka bottle, tipping it slightly to examine its contents. 'And,' he continued, 'because the Americans are moving to establish themselves firmly in Vietnam and Indonesia, we are prepared to overlook the idiosyncrasies of the Indonesian leadership for the time being. Also, we have not been paid and must protect our substantial investments. We have given those people our technology, our money, and our friendship. They have repaid us by refusing to acknowledge their debt and have placed even greater demands on the Soviet Union. Now they want steel mills to be completed in Tjilegon, dams to be constructed throughout the island of Java and many, many more infrastructure investments which run into billions of valuable foreign exchange.

'It is quite apparent to Moscow that, unless there is a clear change in leadership within the Indonesian Military, the Americans will be encouraged to displace our country's interests and Russia will no longer lead the world's communist effort. In the event that Soekarno's Military leadership continues to make overtures to the United States and such efforts remain unchecked, the Americans will develop a defensive strategy involving Vietnam and Indonesia which will result in an American presence in Soekarno's country even before he realises what has happened.'

'Most of the country's generals have already been recruited by the enemy. There is a very strong possibility that they could tear the leadership away from Soekarno. We would prefer that he remain in power, preferably only as a figurehead, even though our best interests are not being served. At least, the Americans would not be able to swoop in and take our rightful place in the country.'

'These officers from the Diponegoro Regiments. Why would you want to support them?' Harry asked, still confused.

'These soldiers have turned against their superiors who have grown fat from the funds sent by the Americans. They have sold their country to the CIA. There are many of these senior officers who sit in Djakarta, enjoying their large houses and cars, sniffing around after the Americans who inundate the capital as we speak. We must support these soldiers. They are our only choice. Without them Russia will have no future not just in Indonesia, but all of Asia. Should the Americans gain a foothold there, it will be impossible to maintain our relationship with these people. Already we have seen the British remove the Communist Party from Malaysia and even Singapore. Next, the Americans will endeavour to support the South Vietnamese until even Ho Chi Minh is forced back into the mountains of North Vietnam. No! Mother Russia has decreed that this will not happen.'

'What makes you believe that the Diponegoro Command, assuming what is in this report is reliable, will agree to any relationship with the Russians?'

'We have no idea whatsoever what their reaction would be.' He hesitated, and immediately Harry felt that Konstantinov was lying. He was hiding something. 'We have decided that there is no real risk. It would be just as favourable for us should they be successful in eliminating the pro-American lobby. That will give us the opportunity to reassess our approach and commitments in order to consolidate our presence in the country. The pro-American generals must go! We are fortunate that the opportunity has arisen,' he said, once again pointing at the file, 'and we may be able to accelerate their removal. You must go to Indonesia and talk to these men.'

Harry looked at the colonel. The alcohol's effects had caused a slight dull ache at the base of his neck and shoulders. He straightened his back and rolled his head gently, collecting his thoughts.

'And just what am I to say to these men when I meet them for the first time? Hello, there, I have a message from Boris, we want to support your impossible efforts to overthrow the government? For Chrissakes, colonel, who's responsible for this idiocy?' he snapped, not caring that he may have overstepped the mark. The Russian's suggestion that he go to Indonesia and even attempt such a poorly-conceived attempt to win over the isolated group was beyond comprehension. Konstantinov's eyes narrowed as he glared at the ASIS Chief.

'You are no fool, yet you talk like one,' he admonished. 'Take the file, read it then return when you have formulated your approach. You are not merely being asked to carry out this task, Comrade Director, it is not as if you have a choice.'

Harry resisted responding. His temples thumped adrenaline. He felt the rage but managed to contain his feelings. What he had been instructed to do was impossible! Konstantinov had placed him in a no-win situation. If he refused, he would be exposed. If he accepted, his relationship with the Indonesians could be at risk. What if they refused to deal with him again after he revealed the information he had obtained concerning their subversive activities? What if they exposed him to any one of the 'friendly' operatives already established within the target area? His life would be hanging by a thread. Harry rose to his feet, his heart filled with hate. He lifted the file and placed it almost casually, under his arm.

'Good!' The colonel exclaimed, as he also dragged himself upright. He reached into his coat pocket and extracted an envelope. 'Expenses,' he merely said, extending his arm.

Harry glared at the Russian. How he despised this man. He hated Konstantinov for what he was and for the power he exerted over him. But he despised himself even more. He took the envelope and buried it inside his coat. An hour later Harry Bradshaw returned to Melbourne.

* * * * * *

Melbourne

'We are acting alone on this one,' Harry advised the surprised Director of Military Intelligence. 'The Prime Minister has agreed.'

158

The statement required no response; the DMI understood that the PM's concurrence was sufficient.

'May I ask why, Harry?' General Thorpe asked, knowing that whatever the response from the cloak and dagger Chief, the answer would most likely be a deliberately distorted truth. He sometimes wondered why he even bothered.

'John,' Harry started, clasping his hands together while preparing his response. He needed the DMI's support which, he knew, would not be forthcoming unless he could convince the Army Director that what he was being asked to do would not compromise his own Department. Harry had not endeavoured to establish any real personal relationship with any of the three Military Intelligence Directors. He considered these men as necessary conduits for the dissemination of intelligence material but, as they were not directly involved in the direct collection of intelligence as were his field operatives, Harry encountered considerable difficulty when seeking their support for his clandestine operations. Australia's signals intelligence was virtually under the direct control of the man sitting across the highly polished mahogany table but it was not this area of support the ASIS Chief needed.

'The PM agrees that our activities should be more in support of our Commonwealth interests than, say, our American cousins. The US sees global interests only in terms of themselves against the Soviets. They really don't give a damn in respect to Australia's own position. Their world revolves around the US of A. The PM is quite adamant. We will do this one alone because, if we don't, our national interests will be damaged beyond repair. You know yourself, John, how bloody casual the Americans can be about Australia's interests. They have been beating their own drum ever since they pushed the Japs back from our shores.' Harry rubbed his face with one hand; he was tired. It was not obligatory that he explain to the DMI. He knew that it was just good politics to do so.

'The Americans want control over all of our Intelligence in the target area,' he lied, knowing that this would be sufficient for full DMI support. None of the agencies would stand for such a development. S.E. Asia was Australia's backyard and the Military would insist that they maintain some semblance of independence in the region.

'And you have convinced the PM that we could end up out in

the cold again?' The DMI's reference was to Vietnam. The Australian Forces had only been involved after the Americans required international support for their continuing presence in Indochina. The Australian Military had wanted to send their own advisers years before but the Americans had politely refused. Now, it appeared, the Yanks wanted control over Australia's intelligence gathering services in Indonesia. No, the DMI concluded, not while he had any influence in the matter.

'Exactly,' Harry lied again, while nodding his head.

'Well that's it then, as far as I'm concerned. You'll have your request, Harry.'

'Thanks, John. Knew we could count on your co-operation. I will inform the PM,' he added, both men rising to their feet and shaking hands. The DMI departed leaving Harry to sit and contemplate on his next course of action. He returned to his desk and commenced preparations for the next step in his complicated scheme. Now that he had secured the services of the Army's Military Attaché in Djakarta as an acceptable cover, he believed that what he planned was achievable.

Harry rose and went to his own safe and played with the double tumbler action until both combinations permitted the heavy handle to open, revealing the most secret papers he hoarded there. Selecting a thin brown file without any security markings to designate its sensitivity, Harry informed his secretary that he was not to be disturbed until lunch. Then he sat down and read the file once again, brooding over the damaging contents. It seemed as if only minutes had passed when his secretary, Madge, buzzed to advise him it was time for his luncheon appointment with his deputy, Anderson.

Harry returned the file and re-locked the safe. As he tested the handle to ensure that the contents were indeed securely hidden, Harry knew he would not have much time to implement his plan. He thought about those around him who would be essential to its successful realisation and sighed deeply. He hoped he could still rely on young Murray.

* * * * * *

FREEDOM (MERDEKA) SQUARE

Djakarta

The first riots occurred along Djalan Nusantara, across the canal from Pasar Baru where the majority of Djakarta's foreigners shopped. Several thousand students pushed and shoved their way along the street towards the Palace grounds, chanting as they held placards high above their heads.

'PKI, PKI,' the students sang, waving to their fellow citizens who merely moved away from the oncoming crowd of communist students from the University of Indonesia. There had been rallies all over the city, supported strongly by their Party. Chairman Aidit had encouraged the students to go to the streets and show the people just how large their numbers had grown. It was an attempt to intimidate, the populace knew, and reacted accordingly. As the large crowd dressed in white cotton uniforms and red bandannas moved toward the fringe of Pasar Baru, the Chinese shopkeepers immediately closed their premises and boarded the shop fronts to prevent pillaging. They had seen this all before and most were concerned with the growing frequency of such demonstrations.

As the young communists moved en masse along the main road chanting 'PKI, PKI' their voices could be heard across the other side of the city block, and as far as the radio station. They approached the high white-washed walls outside of which the Presidential Guards stood and watched, prepared to move should the students provoke a response. The crowd continued to move towards the main gate and the Guard Commander issued the order for the soldiers to cock their weapons. They knew that standing orders required that the first volley be fired over the demonstrators' heads but the contingent were all just as prepared to fire directly into the crowd should they attempt to enter the Palace grounds.

The communist students came slowly to a halt outside the President's offices and continued to chant, drowning out all other sounds as they called their Party's name. The soldiers stood tense, waiting for the inevitable rocks to be thrown. Minutes passed and the students moved closer to the gates, annoyed with the lack of response from within. As the students became bored with the inaction and their chanting lost rhythm, another sound could be heard faintly above the noisy mob. It was another large crowd of students, apparently moving towards the Palace gates as well, chanting loudly. The first group turned to greet their fellow students and immediately there were angry shouts as they discovered that these were not from their student union.

'*Abolish the Communist Party,*' the newcomers cried loudly, '*Down with Aidit!*' they challenged, moving towards the PKI supporters. As the large numbers of students approached, it became evident to those who watched from across the street that there would be serious trouble as the two rival factions clashed. The anti-Communist students moved forward into direct confrontation with the PKI demonstrators. Immediately, all hell broke loose as the opposing groups ran towards each other, brandishing their placards as weapons. The Palace Guards braced themselves for the inevitable. And then the rock throwing commenced.

Students reached down and picked up lumps of tar and rock which lay alongside the broken edges of the road, then hurled these with all their force at the opposing students. Within an incredibly brief period of time, the street was transformed by the savage riot. Students punched and kicked at each other brutally, boys and girls fell unseen, their agonising screams smothered by the tumultuous roar. Rocks and other missiles thrown without aim cracked heads indiscriminately, and as the injured fell they were in danger of being trampled to death.

It became impossible to distinguish between adversary and friend. The main body of rioters crushed and trampled students in the centre as it gathered momentum towards the Palace gates.

The officer of the guard shouted a command and instantly shots were fired into the air. For a brief moment there was a stunned silence, followed immediately by a roar as the students turned on the soldiers, pushing forward without fear. Incredibly, they seemed to amalgamate as one body and turned on the green-uniformed guards. As they surged towards the small contingent of guards, a hail of rocks sailed through the air, injuring several of the soldiers. Instantly, they retaliated. The second volley of shots ripped through the front line of students tearing through clothes and young bodies. Bullets penetrated deep into the astonished crowd and the air was choked with screams and gunfire. Panic-driven students fell over each other in a futile attempt to escape. But the soldiers did not stop firing, and scores of students fell with each volley. Suddenly the ear-piercing rapid fire ceased. The soldiers had run out of ammunition.

The more fortunate students stumbled in terror, away from the bloody killing ground, anxious to flee before the soldiers changed magazines and recommenced firing. Those who could ran without looking back, knowing that they were leaving friends behind, friends who still screamed in fear for their lives. Friends who would surely die when the soldiers opened fire once again. A loud shout shook those who remained and they tensed, waiting for the next barrage of bullets. Another shout, this time louder, and the soldiers obeyed the command. The officer stepped forward and positioned himself directly in front of his men and barked another order, removing the automatic from its holster to ensure compliance to his command.

The disgruntled guards paused, considering their positions; then turned and moved back inside the Palace grounds. Their Captain moved swiftly, re-locking the large iron gates as he issued more orders to the men. He then turned and viewed the scene before him. He attempted to count the bodies which lay spread across the wide road. There were several mounds he could see, where students had fallen to the ground together, dead as they hit the road. When the young officer counted thirty, he swallowed, with great difficulty, then continued the bloody task. It was difficult to know how many had died from being crushed in the panic to escape, but the Guard officer understood that protocol dictated his report should only apportion the most conservative number of dead to gun fire.

Later he would indicate in his report that two students had been accidentally shot as they had grabbed the guards' weapons while the rest had died as a direct result of the bloody clash between the opposing factions. The bodies had been quickly collected by an Army detail and disposed of without ceremony behind the city's notorious Senen Prison. Grieving families and friends would be told that many of the bodies had been so badly mutilated that identification had been impossible. They would never see their children again.

* * * * * *

Murray had moved quickly to investigate the demonstrations once word had arrived at the Embassy. This was one of his functions. Being fluent in *Bahasa Indonesia*, he was considered the only appropriate officer to send out whenever these disturbances occurred. Murray would take one of the Embassy Holdens and drive directly to wherever the students held their rallies. Often he would walk alongside their flank, talking to them and getting a feel of what the rank and file really thought they were achieving with their demonstrations. This provided Murray with the opportunity to photograph student leaders in action.

Although many of the faces he identified were those of friends he had made over the years, he soon discovered there were now many more he could not recognise, who had become prominent with the accelerated spread of communism throughout the Republic. Murray was disciplined and understood that his role was that of an observer. It was essential that he not become embroiled in any of the student activities. He was now a diplomatic officer and could not demonstrate allegiance to any of the participating factions. He was there only to collect information and then provide an assessment of the situation. The intelligence reports detailing his observations would be his sole responsibility.

Murray had instructed the driver to pull over near Djalan Veteran, from where he walked the remaining few hundred metres towards Djalan Nusantara. The driver was relieved that the *tuan* had not insisted on taking the vehicle any further.

'*Aduh,*' he had thought when ordered to take *Tuan* Murray down past Merdeka Square. The entire driver pool had heard the news about the latest demonstration and none wished to venture outside. Often their cars were stopped by the demonstrators then wrecked. It was a terrifying experience, Achmad knew. He had already been caught twice and was extremely nervous, knowing that he was to take the young *tuan* down to take a look at the excitement. Achmad just couldn't understand why this *tuan* always went out in search of trouble.

'*Achmad. You wait here for me, understand?*' he had instructed the agitated driver. '*Tentu sadja, tuan!*' he had responded. '*Of course I'll wait here,*' he thought to himself silently, '*only a fool would proceed any further.*'

Murray carried the small Minolta in his left hand and walked quickly along the small side street until reaching the corner of Djalan Nusantara. He stood for a few moments observing the military vehicles pouring past, heading west in the direction of the Palace gates. He assumed that the road would be closed off within minutes and so elected to cross the small bridge which led directly down through Pasar Baru. Once on the other side Murray turned to the left and followed the narrow lane bordering the *kali*, and running parallel with Djalan Nusantara which was then on the other side of the canal. He walked quickly, concerned that he had missed the demonstration. Minutes later, he was pleased that he had. As Murray neared the roadway opposite the Palace Guards, he could clearly see the aftermath of what had obviously been a serious clash. Even at that distance he could make out the bodies lying like large broken dolls, scattered across the road and, in some places, already stacked in piles awaiting collection.

He counted the dead as accurately as he could, his task made more difficult by the soldiers as they moved the bodies around, dragging some in one direction while dumping others together. Soon it was almost impossible to differentiate between bodies he had, and had not yet counted. Murray estimated there were approximately fifty to sixty dead. There did not appear to be any wounded. He assumed that they had either escaped or had been taken to hospital by the Military Police who appeared to be actively conducting the clean-up. Murray lifted his camera again and took several more shots before being startled by a soldier who came clearly into his lens view, holding his rifle to his shoulder and peering down the sights directly at Murray.

He froze instantly, perspiration suddenly covering his body as he waited for the crack of the rifle shot. Slowly he lowered the camera and turned away. He knew that the soldier would continue to watch until he moved far enough away to satisfy the man that his presence was not threatening. Although he knew that he needed to get the hell out of there as quickly as possible, Murray also knew that to run would be a major mistake, and would most likely provoke the soldier into taking a shot. He walked slowly, the trickle of sweat flowing down his spine, his body tense with the knowledge that he could be shot in the back at any moment. As he approached the rusty steel pedestrian bridge Murray permitted his head to turn slightly, just enough to provide a quick glance from the corner of his right eye. The soldier was still watching, his rifle resting in a less aggressive stance. Murray decided to leave the scene; his presence was obviously considered provocative to these soldiers who probably wouldn't understand his right to Diplomatic Immunity in the event that they should challenge him again. Most of these men were poorly educated and easily excited.

He elected to return to the car and report back to the Station Chief. A thought crossed his mind and he frowned. He had identified the PKI banners lying around and suddenly wondered if Yanti or any of her group had been involved. Murray sighed. He would drive over to the quarters where she boarded, once he had filed his report. He felt tired and leaned back to rest as they drove back through Tjut Mutiah into Menteng.

It was only when the vehicle entered the Embassy grounds ten minutes later that his hands began to shake. As he climbed out of the back seat, Achmad held the door open, permitting the *tuan* to lurch forward and away from the Holden just in time as he commenced heaving, the shock suddenly taking effect.

'*Tuan Murray,*' the driver called in surprise. It was quite uncommon for the foreigners to become ill in such a short journey, even from his driving. '*Can I help you, tuan?*' he asked sincerely.

Murray remained bent over for some minutes before recovering his composure. As he walked up the steps and into the lobby he realised just how lucky he had been to return unharmed. He went immediately into the inner sanctum and delivered his report directly to the new Station Chief. He did not mention his near fatal encounter and, as he lay awake that night reliving those few terrifying seconds, Murray questioned his own judgement as to why he had omitted this information, but decided that as they had never really established any real rapport, the other man might have just scoffed at his retreat.

Murray could not understand how Alan Davis had managed the promotion. Wells had been a capable and very experienced Station Chief. He was not confident that Davis, now that he had returned to Djakarta to fill the Chief's position, would be able to handle the pressures associated with the job. Unable to sleep, he read until the early hours of the morning when he decided to take his *mandi*, change and go back into the Embassy to catch up on outstanding reports.

As Murray's current position was described as Second Secretary Political, having moved up one level since his arrival, it was essential to his cover that he perform some of the more mundane tasks associated with the position he held. At the moment, he felt inundated with the tedious tasks related to the United Nations Family Planning Programme for which, much to his dismay, he had been delegated the responsibility of maintaining a watching brief for the Australian Government counterpart agencies. This, and similar functions, consumed a considerable portion of his time and he discovered that once backlogged, it was almost impossible to recover from the mountains of reading material which poured incessantly into his receiving tray.

Murray decided to take a *betjak* from his residence on Djalan Serang to the Embassy where he found all the security guards asleep. He just smiled and crept past them quietly, as the duty-driver swung into the driveway and dimmed his lights. He jumped out of the station-wagon, left the engine running and hurried towards Murray.

'Pagi, tuan,' he said, his face reflecting the long night shift he had worked. *'Tuan Murray, would you accept this cable please? It would save me having to drive out to Kebajoran to wake Tuan Evans and then bring him back to the Embassy.'*

Murray willingly accepted, just to help out. He knew what it was like to be the duty officer as the chore came around every two months and created havoc with one's social life. Communications were very poor. Apart from the covert radio installed in the rear of the Naval Attaché's office, there were no direct links to the international community, resulting in an inadequate system of cables and telexes sent on a scheduled basis from governments to their embassies in Indonesia. Even highly classified material was moved in this manner.

The Duty Driver would check the central post office on an hourly basis. Whenever such a communication was received, it was his responsibility to awaken the rostered officer and have him taken to the Embassy immediately to carry out the decoding. The officer would commence deciphering the message in the usual manner in the Central Registry where a number of machines had been installed for this complicated process. The first line of every message identified a name followed by a security classification which would indicate whether the officer may or may not proceed. The double encoding system ensured that the integrity of the signal's contents remain intact.

Murray strolled up the steps, unlocked the front doors, checked his mail box, then went through to his own section, unlocking then relocking doors as he proceeded. Most Embassy staff could enter their own sections at any time, as a series of combination locks provided accessibility only to those who were given the numerical sequences to the tumbler security system. A number of alarms had been installed throughout the old building — not that this would prevent a well-organised band of thieves from breaking through the front doors into the main lobby. Anyway, they would not find anything there. The sensitive sections were buried in the building's bowels, with the walls, floors and ceilings all recently constructed from reinforced concrete. All classified material was locked away in huge, room-size Chubb safes providing a formidable challenge to any who believed they could steal Australia's secrets.

Murray turned lights on as he ventured into his own section, leaving them to burn brightly as he settled down beside the boring unclassified material left to the side of his desk some weeks before. He opened the small envelope and spread the five-digit coded message in front, betting to himself that this was probably another of those 'urgent' messages for the Air Attaché's office merely advising that one of the RAAF aircraft overflying to Vietnam had changed pilots and felt the necessity to advise the Embassy in case, he assumed, the plane fell out of the sky and embarrassed everyone. He muttered to himself, observing the cable, knowing that he would have to go through to the Registry and hook up the machines.

He did this and, fifteen minutes later as the heading was deciphered, he discovered that the first line indicated the message was, coincidentally, addressed to him personally. This required that he return to his own section and insert the relevant tapes into another set of decipher equipment. He patiently threaded the two tapes and punched the start button. As the machines clacked away in unison, interpreting the five-digit code imprinted on the narrow tape in the form of puncture marks, Murray was surprised to see that the message bore the highest clearance and was addressed personally to him. He read the two-part message:

TOP SECRET

First code batch for Registry.
Pass to addressee only for final code.
This communication is for the addressee only:
Sec/Sec/Political. Pls pass urgently.

TOP SECRET
OYSTER - MO9
ADDRESSEE EYES ONLY.
ADDRESSEE: M.I. STEPHENSON
SENDER: DIRECTOR. ASIS
Date: 7th February, 1965

TEXT: YOU ARE TO PROCEED TO SINGAPORE FOR ONE-ON-ONE
DISCUSSIONS STOP MEET NEXT WEEK MAYFAIR HOTEL NOON
12TH STOP NATURE OF MEET MOST SENSITIVE STOP IN CONSE-
QUENCE YOU ARE NOT TO ENTER INTO ANY DIALOGUE WITH
OTHERS IN THE DEPARTMENT STOP WILL ADVISE YOUR SUPERI-
ORS YOU ARE ON PERSONAL LEAVE FOR TWO DAYS THOSE
DATES STOP RGDS STOP HB ENDS
TOP SECRET

Murray re-read the signal and then put the message through
the shredder. He was surprised at the contents but pleased that he
would be able to get out for a few days. He checked his watch and
when he discovered that it was already after six o'clock, he locked
up and went in search of the duty-driver. Murray decided to take
Yanti to breakfast and see what her involvement had been in relation to the ongoing PKI demonstrations that were tearing the city
apart. When he arrived at her lodgings Yanti was not there. The
old *babu* who cleaned and cooked for the students under her care
had just shaken her head when he asked to speak to her.

*'Yanti is not here. Neither are her friends. They have all gone away. I
don't know where they are. You come back tomorrow. Maybe Yanti will
return by then.'* The toothless grey-haired woman closed the door.
Murray heard the lock snap shut as he walked away.

* * * * * *

'*Mahree, you haven't been out to the Community Centre for such a long time!*' Ade admonished. Murray kept his arm around her shoulder as they sat together on his sofa. The residence in Djalan Serang was as grand as any of the other Embassy houses with the exception, of course, of the Ambassador's magnificent mansion on Djalan Teuku Umar. The home contained three bedrooms, all air-conditioned, as were the oversized lounge and dining rooms. Embassy houses were allotted according to rank and position. As a Second Secretary, he was expected to entertain regularly and was provided with a suitable expense account for this purpose. Mainly, whenever Murray did entertain, the majority of his guests were Indonesian, unlike many of his fellow officers in the Embassy who mostly only invited other Europeans to their homes. He could understand their problem filling a guest list which included Indonesian guests as, at that time, very few could comprehend English.

He tickled Ade with his other hand and she responded playfully. '*I don't have as much time as before, manis!*' he said, in response to her complaint about the infrequency of his visits to the SUBUD compound. And this was true, he thought. His days were becoming longer in terms of the number of hours he was putting into building his network while maintain old relationships as well.

'*But it seems you still have time for your Gerwani friends.*' Ade argued.

'*Look,*' he started, not wishing to get into another of these discussions. '*Yanti is my friend also, you know that. I thought we'd agreed not to do this any more? Let's leave it alone, okay?*' Murray knew without looking that by now Ade would be pouting. She always did. '*Okay?*' he asked again, tickling her once again. Ade's small but strong fingers found their way to the fleshy spot under his ribs and pinched his skin fiercely, just to let him know that she was not happy with the ongoing arrangement Murray maintained with Yanti and her friends.

Ade knew that Murray was sleeping with his communist friend but blocked that out of her mind. It was his right, she thought, reluctantly, even though she also spent the night in his bed at least once every week. Ade looked at Murray and decided that, rather than risk losing him altogether by insisting on his disassociation with Yanti and his other communist friends, she would just persevere until she realised that the *Gerwani* were not only dangerous, but also untrustworthy.

'When will you return from your trip?' she asked.

'I'm only going for a few days, manis. I will return from Singapore before the weekend.' Murray knew it was pointless in hiding his destination. These were secrets that were impossible to keep in such a closely-knit community as the Australian Embassy. Once he had booked his ticket, it seemed that everyone in the Chancery knew he was going to Singapore for a few days. Immediately, he was inundated with requests to purchase this and that for wives, as the shopping in Djakarta provided few of the luxury items so readily available in 'Singers' as they affectionately called the shoppers' paradise. Murray accepted the small orders, ranging from lipstick to nail polish, knowing that all Embassy officers given the same opportunity to spend a few days 'out of station' would do likewise.

'Don't forget my oleh-oleh!' Ade reminded him. It was customary to purchase a myriad of small gifts when one was away as these indicated to the recipients, upon return, that they had not been out of mind during the absence, however short this may have been.

'I'll buy you some perfume,' he teased.

'Okay,' Ade replied, surprising him. She left the couch and returned with fifty sen, half of one rupiah. Murray looked at the domino-sized note, worth no more than one cent Australian.

'That won't buy you much!' he laughed, accepting the crumpled note.

'No, Murray, that's not to buy the perfume. It's a token gesture only. It is our custom to always pay a little something for perfume, for we believe that such a gift will cause a break in friendship unless the one you give the perfume to pays something towards its cost.'

Murray smiled again. It seemed that he would never stop learning this country's customs. He squeezed her again, then rose and led her back into his bedroom where they remained through the rest of the afternoon. That evening Murray took the Garuda flight to Singapore and, upon arrival, went directly to the Mayfair Hotel. And Harry Bradshaw.

Chapter 10

Singapore

Murray sat comfortably in the floral-covered chair listening attentively to the Intelligence Director. His mood was solemn. Harry's revelations were, to say the least, startling.

'We have a mole, Murray. I'd never thought it possible but there it is. One of our own.'

'What makes you believe it's Davis?' he asked, still not convinced of the accusations.

'We can never be absolutely sure unless, of course, he stepped forward or confessed when confronted with the charge. It is most unlikely that any of these opportunities will arise. Rest assured, young Murray,' he said, almost paternally, 'we will cover your back at all times. If, in the event that it comes to light that Davis is not our man then, with the arrangements we have made, there would be negligible damage to the Service and, of course, Davis' career.'

'Why don't we just confront him then?' Murray asked, confused as hell. He still refused to accept that his current Station Chief was responsible for the leaks mentioned by the Director. Davis had returned to Head Office for a few short months before being selected to replace Keith Wells as Djakarta Station Chief. Although Murray disliked the man and believed him to be bigoted, these were not sufficient grounds to distrust him. He looked at Harold Bradshaw. The Director looked exhausted, the crows' feet lines now more obvious, spread like deep scars around the corner of his puffy eyes. His hair had thinned considerably since they had last met, just a few months before. Murray noticed the heavy stained fingers, evidence of the three packets of cigarettes the ASIS Chief consumed daily. He watched Harry light the smoke and draw heavily.

'What would you do in his place?' the Director asked. 'Would you just step forward and calmly place yourself in the care of Her Majesty's prisons for at least thirty years? Or would you deny any charges of impropriety, placing the onus on your accusers to produce evidence? Come on, Murray, don't you see just how bloody impossible the situation is?'

'So you intend leaving him in situ, knowing that he may be responsible for compromising the Service?' he asked disbelievingly. 'It sure as hell doesn't build confidence, Harry. That's my arse sitting over there in a sling with Davis!'

'Now you appreciate the importance of keeping him out of the information loop with what we have discussed. It is imperative that he not have access to this intelligence. Do I make myself very clear, Murray?'

'Sure,' he answered, not entirely happy with his predicament. The Intelligence Director had explained that he had already arranged through DMI in Melbourne for the Military Attaché to request Murray's services as interpreter to accompany the colonel on a brief tour through Java, visiting Indonesia's Military Commands. The request to visit had already received official HANKAM approval. The Australian colonel was not briefed on the reasons for Stephenson's accompanying him on the tour, merely that it would be so. The Embassy interpreter would be called away for the duration to create the necessary request for Murray's assistance. This would be sufficient to convince the Station Chief, Davis, that all was above board and not arouse his suspicions as to the real purpose of his Second Secretary's being seconded to the Military Attaché's office.

'Let's go over it again, Murray. I know I don't need to tell you just how damn important this is to us in Central Plans. Our necks are stretched way the hell out on this one. If we pull it off without complications, you could easily find yourself sitting in Davis' chair before the end of the year.' Murray's eyes widened. Now that was something he'd not expected to hear.

'Let's see,' he started, recalling the early morning brief. They had breakfast in Harry's room and commenced immediately after room service had responded to their request to clear the trays. 'Colonel Sulistio was trained in the States. It appears that he was recruited by the boys from Langley during his tour Stateside. He returned to his Division in Semarang and moved quickly into Diponegoro Command HQ. Since then, he has maintained a steady stream of intelligence flowing back to Langley. He claims,' Murray recited from memory, emphasising claims as information that had yet to be substantiated, 'that the middle ranking officers of Diponegoro have established their own unit within their Command to effect a military coup d'etat against the most senior generals in Djakarta. Sorry, Harry, I'm still having trouble with this. It just doesn't jell for me.' He paused, leaned down and rubbed his left foot which had fallen asleep. 'Why? The Diponegoro Command is one of the most highly respected of all the Indonesian Commands. Why would they insist on removing their own generals?'

'Murray, listen. I have already explained that their mood is indicative of what is happening through the Armed Forces. The field officers look to their generals in Djakarta and all they see is men whom they once admired, sitting back, permitting the Communist Party to make incredible inroads while they get fat on their backsides, enjoying life in the Capital, lining their pockets while their rank and file continue to experience incredible hardships. You know only too well what has happened to their 'Crush Malaysia' programme. I can confirm that they have lost literally thousands to our SAS boys operating in Malaysian Borneo. This so-called unofficial war has cost them more than just men and equipment. Their President's standing has deteriorated. There are strong rumblings throughout their defence corridors that Soekarno should go and, even though we strongly support such sentiment, only the Diponegoro officers have actually developed a workable plan to rid us all of their pro-communist President.' He stretched his legs across the bed and moved his toes to improve circulation. 'This group that call themselves the Council of Generals. Who do you think is behind it?' he asked.

'Seems little doubt that it's Nasution. My guess is that Yani would be involved, along with most of his supporters. Surprisingly, there's not much leaking out. Could be just another of Nasution's moves to protect the Army from further encroachment by Aidit and Soebandrio. Those two have hurt the Military's power base drastically over the past year. Wouldn't surprise me if the Council is just a club of senior officers looking for a forum to air their many grievances against Soekarno's NASAKOM. Not that the Army seem to be in a hurry to withdraw support for the Crush Malaysia effort. Most of these guys are getting fat off the proceeds generated by the conflict.'

'Exactly!' Harry interrupted. 'This is one of the prime factors behind the resentment expressed by the officers in Semarang. They want a change in their Military leadership and we intend supporting them. We must convince them that it would be in their interests to discontinue this ridiculous war effort of theirs. Surely they must realise just how futile their efforts have been against the Brits and our own boys? Christ, we've taken no prisoners during the Sarawak action and Soekarno is being told that these dead soldiers, reported as having disappeared, were purely deserters who have run into the jungle to hide! Surely the man couldn't be that naive?'

'Okay, Harry, so we approach the Diponegoro boys and offer our support. Why would they want anything to do with us?' he asked, rubbing his foot again as an ache developed from the uncomfortable position.

'The PM has agreed that we may offer some attractive incentives. Firstly, providing they take Soekarno out and put the reins back on the PKI, we would be receptive to guaranteeing our full support in the United Nations for their legitimate acquisition of West New Guinea.' Harry saw the look of surprise on the younger man's face. 'It is a foregone conclusion, Murray,' he said, displaying the open palms of both hands. 'The Indonesians will take it anyway. Any United Nations efforts to implement a referendum there would, in our opinion, be compromised by the Indonesians building a substantial non-indigenous population during the lead-up, moving tens of thousands of Javanese across to settle before any vote could be called. So we can't do much to prevent it and might as well take advantage of the situation.'

Harry reached for another cigarette, ignoring the half-finished stick still smouldering in the bedside ashtray. As he inhaled, the effort caused him to cough harshly. 'Secondly,' he continued, rubbing an itchy right eye with the back of his free hand, 'we'll guarantee them asylum if they screw it all up. This would be an unconditional offer.' Harry's voice reflected his fatigue. He had not had much rest during the past two nights. Particularly the evening before, in Bangkok. He aborted his customary appointment when he discovered he was being followed. It had shaken him badly.

'Seems reasonable. They may just take it.' Murray mused. An escape to Australia should the officers fail. He wondered how many would actually make it and decided that the offer had no real downside for the Australians as it would be unlikely that any of the conspirators would survive. They rarely did.

'You are to target the officers whose names are listed here,' Harry indicated, pointing to the file left on the round glass covered coffee table. It bore no markings to identify the volatile contents. 'Go with the Military Attaché, have a good time in Bandung and Surabaja. But when you hit Semarang, Murray, do what must be done. Identify those officers, spend time with them alone, if possible. You understand their language; they'll warm to you. Don't under any circumstances even consider broaching the subject we have discussed. You're to establish direct contact with these men and, upon your return to Djakarta once the tour is finished, contact them again and foster whatever communication there is between yourself and the men we have targeted here,' he instructed, pointing again at the manila folder.

'And then?' Murray asked, already guessing what the other man's response would be.

'Then, Murray, my man, you will arrange another meeting for yourself to visit Semarang independently, only this time I will accompany you.'

'Could take some time,' Murray suggested.

'Time,' Harry sighed, 'time, unfortunately, we don't have. I need to be able to return and meet with these officers in less than three weeks. Events could easily overtake us all, Murray, and that could be disastrous.' The Director sighed again. He had to have everything in place before the Americans became aware of what was happening.

'Three weeks!' he protested. The time-frame was impossibly short.

'Sorry, chum. That's all you get.'

'And you'll take care of Davis and the other arrangements?' he asked.

'All of it. I just want you to remember how crucial your developing contact with these officers is to the play we are about to make. We can't afford to screw this one up, Murray. It would be disastrous.'

Murray sat silently considering that possibility. It would be dangerous, he knew. 'Okay, Harry,' he said, understanding the extent of the commitment he had just made.

'Thanks, Murray,' the Director beamed. 'I knew I could count on you.'

* * * * * *

Indonesia — Java

They were both tired. The evening before, their Bandung hosts had insisted on entertaining the Australians. Following an early dinner courtesy of the local Chinese restaurant, the visitors were escorted down to a grotty place well-hidden behind the officers' mess. The moment they entered the dismally lighted room the Military Attaché turned to Murray and shook his head. He was not having any of this! A selection of poorly-dressed village girls sat quietly, their features barely visible in the low-wattage light. One of the girls said something and the others laughed nervously. Another rose and walked towards the foreigners, then said something in their local dialect. Murray could not understand the girl, but when she stood alongside Colonel Wharton, the Military Attaché and made a motion with her hands attracting even more nervous laughs, it became clear that the colonel's large frame was the object of their fascination. The Attaché towered over the others present, and the young prostitutes were obviously concerned as to who would have to partner the *bule* visitors.

'Murray, I don't care how you do it, but get us, or at least me, out of here.'

'Give it a few minutes, George.' he had replied. 'We'll sit and keep them company for a while then drift back to the guest house. I'll talk to them. You can just sit there and continue to frighten the hell out of them.' The colonel agreed. He understood the importance of face. It was just so damn annoying that he could not communicate. Not having control of the situation was absolutely alien to his nature and military training.

He squatted down on one of the short stools so as not to intimidate the girls further and listened as Stephenson entertained them. The village girls were obviously surprised that he could speak their language. After a reasonable time had elapsed, impatient to retire in preparation for the long gruelling next day's drive, the colonel checked his watch and indicated to Murray he thought they should leave. As soon as both men emerged from the unofficial brothel, their hosts reappeared smiling, and then insisted on accompanying their guests back into Bandung to the Savoy Hoyman Hotel. They tried to protest but the Area Commander refused to listen. He had organised for the beer garden to remain open and, he said, the band were also waiting. The Australians had no choice but to agree, returning to their rooms in the Army Guest House well after midnight.

They had little sleep, rising early to tackle the long drive down through the mountains and across to Semarang. Both men sat silently in the rear of the Embassy Holden as it wound its way through the narrow, dangerous road which, in places, was barely wide enough for one vehicle, let alone the buses and trucks which forged recklessly down the mountain pass. The men both felt uncomfortable with the conditions but neither complained. Instead, they kept their eyes glued to the road and the steep embankments where, from time to time, they observed evidence of where some earlier driver had missed a corner, plunging his passengers to their death some hundreds of metres below. The road wound through a dense teak forest, the sun's rays hidden by the trees' thick leafy crowns. Monkeys wrestled together along the roadside oblivious to their dangerous choice of playground, scampering to safety only at the very last moment as cars and trucks approached perilously close. Birds of impossible beauty swooped on injured prey left to die by the passing traffic, their shrieks of warning to the approaching intruders echoing through the canopied jungle. Twice the men spotted brilliant green snakes twisting their way with incredible speed as they fled the oncoming car wheels.

Several hours passed before the driver asked if he could stop for a cigarette. The *tuans* were pleased to do so, stretching their legs as they stood outside in the cool morning setting, enjoying the fresh mountain air. Before the driver could finish his *kretek* with its clove aroma, dozens of villagers appeared out of nowhere and squatted around the two foreigners. The men laughed as they climbed back into the car. There was no village visible and yet, as they had experienced in almost every place they had visited in the country, wherever they stopped there would be a crowd of inquisitive children present, within minutes.

The remainder of the drive to the northern port city was uneventful, just tiring. As protocol dictated that they report upon arrival, the men agreed to go directly to the Diponegoro Command HQ before cleaning up, to advise their hosts of their presence in Semarang. They were warmly welcomed, advised of the programme schedule arranged in honour of the Australian Military Attaché's visit, then escorted by Military Police, sirens whining loudly as they cleared the traffic for the diplomatic car.

That evening, the Diponegoro Commander held a reception at the Hotel Istana, one of the few remaining venues suitable for such purposes. Apart from his senior officers, the general invited a small number of government officials, all military appointees. There were also several local traders present. Murray smiled knowingly when introduced briefly to these men. He knew that the businessmen would be expected to pay for the extravagant function. Murray dressed in formal attire, his white jacket requiring some hasty last-minute attention. Colonel Wharton dressed in formal military evening dress, the gold accoutrements adding to his distinguished bearing. The two rows of decorations for service and courage had already been carefully pinned in place on the white penguin-cut jacket by his wife as she packed the evening uniform prior to her husband's departure.

The colonel was not alone in expressing his pleasure that they were staying in the Hotel. Murray had been through this region many times during his first tour, and had suffered endless sleepless nights whenever obliged to sleep in local bug-infested *losmen*. The reception was to commence at six o'clock. Murray accompanied the colonel downstairs to join their hosts, where they stood alongside the Diponegoro Commander as they were introduced to the other officers and guests. It was then that Murray finally met Lieutenant Colonel Sulistio. The colonel surprised both the Australians with his command of English. Immediately, Murray solicited the soldier's help, suggesting that it would be greatly appreciated should the officer take some of the pressure off him, feigning ignorance to military terminology and therefore difficulty with the interpreting.

'I would be pleased to do so,' the Javanese officer willingly agreed. It was an opportunity for him to flaunt his recently-acquired skills in front of the general. He knew that this couldn't hurt his future prospects. Very few of his peers had acquired this language proficiency, even amongst the several thousands of Indonesians who had been trained by the Americans. Murray was instantly relieved. He would now have an opportunity to speak directly to all of the officers whose names he had memorised. He would return to the CIA mole later, Murray decided, encouraging Colonel Wharton to accept the Javanese officer as his temporary replacement. The Attaché agreed, not displeased with the arrangement. He was not aware of the Indonesian's treasonous relationship with the Americans.

As the reception wore on, Murray was successful in making contact with most of the senior officers listed by his Director. He encouraged their questions and established a strong rapport with the men and their wives. Murray flattered the women, and they responded. Before dinner was served, most of those present knew his name while that of the other Australian was totally lost on them. He spoke at length with the ladies, knowing that they were attracted. This never bothered Murray, who enjoyed the extra attention and used it to his advantage.

As the exotic buffet was replenished with even more seafood and rice dishes, Murray roamed the room, talking to their hosts and other guests, stopping occasionally to chat with the senior officers' wives before moving on to speak briefly with some of the government officials. As the occasion was nearing its close, Murray decided it was time for him to reposition himself beside his Military Attaché.

'Thank you for assisting Colonel Wharton,' he said, shaking Sulistio's hand warmly but not with the customary firm Western grip. *'I would never have had the opportunity to enjoy myself so much had you not come along.'*

'But have you not been here before, tuan Murray?' the *kolonel* asked.

'Yes, several times in fact.' Murray went on to explain his student days prior to his joining the Embassy. *'But I never really had the opportunity to move around this freely.'*

'Ah, yes. Of course. You would not have had the benefit of your current status. Tell me,' he asked, looking directly into Murray's eyes, *'did you have the benefit of a surat djalan at that time?'*

'Not really,' Murray responded. The document to which the *kolonel* had referred was the mandatory travel paper issued to all

181

foreigners when they moved outside the Capital.

'*I had friends in high places,*' he joked, half-expecting the officer to enquire further.

'*Ah, I see. Tuan Murray really does understand how my country works!*' Sulistio smiled. '*And are those friends in high places in the Army?*' he asked, pleasantly, but Murray sensed that he was moving into dangerous ground.

'*Tidak, Pak Kolonel,*' he answered in the officer's own tongue. '*No friends in the Military, I regret to say.*' Having provided the opening, he waited.

Sulistio turned his head from left to right then smiled at Murray. '*Seems that is about to change. You have made many friends here tonight,*' he said, then added in English, 'Especially amongst our ladies!'

They laughed together as the others guests moved to depart. The Australians stood alongside their hosts once again, shaking hands cordially as the evening came to a close. The following morning they were taken to the Army Command Headquarters where they spent the entire day, discussing each other's weaponry and training procedures. The visit went well and by the time they were ready to depart for Djogyakarta and Surabaja the next day, Murray knew that he had achieved what he'd set out to do. One by one, he had approached each of the officers on the ASIS list and they had responded warmly to his attempts to cultivate their friendship. He believed that the next objective would not be difficult and immediately commenced planning how he would approach these men to arrange the following visit. With Harry Bradshaw.

* * * * * *

Canberra — Australia

Konstantinov looked hard at the man he would normally have despised. The Russian usually had little time for such men who, having compromised their own integrity, did not have the intestinal fortitude required to extricate themselves from their predicaments. Still, he above all others in his profession acknowledged that, without such players in his world of intrigue, little would be achieved. Blackmail had become an essential tool in the application of his dangerous trade. Harry was different and, Konstantinov, for reasons unknown even to him, respected the ageing spy.

'Why do you wish to continue with the original assignment. Surely this changes everything?' Harry asked. He had just finished rubbing his brow but, for some reason, the tension remained. He rubbed the area briskly, again. 'How reliable is this information? It seems just a little fortuitous to me!'

'Totally reliable, Comrade, totally reliable, I can assure you.'

'Well?' Harry waited. The situation was verging on the chaotic. It had suddenly become very dangerous for those involved in the rapidly-changing scenario.

'You should still proceed with the original plan. Only now, you will have more to offer. Once you have disclosed this information to the Diponegoro officers they will have no choice but to trust you in the future.'

'Colonel,' he started, still confused by the dramatic changes in events, 'please explain why it is that Moscow wishes to reveal this information? Surely it would mean the end of your only foothold in the country?'

'We expect that once you reveal what the Indonesian Communist Party has planned, the Semarang officers will move to preempt such foolishness. This would not only diffuse a volatile situation but most probably result in the Communist Party surviving for the future. The PKI leadership would most certainly be removed, paving the way for more moderate thinking. We believe this would precipitate a return to the Moscow Line and sever the proposed alliance between the Indonesian, Vietnamese and Mao communists.'

'But what if it goes too far? What if they completely eliminate the PKI or simply just ban its activities?'

'Moscow will not permit that to happen.'

'How?' he asked, almost angrily. The scheme bordered on the insane.

'That is not for us to argue, Comrade. Besides, do you really believe that any group is strong enough to completely wipe out Indonesia's millions already dedicated to the principles of communism? Comrade, the suggestion is ridiculous.'

'My God, colonel,' he whispered hoarsely at the ramifications of what was planned. 'This could so easily back-fire. It's too risky!'

The ache in his forehead had moved. His temples throbbed fiercely as he attempted to convince the Russian that what they proposed bordered on lunacy. Konstantinov glared at the Intelligence Chief.

'You know what you must do, Comrade. Just do it!' The discussion had ended. There was nothing left for the ASIS Director to say.

Harry Bradshaw left the Russian Embassy and returned to Melbourne immediately. He filed one report of his visit to the Soviet Embassy with Anderson, his Deputy, and then went about making final arrangements for his imminent visit to Indonesia. He sent out the relevant communications advising of his movements, then left the Head Office and went directly to the Intercontinental Hotel. There he used the concierge to send an international cable. It was addressed to Bangkok. The next morning, an hour after the message was delivered, the recipient made a brief and enigmatic call within the Thai capital then hung up.

'It's Piya,' the boy's voice had said, 'he's coming!'

* * * * * *

Semarang — Central Java

Due to time constraints, Harry had insisted they fly to Semarang. Murray attempted to convince his Director that it would probably be as fast driving the four hundred kilometres, in spite of the road conditions, as it would using the domestic airways. Then there was the safety factor. These short domestic runs by ageing Dakota were extremely bumpy at this time of the year. Murray, for one, hated the idea of flying through the cunimbulus clouds almost at eye level with the smouldering volcanoes that lay in the flight path.

Murray calculated that, considering the taxi rides at both ends, the three-hour delay when Garuda couldn't find the mandatory missing aircraft, the actual flight time virtually amounted to the driving time. But the obstinate Director refused to listen to him.

They arrived during the tail-end of a local thunderstorm. The aircraft was easily buffeted at the restricted altitudes they flew, sending people lurching into the cluttered aisle, gripping their seats each time the plane dropped suddenly. The cabin was choked to capacity as four more passengers than seats stood bravely in the aisle. At the rear of the converted freighter, the ground crew had placed crates containing two of the largest white pigs Murray had ever seen. Another passenger had brought his fighting cocks along. These stood restlessly in cages, blocking the side exit. As the aircraft commenced its final approach, one of the children sitting up forward retched, setting off a chain reaction. When the Dakota taxied to a halt, both Murray and Harry helped open the doors then jumped before being totally overcome by the foul air inside.

They checked into the Hotel Istana. The reception clerk remembered Murray who requested a double room for them both. This avoided the problems with Harry's travel documents. He did not carry a diplomatic passport. Neither did he possess a *surat-djalan* travel pass. Prior to Harry's arrival, Murray had confirmed arrangements with the officers he had contacted. They had expressed surprise that he was returning this soon, but quickly extended an invitation to meet and *makan* together. Murray dressed casually, wearing an open-neck short-sleeve shirt while Harry changed into his safari suit.

It had been difficult for Murray to orchestrate a meeting with the specific officers whose involvement in the planned coup d'etat had come to his Director's attention. During their meeting in Singapore, Harry had concocted an acceptable story, explaining to Murray that the information had been released by their counterparts in Langley on a Director-to-Director basis. Due to Murray's immediate superior being under a cloud himself, it had been decided that he would be left out of the information loop until such times as his position could be clarified beyond doubt. Murray accepted the plausible explanation. Upon his return to Djakarta with Colonel Wharton, he had contacted the Diponegoro officers and expressed his gratitude for their hospitality and suggested that he might return the following week on a private visit, en route to Bali. He had asked for the opportunity to reciprocate their kindness, suggesting another meal at the Hotel Istana, knowing that it would be unlikely for the soldiers to refuse such an invitation. The problem he had was resolving how to cull out the officers they did not wish to meet. In the end, Harry suggested that they arrange a later meeting with the officers concerned, and that this could be organised during the dinner. It was messy, and neither felt relaxed about the tedious but dangerous task which faced them.

Murray was disappointed that almost a dozen of the officers attended the dinner, including Colonel Sulistio. Harry appeared apprehensive when first introduced to the American-trained soldier but Murray decided that the Director, with his extensive field experience, could handle anything which might arise during the evening. And he did.

Once Murray was convinced that Harry had remembered which of the men present were those he wished to meet discreetly, he went about directing the conversations to those officers. It went smoothly and, as coffee was served, Harry excused himself, went to his room and returned with a box of cigars which were quickly opened and handed around the table. Murray was impressed with his style. He watched Harry smiling and laughing with the Indonesian soldiers, never once indicating that the language barrier posed any problem. From time to time, Colonel Sulistio joined in interpreting for the group, permitting Murray the opportunity to initiate separate conversations.

Only a few of the officers drank alcohol, which suited the agents. They knew that these men were unaccustomed to spirits and even one or two beers would normally make them ill. As ten o'clock approached, the soldiers indicated that they thought it time to return to their respective quarters. It appeared that there would be no opportunity to speak to even one of the targeted officers privately. The group started to break up when suddenly one of their number decided to use the toilets before departing. Murray took the initiative and followed the brigadier general through the lobby and out into the toilet area. He waited for the officer to step back out into the rear courtyard.

'*Pak Djenderal,*' he commenced, knowing that he might have only this one opportunity to make his pitch. '*Pak Djenderal, there is something very important that we wish to discuss with you in private.*' The brigadier general stopped, surprised at the statement.

'*What is it?*' he asked, curious as to the foreigner's behaviour. Normally when these people wanted a favour, they would have one of the junior officers make the approach.

'*Pak Djenderal, we wish to meet with you in private. It is most urgent.*'

'*What is there to discuss? I have no business with you or your friend.*'

'*Pak Djenderal,*' Murray again tried, feeling the opportunity slipping away from him. *'What we wish to discuss cannot be said here, nor do I think would you want it to be said in front of the others.'* The Indonesian bristled and began to move away, angry with the arrogance of such an intrusion. These *bangsat* are all the same, he thought angrily.

'Make an appointment with the Kolonel. Then I will see if it is a matter for our further discussion.' He turned and had walked no more than three paces when Murray caught up and whispered urgently, bringing the general to an abrupt halt.

'Diponegoro mau kudeta,' he whispered just loudly enough for the startled officer to hear. Immediately the general turned and snarled at the accusation that his Command was involved in planning a coup d'etat.

'That is a very dangerous statement,' he said, glaring at the *bule*. Murray took a chance. He knew he had to go in all the way. There was no turning back.

'It is only dangerous to those who plot such an action, Pak Djenderal.' he said, knowing that the Javanese was looking for more before he could respond. *'We have information relating to the plan,'* he added quickly, taking the offensive. *'It is this which we must discuss with you in private, Pak Djenderal.'*

'Who are you?' the shocked general asked, his voice almost choking with rage. *'Who are you who dares to insult me in this way?'* he stammered, while clenching his fists.

'Pak Djenderal,' Murray spoke softly, *'we are here to support you.'* For several moments he waited, expecting the other man to scream for his junior officers to join him. Christ! Murray suddenly thought, what if someone had made a colossal mistake? What if he had just approached the wrong man? He tensed.

What seemed like an eternity passed as the two men faced each other. The general continued to stare fiercely at the foreigner who had made the wild innuendo, while the other stood firmly, his hands deliberately loose at his sides. Suddenly the Indonesian spoke.

'We will talk now. Follow me,' he ordered as the relieved agent did as he was instructed. They returned to the lobby where the other officers waited. The general barked at his aide and nodded to the other officers who immediately came to attention, bade farewell to their hosts and departed quickly. Only one other remained behind.

'Pak Djenderal, may I stay and offer my assistance?' *Kolonel* Sulistio

said. Murray watched Harry stiffen as the exchange took place. He guessed what might have been said. The Commander looked at his officer and attempted a smile.

'I will be all right by myself,' he said, obviously pleased with this officer's response.

'But Pak Djenderal,' Sulistio insisted, incurring a look of dismissal which he clearly understood. *'Kalau begitu, selamat malam, Pak,'* he said, acquiescing then bidding his superior goodnight. He turned to the Australians. *'Good evening, gentlemen,'* he said, a little too officiously, *'please take good care of our Commander.'* with which he stepped back and saluted instead of shaking their hands, then marched away stiffly.

'Seems we have upset that one,' Harry said to the general, which Murray considered inappropriate and neglected to translate.

'Yes, you have,' the Commander said sternly to the two shocked Australians. Then he looked at their expressions and smiled resignedly. 'Yes, gentlemen, I do speak some English. Come, we will talk. But not here,' with which he turned, and the others followed the general outside, where his aide waited patiently beside the Commander's Jeep. He motioned for the Australians to climb into his vehicle. Murray was not sure that this was such a good idea, considering they had just alerted the officer in charge to the fact that they were aware of his complicity in an anti-government plot. Harry nodded and Murray climbed aboard with the others.

They remained in silence as the Jeep bumped its way back towards the Divisional Headquarter. Just before the main entrance, the aide turned left and drove down several streets before turning once more and coming to a stop outside a large two-storey building. He flashed the Jeep's lights. Two armed soldiers appeared, rifles held in the ready position while they checked the Army vehicle. Satisfied that it was their Commander, they then opened the heavy iron gates and ushered them inside.

'My home,' was all the general said, climbing out of the uncomfortable Jeep and walking directly into his house. Minutes later, Harry sat opposite the general in his study, with Murray on his left. The room was not large, nor was it air-conditioned. The general waited until his staff had placed coffee in front of his guests and left the room, closing the tall green doors behind. Murray detected a mustiness in these quarters, as if the room was rarely used.

He noticed the photographs hanging on two of the cream walls. Neither were of faces he could recognise. An outdated calendar displayed a painting of the Borobudur temple.

He glanced at the ceiling and spotted the tell-tale water marks where rain had poured through from the broken roof tiles above. Several flags hung listlessly in the corners as if waiting for some breath of fresh air to bring them to life. A wash-basin rested against the far wall, confirming the original designer to be Dutch. Water dripped from the single tap, following a permanent brown stain that no-one had bothered to remove. The room's appearance reflected an absence of wealth, of power. Considering the tenant's position, Murray had not expected such obvious neglect. It was certainly out of character for what he considered to be the norm with other high ranking officials. The general indicated that they should commence.

'We speak English. Later, if too difficult, he can speak for both of us,' the officer suggested, pointing at Murray.

'Fine. Then perhaps I should begin,' Harry remarked, anxious to control the direction of the conversation from the outset. 'Firstly, general, I should clarify just who I am but, before doing this, I must have your assurance that what I am about to tell you must, for the moment, remain with you only. Is that agreed?' The Javanese listened, then indicated that he understood.

'General, I work with the Australian Government. Murray here is my official interpreter and is privy to the information I am about to disclose to you.' The brigadier general held his hand up and looked at Murray who immediately translated what had been said. 'I wish to assure you that the purpose of my visit is to help, not to create problems for you or those in your Command.' Harry waited to see if his host had understood before continuing. 'What I am about to show you will prove that we are genuine friends and look to you for your trust.' Harry extracted a sealed envelope from his pocket and ripped the seal off before removing the contents. He then placed two pages in front of the general. Minutes passed before the officer had completed reading the information. He looked up at the ASIS Director.

'Who wrote this report?' he asked. Harry did not hesitate. Looking sideways at Murray he stated clearly, 'One of your own officers, general!' Murray's cheek muscles tensed. Surely they weren't going to expose the American agent?

'Which man wrote this?' he asked again, slowly, obviously determined to discover the identity of his own enemy within, his *musuh dalam selimut*. He was shocked, given the knowledge that one of his close officers had betrayed him. Immediately the brigadier general showed signs of losing control. 'You must tell me!' he demanded, his voice rising almost to a shout. Murray looked helplessly at his superior. What the hell was going on? he thought.

'The man's name is the officer we met tonight named Sulistio. His name is Kolonel Sulistio.' For a moment there was complete silence. Murray was speechless. God! he thought, the bastard's compromised a friendly agent! What in the hell is Bradshaw up to? he struggled to understand.

'You lie!' the general shouted, then looked at the other man. '*Bohong!*' he repeated in Indonesian.

'No, general. I'm sorry, but it's true. Your man was already in the pay of the Americans well before your plans were even discussed. He willingly became one of their agents while undergoing training in the States. It is always difficult when these disclosures are made, general. Believe me, I know. The fact is, the officer has been reporting regularly exactly what you and your officers have planned to remove the senior Military Establishment in Djakarta.'

'I do not believe you. Why do you not help him if he is working for the Americans? Why come to me with this story? The Australians and Americans are allies! No, you lie!'

'There is more that I must tell you, general. Of course, we are friendly with the Americans and it is true that they are our ally.' Harry paused to ensure that the officer had understood. 'General, although to you it is already a very serious charge that one of your men has been providing secret information to the Americans, there is something far more serious. That matter is the real reason for my meeting with you.' Murray listened intently. He had no idea what the hell was going on.

'What can be more serious than your accusations?' the general snapped.

'General, listen. Please listen to what I am about to say, General, the Australian and British have confirmed reports that the Indonesian Communist Party, your PKI, plans to overthrow your government!' Harry said, dropping the bombshell in a clear and precise manner. There was a moment of silence before the general slapped the table loudly, then scoffed.

'*The PKI ?*' he repeated, snorting as he spat the words scornfully. '*The PKI could not put out their children's washing without falling all over themselves. Why do you come to me with this nonsense?*' he demanded, reverting to his own language. Murray quickly translated for Bradshaw.

'General. Your superiors in Djakarta have already been approached by their American associates. We don't need to discuss that issue here but you are fully aware that your Military leadership has already moved into the American camp. As Australians, I must admit that we are not unhappy about this. The problem is that neither the Americans nor your senior generals believe that the PKI are planning such a move against your people, Now that does concern Australia. It would seem to us that we have a common interest. Since your own leadership prefers to ignore this danger, then we would be pleased to support any intent you have in moving first to establish control.'

'You can understand my own government's predicament. Yes, we are allies with the Americans, but please consider the risk my Government has taken in jeopardising that relationship, here today. Should the Americans become aware of our support for the Diponegoro Command to assume leadership control in lieu of their own preferred faction, it would be disastrous for all concerned. In short, the Americans would never support your efforts, preferring to maintain a strong relationship with your existing leadership who refuse to accept, as you just have, the possibility that Mr. Aidit and his gang are planning their own party. General, this is why it was imperative that I met with you and explained about Sulistio first. Whatever you have discussed, whatever you have been planning, even whoever is involved with you, all this information is now in the hands of the Americans.'

The brigadier general appeared to understand.

'If this is true, why haven't the Americans already informed Djakarta?' he challenged.

'They most probably have. If your superiors refuse to accept that the PKI is plotting to overthrow the government, then why would they believe that their own highly esteemed Diponegoro Command could even consider such an outrageous suggestion?

Have there been any recent transfers of those involved?' Murray, stunned also by these revelations, watched to see if the general had understood the damning information revealed by the ASIS Director.

The general thought for a moment then frowned. Three of his more senior officers had been moved to other Commands during the past month and all were supporters of his covert actions. Slowly, the skin around his mouth tightened with anger as he realized that his entire operation may have already been compromised by one of his own.

'Give me proof,' the Commander challenged. Harry had anticipated this request and had already removed another document from the pocket of his safari jacket. He placed the page next to the other documents.

'There, general, is your proof,' he said, pointing to a line in the centre of the page. 'You can see, sir, this is an extract of a CIA report. It clearly mentions that Lieutenant Colonel Sulistio of the Diponegoro Command is the source of the information contained in the other documents. You will also recognise, general, that this report is stamped 'Top Secret' and, by showing this to you, my country has placed itself in a most difficult position, not to mention that I and my interpreter here would forfeit our careers should the Americans discover that we have passed this very sensitive material to you.' Harry looked to Murray and nodded. Murray repeated all that had just been said in the general's own language. As he did so, the officer looked from one page to the next and then back again, as if cross-referencing the contents. He shook his head in disbelief. Murray looked at the soldier sympathetically while wondering if it had also crossed the general's mind that Sulistio may have more than one master. The very thought that the Diponegoro plans may already be known in Djakarta seemed an obvious possibility to him. The general rose to his feet.

'You go back to the Hotel Istana now. We will check with Sulistio. If what you say and have shown me is true, then I will meet you again tomorrow. If it is not true ...' he left the sentence unfinished but the threat was clear.

'General. I don't want to tell you your business but it is essential that you move to contain this officer by removing him from sensitive positions. We don't want this man to be hurt in any way. That should not be necessary. We ask that you consider this.' Harry looked at Murray as he spoke then quickly glanced away again.

'We will meet tomorrow. Please go now.' He walked out of the room and stood silently beside the large side doors through which they had entered earlier. He did not offer his hand as they departed, and only grunted when both thanked him for the meeting. They returned to their hotel in the Jeep and Harry cautioned Murray with his hand, indicating that they should not go to their room immediately. They found one of the staff and ordered a bottle of *Bir Bintang* which was served warm over brown-speckled ice. They walked out to the small beer garden and sat, quietly discussing what had just transpired.

'Harry, you just burned a friendly! What's going on? Is this something to do with Dirty Tricks?' he asked, referring to the Secret Service's department which specialised in operations of this nature. 'If so, don't you think I should have been told before letting me walk into the crap I just witnessed back there?'

'It's not crap, Murray. We have confirmation that the Indonesian Communist Party is definitely planning a move. We just don't know when. As for their man Sulistio, well,' he lied, 'the Yanks were going to dump him anyway. Seems he has strayed a little from their camp as well.'

'What then is our game plan Harry?' Murray asked again. 'And how does Central Plans suddenly develop resources that the Yanks don't have? How did we manage to confirm the PKI's intentions?' he asked, looking directly at the Intelligence Chief. Harry Bradshaw just stared back at the younger man. He could see the fire in Murray's eyes and suddenly he remembered a time when he, too, experienced those very same emotions.

'Let's just say that we have a man who is very friendly with the Russkies,' he said tiredly and rose, indicating that he wished to go inside. Murray walked with him as far as the lobby, permitting the older man to enter their room and use the bathroom first. As Harry climbed the wide wooden staircase, Murray observed the slowness of his gait, watching the man until he disappeared from view.

He stood there for a moment, staring up at the empty space, wondering who it was the Director had referred to as being so close to the Soviets he was able to produce such incredible intelligence. Murray shivered in the warm tropical night. In a way, he didn't really want to know.

* * * * * *

It was still dark when the Jeep left with the small group and drove thirty kilometres away from the city, heading into the hinterland once they'd crossed the first line of hills overlooking Semarang. There were five of them including the driver. The driver turned off the sealed macadam and followed a dirt road for a further twenty minutes before the track disappeared altogether. They left the Jeep and moved down to the edge of the swift flowing stream where they squatted, smoking *kretek* cigarettes together. The general turned to Sulistio and stared into the man's eyes. The *kolonel* raised the cigarette to his mouth and drew deeply, then sighed, resting his head between his knees. He heard the men move to stand and knew that this was the end. He closed his eyes and refused to whimper or beg forgiveness. He was a Diponegoro *kolonel* and would die like one! Sulistio knew that the man standing behind him would be the djenderal. His Commander always insisted that a good officer should never shirk his responsibilities he remembered, and ...

The single shot to the side of his skull exploded through the stillness of the night, tearing away his face. As the brigadier general stepped away from the body, the other officers moved in quickly, stripping clothes and other identification from the dead officer's remains. Satisfied that they had missed nothing, they then pushed their former comrade's body into the stream.

The following morning the Commander sent for the two Australians.

* * * * * *

The meeting took place in the general's villa. Once again, only Murray and his Director were present. Neither had slept, apprehensive as to the outcome of their earlier discussions. The Commander commenced the conversation by indicating that he accepted the information passed to him the previous evening. The Australians looked quickly at each other.

'And Sulistio?' Harry asked. The general frowned and flipped his right hand casually.

'He has been dealt with.' Both men understood the ominous

gesture and response. Murray chewed the inside of his lower lip. There had never been any doubt in his mind that Harry had antici- pated such a reaction. The general had no choice, given that his own officer had betrayed them all. Harry Bradshaw immediately used the opportunity to raise some of the issues he believed should be resolved when the leadership changed. They discussed the sup- port Australia would provide with respect to Irian Barat and fu- ture joint defence co-operation. The general was pleased. Harry moved on to more current problems.

'General, my government would appreciate your assurance that, when the situation changes, you and your associates will support a full cessation of hostilities against Malaysia.'

'We would agree to this. The Crush Malaysia strategy was de- signed by the communists. We are not interested in carrying on with this fruitless action. Many of us have worked towards con- vincing our superiors in Djakarta that the war is senseless and should be stopped. They have ignored our Armed Forces losses and continue to send our men into the jungles of Kalimantan where already we have lost thousands. You may tell your Government that we will stop the *Ganjang Malaysia* action as soon as we remove those who support it.'

'General, just who are the members of this Council of Gener- als?' Harry asked. The general was very surprised by the question. He smiled thinly at the Australian.

'It would seem that you are very well-informed!' he said. 'Most believe that there is no such group, that it is just rumour, nonsense, so to speak.'

'Would it not be reasonable for us to assume that these officers are the same men you referred to earlier?' Harry pressed.

'It would be reasonable for me to suggest to you who is and who is not a member of the exclusive group,' the Commander re- plied, uncomfortable with the knowledge that the foreigners ap- peared to know a great deal more about the inner machinations of the Indonesian Armed Forces than they should. Harry Bradshaw understood. He withdraw a notebook from his safari jacket and commenced writing. The general sat silently, and would have nor- mally been amused with this behaviour had the situation been dif- ferent. Murray knew what his associate was writing. He acknowl- edged Harry's quick thinking although he did not believe that it would be successful.

'General, I have made a list of the senior officers in Djakarta whom we believe are members of the Council. You understand that this information is indeed relevant to our own position. The Australian Government would not wish to continue developing relationships with those who may, in the future, have little say in Indonesia's leadership.' Harry removed the small page from his notebook and passed it to the general. The Commander read down the list quickly. He looked up at the Intelligence Chief.

'I can't be entirely sure about these,' he said, pointing to the names, one by one. 'This one, however, I am certain would not be involved with the Dewan Djenderal. This, is a good man,' the general said sombrely. 'He once worked here.' The Commander removed his own pen and ran a line through the name before passing the list back to Harry.

'Thank you, general,' he said, smiling confidently. They talked for another hour before the meeting broke up, both sides apparently pleased with what had been achieved. The visitors were driven back to the Hotel Istana where they prepared for their return to the capital. Shortly after noon, the Garuda DC-3 departed, surprisingly, almost on schedule, beating the afternoon storms which approached the coastal city at alarming speed.

As they flew along the muddy coastline, Murray remained silent, pleased that the weather was reasonably calm. He looked at his co-passenger and smiled knowingly. Although there were still many questions he felt were left unanswered, Murray believed that what had transpired during the past twenty-four hours had tremendous significance in terms of future Indonesian-Australian relations. He admitted that many aspects of the discussions he had attended were still unclear in his mind, but of one thing he was certain; Harry Bradshaw was one hell of a negotiator. Murray suddenly felt a sense of pride and gratitude at having been accepted into the Director's confidence. He turned and smiled at the older man.

'Is that the list?' he asked. Harry had the page in his right hand and was staring at the names he had written.

'What?' he responded, startled. His mind had wandered, his thoughts preoccupied with other issues. 'The list?' he asked, remembering where he was, 'Yes. This is the list.' He passed it to

Murray and watched the younger man's expression as he examined the names. Murray thought about the senior officers mentioned and made no comment. He passed the page back to his Director, who seemed distracted.

The aircraft commenced losing altitude as it approached Kemayoran Airport. As the small twin-engined plane circled over Tandjung Priok Harbour before lining up against the sea breeze to land, Murray's thoughts remained on the list he had read, and that also of the recently-appointed major general whose name had been scratched off by the brigadier. He was deep in thought as the aircraft's tyres bit savagely at the runway and screamed, jolting his memory. Then he remembered. The officer whose name had been removed was also a former Diponegoro Commander. Now he held one of the most powerful positions in Djakarta, as the Commander of KOSTRAD, the Army's Strategic Reserve Command. And his headquarters were located on Merdeka Square.

Book two

1965, January to August

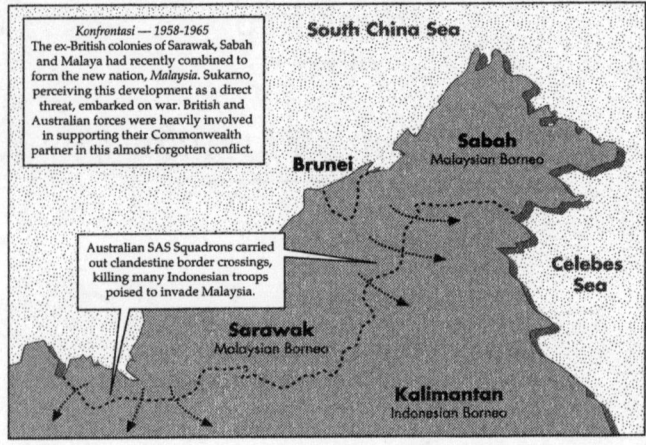

Konfrontasi — 1958-1965
The ex-British colonies of Sarawak, Sabah and Malaya had recently combined to form the new nation, *Malaysia*. Sukarno, perceiving this development as a direct threat, embarked on war. British and Australian forces were heavily involved in supporting their Commonwealth partner in this almost-forgotten conflict.

South China Sea

Brunei

Sabah
Malaysian Borneo

Celebes Sea

Australian SAS Squadrons carried out clandestine border crossings, killing many Indonesian troops poised to invade Malaysia.

Sarawak
Malaysian Borneo

Kalimantan
Indonesian Borneo

Chapter 11

Sarawak — Malaysia — Borneo

Major Zach wanted to slap the mosquito as it sucked blood through the side of his neck but dared not move. He watched through his open sights as the soldier on point headed directly towards him. He held the SLR Armalite rifle firmly as rain fell incessantly, drenching the weapon's stock, covering the open aperture, making it almost impossible to maintain a clear shot. It was his imagination, Zach knew. Mosquitoes would disappear in such torrential downpour. Slowly he bit into his left cheek, forcing his concentration to return. The sudden salty taste of his own blood cleared his thoughts.

Again, he peered down the blurred corridor, the thin dark metal points confused by droplets of rain which clung to the sights. The soldier raised his head not more than a few centimetres, silently cursing the conditions. The rain never ceased, the mud clung at his boots sucking his feet down into the jungle's quagmire, while vines and other thick foliage pulled at his camouflaged clothes and weapon. Still, Zach dared not move. There were others. He knew, without doubt, that the sergeant would be ready over on his right flank, even though he couldn't be seen. The area off to his left had been left clear. This is where they would pause, uncertain, listening as the rain thundered down, making it impossible to distinguish between the jungle's natural sounds and those which could warn them of impending death.

Lightning flashed, followed immediately by a thunderous clap which shook their surrounds. The enemy paused as their platoon commander moved his hand ever so slightly indicating that they were to remain still. He watched; and waited. His breathing slowed, as the forward soldier stood less than fifteen metres directly in his sights, and turned his head, as if suddenly aware of a foreign presence. The major's finger flexed, squeezing softly as he peered over the rifle, his target so close the blurred vision no longer mattered. His could see the Indonesian corporal's eyes, as the soldier peered cautiously into the heavy foliage ahead. The major exhaled slowly as he continued to squeeze the Armalite's fine trigger.

Suddenly, the world erupted around them as the other SAS soldiers followed his signal, releasing hundreds of rounds of ammunition before the Indonesian point man's shattered body had hit the soggy ground. Camouflaged soldiers leaped forward, shooting at the Indonesian patrol as they swooped down the slight incline, struggling to maintain balance on the slippery jungle floor, heedless of the thorny undergrowth which ripped flesh from hands and stung faces fiercely.

The Indonesians, caught by surprise, barely had time to return their enemy's fire before it was all over. The eight-man patrol had been annihilated in less than three minutes.

The savage noise of gunfire was followed by a moment of deafening stillness. Then, suddenly, the forest's creatures shattered the tropical air with screams of terror as monkeys, birds, and other creatures fled to safety.

The major crawled towards his first kill, and crouched over the dead soldier. It was almost impossible to distinguish the officer's form shrouded in camouflage, his tools of war deliberately darkened so as not to betray him, his face blackened to blend with the surrounding forest. He paused, signalled to his NCO, then continued forward. Together they counted the dead. There were seven. Quickly, almost silently, the men moved from body to body removing whatever they found. Letters, identification, paper money. It was all collected. The rain eased momentarily.

The surviving soldier had been hit in the stomach and lay in shock. Corporal Lewis moved towards the wounded Indonesian to complete the kill. He grabbed the soldier's head expertly with his left hand, pulling the man's chin in an upwards motion as his knife commenced its path across the terrified Sumatran's throat.

'Wait!' a voice hissed urgently. Corporal Lewis remained in position, fighting the adrenaline charge. His blade remained at the soldier's neck. 'Lewis!' the voice called again and he stopped, tilting his head sideways to check. It was the major. Lewis kept the knife at his prisoner's throat. 'Lewis, how bad is he?' the officer asked.

'One through the side of the stomach. He'll bleed to death,' the corporal whispered.

'Wait!' the major ordered, then turned and signalled to his sergeant. The NCO scrambled across quickly. 'Give him a shot,' the officer instructed, 'then drag him over there,' he said, indicating a huge decaying tree trunk covered in moss and vines. The sergeant positioned himself alongside the wounded soldier and glared at Lewis. The corporal glared back then withdrew the blade. They dragged the bleeding man over to the dead tree and lifted him slightly so that he leaned against the rotting trunk. Another soldier joined them and ripped the Indonesian's bloodied uniform away to expose the gaping wound. He looked at the major and shook his head. Under normal circumstances the man could be saved. Here, in the jungle, the soldier would die within hours. The morphine was injected unceremoniously as the officer crouched down beside their prisoner and spoke.

'*What is your name, mas?*' he demanded. '*Siapa namamu?*' The wounded soldier stared at the white man before him in disbelief.

'*Sekali lagi, siapa namamu?*' the major asked for his name again. The NCO raised a water can to the man's parched mouth and tipped the aluminium container slightly. The soldier attempted to move but couldn't.

'*Tolong, tolong,*' he cried, pleading for help.

'What is your name, you bastard!' the officer hissed. '*Tell me your name or I will cut you with this,*' he threatened, holding his blade in front of the man's face. The solider sobbed.

'*Hartono, tuan,*' he answered, eyes wide in fear. '*My name is Hartono.*'

'What unit do you belong to?' the major demanded, moving the knife slowly before the soldier's face.

'*Regu Harimau, tuan,*' he responded, informing the white soldier that he was part of the Tiger Team. A soldier behind swore. These were communist bandits, not even regular soldiers. The major glared over his shoulder at the Corporal. Three of his men understood the bastardised form of Malay. They had picked up their experience killing communists during the Malay Emergency.

'*Why aren't you wearing uniforms?*' the officer asked, impatiently.

'We changed before leaving Kampung Saleh.' the Sumatran replied, before breaking into a coughing fit which almost choked him. He was given another sip of water.

'What were your orders?' he was asked.

'We were moving towards Kampung Tanah Tinggi. Our orders were to kidnap some of the villagers. I don't know which ones.'

The major stared down at the soldier. His clothes were obviously Army issue, but neither he nor his dead friends wore any distinguishing flashes. Not even name tags. The sergeant leaned over and tapped his wrist watch. They were running out of time. The major nodded.

'Which one of these is your officer?' he asked, moving his hand in an arc covering the bodies which had been dragged into one area as he questioned the prisoner. Major Zach glared at the Indonesian. The young soldier was probably about twenty, he thought. He asked the question again.

'I don't know, which one, tuan, I can't see from here!'

'What was his name?' he growled, conscious of the dangers in remaining where they were after the ambush.

'Bhakti, tuan. His name is Comrade Bhakti.' His answer was followed by another grunt from the corporal. The sergeant waved his wrist at the officer and shook his head. The major sighed, and rose to his feet. He nodded and moved away. The SNCO stood beside the wounded man and gestured for his men to move out.

'It's okay, Sarge,' Lewis said, his hand ready with the razor sharp weapon. The sergeant stared at the corporal. They had worked together in Malaya when the communists were pushing the British soldiers around the plantations north along the Thai border. He stepped away and made room for the other soldier. Immediately, the Indonesian realised what was about to happen and sobbed. He started to scream as Corporal Lewis bent down and grinned as he displayed the knife. He held the man's head as before, turning his body slightly away. Weakened by the loss of blood, the Sumatran offered little resistance.

'Tuhan, tolong! God help me ...!' he screamed, his cry for help cut short as the SAS Corporal's knife severed his throat.

'Filthy bloody commo,' Lewis spat as he pushed himself away from the pumping blood, wiping the blade on the dying soldier's torn clothing. He joined the others. Major Zach motioned with his hand and the SAS team moved out, covering as much ground as possible. They knew it would be folly to remain. Knowledge of the encounter would already be spreading through the surrounding villages. The sergeant checked his bearings and indicated the direction to those behind. Rain started to fall again, but the soldiers maintained their gruelling pace through the thick jungle. It would have been faster following the tracks, but they didn't dare. If they were observed, their standing orders were to kill those who might identify them for what they were.

Three hours passed, the soldiers refusing to rest as they continued their forced march through the extreme conditions, pushing on towards their destination. By late afternoon they reached the edge of the jungle, and their camp, ten kilometres from Simanggang. Exhausted, they went about cleaning their weapons before bathing in the jungle stream and taking their rations.

Across the river from their camp, villagers went about their lives, as if it were normal for these foreigners to be present on their primitive doorstep. From time to time the soldiers would return a wave, acknowledging the fiercely proud people who tolerated the Australians within their close proximity. These were people of the Dayak tribes, whose ancestors, and theirs before them, had hunted, fished and borne families along these rivers long before migratory tribes had encroached upon their territory. They were allies of the Australians primarily because of the common enemy, Indonesia.

This ancient ethnic group understood what was happening to their people, their communities isolated by political lines drawn by others without knowledge of ancestral ties or responsibilities. The Dayaks were the rightful inhabitants of Borneo. Their families had grown throughout the centuries, spreading along the river shores throughout the incredibly large island. They knew what would be lost if the tribes from the southern islands established control over their land. The Australian soldiers were careful when dealing with the smiling river people. They were known to eat their enemies.

The men ate, talked quietly and listened to their officer outlining the following day's activities. There were smiles all around when the major announced that they were not crossing the Indonesian border again the following day. Instead, the SAS soldiers had been ordered to return to Company Headquarters. Zach grinned at the SNCO and the sergeant returned his smile. The special unit had been out in the jungle for twenty-one days straight, crossed into Indonesia more than a dozen times and killed more than one hundred Indonesian soldiers before these intruders could enter Malaysian Sarawak. It did not bother the Australian soldiers that they had violated another country's sovereignty and killed its people. Theirs was an undeclared war. There were no rules, only enemies. The SAS had been ordered to cross the imaginary lines which officially separated British Commonwealth Malaysia from its aggressive neighbour, Indonesia, and prevent Soekarno's terrorists from infiltrating into the newly-created federation where they murdered villagers and kidnapped children, before escaping to the sanctuary of Indonesian Kalimantan.

The Australian soldiers wore no identification which would have compromised their country in the event of their capture. These men understood the enormous responsibility they carried into Borneo's jungle. They reluctantly removed their insignia and the highly-regarded shoulder flashes, knowing that these would be worn again, soon, once they returned to their regiment.

Major Zach rested well that evening. They had not lost a man. At least, not during this expedition. As he closed his eyes, he thought about the others who had not been so lucky, and immediately blocked these memories from his mind. His tour was almost over. He would be happy to return to Australia for a little R& R, go and visit family, get away from the Regiment for a few weeks and find somewhere with a decent bath. Maybe he would drive up to the snow for a week, he thought, enjoy the cold and the beauty of the mountains, get his mind off the jungle. As these thoughts occupied his mind, Major Steven Zach, SAS, slipped into a restless sleep.

When morning arrived, the Australian soldiers broke camp and moved across the river. There they negotiated with the Dayak elders, sitting cross-legged in the long house as terms were negotiated and arrangements put in place. As the morning sun beat down on the soldiers, their impatience was obvious and tempers grew thin. The villagers pushed their boats into the river and primed their powerful outboard motors in preparation to take them on the six-hour journey downstream.

* * * * * *

'You're going home, Steve.' Colonel Peter Jones smiled, handing the can of Victorian Bitter to his friend, and junior officer. He was pleased that Zach was there. That he was safe. They had been close friends for some time. And, of course, he was particularly pleased with the major's promotion. Zach was the only SAS officer of his rank still permitted to actively participate in the patrols. This was normally left to more junior officers but, due to his uncanny skills in the jungle, his request to remain directly involved in the border crossings was reluctantly approved. 'Well, colonel,' Jones laughed, lifting his own can in recognition of what he believed to be a fine decision by the Army Board back in Canberra.

The Hungarian-born Australian SAS officer laughed and lifted his own can in salute. Lieutenant Colonel Zach, Steve thought. It had a good sound to it.

'Do the lads know?' Jones asked, referring to Zach's men.

'The sergeant major is probably down in the Mess telling your SNCO as we speak.' The Commanding Officer wandered across the raised timber floor and looked over the damp ground towards the other barracks. 'Your men will miss you, Steve,' he said, knowing that he would also. Steven Zach was one of the finest men he had known: not just as a friend, but as a professional soldier. The man had commitment and integrity. His men followed him almost without question.

'I'll drop down for farewells before heading off. They're good men, Peter,' he stated, although he knew he didn't have to tell his colonel this. Their successful patrols spoke for his men's professionalism in the field. Zach had been lucky. During a patrol earlier in his tour, he had lost five of his men in a crossfire ambush to RPKAD troops. These were the Indonesian Army Paracommando forces. There had been no court-martial. The British intelligence had been totally screwed up, placing Zach and his men in extreme jeopardy. They had virtually been ordered to cross into a 'hot zone' which had been cleared by Intelligence as safe. When Zach's men were knee-deep and half-way across the swift flowing stream, the Indonesians had opened fire, killing three of his patrol in the first seconds. The survivors fought their way out of the devastating ambush, refusing to withdraw until they had managed to recover their fallen comrades' bodies. These they dragged back across the river, fighting as they withdrew. Two more men died before they reached the river's embankment. Zach's remaining men carried their dead into the heavy jungle where they remained until a SAS support team arrived and transported the bodies back to their base.

Zach had then returned to the river with his remaining men and, armed with the knowledge that the other embankment was in enemy hands, encircled their encampment and mounted his own cross-fire, placing the Indonesians between his handful of men and the river. They killed more than thirty RPKAD regular Indonesian troops in the brief but savage encounter before slipping quietly away, recrossing the river and returning to base camp. From that moment on, Major Steve Zach's star was on the ascent. His men trusted him, and his peers respected the man who had shown them all the qualities an officer should have. He had come a long way from the horrors of Occupation, first by the Germans and then in 1956 the Russians, when they stormed into his country in one final attempt to destroy the very soul of the Hungarian people. Although his great-grandfather had been German, Zach had considered himself only as Hungarian. Now he was an Australian.

As Steven Zach threw the empty can expertly across the quarters into the designated bin, he experienced a sense of achievement, of success. He was pleased with himself. And why not? he thought. He had just been promoted and ordered back to Australia. There would be no more patrols, and this particularly pleased him. No more ploughing through thick jungle, living in the same clothes for weeks on end. At last he would be leaving the filth and insects which had nearly driven him crazy during those first months, and the monotonous humidity which permanently saturated one's clothes. Yes, he thought, it would be just great to be back in Australia for a change.

The following morning the newly promoted Zach boarded the helicopter and headed for Kuching. From there he was transported by British RAF Andover to the military field in Changi, Singapore. The same day, he caught the QANTAS Boeing 707 directly to Sydney where Movements Control had arranged an interconnecting flight to Melbourne for debriefing. Zach was required to dedicate considerable time being prepared for his next posting. Due to the nature of the position and the sensitivity of access, Steven Zach was obliged to submit to a further security clearance before he could proceed any further. It was towards the end of his stay that he was briefed regarding the existence of ASIS, and met with Harry Bradshaw.

Two months later, Lieutenant Colonel Steven Zach boarded yet another QANTAS flight and headed north, to Asia, once again. Only this time he would not be returning to fight in the jungles of Malaysia. Instead, he would be living amongst the very people he had fought, whose brothers and sons he had taken in battle, extinguishing their lives without remorse. Now, he would offer these people his hand, and develop relationships within their community. It was not what he personally wanted, but what was expected of him. He had been posted to Djakarta. When he passed his diplomatic passport to the Immigration desk at Kemayoran Airport, the official made a note for BAKIN, Indonesia's equivalent to the CIA, that Australia's new Military Attaché to the Republic of Indonesia had finally arrived. Steven Zach was now in the land of the enemy.

* * * * * *

Djakarta

Murray scratched his crotch and made a mental note to stop his new *babu tjutji* from starching his underclothes. His previous washwoman had not returned from the *Hari Raja* holidays. Many of the servants changed jobs at this time in the year, he knew. Once they had received the customary additional month's rice and salary for the *Idulfitri* period, some would go home to their *kampungs* and would not return, while others merely changed households without telling their former employers.

He was looking forward to the weekend away from the city, his first in more than two months. Now his section had additional staff, Murray decided to take advantage of an invitation and fly to Djogyakarta. Tickets and hotel confirmation slips lay on the glass-topped desk. He had little difficulty in arranging accommodation at the Ambarukmo Hotel, occupancy rates being what they were. Foreign tourists avoided Indonesia, what with the ongoing street violence and poor infrastructure. Not to mention the confusing two-tier currency exchange system which made staying at one of the four Intercontinental Hotels expensive, by Australian standards.

Murray checked his room-rate and made a clicking sound of dis-approval. Even with the Embassy discount, he would be charged 32 American dollars for each night. On top of this, there would be food and bar bills to cover. Murray wondered just how many tourists fell off their bar stools when they discovered that a beer in the Government hotels could cost as much as a dollar Australian. Hell, he thought, gasoline was only fifteen cents a gallon, his cook only cost him a dollar per month for salary on top of the thirty kilos of *beras* she received from the Embassy, and yet the Government insisted on charging these exorbitant prices in their four-star hotels.

He reminded himself to take plenty of rupiah. The exchange rate was always lower in the provinces. Murray knew that he could have stayed at the Ramayana Hotel or even one of the other cheaper hotels but he had decided not to on this trip. This time he would stay at the recently-constructed Ambarukmo, built with Japanese War Reparation funds.

Ade had asked him to join her to visit some of her SUBUD friends in Djogyakarta. He had jumped at the opportunity to escape Djakarta's monotonous routine, agreeing on the condition that they fly down together on the Friday afternoon. Murray knew that this would appeal to her. They had spent very little time together recently and he was intrigued with the suggestion that her friends would take them both on a journey neither, she promised, would ever forget. He had informed Davis, his Station Chief, and relegated some of the minor tasks to the new Third Secretary.

'Who are you going with?' Davis had wanted to know. Their relationship had not improved much beyond that when Murray still attended Universitas Indonesia. Murray still wondered how this man could have been selected to become Station Chief. His character flaws were obvious not just to those who worked with the First Secretary, but to the others within the Chancery. When Davis had completed his first tour, there had been no traditional farewell function. Almost everyone had been relieved that he was leaving. To their dismay, Davis returned within months to fill the void created by Keith Wells' departure as First Secretary.

'Haven't decided yet,' he lied. Ade was private time.

Yanti, however, was a different matter altogether. Murray religiously submitted reports regarding their relationship, their discussions and any meetings that occurred. Yanti was business, and he understood the necessity of maintaining their close bond in the interests of their ever-demanding intelligence gathering requirements.

'Taking one of the round eyes?' Davis enquired in his typically derogatory fashion.

'Maybe,' Murray replied, not really wanting to get into another of these discussions with Davis. The First Secretary was still unpopular with both the Australian and Indonesian women on staff. Rumours persisted relating to his extra-curricula sexual activities but Murray no longer cared. There were far greater concerns regarding his Intelligence associate. Ever since Harry Bradshaw's startling revelations, suggesting that Davis could possibly be involved in leaking information, Murray had established a direct operational link with the ASIS Director, by-passing his Station Chief whenever necessary. He could not understand why Davis continued in his post if there was, in fact, substance to the allegations that he had compromised the Service. It made it bloody difficult to function effectively, he thought. He was angry with Bradshaw for not rectifying the problem by removing the agent.

It was apparent that Central Plans had no hard evidence on Davis. Murray sensed that there had to be another agenda. He refused to accept that Head Office would leave Davis in place unless they were uncertain of their suspicions or, as he was more inclined to believe, there was another game afoot and Davis was to play some part without his knowledge. And this would be just the way Bradshaw would operate. Bradshaw's reputation as an experienced field agent was legendary. His uncanny ability to anticipate and resolve complicated problems was equally matched by a deviousness which often startled even the most hardened agents. Murray understood the enormous respect the other officers felt for their Director. There were few who did not admire this man whose valuable empirical knowledge was so envied by others in the Service. At times, his own relationship with the Bradshaws had been a burden. Murray's initial encounter with Susan Bradshaw had later left him feeling confused and disloyal. His earlier concerns that Harry would discover his wife's infidelity and the outcome of that liaison had gradually disappeared as it became apparent that Susan's indiscretion would remain their secret. Murray was grateful that the status quo would remain unchanged. He had the greatest admiration for Harry Bradshaw who, in many ways, had become more than his mentor.

Murray Stephenson's rapid progress within the Service was a direct result of his dedication and talent. That he had been appointed to his current position merely underscored the ASIS Chief's confidence in his ability to execute his duties in a professional manner. Although there were those who whispered that Stephenson's relationship with their Director ensured his ascendancy within Central Plans, the majority acknowledged their fellow agent's abilities and ignored the innuendo. Murray knew that Davis could be included in the minority of people who saw his friendship with the Bradshaws as being the main contributing factor supporting his career. It didn't bother him, especially coming from Davis.

'When will you be back?' Davis asked, annoyed that Murray could be confident of having female company whenever he wished.

'Late Sunday night, Alan,' Murray answered, irritated by the man's persistence.

'Good!' Davis said, as if this fitted into his own plans. 'We have a two-hour briefing session first thing Monday morning.'

Murray raised one eyebrow slightly. 'What's on?' he asked.

'We're having a one-on-one with the incoming Military Attaché,' Davis responded, peering at the single-sheet classified memo in his hand. 'Seems he has quite an impressive record,' he added, squinting to read as he spoke.

'Great,' Murray replied, wishing the other man would return to his own office. 'Could do with some style around here.' Davis looked quickly to determine whether or not the comment was directed at him. Unsure if he had detected sarcasm in Stephenson's voice, he turned and walked slowly back to the adjacent office.

Davis set about re-reading the new Military Attaché's ASIS profile. As he studied the supporting documentation, he discovered that the career officer's records indicated that the half colonel was fluent in four languages, including Bahasa Indonesia. A smile crossed the First Secretary's face as he examined the officer's file photograph. Steven Zach presented well, he observed, surprised that the handsome Attaché was unmarried.

Another thought crossed his mind as the aristocratic features stared back at him. Davis decided he would enjoy having the new Military Attaché around, pleased that Stephenson might finally have some competition around the Embassy. He returned Steven Zach's dossier to his own registry safe, reminding himself to invite the newcomer to dinner as soon as was appropriate.

* * * * * *

Djogyakarta

'Can't you feel the mystique all around?' she asked, holding his hand tightly as they stood on the final level surrounded by huge stone bell formations. It was as if they were suspended by the clouds resting gently on the temple's roof. The climb had not been difficult although many of the original stones had broken away, leaving sections exposed to the weather. As they reached the top, Ade moaned as she peered down the multitude of steep steps, almost wishing she had remained below. Minutes later, as they walked carefully around the magnificent temple's crown, the view unfolding before them, Ade knew that the climb had been worth the effort. They rested there, leaning against one of the intricately carved *stupas*, the cool morning breeze on their faces, the soft sounds of children's voices drifting up as they played far below. Murray opened the tin he had purchased as they entered the temple grounds and extracted a flat piece of what appeared to be tobacco leaf. Ade seized the *dendeng* playfully, and snapped the dried beef into manageable sections before stuffing several of these into her mouth. Murray nodded silently as he chewed the chilli-flavoured meat, smiling at her.

Although they would soon return to Djakarta, Ade was extremely happy. The weekend together had been a wonderful experience for them both, and she felt that their relationship had reached a new level of understanding, of compatability. She was delighted that Murray enjoyed her friends' company. Ade was surprised that he even participated in the rituals, not making light of their beliefs as their group camped for part of the previous night around the ancient Buddhist temple.

Ade explained that this area was considered a holy place, not just by those involved in the SUBUD following, but also by many of the Central Javanese. *Tjandi Borobudur* was visited by many who believed that they could be purified by the mystical atmosphere

213

which surrounded the thousand year old structure.

'This is where we believe our culture was born, Mahree,' Ade had explained. *'We believe that there is a triangle which stretches from here to the ancient feudal courts of Djogyakarta and Surakarta within which there is a powerful vortex of psychic forces. We believe in the sanctity of these forces and often some of the younger Moslem boys sleep here, in search for answers through their dreams.'*

Murray had listened intently, admiring Ade for the strength of her convictions. He envied the Javanese girl her cultural heritage. She explained the significance of mysticism and spoke of Subuh in terms of reverence. As she spoke, the soft musical tones of her voice captured Murray's thoughts. He experienced a sensation of tranquillity he had hitherto not believed possible as Ade explained why they worshipped this special place. His thoughts drifted as the others joined in the gentle discussion, and eventually he fell asleep under the watchful eyes of Borobudur's guardians. The moon silhouetted the temple, casting a spell over them all.

Later, as they returned to their hotel, Ade teased Murray. Earlier, her friends had all laughed when Murray had suddenly sat up straight and smiled, not conscious that he had been asleep for several hours. The sensation he recalled before losing consciousness remained with him throughout the following day. It was later, when he stood together with Ade atop the Borobudur Temple, enjoying the mood which lifted his spirits to new heights, that Murray remembered the floating state which engulfed his being the evening before. He was surprised that he had not recognised the sensation earlier. Concerned with the consequences of what could transpire during these sessions, Murray decided to be more circumspect when exposed to the influence of these group meetings.

His mood suddenly changed as he tried to recall what had transpired during his first experience with the religious sect, and when he couldn't, Murray silently admonished himself for permitting circumstances to evolve outside of his control. Considering the nature of his profession, he realised just how stupid he had been. He would definitely not, he decided, attend any more *latihan* with the others. It was just too risky. He would find a suitable excuse next time Ade asked him to the meditation exercises.

* * * * * *

FREEDOM (MERDEKA) SQUARE

Djakarta

As the cocktails flowed, the level of conversation increased. Alan Davis leaned forward on tip-toe in search of the guest of honour. There were at least a hundred guests present. It was traditional for the outgoing Attaché to host at least one function to introduce the incoming officer and, on this occasion, even the Indonesian soldiers were accompanied by their ladies.

Davis looked around with hidden contempt. One would never really know, he thought, whether the women present were wives or current girlfriends, as many of the Army officers present had an adequate supply of both. As several of the guests shuffled away from him, Davis spotted Steven Zach talking to the Indian Military Attaché. The new arrival had not attended his briefing as arranged. Davis was concerned. As Station Chief it was imperative that the Military understood where they sat in terms of intelligence gathering.

He moved towards the officers. He winced as he overheard yet another Embassy wife complaining about her own domestic incidents and other menial problems. These women seemed to thrive on useless chatter, he thought, pushing between two of the more buxom Indian ladies who stood directly in his path.

'Davis,' he said, finally making it to the corner where the men stood. The Indian Colonel smiled and shook the shorter man's hand.

'Subramanium,' the Military Attaché replied, smiling broadly, displaying his startlingly white teeth under a thick walrus moustache. Davis viewed the four rows of campaign ribbons and was impressed. He hoped he would not be required to repeat the man's name.

'Hello, Alan,' the other officer said. 'Quite a bash.'

'You'll get used to it,' Davis replied in patronising manner while wishing the Indian with the unpronounceable name would move on.

'No doubt I will,' Zach replied, immediately identifying the man as obnoxious. He had obviously signalled his dislike because Davis looked slightly perplexed by his response. Steven understood that, as the new boy in town, he didn't need to start life in this closely-knit community by putting this man down. 'Perhaps you would be kind enough to give me a few pointers when the opportunity arises,' he suggested, hoping this would be enough to mollify, remembering his earlier coolness.

Davis was immediately placated. 'Steven,' he said, 'I would be delighted to show you the ropes.' He then moved in closer and half-whispered. 'Sorry you couldn't make it to last Monday's briefing. You should sit down with us within the next few days.'

Zach looked at the man with hidden contempt. Up until five weeks before, he had known nothing of the existence of the Australian Secret Service. He had almost choked laughing when the DMI had explained that the original name was only changed by adding the word 'intelligence' to avoid being referred to as ASS. Steven Zach felt it was fitting that this 'ass' was their senior representative in Djakarta.

'Other priorities, I'm afraid, ...' he answered, groping for the First Secretary's first name.

'Alan,' he said, not at all offended. 'It's Alan.' In fact, he was quite pleased that the colonel had made the attempt. So few others did. 'You really must arrange some time so that we can brief you on our side of things.'

'Okay, Alan. I understand. I'm sure that you'll also appreciate the pressure I'm under to participate in all of these handover-takeover functions. What about you and I having lunch as soon as Colonel Wharton leaves?'

Davis smiled. 'Great,' he responded warmly, believing he had established rapport with the new colonel. 'I'll look forward to that.' Zach then smiled and apologised, excusing himself as he responded with a wave to an imaginary person across the room. He squeezed Davis on the side of the shoulder as he moved away. The Station Chief was happy. The natural order of things had been put right and the colonel clearly understood his position. The First Secretary wandered back through the room, selecting a whisky soda as one of the houseboys passed carrying a mixture of cocktails. He sipped the double and winced.

'Have to watch old Ali there, Alan,' Stephenson said, smiling at his superior. The senior *djongos* had a reputation for spiking the *tuans'* drinks. He knew that Ali acted under the misconception that an intoxicated *tuan* would be grateful for the additional strength pourings and remember always to put a good word in for the ageing houseboy.

'Murray,' was all Davis could muster. He had quickly fallen from his momentary high.

'Have you arranged a revised meet?' Murray asked, referring to the failed first briefing attempt with Zach.

'All arranged. I'll let you know,' he added. Murray smiled. 'Supercilious little prick', he thought, struggling to let the remark go by in the interests of harmony.

'Okay, Alan, you do that,' he said, moving swiftly away and was immediately welcomed by the couple standing nearby. Murray was a popular figure. Davis despised him for that.

The outgoing Military Attaché was obviously enjoying himself. His tour was over. Three years 'in-country' had taken its toll, and both he and his wife were not unhappy with the prospect of one more posting until his retirement. As Murray approached, Colonel Wharton's wife turned and took him by the arm.

'Well, didn't think you were going to make it!' she exclaimed, pleased that he had.

'What, miss saying goodbye to the best-looking woman in Djakarta?' he teased.

'Murray, my dear, I am going to miss you very, very much!' she laughed, flattered, wishing that she had been twenty years younger. Dorothy Wharton continued to hold his arm, waiting for the opportunity to break into her husband's diatribe. He was lecturing his replacement on how to do things in this country. She waited patiently, accustomed to playing her role. Mrs. Wharton continued to smile, squeezing Murray's arm as they both stood, attentively, listening alongside the two colonels. She had heard it all before. For a moment, Dorothy Wharton felt relieved that it was finally over, although she had reached this moment with mixed emotions. Life had been good to them here. Her husband had held a position of respect, while she had survived with servants and a reasonable social life. Apart from the occasional altercation caused when the colonel became over enamoured with the *babu dalam*, or one of the other female servants, their lives had, for the most part, survived in almost perfect harmony. She was not entirely unhappy with the prospect of returning home. At least, people used toilet paper there, she thought, not really knowing what the local ablutionary habits might have been. The colonel's wife had never visited an Indonesian household in the three years she had lived 'in-country'.

'Thank God you two have run out of breath,' she exclaimed, launching herself into the conversation as one of the men paused to respond to the other's question. 'Steven, have you met Murray?' she asked, moving to one side, pleased with herself to be standing with the three men while some of the other ladies looked on enviously. She knew that the gin-and-tonic had tasted a little too strong and could feel its warming effects flowing through her body. She turned while maintaining her hold on Murray, looking for the culprit. Her husband's handsome replacement spoke before she could spot old Pak Ali.

'Yes, we have met briefly,' Zach replied, holding out his hand. 'How are you, Murray?' he asked politely.

'Hello, Steve. See the colonel has your ear. We'll have time to catch up later, enjoy!' he said, shaking the new colonel's hand warmly before turning to leave them to continue their discussion. Dorothy Wharton continued to cling to his arm.

'Take me over there, Murray,' she instructed, her syllables now noticeably slurred. He permitted the woman to guide them towards the terrace. It didn't bother him that she was tipsy. Most of the wives spent their time drinking themselves into oblivion while their husbands were preoccupied either with the business of the day or some sweet and discreet interlude which offered a refreshing change to what was waiting for them in their palatial residences.

They stepped outside and immediately Murray identified the tantalising smell of barbecued chicken. The aroma of *sate* drifted across the small garden area as the vendor's sing-song voice cried out, *te, te,* tempting those who could hear, to buy his charcoal-cooked chicken sticks. He breathed deeply. Dorothy laughed and squeezed his arm tightly.

'You're something else, Murray' she complained, not unhappily. 'Inside we have smoked salmon, caviar and quail eggs and yet you still pine for the local food. Little wonder none of the foreign girls have managed to get their hooks into you.' She turned and was about to move back into the main room when two others joined them on the terrace.

Murray immediately went on the defensive. One of the men was the Military Attaché from the Soviet Embassy who had enjoyed the position for some years. The position designated the colonel as an active member of the KGB. Murray looked at the other man. He was tall, thin and very distinguished in appearance. There was something familiar about the man but Murray could not immediately recall what it was. He started to move inside, nodding as a matter of courtesy, as he went past.

'Good evening,' the thin man offered, partly extending his hand towards Murray. 'I'm Eric Whitehead. This is Colonel Kololotov.' He smiled at Dorothy. 'Mrs. Wharton,' he acknowledged his hostess before turning to the other men present. 'And you are ..?'

Murray had no choice. He took Whitehead's hand and pumped it quickly, before briefly shaking the KGB colonel's hand. Why did Whitehead look familiar? Murray tried to recall if he'd seen this man around the Embassy recently.

'Murray Stephenson,' was all he offered. He was very familiar with the Russian. Kololotov was listed in the protocol sheets as the longest-serving foreign Attaché in Indonesia. This remarkable achievement placed him at the head of the Attaché Corps which held monthly functions for all Military Attachés, regardless of their political affiliations. What the public did not know was that this man was one of the most senior KGB members in the Soviet Service, and the first to achieve the rank of general while serving overseas.

'I'm an Australian here on business,' Whitehead offered. 'The colonel is with the Soviet Embassy.' Murray looked at Dorothy who, in spite of her alcoholic intake, recognised the sudden change in Stephenson's demeanour.

'I'll be back in a moment,' she promised, moving away and into the crowded room.

'Don't forget my *sate*,' he called after her, wishing Dorothy had remained.

'You're with the Australian Embassy, aren't you?' Whitehead asked. Instantly Murray wished he had followed Dorothy Wharton inside. 'Haven't we met before?' he persisted.

'I don't think so. And who do you work with?' Murray decided to change to the offensive. It normally worked.

'Oh, I work for myself, Murray. Haven't you heard of Eric Whitehead and Associates? We are very prominent in the public relations arena.'

Murray cursed himself. Of course! He should have known. Eric Whitehead was virtually the commercial front for Central Plans'

South-East Asian operations. He had not met the man personally until now. Murray then remembered where he had seen the prominent well-groomed Australian before. He had seen the senior consultant sitting tete-a-tete around the pool a few days earlier. With Alan Davis.

'No, I'm sorry,' he replied a little too hastily. 'But please don't be offended by that. I've spent most of my adult career overseas. How does public relations work?' Murray asked clumsily as he groped for a reasonable response. Whitehead was about to explain when Dorothy Wharton reappeared.

'Gentlemen,' she interrupted, 'have you met our new Military Attaché?' Murray was instantly relieved. He wanted to grab the woman and hug her. Dorothy smiled coyly in his direction and left the men to carry on alone.

'I'm sorry, colonel,' Whitehead said. 'You were preoccupied when we arrived. I'm Eric Whitehead, this is Colonel Kololotov and our fellow Australian here is Murray ...' he trailed off, having forgotten Murray's surname.

'Good evening, Mr. Whitehead,' Zach responded formally. 'Murray,' he said, smiling, and then turned to the third man present. *'Good evening Colonel,'* he said, addressing the Soviet Attaché in perfect Russian. There was a hushed silence. Even the KGB officer was stunned. *'Forgive me if I do not address you as Comrade!'* Moments passed before the Russian could regain his composure.

'Good evening, Colonel. Your Russian is excellent! Where did you learn to speak our language so well?' he enquired, while both Whitehead and Stephenson stood silent, not understanding the exchange.

'A peasant language is not difficult to learn,' he answered, forcing a smile for the others present.

'Ah, I see,' Kololotov responded, nodding his head in an almost condescending manner. *'You are not an Australian at all. Let me guess where you were born.'* For several moments there was an uncomfortable silence as the other Australians waited, not knowing what was transpiring between the other two. *'My guess is, let's see ... German? No,'* he answered his own question, *'more likely you are from Lithuania? Perhaps Czechoslovakia?'*

'Let me save you the effort, Colonel. I am a Hungarian Australian.' Zach said coldly.

'Very good, Colonel. Very good. And how did you manage to crawl

out of that dung heap all the way to Australia?'

Zach's hands immediately turned into fists. Stephenson realised what was happening and stepped between the two men.

'Gentlemen,' was all he said. Murray stared challengingly into the Russian's eyes. He remained in this position until the Russian suddenly broke out into laughter and slapped Eric Whitehead on the back.

'You are new here, Colonel. You should learn some manners,' he said, smiling for the benefit of the others.

'And how would the Colonel be able to identify this change?' Zach replied, also smiling as if their interchange was hospitable. *'Since when does a Russian understand the meaning of manners?'* he added, hoping the barb would score.

'I will leave you here with your friends, Comrade,' Kololotov knew that this would earn a response.

'Go screw yourself, pig,' Steven Zach replied, smiling benevolently as he stood his ground and waited for the infuriated Soviet Attaché to storm back into the main body of guests. The public relations consultant frowned at the other Australians then turned to follow the Russian inside.

'Shit,' Murray said. 'I'm impressed!'

Steven Zach laughed, almost sincerely. 'Sorry,' was all he said. Stephenson knew that the exchange had been volatile. He wished he had understood what had precipitated the hostility. Zach had an impressive service record, he knew, having read the officer's profile on the morning their briefing had been postponed. Steven Zach had telephoned on Wednesday and asked Murray across to the Army Attaché's office. They met informally, and held a general discussion regarding Djakarta and Embassy life. They had agreed to meet again, privately, once the formalities of the colonel's first week had been attended to and his schedule permitted. Murray had made himself available to assist Zach with his settling-in period. The offer had been warmly acknowledged, both men obviously taking an instant liking to the other. As Military Attaché in this post, Steven Zach was privy to the knowledge of not only the existence of the Australian Secret Intelligence Service but who the station operatives were.

Murray looked at the other man. They were about the same height and build, but the colonel was more than five years his senior.

The good-looking officer was not married and there was nothing in his dossier to suggest that there had once been a Mrs. Zach, Murray had noted, as he perused the newcomer's documents. It was not unusual for an ambitious career officer to remain single, in fact maintaining single status was particularly relevant to active field officers in his line of employment. Murray waved to a passing *djongos* carrying an assortment of canapes and removed two before the houseboy offered the tray to Zach.

'*Tidak, terima kasih,*' the colonel refused the finger-food. '*It looks good, perhaps I will have some later. Can you find me another drink?*' he asked the surprised *djongos*.

'I heard you were bilingual,' Murray said as the servant went in search of the drink-waiter. 'In fact, the staff tell me you are fluent in the local lingo,' he lied. It was less embarrassing than revealing that he had found this information in a highly classified report attached to the colonel's ASIS profile.

'They tell me the same thing about you,' he smiled, pleased the incident with the Russian had gone no further. Zach was angry with himself for permitting the Soviet to bait him as he had. In the past, when confronted with similar situations, mostly Zach had been able to resist such displays of animosity. Sometimes he just could not control the hatred which had consumed most of his conscious hours for almost twenty years. The Hungarian-born officer had once sworn to kill all Russians for what they had done to his country. And his family.

'What other skills do you have that we should know about?' Murray asked, politely.

'Thought you would probably already know that, Murray,' he responded, inferring that his personal papers would most certainly be known to the clandestine service, operating under cover in the Embassy. He didn't mind. Considering he was born in a foreign country, one which was now a Communist satellite state, Zach found it difficult to believe that he had successfully crossed that bridge of suspicion which almost always precluded foreign nationals from obtaining security clearance to sensitive posts.

'Ouch,' Murray grinned, remembering not to underestimate this fine soldier.

'It's okay, Murray,' Steven said, smiling genuinely. He approved of the other man. Zach had been well briefed by the Director of

Military Intelligence in Melbourne before leaving for Indonesia. 'Stephenson's all right', the general had advised, 'but watch the Station Chief, Davis. The man is out of his depth. Best you deal with Stephenson anyway, he is well-wired to the top and is going places. He has established himself as a sound and competent officer, and has an intelligent understanding of what is really going on in Soekarno-land.'

'Want to tell me what just happened back there?' Murray asked, curious as to what had transpired. It was obvious that the Russian had lost his cool. Not bad, he thought, Zach had managed to alienate the Dean of the Attaché Corps in his first week.

Zach looked at Murray and the younger man immediately wished he hadn't pried. Murray identified the cold, steel, penetrating look in the colonel's eyes. He had seen it once before. In Semarang. When the Diponegoro Commander learned of his junior officer's betrayal.

'Why not,' Zach said suddenly, to Stephenson's relief. 'The Russian insulted my heritage and I responded accordingly. You might as well get used to it, Murray, I just can't stand the bastards!'

'Shit, Steve, who can?' he agreed, just as the drinks arrived. Murray waited for Zach to select his cocktail first before deciding on the Bacardi and Coke. He checked the ice before the *djongos* was permitted to pour the mix. 'Anyway,' he continued, as the waiter disappeared, 'Kololotov shouldn't be around too much longer, from what I hear. Rumour has it he's about to be promoted and that, my friend, would mean Moscow for Boris.' Murray smiled, hoping to take some of the remaining tension out of the air.

'I really don't care one way or the other. He can stay or go.' Zach then stepped closer to Murray and lowered his voice. 'Maybe you can expand my briefing when we finally sit down together. I would appreciate an update of their activities.' Murray was surprised and Zach noticed the raised eyebrow.

'Spare-parts, Murray, spare-parts. Looks like Boris is about to negotiate a new deal with the Government to recommence supply. Seems there is a thawing in their relationship and, if this is to happen, we'll want to know bloody quick which of their armoured divisions would have the capacity to back up their Malaysian campaign.' Zach noticed Whitehead approaching. 'We'll talk later,' he suggested, with a conspirator's wink.

'Gentlemen,' the distinguished figure said. Minutes before, when the slight altercation had broken out between the Russian and Steven Zach, Whitehead had felt it diplomatic to accompany what he considered to be the offended party inside. His company, Eric Whitehead and Associates, had grown into one of the largest public relations groups in Australasia. Now he was in the process of establishing offices throughout South-East Asia, supported strongly by the Australian Government. The quid pro quo being that many of his country managers sent from Australia were, in fact, ASIS operatives who gained a direct entree into the target countries by utilising his company's established infrastructure and resources. He enjoyed considerable access to Government contracts back in Australia in consideration of his support. The public relations executive was not, fortunately, privy to more than the knowledge that Australia wished to collect intelligence in those countries where he had established his promotional activities. Harry Bradshaw had refused to give the civilian information which would reveal the existence of Central Plans.

Soon after the arrangements had commenced, the company developed the reputation for having an exceptionally high staff turnover, particularly with its overseas representatives, as many of these either refused to return at the end of their assignments, or merely resigned while they were 'in-country'. Now, it appeared he had plans to expand his activities in Djakarta.

'Gentlemen,' he said again, as the three stood alone. 'I must express my surprise at your treatment of Colonel Kololotov, especially you, Colonel,' he continued, pointing with the hand which held his drink, one finger extended. Murray waited. He could not believe that the public relations entrepreneur was venturing down this path.

'What?' Zach asked, frowning at the older man.

'Mr. Whitehead,' Murray interceded, 'perhaps we could let it drop for some other time?' he suggested. 'After all, neither you nor I have any idea as to what really occurred between the two officers. Let's just let it go. Okay?' He didn't like these amateurs and was as concerned as the other agents that people such as Whitehead were a little too close to their activities. Murray believed that these 'fringe dwellers' were totally unreliable as they were motivated by financial gain and often destroyed entire networks with their amateurish antics. Whitehead looked at Stephenson, trying to establish who he was and what his position may have been in the Embassy. Before he could respond, Murray took Steven Zach by the elbow and started to move away from the inebriated guest.

'Mr. Whitehead, the colonel must attend to his duties. He is the guest of honour here tonight, or perhaps you have forgotten?' said Murray. Zach permitted Murray to lead him back into the crowd of tipsy expatriates. The few Indonesian officers who had attended had left immediately after the buffet had finished.

'Ah, there you are,' their hostess cried, 'thought you'd been kidnapped! Come along, now, Steven, these are people you must talk to,' she said, taking her husband's replacement by the arm, and ushering him towards the noisy group standing beside the temporary bar.

'Oh, Murray,' a voice called, and he turned to see Davis moving in his direction. He could see that the Station Chief had also had a few too many. Seemed as if most of the guests had decided to lay one on for the evening. 'Want you to meet a very interesting guy I spoke to earlier,' his voice slurred. Murray looked for an excuse to escape but it was too late. Davis looked around and suddenly identified the object of his earlier attention. 'There he is now. Let's have a few words together,' the Station Chief insisted, walking back towards Whitehead from whom Murray had just, with difficulty, extricated himself.

'Not a good idea, Alan,' Murray resisted. He was annoyed that Davis had not identified the man for who he was. It was not considered to be in their best interests to develop any public relationship with this man.

'Hello there again,' Davis called, 'have you met Murray Stephenson?'

'Yes, I have. Do you two work together?' he asked, causing Murray concern.

Davis answered. 'Yes, First and Second Secretary, Political Section.' These positions would have meant little to Whitehead. He was unaware of their covert activities. 'Murray, Eric here was explaining to me earlier that he is in the process of making application to expand his operations into Moscow. Can you believe that?' Murray looked at the entrepreneur and understood why he had been so put out earlier, when they had first met. Whitehead needed

Kololotov to provide an entree into Moscow. Murray suddenly wanted to smile. Instead, he encouraged the man to discuss his activities and plans for their Djakarta office, leading the conversation away from their own functions in the event Davis screwed it up. Finally, identifying an opportunity to move on, he excused himself and asked to speak to his Station Chief in private. They walked outside and stood alone on the terrace.

'Alan, don't you remember who that guy really is?' he asked, still concerned that Davis had consumed too many whiskies. 'Doesn't the name Eric Whitehead and Associates mean anything to you?' he asked incredulously.

'Sure, Murray,' he answered, looking smugly up at his subordinate's face. 'I remember exactly who he is. Eric Whitehead is the man who might just become my new employer,' he grinned, enjoying the expression on Stephenson's face. 'We have already had discussions, Murray. The position offers double what I'm making now, and the opportunity down the track to earn share options in their company structure. What do you thing about that!' he said, poking his finger into Murray's chest, almost aggressively.

'I think you're a little pissed, that's what I think,' he answered, angry with the absurd proposition. He was convinced that Davis had lost it, and obviously had no recollection whatsoever as to the relationship the Service enjoyed with the public relations firm. 'Tell you what, Alan,' he said, his tone more friendly than before, 'why don't you and I go down to Mamas' place now, just slip out and look for some real company?' Davis stared back at the suggestion. They had never been out together before. Never. The idea of accompanying Murray appealed to him and he agreed.

'Okay, let's go,' he suggested. Relieved, Murray steered Davis quickly outside, placed him in the care of his driver, then returned to thank his hosts. Twenty minutes later he held his Station Chief with one hand while Davis yelled and screamed obscenities as the cold shower continued to pound his head. Murray cursed the man when he had stumbled, and thrown up in the shower cubicle. He left him there in his own mess, the shower still running, while he sat in Davis' lounge listening to his record collection and sipping the expensive cognac he had found buried behind the bar.

Some time passed, the fourth LP fell noisily onto the turntable and started playing a Cliff Richard album when Murray decided that Davis had probably recovered enough to understand what he needed to say. He went back into the bathroom and was surprised to hear the shower still running. He peered in though the shower curtains but there was no one inside. Murray took the three steps required to bring him to the en suite toilet and knocked. There was no answer there either. He pulled the door open and found Davis lying prostrate on the floor. He was dead. The Station Chief had choked on his own vomit and died.

* * * * * *

Melbourne

The Secretary to the Minister for External Affairs reviewed the reports for the umpteenth time and was convinced that what had happened, although tragic, required no further action from his Department. After all, he considered, the man did not really belong to their Foreign Affairs Department and there were strict guidelines as to how his Department should act under these special circumstances. He signed the report off, indicating that no further action was required, with the annotation that the file was to be returned to him personally, once the Attorney-General's office had accepted his findings.

The file was then delivered by security courier directly to the Attorney-General. His office gave the contents a cursory perusal, before onforwarding the findings to Melbourne. Once the documents had been received there, they were personally carried through the maze of offices along St. Kilda Road and delivered under signature to the Director. Central Plans had grown considerably during these two years. Harry Bradshaw relished playing the role of its Head, the Chief of the Australian Secret Service, ASIS.

He gave the report a perfunctory read before signing the document off for return to Central Registry. There was nothing contained in the highly classified document which he had not already known. Davis' death had been treated as an accident, his body returned to Australia within days of his demise, and buried quietly in his home town in Tasmania.

The Director sat looking at the brown file stamped in oversized red letters designating Central Plans' identification codes. Harry had no feelings for the loss of Alan Davis. There was now no risk of complications developing, despite the Director's suggestion that the incompetent Station Chief may have been involved in questionable relationships or that he may even have been compromised. Opportunity had provided Harry Bradshaw with a choice; he could place a temporary senior in Djakarta, or risk rank and file criticism by following his first instincts.

He wrote the message and buzzed his assistant. The signal was encoded and despatched. Within the hour, the message was taken by a supervisor and matched with the coded reference numbers. She checked the unreadable five letter word groupings in the original telex and aligned this yet again for further encryption. As the telex machines clacked away together in unison, she held the thin paper tapes punched full of identification holes, feeling the gaps pass over her experienced fingers. Satisfied that the commencement points had been aligned correctly and that the message had been prepared in accordance with Cipher Centre instructions, the supervisor removed the new tape and placed this on her international machine. She then dialled, by-passing the Australian operator, identifying the correct recognition answer back code of her first addressee, then squeezed the activate button, sending her machine through the thousands of randomly punched holes in her tape. Ten minutes later, the garbled five letter message was received in full by the Indonesian *Pos Telegrap dan Telepon*. Once the P.T.T. supervisor had ensured that the duplicate had been retained, the original was then placed in the appropriate box for collection.

Almost an hour passed before the Embassy driver picked up his hourly collection for delivery to his employers. Another hour passed before Murray, to whom the priority message was addressed, could be located and driven to the Embassy. There, once he had discovered the secret nature of the initial text, he moved to more secure premises. There, he removed the tapes and returned to his own section where a duplicate, but far more classified arrangement, was in place. He placed the tapes on the matching decoder machines and listened as they clattered away, almost in harmony. The noise stopped and the officer tore the text from the top of the Navy grey deciphers. He read the message slowly, then smiled. It was from Harry Bradshaw. He read the signal again. Murray laughed loudly in the huge lead-lined cavern as he spun the swivel chair around in excitement. They wanted him back in Melbourne immediately.

He had just been appointed Chief of Station, Djakarta.

Chapter 12

Melbourne

Susan enjoyed having her friends visit once again. She sat, dabbing her face lightly with the damp cloth, removing the small line of perspiration which had appeared on her forehead. The weather had been excellent, providing their guests with an opportunity to play several sets before the wind suddenly came in from the west, making conditions difficult on the court. Disappointed, they had ceased play and showered, only to discover that the inclement weather had moved on in that brief time, leaving a warm but gentle breeze to tempt them outside once more.

Murray had brought a New Zealand girl along as his partner. Susan would not have expected the young woman except Harry had informed his wife just hours before they were expected. She was not upset. Although Susan had regretted her indiscretion with Muriel's son, she was more than pleased that her moment of passion had not deprived either her or Murray of their friendship, and that the delayed fruits of their brief coupling had not resulted in some contentious dispute between those involved.

Susan had not been overly concerned that her husband was obviously aware that he was not the child's father. She was pleased that the issue never arose and was delighted that Harry eventually came to enjoy his role as father. Or at least, he appeared to, when others were around. Harry continued to be preoccupied with his work which, to her relief, required considerable travel. Her husband had become more and more secretive over the past year, making communication almost impossible between them. Susan maintained her circle of friends and, of course, there was her son to consider. He had already commenced kindergarten, creating yet another void in a life which already had far too many empty hours.

She knew that she could not go on like this forever, just marking time.

These occasional weekends filled with visiting friends helped Susan maintain her balance with reality and forget, briefly, that her life had become dull, even monotonous, to the point of despair. 'Thank God for Muriel Stephenson,' she thought. Often, whenever she felt really depressed, a simple telephone conversation would be enough to raise her spirits. She smiled, knowing that her boy was in good hands. Murray's mother had volunteered to watch the child and they were, at that moment, watching the Mickey Mouse Show together in his room.

Susan Bradshaw smiled as Murray returned from the room he always occupied whenever visiting their cottage. She admired his tall, athletic body, sun-tanned from his years in the tropics. Betty, the young woman who had accompanied Murray, was attractive. As they walked out together, she slipped her arm around his waist. Susan looked on, with a twinge of jealousy.

'Ready for another set?' she called, surprised by this brief sensation. There had never been any further sexual contact with Murray after that one brief encounter. Susan had strived to maintain a relationship between them both which not only preserved their friendship, but also protected their secret.

'Not for me,' Murray replied. 'Have to keep my strength,' he joked, winking at Susan. 'Why don't you two girls have a game?' he suggested, flopping down into one of the deck chairs beside the pool.

'Actually, I would prefer a swim now if you don't mind, Susan,' Betty said.

'Good idea,' she responded, pleased at not having to play alone with the younger woman. They rearranged the heavy poolside chairs to face the afternoon sun. Susan then disappeared inside, in search of the others. She found her husband proudly displaying his most recent acquisition, an opium pipe from China. The other guests stood around feigning interest in the item. Susan identified the bored looks and went immediately to their rescue.

'Come on, people, drinks,' she called, taking the younger couple and leading them back to the terrace which overlooked the kidney-shaped pool. Harry turned and followed, passing by the bar where he stopped briefly and collected the bottle of Moet Chandon, which had been resting in ice. The group settled around the pool, sipping the champagne as the rays of the afternoon sun warmed their bodies. They talked, laughed and enjoyed each other's company. Harry related an anecdote he had heard during his most recent trip into Asia, causing the men to roar heartily while the women almost choked in their attempts to resist laughing along with the others, as the raucous story ended.

'Why don't you go along on one of Harry's trips?' Anne Lawson asked. This was her first weekend invitation to visit the seaside home. Her husband had recently commenced working for the Government. Something or other to do with Planning, she thought, knowing that Government jobs were all a little vague, and boring. The men exchanged quick glances.

'Now there's a good question,' Susan agreed, clapping her hands together in appreciation of the suggestion being raised. She looked across at her husband to watch his reaction.

'It most certainly is, young lady,' Harry laughed, surprising all present. 'Why don't you join me on one of my excursions, darling?' he asked, seriously, reaching for the flute of wine. The glass was Bohemian crystal. It was all he had kept from those earlier times.

'I can't imagine myself gallivanting around with you in Asia, Harry,' Susan responded, smiling at the guests. 'You're always complaining that you don't have sufficient time in any of the places you visit. What would be the point?'

'Right again, my dear.' Harry laughed. 'Perhaps we should just send you off to one of the more exotic places by yourself.'

'Now that is a very good idea,' Susan agreed. 'How about leaving your wallet out Harry, and I'll go shopping in Hong Kong?' she teased, although the idea was appealing.

'Best to do your shopping in Singapore, Susan,' Murray advised. 'You would be guaranteed better quality and the prices are much more competitive. We all use Peter Chew's on High Street. He has never let any of the Embassy people down and will even arrange to have you met and escorted to his shop.' The group laughed, enjoying the thought that one could find such service anywhere these days.

'And you could just drop down and have a look around Djakarta and Bali while you're in the area,' Lawson offered, joining in with his unsolicited advice. 'It's only an hour's flight, and you have friends on the ground there,' he added, pleased that he had been able to contribute. Murray frowned and looked across at his host.

'Normally I would probably agree,' he tried to make light of the conversation. 'But Djakarta is no place for a woman and child, I'm afraid.'

'Oh, nonsense, Murray,' Susan interjected, 'all I have heard from the two of you has been nothing but talk of islands and beaches. I think it's a fabulous suggestion. Don't you Harry?'

'Murray's right, my dear. Djakarta is not exactly an appropriate tourist destination at this time, student demonstrations and all that,' Harry answered, certain that foreign women were rarely in danger in Indonesia. Apart from the street urchins and thieves who preyed on unsuspecting visitors for the most part, it was reasonably safe to wander around the country. The ongoing student demonstrations would be of concern though, he thought.

'But surely these are confined to the city, right, Murray?' She looked to him for help, suddenly determined to at least have the option to visit, even if only for a few days. 'Harry, this is a wonderful idea,' she said, leaning over and running her hand down his forearm. Susan then looked across at Murray. 'Well, am I invited or not?' she challenged. Bradshaw thought quickly. It wasn't such a bad idea. He nodded his head slightly, as he considered the request. As he looked around the circle of guests, Harry suddenly laughed, recognising that they were patiently waiting for his response.

'Harry, I don't think ...' Murray started to say before Susan interrupted again.

'Wait,' she asked, rising to her feet. 'No decisions yet. I will be back shortly,' with which Susan Bradshaw left her guests and entered the cottage.

'Harry,' Murray started again, 'it's no place for Susan right now. Especially with a young child,' he added.

'What if we just send her off to Bali and Djogyakarta for a week?' Harry suggested. 'Susan would be in raptures, I'm sure.' Murray was surprised with the response although he had to admit that travelling through the outlying areas and provincial capitals could be a pleasurable experience. Political unrest was mainly concentrated in Djakarta although he believed that it could spread at any time. Violence lay perilously close to the surface in Asia. Murray knew. He had been exposed to the sudden and violent eruptions which predicated massive unrest and destruction.

'Perhaps, if Susan were to just visit Bali?' Murray suggested as Bradshaw's wife rejoined the group.

'I thought we'd agreed to hold the discussion until I returned?' she asked. 'Harry,' she continued, smiling with enthusiasm, 'Muriel has agreed to look after Michael if I decide to go. So, now it's just a matter of where, and when. What do you really think?' Again she placed her hand softly on her husband's arm. Harry felt the warmth of her touch and rested his own hand on hers. He looked across at Murray for support.

'Susan, if you really want to go, then by all means go. I'm sure Murray would be only too happy to provide you with whatever assistance you'd need.'

'Of course. That goes without saying. Susan, we'd be delighted to have you visit. If you wish, I could probably arrange for you to visit the Thousand Islands while you're in Djakarta.' Harry Bradshaw was not displeased with the outcome. He knew that he could depend on their friendship to ensure that Susan would be adequately cared for during her visit. He smiled in appreciation as Murray glanced in his direction. The ASIS Director was confident that his new Djakarta Station Chief would have little difficulty in being able to make the necessary arrangements.

The following Monday, Susan Bradshaw filed an application for her passport. Three weeks later, bogged down since his return to Djakarta with the additional responsibilities of First Secretary, Murray Stephenson sighed heavily as he read the coded personal message from his Director. Susan Bradshaw had obtained her visa and was scheduled to arrive within days. He looked at the unfinished mound of files and shook his head, remembering his other mounting commitments. Murray was disappointed that she was arriving at this time. Everything seemed to be happening at once.

He thought through his problem and an idea came to mind. He then raised the receiver and punched the internal dialling codes through to the Defence section. An assistant answered and he asked to be connected to the Attaché. Moments passed before the familiar voice answered the phone.

'Zach.' The colonel had not meant to be abrupt. Murray smiled tiredly at the familiar voice.

'Steve, it's Murray. I need a special favour.'

* * * * * *

Djakarta

The crowd roared when the roof finally burst into flames. As the chanting continued, black smoke poured from the building and rose quickly into the breezeless sky. Across the city, other fires were developing quickly. The students had commenced their campaign of terror against the American offices, before focusing their attention on the various United States Aid agencies. The police stood by and watched, almost disinterested, as the devastation took place, often laughing as foreign representatives fled their buildings under a barrage of verbal abuse.

Heat emanating from the building finally forced the crowd back. Dried timbers exploded noisily as the fire raged unchecked. Fire engines had arrived but were blocked by militant students. The men stood and watched, as the building finally collapsed on itself, testimony to their helplessness. The brigade officer knew that any attempt to force his way through the onlookers would have resulted in his tender being destroyed. A thousand hands could lift even the heaviest of his fire-fighting trucks and smash it to the ground, rendering the equipment useless. A loud explosion was greeted with yet another cheer as the remaining wall collapsed upon itself sending a wave of hot ash and cinders into the crowd of onlookers. Startled, they moved back and waited, expecting some exciting finale, but there was none. The fire died down quickly, having exhausted the dry timber and other fuel within minutes.

The mob became impatient, disappointed that the excitement had finished. Someone threw a rock through the air, smashing one of the American cars parked down the street. A loud murmur of approval rose from the students and, within seconds, they turned their attention to the vehicles parked along that street. Shouts of encouragement filled the air as the crowd lost direction, swelling in ranks at great speed as people spilled into the streets and joined in the mass demonstration. Gradually, the crowd grew into an uncontrollable mob, spilling down into the side alleys, chanting and screaming slogans as they went.

A roar of approval thundered through the morning air as several houses fell victim to indiscriminate fire-bombs thrown randomly into the air.

'*Lagi dong!*' a young girl screamed in excitement as Yanti's throw burst through a window, exploding as it entered the second-storey window. Yanti turned and accepted another Molotov cocktail, waiting for the dirty rag hanging from the top of the beer bottle to be ignited. She held the bomb at arm's length as a comrade lighted the cloth wick then suddenly, satisfied that the simple but deadly incendiary was ready, Yanti hurled the bottle over the heads of the screaming mob directly into the building's entrance, where it exploded fiercely in flames. '*Another,*' her friend urged, thrusting a third bottle into Yanti's eager hands. This too was lit and thrown, landing directly where flames from her previous attempt had now engulfed the structure's entire front. The crowd cheered as an upstairs window shattered. Then suddenly they stopped and there was a hush as they stared in horror at two children who screamed at them for assistance, their small bodies framed by the gaping hole, as flames licked precariously around the second level.

'*Ada anak!*' a woman screamed loudly, pointing to the terrified pair. '*There are children up there!*'

'*Bantu'in, dong!*' another cried, insisting they be saved, but the onlookers stood petrified at the spectacle. By now the fire had broken through to the roof and black smoke billowed from the entire building. The firemen stood helpless. Their equipment was inadequate and none dared brave the blazing home, then totally engulfed by flame. One of the children disappeared from sight, having fallen to the floor of her room overcome by heat and smoke. The other child continued to scream and attempted to crawl from the window but could not, her escape blocked by remnants of shattered, razor-sharp glass still embedded in the wooden window sash. A woman in the street screamed as the young girl finally collapsed also, lost to the fire. Immediately the crowd's mood turned even more ugly but now it was directed at the elements responsible for the children's demise.

'*They did it!*' a voice screamed, pointing at the group of *Gerwani* women.

'*Grab them, somebody!*' another voice demanded as others yelled curses at the group of PKI rioters.

'Yanti, quick! Let's get out of here, now!' a friend hissed, sensing their danger. Yanti yelled a command to her group and they obeyed immediately, running down the street away from the angry crowd. Unable to keep up with the others, several of her slower comrades fell as rocks took their toll. They were left to fend for themselves. That was the rule.

'Run!' she screamed as her girls began to slow, and another fell. Yanti heard the shot and knew that somewhere behind, the rifle would be taking aim for a further kill. *'Run faster! They're shooting!'* she yelled, almost out of breath as they neared the small intersection. *'Keep going, around to the right!'* she ordered as her communist gang reached the corner. Terrified, they ran on, then turned as instructed, hoping to flee the deadly rifle fire. Yanti pushed them on, screaming at them not to stop as several of her troops slowed, already exhausted.

'Stop here and you will die!' she warned, grabbing one of the young women by the arm and forcing her to continue down the narrow street towards safety. Minutes passed before the weary women were able to change direction once again and slow to an exhausted walk. Yanti led them away, not stopping to rest until she was absolutely certain that they had not been followed.

* * * * * *

To the south, guests and staff of the Hotel Indonesia stood watching the billowing smoke fill the uptown sky. Although the Nirwana Supper Club was closed for lunch, guests had little difficulty accessing the well-appointed restaurant, permitting a clearer view of the riots below. Sirens wailed as military vehicles sped dangerously through the streets, one having already flipped over as it failed to negotiate the *Selamat Datang* roundabout directly below. A number of BTR-40 Soviet APC's poured into Djalan Thamrin from both Imam Bondjol and Djenderal Sudirman, slowing as they converged on the major intersection. Shots were fired into the air to disperse the demonstrators whose numbers had grown into tens of thousands around the city's new centre.

The angry mob was out of control and surged towards the army vehicles, ignoring the dangerous weapons mounted on the APCs.

Another round of shots was fired. The crowd roared its

disapproval. Suddenly the scene turned even more ugly, the air filled with screams and shouts as rocks were hurled. The soldiers did not hesitate. They fired directly into the mob, killing indiscriminately.

Alarmed, the crowd panicked and fled in all directions, trampling those before them. The violence continued as both soldiers and demonstrators became confused in the melee. More shots were fired, then again, until most of the crowd cleared the area.

Susan watched in horror, transfixed by the brutality of the moment. She hadn't meant to stay, watching the bloody scene. Something had held her there as the violence unfolded in the streets below.

'Wished you stayed home?' Zach asked. He could see just how distressed she was.

'Not exactly what I'd expected,' she said, standing with her arms crossed, still confused by the violence. 'Now I wish I'd listened to Murray,' she added, distressed by the sight of the bodies lying where the panic-driven crowd had trampled them.

'Why did you continue to watch this then?' he asked. Susan didn't respond. Steven was pleased he had decided to arrive earlier than agreed. He was to take her to lunch in the Tjahaja Kota, promising the finest froglegs in town. They had talked to fill in time and were preparing to depart when the streets outside suddenly became congested and an enormous crowd had gathered. Sensing the danger, Steven had suggested they remain in the hotel. When the rioting commenced, he'd escorted Susan to the observation point in the west wing, where they witnessed the partial siege of the city. Zach knew that Susan had never been exposed to such violence before and understood how distressing the scene below must be for her.

'We should move back inside, Susan,' Steven suggested, concerned. Susan turned and shook her head.

'No, I'll stay,' she replied, forcing a smile. Nothing like the mountains, is it?'

* * * * * *

At first, when Murray had requested his assistance, the colonel had been less than enthusiastic. Agreeing to escort an unseen partner had its pitfalls, Zach explained. When it seemed that Susan might be left unescorted, Zach changed his mind and volunteered to assist. Murray had hosted a small dinner party, introducing his guest to a few close friends. Steven had smiled in approval as Susan was introduced. As he observed Murray's attractive house guest during the course of dinner, Steven Zach wondered how she came to marry Harry Bradshaw. He put the thought out of his mind, deciding it was not really any of his concern but, as the evening progressed, the question remained in his thoughts.

Murray was obviously relieved that Zach would shoulder some of the responsibility in ensuring Susan Bradshaw remained occupied during her visit. Murray forewent his rostered turn for an Embassy bungalow in Tugu, offering his weekend allocation to the Military Attaché. Zach jumped at the opportunity, and arranged for a small group to accompany Susan to the hill station. Once she had seen the small cluster of cottages nestled amongst the tea plantations, Susan began to unwind, pleased that she had not balked and refused the invitation. At first, she had felt uncomfortable that Murray would not be joining them but, when the others arrived, Susan quickly settled down and enjoyed the mountain air.

The evening was special. Gone was the sticky, humid weather of the capital. Here, at more than one thousand metres, the temperatures dropped just enough for the guests to enjoy an open fire. The *djongos* burned small tea tree logs and, as the aromatic smoke lingered in the air, Susan detected faint evening sounds emanating from the distant village, further adding to the tropical ambience. The evening passed too quickly for Susan. She experienced a genuine warmth in those around her, and realised just how long it had been since she had relaxed in the company of those her own age.

Late the next morning, Steven convinced Susan to join him for a long walk through the adjacent tea plantation. They strolled slowly through the green maze, Steven explaining how the planting cycle was maintained, and how the fields were first planted hundreds of years before. Susan listened attentively, occasionally asking an appropriate question, pleased with his company. The hours slipped by without their noticing the time. They rested in a small clearing and watched the plantation workers move in line across the difficult slopes, picking the finely-coloured leaves to shape the bushes. Susan could just see their bungalow's roof-line in the distance, partly obscured by a tall, thick stand of bamboo. Towards the west, the sun had moved behind Gunung Salak, indicating that the day was almost spent.

'It's so beautiful,' Susan said, admiring the orderly rows stretched out as far as she could see. 'This is how I pictured Indonesia would be.' She turned to Steven and placed her hand on his arm. 'Thank you for bringing me here, Steven. It will be a memory I will cherish.' Steven accepted the gesture for what it really was, a friendly touch which required no response. He smiled at her.

'Gets better as you go further away from the cities.' Steven rose and pulled Susan to her feet. 'Better be heading back,' he said, pointing to the low cloud rolling down the mountain side. Although the distance was not overly far, Zach knew that it would take almost an hour for them to make it back. As they walked through the well manicured rows, the wind grew in strength, signalling a mountain squall. Steve steered them both towards a simple structure which had been erected as a rest post for the plantation workers, to shield them from the heat of the tropical midday sun. No sooner had they crept under the simple cover when the light squall struck, thrashing the air with heavy rain.

The timber construction was barely three metres long and, having no walls, provided little protection from the horizontal rain as it cut across the mountain slope, stinging their faces and arms. They remained there until the wind abated, imprisoned by the heavy deluge. The sky remained black and threatening, lightning flashing all around as thunderclaps shook the mountain sides. Steven had stood with his back to the initial gusts of wind, protecting Susan from most of the heavy rain. He looked at her and Susan tensed, holding her closed fists to her mouth as a sudden flash signalled another close strike. She attempted to cover her ears, petrified by the ear-splitting thunderclap she knew would follow.

Steven moved closer to her side and placed his arms around the trembling woman. He didn't speak, but merely held her to provide comfort in her moment of fear. Zach could see that she was terrified by the sharp crashing sounds accompanying the tropical storm. He felt her tremble, then turn and bury her face in his chest, and cry out as another brilliant flash heralded the dangerous lightning which seemed to strike the village across the nearby field. Susan trembled and he held her tightly, telling her that she would be all right, as she clung to him in fear.

The tropical mountain storm was typically brief and, as the thunder and lightning dissipated, leaving the reluctant rain behind, Steven continued to hold Susan firmly. They were both saturated but neither felt the slight chill which followed the squall. As the rain eased, the sun broke through distant clouds to the west, casting beams of sunlight over the valley far below. Rain dripped through the weather-worn roof, finding a path down Susan's back, causing her to shiver slightly. She leaned back looked directly up into Steven's eyes.

His masculine smell touched her senses gently, causing an awareness inside that warmed her body, as he continued to hold her reassuringly. Susan tilted her head back slowly, her eyes closing softly as she parted her lips, and lifted her face to his. Steven looked down into her beautiful face and hesitated, kissed her gently, pulling her closer to his body. Susan moaned, her mouth becoming more passionate as they held each other tightly. Moments passed and they separated, staring at each other in surprise. Neither spoke as they stood there, holding each other.

It was Steven who broke the silence. As he spoke, quietly, his fingers drifted softly across her cheeks. She listened as he talked, and held her close. He started to apologise and she placed a finger on his lips to silence his words.

'Don't say anymore, Steven,' she whispered. He looked at her and slowly moved his head from side to side. They had been foolish, and caught by the moment, he felt. Steven smiled sadly and took her arms in his hands, slowly pushing her away.

'This can't happen, Susan,' he said, holding her at arms' length. 'I'm sorry.'

'Sorry? Why be sorry, Steven. I'm not,' with which she crossed her arms quickly and lowered her eyes, embarrassed.

'Susan?' The colonel placed his hand under her chin so that she would look at him.

'It's all right,' she murmured, searching for words to hide her disappointment. 'I suppose you think ....' she hesitated, her lips trembling as she fought back the tears.

'Shh!' he said, moving to draw her back to him, to comfort her as the tears rolled down her cheeks. 'It's okay, Susan. It's okay,' he said soothingly. Susan let him hold her for a few moments before she broke loose and turned away.

'I'm sorry also, Steven,' her voice choking as she fought against the tears. Susan turned and walked quickly away, in the direction of the bungalow.

'Susan,' he called, 'wait!' but she ignored the call. She stumbled, then regained her footing, then proceeded to walk quickly away, wiping her eyes with the back of her hands. He watched her go. Steven knew that he should follow, but felt that she would be best left alone. He stared after her, cursing himself for what had just happened. Steven watched Susan moving quickly along the plantation tracks, until the outline of her figure became smaller, then finally disappeared along the narrow path, through the hibiscus hedge leading to the bungalows. Satisfied that she was safe, he strolled slowly back in the same direction.

That evening, the atmosphere was more subdued. Fortunately the other guests were still present, agreeing to remain until early Monday morning when the traffic would not be as heavy. During a lull in the dinner conversation, Steven smiled as he caught Susan's eye which she rewarded with a playful kick under the table in response. Steven was instantly relieved, pleased that their relationship could continue on an amicable basis. They had returned to Djakarta early the next morning, Steven promising to take Susan for an experience he boasted she would never forget.

'Frogs' legs, Susan,' he had said, indicating the size with both hands. 'Best I have ever eaten.' She laughed as his car drove away, already looking forward to their luncheon appointment. Susan was pleased she had moved into the hotel. She sensed that Murray was uncomfortable having her stay alone in his villa, and knew he was relieved when she opted to move to where, she suggested, there was a splendid pool and other women to talk to.

Now, as she stood high above the city centre, Susan wished they had remained in the mountains. The contrast between the tranquil hill station bungalow setting and the chaotic scene below was almost incomprehensible to the young woman. As she stood overlooking the carnage below, a number of two-man Scout cars suddenly poured onto the roundabout and opened fire on the few remaining onlookers with their deadly 7.62mm guns. Susan caught her breath sharply as she witnessed a group of stragglers collapse to the ground like oversized rag dolls. Shocked, she turned away sharply.

'Okay, that's enough! Please take me back to my room, Steven.' He did so, insisting that she remain there until he returned. 'Where are you going?' she asked, concerned.

'I must go the Embassy, Susan. They will be looking for me there. I'm sorry, it's bad luck. I will try to get back in a few hours. Providing the phones are still working, I'll ring you in, say,' he said, checking his watch, 'two hours.' He looked at her worried expression and smiled. 'It's okay. I'll be back before you know it.' Steven Zach left. Minutes later, he found himself standing behind other hotel guests blocking the lobby as they watched the end to the violence not fifty metres from the hotel driveway.

Steven exited via the northern wing rear entrance and crossed the car park. He walked through the Karya Wisata Hotel, out through the service area and across the small pedestrian bridge which brought him to Djalan Teluk Bitung. He walked quickly back towards Djalan Djenderal Sudirman and turned right, hurrying away from the hotel roundabout until reaching the Djalan Blora underpass, some three hundred metres from where he had started. There he found a *betjak* driver who, having been offered twice the normal fare, agreed to take Zach to the Embassy on Pegangsaan, by following the railway track. Twice they were forced off the small road by speeding Ferret Scouts as they, too, were obliged to seek alternative routes down to the riot centre. Fifteen minutes passed before the *betjak* delivered the shaken colonel to his Embassy. Zach went directly inside, where his assistant, an Army Warrant Officer, was obviously relieved that his colonel had returned.

'They're holding a prayer meeting extraordinary, now, sir,' he advised the Military Attaché. Zach merely nodded and left. He had expected as much. 'Prayers' were normally held Tuesday mornings, and were attended by the three Military Attachés, the Ambassador, his Counsellor and ASIS Station Chief. The riots had obviously demanded an urgent session be called to determine what course of action the Embassy might take, if deemed necessary. The Ambassador's secretary escorted Zach into the room.

'Gentlemen,' he said, nodding first to the Ambassador as the ranking officer present, and then to the others.

'Pleased you could make it, Steven,' the Head of Mission announced in a patronising tone. His deep resonant voice always surprised first-timers. The Ambassador stood not much taller than the exquisite mahogany desk behind which he ruled his miniature kingdom. The Military Attachés only gave the posturing Ambassador such respect as his position demanded, while normally ignoring whatever suggestions the undersized tyrant proffered during these sessions. Zach thought it quite appropriate, that, in his absence, the Ambassador was regualrly referred to as the King from *The Wizard of Id*. 'Our political section was in the process of briefing us,' he said. 'Please continue, Mr. Stephenson,' he ordered, waving a small podgy hand through the air.

'Thank you, Mr. Lovenight,' Murray responded. He disliked the little man immensely and refused to refer to him directly as Ambassador, electing instead to use the man's surname. 'I'd only just commenced, colonel,' he stated, formally. 'The position report is basically this. There are at least three major demonstration points. The worst appears to be centred around Djalan Thamrin leading up to the Hotel Indonesia. The city's Garrison Commander has placed a ring of troops around the embassies located off Iman Bondjol and behind Djalan Madura. They don't want the demonstrators to hit any more embassies although the Brits are not convinced that they won't be targeted yet again.' Those present were painfully aware of how the British Embassy had recently been gutted by fire, a result of past demonstrations. There were at least ten foreign legations situated within the danger area, including the Soviet, the New Zealand and what was left of the British Embassy.

'American offices are taking a pounding,' he continued. 'None of their citizens have been injured, although a number of local employees have been reported killed or are suffering serious injuries. It would seem that they are taking the brunt of the demonstrations. There are other and less serious reports of riots, but the majority of these appear to be strictly incidences of looting. We have estimates of around three hundred dead with no less than fifteen foreign offices and homes destroyed.'

'What's happening outside Djakarta?' asked the Air Attaché, explaining that he planned a visit to Sulawesi as part of his annual tour around the archipelago.

'So far, it seems, nothing,' Murray replied. 'But don't count on that situation continuing, Group Captain. Our information is a little loose out there in the provinces but it would seem that there definitely is a groundswell building. My advice would be to post-pone, or even cancel, your journey for a few weeks, at least. There is pressure mounting on the Military to prevent these communist demonstrations and we should not be surprised if they do take some action. Soebandrio's power play must have them concerned. After his recent appointment as Deputy Prime Minister, we have confirmed reports that the PKI have been told that their represen-tation in Cabinet will shortly be increased, to the detriment of the Army and Police. It seems that their Airforce, AURI, has made con-siderable inroads into the Army's traditional power base. Seems there's to be a major visit to China within weeks.'

The Attachés discussed the situation at length, agreeing to con-tribute to a final situation report which would be radioed within the hour to Canberra. As the meeting concluded, Murray took Zach aside as the others returned to their offices.

'How's Susan?' he asked anxiously.

'Still in the hotel. Agitated, distressed, but we shouldn't expect less. She watched the Ferrets open fire on the crowd. I told her to stay put until I returned. How are the phones?' Murray grimaced.

'Useless,' he answered.

'Okay, then. I'll prepare my contribution for the situation report and send it over to the Counsellor. Then I'll shoot back to the ho-tel.' Zach looked at his watch and swore.

'Tell Susan I'll call by later. And Steve,' he said, placing his hand on the other man's shoulder, 'thanks!'

Zach smiled and nodded, then returned to his office. A further two hours passed before he could leave the building. He took one of the Embassy vehicles down along the circuitous route he'd taken by *betjak*, instructing the relieved driver to drop him near Djalan Blora. From there he walked towards the Hotel Indonesia, surprised to see the area cleared of demonstrators, although two menacing BRDM Soviet Scout cars remained on both sides of the rounda-bout, maintaining an ominous presence. Further down the proto-col avenue smoke was still evident, and black clouds reached high into the air behind Sarinah, Djakarta's only department store.

He telephoned from the lobby then went directly to Susan's room. She refused to leave the hotel but did agree to join him down-stairs for cocktails. Steven escorted her down to the Baris Lounge Bar which, by then, was packed with guests and foreign journalists.

'I'm ready to return home,' Susan announced. Steven was not surprised. He had half expected this reaction. 'Would it be possible for me to leave tomorrow?' she asked.

'We could try, Susan. It won't be easy, the few flights to Singapore will undoubtedly be full. Wait for Murray to arrive. He should be here around five. Maybe he'll be able to call in a few favours if you're really determined to leave.'

'I couldn't stand another day like today,' she admitted, moving the small candlelight away from the centre of the low table. She looked at the *katjang goreng* and, deciding that the peanuts had been cooked in too much salt, pushed these to the side. Steven watched her. She was suffering from shock. She talked without listening, preoccupied with her own thoughts, the day's violence obviously heavy in her mind. He had seen this reaction before, but on a more exaggerated scale. Often, soldiers returning from their first confrontation with the enemy would either remain silent for days, or babble on incessantly like some excited child.

The bar lounge lighting was deliberately soft as this was where most foreign couples congregated during the early evening. It really didn't seem to matter whether it was early afternoon or late evening as the lighting never changed. Small smokeless candles set snugly in *bangka* tin holders provided flickers of light, further diminished by delicately-made red light shades. Even in this subdued light, Steven could see the anguish in her eyes.

Steven felt bad about Susan. In less than a week she had travelled from what was a relatively parochial society into a world where violence lay just below the surface at all times. He was annoyed that her husband had not, with his obvious understanding of the region, prevented her from travelling to Indonesia at this time. And, of course, there was Murray, he thought. Surely he could have dissuaded Susan from venturing into the country knowing just how volatile the political atmosphere had become. He leaned across and placed his hand over hers. Susan looked up into his eyes and smiled, just as Murray entered the bar and made his way over to where they sat. One of the waiters carried a low stool over for the familiar figure. Murray joked with the man, then ordered a Bacardi and Coke. He looked at his friends and immediately sensed the woman's tense mood.

'Looks like the worst is over.' He looked at Susan Bradshaw.

'Hear you had a bad time. Are you okay?' he asked, gently stroking her arm.

'Susan wants to go home, Murray. Tomorrow, if possible,' Zach informed him. Murray peered across at his friend in the dimly-lit lounge.

'Well, that's a pity, Susan,' he said, almost nonchalantly. 'I have managed to arrange a few days out on the islands for you, as promised. Do you remember what I told you about the Pulau Putri group of coral atolls?' he asked, sure that he had recounted stories about the Thousand Islands to Susan over the past few years. Murray sensed the mood and tried to lift her spirits. 'Hey, Susan,' he said, 'we are talking about crayfish, white sand, blue water and coconut palms!'

'And what else?' she asked, guardedly.

'It's a different world, Susan. And totally safe, I can assure you. Besides, today's violence is already history. Trust me, Susan, you wouldn't forgive yourself if you passed up this opportunity.' Murray looked to Zach for help but found none there. Steven Zach was disturbed by the fact that Stephenson seemed so cavalier about what was happening around the city.

'Murray, I think Susan has made up her mind,' he said, looking at them both. 'There has been a suggestion that even tomorrow wouldn't be too early.' Murray had expected this response. He looked across at Steven Zach but the lighting did not provide the opportunity for Murray to signal his friend. He tried another tack so as not to appear obvious. Hell, he thought, Zach was not to know that all international flights had been grounded for at least another forty-eight hours and there was no point in further panicking Susan with this detail. When he had discovered the airport's temporary closure, Murray considered the options. Susan could remain penned up in the hotel until flights returned to normal, or he could arrange for her to visit the idyllic islands just a few hours by power boat from Djakarta's harbour. A cruise out to the islands where he knew it would be completely safe would not only remove Susan from the dangerous city, but also from his immediate concern. There was no guarantee that, should she refuse, Susan would not become bored and venture out into the unsettled surroundings. He knew her well enough to be concerned about this.

'Susan, you really should consider this trip. Okay?' Murray

asked, wishing that Zach would support him. 'Tell you what,' he added, before she could refuse, 'if you agree to go, I will personally guarantee you the largest green crayfish you have ever seen. Okay?' he tried again. Steven looked across at Susan and was surprised that she appeared to be considering the offer. He frowned, then stared at Murray in the difficult light, trying to attract his attention without alerting Susan.

'Back in a moment,' Zach said, finally catching Murray's eye, as he excused himself and walked in the direction of the toilets. Several minutes passed before Stephenson entered the men's area and discovered Steven waiting patiently beside the wash basins.

'Took your bloody time! I was getting dish-hands wiping the damn things every time someone walked in or out of the place,' he complained. 'What's going on, Murray? Why the push for the islands?' Murray brought Zach up to date on what had happened at Kemayoran Airport. He shook his head and cursed the airlines, as he listened to the Station Chief justify his suggestion for Susan to spend the next few days out on Pulau Putri. They discussed the alternatives briefly, then Zach returned to the bar lounge. Susan gave him an enquiring look.

'I had to check in with the Embassy, sorry,' he lied. Then he leaned over the low table and asked, 'Are you seriously considering the island trip, Susan?'

'Could I still leave for Sydney tomorrow if I decided against the boat trip?' she asked. Steven looked directly at Susan. She was obviously not to be fooled and he decided to be frank with her.

'It may be some days before we could get you out via Kemayoran Airport anyway, as flight restrictions have been imposed. I agree with Murray. You could either stay here in the hotel bored to death, or go swimming out on the beautiful islands.'

'Alone?' she asked, now tempted to go, but not by herself.

'Of course not,' Zach replied. 'We'll make a few calls and see who amongst the wives would like to join you. Our Naval Attaché has his own thirty-footer complete with boat-boys. His wife is a water freak and would jump at the opportunity to take you out with some of her friends. Actually, the more I think of it the better this excursion sounds. You would be in safe hands and out of this confusion. Okay?' Susan thought for a moment and sighed. It would be better than sitting around the hotel pool there, she agreed.

'Could you both join us?' she asked, hopefully.

Zach frowned again. It would be impossible with the current situation and the monitoring requirements. 'We'll try to make it out on Friday. That way we could all come back together on the Sunday afternoon. I'll speak to Murray. If we can't make it, we'll let you know. The captain's boat is fitted with SSB which will keep everyone in touch.'

'SSB?' she asked as Murray returned to their table.

'Single-Side-Band radio,' he answered simply. Zach looked at Murray. 'Well, looks like we have a starter,' he said, now feeling more comfortable with the arrangements. Murray checked his watch and pulled a face. He finished his drink and rose, leaned over and kissed Susan on the cheek.

'Sorry, must be off. Besides, have to catch up with our friendly Navy Attaché and get things organised for this trip. Will you be all right?' he asked Susan as he stood, preparing to leave.

'Not if you're both deserting me,' she smiled, and looked questioningly at Zach.

'Of course not,' he laughed, waving to the waiter for drinks. Murray nodded, and left his friends while he returned to the Embassy and made the necessary arrangements for the island excursion. It was already late but he knew that the captain would probably still be in his office. While Zach entertained Susan Bradshaw, Murray went about organising the trip, driving out to the captain's house to speak with the Attaché's wife, and then despatching his driver down to the harbour area to alert the two-man crew that they would be departing the following afternoon. By ten o'clock that night, everything was in place, right down to the captain's wife having arranged for another of the wives to join in the boat trip. Provisions were not a problem; she merely drew on the substantial stocks in their store.

The three ladies were driven to Tandjung Priok by the colonel's driver the following day, where they boarded the captain's private launch and immediately went about covering their bodies with suntan oil. As they passed through the harbour's entrance just after midday, sipping gin tonics, and laughing at each other as they stumbled around the boat, the powerful twin Evinrude outboard engines pushed the launch through the calm seas at more than twenty knots, and took a heading for the farthest point in

The Thousand Islands.

The women settled down to enjoy the voyage and, within minutes, as they approached the first of the small coral atolls in the chain, Susan felt as if they had entered another world. She looked back towards the city, almost hidden beneath the heavy smog fed by diesel-driven buses and trucks, and immediately experienced a sense of release from the devastating events of the previous day. As the senior boat-boy steered the vessel around Pulau Edam with its historic lighthouse, Susan caught one last glimpse of Djakarta's distorted skyline through the distant haze and sighed, raising her glass in salute to the men she had left behind.

* * * * * *

Semarang

General Prajogo, the Diponegoro Commander, stared at the intelligence report in disbelief. It had taken months to acquire and, even then, the damning document left numerous questions unanswered. He rose from behind the heavy teak desk and moved to the window. His thoughts were clouded with the information contained in the BAKIN foreigners' desk file, a copy of which now lay open on his desk. His own Intelligence Officer had taken the initiative in the end, visiting the Indonesian Intelligence Co-ordinating Agency in Djakarta where, subjected to considerable persuasion, his brother-in-law had permitted him access to the sensitive files.

The general felt betrayed. But this was not a new sensation for the veteran army officer, as he considered the very existence of the Council of Generals a clear indictment of the senior Military leadership's intention to move his country away from the preferred policy of non-alignment, and deliver his people into the hands of the Americans. Not that he had any time for the Soviets, either! And then, of course, there was the other imminent threat of the communists moving to take control. The general cursed the PKI under his breath as he considered the unexpected complication disclosed in the folder lying on his desk.

He knew that the success or failure of their plan would be in the timing and now, with the evidence he had received, the general was convinced that their plans would most certainly fail should

251

they continue as originally scheduled. No, he thought, he would not lead his men into the well-prepared trap. He and his officers were certain that the PKI must be close to finalising their plans as their presence in the capital had grown considerably, fuelling speculation that their move to take control was imminent.

Having considered all of these matters, the Commander decided to take the Javanese approach to the problem, preferring to see how the situation developed first, before launching his own plan to wrestle control from the Council of Generals. A window of opportunity had opened and he now knew what it was that he must do. No, he decided, the Diponegoro Command would not move first to snatch the reins of government from those in power! Instead, he would wait for the communists to first make their move and then thrust his soldiers into the arena to challenge the PKI leadership. It would all come together perfectly, he believed, just as long as they were patient. His men would defeat the communists' attempt to snatch control and, while this was happening, his officers would ensure the removal of the members of this so-called Dewan Djenderal, who sat around idly ignoring the obvious as they grew fatter with the help of their American friends.

The Commander was convinced also that the people of Indonesia would applaud his actions in restoring the Government and dealing with those responsible. The *rakjat* would support the Diponegoro Commander when he explained why it had been necessary to remove the current military leadership. The people, his *rakjat*, would understand. Of that he was certain.

The general turned back to the folder which had, once he had discovered its secrets, resulted in his drastic decision to place his own plans in abeyance until the communists made the first move. He looked down at the report and shook his head once again at the annotations made by the senior Intelligence officer responsible for the contents. He just couldn't understand how this man had so obviously fooled even his own Government and still managed to maintain such a senior position. There was little doubt in the Commander's mind that his Command had been compromised by the foreigner mentioned in the file. It was obvious, he concluded, having read of the man's constant association with the communists. Most likely, the PKI were just waiting for the generals to move first and had prior knowledge of his intentions. The communists were clever. They could then use this in their favour to gain even greater control over the President and the country. No, the Diponegoro Divisions would wait. He would play their game and see, just who would win the final play!

General Prajogo looked disapprovingly at the passport sized photograph taken from their Immigration files and attached to the report. His fingers scratched at an irritation on the crown of his head. Then, almost absent-mindedly, the Commander cleaned the dead tissue from under his fingernails with the *Djogya* silver letter- opener, a gift he had received from his fellow officers. Still deeply disturbed by the revelations disclosed in the open folder lying across the large sheet of blotting paper, he frowned once more then drove the sharp point directly through the photograph of the man he considered responsible for the major shift in his strategy.

'Bangsat!' he growled, looking down at the folder, but Murray Stephenson's face just smiled back at him, mockingly.

* * * * * *

The Assistant to the Naval Attaché, Chief Petty Officer Ron Brindles, himself a Milne Bay veteran, stared through bloodshot eyes as he assured Colonel Zach that the crew had understood the captain's instructions clearly. His condition was more a result of his alcoholism than time put in behind the unofficial Embassy radio. The vessel would be standing by in Tandjung Priok Harbour at 0800 hours on Saturday morning, to transport the Military Attaché and other guests to Pulau Putri, the Chief had said. The ladies would remain on the island while the launch returned to fetch those passengers intending to spend the weekend on the coral atoll. Chief Brindles relayed the information as if he were reading the departure details to the passengers of some ocean-going liner. As it turned out, there were only two. The captain had decided that as the Indonesian Navy did not appear to be involved in the political disturbances, there would be little point in his forgoing an opportunity to spend time out on the islands. Armed with additional supplies, the two officers boarded the vessel, which covered the forty nautical miles in two hours and arrived at their destination as the women were preparing an early lunch.

ALRI, the Indonesian Navy, controlled these islands, most of which were uninhabited and covered with thick stands of coconut trees. Fisherman landed from time to time, mainly out of curiosity or to sell their catch to the few foreigners who occasionally visited the small paradise. A makeshift jetty had been constructed although the captain still preferred mooring away from the shore. Two timber shacks had been erected and the women had established possession of these with just a few rupiah. At the rear of the dwelling a western toilet had been installed adjacent to the *mandi*, where one could bathe with fresh water, providing the overhead tanks had recently benefited from rain. A cooking pit prepared with coral lay between the beach bungalows and the lagoon. It was an idyllic place.

Zach could not believe the magnificent setting as their vessel turned carefully into the wide lagoon. At first, he thought their destination was the centre of the beautiful, elongated crescent-shaped island directly in their path. The water was clear to incredible depths, reminiscent, he thought, of Australia's north-eastern coastline. A pod of dolphins lept out of the water, leading the way through the narrow channels and brilliantly-coloured coral reef. As their launch moved farther into the setting, Steven discovered that, what he had believed to be one long island suddenly fractured into a chain of tiny coral atolls, numbering more than fifty. Each of these minute islands was smothered with coconut trees, which swayed gently in the tropical sea-breeze. Zach saw as the launch glided past that the palms were thick with bunches of yellow and green coconuts. It was as if they had entered an untouched world, Zach thought, almost at a loss for words as they became encircled by the beautiful group of islands.

The women waved as they wandered down to the water's edge, watching the vessel moor alongside the shaky jetty. The men stepped ashore, leaving the crew to manage the supplies and start up the small diesel generator to prevent the perishables from spoiling, and prevent the ice from melting further in the ship's oversized freezer.

'Well, we made it!' Steven smiled, removing his sneakers. The fine white sand felt great beneath his feet. He removed his shirt and sat on the narrow beach. 'Think I'll move the office out here!' he joked. He looked up at Susan who seemed totally relaxed. Zach was pleased. 'Have you learned how to scamper up one of those yet?' he asked, pointing to the coconuts high above their heads.

'Sure,' she replied, also laughing. 'We did that first thing this morning when we discovered the men were coming.' She was obviously in good spirits, he thought, relieved that sending her out with the others had not been an error in judgement.

'Murray said to say 'hello'. Obviously, he couldn't make it.'

'What's happening back in Djakarta?' she asked, some hint of weariness in her voice.

'It has quietened down, thank God.' Steven watched her face. 'Airlines have space available if you wish to return on Monday.' Susan looked down at the sand and moved her toe around, doodling.

'And if I say yes?' she asked, digging into the sand with the heel of her foot.

'It would be easy enough. We could just radio the Embassy and the Duty Officer would make the arrangements over the weekend for you.' He watched her move sand around unconsciously. 'That is, if you really want to go on Monday,' he added.

Susan seemed to be deep in thought. She looked up and smiled. 'We don't have to make that decision immediately, do we?' she asked.

'No, of course not.' Steven replied, rising to his feet. 'Now, Jane, how about some food for Tarzan,' he joked, making light of the moment. It worked, Susan entered into the spirit of his mood as she led him to the bungalow and made them both a vodka mixed with canned orange juice. They sat outside on the narrow stretch of sand leading down to the lagoon where occasional ripples broke the glass like appearance of the water's surface. The sun warmed their bodies as they sat, quietly enjoying the tropical ambience. Steven could see the tips of coral exposed as the tide receded. Before he had finished the vodka, reef was evident all around. He watched, fascinated, as an area almost the size of a football field slowly appeared, exposing sea life of considerable variety. Coral fish continued their dangerous adventure, swimming through the now shallow waters in search of food, oblivious to the sharp-eyed prey waiting high above for an opportunity to pounce. Crabs scurried around, playing hide-and-seek between the outcrops while sea-slugs, those succulent, cucumber-shaped tropical delicacies, lay indolently just below the surface. Soon, Steven could see that it would be possible to walk most of the one hundred metres across to the adjacent island, in the ankle-deep lagoon. Just a few steps to either side of the natural causeway, Steven observed how quickly the shelf fell away to much greater depths where larger fish fed lazily off the rich coral reef.

They remained there, together, enjoying the atmosphere and each other's company as the others, drinks in hand, wandered down to join them. As the sun reached its zenith, the men entered the deeper waters and snorkelled, while the women stood, waist deep, holding their drinks and chatting contentedly.

As the day wore on, they continued to enjoy the setting, eating crayfish and crab bought from passing fishermen for lunch, while consuming what appeared to be a never-ending flow of cocktails. By evening, the men were hungry again, insisting that they break out the steaks. The meal was cooked and consumed, along with several bottles of Italian wine obtained from some dubious supplier back in the capital.

Steven rose to his feet and stretched. They had finished eating and he'd had more than enough to drink. He strolled slowly down to the water's edge and remained there, admiring the evening sky. The lagoon remained dead calm, untouched by the soft breeze which moved, unnoticed, as it gently touched the tall palms standing like self-appointed guardians over the island and its tenants. He yawned, but he was not tired. Zach breathed deeply, savouring the tropical salt air. There were few clouds and, as the moon suddenly broke loose casting its golden spell across the waters, he became mesmerised by the magical setting.

He sensed someone moving close but did not turn to look. Nor did he flinch when she placed her arm around his.

'It's so incredibly beautiful,' she whispered. Zach remained silent, as he knew words were not necessary. They stood, together, captivated by the balmy tropical evening. 'Let's walk,' she suggested, encouraging Zach to follow as she moved away, holding onto his arm. They stepped into the tepid water and strolled slowly, away from the bungalow's lanterns and the others. They followed the sandy shoreline where phospherescence sparkled as their feet stirred the shallows. As they moved together, their arms locked around each other's waists, Susan rested her head on Zach's shoulder. Out of view, they stopped momentarily, under a tall stand of coconut palms. They didn't speak. It wasn't necessary and, as Susan lifted her mouth to his, Steven responded with a tenderness she had forgotten was possible. The warmth of his kiss engulfed her, and she pressed for more. Steven reached down and lifted Susan into his strong arms, moving towards the palms. He placed her gently on the sand, continuing to kiss her softly as his hands found their way over her body. He removed her clothes, then his, kissing the soft white areas as she encouraged him with her hands. She kissed him again, urgently, and Steven responded, almost impatiently, causing her pain which went unheeded as they joined passionately. Suddenly, Steven moaned and Susan cried out, her body arched and trembling in ecstasy. Then it was over.

They lay in each other's arms, resting, Susan stroking her lover's back as he kissed her mouth, then neck, softly.

'Steven,' she started, but he kissed her again, silencing her voice. As the warm air washed over their bodies, and the soft moonlight occasionally broke through the tall palms, casting shadows across them, they fell asleep. Clouds moved lazily across the evening sky blotting out the light, as Susan and her lover lay together. A gecko lizard scurried across a fallen coconut trunk, seeking refuge from birds it sensed watching in the darkness. Soon, the morning stars brought a colder breeze.

Steven woke, and shook his companion gently. Susan lay quietly listening to the ocean's sounds as the tide encroached. She placed her hands on Steven's face and whispered his name. They embraced, then kissed, and as Susan moved her hands across his body Steven became aroused, touching her body softly, caringly. As they made love again, this time with greater tenderness than before, Susan closed her eyes and wished that the moment would never cease; that the indescribable warmth which flowed though her body would never end and, as their bodies slowed, she sighed, deeply, in contentment.

As the morning sun threatened to spill over the early horizon and the evening hunters returned to the sanctuary of their nests, Steven and Susan walked slowly back to their bungalow, and their friends. Neither spoke, for there was little left to say.

They both understood what had happened and the consequences of their actions. But, at that moment, neither seemed to care.

Chapter 13

Presidential Palace
Djakarta

Bung Karno stood facing the northerly aspect of the Palace grounds. He had a great deal on his mind. Below, he observed a Toyota jeep enter through the main gate. From it emerged the figure of a man he had grown to despise. Soekarno snorted. His military now boasted almost four hundred officers of general rank amongst whom, he felt, to his dismay, less than a handful could be trusted. The President stepped back from the tall window and withdrew to the small ante-chamber where he normally rested. He would make the general wait. Soekarno looked at the Dutch grandfather clock and noted the time, before disappearing into the adjacent room. There, he removed his shoes and lay on the couch, closing his eyes permitting his thoughts to flow freely as he waited, anticipating his personal assistant's announcement that Nasution had arrived. Soekarno closed his eyes willing the pressure at his temples, to go away.

His dream of a non-aligned nation was quickly dissipating, forced into oblivion by the British, who were using regional conflict to reassert their colonial presence. He wondered if Nasution was part of this latest conspiracy. He sighed. If only the British would leave well enough alone, he thought. It seemed that they were determined to force the issue over the Federation of Malaysia up to the very end. The British had mobilised forces far beyond what he and his advisers had envisaged. None could have anticipated their transporting so many of their soldiers from Europe into Malaysia to support the newly-created Federation of Malaysia with its eastern alliances. At least Brunei remained outside the British-conceived amalgamation. Singapore too had been obliged to reconsider its position.

He was pleased, at least, with this development. The Singaporeans were, in his opinion, astute and their neutrality essential to the ultimate realisation of a Pan Indonesia.

He knew that his authority and stature had grown as a result of his non-aligned policy. Soekarno believed that the new emerging nations needed to position themselves on the international dais using their collective voice to demonstrate to the neo-colonial powers that the world had changed. He urged the other newly independent nations to emulate Indonesia, unified under a common philosophical front, to shun British and American overtures to surrender their political independence in exchange for economic bondage. He had a greater dream for his people, one which would provide not only an independence to achieve those freedoms denied under Colonial Rule, but one which would also guarantee their right to exist without the fear of reprisal from the British and Americans for Indonesia's stance on non-alignment.

He felt tired. It had been only six years since the Americans had positioned their Seventh Fleet in Singapore, in preparation of their Sumatran invasion, a move he had recognised at the time as being intended to split the fledgling nation into chaotic and more easily influenced states. The Americans had, of course, failed. Now he was faced with another attempt by an old rival to challenge his power. The British had embarked on a course which, having been discovered, proved beyond doubt that they would never accept an Indonesia under his leadership. A telegram addressed to the British Foreign Office and signed by the British Ambassador, Andrew Gilchrist, lay on his desk. It was the most damning indication yet that the British would stop at nothing to subvert his Government. His Deputy Prime Minister, Dr. Soebandrio, had produced the letter which contained documentary evidence of a plot against both himself and his Foreign Minister. The communication was proof that the British had established close connections with local army elements who would support the overthrow of Soekarno and his Government.

The President knew that Chou En-Lai's visit had ruffled feathers in the West. When the Chinese visited in April to participate in his tenth anniversary celebrations of the Bandung Conference, Soekarno realised also that anti-communist factions within his Military had deliberately boycotted the ceremonies to demonstrate their displeasure at having Mao Tse Tung's right hand man present. He knew that his generals suspected Soebandrio of arranging arms for the purpose of creating a Fifth Force in Indonesia, to be called upon in the event the communists gained control of the Government. When he had urged his Commanders to give this 'Fifth Force' serious consideration their reactions were, as he had anticipated. Nasution had excused himself from the meeting and had not returned. Several of the others present were obviously agitated by his suggestion but not prepared to display their displeasure openly. These, he believed, were the nucleus of what was deemed to be the secret Council of Generals. Soekarno smiled as he considered his provocative proposal to develop a fully armed party to counterbalance his own Military. It was, in fact, just a ploy. But he knew that his generals had not understood the tactic. Instead, they viewed his proposal as one which would undermine their own powerful positions. His thoughts returned to the man who would now be waiting outside, angry with being deliberately kept cooling his heels. Soekarno knew what Nasution wished to discuss. No, not discuss, he thought, it would be more like a confrontation, again. Someone inside the Palace had apparently informed General Nasution that he had sent Omar Dhani to Peking to negotiate a secret small-arms deal. An aide had reported that the senior general had been livid when he discovered that the communists were arranging for weapons to be delivered covertly into the Republic. Soekarno realised that Aidit, as Chairman of the Communist Party, had overstepped the mark recently, publicly announcing that they would arm five million communist workers and up to ten million peasants to carry on the war against Malaysia, should the TNI continue to fail in this mission. Aidit had created even more enemies amongst the Indonesian Armed Forces with that outlandish statement, Soekarno knew.

In order to appear impartial, he decided to maintain an ambiguous position, openly favouring the creation of such a Fifth Force while never really moving to introduce such an ambitious plan. He had to be seen to be still in charge of the powerful factions. It was, he felt, the most difficult balancing act he had yet attempted in his political career. On one hand he was faced with the monster of his own creation, a mass of more than twenty million workers who could clearly overwhelm the military should they become armed. Their union movement, SOBSI, had volunteered to fight alongside Indonesia's regular forces if the country were ever subjected to aggression. On the other side of the coin, he was faced with the Military and its many factions. Soekarno thought solemnly for a moment. This Dewan Djenderal was a real threat, and he had little doubt that those involved in the secret Council of generals were receiving support not only from the Americans, but also from the British. That damn letter sent by Ambassador Gilchrist was proof! There was a knock at the door as his aide peeked into the chamber. Soekarno waved impatiently for him to enter.

'Bapak, Djenderal Nasution still waits,' he said, almost timidly. The Palace staff were all aware of the differences which existed between their President and the Sumatran general. Soekarno lowered his feet to the floor and rubbed his feet on the Persian carpet.

'Tell him I will be there shortly,' he instructed, sending the young officer away. He dressed slowly, then checked himself in the long mirror, ensuring that his many rows of military campaign ribbons were straight. Satisfied, he smiled at his reflection and marched out into the formal office area to greet his most senior military officer. Nasution rose to attention as Soekarno entered.

'Bapak,' he said, the obvious lack of deference evident in his eyes. The President indicated that Nasution should sit again, as he selected a large, ornately carved chair for himself. Soekarno then crossed his legs, permitting the toe of his highly polished shoes to point in the officer's direction. Nasution observed the offensive movement, leaned back into his own seat and emulated the President's behaviour. There was then a moment of silence as they viewed each other, before the general finally spoke.

'No doubt you know why I am here, Bapak,' he commenced.

Soekarno remained perfectly still, without responding. Nasution sighed silently. It was going to be as difficult as every other time they had met, he felt immediately. He looked directly at his President. What is really going on in the man's mind? he wondered. How can he continue this madness against Malaysia, with the incredible losses their men had suffered at the hands of the British and Australian SAS in Sarawak? Why is he permitting the communists to arm? Surely he must expect the Armed Forces to react to such a provocative step? As these questions ran through his mind for the umpteenth time, still there were no answers.

'*Bung Karno,*' he started again, selecting the form of address he knew Soekarno would appreciate. He had to try to convince the President to cease supporting the communists openly against the Military. It was flirting with disaster, he knew for certain. Many of his officers had already expressed a desire to ban the Communist Party. Like him, they also could not understand why their President had permitted the communists so much power within the Government. Their representation was directly disproportionate to the *rakjat's* wishes. This had been clearly demonstrated and still the Great Leader of the Revolution failed to recognise just how much power he had already given Soebandrio and Aidit.

'*Bung Karno, I have come to seek your assurance that you will not support the arming of the PKI,*' he said. '*There is considerable unrest amongst the Military at the suggestion that this so-called Fifth Force has your blessing. We have been informed that you have sent senior AURI officers to China to arrange for the purchase of weapons.*' He paused, looking to see if Soekarno had registered the fact that knowledge of the Air Force contingent's mission had leaked from the Palace. '*I have come here today to seek clarification of this matter.*'

Soekarno uncrossed his legs and leaned forward as one of the Palace household staff entered and made his way towards the country's two most senior men. In Javanese style, the old man bent forward, so that his head would be lower than that of the President and his guest. Incredibly, the ageing *djongos* managed to balance the silver tray with its load of drinks and *makanan ketjil* without spilling either the cold coffee or the sweet sickly cakes, as he knelt on the floor and served.

'*Dhani's trip to China was simply within the framework of responding to an invitation extended by Chou En-lai during his visit. It is nonsense that the purpose of his visit is to secure weapons for the communists.*'

'*Bapak President,*' Nasution responded, careful not to permit his anger from becoming evident. '*It would be inappropriate for Dhani to enter into any agreements with the Chinese without first obtaining approval from the Armed Forces' Chiefs of Staff.*' He avoided accusing Soekarno of lying, even though the President's lack of candour was obvious to Nasution.

He waited for a response but Soekarno remained still, as if considering his reply. Then the President looked at his highly polished shoes, almost as if disinterested in continuing the discussion. The powerful men sat facing each other for several more moments while a Dutch grandfather clock standing in the near corner ticked away the seconds. Suddenly Soekarno rose to his feet and walked slowly towards the steel-framed window overlooking the palace's southerly aspect. He stood still, hands clasped behind his back as he stared at the activity in the courtyard below.

'Dhani will provide a full report concerning his activities upon his return. He is not on a mission to purchase weapons from our Chinese friends.' The President then turned and smiled at Nasution. *'You have my word,'* he added.

Nasution then rose to his feet also and looked directly at his Commander-in-Chief. He knew that Soekarno was lying and wished it were otherwise. In spite of their differences, the Sumatran acknowledged that his President had made considerable contribution to their country. If only the man had not permitted the communists to grow into the force they had become, threatening the very existence of the *Republik*. He knew it would be unwise to challenge the President's integrity as such a move could only result in a further deterioration of his position as the Military's most influential general.

He sighed silently, disappointed once again with Soekarno's obvious attempts to disguise whatever scheme the Airforce Chief of Staff had initiated during his current visit to China. Nasution was certain that the information he had obtained was reliable. Realising that the President was determined not to reveal anything relating to the covert arms purchase, he decided to leave. Even before he had sought this audience, Nasution had somehow known that any attempt to dissuade Soekarno might fail, and would not deter the President from the dangerous course the country had now taken. He stared at the man he'd once admired and suddenly knew what had to be done.

'Then I will inform the other Chiefs of Staff that Dhani's journey to Beijing is merely one of Muhibah,' Nasution stated, indicating he had accepted the explanation that the Airforce general's visit was one of a goodwill nature. Soekarno looked directly at his senior general and their eyes locked momentarily. Both men knew that the other had lied. There was nothing left to be said. Nasution nodded slightly in the President's direction.

'*Bapak,*' he said politely, then came to attention, retrieved his cap and marched from the regal setting. Soekarno turned back to the window as if disinterested and observed the scene below. Moments later, he watched Nasution emerge from the building and walk determinedly across the court-yard to his jeep. As the Army vehicle sped away almost injuring one of the palace guards who had foolishly failed to identify the four-star general, the President frowned. He was annoyed with the information leaks from within his own close circle. It was almost impossible to maintain any secrecy these days, he thought angrily, turning away from the window as he wondered whom amongst his trusted confidants had betrayed the real purpose of Dhani's mission to China.

His mind clouded with these worrying thoughts, the President instructed his aide to inform his Japanese wife, Dewi, that he would not be visiting that evening. Already he had become bored with his Japanese acquisition. Instead, he would visit his most recent conquest and spend the hours with her instead. He needed to experience the luxury of the girl's innocence and youth. Suddenly the pressures of the moment disappeared as an image of the young Javanese girl entered his thoughts and he smiled, delighted with his decision. The heavy matters of state could wait, he decided, anticipating an evening of pleasure with yet another of the willing students only too eager to discover for themselves the truth of the President's legendary sexual prowess.

The Indonesian President stretched as he made his way back to the private chamber, removing his clothes as he went. Having removed all of these, he then stepped into his favourite sarong, pulling this up loosely around his waist and climbed onto the hard four-poster bed. Then he closed his eyes to rest in preparation for the evening's activities and, moments later, he felt the tensions of the day fade away. Soekarno fell into a deep and comfortable sleep, unaware of the dangerous elements which were moving to engulf his Presidency.

And the people of Indonesia.

* * * * * *

KERRY B.COLLISON

Lembah Njiur (Bogor)

It was apparent from the mood that not all of those present were happy with having been summoned to the secret hillside rendezvous on such short notice. Major Djenderal Harjono moved to console the other senior officers as they waited impatiently for Nasution to arrive. He observed Parman and Soeprapto, and was concerned. The generals' faces reflected the constant stress under which they were obliged to operate. Both men had been working to maintain some semblance of authority within their own Commands whilst the communists continually destabilised their power base. It was apparent that they were all deeply worried by the intensity of the communist elements encroachment throughout the Military. It seemed as if overnight, many of the middle-ranking officers had shifted their loyalty to the communists, challenging the once firmly ensconced TNI leadership. The PKI had indeed become a major force within the Military and, as their numbers grew, the communist officers became even more apparent, often showing open disdain for their senior officers who had refused to identify with the powerful political party.

Worn brakes indicated the arrival of another vehicle as the jeep came to a noisy and abrupt halt outside the bungalow. They all knew it would be Nasution. They listened as a door opened, then closed. There was a brief but muffled exchange then he entered, and they all rose to greet their leader. Without exception, those present admired and respected the Sumatran general. He was an honest man. A hero. He had assumed leadership when General Sudirman had passed away, leaving the fledgling Republic's Military in Nasution's capable hands.

As he entered they could see that he too displayed signs of exhaustion. Tired as he was, Djenderal Nasution smiled at each one in turn, shaking their hands as he moved amongst their number. They were all quietly relieved. None had dared say it, but there was not one present who had not feared that Nasution's delay may have been at the hands of their enemies, for these men understood the ruthlessness of those dedicated to destroying the anti-Communist officers within the military.

The men waited for Nasution to sit before they too returned to their chairs. Yani knew from his friend's weary features that their position had become critical. Nasution had aged dramatically over the past months. Yani admitted silently that none of them would survive Soebandrio's machinations if they delayed longer. Of this he was certain. General Nasution spoke.

'Well, my friends,' he commenced in sombre voice, 'I can confirm that Dhani is on a mission to purchase arms for the communists.' The four-star general looked directly at Yani, his closest ally amongst those present. 'Your intelligence has now been confirmed. Soekarno all but admitted that our Airforce colleague is, as we speak, licking Chou En-Lai's feet and arranging for the Red Chinese to ship weapons to the Indo-nesian Communist Party.' Nasution observed the faces of his Council. Major General Harjono merely shook his head in disgust. He had developed a deep distrust for the Airforce general ever since the President appointed Dhani to KOGA, the Komando Siaga, an inter-service body formed to wrest control of the Malaysian campaign away from the Army. He had been instrumental in foiling Dhani's attempts. Nasution went on. 'We must now assume the worst, gentlemen. The PKI is moving to arm its cadres and that, we must be-lieve, will result in armed insurrection and a communist take-over.' He paused, sipped the cold thick coffee, then placed the heavy glass back on the aluminium coaster. 'We must now agree to pre-empt such action. We must move before they are armed.'

'When will these shipments arrive?' General Parman asked, con-cerned that the weapons may already be in the Tandjung Priok Harbour.

'Within the month,' Nasution replied.

'But that leaves us little time to prepare!' Soeprapto exploded. He, more so than the others, understood the logistical problems which faced the Armed Forces at that time.

'This is why I summoned you here tonight. We cannot wait any longer. I have appealed to Bung Karno but he remains deaf to our suggestions. I have no doubt that our President supports the arming of this so-called Fifth Force as a counter-balance to the Military. He is a fool. Soekarno has developed other appetites which distract his attention from the guardian-ship of our country.'

'We are not ready. We need more time to prepare,' Soeprapto com-plained again, still concerned with the complex arrangements he would be responsible for when they made their move against the communists.

'We must determine a date, now!' Nasution demanded. 'We can't delay any further.'

Yani rubbed his face to assist with the circulation. Like the others, he too was tired. He wished the problems they faced would disappear without the inevitable confrontation which he knew would throw the country into further turmoil.

'We need an appropriate opportunity to disguise any sudden troop build-up within the capital,' he suggested. 'Why not take advantage of the Fifth of October?'

Soeprapto raised his eyebrows at Yani's idea. Then he slowly nodded in agreement. There would be adequate time for him and the others to prepare their Commands. The date suggested was appropriate. The Fifth of October was Armed Forces Day, which required substantial increased military presence to accommodate the demands for the many parades which traditionally took place around the city on that day. Soeprapto almost smiled at the thought of moving additional men and equipment into Djakarta without raising suspicion. He nodded in consent, again, in the direction of the astute Army Commander. The others also warmed to Yani's suggestion, pleased that they would not have to fight their way into the city through a mass of communist supporters.

The meeting continued for several hours before the men returned to Djakarta. As each sat silently contemplating the evening's events, not one amongst their number was in the least concerned that their actions did, in fact, amount to treason. Without exception, they were convinced that their proposed actions were in the national interests, and that as guardians of the *Republik*, it was their duty to take whatever steps were necessary to ensure the stability of their nation. The communists had to go. And along with them, the Great Leader of the Revolution, President Soekarno.

* * * * * *

Djakarta

Major General Soeharto looked at the report and frowned. He understood that past personal differences might justify his not being included in whatever Nasution and Yani were up to but, as a matter of principle, he believed his exclusion from the Council of

Generals represented a deliberate attempt to isolate him from any chance of achieving the Army's top post. Being Javanese, the thought of a direct approach to those he believed to be members of this Dewan Djenderal just did not enter his mind. To do so would be too confrontationalist and out of character. He considered the conundrum and decided to attack the problem from another angle. The KOSTRAD Commander removed the intelligence report from the other sensitive documents and placed this in his jacket pocket. He would wait to see just what Nasution and his crowd were up to before making his move. The situation was becoming even more confused, he felt, the capital tense with rumours spreading quickly suggesting the President was very ill, even dying, and that Dr. Soebandrio and his fellow communists were preparing to arm themselves in the event of Soekarno's death.

The general rose from his desk and moved to the window to think, as he had so often done before when confronted with a difficult decision. As he peered across towards the United States Embassy, a thought suddenly entered his mind which caused him to smile. He had been invited to join the American Ambassador for dinner that evening and had accepted, knowing that this would provide an opportunity for him to consolidate his position even further with the United States defence establishment. He had elected to develop these lines of communication realising that the Soviets would soon cease most of their military support for his country and, when that time arrived, his keen political sense told him that only the Americans would be able to fill the void created when the Soviets reneged on their commitments.

He returned to his desk and locked the confidential file in the top drawer. The general them summoned his aide and issued instructions before leaving his office and driving down to old Kota. He had to visit his old friend. There was much to discuss and these conversations were best held discreetly. Soeharto understood that it would not be wise to have the Chinaman visit his office on Merdeka Square.

Chapter 14

Djakarta

Murray was concerned when Susan expressed reluctance in leaving Djakarta. Later, during the course of the dinner at Steven Zach's residence, he was horrified to discover that they were obviously having an affair. He sat in disbelief, observing their glances and listening to their light-hearted banter on the weekend on Pulau Putri.

'Then he almost drowned me!' Susan said in mock reproach. Murray pretended to be attentive while she laughed and described how Steven, while showing off to the others, had tipped the rubber Zenith dinghy over, almost drowning them both. Murray could not imagine the Military Attaché behaving in this manner.

'Guess you'll be returning to Melbourne soon?' he asked. They sat sipping coffee and liqueurs in the corner bar in the main guest area. Immediately, he sensed the mood change as both Zach and Susan became silent. 'Just let me know, if you wish, and I'll organise the flight for you.'

'I'll do that, thanks Murray,' Zach replied. He looked directly at the Station Chief. 'Susan thought she may spend a few more days here before returning home,' he added, turning to her and smiling lightly. She responded, leaning across and placing her hand briefly on his.

'It's okay, Murray,' she said, unconvincingly. 'I will ask for your assistance though, if you wouldn't mind.'

'Sure,' Murray answered, his stomach sinking at the evident warmth his friends displayed for each other. 'What did you have in mind?'

Susan sat thoughtfully before responding. 'I have known you for some time, Murray. I believe that we have been more than just close friends.' She leaned over and took Steven's hand in hers. 'Don't be alarmed,' Susan said, observing the sudden frown which had appeared on Murray's brow. 'Without going into any detail, I just wanted you to know that I will not be returning to Harry.' The words hung momentarily in the air and the room seemed to become quiet. Murray could hear the soft humming airconditioner as the compressor cut in sending cool air in their direction. A gecko's throaty call broke the silence.

'Have you told him yet?' he asked, a little too loudly.

'No,' she answered, 'I haven't had the opportunity. Besides, these things are best discussed in person.' Susan continued to hold Steven's hand as she spoke. 'Murray, I know that this is difficult for you. Please understand,' she asked, touching his arm with her free hand. Murray didn't know what to say. He just smiled at his two close friends then raised his glass.

'Well, whatever the outcome ...' he said, draining the glass quickly. He suddenly felt the need to leave.

'Murray,' Susan started, seeing that he was uncomfortable. She slid off the bar stool and stood alongside Stephenson, taking his hand and squeezing it firmly. 'Murray, please,' Susan pleaded, hoping he would understand. He smiled without warmth and rose to his feet.

'Best be going,' was all he could manage. He shook hands with Zach and kissed Susan lightly on the cheek.

'Will you join us tomorrow?' she asked, now agitated by the strength of his reaction.

'Probably not,' Murray replied, abruptly, as he strolled towards the door. 'I'll no doubt see you in the morning, Steve. Goodnight,' he said, forcing a smile for the houseboy who had suddenly appeared from nowhere to open the door. He walked quickly to his car and barked at the driver. Murray was unusually silent as they drove towards his house in Djalan Serang in the elite suburb of Menteng. He could not believe that Susan had been so rash, and Zach! Murray felt overwhelmed with disappointment. For some reason he could not explain, he felt betrayed by his two friends. And then there was Harry. How was he going to react to the news that his wife had decided to leave him?

'God,' Murray thought, 'what a bloody mess!'

As they pulled away from the Military Attaché's residence,

Murray had been too preoccupied with Susan's disturbing revelations to notice the Chevrolet which had pulled in behind the Australian Embassy Holden and remained there as they wound their way through the streets of Kebajoran. It was only after he had noticed his driver altering his rear-vision mirror several times to deflect the other car's lights that Murray recognised the surveillance vehicle for what it was. He instructed the driver to return to the Military Attaché's home and, as the other vehicle continued to follow, Murray was then certain that he was, in fact, being tailed.

'I've changed my mind,' he advised the driver, *'I've found my wallet, it was in my pocket all the time,'* he lied. *'Let's just go home.'* The *supir* remained silent. He really did not mind driving the *tuan* around, even if he did wish to travel around in circles. The driver did as ordered and entered the Prapantja Roundabout once again before joining Djalan Djenderal Sudirman. Again he adjusted his mirror, cursing silently as the other vehicle's lights blinded his vision. Murray did not attempt to identify the other vehicle. It was not so unusual to be followed, he knew from experience. Mostly it was just inconvenient and bloody annoying. When they approached the Embassy villa, the driver was obliged to slow down considerably as armed soldiers partially blocked the small road. The driver knew that one of the more important generals lived close by in this street. He stopped, moved the stick into first gear then proceeded carefully so as not to alarm the trigger-happy guards.

It was then that Murray turned quickly to see if he could recognise the other vehicle which had stopped just far enough back to prevent identification. He squinted though the glare as the Chevrolet reversed a few metres then turned and sped away as his own driver slowed to avoid the military barricades strung along this street. He rubbed his eyes briefly then touched his driver on his left shoulder, instructing him to stop. Murray had identified several of the soldiers and, as his villa was only a few doors down the quiet street, he decided to walk, hoping to shake the cloud of depression he felt descending.

'I'll get out here. Terima kasih, Mas,' he said, as he opened the door and left the driver to return to the Embassy compound. Murray walked the remaining distance to his villa, past the familiar barb-wire blockade surrounding his neighbour's house. He

stopped, opened a packet of *Gudang Garam* cigarettes, lit one, then offered the remaining packet to the soldiers. They didn't hesitate, smiling as they accepted the near-full packet.

'*Terima kasih,*' they called, as Murray continued on his way, waving one hand in acknowledgement to those he had left behind. His *djaga* opened the heavy sliding gate, permitting him to enter.

'*Selamat malam, tuan,*' the security guard welcomed, smiling as Murray touched him gently on the shoulder.

'*Ya,*' he responded, '*Selamat malam.*' He really did not feel like entering into his usual discourse with the servant, continuing on his way into the magnificent residence. The other servants all scurried into the lounge as he entered. It was always the same. The cook would lead, followed by his *djongos* and then the other servants. Murray's depression lifted immediately. 'How could one remain unhappy surrounded by people such as these?' he thought.

The *koki* insisted that he have something to eat. Murray knew that she would have been aware that he would have already eaten elsewhere. There were no secrets from the servants. He accepted a small dish of *bakso* and consumed just enough to satisfy the cook. It was a game they all played. But it was an important gesture, Murray understood.

He then showered, standing under the hot stinging water, mulling over the bombshell Susan and Steve had dropped on him. He breathed deeply, running his hands slowly through his thick hair, enjoying the warmth of the shower as the water stung his skin. He opened his mouth, permitting the spray to touch his tongue and, enjoying the sensation, he moved his face slowly from side to side as the water pellets massaged imaginary pressures from his head. A noise suddenly made him stiffen then, identifying the familiar sound and scent, Murray relaxed. He held his hand over the shower head as the girl closed the screen door behind and placed her arms around his waist.

'Allo, Mahree,' Ade said, smiling as she stood on her toes and kissed Murray sweetly. The water cascaded down over her thick, shining black hair as he knelt, placing his arms under hers, lifting her off the shower floor.

'Allo yourself,' was all he said, savouring the moment. He kissed her gently as he relaxed his hold, permitting Ade to slide back onto her feet. She laughed, then slapped him playfully on the thigh.

They showered together, taking turns to rub the other's back as they bathed, laughing as their hands ventured into sensitive areas. They did not make love. Instead, once they had changed into sarongs, Ade sat on his bed and commenced brushing her hair. Murray sat next to her and gently rubbed her shoulders and neck.

'*Awaslu!*' she warned, happily, enjoying the sensation. A soft knock on the bedroom door interrupted the moment.

'*Maaf, tuan,*' the *djongos* apologised, '*there is a driver here for you from the Embassy,*' he whispered hoarsely. Murray checked his watch and swore. He changed quickly and left, first kissing Ade softly on her forehead.

'*Won't be long,*' he promised, escaping before she succeeded in pinching his stomach playfully. As he appeared, the driver handed the message directly to him. He sighed, resenting the tedious task ahead. Murray left the villa, waved to the soldiers outside and was immediately driven to the Embassy. He checked to see if he had been followed again but the streets were already devoid of traffic. Once at the Embassy, he went through the monotonous routines which consumed most of an hour before he was able to decipher the incoming communication. It was from Harold Bradshaw, his Director. He read though the text quickly and decided that a response could wait until the following morning, remembering that it was already early evening back in Melbourne anyway. He placed the decoded message carefully inside his wallet, then secured the communications centre and locked the building behind as he left, anxious to return to his villa.

As they drove the short distance back to his villa, Murray frowned when he observed the duty-driver adjust his rear-vision mirror. He turned quickly and identified the Chevrolet which had followed him home earlier in the evening. As his vehicle approached Djalan Serang once again Murray elected to walk through the barricaded street rather than have the soldiers move the obstacles aside for the diplomatic sedan. After his driver sped away, he remained standing on the side of the road, staring back around the corner at the long dark sedan with oversized tail wings. The driver had killed his lights and parked not a hundred metres down the road. Murray turned and walked towards the Chevrolet. Annoyed, he wanted to know who they were.

As he approached, he heard the engine roar into life as the driver flattened his gas-pedal to the floor, powering the eight-cylinder machine forward with incredible speed. Immediately he realised that he had been foolish and turned to escape. As his legs carried him back towards the junction, he looked desperately for a means to evade the oncoming car but the surrounding houses all lay behind high walls covered with barbed-wire and broken glass to prevent such intrusion. Only seconds had passed when he accepted that he would not make it, the vehicle's brilliant headlights silhouetting his frame as his feet pounded the footpath. Murray had only a few metres to cover before reaching the corner when the Chevrolet's off-side wheels mounted the footpath directly behind and swerved towards him. As the engine's roar filled his ears, Murray panicked, and lept desperately for the top of the adjacent wall. The machine seemed to leap after him and smashed into the concrete perimeter fence, before continuing along the footpath amidst the screams of tearing metal.

He screamed in pain then fell hard to the ground and rolled, unable to avoid the broken curb-side rubble. His head struck the ground savagely, stunning him. Dazed, he struggled to his feet before his attackers could return and complete their mission. Pain stabbed at his ankle as he staggered back towards his street, his bleeding right hand raised to the wall for support. He heard the squealing tires as the heavy sedan turned violently, and he cried out in pain as he forced his twisted ankle to carry him back to safety.

He heard the car approach and Murray knew that he would not be able to reach the corner in time. The engine screamed, locked in second gear as its driver bore down on him again. Murray half-turned. Immediately blinded by the light's high-beam, he lifted his uninjured hand to lessen the glare. He held his breath, waiting, as the car roared towards where he leaned against the wall. He cursed out loud; the corner was only metres away. The glare blinded his vision but he identified the clunking noise as once again his attackers steered their vehicle up onto the footpath. He braced for the impact. Suddenly his world exploded into sounds of screaming metal and rapid fire as the machine-pistol's bullets punched through the air sending shock waves, slapping his eardrums fiercely. In the moment Murray fell to the ground, he caught a glimpse of the soldier standing almost alongside, and he heard the staccato sounds continue as the machine-gun punctured the night, shattering glass and piercing metal as the oncoming sedan suddenly swerved violently away.

The general's guard continued to fire from the hip as the Chevrolet suddenly swerved, the driver fighting for control as he turned sharply and gunned his engine even harder than before. Murray lifted his head and peered in the direction of the escaping vehicle. He breathed deeply and pushed himself upright. A hand gripped him roughly under his shoulder, and he succeeded in making it to his feet. Barely seconds had passed before he was surrounded by more than a dozen soldiers who half-carried, half-dragged the Australian back to his villa where he was taken inside and deposited safely on his lounge. Convinced that the foreigner's injuries were superficial, they then left him alone with his servants and returned to their duties outside, as if nothing had happened. They were accustomed to such incidents and were not overly concerned. The attack had not been directed at their general and he was not even there at that time. They would not even file a report unless asked to do so. The soldiers knew that even if they did, the incident would most probably be ignored at higher levels.

Murray sat on the lounge and removed his shoes and socks, exposing the damaged ankle. His hand was bleeding profusely. His servants fussed over him, believing that he had fallen on the broken footpath. They had not witnessed the attack and he did not wish to alarm these easily frightened people. Although they had heard the gunfire, none had associated the two incidents as the sound of weapon fire was commonplace throughout the capital. Often the soldiers would just fire into the sky out of boredom. The houseboy tended to his cuts and bruises. Murray's hand continued to bleed. He knew that the wound should have been stitched but decided against alerting the Embassy doctor. He would keep a close watch on the wound himself. The old cook could see that he was badly shaken. She had the *djongos* pour Murray a large whiskey which he thankfully drank. Soon he stopped shaking.

Murray then remembered his house guest and limped painfully into the bedroom. He entered quietly, and found Ade curled in the foetal position, eyes closed and hands clasped almost as if in prayer. She had slept through the noise and gunfire. He looked down at her and shook his head in wonder at this realisation. He limped into the bathroom and undressed, checking bruises and torn skin.

The area surrounding his temples ached and, as his hands explored the skin under his thick crown of hair, he discovered a tender lump where his head had hit the pavement earlier. Murray ran the bath and soaked himself, holding his injured hand and leg outside the tub as he scrubbed the other parts of his body. The warm water almost put him to sleep as he lay there quietly, reviewing the attack on his life. He wondered if he was responsible for provoking the men who had followed him earlier. Would they have gone about their business had he not approached their vehicle, or would they have waited for a similar opportunity to do him harm? Who were they?

He levered himself out of the *mandi* carefully, then dried himself slowly. He was just too tired to think. As he re-entered his bedroom, Murray looked at the beautiful woman in his bed and was pleased that she was still there. He lowered himself onto the bed carefully so as not to wake her. He lay on the sheets, his head nestled against the soft pillows, and closed his eyes. Ade sensed his presence and moved closer, still half-asleep, nestling gently alongside so as not to disturb her lover. Murray lay quietly watching as her chest moved slowly, the soft sounds of her breathing blended with the muffled tropical calls of deep-throated bull frogs and geckos. The airconditioner hummed through the night, wafting the artificial breeze around the room. As he slid gratefully into the sheets, Ade moved her arm across his chest, almost possessively. Finally, he fell into a restless sleep.

The night passed without further event and, as the early morning brought familiar sounds of the new day, Murray remained in a deep sleep. Later, when most of Djakarta's citizens had already risen and completed their ablutions, Murray was finally awakened by his throbbing injuries. He sat upright slowly and then reached for the beautiful young woman beside him. But Ade was no longer there. Instantly, the recollections of his near encounter with death flooded his mind and he lept out of bed only to curse himself as the pain shot though his lower leg. Murray sat back down on the bed and rubbed his face and, as if by signal, immediately his head began to ache. He groaned, then made his way into the bathroom and, as he stood in front of the mirror examining his face and bruised torso, a thought flashed though his mind.

In pain, he hobbled back into his bedroom and searched for his trousers. For a moment he could not remember where he had placed them. Then he remembered. They were still on the floor lying half-hidden under the bed. Murray bent down and retrieved the cotton slacks and immediately his hand went anxiously to the back pocket. He checked again. Nothing. He then checked the other pockets and discovered that these too were empty. Murray lowered himself painfully to the floor where he looked under the bed. Still nothing. He searched around the room with a similar result and, struggling into his sarong, he went out and called his servants. He instructed his houseboy to search the lounge where he had rested while bathing his injured foot and then outside along the street, but still there was nothing.

He cursed himself for his stupidity. He had lost his wallet. And the sensitive contents which should never have left the Embassy restricted area. Murray returned to his bedroom and sat alone on the bed, his hands gripping his pounding head as he struggled to collect his thoughts. The seriousness of his security breach and the possible ramifications of his stupidity grew in his mind as he recalled sections of the decoded communication from the Head of Australia's Secret Service.

Somewhere in the city someone now possessed a most incriminating document. And then, as he sat there on the cold linen sheets, another thought crossed his mind which he immediately tried to dismiss. Why had Ade left so early without saying goodbye?

* * * * * *

Their numbers had grown dramatically over the past months. The holy man was most pleased. Each day he would dedicate as much time as possible to speaking directly to the new converts who came from many parts of the globe. Bapak Subuh was most pleased that his teachings had spread so far. And so quickly. Followers of his philosophy visited from countries even he had not envisaged and, without design, SUBUD had grown into a formidable sect with an enviable financial base. Many of his foreign followers were middle-class men and women whose careers covered the professional spectrum.

Even he had been amazed at the number of lawyers, doctors, accountants and engineers who had flocked to hear him preach his philosophy, which embraced all cultures, all religions, and all political leanings. He knew that there were many sceptics amongst those who visited. But he also knew that none of these departed a lesser person for, once they had met with the man who provided them with the opportunity to reach though the window into their souls, their noble natures invariably capitulated to their new capacity for love and understanding. And then they accepted his teachings.

On this day, he felt troubled. A recurring dream had dominated his thoughts throughout recent weeks, and now he believed that his interpretation of the events which presented themselves clearly as he slept, predicted dark days ahead. He decided to seek a further meeting with the man whose spirit occupied so many of his sleeping hours. Even he sometimes did not understand how the universe moved and controlled their lives, although it was clear that there was a sequence to everything that mattered, and that he played but a minor role in the Greater Order.

As he sat deep in thought, contemplating his troubled interpretations, Subuh suddenly smiled as he recalled the first time he had encountered the young sickly child in Semarang. He knew that their meeting had been prearranged. It was just a matter of destiny. Then his smile faded as quickly as it had appeared as he remembered the ominous visions which had continuously invaded his dreams. The holy man willed his anxiety to retreat, providing a purer path for his mind to deal with the demons which threatened to take control of his consciousness. He closed his eyes and moved his being onto another level, another plane, as his physical presence began to separate from his spiritual core.

An hour had passed before Subuh suddenly opened his eyes, totally refreshed from the *latihan*. His first thoughts were to make arrangements to meet with the younger man. The spiritual leader smiled in anticipation as he rose to send a short personal note requesting yet another meeting with his friend: a friend who had grown not only in stature amongst his peers, but whose character reflected the very substance of Javanese tradition. He was delighted with what this man had become. The words of request flowed from his pen with humility and respect. When he was finished, he sealed his letter. Subuh then wrote carefully across the envelope, and placed the letter carefully inside a small folder, calling for one of his attendants.

That evening, as he sat alone in his home along Djalan Tjendana, the recipient read the letter over and over again. He was not displeased with the contents, only concerned that they had not met in person to discuss the holy man's interpretations in greater depth. The general took the letter and placed it inside his desk drawer, knowing that it would not be disturbed there. He decided to make time and meet discreetly with the respected spiritualist. The general acknowledged that it would be in his best interests to heed the warning contained in the letter. But he needed to know more. He sensed that the communication left a great deal unsaid, and this was of immediate concern to him. The city was rife with rumours and he understood clearly that there were undercurrents flowing which could, if he was not careful, drag him and many others away into a dangerous sea of conflict. He reached across his teak desk and smiled at his mother's photograph. And then, as always, the memories of early childhood came flooding back as Soeharto remembered those difficult early childhood days when he had first encountered Subuh in Semarang.

* * * * * *

United States Embassy, Djakarta

The flag moved listlessly as the Marine Guard ceremoniously raised the colours. The day was already suffocatingly hot, and the American could feel sweat rolling down his back as he slowly pulled the cord through white-gloved hands. Black residual lines appeared on his gloves: proof, he thought, that living in Indonesia's polluted capital was dangerous for one's health.

Inside the United States Embassy, there was already a flurry of activity, even at this early hour. In all, the total complement of American citizens officially accredited to this mission numbered sixty-two: in reality, more than three hundred operated out of these facilities, making it the largest foreign representation in the country. Apart from the diplomatic officers and their families, the complex housed a myriad of small offices which accommodated United States Navy, Army, Air Force, Marine and other Defence personnel. The congested building was like a rabbit warren. Its occupants moved around their tight quarters, squeezing past each other through the narrow corridors which connected the complicated maze of offices.

Marine Guards working in shifts around the clock manned positions throughout the complex, and it was not possible to pass through the different levels or sections without every movement being monitored. The steps to the immediate right of the foyer entrance led to the first level. There, yet more tireless watchers maintained close scrutiny of the pedestrian traffic which passed through the Defence Attaché's offices.

The corporal smiled as he recognised the approaching civilian and rose to his feet as the CIA Station Chief, Samuel Preston, passed his security post. The tall fair-haired Chief merely nodded at the guard as he strolled past, continuing along the passageway until arriving at the colonel's office. He knocked then entered without waiting for a response. He was expected.

'Frank, Pete,' he said, nodding to the two men who remained seated as he lowered himself into one of the under-sized chairs. It seemed that everything in this wing had been miniaturised to accommodate their swelling numbers. He was unable to cross his legs comfortably in the restricted space. 'What's up?' Preston asked, as he moved around in the rattan chair trying to find a comfortable position for his large frame.

'Thought you should see this,' the colonel remarked, handing a folder across to the CIA Djakarta Chief. The file cover was crossed with a thick red band marked 'Top Secret'. He opened the file and read the document while the others remained silent. As he came to the end of the first page the experienced agent let out a soft whistle then looked up at the colonel.

'Source?' he asked, handing the sensitive material back. The colonel accepted the file then threw it casually over onto his desk. He looked at the officer his men referred to as the Chief Spook and immediately wondered just how much mileage he could get out of the situation. The fine line which separated Military Intelligence from their country's more clandestine service often provided for territorial jealousies, and the colonel believed that he had scored heavily by securing the document.

'Not able to say, Sam. At least, not right now,' the colonel answered, his smile not evident as he sat there enjoying this rare opportunity to play advantage over the CIA. The Station Chief stared at the colonel through thick heavy-framed bifocals and tilted his head.

'How can we verify its authenticity, Frank?' he asked, not quite testily, but close. 'You don't have the in-country resources to substantiate that,' he said, pointing directly at the file. 'My Director in Langley would insist that I verify the document. That means disclosing the source, Frank,' he insisted. The colonel leaned over and recovered the folder and opened the file. He looked at the document as if deciding whether or not to reveal how the information came into his possession. Then he threw the file back onto his desk. He had scored enough points and knew that, ultimately, he would be obliged to surrender the detail the senior agent demanded.

'To tell you the truth, Sam, we're not absolutely sure,' he admitted.

'Come on, Frank,' he coaxed. 'We're on the same team here.' The Station Chief could have said almost anything else and not rattle the officer. The colonel's face reddened but he managed to keep himself in check. He hated being patronised.

'Pete here believes it came from someone in BAKIN,' he responded, indicating the Major with a nod of his head.

'BAKIN?' the Chief said in surprise. He was tempted to scoff at the suggestion that the Indonesian counter-part agency to the CIA was responsible for providing the sensitive material.

'Pete, you'd best fill Sam in,' he ordered. Major Peter O'Brien cleared his throat and commenced.

'I attended a briefing with our Defence Co-operation team over at BAKIN late yesterday. We were there for a couple of hours discussing matters of mutual interest.' He hesitated, embarrassed. 'During the course of our visit, there must have been at least twenty or more of their people in and out of the conference room throughout the afternoon. Most of us left the session for a leak at least once during the discussions, although I'm certain that our team never left our files unattended at any time. Not that these contained anything of a sensitive nature. We always follow the guidelines.'

'And?' the CIA Chief prompted, impatiently.

'Well,' the major answered, obviously bewildered by what had transpired, 'when we returned, I passed my papers to Meyers for filing and it was he who discovered the document at the bottom of my folder. Somehow I must have picked it up by mistake while we were there, or one of the Indonesians slipped it into my papers, although I can't see how.' He looked down at the floor briefly and coughed again, nervously. 'As soon as Sergeant Meyers gave the document to me, I immediately called the colonel here.'

'And so we are unable to confirm its source,' Sam stated, almost accusingly. 'That doesn't give the information much credibility, gentlemen.' The three men sat quietly, thinking.

'Why would the Indonesians pass such information to us?' the Defence Attaché colonel asked. Preston paused, considering just how much information to reveal regarding CIA covert operations within the country.

'It's quite possible that one of our people inside BAKIN took advantage of your visit to make the drop. It is also possible that one of their Intelligence officers decided to initiate a play of his own. Without knowing who is responsible, then I'm afraid, gentlemen, the contents must remain suspect. Having said that, I would appreciate the original for onforwarding to Langley. I'd suggest that you warn the sergeant not to discuss the document with anyone else and shred any copies that have been made. If the information proves not to be false then we wouldn't want half the world to be in on it. Okay?' The two Army officers knew that this was not a request. The Station Chief had the authority and they knew that his instructions were appropriate.

'There are no copies, Sam,' the colonel stated, reaching for the file once again and passing the folder to the CIA Chief who struggled out of his chair, preparing to leave. He smiled briefly and nodded at them both.

'Thanks for your co-operation, gentlemen,' he said, then left. The Station Chief then returned to his own office and worded a brief communication to Langley. He took this personally up to communications where the message was encrypted by one of his own men and then despatched immediately. Within minutes, the information had been passed to the senior desk officer, who read the signal and, in turn, telephoned upstairs to request a meeting with Richards, the Australian Area Operations Desk Officer.

Less than an hour had passed when Senior Agent Richards made the necessary amendments to the profile, then buzzed the registry clerk to retrieve the thick folder and re-file the report under its revised classification. The Top Secret documents titled STEPHENSON, M.L. had been updated and reclassified. His file had been removed from the 'possibles' section into his new category. The CIA had now confirmed Murray as an active agent working together with Harold Bradshaw. The only question which remained in the American Intelligence Agency's mind was his role and relationship with the Indonesian communists. Senior Agent Richards had underlined the grading classification in red and annotated, 'possible double' due to Murray's association with the Partai Komunis Indonesia.

* * * * * *

Melbourne

Harry Bradshaw was miffed with the news that Susan had elected to remain in Djakarta yet another week. and the fact that this information had been received via an impersonal telex sent from the Embassy. It was not so much that he needed her around, or that he missed her company. Harry was just annoyed that he had not been consulted before she had arbitrarily made the decision to remain.

Harry had phoned Muriel to see how young Michael was faring. He knew that the woman was extremely fond of the boy. Harry thought about the child who carried his name, and wondered if he had been correct in assuming who his real father had been. Harry knew that the child could not have been his own son but having Michael in his family contributed conveniently to the image he wished to project. Although earlier concerns had diminished with time, he still wished he could be certain about who had really fathered his son.

He considered Susan's extended stay, then carefully penned an acknowledgement, thanking Susan for the message and wishing her an enjoyable stay. Harry then wrote a brief message to Murray and marked the despatch for encryption. He then checked his watch and made a mental note of the time, planning his day to accommodate an early morning departure the following day to Canberra.

The Secret Service Director chewed at his upper lip as his thoughts turned to the Russian. He wondered why Konstantinov had advanced their scheduled meeting by almost two weeks. It was obviously important enough for the Russian to ignore established contact regimes. Harry had been deeply disturbed when the enigmatic message had been relayed to him at the Toorak Club. Harold Bradshaw was completely conscious of the dangerous possibility that he could, at any moment, be compromised by such amateur behaviour. He also knew that, should his betrayal be discovered, it would be most unlikely that he would ever face the courts. As for Konstantinov, the Australian Government would merely make him persona non grata, upon which the KGB officer would most probably retire to some lakeside *dacha* and be rewarded with an overly adequate pension for his years of service to the Kremlin.

Harry had decided that the Soviet ploy involving the Diponegoro Command went much farther than the Russian revealed. He was certain that, as Moscow supported the Central Javanese Command, it would be logical that they had identified 'friendly' senior officers within that Command. They knew who was prepared to maintain an ongoing relationship with the Soviet Union once the senior echelon of officers currently ensconced in the nation's capital had been successfully removed. This made sense to the Director. What concerned him most about this precarious scheme was the inherent danger always evident when there were two or more players in the game. Bradshaw wished there were some means whereby he could identify which of the Diponegoro officers were pro-West, and which were plotting to betray their own men by delivering their country into the hands of the Soviets. Harry also realised that these conclusions could not be raised with Konstantinov. He had no choice but to go with the flow, so to speak, and wait for developments to direct his course of action. There was little doubt in his mind that the stakes were enormous. His own position could easily be sacrificed should Moscow consider this to be to their advantage. He shuddered involuntarily at this unpleasant thought.

The information flow originating from Djakarta Station and roving agents all indicated that the situation in Indonesia was becoming more and more tense. It was obvious that the communists were getting closer to making a move. Reports concerning the Indonesian Airforce Chief, Omar Dhani, and his so-called goodwill visit to Mainland China convinced his fellow Intelligence associates that arms shipments for the Indonesian communists were imminent, and once these had been completed, Dr. Soebandrio and Aidit would most surely make their move. The conundrum was: who amongst the established members of the Indonesian Armed Forces, the TNI, would support a communist take-over?

As Director of the Australian Secret Intelligence Service, Harold Bradshaw was privy to considerable American intelligence which flowed regularly from Langley to Central Plans. He had become concerned about the deterioration in the quality of this information exchange during the past six months. At first, Harry had put this down to the fact that the Americans had become bogged down in establishing further networks throughout Indochina as a result of the escalation of their involvement in Vietnam. But after challenging the veracity of several CIA-sourced reports relating to the Council of Generals, Harry began to sense that there was a deliberate effort afoot to reduce the information flow through the Australian Intelligence agencies. He believed that the Americans were increasing pressure on some of the generals to arrest Soekarno and seize power, presumably because they were concerned with the Indonesian President's proposed alliance with their new enemy, Ho Chi Minh.

It was apparent to the Australians that the Americans believed there was an imminent danger that Soekarno would open a second front. They feared he would further escalate the regional conflict by moving against the Philippines, even though his *Crush Malaysia* campaign was rapidly losing steam. The Australian Prime Minister had become alarmed when Harry learned that the American President, Lyndon B. Johnson, was considering an option to drop 'the big one' on Hanoi or even Djakarta. Bradshaw's office also alerted MI6 in London, and the British responded by warning the Americans that they could not support such extreme action. Their view was that such a drastic response would be likely to drive many millions more into the arms of the region's communist leaders.

It seemed to Harry that the West was rapidly losing whatever influence it may have had over the Asian states. This would, he expected, delight his Russian masters as they too manoeuvred to expand their sphere throughout the region. Harry sighed. His life had become dangerously complicated, and he wondered how much longer he could continue as events gathered momentum around him, threatening his very existence. He wished he could get away for a few days. Perhaps even visit Thailand. And Piya. It had been too many months since his last visit. Harry reluctantly dismissed these pleasant thoughts and returned to the matters at hand. He busied himself with arrangements for his following day's flight to Canberra. And his appointment with Konstantinov.

* * * * * *

Semarang

General Prajogo listened attentively as the two men delivered their report. His firm Javanese features in no way betrayed his feelings. He was not angry with his men. They were excellent soldiers and had proved their loyalty to him time and time again. He accepted what they had said as unblemished truth. When they had finished, both men stood silently, their berets tucked neatly under their left shoulder epaulette, waiting for the general's admonishment over their failure. Instead, their Commander simply nodded and thanked them for their report, then moved outside to inspect the damage.

He walked around inside the high-walled enclosure several times then grunted. He had seen worse. The general barked an order and his small team of men immediately went to work repairing the vehicle. It would take weeks, he knew, and possibly longer if they were unable to source parts for the damaged bodywork. The left-hand drive sedan was badly damaged along its entire off side. The right-side double headlights had disappeared and most of the side panels had been ripped viciously away. Only two of the side windows remained intact, while shattered pieces of the windscreens were spread throughout the car's interior.

The general was amazed that neither of the men had been injured. It was a sign, he believed, as he moved closer to the Chevrolet and counted the rows of holes which ran up the bonnet and across the solid roof. Relieved that they had not been caught, he turned and smiled at his two soldiers and nodded in quiet admiration at their lucky escape. Then his mood changed as he remembered the object of their failed mission and swore silently to himself that their enemy would not be as fortunate in the next encounter. Of that he was certain. Even if he was obliged to kill the Australian himself.

* * * * * *

Canberra

The KGB had never been known for its subtlety. Harry knew that. As his driver took him back to the Fairbairn Airport terminal, he decided that the visit had been a total waste of time. His meeting with Konstantinov had lasted less than fifteen minutes and, for the first time since he could remember, there was no vodka.

He had been ushered upstairs in typical style and unceremoniously left alone to wait until Konstantinov suddenly appeared, flushed from some tete-a-tete in the Soviet Embassy. Harry wasn't at all annoyed, just bored.

Konstantinov had been full of his customary bonhomie, perhaps even more so as he cracked jokes about Lyndon Johnson and offered the ASIS Director a cigar, forgetting that Harry had long given the habit away. The Intelligence Chief had observed the heavy-set Russian's flushed, jowly cheeks, and decided that this accounted for the lack of vodka. Harry did not object. Sometimes the effects of these sessions with the great bear sized Russian would remain with him for days once he had returned to Melbourne.

They had spoken briefly of events generally before the KGB Attaché moved the conversation to Indonesia, and the Diponegoro 7th Division. Harry had reiterated most of what he had disclosed before, and was surprised that Konstantinov had insisted that Harry identify, again, the list of officers the Diponegoro Commander had written down as possible members of the so-called Council of Generals.

'I have given this to you already, once before,' Harry suggested, thinking that in typical Soviet style he was being tested as to the accuracy of earlier reporting. Sometimes, he thought, they acted like children. He then wrote the names down again, knowing that Russian sources within the Indonesian Military would already have provided such information. Nasution's membership had grown and, with that, the rumours of just who were members of his clique.

As he was about to leave, Harry was surprised by Konstantinov's unfamiliar display of friendship. The man had grabbed him in a suffocating embrace and promised him that soon things would be different. As the ASIS Chief climbed aboard the Australian Airlines Fokker and took his seat in first class, he remembered the Russian's foul-smelling breath and deep, thick body odour. Suddenly Harry shivered, and he looked up to see if the plane's air-vent was blowing directly at him. It wasn't.

Chapter 15

PKI-Gerwani Training Camp
Sukabumi, Java

Yanti looked with admiration as her trainees came to attention. The hour was late and they were all tired. She could see that this had been one of the better intakes as most of the young women had been able to complete the physical training without any serious incidents. The Gerwani had indeed become a force to be reckoned with. Many more thousands of young women had joined the Communist Women's Movement and participated in combat training camps. At first, Yanti ignored the soldiers as they laughed at their female comrades struggling to complete their physical training exercises but, as her own skills developed, she often challenged the men, displaying a deadly accuracy with handguns.

The women were not issued with standard weapons. Only senior members such as Yanti were permitted sidearms and even then, these were handed back into the store before leaving the camp training area. The others were trained to use the simple farmers' *golok*, the deadly sharp-bladed tool which, when wielded as instructed, could separate an enemy's head from his shoulders with one swipe. For uniforms, they dressed in dark pyjama clothing and wore white bandannas around their foreheads. These made them appear most threatening as they leaped forward, then back, then forward again, brandishing their deadly blades in practised movements.

Yanti had been away from Djakarta for more than a month. She missed seeing Murray and was eager to finish training this last group and return to the capital. There was an air of excitement as their *Komandan* had alerted them to the possibility that they would soon be called upon to demonstrate what they had learned at basic training. Yanti believed that she would be given a prominent role to play in whatever was planned, as she had excelled as one of the more senior members of the Gerwani. Although she wished to put the incident behind her now, she had even proven her loyalty by submitting to the requests made of her just the week before when their camp had been privileged by a visit from Comrade Aidit himself.

The unexpected surprise had come as they had finished their evening meal of rice and salted fish. Their *Komandan* had called the young women to assembly and advised them to remain silent as they were addressed by their country's most senior communist, their Chairman. The girls were ecstatic. Few had ever seen their leader and, when he arrived accompanied by a dozen or so soldiers, they had all cheered and clapped as Aidit had stood before them and told them just how proud he was of their contribution to the cause. Yanti had enjoyed meeting the man and was even impressed with the officers who accompanied their Chairman, although she was surprised to see several officers wearing the regimental colours for the President's own guard, the elite *Tjakrabirawa*. Later, when her trainees had moved into their quarters, Yanti had been summoned by her *Komandan*. Without any subtlety whatsoever, she was told that the Chairman and his soldiers expected to have company during their brief visit. Yanti was not only surprised, but offended. At first, she refused. How could she possibly ask her girls to do such a thing, she argued, but the *Komandan* was adamant.

He explained that it was expected of them and that to refuse would not only be a direct insult to the Chairman, but to their cause. Yanti had argued against their demands, unsuccessfully. The *Komandan* had insisted that she was over reacting to what was considered quite acceptable behaviour. Then she was warned that her failure to co-operate would most certainly end in her being overlooked in the future, when the Party would need women of her calibre. Yanti had finally agreed. She had returned and discussed the demands with her group and was astonished to discover that most of the girls were not unhappy with the proposition. Yanti escorted ten of her volunteers back to where their guests were temporarily billeted and left them to entertain these visitors. No sooner had Yanti returned to her own quarters when she heard her door opened and two of the *Tjakra* soldiers brazenly marched in and started undressing. She did not resist. Yanti knew to do so would only be folly. Instead, she lay there until the men were finished and had left. When she was certain they had gone, Yanti ran to the end of the line of simple huts and remained there, washing herself in the *mandi* until she felt clean once again. Then she returned to her bed where she sat, cross-legged, angry and belittled.

A week had since passed and Yanti had managed to come to terms with what had happened. She decided to erase the incident from her mind and, to a greater extent, her strong Sundanese will succeeded. As a result of the encounter, Yanti's dedication to the cause grew. She felt that she had now given all that she had to her country, and that one day she would be rewarded for her unselfishness and loyalty. Yanti pushed ahead with the last few days of the demanding course, pleased that she would soon be in back in Djakarta, and in Murray's comforting arms.

* * * * * *

Melbourne

Harry seemed confused by the discussion. It was almost as if he had not understood the import of what she had said. Susan stopped talking and looked at her husband.

'Harry, do you understand what this all means?' she asked. Harry crossed his legs and remained silent. Damn her to hell! he thought, deciding that Susan could not have selected a more inappropriate time to announce a separation. His whole world had started to crumble. He stared out through the colonial glass window towards their deserted tennis court. Susan had selected the venue. She had telephoned upon her return from Indonesia and advised his secretary that she would not be available for a few days, and would contact Harry when she had recovered from her trip. When he had received the ominous message, Harry already feared that he had lost her.

Somehow he had always known that this day would arrive. He had been a fool to expect Susan to continue their relationship with the constraints they both endured. She was still young, and needed more in her life than he could provide for her. Harry turned back to listen.

'... and we should do this, Harry. Please, listen to me!' she pleaded, determined not to cry. Susan felt drained. She still adored Harry dearly but he could not give her the physical attention she so desperately needed. Why couldn't he understand this?

'Susan,' he started, leaning forward and taking her hands in his. 'I would be lying if I said that it's all right. I admit that I have taken so much for granted over the past years but, is there no way I can persuade you to just take some time to consider your decision first? Aren't you being just a little too hasty?'

'Harry, there is someone else,' Susan said, knowing that this would hurt him deeply, and wishing there was some other way to bring their discussions to a head. 'I'm in love with someone else, Harry. I'm sorry.' She lowered her head, not from shame but because she suddenly felt drained of all energy. She had known it would be difficult, but not like this.

'Is it Murray?' he asked, his voice almost a whisper.

'Good grief no!' Susan replied, a little too quickly and then added, 'how could you even suggest ...?'

'Well, who, then?' he demanded, but not angrily. Already he felt very tired and wished the discussion finished so that they could talk about other things.

'Harry,' Susan started, not wanting to get any further into this. She was concerned that her husband may become irrational. There was something obviously wrong. He was not responding as Susan had expected. She tried again. 'It doesn't matter who. What is important is that we must settle how best to end our marriage and, if possible, Harry, in the most amicable way.' She looked at her husband closely, concerned with the almost vacant response. 'Harry?' she asked, frustrated by his unexpected loss of concentration.

'I'm still here, Susan,' he said, 'I'm still here.'

'Well?' she demanded.

'What about Michael? What will happen to him?' he asked, hoping this might change her decision.

'Michael is my problem. I will take care of him. You know that.'

'But it wouldn't be fair to him,' he argued.

'Harry, you know he's not your child. Let's not make this messier than it already is. Please!'

Harry sat holding her hands, knowing that their relationship had ended.

'Harry?' Susan asked again.

Harry then shook his head sadly and released her hands. 'Do whatever you must, my dear, but please keep it as discreet as possible.' He then smiled thinly. 'You know I don't want this. Isn't there anything I can do to resolve the differences? If I agreed that you could continue your relationship with whoever you've found, without a divorce, could you live with this, say, for another year or so?' he felt, desperate that Susan should not cut him off without the opportunity to prepare himself for such a dramatic change.

Susan shook her head. 'No, Harry. I'm sorry.' She then rose and moved across to the cocktail cabinet and poured herself a stiff shot of vodka. She turned and raised her eyebrows but Harry merely shook his head. He had never seen her take a drink by herself before. He felt desperately tired but steeled himself to complete the grisly details.

'Okay, Susan. How do we do this?' he asked, his voice but a whisper.

Susan placed her drink down and moved quickly across the room and knelt beside her husband. She gripped his hands and kissed him lightly on the cheek, then rose and returned to where she had placed her vodka.

'I believe that we both deserve for this to be kept as civilised as possible. What would you accept as a fair arrangement, Harry?' she asked. Harold Bradshaw wanted to laugh but couldn't. He had lost his wife to another man and traded his soul to another government. He had no children, no future, and soon, if he was not extremely cautious, possibly no life. He looked up at Susan and didn't know what to say.

'I would like to keep the bungalow,' she said, awkwardly. 'After all, I have spent far more time here than you.' She looked carefully across the room for his response.

'Whatever, Susan. If you want it, take it,' he answered in a tired voice. 'Why don't you just tell me what you want and how you wish to settle the whole mess?'

'Fine, Harry,' Susan replied, strangely angry that he had not even attempted to fight for the home they had made together. 'How about we have something drawn up by your solicitor?'

'Fine by me,' he answered wearily, rising unsteadily to his feet. 'Well, guess that's about it then?' with which he picked up his keys and moved towards the door. 'Be a darling and pack my things for me, Susan?' he asked, his face now pale as he forced a brave smile. 'Best send them over to the Toorak apartment. I'll stay there until things are settled.'

'Of course, Harry. I'll attend to that. You don't have to go now, you know,' she said, unconvincingly. He walked slowly to her side and took her hand softly, then kissed her gently on the forehead as he had so many times before.

'Goodbye, Susan,' he whispered, and squeezed her hand softly. He smiled and moved towards the door, then hesitated. 'If it doesn't work out ...' he started, pausing as he opened the door. He stared at his wife and forced one last smile, offered a slight wave, then turned and closed the door quietly behind. Minutes passed, and then in the sudden emptiness, she cried.

Book three

1965, coup and counter-coup

Kerry B.Collison

Chapter 16

Djakarta,
early September

The general mood in the capital was solemn. Another bloody day of rioting had ended with hundreds lying dead. Once again the people had flooded into the streets to protest escalating prices and rice shortages. When the crowds gathered around the Palace, elements of communist units had infiltrated the demonstrators' numbers and started their familiar chanting, demanding food for the people. Within minutes, the crowd had been turned into an unruly mob and, as the soldiers and police moved to disperse the angry gathering, they were met with a hail of rocks. At first, batons were used to force the demonstrators back from the main gates, but these were not enough to deter the crowd. As their numbers grew, they surged forward, crushing the Palace guards.

The first volley of shots was fired directly into those immediately in front of the main gates but, to the astonishment of the Guard Commander, the crowd merely surged forward again. He yelled for a second volley and pointed his own revolver at the sea of screaming faces pushed hard up against the gates. As the shots reverberated through the Palace buildings, those inside prepared to barricade the doors and windows. The Tjakrabirawa Guards were likely to have great difficulty in preventing the demonstrators from entering the grounds.

The President was not present. He had presented yet another radio broadcast from the nation's central broadcast station, Radio Republik Indonesia. He appealed for patience while the Government endeavoured to correct the immediate problems of food shortages. As he spoke, elements of the communist PKI moved to a number of other locations around the city, and commenced throwing stones through Chinese shop windows, exacerbating the capital's security problems on all fronts.

The Council of Generals continued to meet covertly to discuss preparations for the Armed Forces Day on the Fifth of October, and their secret agenda. They had quietly permitted the rioting crowds to have their way, letting off steam as the Military prepared to mobilise its forces to move into the city, ostensibly as a prelude to the massive parades planned for the year's celebrations. The generals had laughed together when Yani related details of his conversation with Soekarno, and how pleased the President had appeared when he was advised that this year, the Tentara Nasional Indonesia would present the people of Indonesia with a parade they would never forget. The President had eagerly agreed to the massive demonstration of military power to be held along the capital's protocol roads, believing that this would distract the hungry masses from their more immediate problems, and even intimidate those who continuously moved to destabilise his Government.

Soekarno had made a number of public appearances to eliminate ongoing speculation regarding his health. It was true that he had been seriously ill, and still suffered fatigue from the debilitating kidney complaint, however Chinese doctors flown from Beijing had managed to remove some of the painful stones with their time-proven herbs and elixirs. During his brief recuperation, the President continued to depend heavily on his trusted confident, Foreign Minister and Deputy Prime Minister, Dr. Soebandrio, who continued to act as the catalyst for the growing bond between the Government and the Indonesian Communist Party.

Chairman Aidit now believed that he had the numbers to force the Indonesian Military to bend to his Party's wishes, and sufficient influence over Soekarno to ensure his support. Arms shipments from Mainland China had commenced and he expected that sufficient numbers within the PKI would be fully armed and ready within three months.

The Commander of the Dioponegoro 7th Division in Central Java waited patiently as the country slowly moved to the boil, maintaining his Command's preparedness for the moment he knew would surely arrive. The general was resolute in his plan to save his country, as Indonesia moved closer to the brink of chaos.

* * * * * *

Murray Stephenson walked slowly from the car towards the Embassy steps. The airconditioner had failed and his mood reflected the discomfort he felt as the hot, sticky weather caused streams of perspiration to run down his back, causing damp patches on his clothing. It was mercifully cooler inside the building, and he checked his watch with the large clock which hung behind the Consulate reception, noticing that one of the two was incorrect. Murray made a mental note to check again later, when he listened to the Radio Australia Broadcasts from Melbourne.

He moved through the maze of corridors until he reached his own section, buried well behind the main entrance. He nodded at other officers as he loosened his tie and unbuttoned his collar. His Number Two opened the final access door after he had punched the buzzer impatiently. Murray had looked at the Second Secretary and thrown his jacket across the room aiming for the corner chair. He then stood directly in front of the Carrier window-unit airconditioner and unbuttoned the rest of his shirt, permitting the refrigerated air to cool his body. He looked back at the other man and noticed his look of concern.

'Don't ask,' he said, kicking his shoes off. He removed his trousers and placed these on a hook close to the cool artificial breeze. During the previous Station Chief's tenure, there had been a painting of Sir Robert Menzies' stern face hanging there. Murray had removed the Prime Minister's picture as he had discovered a more practical use for the wall hook.

'Aircon gone again?' the agent asked. Murray nodded as he continued to undress, removing his socks.

'You'd think they'd fill the bloody things with freon from time to time,' he complained. Embassy maintenance had gone to hell once the new man had arrived. Murray had seen it all before. Some of the expatriates just could not handle being stationed overseas, let alone in a difficult post like Djakarta. The new maintenance officer just could not assimilate, running around screaming at his local staff and, in frustration, attempting to carry out the work by himself rather than entrust the task to his quite capable Indonesian technicians. The end result was a substantial back-load of job orders which had become unmanageable. Murray had suggested to the Consul that the car-pool maintenance be given to Sjaiful, a particularly competent supervisor who probably knew more about mechanical repairs than anyone else, including the Australian, but he was politely reminded that this was not his domain. As a result, more than half the Embassy fleet ran without adequate air-conditioning. The high ambient temperatures and extreme humidity took their toll. Tempers were often frayed and the atmosphere amongst the small community suffered as the country prepared itself for the imminent monsoons.

'There's a 'priority' signal for you, Murray,' the agent advised, handing the message to Murray who now stood almost naked, scratching at a spot on his behind. He read the heading, checked the references and dropped it on his desk. He would decipher it when his clothes were dry. He felt his backside stinging from where he had scratched the skin.

'Shit,' he muttered through clenched teeth, 'it never fails. Every time I visit those bloody offices my backside ends up feeling like I've sat in stinging nettle. You'd think the Indonesians would spray those stinking rattan chairs. Christ!' he exclaimed, stretching to see the large welt as he pulled at the skin around his buttocks. He had been bitten by the tropical lice which thrived in the rattan chairs commonly used in government offices. Dust accumulated between the layers providing a suitable breeding ground for the savage bugs. He cursed, knowing that the severe itch would remain for hours, leaving welts the size of a two-shilling coin. He resisted scratching the bites further.

'What's your schedule for today?' he asked.

'Wanted to check with you first,' the agent replied. 'Colonel Zach has asked if we want to sit in on his discussions with the Indonesian Army. If the answer is yes, I'd best make a move as their meeting has been set up for twelve.'

'What's in it for us?' he asked. Many of the discussions were merely an excuse for the Indonesian officers to put their hands out, often providing nothing in return.

'Zach thought you might be interested. Says he is meeting with one of the team leaders who recently returned from Kalimantan.'

Murray smiled. 'Should be an interesting meet. This time last year the colonel was over there knocking those bastards off!' Doesn't seem to be of particular concern to us. Got anything else pressing?'

'No.'

'Might as well accompany the good colonel then. I'll be here when you return.' The other man nodded then left. Murray then removed his underpants and inspected the welts. He removed his trousers and replaced these with the cotton underclothes. He was confident that he would not be disturbed, as this was the most secure office in the entire building, access only being given to his Number Two and visiting agents. Murray towelled himself and checked his drawer for something to ease the itch. He found an opened tube of cream left from previous attacks and rubbed this into the area affected. He then stood, thinking about his current activities and the deteriorating political scene.

Murray also thought about his friend Zach, and Susan Bradshaw. He shook his head in disbelief. Even after almost two months he still had difficulty coming to term with the fact that his Director's wife had entered into a relationship with Steven Zach. Having examined his own feelings, Murray admitted that he had been disappointed only because there had existed a bond directly between himself and the others, and that the nature of this relationship had automatically changed the instant Steven and Susan had entered into their affair. He was still fond of Susan and continued to be Zach's friend even though this did, from time to time, prove to be awkward. They had set aside some private time and talked it through and Murray was pleased that Zach understood his predicament. But he never mentioned the child.

Susan had not returned to Djakarta although Murray was certain that she maintained close contact with Steven. She had written to him explaining what steps were being taken regarding her marriage to Harry. Murray had been saddened when he read the letter. He decided against communicating a personal message to Bradshaw. He thought it best to wait until they met and Harry had the opportunity to tell him in person when he next visited Djakarta.

Murray's eyes dropped to his right hand and he clenched his fist, then opened his hand to check the red scar tissue. The wounds had taken weeks to heal, requiring stitches across his right palm and most of his fingers. He winced as he remembered grabbing for the top of the wall, his left hand grasping the edge as his right struck the row of broken glass embedded along the top of the cement to prevent intruders. He knew he had been extremely lucky.

Not only could he have lost his hand but his life as well. Murray was most indebted to the soldier who had been guarding his general's house just down the street when his attackers moved in for their kill. There had been no incident recorded. Murray had decided against this as he could see no benefit in alarming others. Instead, he later communicated the incident directly to Central Plans in Melbourne, on an 'eyes only' basis for Harold Bradshaw, his Director. Murray did not disclose the fact that he had broken with procedure and removed sensitive material from the security of the Embassy as he assumed that his wallet, and its contents, would have been thrown away once the money inside had been removed. He believed that it had fallen out of his trousers during the attack, and had most probably been recovered by one of the numerous itinerants who could have passed by any time before he had discovered his loss.

As for his attackers, Murray had no idea whatsoever who they might have been. Nevertheless, he increased security at his residence by employing an additional *djaga* and, whenever he moved around the city Murray did so with extreme caution. He had made a serious enemy out there somewhere, and he was determined not to make their tasks any easier. Murray couldn't be sure that he had not provoked the attack by confronting them in their car.

Although he believed that was possible, why did they return for a second attempt? Was it just a rush of blood on the driver's part or had there been others in the vehicle directing the operation? These, and many other unanswered questions, continued to occupy his thoughts as he went about his activities. He understood that the very nature of his position could have resulted in the attempt on his life. The attack could have been related to any of his clandestine activities as Station Chief. After all, that's what he had been trained to do. He just wished there weren't so many damn restrictions relating to his carrying a weapon. The Agency directive was quite explicit. Unless extreme prejudice was evident, agents were to store their weapons by the most secure means available. In Murray's case, this clearly meant leaving his automatic locked in the small office safe along with his other tools of trade. Unconsciously, he massaged his right hand as the image of his P9S crossed his mind. To hell with the standing orders. They should all be armed when moving around this city, he thought.

Murray checked his watch again and decided to listen to the half-hour news broadcasts. When these were finished, he adjusted his watch, dressed and went over to central registry, clearing the inner decoding safe of other officers as he set about deciphering the message he had received an hour earlier. Murray stood in front of the telex machines as they rattled away noisily, spewing tape down onto the floor as the message took readable form. When the clatter had finished, he reached up and tore the paper from the machine. Murray had already read the detail as each word had formed during the decoding process. He then extracted the two tapes and locked these away, ensuring that he had not left the carbon copy on the machine. He then re-read the signal, memorising its content before he ran both copies through the shredder. As an additional precaution, he removed parts of the finely-cut paper and placed these in an adjacent shredder's bin, knowing that one could never be too careful. Murray then returned to his own section and considered the information contained in the document he'd just destroyed. He frowned. Harold Bradshaw was on his way to visit the Djakarta Station. Murray thought about this and wondered if the visit was personal or professional. Then he shrugged his shoulders and decided it was probably both.

* * * * * *

Changi Airforce Base, Royal Air Force, Singapore

The second pilot indicated with a thumbs up and immediately commenced rolling the deadly bomber in tandem with his team member. Both aircraft moved swiftly across the concrete tarmac as they taxied from the hard-standing area reserved for their squadron, across from the row of hangers and then waited for clearance before moving out onto the runway. There was considerable traffic overhead and both crews listened as other aircraft communicated with their respective towers. The three main operational fields on the small island led to considerable congestion. Changi housed the largest contingent of British aircraft and personnel. The RAF had more than doubled their presence two years before, when the Indonesian President embarked on his crusade to destroy the fledgling Federation of Malaysia.

Other aircraft, including several squadrons of SAR helicopters which could double as gun-ships, were located in both Seleta Airforce Base on the other side of the island and Changi Field. The commercial airstrip at Paya Lebar continued to accommodate the world's airlines, bringing thousands of tourists to the friendly Singaporeans.

As the pilots of both aircraft waited patiently for their final clearance, they observed the distorted perspective created along the runway as the tropical sun baked the airfield's surface, covering the long stretch of concrete with layers of imaginary water. As the minutes ticked by, the pilots offered their silent gratitude to the British engineers who had designed their aircraft and support systems. The temperatures inside the cockpit would have been unbearable had it not been for the airconditioned suits. As the flight commander looked over his left shoulder, his radio crackled and they received clearance for take-off on the main runway. Winds were light and weather over Singapore was still fine, although late afternoon thunderstorms would roll in and dump their rain before the aircraft had completed the first leg of their mission.

Both pilots responded to the tower with a 'roger' and immediately commenced rolling onto the main runway. They lined up their aircraft and released the thousands of horsepower required to thrust the sophisticated aircraft into the sky. Within two minutes, both aircraft had left the military field behind and climbed at an incredible rate as they followed a heading away from the Indonesian islands just a few nautical miles to the south. They eased their noses around to the north, then west, then south again as they gained sufficient altitude to make their run. Fifteen minutes later, as the aircraft reached fifty-thousand feet some one hundred and fifty nautical miles north-east of Singapore and over the Malaysian islands of Anambas in the South China Sea, they turned, and marked their new direction as the crews went into full battle alert.

Minutes later, the aircraft entered Indonesian air as they crossed the Equator and the pilot snapped an order to both crews. There was a moment of turbulence as the cockpit indicator flashed, acknowledging that the mechanisms had functioned. He glanced over at his wing man and confirmed that the other aircraft had followed suit and was in the correct mode. Both aircraft then flew with their bomb-bay doors open. Their bomb load was armed with atomic warheads as instructed, to deter the Indonesian Government from launching any attack with their recently-acquired Bear Bombers which, at that moment, sat quietly along the runway at the AURI Airforce Base in Madiun in East Java. The RAF Vulcan bombers then commenced the first leg of their run through enemy territory, conscious of the SAM missiles which no doubt lay on their revetments waiting for the command to launch. There was little comfort, these pilots knew, that the Soviet SAM's strike capability lay between six and forty-five thousand feet. They had been known to reach greater altitudes, although the airmen knew that the SAM's accuracy went to hell once it pushed past its recommended threshold.

Fifteen minutes passed and the bombers crossed the island of Bangka, maintaining their heading for the Indonesian capital. Another twenty minutes had ticked by when the Royal Air Force pilots banked to port and corrected their heading to fly almost due east. They were now on their second leg, which would take them directly over the squadrons of Soviet TU-16 bombers, the Russian answer to the American B-52's currently bombing the hell out of North Vietnam. The pilots could not see the Java coastline but they knew the cities below by rote, as their squadron had flown almost identical missions twice weekly, over the past two years. In every instance, the Vulcans had been armed with atomic warheads and the aircraft flew with their bomb-bay doors in the operational ready mode.

As they checked their instruments, the aircraft passed over Tjirebon, Pekalongan and Semarang where a further course correction was made to the south-east to enable the deadly loads to fly directly over the huge Soviet aircraft based below near Surakarta. Turbulence rocked the aircraft as they crossed the string of active volcanoes, their craters up to seventeen thousand feet above the sea. The flight commander checked his instruments and alerted the crews. They then changed course for their final leg and closed the bomb-bay doors. Two hours later, the aircraft had landed in Darwin and were already being refuelled for their return run.

The crews remained in the immediate area as this process took place. Then, as they carried out their final checks, the RAF crews waved to their Australian counterparts and flew out of the Darwin base under cover of darkness. They retraced their steps over Indonesia, covering the same targets again, before returning to Changi Field.

President Soekarno went to great lengths to ensure that only a limited number of his Military and Cabinet were advised of these flights. It was humiliating. He was painfully aware of the commitment the British had given the Malaysian and Singaporean Governments and, in fact, he had been personally advised by the British Ambassador that these flights would continue as long as the Indonesian President persisted in his attempts to invade either of those two British Commonwealth countries. A direct warning was given to the President that his Airforce was being continuously monitored and, in the event any of the Indonesian Airforce Tupolov long-range bombers so much as strayed outside the immediate surrounds of Madiun, he could expect that either Djakarta or Surabaja would be subjected to a pre-emptive strike by aircraft armed with atomic warheads.

At first Soekarno thought it was all bluff until he was shown the radar tracking reports. He was livid and delivered a stinging attack on British Imperialism to his followers during that year's Independence Day celebrations. He then ordered that the flights be kept from the Indonesian people. Soekarno believed that his *rakjat* would never believe that, even with the sophisticated weaponry introduced by the Soviets, they were still unable to prevent the West from violating their airspace at will. The flights continued and Soekarno issued direct instructions to Omar Dhani that the TU-16's were to remain grounded.

* * * * * *

Clarke Airforce Base,
United States Airforce, Philippines

The American Airforce general removed his shields and rubbed both eyes slowly. He was tired and ready for some shut-eye. He glanced over the data recorded on the 'flights in progress' board and shook his head in disgust. There was one still out somewhere, and there had been no radio contact for well over an hour. He knew his arse would be in a sling if they had a repeat of the Pope flight although he did not believe that they were faced with a similar problem.

The general appreciated that things had changed considerably since then, what with the continuous bombing runs on 'Nam which originated from his field here in the Philippines. The one-star general straightened and drew in several deep breaths before rubbing his face again. Suddenly, the radio, set on the specific frequency allocated to the southbound incursion, came to life. Immediately all signs of fatigue disappeared as the pilot identified his position and advised that they had suffered some light ground fire. This had interfered with their earlier transmissions as they were completing their final drop near Makassar. Now they had completed their mission and were over the Sulu Sea off the west coast of the central Philippine islands. They reported that their run had been successful and that only minor damage had been sustained.

The general was pleased. He disliked lending his boys to the Air America flights but he accepted that they were all on the same side. He knew that his pilots enjoyed these missions, even though no record of their flights and hours in the air was recorded in their log books. Neither did they wear uniforms or dog-tags whilst on these flights. The up-side was that the CIA Station Chief paid each of his men a cool grand for each mission, and that was big money in anyone's book. He had to be selective when choosing pilots for these clandestine runs over Indonesia. Married men were never selected. He preferred the boys who had already scored time over 'Nam as they wouldn't be gun shy if things came unstuck. As for the aircraft they flew, that was another consideration. The general disliked using vintage aircraft. They had been good in their day but, as he had discovered himself when having to ditch one of the old ladies just the year before, those C-47's were definitely ageing, and really should not be used for covert flights.

The men were never briefed as to who were the beneficiaries of the night cargo drops. He could only speculate as to the purpose of the tonnes of weapons tied to darkened parachutes that his men alone had thrown out of the ancient cargo planes. Suddenly he chuckled as he envisaged these dangerous loads swinging through the evening sky and landing, as they often did, on village roofs or even on people in the streets. It didn't concern him. They were dropping shitloads of high explosives to the north all over 'Nam.

Why shouldn't this asshole Soekarno, get some too? They were surrounded by commies everywhere, he decided, wishing he could return to active flying duties. He really missed those missions. The movements officer approached and then waited at an appropriate distance until his general waved him over.

'Whattaya got?' he demanded, taking the clipboard from the major before he could refer to the data annotated there. The general shook his head and swore. 'Goddamn it, Major, we have one of those old birds limping its way back in as we speak. Now what do they want?' he snapped. The junior officer took a deep breath.

'The spooks have asked for fifteen more flights before the end of the month, General. That will mean utilising the other two birds in hangar two-two. I need your authorisation to ask the colonel over there to give us some urgent support crews to bring them on line again.'

'How deep are the targets?' the general asked, angry with the additional demands being made by the Station CIA Chief. They must have something really hot on their plates, he thought.

'All the way, General. All the way.'

'For Chrissakes,' he spat, knowing that he would be especially tight for crews. 'Get onto the rosters and tell the boys the bad news. Give me a list of those who've already had more than two runs this month. Don't want them to get too greedy,' he ordered. The major turned and disappeared quickly while his CO continued to monitor the days' flights over Hai Phong in North Vietnam. The officers all knew that their Commanding Officer had their best interests in mind and always took their position whenever it came to it. Just the week before, his men had been dragged over the carpet for dropping their load too close to the British freighters in the North Vietnamese harbour. The general had cursed and shouted, furious that his men were obliged to avoid hitting the limey ships delivering much-needed supplies to Ho Chi Minh. He just could not understand what the Brits were doing there. Weren't they supposed to be America's allies?

As he glared out through the thick plate-glass windows overlooking Clarke Field Airforce Base, the general snorted in contempt and muttered something unintelligible to himself. Then he remembered the additional flights requested into Indonesia and his face became even more serious.

All the way, the major had said. And he knew only too well what that meant.

* * * * * *

DJJakarta

Aidit listen intently as the other members of his *Dewan Revolusi* spoke. Soebandrio was present and was a senior member of this Revolutionary Council. Aidit looked around the room and felt confident that their plans would be realised. And soon.

For he now believed that he had the support necessary to effect a successful coup d'etat against the Council of Generals before they acted first. He had been informed that news of Air Marshall Omar Dhani's real purpose in visiting Red China had reached Nasution. Aidit was most concerned that the arms shipments would be interrupted by the anti-Communist TNI generals. As he listened to Untung outline specific responsibilities for the Military officers present, the Chairman of Indonesia's Communist Party watched the effect the lieutenant colonel was having on the others as he assumed control over the meeting.

The gathering consisted of members of almost every facet of Indonesia's multi-layered society. Apart from Colonel Untung, Brigadier General Soepardjo was present, as well as Colonel Latief and Majors Soejono and Agus Sigit who would all play significant roles when the time arrived. Aidit considered their ongoing need for President Soekarno's support although, at times, even he seemed to waver. Aidit accepted that there had been compromise and the necessity to identify his own interpretation of Communism as the accepted ideology within his Party. In securing Soekarno's protection, Aidit realised that the PKI had lost much of its doctrinal purity, not to mention its revolutionary will. Still, he believed, in typically pragmatic fashion, that it was imperative that he adjust the basic philosophy to accommodate the Indonesian mentality. The Party Chairman looked across at their host.

The house where they congregated belonged to Wahjudi, one of Aidit's most devout supporters. They all wore civilian clothes to avoid detection as the members were obliged to pass through a narrow gang in order to access this meeting place, which was located directly behind another building with no vehicular access. The members of the Revolutionary Council were aware that their plans had moved into a critical phase and, even more so than before, they had to be careful. Aidit sensed that they were near to achieving their goals and cautioned his inner circle of conspirators to maintain diligence at all times, fearing that the slightest slip would tear their dream of a communist state asunder.

Latief had proposed that they establish a Central Command within the Revolutionary Council, to be headed jointly by Untung and Soepardjo. They had all agreed. Next, they finalised the list of all those units which could most definitely be counted on to support their actions. Aidit listened excitedly as even he was surprised at the number of companies and units which had already committed themselves to the movement. Ever since their President's health had deteriorated, their rank and file had become seriously concerned that, should he die, there would be no-one left to protect the communists from the Council of Generals, the members of which were either known or assumed to be known to Soebandrio and Aidit. These senior Party officials warned that, in the event Soekarno passed away, these senior Military officers had made it quite clear that they would not only abolish the Indonesian Communist Party, but had promised to incarcerate its prominent membership. Aidit continued to listen as Untung spoke.

'That leaves us with a target date to determine. We should agree on that now,' he suggested. Those present immediately looked towards Aidit who nodded in affirmation.

'I agree. We must select the most opportune date for our move. What are your suggestions?' he asked. The members discussed this important issue for almost an hour until they reached agreement. They decided on the tenth day in November. It was the national holiday which celebrated the Heroes of the Revolution. Not long thereafter, the meeting broke up and they returned to their homes. Aidit had remained behind to speak with the Tjakrabirawa colonel.

'Comrade Untung,' he addressed the Palace Guard officer, *'we should speak more about Nasution and his Council. I believe that you and I have a clearer understanding of what their fate must be if we are to be successful in our efforts to take full control of the Military?'*

Colonel Untung smiled at Aidit. He had been promised an appointment as the new Armed Forces Chief once the communists had taken full control of the Government. Under the new regime, there would be no rank higher than that of colonel. There would be an immediate rationalisation of officers and their ranks. He, in turn, would be promoted to this most senior Military position over his superiors, in consideration for his loyalty. He relished the thought of eliminating the current *TNI* leadership. The colonel then extracted the list of officers who had been targeted for immediate arrest. There had been considerable debate concerning which of the generals belonged on the list. They had agreed that all of Nasution's so-called Council had to be included. There were others, but these had been discussed at length and removed from the final list.

Aidit addressed the Deputy Prime Minister, Dr. Soebandrio. *'I'm not entirely comfortable leaving him out,'* he argued, referring to Soeharto, the Strategic Reserve Forces Commander. *'Although your arguments are strong, we must remember that he would be one of the most senior ranking officers once Yani and Nasution are removed.'*

'Not under our proposed reorganisation of the Military. Besides, it is a known fact that he and Nasution have been feuding for years. Also, he is not a member of the Council of Generals. We would do well to remember that, once we've taken power, we will need to maintain strong relationships with the Chinese, both politically and commercially. This man has developed considerable strengths within the local Chinese community. I recommend that his name is removed.'

After further debate, they all agreed. In the end it was decided that providing the most senior officers were arrested, the others would fall into line. After all, they had their President's blessing, he argued.

'It would be detrimental to our maintaining leadership should these officers remain alive. There would always be the danger that they may gather enough support to move against us in the future. Besides, should they be swept away in the excitement, their supporters would be like a dragon with no head. We should eliminate these men immediately upon our units moving into the capital. You would need to think through this very carefully. We need to have at least one team dedicated to this important task. A team which we could totally depend upon to carry out the necessary executions,' Aidit insisted.

'I will make the arrangements, Comrade Aidit. In fact, we already have such a unit which would be well-suited for this mission. They are

completely trustworthy and have already proven themselves to the Party,'
Untung advised.

'Then I will leave this in your capable hands, Comrade,' the Chairman smiled, satisfied that the powerful members of the Military
leadership would be dealt with as he seized control of the Government. They talked a while longer; then, so as not to attract attention, left separately to attend to their other duties.

Several days passed before Lieutenant Colonel Untung made
his final decision. He selected several units from the Gerwani to
assist in accommodating the Party Chairman's request. He had
seen these young women as they trained and was convinced that
they would carry out the executions when the time arrived. He
searched his mind for the team leaders he had encountered in
Sukabumi when he and the others visited the field training camp.
Then he remembered and made a note to make direct contact during the next few days. He wrote in his diary, *Gerwani — Sukabumi
— Check names of the team leaders.*

The following Monday, Yanti was summoned to PKI Headquarters.

* * * * * *

Bangkok

Harry sat uncomfortably in the back of the airport taxi as the
traffic ground to a halt. He leaned forward and peered ahead
through the heavy downpour. The intersection was blocked by
stranded vehicles, unable to move further when their saturated
distributors had ceased to function under the waves of water which
inundated the capital's roads whenever it rained. He looked out
through the side window and estimated the filthy water to be at
least knee-deep.

Harry knew the city well and, considering the remaining distance to his hotel, decided that he would wait until the driver
managed to extricate them from the congestion rather than wade
through what was probably a combination of rain water and raw
sewerage. There was a *klong* not two hundred metres off to their
right and he had little doubt that this canal would already have
spilled its filthy effluent into the lower areas. It seemed that

Bangkok was sinking. Almost every visit he had made had resulted in his being bogged down in the rain somewhere on the city's over-crowded roads.

An hour passed. The driver had killed the engine as he was running short of gas. The man turned and smiled through irregular yellow teeth, and offered Harry a cigarette. Harry declined, wishing his command of the language was good enough to tell the man not to light-up in the confined taxi's interior. As the smoke drifted across to the rear seat, Harry quickly opened both windows but this made little difference. The driver waved the cigarette around as he fidgeted impatiently, tapping his fingers on the steering wheel to the beat of some imaginary song. Another hour had passed before the police had cleared the congested intersection and they were able to proceed. By then, the Director's clothes were saturated by the suffocating humidity and heat. The driver lit another cigarette just after Harry had closed the rear windows to benefit from the airconditioner. Then the taxi moved slowly forward into the stream of down-town traffic, the driver touching his brake, then accelerating, then braking again, riding his clutch and making Harry feel distinctly nauseous.

When they finally arrived at the Intercontinental Hotel, Harry checked his watch and was dismayed that the entire trip from the airport had taken most of four hours. He completed the registration formalities, went immediately to his room and showered. Then he dialled the local number and waited. As he listened to the dial tone ringing, unanswered, Harry became concerned. He acknowledged that he was late, but that had never been a problem in the past as Bangkok residents were quite relaxed about appointment times, due to the city's notorious traffic problems. The tone changed indicating that there was no one there. Harry dialled again, with a similar result. He frowned. As was his custom, he had sent a cable advising details of his arrival although he couldn't be sure that this had not gone astray.

Suddenly, Harry felt the skin on his neck prickle. Immediately, he became even more alert. His years in the field and inner senses told him that something had gone wrong. He knew from experience that it was most out of character for Piya not to wait. He decided to go down and check the premises for himself. Clearing the round coffee table, he placed his briefcase down flat, then extracted a small nail-file from his personal vanity set. He removed four brass screws which held the lower section of his well-worn leather case, then separated the two sections. Harry pulled one of the chairs closer and made himself comfortable while he examined the contents exposed in the hidden compartment. He removed the short cylinder and inspected this first, before placing it back in the indentation designed to hold it secure. He then coaxed the 7.62 mm pistol from its own slot and checked the Soviet Tula Tokarev's eight-round magazine.

Memories came flooding back as he held the pistol confidently. He had opted for this weapon specifically when he first arrived in Berlin as it was standard issue in the Soviet Army and, as he spent most of his time in their territory, Harry felt more comfortable carrying one of their handguns. He knew that the TT pistol was common throughout the Russian satellite states. It suited his hands, weighing less than two pounds. He was not concerned with its range, believing that no one in their right mind should attempt to take out a handgun target in excess of fifty metres.

Harry extracted another clip containing gilded steel-jacketed bullets and placed this in his back pocket. He removed the small cylinder once again and connected this to the pistol. Satisfied, he unlocked the silencer and placed this in his side pocket. He then changed shirts, selecting one which he could wear, hanging outside his trousers. The automatic under his belt was well hidden behind the curve in the small of his back, and covered by his loose fitting shirt. He checked himself in the full length mirror. He was ready.

Harry left his poolside suite and returned to the lobby to check personally for messages. There were none. Ignoring the concierge's attempts to steer him towards the hotel taxi service, Harry elected instead to walk the short distance to the main entrance where he hailed a private taxi and issued directions for the driver to follow.

Unknown to Harold Bradshaw, his movements had been closely monitored. As the unmarked pirate taxi pulled out into the traffic, an inconspicuous figure hurried across the hotel car-park and hissed at his companion to hurry. Moments later, the relatively new Fiat leaped into life as the driver accelerated quickly and followed the Intelligence Chief on his journey across the city, to meet his lover. It soon became obvious that the Australian was heading for the destination about which they had been briefed, and that their quarry was taking evasive surveillance measures. They decided to drive directly to Piya's small flat, convinced that Harry Bradshaw would soon appear for a rendevous with his young friend. They arrived not moments after the Russians had left, having baited their trap. The CIA agents remained outside, well hidden in the shadows, waiting.

* * * * * *

Piya had watched in fear as the telephone continued to ring. He glanced up at the two men who stood, menacingly, their huge frames filling the room. He shivered and looked at the window airconditioner unit to see if he had remembered to turn it down, then realised that it was fear that was responsible for the chill in his spine. He needed to use the bathroom, desperately. Piya inadvertently made eye contact with one of the men and immediately wished he hadn't. His stomach churned as he remembered their earlier visit. And the beating.

He closed his eyes and prayed to his gods. Piya could not understand why he deserved so much unwarranted attention. First, he had been beaten by the American. But that had been months ago. He had thought they had forgotten about him. Now there were others, with accents he did not understand at all. He was consumed with fear. He could hear the television in the adjoining apartment as his neighbours' children played with the volume controls. Piya wished he could call out but realised to do so would only hasten his demise. He sniffed, fighting back the tears, which earlier had earned him a stinging slap to the side of the head. He glanced at the bedside clock. It had been a gift from the man Piya knew had just telephoned. He bit his lip, fighting to control his tears and, as an uncontrollable sob escaped from deep in his chest, his head exploded with a flash, and he fell to the floor stunned by the blow. He lay there, terrified, waiting for the vicious kick, covering his head with both hands.

'Get up, you little whore,' a voice snarled at him. He struggled to his feet and sat back on the side of the bed. 'And stop your snivelling!' The one who spoke then checked his wrist-watch and cursed. 'He's not coming.'

'Give it another thirty minutes. He'll come,' the other man said confidently, 'he'll come to see his little friend here. I guarantee it.'

'No more than thirty minutes, okay? And then I get to carve this little piece of shit into dog meat!' he grinned cruelly as Piya's eyes opened wide. The other man smiled knowingly at the suggestion and winked at his accomplice.

'Sure, why not?' he agreed, enjoying the fear on the young Thai's face. They then both remained silent as they waited, tensing from time to time as occasional pedestrian traffic passed close to the apartment's entrance, before moving away. Piya stared at the clock unable to control his fear. There was little time left. Would Harry come, he wondered? Again, he closed his eyes and prayed, pleading that someone would make these men go away.

* * * * * *

Harry waited in the taxi for some time, until certain that he had not been followed. Then he paid the taxi and walked the remaining distance towards Piya's flat. He stopped half a dozen times and checked over his shoulder but could still not detect anyone following. Strange, he thought, he just had that feeling. He knew he should slow down, double check, anticipate. Harry deliberately dallied on the last corner, feigning confusion as to his whereabouts. He could not identify anything out of the ordinary but, there again, he realised anything could go unnoticed in Bangkok's sleazy backstreets. He noticed the Fiat down the street but decided that its presence was not threatening. The car's occupants had slid, unobserved, low into their seats as Harry had arrived.

He stood across from the apartment and observed the building and its neighbouring structure. Harry could not see any movement amongst the street's shadows. Again, nothing appeared out of the ordinary except the absence of the welcome light which Piya would normally leave on when expecting his visit. Harry discounted this, now almost convinced that his cable had not been received, accounting for Piya's obvious absence. He moved closer to the building, then stiffened. The airconditioning unit hung out over the footpath where it had been ever since he had first visited this location. He looked up and listened to its hum and observed a few drops of condensation fall close to where he stood.

Immediately he sensed that there was something wrong. Piya would never have left his apartment, not even for five minutes, without first turning the airconditioner off. It was just one of young Piya's many idiosyncrasies. Harry knew that someone waited inside.

He paused outside and considered his options. Whoever occupied the apartment would not expect him to be armed. He decided to force the confrontation. A couple approached and he waited for them to pass and turn the corner before he climbed the narrow steps and knocked loudly on the solid timber door. There was no answer. He knocked again as he gripped the door handle and turned the knob, pushing quickly with his left hand while holding the Tula Tokarev with his right.

The door flew open into darkness. Harry threw himself to the left and extended his right arm preparing to shoot. Dim light fell through the open doorway as he stood still, his senses alive, his finger tensed on the pistol's trigger. He realised that he had stopped breathing. Slowly he released the breath he had been holding and sucked fresh air in through his dry mouth. He cursed silently as his fingers groped along the wall for the light switch near the door.

'Piya?' he whispered hoarsely, suddenly identifying the fierce stench in the room. 'Piya?' he called again, his fingers locating the switch as he flicked the lights on and dropped to the floor, his weapon still extended towards the centre of the room. He sat crouched in this position looking directly across to the large double bed as his eyes adjusted to the sudden infusion of light. Suddenly, he groaned and cried out loudly, as he sprang to his feet then turned pointing the automatic around the room in search of others present. But there were none. Only Piya. He lay spread across the length of the oversized bed, his legs dangling across the side as if he had been doing exercises then gone to sleep. But Harry knew that this was not so. The twisted expression on the young man's face told him otherwise.

Harry felt the blood drain from his face as he stared at the once handsome boy. He bent over the body and closed Piya's eyes, unable to avoid looking at the blood-stained torso as he did so. For several minutes Harry stared at the corpse, anger building as it had once before, many years ago. Too late, he remembered the open door and, as he turned to remedy the oversight he just caught a glimpse of the huge fist before it crashed heavily down on the base of his neck, smashing him to the floor. His body buckled with the impact, causing his pistol to fly out across the room where it fell noisily on the polished tiles. That was the last sound he heard.

Below, in the street, the Fiat's driver looked at his passenger and raised his eyebrows when the Russians slipped into the apartment. They had not expected to see them there.

'Wait,' the other man ordered, gripping his associate's arm to prevent him from leaving the vehicle.

'You didn't recognise those gorillas?' the driver asked incredulously.

'Sure,' his partner answered, 'that's why we should wait. Let's see what Boris is up to first before we make out like the cavalry.' The driver killed the engine and they sat quietly waiting for the Russians to leave.

'What do you think he's doing meeting with KGB?' The taller man looked across at his partner sitting behind the wheel. Sometimes he wondered how the man qualified as a field agent. Langley must really have screwed up with this one, he thought.

'Maybe they've organised a gang-bang together, Jerry. Shit, man, how the hell would I know what those mothers are doing there with the target.'

'We should take some shots. The boss will ask us why we didn't take any shots.'

The other agent thought about Jerry's suggestion and admitted that he was right. He rummaged around on the rear seat, then dragged the entire assembly across and onto his lap. There he rearranged the lens, replaced the film to compensate for the light and adjusted the focus. The agent activated the shutter release several times to ensure that the film had been picked up by the sprockets. Then they waited.

When the door finally opened only one of the oversized bear-shaped Russians re-appeared. The Americans watched as he walked away and disappeared around the corner, but not before they had shot several frames of the huge man as he was caught in the brief shaft of light from the doorway.

Jerry looked across at his partner and raised his eyebrows, then turned his attention back to the apartment's entrance, waiting for the second man to leave also. He didn't. Jerry was becoming restless when the dark-coloured Mercedes 180 slowed then stopped directly outside the target's apartment. The driver left the engine running and moved to the rear of the sedan, opening the trunk. The two CIA agents were almost caught off-guard when the door opened quickly and the Russian ran down the steps carrying a large bundle over his shoulder, which he unceremoniously heaved into the Mercedes' open trunk. The agents continued filming as both men lept into the sedan and drove quickly away.

The Americans looked at each other and, without speaking, sprang from their Fiat and ran up the steps and into the apartment. Moments later the one called Jerry was doubled over the bathroom basin heaving from the sight of the bloody and mutilated corpse they discovered lying on the bed.

'Come on Jerry, let's go, man!' his partner called, cursing as he attempted to drag his associate up off the floor. 'If we get caught in this shit, man, we'll end up wishing that was us,' he hissed, pointing to the body as he dragged Jerry out of the apartment. Suddenly he paused, saw Harry's weapon and bent down to retrieve the automatic, shoving it quickly inside his belt as he continued to push the other agent out of the building. They ran back to their car and left the scene quickly, before someone called the police. Above all else, it was their duty not to be compromised by these situations. Both men reported directly to the CIA Station Chief at home, who instructed his agents to go directly to the U.S. Embassy, develop their film and complete their reports. He told them to wait there until he arrived.

Later, he listened to their observations, read through their reports and checked the photographs. The image was not as clear as he would have liked but, he acknowledged, the photographs were good enough to identify the Russians at work. The CIA Chief scratched his head as he examined the picture showing the one Soviet agent carrying a bundle in what appeared to be a carpet or something similar. There had been no evidence that Harold Bradshaw, or 'Finger Jar', was dead, he thought; otherwise, why would the Russkies bother to remove the Australian's body?

He completed his own analysis and sent the entire report up to communications for encryption and despatch. Let Langley work this one out, he decided, knowing that the lights would burn throughout the night when news of Harry Bradshaw's abduction reached the Director's desk back in Virginia.

* * * * * *

He couldn't breathe. His tried to free himself from inside the carpet but discovered that his hands had been tied. Harry could smell the exhaust fumes as the deadly smoke leaked into the trunk compartment. His throat was hoarse from coughing. They had tied something around his mouth to prevent his calling out. He knew that if they did not stop and attend to him soon, he would die from asphyxiation, or at least carbon monoxide poisoning.

Harry had regained consciousness only to pass out again. He had no idea whatsoever where he was until he identified the poisonous fumes and then cold realisation returned. He had been kidnapped. But, by whom? Rational thought dictated that there had to have been a mistake. Why would he be kidnapped? It most certainly would not be the Soviets, his mind argued, nor the Americans or Brits! What would be their benefit? Obviously, someone wanted something from him. And in earnest, he admitted, remembering the body left behind which had been used as bait. He had been professionally set-up, this he knew. Someone had gone to extreme lengths to arrange for his abduction. Someone, again obviously, who was familiar with his secret liaison with Piya. Harry winced with pain as the car hit a pot-hole somewhere, driving his head hard against something solid. The fumes seemed to increase as the car reduced speed, turning left, then right, then left again, then slowing to a stop. He could hear voices, then the vehicles moved forward again, but not too far before it came to a halt and the engine noise died.

He heard men's voices, then a rattling sound as the trunk was opened and he was lifted bodily from the suffocating hole. The carpet was removed and he squinted as bright lights attacked his eyes. His hands and feet were untied leaving him to stand groggily in the basement garage. One of the huge men dragged him by the shoulder, forcing Harry to follow quietly. Immediately he recognised these men for what they were, and was confused. He could see from their features that they were Russians. They even smelled like Russians, he thought bitterly, as he stumbled, cracking his knee on the first of the steps which led to the building's ground floor.

They passed through several fire exits before he was ushered into a lift which took the three men to the third floor.

Harry identified the building as the Soviet Embassy. Now he was even more confused, although feeling slightly more confident. Surely if they wanted him dead, he would have been killed already and left beside Piya? They entered a small room devoid of anything on the walls. It was an interrogation room. He had used them himself, in the past. His two guards then left, leaving him alone with his thoughts and the two chairs which had been positioned facing each other. The door opened and he turned.

'Hello Comrade Director,' Konstantinov bellowed, enjoying what he perceived to be an amusing moment for all. 'Sit down, Comrade, sit,' he ordered, placing his huge frame on one of the chairs. Harry sighed and did as instructed. The door opened and an unfamiliar face entered, carrying a tray with two glasses and a bottle of vodka. He looked at the KGB officer and accepted one of the glasses as it was poured. Both men swallowed the contents without hesitation. The glasses were then refilled and the attendant retired, leaving the men alone. Konstantinov swallowed the second shot and kept his empty glass raised until the Australian followed suit. Harry coughed as the spirits burned all the way down, sending a pleasurable flush through his tired and battered body.

He looked at the Russian and waited. He knew that Konstantinov would get to the point soon enough. Harry felt that he had experienced enough surprises to fill a life-time already. What was the KGB man doing here in Bangkok? And why had he orchestrated his kidnapping?

'Well, Comrade, seems that you have been overcome by events,' the Soviet spy-master commenced. His mood was convivial as he refilled both glasses. Harry waited. There seemed little point in interrupting. He wanted Konstantinov to get to the point quickly, and tell his story. Especially the part which finished ... and that's why we killed Piya. He lifted the glass and swallowed its contents in one swig. Konstantinov was impressed.

'Harry,' the Russian started again, this time sending a cold chill through the ASIS Chief's body. He had never called him that before. 'Harry, I believe I have some good news for you. Or at least, I would hope you will consider it good news.' Konstantinov smiled, almost benevolently, as he held his fourth glass of vodka steady, then raised it in salute before finishing it quickly. Harry waited.

'The good news is you are going home, Comrade,' the Russian said, pleased with the announcement. Harry looked at the KGB officer suspiciously. Why kidnap him to tell him that?

'You will leave tomorrow morning with some of the Soviet staff and families who are returning to Moscow by Aeroflot,' he announced. Harry was stunned by the statement. Home? To the Kremlin? Konstantinov must have flipped! His mind raced as the implications of what had just been said dawned on him. My God, he thought, they want me to do a Philby!

'I see you are pleased, Comrade. This is good. You see, there are those in Moscow who wished to terminate our relationship with you in a less friendly fashion. I argued on your behalf. They now all agree. You have been a faithful warrior to the Kremlin and now you are to be rewarded. You will be given an apartment in Moscow, treated with respect, permitted to travel freely within the Soviet Union and even an adequate pension.' Konstantinov paused to examine Bradshaw's reaction.

'Why?' he asked, still stunned by the news. He felt as if someone had gripped his guts with ice-cold hands and would not let go. His mind raced, searching for answers but there were none there. 'Why Moscow?' he asked in disbelief.

'Why?' Konstantinov responded. 'I would have thought that quite clear, Comrade Harry,' he smiled, pleased with their new relationship. 'You are being retired. And in a pleasant way.' There was a hint of menace in his voice. Harry was almost lost for words. What in the hell was going on here?

'Why can't I just retire in Australia?' he asked, fearing that he already knew the answer. Konstantinov looked at Harry's drink and observed that it was empty. He refilled both glasses.

'Because if you return to Australia, my friend, you will most surely die,' he said solemnly. Somehow Harry had anticipated the answer although he was still confused. 'Our masters in Dzerdzhinsky Square have decided to put you out to pasture, Harry. The reasons are many and complicated. I can tell you, though, it is because of what is taking place in Indonesia that you are to withdraw from your own country's involvement there as our interests will most certainly be compromised should you remain in the game. Remember, Harry, it could have been worse. There are still those who would feel more comfortable knowing

324

that your retirement was more, ... let's say, permanent.'

Konstantinov explained how he had argued on Bradshaw's behalf, stating that the Australian Intelligence Chief would be a considerable asset in terms of propaganda alone. The West would be stunned to discover that one of their most respected officers had defected. Konstantinov relished the idea of such a disclosure, coming not so many years after the British scandals involving McLean, Burgess and, of course, Kim Philby.

And then, of course, there was the immediate risk. The Kremlin would be vulnerable if the man they had turned remained within reach of the discretionary powers of his own Government. Moscow had been emphatic. Repatriate or remove Bradshaw, and quickly. It had taken years for the KGB to successfully infiltrate the American Central Intelligence Agency and now, with one of their deep-cover agents positioned close to the decision-makers in Langley, they had discovered that Harold Bradshaw's activities had already been known, and he was currently suspected by his Western ally of having been compromised in some manner. Their mole had even verified the Australian's allocated code-name within the CIA: Finger Jar. Moscow insisted that he be removed from the arena immediately, convinced that he could be turned again at any time, by the Americans. There was too much at stake to consider the interests of just one man. Now Konstantinov was not certain that he had taken the appropriate position by supporting Bradshaw's repatriation to the Soviet Union.

'Why didn't you discuss this with me during our last meeting in Canberra? Harry asked. 'Why was it necessary to go to these elaborate steps here in Bangkok?' He paused. 'Your men were excessive,' he added, almost sullenly. The Russian looked at the Australian and smiled.

'Come, Comrade. Would you have entertained leaving Australia if we'd asked? Also, you must admit, these things are more easily arranged from Bangkok than say, Canberra, no?' The Russian continued to observe the other man's reactions. 'We decided that, as you were already here, the most difficult step had already been overcome by your leaving your own country voluntarily. After all, Harry, we wouldn't want the embarrassment of repeating the Petrov fiasco.'

Harry was stunned. His mind raced but he knew that this

decision was already a fait accompli. The Russian had obviously taken steps to ensure he would not return to Australia. What had they done? He understood that retirement to the Kremlin may be his only choice. The alternative was patently clear. Harry looked hard at the Russian facing him. The jovial expression betrayed only by the cold, piercing eyes. Harry could not believe this was happening to him. Desperately he decided on one last course of action. He paused then raised his glass.

'When did you say I'd be leaving?'

'Tomorrow, Harry,' Konstantinov answered, 'tomorrow,' raising his glass in a toast. 'I will now tell you how pleased I am that you have made the correct decision, my friend. Had you refused ...' he left the words hanging. Harry thought for a moment.

'Am I permitted one last night on the town?' he asked, forcing a mischievous grin. For a moment he thought he had gone too far, as he observed the flicker in Konstantinov's eyes as they momentarily clouded over. The KGB officer didn't answer immediately, pouring the remnants from the bottle into his own glass, then spilling half of this into Harry's.

He had suggested to Moscow that, should Bradshaw clearly be receptive to his being repatriated to Moscow, then this would be the preferred course of action. Konstantinov had been instructed that, should there be the slightest hesitation evident in Harry's response, then the Australian was to be eliminated. There had been considerable resistance to the idea of having the Australian living in Russia. Several had argued that, at some point in the future, Harry would become a major liability if he was not totally receptive to the idea of spending the rest of his days behind the Iron Curtain. Konstantinov had agreed to test Harry Bradshaw's response, and accepted responsibility for the final decision. It now appeared that he had little choice. In his own way, Konstantinov felt a little saddened by the decision he knew he must make. He had given the Australian his chance and the KGB general now decided to correct an earlier error in judgement. It just never paid to be sentimental, he knew. Especially when one's own position may be at risk.

'I don't see why you shouldn't have one last fling in the decadent West,' he smiled, then added, 'or in this case, the decadent East.' They both laughed. Harry looked at the other man and rose to his feet.

'I would appreciate just a few hours to pick up my things from the hotel, have a few quiet drinks at the bar. You know, sort of say goodbye by myself.' Konstantinov looked at the Australian, then nodded.

'I can't let you go alone, Harry. You know that.' He then rose to his feet also and extended his hand. 'I will send one of my men to escort you. Sort of keep you out of further trouble, yes?' He smiled as they shook hands. 'You must now remember that you are a member of the greater communist community, Harry,' he said, pumping his hand. Harry considered this and smiled through the alcoholic haze and assured the Russian he would do so. As they laughed together, the attendant appeared and cleared the empty bottle and glasses. Konstantinov then told him to wait. Minutes passed and Harry struggled to clear his head. The door opened and one of the guards motioned for him to follow. Pleased to be given the opportunity to leave, Harry followed. Konstantinov was waiting outside. They shook hands once more, and Harry turned to follow the enormous mountain of a man who was to accompany him.

As they walked away, Konstantinov's cold eyes followed. He had waited for the man to become indignant at the murder of his friend, and he hadn't. He had waited also for Harry to try to negotiate a deal which would have been more in character. Instead, he lied. Konstantinov had then known that Harold Bradshaw had no intention of living in the Soviet Union. Anyway, Harry would have been a tiresome problem for the rest of his days and it would have been on his head for recommending that the Kremlin accept him in consideration of his years of service. Konstantinov heard the heavy steel exit doors close behind the departing Intelligence Chief, and knew that he would never see the man again.

* * * * * *

The thick set guard sat in the back of the sedan as the Mercedes left the Soviet Embassy compound and headed back towards the King's Palace grounds. The Intercontinental Hotel occupied a large section of the Royal property and provided its guests with magnificent gardens and walkways across small streams which meandered through well-manicured lawns. When the driver reached the intersection, he continued on through instead of turning towards the hotel.

Harry lay unconscious in the vehicle's trunk. He hadn't expected the expertly-delivered blow he received as he bent to enter the car. They had not even bothered to tie his hands or feet. He had been tossed, once again, into the rear of the sedan as it was parked in the garage basement. Although Harry was well past his prime, the Russians took no chances. They wanted him alive when he hit the *klong*. A post-mortem would reveal the excessive amounts of alcohol in his blood, and this would be considered a contributing factor in his drowning.

The car continued through the city, leaving the outskirts of the capital until the bright lights all but disappeared. Traffic thinned as they moved into the rural area and still they drove on, stopping only when they arrived at the river junction which was fed by deep flowing streams. The driver remained in the vehicle as the KGB guard removed Harry's limp body from the trunk and carried him down to the *klong*. There he placed the unconscious man beside the muddy river and lowered his head into the water, gripping his victim's wrists from behind. At that moment, the water partly revived him and Harry opened his eyes under the murky waters. He panicked, and coughed as water flowed into his lungs. He struggled vainly, kicking with no effect, as his killer held him down. Slowly, he lost consciousness. The Russian continued to hold Harry's head underwater, even after his victim's efforts to resist had ceased. Within minutes it was all over.

The killer checked Harry's pulse then, having ascertained that the Intelligence Chief was dead, he pushed the corpse further out into the dark *klong's* current. He watched until he was satisfied that the body would drift downstream towards the city, where, hopefully, it would be discovered. The authorities would report the death as a tragic accident.

Satisfied that he could contribute nothing more, the KGB killer moved quietly back into the darkness. Rain began to fall as the Mercedes sped towards the Soviet Embassy and, within the hour, Bangkok's canal system was once more subject to a tropical downpour which filled every available catchment area, then spilled over, flooding the capital yet again.

The body rolled, and turned, before finally disappearing under the swift and muddy torrent. In the morning, it swept past unsuspecting villagers as they squatted alongside the embankments washing clothes. The corpse travelled on, past the floating markets, and finally drifted out into the sea.

Chapter 16

Melbourne
mid-September

The Deputy Director, John Anderson, sat quietly observing his Regional and Station Chiefs as the meeting was called to order. Conversation died as he stood, tall and gaunt, at the end of the long conference table and placed his hands in his pockets. He did this out of habit, and all present were familiar with his mannerisms. Anderson was popular within the Service, although he had bruised enough politicians in Canberra to warrant more than his share of criticism for the invariably tough position he took in relation to Australia's security.

Anderson was generally admired by the Intelligence community for his unique ability to cut directly to the core of a problem. He was known for the contempt he held for politicians, which often brought him as second most powerful Intelligence officer in Australia, into direct confrontation with members of Cabinet. When his name was mooted as a temporary successor to the missing ASIS Chief, there was considerable resistance in Canberra. Fortunately, he had the support of not only the Military Intelligence Directors, but also the Head of ASIO and the Attorney-General's permanent Secretary. Within two weeks of Harold Bradshaw's disappearance, Anderson had assumed the mantle of the missing Director.

There had been an immediate inquiry. Ultimately, the Prime Minister's office had decided that, because of the sensitivity of the position Bradshaw held, his disappearance should be investigated internally with all findings to be delivered directly to his office. Two teams were established for this purpose, one of which spent just two days in Thailand, where they held confidential discussions with the local police before returning home to Melbourne.

Most of the investigation was perfunctory. Anderson had

personally briefed the Prime Minister in relation to the personal discussions he had with Langley's Chief of Station in Australia. The Deputy Director had been shown copies of the reports filed from their Embassy in Thailand. Anderson immediately moved to have the investigation severely curtailed to avoid further embarrassment to the Australian Secret Intelligence Service. Bradshaw's sexual preferences had not been a well-kept secret. The Americans had returned Harry's unfired weapon, which ASIS confirmed through forensics as being his automatic. The Director's fingerprints were all over the Soviet pistol. The Thai police had co-operated fully, discreetly shredding all official evidence which implicated the Australian in the murder of one of their nationals. Anderson had personally approved the substantial payment made to the Thai investigators, although he had scoffed at the suggestion that these funds would be passed on to the dead boy's family in Chiang Mai.

There was no commemoration of his passing, not even a memorial service, as Harold Bradshaw was merely missing, not dead. Anderson had informed Susan Bradshaw of her husband's demise and was impressed with her stoic acceptance that Harry may have disappeared from her life forever. The Deputy Director had confirmed that, although Harry was officially considered only missing, the Government would ensure that Susan and her son would continue to receive whatever benefits they were entitled to under the Act. The room became quiet as Anderson withdrew one hand from his pocket and coughed, signalling that the meeting had commenced. He looked at the members of his inner sanctum and cleared his voice.

'Before we start, we'll have a moment of silence so that we may pay our respects to Director Bradshaw. I'm confident that there is not an officer here who has not, in some way, been touched by Harold Bradshaw. He served our country to the full.' Anderson hesitated, permitting Wells the opportunity to recover from his sudden coughing fit. The senior Intelligence officer almost choked, suppressing an attack of laughter as Anderson mentioned the word 'touched'.

Anderson shot a severe glance at him and Wells regained control. The Director lowered his head and uttered a silent prayer. He then tilted his head and swept the room with an authoritative look.

'Gentlemen, let's not allow our former Chief's demise to affect our judgement and good sense. Suffice to say, we have all suffered a great loss and I wish to remind you that he did leave a family behind. I will be speaking to you on an individual basis concerning Director Bradshaw's disappearance. In the interests of Central Plans and the security of our country, I wish to reiterate that rumour-mongering in any form will not be tolerated. Our jobs are difficult enough without creating internal conflicts.' Anderson then lowered his voice as if others may be listening. The officers leaned forward as he continued. 'We must assume that Harry is dead, and get on with business. Most of you are already aware that I have been appointed Chief pro tem. The Prime Minister has suggested that we maintain this position for at least six months considering the circumstances surrounding Harold Bradshaw's disappearance.' The acting Chief then looked around those present, pleased to see from their expressions that they appeared to support his appointment.

'I want you all to feel confident that there will be very few immediate changes within Central Plans. This meeting was not designed to be a briefing session, but merely an informal discussion with you all as the new Head of our Service. However, if any of you wish to take this opportunity for general discussion, then I invite you to do so.' Anderson looked around those present, his eyes coming to rest on Murray Stephenson sitting opposite Wells.

'Will we have access to the Bradshaw files?' Stephenson asked. This drew a surprised glance from others present. Anderson frowned slightly. The directness of the question had caught him off-guard.

'Limited access only,' he replied, moving on to another officer in an attempt to cut short further discussion of the missing Director.

'Will the current policy on overseas travel be maintained in view of what happened?' the second officer asked. Anderson indicated that this would be so.

'Considering that Station Chiefs must continue with whatever they had in play when Harry disappeared, wouldn't it be more appropriate that we have complete and immediate access to his files?' Stephenson asked, refusing to let Anderson stone-wall him again. 'My sector has ongoing operations which could be seriously jeopardised, even terminated, unless we move quickly to restore direction and continuity. We are operating under the most difficult circumstances in an extremely hostile environment. May I ask again, if the Director's files will be made available to me, as Station Chief?'

Anderson moved to block the challenge. It was no secret that this officer had developed an advantage over his peers due to his close personal relationship with Bradshaw. Anderson felt that Stephenson's demands were an attempt to challenge his authority while revealing what many of those present had long suspected. The Acting Chief had not always been fully briefed by Harry Bradshaw who, much to the chagrin of his Deputy, had conducted many of the covert operations without revealing any detail whatsoever of his clandestine activities. Murray observed his new Chief's reactions, convinced that Anderson really had no knowledge at all of the sensitive operation he and the missing ASIS Director had initiated.

'My position remains unchanged. Limited access will apply. Even to the most senior operatives who may believe that there are special circumstances which may dictate otherwise.'

The room became quiet as the other officers identified the poorly-disguised reprimand. Although there were some who disliked Murray because of his relationship with the Bradshaws, most considered him to be one of their finest officers and were surprised at the evident personality clash which had just occurred before them. Anderson then asked if there were any other questions and, when there were none, closed the meeting and left without muttering another word. He was furious with the Djakarta Station Chief and, once he had regained his composure, he had his secretary, Madge, send for Stephenson immediately. Anderson knew that he had to place his stamp on the whole Service quickly. He could not afford to have his authority challenged in any way. Even if this resulted in his losing some of his senior operatives. And this included Murray Stephenson.

* * * * * *

Djakarta

Colonel Steven Zach completed reading the file, adding his comments in a hand-written memorandum for the other Attachés and then called his assistant. The thick folder contained information relating to Indonesia's ORBAT, or Order of Battle, an information schedule which listed the Military's armaments. His eyes were tired from checking through the fine detail which covered the Republic's military hardware purchases over the past seven years. Zach never ceased to be surprised at the incredible sums this country had expended on arms purchases.

He read the Pentagon report which detailed Indonesia's acquisitions from the Eastern Bloc. Had the man on the street back home in Australia been aware of the substantial military build-up just off their shores, he felt sure there would have been fewer anti-conscription demonstrations in his adopted country. The figures were boggling. He wondered how Soekarno had intended paying for the 275 tanks and armoured cars, the four destroyers and 24 torpedo boats and submarine chasers, not to mention the submarines and sophisticated fighters and bombers which now graced the country's military airfields. Zach compared Australia's paltry Airforce with Indonesia's AURI. How could Australia defend itself against squadrons which boasted fifty jet interceptors, forty jet and piston trainers, twenty long-range bombers and as many transport aircraft which gave support to Indonesia's massive number of ground troops? Zach shook his head at the American allies. The United States had run dangerously hot and cold in their relationship with Soekarno. He hoped the Americans would not regret their military aid package which provided weapons for 20 of Soekarno's infantry battalions, along with trucks, radio equipment and small ships for the Navy. They had also given them enough equipment for a company of Indonesian Marines, complete with a 60 mm mortar section. On top of all of this , the Americans had recommended pilot training for the AURI pilots.

Steven Zach was, in a way, pleased that he was in the Military and not one of the civilians responsible for the present convoluted political situation in Indonesia. Even with his background, he found it most difficult to understand Soekarno's non-alignment policy. How had he managed to successfully seduce both the Soviets and the Americans as he reconstructed his country's Military strength! The clever dictator had developed alliances which clearly associated the Indonesians with all that was considered unholy by the West.

The Warrant Officer entered, listened to his instructions, then left with the classified file. Zach leaned back in his swivel chair and stretched. His thoughts moved to Susan's letter, which had arrived just days before Murray had told him of Bradshaw's sudden disappearance. He wished he could be with her in Melbourne. Apart from Murray, they had not discussed their relationship with others, although naturally the Attaché wives had gossiped after their return from the Pulau Putri weekend. Zach had sent her a cable, offering his condolences. Not sure who else might see the communication, he remained discreet, electing not to mention anything which could compromise her at this difficult time. At least Murray would have the opportunity to look in on her during his rush visit to Melbourne. Zach knew why Stephenson had needed to go to Australia. It seemed appalling that Bradshaw could disappear without trace, and he had suggested to Murray at the time how improbable it was that an official of Harry's experience could vanish without leaving some trail. The Station Chief had wanted to leave then and there for Thailand but, Zach knew, something on the boil in Djakarta had prevented Stephenson from visiting Bangkok before leaving for Australia.

* * * * * *

Bangkok
United States Embassy

The officers had been ushered into the Ambassador's private quarters and treated to lavish servings of American ice-cream and apple pie. The United States officials went out of their way to make the small delegation comfortable. The three Indonesian officers were suitably impressed, reacting warmly to the Ambassador's friendly manner and sincere interest in the proposal they carried.

Each of these officers had been hand selected by Major General Soeharto. They had served with him in Java and Sulawesi, and their loyalty to him was beyond question. This was their second visit.

The first had occurred only weeks before, during which they laid the groundwork for these current discussions. They had not been presented to the Ambassador during their previous meetings. Instead, these emissaries first met with the Defence Attaché who, in turn, introduced the officers to members of the State Department.

The discussions had been warm and friendly, establishing a basis for further exchanges. To date, these trusted men had already met in secret with Malaysian and Singaporean officials. The common ground, upon which Soeharto wished to initiate a rapprochement with his President's declared enemies, had been established. At first they had been treated with extreme suspicion. The Federation of Malaysia had been at war with its giant neighbour for almost two years and there was considerable fence-mending required before the officers could make any real headway. Eventually, as the Malaysians genuinely desired restoration of former relationships across the Straits, they accepted the messages of hope, indicating that there would soon be moves to end Confrontation.

As the afternoon progressed, each of the officers had been taken quietly aside by the CIA Station Chief and given envelopes as a token of America's gratitude for their contribution in restoring dialogue with the West. The men were ecstatic with the reception, and the obvious support for their endeavours. The Ambassador repeated his Defence Attaché's commitment, undertaking to provide support to the Indonesians when the time arrived. The colonel heading the delegation was then given a sealed envelope to be delivered to his commander, and the officers were escorted back to the airport where they were flown to Singapore. Once there, still dressed in their civilian attire, the men caught the Cathay Pacific flight home to Djakarta.

That evening, Major General Soeharto sat quietly reading the letter he had been given by his emissaries. He was pleased. It had been his own initiative to establish contact secretly with the Malaysians and Singaporeans to allay their fears that there would be increased military activity in the future. He expected that his approach would be treated cynically, as he was, after all, the Deputy Commander of the Crush Malaysia campaign. Soeharto understood that their attempts to threaten their neighbours had been futile. Due to heavy losses in Sarawak, the Army had resisted sending paratroopers in support of Soekarno's request for massive airdrops over Malaysia. Instead, the Airforce were obliged to wear the brunt of the exercise, which failed miserably. Dissent had grown dramatically during the past months, resulting in his decision to establish contact with the opposing forces.

The general read through the contents one more time and,

satisfied with the support he had received from the Americans, destroyed the letter carefully. He closed his eyes and smiled. Time was running out for them all. And only he would be prepared when the moment finally arrived.

* * * * * *

Semarang

General Prajogo, the Diponegoro Commander, walked together with his old friend, listening, deeply disturbed by what the other man imparted. They had left the Command Headquarters and walked away from the other officers as his colleague had indicated that he wished to speak privately to his fellow general.

'We have always been able to share a confidence, Mas,' the visiting Brigadier General had stated, *'but what I'm about to disclose to you must remain only with you. It could mean my career, perhaps even my life. Do you understand?'*

'Sounds very intriguing indeed.' The Diponegoro Commander smiled. His friend had always enjoyed the melodramatic, ever since they had attended basic training together.

The general looked back sharply. *'No, Mas,'* he insisted, *'this is really the most serious discussion you and I might ever have. I must have your word that, whatever I say to you, under no circumstances will you repeat this information, for whatever reason. Do you agree?'* The commander looked closely at the other man and was surprised at the concern in his old friend's voice. He thought for a moment before answering.

'Only if what you tell me doesn't compromise me in any way, or commits me to something I may disagree with.' Then he smiled again, just to ease some of the tension between them. After all, they were practically brothers. Their careers had taken similar paths, both had achieved their first stars in the same year.

'I am taking you into my confidence, Mas, as I expect that you, of all people, should have been invited to participate in what is planned. I don't understand why you have not already been approached.' The commander listened, concerned with the direction their conversation was taking.

'Go on,' he urged, suddenly eager for the rest.

'As you know, Mas, I have been seconded to Pak Yani's staff in

338

Djakarta.'

'Yes, I had heard,' the commander said, a little impatiently. General Yani's position as Chief of Army Staff was one of the most powerful in the country. The commander did not believe the position should be Yani's. In his opinion, there had been others more deserving.

'Have you heard mention of the Dewan Djenderal, Mas?' the other officer suddenly asked, almost in a whisper. The commander immediately stiffened at the mention of the Council of Generals. As far as he was concerned, these generals had grown fat at their country's expense and represented the very epitome of corruption at the top.

'I have heard some rumours. Why?' he asked, cautiously. They were treading on very dangerous ground, even for two men who had known each other so well.

The visiting general hesitated, then continued. *'Mas, once again I must remind you that you can not repeat anything of what I'm about to reveal to you.'* He then looked at the Diponegoro Commander enquiringly, who had stopped and turned to his companion, curiosity aroused.

'Agreed. Now what about this so called Council of Generals, what are they up to?' he asked, attempting a weak smile.

'Over the past weeks the generals have solicited support from officers they believe they can trust. I have only just been approached. And by Pak Yani personally! It would appear that they have been successful in their recruitment as they are confident that the majority of all the Army's field officers will move with them.'

'Move? Move where?' the commander asked.

'No, no, Mas. Not move, mobilise. The Council is going to sack Bung Karno and move against the PKI!' he answered, bubbling with excitement, unable to contain the information any longer. *'We're going to sack the President and abolish the Communist Party, Mas,* he repeated, grinning from ear to ear in satisfaction, as if it were his own idea, *'and then we're going to put this country back in order.'*

The commander froze where he stood, shocked by the revelation. Was this really possible? He stared at his visitor, almost disbelievingly. When he observed the other man's excitement, he realised it was true.

'When?' he asked with difficulty, his mouth dry. Why hadn't he

been approached before this? Had he and his Command been deliberately overlooked, until now?

'*Remember, Mas, only a select few are to know. I will advise the Council when I return that they can count on your Command for support. There will be much more information to follow. The most important point is that you are prepared to move on the day, with the rest of us. Will you be ready?*' he asked, forgetting to reveal the target date in his excitement. The commander thought quickly. Of course he must commit as a matter of self-preservation. He did not hesitate.

'*The 7th Division of the Diponegoro Command will be ready. When do we move?*'

'*The Fifth of October, Mas,*' he laughed, pleased with the surprised look on the other man's face. '*That's right, Mas,*' he repeated, in a conspiratorial voice, '*Armed Forces Day. It will be so simple. Our Military will summon only those Commands which support the Council, to attend the parades scheduled to be held throughout the capital. Even Soekarno has given his blessing to making this year's effort greater than previous celebrations. He thinks this will distract the rakjat from their empty bellies as our tanks rumble through the streets. There should be little or no bloodshed. Our troops will control the city from the moment they enter Djakarta. The entire concept is brilliant,*' he boasted, proud to be part of the planned revolt.

The two generals discussed which Army units had already committed to the coup attempt. By late afternoon, the Diponegoro Commander had memorised most of the detail he had heard. Later, after his visitor had departed, convinced of his friend's loyalty, the commander returned to his home where he remained alone, brooding over the day's startling events. By morning, having not slept throughout the night, he had considered all of his options then made his decision. The only common ground he could identify with the conspirators was the fact that both he and the Council would eventually abolish the Indonesian Communist Party.

He considered how his Army superiors were slowly but surely delivering their country to the Americans. This, more than the knowledge that these men had grown fat at others' expense, raised the fire in his stomach. He could not understand how they could betray the *Republik* knowing that just a few short years before, the United States financed teams from Taiwan and South Korea which occupied Indonesian territory, joined rebel movements and endeavoured to destroy national unity. How could they have forgotten the aerial attacks flown from American bases in the Philippines and the thousands who died defending Indonesia against the American-sponsored uprisings? He believed he had no other choice, for failure to move quickly would ultimately result in the very men he despised taking control of the *Republik*. The decision to inform his other enemies, the communists, of the proposed move by the Council on the Fifth of October did not sit well on his mind.

General Prajogo still believed that his President's position of non-alignment was the only acceptable political position to take, ignoring the overtures of the Americans and Soviets. As for the communists, well, once he had moved to Djakarta and left the Diponegoro Conmmand in the hands of his trustworthy officers, he would use the Communists as they had used others. He would have their leaders removed and the PKI abolished. But first, it was imperative to his own strategy that the PKI make the first move and pre-empt the others. Prajogo had to find some means whereby the communist leadership could be alerted to what was happening in the Nasution camp.

Before the late-morning *lohor* prayers had commenced, the commander had put his own play in effect. He now realised that the task ahead was too great for him to carry out alone. He would go to Djakarta in search of the one man who still commanded his deepest respect. A man who had also once been the ranking officer commanding the Diponegoro Divisions, and a man he knew he could trust to support a fellow general's pursuit for a better Indonesia. He would seek this man's assistance. But first, there was another matter he must attend to.

The Commander called his aide and instructed the officer to summon Colonel Sutarmin. He had a mission for the veteran who had just recently returned from the jungles of Kalimantan. A mission which the combat-hardened colonel would most surely relish. One which would provide an opportunity to partly repay the Australians for the thousands of Indonesian soldiers who had perished, slaughtered by their SAS during their illegal raids over Indonesian soil.

* * * * * *

Kerry B.Collison

Indonesian Airforce General Omar Dhani listened in dismay as China's powerful Chou En Lai carefully laid the information before him. The second most powerful man in China after Chairman Mao Tse Tung, refrained from clucking at the man's ignorance. It was obvious that the Indonesian general before him had very little appreciation of what was really taking place in his own country. With the assistance of an interpreter, senior Minister Chou En Lai explained to Dhani, for the third time, how the information came to him.

The Indonesian Airforce Chief of Staff was confused. Why did these people always have to talk in riddles, he wondered? The information the Chinese had insisted was absolutely accurate alarmed him greatly. Dhani knew that the Army had been planning something because they had gone to incredible lengths to exclude him and the Navy from their secret meetings. Even so, the Airforce general had great difficulty in accepting Chou En Lai's startling information, which suggested that Nasution's Council of Generals would effect what amounted to a coup d'etat in less than three weeks. In his mind, the idea was preposterous, or it had been until the Minister then went on to substantiate the claim, with damning evidence.

'Should they succeed, General Dhani, the first to go will be our dear friend Soekarno. There is no doubt in our minds that the Council would then move to eradicate the Communist Party in your country, sparing none.' This had sent a shiver down Dhani's spine. He was painfully aware that should such a situation evolve, he would be one of the first to be incarcerated by the Army generals. Chou En Lai then went on. *'Here is proof of the Americans' involvement in the subversive attempt not just to destroy President Soekarno and Aidit's Party, but also to provide the means for the West to completely ensconce their own Military in the Indonesian Republic.'* The Chinese Minister paused for effect. *'The Americans are even more imperialistic in their foreign policy than the British,'* he said, uncertain that the man before him would understand, but he continued anyway in the hope that Dhani might learn at least something from the people who were currently providing the necessary support to his associates in the PKI.

'First, they attempted to take China and our great Chairman chased their puppets' tails across the sea to Taiwan. Then they tried Korea, even sending tens of thousands of Chiang Kai Shek's so-called National Army into Burma to bark at our heels. This too failed, leaving their soldiers nothing but access to the white powder which destroys their brains. Now they are at war with Ho Chi Minh and it is inevitable that the Americans must lose. Make no mistake, General, this information is real and you would do well by your country to leave here immediately and return home, where you will then be in a position to prevent what is planned.'

Omar Dhani examined the information again. He did not wish to challenge the detail offered and could find no reason to do so. Suddenly he was pleased that these people were his friends. He admired their uncanny ability to survive, wherever they established their communities. And now, because one of his fellow officers had developed strong personal and commercial ties with a Chinese back in Djakarta, ties which had resulted in the flow of information at hand, Dhani believed that he had been given the opportunity to pre-empt the moves of others. Moves which would, undoubtedly, have resulted in his own death, had they been successful.

Dhani and most of his contemporaries had similar relationships to that described between the major general and the Chinese trader mentioned in the report. The expatriate Chinaman had been clever, following the Army officer's career through the years. They had remained loyal to each other and enjoyed the fruits of their relationship. Now, unwittingly, that very same relationship had provided the means whereby the Indonesian Communist Party could advance its own cause by pre-empting the Council of Generals move to topple the popular President and deliver their country to the Americans.

Dhani read through the information again and shook his head. Apparently the major general had held in-depth discussions with one of his own, which resulted in the disclosure that Nasution and his secret Council intended moving against the Government on Armed Forces Day, the Fifth of October. It appeared that the general had decided that there was little he could do to prevent the more powerful faction from effecting their move. Instead, understanding the ramifications of such a successful action, he had discussed the intended coup in depth with his close Chinese friend who participated in his *kongsi*, their business house, and suggested

343

that he and his family ensure that they remove themselves from any possible harm which may result from the power struggle.

The report made it clear that the major general had been given an assurance that the information he had passed to his old Chinese friend would, in no way, be revealed to others. The Chinese trader had been grateful for the warning and moved quickly to protect not just his family and friends, but, in typical style, his business interests as well. The closely-guarded secret was passed from trader to trader within hours until finally, the Chinese Embassy in Djalan Hajam Wuruk was abuzz with the facts.

The Ambassador had apparently wasted little time in telexing this incredible information directly to the Minister in Beijing requesting advice as to what action should be taken by the Embassy and staff, knowing that when Nasution and his generals took control, the Chinese would, once again, be punished for whatever ills prevailed at that time. The Ambassador had pointed out that Nasution had arrested many Chinese merchants just a few years before, and seized their businesses on the pretext that they had been involved in supplying arms and providing support to the rebels.

Following Chou En Lai's advice, Omar Dhani departed immediately for Djakarta, flying directly in on of his own Airforce jets. He arrived early the following morning and went directly to Aidit and Soebandrio where he delivered the incredible news. The three spent the day closely locked in secret at Colonel Latief's house, as they formulated their own plan to circumvent Nasution's move to take control of the country.

'We have no choice but to advance our own plans,' Aidit insisted.

'But how?' Soebandrio complained, understanding the logistical nightmare in bringing their people together a month before the scheduled seizure of power from the Military.

'We will just have to move with what we have and trust that the element of surprise will still be to our advantage. Also, it is now more imperative than ever that, when our troops move into the city, they first must take every member of the Council and place them under immediate arrest.'

'But what about their personal security?' Dhani asked. All the generals would be well protected by their own trusted guards.

'We will use the Tjakrabirawa teams supported by the Gerwani. The

original plan has not changed, it's only a matter of advancing the timing. It will still work, as planned,' Aidit insisted.

'And we should make this move when?' Soebandrio asked. He would not be involved in the actual attack. His role would be to muster provincial support as the movement gained momentum once they had established control over the capital.

Aidit thought for a while then smiled. *'We are most indebted to our Chinese friends. As we must make the move before the Fifth of October, why not agree to enter the city and arrest the Council on the anniversary of the People's Republic of China?'* Both Soebandrio and Dhani were supportive of the suggestion. It did not leave much time but, there again, there was little choice. If they failed to move quickly, then all would be lost. They agreed. The plan would be known as *'Gerakan 30 September'*, the 30th September Movement, even though the actual attack was planned for the early hours on the morning of the following day. Their commanders were all summoned and briefed.

The communists would make their move to take control over the capital and the Military, on the morning of the Anniversary of the People's Republic of China. Each and every person involved in the operation clearly understood that they had very little time left in which to implement their strategies if they were to be ready to move on that momentous day, the First of October.

Chapter 18

Susan stared at the walls and wondered why she had insisted that Harry give her the bungalow. Now she couldn't stand the place. Everywhere she looked, memories interrupted the tranquillity she needed so desperately. She couldn't even be sure that he wouldn't just reappear, and offer one of his casual explanations as he had so often in their past. She prayed desperately for some evidence that he was really dead. How long could she be expected to carry on like this, not quite a widow? The thought crossed her mind momentarily that he had done this just to punish her.

Susan read Zach's almost impersonal cable again and then crumpled it in her hands. At least she'd had the company of Murray for lunch when he was in town. Apart from Muriel Stephenson, there had been few visitors. Most did not offer condolences, she noticed, just support. Muriel had stayed over twice. She was a godsend, always there, assisting with the child without being asked. Susan rose and moved over to the cocktail cabinet and made another drink. She grimaced as she swallowed, the alcohol biting hard. It was her sixth for the day and it wasn't even five o'clock, she noticed. What the hell, she thought, angry with Steven's almost impersonal letter. Susan then wandered around the lounge area, moodily, lifting cushions and throwing them back onto the cane settee. As she passed the painting to the left of the bar one more time, Susan stopped and examined the lush island vegetation against a full tropical sunset. She stared at the picture for several minutes. It was the trigger she needed.

Without thinking further, she raced into her bedroom and checked inside the cupboard for cash and, satisfied there were sufficient funds, she dialled information and scribbled down the numbers. Then Susan phoned Muriel Stephenson and pleaded for her to keep her son for another week. Murray's mother was only too happy to do so. Two, three weeks, she laughed, suggesting that Susan should take a complete break away from the uncertainty which surrounded her life at present.

Muriel was surprised that she had grown fond of Susan Bradshaw. And it was not just because she suspected that the child was her grandson, but more because, considering the circumstances under which the lonely woman lived, Susan had consistently displayed a resilience Muriel had not thought possible. She thought her own son a fool, but had forgiven him his indiscretion. The matter had never been raised, not since the christening.

Susan made two more calls, then danced into the bedroom and packed. She had a flight to Singapore and it departed in less than four hours. There was so much to do. She remembered her passport and that there was no valid visa for Indonesia. Deciding that this could be arranged in Singapore upon arrival, Susan completed her packing, then bathed. Thirty minutes later, she phoned the overseas cable service and dictated a message, which the operator confirmed would arrive the following day at its destination. She listened as the woman read her cable back before advising of the charges. Susan smiled as she replaced the receiver, knowing that her impetuous behaviour would, no doubt, attract strong criticism from her circle of friends. She shrugged her shoulders at this thought and then locked the house and drove back up to Melbourne and Essendon Airport.

The Qantas 707 four engined jet deposited her in Singapore in the sleepy morning hours where, to her dismay, Susan discovered that her passport had to be sent to Djakarta for endorsement, due to confusion resulting from the *konfrontasi* conflict. Disappointed, she checked into the Raffles Hotel and waited, while the High Commission assisted with her travel documents.

When she received the call, Susan was ready to leave but unable to get a seat on the overcrowded flights. It seemed that suddenly everyone was heading into Indonesia. She had already spent four days by herself, wandering through Collyer Quay and its quaint Change Alley more times than she cared to count. She had visited Robinson's Department Store and marvelled at their displays, and sampled the extraordinary choices of Asian cuisine unique to the crossroads city, before returning exhausted to the colonial splendour of her magnificent Raffles suite.

The next day, Susan Bradshaw managed to catch a Cathay Pacific flight to the Indonesian capital. As the aircraft banked, then turned on its final approach into Kemayoran Airport, Susan smiled as she recognised the harbour below. She remembered her first visit and the violence she had witnessed and, for the first time since leaving Australia, Susan wondered if she had made the correct decision in returning to Indonesia.

The Boeing's undercarriage groaned as hydraulics completed the procedure locking the wheels into place, and Susan managed to complete the last of her complicated arrival forms as the tyres screamed, announcing their arrival. As the aircraft came to a halt outside the terminal, she checked the forms once again and sighed at the date. It was almost the end of another month. She looked out through the porthole at the dilapidated buildings and was suddenly overcome by a feeling of helplessness. An ominous hiss indicated that the passenger exit door had been opened. Susan took a deep breath, then stepped from the aircraft.

* * * * * *

Djakarta, Tuesday, 28th September

Murray received the call via the Embassy switchboard. Once he had replaced the receiver, he cursed loudly at the woman's stupidity then went directly in search of Steven Zach. Susan had said that she had already tried to speak to Steven, and had been advised that he was still on his round of morning appointments.

He discovered Zach in the Embassy foyer talking to one of the other Attachés.

'Steven,' Murray called, his voice urgent, 'sorry to butt in. It's important.' He smiled at the Air Attaché and led Zach away by the arm.

'Well, what's up?' Zach asked, concerned by Murray's sombre expression. He listened, his face growing dark with the news. 'Why the hell didn't she let us know?' he asked. They both knew that this was no time to be distracted from their responsibilities. Something was brewing out there on the streets and both men believed that trouble was imminent. There had been rolling demonstrations every day, clouds of dark smoke rising high into the city's sky, identifying the hot spots. Their latest estimates indicated that in the course of the past month alone, more than six hundred had been killed as a direct result of demonstrations and looting in the capital.

'Beats me, she's booked into the Hotel Indonesia. Guess she wants you to hold her hand,' Murray said. Zach looked at his friend sharply, then accepted that the comment was not meant unkindly.

'I'll ring her right away. Thanks, Murray,' Zach said, patting the Station Chief's arm. 'Did she say how long she was staying?'

'Sounded pretty much open-ended.' Murray hesitated before continuing, then decided to say it anyway. 'It's tricky, Steve. She shouldn't be here right now and you're probably the only one who can tell her that.' Zach nodded in agreement.

'I'll ring her first, then shoot down to the hotel. Catch you later,' he said, leaving Murray alone in the Chancery lobby. Then he frowned. Why hadn't his own people picked this up? Her name should have triggered all sorts of alarm bells when she had departed Australia. How did she manage a visa?

Returning to the security wing behind the Consulate section, he went into his Number Two's room and briefed the agent on the woman's presence. It was protocol. The Second Secretary merely nodded and offered to keep an eye on her should the Station Chief consider this necessary.

'No,' Murray had said, 'let's see how long she's staying first,' hoping silently that Susan would listen to common sense and leave the troubled city. He then telephoned the operator and advised her to take messages for the rest of the day as he would be out of his office. Murray left for his appointment with the lieutenant colonel from Semarang, his thoughts pre-occupied with the brief and enigmatic telephone conversation they'd had the day before. Murray could not recall the officer from his earlier visits to the Central Javanese city, although the suggestion that the man had information vital to Murray's personal safety was sufficient to interest him. He had asked for more detail on the telephone but the officer insisted that they meet in person. Intrigued, he had agreed to meet at the location nominated. But before doing so, Murray removed his P9S automatic with its double-action lock from the safe, checked the nine-round magazine, and placed the German weapon inside his briefcase. These were dangerous times in Indonesia, he knew, and to attend a meeting so shrouded in secrecy, unarmed, would be extreme folly.

* * * * * *

'No, I did not receive your cable. And, quite frankly Susan, if I had, then you would not be here,' Zach said sternly. Susan pouted.

'You aren't pleased to see me, Steven?' she asked, feeling foolish. Perhaps her visit may have been just a little too reckless.

'Of course I'm pleased to see you. He ran his fingers through his hair and looked at her in exasperation. 'It's just that you couldn't have picked a worse time. Susan, didn't you notice anything on your way in from the airport? Didn't you see what is happening out there?' he jabbed his finger emphatically in the direction of the hotel's window. Susan's eyes followed the movement. It all seemed normal enough outside. And she hadn't seen anything unusual on her way into town.

'Look, Steven,' she started, 'I won't be in your way. I needed to get out of Melbourne and I thought you might be pleased to see me.' She searched his eyes. 'It's been hell, Steven,' she said, struggling to contain the tears. 'You have no idea what I've been through. They don't even know if he's dead!' She began to look down at the floor like some scolded child. It was too much for Zach. He stepped forward and lifted her off the couch and into his arms, holding her close and whispering soothing words.

'I'll leave immediately, Steven, if that's what you wish,' she mumbled, hoarsely into his chest. Then she pushed away slowly and looked into his eyes. 'Is that what you want, Steven?'

'No. No, it's not what I want,' he replied, 'it's just that the city is no place for you to be right now, Susan.' He then thought for a moment before continuing. 'If you do stay, then you must agree to listen and abide by what I'm about to say. Okay?' Immediately, she moved back closer and placed her head on his shoulder. Zach couldn't see the almost childish smile.

'Okay,' Susan agreed. 'You lay the ground rules and I'll follow.' He had acquiesced. It had not been as difficult as she had anticipated. Susan stroked the rough beginnings of stubble on his cheek.

'Good, then here's rule one. Stay in the hotel until I return. I don't want you wandering around outside under any circumstances, especially alone.' He held her away and smiled. 'Now, I must return to the Embassy. I'll try to be back before six o'clock. Okay?'

'Fine by me, darling. I'll just sit around the pool and read or something.' She looked at him and smiled. 'Thank you, Steven,' she said, rising up onto her heels and kissing him softly. The warmth of her mouth made him want to linger but he pushed her gently away. He had to go. He squeezed her hand and left, hurrying back to the Embassy.

When he got there, his assistant greeted him with a number of priority signals which had been received during his brief absence. He went to work immediately, examining the information that had been forwarded from the Directorate of Army Intelligence in Australia. An hour later, Zach also left the Embassy to attend an urgent conference at the United States Embassy where he spent most of the remaining day deep in discussions. It was during this meeting that Zach decided to take at least one night off and spend it with Susan up in the Puncak Pass before sending her back to Australia. He believed that she would be more receptive to his suggestions to return home once they were together in the hill bungalows, where they had first become involved. He knew she should leave as soon as possible but decided that, as long as she boarded her flight before the forthcoming Military parades, she would be relatively safe.

Zach checked the bungalow roster upon his return to the Embassy, then telephoned around in an attempt to locate one of the other Embassy members who might be receptive to his request to exchange their rostered turns in the mountain resort area. It seemed that many of the wives had prearranged parties and guests right through until the following weekend. They too had decided to stay away from the city as troops continued to pour into the capital in preparation for the Fifth of October parades.

There was only one opportunity and it was late-midweek. Steven checked his schedule and found that he could afford the one night away. It was in just a few more days. He then checked the airline flights and booked Susan out for the afternoon following their return from the mountain retreat. He circled the calendar on his desk, and wrote 'Susan leaves' alongside the date. It was the coming

Friday. He then telephoned Susan to tell her of the arrangements. She was thrilled with the opportunity to return to the cool mountain lodge. As it was already Tuesday, she was pleased that they would be in the mountains alone together, in just two more days.

* * * * * *

Tandjung Priok Harbour

Murray directed the driver towards the row of long *godowns* which blocked the view into Djakarta's filthy harbour. He instructed the driver to stop alongside the perimeter fence and examined the faded notice, still hanging where it had been placed many years before. He checked his watch and observed that he was only a few minutes late. Murray knew that this would have little significance in a land which practised *djam karet*, or rubber time, as a matter of course.

'Stay here,' he ordered the driver, opening the rear door. He was assailed by a wave of heat as he climbed out of the airconditioned vehicle. The driver's pained expression immediately changed to relief as he realised that he would not be expected to accompany the *tuan* down the narrow gang between the old port warehouses. *'I'll be back in half an hour so you'd better kill the engine,'* Murray suggested, then left his driver alone. As soon as Murray disappeared down the narrow lane, the driver looked back over his shoulder, checked the rear-vision mirrors and wriggled uncomfortably in his seat. Remembering where he was, the driver then reached over behind and locked the rear doors first, before checking those in front. *'Tuan Murray must be a little crazy,'* he thought, but most of the drivers already knew this.

Murray continued down through the maze of dilapidated buildings, checking the oversized numbers painted on stained cream walls. The warehouses all appeared empty as he continued to move through the neglected site, searching for the *gudang* number which would lead him to his designated meeting place. There didn't seem to be any security around, and this surprised the Station Chief. Then he shrugged this off, assuming that the security would most likely be asleep, resting from the stifling midday heat.

He continued his search. There appeared to be no sequence to the numbering of buildings. Murray looked back and checked again to confirm the random figures painted on both sides of the huge open doorways and, quite by accident, noticed the number he had been searching for just a few metres back. He turned and walked over to the building; then stopped and opened his case. He placed the automatic inside his belt, then held the light case directly in front of his body as he entered the long silent warehouse.

'*Kolonel*,' he called out, remaining near to the entrance, scanning the huge empty expanse inside the old storage centre. There was no response. He called out again, '*Kolonel, it's Stephenson.*' Still there was no answer. Murray walked deep into the building, and came to a halt almost directly in the middle of the dust-covered concrete floor. He could see that little, if any, traffic had disturbed the dust at his feet. He peered down the length of the building. Murray estimated that the far wall was more than one hundred metres from where he stood. Pencils of light pierced the stillness as the midday sun penetrated the rusting galvanised roof overhead. He called out again, then waited. Suddenly he heard a slight noise in the distance. He checked his watch and turned. The colonel was only fifteen minutes late. Nothing, really, in this country, where even soldiers could not be relied upon to be punctual.

The ambient temperature in the old warehouse was most probably ten degrees hotter than outside, and the perspiration was drenching his body. He decided to move back to the entrance where it was slightly cooler. As he turned, he heard the unfamiliar sounds again and decided that this, at last, must be the colonel. He walked slowly towards the entrance and, when he was within fifty metres of the huge sliding doors, a figure appeared, framed by the open space.

'*Tuan Stephenson?*' the man called, his voice echoing through the empty building. Murray stopped, not forty metres from the figure and answered.

'*Yes, I'm Stephenson. Are you Kolonel ...*' he started to ask but stopped in mid-sentence as he identified the swift movement and the weapon's silhouette. He dropped his brief-case and rolled to his right as the world exploded all around. The first bullets punched through the short distance to where he had stood, their velocity so great Murray could feel the shock waves against his body. He came up to his feet still holding the P9S fully extended, fired the first three rounds without aiming, then threw himself hard to his left, ignoring the sharp jabbing pain which stabbed his knee as it hit the concrete. Murray fired again, then again, before taking more deliberate aim at his attacker. He heard the man scream. Murray fired again, recognising the dull thudding sound bullets make when they hit a man's body. He saw the killer's arm swing, bringing the deadly weapon to bear and so he rolled once more, this time again to the left.

The air was shattered with a screaming staccato of bullets as they hit the ground to ricochet around the *gudang*. In desperation, Murray fired his last three rounds, cursing himself for not bringing a spare magazine. His assailant, wounded at least once, turned to flee but buckled, staggered, and then collapsed into a heap, his weapon still clasped firmly as he fell. Murray waited, trying to determine whether the man could still return fire. Had his last shot found its mark? He ran across to his right, watching for movement. He approached the crumpled figure from the side, remaining half crouched, expecting the soldier to turn at any moment and recommence firing. But there was no further movement from the fallen man. Murray had hit twice. His first bullet had merely grazed the soldier's arm but the second had entered through the stomach and shattered the man's spine.

He knew it wasn't necessary to check for a pulse. Quickly and with expert hands, the Station Chief examined the dead man's pockets. He removed the contents. Apart from some identification there was little of significance to find. The soldier was wearing a non-issue tunic. Murray unzipped the thin jacket to reveal the soldier's uniform and immediately recognised the identifying flashes of the Diponegoro 7th Division based in Semarang. He checked the dead soldier's weapon. It was a Swedish 9mm M-45 Carl-Gustaf automatic machine gun. Murray pried it out of the dead man's hands and then realised just how close he had been to death. He knew that this weapon's rate of fire was controlled by finger action and not by fire control. Had it been otherwise, his killer might have succeeded. Almost half of the magazine's 36 rounds remained intact.

Murray left the body and peered outside. He couldn't be certain, but it appeared that the soldier had acted alone. He then retrieved his brief-case, and found the leather torn where one of the 9mm rounds had grazed the surface, searing a path from one end to the other. He placed his automatic back inside the case and, checking outside once again, walked quickly back along the narrow lane and across to where his driver waited.

They drove back in silence. Murray felt it best not to raise the question of gun-fire and he knew that, with any luck, the driver would not have necessarily associated the brief bursts with his *tuan's* presence in the harbour area. Gunfire was not unusual in Djakarta. Anyway, from the stuffy odour which greeted him inside the car, it was fairly obvious that the driver had kept all of the windows closed during his *tuan's* absence, further reducing the likelihood that his driver had heard anything. He instructed the driver to return to the Embassy. As he sat in the rear of the sedan, even he was surprised at how coolly he had reacted. He looked at his hands and smiled. They were not shaking. He felt absurdly like laughing out loud.

When Murray arrived, his Number Two handed him several incoming messages, which he knew could wait until the following day. He opened his safe and extracted the spare clip of 9mm rounds and slipped it into his pocket. He had already decided on his way back to the Embassy that he would never again venture outside without at least one spare clip for his P9S. He had been lucky and he knew it. Next time — and he now believed there would be a next time — he would be better prepared.

There had now been two attempts on his life, and both carried out, in all probability, by members of the 7th Diponegoro Division. As he was driven to his residence, Murray recalled his visits to Semarang and the discussions that had taken place with Harry Bradshaw and the general. Suddenly a thought crossed his mind. Surely the attempts on his life had to be related to the information the former ASIS Chief had given the general concerning his man Sulistio! They had accused the man of betraying the general. Now, he believed, he was being held to account for Sulistio's death. Murray considered this scenario and believed that he was on the right track. He had to be, he thought. What other possible explanation could there be for elements of the Diponegoro Command to want him dead?

* * * * * *

FREEDOM (MERDEKA) SQUARE

Halim Perdanakusama Airforce Base, Djakarta

Yanti settled down with the other Gerwani women and tried to sleep. They had been gathering here, at the AURI Airforce Base, over the past two weeks. She had counted almost 2,000 volunteers for the permanent troops; all had joined under the newly-created communist Central Command. There was a strong feeling of pride as the young men and women gathered in their makeshift billets, preparing their weapons, ready for the imminent orders to move into the capital.

Yanti was particularly proud. She had been promoted and selected to head the Gerwani assault teams which would accompany other units, consisting of the Tjakrabirawa Palace Guards, the Pasopati troops, the KODAM V Djaya Infantry Brigade, the AURI Kavaleri and Pasukan Gerak Tjepat units, as well as two companies from the Bhimasakti which stood ready, under the command of Captain Soeradi. Yanti's Gerwani were ordered to accompany the Pasopati troops, because they had been assigned probably the most important task when the moment came. They were to arrest the Council of Generals and bring them, dead or alive, back to the Halim Airforce Base. They were to be part of the operation designated 'Takari'.

The strategic Airforce base had been chosen as the final staging point for the communist forces. The Airforce Chief of Staff, Omar Dhani, had approved the use of his facilities for this purpose well before he had departed for Mainland China to organise the armament shipments which had now all but been completed. When questioned by his peers as to why there were so many non-Airforce personnel occupying the base, Dhani had easily convinced his fellow officers that the additional ground forces had been brought in as part of the airfield defence exercises aimed at preparing for the possibility of a Malaysian air attack on the capital. On the 26th of September, the majority of the volunteers, spawned by the Pemuda Rakjat, the BTI, Gerwani and SOBSI moved into the Halim Airforce Base as part of the ground defence exercise named *Lubang Buaya*, or Crocodile Hole. Airforce officers carried out the training as instructed by their Chief of Staff and cleverly disguised the substantial build-up of communist forces within the military complex.

The mood was restless as they waited for the final command. Yanti knew that this was imminent, as she had heard that almost all of the senior Communist Party officials had already departed, as planned, for selected provincial centres where they would provide additional support to PKI followers in those distant locations. Comrade Aidit had decided that he should remain in Djakarta until power had been successfully seized. The others, including Dr. Soebandrio, had already left for their destinations where they would remain, until word of the successful coup d'etat signalled the planned move throughout the entire archipelago, to seize power from all the provincial authorities. There had been almost a mass exodus of senior Communist Party officials over the past two days. Yanti had seen many of them depart directly from the Halim Airforce base. She had not been surprised that the majority of the Airforce personnel had, in fact, joined the communist cause. Yanti believed that most of their Navy had done likewise. They had both borne the brunt of most of the fighting over the past two years and wished now to take revenge on the Army and its demanding generals.

Yanti was tired but had difficulty sleeping. She wished she had had more time with Murray the week before but he too had been extremely busy with his responsibilities at the Embassy and could not spend more than the one evening with her. She smiled. The memory of their last night together comforted her as she lay in the overcrowded quarters. Images of their love-making gradually soothed her tension and, as the rhythm of her breathing changed, Yanti finally drifted off to sleep.

* * * * * *

Presidential Palace

Soekarno stood silently, deep in thought. He felt tired, and knew that the accumulated effect of the medications he had been given by the doctors for his kidney ailment, only partly contributed to the general feeling of malaise he now experienced. As President, he felt saddened by the decision he had been obliged to take.

He loved his people dearly and had endeavoured to provide the leadership they so desperately needed. Now, it would seem, there was to be even more bloodshed as elements within his Government prepared to push their *Republik* even closer to the edge of chaos and disaster.

He had listened as Aidit and Soebandrio had provided details of the Council of Generals' treacherous plan to move, within days, on the Palace. Soekarno now understood that he had been deceived by his Military, aware that 20,000 soldiers had been camped around the Senajan Sports Complex in preparation for the Armed Forces Day parade, and that these additional units had added to the largest military gathering ever seen in the capital.

Soekarno was bitter as he recalled the many conversations he had held with the Military leadership, the last only days before when he had demanded that General Yani disclose the real purpose of the secret Dewan Djenderal. He remembered that Yani had been adamant, admitting that there was a group of his fellow senior officers which had been casually referred to as a Council of sorts. However, he had insisted, the membership consisted only of senior command officers who met to discuss military matters in private. Yani had sworn to him that he and his fellow officers had no secret agenda and now, the PKI Chairman and his Deputy First Prime Minister were telling him that Yani had been lying. Soekarno had cursed his Army Chief of Staff for his apparent disloyalty.

As President, he believed that it was imperative that he maintain a balance between the political parties and his country's military establishment. Now, as he listened, Soekarno realised that he had failed. There was no other choice. He approved the plan in principle, believing that the Council of Generals had, at all costs, to be prevented from succeeding with their plan to overthrow the Government and establish their own military dictatorship. Soekarno snorted at the thought of Nasution being welcomed at the White House by a grateful American President. No, he thought bitterly, he would never permit this to happen. He and his people had struggled far too long against the neo-colonialists and old guard imperialists to throw it all away now. Nasution and his crowd had to be stopped. Aidit's strategy seemed sound and Soekarno had given it his blessing.

Soekarno bade farewell to his two senior advisers and slumped in his chair. He loosened the top button of his tunic and wiped the sweat from his face. Although he had hidden it from the eyes of his subordinates he had been suffering increasing nausea and dizziness as the meeting progressed. He reached out for the bell to summon an attendant for some water and, seconds later, he reeled sideways from his chair and slid heavily to the floor. He was rushed to his Japanese wife's home in Selipi where the resident Chinese doctors quickly took charge.

Soekarno could not know that the plan to which he had so cordially given his blessing at his last meeting was in fact a plan to arrest the country's most senior generals. He would never have approved such drastic measures.

As Aidit well knew.

* * * * * *

Philippines
U.S. Airforce Base, Clarke Field

The barometer had been falling for over an hour as the Flight Control Officer made his way up the steep stairwell and into the Officer Commanding's presence. The Airforce general snatched the clipboard impatiently and quickly examined the list, then cursed.

'Goddamn mothers,' he snarled, chewing through the sloppy end of his Havana cigar. He pulled it away from his mouth and spat into the waste-paper receptacle. He passed the clipboard back to his major and snarled. 'How reliable is this intelligence?' The major was not offended by the suggestion that his report may be suspect. He could only provide interpretations and evaluations on the information given without wandering into the world of supposition. The major, like most experienced Intelligence officers, was painfully aware that those who collected intelligence information operated under the most difficult conditions, and often opted to provide what their masters wanted to hear, and not what was necessarily an accurate assessment of a true situation in the field.

'We couldn't get any photography, General, but subsequent overflys confirmed the situation.' The OC snarled at no-one in particular. The drops had been a disaster and he could only blame the incompetents in the meteorological station. Their weather forecasts had been disastrous. The unseasonal hurricane had presented his boys with one hell of a curly flight plan. Weather over the past week had all but cancelled most of his flights south into Indonesia and, as the weather seemed to break creating a window for his pilots, he had stacked the backlogged flights, and sent them all down within a twelve-hour time frame in order to meet the drop deadline. Weston, one of his most experienced pilots, had led the first mission and dropped his cargo along with signal beacons for the other flights to follow. Weston had missed his target by more than fifteen miles, and seven more loads were then dumped all over the rough terrain. They had dropped enough weapons and ammunition to equip a small army.

And over the wrong target.

* * * * * *

A village in Java

Throughout the following day, the villagers collected the weapons and boxes of ammunition that had curiously arrived during the night. They had heard the sounds of aircraft flying overhead and even sighted one of the twin-engined planes during the morning and wondered why they had been given so many rifles and bullets. The village *lurah*, as the *kampung's* elected head, had ordered that the parachutes be collected along with their cargo and delivered to the *balai kampung*, as this meeting hall was the only building which could house so many boxes.

This isolated *kampung* had remained almost untouched by outside influence for hundreds of years. Almost, that is, except by the encroaching influence introduced by the people from Kampung Kali Ketjil, the adjacent villagers who lived nearer the sea and followed the teachings of their Christian God. As in many other villages, there was but one radio around which these simple people would gather with their children, to listen whenever their President addressed his people. They adored Bung Karno, although they had never seen the Great Leader of the Revolution. He was one of them, and a true believer.

The village chief addressed his fellow villagers and explained that the weapons were a gift from *Allah, The One and Only True God*, and that they should all consider the delivery as a very special sign. He led them in prayer in accordance with the fundamental teachings of the Prophet Mohammed, as they prayed for guidance and direction. The *lurah* then ordered that the arsenal be guarded as he and the other devout Moslem villagers waited patiently for a sign which would enlighten them all.

It was Tuesday morning, the 29th of September.

* * * * * *

Lembah Njiur

They all laughed as Brigadier General Sujoto finished telling his story. Major General Parman leaned over and slapped his friend's leg playfully, enjoying the anecdote as related by the younger officer. The mood was almost festive as they had finished their meeting, confident that all was in place for the following Monday's momentous occasion. Harjono smiled at Pandjaitan, then winked at Suprapto. They were on the final countdown, with just six days to go.

The full Council had gathered. It was to be their last meeting before the Monday parades when they would lead their men down through the streets of the capital as teams of select men and officers occupied the Palace and placed Soekarno under arrest. They were not surprised at just how easy it had all been, to muster such incredible numbers around the city under the guise of preparing for the Armed Forces Day celebrations. As far as they were concerned, it was already a fait accompli. They believed that it was not even necessary to wait for the following week as they had already successfully occupied the nation's capital. Within the week, the country would be under their direct control and there would be a new President. The Communist Party would be banned and any Fifth Force resistance would be dealt with severely. Brigadier General Pandjaitan burst out laughing again as Sujoto repeated his story, feigning a serious face as he recounted his meeting with the *Tjakrabirawa* colonel.

The Palace Guard officer had insisted that his information was accurate and was furious with the general for not giving any credence to his report. He was adamant and almost on the verge of tears when Sujoto had suddenly burst into laughter at the suggestion. The brigadier was then obliged to reprimand his colonel for carrying such ridiculous stories out of the Palace. He had sent the officer away, suitably chagrined by the admonishment he had received from the general.

'Oh, I agree, said Soekarno. *Let's attack the Military before they can do us any harm,'* Sujoto repeated, bringing tears to the eyes of the others present as he mocked the colonel's story, suggesting that he had overheard a conversation which supposedly took place between Aidit, Soebandrio and their erstwhile President. *'And then Aidit said, aduh, Bung, I would be proud to lead the PKI against the treasonous Yani and his generals!'* with which the room broke immediately into raucous laughter at the very suggestion that Aidit could muster enough support to even consider challenging the might of the Military leadership.

The meeting then broke up as it had commenced, in fine spirits. Soon the whole world would know all of their names.

Chapter 19

30th September 1965
0500 Hours

The first morning prayers had come and gone. Subuh stretched, preparing himself for the rituals he had followed for most of his sixty-four years. Then the holy man prayed. There were no intonations, no vocal prayers. Instead, there was silence as the *maha guru* transcended to a higher level. The Master remained still.

His physical being receded as he concentrated on his inner self, enjoying the floating sensation of separation as the *latihan* commenced. After many years of dedication, he no longer experienced the urgency which had accompanied the first transition as his consciousness distanced itself from his mortal presence.

The holy man's inner being settled peacefully into its own plane. He was only conscious of thought patterns established through years of dedicated compliance. Then suddenly, the ugly images reappeared, threatening the tranquillity of the moment and, as the *maha guru* summoned all of his powers, he feared, for the first time, that he would lose this struggle.

The world appeared before him, confused and in disarray. As his spirit passed through the many-dimensional barriers, he encountered the most terrifying scenes. Voices echoed through the darkness as images of familiar faces flashed across his mind like splinters of light. He had transcended into a world of terror and destruction. As his soul prepared itself against the onslaught of evil, he recognised a fierce, distant voice. In that moment, shadows twisted and changed as darkness gave way to light, and he immediately identified the face of the man who had been summoned to act against the powers of evil.

When he awoke, the spiritual leader was surrounded by a sea of concerned faces. He smiled, absorbing their warmth, and rose slowly. Upon discovering his unconscious body, his followers had carried him carefully to his protected chamber. He, however, refused to be pampered, insisting instead that he be driven into the city for a most important meeting. Reluctantly, the guru's most senior followers acquiesced, and drove their master to the destination in Menteng. Upon arrival, he once again refused their assistance as he climbed with obvious difficulty out of the car and entered the house alone. The armed guards recognised the man and bowed in deference as he shuffled through the barbed wire gate towards the main house. He knew that his presence required no formal announcement.

Subuh remained inside briefly, politely refusing the proffered refreshments as he spoke quietly to the solemn-faced Javanese general. An hour passed before the holy man emerged, smiling wearily at the armed sentries as he moved slowly down the pathway into the waiting sedan. The soldiers guarding the residence on Djalan Waringan watched his car disappear round the corner.

Inside, Major General Soeharto sat reviewing the vision seen by the *maha guru*. Suddenly, he too felt the heavy burden of responsibility. Being Javanese, he understood that his people had long developed psychic faculties and it was not uncommon for such visions to be seen. He sensed that to ignore the dream and its interpretations would most certainly invite disaster.

He sincerely believed that the holy man had been destined to shape his life. Was it not Subuh who had precipitated the changes which had influenced his early childhood years? Now the guru had returned to warn him of impending danger. The Javanese general believed that his world had been shaped not by mortal hands, but by the gods who had created the heavens and earth. He closed his eyes and offered his thanks to those powers which continued to steer him safely through life's maze. He remembered his wife and children, and asked that he and his family be protected from the approaching evil which, he could now sense, endangered them all.

The general's thoughts were interrupted as his wife, Tien, entered the room and reminded him that she wished to leave early to take their son to the hospital. The boy's condition had deteriorated during the night and, having already bathed and fed the youngest of her six children, she was ready to leave with him. The general watched as they were driven away, and then he too departed, arriving at his KOSTRAD offices well after the Thursday morning parade was over.

* * * * * *

1030 Hours

Murray thanked the Military Attaché's assistant for the coffee, then waited for the Warrant Officer to leave his colonel's office before continuing their conversation.

'I'm pleased she's agreed to return to Melbourne, Steve. This is no place for her right now, as you know,' he said, relieved. He knew how distracting having a woman around could be. Earlier, he had left Ade still dressing as he had dashed to the Embassy just in time for his first appointment. It always seemed to happen whenever Ade stayed over, although he was not complaining. She filled a void in his life and Murray had appreciated her company, particularly over the past two days. On Tuesday night, when Ade had arrived unannounced, she discovered him sitting alone in the bedroom, half-undressed, his whole body shaking. Quickly she had finished removing his clothes and forced Murray to lie down while she went in search of a sponge and water. She was very worried and wanted to call the Embassy doctor but he had insisted that it was nothing, citing a reccurring attack of malaria. By the time Ade had returned to the bedroom, he had ceased shaking. The delayed shock from events of a few hours before had finally surfaced, and, what is more, he knew that he was still not out of danger.

Murray had slept in late that morning, electing to arrive at the Embassy just in time for the weekly prayers meeting which was always scheduled for ten o'clock Wednesday morning. The session had dragged on for almost two hours as the Ambassador listened to the Attachés brief his Counsellor regarding the rapidly deteriorating military situation. The Station Chief had then spent a few hours in his own office, catching up on the sudden increase in communications traffic which threatened to bury his desk. By early afternoon, he'd had enough. He telephoned the hotel and spoke briefly with Susan, then left the Embassy compound, swinging by his house for a change of clothes. An hour later, as he completed his workout, Murray climbed out of the hotel pool and joined Susan as she sat sunning herself in the late afternoon sun. He remained only long enough to greet Zach when he arrived, then returned to his residence on Djalan Serang, where he knew Ade would be waiting.

The servants had prepared dinner and they remained indoors. He believed that whoever wanted him dead would wait for an opportunity when he strayed away from locations which were well frequented by other expatriates. In the meantime, Murray kept his P9S close at hand, although away from Ade's curious eye. As he had rushed out the door earlier, she had called out to remind him that she would not be staying over again that night, promising to come back before the weekend. He had blown her a kiss and hurried away, missing another breakfast as well.

His thoughts returned to Susan and Zach, as he sipped the strong Arabica coffee.

'When is she leaving?' he asked. Zach moved uncomfortably in his swivel chair then raised his own cup, sipping the aromatic brew.

'Hopefully, Friday afternoon,' he answered. Murray raised his eyebrows and placed his coffee down.

'What in the hell does that mean?' he asked, surprised at Zach's response.

'I'm taking Susan back up to the bungalows late this afternoon. We'll spend the night. I'll break the news to her then.' Steven looked directly at his friend, who merely shrugged.

'Better you than me,' Murray said, anticipating Susan's resistance. He had seen her stubborn streak before. 'When are you leaving for the hills?' he enquired. Come to think of it, it wasn't such a bad idea taking her to the mountains, as she had been stuck in the hotel grounds for more than two days now.

'We'll get away about three and return first thing in the morning. I have her booked out on the last flight,' Zach advised.

'Best get away early, Steve. The military traffic could slow you down somewhat.' They went on to discuss the substantial build-up of troops around the Senajan Sports Complex and arrangements for the following Tuesday's celebrations.

All embassy officials were expected to attend the parades. Invitations had begun to flow in days before, requesting their presence at a number of official venues during the celebrations. It was considered mandatory that all Military Attachés attend. Murray left Zach and returned to his mountain of paperwork, striving to clear his desk as the other Embassy officers had begun to leave for the day. It was just after two in the afternoon.

* * * * * *

Halim Perdanakusumah Airforce Base, 1430 Hours

Yanti smiled sweetly at the driver as she climbed into the truck and slammed the door firmly. Her features did not betray her excitement as the heavy troop vehicle rumbled through the main security gates and headed towards the by-pass road. She held on to the cabin strap as the truck made its way through the broken macadam, lurching over the large pot-holes.

Yanti checked her watch again, impatiently. She knew there was very little time left. She also knew that all hell would break loose if the other team leaders became aware of her absence from the exclusive compound, which now housed all of the Gerwani units. Yanti and her command had been placed on full alert just hours before. The moment had come.

Yanti's team had received their orders and been secretly briefed. They were to accompany several of the Pasopati units on their mission to arrest the members of the Council of Generals, and take them back to their compound in the Halim Airforce Base. They would depart not long after midnight, when they would be briefed for the final time, then covering the 25 kilometres into the city in two columns before dispersing into five attack groups. They, in turn, would be followed by units of the Tjakrabirawa Palace Guards whose deadly purpose would be to secure the inner city areas of Menteng and Tjikini where most of the senior Military officers lived and certainly the majority of all foreigners.

Yanti had listened in disbelief when their leader, Colonel Untung had casually remarked that he had given explicit orders to the Palace Guard troops to shoot and kill any foreigners who might attempt to leave their houses for their Embassies.

It was imperative, he emphasised, that the foreigners not be permitted to alert their own missions once the attack had commenced. He warned that there were many foreign elements present in Djakarta whose sole aim was to support the Council of Generals Westernization of their *Republik*, and that any interference would not be tolerated. Hence his orders to shoot any foreigners they encountered, on sight. He had smiled, then suggesting that foreigners should not be out on the streets at all, considering the hour. Didn't they know that Djakarta's streets were considered dangerous at night? Many of those present at the briefing had laughed, some, including Yanti, nervously. Murray had to be warned. She knew what he was like, staying out with his friends to all hours of the morning. He would be in danger. She had to tell him to stay indoors.

As the truck bumped along then came to a halt at the by-pass intersection, Yanti looked sternly at the driver. What was he waiting for, she thought impatiently, urging the man to hurry. The soldier smiled at the attractive Sundanese girl, then slowly removed his foot from the clutch. The truck lurched forward and stalled, immediately blocking the southbound traffic. The driver cursed and shuffled the gears while leaning on the starter and, reluctantly, the old cylinders sprang to life, in a cloud of smoke. Ignoring the cacophonous sounds blasting from horns all around, he guided the truck across the main road and down onto Djalan Gatot Subroto. As they passed the Airforce Headquarters, Yanti checked her watch again and knew that Murray would already be home. She hoped fervently that this would be one of those rare occasions when he would not go visiting.

Yanti knew most of the places Murray frequented and shook her head at the thought that she might have to go searching for him without the benefit of transport. The soldier had only agreed to drop her near to the Senajan Complex where his own unit was billeted. Yanti knew she could jump on a bus along Djalan Djenderal Sudirman, then take a *betjak* the short distance through Menteng to Murray's house. Impatiently she looked at her watch yet again. She hardly had time to get to his house and back to Halim, before she was missed. They crossed the clover-leaf-shaped junction and Yanti asked the driver to stop and let her out. She jumped out of the high cabin and ran down to the divided road, searching the oncoming traffic for signs of a bus. Yanti started walking towards the city. It was only a few kilometres and she could easily identify the Intercontinental Hotel in the distance. She rubbed her watch nervously, refusing to look as valuable seconds ticked by. As she walked on, Yanti looked back over her shoulder and was relieved to see a yellow bus moving towards her, and she waved it down. Yanti jumped onto the step, unable to go any further as the bus was already jammed full. The bus then groaned and moved forward, painfully slowly, belching its poisonous fumes in the faces of pedestrians by the roadside. Yanti wanted to scream. It would have been faster to walk. She glanced at her watch. *Aduh!* She wasn't going to make it.

* * * * * *

The bus carrying Yanti rolled slowly towards the Welcome Roundabout and she could clearly see the Selamat Datang statues standing high in the air, their arms frozen in gestures of greeting. As Yanti stepped down, a blue and white Holden passed her heading in the other direction. The Embassy driver leaned on the car's horn to clear a path ahead as he sped south and away from the Hotel Indonesia.

'When do you expect we'll arrive, Steven?' Susan asked, in reply to Steven's explanation that the traffic was particularly heavy due to the Armed Forces' celebrations, which were crowding the streets with endless convoys of soldiers.

'It will probably take most of three hours. Sorry,' he apologised, annoyed about losing valuable time in the mountains together. He had hoped they would have the opportunity to take a walk in the tea plantation, as they had once before. It was there that he hoped to encourage Susan to leave the following day. The driver expertly wove through the heavy traffic, blowing the horn even more so than before.

Steven's estimate had been accurate and the couple arrived at the hill station bungalows just before six. As they gratefully climbed from the vehicle, the air was filled with the *Mahgrib*, the Moslem evening call to prayer, and they both hurried inside where they were greeted by the old woman who cleaned and cooked for the white *tuans*. 'How lovely!' Susan had exclaimed, rushing over to the fire which had been lit as the sun went down. They opened the small box containing supplies and gave the food to the cook, then settled down to sip their glasses of Mouton Cadet. They smiled at each other, and suddenly Steven didn't have the heart to broach the subject of her departure. He decided to leave it until later, or even the following morning.

Susan kicked her shoes away and made herself more comfortable on the large colourful floor cushions. She smiled as Steven joined her, placing his wine on the floor beside hers. He placed his arm around her shoulders and pulled her gently towards him. They embraced, then kissed. As Steven stroked her hair, Susan sighed softly in contentment. There was no other place in the whole world she would rather be than here, with Steven, in these tranquil mountains outside Djakarta.

* * * * * *

1730 Hours

Yanti had missed Murray by only a few minutes. His servants had no idea where he had gone and she decided that it would be futile to go searching for him. Yanti was almost beside herself. Common sense dictated that she should leave without wasting another moment. If she failed to return before the next scheduled check, her absence would most certainly trigger a search and then, she was certain, alarm. Reckless of her own peril, she elected to remain at the villa and wait for Murray to return. An hour passed, then two. Then the phone rang and Yanti sprang to grab the receiver.

'Allo,' she answered, expecting the voice to be that of Murray's. Instead, there was a brief pause before the other party spoke.

'Who is that?' the woman asked. Yanti knew immediately that it was Ade.

'It's Yanti,' she said, hoping that Ade would be annoyed with her being at Murray's house.

'Let me speak to Murray,' Ade demanded. She hated the Gerwani woman.

'Murray's not here, Ade,' Yanti replied, knowing that the other woman would not believe her. The line went dead as Ade banged her phone down. The momentary distraction did little to alleviate Yanti's fears that Murray would not come. By the time she heard the amplified prayer call from the Mosque, Yanti began to panic. She telephoned the Embassy but no one answered her call.

The minutes continued to tick by. Where in the hell is he? she thought wildly. It started to rain and she knew that this too would hinder her return to Halim. And then she heard the heavy iron gates as the *djaga* opened the way for someone to enter. *'Let it be Murray,'* she pleaded running out through the main door as he stepped out of the car.

'Quickly, Mahree,' Yanti called excitedly, *'we don't have much time.'* Murray laughed as he hurried out of the rain and stepped inside. He was surprised to see her and, at the same time, relieved that Ade had not remained for another night.

'What are you doing here?' he asked, picking her up and giving her a playful hug. *'I thought you might have run away with someone else,'* he teased. He knew of her involvement with training the new Gerwani recruits. Sometimes he just could not bring himself to believe that the beautiful young woman who was so loving and exciting in bed could actually be a member of the hardened communist women's brigade.

'Mahree, we must talk,' she whispered, leading him into the bedroom. *'I really don't have much time.'* As they closed the door behind them, she observed that he had cleared the bedside table and placed his brief-case there. She had never seen him take work into the bedroom before.

'Okay, manis, let's talk,' Murray said, undressing quickly. Yanti frowned. She knew that she had to approach this situation carefully. *'If only there was more time,'* she thought, bitterly.

'Come on manis, are we going to talk or just play?' he laughed, reaching for her arm and pulling her down to the bed. Suddenly she decided that perhaps it was best to do this first. Quickly, Yanti removed her own clothes and rolled onto the bed beside him, and kissed him playfully on his hardened stomach, then stroked him as she had so many times before as they prepared each other for what was to follow. Yanti moved with a sense of urgency, surprising Murray with her impatient love-play. As they moved together, he sensed her mood and became excited by her demanding rhythm, losing control of the love-making as Yanti rolled, moving herself in the dominant position. Within moments it was all over. As they lay together, Murray looked down and was surprised to see her eyes filled with tears. Yanti had never cried. Ade, yes, but not Yanti, not that he could recall. He sat up and rolled her over to face him.

'*Mahree, I love you,*' she said, while pushing herself into a sitting position on the bed. '*I love you enough to care what happens to you.*' Murray had never seen her as serious as this before. Something was troubling her deeply.

'*Sure, Yanti, I know. But nothing's going to happen to me, okay?*' he said, wondering what Yanti would say if she knew of what had happened just two days before. A thought crossed his mind but he immediately dismissed it. There could not possibly be any connection between what had happened at the harbour and Yanti's strange behaviour now.

'*Mahree, if I tell you something which would get me into the most serious trouble should others know, would you promise not to mention it to anyone?*' Murray cocked his head and looked directly at her beautiful serious face.

'*Of course, Yanti,*' he replied, becoming concerned with her strange behaviour. She hesitated, then took both of his hands in hers.

'*Mahree, if I asked you to stay here all night tonight would you promise me you would, without asking why?*' He looked at her pleading expression and wanted to smile. Yanti was up to one of her little games she often played. He decided to go along with it.

'*Okay, sure,*' he promised, keeping a straight face, and wondering what she would do next. Yanti's face clouded over. She could see that he was not taking her seriously.

'*Mahree, listen. You must promise, okay?*' she asked, her voice almost breaking into sobs. '*I want you to promise me that after I leave here tonight, soon, you will remain inside until I phone you in the morning. Promise me Murray, okay?*' He looked at her face. This was no game.

'*And if I asked you why...?*'

'*You can't. You must not. I will not tell, even if you do.*'

'*If it means that much to you, of course I'll stay. I hadn't any plans to go out anyway.*'

'*Do you really promise?*' she insisted, squeezing his hands as one of her nails dug deeply. '*Please don't make a joke of this, Mahree. It is very important. Tomorrow I will explain. Okay?*'

'*Okay, manis,*' he sighed and threw the sheet back as he slid off the bed.

'*No, Mahree, I'm late. Let me go first, please,*' she said, jumping off the bed quickly and running into the ensuite. He heard the shower and got up to join her there. Murray enjoyed having his back scrubbed. He did not believe that she really had to leave in such a rush. Indonesians rarely hurried. Time was always flexible. As he moved to the end of the bed he reached down and retrieved Yanti's clothes, which had fallen to the floor during their brief tryst. Murray smiled at the camouflage-coloured uniform. He remembered this as the regular Gerwani dress which they often wore to parades. Getting ready for Monday's parades, he thought, throwing the clothes onto the rattan chair and, as he did so, the contents of her unbuttoned jacket pocket spilled onto the carpet runner. It was a note book.

He bent down again and was about to place this on top of her clothes, when he recognised something of what had been written on the exposed notebook page. He frowned, then flicked through the rest of the small pages. These were full of annotations relating to units with times and names scribbled inside. He couldn't make head nor tail of what she had written. Murray then flicked back to the first page and looked at what Yanti had written there and suddenly a chill passed through him. It was a list of names. He had seen it before, or at least one very much like it. Murray heard the shower door open, then close. He read through the list quickly, trying to memorize what he could before Yanti returned from the bathroom but she stepped back into the bedroom, still towelling her body, before he could return the pocketbook to her jacket.

Murray looked up in surprise then, as casually as he could, flicked the small book onto her clothes. Yanti remained still, staring at him as she dripped water onto the floor. He could see from her eyes that she knew he had seen was written in her secret notes. She lunged forward and snatched the book up and opened the pages as if there would be evidence of his invasion of her privacy. She turned sharply and glared.

'What did you read, Mahree?' she demanded, the softness all gone. *'Why did you read my personal letters?'* she challenged.

'It fell out, Yanti. Your book just fell out when I picked your clothes off the floor. Why are you so upset?'

'Did you read it all, Mahree?' she asked again, knowing that he would have. There had been enough time.

'Some,' he replied, gauging her reaction to this admission. *'It

just caught my eye, that's all,' he lied. *'What's the list for, Yanti?'* he asked, still watching her eyes as they narrowed slightly then looked away from his gaze.

'What list?' she answered, sharply.

'The list of generals. The list in the front of your notes. That list!'

'It's not a list,' she snapped back angrily. *'These are just notes for Monday's parades,'* she lied. *'The Gerwani will be participating in the parades, Mahree. These are just my notes concerning what I must do as one of the team leaders.'*

Murray walked over to her and said quietly, *'Tell me, manis, why have you listed those generals in your book. And why do you insist that I remain here tonight?'* he watched her as she commenced towelling herself again quickly. She ignored the questions and grabbed her clothes. Dressing quickly, she prepared to leave the room. Her eyes softened and she turned back to Murray and touched his arm with her hand.

'Remember what I said, please Mahree. Stay home tonight. If you don't, it could be dangerous. I can say no more,' with which she reached up and kissed him on the cheek. Murray tried to stop her from leaving but she pulled away angrily and opened the bedroom and turned. *'I came here tonight at great risk to myself because I love you, Mahree. Don't betray me. And please, please listen to my warning. Stay home tonight. The streets are going to be very dangerous!'*

'Yanti,' he called but she moved too quickly. He grabbed at the sheet and pulled this around his body, chasing after her, calling for her to wait. But she was gone even before he could make it to the front door. Murray stared out into the drizzle and cursed. He showered and dressed hurriedly, then telephoned the duty officer and requested that his car be sent immediately to take him to the Embassy. The rostered official responded to the urgency in the First Secretary's voice and sent the duty driver around immediately.

Twenty minutes later, Murray sat in his office examining a file to which only he had access. These were his Diponegoro notes and assumptions. The only other ASIS officer to have had access was now missing, perhaps even dead.

He flipped through the documents, searching for the one loose page he had placed there after he and Harry Bradshaw had visited Semarang together. Murray swore as he flipped through the pages, searching frantically. At last, with a triumphant cry he discovered that it was still there and, as he extracted the single sheet and placed it under the light, he stared at the names in disbelief. The list was almost identical to that of Yanti's. Murray stared at one of the names which had been crossed out. The name of the major general who led the Army Strategic Reserve Command, KOSTRAD.

He sat there stunned, staring at the damning evidence, confused by the information which had fallen into his hands. Then, as the cold realisation of what was planned swept across his mind, Murray raced into the Registry, unlocking doors as he went, and leaving these open behind. He entered the main safe and turned the telex machines on to warm them up then suddenly had another idea. The radio! He fumbled through the Embassy telephone directory until he located the Assistant Naval Attaché's number. Then he grabbed the nearest telephone and dialled out. A voice answered, but it was not the Chief Petty Officer. His *djongos* advised that the *tuan* was out and was not expected until late. Sometimes his tuan stayed over at his friends house. No, he did not know where his *tuan's* friend lived. Murray thanked the houseboy, then swore at the system which provided only one qualified radio operator for the clandestine transmitter. The communications aerial farm which hung all over the Embassy was so obvious, he had often wondered why the Indonesian Foreign Office had not already ordered the illegal facility to be taken down.

The Station Chief knew that even the highest priority message would be dependent on just how quickly the Indonesian postal services would respond and onforward the encrypted five-group-worded message. He knew from experience that this could range from three hours to three days. Murray was no longer sure just where the Americans or the Brits would sit when the communists made their move. And he had no real hard evidence to support his conclusions. He was not entirely sure that they would give him access to their own networks, as his country's allies could easily have their own agenda. Even so, protocol demanded that he first communicate directly with ASIS and Central Plans. The rest would be up to them. Frustrated by this knowledge, he had no other choice but to drag the only other man back who, due to his active operational experience in the jungles of Borneo, could operate the damn complicated apparatus. Even then Murray was not certain that he had sufficient time. He could feel it in his bones.

He knew the communists were going to make a move. And the information which he had gleaned from Yanti's notes, and her warning for him to remain inside, indicated in every way that this was the night. He had to get Zach back. Immediately.

* * * * * *

Senajan Sports Stadium, 1900 Hours

Aidit, the Communist Party Chairman, was pleased that Soekarno had recovered enough to attend the rally, as it was essential to his general plan. He stood alongside the President as Soekarno addressed the gathering of Indonesian technicians who were members of the communist-backed labour movement. Aidit smiled as his leader spoke. Soekarno was in his element, his charismatic style captivating all who listened. The Great Leader of the Revolution, and President for Life spoke without the assistance of a prepared speech. As the loyal followers listened and watched, they gasped in surprise when the President suddenly stopped halfway through his speech and clutched at his chest. In pain, he was assisted back to his chair as the crowd surged forward only to be pushed back by the Tjakrabirawa Palace Guards. Many broke into tears as they watched their President grimace, in obvious pain as he clutched at his chest.

Aidit and the other committee members crowded around, loosening Soekarno's tie and rubbing his chest with ice. The crowd was hushed as those surrounding their President moved slowly away, exposing their leader as he rose weakly and raised his hands in salute. He had suffered from an extreme attack of heartburn and, once it had passed, Soekarno smiled at his audience and continued with his speech. When he finished, the crowd roared their approval for the sixty-four year-old hero. They chanted his name as he left the stadium, and touched the hands of all those closest as he passed among them along the exit route. He was loved. He was their President. And the morrow would see those who disagreed removed from the very institutions they led against him. He entered the Presidential limousine and returned to Sari Dewi's house in Selipi to spend the night in the arms of his Japanese wife.

* * * * * *

FREEDOM (MERDEKA) SQUARE

Yanti had to stop and regain her breath. She had run across the airfield, then behind the enormous aircraft hangers until reaching the area across from where her strike teams were billeted. She knew that there would be perimeter security watching and she walked the remaining two hundred metres knowing that she would be observed.

'Halt!' the soldier called, advancing towards her with his rifle extended in her direction. She stopped, her heart beating furiously. As he approached and identified her clothing, the soldier demanded to know what she was doing outside the secured area. She had already prepared her response, knowing she would be challenged.

'Kolonel Untung had sent for me earlier,' she lied, knowing that this soldier would not know whether this was true or not. He advanced closer, suspicious.

'Why have you returned from this direction?' he challenged, looking past her to see if she had been with any others. Yanti moved towards the soldier and let him see the unbuttoned jacket. She was not wearing anything underneath. The soldier grinned as he could see most of one of her breasts from the side.

'The kolonel wanted to be discreet,' Yanti replied, moving slightly to the side so that he could have the benefit of the overhead perimeter lights. The soldier lowered his weapon and moved closer.

'And where is your kolonel now?' he asked, standing very close. He smiled at her and placed his hand on her shoulder. When she offered no resistance, he moved to place his hand inside her jacket. As he leaned forward, Yanti placed her right hand around his free wrist, leaned backwards as she turned and rolled the guard over onto his back. The movement was quick and very professional. The soldier lay stunned, and embarrassed, his weapon already in her hands as she stood over him.

'My kolonel is probably back in bed already. Where you should be. He would be furious that one of his soldiers had been so easily unarmed by a mere Gerwani,' she teased, before stepping back from the prostrate figure. At the mention of the colonel, he jumped back to his feet and brushed himself off quickly. Yanti returned his rifle and walked on towards her own barracks leaving the soldier wishing he had smashed her to the ground.

As she entered her compound, Yanti was relieved to see that the second briefing had not commenced as her companions were still milling around waiting to be summoned. She moved amongst her women and offered reassurances where needed. Yanti could see the excitement building as the AURI Cavalry mingled with the several companies of the Airforce's Rapid Deployment troops. She overheard grumblings of disapproval from a group of angry Tjakrabirawa soldiers when they were informed that the Bandung Cavalry contingent would not be coming. For some reason yet to be discovered, both companies' loyal communist officers were replaced on that very day.

A whistle sounded, calling all section commanders to their second briefing. They gathered inside the Central Command quarters and listened attentively as colonel Untung and his commanders briefed those present. As she listened to the colonel praising his officers for their dedication to the Party and cause, Yanti was pleased that she had been chosen to lead the two teams of Gerwani in what had been named Operation Takari. Their forces consisted of three commands, each broken down into four teams. Yanti's team were in the First Command, which had been given the responsibility of assisting with the kidnappings and transportation of the generals back to Halim. Each of these targets were given code names to be used during radio communication. They had all been expected to memorise the codes and, as Yanti prepared for the signal to move, she ran these through her mind so as not to forget. Nasution's code was 'Nurdin' she remembered, while General Pandjaitan's was 'Singer' and General Sutojo's was 'Toyota'. Yanti ran the others through her mind, recognising that one was missing. She searched her memory for the remaining code on her list which correlated to General Yani's name, and was relieved when she also remembered that the Army Chief of Staff had been designated 'Jonson'. It was then that Yanti, along with the other section commanders, was instructed by Colonel Untung that the generals were to be taken, dead or alive. This startled Yanti.

She had realised from the very beginning that she might be required to kill and could even be killed herself. She felt a sense of doubt. Faced with the reality of her own involvement, Yanti's mind wandered. She wondered what Murray might think of a woman who had blood on her hands. Immediately she struggled to refocus her attention on the important information being given at the briefing. Yanti forced herself to regain her composure and listen as the team leaders were instructed in communication procedures.

They then rehearsed identification codes and signals. Yanti's teams were to answer *'Takari'* whenever challenged by the call *'Ampera'*, and were instructed to blow their horns three times in response to any challenge of two blasts from any of their number. The Operation Takari Commander, First Lieutenant Dul Arief, insisted that they continue to rehearse this information in their minds knowing that it would be difficult, later in the dark, to distinguish friend from foe.

The excitement continued to build and Yanti suddenly discovered that she had her hands full overseeing preparations for the early morning attack. Preoccupied with her troops, Yanti had little time to reflect on Murray's earlier reaction to information in her notebook. She had wondered, briefly, whether or not the small pad had in fact accidentally fallen from her jacket, or whether he had gone through her pockets. His curiosity had been aroused and, the more she considered the incident, the more Yanti felt uneasy with the knowledge that he seen the list. She hoped that her lover would be unable to relate these to anything more sinister than the explanation she had given to him. Not, that is, until they had completed their mission. Only then, she was sure, would Murray associate the names mentioned in her book as belonging to those senior officers who would, by then, be in custody at the Halim Airforce Base. With a wry smile, she wondered how Murray would react, when he learned that his Yanti had been partly responsible for the operation which kidnapped the entire Council of Generals, and had carried them all away.

* * * * * *

2100 Hours

Murray checked his watch and resisted the temptation to push the driver any harder. As it was, the man had almost killed them twice already. The Station Chief moved around uncomfortably. He adjusted his automatic under his batik shirt.

There were no white lines, no warning signs or other aids on these roads to assist the drivers. Trucks, buses and even armoured vehicles tore through the night, often without headlights to warn oncoming traffic. As they had followed the dark road around one corner, Murray yelled, warning the driver in time to avoid the truck parked without lights, broken down in the middle of the main highway. They had swerved in time, barely missing the men who sat repairing the truck's differential. Once they reached Bogor, the road narrowed even more. As they commenced the climb through the foothills, Murray checked his watch again. They were losing more time than he could afford.

On they drove, passing other vehicles on dangerous curves, overtaking buses and trucks as they struggled up the steep incline. As they neared the turnoff halfway up the mountain, the driver pulled out and overtook a slower sedan, only to be run off the road by an oncoming Army truck. The Holden swerved and slipped as the driver's side wheels lost traction along the soft shoulder.The inept *supir* panicked and overcompensated, causing Murray to stifle a cry as they came perilously close to overturning and rolling down the steep incline. Enough was enough. Murray ordered the driver out of his seat and took charge. He gunned the engine, spinning the wheels on the soft damp soil, correcting the car's path, powering them forward onto the bitumen.

After several kilometres, Murray turned the wheel abruptly, leaving the main highway to Bandung and followed the gravel road up into the Embassy compound. He killed the engine, ran up the bungalow steps and knocked loudly. A frightened old woman appeared, who, on discovering Murray's familiar face, broke into a toothless smile.

'What's wrong tuan Murray?' she asked, unlocking the porch doors with an old key.

'It's okay, 'bu,' he reassured her, moving quickly to the door he knew would lead to the master bedroom. He knocked loudly.

'Steve, it's Murray. Sorry, but it's really very urgent,' he called, continuing to knock. Steve opened the door abruptly, dressed only in a towel. He looked at Murray and scowled.

'For Chrissakes, what's the racket all about?' he demanded, squinting at the light. 'What are you doing here, Murray?'

'We don't have time to talk. Grab your clothes and you can dress in the car,' he said, moving into the room uninvited and switching the light on. Immediately Susan pulled the sheets even higher to hide her naked body. Shocked by the intrusion, she glared at their friend.

'What is it, Murray?' she also demanded, embarrassed and angry.

He thought quickly. They couldn't leave her there as it might be too dangerous. He decided to take her with them. At least he could put her back in the hotel where she would be safe.

'Get dressed,' he barked, startling his friends. 'I don't have time to explain. Just do as I say, please. Get dressed and, if you can't find something, leave it behind. Come on, let's go, quickly,' he ordered, leaving them to dress. Zach knew from Murray's tone that they should do as he said. His mind raced as they searched for clothes which had been thrown around the room at random.

The Station Chief had them dressed, packed and in the vehicle in less than five minutes. He glared at the driver, telling him to remain behind as Murray desperately needed to talk to the Military Attaché in secrecy. At first, the *supir* had ignored the *tuan* and started to argue until the *tuan* clenched his fists and took several steps towards him. At that, the driver had then shrugged his shoulders, reached back into the car to retrieve his cigarettes, then held the door open for Susan.

'*Go back to the Embassy with the kolonel's driver tomorrow morning,*' Murray called to his driver as he slipped behind the wheel and reversed savagely out of the driveway, then headed back down the narrow dirt track towards the mountain highway. Steven sat alongside Murray as they re-joined the sealed macadam and turned towards Djakarta. He finished lacing his shoes and looked across at the Station Chief.

'Well?' Zach asked, waiting for an explanation. Murray looked into his rear-vision mirror and observed Susan combing her untidy hair. She looked distressed. He was concerned that she would hear everything he had to say and, with that in mind, Murray cautioned Zach with a brief hand signal. He leaned back slightly and lifted his shirt with his free hand to remove the uncomfortable weapon which he placed on the seat. Zach's eyes narrowed. He had not known that the Station Chief was carrying the P9S.

'I have every reason to believe that the communists are planning to make a move on the Government, Steve,' he started, holding the steering wheel tightly as he was forced to swing wide to avoid something which had moved along the dark roadside. Steven said nothing, waiting for him to continue. 'I need your help. I don't know where the hell the radio operator is, and I couldn't think of anyone else who could punch the signals out in his place.'

'Shit! How soon?' Zach asked. Murray was the senior Intelligence officer and he respected his judgement. If Murray Stephenson said there was going to be a move on the Government, it was good enough for him. Murray would never speculate without sound fact to support his observations. The communists' move probably would not amount to much, he thought, having seen recent evaluations of their strengths and weaknesses. Zach knew that his Director of Military Intelligence in Melbourne thought that the PKI were lacking in experienced military leadership, in spite of the Navy and Airforce being predominantly communist at the top.

'As we speak, I'm afraid,' Murray answered, braking to avoid running into an oncoming vehicle which had pulled out to overtake yet another stalled truck. Susan cried out as she lost her balance and bumped her head on the side window.

'Do we have to go this fast?' she called out angrily, but was ignored by both men.

'So, what's happening?' the colonel asked, glancing at Susan through the corner of his eye as they spoke. She was busy with the buttons on her blouse.

'They have a list, Steve. A bloody hit list!' he said, dropping his voice a little. 'If I'm not wrong, they're going to take a crack at the members of Nasution's Council of Generals and, once they've succeeded, they'll most likely grab the Palace as well.' Zach was a man not normally given to surprise, but in this instance he frowned and stared back at Stephenson. Was it possible that the communists would have any chance of succeeding against Nasution and his powerful associates? Obviously Stephenson thought so.

'I won't ask you how you came by this information Murray but, for Chrissakes, are you absolutely certain?' Zach asked. 'If we're going to hit the air-waves, my friend, we'd bloody well better be confident that you are right. You're talking about a possible coup d'etat here Murray. And against the Indonesian Military! Jesus, Murray, I hope you've got something to back this up.'

'Sure,' was all Murray said. Zach did not have to know that Murray was acting primarily on a gut feeling, and a voice in the back of his head which kept telling him that, somehow, Harold Bradshaw's disappearance had something to do with all of this. The list was the common denominator. Murray looked across at his friend. He knew that once they had successfully signalled his Director in Melbourne, the contents would be disseminated within the hour to all friendly countries which, in turn, would communicate directly with their own embassies and consulates in Djakarta. He was simply taking a short-cut.

Murray knew that raising the alarm via Australia would carry more credence than if the news first broke via dubious Indonesian sources. Lives could be saved, as long as he could have Zach back in the radio room before the situation deteriorated further. There was no way of determining just how the communist move might affect the security of foreigners throughout the country, once the blood-letting commenced.

'I'll let you have a look at what I have when we get back,' he said to Zach, hitting the brake pedal again as they rounded a corner and were confronted with two oncoming trucks occupying both sides of the road. He managed to pull off the road in time to avoid a collision.

'All right?' Zach asked, reaching over to Susan and placing his hand on her knee. She grabbed his hand and held it tightly. She had been petrified from the moment they had left the bungalow. Zach squeezed her hand firmly, then released his grip and turned back to Stephenson, who had already brought the car's speed back to a dangerous level. He glanced at his friend's features, and was reminded of the grim, determined men with whom he had fought alongside against the Indonesian soldiers in Kalimantan.

Zach decided not to distract Stephenson any further. The road was dangerous and he was impressed by his friend's driving skills, glad that it was not he who sat behind the wheel. Zach looked at his watch and noted that it was well after midnight. He wondered what the new day would bring.

* * * * * *

Friday, 1st October, 1965, 0130 Hours

Yanti walked to the back of the truck second in line and checked that her teams were all settled. They had boarded the trucks almost half an hour before and had already become restless with the inactivity. She told them to quieten down, then moved on to the third vehicle, climbed into the driver's cabin and waited for the signal to roll. Moments ticked by and suddenly she saw officers from their Central Command walk by briskly. They were led by Brigadier General Supardjo. As she watched, the soldiers came to a halt and dispersed. Colonel Latief moved towards the other column while Major Gatot Sukresno continued to follow the other officers, Supeno and Suradi. There was a hushed excitement in the air as she looked across at the parallel convoy and knew that the soldiers there were ready.

Yanti was scared, but was careful not to show any outward sign. She hoped the uneasy sensation in her stomach would pass once they were under way. The Gerakan 30 September forces had drawn units from all sections of the Indonesian Armed Forces. Yanti had seen regimental flashes on soldiers shoulders identifying units from the Tjakribirawa, Brawidjaja and AURI Commands. She was particularly surprised to see soldiers strutting around from the 454th Company, which she knew was one of the Diponegoro Command's best units. It seemed that the Indonesian Communist Party had been successful in securing support from a major cross-section of the country's military, the *Tentara Nasional Indonesia*.

She returned a wave from one of the commanders as he walked past. Yanti remembered that this officer would take two units and occupy the telecommunications centre, then move on to secure the radio and television stations. They knew that their task had been made less difficult by commencing their attack when most of the city's inhabitants slept. Their Central Command had planned the strike to take place well before the capital stirred as first prayers were called in the early morning darkness. Nervous, Yanti was disappointed to see that the hands on her watch had hardly advanced since she had last checked. Suddenly, she saw two men run up to the lead truck and hit the driver's door firmly, before continuing onto the next truck loaded with armed Airforce troops, and repeating the signal. Her heart leaped into her mouth as the driver alongside her hit the starter and their engine roared into life. It had started and they were on their way into the city. Suddenly she opened her window and vomited violently. The driver leaned across and slapped her lightly across her back and, as their truck groaned slowly forward, she turned, and looked with embarrassment at the seasoned soldier.

'*Tidak apa-apa,*' the Malaysian campaign veteran offered, telling her it was all right. Yanti grinned gratefully and returned to concentrate on her Gerwani's role in the attack.

The trucks rolled slowly along the airfield's dirt roads, crossing the concrete hard-standing area past a selection of unserviceable American Hercules transports, and continued on past a row of empty aircraft hangers, then down to the western perimeter gates where they stopped. Security checked the convoy one last time. They were joined by a number of Toyota jeeps carrying mobile radio equipment ,and another jeep which had just returned from reconnaissance, where Sergeant Major Sulaiman was familiarized with General Suprapto's house in Djalan Besuki. The barbed-wire-covered gates were slowly drawn open and the lead vehicle lurched forward.

* * * * * *

Djakarta, 0200 Hours

They drove on in silence. Murray had managed to get them back to within twenty kilometres of the city well before two o'clock. He slowed at the junction to the west of the huge Halim Airforce Base and turned towards the city. He was pushing the engine to its limits along Djenderal Gatot Subroto, when he came up behind an Army convoy and was obliged to slow abruptly. He could not overtake. The soldiers standing in the rear truck indicated with a wave that he was to remain behind. Murray was tempted to blow the horn but resisted, knowing that this was an offence and could get him into trouble with the soldiers ahead. He fumed, angry that they had managed to make reasonable time on the return trip only to be delayed now.

When they reached the first roundabout, Murray decided to turn right and save time by cutting back behind the eastern suburbs and enter Menteng via Tjikini and the Senen roads. They followed the circle around and Murray caught a glimpse of the full convoy as it continued on towards Senajan. In those brief moments as a dark cloud passed across the sky, smothering the moon's rays, he could just make out that all the trucks were loaded with soldiers. The thought never occurred to him that the convoy might be part of the communist contingent, heading into the city, on their way to create a new chapter in Indonesia's history.

* * * * * *

0215 Hours

The air was still as the President moved outside and away from the air-conditioning. He had never really enjoyed the artificial cooling, preferring instead the soft breeze of an overhead fan. His lower back ached. He bent and rubbed the area surrounding his right side, knowing that it would make little difference. The kidney stones remained and reminded him of his failure to heed advice given many years before concerning his diet.

Soekarno moved slowly across the terrace and stood in the partial darkness observing the sky. On the far side of the courtyard he could see the glow of a clove *kretek* cigarette being smoked by one of his Tjakrabirawa Palace Guards. He raised his head, thinking he had heard the cry of a bird, then sadly remembered just how long it had been since he had heard the cry of anything wild, or free. A soft puff of wind fanned across his face and he looked to the heavens where thick dark clouds crossed the sky heralding further rain. The Wet Season was gaining momentum.

He had not been able to sleep. His mind was filled with the events which had overtaken his life, his Presidency, his people. He felt he had been betrayed by those closest to him. He had refused to entertain any discussion about what would happen to those who had plotted his overthrow. It was sufficient that they had been discovered in time and he, as President, had once again been given the opportunity to act, in the interests of his people. Soekarno loved his *rakjat*. In the twenty years of his Presidency, not once had he taken from the people. He had fought for them, then struggled for them and been imprisoned for them. The years of sacrifice had thankfully ended in independence for the Indonesian people. In material terms he had nothing. His wives and children lived simply. They had never once taken advantage of his position nor his power, for these things had little value in his world. He had struggled to introduce the basic principles of Pantja Sila, so that the people of his great country would have a set of values to guide them through life, and remind them of who and what they were. Diversified they might be, he thought, but at least after this night they would remain united. The Council of Generals would be destroyed forever and, in their ashes, a new generation would grow. He and those who had supported the principles of *Merdeka*, of freedom, had done so to protect their generation and those which followed.

Soekarno turned and shuffled across the terrace into the magnificently-appointed bedroom where he edged towards his bed. He was still in considerable pain and so placed his arms behind, then carefully lowered himself down onto the pillows. Suddenly he felt a little better and looked across at the Japanese woman sleeping by his side. He smiled. Dewi remained asleep, and he was pleased that this was so. Sometimes, he admitted silently, the former hostess could be very demanding.

* * * * * *

Murray had dropped Susan at the Hotel Indonesia first, then he and Zach swung back round the quiet roundabout and down Djalan Iman Bondjol towards Tjikini and Djalan Pegangsaan Timur and the Australian Embassy. He was exhausted.

Zach remained deep in thought as they sped down the deserted road lined with an unkempt nature strip where itinerants huddled together in sleep.

'Doesn't exactly look like they've started beating the drums,' Zach said. But as an experienced field soldier he was more than aware that an enemy rarely saw the first strike.

'Don't wish for something we don't need,' Murray muttered, blinking. His eyes felt gritty with fatigue. They arrived at the Embassy, gave the *djaga* on duty a perfunctory wave and hurried into the Embassy, unlocking and relocking doors with Murray's keys as they went. They opened the restricted access door leading into the radio room and searched for the light switch. Zach cursed loudly as he cracked his head on a protruding shelf hidden in the dark. Murray located the lights and Zach set about warming up the radio while Murray returned to the Registry and encrypted the message. He rushed back to Zach who had established direct contact with the Australian spy-ship positioned in the South China Sea, and had requested its officers to stand by. He would send a confirmation copy to the secret signals listening base in Singapore as well. Murray returned and handed the encrypted message to Zach for despatch. It hadn't been too long since the colonel had used Morse code, and he managed to complete the transmission in less than twelve minutes, then closed the station having received acknowledgement from the receiving operator. Zach rubbed his right hand as it had begun to cramp, then turned to Murray.

'What's next?' he asked, flexing his fingers.

'I'm going to try to warn the generals,' Murray replied. Zach immediately shook his head.

'Don't do it. Don't get involved,' he warned. 'They are all well guarded, Murray. Who knows, perhaps they'll snuff this whole thing out even before it starts.'

'I have to at least give it a try,' the Station Chief replied, lifting the automatic and placing it back in his belt. Zach observed the movement and shook his head.

'I think you're being foolish,' Zach said. 'Just what do you think you can do at this late hour?' He then paused. 'You might already be too late.'

'Well, it would be useless trying to ring them, that's for sure. Even if someone did answer at this hour, do you think a servant would take it upon himself to wake his general on the advice of a telephone call from a foreigner? I don't think so. No, there's no other choice. They must be warned.'

Steven Zach looked at the Station Chief's determined face and knew there was no point in arguing any further.

'Okay, Murray,' he said, wearily, 'let's go.' Stephenson hesitated at the Military Attaché's offer to assist. Should their attempts to warn the men on the list fail and the Indonesians later discovered that an Australian Army officer had been involved, he knew that such ramifications would be most damaging to their country's relationship with its giant neighbour.

On the other hand, Zach was a most competent officer, and

Murray was pleased that he had offered.

'We'll start with General Harjono as he lives just a few doors down from my place. We've spoken once or twice. If we can get him to listen, maybe he'll believe us and contact the others.' Zach agreed and they left the building hurriedly.

It was just after three o'clock in the morning.

* * * * * *

The Australian spy-ship had been positioned in these waters throughout the duration of the Crush Malaysia campaign, and remained in the area specifically to accept all radio transmissions from South-East Asian stations. Once the ship had received the coded signal, the communication was then pumped into the atmosphere through a powerful transmitter, and received via the Australian Army secret intelligence listening post in Toowoomba, Queensland. This listening station, located in the most unlikely of places, was manned by a battery of highly qualified signals specialists whose life was dedicated to picking the air clean of all radio transmissions which emanated from Asia.

Army Warrant Officer Nicholas 'Nicko' Denison listened intently, writing the Morse code down faster than many clerks could type. He acknowledged the message and tore his headset off and ran to the command desk. The officer of the day took one look at the highly sensitive classification and telephoned Melbourne to alert the early morning watch that he was about to despatch a signal bearing 'eyes only' classification. He then moved to the bank of antiquated telex machines and instructed an operator to send the message as it appeared on the written receiving report.

The typist-cum-telex operator punched the keyboard sending the five letter coded message directly to a similar machine in Melbourne. She had to slow her typing movements as the machine could not accommodate her speed and started to choke. Five minutes passed before the duty officer was able to place the long thin tape punctured with thousands of tiny holes, alongside a matching tape which acted as the deciphering 'twin', As the deciphering mechanisms clattered away, the officer on duty in what they called The Factory, observed the initial notification which stated, 'Eyes Only OYSTER' followed by the signal's priority. In the young officer's short career he had never seen any communication which had been graded 'FLASH' before. Immediately he called his superior. This grading was only used by troops fighting on the front line when they first sighted the enemy. He knew there had to be something wrong.

The Melbourne-based Officer Commanding, Colonel Sharpe, was summoned from his quarters, near St. Kilda Road. A further fifteen minutes passed before he read the communication, then phoned Canberra. After this, the colonel telephoned ASIS Acting Director Anderson at his home in Melbourne, apologised for the hour, then requested the Intelligence Chief's immediate presence.

Less than twenty minutes later, Anderson climbed wearily from his ageing Ford Customline and made his way into the dark, well-disguised buildings. He joined the others where they sat, sipping instant coffee. He cursed Stephenson. Why hadn't he taken steps to remove the Djakarta Station Chief when the opportunity had first arisen? Anderson read the signals and snorted contemptuously. In his own opinion, there was no valid reason to suggest that the Indonesian communists could possibly effect a successful coup d'etat. The ASIS Director believed that the Djakarta Station Chief was grandstanding and his behaviour was most probably related in some way to the disappearance of Harold Bradshaw. This message only confirmed his suspicions. Murray Stephenson had been in Indonesia far too long.

As Acting ASIS Chief, he had discussed the Indonesian situation just the day before with Agency representatives in the American Embassy in Canberra. There had been no suggestion that the PKI was in any position to carry out such a grandiose scheme. In fact, he had been given access to sensitive information which totally contradicted what Stephenson was now suggesting. During the one-on-one meeting with the CIA Director, he had been informed that the United States had entered into an understanding with senior officers of the Indonesian Military to support their move to take control of the Government, and this was only a matter of days away. The generals had agreed to dismiss Soekarno and dismantle the complex political system which had enabled the communists to consolidate their position in Indonesia. The ASIS Chief undertook to protect the integrity of this information, agreeing not to disseminate any of the intelligence to other agencies until cleared by his counterpart. It was apparent to Anderson that whatever Stephenson had seen was merely one piece of the overall strategy being put into place by the American initiatives in Djakarta. He knew that Stephenson had misread the situation.

Anderson advised the other Intelligence officers who had also been called in urgently that he would personally take charge of the situation. He pocketed the communication and thanked the surprised group of analysts, then returned to his well-appointed accommodation. As his head touched the pillow, Anderson already knew what his first business of the day would be, when he arrived at his office in Central Plans the next morning. The Acting Director smiled, as he easily gave way to sleep, pleased that he would soon be rid of his predecessor's protegé.

Chapter 20

0310 Hours

The Embassy guards waved as they drove through the gates and headed towards Murray's residence. He turned into Djalan Professor Moh Yamin and drove towards the Intercontinental Hotel for two blocks, then turned left into Djalan Tjik Ditiro as the engine spluttered, then died. Murray turned the starter as he peered at the dash instruments then swore, realising that they had run out of gas. Immediately, both men jumped out and jogged towards the villa on Djalan Serang. They had less than four hundred metres to cover now. They had just turned the corner together when Murray pulled Zach urgently to the side of the broken footpath.

'We're too late!' he hissed, bending low to the ground, watching the fury of activity less than a hundred metres away. Soldiers poured out of the three trucks and ran along the road while others forced their way past the alarmed sentries guarding Major General Harjono's house and family. Murray was within twenty metres of his own villa. He realised that there was little they could do for his important neighbour. He looked at Zach and signalled, pointing across at his residence.

'Let's get to a bloody phone, and quick. We must alert the Ambassador and the other Attachés now we have solid evidence of what's happening. Also anyone else we can contact. There's nothing we can do now, for them,' he nodded in the direction of where the soldiers had congregated. They could hear shouts and signs of resistance as the communist Takari teams easily overran Harjono's own security. They rose from their crouched positions and started across the street. Suddenly, a soldier shouted and they knew, instantly, they had been spotted.

'*Stop!*' the voice demanded. Zach and Murray both froze.

'*Stop!*' the soldier screamed and raised his weapon at them where they stood half-way across the road. Suddenly, Zach realised the soldier was going to shoot.

'Run!' he yelled, and Murray sprang into action and legged it across the road as fast as he could.

'Keep going!' Zach yelled, bending down to reduce the target. They had just about made it to the other side of the road when the soldier began shooting, sending a spray of automatic fire in their direction. The first bullets hit the footpath ahead and ricocheted into the night. They both turned away from the onslaught and ran furiously back across from where they came, bullets following their pounding footsteps. Suddenly the whole street seemed to come alive as the soldier was joined by his comrades, shooting wildly at the running figures.

'Shit,' Murray called loudly, 'the bastards are trying to kill us!'

'Then for Chrissakes man, run!' Zach ordered. Murray didn't know how they managed to make it back to the corner unscathed. They ran as fast as their legs would carry them, crossing Djalan Tjik Ditiro. The sounds of running soldiers signalled that they were not too far behind. Just then, Murray fell, and as he hit the ground bullets whipped dangerously close to where he lay. He screamed in pain and Zach thought the Station Chief had been hit. Instead, it was an old injury, come back to haunt him. Murray knew, as he struggled to his feet that the excruciating pain in his ankle would foil their attempts to escape. Zach saw the problem and pulled Murray to his feet, scooping his friend up effortlessly as the soldiers approached closer. Bullets broke the air around their heads and Zach was forced to throw them both to the ground, causing Murray to scream in pain.

'Give me the gun,' he hissed, groping for the automatic Murray carried.

'No, hell no!' Murray yelled, fighting against Zach as the colonel gripped the P9S and pulled the handgun free. 'They'll shoot you dead if they see you armed!' he shouted, not realising how ridiculous this sounded to the seasoned veteran.

'Shit, Murray, what the hell do you think the bastards have just tried to do?,' Zach hissed, turning with the weapon and pointing it directly at the approaching soldiers. There were three of them, all dressed in battle fatigues and armed with what Zach guessed from the rapid fire would be either Soviet Sudarevs or Spaghins sub-machine guns. The weapons could even be Stens, he thought. It really didn't matter. He knew from his anti-guerrilla sweeps in the jungles of Sarawak that the Indonesians had both. The leading soldier fired from the hip as he crossed to their side of the road, sending a spray of bullets just off to their right, ripping chunks of cement from the adjacent wall. Zach believed he had no choice. He aimed the pistol and fired three shots in rapid succession. The soldiers behind threw themselves to the ground as one of Zach's bullets found its target. The Indonesian soldier's body jerked back, and then sideways, and he was dead before he even hit the ground. Zach then charged towards the other two startled soldiers, and fired two shots as he scrambled towards their fallen comrade.

Zach dropped down heavily beside the dead man, using the body for cover. He stuck the P9S into his belt. There were still four rounds left in the automatic's magazine. He ripped the sub-machine gun from the soldier's hands and pointed the Soviet PPS at the other two soldiers and squeezed the trigger. The SMG Sudarev pulled to the right as the remainder of the thirty-five 7.62 mm rounds tore from the barrel, sending flames out the side of the weapon's circular cooling holes. Both soldiers scrambled in a vain attempt to escape, their faces twisted as they fell in the fierce hail of bullets.

Zach ran across to where they lay, and crouched beside them. He removed one of the weapons, checked the curved box magazine and threw the empty Sudarev aside in disgust. Damned obsolete Soviet junk, he thought. He rolled over the other body and checked the second machine-gun. There were still rounds in the magazine so he grabbed the weapon and ran to the injured Murray.

Zach responded to Murray's enquiring look with a quick shake of his head, indicating that the men were all dead. Murray knew that the colonel had had little choice. They could not afford to leave any witnesses who could identify them as having exchanged fire with the Indonesian soldiers. Zach pulled Murray to his feet, then put his head under the injured man's arm and half-carried, half-dragged him away from the scene of carnage.

As they struggled along, Murray kept looking over his shoulder, expecting another attack from behind. But none came. Instead, the remaining soldiers concentrated on their task at hand, the immediate capture and arrest of Major General Harjono. Zach checked the automatic. It was too obvious, he knew. He buried it inside his shirt, still held in place by his belt. They hobbled along, careful of the broken pavement, Zach acting as Murray's crutch. The men pushed on until reaching the junction of Prof. Mohamad Yamin and Tjik Ditiro. They rested, and Zach waved at a passing *betjak* which stopped and accepted the fare from what he believed were two drunken *tuans*. Murray Stephenson and Colonel Steven Zach were already well out of earshot when the staccato sounds of Sten fire pierced the air along the street known as Djalan Serang.

* * * * * *

0320 Hours

When their contingent had first arrived, Sergeant Major Bungkus, as team leader, had jumped down from his jeep and disposed of the sleeping security without effort. He had then run to the front door and banged loudly, calling out to those inside. Mrs. Harjono awoke with a start and left their bedroom, passing through the family room and across to the side entrance where she peered through the curtains. She was startled to see soldiers dressed in Tjakrabirawa Palace Guard uniforms. Others were gathering in her front yard and she immediately became concerned. She stepped out through the side door and confronted the men there.

'*I must speak to Bapak Djenderal Harjono,*' the sergeant demanded. Harjono's wife gasped at the NCO's insolent attitude.

'*The Djenderal is asleep,*' she replied defiantly, but Sergeant Major Bungkus knew this not to be so. He suspected that the general was awake and had sent the woman out to investigate. '*What are you doing here?*' she then demanded.

'*The Bapak Djenderal has been called urgently by the President,*' Sergeant Major Bungkus lied.

'*Stay where you are. I will inform the Djenderal,*' Ibu Harjono instructed the soldier. She returned inside, leaving the side door open, then hurried into her bedroom. '*Pak, Pak,*' she whispered urgently, '*there are Tjakra Palace Guards outside insisting that you go with them. They said that they are to take you to see the President!*' Djenderal Harjono was alarmed by his wife's wild-eyed expression.

'Tell them to leave immediately,' he asked his wife, then added, *'and tell them to come back in the morning. At 0800 Hours.'* They both listened to the distant gunfire and became even more alarmed. Ibu Harjono did as asked, returning downstairs to confront the soldiers who waited there.

'You are to return tomorrow morning,' she called to the men outside through a half-opened door.

'The Bapak is to come with us now!' the sergeant outside demanded once more. She was shocked by his insolence.

'The Bapak Djenderal is not well,' she lied. *'Come back in the morning as he has ordered.'* For a brief moment there was silence, and then Ibu Harjono thought she could hear the soldiers outside talking.

'Go away,' she called through the small opening, wishing that the general's own men had been present. She listened but there was no response. Ibu Harjono then proceeded to close and lock the front door. Suddenly she was startled by a loud banging noise as the door's timbers screamed under the soldier's onslaught.

'Aduh, aduh,' she cried in alarm, running back to her bedroom.

'What is happening?' the general asked, panic rising in his voice.

'They refuse to go, Pak,' replied the anguished Ibu Harjono. *'They tried to break into our house!'*

General Harjono suddenly realised that he was in grave danger, and that the men outside were there to take his life. *'Get the children. Quickly!'* he ordered. Ibu Harjono started to cry, lost in the sudden turmoil. She put her hands to her face.

'What do they want?' she cried, fearing that she already knew the answer.

'Do as I say, now. Get the children and stay with them in the next room. Lock the door. I will go and talk to the men and then send them away.' As he spoke, they both heard Sergeant Bungkus scream angrily.

'Come out now, Djenderal, or we will kill your whole family!' General Harjono knew then that he was to die. He turned to his wife and held her tightly.

'Go. Now. Get the children as I asked. Take them into the next room and stay there. You will be safe. I promise you.' He attempted a smile as he quickly touched his wife's face. She turned and hurried away to do as her husband had instructed. Ibu Harjono knew that it was

now her responsibility to ensure the safety of their children. She didn't look back at her husband of thirty-one years as she hurried to the other room.

'Come down, Djenderal!' she heard the soldiers demand menacingly. Suddenly there was a burst of machine-gun fire. She grabbed the children, fled to the safety of the back room, and bolted the door behind, leaving her husband cut off from his family. Ibu Harjono could hear the general moving around. It seemed that he was moving their furniture in the bedroom.

Sergeant Arlian opened fire with his Sten while Private Subakir half-emptied his own Sten's magazine, shooting through the thick teak door. Bungkus then burst through the doorway and found the room in darkness.

'Get some light in here!' Bungkus yelled. Immediately, one of the soldiers set fire to some loose newspaper sheets and threw this inside the large room. They then entered as the flames flickered, casting an eerie light through the darkness. Something moved, catching the intruders off-guard. It was Djenderal Harjono.

'You bastards!' he screamed, lunging forward to attack with only his fists. He had been unable to find a weapon in the bedroom. He leapt forward and wrestled with one of the soldiers, throwing Private Subakir to the floor. He groped for the man's weapon unsuccessfully, and, as flames died out, returning the room to darkness, he moved to the farthest corner, crouching beside a built-in cupboard. Private Subakir was back on his feet within moments.

'Kill him!' a voice commanded from somewhere behind in the darkness. Immediately, Subakir unleashed a hail of bullets sending the heavy-set general crashing to the ground.

In the adjacent room his wife and children screamed loudly, crying for help as they heard the bullets rip through the walls.

'Shut up in there or we will kill all of you as well!' Bungkus threatened. The children huddled together, petrified. Suddenly they heard another burst of fire from one of the Stens and they whimpered, knowing that it was all over. General Harjono was dead.

The communists dragged the half-dressed body out into the family room. Harjono's singlet and short pants were smothered in blood and, as he was unceremoniously dragged outside, over the terrace and through the front garden, his body left an ugly trail of blood. Sergeant Major Bungkus, assisted by Subakir, Wagirem, and some of

Yanti's Gerwani, threw the general's corpse into the waiting truck. The Gerwani women shrieked with pleasure at their unit's success.

One of Harjono's children raced outside to be confronted by the grisly spectacle.

'Bapak! Bapak!' the child called out in anguish at the sight.

'I said shut up!' Private Wagirem screamed as he knocked the child unconscious with a vicious blow from the butt of his machine-gun. The soldiers then all boarded their truck and drove away. As soon as she realised that they had gone, Ibu Harjono fled into the darkness outside. She cried out loudly for assistance as she ran to the homes of General Parman and her husband's other close friend, General Suprapto. But she was too late.

* * * * * *

And so it went on. As the attack had commenced against General Harjono, the houses of the other generals had also come under siege. Major General Parman and his wife were awoken by sounds of movement outside and, suspecting that the neighbours on their right were being burgled, the general went outside to investigate and, if necessary, lend assistance to his friends next door.

'Who's there?' Parman challenged, but there was no reply. His wife had remained inside. *'Ada siapa?'* he called again, but still there was no response. Suddenly he recognized the sound of army boots hitting the ground somewhere nearby.

'Who is there?' he challenged once more, now wishing he had carried his revolver with him. Within seconds he was surrounded. Parman knew instantly what was happening. What a fool he had been! He had left his family unprotected.

The soldiers had been obliged to jump the small iron garden gate as this had been locked by the security guard earlier. At first General Parman was relieved, as he identified the uniform of the Tjakrabirawa Palace Guards. His fears were allayed. He had no way of seeing the Gerwani women soldiers who were hidden, out of sight, in the truck parked outside.

'What are you men doing here?' he demanded to know. The group's leader, Sergeant Major Satar came to attention and saluted convincingly.

'Bapak Djenderal, we have been sent to escort you to the Palace. The

President has asked that you come immediately, as it concerns national security. President Soekarno has instructed us to inform you, sir, that it is very important that you come.' Sergeant Major Satar lied very convincingly. As he peered over the sergeant's shoulder, General Parman briefly caught a glimpse of a man standing there, almost in the shadows. For a moment, Parman thought he recognised the face but then decided that it could not be the same man, as this one wore the 'Tjakra' uniform. He started to call out to him but then hesitated. The man he remembered was still serving in Semarang, with the Diponegoro Divisions. No, he thought, it couldn't be him.

General Parman's role as the most senior Intelligence general often demanded his presence at the oddest of times, and he was accustomed to being called to the Palace by the President. Parman was an exceptionally good officer. He loved his country and remained loyal to his President even though others in the Council did not.

'I will not be long,' he said to the sergeant, turning to re-enter his house while permitting the Tjakrabirawa guards to follow. He believed there was nothing amiss.Two soldiers also entered, their weapons bearing fixed bayonets. Ibu Parman, also awakened by the noise, was shocked by this presumptuous invasion.

'Where are your written orders?' the outspoken woman demanded. She was not accustomed to such behaviour in her home.

'The NCO outside has these, ibu,' they had lied in response.

'Then go and get it for me,' she ordered, but the soldiers did not budge. The soldiers started to follow her around the house. Suddenly her temper flared.

'Why are you following me? Stop this behaviour and leave my home immediately!' she demanded.

'Sudahlah,' the soldier responded, telling her that he would accept no more of her manner. She was shocked.

'What are you doing here,' she cried, alarmed as other soldiers entered the room. Her husband could not hear the exchange as he was in the bathroom washing his face and changing into his dress uniform to meet the President. When he reappeared he sensed that something was gravely wrong. General Parman saw the look of terror growing on his wife's face and he turned to re-enter their bedroom.

'Cigarettes,' he called, searching for an excuse, leaving the room only to be followed by one of the bayonet-wielding soldiers.

'You must hurry,' the soldier insisted. Parman became enraged at the man's insolence.

'Get out of my room! Immediately!' he demanded. When the corporal merely laughed, General Parman knew instantly that his situation was hopeless. He shook his head in dismay.

'Wait outside,' he ordered, but the soldier simply smiled and grabbed him roughly by the arm and escorted the general out of the house. When Parman reached the front door, he turned and looked back at his wife and then smiled.

'Call General Yani and tell him that I have been summoned by the President,' he asked. Immediately his wife moved towards the telephone to do as her husband had instructed. *'Stop!'* Corporal Chairuman cried, as he leapt across the room, smashed the telephone to the floor, then ripped the line from the wall.

'Outside!' the sergeant barked, enjoying the role reversal. Parman stood in the doorway refusing to move further. Corporal Chairuman took two quick steps and hit the general brutally with his rifle stock. As he doubled over, the other soldiers moved to his side and ushered their captive outside.

'No! Please no!' Ibu Parman cried in desperation. What was happening here? How could this be happening to them? Sergeant Major Satar turned and grinned sardonically. He was enjoying all of this.

'We will take good care of the Bapak. Don't you worry, 'bu!' he said, his voice full of sarcasm as he too then marched out into the courtyard to oversee his troops. Ibu Parman followed outside, too scared to cry. She witnessed her husband being thrown into the lead truck.

'Parman! Parman!' she called in desperation after her husband, then fled inside as one of the soldiers turned towards her, hate in his eyes. Before she aware of it, they were gone. The communist contingent sped through the quiet city, on their way back to the place they called Crocodile Hole, where they had planned to detain their captives inside the Halim Airforce Base.

Only minutes had passed when Ibu Harjono suddenly appeared at the Parman residence. Sobbing uncontrollably, she told the terrified Ibu Parman that General Harjono had just been shot and that his body had been taken away. Ibu Parman collapsed.

* * * * * *

0345 Hours

Zach provided support to Murray as they hopped up the Hotel Indonesia steps. They had decided to return there, as the hotel's phones would probably still be working. Zach had suggested that the communists had probably cut all Embassy and other foreign communications, but he doubted if they would have attempted to disrupt the Hotel Indonesia's lines, as this may have alerted others to their game. They went immediately to Susan's room and knocked loudly on her door. Susan looked tired and scared as she opened the door.

'My God!' she gasped, alarmed at their dishevelled appearance. 'What happened?'

'Later, Susan. Later. Just help me get him inside,' Zach said. She held Murray carefully and helped as he hobbled into the room. Murray sat on the bed by the telephone and started dialling. Susan clucked admonishingly, believing that he should at least rest for a while. Murray ignored her and continued with the task at hand. He could remember only a handful of the residential numbers and, in each case, no-one answered. It was just too damn early in the morning, he thought angrily, wishing they had gone to the Embassy where all the numbers were stored.

'Steve, this is no good. I'm not getting anywhere. We have to go to the Embassy and try from there. If the phones are out as you suggest, at least we can grab the staff directory then beat it back here. What do you say?' he asked, pulling himself to his feet, wincing with pain. Zach knew that Murray was in no shape to venture back outside. He would only slow him down.

'You stay here. There's no need for both of us to go. Give me your keys, Murray. Besides, you can't even walk, let alone run.' He looked at Susan and smiled, anticipating her objection. 'I wont be long. Why don't you rustle up some room service for, say, five o'clock, and we'll all have breakfast when I return?' Zach took Susan in his arms briefly and kissed her cheek. She stiffened, then stepped back and lifted his shirt, exposing the P9S automatic. There was a moment of silence in the room as she looked up into his eyes, then turned questioningly towards Murray. Knowing that an explanation would be too difficult, Zach then left, promising to return within the hour.

* * * * * *

Yanti stood alongside the soldier as they prepared to enter General Suprapto's home. She had watched the general's arrival prior to the 'Tjakra' team's departure from Halim.

The procedure was much the same as when General Parman was successfully captured. The team was fortunate that Suprapto had suffered severe toothache through the night and had risen from his bed to paint, as a means of distraction. He was extremely tired.

The team had waited outside where through the windows, they could see Suprapto work until the early hours of the morning on a painting. Yanti knew Suprapto was an artist of some standing. She had seen his work on the walls of the Djakarta Art Gallery and was aware from newspaper reports that he had arranged to have his paintings displayed in the Djogyakarta Museum. At about four o'clock they saw him put down his brushes and retire to his bedroom. They waited, giving the general time to fall to sleep. Then it was time to move.

As the assault team crossed into Suprapto's front yard, the neighbour's dog heard their movements and started to bark. The general awoke with a start. Within moments he was joined by his wife. They peered outside and identified the Tjakrabirawa Palace Guards.

'What are you doing here at this time of the day?' he challenged, calling to the soldiers through the open window.

'The President has instructed us to escort you to the Palace, Pak Djenderal. The President has asked that you come immediately as the situation is urgent.' Suprapto shook his head and made his way down to the front of the house and unlocked the front door. Immediately, he was confronted by Sergeant Sulaiman, the team leader. General Suprapto looked across at the men assembled there and, for a moment, thought he had spotted a familiar face. When he looked again, it was gone.

'Djoko?' he called, but the face had disappeared. What was he doing in Djakarta? he wondered.

The general always obeyed his superiors. His President was the Commander-in-Chief, and had ordered him to the Palace. That was sufficient. He nodded to the sergeant, accepting that he would have to go.

'Wait here,' he ordered, 'I will first change into my uniform.'

'No, there isn't time,' the sergeant insisted and, at that moment, they lowered their bayonets at his stomach.

'What ...' Suprapto called in surprise, but had no further chance to summon help as the soldiers pounced heavily and threw him down. As his head smashed against the marble floor, he uttered a muffled scream.

'Tie him up!' the team leader ordered.

Yanti motioned to the other Gerwani women and they ran forward. The general was hauled outside through his front garden and thrown into the waiting truck. The women climbed aboard, kicking and punching the terrified man until he lost consciousness. Then they drove through the sleeping city and out to the Crocodile Hole in Halim Airforce Base.

The general's wife, alarmed at the commotion, had ventured cautitously back into their living room. Immediately she was confronted by a dozen or more soldiers. Ibu Suprapto didn't hesitate, making a grab for the telephone.

' Kill her!' one of the soldiers shouted, but one of Yanti's troops stepped forward and struck the woman hard, across the face. She fell, then rose and scrambled away from her attackers.

'No! Don't kill me!' she cried, falling to her knees as she tried to escape. The soldier ripped the telephone from its wires and threw it across the room. He looked at his sergeant who shook his head, indicating that the woman was not to be harmed further.

Struggling to her feet, Ibu Suprapto fled back into her bedroom and opened the windows there. Bravely, she leaned out and could see the garden full of soldiers in red berets, wearing the uniform of the Palace Guard.

Ibu Suprapto could not believe the treacherous behaviour of President Soekarno's own personal guards. She watched and listened as the kidnappers departed. When she was certain that they had all left, Ibu Suprapto ran to the front of her house and slammed the doors firmly shut. Her heart was still pounding and she felt faint. Forcing herself to the study, she scribbled a note for General Parman, hoping that he would be able to help her husband who had just been kidnapped from his home. She sealed the envelope and went in search of one of her servants. They lived behind in separate quarters and, surprisingly, seemed to be unaware of what had just transpired. She was about to send one of her servants out into the night when there was a knock at her door.

'Bu?' the voice called, but she did not dare to open the door. Fearing for her life, she refused to answer. Finally, she checked from the upstairs window and was relieved to discover that her caller was alone.

'Who's there?' she asked, unable to see the woman clearly.

'They have killed my husband, Djenderal Harjono!' the woman cried out. Stunned by this news, she hurriedly let Ibu Harjono in and the terrified women clung to each other. Both described the horror which had occurred in their houses.

'There is no use in sending your note to Pak Parman,' Ibu Harjono told General Suprapto's wife. *'He too has been kidnapped.'* The women then locked the doors just in case the soldiers returned to kill them also. After all, they were witnesses.

* * * * * *

0425 Hours

Zach cursed as he sorted through the keys. He had taken a *betjak* from the hotel and arrived at the Embassy in less than ten minutes. As he passed through the front gate, he stopped and gave one of the guards a handful of rupiah and explained where the unguarded Embassy car could be found. Rostered drivers would start their day within the hour and he assumed they would have fuel in the workshop. He then went about unlocking the Embassy, wishing that he had asked Murray to identify which keys he would need, thereby saving precious time.

Zach wasted fifteen minutes making his way into the Consulate section where lists of all staff were pinned to the Consul's inside wall. He commenced dialling, first the Ambassador, then the Counsellor, making his way down the list according to seniority. When a telephone continued to ring unanswered for more than twenty seconds, he moved to the next number on the list. Within twenty minutes, he had managed to contact eleven of the fifteen permanent Embassy officers. Satisfied that there was little else he could achieve, Steven Zach returned to the hotel.

* * * * * *

While the Australian Military Attaché was in the process of alerting Embassy officers, one of the Takari kidnap teams arrived at the home of General Sutojo Siswomihardjo and knocked brazenly on the general's front door. Meanwhile, members of the communist team slipped quietly down the side of his home and seized his houseboy, threatening him with their bayonets. Petrified, the ageing *djongos* unlocked the rear doors which led directly into the main house. General Sutojo heard the noise and went directly to his front door.

'*Who are you?*' he demanded, annoyed that his security had not prevented whoever it was from disturbing him at such an ungodly hour.

'*It's Gondo from Malang,*' the soldier answered. His curiosity aroused, Sutojo foolishly opened the door. He stood there for a moment trying to identify the soldier. Suddenly, he was attacked.

'*What the hell ...!*' Sutojo yelled, as he was seized by two of the kidnappers.

'*Gag him, quickly!*' the team leader ordered, then delivered several punishing blows to the general's head. As they dragged the unconscious general away, Ibu Sutojo emerged from their bedroom, alarmed at the noise. She was terrified, believing that they had been invaded by robbers, a not-uncommon event around the city. At that moment, soldiers entered from the rear of her house. She stood, stunned, as they went about destroying everything in her home.

'*No!*' she cried, as the soldiers moved around the lounge room hurling loose furniture around, ignoring her presence.

'*No!*' Ibu Sutojo cried aloud in anguish,'*not that!*' as one of the men use his rifle butt to destory her prized Ming vase. She collapsed to the floor as the rampage continued. Glasses were smashed, plates thrown to the floor and family pictures destroyed. Ibu Sutojo pleaded with the men to stop, but they ignored her, continuing to smash everything in sight. She ran to the front door only to catch a glimpse of her husband being lifted into one of the two trucks which had brought the kidnappers to her home.

She tried to cry out, but choked in fear as one of their attackers suddenly appeared, menacingly, and pointed his bayonet at her. She listened in silence to the shrill cries of the Gerwani women as they kicked and punched her husband insensible.

Ibu Sutojo moved slowly away from the threatening soldier and turned, re-entering her home. Amidst the incredible scene of soldiers laughing and smashing her prized possessions, she had the presence of mind to slip back into her bedroom and lock the door. There was an extension in her room. She grabbed the phone and dialled. It seemed to ring and ring for ages, unanswered. She was about to place the telephone down when, suddenly, she heard a voice.

'Siapa ini?' someone asked. Immediately Ibu Sutojo held the telephone closer and whispered urgently.

'This is Djenderal Sutojo's wife. Call Bapak Suthardio, quickly! Someone here is trying to kill us!' She had connected to the home of the Minister for Justice, Brigadier General Suthardio, who also acted as the country's Attorney General.

'The Bapak is still ...' Suddenly, as she was speaking to Suthardio's servant, the line was broken. The kidnappers had ripped the wires from the wall in the living room. She sat there in the dark and held her breath, believing she could hear footsteps approaching. Then, after what seemed to be an immeasurable time, there was silence. She waited, listening to what was happening outside her room. Suddenly, she remembered. The children! Ibu Sutojo jumped to her feet and darted from the dark room, hitting furniture as she made her way towards the children's room. She heard a noise. Alarmed, she stopped and listened. Then, deciding that it was safe, she continued on, reaching her children's room safely. There, she was relieved to discover them unharmed. She gathered them together and ran down the road to the Attorney-General's house.

Upon arrival, Sutojo's wife explained to Suthardio what had happened, deposited her children, then hurried off to her other friend's home only to discover that General Parman had also been taken. Ibu Sutojo remained with Ibu Parman and prayed. Their world had been irrevocably destroyed.

* * * * * *

Less than one kilometre away, another Takari team entered General Pandjaitan's front yard and moved to the rear of the two-storey home. There they discovered a connecting pavilion, and attempted to break through the small building's door. Inside there were three young men sleeping. These were the general's nephews.

'What the ...' the oldest called, startled by the noise.

'Open the door!' a voice from outside demanded. The older boys were not impressed. Their uncle was a general. And they had their own guns.

'Who the hell is it?' they demanded, searching around in the darkened room for clothes. The youngest boy buried his head under the sheets of the top bunk where he had been sleeping, as the two older brothers jumped out of their beds. One of the nephews groped in the dark for the revolver he kept hidden in the closet.

'Open this door or we will shoot!' the menacing voice called.

'Go away!' the second eldest called, frightened. 'Don't you know that this is Bapak Djenderal Pandjaitan's house?' As this was followed by a few moments of silence the nephews felt that this had worked. Obviously the men outside were thieves. 'Wait 'til the general's security catches these arseholes!' they sniggered amongst themselves, envisaging their attackers fleeing at the discovery that they had mistakenly attacked such a place. The oldest boy still searched around in the dark for the revolver he had hidden. Where in the hell had he put the bloody thing?.

Before he could arm himself, the door crashed open. Two NCO's stepped inside and opened fire at point-blank range, killing both the young men instantly. The third boy remained hidden, his fear almost giving him away as the soldiers then filed through the pavilion, gaining access to the main house. Meanwhile, several of the soldiers outside fired directly into the upstairs windows, breaking all the glass and smashing the light which had just been switched on. Sergeant Sukardjo led the first assault into the house. He ran to the bottom of the stairs and yelled loudly.

'Bapak Djenderal, you must come downstairs,' Sukardjo ordered. He then took several steps and looked further up into the second storey but couldn't see too much there as the upstairs hallway was in darkness.

'Who are you? What do you want?' General Pandjaitan shouted, his head protruding from the master-bedroom door. The shots had smashed through his room but fortunately only damaged the furnishings. He looked at his wife. She sat on the bed, her hands covering her face in shock. And then he thought of his children. They were in the adjacent bedrooms. His mind raced. His gun was downstairs locked inside his desk.

'General, we have been sent here by the President. You are to come with us immediately.' Sergeant Sukardjo was quickly losing patience and signalled to the others that he would move up the stairs, ordering them to remain below. 'General,' he called again, 'General, we are from the Tjakrabirawa Regiment. The President has instructed us to escort you to the Palace. It is urgent.' Seconds ticked by and there was no response. Sukardjo started moving up the stairs when Pandjaitan suddenly called out, telling them to wait while he changed. More minutes passed and, to their surprise, the general emerged, dressed in his parade uniform complete with medals and ribbons. He walked down the stairs and into the family room. The kidnap team circled the general with their bayonets and in that moment, he knew that he would die.

'Move,' Corporal Dikin ordered, shoving the high-ranking officer roughly towards the open front door. 'I said, move!' the young Corporal screamed, and kicked the general in the knee savagely. Pandjaitan was led out into the front garden where Dikin, with several cruel blows to the back of the general's head, sent him crashing to the ground. Pandjaitan lay there groaning. Dazed, he looked up but instantly knew that these soldiers were there to kill him. As the man attempted to rise to his knees and pray, both the young corporals opened fire with their Thompsons and Stens, shooting at point-blank range. His head exploded, throwing hideous lumps of bone and tissue around the garden. The kidnappers then threw his body over the fence onto the footpath, where others loaded it into the waiting truck. They too then returned to the Halim Airforce Base. Another mission successfully accomplished.

* * * * * *

Over at Lieutenant General Yani's house in Djalan Lembang, soldiers from the Presidential Guard poured into the Chief of Army Staff's driveway, where the general's security guards greeted the kidnappers cordially, recognising the respected Tjakribirawa uniforms. The unsuspecting guards were easily overpowered and the communist team, led by Sergeant Major Raswad, moved directly into the general's house.

Yani's seven-year-old daughter had woken and was in the process of wandering around her home in search of her mother. She had forgotten that the following day would be her mother's birthday, and that Ibu Yani had spent the night in her husband's official residence over at Taman Surapati. The child was the first to encounter the soldiers who had stormed into her home.

'Where is your father?' Sergeant Raswad asked the child. He had a daughter of his own.

'He's still asleep,' the young girl replied, not in the least concerned. Her father was the Army Chief and she was used to soldiers being present in their house at all hours of the day.

'Would you go and wake your father, please,' he coaxed the girl, 'and tell him that Bapak President wishes to speak to him urgently.' She smiled at the soldier and went to her father's room to do as she was asked. Meanwhile, Yani's second daughter had woken, startled by the noises outside. She woke her eleven-year-old brother and, frightened by the strange sounds, they also ran to their father's room.

When General Yani emerged, he was still dressed in his pyjamas. He was furious that someone had so easily compromised his security and entered his home.

'What are you doing in my home?' he yelled at the men as they moved towards him.

'President Soekarno has instructed us to take you to him,' came the rehearsed reply. General Yani was livid. He detected the insolence in the sergeant's manner. He continued to stare angrily at the intruders, then turned to re-enter his room.

'Wait outside. I will bathe first then change,' he ordered. Raswad stepped forward and raised the muzzle of his weapon.

'That won't be necessary,' he sneered, and turned to smile at his comrades just as General Yani stepped closer to the soldier and hit him with all of his strength. The Palace Guard fell heavily to the marble floor. Yani recognised his peril and turned to flee. He ran through the kitchen and managed to reach the rear door when he heard the shouts from behind.

'Gijadi, shoot!' Raswad screamed at his comrade who was blocking the other's line of fire. Immediately, Gijadi opened fire, spraying bullets along the corridor and through the glass doors as the Thompson jerked in his hands. General Yani died instantly, seven of the bullets reaching their target. The children had remained in their father's room, as ordered. Now, huddled together as the sound of machine-gun fire ripped through their home, they trembled in fear and began to cry.

Their father's body was dragged through the house and out through the front door. His blood stained the entire length of the house as the killers carelessly rolled his corpse out into the front yard. Members of the Communist Youth Movement then took over and threw Yani's body into one of the waiting Toyota jeeps. A solitary figure moved out of the deep shadows and climbed into the truck to examine the body. Satisfied, he leaped from the back of the vehicle and vanished back into the night. The sergeant barked at the rest of his troops and they boarded the truck. Then they too returned to their headquarters at Halim.

* * * * * *

0435 Hours

The conspirators were aware that their plan to overthrow the Military could fail if they missed their most important target, Indonesia's most senior and respected general, Abdul Haris Nasution. The man was a legend throughout the country, and was greatly admired by the people of Indonesia. The communists knew that his capture would have to be executed with precision as Nasution was always surrounded by well-disciplined soldiers who would give their lives to protect their national hero. It was for this reason that a full company of soldiers was designated the responsibility of kidnapping this powerful officer, the nation's Minister for Defence.

Before moving on Nasution's home, the kidnappers disarmed soldiers and guards down the road at the Deputy Prime Minister's residence. There, the Tjakrabirawa soldiers encountered resistance, resulting in the death of a senior police officer, Brigadier Satsuit Tubun. The communist soldiers then moved quickly to complete their mission, disarming Nasution's own guards and forcing their way into his home. The intruders smashed their way through doors and windows in search of the general. Ibu Nasution urged her husband to flee immediately and, reluctantly, he hurried out through the rear of their home and into a neighbouring yard, where he hid behind the pump house. The residence was protected by diplomatic privilege, being the home of one of the Iranian Charge d'Affaires in Djakarta.

Moments later, the Tjakrabirawa soldiers opened fire, shattering the bedroom door behind which Nasution's wife hid in terror. A hail of bullets tore through the wooden louvered door but, incredibly, Ibu Nasution remained unharmed.

The nanny screamed in terror as the entire house exploded with the sounds of machine-gun fire. She grabbed the child and ran through the house, screaming as bullets punctured the walls and ceilings. Several finally found their mark as the woman fell, still holding the little girl tightly in her arms. Corporal Hargijono's orders had been to kill the general. Instead, three of his bullets ripped through the five-year-old girl's tiny frame, tearing through flesh and bone as they exited, breaking her spine. The nanny was wounded, two of the bullets passing through her hand before entering the child she had tried to protect. Irma Surjani Nasution died instantly, her young life snuffed out even before she had seen her sixth birthday.

In a small pavilion located at the rear of the house, two officers leaped from their beds, startled by the sounds of gunfire. Both men were Nasution's adjutants and were quartered there in the small building.

Lieutenant Tendean ran outside, armed with his revolver, while Hamdan, his police offsider, remained inside still searching for his weapon. The Army adjutant was immediately confronted by the Palace Guard troops and disarmed. Suddenly, an unfamiliar officer appeared and took charge. He looked at the adjutant's face and smiled. Tendean bore a remarkable resemblance to Nasution, and in the dark yard he was mistakenly taken for his superior. He was immediately arrested and dragged outside, where he was bound and placed on the floor of the team leader's jeep. Satisfied that they had captured General Nasution, the soldiers drove their prisoner directly to Halim, believing that Operation Takari had been successfully completed. The Council of Generals had been destroyed. Indonesia was now in the hands of the communists.

Concealed behind the overgrown structure built over his neighbour's well, Nasution thought he recognised the voice of the officer who had appeared and ordered the arrest of his adjutant. He shook his head, confused. It had sounded like Djoko! But he knew this could not be. The Diponegoro officer was supposed to be in Semarang, looking after things in Central Java. As he sat alone, the cold realisation of what was really happening suddenly occurred to him. He closed his eyes and prayed, shocked that he had been betrayed. Nasution then knew, that if he was to survive, he dare not reveal his whereabouts to anyone.

* * * * * *

Lubang Buaja -Halim Alirforce Base, 0530 Hours

The atmosphere surrounding the return of the last contingent was euphoric, as the team leaders gathered to see Nasution. The other captives, Generals Parman, Sutojo, Suprapto and Lieutenant Tendean had been tied together, and placed alongside the bodies of the other generals, Harjono, Pandjaitan and the Army Chief of Staff, General Yani, whose bloody corpse remained dressed in pyjamas.

Their success had driven the Gerwani women into a frenzy. Someone had produced a bottle of *arak*, a dangerously overproof extract derived from palm fruit, and toasted the success of the 30th September Movement and their comrades. Exaggerated tales of bravery and cunning were swapped around the fire as news of each successful kidnapping was announced. One by one, the units returned carrying bodies or prisoners. The bodies of the three dead generals had been laid out for all to see. Some of the Gerwani women, intoxicated by the deadly mixture of *arak* and the euphoria of bloody success, danced around the fire's flames laughing, singing, and mocking the once powerful men before them. Then, as the occasion deteriorated even further, the women began to chant, and shout obscenities at their prisoners.

Yanti walked proudly amongst her troops as they enjoyed their moment of triumph. The *arak* had helped. As she swallowed her first sip and felt the fire touch her insides, Yanti let out a yell of joy, and danced around with her friends as they shared the bottle of powerful spirits. Very few of their number had ever taken alcohol before. Someone added more fuel to the bonfire around which more than two hundred had gathered to celebrate the mission, the first step in achieving their Party's goals.

The prostrate forms of the three dead generals seemed to bother no-one. Some of the women, in unaccustomed alcoholic frenzy, tore their clothes away and danced, naked. An older woman spat on the corpse closest to where she stood and her friends laughed, teasing her that she was still frightened of the dead, whereapon she stepped forward quickly and kicked the body to prove that she was not afraid. The others laughed and so did she, warmed by the alcohol and the camaraderie. Another women, not to be outdone, took one of the soldier's bayonets from his scabbard and drove the steel blade into the dead man's chest. For a moment there was silence as they watched the woman extract the blade and hold the bayonet up for them to see.

Yanti did not like the way the mood was changing and held her breath in apprehension. Suddenly a loud cheer filled the early morning air as the women scrambled to see who could desecrate the other bodies first. Within moments there was pandemonium as they struggled with each other to see who could do the most damage. They kicked and pushed, tore at each other's eyes, screamed obscenities and even drew blood as teeth sank deep into an adversary's limb. Yanti could see that they had lost control. There was only one thing that she could do. The violence was escalating dangerously quickly as some of the soldiers joined in the melee when Yanti's shot rang out, bringing the violence to an end.

'Why are you doing this to each other?' she screamed angrily, still holding the gun in her shaking hand. 'They're the ones who are your enemy,' Yanti yelled loudly pointing at the three men who had been tied and gagged then left to await their own fate. Lieutenant Tendean, the officer who had been mistaken for General Nasution, watched the young woman walk across to where he lay. The camp was suddenly silent. Tendean shuddered at the sound of the metallic click as the hammer of the revolver was slowly pulled back into place. He closed his eyes and whispered a prayer. Then he heard the whispering metallic sound of the action as Yanti pulled the Colt .38 trigger, sending the hammer roaring back into contact with the cartridge.

The bullet's impact brought an immediate roar of approval from her comrades. Yanti believed she had executed the country's most powerful solider, General Nasution. She threw the weapon to one of her team, who walked across and pointed the gun at the other prisoners. The young woman teased by pointing the gun first at one, then another, then shot General Parman through the eye. The communist soldiers and women roared again, and joined in the executions of the last two captives, Suprapto and Sutojo. The two remaining generals were trampled, beaten and gouged to death as the women fought over who would deliver the final blow to the former Military leaders.

The frenzy continued as the generals' bodies were further mutilated. Finally they were carried across the yard and thrown into the deep dry well behind the Gerwani billet. And then, as suddenly as they had started, the celebrations ceased.

* * * * * *

Lieutenant General Nasution was not aware that his six year old daughter had died in the attack. As the main body of communist soldiers departed, Nasution continued to hide in his neighbour's yard. He could still see Tjakrabirawa soldiers wandering around nearby. Reports of the attack on his home finally reached the Fifth Military Area Commander, General Umar Wirahadikusumah, who despatched a number of light tanks to the scene. It was not until well after six o'clock that Nasution was able to move to a safer location, assisted by Lieutenant Colonel Hidajat Wirasondjaja. Less than an hour later, he heard the radio broadcasts announcing the coup, and Nasution immediately contacted the Strategic Reserves Commander, Major General Soeharto, who had just arrived at his own headquarters along Merdeka Square. Immediately, Soeharto went in search of his President. But Soekarno was nowhere to be found.

Chapter 21

One could not blame a casual observer for thinking that nothing had really changed in the capital. Clouds cleared and the sun rose over Djakarta while its inhabitants went about their chores, as they had for as long as they could remember. The communist forces had taken several strategic locations around the city, successfully occupying the radio, television and other communication stations even before first prayers had been called for the day. Captain Soeradi's communist soldiers had taken most of the strategic buildings around Merdeka Square, without any real resistance.

The two Australians had hired a pirate taxi from outside the hotel and instructed the driver to take them down town. At first, Murray could not see anything which would indicate that a military coup d'etat was well under way until Zach pointed at the two Armed Personnel Carriers of British origin positioned where they could control all traffic moving towards Radio Republik Indonesia, the national broadcast station.

'First time I've seen them bring out the Saracens, Zach whispered, indicating the two APC's. 'The Brits would be pleased to see their export drive making inroads at last,' he joked weakly. They were tired.

'Over there,' he said, pointing across Murray's side of the car. 'Soviet APCs,' he said. 'They're fully amphibious,' Zach added, making a face, then indicated to the driver that he should slow down. They drove past the Soviet BTR-50Ps and Murray could see at least half a dozen soldiers standing ready, inside the open top.

'They're new additions too,' Zach commented, nodding in the direction of the pile of sandbags which had been stacked around what appeared to be a heavy machine-gun battery. Murray squinted through the window, his vision slightly impaired by the early morning sun. 'You wouldn't want to be in their line of fire,' Zach continued. 'Those Czech guns spew out 12.7 mm bullets at a rate of eighty rounds per minute. And they have four barrels.' Zach then scratched his head. 'They're mainly used for anti-aircraft purposes,' he said, 'doesn't make much sense having them here unless it's mainly for show.' Murray knew that the Military Attaché was suggesting that the Indonesian Airforce would not attack the communist position. They then attempted to drive around the National Monument but were prevented from doing so. Soldiers had begun to blockade the western access to the Square.

'Communists?' Murray asked, unable to determine which faction was in control of the military there. Zach stared across at the men in uniform and shook his head.

'Impossible to tell.' Zach went on. 'They could be Government forces but I'm not sure. Let's drive down towards the Palace and see what's happening there.' Murray agreed, and ordered the driver to turn into Djalan Veteran then down Djalan Nusantara towards the Presidential Palace.

The driver followed their directions, taking the tuans past the Palace before turning into the main arterial road which led down Kota, Djakarta's Chinatown. The traffic had already become congested here as thousands of bicycles and *betjak* joined the vehicles thronging the narrow road.

Zach noticed that the foreign mainland Chinese community had wasted little time in commencing celebrations for their national day. Red Chinese flags, signalling the beginning of the October First Chinese anniversary activities, had already been raised along most of Djalan Hajam Wuruk and, as the morning sea breeze floated in from the north, the colourful flags danced. Satisfied that all appeared normal around the old city quarter, Murray then instructed the driver to take them out to the Senajan Sports Stadium. They were surprised to discover that the scene here too appeared normal. The tens of thousands of troops had already risen and were casually attending to their early morning ablutions as the Australians drove slowly by.

'It almost seems as if someone has forgotten to tell them what's going on,' Murray remarked. Everything just seemed too normal. He checked the time and suggested they go to the Embassy. Zach agreed, stopping off at his villa for a quick shower and change of clothes while Murray made his way to his own house to do likewise. The driver turned off Djalan Iman Bondjol and into Tjik Ditiro, then stopped. Murray could see that the road had been barricaded where it intersected with his street, Djalan Serang. There were soldiers running around everywhere, fully armed and looking very menacing. He told the driver to wait, climbed out of the taxi and started limping in the direction of the junction where he had almost been shot just hours before. As he approached the corner, two soldiers jumped forward and pointed their weapons directly at his chest. Murray sighed. His ankle hurt, his head ached, and the last thing he needed then was to be refused entry to his own home.

'I live in that house over there,' he told the soldiers, pointing at his villa.

'What is your name? Which country are you from?' was the terse demand. Murray could see that these men were agitated, armed, and ready to fire. So, tired as he was, Murray forced a smile.

'I'm Australian. I work at the Embassy. That is my home over there. Please let me through.' The soldiers were still not sure. One of them turned and went in search of an officer, returning with his Captain. Murray repeated what he'd just explained to the other soldier and, accompanied by the officer, was escorted down the street into his villa.

Exhausted, he dragged himself slowly into the house where his surprised servants fussed over him. They had been worried about their *tuan* when they too discovered what had occurred along their street just hours before. He stripped and bathed, standing uncomfortably on one leg, but enjoying the luxury of the luke-warm shower. Murray closed his eyes. He could still visualise the soldiers running after them, shooting wildly as both he and Zach ran for their lives. He wondered how the generals had all fared, and how many of those on the list he had seen had been able to defend themselves or avoid whatever the communists had planned for them. As the dull ache across his temples slowly disappeared, Murray felt the waves of fatigue take over. He limped from the shower and towelled himself dry in the airconditioned bedroom, then sat naked on the soft, cool double bed. Before he was aware of what was happening, he placed his head on the tempting feather pillows and closed his eyes for a moment's rest. Exhausted, he fell deeply asleep, unaware that Zach had been trying to contact him by telephone.

As he waited for Murray to return, Zach listened to Djakarta's central radio station and caught the broadcast announcing Untung's successful arrest of the entire Council of Generals. Unable to communicate this information due to the disrupted telephone system, Zach left a message with his own servants for when Murray returned, then left his residence and hailed a *betjak* to take him to the Embassy. Zach had little doubt that once foreign governments were alerted to the dangerous turn of events, many, including the Australian Forces, would go immediately onto full war alert. As Military Attaché, his presence in the Embassy would be crucial to the decision-making process which would undoubtedly follow. He would catch up with the Station Chief later.

* * * * * *

0700 Hours

Djakarta's inhabitants had no idea that there had been an attempted coup d'etat until Radio Republik Indonesia's early morning broadcasts announced that Lieutenant Colonel Untung had arrested several high-ranking Army officers. The surprise announcement went on to advise that Untung had initiated these steps to pre-empt similar action by the Council of Generals themselves. The capital was stunned to discover that those responsible, acting under the banner of the 30th September Movement, had already taken control of many strategic positions in and around the city. The station's listeners were then advised that there would be a Revolutionary Council established to take control of government. A decree was then issued, the first of several, abolishing the Dwikora Cabinet and demanding that all officers who previously held the rank of lieutenant colonel or higher, write immediately to the Revolutionary Council, pledging their loyalty to the new authority.

It became apparent that the communists had successfully executed their coup d'etat and were now in full control of the city, if not the whole country. As the capital's population became aware of the ramifications relating to the communist take-over, so did the rest of the world. Communication centres around the globe became alive with the news that the world's fifth largest population had suddenly fallen under the control of Chairman Aidit and his Communist Party.

The Naval Chief Petty Officer had arrived at the Embassy and immediately realized from the activity that he should have maintained contact. He was rushed into the radio room where he was greeted by a mountain of priority signals requiring immediate despatch. The Chief threw himself into the task and, within five minutes, no less than five listening stations had caught his signals. The first of these was an Army NCO who was about to go off shift from what had been another relatively boring night at his station in 7 Signals Regiment in Toowoomba. He was looking forward to the weekend and, when he picked up the tiny radio beeps, he looked around the section quickly, believing at first that someone was playing a prank. Then he wrote the code down quickly. The signal had been designated 'FLASH' in terms of priority. As the entire text became clear, the corporal tore the message from his pad and raced this quickly to the officer on duty who grabbed the red telephone, and within seconds was communicating directly with the Director of Military Intelligence in Melbourne.

Around the world, signals intelligence intensified as, station by station, codes were decyphered and verification was sought of the alarming news. In Singapore, all leave was cancelled as the British Forces went directly to full alert. The Vulcan bombers, having returned but a few hours before from a run over the archipelago, were refuelled and sent back into the air as the crews awaited further instructions. At Butterworth in Malaysia, the RAAF went to red alert status, as the squadron of Sabres was moved out of the hangars. RAAF Central Command in Canberra flashed signals around the country placing Australia's limited Airforce, too, on red alert. A squadron of Mirage jets left the ground from Williamstown and headed directly for Darwin.

The United States Airforce Commander at Clarke Field read his revised orders for the day and swore. They had already scheduled fifteen more flights into 'Nam for the day and now he had been asked to place one squadron on stand-by in the event that these B-52's may be required to strike at the Madiun Airforce Base where the Indonesian TU-16's sat threateningly, ready for flight. By 0900 hours, the West was ready. All that remained was to wait and see which way the communists would move.

* * * * * *

1000 Hours

Those few members of the Communist planning committee who understood something of military strategy had always suspected that their only weakness would be the lack of experienced military leadership within their ranks, once the coup had commenced. Their initial putsch had, indeed, been relatively successful, considering that many units committed earlier had failed to appear. As the morning progressed, the Communists were elated to discover that they had, in fact, achieved control. Radio broadcasts convinced the populace that the PKI had taken over the Government, and Military Commanders throughout the country waited for orders as confusion continued, due to the loss of their most senior officers. Communist elements within regional Military posts moved quickly to establish control, removing officers and disarming those who were not supportive of the 30th September Movement. And then, due to lack of direction, the Communists vacillated.

Chairman Aidit had always believed that, once his forces had established control over strategic targets within the capital and arrested or removed the members of Nasution's Council, the President would then throw his support behind their Movement and the battle would be won. When Soekarno left his wife Dewi's house in Selipi that morning, he drove directly to the Halim Airforce Base to meet with the coup leaders. He remained there throughout the morning and it was at this time that he was informed that Operation Takari had not been as successful as was first reported. Reluctantly, the communist officers revealed to Soekarno that they had mistakenly kidnapped one of Nasution's adjutants, believing that the officer was in fact the four-star general.

The President was livid. Immediately, he knew that the communists could not win, as Nasution could easily rally the Army behind him and, once this happened, he had no doubt that his old foe would initiate steps to remove him as President. Soekarno decided to cut his and the PKI's losses. He ordered General Soepardjo to cease all military action in support of the coup to avoid further bloodshed. The general refused, knowing that once a military operation lost momentum, it would most certainly fail. Many within the PKI leadership elected to ignore the President's demands, although Colonel Untung feared that by doing so the Communists could not achieve the level of support they desperately needed to maintain control. The Revolutionary Council entered into heated debate and, incredibly, the leadership collapsed and the coup fell into limbo.

Untung believed that not having captured General Nasution was the major contributing factor behind his President's failure to continue support for their cause. In consequence, he despatched elements from the 530th Battalion to return to the city and search for the missing general. Soekarno then announced the appointment of a caretaker Chief of Army Staff, naming Major General Pranoto to replace Yani. The President believed that he could trust Pranoto as the man was known to have close relationships with the PKI leadership. Before six o'clock that afternoon, another decree was broadcast advising that the President was well, and had assumed leadership of the Armed Forces as well. A signed copy of this decree and that of General Pranoto's appointment was then sent by messenger to the Strategic Reserve Forces' Commander, Major General Soeharto.

Soeharto was advised that the President required the presence of Pranoto immediately, at Halim. Although Soeharto was junior to Pranoto, he was the KOSTRAD Commander and refused to permit the officer to leave, resulting in a stand-off. Thirty minutes later, still suffering from the shock of his daughter's death and his spirit near broken, Nasution arrived at the KOSTRAD headquarters. He had remained hidden in the home of his neighbour, the Iranian Charge de Affaires until he was satisfied that it was safe to venture outside these premises which were protected by diplomatic privelege. But before leaving this sanctuary, he held secret talks with members of the American Embassy whom he had alerted as to his predicament. It was the Americans who later informed him of his daughter's demise.

At KOSTRAD Headquarters, Nasution discussed the tense situation with Soeharto. They had both been informed that the

President had summoned others to join him at Halim, in a show of solidarity. Helicopters had arrived carrying the Minister and Chief of Police, Inspector General Sutjipto Judodihardjo and the Minister and Chief of Naval Staff, Admiral Martadinata. There were others too, who had heeded their President's call, including the Deputy Prime Minister, Dr. Leimena. It was obvious to Nasution and Soeharto that these men were communist supporters, and that their presence was an attempt to consolidate the PKI's power.

An hour later, an ultimatum was delivered to the communist forces at Halim to either surrender, or prepare to be attacked by the full might of Soeharto's Strategic Reserve Forces Command. The message was ignored. Soeharto then sent one of the President's adjutants with a letter in which he advised that he, and not Pranoto, would assume leadership of the Army. Soeharto also advised Soekarno that he should deal only through him, and that it would be best if Soekarno left Halim immediately as KOSTRAD was preparing to attack the communist forces at the Airforce base.

Major General Soeharto then ordered the RPKAD, the Army's Paratroop Regiment, to retake and occupy all positions which had fallen to the communists. In less than an hour, Soeharto's soldiers had routed the enemy forces and retaken the radio, television and other communication centres. The coup was all but over. Soekarno reiterated his demands that the communists cease any further attempts to take control, and then left Halim before it came under attack. The Airforce Chief of Staff, Air Marshall Omar Dhani attempted to convince Soekarno to follow him to Central Java but the President refused, recognising that he should remain close to the capital. Just before midnight on the first day of the failed coup d'etat, President Soekarno left Halim Airforce Base by car and was driven directly to the Bogor Summer Palace. Upon arrival, his adjutant phoned General Soeharto who acknowledged the President's whereabouts. Soeharto then moved on the collapsing communist forces at Halim. He attacked at 0300 hours on the morning of the second day of October, less than twenty-four hours after the communists had made their first move on the Council of Generals.

Just one hour before the Government forces attacked, the Chairman of the Indonesian Communist Party, Comrade Aidit, climbed aboard an AURI aircraft and fled Halim Airforce Base, for Djogyakarta in Central Java, leaving behind remnants of his shattered dream for a communist state. Brigadier General Supardjo proposed that their forces remain and defend Halim, to the death, against Nasution and Soeharto. Air Marshall Omar Dhani suggested to Colonel Untung and his right hand man, Latief, that AURI and the 30th September Movement integrate their forces to protect Halim, but the Airforce Chief was left alone as Untung and Latief fled, also to Central Java. The dispirited soldiers watched in dismay as their officers deserted, many changing into civilian dress as they fled from the Halim camp known as Lubang Buaja, the Crocodile Hole, where Yanti and her Gerwani troops remained, ready to fight.

* * * * * *

1100 Hours

Murray woke with a start, his heart racing as he sat upright in the bed.

'Tuan Mahree, bangun! You must wake up!' the voice called, somewhere in the back of his brain. Suddenly he realised that it was the *djongos* calling from outside his bedroom door. He jumped out of bed quickly and tore the door open, not quite knowing what to expect. His ankle throbbed painfully.

'Tuan, there is a driver outside. You must go to the Embassy now, it is urgent,' his houseboy explained, concerned that he had woken the tuan when he so obviously needed rest. Murray thanked the man, threw water quickly over his face and changed. He looked at his watch and swore loudly. On his way through the house he checked the phone and found that the lines were still out of order. Murray hobbled out to the waiting car and climbed in as the driver gunned it recklessly. It wasn't until they'd reached the corner that Murray realised the barricades were gone. He turned quickly, and observed that the street which had been full of soldiers just hours before, was now deserted.

He ordered the driver to stop, then reverse the vehicle back down the street. The driver slowed when they came up to his gates, thinking the tuan may have forgotten something, but Murray insisted that they continue backing down the narrow street past his own villa. When they came to where General Harjono lived, Murray ordered the driver to stop. From inside where he sat, he inspected the area surrounding Harjono's house. It was deserted.

'*Sudah pergi, tuan, semua,*' the driver said, explaining that the occupants had all vacated the villa. Murray thought about this for several moments then instructed the driver to return to the Embassy. During the short time he had slept, life in the city had moved on, and quickly, he observed. The general's family must have been moved. Murray then realized that this would explain why security had suddenly disappeared from his street. He looked at the driver and smiled dryly, remembering just how quickly information passed through the drivers' network. He took advantage of this to bring himself up to date on events as they made their way to the Embassy.

The Embassy was alive with activity as officers scurried around their sections, yelling at each other, frustrated by the congested communications system, and the absence of many of the local staff who had opted to remain home with their families. The Consul waddled around officiously calling out to all, reminding them of the standing orders governing behaviour during such crises. It was his responsibility to contact all registered members of the Australian community and warn them of the dangers of leaving their homes. The telephones were a disaster and, in the absence of sufficient drivers to convey messages by car, the Consul had no idea how he could carry out his duties effectively.

'Oh, Murray,' he called, spotting the First Secretary on his way through the lobby. 'You are wanted in the Ambassador's office. There is a prayer session under way,' he said, checking his watch as he spoke, 'and they've been at it for more than an hour already.'

'Damn!' Murray muttered under his breath, changed direction and went straight to where the other senior Attachés had gathered. The Ambassador's secretary spotted him approaching and rose from her desk to escort him into the meeting.

'You're very late,' she whispered as he smiled tiredly at her.

'Slept in again,' he said, grinning, knowing that she would not believe this possible at this time.

The secretary knocked softly, then opened the door permitting Murray to enter the inner sanctum. All heads turned as he limped in, acknowledging his presence with a nod or a mumbled greeting. The Ambassador peered over the top of his glasses at the man he disliked most in the entire Embassy.

'Where have you been? All departments were advised of this meeting more than two hours ago,' the Ambassador complained. Murray deliberately ignored the senior public servant and apologised instead to the others.

'Sorry gentlemen,' he said, 'have I missed much?' Zach jumped to his defence.

'I can fill you in later. Right now we are trying to assess where we're at, in terms of the communists' strengths and whether or not they will be able to hold onto the gains they've made. As Army Attaché, I have to say that I'd never have believed it possible for the communists to take the city as quickly as this.' The colonel pointed to the map of Djakarta on which some of the known communist positions had been marked. 'What is surprising,' he went on, 'is that there has been no apparent counter-attack from any of the TNI forces. It's almost as if there is no opposition.' He then looked at Murray and, recognising the signal, passed the floor to him.

'Gentlemen, the lack of opposition is probably a result of Government troops not having commanders.' He had their attention. Even the Ambassador frowned, confused by the statement. 'There is strong evidence to suggest that the communists have been very clever indeed. I believe that they first moved to remove most of the Military's senior officers even before occupying these positions in the city,' he nodded in the direction of the map. There was a brief silence as those present considered his opinion. Then the Consul spoke.

'What evidence would that be, Murray?' he asked. Murray cleared his throat before answering.

'Our intelligence suggests that the PKI made a move late last night to arrest members of Nasution's Council of Generals, and perhaps other high-ranking officers as well. We know there was an attempt on General Harjono's life during the early hours of this morning. There is sufficient evidence to suggest that others, including Nasution himself, could already be in communist hands.' Murray turned to the Military Attaché. 'Wouldn't this account for the fact that there has been no response from the Government troops? Why hasn't Nasution appeared to reassure the public, and where is their Army Chief, Yani?'

They considered what the Station Chief said. Was it possible? It sounded highly improbable that such senior officers could be taken as easily as Murray suggested. Some voiced doubts.

'The radio broadcasts confirm that the communists are in control of communications, radio, television and lord knows what else. If Yani and Nasution are still around, why don't they just take those positions back?' Murray repeated, feeling a sense of frustration at the inability of the others to understand what was happening. There was a knock at the door and the secretary interrupted.

'Group Captain,' she said, addressing the Air Attaché, 'I have been asked by your Assistant, Sergeant Cooke, to advise you that there has been a further broadcast from Radio Indonesia. He says that the general text of the message is another Revolutionary Council decree stating that the ...' she hesitated, checking her notes, 'ah, the Dwikora Cabinet has been declared officially disbanded, and that the Communist Party has President Soekarno at Halim. The President is reported to be safe and well, and continues to direct the affairs of the Government on behalf of the people.' She finished reading the message, then slipped quietly away.

'Seems that Soekarno has thrown his lot in with the Communists,' the Counsellor suggested, breaking the silence. The others in the room merely nodded, considering the enormous implications of this information. They all knew that the situation was bloody serious. Soekarno's open support for the Communists against his own Military could tear the country apart. In the light of this news they discussed, for some time, the final format of a communiqué to be sent to Canberra, the essence of which contained the respective opinions and recommendations of the joint military Attaché's, diplomatic and political sections. A final draft was circulated early in the afternoon and Zach and Murray, who had eaten nothing all day, sent one of the drivers out to buy *nasi goreng* with *sate*. They ate the roadside food straight from the banana leaf packets, understanding the risks, but too preoccupied to care. As the afternoon progressed, the mass of intelligence matter had grown. They remained huddled together, listening to communist radio broadcasts while they re-examined the data from reports flowing in from friendly stations around the globe. Hours passed without the men becoming conscious that night had fallen. Zach suddenly said something which caught Murray by surprise.

'They've blown it, Murray! The communists have lost the initiative. Look at this!' he said, showing Murray the British Embassy report compiled by their own Defence Attachés. It showed quite clearly that, having ensconced themselves in the major centres, the Communists had done nothing with their military gains and had, in fact, withdrawn from several strategic locations due to lack of logistic support. The coup was already crumbling. British listening stations in Singapore and Malaysia confirmed that the Indonesian Army signal traffic had been sent in clear language, and most indicated that the Strategic Forces along with the Army's para-commandoes were preparing a counter attack. It seemed to be an incredible turnaround in just a few hours. What would happen now? Another hour passed as they mulled over possible outcomes. Finally Murray leaned back in his chair and rubbed his face vigorously. He was tired. And annoyed.

There had been nothing back from Central Plans and he could not understand why. The city's postal communication services had all but collapsed but the Embassy still had its radio channel open. ASIS traffic would have been awarded first priority, Murray knew. There had been no response whatsoever from down south and he was annoyed with the breakdown in communications. He was surprised to see that it was already well into the evening. Murray gazed across at his companion. Zach looked like he had not slept for days.

'That's it,' Murray said, pushing his chair back from the desk and stretching. 'I'm away from here. Do you want a lift down to the hotel?' he asked, hoping Zach would refuse. There were no drivers available and he really did not want to be stuck entertaining Susan. Steven Zach smiled and said nothing. He too stood, stretched and then smothered a yawn. He placed his hand on Murray's shoulder, then left the building. It was almost midnight, too late to telephone Susan. Zach went home to catch up on some well-deserved sleep.

Murray followed not far behind the colonel as he too signalled a *betjak*. He listened as they moved slowly along the street where Zach had saved his life just the evening before, amazed that so much had happened in such a short time, and without leaving any signs of what had transpired. As the *betjak* driver turned into Djalan Serang, it seemed impossibly quiet. Murray climbed down from his ride and looked in amazement down the deadly silent street.

He had lived in Indonesia long enough to know that violence lay waiting, just below the fragile surface. The *betjak* peddled away with an occasional clang as the driver warned others of his presence. His gaze then returned to the scene where he had almost lost his life. Twice. Then he looked back down towards General Harjono's deserted home and wondered if, in the future, anyone would remember that this street had been the scene of the start of the Communists' attempt to seize control of the country.

* * * * * *

1600 Hours

The Gerwani women had slept well into late morning, by which time the euphoria of earlier events had passed away. Hungover and tired, Yanti and her colleagues moved around slowly, listlessly, almost without direction as the general mood throughout the camp changed to one of deep depression. The women experienced an emptiness as they waited for word from their leaders that it was time for them to leave their camp and return to their homes. But, as the day progressed, the word never came. Instead, they watched in disbelief as their President came, then left, and their leaders argued amongst themselves. Night came and, to their dismay, they were suddenly urged to flee. Until that moment, Yanti and the others had no idea that their coup had failed. By the time they were alerted to the fact that Government forces were on their way, it was already too late for many of their number. When the Red Berets attacked, dozens of the young Gerwani girls were simply bayoneted to death as the soldiers stormed through. The brutal attack lasted less than three hours and, as the first rays pierced the dull morning sky, it was all over.

When it was obvious that they were doomed, Yanti had escaped with a small group of her friends along the very same path that she had taken the day before. She led the three young women across the fields, away from the onslaught of Soeharto's forces. The women had discarded their uniform jackets and made their way along the airfield perimeter fence, to an area where Yanti knew it would be safe to hide. There the group remained all through the day, terrified that they would be discovered. Night fell. They had been without food and water since the bloody festivities of the night before. Under cover of darkness, they made their way towards a small group of huts occupied by itinerant workers, and begged for food, but were turned away. Yanti suggested that they separate and make their own way back to their villages as best they could. Two of the girls agreed but the third clung to Yanti, refusing to leave. She had no place to go and insisted on staying with her leader.

The two walked through the night. They had no money, no food, and were in danger of being arrested at any moment by any one of the many passing military vehicles. Their world had been turned upside down and they were lost, with nowhere to go and no-one to go to. And then Yanti made her decision. It would be a long walk, almost twenty more kilometres, but she knew there was little choice. The pair set out together and headed into the city. Yanti knew, that providing they walked through the night, it was possible to reach their destination before morning and, hopefully, before he went to the office. She took her companion by the arm and started to walk, hoping that Murray would not be too upset that she had brought a friend.

* * * * * *

1700 Hours

Susan was in two minds about having missed the flight. She wanted to go but did not wish to leave Steven behind. What had been annoying though, she felt, was being left alone at the hotel. There was little else to do except sit around the swimming pool and eat. When Steven finally managed to call, their conversation was abruptly disconnected by the operator. Susan had finally given up in frustration and left a message with both the operator and reception that she could be located at the pool. By late afternoon she was bored and a little put out that neither Steven nor Murray had made any further attempt to contact her again.

There had been little information available as to what the latest developments were, outside in the streets. Susan decided that she would wait and hear what it had all been about, first hand, once Steven arrived. She ordered another gin and tonic and settled back to enjoy the afternoon rays as the sun galloped on its way to the west. At six o'clock she showered, changed and returned to the lobby, then settled down in the Baris Lounge Bar to wait. By late evening, Susan was more than a little tipsy and decided to return to her room, bored and annoyed with her most monotonous day. All in all, Susan felt, she could not have been abandoned in a more unexciting place. She fell asleep, not knowing that at that precise moment, Major General Soeharto's troops had left the city, and were, at that very moment, on their way to place their stamp on Halim.

And history.

Chapter 22

Friday 2nd October

Yanti told her friend to be quiet. She knew that soon the morning light would remove the advantage of darkness so they hurried through the city's outskirts, along the secondary roads, arriving at last at Tjikini. Yanti knew that their clothing would probably be enough to warrant closer inspection should they be spotted by the roving military police. She warned her friend, Erika, to be quiet as a foot patrol passed nearby.

When she considered it safe, Yanti grabbed her tired friend's wrist, dragging her across the railway crossing and down the street following the canal. If necessary, Yanti was prepared to throw herself over into the filthy *kali* to avoid arrest. They continued along the street, conscious of the aggressive looks from the many itinerants who lived along the canal's banks. Yanti had counted on their presence, prepared to move amongst their number to disguise their own presence if they should encounter passing patrols. She knew that if they were stopped and questioned, it would be all over for them. They had thrown all of their identification away, knowing that these would most certainly incriminate them if they were caught.

They arrived, exhausted, outside Murray's house just as the night *djaga* was leaving his security post to return home. Yanti held her friend's hand and waited for the servant to pedal off down the street. Then they slipped into the grounds, moving down the side of the building, using the servants' access to the kitchen and laundry area. Yanti knew that the servants did not like her, probably due to Ade's influence. It was still early and Yanti knew that the cook would not have arrived for work, and the other servant who slept behind the laundry would still be asleep.

She opened the side door which was always left unlocked to permit the servants access into the main house. Yanti held her finger to her mouth urging Erika to be silent. Then, opening the interconnecting door to the main guest room, she peered inside.

Satisfied that there were no others present, she then tugged her friend's hand, and went inside. She whispered to Erika to remain where she was, then carefully opened the door leading into Murray's room. As she slowly opened the door, and slipped through the narrow space she had created for herself, Yanti felt the rush of cold air from the air-conditioned room.

The force of the blow as Murray's fist smashed through the darkness almost ripped her head from the rest of her body. The impact threw Yanti back into the wall, knocking her unconscious. She collapsed to the floor. Seconds passed, and Murray had already jumped back waiting for what might follow. He heard someone running towards his bedroom and, as the footsteps approached, he flung the door open quickly, then slammed it shut, with the full force of his body. He felt the heavy door wobble, almost springing back on itself. He heard the muffled cry of pain, and pulled the door back open quickly, ready to kick at whoever was there.

The crumpled body of a girl lay unconscious where she had fallen. Murray, nonplussed at the sight, moved back behind the doorway, listening for any other attackers who might be following. He knelt down in the semi-darkness, moving his hands over the first intruder's body. Surprised, he rose and flicked the light switch.

'Yanti! What the...' Quickly, he scooped Yanti's unconscious body up and placed her on his bed. Then he reopened the bedroom door and examined the other young woman lying there. He lifted her too, and placed her alongside Yanti on the bed.

For a brief moment, Murray stood back and observed the two women. He could judge from their appearance that they had been in trouble. Then he stared closely at Yanti and wondered just what his young friend's contribution may have been towards the communists' attempt to take control over the country. He frowned at the two and shook his head as one would at errant children. He went in search of his servants to have them take care of his two intruders. Murray could have no knowledge that the young women who lay on his bed had played their part in the kidnapping, mutilation, and eventual death of the missing generals.

* * * * * *

Colonel Suhendra parked his jeep so as not to be conspicuous. He was tired and knew it would be extremely difficult to remain alert. The journey from Semarang had taken much longer than anticipated, due to the numerous road blocks already in place as a result of the communist uprising. He had dropped General Prajogo at Djalan Tjendana, not far from where he now rested. The Diponegoro colonel settled back and closed his eyes for a few minutes. He doubted if the people inside would emerge before he could snatch a few minutes rest. He looked across the dark intersection and noticed the movement from the corner of his eye. He sighed, and stretched. As he watched the two wretches cross the road and enter the foreigner's house he suddenly frowned. Then he smiled, wondering just what the two would steal from the Australian's house while he slept inside.

* * * * * *

Meanwhile, Soeharto's Strategic Reserves together with the RPKAD had met with little resistance as they swept across the Halim Airforce Base. When a number of PT-76 tanks trundled across the main runway, the 'Tjakra' battalions retreated without a fight. Then the rest of the communist forces collapsed and ran, terrified as Red Beret troops attacked, swarming all over their enemy's positions. Most of the heavy fighting was all over within hours and the Government troops swept through the area mopping up what was left of the communist resistance. By late afternoon on the following day, Halim had been re-taken and the communist forces completely routed.

President Soekarno remained in Bogor, directing the country's affairs from the safety of his Summer Palace. At no time did he divulge any information as to his knowledge of the whereabouts of the missing generals, although he was most curious as to why he had not been asked. He listened to the Radio Indonesia broadcasts, then back in its rightful hands, and not once had any of the announcers alluded to the fact that Yani and his fellow officers might be dead. The Army had retaken control of the capital, and it appeared that the memory of the communists' unsuccessful coup d'etat would quickly fade away.

* * * * * *

On the other side of the city, Ade sat and listened attentively to the radio broadcast announcing the re-taking of the communications station. She thought about what had taken place throughout the capital and wondered how her friends had fared. She was still annoyed that Murray had made no attempt to contact her. She assumed that his communist friend, Yanti, would have fled the city along with all of her comrades now that they had failed in their attempts to take power from the Government. In a way, Ade was pleased. At least she would not have to compete with her any longer and, with these thoughts in mind, the young Javanese woman continued on her way out to meet with some of her friends. They had all agreed to attend the *latihan* sessions at Subud together. At this terrible time they felt the need for spiritual support. There was another scheduled for the following day, Saturday, and Ade decided that once the group session had finished, she would catch a bus into the city and drop in on Murray. It had been more than a week and she just knew that he would be pleased to see her.

* * * * * *

Murray had left instructions with his servants to let the two girls sleep and, when they awoke, the *koki* was to feed them. The old woman accepted her *tuan's* instructions although she was not all that happy having Yanti in the house. Along with the other servants, she believed that Yanti's presence could only bring trouble. They all knew that it would only be a matter of time before the hunt would start for those who participated in the abortive coup. Servants had their own lines of communication and often they knew what was going on even before their *tuans*.

Murray once again spent most of his day at the Embassy with Zach and the others, discussing intelligence material which had been made available from friendly sources, and generally following through with his own reporting for the teams in Central Plans. He had been surprised, however, that there was only one brief message from Anderson. The tersely-worded text, once deciphered, left little doubt in Murray's mind that the new ASIS Director disliked him.

Murray thought about this as he sipped his cup of Robusta coffee back in his own office. He was growing tired of the whole damned business. Now that Harry was no longer the head of Central Plans, he was somehow unable to maintain the same level of interest and loyalty to the organisation. Ever since his old friend's unexplained disappearance, Murray had been toying with the possibility of moving on, and creating a new career for himself. It was an attractive idea. He had few ties left in Australia and the contacts he had developed over his years as a result of his time in Indonesia would stand him in good stead. Murray decided that, once the pressure was off and the excitement surrounding the communists' failed move on the Government paled with time, he would give the matter some serious thought.

Right now, though, he had to stay on top of what was happening. Or rather what was not happening. He could not understand why there had not been anything in the media concerning the generals who had been captured by the communists more than two days before. Murray suspected that they were most probably still being held as hostages to afford Chairman Aidit and his followers some negotiating power. None of the men had come forward since their disappearance, adding evidence to this supposition. He completed his report which highlighted this conclusion then took it over to Zach's office before he sent it to Melbourne. The communications centre in Australia worked a seven day schedule. Even though this was a Saturday, their messages would be treated as if it were any other work day. They went over the contents together.

Zach read the first part of the report and smiled. 'You're right! These guys have never missed an opportunity to have their pictures in the paper. Suddenly, their names aren't even being mentioned. Something's going on, Murray, and I'll bet your evaluation is spot on. The bastards still have Yani and his mates locked up somewhere and are using them to negotiate themselves out of the mess they have created for themselves.'

'It's interesting that Soeharto seems to have stepped in and is taking a strong position against the communists. Considering their relationship in the past, why do you think Nasution let Soeharto pick up the ball, virtually by himself and run with it?' Murray asked. This question had been on everyone's mind.

'Could be that he's just doing what a good Commander would

do when the other senior officers are missing. Soeharto reports to Yani. The Army Chief of Staff is being held, or so we believe, in-communicado somewhere. Nasution narrowly escapes death and discovers that his fellow members of the so-called Council of Generals have all disappeared as well. Who else could he turn to?' Zach asked rhetorically.

'I don't know, Steve,' Murray said, almost contemplatively. 'When we remember that Nasution is still the senior officer and has the support of the people, why wouldn't he have taken control of the Halim attack?'

'We shouldn't forget that he lost a very young daughter during the bungled kidnapping. Who knows just how much influence this may have had on his own judgement at the time. It is Soeharto's responsibility, as Commander of the Strategic Reserves, to move as Nasution directs. Perhaps we'll understand more as time goes by, Murray. It's bloody difficult to speculate about what is really going through their minds. Let's see what happens when Yani returns. It's my bet that nothing much will change because Nasution's fellow Council members have substantial support from within the Army.' Zach thought for a moment then added, 'I wouldn't say the same for the President, though. He's really screwed up in a big way, this time. Word is, even the junior officers in the Army are yelling for his guts. In my opinion, Soekarno committed a major political error in moving out to Halim with the communists. I was stunned when the news broke on radio, yesterday. It is obvious that he's somehow involved in the 30th September Movement or, at least, he was aware of what the communists had planned.'

'Seems he's set up camp in Bogor. That's more than a little ironic. Nasution once drove a tank up to the Palace steps there and demanded that Soekarno step down as President. Bung Karno talked him out of it!' Murray laughed lightly at the fact that circumstances had almost gone full circle. Nasution was in the capital cleaning up after another of the Great Leader's misadventures. As the ranking officer, it would seem that General Nasution would once again be obliged to confront his President as he had done before. On the steps of the Bogor Palace. Their conversation then turned briefly to Susan.

Zach said, 'I have her booked out tomorrow. You can imagine the trouble we've had trying to get a flight. The airport is jammed with locals with fistfuls of dollars ready to pay any amount to get out. Probably most of them have had some sort of relationship with the commies, and don't wish to stay around. Can't say I blame them. Anyway, the important thing is we'll have Susan out of here by tomorrow night.'

'Great. I'll try and drop in before she leaves.' Murray then left Zach alone and, as it was again already late, he called for a motor-pool driver to take him home. As they drove the short distance to his villa, Murray had little time to reflect on the day's events. The driver turned into Tjik Ditiro and headed for Djalan Serang. Murray observed that traffic was unusually light and, as they turned into his street and pulled up outside his house, he failed to notice the Toyota jeep still parked across the intersection. It had been there all day. He climbed out of the Embassy car and walked down through the servants' entrance, as he had done so many times before. Yanti and her friend Erika were sitting with the cook, eating together. When she saw him, Yanti jumped up to greet Murray and squeezed him tightly as the old *koki* shook her head and walked out of the kitchen.

'*Mahree, you're so late,*' Yanti said, her strong arms encircling his body. He laughed and broke her grip, pushing her back to the seat and the unfinished meal. Although they had obviously washed the clothes they had worn to his house the evening before, Murray could see that they belonged in the rubbish bin. Apart from a slight swelling on the side of her jaw, Yanti seemed none the worse for wear. He looked closely at Erika and decided that she too had been extremely fortunate not to have suffered more serious injuries from his blows.

'*Mahree, do you want something to eat? Erika is a fantastic cook,*' she said, pointing at the other and younger girl with her spoon.

'*No thanks,*' he said, not wanting to cause trouble with his cook. Leaving the two alone to finish their meal, he showered. As the water washed away the day's accumulated tiredness, he thought about what he should do with Yanti and her friend. Murray knew they should leave. But it would make little difference if they stayed another day. It might even give him the opportunity to talk to them about what they had been up to and what they saw at Halim. He towelled himself dry and wrapped a batik sarong around his waist. Then he called the girls into his room to avoid having his servants

441

overhear their conversation.

The girls were relieved when Murray told them they could stay over for another night. This had been in their thoughts all day. They were still scared. He gave Yanti a handful of rupiah and told her to send one of the female servants out to the evening market to buy some clothes. He then spoke to the cook who burst into a toothless smile when he told her to prepare something for him. The two young women went off to inspect their temporary quarters.

When he had finished eating, Murray checked his telephone. The lines were still down somewhere. His telephone call to Susan could wait until tomorrow. Right then he was just too tired to go out again. Murray went to the refrigerator beside his small bamboo bar and grabbed one of the huge cans of Victorian Bitter. He then moved back into his bedroom, and lay on the wide double bed, falling asleep before he could finish the beer.

Some hours had passed when Murray was awakened by an unfamiliar sound. He pulled the bedside drawer open quickly and extracted the P9S. He slipped from the bed and moved through the dark room, then carefully, and slowly, turned the door handle and peered into the dimly lit guest room. Both Yanti and her friend sat cross-legged in the middle of the large room, and Murray could hear that the younger girl, Erika, was crying. He opened the door wider and approached the two sitting on the carpet square, directly under the overhead fan. Yanti turned and saw Murray and immediately jumped to her feet.

'Maaf, Mahree. I'm sorry. We woke you.' It was a simple statement but Murray identified her sincerity. 'We're scared, Mahree,' she said, then bent down and placed her arm around her friend. Erika looked up then also climbed to her feet.

'I'm sorry too Mahree,' she cried, choking on the sobs as she spoke. Murray looked at them both and realised that the women were not just scared. They were traumatised by the events of the past days. He stepped closer to the two and wrapped his arms around them both, drawing them to his chest.

'Why are you still frightened?' he asked, although he suspected he already knew why.

'Mahree, the servants don't like us being here. We're worried that they will tell the police,' Yanti said. After Murray had retired, she said, the cook had snapped at them both and asked when they would be leaving. Yanti then forced a sad smile and looked up at Murray. *'We are scared, Murray. You don't understand what has happened. If they inform the police it will be very bad for us. Very bad,'* she repeated.

Murray looked at their worried faces and attempted a reassuring smile. He took them by the hand and led them both back into his bedroom. He knew that this would be sufficient to silence the servants. They would be miffed by the girls' presence but would not even consider informing the police while there was any chance that their *tuan* still enjoyed their company. The two girls undressed and climbed into the huge bed, enjoying the feel of the cool sheets as they slipped between these quietly. He then climbed in alongside Yanti who lay in the middle of the bed. Murray reached for his unfinished beer. The contents were warm but he drank anyway, sipping slowly as his thoughts returned to the warning Yanti had given him, just days before. And then he understood just what Yanti had done for him. She had taken grave risks in order to warn him from venturing outside his villa that night. She had known that there would be troops in his street during the time the Communists planned to kidnap his neighbour, General Harjono. She had also known that he would most probably have been awakened by what was taking place outside and, as a matter of course, would have wandered outside and into the street. She had saved his life. Murray thought about this as he rolled onto his side and prepared for sleep. Soon his thoughts cleared and his breathing fell into a soft deep rhythm. The girls too slept, comforted by Murray's presence. The streets outside also became quiet as the city's inhabitants retired for the day, locking their doors and windows as they went about securing their homes in preparation for the night ahead.

* * * * * *

A hundred metres down the road from where the Australian slept soundly, a car engine broke through the stillness. Kolonel Suhendra then gunned the jeep's engine and drove away, disappointed that he had so little to report. He drove towards the barracks where he knew there would be a bed. He would stop along the roadside and buy something to eat. Then he would rest for a few hours before returning to his post to wait for the Australian to leave his villa alone. The colonel thought about this as he drove away in search of a roadside *martabak* stall. He hoped that this mission would not take too long, as his presence was required back in Semarang.

* * * * * *

Halim Airforce Base, Sunday 3rd October

Government troops were in the process of completing their final sweep through the remnants of the area known as the Crocodile Hole, when they discovered a dry well covered with leaves and branches. Suspecting this was used to hide weapons, the soldiers cleared the well. There, in the gloom, tumbled together like discarded sacks of refuse lay the bodies of their missing officers. News of the discovery swept the capital. And then the whole country. The corpses were removed and photographed, and these in turn were published in every newspaper throughout Indonesia. The people were shocked at the condition of the dead bodies. The suffering of the men before they died was unimaginable. Evidence of the mutilations, some showing testicles removed and eyes gouged from their sockets, proved to be too much for the Indonesian people. The country roared its disapproval, and the Communists were immediately held responsible for the atrocities carried out at Lubang Buaja. When interrogated, the captured Communist soldiers immediately blamed the excesses on the Gerwani women.

As the city awoke to the news of the slaughter of General Yani and his fellow officers, anti-Communist factions hit the streets demanding revenge for what had happened. Within hours, the city streets swelled with incredible numbers of students chanting for the removal of their President for permitting such atrocities to happen under his guardianship. The mood was violent. The people demanded revenge. Terrified by their sudden change in fortunes, the Communists and their supporters immediately went to ground. Known Communist sympathisers were dragged out of their houses and killed. Teachers identified as being sympathetic to the PKI were stoned as they arrived at their schools. Violence continued to erupt throughout the city and finally spilled over into the countryside.

In the first hours following the broadcasts, thousands upon

thousands died. Few of these were true Communists.

* * * * * *

At first, when Ade had been shown the early morning newspaper, she refused to believe that Indonesians could do such things to each other. The photographs were most explicit and, as she stared at the mutilated corpses and read the names of the men who had been tortured before they died, Ade cried. Depressed by these atrocities, she felt she could not go to the *latihan* sessions and elected instead to go directly to Murray. She needed desperately to be with him. Ade caught the bus from the station at Blok M, and then a *betjak* from outside the Intercontinental Hotel. It was not until nine o'clock on Sunday morning that Ade walked into the front yard and peered down the small access used by Murray's servants. She hesitated, then decided to enter via the kitchen as she had so many times before.

'*Pagi, ibu,*' she said kindly, spotting the old cook pottering around in her kitchen. The toothless woman looked up, startled, and did not know what to say to the unexpected visitor. Ade sensed that there was something a little strange about her behaviour but just smiled as she continued through the house towards Murray's bedroom. The old cook shuffled outside and called the other servants and explained excitedly what was happening. They all gathered in the kitchen and listened, holding the servery door open just enough so they could hear.

Ade opened the bedroom door and closed it behind her, softly. It seemed that Murray had slept in. He often did on a Sunday. She tip-toed across the dark, windowless room and went into the bathroom. There were no public conveniences anywhere in the city and she had waited a little longer than expected for her bus to arrive. Hearing the noise, Murray awoke with a start, reached for the beside light and then remembered what had happened before falling asleep the night before. He looked across at the two women. They were still sound asleep. Yanti had pulled the sheets across the bed exposing Erika's naked body to the cold air. Murray slipped his feet out of bed and was about to go to the bathroom himself when he heard the toilet flush. He turned and looked at the two girls lying on his bed, and was confused. Then Ade opened the bathroom door and walked into his bedroom.

At first she faltered, then remained still, in shock. Yanti and another young woman lay on Murray's bed, both obviously naked. She looked at Murray, her face reflecting the disbelief that he could do such a thing, that he could have these types of women in house, let alone his bed. Ade shouted at him as he stepped forward and raised both fists and pounded his naked chest, cursing Murray in Javanese. Both the girls jumped up, startled by the screams in the confined space. As soon as Yanti realised what had happened, she grabbed Erika's arm and dragged her into the bathroom, past the screaming Ade, and locked the door behind them.

'Mahree, how could you do this?' Ade screamed, her hands now held in Murray's firm grip to prevent further blows. He could not believe what was happening. Why did she have to pick this, of all times, to visit, he thought angrily. He hadn't even slept with the women! Or, at least, not with Erika.

'Take it easy, Ade. Just cool down. You know we have an agreement. You shouldn't get angry. Okay?' he asked, releasing his grip, hoping she had settled down.

'Mahree,' she cried out loudly, *'you don't understand. Yanti and her Gerwani friends are all murderers. They killed Bapak Yani and the other generals!'* Suddenly Murray's stomach felt as if a cold hand had gripped it. He grabbed Ade by the shoulders and shook her roughly.

'What do you mean? How do you know this, Ade?' he asked quickly, as she began to sob. Not now, Ade, he thought, not now, hoping that she wouldn't lose it altogether. *'Tell me, Ade, what do you know about Yanti and her friends?'* She grabbed his wrists. Murray was hurting her as he continued to shake her shoulders.

'Ask your servants to get you a newspaper. Better still, listen to the radio. The reports are all over the news. They killed the generals, Mahree,' she yelled loudly, *'and they even murdered Bapak Nasution's five-year-old daughter!'* she added, before losing control and breaking into chest-heaving sobs. Behind the bathroom door, Yanti and Erika looked at each other, their faces covered with fear.

'Are all the generals dead?' Murray asked stunned by Ade's revelation.

'Yes, Mahree, yes. And you have let that filth stay here, hiding in your house,' she cried, accusingly. *'How could you have done such a thing?'* She felt weak. Murray caught her as she fainted. He lifted her eas-

ily and placed her on the bed. Then he grabbed at the bathroom door handle and pulled angrily.

'*Okay, get dressed. Quickly!*' he hissed as both women rushed past and hurriedly searched for their clothes.

'*Mahree, I'm sorry,*' Yanti started to say but stopped when she caught the look in his eyes. Suddenly she was even more frightened than before.

'*Get dressed,*' he snapped angrily, moving towards the bedroom door, '*then get out there and wait. Don't move from those chairs until I tell you, Yanti or so help me, I will call the police myself!*' Erika grabbed her shoes and fled from the room. Yanti followed as soon as she finished dressing. Murray called to his houseboy and told him to watch the girls. Yanti and her friend were not to leave, he told his excited servants. Then he returned to Ade who, by this time, had begun to recover. He helped her sit up, then rubbed the back of her neck.

'*Are they gone?*' she asked, looking around the room.

'*I told them to wait outside ...*'

'*Mahree, you can't let them stay. You just can't!*' she pleaded, gripping his arm tightly. He felt the nails biting into his flesh.

'*It's okay, Ade. It's okay. I will send them away just as soon as it's safe. You wouldn't want them being caught as they left here, would you?*' he suggested, knowing that what he said made sense. Murray wanted the opportunity to speak to the girls alone. He needed to find out more about what happened at Halim. He dressed quickly and told Ade to remain in the bedroom. Then he went outside and sat with the distressed pair who were, by now, also near to tears. He understood that they probably already knew what would be in store for them once they were caught and taken away to prison. If they were lucky, that is.

'*Okay, Yanti,*' he started, '*I want to hear the whole story. No lies, no embellishments, just what happened.*' She looked at him, fighting back the tears. She hadn't cried for such a long, long time. '*Yanti,*' he said, leaning across and placing his hand on her shoulder, '*I know you probably saved my life the other night. For that alone, I will help you both as much as I can. But you must tell me exactly everything that happened. Okay?*' He waited for her to respond and, catching his servants hanging around in the kitchen with the door slightly ajar, he called his *djongos* and told the houseboy to bring coffee and rice porridge for them all.

They sat together and talked. Murray listened, prompting only when he could see that they had left something out. The girls explained their role in the kidnappings and how the prisoners were taken to the Crocodile Hole at Halim. They lied, blaming others for the mutilations and executions knowing that to do otherwise would not serve their cause. They described how the bodies were thrown down the old dry well, and then covered with leaves and branches.

Erika cried as she told how the Red Berets had killed the Gerwani women. Then they explained how they had managed to escape and seek safety with Murray. When they had finished, Murray went back into the bedroom and spoke briefly to Ade. He told her to remain where she was until the others had left. Reluctantly, she agreed. He then called his servants and warned them not to say anything to anyone, and suggested that if they did and this resulted in the police coming to his home, then they too would most surely be suspected of hiding the girls. When the old cook heard this, she wanted to leave immediately, but Murray managed to convince her that it would be safe, in the long run, to remain. He then sent the *djongos* out to find a pirate taxi, and have the driver park his car inside the yard. Then they waited.

'Where will we go, Mahree?' the girl called Erika asked. Murray looked at her and attempted a smile. He had decided on a course of action which, he knew, depended on assistance from others whom he really had no right to ask. Almost an hour passed before they heard the car pull up outside and the creak of the front gates as the houseboy returned. Murray bundled them into the American sedan and told them to sit down low in the seat without creating the impression that they were hiding. He wanted anyone along the street who may have been watching to observe the vehicle departing with passengers. Murray only hoped that the servants' gossip had not been overly explicit. He had listened to the eleven o'clock broadcast and knew that it would not take too much for even the back streets of Djakarta to burst into violence.

He called Yanti and told her to take the letter he had written, and give it only to the man whose name appeared on the envelope. She had reached up and kissed him but Murray could not bring himself to respond. He knew her account of the deaths of the country's military leaders was essentially a lie. He then gave the driver an excessive amount of rupiah and sent the two former Gerwani women on their way.

* * * * * *

Colonel Suhendra watched with interest as an old Buick pulled up outside the Australian's house, then backed into the driveway. He assumed that the car would remain as the servants had then closed the iron gates. He had seen the attractive young Indonesian girl enter more than an hour before and assumed that she was involved somehow with the foreigner. Then he recalled the unkempt women who, some hours earlier, he had seen slip like thieves into the yard. When he had driven away late the night before, Suhendra had assumed that the two women, after getting what they could, had slipped out again and moved down the street out of his sight.

The scraping sound of metal on metal alerted him. The colonel watched as the gates were opened and the Buick pulled out of the driveway and turned in his direction. He could see that there were at least two passengers in the back seat. He started the jeep and waited for them to pass, then he followed the illegal taxi as it moved sluggishly down the street.

* * * * * *

Zach sat opposite Susan as they ate their way through lunch. He had already finished and she felt he had rushed his meal. Suddenly it seemed that everything was going wrong again, just as before. Her flight was scheduled to depart at five-thirty. Susan thought that he was overly preoccupied with whatever was happening outside.

'Is it really that serious?' she had asked in response to his comment that they should leave plenty of time to get to the airport due to the unrest.

'Worse,' he had replied, abruptly.

'Do you want to leave now?' Susan asked. There seemed little point in his staying. They still had most of the afternoon to kill and it was noisy around the pool. Sundays attracted a larger crowd than usual and Zach would have known most of the faces present.

He ordered another drink as the waiter passed by and tilted his head politely in Susan's direction to see if she too wanted her drink topped up. She nodded, lifted her half-finished gin and tonic and finished the remains of her fifth drink for the day. Susan was not happy.

Actually, she thought that he should be punished. After all, Steven had shown her so little attention since her arrival, leaving her to spend so much time alone. All in all, she thought, the trip had not had the remedial effect that she had anticipated. She looked across at Zach and wished she could read his thoughts. She noticed other women casting admiring looks. He was handsome, intelligent and she cared for him. But she was annoyed. He seemed to be so distant. There had been little opportunity for them to have any real time together on this trip. Susan was not impressed with the excuses he had given. The streets had seemed relatively quiet. The stories of some coup and the country's upheaval were all lost on her. It seemed to her that there had been far more street violence the last time she had visited than what was evident now. Maybe he had already become bored with the relationship, and was too embarrassed to say. Susan knew she was becoming tipsy, but didn't care. She looked at him and suddenly realised that their romance had mainly been the result of her own loneliness. Then she thought of Harry and wondered if he was really dead, or had he just run away? Susan knew that it wouldn't have been another woman in Harry's case but felt bitter about the way she had been left in limbo. She smiled at Steven and wished that they had met elsewhere and under entirely different circumstances. Her own world was full of uncertainties. She wasn't even sure if she was still legally married or even had a husband. Somewhere.

Their drinks arrived and Susan finished hers before Zach was halfway though his. Then she stood and asked Steven to take her back to her room. Somehow the magic had vanished and she wanted to leave. The special moments they had enjoyed together would always be just that. An interlude. Steven Zach had merely filled a vacuum in her life, although looking across at the handsome man, Susan knew that it would be most unlikely she would be attracted to anyone as powerfully again. In that instant, she knew what she must do. Susan smiled and placed her hand on his. He looked at her and smiled back. Had he read her thoughts? Then they strolled slowly back to her suite and waited together through the afternoon until it was time to leave. There was no suggestion that they would make love. Later, when there was nothing left to say to each other, Zach escorted Susan to the airport.

* * * * * *

Murray had not told Ade where he had sent Yanti and her friend, and she didn't ask. Satisfied that they were gone forever, Ade had eventually left his bedroom and wandered around the house, letting the servants see that she was still there, and very much in control of the situation.

Almost 12 kilometres to the south, the ageing Buick coughed and hesitated as the poorly-maintained fuel lines restricted the flow of fuel to the engine. The passengers sat quietly in the back of the sedan while the driver worked on the problem. An hour later they continued on their way, and were pleased to discover that their destination was not all that far from where the car had broken down. The driver entered the compound and stopped directly inside the front gates. He had already been paid by Murray, but this was as far as he wanted to go. The two girls scrambled from the taxi and went in search of the man whose name was on the envelope Yanti carried.

Outside the entrance to the Subud complex, Suhendra stopped his jeep and left it alongside the road. He then entered the unguarded centre and followed the two women he had seen leave the Buick. It was obvious to him that they had never been there before. They appeared lost. After some minutes he observed that they were met and taken across a small parking area surrounded by Banyan trees. Then they were ushered inside a chapel-like building. He waited. The afternoon dragged on slowly and he became restless with the inactivity. It seemed to him that the two he had followed would not reappear. Then, when he was about to leave, suddenly, they both emerged. For a moment they stood talking to an old man dressed in white robes. They walked towards the compound's main entrance. He followed.

* * * * * *

Yanti and Erika had spent the time inside waiting for Murray's

451

letter to be delivered, and read. As the afternoon slowly passed they had become increasingly worried, at the uncertainty of their situation. Finally, they were escorted through the building and across a garden to a small pavilion set in a pleasant landscape. They removed their shoes before entering, and were ushered into a small room, devoid of furnishings. Inside, they discovered an old man, sitting alone, as if in prayer. He looked up and smiled, then indicated that they too should sit on the *tikar* carpet. They did as instructed. Immediately, Yanti felt at ease in the presence of the guru. She sensed a warmth emanating from him and, without knowing why, knew that they would be safe in his care.

She had taken Erika's hand and sat, cross-legged, and watched as the old man had taken Murray's letter and read it slowly. After a time, he rose and smiled at them both, without speaking. It had felt as if they had only been in his presence for no more than a few minutes but, when he ushered them outside, Yanti looked at her watch and was startled to see that they had been sitting there, alone and at peace, for more than an hour. Neither of the two could remember speaking during their time in the small chamber, and yet both recognised that some exchange had taken place. As they bid farewell to the guru, they were given directions for where they should go next.

When they left, Yanti and Erika walked from the compound and looked for some form of transport. They had been instructed to stay with a family on the outskirts of the city and were also given a letter for the people who would take care of them until the situation changed, permitting their return to their own villages. As they waited, they were observed. Suhendra watched as they looked around for transport, and waited. Two hours later, he followed them to the small house on the road to Bogor, and concluded that this where they would remain. He then returned to Djakarta, and reported what had transpired.

During the early evening, a team of Red Beret soldiers raided the house and arrested all of those present. When the owner resisted, he was shot. Then his wife screamed at the soldiers and she too was silenced as they beat her to the ground with the stocks of their rifles. The two women who had been followed from the Australian's house were taken into custody and escorted to the Military detention centre, where they were interrogated. They were beaten with a rattan cane until their bodies were covered with blood. The questions continued. Erika, nowhere near as resilient as Yanti, broke first. As she cried out in pain and finally admitted to their complicity in the kidnappings, Yanti knew it was all over. She was taken into the adjoining cell where the punishing interrogation continued. Each time she regained consciousness, Yanti would be thrashed again, the strokes ripping through her flesh.

She collapsed in agony, only to be revived by her interrogators. They wanted her to tell them about the Australian but she had nothing to tell. She sobbed, choking on her own blood in a valiant attempt to convince them that they were only lovers, and that he was not involved with the Communists. They refused to believe her, continuing with the brutal flogging until finally, unable to withstand any further punishment, Yanti bit through her own tongue then collapsed. The interrogator rushed outside, then returned before she could choke on her own blood and pierced Yanti's tongue with the piece of wire, then ran this through her cheek to prevent her from swallowing the muscle. Yanti never regained consciousness. When it became obvious that neither of the two Gerwani detainees could be of further use, their battered and bruised bodies were dragged from the interrogation centre and they were placed with a number of other prisoners.

As the first morning prayers were called, the ten-man squad took their positions and waited for the command to fire. They raised their automatic weapons and looked down through the sights at the seven women who lay on the ground not twenty metres away. In the distance a voice carried through the air, breaking the morning silence, calling the faithful to prayer. As the words *Allahu Akhbar* reached the ears of those who believed and followed the teachings of *The Merciful One*, the morning air exploded with sounds of rapid fire as the soldiers squeezed the triggers of their recently-acquired American rifles.

As the sun forced its way into the sky and the morning light touched the trees, then roof tops across the city, Ade murmured softly and moved her body closer to the warmth of the man she loved.

Chapter 23

Djakarta

It was appropriate that the murdered soldiers be buried on the very day normally reserved for parades and celebrations to mark Armed Forces Day. The city's inhabitants flocked to the main thoroughfare to observe the funeral procession as it passed on its way to the Heroes' Cemetery, Kalibata. There was an eerie silence as the six caskets were paraded slowly through the capital. But the city would have little time to mourn. The morning papers carried more photographs of the murdered generals, which further inflamed the people against the PKI and those associated with the 30th September Movement. Accusations were made suggesting that Indonesia's minority Chinese population had prior knowledge of the PKI's plans, and these were underlined by the fact that the attempted coup d'etat coincided with the anniversary of Mao Tse Tung's People's Republic of China. A groundswell of anti-Chinese feeling grew quickly, fuelled further by leaked reports relating to the secret arms supply agreement put in place by the Air Force Chief, Omar Dhani. As demonstrations continued to sweep the country, the Chinese locked their shops, barricaded their homes, and prepared for the worst blood-letting the country had ever known.

Reports of the President's meeting in Bogor had already filtered back to the capital. Soekarno had summoned the nation's leaders in an attempt to restore solidarity amongst the warring factions, but he had failed. The President had then issued a statement condemning the 30th September Movement, and called for a day of national mourning for the slain officers who were the first victims of the failed coup. The six officers were then officially declared Heroes of the Revolution.

Two more days passed before Soekarno called an interim Cabinet meeting. A further statement was then issued further condemning the Communists and their Revolutionary Council, while appealing to the nation for calm and continued support for the real Revolution against Neo-colonialism. On the ninth day of October, just eight days after he had fled Halim, President Soekarno left the safety of the Bogor Palace and was flown by helicopter back to Djakarta. At all times, the responsibility for his safety remained with units of the tarnished Tjakrabirawa Guards. Soekarno then attempted to restore the country's leadership to what it had been prior to the failed communist movement, but discovered a formidable opponent who refused to permit the re-instatement of left-wing elements into the Government. A struggle for power commenced behind closed doors and, on the 14th day of October, two weeks from the day of General Yani's murder, Major General Soeharto took his place as Chief, and Minister of the Indonesian Army.

* * * * * *

A remote village in Java

The villagers all gathered to hear what their *lurah* had to say. As they assembled together in the *balai kampung*, the village meeting place was unable to accommodate everyone, compelling many to stand outside. This was the third such meeting called by their leader. Following both the first and second assemblies, there had been discussions as to what they should do and, unable to reach their traditional form of consensus, a further meeting was agreed upon to provide the entire village with the opportunity to have their say. Outside, stacked in rows for the gathering to see, was the arsenal of American weapons sent to them from the sky. The head man had ordered that the boxes be moved out of the village meeting hall and opened, for his villagers to see.

Mothers, delicately balancing baskets of cloves, garlic and peanuts on their heads, stood, holding their children. Most of the older women chewed betel-nut as they listened to the village elders have their say. The well-worn dirt yard which was the *kampung* square was dotted with blood-red lumps where the women had spat out the glutinous remains of the mixture of chalk, tobacco and *gambir* nuts. Produce was left unguarded across the square where their central market provided a communal outlet for all their needs. It would be a rare thing for someone to steal from another in this village. They lived together peacefully as had their parents before them. And, like their forebears, these people followed the strict teachings of the Prophet Mohammad and the Holy Koran.

There was a hush as the *lurah* called out to the villagers to listen. He was their unchallenged leader. He could read and write, and knew more about the outside world than any of their number. More importantly, he ensured that the people followed the dictates of their faith. He raised his right hand and indicated to the villagers that the meeting had commenced.

'We have heard from the elders and now you must have your say as well. Many of you sat with me and listened to Bung Karno as he spoke of the evils of those who would destroy our land. These people are called communists,' he said fiercely, then even louder, 'and we all know where they live.' The lurah's statement was met with a roar of approval for they knew just who he was referring to. The people who lived over the mountain in the village they called Kampung Kali Ketjil were obviously all involved with what had happened. They prayed to a different god and had even attempted to bring that influence into this village.

'Last night we listened to the radio and heard how the evil these communists have introduced to our land has spread through the country. We heard our leaders tell us that we must help them prevent their influence from growing further. We also heard them say that the only way to ensure that we remain safe from the terrible influences of these godless people was to remove the evil from our soil, as one would tear a diseased plant from the ground.' The villagers murmured loudly in support.

'We have been warned. There will be no further harvests unless we act now to remove these weeds which threaten our families and children. And like the diseased plant that would spoil the others we must act and follow what has been said. We must tear these plants from the ground, right down to their diseased roots!' The villagers roared again.

He continued to speak, and the people became even more excited. Their anger grew, and the mood became violent. Several of the village men started shouting that it was time to act, and a loud cheer followed the suggestion that they take the weapons and chase the Communists and sympathisers away. The villagers' appetite whetted, and consensus finally reached, the *lurah* agreed to lead the men on an armed attack across the mountain, and into the nearest village.

The following morning, as women prepared for the day and children played in the dirt outside their modest dwellings, the people of Kampung Kali Ketjil were attacked by the neighbouring villagers. The small Catholic church was razed to the ground and the priest's decapitated head was placed on a pole outside his place of worship. Volley after volley of gunfire could be heard reverberating along the small river as men, women and children were slaughtered during the raid. The village was then burned to the ground and the river boats destroyed. The attack had lasted no more than two hours. The last survivors were dragged from their hiding places, dismembered and left in the village square as a warning. Then the *lurah* led his men back across the mountain. The following week they mounted yet another attack, venturing much farther afield, where they again destroyed an entire community simply because some of the villagers had converted to Christianity.

Across the nation the story was much the same. As the weeks progressed, reports of mass slaughter and terror reached the cities. The entire archipelago erupted into an horrific nightmare of blood feuds and genocide, fuelled also by the likes of Colonel Sarwo Edhi who moved his RPKAD troops through Central Java, destroying villages and whole communities suspected of being communist or sympathetic to their cause. And, as civil war continued, tens of thousands of young children fell victim to the policy of destroying communism down to its very roots. Most were murdered simply because one of the members of their family might have been seen in the company of a known communist. Villages attacked each other settling old scores, families attacked neighbours over the most minor of disputes, and brother killed brother out of sheer sibling rivalry.

In Bali, the people living on the Island of the Gods moved quickly, slaughtering a greater proportion of the population than in any other part of Indonesia. They killed many of their own, but also took advantage of the situation to remove all signs of Javanese presence from their island. The carnage was to continue unabated, finally dribbling to a close more than one year later, leaving in its trail more than half a million dead and many more maimed or scarred for the rest of their lives. Even Djakarta City was not spared the marauding gangs. They plundered the countryside, running amok as they broke into houses, killing the occupants and burning their homes to the ground. Not even houses under the umbrella of diplomatic status were safe. Several of the foreign legations lodged official complaints concerning attempts on their staff.

It was on the evening following the announcement of Soeharto's appointment as the new Army Chief that Murray learned just what it was like, to wake suddenly in the dark, and discover that one's house was on fire.

* * * * * *

It was the smoke which first alerted Murray. He coughed, waking immediately to the acrid smell that had crept under the door and slowly enveloped the room. He fumbled for the bedside light and squeezed the switch. Nothing happened. The air inside the room was sticky and then he realised that the airconditioner was also not working. He moved through the dark and unlocked his bedroom door. A cloud of smoke billowed through the doorway followed by flames. Shocked, he closed the door. Fighting down the rising panic, he stumbled through to the ensuite bathroom and turned the tap. Nothing. He cursed. The water pump would have ceased functioning the moment power had stopped flowing. His mind raced quickly.

Murray moved back into his bedroom and groped for the bedside table. He opened the drawer, located his wallet and passport and placed these on top of the table. Then he extracted the P9S from the back of the drawer. Valuable seconds were lost as he stumbled around in the dark, finding the wardrobe, where he quickly ran his fingers over the clothing. He pulled at the denims and put these on. Then he took one of his T-shirts and made his way back into the bathroom, removed the top of the water cistern, then dipped the shirt. He threw some of the water over his face and body, then slipped into the wet clothing. Making his way back into the bedroom, Murray shoved his documents inside his back pocket and the automatic inside the waistband of his jeans. Feeling around on the floor, he discovered the casuals he had worn the day before. He slipped these on as well, then readied himself for what he knew was waiting outside.

As Murray opened the solid teak door he was hit with the full force of the fire. The heat was incredible and he held his hand up to cover his face as the searing blast of air sucked the oxygen from the room. He slammed the door shut again, and groped around for the towel he had thrown down after showering the night before. Murray grabbed it, then ran back into the bathroom and immersed it in the remaining cistern water. He wound the towel around his head and neck, then opened the door once more, and, without hesitating, ran blindly through the area of the house which he knew like the back of his hand. The heat sucked the air from his lungs but he continued through the smoke-filled room as the ceiling collapsed above the wall adjoining the kitchen. He grabbed at the door handle, screaming in pain when the metal burned deeply through flesh.

Fear gripped him, but he stepped back and then lunged forward, smashing the door with all the force he could muster. There was no air and Murray knew that he was about to pass out. He threw himself through the kitchen and kicked furiously at the external door, bursting thankfully out onto the small pathway alongside the house as the door timbers folded under his weight. He struggled to his feet and stumbled the few metres down to the servants quarters where he found his houseboy lying on the floor. He staggered around feeling for others who might have stayed over with his *djongos*. Satisfied that he had been alone, Murray lifted the small frame and threw him over his shoulder. Then he headed out along the narrow passage used mainly by his servants, until reaching the front garden. He stumbled, regained his footing, then fell again. Murray reached down and grabbed the houseboy by the arm and dragged him the rest of the short distance out onto the street where a large crowd had already gathered.

He dropped his houseboy on the far side of the street and then fell to the ground, sucking in deep breaths of air. He looked for his security guard amongst the onlookers but could not see him anywhere. Murray shook his head knowing that the man would have disappeared to avoid being blamed. He had probably fallen asleep, Murray guessed, and had panicked when the fire had broken out.

There was an explosion somewhere out the back of the villa and the crowd ducked as flying debris landed near where they stood. Murray guessed that there would be more, knowing that there were at least three gas bottles stored behind the building. A servant from down the street who was friendly with Murray's *djongos*, tugged at his arm and drew his attention back to the unconscious servant. Murray asked the young man to take his injured friend down to his *tuan's* house and care for him there, away from the fire. The flames had reached well into the sky, lighting the whole area as Murray watched the roof cave in. The neighbours had already left their house waiting anxiously to see if the fire would spread. It didn't. By morning it had burned itself out, leaving only the brick walls standing as evidence.

Murray had remained around until the fire had burned itself out. He had no telephone, no car, and no servants. Or at least, not until his old cook had arrived and, even then, once *koki* discovered that her place of employment had been destroyed, she too had to be assisted, overcome by shock. He then went down the street to check on his *djongos*. Murray was worried that the houseboy had not reappeared that morning. They had been together for some years and Murray treated him, as he did the old cook, almost as if they were family. He approached the house and could see that a number of other servants from along the street had gathered to check on their friend. As Murray moved into the driveway, he sensed that something was wrong. He pushed past the servants blocking the side entrance and entered the small room. His *djongos* lay on his back on the narrow bed. He was dead. Murray moved across to the body and bent down to examine his small friend. In the early morning light he could see the look of anguish on the man's face. One of the servants pointed to a minute puncture hole low on the houseboy's back.

Murray checked the small wound and concluded that the weapon used was probably a knitting needle. Murray had heard of similar killings before. He knew this style of killing was quite common amongst the cross-boy gangs which had suddenly emerged during the past weeks. One of their number would merely walk up behind their intended victim and drive a knitting needle deep into the lower back, leaving only the smallest of puncture holes as evidence of an attack. Often the victims would feel a sharp stabbing pain and continue walking without realising that they had been seriously wounded, until finally collapsing, as their insides filled with blood from the wound. Then, like Murray's houseboy, they would die. The Station Chief rose and placed his hand on the body, nodded silently at the still face of his servant, and friend. He clenched his fists and swore silently, knowing that the man before him had been murdered. Somehow, he had to put an end to his feud with the Diponegoro soldiers, even if it meant going back to Semarang to speak to the men there.

He stepped outside and spoke quietly to the owner of the house. Murray thanked his neighbour and assured them that he would bear the cost of funeral arrangements. Then he walked down the street watching for a passing *betjak*. As he stood on the intersection of his street and Tjik Ditiro, he noticed that something was out of place. Tired and distressed by what had happened, Murray shook his head and, out of habit, rubbed his face.

He heard the clanging bell of an approaching *betjak* and waved. He then climbed aboard. As his driver peddled slowly away, Murray turned back and looked across his shoulder, without knowing why. Suddenly he remembered what it was that didn't fit in the scene back at the intersection. It was the jeep. The jeep was missing. And then the thought struck him. Every day, as he had been driven to the Embassy over the past week, he had noticed the Army vehicle as the Embassy driver had slowed each time before turning into Tjik Ditiro. It had not really registered before. There had been too much else on his mind.

He tried to recall returning to his villa each night, and whether or not he had sighted the jeep as his driver turned into Djalan Serang. The more he thought about it, the more convinced he became that there had been something there, waiting. Waiting for him. Suddenly he experienced a familiar chill pass down his back. He leaned forward to see if anyone followed. Then he felt for the automatic, still tucked away inside his jeans.

* * * * * *

Murray was surprised when he detected the hesitation in Zach's response. He had telephoned and asked if it would be all right for him to bed down at his house until the Embassy could find somewhere suitable for him to stay. He had spent his first hours cleaning up at the Hotel Indonesia. Then he had gone directly to the Embassy and submitted his report to the Ambassador, through the Consul. Murray had reported that the fire was accidental, caused by a leaking LPG bottle. A more detailed copy was then despatched through his own channels directly to Central Plans in Melbourne. He still did not reveal that there had been another attempt on his life.

Before heading off to replace his sparse wardrobe, Murray dialled the colonel's extension. He had expected a warmer response to his suggestion and immediately regretted having asked. He really needed a friend right then and was disappointed with Zach's obvious reluctance to have him around.

'Anytime after tomorrow, Murray, okay?' Zach had said. 'I've got something on my plate right now. Anyway, a night in the hotel won't do you any harm.'

'That's fine, Steve,' Murray had replied, wondering why he couldn't move directly into one of the three empty bedrooms in the Military Attaché's residence. Then the thought struck him that Steve probably had a woman staying over and was embarrassed because of Susan. Murray smiled and shook his head. The following day, Murray moved into Zach's residence.

* * * * * *

The United States Embassy

The resident CIA Station Chief, Samuel Preston, was not at all happy. He read through the classified reports and shook his head at the incompetence of the so-called Military advisers on Embassy staff. These were the same so-called experts who had been unable to ascertain who was doing what to whom over at Halim when the commies had taken charge, and then told the Ambassador that General Yani and the others were most probably alive and only being held as hostages. And, before that, dropped weapons into unfriendly hands, delivered equipment mistakenly to the communists and, if all that wasn't enough, had five of their number arrested and thrown into jail for breaking the goddamn local curfew! He chewed angrily on his unlit Havana, reading through the remaining reports.

When he came to the blue-coded files, he pushed everything else aside and snapped the cover of the first document open. There was a recent photograph attached to the inside cover sheet. He examined the man's face, and then eyes. First he read the running observation report on Colonel Steven Zach. Then he read the recent communications on Stephenson. When he had finished, he took the files and personally returned the sensitive documents to CIA/Per/Only registry and lodged a security error breach against the officer who had left the highly-classified documents on his desk unattended. Then Preston bit through the soggy tip of the cigar and spat into the rubbish bin beside his desk. With a well-rehearsed movement, the Chief flicked his Zippo lighter and held the flame to his Havana. He drew on the cigar until the tip glowed, then inhaled deeply. Satisfied, he went on with business.

Over in the adjacent building, the United States Ambassador to Indonesia sat across from the major general and nodded to his interpreter. The young State Department officer, not quite equipped for the idiosyncrasies of the Indonesian language struggled, as he attempted to pass the gist of what his Ambassador had said to the Indonesian officer. They had picked him to act as interpreter only because of his security clearance. There was no-one in the entire Embassy capable of interpreting fluently at this level. His head ached. They had been at it for over an hour.

'General, the United States Government wishes to thank you for what you have said today.' He then checked his notes. 'Hmmm... We wish to say that we applaud your efforts in removing the communists who threaten your country. Hmm...We wish also to say that although we have heard conflicting reports concerning the.... the exaggerated numbers of dead, the United States Government have no... sympathy for those people and we... encourage your Government' to continue with its valiant efforts to...' again, he checked his notes — 'continue to... eradicate the communists. We pledge our support to you, and send our President's personal congratulations to you on your recent appointment. We look forward to the future and a time when we are able to discuss more...hmmm... concrete proposals concerning Defence Co-operation. Thank you.'

Major General Soeharto merely smiled. These were the words he had expected to hear. There would be more accolades, he knew, but not at this time. He rose, shook hands with the Ambassador, and was escorted down through the private access used for moments such as these. The Ambassador then called his secretary and asked for a few minutes before his next appointment. He spent a few quite moments alone, thinking. He mumbled a short prayer while holding his father's Bible, which had been passed down to him when his father had retired from the ministry. He then spent a short time washing his face and hands before returning to his desk. Refreshed, he signalled his secretary that he was ready.

When his next guest shuffled into the private reception area, the Ambassador stood until the older man had settled comfortably in the matching deerskin-covered chairs. They talked for more than an hour together before the guru rose and smiled at the American, then shuffled back out of the magnificently appointed chamber.

The Ambassador leaned back in his thick leather chair and reflected on his two recent visitors. It was obvious that both were leaders with strong convictions. He was convinced that each would achieve a very strong following some time in the future.

As he recalled their responses and reactions during the private discussions, the Ambassador was amused to discover that his two visitors were actually very much alike. He stretched, then leaned forward and lifted the photograph on his desk. Then he looked across at the wall decorated with flags and a photograph of Lyndon B. Johnson watching from the wall, and smiled. The President was preoccupied with his escalating war in Vietnam. That left the team from the State Department to do practically whatever it wished in Soekarno's Indonesia.

Chapter 24

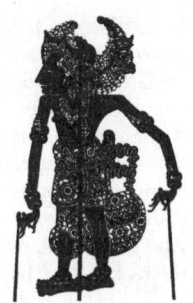

The agent was burdened with the knowledge that his KGB masters would believe that he had revealed details of the Soviet network inside the CIA. Interrogation techniques could easily extract such information. The mole also knew that the KGB would use him as an example and punish his son who still lived in Moscow.

If it had not been for the ongoing background noise which always affected those working on this level, many more agents would have heard the shouts, moments before the loud shot. Instead of throwing themselves to the floor as they were trained, the few amongst their number who immediately recognised the sound for what it was, turned towards the gunshot and stared in disbelief. Senior Agent Richards along with several others had yelled as the officer jumped to his feet, placed the .38 Police Special to his mouth and pulled the trigger. Immediately, the senior administrators moved to damage control.

The dead agent had known the moment he had been confronted with the evidence. Intuition had told him that there was something wrong. He had sensed it for days. And then, out of the blue, he knew he had finally been discovered. He elected not to face the mandatory weeks of interrogation. Consequently, he took the only steps which he believed would convince his superiors back in the Kremlin that he had not betrayed his country. His son would be safe.

Senior Agent Richards had moved quickly to quash all speculation about the man's motives, citing a terminal disease and associated stress. The Director had called an urgent meeting of his departmental heads to review their options. The active operations which had been running at the time of the Soviet mole's suicide were discussed. As a result of the agent's suicide, the CIA had discovered that an operation, similar to their own, had already been initiated by the Soviets. Only the targets were different. Any such action by the Russians had the potential of jeopardising years of American planning. The United States Government's most valuable resource within the Indonesian Military had come under threat. Someone had given the order to kill Soeharto, a leader who had suddenly become one of the most powerful men in his country. And if he died, responsibility for his death might well be laid at the feet of the CIA.

* * * * * *

Semarang

The Siliwangi and Dipongoro Commands had worked together planning their operation to support the anti-Communist sweep through the island of Java. In the first few weeks following the failed coup, Colonel Sarwo Edhi had already cut and slashed his way through most of what he claimed were Communist communities. Reports of his RPKAD Para-commandoes cleansing operations had already accounted for tens of thousands of so-called 'enemies'.

Brigadier General Prajogo was pleased with the course of events. The communists had made their move first and failed. Now, under new leadership, the Army would see that the PKI would be removed from the country forever. He thought about the Council of Generals and the deaths of the six officers. Although saddened, he now believed that their demise had served their country well, creating the necessary groundswell required to move against the communists in the harshest way. He was particularly saddened by the news of the death of Nasution's daughter and was pleased that officers such as Sarwo Edhi had extracted their revenge on those who had supported the treacherous PKI.

His thoughts turned to the Australian who apparently led a most charmed life. The general firmly believed that the Communist threat was still very real, and as long as elements existed which continued to support Soekarno's soft stand against the Left, the Republic would remain in danger. He looked at the daily reports and re-examined the annotations made by his aides. There was a request to accept a courtesy call from a visiting foreign officer on tour through Java. The general knew what that really meant.

The foreigners were becoming restless with the reports that Sarwo Edhi's cleansing campaign had been excessive. He had read several of the foreign press clippings charging that the Indonesian Army had embarked on a campaign of genocide, spear-headed by the RPKAD colonel. The request to visit had been accompanied by the Deputy Chief of Army Staff's recommendation supporting the tour and, in consequence, the general had little choice but to agree, even though it conflicted with other arrangements, already in place. He signed his name approving the Military Attaché's visit, then read the BAKIN intelligence report on the officer, Colonel Steven Zach.

* * * * * *

Djakarta

Zach could tell that Murray was keeping something back. He looked across the table at his friend and waited, but the Station Chief remained silent. When Zach had advised those present at the Wednesday prayers meeting that he had received approval to tour Central Java, Murray's initial reaction had been very supportive, but later had turned to one of concern. They had just finished dinner. The Embassy still hadn't found suitable accommodation for Murray and he had remained at Zach's house while the search went on.

'Why don't you come with me?' Zach suggested. 'I'll only be gone for ten days or so.'

Murray looked at the other man and seemed to be considering the idea. He played with a toothpick.

'I could do with a first-hand assessment of what's really going on around Solo and Surakarta,' he said, then added, 'They got Aidit today. The info came in just after you left.' Zach hadn't heard. Without their Chairman, the PKI had no real leadership left.

'I'd like to be present when they interrogate him,' the colonel smiled, knowing just how impossible that would be.

'He's dead. They took him out as soon as they discovered who he was,' Murray said.

'I'm not surprised. There were most probably standing orders from above to ensure his silence. Aidit would have had information on many of the boys still sitting close to the top. They'll be running scared until this business is over, once and for all.' Zach poured himself some more coffee.

'Soekarno is keeping the game alive, Steve,' Murray said, discarding the broken toothpick. 'Don't hold your breath waiting for the Communists to just give up and go away. They know that their very survival might depend on the President's goodwill. Or even on those who secretly supported their Movement but now find themselves between a rock and the proverbial.' Zach listened to Murray. The man's understanding of how the Indonesians thought was second to none in the Intelligence community.

'Will you think about coming with me? It'll give you the chance to show off some of those places you're always bragging about.' said Zach, urging Murray to agree. 'We could swing back through Bandung on the way back from Semarang instead of going along the coast.' At the suggestion of the port city, Murray looked up quickly. He thought he'd caught a flicker in his friend's eyes. He was tempted to accept.

Murray knew that he had to resolve the ongoing problem with the Diponegor officers in Semarang. If only he could sit down and talk with them, he just might be able to settle their differences. He was sick to death of peering over his shoulder the whole time. Since the fire, he had not noticed any further surveillance of his movements. Perhaps whoever was directing the feud had decided that enough was enough, although Murray knew that this was probably wishful thinking on his part. He sat thinking about Zach's offer. If they were together, Murray believed that he would be safe, although he was not entirely comfortable with the prospect of taking the chance just to find out.

'And you won't even have to interpret for me,' Zach was saying, as Murray half-listened to the other man's encouragement. It might be the solution to his problem. He had an idea.

'If we're going together, best put my name down as your official interpreter. If the Army approves my travel, I'll go.' Murray then looked up and smiled at the grin on Zach's face. They had become good friends. Murray trusted the man.

'Great,' the colonel responded, grinning broadly. 'I'll have the W.O. process the request first thing tomorrow morning.' He clapped his hands together, then went in search for one of the servants. They needed more wine. As Steven Zach wandered out of the dining room, Murray considered his decision and hoped he had not been too adventurous in electing to throw himself into the enemy's camp. Zach returned with another bottle of claret and they sat together talking, sipping the red wine, while the servants cleared the table. When they had finished, the men went to their respective rooms and threw themselves into bed. Having consumed his fair share of the wine, Murray had little difficulty sleeping. Within moments of closing his eyes, the gentle hum of the airconditioner lulled him to sleep, and he dreamed of his first trip to the magical islands surrounding Pulau Putri, and the special moments he had enjoyed while still a student at the university. Then his dream twisted, becoming convoluted, and the mood changed. Suddenly he could see Yanti running along the sand, calling to him as she was chased by soldiers, but he was unable to help. His feet were being held as he tried to swim the few metres back to the beach to help her, and each time he attempted to kick free, his body would sink a little further into the deep water. And then he was cold. Very cold. And the dream changed as he was chased down the street by a crowd of servants who had gathered and called out to him, accusing him of killing his houseboy and, as he ran to escape, his path was blocked by a row of soldiers wearing the insignia of the Diponegoro 7th Regiment. And then he began screaming ...

Murray awoke with a start. He was covered in sweat yet the cold air-conditioned air continued to blow across his body. He sat up and shivered, then the waves of nausea rose through his stomach and he knew that he was going to be ill.

The following morning he had recovered from the attack but still appeared grey around the face when Zach sat down to have coffee with him. They rarely ate a real breakfast, not that Murray was in any condition to do so this day. Zach shot an inquiring look across at the Station Chief but Murray recognising the look, just shook his head in disgust.

'I was going to suggest you shoot your cook,' Murray attempted to make light of his debilitating attack. Few expatriates successfully completed a tour of the country without at least one serious illness during their stay. Zach smiled knowingly and left Murray behind, offering to send the driver back later. At ten o'clock Zach telephoned to see how he was.

'Are you up to some good news?' he asked, pleased that his assistant had been able to wait for the approval and return with the travel warrant already signed. The Army protocol section had merely added Murray's name to the colonel's already approved tour, as he was listed as the Military Attaché's interpreter. No other formal clearance had been necessary. Zach promised to send the driver straight around to bring Murray to the Embassy.

He went back into his bedroom to change, while thinking about the tour with Zach which would take him back to Semarang, and the Diponegoro officers. He knew that his dream had been a result of the seafood they had eaten but couldn't help thinking that perhaps there was an omen there somewhere. 'Omen indeed! You've been here too long, my friend,' he said to his reflection as he dressed in front of the mirror.

* * * * * *

Murray knew that it would not be appropriate for him to have Ade stay while he remained in Zach's house. He had no doubt that the colonel would have agreed had he asked but, understanding how the Military functioned, Murray believed that having an Indonesian girl stay over at the Attaché's house would most definitely be frowned upon by the wives. He knew that gossip had ruined more than one officer's career over the years.

There had been little opportunity for Murray to take time to catch up with Ade since his house had been burned. She had discovered what happened only days after his narrow escape, and had telephoned him at the Embassy to see that he was unharmed. He had taken her to the Tjahaja Kota restaurant twice but they had not been able to spend the night together. Neither had mentioned Yanti's name although Murray wondered how she had fared. He thought it probable that she had managed to return to her village and remained in hiding, out of reach of those who continued to search for all who were involved in the Crocodile Hole massacre. Murray hoped that she was safe. He could not understand what had driven Yanti to be party to the mutilations at Halim. Ade, on the other hand, tried not to think about her. Secretly, she hoped that Yanti was dead.

As he would be departing for Semarang within a few days, Murray sent her a letter with one of the drivers, suggesting that they meet at the Hotel Duta for an early dinner. He would rent one of their rooms and then spend what he could of the evening with her. The driver returned within the hour with her reply. She would meet with him at the hotel.

That evening, as they lay awake together, Murray told Ade that he would be going away with Zach on a tour through Central Java.

'Why are you going, Mahree, isn't it still too dangerous?' she asked. There were reports of continued fighting between the Army and the communists.

'Well, Zach asked me to go, and I agreed. Besides, his Indonesian is not as good as he thinks,' Murray lied. He had to provide some reason for accompanying the Military Attaché. Ade appeared to accept this and he changed the direction of their conversation, knowing that it was difficult for him to justify venturing through Central Java when fighting had been reported as being so heavy. He needed to establish just how strong the Communist resistance really was, as Central Plans had expressed concern that the information being passed out by the Indonesian authorities had been drastically altered in their favour. Once Murray had alerted Melbourne that he would accompany the Military Attaché on a tour through the area, he was immediately given a list of target information requirements from his superiors.

They left the hotel together before midnight, promising to meet as soon as Murray returned from his tour with Zach. He was pleased that he had made the extra effort to spend the evening with Ade, deciding that all in all, he was very lucky to have her around.

* * * * * *

Embassy of the Union of the
Soviet Socialists Republic, Djakarta

Colonel Kololotov sat thinking about the last directive he had received from Moscow. The report had been hand-delivered by courier and included recommendations from the Head of KGB activities for S.E. Asia, General Konstantinov. The former Canberra-based Russian spy chief had become the first senior KGB officer to be promoted to that rank while still serving outside the USSR and, as Kololotov knew, this made the regional head one of the most influential members of the *Komissia Gosudarstvennoy Bezopasnosti*, the KGB.

The colonel was concerned about his career. Being stuck in Dja-karta during the current problems was proving to be disastrous for him. Chairman Aidit's premature move against the American supported Council of Generals had not only resulted in the demise of the Indonesian Communist Party, but had greatly strengthened America's position in influencing Indonesian affairs. Senior Military officers on whom the Soviets had pinned their hopes to move their Government back into the Kremlin's fold had suddenly been removed or shuffled away from positions of any real power. Years of building relationships with the Indonesians had all but been lost. The PKI's failure to remove General Nasution and the death of the others had only precipitated a sudden rise in anti-Communist feeling throughout the country. To the Soviets' dismay, much of this was also directed at the USSR. When mobs of angry demonstrators crowded their Embassy, the Kremlin had been furious. At least they had not burned the building, Kololotov thought, remembering the damage done to the Chinese Embassy days before. Yes, his masters in Moscow were most unhappy with the current state of affairs in Indonesia. Alarmed by the sudden swing towards their enemy's camp, the Russians had demanded that swift action be taken to correct American initiatives to subvert Soviet influence in the Republic. Kololotov had been ordered to follow the directive now sitting in the folder on his desk.

He sighed, knowing that what they had asked would most probably cost him his career if he failed. And his life, if he was not careful. With this thought, he unlocked the top drawer of his desk and checked that the 7.63 Mauser was fully loaded. The German automatic lay there with its spare ten-round magazine. He lifted the heavy weapon as if gauging its suitability for what he had in mind, moved the safety with his right thumb, then laid it gently back in the drawer. Kololotov then re-locked the desk and leaned back in his chair, looking over his left shoulder into Djalan Iman Bondjol where he could see a convoy of military vehicles moving towards the roundabout.

The Embassy's double-glazed windows all but eliminated the siren's sounds as he observed two military police motorbikes clearing the way for the speeding vehicles behind. Kololotov snorted in disgust as he recognised the assortment of Soviet, American and Japanese equipment knowing that there had been a shift away from using his country's hardware only because the Indonesians could not pay the country's massive debt to their Soviet benefactors. He watched as the convoy entered the roundabout and then cut across the road directly into the Hotel Indonesia. Surprised, the KGB officer unlocked his desk again and reached for the binoculars there. He turned back quickly and adjusted the focus slightly, just as the well-guarded figure emerged from the second vehicle, and walked confidently up the Intercontinental's steps before disappearing from view. Kololotov leaned back in his chair again, unconsciously chewing the binoculars strap as he wondered about the man's sudden rise to the Army's most senior post. Then, he shrugged to himself and reached back into the desk to replace the glasses knowing, that in a few more days, it would no longer be an issue. Kololotov recalled the Kremlin's conclusions as to how this officer's name might have been overlooked on the night of the kidnappings. But he could not support their findings. Nobody, he believed, could really be that stupid. The colonel had lived in the dark world of subterfuge and lies long enough to realise that even in a land where people thrived on the mystique, the simple explanation of how that general managed to be overlooked on that fateful night just did not wash with him. He was convinced that there had to have been another agenda, and that it was most unlikely that he, or any other than those directly involved, would ever know the truth of what really transpired during that night.

Suddenly, he sighed. These thoughts were taking him nowhere. Kololotov pushed the subject aside and returned to the tasks before him. He had much to do before leaving on his trip. The KGB colonel telephoned downstairs and confirmed that he would be requiring one of the unmarked Embassy sedans. Then he picked the dossier and file up from his desk and went down the passageway to discuss his journey with the Political Counsellor. He would require his assistance in accessing the huge safe in the Ambassador's office where funds for all covert missions were kept under lock and key. Kololotov knew that the Counsellor would require time to arrange the cash and have it all checked, before surrendering such a large amount to him. As he made his way through the second storey of the Embassy, the KGB colonel wondered if things would really change once he had effected payment to the man. His superiors on Dzerdzhinsky Square obviously thought so, believing that they really had very few other options. They had proposed the plan and left the details for him to arrange. He had cursed them all when he had first been advised. The task they had given him was practically suicidal. Security around the capital had become virtually impenetrable since the kidnappings. The KGB colonel had instructed his source inside Army Headquarters to keep him informed, and finally the news he had hoped for, came. There would be a brief tour outside the city. He knew that they must take this opportunity, away from the watchful eyes of his bodyguards. The Americans would then be blamed.

Kololotov knocked, then entered as the voice inside answered. He then went together with the Counsellor to make arrangements for the US Dollars he had been instructed to deliver to the officer in Semarang, wondering as he did so whether their man in the Diponegoro really had what it took to see the assassination through.

* * * * * *

CIA Headquarters, Langley, Virginia

Senior Agent Richards left the meeting with the Director and immediately returned to his own office where he drafted messages to his Station Chiefs in Djakarta and Australia. When he had finished, he personally carried the signals over to the communications centre where he identified a familiar face and motioned for the cipher clerk to approach.

'I'll wait while you do these,' Richards advised, handing the messages to the woman. 'And Jean,' he added, before releasing the pages, 'there will be no copies and no logged despatch for these. Okay?' The request was unusual and she raised an eyebrow in surprise. Richards had anticipated her reaction. She was one of the centre's best operators and knew how to keep her mouth buttoned. 'Director's orders,' he said, releasing the pages into her hands. Jean then went to work and, less than fifteen minutes later, both signals had been despatched to their addressees. These were not recorded in her work log, and she returned the hand-written pages to the senior agent. Richards thanked the operator and returned to his own office where he shredded the two signals.

Across the globe, the messages were received and passed to their respective communications officers who, upon sighting the addressee's name, alerted the officer designated that there was an encrypted and urgent signal waiting for him in the Embassy. Within half an hour, the messages had been read then destroyed in both Djakarta, and Canberra. The United States CIA Station Chief in the Indonesian capital phoned BAKIN and made arrangements with his contact to meet later that day.

In Canberra, a similar conversation took place and a meeting was set up for the next morning. As soon as he had replaced the receiver, Anderson buzzed his secretary, Madge, and instructed her to book a flight for him to Canberra. Then he sat in deep thought trying to untangle the enigmatic message that had been passed to him, and wondered just what his Djakarta Station Chief had done that had ruffled their American cousins' feathers so.

Chapter 25

Java

Zach leaned forward and attempted to stretch. He was uncomfortable from the many hours of just sitting, with Murray, in the rear of the Holden. They had just finished their brief one-day stopover at Solo, during which time Zach paid a courtesy call on the local Army commander. They discovered there, too, that the story was the same as it had been wherever they had stopped. It was obvious that the local commanders had all been given an identical brief on how to respond during conversations with the visiting Military Attaché. They had learned very little from these officers. Instead, evidence of what was really taking place could be seen along the roadside as they passed through the densely populated centres.

Their tour had taken them up along the central highlands, through Bandung down to Tjilatjap and back up into Djogyakarta. They had spent almost five days on the road before reaching the special area still ruled by the Sultan. Zach had been invited to a small gathering hosted by Hamengkubuwono, the Ninth Sultan who, until recently, had served as a member of Soekarno's Cabinet. Zach had been keen to meet with the Sultan as he believed that they would glean more from any discussion with him than they might from the local garrison commanders.

It had been a frustrating week. They could see that Central Java had suffered badly from the ongoing civil war. When they had stopped at a roadside stall not far from the southern coastal port of Tjtjalap, the *nasi goreng* vendor had talked enthusiastically of the ongoing slaughter of Communists in the neighbouring villages. Zach had not been overly keen when Murray had pushed for a slight detour, one which would take them through the turbulent area.

Ten kilometres down the narrow provincial road, the driver had suddenly braked, refusing to continue. At first, neither of the passengers understood until Zach swore and yelled at the driver to go forward to the next side road, and turn around. Murray reached for his brief-case, reacting to the possibility of danger.

Alongside the red dirt road, stacked as if they were piles of logs, were rows upon rows of bodies. These had been placed, Zach thought, to assist with the count. In places, the piles were stacked more than four to five bodies high, and the rows continued along the village road, almost as far as they could see. Neither spoke. Murray silently photographed the terrifying scene. Zach later said that he had carried out a quick count as they had driven by, estimating that there were at least a thousand dead, stacked off to the side of the road, only partly hidden in the knee-length grass. And these weren't just the bodies of men. Murray's jaw tightened as he identified the bodies of children amongst those thrown onto the piles of dead. It was a grisly discovery.

The driver started to drive faster, as more and more bodies came into view. Neither of the two *tuans* prevented him from doing so. They had seen enough. More than enough, Murray felt, sick to the stomach fighting back waves of despair. It reminded him of images of a Hitler death camp. As they drove away, Murray wondered just how many more would die before the President called a halt to the genocide.

A few days later, they had met with Hamengkubuwono, briefly, in the royal court, and warmed to the Sultan immediately. He asked had they driven through the areas where fighting continued. When he discovered they had, Murray saw a look of concern cross the ageing Sultan's face as Zach described what they had seen. The Australians knew that there was little that the royal leader could do to rectify the situation. His authority as Sultan was severely restricted to the special area of Djogyakarta and its surrounds and, although greatly respected by the people of Indonesia, he was unable to exert any real influence over the Government. Hospitable and gracious, the Sultan had provided escorts while the men remained within his domain. The following day, they left for Semarang.

* * * * * *

FREEDOM (MERDEKA) SQUARE

Semarang

Pak Didi, the Hotel Istana manager, was excited with the sudden surge in the number of guests. The past month had been disastrous, since few were willing to travel through the country due to the ongoing political unrest. He went through the bookings and checked the names and nationalities against the rooms allocated. Satisfied that all was in order, he then completed the mandatory daily police report and instructed one of his staff to take this down to the station.

The authorities insisted on keeping tabs on all visitors, not just the occasional foreigner who might be passing through. Pak Didi sighed. He had wished that the town had more to offer than just being on the road to Borobudur and Djogya. It seemed that the port city had so little to offer the tourists. Rarely did his guests stay more than one night, using the Istana Hotel merely as a way-station. At least, he thought, collecting a copy of the guest list for his file, there were still some foreign guests willing to brave the countryside and visit.

He then went about arranging for fruit baskets to be placed in the rooms to welcome his foreign guests. It was a thoughtful touch, he knew. Deciding to check on the arrangements himself, the fastidious manager climbed the staircase. He checked the first two overlooking the garden, which he had allocated to the Australian group, and was satisfied that all was in order. Then he moved along the passageway and inspected the smaller room facing the street. He stepped inside and looked around. Pak Didi then turned and left, closing the door behind him as he did so.

Then, with a slight display of arrogance, and knowing that he would not be seen, the manager made a face as he walked back down the passageway. Pak Didi resented the fact that he had a Russian booked into his hotel room. In his experience, they had never shown any gratitude for his gestures of hospitality, and besides, he thought they were generally uncouth. Pak Didi knew that, had it not been for the fact that the Istana Hotel was the only recognised accommodations where foreigners were permitted to stay, the Russian would most probably have been just as comfortable staying in one of the local *losmen*. With this thought, Pak Didi went down to the kitchen and cancelled the fruit basket for room 208.

* * * * * *

Diponegoro Headquarters

Colonel Suhendra's stomach growled as he sat nervously, considering how he would have to change his rostered duties with one of the others officers, to enable him to slip away in time to meet with Kololotov. He had been surprised when the Russian had contacted him by telephone. Suhendra lived in continuing fear that he would, some day, be compromised by his Soviet colleagues through their often amateurish ways. He had discovered, much to his dismay, that whenever the Russians had attempted to communicate with him, over the past four years, their clumsy methods had almost cost him his life. Suhendra recalled an earlier meeting with his Soviet Embassy contact some months before. The stupid fool had simply sent a letter to Suhendra's home instructing him to meet with the Russian in a popular beer garden. When the note had arrived, his wife had opened the envelope and, unable to understand the contents, accused her husband of having an affair. Later, he had still met with his contact. But not at the predetermined location. It was just too risky.

Suhendra had been responsible for revealing Colonel Sulistio's relationship with the Americans. Subsequently, when Lieutenant Colonel Sulistio did not return from one of his evening patrols, Suhendra knew immediately that the information he had passed to his Soviet controller had been effective. They had obviously wasted little time in orchestrating the colonel's demise and, at the time, he was relieved that the American sympathiser was no longer around to complicate his life. This had been difficult enough, what with the frequent visits his Commander made to Djakarta, often insisting that he drive with the general. At least he had been able to do something constructive during the last visit. Suddenly Suhendra smiled as he recalled the success he'd had in observing the Australian's activities during Prajogo's recent visit to the capital. It hadn't bothered him when, after their arrest, he had discovered that the two detainees were members of Gerwani. He had no time for this women's group, even though they were pro-Communist.

Suhendra had been recruited by Kololotov's over-zealous predecessor in 1958, when, along with many others, the Javanese officer had become disillusioned with his country's unsuccessful attempts to prevent the Americans' ongoing intrusions into Indonesian territory. It had not been difficult to influence the young Lieutenant, whose brother had been killed in Sumatra during a coastal patrol off Padang. Indonesian Intelligence had been informed by Soviet sources that the Americans had been offloading tons of ammunition from two submarines along the Sumatran coast. Sadly for Suhendra's brother and most members of his marine patrol, their craft came under fire and was sunk during one such US Navy mission.

Survivors had confirmed sighting the submarines, although the United States Government hotly denied the claims. Suhendra's father had been a communist. He had died in late 1948, during the fierce fighting in Madiun when the TNI brutally prevented a Communist uprising from succeeding. He and his brother had been orphaned. They had barely survived, living hand-to-mouth, along with millions of others. When the time came, they joined the Military. After their country gained formal recognition of its Independence, political infighting had started, throwing the country into disarray. They learned quickly, understanding that they had to be circumspect regarding their political affiliations. Promotions were overlooked by those who were anti-Communist. The young officers both maintained their father's political convictions. However, neither registered as members of the PKI.

At the time they were still young officers, the Americans moved to create a major split in the Republic. Rebellion broke out on several fronts, and Suhendra was soon dragged into the conflict, as was his brother, as members of the fledgling Armed Forces. It was then, as a junior Intelligence officer, that the young lieutenant discovered just how serious the Americans had become in their efforts not only to destabilise the Republic, but to create three separate and independent states under their influence. Then he lost his brother.

Suhendra had been bitterly disappointed with Soekarno's permissive attitude towards those who would drag his country into a pro-Peking communist alliance. He strongly believed that his country needed to remain ideologically identified with the Soviets. Suhendra was convinced that the Indonesian Communist Party would deliver his people into the hands of the Chinese. When news first broke of the Halim massacres, he too wanted to rush out to join in the search for those who had kidnapped and mutilated their own people. But later, he realised that the PKI had, in fact, assisted his own ally's cause by removing those who had steered Indonesia towards American control. And now even the PKI had failed.

Suhendra understood that the events surrounding the 30th September Movement had driven his country's leadership further away from Communism, and that those who now influenced the Government had made it quite clear that Indonesia would never tolerate any re-emergence of the Left in any form. Suhendra fiercely believed that those who had taken charge since the abortive coup d'etat, should be prevented from delivering the country back into the hands of the neo-colonialists. Also, there were the financial considerations. Even a good Communist needed money. He had agreed to participate in the plot which would follow through from where the PKI had failed. Only, this time, he was determined that no-one from their list would survive.

* * * * * *

Army Chief of Staff Offices, Djakarta

Arrangements had been confirmed for Soeharto's flight. At first, he had been reluctant to ask AURI for the use of one of their aircraft, knowing that many of the Indonesian Airforce officers were still loyal to Air Marshall Omar Dhani and the PKI. It was only after he was assured that the crew had been hand-selected by Army Intelligence that the Chief of Staff agreed to fly. His schedule would first take him down to Djogyakarta from where he would then proceed by staff car to Solo and Surakarta. The general wished to see what was happening for himself. In view of this, he would return to Djogyakarta and fly the short distance across the fertile plains, before dropping down to visit old friends. He was looking forward to seeing his former Command, and the officers of the Diponegoro Divisions based in Semarang.

* * * * * *

FREEDOM (MERDEKA) SQUARE

Melbourne

Director Anderson sat stunned, his face grave as his visitor revealed the startling evidence with its damning implications. He glared at the document holder stamped 'Most Secret - C.I.A. Director Only' across the face.

'I'm sorry,' the American said, sincerely. He had flown down from Canberra then gone directly to the address in St. Kilda Road. The CIA Station Chief looked at the grey-headed Australian and genuinely felt sorry for him. The flurry of activity generated by the contents of the report he carried was nothing when compared with the accusations and soul-searching that had taken place back in Langley, after the suicide. The experienced Chief also knew that if the Australians refused to rectify the problem immediately, then his own people would not hesitate to remove the danger themselves.

'I can't accept this as irrefutable proof that Stephenson is one of theirs,' Anderson said a little too sharply. The American knew that this was going to be tough. No one wanted to hear that they had been betrayed. 'Shit,' he thought, 'if only this man knew the whole goddamn story!' He sat quietly, waiting for the Australian Intelligence Head to get it all out, as he knew he would.

'Granted, Stephenson's been known to be a little unorthodox from time to time in the way he handles his duties,' Anderson went on, 'but we've never been given any reason whatsoever to suspect that he has, in any way, compromised this agency.' The American waited. He knew there would be more before the recriminations started. 'It should be clear to your people that his relationship with elements of the Indonesian Communist Party were a result of directives from this office.'

'Our sources in Indonesia are beyond reproach. There is more than sufficient evidence to support Langley's conclusions. Otherwise, why would we be having this conversation?' he suggested.

'Murray Stephenson is our Station Chief. Langley knows that. Situations are rarely as clear-cut as they appear to be. Aside from his instructions to associate with the communist students and elements of the PKI as an integral part of his cover, Murray Stephenson has never been associated with anyone who could even be considered 'pro-Soviet.' He paused, collecting his thoughts.

'The suggestion that Stephenson might be a threat to Soeharto is, quite frankly, absurd.' He was angry not only at the suggestion that one of his agents may be involved in some plot to remove one of Indonesia's brightest stars, but also because his anger was evident. He had meant to keep his temper.

'I'm sorry, but the evidence does point to his involvement. Even if you're not convinced, our agency is. We should accept their findings,' the American said, not offhandedly. He found it difficult dealing with people who failed to understand that the United States was working in their interests, too. Seemed to him that half of the goddamn world failed to appreciate this. He had been instructed by his Director not to reveal the additional information he carried unless it became apparent that the Australians were reluctant to accept the American findings.

'Your predecessor, Bradshaw, recruited Stephenson, I believe?' he asked, already knowing that this was true. Anderson frowned and nodded, anxious as he watched his visitor push yet another folder across the table. It had the same security warnings blazened across the cover as the other. Suddenly Anderson didn't want to know what was contained in this second folder. He looked at the other man. His eyes narrowed as his stomach tightened. There was silence. Then the ASIS Director snapped the binding away from the document and opened the report.

The inside covering sheet contained a full head and shoulders photograph of his predecessor, smiling as if he'd posed for the shot. For a brief moment, Anderson was taken aback, having already forgotten just how charming Harry Bradshaw could be. He flipped through the preamble and commenced reading the CIA profile report on the man who had been Australia's most experienced field agent and, later, Head of its clandestine Intelligence forces. As he read through the file, even he was surprised at the depth of the information contained in the document. Harry's early life and associates were all well-documented, including extracts of Soviet reports relating to his activities when employed by the British MI6. Anderson paused, removed his glasses and rubbed an itchy eye before returning to the fascinating reading. Then he paled. As he turned the following page, there was another photograph. And another. These showed a considerably younger Harry in Berlin. Anderson was embarrassed by what these photographs obviously inferred. Then he was angry. Why hadn't their allies produced these damning reports before? Why wait until the man was missing, probably dead, before they revealed what they had? Had Harry been compromised by the Americans? Had they been using him as well? These and other questions raced through the Director's mind as he turned the pages, one by one, following the damaging evidence of Harry's dark secrets. He stopped and rose slowly from the long mahogany table and shuffled like an old man over to where coffee and biscuits had been left by his secretary. He poured the coffee and turned back to his visitor. The American nodded. Anderson then returned to the table and placed one of the cups in front of his visitor.

'How long has the Agency had this file on Bradshaw?' he asked, almost casually. The American sipped the dark liquid. He thought it tasted like crap.

'You know how it goes. Everyone keeps tabs on everyone else. In Bradshaw's case, we had him on file ever since he was working with the Brits. You probably don't know this but our boys are paranoid about giving anything to the limeys, and that goes back even before the shit hit the fan with Philby, Burgess and Maclean, just to mention a few. Their MI6 is like a ship full of leaks. Hell, no one wants to deal with them anymore. Bradshaw came to our attention when he worked for MI6. They had him over in Berlin. But you know all about that. To be honest, we didn't know about his little idiosyncrasies until we caught him in Bangkok. Then, due to the sensitivity of our relationships with Australia, we decided to keep him in check just in case your own people weren't doing their job.'

'What happened to him?' Anderson asked, knowing that the Americans had the answer. The CIA officer was taken aback at the bluntness and waited for a time before replying. There was still a great deal more on file which wasn't revealed here in the documents he'd shown Anderson. He crossed his arms and looked down at the table.

'We believe that Boris got him,' was all he said. It was Anderson's turn to be surprised. He had believed his department's conclusion that Harry had fallen victim to one of the groups of thieves which thrived in Thailand by robbing tourists. His body had obviously been dumped somewhere discreet. 'Perhaps even in the crocodile farms on the outskirts of the city,' he suddenly thought.

'The Russians?' he asked, disbelievingly. The American nodded slowly and leaned across to check the second file Anderson had been reading. He found what he'd been looking for and showed the report to the ASIS Chief. Again, there were photographs attached. Anderson read through the pages and then leaned back in his chair.

'We know all about those visits. They were all well-documented at his request. It was, he said, his way of maintaining civilised communications with the Kremlin. I could show you these if you feel they're important. Personally, I believed at the time that Harry should have left the ongoing contact well enough alone, but he was the Director and dictated most of the policy around here while he was in the chair. No, I don't accept that there was anything sinister in these visits.' Then looked across the table. 'Why does the CIA believe otherwise?' he asked, watching the American's face to see if there was anything there which might indicate just how much more they knew. That they weren't telling. Anderson understood how the game worked. His visitor unlocked his arms and placed his hands on the table. Anderson was then certain that there was, indeed, a great deal more that hadn't been disclosed.

'You'll have to leave that with us for the time being. We have something in play, as we speak. When it's finished, I'm sure my Director would be happy to discuss this with you further. In the meantime, he's looking for a reassurance that your man Stephenson will be removed from the area, at least until we can clarify the situation.' Anderson understood quite clearly that this was not a request. He was furious that he would be obliged to agree to their demands. He did not accept their suppositions based on Stephenson's known relationship with the former Director. What they were suggesting was absurd. Ludicrous! But he would have to comply, knowing that to refuse could jeopardise their close working relationship with the American Intelligence Services. Not to mention the danger Stephenson would then be in. Anderson knew that it wouldn't be the first time the Americans had taken out one of their own friendlies whose presence interfered with one of their own operations.

'Stephenson will be told,' Anderson said, unhappy with his own response. His visitor immediately smiled, then rose. He retrieved both the document holders and extended his hand.

'The Director will be very pleased. I will inform him of your co-operation.' They shook hands. Nothing further was said. Anderson walked with the American as far as the first security level and passed him on to his secretary, then returned to his office and thought through his meeting with the Agency representative. Then he waited for his secretary to return to take his instructions. Within the hour, two messages had been encrypted and sent across to communications for despatch. These were passed through the enciphering machines and coded, then directed through the central despatch unit located in Canberra.

At the post office in Djakarta, the messages were placed inside small envelopes, and placed in the Australian Embassy box. An hour passed before one of the drivers arrived and cleared the messages, taking these directly to the rostered duty-officer. He, in turn, went immediately to the Embassy and passed the signals through the first stage of decipher, which indicated that the signals were for the political section. The officer telephoned around to locate those concerned, and found the Second Secretary at home. Murray Stephenson, he said, would not be at the colonel's house as they had both left that afternoon by car for Central Java.

The officer went directly into the Embassy and went through the complicated process of deciphering one of the messages as it was, in fact, addressed to him anyway. He placed the other on the First Secretary's desk for when he returned. Only Murray would be able to decipher that particular message as each had their own codes locked in individual safes. Half an hour later, having read his own message, Murray's Number Two went in search for the Chief Petty Officer to see if he could send a most urgent despatch by radio back to Central Plans in Melbourne. He had to inform the Director that Stephenson had left on his trip, and that it would be most unlikely that either he or the Military Attaché would be contactable due to the current crisis. Even at the best of times, telephones rarely worked in the countryside.

At ten o'clock that evening, Anderson sat behind his desk glaring at the incoming signal. There was no way he could now prevent the Americans from taking remedial action, which is precisely what they would do once they discovered Murray was already on his way to Central Java and could not be recalled. Anderson summoned one of the night-duty secretaries and dictated a message to Langley. He informed the CIA that Murray had been contacted and would be returning to Djakarta.

That night, before he closed his eyes and wished for sleep, the Director considered his decision to mislead the Americans. He'd really had no choice. Stephenson was far from being Anderson's first choice as Station Chief in Djakarta, and he had often held his own reservations as to the man's integrity. Nevertheless, he found the accusation that Murray Stephenson had embarked on a mission to assist with the assassination of the new Indonesian Chief of Army Staff, Major General Soeharto, absolutely incomprehensible.

Chapter 26

Semarang

Zach stepped out of the car and smiled at the porters who hurried out to assist with the luggage. He was pleased to be in Semarang, as it was the last military post he was to visit on the tour. There would be a number of courtesy calls to be made and then, with a little luck, he expected to be back in Djakarta before the end of the week.

'Pagi, tuan,' the porters called, almost in unison as they waited for the driver to open the rear of the sedan. The porters were all dressed in white trousers and jackets, with the familiar black *pitji* sitting on their heads. Zach and Murray left them to take care of their luggage and strolled into the large open foyer where they were met by the ebullient manager, Pak Didi.

'Welcome, gentlemen,' he said, smiling profusely, waiting to see whether or not he should shake their hands. Many foreigners, he knew from experience, didn't care to do so. Murray stepped forward and extended his hand. Pak Didi was pleased. He had always liked Australians. *'I have arranged two suites as requested by your Embassy. These are adjacent, on the second floor.'* They thanked the manager and then moved to the reception desk where they were required to show not only their passports but also the travel pass issued by Army Headquarters in Djakarta. They registered, then went to their rooms to clean up before lunch. Zach had meetings arranged for the afternoon and asked Murray if he wished to accompany him.

Murray had thought long and hard about his position, and the danger he would be in once his presence in the coastal town was known. He realised that this would be only a matter of hours, as a copy of the colonel's travel warrant would soon pass from the hotel registry desk to the local police station. From there, they would telephone and inform the local Army garrison of the Military

491

Attaché's arrival. Chances were, his name might not be mentioned as the accompanying interpreter, and he hoped that this would be so. Murray was anxious to meet with the Commander and establish some dialogue with the man.

He had to convince the brigadier somehow, that he should not be held responsible for the circumstances which led to Colonel Sulistio's demise. He knew that this was imperative for his own safety. The problem was how, as Murray really didn't wish to float in with Zach, unannounced, and place his friend in a difficult position. He had also thought about Steven Zach as they had driven through Java together. He admired the man and respected their friendship. A strong bond had developed between them and, apart from the early discomfort he'd felt concerning Zach's affair with Susan, Murray believed that their relationship had strengthened considerably over the past months. Zach had explained what had happened the day Susan departed. He explained that, afterwards, he'd felt a little guilty at being relieved that she had gone.

It was then that Murray understood Zach's earlier reluctance to have him stay at his house. An embarrassed Zach admitted that he had invited the Ambassador's secretary around to his villa twice, although nothing had come out of the discreet encounters. Later, he had even suggested that he might give their relationship another try, once things had settled down in Indonesia and he could take some real time away and visit Susan in Melbourne. Murray was pleased with this. He understood just how difficult it would be for them both, considering Harry Bradshaw's disappearance. Murray believed that if he was to secure his friend's total support, he would have no choice but to disclose how he had nearly been killed in the harbour warehouse, and circumstances relating to the other attacks. He thought about this throughout their long drive together and finally decided, as they neared Semarang, that he would explain what had happened, and leave it up to Zach to decide whether or not Murray should accompany him to meet the general.

Murray knew that it would be most unlikely for the Diponegoro Commander to agree to meet with the man his troops had attempted to kill. Murray wished he could resolve his problem alone but realised that he really had no choice but to seek Zach's assistance.

* * * * * *

FREEDOM (MERDEKA) SQUARE

MOSCOW

It was obvious that they had lost one of their most valuable assets. Fortunately, he was not alone in his service to the USSR for, over the years, there had been many within the American Government who were receptive to payments in exchange for information. When their senior agent failed to communicate later that day, the alarms went off, causing officers in the Soviet Embassy in Washington to work through the night.

By mid-morning, their worst fears were founded. Their deep-cover operative had been uncovered. When the news was announced during an urgently-called Intelligence briefing, not one of the officers present even thought to commend their patriot's actions in taking his own life. Instead, they were angry. Coded messages passed back and forth until it was decided that the mission previously ordered to be implemented by General Konstantinov, should be temporarily put on hold. The Soviets suspected that their plans had been compromised. Their mole had been unable to protect the integrity of the mission. They assumed that the Americans had been alerted. The assassination attempt was not to proceed as they then believed that discovery of their involvement would be inevitable. The KGB immediately communicated this decision to their agent at the Soviet Embassy in Djakarta. Colonel Kololotov was already preparing to leave Semarang and return to Djakarta when he received his new instructions. He cursed them all, knowing that he might not be able to contact Major Suhendra again, or in time.

* * * * * *

Diponegoro Headquarters

The Commander smiled cordially as they shook hands. Zach was then introduced to the other senior officers present, including Colonel Suhendra. The courtesy call went well, Zach deciding to avoid any further attempts to pry information from the Central Java commands as to what the status really was in respect to the Communist clean-up. He knew that they would deliberately mislead him and believed that he had already acquired sufficient information for his final report. During the course of their conversations Zach heard the distant sounds of sirens approaching. When it became obvious that his host had another guest, he suggested that he return when it was more convenient for the officer.

'No, please stay, Kolonel,' the Commander had insisted. He was impressed with the Australian who spoke their language, acknowledging the effort it would have taken. *'But you will excuse me while I greet my other guest.'* Zach was then entertained by the other officers for almost half an hour as he sat wondering who was with their Commanding Officer in the adjacent building. He was about to leave when the door opened and the Commander returned. He entered the room smiling, obviously pleased with himself.

'Kolonel, have you met my guest before?' he asked, stepping aside as all the officers present jumped to their feet. Momentarily surprised, Zach had done likewise, standing at attention as a sign of respect to the Chief of Army Staff who had entered.

'Pak General,' he said, waiting for the distinguished officer to make the first move. Major General Soeharto smiled and stepped forward, offering his hand to Zach. They exchanged greetings, then the general turned to the other officers and merely nodded for them to sit.

'So, Kolonel Zach,' the Chief of Staff said, still smiling at the Australian, *'you have been touring through Java. What do you think?'* Zach was surprised by the question and wasn't quite sure how to respond. He smiled back.

'I think your country is very beautiful. I would like to see more,' he replied diplomatically. His answer was well-received. The Major General then turned and spoke to his fellow officer in his own dialect. Zach at first thought this rude, then he remembered that all of the officers present were Javanese.

'Kolonel, you have been invited to join us tonight. We are having a small reception for Djenderal Soeharto.' Zach accepted immediately, acknowledging the honour of being invited to join these men during their private dinner. The function would be held at the hotel where he was staying. Zach was later to discover from Murray that this was the only real venue in town, and that any function held by the Army would most probably be paid for by the local merchants.

They talked for a while longer then, knowing when to leave,

Zach apologised to the officers and departed, returning to the hotel to catch up with Murray. He was escorted to his car by Colonel Suhendra. Zach's driver saw him coming and started the engine to cool the vehicle's interior. The officers saluted each other.

'*Thank you for your hospitality, Kolonel,*' Zach said, sincerely. '*If you come to Djakarta please contact me at the Embassy. I would be delighted to see you again.*'

'*Oh, you'll see me before then,*' Suhendra suggested, smiling at the confused look on the other man's face. '*I will also be attending the function tonight at your hotel. It is a command performance. All of the senior Diponegoro officers must attend.*' Zach laughed, knowing from his own experience what they meant in military terms. They then shook hands and parted, agreeing to speak again later that evening.

Zach's car left the compound and the Indonesian soldier's smile vanished. As he stared after the departing vehicle he wondered how the Australian's presence that evening might interfere with his plans. Suhendra returned to his own office to consider how best to ensure that the foreign Military Attaché's presence later that day would not jeopardise his preparations in any way. It was not in his plans that a foreigner should die. But if he had no other choice, then the visiting colonel would become one of the unfortunate casualties.

* * * * * *

Hotel Istana, Semarang

Murray sat sipping his second beer, enjoying the lobby setting. Overhead fans turned slowly, moving the air gently around the old colonial structure. Rattan chairs, with high and intricately woven backs, were positioned in pairs, facing oval-shaped tables. Orchids sprinkled with deep violet colours decorated the tall columns, while arrangements of hibiscus were carefully placed at each end of the bar. Had it not been for the threatening cloud of depression hanging around as he waited for Zach to return, Murray would almost have been happy.

They had discussed his predicament at lunch that day. Zach had expressed surprise that he'd waited so long to reveal the situation, reminding that the violence could have followed when Murray moved in with him. At first, Steven Zach had been quite annoyed that he hadn't been told. Then, as Murray explained the complicated relationship he'd had with Bradshaw and Central Plans, Zach began to understand why Murray had concealed what had happened from his new Director in Melbourne. They had ordered lunch but neither had eaten. Murray knew that Zach's trust was imperative, and even though Zach had not responded warmly at first, for the first time he felt comfortable with the knowledge that someone else was also aware of the threats on his life.

Steven Zach had been adamant. He could see no advantage to either of them should Murray accompany him during his courtesy call on the local military authorities. They had discussed this at length until both reached the same conclusion. Any approach by Murray would be treated with contempt, as long as the Diponegoro officers still believed that he was involved with the Communists, and may have been responsible for the demise of their Lieutenant Colonel, Sulistio. Finally, Murray accepted, albeit unwillingly, his friend's advice not to attend Zach's meetings with the Army. He remained behind, settled down with a bottle of Bir Bintang and waited for the Military Attaché to return.

Towards two o'clock, he heard a Russian voice echoing through the empty, high-ceilinged lobby. Murray had turned around and spotted Kololotov immediately. Kololotov had been trying to telephone his Embassy in Djakarta and had been disconnected several times while attempting to do so. He had stormed down to the reception and accused the operator of eavesdropping. Murray attempted to look away quickly. But not before Kololotov had caught the look in the Australian agent's eye which told him instantly that he had been observed by the enemy.

The Djakarta-based KGB operative was obliged to leave the hotel and place his call directly from the local P.T.T. When he returned, he passed back through the hotel lobby and observed that the other foreigner was still sitting alone, drinking. Recalling the annoying conversation he'd had with the Counsellor, Kololotov approached reception and informed the staff he might be staying yet another day. Then he went to his room to consider just how he could contact Colonel Suhendra again, knowing that the officer would have left the compound along with the others at three o'clock. He checked his watch and swore to himself. Had communications been what they should, he would have been able to telephone the colonel in time and arrange a meeting during the afternoon. Now he had no other choice. Kololotov knew that Suhendra would arrive at the Hotel Istana around six o'clock for the function. He would wait and speak to him then.

Murray watched the Russian from the corner of his eye and wondered what the Station KGB Chief would be doing in such a place. Certainly there was little for the Soviets here, he thought, remembering the deep anti-Communist feelings which ran through the local community. He considered asking the reception how long Kololotov had been there when he spotted Zach walking up the steps into the lobby.

* * * * * *

'How did it go?' he asked, noticing his friend's discomfort with the heat. There were damp spots under Zach's armpits.

'Better than expected,' he replied, nodding to the waiter who had suddenly appeared. He pointed to Murray's bottle of beer. 'Met Soeharto,' he said, resisting the temptation to smile as he watched his friend's reaction.

'Sure you did,' Murray responded, sceptically. Then he saw from Steven's expression that he was indeed serious. 'No bullshit?' His friend played with him for a moment, almost ignoring the response. He accepted the glass of beer, sipped the thin layer of froth, then placed his glass back onto the round rattan table before replying. He knew Murray would find this annoying.

'No bullshit,' he said, smiling, as he wiped his mouth with the paper serviette. Then he continued to play the game. 'What have you been doing with yourself while I was away?' Murray leaned over and shook his fist playfully.

'Come on, Steve, give. What happened. Did you have a chance to talk to the Commander privately?' Suddenly Zach remembered the seriousness of Murray's situation and dropped the game.

'No, Murray, I'm sorry. Soeharto arrived just as I was building up to asking for some private time. But don't be too alarmed. I have been invited to attend their cosy little gathering here, tonight. Right here, Murray, in the Istana Hotel.' Murray listened intently. He wasn't overly distressed by this news. Perhaps an opportunity would present itself to manipulate a meeting with the general, somehow. He considered that possibility.

'Can you get me an invite?' he asked, knowing that this was most unlikely. Zach looked at his friend, knowing what might be going through his mind. He had to do whatever he could to help clear the dangerous problem. Zach understood the stakes that were involved.

'How about you just turn up,' he said, then waved his hand knowing that this would not be acceptable. 'What if I phone and ask if I may bring my interpreter,' he suggested, thinking quickly, before shaking his head as he realised that this also wouldn't work. 'No, that's no good either. They already know I speak their language.'

'How about we wait for me to pass through the lobby at an opportune time, and you can step forward and pretend we've just bumped into each other?' Murray asked, knowing that there was always the possibility that he had already been spotted. Or the receptionist's report would have reached the Army Intelligence desk officer of the day and someone there might have remembered Murray's name. It was possible, Murray thought, he had been there before. And now he was well-known to the Diponegoro officers. At least, to some of them. Suddenly the idea lost its appeal. Murray began to think that perhaps the only solution would be to approach the problem through Djakarta contacts. The trip had been an error in judgement. Or at least the visit to Semarang was, he now believed.

'Maybe I'd best give it a miss. It wasn't one of my best ideas,' he said, rather despondently. He raised the beer to his mouth and took a long swallow. 'Let's cut our losses. Why don't you attend alone, then we'll head back early tomorrow?' Zach considered what he'd said.

'Okay. But we'll still have to work on your problem.' He looked at Murray with a sympathetic smile.

'By the way,' Murray said, nodding over his shoulder without looking, 'there's a Boris running around the hotel yelling at the staff.' Zach lifted his head but couldn't see anyone resembling a foreigner.

'There's thousands of them. Probably an agent for one of their ships.'

'No, this one is on our lists. It's Kololotov.' Suddenly Zach was interested. He was familiar with the name and what he represented. The KGB had never been overly clever, nor discreet, when it came to disguising their agents.

'Are you sure?' he challenged.

'Sure? Of course I'm sure. He virtually threw a tantrum right over there within earshot. Seems his phone wasn't working in his room and he'd missed reporting in to Big Boris, or something like that.' Murray had been drinking a little longer than he normally would at this time of the day. He was becoming a little aggressive. Zach finished his beer and rose. Murray didn't move. He had no reason to. Zach looked up at the lobby clock which informed the hotel guests helpfully what the time might have been in Moscow and Tokyo. It was apparent no-one liked the Americans. Not that it would have mattered as all three clocks had stopped. He checked his wrist-watch. There was still an hour or more to go before he would have to dress for dinner. He told Murray to take it easy and left him alone, hoping that his friend knew it was time to take a quick afternoon nap. As one would do in Djakarta, under the same circumstances. Then Zach went for a stroll outside.

* * * * * *

Semarang Harbour

Kololotov sat alone listening to the filthy harbour water slapping against the wooden poles which supported the small seafood restaurant. The thick, foul-smelling combination of rotting seaweed, discharge from ships' tanks and whatever waste fifty-thousand port-dwellers had hurled into the dark waters did not bother the Russian. The KGB colonel waited in the small shanty-styled structure, irritated that he was there and not already on his way back to Djakarta.

He had been unable to telephone Suhendra, and now he was really concerned. He had sent a rather ambiguous note to the officer by hotel taxi, hoping that someone over at the Army base would have enough initiative to take the two dollars affixed to the envelope and pass it on to the colonel, wherever he was now billeted. Kololotov then caught a *betjak* down to the harbour and waited, on the assumption that the letter would be delivered, and understood. He had argued with the driver over the fare. He despised these people, they were always wanting more. Finally, and to avoid becoming overly conspicuous, Kololotov had paid the additional two-and-a-half rupiah, throwing the note to the ground in anger. He had then entered the shanty-styled structure to wait.

The two hours dragged by slowly. Finally, the Russian accepted that his man had not received his note. He left the small restaurant and looked for a ride. Outside, he noticed the man who had peddled him down to the harbour earlier, waiting with some others. The group of *betjak* drivers sat atop their machines and ignored the Soviet. Even they had their pride. He then started the long walk back to the Istana Hotel.

* * * * * *

Diponegoro Army Married Quarters
Barracks, Semarang

Suhendra's wife received the note and sent the driver away. Her husband was not there. She opened the envelope and frowned at the writing, wondering if the note could be from another woman. She had never studied foreign languages and certainly could not understand whatever was written there. Anyway, she wasn't overly fussed. Her husband had already left, missing his customary afternoon nap. She made a face, remembering how he had returned to their quarters briefly, undressed and taken a quick *mandi,* then changed into his dress uniform before disappearing again, while muttering something about looking after visiting dignitaries.

She really didn't feel too annoyed. These days one was fortunate to be still considered one of the 'active' wives. Her husband had been married twice already and, somehow, with the number of nights when he stayed away until late becoming ever more frequent, she assumed the worst. He was probably going to take a third wife. She sighed and looked out the window at their three children, all still in primary school. Then she cleared her head of these negative thoughts and went about preparing the evening meal, knowing that no good could possibly come from worrying about what her husband may be doing.

* * * * * *

FREEDOM (MERDEKA) SQUARE

Diponegoro Ordnance Depot

Suhendra took the key and opened the third door to his left. As the senior officer, he had not been questioned when he walked past the drowsy guards and entered the storage facility which was located as far away from the other buildings as could be managed. He walked down the musty corridors covered on both sides with chicken wire to permit ventilation through the dangerous stores. He looked up. The plastic skylights were dirty, restricting the necessary natural light into the explosive goods area. He made a mental note to have the roof cleaned and proceeded along the four-metre-high racks of explosive devices and weapons. Suhendra was happy here. He understood the complicated weapons and explosives which were laid out here in the central store, under his control. His responsibility.

He knew the neatly-arranged items almost as if he had created them. Suhendra knew that he could come and go, remove almost anything he wished without the other officers questioning his access. And Suhendra was pleased that this was so, for it was here that he had hidden his money, knowing that the bundle of cash would be safe, buried under the explosives.

He stopped to examine the new storage bins he'd introduced to accommodate the various mortars his Government had purchased. The colonel nodded confidently as he sighted the boxes containing the Danish Madsen 51mm mortars, and then, alongside, the British hand-held two inch weapons. He snorted, looking beyond to the Soviet M1938s sitting beside the smaller American version, knowing that most of the Soviet equipment would soon be replaced if he was unsuccessful in his mission.

Suhendra was immediately reminded of his purpose in entering the huge weapons facility. He quickened his pace, knowing exactly where to go. He turned to his left past a number of unopened cases of Italian 7.62 BM59 Berettas which were awaiting despatch, and moved across to 'G' section. There he found what he wanted. He placed the detonator and timer inside his trouser pocket and continued on his search.

Suhendra smiled, stopped, then picked up the block of TM-200 explosive. It originated from Czechoslovakia, he knew. He had selected the area under where the explosives were stored to hide the money the Russians always gave him, knowing that even the most inquisitive of his fellow officers would not dare venture this far into the dangerous storage area. Let alone check under the supply of TM-200!

He placed the explosives inside his case casually, before running his hands across the adjacent boxes. These contained grenades. Again, the colonel knew that he had an ample choice here. There had been no shortage of suppliers eager to fill his country's warehouses with their expensive tools of war. The boxes had all been opened and the covers discarded. The first contained the British 36-M anti-personnel grenades. He passed over these quickly, not because they were not efficient, but because they did not fit his plan. Then he stopped and picked up one of his old favourites, the Soviet RDG-33. A soldier could throw that a long way, he thought, holding the torch-like shape as if it were just a toy. Finally, he hesitated alongside the box which contained the American MK2 fragmentation grenade.

Suhendra took one of the half-kilo olive-drab weights and threw it casually into the air before catching it again. He thought that it would only be fitting for the assassination to be carried out with at least some American components, as he knew that most of these had been given, not only covertly to his superiors, but also without cost, even though eventually many had benefited financially along the way. He ran his hands across the raised criss-crossed bumps on the grenade's surface, and the thought crossed his mind that these may even be remnants of the shipments his brother had died for, when he had been ordered to search for the American submarines along the Sumatran coast just a few years before. His face clouded with the memory and he turned to leave.

He stopped suddenly, as if unsure of what he'd taken from the case. He rubbed his hand across the plastic cover, checking that the explosive was there. Suhendra knew that these this would do the job. Then his mind turned to the grenade still gripped tightly in his hand. The compact explosives were wrapped in a deeply grooved cast iron body, criss-crossed for maximum effect. After detonation, anyone within ten metres of the explosion would suffer severe injuries. He knew this from experience. Some of his men had used these on the range against PKI detainees. He returned the grenade to its case. Satisfied that he had all he needed, Colonel

Suhendra then left the munitions warehouse as easily as he had entered. He headed towards the reception for the Chief of Staff at the Istana Hotel. At that time, he still had not received Colonel Kololotov's message.

* * * * * *

Hotel Istana

Zach walked back in the direction of his hotel, deep in thought. He was concerned for Murray, convinced that the local Army garrison had to be approached by a third party to convince them that their position regarding the Station Chief was all wrong. He turned the corner and waited for the oncoming group of *betjak* to pass before attempting to cross the wide street. Then he noticed the tall foreigner, dressed in light-coloured trousers and short sleeves, walking quickly towards the Istana Hotel. Zach remained where he was on the side of the road, watching. When he observed the man swing determinedly into the hotel drive, Zach decided that this would have to be the Russian, Kololotov. He followed, also entering via the hotel's main driveway.

When he entered the lobby, the Australian was surprised at the transformation that had taken place in his brief absence. The columns had already been decorated with palm leaves, tied across at the top presenting an appearance similar to a bridal path formed by green and yellow tinted branches. The lounge chairs had been moved closer to the reception area while at the other end, staff were furiously running around throwing white tablecloths over the long collapsible tables, now standing in one line.

Flower arrangements had started to arrive. Zach looked at several of these tall, almost wreath-like displays of lilies and smiled, observing that the local merchants had not been backward in demonstrating that it was they who were funding the evening's festivities. He was surprised also at the number of guests expected. Zach had envisaged that there would be only a few tables, mainly to accommodate the senior officers, but he could see that there would be many more. To Zach, it appeared almost as if the function was still growing in numbers as the hotel manager fussed around checking the arrangements, obviously not really prepared for the additional catering he would be obliged to provide. Zach estimated that there would be no less than a hundred guests expected: many more than even he had anticipated. He wandered over to the reception and asked for his key. It was then that the electricity died. Zach sighed, walked slowly up to his room and entered. He went directly to the windows and opened them, knowing that it would probably be some time before the power was restored. He looked at the silent airconditioner and shook his head. The country had some very serious infrastructure problems, he knew, and electricity supply definitely headed the list.

Zach sat on his bed waiting for power to return before showering. Without the airconditioner it would merely be a waste of time. He undid his shirt and strolled back to the window overlooking the secluded beer garden and stood, willing whatever breeze was out there to cool his sweaty chest. He looked down to the courtyard covered with moss-coloured bricks and near the corner he noticed figures, partly covered by the thick-leaved frangipani tree. Then one of the figures moved and he could see that it was the Russian, Kololotov. He leaned out of the window then tilted his head to the side. Zach could then see that the other man was an Indonesian Army officer, and obviously one of the evening's guests as the soldier was wearing the white officer's formal attire. Zach moved back slightly, to avoid being observed. Then he listened, catching only a few words of the sharp exchange. They spoke in Russian. Zach was surprised, as he caught some of their conversation.

'You will do as I say, if you...' the speaker's voice was muffled and Zach was unable to hear all they said. *'... then you will compromise us all!'* he heard, barely catching the hissed words. He could tell that this had been the Russian speaking. He strained for more.

'... talk to me in this manner. I am... and this is still my country!' the other man had replied, with a similar amount of venom. The exchange was heated, he could tell. Suddenly, Kololotov swore at the other man, which resulted in a slight scuffle. The Indonesian cursed back and threatened him. The Russian swore again, followed by silence and what he thought were footsteps. Then he could not hear either of the men at all. Zach leaned out of the window again and was surprised to see that the Russian had gone. The other man had remained, and was standing alone, straightening his uniform.

Zach could then clearly see the face of the soldier. It was Colonel Suhendra, and he was obviously very, very angry. As quietly as he could, Zach leaned back into his room and snatched his shirt from the back of the chair. He hurried down the hallway as he buttoned his clothing, and followed the steps down into the lobby, ignoring Kololotov as they passed on the stairs. He walked directly out into the rear garden area to find the Indonesian, but he had already slipped away. Surprised and disappointed, he turned and re-entered the lobby, only to find that Murray, who had been having a sleep, had reappeared. Zach told the Station Chief what he'd seen.

'What do you read into it?' Murray asked.

'Obviously Suhendra is their man here. Or at least one of them. Boris would normally have more but I'd be surprised if there are others of the colonel's rank down here. The Diponegoro boys may not be overly fond of the Americans themselves, but having said that, we shouldn't forget that it's here, in this province, that the communists are taking their worst hiding.'

'What do you think they're up to?'

Zach remained deep in thought. The exchange he'd overheard had most definitely been vitriolic. There were possibly even blows exchanged, or at least some serious shoving.

'Got to admit, I really have no idea what it's all about,' he answered.

'Let's talk to the reception and see how long Kololotov intends staying. Maybe we could stay over another day ourselves. I'm still in two minds about leaving here without first settling my problems with the Army.' Zach considered this and nodded. Murray then wandered over to the reception and started talking casually to the staff. Zach could see them talking and smiling. He knew that the staff would tell him what he wanted to know, seeing them warm to Murray's friendly face. Murray strolled back to the bar where Zach was sipping a whisky.

'Seems that our friend has already booked out once today. Curious, he hasn't checked back in yet, but the staff seem to think that he might stay another night. He's still upstairs in his room,' Murray reported. Suddenly, lights blinked in the fading sunlight. Assorted mechanical whirring noises indicated that the power had been restored. They both moved upstairs to shower and, in Zach's case, to prepare for the function which would soon commence. He entered his room and went immediately to the windows, closing them before undressing then showering in the antiquated bathroom.

* * * * * *

Kololotov was livid. He remained in his room trying to decide what course of action to take next. It had never been his plan to remain another night, but he now believed that it was imperative that he do so. He thought back over the altercation. Colonel Suhendra had become unreasonable. No, more than that, he decided. The colonel had become irrational. When he'd been informed that the operation was cancelled, Kololotov had been shocked with the response ...

'It's too late to change your minds now,' Suhendra said, anger evident in his voice.

'You must also return the money,' Kololotov insisted. His masters would never believe that he had been unable to recover the funds once the mission had been aborted. He had to take the money back to the Counsellor.

'No!' Suhendra hissed, his voice rising, *'The money is mine to keep. I will have expenses,'* he demanded. Kololotov's own anger flared.

'You will do as I say. If you continue with the original plan it will most certainly fail. Then you will compromise us all!' the Russian hissed back at the stubborn Indonesian.

'You have no right to talk to me in this manner. I am an officer of the Army and you are nothing.' He dropped his voice even further, *'We must continue with the plan. It is for the good of my people. You don't understand. We must proceed. I am making this decision myself now, and this is still my country.'*

'You are a fool!' Kololotov accused harshly, knowing then that it was unlikely that he was going to recover the funds. He would have great difficulty convincing his superiors that the money had, in fact, been paid. *'I will abandon you now and inform my people that you are no longer to be trusted,'* he hissed again, moving closer, Suhendra recoiling from the bad breath.

'You are a pig,' the Indonesian spat angrily at the Russian.

Kololotov grabbed the front of his uniform and jerked his arm upwards, lifting the smaller man almost off the ground. They scuffled briefly then froze, as one of the staff passed by almost within view. The Russian whispered threateningly into the colonel's ear, then stomped away in anger, returning to his room to think things through. His hands were tied. Somehow he must take steps to prevent the assassination attempt from continuing as planned.

* * * * * *

Suhendra remained behind, shaking in rage. He hated the man who had so easily intimidated him. Had he been in possession of his dangerous package right then, he would have willingly selected a new target and forgone the other, just to repay the Russian for this confrontation. Looking down he saw that his uniform had been rumpled and, straightening the jacket, he walked quickly away. How he wished he had not informed Kololotov about the function that would take place in the hotel later. He had to think. And he knew that he also had to regain his composure. Suhendra moved through the rear of the garden and sought out his jeep. His hands were still shaking when he leaned behind the seat and checked that the metal box he'd placed there earlier that afternoon had not been disturbed. He sat alone for some minutes, considering his options now that the Soviets had aborted the original plan. It took but a few moments before Suhendra decided that it would still be in his interests to proceed. Only now he would modify his plan to accommodate his target's revised itinerary.

When Suhendra's Commander had informed his staff that the new Chief of Staff would visit, the Army's own guest house, maintained only for VIP visits, was immediately prepared. Suhendra had planned to place the explosive in the major general's quarters before he retired. When the explosion took place, he would be back in his own quarters, asleep. Now, as the general had decided not to remain overnight, Suhendra's options had been severely restricted. He had thought about the limited time left, and even considered placing the explosives close to where his target would sit during the function. Suhendra knew that his own Commander was not one of the American supporters. Suhendra admired the man and decided that he would not be responsible for his death as well. The function as a possible venue for Soeharto's assassination was therefore discounted completely. There would be no other opportunity, he felt, apart from the general's transport. Suhendra knew that it would be almost impossible for him to place the explosives in the correct vehicle, and at the right time. There were just too many unknown factors involved for him to take that risk. Finally he had decided to place the device on board the departing aircraft, which would transport Indonesia's most powerful soldier back to the capital. Once the man was dead, others who waited in the wings would not hesitate. Even Nasution would not be missed this time.

He thought about what he must do, when the time arrived. As a member of the Commander's personal staff, he would have little difficulty in boarding the airplane prior to its departure. Then he would set the timer and place the package on the aircraft. The explosion would do the rest. Satisfied that the changes to his plan would not be difficult to incorporate, he waited inside his jeep for other invitees to arrive.

Chapter 27

Semarang

Kololotov remained in his room until well after the loud music had started downstairs. Then he remembered that he had not confirmed with reception that he would be staying for another night. He had to remain, there was no other choice. When the situation presented itself, he would go downstairs and confront Suhendra again, if possible, and convince him to reconsider. He must find some way of attracting the colonel's attention during the function without being overly obvious to the other guests. Only then could he consider leaving the city and driving back to Djakarta. Kololotov bathed and changed into a long-sleeve white shirt and dark trousers, so as not to appear too conspicuous once he had moved down amongst the many guests. He knew that his presence would not be challenged. The Indonesians were too polite for that. Instead, those present would assume that either he was an invited guest or as a resident in-house, had wandered into the function believing that it was open to all the hotel guests.

* * * * * *

Murray was unhappy with the commitment he had given Zach to remain out of sight in his room. But both understood that he would be recognised once a few of the Diponegoro officers remembered his face from earlier visits. So, reluctantly, he had agreed. Zach had undertaken to make a concerted effort to deal with Murray's problem the next day.

Murray had ordered a half of Scotch and settled back with a generous serving of local dishes to keep himself occupied. Within the hour, he had become restless and bored. The music teased as he listened to the orchestra play, and he was fascinated by the number of string instruments supporting the traditional, almost calypso-style music which filled the tropical night. Murray turned his airconditioner off, then opened his windows to allow the sounds to filter through. He ignored the mosquitoes which flowed through the large opening. Even with almost a quarter of the bottle already under his belt he was not relaxed. Murray moved to his bed and lay back in the darkened room, listening.

* * * * * *

The lobby filled quickly as guests flowed into the large high-ceilinged space, their voices carrying through the building. The manager, Pak Didi, ran around nervously, watching as the mixture of local merchants and military crowded into the reception area. He looked across at the receiving line and was pleased that he had managed to arrange everything in time considering the incredibly short notice he had been given. The men who stood waiting together, as hosts, were amongst the most powerful in his country. Suddenly he felt his chest swell with pride as he danced quickly towards the kitchen.

Zach entered the lobby and accepted a warm beer poured over ice. When the next waiter passed, he exchanged this quickly for what appeared to be whisky, then stood observing the other guests as they formed small groups and conversed. The noise level rose quickly and, as he mingled with some of the Indonesian officers and their wives, he spotted Colonel Suhendra standing alone. He moved towards the man immediately.

'Hello, and *selamat malam, Kolonel,*' he said, wishing the officer a good evening. They didn't shake hands. Both men had already spoken during the course of his meeting earlier in the day. '*This is quite a function,*' he stated, hoping to engage the colonel in conversation.

'*Yes, it is,*' replied the colonel, matter-of-factly, as if such occasions were common in his city.

'*There are not many foreigners present,*' Zach suggested, directing the conversation.

'*There not too many who would be welcome at such a gathering,*' Suhendra replied. Zach detected an air of hostility. '*It is difficult these days for my Government to know who to trust.'*

'I hope you don't include the Australians in that observation,' Zach parried. Now that Suhendra was apart from his peers his prickly attitude was more apparent. Zach pushed ahead.

'I believe I saw you here earlier,' he said, watching for a reaction, *'out in that magnificent rear garden setting.'* He observed Suhendra's reaction. The colonel's face froze as his eyes moved to stare aggressively into Zach's. This, Zach knew, was considered confrontationalist in this country. He knew he had hit a nerve.

'I think you must be mistaken,' the colonel responded, emphatically. He then waved at someone across the room and forced a smile. *'Excuse me, I am called,'* with which he quickly walked away and through the crowded lobby.

The Australian Military Attaché lifted himself unobtrusively onto tiptoe and glanced in the direction the man had taken to see if he had, in fact, been summoned. Suhendra had already disappeared from sight. Zach then strolled across to another group and introduced himself, hoping to speak again with the colonel later. As he was speaking to the wife of one of the other guests, a loud gong sounded the buffet's commencement. Zach stepped back, knowing that there would be a rush.

The buffet came under attack as the guests filled their plates with the fine assortment of food which had been prepared for them at the local traders' expense. He waited before taking a small plate of *sate*, then stepped back to watch the other guests enjoy themselves. As he pulled the charcoal-cooked chicken meat off the skewer with his teeth, careful not to drip the soya sauce, he spotted Kololotov standing at the bar section, looking like some imported foreign bartender who had lost his way. Zach moved slightly, standing almost out of view behind a group of younger officers. He observed the KGB officer staring across the room. Zach followed the Russian's line of sight and discovered that Suhendra had returned. He continued to watch the two, as Kololotov's efforts to attract the other man's attention were obviously being ignored by the Indonesian officer. Then he watched with interest as the poorly-dressed Soviet attempted to move through the throng of guests, heading directly towards the man who refused to recognise what Zach had thought were obvious signals to talk, or meet outside. He continued to observe the move, and was not surprised when he saw the Indonesian turn suddenly and walk away from what might have been a confrontation, towards the far end of the lobby. Then he noticed Kololotov pause before following the other man who had exited in the direction of the toilets.

Zach made his way to the far end of the lobby and stood so that his view of the reception area was unhindered. Minutes passed, then, as he anticipated, first one of the men re-appeared, followed by the other at a respectable interval. Zach was caught off-guard when the Russian returned to the lobby, but instead of rejoining the gathering, he turned to his left and climbed the staircase, obviously heading for his room. Zack moved back and stood alongside a small group of smiling local businessmen who had finished eating, but remained standing around talking not far from the other guests. Zach smiled, introduced himself, and started to talk to one of the merchants when he observed Suhenra trying to look inconspicuous. Zach understood the movements. He apologised, mentioning he had forgotten something and moved away, just as Suhendra turned from where he was standing close to the stairwell, and climbed the carpeted stairs. Zach noted his exit then returned to the guests at hand. He remained close to this station waiting for the Indonesian colonel to re-appear. Some minutes later, he felt a hand on his arm and turned to see the commander smiling at him.

'You are enjoying our reception for the Chief of Staff?' he asked, not insincerely.

'I am. Very much. Thank you for the honour of the invitation,' Zach replied. He wanted to move slightly so as to keep his peripheral vision open to the staircase leading upstairs.

'You are driving back tomorrow?' the Commander asked, knowing that this was fact.

'Yes, unfortunately,' Zach responded again. Then he remembered Murray. 'I might stay over another day, if there was an opportunity to meet with you, Bapak,' he said, using the term of respect which was not lost on the senior officer. The Indonesian smiled at him.

'I will not be here. Pak Soeharto has asked me to join him tonight on his flight back to Djakarta.' The Commander seemed pleased that he would be leaving with his old friend. He had yet to announce his departure to those other than his aides and senior officers. He would do this shortly.

'Ah,' Zach said, making small talk, *'then you will arrive back in the capital even before I leave the province.'* The general smiled again and nodded in affirmation. Then he suddenly became serious.

'Wait here,' he ordered, leaving Zach standing alone. Only moments had passed when a captain walked over and took him by his elbow.

'Pak Kolonel,' he said to the surprised Attaché, *'the Bapak wishes to speak to you.'* Zach followed, conscious of the stares as he did so. The young officer took him through the congested hall, holding his hand in front as he made way for them both until they reached the hosts who were seated off to one side. The general indicated that he should sit.

'I hear that you don't enjoy driving so much?' Soeharto asked. The others in his group smiled knowingly. One of the ladies even giggled. Zach felt slightly embarrassed.

'It isn't that I don't enjoy the beautiful countryside,' he said, searching for the more difficult words, *'it is that sometimes I become impatient to be at my next destination.'* The group were flattered with his reply. They had all, at some time or another, travelled the long journey across the broken roads to their villages. Here was a foreigner who really understood how to behave. They were impressed.

'You are invited to join us tonight, if you wish,' the general offered. Zach was caught off-guard again and, for once, wasn't quite sure how to respond. If the invitation was sincere, he would have to go. There would be the added advantage that he may be given the opportunity to speak to the other officer, alone. On the other hand, had the general's invitation merely been a polite gesture, he should find an acceptable way to refuse.

'You are very kind, General.' Zach replied, knowing that they were all watching to see how he would respond. *'I would be pleased to join you on your flight. Terima kasih,'* he said, hoping that he had made the correct decision. The wives clapped their hands as one would expect young school girls to react. The two generals smiled.

'Well, that's it then,' the Commander said, *'Captain Suhardjo there will take care of the arrangements.'* Zach decided that this was his signal to leave. He excused himself, thanked the generals again, and walked away followed by envious eyes. He mingled with the officers who seemed suddenly eager to be seen talking to the foreigner who had found the ear of their commander. And the new

Chief of Army Staff. Zach laughed and talked, enjoying the moment. He didn't even notice when Colonel Suhendra surreptitiously rejoined the party.

* * * * * *

Murray felt drowsy. Although the windows were open and the music continued to drift into his room, he could still hear the sounds of staff as they walked along the corridor. There had been a lull in the noise when the band had taken a short break. He felt his eyes closing as the soft breath of the evening sea-breeze wafted gently through the open windows. He had finished almost half of the whisky and, when he at first heard the sounds, thought nothing of them. Then he heard the noises again, and sat up immediately, alert. Surely the noise had been a cry of pain?

He moved through the semi-darkness and placed his hand inside the case, removing the automatic and checking the magazine as a matter of habit. He stood by the door and listened. There! He was sure he'd heard it again. There was little to be heard but the sounds downstairs, as the guests went about jostling each other over the buffet. Minutes passed, and Murray waited. But he could hear nothing more. Slowly he lowered himself back onto the bed and closed his eyes, listening. Then he drifted back to sleep.

* * * * * *

Suhendra had followed Kololotov upstairs to his room. They had quarrelled.

'You must not execute the plan. If you do, it will be the end of both of us,' the Russian had warned. Why wouldn't this man listen? 'I will wait here until tomorrow, Kolonel. The money I gave you must be returned.'

'This is no longer your plan,' Suhendra spat at the KGB officer. 'The major general isn't even staying here. Your plan would have failed. Tell me, would you still have demanded the money be returned had I destroyed an empty guest house?' he asked sarcastically.

'It was your information we had acted on. You cannot blame anyone but yourself. You have no choice, return the money!' Kololotov demanded, once again.

'I will keep the money. I will also complete the mission. For me, nothing has changed.' Suhendra said, with a menacing smile. *'If you threaten me with exposure, then you only threaten yourself. You cannot accuse me without involving your own Government.'* The Russian's face muscles tightened as his eyes narrowed.

'You are a fool, Kolonel,' he growled. *'I am covered by diplomatic privilege. You, on the other hand, are not.'* Suhendra thought quickly about this. What the Russian had said was true. Would the Russian go that far to ensure that the mission was cancelled? Suddenly the possibility seemed real. Suhendra attempted another approach.

'Listen. I have already made the arrangements. It will be merely a simple matter of the general's aircraft disappearing on its return flight to the capital. No one will suspect. There will be no danger for you or your Government.' Kololotov understood immediately. The colonel was going to place explosives on board the aircraft before it departed. He had to find out more. The Russian attempted a knowing smile. One of a fellow conspirator.

'When will you do this?' he asked, as if receptive to the plan. He observed the Indonesian officer closely, watching his eyes as he replied.

'He intends returning once the function downstairs is finished. I will accompany the other officers as they escort the Chief of Staff out to the airfield. I will board the aircraft and place the explosives to the rear of the cabin. I will set the timer as soon as he leaves the hotel. It will not be difficult to accomplish.' Suhendra appeared calm. He apparently cared nothing for the crew and other passengers on that return flight to Djakarta. But Kololotov understood clearly how these men would die. Those who survived the blast would probably live long enough to experience the terror of falling from the sky, knowing as they screamed that nothing could save them from certain death. How they died was not of any great import to him. Who was killed in the accident was his only consideration at this time.

'I order you not to proceed with this plan,' he snapped, surprising the colonel. There was a moment when silence engulfed the room, before Suhendra realised that he had been tricked. He glared at the Russian and turned to leave. Kololotov lunged across the narrow space, losing his footing on the loose bedside carpet. He crashed face-down onto the wooden floor, stunned. Suhendra recognised his opportunity but stopped as he was about to flee. The burly

Russian had already begun to rise groggily to his knees.

Suhendra's mind raced. He reached across and lifted the thick, solid glass ashtray and smashed it with all of his force against the side of the Russian's head. Kololotov collapsed to the floor again, screaming in pain, blood pouring from the wound. Suhendra stepped back. He was shaking all over. The ashtray slipped from his hands. The screams became indistinct, died away, but had they been overheard?

He bent down cautiously and inspected the body and, as he did so, Kololotov moved and groaned. Alarmed, Suhendra sprang back, watching, horrified as the injured man moved slightly, then lifted his head. Colonel Suhendra panicked, retrieved the glass weapon then wielded it savagely, again and again, smashing the man's head. Suddenly he stopped, out of breath, glaring down at the prostrate body. Kololotov appeared to be dead.

Suhendra raised his head and listened to the sounds from below. The band had begun playing again. Startled, he checked his watch. He had been away from the function for almost half an hour. Standing up quickly, he checked his uniform for blood and, satisfied there was none, straightened his clothes and left quietly down the long corridor which led to the stairs. Minutes later, he stood amongst the other guests and officers, holding a small plate of food in his hands. He looked down at his hands. They had nearly stopped shaking. Everything was going to be all right.

* * * * * *

Captain Suhardjo found the Australian Military Attaché engrossed in conversation with several of his fellow officers and wives. He waited for the officer to finish speaking before he moved forward and interrupted.

'Kolonel Zach, I am to inform you that the general's party will leave in fifteen minutes. If you have luggage you wish to take, I will wait for you just outside, over there,' he indicated a tall tree behind which Zach could see the white painted lines on the helmets of the military police. He thanked the officer and excused himself from the group, and went directly upstairs. There wasn't much to pack. Then he knocked rather loudly on Murray's door and waited. Moments later, a tired Station Chief opened the door, still rubbing his eyes.

'Well, how was the bash?' Murray asked, relocking the door behind Zach and indicating that he should sit. He yawned, looked at his wrist watch and clicked his tongue in annoyance at having fallen asleep so early.

'I'm off, Murray,' Zach said, and explained what had taken place downstairs. Murray seemed annoyed at first, until Zach said it would be an excellent opportunity to talk directly to the Commander about Murray during the flight. Murray thought about this and nodded his head in agreement.

'There's not much point in trying for an appointment tomorrow now that he's going to be leaving on that flight. You may as well go with him, Steve. At least, that way something might just come out of it.'

'When will you head back, yourself?' Zach asked. Murray thought for only a few moments before replying.

'First light. I really don't want to stay around here any longer than I have to. There's no reason to hang around.' Then he remembered. 'Will you let the reception and our driver know?' he asked, wishing to avoid going back down to the lobby while the Army personnel were still there. Zach agreed. He then left Murray, checking first to see if there was anything he could do before leaving.

'No, Steve, thanks. Think I'll give food a miss and just crash again. It's a hell of drive back tomorrow.' Zach nodded, then went down to the reception to inform them that he was leaving and ask that the account be presented to his friend in room 201. He asked for his luggage to be brought down while he went in search of their driver. Zach stepped out into the musty evening air and peered through the carpark. It was packed full of vehicles, most of which belonged to the Army. There were soldiers and drivers milling around everywhere. He could see four jeeps lined up together, and recognised the gold stars attached to the rear number-plates indicating that these were the general's transport. Zach walked over to a group of men squatting under one of the palms and asked if they had seen his driver. They called out in the partially-lighted area and, within a few minutes, the man appeared. Zach gave him Murray's message and, as he turned to leave, he spotted one of the mobile roadside vendors cooking inside the hotel grounds, serving food to the soldiers and drivers. Zach smiled, knowing that the *martabak* was one of Murray's favourites.

'Get one of those for yourself, and one for tuan Murray. Okay?' he instructed the driver, while digging into his wallet for small notes. He pulled out a one hundred rupiah note, 'Give tuan Murray the change,' he insisted, then gave a wave as he then went in search of Captain Suhardjo. When he caught up with the aide, the officer was busy organising the general's departure. Zach's one piece of luggage arrived, and this was stored in the rear of one of the jeeps while he remained there, in the carpark, wondering how much longer he would have to wait. He saw the driver collect the large Indian omelette filled with chillies, and walk towards the hotel. Zach smiled knowing that Murray would probably curse the intrusion as first, then thank him once he discovered the food. Then the two generals appeared, smiling and shaking hands as they bid farewell to the officers and wives who would not accompany them to the airport. Zach joined the senior officers and, twenty minutes later, the military motorcade entered the Semarang airport and crossed the field to the AURI hangers where the C-47 transport waited.

Zach stood by the aircraft, and to the side, as the Indonesian officers talked amongst themselves on the tarmac. He observed some of the crew moving around the twin-engined plane and saw Colonel Suhendra board, then leave some minutes later. He waved to the colonel as the Indonesian climbed down from the aircraft and waited beside the steps as the commander continued talking to the major general and others, just out of earshot. Then they were given the signal to depart. Zach waited until the Commander and General Soeharto boarded, and then he followed. As he stepped into the aircraft, he turned and waved once again to the colonel standing outside, smiling as he did so. Suhendra returned the smile and stepped away as the starboard engine started, blasting a tunnel of smoke in his direction. Then Zach heard the cabin door locked. They were ready to depart.

* * * * * *

The driver was prevented from entering the hotel lobby through the main entrance because of the presence of VIP's. Instead, he was redirected around the main building and told to use the side access which took him through the rear garden. He passed through a short walkway and into the reception. He knew that he should not be there and attempted to attract the attention of one of the waiters to take the food up to the *tuan*. The manager passed close by but did not notice the Embassy driver for, at that moment, he heard the whistles outside, alerting the police and military escorts to the general's imminent departure. Finally the driver caught the eye of one of the waiters.

'What do you want in here?' the waiter demanded, officiously, looking over his shoulder in case he was seen by Pak Didi. It was against the rules for a driver to be in this part of the hotel.

'I have a martabak for tuan Murray, upstairs. Would you take this up to him for me?' he asked. The waiter looked concerned. He was not permitted upstairs. That responsibility rested with the kitchen waiters. He belonged to the lobby bar service area where Pak Didi had first placed him, almost two years before. He shook his head.

'No, I can't. Ask one of the kitchen waiters,' he suggested, wishing that he could have helped as he knew that the foreign *tuans* tipped exceptionally well.

'Look, why don't you just do it. The kitchen staff will only tell me to ask the manager, you know that,' he argued, knowing that the man was only looking for a few rupiah for himself. The waiter could see no value in offering to assist the driver who, as he could see, wasn't even Javanese.

'Give me five rupiah and I'll do it,' he said, glancing around again to ensure that Pak Didi was still preoccupied with the guests outside. The driver was furious. The request was exorbitant. Besides, he had no right to give *tuan* Zach's money away to this man. He refused.

'Then do it yourself,' the waiter retorted, turning away, ignoring remarks which followed him. The driver looked at the omelette wrapped in newspaper and banana leaves. Then he looked up at the stairs. He turned his head and saw quite clearly that almost everyone present had moved away from the reception area and towards the main entrance to farewell the visiting general. He didn't hesitate. Moving up the stairs two steps at a time, he soon covered the short distance arriving at the corridor which led down to the suite rooms. Then he frowned, knowing that he should have first checked to see in which room *tuan* Murray stayed. He walked along the carpeted hallway looking at the bottom of each door to see

which still had lights burning. The driver moved along slowly, checking as he passed room 201, then 203 which had been allotted to the Australians. There were no lights and so he continued down to the end of the corridor where he discovered that the lights to 208 were still burning. He knocked and waited. He knocked loudly, again. Then he heard the loud moan from inside.

* * * * * *

Murray had just drifted into sleep when he thought he heard knocking. He opened his eyes and listened. The sounds were coming from further down the passageway, so Murray closed his eyes again. He felt hungry. Why hadn't he asked Zach to send a platter of food up with one of the waiters?

He heard the loud knocking again. Curious, Murray listened. Suddenly he heard someone call out, *'Tuan, tuan!'* and he threw himself out of bed, unlocked his door and peered cautiously through the narrow gap, preparing himself for danger. He couldn't see anything at all. The shouts came again, calling from somewhere down the hallway. Murray considered grabbing his weapon, but decided to wait until he learned more about what was happening. Then he saw his driver appear from the far room and run in his direction. Murray swung his door open and grabbed the man as he passed, pulling him savagely into the darkened room. He slammed the door shut and flicked the lights on as he held his forearm across the driver's throat.

'What have you been up to?' Murray demanded, relieving some of the pressure against the man's neck. The driver's eyes remained opened wide, filled with terror. He thought he had been attacked by whoever had hurt the other *tuan* down the hall. *'I said, what have you been doing down there?'* Murray hissed at his driver, between clenched teeth. He then shook the man roughly and released his grip. The driver slid to the floor, then raised his hands over his head for protection.

'Nothing, tuan, nothing!' he wailed, horrified with the sudden turn in events. Why had he gone upstairs with the food? Now look at the trouble he was in!

'What happened?' Murray snapped, raising his hands threateningly.

'*Nothing, tuan, nothing. I didn't do anything, I swear!*' he sobbed, curling his feet up underneath his body. '*Tuan Zach told me to buy some martabak for you and I thought you were in the other room,*' he choked, forcing the words out. Then he remembered. '*Tuan! There's a man down there who's hurt badly. It's another tuan,*' he gushed, excitedly. Murray knew immediately who it would be. There had only been three foreigners staying in the hotel and Zach had already departed. He dragged his trousers and shirt off the chair and pulled these on quickly. He shoved his P9S inside his belt. Then he slipped into his shoes and killed the light.

'*Wait here,*' he ordered the driver, before opening the door and moving out into the hallway. He walked slowly towards the far room. Arriving at 208 he found the door ajar. Inside, Kololotov, who was bleeding profusely, had dragged himself up into a half-sitting position. He saw Murray and attempted to crawl towards the bedside table. Murray guessed that the Russian would have a weapon there somewhere. He closed the door with one hand and moved to block the man's path. The Russian slid back to the floor and moaned loudly.

'You, ... who are you?' he asked, his voice barely audible as he dragged himself into a sitting position. His vision seemed impaired. Murray looked at the bloodied mess around the man's face and head. He couldn't understand how he was still conscious having taken such punishment.

'I'm a guest,' he answered slowly. What in the hell had happened here? Murray wondered, glancing around. Then he noticed the ashtray and sucked in air through his teeth. This had been the weapon. 'What happened?' he asked.

Kololotov gasped with pain as he finally managed an upright sitting position, leaning against the bed end. He looked as if he would pass out again at any moment. Murray looked around and spotted the thermos flask filled with boiled drinking water. There was no refrigerator. He moved over and poured a glass of the tepid water and placed this in the Russian's hands, careful not to position himself to his disadvantage. Kololotov took the glass and raised it to his lips, spilling more than he drank. He coughed, and as he did, his face contorted in pain. Murray removed the glass.

'Want to tell me what happened? Should I ask reception to get the police?' he asked, knowing that this would most probably be the last thing the Russian would want. Kololotov appeared to ignore the suggestion. He seemed to be having difficulty maintaining consciousness. 'Has this something to do with your friend, the Diponegoro colonel you were seen with earlier?' Murray went on. Kololotov seemed to understood this. His hands tensed, forming a fist.

Murray moved away as if intending to leave. 'I'll go downstairs and see if someone can find him if you want,' he suggested, realising that the Russian's mind was still confused from the savage bashing he had taken.

'Are they ... still downstairs?' he asked, groaning.

'Who?' Murray asked, his curiosity more than aroused by now. 'Who should be downstairs?' he asked, hoping that the man wouldn't pass out.

'The ... the ... general. Has he ... has he already ... left for ...' He stopped, the pain preventing him from continuing. Murray bent down and placed his hand on the Russian's shoulder. He knew that there would be no danger from this man now. Odds were, from the look of him, he might not make it.

'Left for where?' Murray asked, gripping the man to let him know that he was there to help. 'Where was the general going?' he asked, knowing the answer himself, but curious that this was of interest to a man who might be dying. He wanted to shake the man but knew this would probably kill him. Suddenly there was a loud groan.

'Has ... the ... general gone to ... the airport?' the Russian managed, almost fainting with the exertion. Murray could see where part of the man's head had been opened wide. The sight of the gash made him feel ill.

'What about the general?' Murray tried again, suddenly very concerned. A familiar feeling of dread started down his back. How did the Russian know so much about the general's movements? 'Listen, what about the general?' he asked again, slowly and clearly. He could see that the man was almost gone, his eyes had begun to glaze over.

'Suhendra ...' Kololotov suddenly said, spitting the name out with a groan of agony. He seemed to be trying to form the words but they just wouldn't come. 'Suhendra ... he must not continue ...' again the words fell off. Murray could not quite make out what he was saying. It sounded like someone's name. Who in the hell was he referring to?

'What must he do?' Murray asked almost irritably. Kololotov tried again, and he opened his eyes and blinked. Suddenly it appeared as if he could recognise what was happening in the room and could see the other man clearly.

'Suhendra ... Suhendra ... must cancel ... the mission.' The words were almost indistinguishable now, as his voice slurred. 'Not ...Soeharto,' he said, fighting to stay conscious 'Not ...not ...now.' And then Kololotov died, his body sliding to one side and onto the floor. Murray knelt, then felt his pulse. He knew the man was dead even before he checked, surprised that Kololotov had survived this long. He rose, and stood staring down at the dead KGB officer. Murray frowned, trying to make sense of what the dying man had said. Was he saying Sunda? No, he thought, it sounded more like... and suddenly he realised what the Russian was trying to say. The words raced through his mind and he swore loudly, recognising the name of the colonel that Zach had spotted in the hotel garden.

He turned and raced down the corridor as fast as he could, repeating the words which had so suddenly alarmed him. Airport, Suhendra, mission, Soeharto! He couldn't believe that what he was thinking might be true. The Soviets were involved somehow in a plan which concerned the major general and his aircraft. His mind continued to race with the possibilities. Was there going to be an attempt on the Chief of Staff's life?

He banged his bedroom door open violently and grabbed his driver, half-dragging the frightened man along the corridor with him as he ran down the staircase and through the lobby. There were still a number of guests who had remained behind to enjoy what was left of the buffet and each others company. They heard the shouts and turned, surprised, as the foreigner rushed through the reception dragging his driver behind. The hotel manager stood with his mouth open when the two almost collided with him as they blundered through the lobby and down the steps into the carpark.

Murray took one look and did not need to be told that Zach's party had already departed. He cursed loudly, then yelled at the driver to run faster as they headed for the Embassy car parked across the enclosure. Suddenly there was a shout from behind, as one of the Army officers ran into the carpark yelling to the others waiting there. He had seen the Australian run through the lobby and couldn't believe his eyes. He was certain that it was the same man from Djakarta. What was he doing there?

Murray and his terrified driver made it to their vehicle first. The Embassy driver didn't need to be told to drive quickly: he did, not knowing which direction to take and spinning the car wheels on the loose gravel surface. The engine screamed as the driver pushed the six-cylinder motor past its limits, missing the gear change in panic, expecting the car lights behind to belong to the military police. He thought that he would be accused of harming the injured guest in 208, and that *tuan* Murray was trying to save his life.

'Go straight to the airport,' Murray ordered. The driver looked at him in disbelief.

'But tuan, it would be better if we drove the other way,' he complained, knowing that they would surely be caught if he took that road. *'We are faster. They won't be able to catch us if we just drive to Tjirebon,'* he implored, indicating that they were already being pursued by the other vehicle.

'Just drive as fast as you can to the airport or I'll throw you out here and drive myself, okay, mas?' Murray snapped, cursing for not having taken the wheel himself. He turned in his seat and caught a glimpse of the car behind. *'Go faster!'* he urged, just as the hapless driver hit a large pothole and almost lost control. Murray swore loudly as his head hit the roof. Glancing back he could see that the car following had also plunged one of its wheels into the hole as headlight beams flashed wildly in all directions. Their driver had overcorrected and spun off the road.

'For Chrissakes, go faster can't you!' he screamed at the driver, knowing that this would be their opportunity to lose the others. They accelerated away and within minutes the town lights started to disappear behind. *'Go down there!'* he snapped, pointing to a side road. The driver obeyed, losing a little speed as he threw the sedan into the corner, fishtailing wildly on the dirt track.

'Stop over there, quickly,' Murray ordered. They came to an abrupt halt and a cloud of dust engulfed their vehicle. *'Now get out, mas,'* he said, sliding across and forcing the driver to move away as he leaned over and opened the door. It happened all too quickly for

the surprised driver. He fell out as Murray moved into the driving position and wound the window down.

'Stay here,' he shouted at the stunned man. '*I'll send someone back for you.*'

'No, *tuan*, no! *Please don't leave me here,*' he screamed, but his words were drowned as Murray gunned the engine and turned the wheel, throwing gravel everywhere. He headed back in the direction of the airport, hoping that those who had been following would, by now, assume that he had gone on through the city and was still well ahead of them. Murray looked down at the speed-ometer then back at the narrow road, willing the car to go faster.

He knew that the airport would only be a fifteen minute run at this time of night. The road was quiet due to the curfew. Only a few more minutes had passed when he spotted outlines of the air-port buildings in the distance. As he sped along the perimeter fence road, he couldn't see an aircraft anywhere. He ground his teeth and muttered, hoping that he was not too late. When he reached the turn-off to the airport main entrance, he swung the car into it and drove towards the main guard gate to the joint civilian and military field. The boom was still open but, in the distance, he could see that there were soldiers standing around nearby. He stared down the driveway as he accelerated towards the open gate, will-ing the men not to stand in front of his speeding vehicle, nor to lower the boom. Suddenly, Murray caught the flash of headlights in his rear-vision mirror again. He knew it would be them. He drove the gas-pedal all the way to the floor.

The main-gate guards had been standing around waiting for the vehicles which had entered some time before, to return, so that they could go back to sleep again. The airport had no more than two flights each day, and rarely any at night. There were no night-landing facilities available there, although this never bothered the military flights. Once the general's entourage had departed, they would be able to get back to sleeping until morning, when they would be relieved for the day.

The soldiers looked at the car speeding towards them and won-dered what had been forgotten by the previous group. They could see that this driver was in one hell of a hurry and stood back as the car swept by, throwing a cloud of dust and small pebbles through the air as it did so. The guard officer could see that there were two vehicles, and waited for the second to scream past before stepping back onto the road. He shook his head at the reckless drivers, wondering what would have happened had he insisted that they stop. Then he turned back to talk to one of his men as the two vehicles sped on through the field.

Murray swung the car first to the left and then the right as he looked for a way around the aircraft hangars. He was driving blindly, guessing at where to turn next. As he slowed, the car behind caught up and now he could see that there was not a great deal of distance between the two. He knocked the rear-vision mirror away with his hand to prevent the other car's high-beams from blinding him. Then he began to panic that he had missed the flight. Murray turned once more, and rounded the remaining hangar spotting the line of jeeps waiting on the hardstand surface. These were surrounded by soldiers. He was within a hundred metres and he could see that these soldiers were surprised at the appearance of the two vehicles, one obviously in pursuit of the other. Murray searched for the aircraft and felt his heart sink. He was too late! Then, as he passed another building, he caught a glimpse of the freighter moving towards the main runway, taxi-ing slowly. He didn't hesitate. Aiming his vehicle directly at the runway, he drove across the grass strips and over deep gutters which carried excess rainwater away. He could hear the heavy tearing noises underneath, as exhaust assembly and other parts of the vehicle were ripped away. The soldiers behind remained locked on his tail, their headlights bouncing all over the airfield as they drove across the slight undulations and gutters in full chase. Murray could see the C-47 turn, then face down the main runway, hazard lights blinking. He drove directly at the stationary plane, flashing his lights. There was less than a thousand metres to go.

Inside the cockpit the AURI colonel looked quizzically at his co-pilot.

'What the hell are those two vehicles doing?' the pilot snapped. He watched the two pairs of lights dance across the perimeter until finally turning into his flight path. The co-pilot shook his head, raising his eyebrows to indicate that he too didn't understand. The thought flashed through his mind that these were the jeeps which had brought the generals out to the airfield and might have decided to line the strip providing additional light. He shook his head again, knowing that this was precisely the sort of dangerous cowboy behaviour he had seen so many time before, when flying in and out of the Army-controlled airfields. He moved the stick forward as his CO nodded. The engine pitch immediately changed, sending their screaming messages to those all around that the plane had commenced take-off. Committed, the aircraft started to accelerate forward.

The officer riding in the chase vehicle yelled at the others inside his car when he suddenly realised what the mad Australian was going to do. They had gained on the smaller car and were now alongside. He could see the determined look on the foreigner's face. The crazy fool intended to ram the aircraft with his own car! He screamed at his driver to go faster and force the foreigner off the airstrip. The driver kicked the gas-pedal hard and pulled the heavy eight-cylinder American Plymouth across the gap which separated the two vehicles.

Murray flinched as the sound of screaming metal on metal accompanied the collision, forcing his own car to swerve violently to his left, then right, before losing control as the Plymouth collided again. Suddenly Murray knew that it was all over. The Holden rose on its side and was plunged wildly off the runway as the much heavier vehicle ploughed on through. He felt the wheels leave the ground and, for a brief moment, caught a glimpse of the oncoming aircraft as it too had been forced to swerve from the path of the duelling sedans. In those seconds, as his car rolled and thumped then rolled again, Murray cried out in pain and his body was flung violently around inside. Suddenly, the screams of twisting metal ceased, and his head smashed forward into the steering wheel, bursting the cartilage in his nose and knocking him unconscious.

By now the shocked soldiers who had been standing around waiting for their senior officers to depart had recognised what was happening and driven their jeeps recklessly towards where the aircraft had ground to a halt. They had their weapons ready to shoot. Uncertain as to which of the two vehicles had intended attacking the aircraft they encircled the wrecked cars and pointed their weapons threateningly at those inside. The senior officer jumped down from his jeep and ran across to the aircraft which, by now, had come to a complete standstill askew from the runway. The pilot had kept the engines running waiting to see what developed next.

He cursed the stupidity of the two drivers, thankful that he had braked and kicked the rudder as hard as he had, to move out of the path of the hurtling mass of metal. He had no doubt the oncoming cars would have struck his undercarriage. As he stared back and across at the confused scene, as arriving jeeps focused their lights on the wrecks, he felt a hand touch his shoulder. Turning to the Army officer, he acknowledged the signal and instructed his co-pilot to close the engines down. Then he levered himself out of the captain's seat and went back into the cabin to check on his VIPs.

Zach had already moved amongst the other passengers, confirming that none had been injured when their aircraft had bounced around, then suddenly come to an abrupt halt slightly off the main runway. He peered through the porthole at the wrecked cars.

Suddenly, as one of the approaching jeeps swung towards the damaged vehicles on his left, Zach was stunned. The jeep's headlights picked out the Australian Corps Diplomatique number plate hanging off the back of the car. Without hesitation, he leapt over, snapped the cabin door open, then jumped to the ground. He ran to the wreck and, when he saw the driver, called out for assistance.

'*Get over here, quickly,*' he screamed at the soldiers in the jeeps. '*Give me a hand here!*' he called again, leaning inside to see how best to pull Murray from the wreck. 'Murray, Murray,' he yelled, running his hands over the unconscious body. 'Murray, can you hear me?' He felt around for a pulse. There. He found one. He was still alive. He called again, 'Murray, Murray, can you hear me?' Just then one of the soldiers approached with a torch and shone the light onto the injured foreigner's face. It was covered with blood. The Indonesian soldier called out to the others.

'*Put a guard around this car, quickly,*' he ordered. Zach heard the man's commands but these didn't register. He was too concerned with Murray's condition. Slowly he managed to free the body from inside the wreck and, unaided, drag the unconscious man onto the grass. He ran his hands expertly over his friend's body, relieved to discover that there were no severe injuries. He checked inside his mouth and ears. Then he called for water. There was none on the jeeps.

'*Kolonel,*' he called, addressing one of the guard officers, '*would you please help here. This man needs water. There would be some on the aircraft,*' he suggested, and waited for his assistance. Instead, the officer stepped forward and withdrew his pistol. He didn't wish to go anywhere near the aircraft.

'No water. This man is under arrest,' Suhendra shouted angrily. Zach was dumbfounded.

'Arrest?' he shouted back, rising to his feet, *'What for?'*

He stepped between Murray and the Indonesian colonel.

'He tried to kill the general!' the colonel screamed angrily, then grabbed a pistol from one of the security guards. He waved this threateningly. Steven Zach knew that they were in grave danger. The situation was extremely volatile and he knew whatever he did next might just determine their fate. He looked over and noticed that the VIP passengers had remained close to the waiting aircraft. He raised his hand to wave but there was no response. The Commander was in deep discussion with some of the men who had been pulled from the wrecked Plymouth and Zach could see them pointing in his direction. He turned back to the colonel and Zach's mind flashed back to other images, other times, when he had seen similar looks on men's faces during the heat of battle. There was a loud groan from behind and Zach turned quickly, in time to see Murray open his eyes and cough, as blood had trickled down into his breathing passage.

'Murray, wait,' he said, bending down to help him into a sitting position. If there was any more bleeding this would be more comfortable. 'Take it easy, Murray, it's okay,' Zach said, considering what to do next. He had to remain close to Murray. He could see that Suhendra intended to kill him, given the chance. Murray coughed again and wiped his face with the back of his bloodied hands. These had been cut as he'd been flung around during the crash. His vision was still blurred, but he knew that Zach was there. He gripped Zach's arm and dragged him closer.

'Get away from the plane!' he whispered hoarsely, the urgency in his voice startling Zach. Until then, he hadn't even wondered what the hell Murray was doing there. There hadn't been time for that. He leaned closer and placed his ear near Murray's mouth. 'Get them away from the plane!' Murray repeated, whispering just as hoarsely as before. 'It's going to blow!' he warned, then broke into a heavy cough throwing more blood onto the tarmac. Zach was stunned.

'Jesus, Murray, are you sure?' he whispered back. The injured man coughed, then sucked in as much air as he could, wincing from his bruised ribs.

'Suhendra ...' he gasped, 'it's Suhendra. I think he's interfered with the aircraft somehow.' He coughed again, grimacing with pain.

'How, Murray, for Chrissakes how?' Zach pressed, cradling the injured man.

'I'm not sure ...' Murray replied, taking as small a breath as possible as the sharp jabbing sensation continued around his ribs. 'Kololotov is dead ... Suhendra killed him. Of that ... I'm sure. He said Suhendra's name ... just before he died.' Murray stopped for a moment, to take another small breath. Zach waited impatiently. 'He also mentioned the flight ... and Soeharto.'

'Get away from that man. He is under arrest,' they heard the colonel yell at them. He then screamed at the other soldiers standing with their weapons at the ready. *'Take that man over to my jeep, now!'* Zach was about to stand when Murray gripped his arm and pulled him back.

'Get ... them ... away ... from the bloody aircraft,' he hissed, dragging himself upright.

Zach placed his arm around Murray's back to assist him to his feet. Murray looked at the officer standing directly in front of him and squinted. The jeep headlights presented the colonel merely as a silhouette. Zach suddenly understood why he couldn't permit Suhendra to take charge. He would most certainly kill Murray Stephenson. He looked across to the generals still standing at a distance. Then he called out loudly.

'Commander, this man has just saved your life!' He could see the men break into animated conversation. The officer who had pursued the Australian had raised his voice and was waving his hands around wildly. Zach looked sideways at Suhendra.

'General,' he called out to the Chief of Army Staff who had been surrounded by security just in case his life was further threatened. *'General, this man has saved your life as well. Please, bapak, listen to what he has to say.'* Suhendra started to move forward and raise his gun, pointing it at the two Australians.

'Stop!' a voice commanded, and Suhendra turned slightly to see who had issued the order. He kept his gun pointed directly at the foreigners. Zach could see the finger tightening.

'I said stop!' the deep voice barked again, closer this time as the

men approached. Suhendra turned and saw the group of VIP's moving away from the aircraft. In that moment he knew that he had failed. He tensed, then squeezed the pistol's trigger.

Zach saw the hammer pull back as the weapon cocked to fire and, in that millisecond, he knew Murray was dead. The hammer snapped forward sending the high tensile steel smashing towards the chamber and, even before either of them could scream, the deathly silence exploded with a sharp click. The chamber was empty. Shock and surprise flashed across Suhendra's face as what happened registered in his brain, and he squeezed the pistol again. Zach had already moved, anticipating the colonel's reaction, kicking high and hard as he threw himself into the air, his right shoe heel striking the arm in which the officer held the weapon.

'Stop this! Immediately!,' the Commander yelled, and two of his aides moved quickly to recover the revolver which had spun through the air and landed some metres from where Suhendra stood, holding his wrist in pain. Suhendra knew that this would be the end. He glared at the two Australians. How did they know? The question flashed through his mind. Then he cursed himself for not checking the other soldier's weapon. He stood there, head lowered, knowing that soon he would most certainly die. Suhendra looked back at the aircraft. If only it had taken off just seconds sooner, he thought bitterly.

General Prajogo eyes were filled with hate. After focussing on Suhendra he turned to Murray. *'You have committed a grave act against the Indonesian people,'* the Commander snarled, staring at the face of the man he'd tried to have killed. He could see that his aide had correctly identified the Australian who moved with the Communists. He looked sternly at Zach.

'I know this man, Kolonel Zach. He has been here before. He ...'

'For Chrissakes Steve,' Murray interrupted, his voice still hoarse. 'Tell him about Kololotov. And Suhendra,' he added, still wincing in pain. The general glared at him.

'General,' Zach started, watching Suhendra as he spoke, *'Murray Stephenson did this to stop our plane from departing. What he did might have saved our lives. Will you at least give us the chance to explain. He deserves at least that.'* The Commander started to shake his head when his superior interceded.

'Let him speak. I wish to hear what he has to say,' Soeharto ordered.

Suddenly everyone became quiet. Murray cleared his voice.

'There may be a bomb on your aircraft, bapak. It could detonate at any minute. I believe that this officer knows what I'm talking about,' he said, indicating Suhendra. The Commander stepped closer to his Chief of Staff and whispered something.

'I am told that you are not like Kolonel Zach. The Commander says that you are our enemy. Why should we believe you?' he asked. Murray looked at the serious Javanese and rolled his eyes in exasperation.

'Why then would I do this?' he asked, moving his head from side to side slowly indicating the wrecks.

'It's true, general,' Zach interrupted. *'Why would he have risked his life? What did he have to gain?'* The officers stood waiting. They were still not convinced.

'Ask Suhendra what he did to the plane,' Murray insisted with difficulty, as blood continued to flow from his broken nose. He was angry that they refused to believe him. *'Why not have the plane checked?'* Suhendra was silent, rubbing his injured wrist.

'Suhendra?' the Commander asked, looking at his colonel.

'I don't understand what this foreigner is talking about, Bapak. There could be nothing wrong with the aircraft as the crews themselves had it thoroughly checked. Why am I being accused? Surely it's these foreigners that should be questioned, not me. He's the one who tried to drive his car into your aircraft. Why am I being treated in this way?' he asked. The Diponegoro Commander thought for a moment. Suhendra was one of his finest officers. He trusted him implicitly, and besides, he sounded so convincing.

'Take the Australian, Stephenson, away for questioning. Take him back to the barracks,' he ordered, then he spoke privately to the other general. He nodded. They seemed to be in agreement over whatever he'd said.

'General, you can't do this!' Zach pleaded. He realised immediately what would happen once Murray was out of his sight. *'If you take him, then you must also take me,'* he challenged. The Commander flashed him an angry glare as he turned and took the arm of his friend, and senior officer, then started back towards the aircraft. They would depart as planned. He called out for the crew to remove Zach's luggage. The crew obediently entered the aircraft.

'General,' Zach called as he watched them both move towards the plane. *'Please don't do this,'* he implored, and went to move after

them but stopped when several of the security guards raised their machine pistols at him. He stood there in dismay as one of the other guards motioned with his weapon that they were both to follow him. As they walked over to the jeeps, suddenly he heard shouts coming from the direction of the aircraft. Soldiers ran towards the plane and ushered their senior officers away, providing a protective shield as they did so. The crew, dressed in their orange flying suits, jumped out of the aircraft and started to run. The guards hurried their VIPs towards the waiting jeeps and moved around behind these as a shield. Zach knew instantly that they had discovered something to cause all this panic while searching for his luggage to offload.

'Get down over there,' he yelled, warning Murray. The soldiers guarding them turned and watched the confusion. Zach then yelled at them also. There was another shout and Zach looked up just in time to see Colonel Suhendra running towards the aircraft.

'Stop him,' the Commander roared, and two of his aides jumped to their feet and fired. But they were too late. Suhendra leaped into the open cabin and pulled the door shut behind him, locking it in position. He stood there gripping the handle, then he turned and saw the container lying on the floor. The container which would have changed the course of Indonesia's history had it not been discovered. Suhendra moved slowly towards the metal box and knelt down beside it.

The Indonesians and Australians all remained hidden behind the row of vehicles not one hundred metres from the C-47, waiting. As the minutes dragged by, the tension on the silent airfield grew intense. Zach sat against one of the jeep's wheels wondering what in the hell Suhendra was doing inside. If he was going to blow the plane, why hadn't he already done so? He looked across at Murray and observed that he too was safely positioned behind a wheel waiting for the explosion. Zach looked across at the group of soldiers sitting, half-crouched around their leaders and wondered what was going through their minds right at that moment.

Inside the aircraft, Suhendra had sat down alongside the metal container and placed his hands on his knees and sobbed. From the moment he'd discovered that his Commander would accompany Soeharto on the flight, everything had seemed to go wrong. He cursed Kololotov. When Suhendra had returned to the function and discovered that the generals would be travelling together, his immediate reaction was to cancel his plans. But then he realized that the Russians would discover what had happened in Semarang and would move to take their revenge. Suhendra understood that this would be his one and only opportunity and, although he wished it could be otherwise, his own Commander would die too.

Suhendra looked again at the bomb he had prepared and suddenly his father's image flashed across his mind. The hardship which followed his death. Then he remembered his brother and the resolution he had made when he had been killed by the Americans. The tears stopped and he wiped his eyes with the back of his wrist. He reached down and smiled at the open container, remembering the large amount of money he had hidden away in the ordnance depot. And how he had booby-trapped the box covering his hoard. Then he laughed at his own joke and advanced the timing mechanism manually.

Those surrounding the aircraft had come to suspect that either the bomb was faulty, or Suhendra had changed his mind. When the explosion came, the blast lifted the vehicles some inches off the ground, blasting everyone away from behind their protective wall as the air compressed then expanded under the violent detonation. The aircraft's fuel tanks ignited and contributed to the deafening explosion, throwing huge pieces of the plane across the field in a continuous fiery blaze. The scorched air seared flesh, causing all the men to shield their faces from the heat. Within seconds it was all over.

The men lifted themselves slowly to their feet. They were shocked to see how little was left of the plane. Small fires were evident around the field as parts of the aircraft continued to burn, flames dancing like ghosts wherever the soldiers looked.

* * * * * *

'Murray?' Zach asked, looking in his direction. He was still sitting down, facing away from the blast.

'I'm okay. You?'

'I'm a lot better than I would have been had you not been such a lousy driver,' he answered, forcing a smile. Murray could barely detect the grin in the semi-darkness.

'What about that lot?' he asked, still pissed off that they had to go through all of this. Zach looked over and watched the men climbing into their Jeeps.

'They're okay. Look's like they're leaving. Do we want a ride?' he asked, still grinning. It was good to be alive. As he spoke, the soldiers called to them and Zach helped Murray to his feet.

'*Come, we will take you back to the hotel,*' the Commander said. '*And then we can talk.*' Zach looked at Murray who sighed in relief. It was all over. Now he would be able to walk the streets of Djakarta again without having to look over his shoulder all the time. He couldn't smile but he did the next best thing. He placed his hand on Zach's shoulder, then limped towards one of the waiting jeeps. He started to climb into the Army vehicle.

'*No,*' he heard the officer say, causing him to look up. '*You will ride with us here,*' the major general said. The soldiers all looked at the Australian, then at the two generals. Murray stepped back and moved around to the staff car. He looked up into the faces of two of the most powerful men in the country, and they both smiled. Then he knew that everything was really going to be all right. Suddenly the soldiers all cheered as the Commander offered his hand and assisted Murray into the rear of his jeep.

The four vehicles drove away from the scene of devastation weaving their way through pieces of wreckage and across the airfield. Zach looked back and observed Murray sitting in the rear, disguising his pain as he talked. Throughout his military career, Zach had seen many men risk their lives for others, but Murray's endeavour had indeed been exceptional. He was a true hero. A clandestine warrior of the highest calibre. Zach looked up at the brilliance of the starry sky and smiled.

Chapter 28

Djakarta

Murray looked at the letter delivered by diplomatic courier from Australia. He used the short-bladed letter-opener shaped in the design of a silver *keris* to slice carefully through the end of the envelope. It was stamped on both sides with the appropriate warnings and security classifications. He read the brief enclosure then let it fall back onto the desk. He hadn't expected the official notification of his transfer back to Melbourne for at least another six months. Following his return from Semarang, he had submitted to Central Plans an in-depth report of the political atmosphere and what he had witnessed during his tour through Central Java. Zach had agreed with him that it would not be in their best interests, nor in those of the Indonesians, to disclose the events surrounding the assassination attempt. They understood all too clearly that the current political uncertainty which prevailed could all too easily be manipulated to the disadvantage of the West, and that disclosure of yet another attempt on the country's generals might further inflame the people.

He told curious members of the Embassy that he'd broken his nose in a *betjak* collision, and they'd accepted his explanation without question, although there was the odd knowing wink from some of them. Murray's reputation had long been the subject of embellishment and rumour. He had been invited to Army Headquarters unofficially, where he met again with not only the Chief of Staff, but also his former enemy, the Diponegoro Commander. The three enjoyed an informal discussion and, it appeared, the Semarang Commander was satisfied with the Australian's political position in relation to the Communists. He was not directly asked about his relationship with the PKI students, nor was he questioned in relation to his earlier visits to the Diponegoro Divisional Head-quarters with Harry Bradshaw. Instead, the meeting was conducted in typical Javanese style, with questions presented politely, but obliquely. Murray understood that it would be most unlikely that they would become close friends, even though he had saved the general's life, for there would always be that unanswered question in their minds about Murray's role in those earlier machinations which cost Colonel Sulistio his life. But no further mention was made of the incident, nor the near-fatal attempt on their own lives. And then there was Ade.

Murray had visited the Indonesian Intelligence Agency, BAKIN, within days upon his return to his office. It was a courtesy call, and one which was expected of all foreign Embassy officials who had journeyed through the country in any official status. He had ar-rived almost an hour early for his appointment, hoping that he could clear the mandatory interview earlier than scheduled. Murray's face was known to the desk security officer who, unable to contact the appropriate extension upstairs, escorted the Aus-tralian up to the third level where he was instructed to wait. Murray was aware from previous visits, that this was the section which attempted to maintain surveillance over members of the foreign community, a daunting enough task, he knew, considering BAKIN's limited resources. He heard voices inside, and laughter. Then the door opened and the pair came out together, still smiling at their private joke.

Ade's face froze as Murray looked at her, completely caught by surprise. She tried to speak but the words wouldn't come. Instead, she dropped her eyes and continued past without so much as a sound. The Indonesian Intelligence officer, obviously flustered by the embarrassing encounter, stammered an invitation for Murray to enter his office. He did so, staring back over his shoulder at the woman who had shared his bed all those years. Later, when she telephoned asking if they could meet, Ade explained that she had been down to the Intelligence Agency arranging a security clear-ance for her cousin in Java. But to Murray, the story had no sub-stance. He knew that the office she'd visited was in no way con-cerned with such matters. Instead, he had files in his safe which described quite clearly how the Intelligence Agency had developed a special corps of young women, who were employed to keep tabs on specific foreign targets. It was clear to Murray that Ade had been their conduit for some time.

They did meet, but only for dinner. Murray said it was to say goodbye, as he was returning to Australia. She cried through the meal. Murray felt saddened that even this relationship had been tainted by the devious world in which he had chosen to live. They had parted that evening, not even as friends. Later he would recall the coincidence of her journey to Australia when he returned to Melbourne. Murray's disappointment grew even greater as he came to believe that her placement by his side was far too sophisticated for the Indonesians. Ade had to have been working in conjunction with an outside agency. And he thought he knew which one that would be.

* * * * * *

Melbourne

He walked through the long corridors and observed that nothing had really changed since he was first escorted through these bleak offices by Harold Bradshaw. Anderson's secretary had smiled warmly when he arrived, taking him straight through into the Director's well-appointed chamber. She left, closing the door behind her.

'Well, that's about it then,' Murray said, placing the file on Anderson's desk. It was his final clearance document which had required that he meet and be interviewed by no fewer than twenty other Intelligence offices from various agencies within the Australian Government. Then, as he had completed these sessions, each of the agents had signed him off, but very few bothered to shake his hand and wish him well. Murray had no idea whatsoever how he had become a pariah within his own organisation. He put this down to his allegiance over the years to the former Director who, having been missing for more than a few months, was now considered to be a potential defector. He had heard the rumours. And the whispers when the others had thought he was out of earshot. Now, as of this moment, he was his own man again.

'What are your plans?' Anderson asked. Murray knew they would maintain a file on him and keep it current.

'I have decided to return to Djakarta,' he said, knowing that this would be of concern to all within the ASIS community. Central Plans' personnel would all, no doubt, be briefed as to what they should do in the future if they were to come into contact with the former senior agent. Anderson looked unhappy with this news.

'Do you think that wise?' he enquired.

'Why not? I have sound contacts there and thought I might try my hand at something else for a change.' He knew they would find out eventually. They always did. Anderson shook his head as if in the company of some errant schoolchild. He stood.

'I'll see you out, as it's your last visit,' he said, almost with a tone of regret. Murray turned as Madge entered and raised her eyebrows at her Director. He wondered where Anderson kept the button which had signalled her to come.

'Bye, Madge,' he said, bending down quickly and kissing the surprised woman on the forehead. She clucked her tongue and turned away as the two men left the Director's office and walked slowly down the linoleum-covered passageway. They continued down through the maze of smaller offices, neither speaking as they went. Murray looked directly ahead, ignoring the rows of smaller offices, the nerve centre of the Secret Service. As he walked along the corridor he knew, without looking, that each of the agents there would be aware of his departure and wondered how many of their number had bothered to look up and smile.

They stopped in the central clearance foyer and Anderson extended his hand for the last time. As he did so, a young man entered via the security doors and walked directly towards the two men.

'Good morning,' the newcomer offered with a youthful smile. Murray returned the smile and wondered if he had been that young when he'd first been recruited. Anderson hesitated, then decided that they should be introduced.

'Murray, even though you're returning to Djakarta in your own capacity, I have no doubt that you will wish to keep your finger on the pulse of things. I don't have to remind you that you are, and will continue to be, covered by the Official Secrets Act.' Anderson turned to the young smiling officer who Murray thought could be no more than twenty years old, and placed a paternal hand on the young agent's shoulder. 'This young man is one of our bright new stars. You will see him in Djakarta within the next few months, if you're there. He'll be taking up a position you yourself once held in the Embassy, Second Secretary Political.'

Murray smiled, reminded of his own youthful experiences in Indonesia. He spoke warmly to the younger man.

'Well, when you arrive and get settled, look me up. I'm Murray Stephenson,' he said, extending his hand which the younger man took, then shook cordially as he introduced himself.

'Yes, I've heard a great deal about you,' he said admiringly. 'And thanks, I'll certainly do that.' The young man turned to the Director and said, 'I'll wait in your office,' and smiling, walked away.

Murray watched the agent as he climbed the stairs on the far side of the room. Then he turned, nodded at the Director and passed through the security doors for the very last time.

Anderson watched Stephenson depart. He hadn't liked the former agent, but he had to admit he had been one of the best. He almost grinned in pleasure as he turned away and moved back towards the steps which led up to his office. He would dedicate some hours to briefing the young agent, a man he was convinced would develop into one of ASIS's finest agents. Only an exceptional recruit would have the same instincts and level of commitment as Stephenson, but he was confident the young man waiting for him would be equally willing to commit himself to the demands of the Service.

Satisfied that the day had worked out precisely as he had planned, Director Anderson returned to his office.

The young man's name was Stephen Coleman.

Epilogue

Merdeka Square

There was a moment when the crowd fell silent. For hours they had jostled, pushed, yelled and even laughed, waiting together until their charismatic leader appeared.

A soft breeze touched the faces of the spectators as they waited patiently. Now only a few spoke. They could feel that the moment was near. As the crowd of almost one hundred thousand waited, they observed the evening sky become brighter as the pale moonlight slowly spread across the heavens.

Suddenly there was a cry, followed quickly by others calling loudly as the moon's light struck the figure standing alone on the dais. Within moments the multitude reacted, overwhelmed by the presence of the great man. They called out to their leader, their voices falling into a rhythmic chorus while they chanted his name. Then they commenced swaying together as they chanted, *'Hiduplah Bung Karno, Long Live Bung Karno, Long Live President Soekarno...'*

Their voices reverberated across Merdeka Square and through the buildings surrounding the huge gold-leafed obelisk. Voices rang through the side streets and into the restaurants, even down the main thoroughfare leading into Chinatown until finally, in the distance, their chanting became but a whisper, barely audible at all. And at that moment it was as if the gods had sent a signal to correct the destinies of the two great men, born together to become leaders of the Indonesian Nation.

* * * * * *

As Soekarno's power diminished, the spiritual leadership of Subuh grew in intensity until his star could be seen as brightly as any other in the heavens. It had been ordained. The SUBUD following would grow to be even greater than that of their master's namesake, Soekarno.

Soon the sounds became mere whispers as the Great Leader moved away, his evening shadow all that was left for them to remember him by. As the faithful shuffled across the open field and looked up to where he had once stood, only a few shed tears for what had been, and their glorious past. As the moon crossed the heavens and gave way to the thickening clouds, the bright light quickly faded, moving away out of sight until it disappeared altogether, only to be replaced by another.

Within a few short months, Great Leader of the Revolution, President for Life, Bapak President Soekarno, moved from his Palace of dreams in Djakarta, into his house of exile in Bogor, where he was destined to spend the remaining days of his life. There, he acted out the remaining chapter, playing it through as if it were some intricate part of the shadow plays which had captivated his soul and dominated his thinking since he could first remember. And, in compliance with the prophecies long mooted by those who claimed to hold the keys to understanding the mysterious powers which govern the Javanese culture and mind, the people of Indonesia transferred their love and loyalty to another.

On that violent stormy day in the small town of Bogor, the inhabitants were surprised when the skies cleared overhead, and the wind dropped. They had all looked up in awe as a magnificent rainbow suddenly appeared, displaying a brilliance of colours none of their number had ever witnessed before. The people stood transfixed and their eyes followed the colourful shapes which gently touched the lines of the Summer Palace where their former President remained. A prisoner. They knew it was a sign. An omen. And at that moment, as the rainbow suddenly disappeared and the sky turned ominously dark, a soul moved from earth and took its place in the heavens to wait for the moment when it could return. Inside the Palace, the man who had founded the Indonesian Republic and first enunciated the philosophy of *Pantja Sila* which would continue to guide his people through their lives passed away quietly in his sleep, alone.

Author's Note

Merdeka Square is a work of fiction, written while I lived in Vietnam. It is based on my imagination, on research into historical facts, and my personal recollections from my period of service in Djakarta. As the reader might imagine, there are obvious reasons why I found it necessary to tell the story of this fascinating period in this fictional form.

No doubt many readers , and in particular my critics, will have difficulty in differentiating between what appears to be fiction in the story, and what is undeniable fact. Obviously most of the characters are fictitious, but it is a fact that the Head of the Soviet KGB Station in Indonesia during the time I served in the Australian Embassy was General Konstantinov and, as mentioned in this novel, he was the first KGB officer to be promoted to the rank of general while serving outside the USSR. I met with the man, a leading Soviet spymaster, several times during the course of my service. He was later replaced by Kololotov, with whom I spent many wonderful Sunday afternoons sipping Georgian Brandy up in the Coolibah Estate in the mountains of Puntjak Pass.

Perhaps the most controversial aspect of this account is the murder of the Indonesian generals on that fateful morning of the 1st October 1965. There has been considerable debate as to whether the captured generals had been tortured, and to what extent the Gerwani played a role in these officers' deaths.

The surrounding events have been poorly documented in the West over the years, but I have seen sufficient intelligence material to convince me that the Gerwani did, in fact, play a significant role in what happened to the prisoners once they had been escorted to the Crocodile Hole at Halim. The descriptive passages relating to the kidnapping, murder and frenzied mutilation of the generals and other officers are taken directly from interrogation reports which I have read. I have attempted to maintain the integrity of those real details in the story line.

There are those who maintain that these women were innocent of many of the accusations made about them. I have been present at interviews with those who would refute such claims. Of one thing we can be certain. The Gerwani were present during the last hours of those generals who were dragged from their homes and families in front of their children, only to be brutally murdered at the Halim Air Force Base. Autopsy reports 'discovered' by academics later indicated that the generals had not been tortured.

It would seem most fortuitous that such revealing documents had 'accidentally' been discovered by a foreign academic while sifting through medical records in Indonesia. Such a controversial discovery would obviously benefit the anti-New Order lobby and I have great difficulty in accepting the validity of the documents, although I certainly do not question the integrity of those foreigners who were involved in their discovery or those who differ from my view.

The role of Western powers in these events is also controversial. There is substantial information in the public domain made available by authors such as Brian Toohey in his exposé of the Australian Secret Intelligence Service (ASIS), *Oyster*, in which Toohey tells us how senior Australian agents not only established networks in Indonesia, but also infiltrated the secret religious cult known to many as Subud.

This book is in no way intended to offend the followers of Subuh, nor the association known as SUBUD. The heritage left by Subuh is obviously of great spiritual wealth. The SUBUD following throughout the world is large and influential and is well supported by Western intellectuals. In Australia this little-known sect has a dozen or more chapters and many followers. There is little hard information in the public domain about SUBUD.

It is a fact that the founder of this organisation, the late Bapak Subuh, was born at approximately the same time as Indonesia's charismatic President, Soekarno. The Javanese believe that a man's name is all-important, being directly related to his destiny. It is therefore interesting to note that the spiritualist was born with the name Soekarno, and later changed it to Subuh. Likewise, the man who became Indonesia's first President was born with the name Subuh, and changed this to Soekarno. It seemed that their destinies were to follow a parallel path and only when his namesake fell from power did the spiritual leader's star move to the ascent. Also, we should note that Indonesia's second President was not born with the name Soeharto.

Under the Rules of Disclosure, it is not yet possible to obtain accurate details of the American and Australian Government's involvement in the era known to many as The Years of Living Dangerously. Fortunately, institutions such as Cornell University in the USA have successfully identified substantial pieces of evidence. Their information suggests that the CIA had established dialogue with senior officers of the Central Java Army Division known as the Diponegoro Command in 1965. Their aim was to support a coup d'etat against what they considered to be an anti-American President and his communist friends.

There are still many questions left unanswered as to what role the Western powers actually played in President Soekarno's downfall, and how Australia's spies contributed to the outcome of the complicated power struggle which resulted, subsequently, in the massacre of half a million Indonesian people, most of whom were guilty of nothing more than simple ignorance. There is strong evidence that foreign powers had developed a sophisticated network of Indonesians who were loyal to the concept of destroying their President. Estimates place this number in the thousands, financed mainly by the CIA.

Records tell us that this was once President Soeharto's own Command, from which he was unceremoniously removed by (then) General Nasution. We also now know that at least three of the six assassination attempts made against Soekarno were financed by the CIA. Although there have been strong rumours of attempts made against President Soeharto, none of these have ever been given any credence by the Palace, often the very source of such innuendo.

During post coup trials held in camera, evidence was given by Dr. Soebandrio, Soekarno's Foreign Minister and Deputy Prime Minister, that elements within the powerful Indonesian Military had, at that time, formed a secret group known amongst themselves at the Council of Generals, whose aim was to overthrow Soekarno's Government and destroy the Communists. Soebandrio claimed to be present when the then Army Chief, General Yani, confirmed the covert Council's existence to the President.

Documentary evidence also supports the fact that China's Chou En Lai had commenced sending arms to the Indonesian communists to assist with the creation of a militant Fifth Force within the Republic. We can safely assume that at the time of September 1965, there were at least three plots afoot to overthrow the Government of Indonesia. A great deal more could be said but, due to restrictions placed on the writer, readers will have to wait for more details to be released.

As to events following those described in this book, the people of Indonesia quickly tired of the brutal conflict which cost their country more than half a million lives. Three quarters of a million had been arrested, many never to be seen again. The Indonesian Communist Party, the PKI, had virtually disappeared. Its leaders had either been murdered or jailed. But their ghosts remain with us. Massive demonstrations against the Chinese for their past support of the PKI-Peking Axis seriously affected the nation's security and economy. Emerging student groups, KAMI, and later KAPPI, quickly realised that they had the power to influence national policy and, not unlike the PKI, demonstrated en masse, day after day, until their voices were finally heard.

When President Soekarno moved to have the student groups banned, the country moved back into chaos. During a Cabinet meeting on 11th March 1966, the President's Palace Guard Commander warned his leader that Sarwo Edhi had sent his RPKAD troops against the Palace. Soekarno fled, once again, to Bogor by helicopter. Later that day, confronted by Generals Basuki Rahmat, Amir Machmud and Mohammed Yusuf, the man who had been appointed President for Life surrendered his power to Major General Soeharto.

One year later, Soeharto was appointed Acting President by his supporters. Another year passed and, on 27th March, General Soeharto was officially installed as the second President of Indonesia. A new era for the people of the archipelago had begun.

Finally, for reasons of historical accuracy I have presented all Indonesian words, names and place names in the spelling which was used in those times.

Yes, this book is a work of fiction, but it is very definitely based on historical fact. As to the rest, I will leave you, the reader, to judge.

Kerry B. Collison,Yangon, Myanmar

Glossary of Terms

Although many readers would have visited Indonesia, this simple glossary of the *Bahasa Indonesia* and other words used throughout the novel may assist others who have not yet been fortunate enough to visit the beautiful archipelago and become familiar with its multi-faceted culture and language.

ABRI	Indonesian armed forces
adjal	destiny
aduh	exclamation of complaint
akan	will do
ALRI	Indonesian navy
Antara	Indonesian News Service
Apa kabar?	How are you?
ari-ari	placenta
ASEAN	Association of Southeast Asian Nations
ASIO	Australian Security Intelligence Organisation — the Australian domestic spy service
ASIS	Australian Security Intelligence Service — the Australian overseas spy service
AURI	Indonesian Air Force
awas!	be careful!
babu	old term used to refer to a female servant
bagus	good
Bahasa	language
BAKIN	Badan Koordinasi Intelidjen Indonesia — the Indonesian equivalent of the CIA
balai	hall, meeting place
bangsat	arsehole
Bapak/Pak	a term of respect to an older or more senior person
baru	new
betapa	how
beliau	His Honor, Sir

berita	news
betapa	how
betjak	tricycle taxi
bingung	confused
bioskop	cinema
bisa	can
bohong	liar, lie
brengsek	something/somebody incompatible
bule	derogatory slang for foreigner — 'whitey'
bulu-babi	sea urchin
Bung	older brother
bunuh	kill/murder
CIA	Central Intelligence Agency — US foreign spy service
cinta abadi	eternal love
cyclo	tricycle taxi
desa	small village
dia	he/she
djaga	guard
djahanam	curse/hell
djalan	road
djelaskan	explain
Dji Sam Soe	cigarette brand
djongos	servant (male)
djuga	also
DMI	Directory of Military Intelligence
dukun	witch doctor
dulu	before
enggak/tidak	no
fadjar	dawn/daybreak
gamelan	Indonesian orchestra
ganja	cannabis
ganjang	to chew savagely
GERWANI	Indonesian Women's Movement — Communist-affiliated group
golok	large field knife
gotong-royong	working together
gudang	storage room
gunung	mountain

halaman	garden/court
HANKAM	Department of Defence
hidup	live
hormati	to respect
ibu ('bu)	mother, Mrs, older woman
Idulfitri	end of fasting period feast
itu	that, it
jangan	don't
journos	journalists
kali	stream
KAMI	Student Action Front
KAPPI	Student Action Group
kampung	village
Kapten	Captain
kawin	marry
kenapa	why
kepulauan	island group
kita	we
koki	cook
Konfrontasi	War against Malaysian Federation
kongsi	union/company/society
KOPASGAT	Indonesian SAS
Korp Komando	Indonesian Marines
KOSTRAD	Strategic Reserve Command
krait	deadly poisonous snake
kretek	clove cigarette
ladang	arable land
Laksamana Laut	Vice Admiral
Laksamana Madya	Admiral
langganan	dealer/client
Langley	CIA headquarters, USA
Lebaran	a religious feast
Letnan Satu	First Lieutenant
losmen	housing — barracks
lubang maut	death hole
lurah	village head
maaf	apology
mandi	bath, bathe
manis	term of endearment/sweet

Mas	address to a man
"masuk kandang kambing mengembik"	when in Rome, ...
mati	dead
mengerti	understand
Merdeka	independent, free
mereka	they
MI5	British Secret service, domestic
MI6	British equivalent of CIA and ASIS
mudah	young
nama	name
NASAKOM	Nationalism, Religion and Communism
nasi putih	steamed rice
nenek	grandmother
nenek mojang	ancestors
njonja	address to an older woman, or married woman
obrol-obrol	chatting/gossiping
OPM	Free Papua Movement
OPSUS	Government Special Operations Unit
orang asing	foreigner
pagi	morning
Pantja Sila	the Five Principles of Indonesian National Philosophy
panggil	call
parang	sword
Parlimen	Parliament
pasar	market
pasti	certain, sure
pemerintah	Government
perahu	fishing boat, outrigger canoe
perwira	officer
pitji	black cap worn by men
PKI	Indonesian Communist Party
PLN	Electric Company
Presiden	President
pribumi	indigenous people — 'sons of the soil'
protokol	protocol

PTT	Post, Telegraph and Telephone
pulau	island
rakjat	people, of the country
Ramadhan	the ninth month of the Moslem year
Ramayana	Indonesian epic originally from India
rambutan	red fruit with hairy rind
randjau	landmine
rezeki	good fortune
rendang	spicy meat dish
ringgit	Malaysian currency (dollar)
rotan	rattan, cane
RPKAD	Indonesian Para-Commando Army Regiment
rupiah	Indonesian currency
sabar	patience
sampai	until
sawah	rice fields
saya	I
sedih	sad
sekolah	school
selamat datang	welcome
selamat djalan	goodbye
selamat pagi	good morning
semua	all
serta	with
sialan	damn
siapa namanja?	what's his/her name?
silahkan	please
simpati	sympathy
sisihkan	to put to one side
sop buntut	ox-tail soup
SUBUD	religious cult — Susili Budi Dharma
subuh	dawn, first light
sudah	already
sumpah	swear
tamu	guests
Tandjung Priok	Djakarta harbour
tas	handbag
tenangkan	calmed

tentu sadja	of course
terima kasih	thank you
terpaksa(lah)	forced to
terserah	do as you please
tinggi	high
Tjakrabirawa	Presidential Guard
tjap	stamp
tjengkeh	cloves
tjepat	fast
tjewek	girl
TNI	Indonesian National Forces — military
toko	shop
tua	old
tuan	sir
Tuhan/Allah	God
tukang	labourer/worker
VOC	Dutch East Indies Company
wajang kulit	shadow puppets
walaupun	although
waris	legal heir
warisan	inheritance
yang	which, who